DOVE'S EYES

Kienn

gothic neo western 1

A disgraced detective is hired to investigate a ritualistic killing in an isolated prison town. Falls into the hands of a charming doctor on a crusade to cure mankind of sin.

queer gothic neo western horror mystery | 70k
ergodic literature, religious trauma, psychological horror
adult novel

These characters are flawed and problematic.
Content warnings disclosed at the end of the book.

Ebook Edition
ISBN 9798230080619, ASIN B0FMPGYQKP
Paperback Edition
ISBN 9798348247959, 9798298248488
Hardcover Edition
ISBN 9798298371643, 9798869067647
Text | Cover art | Design | © 2025 by Kienn Nguyen
Pure fiction.
All rights reserved.

Table of Contents

01 | a sprig of hyssop 1
02 | of the lamb 21
03 | water and a rag 42
04 | your eyes will see 72
05 | over the chokecherries 99
06 | the sculpted hands 123
07 | the fallen stars 141
08 | my real face 160
09 | the prince of sand 185
10 | the kiss of death 207
11 | a wooden canary 229
12 | his own damnation 259
13 | sacrifice our sons 276
14 | to be judged 290
15 | to forget himself 306
16 | to suffer for their sins 319
17 | our sole fated death 324
18 | into dust 337
19 | he can see 344
20 | this little communion 368
21 | come back to me 383
22 | in each other's blood 391
author's note 414
content warnings 415
about the author 416
thank you 417

He guides me along the righteous path for his name's sake.

01 | a sprig of hyssop

On the steps of Bentham's psychiatric clinic former detective Corey Handler Delgado sat praying over his father's rosary, melted mascara running down his face as beads of piety cast jadeshine over his gloved hands. A steady breeze battered his fraying gray coat into tattered wings, red sweater a crimson bleed down his throat. Summer sweat had mucked his tawny brown skin all the way from the west coast and dark hair rooted to his shoulders like vines. The doves dotting the sky funneled into a spiral at the push of the wind. He found no penance in them. He was half awake. Reliving his purgatory.

Carbon County, Wyoming, the land of the sunlight clear. Along the river, this ageless sore they called Bentham. Nested between the mountains, shuttered just beyond a fence, the mirage of a town that hovered like a forgotten dream. Old breath and dust specks and the faint glow of lost salvation. A three wheeled motorbike smelling of warm wood spice and pinstriped leather had taken him down an unmarked path to this corroded urban sprawl locked behind a narrow guillotine gate. The clinic a droning concrete monolith, brick and board confined to shadows and forever sealed in stone. If Bentham had a soul, it was trapped. Pinned down by the Wyoming wind. But the town of Bentham didn't exist. And the infamous neuroscientist, Dr. Wayne Sykkes, hadn't been seen alive in years.

Only, yesterday the doctor dialed in. Asked him if he sought salvation. Called him a dog.

A thump and a scatter of feathers. Corey dropped his rosary, dawdled to his bootheels, and found, rigid on the floor, the still-beating body of a rock dove. He bent to scoop it up into the dark of his coat where it lay pliantly blinking under his touch, until a distant shudder caused it to flutter and flee. Gray featherdown tufting in his ivy hair.

The door swung open. The detective glanced up from his stupor and was met by a yellow ascot. The broad chest of a man in his late thirties. Silver frames and a sharp face that betrayed nothing but a serpentine pleasantness. Candle cream skin and gray waves that brushed over his cheeks, drew back into a sculpted mullet. He understood then, eyes lacquered in gold, how the town so sorely mistook him for the son of man.

Another pass and Corey spoke softly, though now he could have painted the man from memory. A strike of red for the stroke of his lips. Light to dark. The same face he had learned all those years ago.

  wayne sykkes.

The doctor's eyes roved down. A whetted smile. He was leaning against the doorframe, waistcoat open and the collar of his shirt undone.

  Ah.
  Doctor. Wayne Sykkes. Yes.
  You must be Corey.

He offered his hand. Fixated on Corey's gloves. He had calculated the exact diameter of the detective's wrists from old photographs. Made no show of knowing it.

Such pretty eyes you have.

His smile widened to a chasm.

Come in, darling.

The former detective stared into him. Lost in the details of his face. A puff and he picked up his rosary and pushed past. The doctor caught his arm. Delicate fingers, faded tips had he been a painting in oil. Azure veins worthy of the highest varnish.

Please.
Stay right beside me.

Corey bristled at the touch. Dared the doctor to remove his hands before breaking his eyes away.
No amount of eyeliner could have protected him from that yellow wallpaper. A suffocating neon that snuffed sentience, shrunk it down to a grit of sand. Blackened mold crept along the edges, walls clawed and shorn in bullet holes.
Chairs lined the lobby floor, a procession of gunmetal headstones marching towards double doors the scrag ewe red of viscera. There labeled, the doctor's operating room. To its right, the front desk. Empty.
A squint but Corey held his tongue. He had skimmed the doctor's literature. Scrutinized the headlines. Aeresolized nanoelectrodes. Neuron pattern maps. Activation adaptive algorithms.

Lovely, isn't it?

The doctor's hand had crept its way back into the crook of his

arm. Stopped him beside a pot of roses. Mustard petals of woven plastic, myrrh and balsam.
what?

>The color yellow.
>Like the streets in heaven. Paved in gold.

The doctor held his arm closer. Giggled slightly.

>I chose the exact pattern and hue when we renovated the place.

>Did you know, that in 1971 the clinic used to be a prison? 1971. And it was an asylum before that. A saloon when it was first constructed. 1868. Old Bentham was just a mining town...

A glance around the empty eminence of the clinic. The front desk could have been a bar top in another life. Wood rot that mellowed with age.
you wanted me to sign something?

>Hm?
>Ah.
>Yes.
>The contract.
>Company policy.

Dr. Sykkes took his wrist and dragged him to the right wing of the clinic, the storage area beyond the bar. Locked behind a palm scan. He pushed him into what looked to be a tight office space and the doctor behind him guided the detective to his desk.

Took one of Corey's gloved hands, spread his fingers, pressed his folder into them.

Each line was a clause of forfeiture. Corey ran a thumb down the length of it.

informed consent?

A glance up. The doctor was right over his shoulder. Iris, sandalwood, clove. Cold fingertips just over his collarbone. Corey swallowed the water over his tongue. Met that piercing hazel glint.

you said i wasn't going to be a part of your experiment.

> The numbers need to match up.

you want me to forfeit my rights.

> It's only a precaution.
> You're free to leave.

The hand snaked down. Drew the folder back.

> An unforgiving summer it is.

Corey's fingers tightened. With a soft chuckle the folder released back into his grasp and the doctor leaned closer. Fingertips carding through the dark rootlets of his hair. Voice sweeter than the flesh of overripe fruit.

> How long has it been since you last bathed?

A graze over his beltline. A familiar yet tainted touch. The stones leavened in his stomach and Corey fell earthly still.

> I can fill you with the seed of faith.
> And you will know no hunger.

what are you-
A drift closer. Grasping Corey's shoulders.

> How much more must you suffer?
> How often must you die for your sins?

He turned his jaw to face him.

> Your soul is in transition.
> Have faith in me.
> I can save you.
> I can make you whole.

Corey wrenched the hand away. Held it at length. The silver edge of the doctor's watch biting into the thin cloth over his palm.
men can't be saved.

> Saving is not done by man.

mm. and what are you?

> The will of God.

the will of god?
tempting.
but-
The doctor held the tip of his pen to his spreading lips. The weight of his father's jade beaded rosary sinking in his pocket. As the doctor watched he spoke, the heat of forty-two summers

burning shame into his skin.

    i don't need saving.

Taking his pen he bent over the desk, cut fresh into the parchment. And all the world was sealed in inkstain.

He was stripped of his remaining possessions. No unauthorized external communications. No unauthorized travel. A guest room had already been cleared out and Corey would be staying with him.
He didn't protest. Turgid sleep tugged at his head but even as he closed his eyes there was no slipping into dream.
Dr. Sykkes checked his wristwatch. Pretty mouth twisted into a small frown.
Unfortunately we don't have time for you to get settled just yet. We have a meeting to attend.
Corey pried himself from the desk. Fixed his sleeves. Cocked a brow.

    a meeting?

Yes. You ought to introduce yourself.
The doctor buttoned up his vest, gestured out the office.
Shall we?
A sigh. Corey followed his motion and wedged open the door.
The doctor drifted by. Eyes fixed to Corey's like a cat.
And Corey caught his arm.

    forgetting something?

The doctor seemed to be enjoying the contact.
Hmm?

    why am i here?

A thin smile. The doctor rolled his shoulders. Stared him down.
Murder.

    murder?

Dr. Sykkes brushed ahead.
Isabella Rivera. Twenty-four.
She was found stabbed to death a week ago.

    she have family?

We were her family.
They made their way across the lobby. Dr. Sykkes palmed the scanner, opened the front door. Corey watched him, the way he slipped by with an unreadable expression.

    what did the authorities find?

We don't have a centralized policing force.

    county sheriff?

As a company town we have earned a special sort of jurisdiction. Our business is our business. The involvement of external authorities, on the county, state, or federal level, is not required. We govern ourselves, and will handle the investigation ourselves. As was meant to be, in true American spirit.

you're stuck.

The doctor cut through the lawn. Walking so briskly he scrambled to catch up.

any witnesses?

No witnesses.

suspects?

We doubt that it was personal.

family?

We were her family.

but you ruled everyone out properly? alibis?

Ruth conducted a number of interviews. I trust her judgement. And Jacobi secured the scene. Conducted the forensic analysis.

they have the training for it?

I have full faith in their abilities.

faith can only get you so far.

A puff in the cold. Corey gathered his coat.

over half of murders go unsolved.
what makes you think i can do any better?

The Lord works in our favor.
Dr. Sykkes had slowed his pace. Watched Corey's face as he rolled up his sleeves.
The person responsible is still in town. I need your eyes.
Corey looked away. Fidgeted with his ring.

> you saw my track record, didn't you?

Compared to averages? You fare quite well.

> i got the wrong guy.

You did.
But it isn't about punishment, dear.
It's about healing. Prevention.
Corey scoffed.

> what does that mean?

What do you think that means? Healing?

> you're just gonna let them go, doc?

Of course not.
There just simply isn't a need for vengeance.

> so you're letting them off easy? for murder?

Do not put words in my mouth. I did not say that.
Healing is reconciliation. In healing you embrace the shadow and reconcile.

mm.

He scuffed the gravel under his boots.

so that's what this is? you're healing these people?

I see you've explored my early research.
Corey scoffed. Averted his eyes.

doctor wayne sykkes. famed neuroscientist and neurosurgeon. thinks he can cure sin.

we know it to be true because god came to him in a dream.

you're sick.

The doctor's smile faded. Gaze sharpened in dangerous hellfire.
Call me whatever you please. But I am not sick.
Corey only chuckled. Took in his surroundings. Cracked turfs and dry rotted porches. Trash left out to be collected torn open by rats.

you tell yourself that. but it's no wonder this place has gone to shit.
giving me a chance ought to be the biggest mistake of your life.

Hm.
Dr. Sykkes loosened his ascot. Smiled sweetly without a single hint of malice.
I'm sure you'll change your mind.

They had walked a mile's length across town. Started up an incline, where a high hill chapel sat. Gleaming white in the midday sun. A picturesque garden of pastels and prayers. Painted so bright he could see the dust scattered in the glare of it. At the steps were oaken doors with gold etched angels wings.
Just follow my lead.
Acquiesce with the people's wishes.
They'll be pleased to have your help, I'm sure of it. They just need to see how desperately we need a fresh pair of eyes.
Dr. Sykkes reached for the door. Corey nodded.

> sykkes.
> Doctor.
> doc.
> fix your helmet hair.

The doctor blinked at him over an extended arm. Hand hovering over the silver knob.

> Pardon?

Corey reached out. Ruffled the doctor's flattened mullet. The cloudy purple of the setting sun lit his glasses, painted his cheeks an early apple red.

> ...Thank you.

He yanked the door open. The red had worsened.

> Don't do that again.

Corey scoffed lightly and pushed past him.

The doors opened up into a hollow auditorium, wooden floors and dandelion walls, the muffled chatter of a hundred heads, scattered chairs scraping. At the front a ragged stage clothed in curtains a clotted red, the podium erected in the center like a pillar. White screens flashing lines from the hymnal choir. Be Thou my Wisdom, and Thou my true Word.
The doctor draped an arm over Corey's shoulder. Nodding to some familiar faces in the crowd as he flashed his brilliantly radiant smile. Corey watched a roach scuttle by with a blank expression. What he would give to bite a chunk out of him.
The speakers crackled. A man had risen to the edge of the podium. Crisp black silk over sand roughed skin and wisps of grey swirled brown. By the weight of the doctor's piercing hazel stare he raised a hand and the sea parted. Chattering choking into silence. All eyes set on the newcomers.
Ah, doctor.
His voice was resonant and warbly.
You're here.
Dr. Sykkes nodded.

    Afternoon, Shepherd.

The Shepherd's gaze landed on Corey. An admonishing look.
Is this poor little thing the reason for our meeting?
The doctor's hand slipped down.

    Yes.
    This is Mis-
corey.

Corey stepped forward. Thumbs in his belt loops. The Shepherd's face rang some semblance of familiarity in his head.

    nice to meet ya.

He caught the doctor's eyes in his peripherals. Elbowed him in a smooth motion concealed by the clasping of his hands behind his back.

    Hm.
    Yes.

A finger tapped his spine.

    This is Corey Handler Delgado. Former detective.

Detective?
The Shepherd straightened over the podium and met the doctor's gaze.
Is he here by your invitation?

    Yes.

    It was of executive opinion that we involve a trained third party investigator.

A laugh. It came from the Shepherd's stomach and leeched in their ears.
Correct me if I'm wrong but as I recall the town voted against hiring a private detective and this action goes well against the majority vote.
At the hush of murmurs Dr. Sykkes stepped forward. Pushed up

his glasses.

Considering the current state of the investigation I thought it necessary. Incidents such as these require extreme diligence and exigence and while I do not make such decisions lightly I always intend to act in the best interest of this town.

Well, doctor, I can't say the town is all too pleased.

Whichever way we may feel about it, the terms are clear-

Cops deserve to be shot.
The gruff voice came from a broad shouldered man with red boiled cheeks, rolled up sleeves and grease behind his ears.
Howdy doc.

... Howdy, Simeon.

Corey was it? Corre corre. Thought he'd be taller.
How do we know he ain't gonna stick his nose where it don't belong?
Corey shot a weathered scowl but Simeon didn't spare him a second glance. Dr. Sykkes tugged on his coattail like the end of a leash.

I will be monitoring his activities diligently to ensure that he acts within the realm of lawfulness and that no rights are violated.

I don't want you to think of him as an enforcer of

the law. He will be serving us within the capacity of a private investigator. He actually shares a similar past with the majority of us.

A survey of the unhappy faces. Simeon shrugged.
If that's what you think.
He had pulled out his pocket knife. Sheathing and unsheathing.
I suppose that's just how the doctor is.
Bet on losing dogs. Forgive sinful women.
Guess we'll have to make room for one more.
Though it don't look like he'll take too much...

Excellent.

The doctor smiled until it cut his cheeks.

I'm glad we could come to an agreement.

...Lust not after her beauty in your heart... neither let her take you with her eyelids...!
A graying woman raised a hand to speak. Dark brown skin a deep pine bark leather. She wore an eyepatch over a cataract and had the mean weathered look of a survivor.
Where's the capital coming from? Emergency fund?
The doctor withdrew. Clapped with enthusiasm.

Ruth. Yes. Excellent question. Thank you. Ehm...

He tilted his head into his hand.

I believe we will have to put a pause on the expansion into a ranch for the moment-

The auditorium bubbled to a clamor and drowned out his voice.
Corey passed an unamused look to the doctor, who looked pleadingly to the Shepherd. The Shepherd raised his blessing.
Have faith in your leaders.
The Lord has brought him to us.
Let us be tried.
He swept his gaze through the souls of his peoples. Simeon slunk back to his table and Ruth shook her head with a sigh. The doctor cleaning his glasses.
We welcome the lamb with open arms.
Teeth sharpened in shadow, the Shepherd extended a hand.
Come forth.
The people were watching. Making him conscious of his own breathing. When the doctor nudged him forward he took a doe step. And with one step taken it would look foolish to turn back.
As we end this period of mourning let us remember. Isabella's death serves as a warning. A warning for all of us.
He who is known as The Devil may come in many forms.
The Shepherd shackled firm the doctor's arm. Gaze set on Corey.
Evil has already claimed one soul.
Let us not lose yours.
Dr. Sykkes picked his hand from Corey's shoulder. The Shepherd took his place in the pulpit.
Let us formally christen a new member into our community.
Raising his blessing, the congregation followed.
O, Lord, we call upon thee, to begin the journey of the purification of the lamb. Here we ask that you, Corey Handler Delgado, confess and be reborn.
A spotlight enveloped him. Swallowed his eyes in fluorescent light. The wave of sleep jettisoned from his veins. Foamy and

dredging.

> what?

Dr. Sykkes watched from the shadowed edge of the circle. An ethereal beauty to him under that sickly yellow light. Like the pale death of consumption.
Confess, child.
The blood must be cleansed.
In this bath of light he knew without seeing that they were watching with unblinking eyes. Corey lowered his gaze and spoke from the dark ichor of his mind.

> your shepherd.
> job kaplin.
> he was sentenced to fifteen years wasn't he?
> yet here he roams free. all of you follow him.

Corey.

> you're all criminals.

The doctor pulled him. Down from his pedestal. Enough to splinter his arm. Still he couldn't see his face. Only a whisper.

> Everyone here is a prisoner under Bentham's privatized system. Everyone here has done something they regret.
>
> Including you.

Corey narrowed his eyes. A curl to his tongue.

you're delusional.
turning sinners into saints.
a girl is dead and you're playing god.
i'm not confessing anything.

Confess.

A wincing breath and he huffed. But the spore of guilt had seeded into the soft of his stomach, drained his skin to feed the foreign innards bonelocked inside.

i've got nothing to say.

The shadows watched. The doctor's looming closest. Lips unmoving.
You waste away on an empty street corner. Face hidden in shame.
You rot alone amongst soiled bed sheets. Eyes shut in fear of the truth.
You lie asleep in purgatory. Soul forever damned.
Is it easier for you to keep yourself shut to The Lord?
Corey's mind blocked the words from registering in his head, stunned him out of jumping awake. And the voices only continued, slight and whispery under his ear.
You are weak.
Confess.
Confess from your mind. Confess from your lips. Confess from your heart.
A ceiling full of light. Corey shut his eyes. Felt for his rosary, a tribute to filial shame. All he had to do was confess, confess for them to judge and they'd leave him to his own misery.

i tried to kill a man.

Silence lapped his ears. Compelled him to speak out of the guilt gorged in his throat. He huffed and with it his shoulders sagged.

    is that what you wanted?

The devil is in you!
Lord, save his soul!
The Shepherd's hiss shocked him into his senses. Vicious spittle from his teeth. Corey stumbled back. Dr. Sykkes firm behind him. Pressed against a wall, and the shadows loomed with fists full of stones. The doctor hushed low over his shoulder.

    You haven't confessed everything, have you?

Fingers twisted into his hair. Pushed him down to his knees. The Shepherd's cry split his ears and the stewards wailed, heat and flesh converging in a spiral, a cocoon of warm bodies and snug arms, one beating, breathing mass, crying and mewling in unison.
The purging flood is upon us.
They raised a basin over him. Gold and sloshing and incensual.
We thank thee, O Lord, for answering the prayers of those under the altar. The unclean lamb shall be reborn. The unclean lamb shall be delivered from evil.
The basin tipped. Drenched skin in perfumed oil. Thick and slippery and clinging. Nails drove his head into the floor, shadows pressing until he choked.
An explosion of glass. Corey jerked upwards, threw his elbows, smashed the Shepherd's nose.

02 | of the lamb

Blood dripped from the Shepherd's fingers, seeped into the cracks in the chapel's foundation. The congregation watched and breathed in silence. A trail of glass cut across the wooden floor and in the shadowed corner lay the little body of a dead mourning dove, open eyed and stiff.
The doctor had Corey pinned by the shoulders, fragmented light filtering in from the broken window over his head. Binding the wrist of the offending hand in his grip. Shallow breaths, oiled droplets falling from his silver hair. And the Shepherd bellowed.
He! He is a demon possessed messenger of Satan!
You, doctor, you have disobeyed the word and you have lost your way!

    i'm sorry,

Dr. Sykkes clamped Corey's mouth shut.

    I sincerely apologize.

The Shepherd laughed. The townspeople parted from the two of them.
You have deceived us.

    I have deceived no one.

You hide your machinations and bring taint into this house.

    Taint?

A glint in his lenses and the doctor's hazel eyes smoldered.

Is he not deserving of salvation?

How can he be saved if he does not let grace into his heart? The sick one denies anointment as a thirsty fool turns away water. Corey struggled beneath him. Dr. Sykkes kept him pinned.

I apologize for the detective's behavior.

However, by principle, I believe him to be deserving of a second chance.

Healing takes time. He has much to recover from. I beg of you to show mercy. Just as you were given.

He will bare his soul, I swear it.

C'mon, Job.
A woman with dark hair drawn back, a gentle smile and sunny brown skin. Shirt printed in tropical flowers. She guided feet away from the shards, a broom handle in her grasp. Sweeping the mess away.
Give him a chance.
The Shepherd shut his eyes, drew a wincing breath. Leaning against Simeon for support.
The Lord tests us.
Let us be tried.
He dismissed them with a hand, holding a rag to his nose, and the eyes of the congregation shied away.
The woman in the tropical shirt approached, passed a towel into the doctor's hands. He murmured to her before seizing Corey's

hand and dragging him out.

> Thank you, Jacobi.

Dr. Sykkes pulled Corey up to a wall. The detective had expected to see anger in the man's face. Towel clenched in his fist. But instead the doctor held him. Soothed him. Pressed the wool over his eyes, wiped the warm oil from his warm skin. He looked more gentle tempered without his glasses. That soft hazel. Muttering to himself. Judas wears the frock of Job.
The back door blew open and a bag hit the foot of the dumpster. Through the film of plastic he could still see, under the Bentham branding stamped over the bag, the open eyes of the dead dove. At Corey's switch Dr. Sykkes paused, the cloth over his cheek.

> Pay no mind to them.

He turned his face back to him.

> They are only startled by recent events.
> Which is why I need you. To clear things up.
> You can do that, can't you?

Corey scoffed.

> i just punched your pastor in the face.
> You were overwhelmed.
> maybe i should punch you next.
> You're getting defensive.

He tilted his chin up. Cleaning around his neck.

Do you not want this case?

i've already fucked up, haven't i? it'd be stupid to keep me around.

You didn't mean to hurt anyone. You admitted that much. Which demonstrates remorse and a possibility for self improvement.

they don't even want me here.

I want you here.

Corey huffed and stopped his hand from dabbing his cheek.

so, what, am i cleansed now? or do i gotta go through another scary ritual?
It is entirely symbolic. True development occurs within.
good little ratlings, are they? you drug them, get them hooked on faith.
On the contrary. They are here because they want to get better.

A wipe over his cheek.

So are you.

Corey looked away. Felt for his rosary. The doctor continued wiping, as though to learn every plane of the detective's face. But the moment the doctor reached Corey's smokey eyes the detective slapped his hand away. And the doctor latched closer.

Why do you wear that?

Corey raised a brow.

just eyeliner.
You shouldn't present yourself in such a deceitful manner.
it's makeup.
I'd prefer to meet people as the Lord fashioned them.

Corey tossed his fluff of hair, flashed a studded ear.

like what you see?
Hardly.
then stop looking at me.
Hey! Everything alright?
Dr. Sykkes straightened and took a step back. The woman in the tropical shirt had popped her head out the door. A shrug and a sympathetic look.
Bit of a rough introduction, eh?
Lighten up! A little attempted murder never killed anyone.
Voices raised from inside the chapel. The doctor sighed.

Jacobi. How are they faring?

You can probably tell by the sound of it.
A grumble in his throat.

He knows what my answer will be.

Then let him hear it. C'mon. Let's talk it over.

Jacobi took Dr. Sykkes by the arm.
Be back in a minute!
And the doctor left him one final command before being swept away.

    Behave.

Corey watched as they got out of earshot, leaned back against the wall, a hand through his hair. Slick to the roots with anointing grease. A great discomfort seeded in his skin, blistered cold in the wind. The lick of a thousand tongues and they all stung.
What did it matter? He bares his soul. They tell him that everyone deserves forgiveness. But it is only after they judge him with their eyes that they satisfy themselves with an illusion. He confesses to dig at the earth packed over his head, it falls from the ceiling and crushes him, nothing but a small disturbance in the dusk, nature deep aslumber. Still yet he dreams of tasting the rain. He does. It floods his crypt and bloats his flesh on sewage and ash. The body rises again, the soul does not.
A thump drew his eyes to the foot of the dumpster. The plastic bag, jumping, writhing. The thing inside smearing clotted blood under the plastic film.
Corey stepped closer. Pinned the bag down with the toe of his boot. It continued to flail. A gurgle from its throat.
He got to his knees. Counted its jumps. Applied some old napkins under his gloves. Unraveled the knot at the top of the bag. Bone and feather mass bumped under his palms. Screamed. It bit his thumb and he shot down the bag and out from the bag whipped a shadow sleek and featherless. It thunked a branch, fell

straight into the thicket. Tumbled down the hill and into the maw of the forest. Leaves shivering.
He stared after it. Rose to his feet. In a stupor he tossed the napkins, the bag full of feathers. Felt over his gloves. His skin was intact but his heart wouldn't stop pacing.
The door swung open behind him.
Hey! All good there?
Wide eyes. He avoided Jacobi's gaze. Pinched his fingers.

> fine.
> where's the doctor?

A shout from inside. Jacobi apologetically closed the door.
Busy.
It's okay. I'll be taking care of you now.
She edged closer. Smile faltering. His brown skin had gone ashy.
You look a little pale.
A small sigh. Her gentle tone reminded him a bit of his sister. Motherly without the sting of expectation but wholly understanding. Corey slowly met her gaze. Grounded himself in the familiar brown of her eyes.

> i'm okay.
> thank you.

A pat over his head. Unfortunately she was taller than him.
The strength of the Lord be with you.
She put on her shades. Late in the afternoon and the sun had already set.
Welp. We ought to get going. Before the doctor comes out fuming.

She walked a slow and even pace. Corey kept beside her. Even in this cold she favored cargo shorts.

> you know the doctor well?

Well enough.
A short chuckle. Nudging her sunglasses.
The man was on a mission.
Got me out of a really bad place.
I owe him a lot.
A brow raise. Corey considered it. The grime of his skin and the hunger he'd known before. Sweet temptations in his ear.

> if it weren't for his voice i never would've believed it was him.

Tell me about it.
And to think Kass agreed to fund it. Pretty radical.
Corey had to laugh. Dry in his throat.

> how stupid. but i wouldn't expect any less from the likes of kassiel more and wayne sykkes.

Jacobi arched a brow.
They're eccentric for sure, but I wouldn't call them stupid.

> you're all criminals. no shit someone got killed.

Everyone here is trying to do better. Have an open mind.
And, for the record, you've probably got the worst charge out of all of us.

    really.
    what did you do?

Jacobi grinned.
Had a run in with ATF.
Not my smartest moment, I will say.

    seriously?

Yep. Squibbed. My gun exploded.
She waggled her fingers, pointed upwards.
All he's looking for is faith and devotion. Each and every one of us, he looked inside and saw worthiness.
A puff. Corey looked away, traced the horizon. The fog rolling in between the mountains.

    why was isabella here?

Belle?
Belle was a survivor.
Bentham gave her new life.

    took her life too.

Halfway across town was the hospital, Bentham General. Unblemished stone that towered. Jacobi led him inside, took him to the second floor, the elevator. Quiet all the way up. When the doors slid open Jacobi made down the hall.
The doctor told you, right? I handled forensics. Not the most qualified. But I suppose I'm the closest we've got.

    not the most qualified?

Took some courses. Shadowed a guy.
Jacobi unlocked a closet. Repurposed into evidence storage.
Listen, we were pressed for time and- Bentham's on its own, y'know? I was careful, came in with my gear, documented everything.

   right.

In the cabinet was a folder. She handed it to him, a nod.
Took a bunch of photos.
Autopsy found a bruise from a workplace related incident, and that stab wound there. Probably done with a kitchen knife. Couldn't find anything in the vicinity though. Spatter pattern in the grass confirms it was pulled out. Returned westwards.
She was dragged and dumped. From where, we're not sure. Last seen at Ruth's store, just at the edge of her time of death window. No prints. But we found a good chunk of DNA under her nails. No flags on CODIS though.
Oh, and hair. Short gray hairs. But it matched Pal's cat, so we ruled that out.
Corey held the folder open. The girl was laid out in the grass amongst the trees. Arms spread. Buried in the underbrush.
In death her skin rusted like daylilies. A gash cut down from the silver cross on her pendant, bled from her pink top into the folds of her dress shirt. Staring up into the sky. A crown of reeds twisted into the curls of her hair. Flowers pressed to her lips. Lavender in color, soaked in red. Isabella Rivera. Only twenty four.

   what's that in her mouth?

Hyssop. We have some growing in the chapel garden. It was submerged in a wine, very mildly aged, with traces of natural resin.
And there were lipids in her wound.
Corey closed the folder. There was a dove in the corner of the widest photo. Head at an odd angle.

> she was crucified.
> myrrh and balsam.
> ritual murder.
> they anointed the blade. posed her body. dressed her up.

Ritual sacrifice, detective?

> religion is irrational.

He thumbed the paper edge.

> was belle a holy person?

Tried to be. She went to church. Participated in the youth group. Worked a stable job with Simeon. Even took the cure, when it got too much for her.

> what did she do?

I suppose she'd lie about things. Make stuff up. Be too loud. And maybe a few affairs.

> far from a saint in their eyes.

A short scoff and he shook his head.

    i don't think this is in mockery of her.

He set the folder down.

    no, not mockery.
    disrespect doesn't look like this.
    mockery doesn't look like this.
    easing her to rest? cleansing her skin? this is veneration. obsession.

Well, we swabbed her skin. Didn't find anything unusual.

    of course not. water and a rag wouldn't leave any residue.
    but there's dirt on her. in her hair. everywhere but her face.
    you die, you shed tears, your makeup runs.
    so they wiped her face. as clean as they could.
    but they missed the corners of her eyes.
    she died. almost as the lord fashioned her.

Faith doesn't drive someone to murder. It's against Scripture. Everyone here knows this.

    you have to accept that someone in town did it.
    and by the looks of it, it was someone in your congregation.
    using faith as a shield.
    sanctification mirroring obsession.

That doesn't narrow it down much. We're a God fearing town.

> someone cared enough to kill her.
> to think it and succeed.

Corey took out the phone Dr. Sykkes had given him.

> i have your contact?

Everyone's in the directory, yep.

> suppose i should speak with ruth next.

A nod.
Ruth knows Belle's network the best. Handled the interviews. But she's probably gone home by now. Or out on patrol. Hopefully she'll be in a better mood by tomorrow morning. You can probably find her at her grocer store. Or the garden.

> i don't want to have to justify myself to her.

Listen, detective.
She loved Belle like a daughter.
Didn't sleep for a week.
You can understand then, how she felt, when the doctor took things over without consulting her. She wants to trust you. But we don't know you.

> i understand.

They meant it, you know. Baring your soul. You need to earn our trust.

A short smile and he tucked his hands behind his back.

> who else was belle close to?
> you mentioned a youth group?

Dani. Her roommate.
She hasn't left her home since. Ruth's been delivering groceries for her.
I'd recommend giving her time. Let her come to you. I'm sure Ruth's told her about you by now.

> i'll keep that in mind.

With a gesture Jacobi led him downstairs. Offered to walk him home. He shook his head.

> i know my way.

You sure?

> yep.

Uhuh.
She spoke again. Slowly.
You sure sure?

> yep.

It's not safe out there. I mean, what if something happens-

> i'll be fine.

Alright.

Jacobi clapped his shoulder.
Just keep an eye out. Stay safe. Stay out of trouble.
Don't be afraid to call. Anything you need.
I'm always here, should you come looking for me.
You'll figure it all out.

    thank you.

He smiled softly. Starting to miss his sister.

    i'll tell the doctor you walked me.

He pushed through the doors, out into the cold night. Bumped straight into someone, tall and unflinching.
The white coat over her shoulders told him she was a doctor. Skin a fair weathered aspen, a light scar over her brow and choppy brown hair. She smiled brightly.
Jacobi in there?
A nod.
She moved to pass but turned. Eyes narrowed and sparkling.
You're the detective Wayne hired aren't you?
Corey, right? I'm Dr. Miranda Olliver.
He shook her hand. It was firm and he was stupid.

    hi.

How's Wayne doing?

    wayne?
    he's fine.

Ah. I see.

Some first day, huh? How was the ceremony? I heard it didn't go so well.

    not really.

Tell me about it.
Always freaked me out.
He must have been standing and staring too rigidly because she laughed and relaxed her shoulders so that she towered slightly less over him. Fidgeting with her carabiner of keys.
Is this at all what you expected? I bet Wayne didn't tell you much coming in.

    no, he didn't.
    you know him well?

I've known him since childhood.
What do you think of his cure?
A smile. It didn't reach her eyes.
I don't like it. One bit.
Corey nodded slowly. Shifted where he stood, tried to make himself taller. Dr. Sykkes had the poise of a snake. Dr. Olliver seemed capable of razing cities.

    i don't think it works.

If it does?

    i don't know.

You don't know?
Dr. Olliver let the door close behind her. Leaned down to face

him.
That feeling in your gut? Remember that.
That's exactly why it's wrong.
Her eyes didn't flinch under his gaze.

> you don't agree with him?

No. I don't.
I've been trying to get testimonies. Proof. That his cure hasn't been working.

> what have you found?

Not enough.
I was close with Belle. Tracking her progress.
It wasn't taking.

> it wasn't?

No. It was killing her. And everyone here knows it.

> could the cure failing be the reason why belle was murdered?

I don't know. It's possible. She had a lot of eyes on her.

> all the eyes in the world. all they see is divine judgement.

Dr. Olliver looked around for a moment. Shifted to whisper in his ear.
Listen. I need you to do something for me.

> yes?

He's put you on the case instead.
I didn't have a chance with Ruth, but I might have a chance with you.
Keep an eye out. Take notes. Anything that proves the cure isn't working.

> how do i know who's on the cure and who isn't?

You don't. Wayne doesn't disclose who sees him. I'm only working with the few that get outed.

> outed?

Made a community concern. Job pushes him to do it. They have a ceremony, hold meetings. He keeps it confidential otherwise.
I suppose he chose the perfect victims. Desperate people.
They worship the cure. Worship it.
So far it's just been Belle who hasn't been taking.
And me, I suppose.

> you?

I asked him to do it. Didn't work. Messed me up.

> he didn't stop?

I didn't tell him.
And now he's about to make the biggest mistake of his life.
She met his eyes.
You signed the contract?

>sort of.

Sort of?
He took out a napkin. Scribbled over it.

>corey handler. right?

... Yeah?

>now squint a little.

Oh.
Dr. Olliver swiped her brow and grinned.
Clever.

>he had no idea.

I like you.
Corey's short smile quirked downwards when his pocket buzzed.
Dr. Olliver chuckled knowingly.
That Wayne?

>yep.

I should let you go then.
Need to catch up with Jacobi anyways.

>right.

She pushed the door open.
Stay safe.
I'm in my office if you ever need anything.

Keep this between us.

    i will.

A smile. Miranda gave him one last wave before receding into the hospital. Cracks in the wall.
Corey dug his hands into his pockets and started walking.

The night was louder than the evening. Singing crickets and the rustle of the wind. A screech. Owl or feline.
A short distance away from the clinic and the lamp ahead of him lit up. Moths gathered below. Shadows quivered.
He stopped in his tracks. Tracing the circle of light. It shouldn't have turned on. Not at this distance.
A step back. Reaching for a gun he didn't have. He bumped against something like stone. Something too fingerlike to be a branch. It moved. He spun to face it and was cut down by a sharp blow to the head.
His back bit the gravel. He crawled. Clawed his way up the steps with his hands to jostle the door knob beat on the metal door press the scanner but the cold red of denial seared the nerves of his eyes and he dropped his hands. Easy answers don't come to godless men.
A fistful of hair and they dragged him through the dirt. Drowned his pupils until all he could see was burned disks and masked faces whispering.
He tore away. Tendrils ripping from his skin. Scaled to the top of a lightpost. Clung against the slip of his gloves until his vision adjusted and he looked down below from his heightened adrenaline.

The shadows had vanished.
From the bushes watched a single mask. A red twisted caricature floating over nothing. And the whispers solidified in his mind like wax.
A bird knocked him from the pole. Body impacting concrete. Bone splintering into open flesh. He watched himself bleed. A slow drip feed appeasing the hunger of the earth. Each drop carried away by the undercurrent of his mind, the hush of a thousand damned. One thought from which everything spiraled, an empty darkness of blackened stars, and the thing inside him stirred.
Sand Prince.

03 | water and a rag

Corey bit him. Hard.
The doctor had only been testing Corey's range of motion, his sensations. Hovering close, bending the other's gloved fingers. Trembling Corey leapt in a gritted scream, clamped down on his shoulder. The doctor pushed him back down, muzzled him.
Hold still, please-
A whine like a wounded mutt but at the doctor's tightening grip he kept still. After a thorough examination they carried him to the hospital where Dr. Olliver pumped him full of anesthetics, picked clean his mangled arm, and sent him home with a splint and a diagnosis for osteoporosis. Brittle bones at age forty-two.
He was lucky that Ruth had found him, unlucky that the patrolmen had missed him entirely on their rounds, coming in only too late. Dr. Sykkes had been none the wiser, only peeking his head out when Ruth shouted. Rushed to the detective's side, half conscious in the dirt.
Dr. Sykkes carried Corey back to the clinic. Too tired to wash and unable to think he collapsed into bed. Sunk into a dark room where his eyes burned and when he rubbed and rubbed out came grits behind his eyes and his skull dissolved into sand.
The detective jolted straight, heaving breaths and heated skin, sweat and a tremor. The doctor hovering over him in the dark. Piercing hazel eyes. He'd left his glasses on his nightstand.
Darling.
Corey tilted his head up at him, a thick swallow. His eyeliner hadn't budged in the slightest and the wallpaper was covered in

spinning rats.

 wayne...?

A small sigh. Wayne sat. Didn't correct him.
You were making disturbances in your sleep.
How is your arm?

 numb.

Corey shifted. Eyes tracing over the other. One side of the doctor's shirt hung open. It slipped down to his elbow, exposed his chest. A bandage stuck over the edge of his collarbone. Corey's doing.

 how's your shoulder?

Wayne gathered up his shirt.
Good.
Thankfully you have a small mouth.
The wound wasn't too deep.
Corey averted his eyes. Even in the dark the doctor could see him smiling.

 couldn't get inside. the door was locked.

Yes. I apologize.

 really ought to give me the key or something.

I understand your concern, but that is something I cannot do. The operations here are very delicate. I have yet to properly integrate you into the town functions.

> so i'm your prisoner.

You are not.

> everyone else is.

He glanced at the clock. Early morning.

> do i at least get something to defend myself?

I am not arming you with a lethal weapon.

> how am i supposed to be in a western if i don't have a gun.

Shoot with your mouth, dear.

> looks like i did just that.

When the other failed to entertain a response Corey leaned even closer, right into his ear. Grinning like the devil.

> maybe i should sneak into your bedroom.
> nab the pistol you keep under your pillow.

Wayne gave no reply, though his nose twitched, not unlike a rabbit's.
If you wish to withdraw I understand completely.
A huff. The glint in the other's eyes made his stomach tighten like a fist. Corey pulled back.

not the type to back out.

Hm.
Wash up. The sun hasn't risen yet. I'll fix you something to eat.
He rose to his feet. Paused. Raised his brows.
Oh dear.
A hand fell to Corey's shoulder.
You're bleeding.
A glance down at the mattress. Splotches of red in the bedding bunched between his ankles.
Corey looked up. A girl in white stared back at him from the doorway.
He snatched the bloodied covers and ran to the bathroom. The tiled room behind the door choked of incense and mirrors and like most men Corey was afraid of his own reflection.
Instead he kept his eyes down, inspected himself. The source of the bleed. His mangled arm.
Throwing the blanket, he peeled off his clothes and knelt over the tub. Scrubbed out the blood stains with his one good arm. When that was done he held himself under the lukewarm water. Wincing as his skin washed of week old sweat.
A basket of feminine products sat next to the towels and sticks of myrrh. He entertained a number of reasons. Dried off and unwrapped one.
He didn't need the doctor's help. Wayne had left him clothes at the foot of the door but that was it. The white blouse clung to his skin in tapers and aspirations but it was designed like a casket. It fit his frame far too neatly because it wasn't meant to be lived in. The doctor on the other hand was pleased to know his measurements had been exact. Even more pleased that breakfast

this morning was deep fried grilled cheese sandwiches. Corey found him in the kitchen, perched at a small dining table of dark polished wood, hand lingering over his holy scripture. Two plates in front of him. Frames crooked atop his sharp nose.
Everything alright, dear?
The detective watched the doctor, his cool demeanor. Fixed his glasses for him, slid into a chair.

 just some stitches that popped open.

A head tilt.
May I see?

 it's fine. stopped bleeding.

Hm.
Well, if it does start bothering you again, you can come to me or Dr. Olliver.

 right.

Corey ruffled his drying hair. Eyes on the sandwich. He was used to going hungry but it was taking his last shred of dignity not to devour the plate entirely. A soft chuckle and the doctor made the slightest adjustments to the placement of his utensils.
You have permission to eat, you know.
We could say grace.
The doctor before him sat polite and kittenlike with a smile.
Unfortunately, I'm out of lemon bars-
Wronged by far too many pigeons Corey crammed the deep fried grilled cheese sandwich into his mouth. The doctor had

only blinked once.
With delicate fingers Wayne cut a bite from his sandwich. The dining room had nothing of interest to focus on so Corey stared at him. Straight into his eyes.
The other smiled uncomfortably enough to get him talking. Kicking his legs up on the table.

>six degrees in six years.
>you seem to know a lot.

A slow nod. With more finesse than necessary the doctor pushed Corey's boots off the table. Corey let him.
I've thought of an answer to everything.

>so. who's the murderer?

I can't say without all the facts.
But my opinion is that it was a mercy killing.

>why do you say that?

The people here are not hateful. They are merciful.

>still killed her.

Corey rolled the red cloth napkin between his fingers.

>your cure drive someone insane or something?

>maybe you paid out the review board, and then the cia stuck their fingers in it.

A waxy smile. Corey noticed his slightly crooked teeth. The doctor kept his eyes.
I didn't take you as someone who jumps to conclusions.

>i tried to kill an innocent man, remember?

The doctor pushed closer. Voice low.
I have discovered the cure for original sin. To separate the mind from the flesh. *Divinity*. No matter what you say or do, it is His will, not mine.

>forcing people to become something they're not?

Wayne looked away and Corey leaned back. Tapping the table top. He could picture, all the things he'd do to those silver waves.

>the soul rots. habits fester.
>they have no one to blame but themselves.

I am not giving up on them.

>i'm willing to bet your cure doesn't work.

>people aren't that simple.

>god sent a great flood but sin still lingered. nothing ever washes away completely. man leaves behind his ghosts.

>i don't believe in second chances, wayne. especially not the kind you're selling.

It's Doctor. I believe I've earned the respect.

    no you haven't, sunshine.

The doctor licked his teeth. Leaned over to whisper.
Why are you here, dove?

    why am i here?

Here. Working this case. If you detest yourself so.
A man who doesn't believe in second chances has no reason to rise come morning.

    i'm selfish.
    i think i own the truth.

Then you admit you don't.

    i own some of it.

    it's all abstraction. everything is what you make of it.
    nothing makes sense.

Oh. Corey.
Wayne chuckled softly and pulled away. Lenses glinting in the light.
The truth is rather simple.
You regret it, don't you? You're here because you're hopeful.
Because Bentham is hope.

    hope?

Corey lunged over the table until his teeth were at the doctor's throat.

> i hate you, wayne. i hope you know that.

Wayne tilted his head. Still nibbling on the cut of sandwich stuck to his fork. The scarcest tremble.
And here I sit and contemplate, the things I've done to deserve your hate.

> it's your fault.
> it's all your fault.
> i tried to kill a man.
> i tried to kill a man and it's your fault.

Corey snatched the fork from Wayne's hand.

> gregory moorhirsch.

> you know how it went.

> at least on paper.

> i went after him. hit my head. woke up finding i lost my job and my freedom.

I'm sorry the system wronged you.
As I understand you were kept apart from other incarcerated persons as a protective measure.
Corey had the other caged between his arms.

> that's a nice way to spell solitary confinement.

I'm sorry.

> five fucking years.
> all that time just thinking.
> i never would've been in that situation if it weren't for you.

The doctor's eyes were averted. Corey didn't care.

> do you even know what you did?

Please. Explain to me and I will listen without judgement.

> funny you say that.

He leaned over until the doctor couldn't turn away.

> some big wig was pushing a bill. they wanted your opinion. you gave it to them. it was the wrong opinion but they still signed it into law.
>
> the kid that got killed?
>
> he was forced to do terrible things to pay for his care.
>
> you're the reason he ended up in a dumpster.
>
> you're the reason the hunt even started.
>
> i've hated you since.

Hesitation. The doctor spoke slow and quiet.
At the beginning of our discussion you said these choices were a

matter of character. That we have no one to blame but ourselves. Yet here you are now saying you blame me.

    never said i wasn't mad at him too.
    never said i didn't blame myself.

You shouldn't.

    you should.

Corey looked out into the foyer. Grinned nice and close.

    dr. wayne sykkes.
    the religious freak on tv with the hair and the smooth talking.
    never expected to find you at my cell door.

The doctor stared into him a long while before breaking into a nervous smile.
Oh?

    it was insulting.

Insulting?

    poking your fingers in the kennel and saying oh ma i want that one.
    as if your charity could ever fix the sorry state of the pound.
    you put me in there. you did.
    when you should've been in there right beside me.

Wayne clasped the top button of his shirt.
I truly wished to see you, darling.
There is a drought of strong will in this modern age. Despite your mistakes your choices demonstrated strong will.
Corey reached out and popped it open again.

> you'll find that my strong will bends the wrong way.
> i wonder, how your will bends.

The doctor met his gaze with such softness it felt undeserved.
You admire me so intensely.
Like a dove.

> and you're eating a cheese sandwich with a fork and a knife.

The detective picked himself off of the doctor's lap. Trotted down to the lobby. Tried the door. It wouldn't budge.
The doctor's voice swung down from above.
You'll need my fingerprints, dove.
Corey grumbled and the other took his leisurely time down the staircase. Pressed his palm to the scanner with a lazy smile.
You're seeing Ruth, I take it? You can find her at her grocery store. Can't miss it. There's always a line.

> thanks.

Behave.
Don't get into trouble.
Corey tilted his head and fluttered his lashes.

> want a kiss goodbye?

The door swung open. Before the detective could depart the doctor took his arm.
May the Lord guide you lest he lay his penance.
A huff. Corey pulled his arm away. Set backwards, eyes on the other.

    pray for yourself first, sunshine.

He returned to the scene of the crime. Sketched it out on some old napkins. The tree had lovers carved into it. M+A. S+I. B+D. Beyond that there was nothing he missed from the photos. The dead dove was gone. A black and silver cat hissed from the bushes. Tore a hole in his sleeve.
Ruth's grocery store was just a short walk from the clinic. She wasn't there. Turns out she was in the garden behind the chapel. A clearing that bled into the forest. Full of wild overgrowth. She knelt at the roots of a chestnut tree. Sifting through seeds. She spoke without looking up.
Handler.

    ruth welles.

I know.
A flower was woven into one of her gray braids. A lily. She raised to her feet, gestured.
Quite the fall.

    was hoping you saw something.

A sigh. She took off her gloves, stuck her hands in her pockets.

Didn't see a thing.
Was between the hospital and the clinic. Didn't even hear you hit the ground.
Thank God the doctor was right there.

    mm.

Corey nodded.

    he didn't know until you called him?

Nope. Looked plenty surprised. I swear he's in his own damn world sometimes.

    need to follow up with everyone else on the patrol.

He retrieved another old napkin from his coat. Clicked his pen.

    could i get their names?

Ruth raised her brows at his sorry state.
Sure.
Simeon Turner. Paladin More. Kraig Cephas Gersch.
Didn't see a thing either.
You ain't suspecting them are ya?
Corey gave her a smile.

    can't rule out the possibility.

Ruth smiled back.
Don't think we didn't hear what you said about us.
We fought long and hard to get where we are now. Don't forget

that.

    i didn't mean any disrespect-

Want to know what I got caught for? Contraband. Did plenty worse on the reservation.
You gonna give me trouble for that?

    no ma'am.

Desperate people don't have the luxury of choosing.
You only turn to the devil when you feel God has turned on you.
Bentham is proof the light of the Lord still burns.
Corey tilted his head.

    you believe in god?

God is survival.
Wyoming births strong women, Handler. God and Wyoming made me strong.
Corey looked away. Saw a single headstone in the distant edge of the clearing. A statue praying over it like an angel.

    could you tell me about belle?

A small sigh. Ruth led him down the path to Belle's grave. Adorned in flowers and covered by the silhouette of a great chestnut tree. The marble statue bore her face. She was the sleeping angel.
Ruth busied herself with the bushes and shrubs at the statue's feet.
Job commissioned the statue. Kraig carved it. Didn't sleep for

days. Just chipping, chipping, chipping. I could hear him, crying.
I cried with him.
We all loved her, detective.
We all wanted what was best for her.

    but not everyone was happy with her.

Hate the sin. Love the sinner.
We tried. Lord knows we tried. But what can be done, when a girl becomes unmanageable?

    you tear off her wings.

Ruth shook her head. Gathered red berries in her palm.
Belle got herself killed.
All she had to do was act proper. All she had to do.
She dropped the berries onto the headstone. Grabbed a rock.
Now I gotta worry about my other girls.
They have me concerned, you know?
The Lilies, they had enough to deal with. Proving themselves to the world.
And she had to come in and ruin it all. That girl, she-
A pound onto stone. The red berries scattered and fractured.
After all the chances she was given.
Another hit.
After all that.
Another.
She was so close.
Another.
So damn close.
The stone was cracking in her fist.

And they done took it away.
The stone shattered. Ruth didn't seem to notice.
They done took my girl away.
She had rendered the berries into a smear of red paste. Blotting out Belle's date of death.
Things weren't okay before she died, detective.
She was struggling.
Struggling hard.
She hit me plenty. Tore up the garden.
Nothing would help her.
The cure was her last hope.

    it didn't take.

It was going to. I know it. If she had more time she would've-
Ruth rose to her feet.
Chokecherries.
She explained.
They're poisonous unless you prepare them right.
Belle loved the jam I'd make for her.
A wipe at her eyes. It choked him cold.
Dammit. God damn it.

    are you sure- i can come back later-

No. You listen to me, detective.
She only continued after he met her eyes.
I spoke to Simeon. Dani. Everyone in between. No way any of them could've done it. Last person to see her was me, at my store. That's all I could find. I am praying to God that your eyes will see differently. That the Lord Himself will guide you.

dani.

The name burst from his mouth before he could stop it.

i need to speak to her.

You leave Danielle out of this.
She's grieving. I'm grieving. You wait for her to come to you. You hear me?

yes ma'am.

Now. You let the chokecherries dry. Don't touch em.

yes ma'am.

One last thing. You ask the doctor why the shipment's late again. It's damn pissing me off.

yes, ma'am.

Ruth rubbed her face and left Belle's grave before the tears got ugly. Left hyssop in her wake.
Corey stayed where he was under that chestnut tree. Sunk his boots into the rot and trash. Wads of paper eaten up by wetness and mold. Folded up into stars. Being the sentimental type he was he stuck some in his pocket. Knelt down to curl up with Belle's monument.
He needed to talk to Dani.

Hey!

A girl in her twenties, sepia brown skin and dark hair braided over her shoulders. She wore a pink bell sleeved top and jeans. Smiled and waved as she ran up to the detective.

    Saw you pick up those paper stars.

He gave a slow nod. Hands still in his pockets. There was something off about her. He couldn't place what.

    yes?
    Belle made them. Did you know that?
    i didn't know.
    i'll put them back.
    No! Keep em. Sorry.
    You're the detective right? Saw you talking to Ruth.
    I'm Lee. Lee Palomo.
    lee.

Corey shook Lee's hand. Soft but firm.

    nice to meet you.

Lagging behind Lee were two others, waving to Ruth. A girl with dark skin a sapphire umber wearing a black vest over white dress, and a blonde boy with gold hair and pale ivory skin under a baby blue button up. Essie and Pal.
The girl in the dress curtsied.
Essie Easley. G'day.
The boy flashed a smile and a shrug. Fixing his black satin tie.
Pal More.

    mm.

Pal chuckled.
Lee. Are you bothering the detective?
Lee smiled brightly, shook her head.

> Nope, I just think he has questions.

She flicked her eyes to him.

> I hope Ruth mentioned us. We're the Lilies. We all knew Belle.

you were friends?

Essie brushed off the edge of her skirt.
Well. Closest thing to it at least.
We want to help. Any way we can.
Pal had his hands in his pockets. A solemn bow of his head.
I prayed for her every day.
Well Pal you pestered her every day too.

> And me! No good morning, just straight to verses and repenting! Gosh, Pal.

Listen, you need faith for the cure to take. If she had been more faithful-
Corey smiled politely as he often did with girls but as Pal spoke Essie's eyes narrowed and she raised her voice.
No. The cure wasn't good for her. She was fine before the doctor tried fixing her.
Essie. She wasn't fine and you know it. Refusing to leave the house, screaming, hitting people. That wasn't her. The doctor was trying to help her. You need to have more faith in Him.

Who got her there? Dr. Sykkes is a sham. He kept saying it would work. It didn't. It only made her worse. You think she was happy, locking herself in her room?
I know it wasn't pretty. But he was in the middle of calibrating it. Which is hard to do when the soul isn't willing. Weak faith is why Isabella died.
She was murdered. All you did was make her miserable.
Pal looked just about to cry. Essie's face softened and she held out her hands.
I didn't mean-
No, you're right, I should've tried harder. It's my fault, my fault, she didn't-
Pal stumbled off. Essie chased after him. Lee took some steps after them before turning to him apologetically.

>Sorry about that.

He was used to it.

>essie said the cure wasn't working?
>Well. The doctor kept saying he was calibrating it.
>No way to know now.

A frown and Lee shrugged. Picking at the pink hem of her shirt.

>I don't think Belle even wanted the cure. Only took it because she had to.

>was pal pressuring her?

>Pal and everyone else. The doctor would stop by and act all concerned. And the Shepherd would call her

up front, preach bad about her.

Simeon just made her miserable.

The amount of times she's had to say no to him.

Corey glanced up from the smear of chokecherries.

he ever hurt her?
Wouldn't put it past him. I didn't notice anything though.
Then again, Belle was pretty good with secrets.

Peering around she leaned closer.

Listen, Ruth probably didn't tell you because Belle would ramble towards the end of it all, but before she stopped going to meetings she said, He's gonna kill me. He's gonna kill me. Didn't say who, and it was the only thing she said, kept saying. No one gave it much thought. She was going crazy after all. But I thought you should know.

A smile. She pulled back, plucked a chokecherry from a shrub and was about to pop it in her mouth when the detective grabbed her arm.

those are poisonous.

A shrug. She ate it. Made a face at the tart taste.

The pit is poison. The flesh is fine.

He waited for her to spit it out. She did.

Kraig Cephas Gersch owned a pet store on the edge of the forest. It was along this unfortunate strip of land he found Belle Rivera's body.
Reviewing the transcripts, Ruth spoke heartfully of Kraig. Kraig was the man who spoke in timid scripture. The man who never lied. He had reported his discovery in a trembling voice, prayed and fasted in the chapel without end. It took him three days to sculpt Belle's likeness. To honor her as a martyr.
Corey stood by the door waiting. Kraig's home was meek and unassuming. Arrested for failing to pay his dues, Bentham took him in by virtue of his faith. He saw God in the doctor and it was then that he devoted his soul.
The door creaked open and Kraig hid behind it. Big weeping eyes and a blue apron. His pet shop drowned in burning incense, divine imagery. The occasional smattering of pet supplies. He didn't speak, bowed his head and eyed the detective nervously. Fresh scratches trailed up his arms and a cat hissed from behind him. Black and silver, droopy ears. The same cat that had shredded Corey's sleeve.
She circled around Corey's leg, batted at his bootlaces, rendered him immobile. Kraig scooped her up, cradled her in his arms. Brushed her cheek to placate her as she tore at his thumbs. A trembly voice, avoiding Corey's eyes.
...He blesses the home of the righteous... Proverbs... three... thirty-three...
Corey did the polite thing. Fixed his gaze on the crucifix over Kraig's shoulder.

detective handler.
you must be kraig gersch.
you found isabella rivera?

A nervous swallow from Kraig's throat. He nodded. Corey gave a small smile of reassurance.

did you see or hear anything unusual?

Kraig shook his head and the mumble spilled from his lips like still water.
...A man's heart plans his way... but the Lord directs his steps... Proverbs...sixteen...nine...

i understand you spoke to ruth.
if you missed anything-

A choke. The cat leapt from Kraig's arms.
Do... you... believe... in God...?

no.
not anymore.

Kraig stared at him. A long fixed stare. Wet eyes unmoving. With a pallid whimper he drew back. Corey offered him some placating words but the man still wouldn't meet his eyes.
...The way of a fool... The companion of fools will be destroyed... The companion of fools will be destroyed... destroyed...
A cry. Kraig buried his wretched face behind his wrists. Whimpering. Muttering. Praying. When he imbibed from his divine flask some ragged thirst, Corey backed off from the door. Sin is a reproach to any people... Proverbs... fourteen...

thirty-four... Sin... is a reproach... to any people... Proverbs... four...teen... thirty...four...
The rosary hung heavy in Corey's pocket. Kraig shut the door.

Corey stood at the steps of the Turner residence. Creaky floorboards and rusted railings. It was one of the nicer, more spacious housing units afforded. Not a container but a mobile home. Converted into both a furniture store and a woodworking station.
He stood ready when the door swung open. Cracked an instant frown.

    simeon turner.

Simeon had himself wedged against the door. Rolled up sleeves and a bottle of cider in his hand.
You again.
A chuckle. Like he'd somehow gotten buzzed on apple juice.
Delgado, right?

    handler.
    i had a few questions-

Hey. I never got to ask. Cause you can never tell these days. They make it so damn complicated.
Are you a man or woman?

    i'm a detective.

A chuckle. Simeon swiped his lip.
Detective. That what you call yourself now?

Got a long way to go.
Corey narrowed his eyes slightly. Wandered over Simeon's shoulder. Dead right into the kitchen. Guts, gore, and blood. All over the counters. Cracked ribs and slabs of meat. Butcher knives and bones. Guns and mirrors.
Simeon followed his eyes. Gave a hearty laugh.
Ever gone hunting, Delgado?
Corey's eyes glittered dark and soulless.

    once.

Well.
Simeon stepped back. Allowed the other into his abode.
I shot this one myself.
Had plenty to carry home between the three of us.
A man takes what he wants. Reaps the rewards. God's gift.

    i'm here to talk to you about belle.
    she was your employee.

Belle? She helped me with my business. Building furniture. One of our number one exports! The doc has the numbers. Man loves his numbers. Sheesh...

    she have any problems?

Aside from the usual? She did good enough work but she spent too much time talking to Dani.

    dani.
    have you spoken to her since?

The smile fell away from Simeon's eyes like meat from a bone.
No. Dani doesn't want to see me.
He cleared his throat. Slammed the bottle down on the bloody counter.
Belle was trouble.

    you two get along?

I was fixin to make her my wife.
Crazy as she was a little lovin would've set her straight.
Even had the Shepherd's blessing.

    heard she didn't take well to you.

She liked the attention.
That's what did her in.
The cure didn't work on her. You had to be willing. She wasn't willing.
A sigh. He wiped his brow. Left a red smear.
All the privilege of being here. Should've given it to someone more deserving.
Corey narrowed his eyes but Simeon didn't notice, didn't care. The bitter cider had loosened his tongue.
Maybe she was rotten. Or maybe, the doctor's cure don't work. Just like Ms. Olliver said.
And now she's dead. And we can't leave or do anything about it.
At that Corey raised a brow.

    you can't leave?

The doc says we can. But really, we can't.

We leave, we lose everything. Owe everything.
Corey had to laugh a little.

> well that's shitty but i'm not surprised.

Ya think? All that praise Bentham shit. Kass More's got some greedy bastards working under him. Guess they outsmarted the good doctor.
He met Corey's eyes. A grin over the rim of his drink.
See, after what happened to Belle the doctor got all jumpy. So we took a closer look at the contract.
Should've known.
Back out and you pay it all back in full. Right back into the slammer.
A swig. He coughed on it. Choked and spat. Wiped his mouth red.
Once I find the sonofabitch that did it, I'll kill him.
Might even earn a bounty for his head.
Corey took a napkin from his pocket. Clicked his pen.

> where were you, the night belle died?

Right here.
Sharpening my tools.
Simeon eyed the detective's gloved hands. Smirked a little.
Are you here to find a suspect or collect evidence?
Corey raised a brow and tucked his notes away.

> there a difference?

Plenty of difference. I suggest you think about it.

He nudged his one arm. Pushed a corked bottle of cider into Corey's free hand.
Some fall you had.
Drink up. It's good for ya. Apple a day keeps the doctor away. Though it seems it'll take a lot more to keep him away from you.
With no space on the counter to put the bottle down Corey clenched it in his hand. Watched him. The way he circled.

    you were on the patrol.

Yep.
Didn't see a thing.
Just like Ruth told ya.
Really wishin I did though. You must've climbed sky high to break your arm like that.
Though I heard, that you just have really fragile bones. Like a bird.
A step closer. Leaning down as he grinned.
Need help opening that?
A lunge. Simeon nabbed the napkins from Corey's pocket before he could stop him. All Corey could do was point the bottle at his throat.

    those are mine.

What, the good doctor sugar couldn't afford you a proper notebook?
Simeon rifled through the napkins. Held them up to the light.
How cute. You made some little drawings.
Corey dropped the bottle. Shattered it over his boots. He stepped up into Simeon's face and snatched his notes back.

who is the sand prince?

The voice was Simeon's. He could've sworn it. But the affront melted into amusement and Simeon guffawed from his belly. What the hell did you just say?

04 | your eyes will see

Corey sat in the shade of the great chestnut tree. Throughout the week he returned to the garden to meditate. Packed mud over the sprawling orange fungus that'd taken root into the bark as stone angels watched over him.
He reviewed once again the files and the notes, but as the sun fell he found nothing of conflict and got to his heels. A distant figure hung over the hill like a smudge of ash and as he neared he recognized that poised and lanky frame. The doctor, kneeling before the chapel doors. Delicate hands folded in his lap, head bent in prayer. Dusk shining his silver hair lavender.
Corey approached slowly. Hovered behind the other man.

> wayne.

The doctor's eyes opened and he turned his head slow.
Corey.
A smile.
I was wondering, where you'd gone.

> i was thinking.

It's not safe staying out so late.
Wayne's eyes traveled up the length of Corey's body. Lingered over his elbow, his hip.
How is your arm faring?

> nothing new.

Has the Lord revealed anything to you?

> that this might be bigger than the both of us.

Corey leaned over his shoulder. A smile as the other caught his eye.

> so what are you doing all the way out here? the lord reveal anything to you?

He told me where to find you.
Wayne nudged his wrist.
Dove. Pray with me.

> no thanks.

You keep your faith in your pocket. Please, share it with your dear friend.
Corey wasn't sure if they were on such intimate terms just yet but the way the doctor looked at him he could almost believe it. He obliged him, squatted down.

> you pray often?

Of course. I am but a sinner.
But I've been praying for Belle as of late. Her soul.
A gentle smile as he regarded the detective's blank face, intense eyes.
Whatever you think of me, I only wanted to save her.

> didn't seem to go so well.

It was a test.
Perhaps you will be the one to show me the answer.

    not so sure about that one, doc.

Corey knelt down beside him. Folding his legs, digging into his coat until the beads tangled his fingers.

    i don't pray out loud.

Quite alright.
Pray as your soul has learned to.
God hears us all the same.
A nod, Corey tilted his head, cheek against the cold jade of his rosary. Eyes cast downwards. Then he dropped it back into his pocket, shook his head.
What did you pray for?

    nothing.

That can't be all.

    i pray that you come to your senses.

A smile and Corey made the sign of the cross. The doctor puffed and straightened until he once again towered over the detective. Roughing his collar.
We have supper with the Kaplins in an hour.

    me and you?

And Miranda.

alright.

Corey ruffled his fluff of hair.

let me wash up.

Of course. And perhaps you could wash that paint from your face,
A scoff and the detective got to his heels.

as if, sunshine.

She was a soft spoken woman, Anna Kaplin. Dark curls protected in a bun, skin woven a russet brown, a yellow sundress swept in rolls and curves. The submissive wife, she put her trust in the men and kept bad days to herself. Tending to guests as Shepherd Job sat at the head of the table. Wayne to his right. Dr. Miranda Olliver at his left.
Job raised his hands in reverence. Supper set on the table. Opaque gelatin a murky yellow, cobbles of meat and blots of orange suspended within. Boiled elk hooves and skin and tendon and bones. Stale like the insides of a fridge.
Before the wall full of crosses the house canary rattled in its cage. The Shepherd attacking the corner of his aspic. A long draw of quiet following the initial formalities.
Doctor.
It was Dr. Sykkes who answered. Adjusting his glasses.

Yes?

I heard from Ruth that the shipment is late again?
A slow nod. Fork tightly clenched.

> Yes. Nothing to worry about.
> Just some supply chain issues.

I see.
A smile from Shepherd Job. Bruising between the eyes. He locked his sights on Corey.
I am pleased to see you've stuck with us a week now.
Have you had any breakthroughs, Mr. Handler?
Corey offered a smile. Just as he practiced.

> no. nothing conclusive just yet.

Ah.
I see.
We had a wonderful service last week. I only wish you had attended.

> mmhm. yeah.

Corey looked away. An attempt to break bread with his one arm. Wayne had to reach over to keep him from making a mess. Miranda offered a smile and Anna kept quiet. Neither of them had spoken up since.
Dr. Sykkes.
Wayne raised his brows.

> Yes?

I had something to ask of you.

A proposal, supported by the majority of the town.
Wayne's shoulders tensed. A light chuckle.

    Is this a matter better suited for town hall?

I thought it would be good to discuss it here.

    Here.
    Of course.

Wiping his hands he took up his fork.

    What is it?

There has been a growing desire, a pressing need, I'd say, to renegotiate the terms of our contract.
The clink of silverware. Porcelain cup spinning.

    The contract?
    Whatever for?

People feel as though the terms of agreement have changed.
That it is no longer safe here.
The Shepherd gazed about the room. Straightened until he loomed at the head of it.
We want the ability to leave town.
The doctor put his fork down. Smiled thinly.

    They are free to leave, are they not?

Probation looms too steep a price. A price most of us cannot afford.

Unfortunately I have no say. The agreement was decreed by Bentham executives.

We understand that but you are our sole link to Bentham Incorporated. The people have turned to you, doctor. And you betrayed our trust in betraying the vote.
A quick and heavy breath. Lenses glinting a dangerous gold.

Betrayed?
Do they not have faith in me?

The Shepherd stanced himself in his chair but a ringing cut his voice. The doctor's phone. He'd been answering more calls as of late. This one came at the right time.

Excuse me. I'll have to take this.

He went straight out the door.
Silence. Anna brushed aside her dark curls and clasped her hands.
Perhaps we should prepare the brownies?
A plate skidded. Miranda was already out of her seat.

Yep. Excuse us.

They filtered out the room.
Corey shoveled food in his mouth. Hoping to join them. But they'd up and left and he was alone with the Shepherd.
His weathered eyes roved over Corey's features. Passing bites of meat jelly into his lips. He thought the detective to be a strange one. Frightful looking, with his dark hair and painted face. Refusing to look anyone in the eyes.

Shepherd Job chuckled.
Enjoying my wife's cooking I hope?

    yes,

A nod and swallow. The suspended meat clumped in his belly.

    very comforting.

Good, good.
I do hope you'll be joining us for service tomorrow. Your presence is lacking.
Corey nodded but his eyes kept flicking towards the kitchen.

    of course.
    i'll consider it.

Hm. A shame to see a man without faith. But, I'm sure you have seen.
A smile. It cut up to his ears.
If the Lord demands blood he shall have it.
A shout and a scream outside the door. Wayne stormed in. Brow fuming.
Job smiled and wiped his mouth.
News?
The detective reached for his arm but the doctor wrenched it away.

    Bentham.

Ah.
The Shepherd clasped his hands.

Did you inquire of the contracts-?
The doctor slammed the table and snarled.

    Enough about the contracts!

The Shepherd unfolded his hands.
Of course. We meant no offense.
Heavy breaths. Wayne sat. Pinched his nose.

    Apologies.
    I didn't receive the best news.

Corey brushed beside him.

    care to share?

    No.

    mm.

    Why don't you go help the girls in the kitchen? I have something to discuss with the Shepherd.

Corey had been more than happy to take his leave but at Wayne's look he quickly excused himself. Gathered his plates and made towards the kitchen. Caught Anna's voice. The house canary screaming at him.
Boysenberries.
A scoff from Miranda. The fridge shutting.

    You don't like boysenberries.

Job is afraid the fruit will spoil.

> Of course.
> Fruit over flesh.

At the silence Corey walked in. The two crowded over the brownies. Anna stirring up a bowl of icing.
I wish I was a rat.
You'd take care of me and Boggles.

> hi.

Anna noticed him first. Miranda quickly hopped back. A gap between herself and Anna.

> Hey- Core-
> mm.
> sorry to intrude.
> boys are out talking.

He set his dishes in the sink. Raised an appreciative gesture towards Anna.

> wanted to thank you. for the food. and the get well presents.

Miranda tried stealing his dirty dishes but he shooed her away.
Anna beamed and dried off her hands.
Yes! Of course!
When I heard the news-
She wiped at her forehead.
All three patrolmen out there, I'm surprised they missed you!

Must be the devil's work.

    mm.

Corey tugged at his cast.

    three?

She shifted nervously on her feet.
Oh. Am I forgetting someone?
I- I don't go to meetings but I was watching out the window.
Ms. Welles, Mr. More, and Mr. Gersch.
All three of them, spaced out, making rounds around town.
I'm forgetting someone aren't I?

    simeon turner.

Corey turned to scrub at the stain on his plate. Jaw set.

    you didn't see him?

Anna raised her brows in concern.
No, I-
As she opened her mouth Shepherd Job's spiteful bark ripped into the candid quiet of the kitchen. Words shooting her gray and ashen.
Doctor! I am offended you would insinuate- and send that witch of a woman-!
Dr. Sykkes turned the corner. He looked rather pleased with himself. Flicked to Corey and Miranda.

    Let's go.

Corey cocked a brow but followed. Glanced over his shoulder. Miranda wouldn't look at either of them.

 is job kaplin going to fly onto the stage?

Miranda snickered and Wayne only squinted. A large crowd had dispersed about the auditorium. Service today was busy.
No.
His gaze skimmed over Corey's shoulder and his eyes widened. He'd spotted Jacobi, gotten to his feet to greet her. Left Corey alone with Miranda.
They hadn't talked about dinner last night. Now was a good time.
Corey got up. Sat down in the seat right next to her.

 what was that?

Miranda had reclined to her elbows against the chair, eyes set dead ahead. A rat poked its head out of her pocket. Disappeared again.

 What was what?
 dinner. with the kaplins.
 you didn't say a word.

A shrug.

 Supper? Neither did you.

At his look she rolled her eyes.

You saw how Wayne was.

It was bad enough with just him talking. I blab and everything goes to shit. Trust me.

The doctor was making his rounds about the aisles. Shaking hands and having some good chuckles.

what did he even say to job to get him so pissed?

Miranda huffed.

It's stupid.
you can tell me.
It's not even true. I haven't- Neither of us have-

A sigh. She shrunk in her seat.

Forget it.
Have you heard anything new? About Belle?

Corey gave her a long look before turning his face away.

everyone keeps saying the calibrations would have set her straight.
no way to know for sure.

Miranda nodded along.

Testimony. That's good.
We need hard evidence-

Corey was attacked from behind. Firm arms around his neck.

Oh, Core! I'm so glad you're here!

jacobi-

The hold relented. Jacobi jumped the chair, plopped down two seats from Miranda.
Wayne stood in the aisle. Neat vest ruffled by one of Jacobi's tackles. Stared down at Miranda's knees, hoping to take his seat past her next to Corey.
Mouse.
Miranda held his eyes and his shoulders slumped. She shoved his forehead backwards as he stumbled over. Jacobi leaned over, voice low.
Where's Anna?
Corey followed Miranda's gaze. Found Anna at the end of it. The doctor spoke briskly, nails digging into her palm.

Up front.

Oh.
At Miranda's gesture Jacobi took the seat that was once meant for Anna. Dr. Sykkes hadn't looked their way once.
As the lights flickered on over the stage the Shepherd emerged, glided slow towards the podium. Corey clutched the jade beaded rosary cold in his pocket. The Shepherd's voice boomed clear across the auditorium.
Welcome, welcome everyone! A full house today. Wonderful, wonderful that you are all here under God's roof. We are blessed to be here. The strength it takes, to remain complacent in his arms. Constant reminders of the terrible sin and the beautiful faith that surrounds us.

As we begin let us meditate upon the verses selected by you in the congregation.

> Proverbs 23:2.
> Put a knife to your throat, if you are given to gluttony.

A slow hymn of weeping strings. The Shepherd cleared his throat and began to hum.
In honor of those who have fallen asleep, let us sing together,

> Come not in terror, as the King of kings,
> But kind and good, with healing in Thy wings,
> Tears for all woes, a heart for every plea,
> Come, Friend of sinners, thus abide with me,

Almighty God, we welcome your presence. May we be filled with faith and devotion worthy of Your love, and may You fortify our souls against wickedness, and lead us into everlasting joy.
Today's scripture reading is Psalms 139, verses 17 to 24.
Read by one of our most faithful clergymen, Kraig Cephas Gersch.
The pet shop owner trembled up the stage, quivered under his blue polo. A swallow. The pages rustling. He spoke in a tight voice. Slowly raising in volume.

> ...How precious to me are your thoughts, God...How vast is the sum of them. Were I to count them.. they would outnumber the grains of sand... when I awake, I am still with you...
>
> If only you, God, would slay... slay the wicked, away

from me, you, you who are bloodthirsty, they speak of you, you, with evil intent, your adversaries, mis-misuse your name, do I not hate those who hate you LORD and abhor those who are in rebellion against you I have nothing but hatred for them I count them my enemies-

A sob. He bowed his head, knuckles clenched white over the podium.

...Search me, God, and know my heart... test me and know my anxious thoughts... See if there is any offensive way in me... and lead me in the way everlasting...

Gasping through tears Kraig peeled himself from the podium. Wandered back down. Sympathetic pats on the shoulder and murmurs of appreciation.
Shepherd Job chuckled, watching Kraig go.
Beautiful. Beautiful reading. Just beautiful.
A laugh. The Shepherd pointed at the empty space upon the stage.
Look! Look upon our icon of faith! The golden glow of angels! Isn't it just beautiful? We, we have been blessed. Blessed with the sight!
The congregation was fixed. A glow pooling in Jacobi's wide eyes. But the center stage remained empty.
Corey murmured.

what are they looking at?

No answer.

The Shepherd's voice continued.

For this sermon, I would like to further meditate on the scripture.

A gaze out into the crowd.

I know we have all felt tempted.

Who here has felt temptation? Don't lie.

The bubble of a murmur. Corey slung an arm over the back of Wayne's chair. Felt the doctor stiffen slightly over his shoulder.

    i'm tempted to punch you in the face right now.

Wayne took a moment to answer. Eyes flickering over his friend.

Likewise, darling.

The murmurs fell away. Shepherd Job belted with passion.

Now! Who here loves God?

Shouts, hollering, applause. Corey could pick out Jacobi's squealing.

We all love God. Of course we do. And He loves us. But sometimes, we falter.

You heard it, didn't you?

Psalms 139.

The desire to eliminate all sin, wickedness, and rebellion.

Pure, honest to God, devotion.

A low chuckle. His eyes settled amongst the congregation.

Now, you know me.

In my sermons I like to call upon our brothers and sisters in need of prayer.

Today is different.

Today I would like to call to attention a brother we should all

model ourselves after. Kraig Cephas Gersch. The rock, the foundation of our community.
A wail. Kraig had keeled forward in his seat. Face buried in his folded hands. Praying.
Look! Look upon him!
Pure, honest to God, devotion!
As we read today's scripture, I found myself reminded of Kraig.
Kraig is a man who has devoted himself to the Lord.
Kraig is a man who has denied all wickedness and turned to Christ.
The Shepherd raised his hands.
Jesus wrote in the sand to preach forgiveness.
That hasn't changed.
Now, we are the sand. We are the sand in which He writes in.
We must make like the sand of the sea.
We must purge ourselves of evil and call upon God for strength.
Under the Lord's touch sand will become rock-
The doors flew open. Lee Palomo had stumbled in. A bottle in her hand. Tipsy. Corey's stomach knotted.

 Hi y'all!

The congregation went silent.
Wayne sucked in a breath.
Oh dear.
Corey leapt to his feet. Pal met his eyes across the room, Essie at his side.
Miranda was already out the walkway.

 Lee. Put that down. Come on. Why don't we get you some water-

Lee screamed and swung.

>No!
>I'm not going! No!

Pal approached from behind.
Lee.
Corey shook his head but Pal kept advancing.
Lee.
Alcohol is a sin.
Did you read the verse I sent you today?
If you are given to gluttony-
Lee cracked the bottle over Pal's head. Essie screamed and dragged Pal out of the way, Jacobi stumbling to look at his wounds.
Pal slurred and shouted.
Sin is a reproach to any people!
Slay the wicked! Pray, Lee, pray! Slay the wickedness in your soul-
Lee sobbed and held the bottle out in front of her.

>My soul is trapped.

Corey snatched her arms. Twisted the broken bottle out of her hand. She thrashed against him.

>My soul, this body,

A soft whisper into her hair as he held her firm.

>lee.
>it's okay.

> relax.
> relax for me.

He locked eyes with Wayne. The doctor's face was expressionless. Miranda nudged his arm. They took Lee down past the doors behind the stage. The back of the chapel, a hallway of closets and empty rooms. In a dark classroom they sat her down on a desk. Dr. Olliver fetched a water bottle and went to check on Pal. Left Lee alone with the detective. Still mumbling as he held her.

> You're going to forget me, aren't you?
> Just like you forgot Belle.
> Can you hear her? She must be crying...

A sigh. Cold around his throat. He wiped the tears from her cheeks.

> lee. i'm gonna need you to drink some water.
> can you do that?

She held his hand tight in her fist. Shaking her head. The sight of her turned stones in his stomach.

> I don't want to end up like Belle,
> I don't want to,
> Please, please, please,

He held the bottle up to her face. A sniffle. She took the water. Choked.

The door swung open. Essie Easley was standing next to the whiteboard. Stressing the ends of her dress.

> essie. how is pal?

Fine. The cuts aren't deep. They just look bad.
Um, Jacobi and Dr. Olliver are taking him to the hospital but they wanted me to stay with Lee.
Is- is she in trouble?

> no.
> she just needs a friend right now.
> can you look after her for me?

A nod. Essie stayed by Lee's side, hand on her shoulder.
In the hallway the Shepherd's voice thrummed the walls. Wayne caught his eye as he slipped in beside him.
Doctor. If this happens again-

> I will start her on a regimen. Yes, I understand.

Might I remind you, the community is already facing extreme distress-

> she doesn't need the cure.

They looked to the detective. The doctor gave a light chuckle.

> I'd beg to differ, but it is her choice.
> And I will begin consultations immediately.

A smile at Job. The Shepherd shook his head, made back down the hall.
God willing, doctor.
The Shepherd disappeared behind the doors.

Corey stepped forward. Brushed over Wayne's hand. He took it.

>don't do it.

The doctor peered down at his friend.
If it is the Lord's will it must be done.
A cold tremor in his chest. He let go. Pretended not to notice.
Quiet had settled in the classroom. Down the hall a spatter of blood. Corey's fingers twitched. A rash over the skin of his back.
He lowered his mutter to a simmer.

>if it weren't for pal no one would've gotten hurt.

Wayne spoke soft. Hushed over his breaths.
He was only trying to help.
A puff. Corey tugged at his cast. A tightness in his throat.

>she was scared. he only made it worse. he moralized her-

A pinch at his neck. Uncomfortable heat bursting in his chest.

>what is he even doing here?
>last i checked he was a free man.

Applause. Wayne looked up from his watch. Silver hands ticking under his lenses.
The town of Bentham owes its existence to Kassiel.
I find it fitting that Pal wishes to offer his service to the town, as the heir.

>so what? we're a charity case?

Corey looked at him. The red of his lips and the deep gold of his hazel eyes.

>you have any idea the things he's done?

A young Saul. I am well aware.
A scoff. Corey ran a hand through his hair. Strands coming off on his gloves.

>how blessed are we. the prodigal son has graced us.

He has atoned for his sins.
Corey looked away. Head pounding with the chanting beating from beyond the doors. Corey could feel them, the heat, the sickness. It rolled from his tongue.

>pal lived on the same street as belle.
>he knew her well enough to text her every morning.
>verses and shame.

The doctor raised his voice in warning.
Corey.

>he's done it before.
>he'll do it again.

A hand grabbed his wrist. Made the skin there burn.
In denying second chances you deny humanity.

>stop trying to play god.

God?

Belle lies asleep in hope of resurrection.
The unclean lamb delivered from evil.
We have purged ourselves of original sin–
A look into Corey's eyes. Lenses a sickly orange.
Do you forsake her?
A final twist of his stomach. Corey tore his arm away. The heat had risen to his eyes and he couldn't see. Stumbled into the men's washroom.
Wayne didn't follow.
Old dogs prefer dying alone and Corey was dying.
Sick.
He felt sick.
It spread from his stomach. Pooled in his throat.
He held over the shattered mirror and the rusted sinks, clenched white the edge of the counter. Bent over the drain. Hacking and coughing. Clutching at his throat. The stale air had no entrance. The muscles refused to contract. Something was stuck there.
Two fingers against the palate of his mouth. He dug past his tongue. Stretched and retched and gagged. There he felt it. In the hollow of his throat. A knob of something wet, fleshy, hard. He fixed his fingers firm around its neck. Dragged it from the apple of his throat. A long thin bone. Rigid and boiled, intact to the cartilage and suspended in phlegm clouded gelatin. It trembled in his hand, light like bird bone and slick in matted natal down.
The thing inside him.
COR
A jump and he dropped the bone where it caught in clumps of hair and clattered down the open drain. He knew not to chase after it. Murmured to himself, something to soothe his racing heart.

i'm awake.

A swallow. His mouth was numb. He couldn't hear himself. He wet his lips, stared down into the clotted chasm of the open drain, raised his voice higher. Cotton sweetness on his tongue.

I'm awake.

A hand clasped over his mouth. He squeaked down his words.
The voice wasn't his. The image in the mirror wasn't his.
She was watching. Eyes duller than pallid death.
Corey left the washroom. The hallway was empty. Wayne had gone.
From the supply closet a mask grinned at him. Red like stripped antlers, like blood.
He could hear them. Hear them crying.
Corey opened his eyes.
Kraig Gersch. A box of venerables in his arms. Simeon Turner with the keys. Speaking with Job and Anna Kaplin.
The words burst from his mouth before he could stop them. The rosary weightless in his coat pocket.

we must make like the sand of the sea.

The Shepherd regarded him with a smile.
Amen.
You enjoyed my sermon, I see?
His heart hadn't stopped racing. Corey spat. Enough to make Kraig jump.

kaplin. you bastard.

Excuse me?

> under the lord's touch sand will become rock. you know who the sand prince is, don't you?

Prince? Detective- The only prince I bow to is the prince of peace.
A hiss and Corey snapped his jaws in his face.

> what are you trying to hide? tell me. who is the sand prince.

The Shepherd's gaze burned into annoyance.
Again, child, I don't understand what you're talking about.

> king of kings. the sand he writes in. quite the coincidence, kaplin.

Even in coincidence there is God's will.

> unless it was intentional. i saw the masks.

Simeon chuckled.
Please. Masks? What is he on about?

> caught you in a lie, that's what. i know simeon wasn't on patrol like he said he was.

A crack of his knuckles. Bones and blood.
On what account, Delgado?
Corey smiled like a rabid dog. Haunches raised.

ruth, pal, and kraig. anna only saw three patrolmen that night.

Anna Kaplin went gray and ashen. Tugging at the collar of her yellow dress.

Are- are you sure you're feeling alright, detective? I don't recall saying that.

A snap. He looked into her eyes. Her anguish. The fruit had spoiled. Fallen from the flesh. She wasn't lying. Submissive wives do not dare to lie.

Corey took a step back. Opened his eyes. Found himself at Belle's grave. On his knees, lips over the chokecherries.

i'm awake.
i'm awake.
i'm awake.

The bleed had started again.

05 | over the chokecherries

One day before Isabella Rivera's twenty-fifth birthday and three months after she passed, Danielle Cardenas Kwan decided to pick up the phone. After months of silence.
Dani said it was because she saw the detective taking care of Lee all those months ago. The way he stuck by her side, worked the garden.
Since then his arm had healed.
His head probably hadn't.
Dreams of drowning in white sand.
Being on call the detective arrived within the hour. Corey Handler Delgado. Just as frayed and ruffled as he'd always been.
To his surprise the little shipping container home was a far cry from the wreck Ruth had described months before. The unit was spotless.
A glance up from the cockatoo cage and he caught Dani obsessively scrubbing a countertop, messy dark hair and a wrinkled sweatshirt. It kept her busy he supposed. Being locked up inside this tin of a house. Lying down meant taking up a fourth of the floor space and Dani didn't like lying down.
One step brought him into the kitchen where Dani offered him a jam sandwich. Another step and he'd already crossed into Belle's room.
Dani didn't want to stay too long. Shut the door behind him. He pulled out some old napkins. Sketched a lay of the room.
There was a mattress on the floor, pushed into the corner against the wall. Just barely enough room to squeeze in a chair and a

nightstand without scraping the edges. Stickers and polaroids to cover up the flaking sores in the walls. A council of stuffed animals reigned over the thinning gray covers.

A short interrogation and they showed him to a tin of mints stuffed under the pillow. Full of paper stars. A scattered mess of pens and to-do lists long overdue just waiting on her nightstand. In the trash decayed a bundle of half dead roses. Crumpled and faded, wilting off the stem. But somewhere amongst the necrosis curled a lick of bright and luscious green.

The door opened and he swung around. Knocked the one chair over. Dani stood, pale skinned and sunken, hands hidden under her sleeves. A small sigh, she helped him tip the chair back up. Letters etched into the foot of it. B+D.

Dani stared a long while. Flipped the chair back over.

Stupid.

Leaving marks on her pieces.

I'm surprised no one's complained about it.

A small push until it lined up with the nightstand.

    she made that?

Dani didn't answer. Eyes set on the stuffed animals. She shot her gaze down to her feet.

This chair was her second.

Her first went to me.

    it's her right then. to mark what is hers.

Corey nodded towards the roses peeking out the disposal.

    any idea who left her those?

If they're in the trash? Simeon.
Dani knelt down. Gathered up the rotting bag.
He say anything about her?

    that she did good work.

Corey straightened. Kept some space between himself and the other.

    that he was gonna marry her.

As if.
Dani tied a knot over the bag. Got up and lugged it behind her. She'd failed to notice that the rotted roses hadn't died.
Corey followed. A step into the open kitchen.

    he ever hurt her?

Dani dropped the bag onto the floor.
No.
He wouldn't.

    she had bruises.

From an accident.

    who reported it?

Dani didn't answer. Bent to pick up the bag again. Corey spoke soft.

    his alibi is weak.

What's his alibi.

    that he was at home.

A sigh. Dani rattled open the kitchen trash. Crammed down some old paper plates. Voice cold.
He didn't do it.
She slammed the lid.
I was with him.
A long stare and a pounding in his head. Eyes trained on her face.

    you were with him.

She didn't meet his eyes. Wiped at her cheek.
He messed with us. Messed with us both.

    he never mentioned this.

Cause he knows it was wrong.
He was promised to Belle. Shepherd's word.
Corey eased the cupboard shut before she could hit her head.

    have you seen him since-

No.
She rinsed off her hands. Snatched a towel.
I couldn't care less what happens to him. I just know he isn't the one.

    mm.

A twist of his ring. He thought back. To the pens and the

shredded paper.

    did belle ever keep a diary?

No.
At his raised brow she shook her head.
I don't think so. But it's nobody's business.
Belle liked to keep to herself.

    i see.

A long look into her tired eyes. Sharp and sweeping like his. She looked away. Swiped at her nose. Opened the fridge so he couldn't see her face.
It was supposed to be me looking after her. Me.
A sniffle. Glassware clinking. She slammed the fridge shut. A glass jar swinging in her hand.
You want to know why the cure wasn't working?
Corey raised his eyes. Dani took a step until she stood toe to toe with him. Leaned down.
Dr. Sykkes was trying to change things about her that didn't need to be changed.
And she had to pretend it worked.
Dani dropped the jar of red jam on the counter.
I can still hear her.
Dark hair fell over her face. She clutched his freshly healed arm.
Promise me.
Promise me you won't stop looking.
A slow nod. Staring into her tired eyes.

    i promise.

Dani held his gaze a moment. Averted her eyes, reached forward, tucked the jar of red into his coat pocket.
Chokecherry jam.
Belle's favorite.
A step back. Tugging her sweater over herself.
You'll be there tomorrow?

>always.

With the jar in his coat Corey gestured to the half dead flowers rotting in the trash.

>they're still alive.
>may i?

Dani had cracked open a jar of jam herself. Tasting chokecherry was like tasting Belle again.
Take them.

That night Corey checked the furniture. Every last piece. Looking for Belle's mark.
The doctor walked in on him with a shriek. He was worried of course. Corey had sleepwalked into the garden. Started bleeding again. Sounds in the night like a woman weeping. Holding up Corey's hair as they flattened over the bathroom floor, vomiting over nothing but morning dew. He had every reason to be concerned, every reason to pray.
Such was the sight of the detective standing in the middle of the room, chairs and tables upturned.
Dove?
A glance up. Corey put the chair down. Grabbed Wayne's hand

and tugged him over.

> look. under the chairs.
> belle left marks on all of them.
> everything in this room.
> she built everything in this room.
> all this. when she had nothing at home.

A hand through his hair. The doctor peered down at his friend.
Cupped his cheek to check the rims of his eyes.
Are you feeling alright, dove?
A few blinks and Corey looked a little less like a lost puppy.
Leaned into his touch, the caress of his thumb.

> yes?

A hum and a nod.
How is Danielle faring?

> good. i think.
> she'll be there.

Good.
Good.
Wayne smiled, a charm over his fingers.
Anything I should know?

> simeon's got a solid alibi now.

I did warn you, the futility of chasing after Mr. Turner.
A brush under his lip. The breath in Corey's chest faltering.
Did she mention anything about Belle?

> mm, no.
> didn't find anything important.
> don't worry.

Ah. I see.
Good.
Good..
A soft smile and Wayne pulled away. Receded into the hallway where he returned toting a gift bag. Corey stood at attention.

> for tomorrow?

Partially.
He gave him eyes in a way that could have been taken as flirtatious.
Or, perhaps, I am rewarding you for coming home on time. For once.

> mm.
> still not forgiving you for that.

Oh, but it was so amusing.
Seeing you on your knees begging to be let in.
But, no, that's not what this is for. And I think you know that.
The detective scoffed and took a step back.

> no.
> you didn't.

The doctor set the bag down over the detective's bed. Took his hand.
New sweaters. Since you insist on wearing your torn one as many

days as you can.

They're red.

How you like them.

Corey shook his head. He wasn't used to receiving gifts. Felt he didn't deserve them. Days like these were usually forgotten. Spent alone.

    no. i can't take this.

Darling.

A small tug at his sleeve.

It's a gift.

    for what? not getting myself killed?

I believe forty-two is something worth celebrating.

A puff. Corey shook out his fluff of hair.

    wait til your back hurts, sunshine.

Do you think me youthful?

    more spry than i am.

I followed you into the world the year the Berlin wall fell. Two days after Bundy was executed and six days after Bush was sworn in.

    mm. the year lovesong scaled the charts.

A trace over the other's features. The hollows of his eyes, the plush of his lips. Crows feet and smile lines and silver hair. The sleepless months showing soft on his face.

    you don't look it.

The pain never dulls but neither does fate.
A hum. The doctor rubbed the curve of his back. A soothing touch.
If you're still hurting my offer still stands.

    i am not getting a massage from you.

You'll take it then?

    the massage?

The sweaters.

    right.

Corey fought himself a moment. Took the bag, threw it behind him, pulled his friend into a hug. Awkward with how much taller the other was. Muffling his voice.

    thank you.

A rigidness to his stance but at that he relaxed.
Of course, darling.
You work yourself far too hard.

    says you.

Corey rested his chin over Wayne's shoulder.

> just keep it to yourself. i don't want to take away from belle's day.

Of course.
A soft smile. He pulled away, dropped his hand from Corey's.
It seems Belle has touched our lives in ways we've never dreamed of knowing.
Wayne adjusted his slipping lenses. Turned his head away. Voice wavering.
She'll be turning twenty-five tomorrow.
Another slip. He refused to meet Corey's eyes even as the detective chased. Corey gave a short laugh.

> are you crying?

Wayne shot him a glare. Eyes glinting.
I am not.
A swallow.
I can't.
He said this but as he turned away his nose twitched and he tore off his glasses and wiped at his eyes.

> sunshine?

A step closer, hovering over his arms.

> hey.
> it's okay.
> just-

The other flinched away.
Dammit, Corey,

Don't touch me.
A pull back. He raised his hands.

    okay. okay. sorry.
    just
    come here.
    sit.

He didn't sit. Just wandered. Corey stayed quiet. Waited for the other to speak. When he did his voice was a whisper.
I could have saved her.
If I had worked quicker I could have saved her.
Corey shifted closer. A tentative hand that hovered but never touched.

    it's not your fault.

It has everything to do with me.
She came to me for help and I failed her.

    you were trying to help.

A huff. The doctor smeared his face. Wrung out his hands and scratched at his wrist. Scratched and scratched and scratched.
What does it matter to you?
Everything we've done. Everything we've built.
They're all irredeemable in your eyes.
You can't even forgive yourself.
A shaky breath. Wrist red and raw.
You never believed.
And you lost everything for it.

Parted lips and a small scoff. Corey brushed over his hand.

    wayne-

A shove and Wayne threw him against the bed. Hissed into his hair.
Every second you deny salvation. You don't even understand. We could lose *everything*.
A breath. Corey fell still beneath him. Still under those gentle fingers.
Wayne swiped at his tears and left.

In fall the garden clothed itself in leaf litter, kept warm the bereaved.
At Belle's feet Dani wept. Burying her face away in her arms like she was sleeping. Through the marble it looked as though Belle were praying over her. Belle, her stone angel.
Ruth stood at the mouth of the clearing. Blocked the sight of it. Kept the gathered away.
They were here to remember her.
Corey made do with the rotted roses in his gloved hands. Peeled back the rot and death. Watched Lee over the wilted petals. He'd made a promise to Ruth. That he'd watch over her. And Essie was flagging him down. Simeon. Tugging at Lee's hair, an arm around her.
Corey clenched a pair of shears in his hands. Lee was laughing brightly, looking around. Eyes wide and darting.

    she's scared.

Wayne was hovering beside him. Also watching. For signs. A

raised brow.
Oh?

> simeon.

Simeon?
A glance. From them to the detective.
She's smiling and laughing.

> he keeps invading her space.
> all she can do is laugh it off. or else she'll cause a scene.

Corey passed Wayne his shears.

> hold this.

Dove?
What are you–
He slid over and pulled Simeon back by the neck.

> quit bothering her.

Lee watched with shining eyes but Simeon only chuckled and brushed him off.
I don't see the problem, officer.

> she's uncomfortable.

What are you, her dad?

> don't cause a scene.

You started it.

maybe you should leave space for jesus.

A scoff. But Simeon locked eyes with the doctor behind the detective. Shoved off, shooting eyes at Lee.
Looks like you got yourself a guardian angel.
A smile and a nervous laugh. Simeon gave one last smirk. Didn't look back. Joined Kraig with the Shepherd.
Lee tackled the detective in a hug.

Thanks Core!

A hand to steady her and a soft chuckle. Lee had changed over the months. Let loose and lopped off those braids of hair. Ruth thought Corey was a bad influence, encouraging it. But Lee had always been meaning to do it.

of course.

A glance over and Wayne was watching, Jacobi talking off his ear. Corey flicked back to Lee. Sights locked on Simeon.

if he gives you trouble you call me.
I will.

Softly smiling. He tilted his head.

how's your painting going?

Lee ran a hand through the choppy ends of her hair.

I'm starting to get a hang of it but I'm not as good as you are-

Lee!
Pal More seized Lee by the arms.
Thank God the detective stepped in. You need to reserve yourself.
Essie scoffed.
Sim was bothering her.
A wry smile. Pal shook his head.
She was encouraging him.
A hand on her shoulder.
Lee. If you keep this up, you'll end up just like Belle.
Clenched teeth. Corey grabbed at him.

> pal.
> quit it.

The boy only shrugged him off. Stepped closer to Lee.
I can see it. Happening all over again.
You're spiraling. Just like Belle.
And yet you still deny the cure.
Why?
Lee shook her head. Trembling.

> I don't-
> I don't want to end up like her-

Then welcome him in! Welcome the new baptism into your heart lest your fate be sealed.
She shut her ears and sobbed.

> You don't understand-
> None of you could hear it-

None of you could hear-

Dani had gotten to her feet. Leaning against Belle's statue. All eyes on Lee.
Jacobi cut into the center. Toting the doctor along.
Pal. Now is not the time.
Pal spat.
There is a wickedness-
Jacobi hushed him.
Faith ain't about pointing fingers.
C'mon.
Back to work on the garden.
Pal opened his mouth. Fell quiet under the doctor's gaze.
Corey gathered Lee into his arms. Hid her away and soothed her hair. A glance at Jacobi and she nodded, herded them off. Lee went to Essie, who let her cling protectively as she murmured softly to her.
Miranda waved the girls over. Sitting with Anna on a blanket in the shade towards the back, twisting flowers into each other's hair.
The detective was alone with the doctor again.

Wayne cocked a brow.
Caused quite a stir, dove.

mm.

A nudge but the other flinched back. Corey pretended not to notice. Looked around without meeting his eyes, fingers tucked into his belt loops and a wry chuckle.

they only seem to listen to you, sunshine.

Everyone but you.
A glance. Wayne stood tall, stoic, hands clasped behind his back. It was the tilt of his nose that betrayed him. Corey pulled him aside.

you upset?

No.
The reply was too curt. Corey kept staring and Wayne sighed.
I'm not, love.
A glance away. Soft eyes don't lie. Corey accepted that.
The doctor raised a hand. Brushed gently over the other's cheek.
I'm sorry about last night.

mm.

Corey held still. The touch burning more than it should have.

i'm surprised it's taken you this long to strangle me.

Corey-

it's okay.

Keeping his eyes to the floor.

you didn't hurt me.

A roll of his shoulders. He leaned closer. The faintest of smiles.

get in a real tussle with me and you're the one who

should be worried.

Wayne frowned. Pinching his fingers as ice flashed before his eyes.
That doesn't excuse what I did.
I should be in control of my own emotions.

    you shouldn't hold it in.

Corey nudged him again.

    you're a shrink. take your own advice.

I'm not a shrink.

    same thing.

Wayne looked down at his hands. Slender and delicate. Corey took them into his own.

    what happened to belle wasn't your fault.
    you were trying to do good.

That's not enough.
Wayne pulled out of his grasp. Turned Corey's hand over. Thumbed his palm. A soft murmur that grazed over the other's fluff of hair.
You don't even believe in me.
A scoff. Corey tugged him closer.

    you're brilliant.
    the cure. it's nothing short of a miracle.

> but it has its limits.

I know that.
I am here to learn them. To overcome them.

> then you should know.

A lean closer. He tilted up the doctor's chin.

> there are things you shouldn't do.

A moment. Lips parted. Captivated by Corey's smokey eyes. He choked on his own words.
I'm helping them.
A swallow.
I am saving them from sin.

> and what is sin to you?

Wayne didn't answer. Losing himself in the brush of Corey's gloved fingers, gaze averted towards the trees where Miranda sat. The Shepherd had beckoned Anna away and Miranda was tearing the grass at her knuckles.

> you were trying to change things that didn't need changing.

Corey's murmur drew his eyes. A circle over his wrist. Spiraling towards the center.

> you changed my mind.
> some people can change.

He laced their fingers. Pulled his hand close.

    lee needs help. she does.

He pressed his lips over the guard of his palm. Cast reverence over his friend.

    but i'm scared. of what you'll change.

Wayne watched him. The angel fallen before his eyes. Still yet he prayed to his wretched idols. Speaking through his lips like frost.
If it is the Lord's will it must be done.
I am trying to save us, darling. All of us.
Corey stared into him. Past that deep hazel and straight into the man trapped inside. Like the lightless depths of the sea. One last squeeze before he let go and looked away. Bent over his rotting rose.

    go on, sunshine. help jacobi babysit.

The doctor left his side.

Ruth was waiting under the chestnut tree. Clearing the leaves from Belle's name, Dani walking with Simeon. Corey stooped to help her. The stone eyes pleading. Coldness tearing his stomach.
The older woman sighed. Gathering up her berries.
Can't keep out of trouble, that Lee.
Corey glanced up at her. Picked at a weed. A puff.

    and pal can't keep his mouth shut.

Ruth didn't meet him. Shook her head.

Nothing that wasn't true. Keep in line detective.
He narrowed his eyes. A prickle along his neck. Getting to his heels.

>you saw what the cure did to belle.

Over the course of a few months? It changed her life. Just a few hitches in the calibration process.

>unless he's lying. maybe it's worse than he let on.

Ruth gave a little chuckle. The orange fungus over her head pulsating.
You.
Have some faith. Take a look around even. Most of the town is on some form of the cure.

>even- even if it does work- what if he's changing things that don't need changing?

A girl like that needs help, detective.

>receiving help doesn't mean changing who she is.

Maybe changing who she is is something she needs to do.
Corey swallowed. Icy blooms clotting his stomach.
It was happening.
It was happening again.
In the clearing the Shepherd leered. Corey didn't move.
Evening. Ruth. Could I borrow you?
The cold in his throat sunk its blistering claws.
Me.

    can
    you
    hear
    me

What?

    did you hear that?

...Hear what?

    the first letter i spoke.
    and the next letter you spoke.
    she's speaking. speaking through us.

Detective... maybe you should sit down.
A pat over Corey's shoulder. When he looked up she had gone. The rosary in his pocket, vanished.
Across the clearing over the praying marble hands, a man in black vestiges, skin soft and white like bloated death. Eyes unmoving.
None of them could hear. None of them could see.
But I can hear.
You can see.
The detective fell over the base of the statue. Clasped the sculpted hands. The sun over Belle's head shined gold. Split into two. Shed light over the pulsating orange fungus.
From the sky a dove descended. The hyssop's reverent fingers raised to the clouds. A lake of fire. Set ablaze by a thousand tongues.
To the hyssop he crawled. Crawled and crawled and crawled and

dug and dug and dug until his nails snagged leather and beneath his hands was a journal and a name.
Isabella Rivera.

06 | the sculpted hands

Dr. Olliver said it would be a good idea to write my thoughts down. She says I can use it to reflect on my feelings or whatever. Get them all out. If I'm being honest I don't know if it'll help much. I don't even know what to write.
Just keep writing until something comes to mind, she said. But that just feels like a waste of space.
Does this count as a feeling?
Meh. I'll just try again tomorrow.
1:4

Dear C,
I think I'm getting a hang of this. The whole writing to myself thing. I'll just talk about my day again. Things have been going better than I thought. I'm meeting new people. Making something of mysel
Oh. Pal just texted again.
Not to be mean or anything but I don't like him at all. He's too intense with the faith stuff. He and the Shepherd. Always preaching my ear off. Jacobi too, but she's nicer about it. She actually tries to understand me. Pal and the Shepherd just nag. Is this blasphemous? I don't know. I just don't like them judging me all the time. Pal, Ruth, the Shepherd.
At least with Pal, Essie is there to tell him off and Lee laughs at him. I like those two. They're like me. Ruth gets cross with all three of us sometimes. I think she just expects too much. I don't want to disappoint her but I need some room to stretch my legs,

y'know?

Dani understands me. Still won't stop calling me Belle though. I don't think I mind it that much. The way she says it is nice. Belle and Danielle. I think I like her. I'm glad to have her as a roommate. She drops everything to call me and we could talk for days.

Simeon hates it, which is good. The thing is, he thinks I'm slacking off and runs to tell Ruth. I'm not slacking off though. I'm trying my hardest, really. But I'm just so bored. Cleaning up after him? I signed up to do more than that. I hope he lets me work. Really work. I want to make something.

At least I can work on the garden though. Me and the Lilies. I feel like I'm doing something good.

Ruth is nagging me again. Who are you, my mother?

That was mean.

She cares about me, I can tell. Plus she brings me jam.

That's all I guess. Also, I hope you don't mind the name. I don't know what it stands for. It just felt right to me. C. The link between B and D.

B

2:1

Dear C,

I finally finished it. It's just a chair but I'm so happy with it. I called Dani right after and she told me she was proud, that this was proof our pasts don't define us. She's right and I couldn't have done it without her. She was the one who convinced Simeon to let me work, made Ruth tell him. So, I want to give this chair to her.

My first paycheck came too. First thing I bought was this bird from Mr. Kraig. I was getting rat food for Dr. Olliver. Walked in, saw this pretty thing. Like a sign from God. Jacobi did say I should treat myself. We don't have much room for animals, but I think we'll make do. Me, Dani, and the bird.

But that's not the best part. Ruth brought me a jar of chokecherry jam and told me she was proud. I've never tasted anything so tart and sweet.

Everything feels right again. I want to make more things, for the Lillies and for Dr. Olliver. I think they'd like that. Something to make Ruth even happier.

Also, the hyssop I planted is growing strong. Ruth said it's all thanks to me.

I think that's it actually. Just... me.

God is smiling.

Simeon can suck it.

B

2:14

Dear C,

Ever since I started working more Simeon keeps bothering me. Keeps trying to flirt or fluster me. Maybe I should like him back with how hard he's trying. He can be sweet I suppose. Picking flowers from the side of the road. He isn't bad looking either. His smile grows on you. And he's really good with his hands. Has a bit of a creative touch, the things he makes. I think about him a lot but I can't tell if that's a good thing or a bad thing. Every morning I kind of dread seeing him. He makes me nervous. But maybe that's how it's supposed to be. Love messing you up. Like God's love. Whatever it is it makes me tired. I just want to go home with Dani. She always makes me feel better. Like everything will be okay.

I did ask Dani about it all, love and stuff. She said that the guy should make you feel safe and happy and giggly or whatever. Not Simeon though. Maybe love is different in Wyoming.

Still finished making all the furniture for Dr. Olliver like I said I would. But after that I've just been distracted. Haven't been doing super well. I just don't want to be around him.

Of course Simeon told Pal and now Pal keeps telling the Shepherd and now they all keep telling me to pray, even Ruth. Ruth is worried. I told her it's nothing. It really is nothing. Dani says it's okay. That it's not my fault. I want to believe her. I want to believe that God can save me.

B

3:9

Simeon said something to me and now I can't stop thinking about it. It's stressing me out. I don't even know if it's safe to write down.

It's messed me up. I'm acting more reckless. Kissing random boys. Anyone but him.

It's gotten so bad that the Shepherd called me up front. Got me on my knees to beg for forgiveness. I called him a sham and a charlatan. Mr. Kraig wouldn't stop screaming and Pal went white. Good. It's better this way. They should see me as a mess and a let down before they get their hopes too high. Before they see who I really am.

Ruth says I should stop. That it'll get me in trouble. She just doesn't understand. I was always going to let her down.

Now Dani is worried. She keeps checking on me, asking what's gotten into me. I don't want to see her. I don't want her to see me.

I hate seeing her.
I'm making paper stars so that I can fold up my feelings and turn them into something pretty.
The Shepherd wants Simeon to fix me. He can't. God knows I am not worthy.
I am not the girl I say I am.
4:0

Dear C,
I'm seeing Dr. Sykkes now because Ruth made me go. I don't want the cure though. I never wanted it. I just said yes to his stupid experiment because it could get me out of jail and working. How stupid. This place is just as much of a prison and I'm still stuck here. I'm stuck here with the Shepherd and Pal and Simeon and all of these freaks.
I said no to the cure. Ruth thinks I should have said yes. Everyone wants me to take it. Everyone wants me to say yes. They all want me to melt my brain and become the perfect girl but she isn't me.
I told Dr. Olliver and she told me not to listen to them. To listen to myself. She's gotten so fed up with Dr. Sykkes that she's moving out to her own place. I'm making more furniture for her. It keeps me away from home.
Maybe the cure can help me. I don't know. I don't know why God made me this way.
Dani still knocks on my door.
I never answer.
I am not the girl I say I am.
B
4:9

I snapped today.

Simeon keeps pushing me, thinking it's his mission to save me or something. I said yes to lunch cause I pity him. He took me to Psalms, the diner Dani works at. It was fine. We talked. Then he tried kissing me. I smacked him. Threw some tables. Broke a lot of stuff. I don't know. I hurt Dani.

Shepherd Job yelled at me during the sermon again. Ruth is ashamed of me. I deserve it.

I still don't want the cure. Dr. Sykkes says it's fine but I know he's disappointed. I wonder if he'll remove me from the program and cancel my contract. I hope he does.

Either way, Dr. Olliver said that it's my choice, and that Simeon was asking for it.

Dani didn't say a word to me.

5:0

I caught Dani with Simeon again.

Now the room is in pieces around me. I don't even remember doing it.

The chair is broken. Leg snapped in half. And the screaming won't stop. My own hateful voice, over and over again. I hate that bird. I never should have bought him. Dragged him with me into this miserable place.

I keep finding notes with verses. I think it's Pal. Always sending texts preaching me. Jacobi says he's trying to help. He isn't. When will they get it? I'm too far gone.

I tear off the margins and make my paper stars. Dani doesn't know what's inside them. What's inside me. She can never know. I am not the girl I say I am.

5:12

The pallets fell on me.
I think it was Simeon. It couldn't have fallen just like that.
He told me something. That if I keep this up Dani will be next.
I told Ruth. She said he wasn't wrong. That my wickedness was tainting everyone. Tainting Dani. Tainting the Lilies. That I need to fix myself or we'll all be damned.
All this time and she still doesn't get it. I got upset, so upset.
The garden is gone now. Torn to pieces.
I used to love that garden. But I put everything into it and for what? They care more about that garden than they care about me.
I see them. All of them. Watching. The Shepherd, the doctor, Ruth.
I am not the girl I say I am. I think they know it.

5:15

C I'm scared I'm so scared They came after me They came to our place and banged on the walls It's my fault It's all my fault And now I've put Dani in danger I hate them I hate them I hate all of them I hate Simeon I hate Pal I hate the Shepherd I hate Dr. Sykkes I hate Ruth I hate Dani I hate Dani I hate Dani I don't want this anymore I don't I don't I don't I'm hurting everyone around me Ruth says I need to take the cure To show them that I can do better I'll do it I have to do it I have to do it for Dani She doesn't deserve this She doesn't deserve any of this Doesn't deserve me I'm a coward Why can't I tell anyone the truth
i am not the girl i say i am

5:22

god
6:5

danidanidanidanidanidani
7:0

fold
folditfolditup
ihopeshe unfolds them for m
7:25

i see him
i see the prince
the prince
the prince
the prince
the prince
the prince
the prince
lust not
after her beauty
in your heart
neither let her
take you
with her
8:15

i took the bird

and squeezed him until he died
took him to mr kraig
and said mr kraig why do you cry?
i don't know why he's crying
the bird is free the soul is free i am free
still he gave another one to me
my mother scorns
my father screams
my brother shakes
now there is only one person who will meet my

-

8:21

proverbs six twenty five l
ust not after her beauty in your heart neither let he
r take you with her eyelids
god wants
a devo
ted daughter sleep sleep sleep wake wake wake c
o
re
y
he's
going
to
kill
me
he's

going
to
kill
me
he's
going
to
kill
me
he's
going
to
kill
me
he's
going
to
kill
me
he's
going
to
kill
m
e

d

a

n

i

song

of

my

soul

my

voice

is

d

The thing inside him stirred.

Dani agreed to meet with him for lunch at Psalms, still wearing her blue work uniform as she sat across from him. The diner fell under her management now. It murmured around her, a cozy venue of light music and candleglow, afternoon sun filtering in through spacious windows.
Corey selected a table in the corner, asked for a coffee. A daze to his avoidant eyes, smoked in shadow and sleeplessness. The journal tucked under his arm.

> i read belle's journal.

Dani spared him a glance from her napkin. Looked away again. Raven black hair spilling over her shoulders like a veil and an edge to her voice.
Leaving it in the garden was a mistake.
She tore at her napkin. One long strip, looping around and around.
Whatever's in there is dangerous. You shouldn't have read it.
He peered at her from over the rim of his mug. Steam curling around her sallow face.

> of all things i would call it. i wouldn't call it dangerous. misunderstood perhaps.
>
> it was just her thoughts. her truths.
>
> speaking to me.

He set the mug down. Folded his hands.

> you buried it. you buried it because it scared you. didn't you?

She didn't answer. He didn't press. Took a spoonful of sugar to his coffee. Watched the lump of saccharides as it sank.

> simeon hurt her.

A stir over the creamer until it spun slow into a spiral.

> he might not be the one, but he's just as responsible.
> they terrorized her.

Dani narrowed her eyes. Voice frigid.
Vermin like him will get what is coming to them.
I will make sure of it.

> explain it to me then.

A tilt of his head. Eyes soft.

> why are you talking to him again? he's dangerous.

Dani tied a knot in her strip of paper. Tugged sharply.
You, me, him.
We all want the same thing.
Justice for Belle.
She pinched the corners, met his gaze. Smoldering and full of rage.
If that means having to deal with him then so be it.
But I won't be forgetting what he did.
Never.

> okay.
> i see.

but,

He brought his cup of coffee to his lips. Just to get its scent.

if he ever gives you any trouble-

She slammed the table. A lean forward and a hiss.
Understand me when I say. I will handle it.

dani-

She got out of her seat. He caught her arm, slid the journal over to the edge of the table.

you should take this.

please.

she would have wanted you to have it. to read it. the things she never got to tell you-

She snatched her arm away.
Are you serious? You want me to read that? What will that change? She's gone. Nothing feels the same or smells the same or tastes the same and nothing is going to fix that.
I'm not reading it.

no-

He leapt to his heels. Caused her to stumble. Stars spilled from her pocket, snow, tears, rain. Dani stooped to pick them up with shaking hands. Plucked them from the floor like berries. Wiped

at her eyes.
I don't want to read it.
Corey knelt to help her. Hovered quiet and breathless. His gaze was fixed on the fallen stars between her fingers. A swirl.

>the stars.

A swallow and a chill over his cheeks. Voice a hush.

>unfold them.

Dani looked up at him. Teary eyed.
What?

>unfold them for her.
>please.

A scoff. She shook her head and looked away. The detective reached into his pocket, picked out the one eaten by rot. Unraveled it. Held it out in his glove palm.
When the words registered in her mind Dani looked down at the paper stars pooled in her hands. Unwrapped the next one. Then the next. And the next.
Each one was a message written for her. The same three words. Over and over again. Folded up and turned into something pretty.
I love you
I love you
I love you
I love you
I love you

I love you
Crumpled over the paper stars she wept. The song carried just over the hill to the chapel and into the garden where the weeping daughter stirred her long dead heart of stone.
    Corey kept beside her. Held out Belle's journal. Pushed it into her trembling grasp.

        please.
        she wants you to take it.

Dani didn't move. A whisper only he could hear and an empty darkness of blackened stars.
Get
out.
In his chest his heart faded. He rose again to his heels. Backed away. Counted the beads of his rosary. When he turned he saw his own eyes in the window.
Isabella Rivera stared back at him.
Carved in stone. Withdrawing slow from his reflection.
Corey followed. Followed until blackened stars swam in his eyes and the sun split into two and all he could see in the negative void was her ragged silhouette. Her. The sleeping daughter.
Stiff in death she turned. Her marble skin crumbled ashen brown and out spilled from the fissures long dark hair and a snow white gown and deep empty eyes like unlit embers. His own eyes.
A hand on his shoulder.
The sky turned over and went dark.
Loose and bloody earth molded beneath his feet, wet and warm. A gush of wind carrying leaf fall and iris. Sweet words husking light over his ear.

Darling.

You're sleepwalking again.

Corey fell into Wayne's arms and began to whimper.

07 | the fallen stars

Winter came with aching bones. The bleed ebbing into a weeping flow.

In the midst of cleaning the doctor found an old napkin inked and scribbled on. Recognized the scratchy penmanship. A soft smile that faded.

wet crevice,
rotten ochre.
it rasps
on earth.
it yields
infects
seeds.
from life to death is life and death
exsanguinated.
the higher you arch
the deeper it digs.

Note in hand, he knocked on the detective's door. Corey peeked through. Fluffy hair a mess. Wearing one of the red sweaters Wayne had gifted him.

The frown on his face eased considerably when he saw Wayne standing there, adjusting his glasses, nose in the napkin.

Oh. Dove. Is this yours?

what?

A flick down at the paper. Skimming the words. Corey held out a gloved hand. Six months and he hadn't taken them off once. Sensitive skin that broke under feather touch. Ghosts grazed his knuckles and the hair of his arms, blood dried in the breeze.

    give me that.

The doctor tilted his head. A bit of a frown.
I've already seen it.
Tell me, what it is.

    nothing.

Corey kept his gaze until the other gave in, pushing the note into the detective's hand.
I wonder what else you keep from me.
Corey rolled his eyes. Receded into his room, rubbing the back of his neck. To his annoyance Wayne followed.
Sore?

    i'm fine.

They stopped at the foot of his bed. Wayne reached out to cup his cheek and Corey caught his wrist in a tangle. An unamused look.

    quit it.

Why the fuss, dear?

    i'm sure you can figure it out, sunshine.

Don't be ridiculous.
Lie down.
A stern gaze, the lance of his frames cutting across his hooked nose. Corey sat himself down with a sigh. Bed sinking beneath his weight. Wayne tilted up his chin. Examined the dark flush beneath his smokey eyes. Blue silver and sleepless death.
Have you been sleepwalking again?
Corey pulled his face away, a grim smile.

> i don't even know if i'm awake.

A brow raise. The doctor's hand fell to his shoulder, a gentle squeeze.
It seems you're in need of rest, my dear.

> it's more than that.

A push and Wayne laid him down. Traced his fingertips over Corey's sides. Corey hesitated, a breath's width from the cool tones of Wayne's cheek. White and soft. Like that of the lifeless man watching from the twin shadows of the churchyard. He dropped his hand from the other's arm, held still.

> see, lately i've been having dreams.

Pressing. His sweet undertaker passed to him a pitiful glance, returned to his work.
Ah... Dreams?

> nobodies in masks.
> dancing until we became sand.
> praying for me. for me to take off my mask.

Remove your mask?
The day began to show its wear as Wayne pulled back. Silver hair falling apart over his face.
Interesting. Interesting. Did you do it?
Corey shifted a knee before the other pushed it back down.

   not wearing one, doc.

Curious.
A small chuckle.
Everyone wears a mask, my dear.
A cold draft snagged his spine and Corey lifted his head to glare at the other.

   i've fought long and hard to wear my real face.

Wayne nudged him back, planted the other's head firmly back into the mattress, ignored the muffle under his palm.
Now. How can you know for sure what's real and what isn't?

   you're not.

Wayne didn't seem to hear him. Drew his touch down, smoothed the taut muscle in Corey's arms with his wiry hands. A tap over his shoulder.
Turn over please. Fold your arms under your chin.
The doctor hovered over him, leaning his weight on one side, head tilted in patience, eyes astray. Corey searched his gaze and found nothing of response. With a frown he rolled onto his stomach, buried his nose as the doctor's fingers brushed through his hair, massaged the base of his skull, a whisper straight into the

locus of his brain.
Brainstem...
A gentle press. Corey huffed into the sheets and the doctor murmured over his ear. Petting and working his shoulder.
Remember to breathe, dove.
His palms fell down Corey's back, kneaded along the spine. Corey held a small grunt, timed the breath in his chest with the hum of Wayne's throat.
Are you still hearing things?
The hands danced lower. Corey flinched, hissed softly.

> i told you. i'm not hearing things.
> you just need to listen.

I am, dove.
Light over his ear. Wayne dug his fingertips into the notch of Corey's tailbone.
Sacrum.
Soft pressure. Left, then right. A whisper. Murmur smooth basalt over supine skin.
On your back now.
Corey pushed himself up to a sitting position, shoulders sagging. At the bright look on Wayne's face he turned away, folded himself onto his back.

> i wish i could show you.

Wayne circled around. Stopped at his head. A brush over his cheek, ghosting, lingering. Voice soft.
Just let me help you.
He slid his hands beneath, the notches of his fingers setting into

the nooks in Corey's neck, dragging even over the other's scalp. Corey shut his eyes, bit his lip.

> what i'm hearing isn't a voice. it's a pattern. if you listened-

The pressure released. Thumbs brushing his jaw. Wayne peered down at him, silver hair spilling over his lenses, mouth turned into a subtle frown. Light refracted from his head in a ring of gold. Corey averted his eyes, eased up to rub his shoulder. The doctor rounded the bed again. Covered his hand.
And if the pattern is merely of your own design?
Stillness. The detective turned his head slow. Met the other's gaze with thinning pupils that drank light like coal.

> my design.

The doctor raised a brow, absorbed in the feeling of the other's knuckles under his thumb. Each ridge, cold and hollow beneath the fabric.
Your poem, dove. Don't think I wouldn't notice.
The first letter of every last word.
He let his hand free, bent to face him. Rolled up his creased and slipping sleeves.
How can you expect me to help you if you hide pieces of yourself like that?
Corey stretched a smile. His eyes didn't blink. Filled to the rims with blackened stars as he teetered closer.

> you can see?

The doctor pulled back and Corey stopped him. Grasped his hand tight under his gloves. Muttering. The ink letters spewing from his mouth like writhing moths dried and shrunken.

> death,
> exsanguinate,
> arch,
> dig,
> i can hear,
> you can see,
> if i can hear and you can see,
> i wonder
> if i've missed

The words trailed off. Corey remained, still and unbreathing and cold. Eyes a pallid marble. Flicking back to the doctor.
Wayne's palms tensed under Corey's stone clasp. He murmured, slow and even.
Corey.
Perhaps the ANNE's can provide you with some relief-

> I wear no mask.

Corey crawled closer. Dying breaths worming against his neck.

> no mask, no mask,
> and belle sings,

Wayne tore out from his grasp. Hand trembling and clenching. A step back.
Corey. Please.

The other sat where he was on the edge of the bed. A smile. Leaning forward. Hands folded.

I read her journal.

Parted lips. Wayne stuttered and Corey watched him, watched him struggle to tame his own breath.
She kept a journal?

mm.
She did.
and i read it.
All of it.

Corey was close enough to drink the soul from his lips. Ash and roses over his skin, dark hair scattered like feathers banished from light.

No living god can absolve you of the truth, Sebastian.
you did this.
you failed her.
you failed *me*.

A flinch. Wayne turned his face away. Rolled up his sleeves.
Get on all fours.
A soft chuckle over his jaw. Corey cooed soft and low. Pierced his side with shame.

Deny me three times. I wonder, what it will take, for you to remove your mask…?

On your knees.

at least buy me a drink first...

Wayne pulled back. Removed his glasses, swiped at his eyes. Sleepy warmth lapsing into lonesome cold. The mumbles of a child's prayer. Sure with a devout certainty that the Devil sat preening himself before him.
He hushed Corey before the other could speak, replacing his lenses as he cradled his partner's face. Thumbs sliding upwards to the corners where Corey's furrowed brows met the gentle slope of his nose. A soft brush.
You're going to feel a slight pressure.
He pressed his thumbs into the hollows of his eyes, the little coves where tears well and collect. Drew his fingertips down his face. Grazed the lips, smoothed the curves of his cheeks, from the back of his head to the edge of his collarbone. Delicate fingers settling like hands on a piano.
Corey's chest had stopped rising some time ago. Deep eyes hollowed out. Wayne pretended not to notice. Examining the emptiness of his partner's irises. The kind he'd only seen in angels.
White lace curled against his hand. Warm like sulfur. He held still as the heat sunk itself into his shoulder. A brush beneath his ear that licked in blue flame.
The doctor crushed the body into the mattress.
The bone mass flailed and jumped and writhed beneath him, skin too soft and too warm and hair too light and too flowy, and the voice he heard was only an imitation, unlived in, dead. Wayne hissed, weight acumber like stones.
To set fire in the land of the plain-
The varnish over Corey's pupils faded. Crumbled to earth as he

blinked away the blackened stars. Corey hacked and scratched at his wrists.

    get off me- wayne- what the hell-?

The doctor snapped him still. Corey in his red sweater and slipping jeans, choking up at him through his smoke. Living, breathing, flushed red. The rot lifted and gave in to roses, sweet in his hair. A thoroughly unamused look like a puppy tumbled down the stairs.
Wayne removed himself from the other's person. Brushed off, turned to the wall, rubbed his face. A long, long exhale.
Why don't we go outside for some fresh air.
Frame bent away in shame. It wasn't a suggestion. A hand over his throat, Corey didn't question it. Glanced about the room. The only sign of struggle the wrinkled sheets beneath him and an old stain of red that wouldn't wash.
The detective creaked to his heels. Lifted his coat off the chair and slung it over his slim shoulders. Wedged the door open, eyes cast down. The doctor pushed past him, descended the stairs into the lobby, palmed the scanner, pushed face first into the frigid nighttime air. Half through the lawn he fell to his knees. Laid himself down and surrendered himself to the earth. After some hesitation Corey curled up next to him. Buried his nose in his elbow.

    i'm sorry.

Wayne didn't meet his eyes. Kept to the night sky and the thinning clouds. Hair ruffled by the undying wind. Some silence steeling himself before he pointed upwards, a soft whisper.

That's Taurus in the sky. Aldebaran is the brightest star you see there. Behind it, the Hyades. The weeping sisters, rain and stardust come winter.

He folded his hands comfortably over his unbuttoned vest, one leg propped over the other. Lenses glinting like watershine in the moonlight. Silver hair curled in seafoam over his cheeks.

Corey wasn't looking at the Hyades.

Wayne had taken a glance at his companion by chance. A cautionary look at first, until he saw him, Corey, watching passively over the crook of his arm. Close enough to touch yet quiet enough to forget. Under the doctor's hazel gaze the detective turned his eyes away, hid behind his dark hair and burrowed into the grass. Wayne's voice rose, soft and whispery like oceantide.

Did I tell you? About the angels?

Corey sunk himself deeper into his elbow. A small nod.

    you do. every night.

A big smile on his face and a chuckle. Wayne turned his face away. Stars in his eyes.

Angels came to me in a dream once.

He sat up. Nudged his partner.

You would weep. Knowing how fervently I prayed.

A lean forward. Hush tickling over his ear.

They delivered me, to this very moment.

Corey huffed. Pinched a blade of grass. Dry fibers snapping between his fingers.

    to do what? piss me off?

To save you.
A glance. His face was a reflection of the moon and the moon was only a reflection of the sun. Corey turned his eyes away.

    i don't need saving.

Wayne shifted closer. Corey silent. He took his arm. A long look over the smoke of his eyes, like he could will it back into palm leaf.
I saw her again.
The angel of my temptations.
Corey kept silent. A stirring in his belly. Wayne reached out. Brushed aside a lock of hair to trace his cheek. Cold fingertips, something bone dry and ancient.
You remind me of my angel. And, my darling, even angels fall.

    what are you-

Corey's voice cut short. The touch had drifted lower. Fingertips dragging down his arm. Wayne slid a hand up his waist. Stopped over the small of his back. Tugged him close. Slipping upwards from the apple of his throat to his cheek. Thumbing the plush of his kiss.
Perhaps I'm holding back.
Corey stared blankly. Dark hair catching over his eyes.

    move your hand or you'll lose it.

A small scoff. Brushing Corey's hair aside and tracing down the curve of his jaw.
Life and its pleasures can be distilled into two components.

Want and need. Body and soul.
His hand settled over Corey's shoulder. A soft squeeze.
One must favor the soul.
Corey grew conscious of his gloved hands, the black ring over his finger. A shrug. He flashed a smile.

> i don't know if anything is ever that simple, doc.

Is it not? Temptations of the flesh.

> flesh doesn't tempt me.

A hum. Wayne dragged his thumb, to the stud of Corey's ear, into his hair.
I find that hard to believe. Someone like you.

> someone like me.

Flesh. Skin.
You do not crave such things?

> i crave soul.

Corey curled a hand through Wayne's hair. Let a trapped moth into his palm.

> cynthia vane,
> sybil shade,
> my dark vanessa.
> i loved her too deeply.
> too brokenly.
> she thought i didn't love her at all.

He set the moth against the breeze. Watched it flutter and drift under the lamp light. At Wayne's fix he dared closer. Drank in his scent, his iris, his sandalwood, his clove.

    and you? does your passion burn differently?

Wayne stared down at his friend. Pushed his hand down.
It burns when it shouldn't.
I am my own desert and my own temptation.
His hazel eyes flicked back upwards. Golden flecks shimmering.
Like he was grieving something better left unsaid.
Dove, when it comes to want and need, your need is salvation.
And yet I am fearful.
There are so many ways I could hurt you, with just my hands.

    and where are your hands now?

A glance down. Arm wrapped snuggly around his friend's waist like a lifeline. Warmth clinging. The doctor removed himself. Pulled back. A cool smile.
I'm fancying a drink. Care to join me?

    that's some way to ask, cowboy.

A chuckle and Wayne helped Corey to his feet. Let the other lean against him for support. They made their way back into the clinic.

Coat in arm, Corey was about to make up the stairs to the kitchen when the doctor disappeared behind the front desk and into his office. He reemerged with two chairs in tow. A gaze up

at his friend.
And where do you think you're going?

    you can't be serious.

A knock on wood. The doctor flashed a smile, leaned against the counter.
It did serve as a bar top in its previous life.
Corey risked a step. Hands in his pockets.

    what do you have?

Just about anything you could thirst for. Only the finest, of course.
I served briefly as a bartender in New Haven, while I was studying under Dr. Archer and Dr. Campbell.

    of course you did.

Corey sat himself at the makeshift bar. Watched the other work, running back and forth between his office and the kitchen. Letting the river flow like the Styx.
The detective had himself sangria. The doctor absinthe.

    nice that you're unwinding for once.

    are you gonna talk to me about rats becoming gay cannibals?

    or maybe we can come up with another excuse for why the shipments are late again. before ruth breaks the door down.

> or you could call jacobi. have her tell us about all those children that got lost in the mines.

Ah. Not this time.
A sip of his green tincture. Watching Corey drink with a diced apple on his tongue, a smile over the rim and a raised brow. The doctor averted his gaze.
Do not misinterpret my intentions.
The smile dropped right into his glass. Corey stared unamused.

> your intentions.
> is it your intention to deny yourself?

Wayne set his chalice down. Templed his fingers.
The Lord is my strength and the Lord has bestowed upon me His cure.
If you allow Him to help you-

> like he helped belle?

The doctor gawked at him like he'd been pierced in the side. Corey took a sip. One leg crossed over the other.

> what would you change about me?

Dove?

> you regret having me, don't you?

Darling. Why would you say that?
Corey picked at a groove in the wood. Deep enough for a bullet, a nail, a finger. A flicker upwards. Wayne leaned close to brush

over his cheek but the other pulled away, reached for his drink, swallowed down the rest of his thickened wine. Silence. Corey tilted the empty glass, watched the red catch dim yellow over the rim.

> you want me to worship. you want me to change who
> i am.
> but i can't do that.
> and that infuriates you, doesn't it?
> that i don't believe in you.
> that i forsake you.

Corey. Please.
The doctor let a breath. Tugged at the collar of his shirt. With a smile Corey pushed his glass aside, leaned closer. Dug a gloved finger into his chest.

> you'd love to fix me.
>
> set me straight.
>
> tear me apart from the inside and turn me into the perfect, submissive wife.

A tremble and the doctor kept him at arm's length but Corey only pressed onward.

> i say i don't want it.
> but what if i need it?
> if i can't bring her justice, who can?
> maybe, if you fix me,

Wayne squeaked. Tension bobbing in his throat. And at his pleading tone Corey smiled, sharp over his ear.

> you like hearing that don't you?
> all my hope going down the drain and into the hands of your god.
> into your hands.

He settled into his lap. Tugged at the ascot around his neck.

> know what i hate most. about you.

> your love.

> your love is vengeful.

> your love is controlling.

> and when it comes to the things you love you destroy what you cannot control.

A swallow. Wayne trembled beneath him. Every ache in his body pulled taut and stiff.
What is it that you want from me?

> i could tell you all things we both want and you'd tell me that all we need is salvation.

A huff and the doctor pushed back his scattered hair.
Tell me what it is that you need and I'll give it to you.

> i want to see your real face.

You'd sooner have me burn.
A lean forward. The sting of wormwood over his breath.

> then you profess your nature. the fall of man into mortal sin.

> you denounce fire and in the formless void and the sleeping face of the deep you let death sink its weary teeth.

Tasting the bitter hyssop on his lips he whispered.

> when you finally prostrate yourself to the holy fire i will say, let there be light.

The doctor didn't say a word. Eyes fixed on the lapse of air between them. Smooth absinthe. Thickened wine.
Corey picked up his coat and left for the stars.

08 | my real face

In the middle of the night Corey received a phone call. He'd been ignoring Wayne but this time it was Lee Palomo. Crying up a panic. He'd dashed onto the premises with a few breaths to spare. Circling before knocking.
The door flung open and Lee crashed into his arms. Trembling and sobbing. He steadied himself, held Lee there a good minute. Small pats. Lee was ruffled but uninjured. The door marred in scarring words a bleeding red.

    Are they gone?

He nodded.

    they're gone.

A sniff. Lee burrowed into his shoulder, warm and clinging. Hair burning like myrrh, balsam.

    I couldn't see their faces. They were wearing masks and they-

Corey rubbed at a smear of gray and off came a thick smudge of ash. Lee peered up at him with wide shimmery eyes. He tucked his gloved hand away. Murmured soft over their hair.

    it's okay. i'll take care of it.

Lee held still against his neck. The thrum of anxiety over his collarbone.

    Do you know who did it?

He soothed their back. Voice drifting like feathers and dreams.

    i have an idea. don't worry about it.

A frown. Clinging tighter.

    It was Pal wasn't it? He must've told the Shepherd and the sandmen-

Corey tucked aside a loose cut of Lee's hair. Tilted down to look at them.

    the sandmen?
    I overheard Ruth saying it.
    mm.
    did you call her?
    No.

Lee peered around, into the dark that clouded their circle of light, the stars over Corey's head.

    You're sure they're gone?
    i'm sure.
    Could you please- stay with me until-
    i'll stay.

A grin of relief. Charming and lopsided. Lee took his hand, pulled him inside.

As with most homes in Bentham the living room spanned a utilitarian stretch of space, furnished in second hand and cramped with how lived in it was. Paintbrushes and cups of dirty water full of pigments. Old clothes and scattered puzzle pieces. Buttons, figures, cards. A Halloween costume Corey had helped Lee with a few months ago, werewolf cowboys and vampire pirates. There was so much of Lee to drown, soul spilled into every clutter in the room. Like some great web of detraction solely to forget for but a moment the ghost of the person it all unraveled from. Every item a thought discarded.
A rustle from the couch drew Corey's eyes. Being the old dog he was he tilted his head and watched. A gray rock dove teetered over the arm of the couch and toppled into a cushion. Corey couldn't help the small chuckle.

    still here?

    Yes!

    His wing healed up fine, it's just that he's gotten too comfortable. Mr. Gersch said I should keep him for a while, until he's ready.

    that's kind of you.

Their small nod came with a flush. Lee let go of his hand and stumbled over to the easel against the wall. A portrait of blocky strokes, warm and full of hues. Corey followed with a slow and sleepy patience.

    I think I should redo it.

I look too boyish.

The detective offered half a shrug and twice a thought.

suits you.
i don't see anyone else in there but you.

Lee shook their head. Ducked their eyes away. A soft glow and the hum of angels.

It's nothing like the face I wear in the mirror.

Corey reached out, pinched at Lee's cheek. Gentle like crumbled earth or stale coffee grounds.

but it's how you feel. who you are.
the face you painted for yourself.
I never wanted a face.

One final trace over the texture of the canvas. Lee turned towards the couch and sat. Scooping up the rock dove like a cup of trembling and petting it. A deep rumbling purr and a chill to the room.

Do you believe in ghosts?

Corey trailed after. Quiet as he leaned against the coffee table. Wood carved in familiar strokes.

i believe in soul.

The dove fluttered upwards. Lee gave a small smile. Eyes flicking to his.

> I can hear them.
> I know you can too.

Their gaze cast down. Thumbing their hands.

> I'm scared, Core. That I'll end up just like them. Because I'm just like her.

A grasp for his pinky. Corey knelt before them. Peeled off the fabric of his gloves. With bare skin he warmed the other's cold fingers, blew softly over them. Kissing the knuckles like a mother kisses the scrapes on her son's knees. Looking into Lee's eyes he saw the person he could have been. Unlit embers lonely and cold and dark.

> i won't let anything happen to you.

Lee pulled a hand away. A swipe over the cheek and a shaky breath.

> I think I deserved it.
> no. you didn't.
> They know I'm wrong. They know.
> And only the doctor can fix me. Make me right.

A scoff and Corey took Lee's hands again.

> lee. sweetheart.

> i love you, but you don't give up on the whole bush for

having a little rot on the edges.

Again Lee pulled away.

You don't understand.

Another shaky breath. Trembling beneath their calloused hands. Fissures behind their eyes.

The soul that rejects its own flesh must be rotten.
then you take the flesh and paint it yours.

Lee didn't answer. Corey knew the pain well enough to feel within himself a helpless sort of guilt. And when Lee refused to look his paternal intuition told him that the other was crying. Crying and quivering. With a tender touch he gathered Lee into his arms. Soothed their hair and cooed, half to Lee, half to himself.

son.
i see you.
all of you.
i won't let anything happen to you.
not again.

He kissed the top of their head. Lee wept soft into his chest.

They passed the rest of the night with charcoal and movies before Corey departed once again, Lee asleep on the couch under his fraying gray coat. Out in the cold with his dull red sweater he made a final circle around the premises, every shadow

in every rusted corner and hedge. The sun rose behind him. Cast red on the porch a jar of chokecherry jam.
A pause by the window. Corey drew his hands from his pockets. Set them on his hips.

ruth.

One of the shadows shifted. Bold and weathered.
Detective.
It was Ruth Welles who stepped out into the morning light. Silvery braids glinting.
She alright?
He held still. Rigid and distrustful.

lee's fine.

A moment to trace her tired features before he averted his eyes. Six months of shame and resentment and the only link between them was a ghost and a half.
Ruth glanced through the window. Lee curled up and snoring.
Has to learn some way or another.
A flicker. Corey tore his gaze from Lee's messy hair. Tensed and untensed his fists with his slowing heartbeat. The accusation written on his face so broken Ruth had to look away, down into the earth at her feet.
Corey murmured soft and low and hollow. Like Lee asleep could hear him through the windowpane.

you were supposed to protect them.

Ruth fixed on Lee's sleeping form. Haggard creases over her

cheeks. Eyes unblinking.
This time will be different.
Corey turned his face away. Kept walking.

He followed the heat in his head towards the sun screaming behind the chapel and past his risen roses where he fell into the shade of the chestnut tree beneath Belle's feet. Heart refusing to pace itself as he stared into the bright and orange fungus. The ache of betrayal yawned pure oxygen into his blood, flashpoint sharp and volatile.
He put his ear to the receiver. It was a salve. It was a need.

    sunshine.

The voice on the other end was deep and rutted with sleep.
Corey, darling...
A rustle and a hush and a soft groan.
Please don't run off again...
Another breath. Corey kept his words short and clipped. Some turmoil beneath he tried to hide. But Wayne knew him all too well.

    lee was attacked.

Oh dear. Is she alright?
Corey slumped against the pedestal. Rested his cheek against the cold marble.

    did you know?

A brief hesitation. Wayne sat straight, murmured low and

soothing.
No. No, darling, I didn't.

    ruth knew.

Corey wedged his shoulder against the cold.
Did they hurt her?

    they left a mark on lee's door. rubbed ash in lee's face.

But she wasn't injured.

    ain't safe either.

Wayne didn't speak a moment. Corey could hear him swallow and mutter to himself on the other line before leaning close into the phone.
And what would you have me do?
Another of Belle's paper stars under his boot. Corey got to his heels, sat in front of his roses. He was starting to beg. But for Lee, he'd give up anything. His coat, his dignity.

    stop them, wayne. lock them up. kick them out. i don't know. something.

They are the foundation of this community. I can speak with them but I won't go as far as removing them.
Corey gave a short laugh. The doctor revealing his hand.

    that's it?

Wayne spoke sweet and even. The same tone he used to lecture

his patients.
Have it in your heart to forgive.
I'm sure they were only trying to help her see.
Let go. Live and let live.
Corey clenched his jaw. Rose steady to his heels. Wind buffeting his hair until it bloomed about his face like a tangle of dark ivy.
No answer.
The doctor laughed softly. A short pause.
Now, dear, don't do anything reckless.
Nothing but the wind and its muffled demented rattle. The doctor gave another laugh. A bit more force to his voice.
Corey?
A shift and the sound of a zipper threading.
Darling?
Corey hung up.

Simeon Turner's Home Improvement opened at the crack of dawn. Tools, furniture, woodware. Bentham had built and refurbished itself from the ground up and this little department store was at the heart of it all. Near empty except for one Kraig Cephas Gersch at the register, picking up an order of wire bird cages. So there would be witnesses.
Corey walked right up to the shelf full of thinner and spray paints. Plucked a canister of red. Simeon Turner rose behind him.
Can I help you. Delgado.
A smile and Corey turned the can over. Read the label. Produced in the USA by Bentham Inc. He flicked his gaze up to Simeon's jutted jaw.

mind getting me a list of guys who bought this?

Simeon grinned. A mouth full of teeth.
According to law that information is private.
Corey popped the cap. Fiddled with the nozzle. The length of it was firm, sturdy in his hand. He matched the other's smile.

sure, sure, but i'm investigating a case of vandalism, and the only store that sells spray paint of any kind is yours.

Keep wasting my time then. I can't help ya.
A click. Shaking the can. Cold over his wrists.

can't or won't?

Simeon didn't answer. Stepped up into Corey's space. Leaned down and clucked his teeth.
Must be tough, running into a dead end.
A clatter on the floor and the cap rolled sideways from his boot. Neither of the men swapped gazes.

i know what you did.
and i know what you did to lee.

Simeon smirked, nodded to Kraig.
Lee was asking for it.
Put a knife to your throat if you are given to gluttony.
But, go on, little lamb. Keep on dreaming about the prince of sand.
A tear in his stomach. The heat sapped from his fingers. Can held so tight that his gloves squeaked from the friction. Liquid

solvent sloshing cold. The detective flipped the can in his hand. Firm. Sturdy. Hefty.

He sprayed a line of red over Simeon's eyes. When he screamed Corey cracked the canister open over his head. It crunched like a gunshot. Burst in hot acrylic. Dull red mixing with dull red.

Beyond the blackened stars a gape in his heart and the echo of a ring in his ears.

Kraig wouldn't stop crying.

Ruth arrived on scene. Had a feeling after Dr. Sykkes called her about Handler. Pushed into Turner's Home Improvement and saw the detective standing over Simeon, bloodied spray can in hand. Neither of them responsive. She marched forward, pried the bent metal from the detective's hand, pushed him back. Slapped Simeon until he groaned weak but alive. Kraig Gersch wailing.

She told Kraig to call Jacobi and Dr. Olliver. With them came Dr. Sykkes and Shepherd Job.

Jacobi helped load Simeon onto a stretcher. Dr. Olliver looking him over as gently as she could. The detective slumped against the wall. Compressed air gushed from the red twisted aluminum crumple on the floor. One long pneumatic hiss.

Kraig stumbled into the Shepherd's arms, gagging and frothing. Shepherd Job's knuckles clenched white. A snarl to the graying woman.

What in God's name happened here?

Ruth wiped a bloody hand with an old rag.

What do you think.

Kraig whimpered into the Shepherd's shoulder, pointed shakily at the detective comatose in the corner before choking holy

water from his flask.
Wrath is cruel…! Wrath is cruel…!
The Shepherd glared, snapped to Dr. Sykkes.
Doctor!
The doctor kept his eyes ahead. As though ignorance would make his predicament go away.

> Fear not. I will make the proper adjustments.

A growl in the Shepherd's sagging throat.
I want him gone.
The doctor only smiled.

> That decision is not yours to make.

So you deny the will of your people in favor of your pet. You fornicate with the devil and all that is unholy.
Doctor.
You forsake us.
The turbulence in the doctor's eyes clashed like wave against cliff eaten rock.

> Better that a man forsake another man than a man forsake his God.

There is no God in you, Sebastian.
Ruth stepped away to fix the messy aisles. Jacobi raised her hands.
Maybe we should sit down and talk about it-
A barking laugh and Jacobi shut her mouth. The doctor pushed up his lenses, flashed his crooked teeth.

Excellent idea.

Why don't we discuss this over dinner?

Another discussion.

Another discussion while the shelves run bare and our people starve and claw to be let from the den of lions.

Have faith in me. I will set you free.

Kraig whined and the Shepherd held him at length. The doctor hummed, gaze flicking over Miranda. She ducked from his eyes.

Surely you wouldn't deny your wife the company.

At that the Shepherd faltered. Deepened to a shade of red brighter than that of the spray can as the doctor only smiled.
My wife?
The temper in his head fizzled from the spit. He smoothed himself over. A tug at his collar. Pallid skin a sweat and an attempt at a smile.
Of course. My wife.
He shrank down, clasped his weary hands.
Very well then.
May the deliberations commence.
Miranda bent to lift the stretcher. The doctor turned to her.

You have Simeon taken care of?

A small nod. She didn't meet his eyes. Said nothing as they carried Simeon away.
Satisfied Dr. Sykkes turned to Jacobi. He hadn't glanced at the detective once.

> Take him back to the clinic.

An obedient lamb, Jacobi did as told. Took the detective by the arm and marched him across town, sat him down at the clinic's steps. Her and her silent prisoner.

> where is lee?

Jacobi raised her brows, leaned closer. The detective sat with his jade beaded rosary pooled in his lap. Mouth moving unintelligibly.
What?
A whimper into his hands. Beads spilling from his fingers. Jacobi fiddled with her scarred thumbs before squeezing Corey's shoulder. Voice gentle.
Lee's at home. Don't worry.

> i need to talk to lee. please.

Jacobi nodded. Tentatively dialed, held up her phone to his ear. To hear Lee's voice. One last time.

> Corey? I heard what happened, are you okay?
> i'm okay.
> i'm okay.
> lee.
> i'm sorry.
> It's okay. You were trying to protect me.
> i couldn't do it.
> i couldn't do it.

> i couldn't

Jacobi murmured a goodbye. Closed the call and tucked it away. Corey's voice died a whisper. Soft and hollow.

> i'm doing it again.

Jacobi wrapped his beads tighter. A sigh.
You did what you thought was right.
His eyes remained unblinking and she pulled him closer but he didn't seem to notice. Mumbling.

> they know.
> they all know.

A mumble over his hair. She took his face into her hands, into prayer. Wrapped his jade rosary around his trembling fingers.
I'm here for you.
She took him into her arms.
He is here for you.
His pupils bloomed clear under her touch and for a moment he was safe from the blackened stars and the forgotten truth that rested on the formless and slumbering face trapped in the great represses of the deep.

Wayne gave Jacobi a call, said he'd be away for the rest of the day. Asked nothing of Corey. No one did until Miranda stopped by. Propping a boot up on the steps.

> How are y'all doing?

Fine. Corey's, uh,

    i'm okay.

He'd been crying but he showed no sign of it. Remembered something only to forget he even forgot it in the first place. Miranda made no comment, raised a brow.

    You're just sitting out here in the cold?

No key.
A sigh and Miranda plopped down. Boggles peeking out of her pocket.

    Wayne didn't invite me to supper.

Corey warmed his hands, held her satchel for her. She retrieved from it some tupperware.

    They're planning something.
    Keeping me away from Anna.

Over her knee the lid popped open with a snap. A stab of her fork. She bit and chewed with narrowed eyes.

    Corey. I need you to get a copy of his patient files. The ones locked away in his office.

    Do this for me and I can try to get you into a meeting with the sandmen.

Now, hold on–

You know what we need to do, Jacobi.

Corey hugged his arms. Leaned back against the wood rail. Rot bending under his weight.

i'll do it.

Wayne returned home in the middle of the night. Didn't say a word. The look of victory vanishing from his face the moment the other dropped in for breakfast. The doctor refused to speak, staring down at his thumbs and fuming silently the whole time Corey was there, despite his incessant prodding. And the new day came and went just like that. Excruciating nothing. Not even a sweet dreams before bed.
But that wasn't important at the moment.
Miranda enlisted the tech genius of Essie Easley to get the door open just before midnight on the eve of the next day's security patch. Of course Wayne was still up at that time, the light to his room still on, shadow pacing back and forth beneath the door. Busy leaving threatening voicemails on the phone.
Corey watched the clock. Crept down the stairs, ducked behind the front desk. Three seconds and the door to the doctor's office clicked open with a hiss. The detective slipped inside, eased the door shut to a sliver.
The air sealed within bloated warm and stale, tasted of copper coated tongues and fresh metal. Low light gathered around two dark shapes in the room. A desk of handbrushed steel and a filing cabinet with a cracking face.
Corey stooped over the desk. Shook the monitor awake. The doctor had an old email open. Dull white washing the walls

pallid.

Members of the board,
Salutations.
Below is our quarterly report, including findings, concerns, and proposed courses of action.
In short, continued treatment has demonstrated marked improvements and previous complications have been mitigated. Therefore, it is my projection is that as methods are continually refined the failure rate proceeding the early stages of the trial will be reduced substantially.
Complicating matters however is our current operational budget and I would like to confirm whether our request for expansion has been received as per previous correspondence.
Hope and health, your diligence is appreciated.
Best,
Dr. Wayne Sykkes, MD PhD.
Head of Clinical Research, ANNE's Division
Bentham Systems Inc.
wssykkes@annes.bentham.tech

The thread stretched long. Weeks of follow up unanswered.
A puff. The detective searched the rest of the computer, rifled through the drawer. The false bottom hid an accounting book. A decoy. But the lid of that false bottom was covered in smudged fingerprints and the fingerprints pointed towards a crack along the edge of the panel and the crack in that lid split open into two halves. One of those two halves held a ring of four keys. Each shelf in the filing cabinet had a key and each shelf was dedicated to one color, color coded folders green yellow and red, and each

folder had a name. Alphabetical order, from Armas to Welles. Anna Kaplin's folder sat in the bottom drawer, laid out over the rest. Tabbed in red. They were all tabbed in red. Handler, Olliver, Palomo. Red tab by red tab. The rest a slow yellow in the drawer above or a happy green in the drawer on top.
Every skim over brought up his own name in crimson. Sykkes in gold.
The one folder he was looking for was missing.
He opened his own folder. Found that the doctor had been watching him from the beginning. Before he even arrived in Bentham. Everything about him. Right down to the diameter of his wrists. In red pen a question. A name.
And that was the last item on the last blank page inside his folder.
A hand clasped his shoulder. Pulled him up to his feet. Corey grinned, leaned against his friend.

 morning, sunshine.

The other broke his vow of silence. Despite the edge Corey missed his voice.
What are you doing in my office?
Corey hummed to himself and stretched. A yawn.

 was looking for a drink.

Wayne shoved him face first into the wall, caused him to yelp. A press forward and a hiss. Caging him in.
You are in so much trouble you cannot even begin to comprehend it!
Corey clenched his hands and gritted. Cheek against the sapping

yellow of the wallpaper.

    something you wanna tell me?

Heavy breaths down his neck. Wayne's nails tearing scars into the floral pattern beside his head. Corey threw an elbow and was knocked forward, continuing to struggle until an arm clamped around his waist. The doctor growling harsh into his hair.
Hold. Still.
The detective straightened up against him. Puffed through the hair scattered over his face.

    where are belle's records?

As they swayed against the wall Corey leaned back against Wayne's shoulder. Breaths matching the heart pressed to his back.

    not going to answer me, sweetheart?

A tug backwards and the doctor threw him onto his desk, legs kicking. Sharpness over his teeth.
How did you gain access to my office?
Corey gave a short laugh. Shifted his hips. Like he could taste the desperation.

    cool it, cowboy.

The doctor shoved him back and his head hit the desk. He pinned him down by the shoulders.
Speak or so help me God will speak for you.
Corey glared at him.

you left the door open.

Wayne dragged him down by the leg until he was eye level.
Why must you defy me?
I have given up everything for you.
I cleaned up after you, cared for you, consoled you.
Still yet you deny my hand.

never asked for it.

The doctor laughed softly, some morbid jest he couldn't contain but would never be able to tell. Running his fingertips down Corey's face.
Everything is falling apart.
Can't you feel it?

i know something is wrong.

The detective leaned forward.

something you're not telling me.

This is about Miranda isn't it?

miranda?

Corey narrowed his smokey eyes.

what?

You think I wouldn't know?
He grasped the edge of Corey's hip, tight and splintering. A

surge in his hazel eyes that stung deeper than seawater.
You lost everything to betray me.

> you betrayed me first.

Corey pushed against him, up into his space.

> how lucky am i. that red is my favorite color.

Wayne's voice shattered weak over his ear.
Dove. I only wanted to help you.

> you want to fix me.
> you've always wanted to fix me.

A hiss. Teeth inches from his mouth.

> go on then.
> do it.

A shove. Rough and hard and hateful.

> fix me.

Another shove.

> turn me into someone you can love.

Another.

> come on sunshine, what's the matter?

Another. Knee grinding into his stomach.

if you wanna dance, let's dance.

Corey.
Wayne's knuckles tightened white around his wrists.
Hold still.

make me.

I am not fighting you.

mm.
why not?
scared i'll break your pretty face?

You're fragile.

mind or body?

Corey-
A twist and Corey flipped the other onto the ground. Pinned him with a knee. Wayne was big and clumsy and slow and he didn't fight it. Stared up at the other panting over him, leaning down, closer and closer. Silver hair scattered over his eyes. The doctor tilted up until their noses brushed. The detective stopped him. A finger to the plush of his lips.
Dove.

you can't save me.
you can't make me yours.

Corey leaned closer. Grazing just under his jaw. Gloved hand over his throat.

say you don't want me here.
say it.

Wayne didn't move. Laid his head back. Limbs limp. Like a body adrift, plump face rising just below the surface. Skin washed turgid and white. Corey rolled off of him. Swiped at his face. Heat pricked his neck and thighs and a dull ache boiled soft his old bones, born from his hips and the endless bleed welling in his stomach. In the dark he heard Wayne murmur.
I could love you so hatefully.
The air shifted beside him. The doctor took the detective's face into his hand. Corey murmured, no louder than a death rattle.

you cannot love what is dead.

And the night became nothing more than a regretful, hateful memory. Never to be spoken of again.

09 | the prince of sand

The detective found Dr. Olliver's office in Bentham General. Reported what findings he had. The missing folders. Anna's name. His name.

Miranda slumped at her desk. Caramel curls scattering over her face, her white coat heavy on her shoulders.

> I suppose it was only a matter of time.
> mm.
> and simeon won't even look at me.
> whatever he said to job stunned them cold.

Miranda sunk her head in her arms. A long, deflating sigh, creases and stresses along her form. Then she sat back up at attention, rubbed her face, fixed her hair.

> That's everything?

Corey nodded. The tissue in his hands torn to shreds, scattering in his lap and over Boggles. Miranda scooped the nibbling rat from his knee. Face papery like she'd been buffeted in the wind rattling just outside the window.

> You did what you could.

A shadow crossed over her face. She swept her hair aside.

> I'll fulfill my end of the bargain.

One last pet over her rat. The thin whiskers quivering against her palm. She tilted her head.

> How's the dosage, by the way?
> fine.
> i'm hungrier but i'm fine.
> how was lee?
> You're seeing Lee later aren't you?
> the christmas party? i suppose.
> You can ask Lee then.

Miranda offered a smile.

> Is Wayne giving you trouble at all?

Corey took a moment to respond. Hiding behind his dark hair, tossing the scraps of tissue.

> ...no.
> Good.

Miranda gave a mirthy chuckle. Clicked a plastic pen, scratched over a clipboard.

> I think he likes you.

A weary sigh. The smile faded. Amber eyes flicking up to meet his.

> More than he wants to admit.

Heels clacked down the hallway just outside the door. A smooth

voice with a saccharine tone.
What are you doing here?
Dr. Wayne Sykkes. The door to Dr. Olliver's office cracked open, his silver head peeking in. He had heard Corey's drawl from down the hallway, soft and low. Drawn to it like the tide is drawn to the sun behind the moon.

Speak of the devil.

Miranda dropped Boggles in her pocket. Folded her hands businesslike over the desk. Raised brows.

Just talking.

Just talking.
Wayne's eyes flicked between her and Corey. He stepped in, eased the door shut behind him. As though that would lock in the sharpness of his tongue.
It was you, wasn't it.
The other doctor only smiled politely, tilted her head.

Me who?

Why do you insist on taking issue with my work.
I told you already.
Psychiatry isn't social control.

I know.

My work seeks to reduce harmful behaviors.
Miranda laughed softly, got to her feet and perused her library.

> Harm as a result of social pressure.

I beg to differ.
Wayne gritted his teeth.
It isn't healthy. It's unnatural.
Miranda slid a book from the shelf. A heavy tome that weighed down her wrist. Flipped it open.

> Maybe it's your cure that's unnatural.

Wayne snatched the book from her hand.
I am trying to help people!
A scoff. Miranda tugged the book back.

> There is help and there is hubris.

She held it to his throat.

> Do you want to end up like Henry? Victor? Walter?

Do not compare me to them.

> It's the same story, is it not?

She spun the book on its spine. Underlined the cover. The Last Resort.

> You think you've found your solution. Your great and desperate cure. You abuse it. Your own pride has shunted you.

Wayne stepped up close. Leaned down into her ear. Took her

wrist in a gentle, gentle whisper.
Follow me or forsake me. Stand in my way and I will choose the Lord.

    wayne.

A glance. Wayne seized Corey's arm. Wrenched the door open. Miranda called after him a ring of thorns in her throat.

    You abandoned me first, Wayne.
    You abandoned *me*.

Wayne kept walking. Didn't turn his cheek. Dragging Corey behind him like a cross over his shoulder.
Around the corner he shoved the other man up against the wall, bearing down his throat.
What do you think you're doing?
The detective cocked a brow.

    am i not allowed to speak with her?

The Devil works hard to take what is mine but I work harder.
The doctor leaned close. Iris and sandalwood and clove on his clothes. Anise on his breath.
Stop making appointments with my wife.

    your wife.

The detective dropped his shoulders. A gloved hand through the dark snaggles of his hair and a brief chuckle.

    you're married?

He slid down the wall. Kicked up a leg. Burned into him with his smoke and bitterness.

    you don't act like a married man.

What are you implying.

    i've known you half a year now and i had no idea you were married.

The detective took the doctor's hand, laced their fingers, thumbed the fourth with interest. A tilt to his head and a smile.

    you don't even wear your ring.

The doctor curled his lip.
It's complicated.
He wrenched his arm away. Jabbed a nail into Corey's collarbone.
Don't you even think about touching her.

    she's my type but i'm not hers.

Corey grinned. A shift against him. The other glaring down.

    same goes for you.

He settled comfortably. Nodded at the mistletoe over their heads. Flashed a smile.

    am i your type?

Wayne pushed off of him. Corey tailed after like a hungry pup.

Sniffing for a hand to tug on.

what? we're not even going to talk about it?

The doctor whipped around. The detective straightening defensively.
Is one peaceful afternoon with you too much to ask for?
A tight smile. Corey didn't move. Wayne rolled his eyes, punched the button to the elevator. Doors sliding open.
Corey remained on his side of the lift. Wayne on the other.

psalms?

Psalms.

Wayne mellowed significantly over their weekly coffee ritual. Affections a slow brew. It must have been the quiet intimacy of it, sitting by the window in slow roast and cream and caramel. The detective leaning against the glass, one leg kicked over the other, eyes trained on the wind. Lost in his own thoughts.
Corey would occasionally peer over his mug to cock a brow at the other. And the doctor would pause his stirring, thickened honey a flotsam lump in his tea, and smile, lips tightly sealed. He knew the twelfth time around, the detective squirming, that Corey would be compelled to speak. Mostly because he couldn't stand just staring at Wayne. The silence exacerbated how long and gangly and awkward the doctor was. Too tall in his seat and slouched as though he felt himself too grand. Slender fingers wrapped around the rim and a sleepy smile on his face. Intrigued what morose and obtuse thoughts the detective had crumpled up in his mind.

Corey adjusted himself in his seat, leaned forward on his elbows, fingertips templed over the table. He wasn't one to talk much. But he never seemed to shut up around Wayne. Probably because he intended to drive the man insane.

>how come you don't sleep with your wife?

The doctor parted his lips. Blinked and scoffed.
I beg of you to choose a more stimulating inquiry.
A grin and a sip. Corey had a tendency to smile at Wayne's expense. Wayne didn't like it.
The question you posit is hinged upon an unconfirmed assumption and quite frankly holds rather unsavory implications surrounding my character.

>it's not that far of a stretch. you don't even live with her. you live with me.

No. You, live with me.
Wayne quit his stirring. Put down his silver spoon, folded his hands neatly in his lap.
I offer you refuge in a place where beds are in very high demand. You should be more grateful.

>doc. we're living on prison grounds.

Would you rather I throw you in a cell? Do you really miss it that much, dear? Or maybe you'd prefer if I chained you to the floor.

>you're avoiding my question.

And what would you have me say? We are busy people. Our

respective choices in housing serve us well.

> i've never seen you kiss. i've known you for, what, six months? and not once have i seen you kiss your wife.

Intimacy is private.
What is it with your questions, dove? Do you have a vested interest in kissing my wife? Because, as I recall, my liaisons with her are not of your concern.
With one hand Corey reached out and grabbed Wayne's face. A habit of the doctor's he'd turned right back against him. And not once did the doctor protest. He was far too distracted. Corey's eyes, so dark they trapped light.

> i am not interested in your wife, wayne.

Not even the slightest temptation?
At Corey's unamused look Wayne straightened. Which was a cute look to pair with his words.
Do not test me.
Corey only looked even more unamused.

> i'm not interested.

Every man feels temptation.

> i don't.
> everyone goes into heat but me.

Corey said it with no hint of embarrassment. He was far too tired nowadays to feel embarrassed.
You deceive yourself.

> why are you trying to convince me that i have a thing for your wife?
> do *you* even have a thing for your wife?

Of course I do. I love her. Dearly.

> then maybe you should listen to her.

Wayne wrenched himself from Corey's hand.
I'd rather not discuss this,
The detective cut the doctor short jamming a boot heel between his knees.

> if you think you deserve peace you won't have it.

I don't. But I appreciate the offer.
Corey scoffed. A wretchedness to his eyes as Wayne became something that wasn't.

> how can you just sit there. after everything that happened belle.

Belle was sick, Corey. So very sick.

> and you made her suffer.

I did what I could.
In the great calculus of emotions I know nothing. But I cannot question what the Lord wills of me.

> what the lord wills of you?

you abuse your gifts and when god shows you your wrongs you spit in his face and claim preference.

Faith is never easy. God finds ways to test you.

and how many tests of faith will it take?
anna.
lee.
me.
when will it be enough for you?

When my work is done.

the devil feeds you his hubris.

Corey. Let me help you.

i don't need your help.

You are so very sick. And you don't even realize it.
Corey made no comment. Licked his teeth and sat back.

i've seen the way you look at me.
can your god fix that?

Wayne pushed his mug aside, rose to his feet. And Corey tailed after him, the sick dog he was.

you are less than a man. crawling away on your belly like a snake.

The doctor stopped in his tracks and Corey crashed into him.

Wayne didn't move. Voice feathering just above a low low whisper.
Corey.
You will hate me for what I have done.
But the last thing I want to do is mourn you.

The Christmas party went as expected. Lee burrowed away in the big sweaters Corey had gifted them, one for their pet rock dove. The Lilies hosted a gift exchange, Jacobi went door to door caroling, Miranda had Boggles perform a rat circus over her rat nativity, and Wayne got drunk off egg nog after gifting Corey a new coat. Six months became nine, spring thawing as Corey bided his time chasing threads. Eventually Miranda gave him the signal. She'd gotten wind of the Sandmen's next congregation and he was to bear witness.
Just before midnight and Corey crept out and down the stairs. Wayne's bedroom dark and silent. On cue the front door swung open. Miranda in her usual covert clothing. Corey gave her a nod, buttoned up his gray coat, and eased the door shut.
Off they went. Down an overgrown path buried in the trees to an opening at the base of the mountain. The old mineshaft. Red rusted door bolted shut. The detective stepped carefully. Took a knee to inspect the dirt.

> that many men and the ground ain't disturbed.
> they're not here.

Miranda shook her head, walked about the clearing, like she'd find something in the shadows to echo back.
Anna said they'd be here.

The detective looked at her.

    anna.

Miranda didn't meet his eyes. Corey lowered his voice.

    miranda-

I know.
Corey didn't push. Got to his heels, grabbed a stone, stood in front of the lock. Miranda held back his wrist.
Don't. The mines are toxic. We should get out of here.
A glance and a slow nod.

    right.

He dropped the stone and they turned back the way they came. Keeping to the shadows, scanning their surroundings. A dark and empty night and Bentham felt like a forgotten dreamscape. Even Miranda beside him seemed nothing more than a shade. Dust and light leak smudged by one too many hands.
So.
A flicker over. Miranda flapped her mouth a few times before she was able to pop the question.
How are you two.

    mm?

You and Wayne.

    me and...
    ...

i didn't know you were married.

Ah. Don't worry about it.
He looked at her quizzically and she raised her hands.
Don't get me wrong, I care about him, I do. And I know he loves me in his own way.
But it was an arrangement of convenience.
A blink. Corey tried to keep his voice low as they approached the neighborhood.

convenience?

For a detective you are damn oblivious.

does he-

No.
You know how I am. And you know damn well how he is.
Corey slowed his pace. Peeked out their cover of trees as he muttered.

i don't know.
he's...
confusing.

Oh it was pretty damn obvious growing up he didn't like girls like me.
Corey gave a little laugh as they stepped out into the open.

oh really?

Miranda chuckled, kicked a twig.

Wayne Sebastian Sykkes. The scrawny farm boy from Nebraska who refused to go outside. He liked his little gadgets more than he liked people.

    look at him now.

Oh, he's the same. Just hides it better. Learned his manners. Read one too many self help books.
A sigh. Ducking behind a building.
His poor folks thought he was a ladies man with how much the girls loved him. Really they just thought he was adorable. Invited him to sleepovers to do his makeup. I don't think he even minded it.

    and you?

I was never invited.
Too busy collecting dead bugs, I guess.

    i never liked sleepovers either.
    preferred my cartoons.

You get it.
Most times I felt more at home with Wayne. Guess that's the reason I agreed to marry him.
But if anyone actually took the time to ask him they'd find he absolutely hated my guts.

    why?

Usurping his primacy.
His words, not mine.

A chuckle. She swiped her lip.
He has trouble accepting things that don't go his way.

> you don't love him?

Not like that.
She met his eyes. Amber brown glinting violet in the moonlight.
Do you love him?

> miranda.

Be honest.
Are you willing to betray him?

> who's to say i already haven't?

Let me ask again.
Are you willing to destroy him?
Everything that he is. Strives to be.

> i've already destroyed him.
> he's just in denial.

Miranda slowed in her step as they approached the hospital.
I remember the first time he smiled at me.
We were fighting over a stuffed animal. Ripped the head off.
Wayne looked oh so guilty, that rascal. I thought he'd run off and tattle on me but he didn't.
He held the head up. I sewed it back together. A shabby job but we did it. I fixed it.
Rubbing her face she leaned against the wall.
I care about him. I do. But sometimes I wonder if he's human.

Me and Anna. We're friends.
She understood me. She saw me.
But Wayne tasted weakness and he pounced.
If he's willing to betray me he's willing to set fire to the world.
And I can't let him do that.

> he's running out of funds.

What?
Corey's eyes fixed on the treeline. The distant sway.

> saw one of his emails.
> begging to up the budget.
> all those calls. all those late shipments. he's running out of time.

Can't keep this up forever.
Miranda straightened. Fist to palm, eyes ablaze.
If we take this to the townspeople-
Corey clasped his hand over Miranda's mouth. At her raised brows he nodded towards a shadow in the distance, driven and spry. The shadow of Danielle Cardenas Kwon.
She sprinted through the night with a mask sliding down her face. Darted straight into the trees. A glance at Miranda and they followed. Disappeared beneath the aspens and the pines. The feline screech of a wildcat splintering the slumbering silence.
Between two tall trunks like a narrow gateway rose thick smoke and a dim fire. Balled up flames spitting and clawing for dry leaf or rag or pine needle. Sins vowed away fluttering towards the sky. Masked faces swayed amongst the embers. They gathered in golden vestments about a monument of half eaten marble,

weathered surface unrefined. Stone chunks of cleaved flesh. Sculpted into a familiar shape unborn and unrealized. That of his dearest and most treasured, Lee Palomo.
With long stalks of hyssop they struck the stone shoulders. Raised a bowl before the formless praying hands. In the center over a cushion of ash and sand burned a hot tablet of charcoal, and on that charcoal pedestal glowed a sparking gurgling nugget of myrrh. White smoke wisping about the unbraided columns of stone.
Masked faces and bodies cut of cloth. The mask is absent soul and to share the same face is to become one empty body. They pour into the still face violent desires and call themselves virtuous for removing it and putting it on. So afraid of what lies beneath.
Here they danced, danced about the hearth and the sleeping daughter carved of stone. They danced and then they teetered to a stop. Craned their heads. A slow turn.
Miranda fell silent beside him. Chest unmoving.
One tall with hair golden raised to point a dry and bony finger.
A crack split his skull. Every thought, every desire, conscience and subconscience, dragged screaming into the great recesses of the formless deep. Thousands of choices and chances and lifetimes flickering in the inverse light of blackened stars. Then, before his eyes, a great stone ceiling. And the corrupted memory vanished.
Corey woke up.
A sharp pain in his neck and the doctor over his ear muzzled him before he could bite.
Dove.
Corey growled beneath his palm. Legs tangled in his bedsheets.

Wayne raised a brow. Lifted his fingers as Corey calmed.
You were crying in your sleep again.
I was worried you'd start walking.
Corey sat up. Hovered over Wayne's shoulder. Made the small puff small dogs make for woes unknown to man.

    where is she?

A pause. Wayne's hand sifting through Corey's hair. Soft and light.
Lee is fine, darling.

    no. miranda.

Miranda?
The doctor offered a smile. Too sweet. Placating.
You've been asleep this whole time.

    no. i was awake. we were in the forest.

If you left I would know.
Corey snagged his phone from his coat pocket. Dialed and pressed it to his ear. Confirmation. He needed confirmation.

    we were in the forest. remember?

Miranda on the other end breathed soft and stunted. A pause before lowering her voice. Throat stiff and restrained.

    ... I don't know what you're talking about.
    Are you alright?

A puff of disbelief. Corey's gloves squeaked as he clenched the receiver. Neck splitting pain and a deep ache spreading through his skull.

> you were there. you were there. why don't you remember? miranda?

Wayne snatched the phone. Cut off her response.
Leave her be.
Corey took Wayne's face into his hands, those wide hazel eyes, a harsh whisper.

> i burn of ash. i reek of fire. can't you smell it?

Your skin blooms of roses and nothing else.

> wayne-

The doctor held him back. A soothing murmur into his hair. You're dreaming, love. I was watching over you as you slept.

> are you lying to me?

Why would I lie to you, darling?

> you're lying to me, aren't you?
> all of you.

The doctor moved away but the detective grabbed him.

> what did you do?

Dove.

> don't lie.
> don't you lie to me.

Wayne tucked a feather of hair behind Corey's ear. Thumbed his cheek.
Whatever you may think, I want you to understand one thing. Everything I do,
I do for you.

> just tell me the truth.
> please.

Goodnight, Corey.
The detective seized his hand. Tight under his gloves. Clinging to life like vine clings to a wall. Tugged Wayne close to beg soft into his chest. Breath a cold rattle.

> wait.
> please.
> just
> stay.
> it's cold.
> stay with me?

Wayne looked at him as though he were only made of dust.
Corey took his hand, a gesture, a reminder. And the doctor moved closer. Shut off the light. Slid in beside him.
Into his arms Wayne gathered him, kindling embers and blooming roses soft and warm and comforting. Like Corey was a dying memory long estranged. Despite everything he wanted nothing more than to hold him one last time. And with the kiss

of death over his cheek the thing inside him split open.
She hovered over his shoulder with sand spilling from her eyes.

10 | the kiss of death

It was the eve of Belle's birthday and Corey sat at the Psalms with a coffee and a sugar packet. Danielle Cardenas Kwon dining across from him, lips chokecherry red. She cut into her chicken fried steak before she even looked at the detective.
I don't know why I asked you here.
He dropped his hand from his neck. Sat straight.

>doesn't have to be a reason.

But there is.
A slow nod.

>there is.

He tapped his fingers. Avoidant eyes angled downwards.

>you read the journal?

I don't want to talk about it.
Another nod. He shifted again in his seat. Crossed one leg over the other.

>you never brought it to the doctor.

He never asked for it.
At the tightness in her voice his eyes flicked upwards.

>are you with them?

I told you already. The things I'm willing to do.
Dani put down her fork. Ruffled her flattened hair.
Detective, I've got a question for you.

> go on.

Do you think she had a chance. Without the cure.
Corey kept his hands folded. The wind battering twists of shadow onto the wall. From his mouth a low whisper. The demon in his chest compelling him.

> i don't know.

Dani barked a laugh. A sharpness to her teeth.
You know what?
She sat straight to hiss. Dark hair sitting like a crown of thorns. Catching whatever remained of the wind's graces.
I'm glad you've declared the case cold.
Because I will find the truth.
With or without you.
Corey bowed his head, murmured an apology, excused himself. On his way out he crossed paths with Ruth. She shook her graying head. Pushed past to sit down with her weeping daughter.

Wayne had been waiting for him. The door swinging open the moment his knuckles rapped metal. The doctor in his nightgown, pins pushed into his silver hair.
Dove.
A sip of his chamomile tea.
You're late again.

Corey raised a brow. Stepped in.

> evening to you too, sunshine.

How was supper with Danielle?

> fine.
> how was miranda.

Good. Good.
The doctor had led the way up the stairs but now he teetered beside the banister. Propped an elbow, teacup hooked under a finger.
What do you think of breakfast at the Psalms tomorrow?
Me, you, Miranda-
Corey pushed past him.

> i am not going back there.

Dove. I'm sure Miranda would love to see you again-

> she doesn't want anything to do with me and you know it.
> i'm surprised she even agreed to meet you.

Wayne stopped him at the door to his room.
Do you at least feel well enough for tomorrow?
Corey managed a dry smile. Crossed his arms, looked up at the other. Into his eyes.

> it's her birthday, wayne.
> i should be staying back with ruth. helping out in the

garden.

We celebrate her memory with a newfound occasion.

by running around the forest with a gun.

Wayne gave pause. Something on his tongue he couldn't shake. He settled for brushing aside a lock of Corey's dark hair.
You don't have to come along, dear.
A scoff. Corey nudged his shoulder, caught the doorknob.

who's gonna watch out for you?

One last smile. Even as he shut the door Wayne still stared after the space he used to be.

Jacobi let him borrow one of her rifles. Carbon fiber stock, fluted barrel, nicely textured grip. Light in his hands, easy to manage, even with his gloves.

you're not coming with?

Even if I wanted to, y'all've already got a good sized camp going.
She strapped his bag shut.
The doc's got everything else covered?
Corey nodded. Took her hand.

look after lee while i'm gone.

Lord knows I'll try.
Jacobi patted his shoulder.
Stay safe out there.

Corey murmured his thanks. Joined Wayne outside. Pack and rifle slung over his shoulder. They found Simeon Turner and Shepherd Job in the chapel garden. Bade farewell to Ruth and Dani before parsing into the thicket, the Shepherd at the head.
Once we reach the ridge we can set up camp. Perhaps part ways.
The men nodded. It was Corey who set what was on his mind.

> where's pal?

In the silence Shepherd Job answered.
Kind Paladin wished to stay back with Lee. He said she was displaying signs of distress.

> i see.

Simeon butted in. Swinging his long rifle under his arm.
Normally we'd bring Kraig along but he couldn't stomach the thought this time around.
You got the guts for it, detective?

> guns are for boys.
> hold a gun with naive hands and it has you thinking you've been made a man.
> wield it enough times and you'll find it makes you less than one.

Simeon only grinned.
So what's all that extra weight for then?
Afraid the Sand Prince will get ya?
He'd gotten bolder since. But at Corey's glare the smile dropped from Simeon's face. A swipe at his nose.

The party trekked long enough that they came upon a ridge with a clear view of the glade. Wind blowing in their faces from the mountain. They sat like that a while. Long enough for Simeon to kick his tripod in impatience.
Elk rut, early morning, not a single bull in sight. Shit.
The Shepherd chuckled. Another piece of jerky between his teeth as he looked through his binoculars.
Even the hunt requires patience.
Fear not. We have a whole day to seize.
Simeon huffed. Glassed through his optics from glade to horizon again.
Easier said than done.
One day is hardly enough.
A glance over at the doctor and the detective. Wayne was whittling away at a wooden canary with a short knife. Corey had his nose in some literature, sketchbook open in his lap, the mountains in front of them penned to the fullest with every line and letter he could muster.
Simeon sat down. Leaned back against his bag.
Look at you two. Sitting around looking pretty.
Splitting in pairs would've covered us more ground.
Why'd you even come along?
Wayne offered a smile. Carving out the tail. He'd char it after. Said it preserved the wood, burning out the dry rot.

I am here to embrace the gifts of God.

Corey didn't glance up. Liked his Camus a little too much.

had a headache.

Simeon tutted. Stretched out his legs, wiggled a bandaged toe.
Any news about the contracts, doc?
A flicker passed between the doctor and the Shepherd. Shepherd Job cleared his throat.
Deliberations with Bentham are still out of effect at this present time.
Simeon fiddled with the strap over his shoulder.
Said that last time.
Bentham give you the cold shoulder or somethin?
A long, heavy sigh. The doctor got to his feet. Simeon frowned, called after him.
Aw come on, doc. Don't go.

> I've been sedentary for quite too long. I am in need of a walk.

The Shepherd waved a hand.
Let him go.
Simeon didn't say anything to that. A low grumble. The doctor skirted down the ridge in his boots. Sunlight glinting off his silver frames.
The moment the doctor passed by Corey eared the page and tucked his book away. Wedged through the thicket after him, bag over his shoulder. He'd made good distance before the doctor stopped in his tracks. Raised his nose.

> Such a loyal pup.
> Following me like your life depends on it.
> mm.

Corey kept his voice to a low monotone.

    i'm such a good boy.

The doctor shot a disapproving look behind him, narrowed his eyes when the offender stuck out his tongue. The midday sun burned the detective's dark hair ember brown, feathers framing his face. A grim smile shadowed his smokey eyes as he slumped forward, spoke soft and close over the other's shoulder.

    i'm resigning.

Dove?

    case is cold.

    i'm batshit insane.

    you just want to keep me around so you can run your little experiments on me.

How corybantic of you. Don't be ridiculous.
You need my help.
And I need yours.
Corey laughed. Warm breath over Wayne's ear. The doctor had to tilt his head away.

    my job ruins lives.

Because you cling to the past.

    i'm a detective. i'm supposed to put people away.

No, dove.

You are without a body. Without hands. All you have to rely on is your sight.
You are my eyes and I move for you.
A soft sigh. Corey leaned closer, into his shoulder.

> i'm indebted to you. for finding me. for saving me.
> but you should've left me to suffer.
> at least then no one else would have died.

Wayne stiffened under the brush of his lips. Turned his head. What are you talking about?

> you need to let me go.

Your work here isn't done.
Corey grasped for his arm, his hand, to clasp his pulse in his own and feather against the tips.

> deep inside my fingers are cold and my heart is rotting.
> i was never meant to be here.

And yet you stand here before me. Warm lips and ember eyes.

> that's a lie and you know it.

When have I ever lied to you?

> you think i don't know when you lie?

> i can hear. i can see.

> the guilt in your eyes. every time you look at me. like my skin is made of sin.

He smoothed his palm over the slope of his chest.

> everything you've built is falling apart.
> you're low on funds.
> your cure isn't working.

Corey leaned close enough that his hair grazed Wayne's cheek. A low hiss.

> belle deserved better.
> just took you and me to fuck up her life.

Wayne's eyes darkened in shadow. A tremor to his voice. How could you say that. Corey.
A trace over the yellow ascot around Wayne's neck. Corey closed his hand, a slow, tight squeeze.

> that's the truth isn't it?
> and now you want to ruin my life too.

A touch just over his jaw and the ghost of his lips in a whisper.

> i'll be the one that got away.
> because you're a coward.

Wayne struck out, scored him right over the mouth. Soft flesh splitting open and running red down his chin. A bloody laugh and Corey knocked Wayne onto his ass, grabbed a fistfull of his hair. The doctor thrashed beneath him, hard body tensed, teeth

bared. Corey bent down. Bent down to bite.
A high pitched scream like a whistle raked the air, on its tail a gulping series of chirps like a chuckle. The tone resonant enough to shake the trees.
Corey tore himself from Wayne's neck. Let his head free.

    the hell was that?

Wayne pushed upright, brushed aside his dented hair and fixed his crooked frames. The midday sun beat down on their heads, heavy palm fronds.
Luck.
Corey followed the sound with his eyes, trained on the distant treeline ahead. Amongst the thin pines shadows twisted under the breeze tall and wraith-like. Clusters of leaves writhing, ragged bundles of earth. He raised to his knees to get a closer look but the doctor snatched him by the lapels, pulled him back down.
Let me see your face.

    it's nothing.

The thumb prying his lip drew blood and a wince. The detective bared an eyetooth, held back the doctor's wrist, ran his tongue over the sore.

    hit harder next time.

Wasn't trying to.

    right.

Wayne sucked his thumb, hefted Corey to his feet with the other hand, a mutter.
You startled me.
A chuckle. Corey nudged him as he brushed past, starting back up the ridge.

    not our first nor our last.

Are you sure you're alright-

    quit fussing, sweetheart.

When the bushes parted and they reemerged Simeon shrugged them off only to turn his head and stare again. Corey, ruffled hair and a busted lip. The doctor checked himself in the reflection of his carving knife before smiling.

    Hello again gentlemen.

You lovers done bickering?
The Shepherd hushed them. Gestured ahead.
There, behind those pines.
Look at him.
What a beauty.
A shape like a boulder, difficult to pick out with the naked eye even as it shifted. A big bull elk, tall and slow, wandered into the clearing. Pronged antlers a spray of points tapering towards the sky. Its underside bobbed as it raised its head to bugle, the high whistle scream and chuckle.
Such a haunting creature. Something to be penned. Even in

death it would not cry unsung. The detective's eyes flickered over the men.

    who's taking the shot.

Simeon grinned. Leaned into his rifle perched on his tripod. Shepherd reckoned that I do it.

    don't we have enough food at home.

Simeon let a breath. Waiting for the bull to quit baying and hold still.
I dunno. Supplies have been running dry lately. Got an answer for that, doc?
Wayne smiled tightly.

    We'll use every part of it. As we promised Ruth.
    seems more like a pride thing.

The doctor's lenses flashed as he lowered his head.

    Corey. Let us have this.

The bull froze and at the Shepherd's gesture Simeon chuckled.
Listen to your boyfriend.
Simeon squeezed the trigger. The bullet soared loud and the bull jumped. Skittered off into a limping trot. And it kept limping and limping and limping.
Is he down?
Still going.
Ah shit.
A resilient creature it is.

And I'm persistent.
The Shepherd hummed. Simeon got up. The doctor put down his binoculars.

    Where do you think you're going.

I nicked it, I'm gotta kill it.

    barrel's no good for timber.

No good my ass.
The Shepherd nodded.
There is a high chance the bull will bed down and run out of blood to bleed.
A small sigh. The doctor didn't protest that.
Simeon unmounted his rifle, folded up his tripod. Gestured to Corey.
Hey, Delgado.
You good at tracking?

    good enough.

Just our luck.
C'mon then pretty boy.
We got a bull to hunt.

The party packed their gear. Made it down the ridge and through the clearing towards the treeline. Creeping slow and quiet through the pines and aspens, looking for spatters or movement.
Corey made a point to brush against the doctor whenever he

could. Occasionally sneaking in a low murmur.

> a coward hides his real face.

When the doctor finally glared the detective added, soft and with a smug smile.

> never signed the contract.

Wayne raised his brows. Ducked slow under a branch Corey cleared easily.

> Yes, you did.
> maybe you should read it again.

Wayne scoffed. Indignance and annoyance. Corey leaned forward.

> can't keep me here forever, sweetheart.
> My hold on you is tighter than you think.
> i will ruin everything you have built.
> Ruin will come from my own hands. Not yours.
> not if you touch lee.

Simeon chirped. Quiet as he could make himself.
Keep it down lovebirds.
The doctor glowered over his shoulder. Pointed his nose ahead.

> Perhaps it would be wise to divide our attentions across a larger area.

A hush drew their heads. Shepherd Job, fist raised. Limbs stiff

and rigid.
Hold.
Behind a bloom of sagebrush, a shape a tan boulder. The flank of a bull. Long antlers curving around the bend like long boned fingers.
Simeon murmured. Rifle under his arm.
That our friend, you reckon?

    there's blood on the sage.

As he spoke the fingers curled. Stilled when the detective continued.

    it's him.

Corey handed Wayne back his binoculars, swiped at his brow.

    mercy says it's only fair you finish what you started.
    And allow him to miss again?

Bullshit.
I hit him square and you know it.

    his shoulder, more like.

Simeon crept around. Trying to get a good angle. Not a single sound and the bull reared up, bounded deeper into the thicket. The men didn't understand why but Corey knew. He'd seen the shadow looming, the shadow of the man from the courtyard. The bull saw him too.
Simeon hissed, lowered his rifle.
Shit.

Corey pinched the back of his neck, shrugged.

> mm.
> must've smelled you.

The Shepherd sighed. Leaned on his old trekking pole.
Don't chase. There's no use.
They stooped to pick up their gear again but at the sound of a rustle they turned their heads. The doctor was gone. The detective running after him.

Corey caught a flash of Wayne's silver blonde. Pushed his legs faster, until he caught his arm.

> wayne. you really think you can outrun a bull?

A glare. Silver hair disheveled. The grime of his sweat had made the crack in his lenses apparent. A thin fracture over his eye. He threw an elbow.
An injured and disoriented one. Yes.
A sigh. The detective looked about them trying to remember the direction he had come from but the shadows had turned their backs and the sun looked to be split in two.

> sit down.
> it's not safe.

Wayne tugged Corey close, a low growl in his chest.
I'd have caught him by now.
But you-

> ruined it?

Corey let his hand, pushed him away. Another rub at the ache in his neck.

> you're so goddamn selfish.

Selfish?
With a swift finger Corey tapped the doctor's chin upwards, looked him in the eyes.

> god gives you visions and you claim them reality.
> when fate decides otherwise, obsession becomes your master.

Gritted teeth. Wayne didn't move. Threw down his bag and his rifle.
If it is the Lord's will it must be done. And I am the Lord's will. I am.

> mm.

Corey dropped his hand. Fixed a sleeve. The doctor leaned close, murmured over his ear.
I am not letting you go.

> then come with me.

There is no elsewhere.
Only you.

> so we're trapped.

you and me.

A distant flutter. Doves taking to the sky, spinning into a spiral at the push of the wind. Corey offered a smile. Stepped away.

i am not the person you want me to be.

Wayne grabbed the detective by the shoulders, took his face like he was some dear precious thing.
You can be.
Corey's ember eyes went cold. Spinning disks of coal and formless blackened stars. He pushed Wayne's wrists down.

i'll shatter in your hands.
like belle shattered in yours.

Wayne hovered over Corey's arms. Brushed shakily over the other's cheek, threaded through his dark hair. Dust. He was only made of dust.
You don't understand.
I can't lose you again.

you've already lost me.

Corey tilted his head. Clasped him against his cold skin. Soft like snowdrift and gunpowder and mouth froth.

don't cling to a ghost, wayne.

The doctor slipped from his grasp. Dropped to his knees. Man prostrated before his living god.
I need you to stay.

He gazed up at him with dull gold, took the detective's hand, murmured over his gloved fingers. A soft kiss over the guard of his palm as his voice wrecked his throat.
I need you.

    you need me.

Corey bent to meet him. Cupped his face.

    then why did you do it?

A brush over the plush of his lips.

    why did you pull the trigger?

Wayne shut his eyes, turned his nose away, Like the morningstar turned from truth. Corey shoved him onto his back, climbed over him, clutched his hand until two fingers pointed at his temple.

    you knew.
    you always knew-

A distant whistle. Drawn and labored. Corey tore himself from the doctor's grasp. Cold tapping his spine with its thin needle picks. When he spun around the ground pitched and the sky went black.
Before his eyes, the pulsating orange fungus. Surface gurgling molten fire, translucent vellum that bulged and split open as two nubs of fingerlike bone pushed out from the inside. The spongy gills sunk deep into the rotting heartwood, peeled tender along the length of the protrusion. Shriveled antlers. Scraped down to

the bleeding bone. Strips of old skin and shed vessel clotted over the blunted tines, balled and thudded wet on the forest floor. They sprouted not from a burred head but from a mouth. A rattling cavity with no teeth. The breath rose from gaseous bloat and bursted organs. Tasted of spoiled chokecherries. And it was then he knew her face.
The shade of Belle Rivera took a backwards step.
Corey Handler followed.
In the lucid light he reached out a hand to touch her, her cracked marble skin and rusted daylily, but no matter the distance she was always too far away. They walked slow and slow until they reached the base of the mountain, the mouth of the mine and the red bolted door. It hung open on a broken hinge, leaked pit water into a shallow stream.
The shade took one last step. Dipped her feet still bound in yellow rags. And as she stooped to wash she collapsed in a shower of sand. Vanished, as she'd always been.
Corey fell to his knees with a soft cry. Clawed after her. Raked the murky water until grits clotted beneath his nails. The reflection warped beneath his fingers and he stopped. Clasped his mouth to stifle his grief. Lee Palomo slept beneath the surface. A hole through the eye.
A rustle. Rushing water, spilling sand. Corey lifted his head.
The bullet pierced his hand, nailed it to the pine. Clean through his side it snapped his twelfth rib in half. A deep bleed ran from his chest down his thighs and when he breathed all he could taste was blood and burning flesh.
He bent prostrate to tear off his gloves. Found his skin blistered open. Body writhing in pupating moths feeding feeding feeding. A gag in prayer but his voice split high and sand spilled from his

lips. Carried his father's rosary into the poisoned stream. And in the pool of water and formless deep his reflection settled. His own eyes staring back at him. Twin suns and blackened stars.
The girl in white.
Cora.

11 | a wooden canary

It must've been the mold. That's what Wayne told him. That through some regrettable quirk in God's plan, Simeon had mistaken the red of Corey's sweater for the bleeding lungs of their prize bull elk, leapt to aim, and fired. That's what Wayne told him.
Thing is, three years from then, he'd wake in heat and sweat and blood, a ritual for each month, as his mind molded like slush and teeth struck from his spine. At the bloated swell in his stomach he'd curl up and sleep in his solitary corner of the couch, and when the doctor asked him so tenderly over his ear what was wrong he would answer that it was only a stomach ache. He'd watch the sand drip from his nails, his gloves as they ossified and dissolved. He'd sit late in his hospital bed, staring Kraig Gersch in the eyes as the holy water the devout one drank every night clouded into golden, weathered, grain, as he moaned and frothed of headaches and divine intervention.
That's what he neglected to tell Wayne. Even as the doctor tended to him and held his hand to pray for weeks on end. Even as the doctor spent all those restless nights in the operating room pleading and pacing and writhing and crying thinking no one would hear him, Corey on the other side of the wall just listening. Because a little sand was better than losing his eyes.
I need you.
That was all it took.
That was all he could cling to.
Once, in a forest, three years ago. It pulsed in his head once a

night.

He only felt it should've been colder.

And now Wayne looked at him with pity.

After three years he had the details of the investigation committed to memory. When that wasn't enough he went stalking through town, scraping for discarded materials of forensic value. By then Jacobi refused him, turned him away, saying it wasn't right, prying into people like that. All hope in him wilted, and with all their sermonizations he stopped attending service entirely.

Instead he went flower picking with Lee every Sunday. That became his worship. The town had turned their backs on them, watching and abstracting with their reverent eyes, but so long as he had Lee to look after, they would be fine.

He knocked gently on the door. It swung open. Lee could always tell, which hands were his. And his child looked tired. Choppy hair uneven as always. A nest for a cooing rock dove.

Corey shouldered his bag, attempted a smile. Only two people he smiled for and Lee was one of them.

> ready?

Lee nodded their head. Eyes straying. A glance back into the kitchen, the pan, the bowls, the whisk, before stepping out of the way.

> Yep.

Corey entered, set his bag on the counter.

> i've got the eggs, flour, and the lemons.

that all?
Yep.
we'll try not to burn the house down.
Mmhm.

He checked the fridge and the pantry, sorted out their butter and sugar. Lee glanced at him.

I've been thinking.

They pushed forward a bowl. Tinkered their hands.

If human bodies don't make sense to me, maybe I was never meant to have one.

Maybe I'm an angel.

an angel?

Angels don't have form. They don't have to worry about human things like flesh. They just are.

Pure consciousness, pure faith.

Corey settled over the sugar. A small smile.

lee.
sweetheart.
Yeah?
you alright?

Lee shrugged and their pet rock dove fluttered.

>Same old.
>Bad dreams.
>Nightmares.

A cloud of white powdered Corey's garments. He had dumped in the sugar and the flour, all regards abandoned in favor of Lee. The rock dove now sitting atop his head.

>is pal bothering you?

Lee gave a short laugh, wiped down his coat.

>No,

They nudged him aside and grabbed the whisk.

>Relax.
>I don't need anyone else worrying about me.

A puff. He poured the butter and Lee mixed the batter. When that was done they spread it across the parchment in the pan.

>how's ruth?
>Why don't you ask her yourself?

At Corey's blank expression mirrored flatly by the dove Lee patted the batter down into a layer of crust.

>She's fine. Fine as she can be, anyways.
>A little upset that I'm not attending service.
>you're under no obligation to.

Grating the lemons, they dusted fine yellow zest over the sugar. Blending it the best they could.

> she cares about you, but sometimes she doesn't understand when she's hurting you.
>
> You don't need to defend her.

The dove leapt from Corey's hair to roost amongst the cupboards. He sifted the flour into the lemon sugar. Set the whisk to it.

> i'm not.
> i'm just saying i understand.
> i know how it feels to hurt and be hurt.
> to be honest i don't know if i'm doing right by you.
> but i'm trying.
> we all are.

Lee crushed a lemon in their fist.

> The difference is that you listen to me.

As he cut the fruit ascorbic bleed stained the cutting board.

> i suppose i can understand you in ways others can't.
> Are we being selfish?
> you shouldn't hurt yourself for their sakes.
> Even if I'm hurting them?
> you're not.
> I am.

The gold tinged juice filled the cup midway. Lee shook their head.

> I'm rotten.

Corey squeezed his half of lemon over the rim and Lee took the other.

> doesn't that make me rotten too?
> Then we're both rotten.

Another split, another squeeze.

> they tell us rot is bad, but,

He held two halves in his gloved hands.

> even a rose can bloom from rot.

Lee took their half, wrung it out, juice raining from their fingers.

> Maybe the rose is just another deception.
> and yet the rose lives.
> it has the right to live, doesn't it?

He split the last lemon. Blade scarring the board.

> lee.
> i want to watch you bloom.
> i want to watch you paint your real face.

Lee squeezed the remainder of the fruit and tossed the rinds. Corey searched for their eyes.

> promise me.

A pop as the egg carton broke open.

> You know I can't.

With their thumbs Lee let the white and gold yolk fall into the lemon sugar and the flour.

> You know.

Corey watched quietly as Lee cracked the shells, one for each apostle.

> but i can still believe. can't i?

Lee didn't meet his eyes.

> I'm a ghost, Corey.
> So are you.

He fell quiet.
In silence they whisked the mixture together, poured it over the crust, let it bake. Cut clean squares and left them to chill in the fridge.
With everything cleaned Corey perched against the door. Gaze wandering slow across the room. Three years and Lee's room remained the same. Three years and Lee's self portrait remained unfinished.
It would be finished. Some day.
Lee locked the dove in its cage and wandered next to him, tugged the elbow of his sleeve. They knew each other without

speaking. They knew that, while the confection cooled and service was over, the two of them would make their way to the garden, gather their flowers, and go home to their rock dove. And everything would be alright.

Late in the evening the doctor found the detective curled up on the couch again. He brushed his sleeping shoulder, tilted his head to peer down at the other.
Darling.
When Corey stirred Wayne knelt, met his partner's tired, smokey eyes.
Evening.
Have you eaten yet?
Corey squinted.

>i was waiting for you.

Oh, dove.

>beef noodles and grilled cheese...

A glance out the window, the dying light. Corey dug into his pocket, a small grumble.

>shit...

Wayne's eyes only looked bigger and sadder behind his lenses.
What's this?

>lemon bars.
>if they're not melted.

From his gloved hands he passed the moistened parchment paper, two squares.

> i should've put them away before i sat down.

Wayne's fingers trembled as he unfolded them. Corey dropped back into his pockets, scanned the doctor's face.

> something wrong?

No. Thank you.

> i remember you saying you liked them. and lee wanted to bake something-

He didn't particularly understand when Wayne pulled him into an embrace. But he didn't mind it. Resting his chin over the other's shoulder, the char of sandalwood and clove in his hair. As he grazed over Wayne's back the doctor flinched. Corey hooked a finger around the collar of his shirt and when the doctor pushed him away the detective held fast to his arm, narrowed his eyes.

> you've been hurting yourself, haven't you?

What?

> don't lie to me.
> i can hear you at night. when you think i'm asleep.

Wayne flattened, turned his nose away. Spoke soft and low. It's prayer.

    it's punishment.

Corey shifted over the cushions, folded his legs beneath him to stare the other in the eyes.

    show me.

I am fully capable of tending to myself.

    not like this.
    where's your first aid kit?

In my room.
Corey pulled him across the foyer, into the bedroom. The doctor grunted as Corey pushed him to sit, the detective kneeling down to fetch the kit under his bed.

    why don't you pray with me instead?

I can't.
Corey unbuttoned his blouse. Flicking up to meet his gaze as the shirt slipped down his shoulder.

    why not?

Wayne's lip trembled and he turned his face away. Then his back. As he heard his partner suck in a shaky breath he bowed his head. Temptation.
Corey traced his gloved fingertips over the nape of Wayne's neck. The sheer width of the wounds washed his skin cold. Shoulder blade to shoulder blade, and the dressing had been applied unevenly, bunched in ridges as the doctor surely twisted to see

his back in the mirror before taping it all down.

    you should've gone to miranda for this.

Corey looked up but Wayne avoided his eyes and he relented. He left the room to remove his gloves, washed his hands and snapped on latex, ignored the suture scars over his palm. When he returned he sat beside the other, slowly peeled the tape and the gauze, murmured soft apologies over each flinch. And with the dressing removed he was finally able to evaluate the broken expanse of Wayne's back. Uneven rows of raised and red skin, some ridges scabbed over.

    it's healing already.

A glance over. Wayne didn't move and all Corey wanted to do was hold him.
He dabbed the wounds clean and dry, spread a thin layer of ointment, pushing the doctor to lay face down that he could stitch together an array of pads too small and tape them down. The work was neat. Because Corey was an artist. He'd made quilts for Lee.
Wayne rose again at the squeeze over his shoulder, Corey pulling off of him to toss the old dressings and the latex, tugging on his worn leather gloves.

    too loose or too tight?

The doctor hugged his arms.
Fine.
He gingerly pulled on his shirt before Corey intervened to help

him.
Thank you.
A light scoff, Corey stopped before him, bent forward to stare down into his eyes.

>promise me you'll stop.

The doctor pointed his nose downwards. Glasses slipping.
Flesh deep isn't enough.
The rot is in my soul.
Another sigh. Again Corey knelt before him, peered up into that gold tinged gaze.

>and what does hurting yourself get you?

It redirects my weakness.

>and what is your weakness?

The doctor met Corey's eyes, tumultuous, wrecked in seafoam. The hand binded to his wrist heavier than chain. Corey remained, legs folded. A glimpse of devotion, the selfless adoration of one committed to service.
You.
The doctor whispered so softly, that he leaned down to hush over his hair.
My fallen angel.
And when the sand began to spill Corey removed his hand, rose to his feet, wandered out the door. The stars in his head made it hard to see.

>i should put away the lemon bars.

That morning Wayne nibbled petitely on his deep fried cheese sandwich as Corey, not hungry, watched him with intimate affection, earned by three years of trying to convince the man not to use his knife. Citing enjoyment over poise.
I've a meeting to attend.

    another?

Corey leaned into his hand, eyes never straying.

    what is it this time, more supply issues?

Worker's compensation.
I must say their persistence is admirable.

    maybe you should listen to them for once.

On the contrary. I need to help them understand the order of things.
The detective drew a long sigh and straightened.

    how long will you be away?

I promised Job I'd dedicate the full day in earnest.
As such deliberations will be occurring in the Kaplin household.
The whole town will be in recess.

    can i come with?

A pause and the doctor wiped the crumbs onto his plate.
I think it'd be better if you stayed home.

right.

I'll see you?
Wayne had shrugged on his coat. Gaze hitched to his partner's face as he awaited his goodbye.
Corey nodded, waved a hand.

later.

Brushing his shoulder as he passed by, the doctor left the detective to the clinic, alone.
And when he was alone the sifting in the walls got louder.
He wanted it to stop.

Corey put his ear to the clinic's bones. A hush within like water or grain, and in the deepest marrow what could pass as faint weeping. Sand trickled from the floorboards, slithered about the corner. He watched and followed as it washed down the steps, slipped between the crack in the door to the doctor's office. Open. Through the sliver, white lace and blue sulfur.
When he entered he found the office empty, clogged in ash and dust and sand. Pneumatic seal broken. Behind the cabinet, spilling faintly against the heavy air like tears, a pale spiral painted in sand.
He pushed the cabinet aside and behind it was a hatch carved into the wall and a single keyhole. It was through that hole that the sand leeched.
The detective turned to the desk, drew the drawer open, clawed up the false bottom, cracked it down the seam. The half that held the keys to the cabinet hid four keys. That night in Wayne's

office, he had only used three of them.

He slipped the teeth past the sand grits and twisted. The panel opened up into a cold darkness and he switched on his light and raised it over his head, the scatterback of stone walls and endless tunnel and a slope downwards into the unyielding black. He got on his hands and knees. Crawled inside the clinic's underwomb. With the light in his mouth he followed the twist of sand down a narrow corridor choked in sulfuric air, ceiling glutted in rust and cobwebs. As his shoulders scraped the walls clean filth mucked his hair and hardened dust rained over his cheeks. He lifted the neck of his sweater and covered his nose, choosing to dwell in his own rankness rather than the scum over his head.

When the floor evened out and the clearance over him raised he got to his feet. The maw of the endless dark tunnel ahead faintly illuminated. The throat beyond a thrumming darkness, gurgling with illusions and reflections. Glancing back at the hole he had emerged from, he swept his gaze over the great stone ceiling arched above. Skull splitting recognition and a stab in his neck. The space was no larger than his cell had been. Able to trace the cracks in the ceiling with his elbow half extended.

He dropped his eyes and pressed forward.

Every five paces he lit his light. Glanced around. Attributed the noises to slow drips echoing and latent concrete moans. Anything to ignore the weeping.

The air in this pulmonary vein was old, dusted in long dead spores dying to awaken. The bloom in his stomach yawned to rend it.

He pressed over his abdomen. Twisted his rosary tight between his fingers, kissed it in the dark. Faith, now, was more comforting than sight.

He came across the first branch in the tunnel. A small funnel not unlike the one he'd crawled from. But in this system he was nothing more than a cramp. Haunting the threshold, bog damp hair clinging to his skin, he pushed his head into the orifice, then squeezed the rest of his body, and the walls spasmed about him.
Still water slushed beneath his palms and the ropes of his shoulders ached. His spine cracked as he twisted himself about a bend. Chasing the slight incline beneath his fingers, the tilt of fluid in his ears. His coat snagged on nails, tears coated in rust. He nearly cracked his teeth with how tightly he clenched the light in his mouth.
All to surge forward at the sight of the end.
He felt over the hatch. Threw his shoulder against it. Clawed at the edges of the panel with his nails. But like the one he'd come from, this one had been locked.
There he slumped. Caught his breath, rancid air necrotizing his throat and spiking his lungs. He had to turn back.
Shutting his light he felt his way through, sliding slow down the slope, until the ground vanished beneath him and he tumbled out into the main tunnel, where he lay, soaking in the drivel of the earth.
The system was making him sick.
But the sand beckoned him to continue.
He rose to his feet.
Affixed to one side he traveled, discovered the next branch, and the next. Sketching each point in the dim light, he had in his hands an approximate map of tunnels veined beneath the bones of the town. The branches tapered off from the main tendril extending from the base of the clinic, across the length of the town, to the womb low cavern of block cut pillars. Unlit lamps

and splintered wooden beams.

The old mine. Coal, then uranium, when they figured out how to sift the yellow from the pitchblende. They heralded the scar as a miracle, before the town died.

The sand pooled at his feet and went still. A lightness to his head. It dragged his eyes upwards, to the stone fixture of the ceiling, and in the blackdamp air he remembered.

Three years ago, they put something inside of him.

The worm in his stomach inched a fraction upwards and he folded over to retch. Red stringed mucus, curdled in feathers. Dead rot expelled to the air. With ragged breaths he straightened his bones, turned around, and walked back.

The weeping had gotten louder.

He chose to ignore it.

In the dark he stumbled, swatted roaches from his collarbone, raked muck from his cheeks. Counting each opening as he passed. One for each apostle.

He stopped at the thirteenth. The passageway leading back to the clinic. Because in the sleeping face of the deep he saw, two eyes, warm brown.

His own eyes.

He flashed the light. When his brain failed to register the sight he threw darkness back over his head and squeezed forward, eyes first, to sink back into the length of the clinic's womb. The walls wrapped warmly around him.

As he crawled a voice stirred from behind. Uttered a name long deceased. A lure. A lie.

Each step drove his stomach against his spine but it was only at the threshold between filth and cleansing that he turned to face the formless void. Turned on his light.

Belle stared back at him. Velvet shed skin full of necrotic blood and a rattle in her chest. The sand emerged from the gaping cavity of her mouth and swallowed her eyes and his light went out.
From behind a hand on his head and an arm securing around his waist. Corey jolted straight and was met by a familiar softness against his back. The cool rush of breath rich in oxygen.
Corey.
The detective slowly untensed himself. Wiped the grime from his eyes, glanced over his shoulder. As his disorientation cleared he caught the acrid sillage of char in the air. On the doctor's red singed skin, blackened pigment like ash.

> wayne?

He turned to face him, wiped a thumb over the other's cheek.

> what happened?

Wayne caught his wrist. Took in the shredded state of the detective's clothes, the grot in his hair, the mire, the drain.
What were you doing?

> i was- i just discovered these tunnels.
> what happened?

Someone set fire to the chapel.

> what?

In the midst of deliberations Jacobi noticed the blaze on the hill. When we arrived the chapel was only half standing. We found canisters of gasoline abandoned in the wreckage.

    did anyone see anything?

Ruth is investigating.
The doctor scanned Corey's figure, pinched a lock of his dark hair.
You were in the tunnels the whole time?

    i was.

What were you thinking.

    i wasn't.

We secured all entry and exit points to the underground system out of concerns for safety.

    so you knew about the tunnels.

I didn't think they were worth mentioning.
The doctor held him back by the shoulders.
How did you even get into my office?

    the door was unlocked.

Corey.
Wayne tightened his grip, leaned down.
I haven't the patience for your deceptions.

    this isn't a deception.

Do you honestly take me for a fool?

Wayne puffed and pushed himself off of the other.
I thought you were done being reckless. Done trying to take away everything I've worked for.
But here you are. The same man.

    wayne-

Enough.
We have a fire to investigate.
He'd turned away before Corey could protest.

The fire was still raging when they got there, the crowd gathered a short distance from the smoldering rubble. Men passed buckets of water and spit into the flame, the old firetruck sitting lonely, the nearest water line drained empty. Miranda and Anna tended dutifully to the burn wounds, Anna Kaplin ashen skinned and quiet as she kept her distance from the doctor, who was keeping audience with Shepherd Job.
Let me through- Doc!
Simeon Turner tore from the crowd. Danielle Cardenas Kwon holding him back by the arm before Paladin More pried her from him.
Dr. Sykkes regarded the young man, the sparks and cinders in his teeth.
Everything alright, Simeon?
Even better.
A huff.
Dani saw who did it.
Corey looked to Dani, her sharp and weepy eyes, and she turned her face away.

The detective stepped closer. Dani avoided his gaze.

> please. dani. what did you see?

Already told him, it's nothing we can work off of.
Simeon pushed into the detective's face. A grin.
Lee.
His grin stretched wider.
It was Lee.
Your kid.
Dani here saw her leaving the scene of the crime.
Corey stared dully. Turned his face away.

> objectionable evidence. not enough to act on.

Dani reined Simeon in. Grip cold and merciless.
My thoughts exactly.
Seeing someone leave is hardly conclusive.
Simeon glared.
Oh yeah? How do you explain her being there, then?
The detective ran a hand through his mess of hair. Eyes painting the crowd. Anything to avoid his own damnation. Wayne stood over the rubble, drawn to the fire, back turned.

> i'll talk to lee.

I already talked to her.
A glance. Ruth stood, a shade against the burnt beams jutting against the sky, clouds closing in from the horizon. Under her arm, Lee Palomo, sobbing quietly. Essie worrying her skirt a distance away.

Ruth sighed, shook her head.
Can't shield her from everything, detective.
Corey narrowed his eyes.

    there isn't sufficient evidence.

Lee looked up with bleary eyes, runny and redfaced, gasping between chokes. Reaching for him, when he was too far away. He would've moved closer, if it weren't for his own filth.

    I didn't do it. I swear.

She's lying.

    how can you be sure?

As much as I love the girl you know how she is.
And Dani saw her.
Seems open and shut to me.
Dani looked with pleading eyes and Corey shook his head.

    dani saw lee leave. that's all we know.
    hell, lee was probably in the garden when the fire started.

Dr. Sykkes raised his voice. He'd drifted with the smoke. Knelt wrapping gauze about Jacobi's hand.
Regardless of her culpability, the fact remains that Lee's destructive behavior needs to be addressed.
The fire, whether Lee is the arson or not, is far from the only concerning matter the girl has been involved in.
You told me so yourself, detective.

Corey was unable to catch his eyes. But by God he wanted to rip his pretty throat.
With a small cry Lee tore away from Ruth and flung headfirst into Corey's arms. Clinging to his neck and smothering his shoulder in tears.

> I'm sorry,
> I should've listened to them,
> I should've listened,

He took a moment to untense himself. But there he realized, at least he was here. Petting Lee softly, murmuring into their hair.

> it's okay. i believe you. i won't let anything happen to you.

Lee shuddered. Raised their eyes to look up at him. Ash crusting their lashes.

> Corey.
> I'm going to die like her.

He stared into them pitifully. He'd split his own heart, tear the skin from his face, gorge on what failed to be a part of him, over and over again, if it meant keeping Lee safe.
Simeon hacked a spittle, kicked dirt over it. Pushed past as he wiped his peeling nose.
You fed a hysterical woman delusions.
I hope you regret it now.
Paladin More followed, shepherding his sheep. A golden halo over his hair.

Pray, detective. The doctor will save her.
Corey met his gaze from over Lee's head. Cold sapping from his fingers. He looked to Essie.

    can you take lee home for me?

The firelight on her dark skin made her look almost sickly but she nodded. Took her friend by the hand. Corey squeezed Lee's shoulder and told them, gently as he could, to rest. A rag in the breeze, he watched them go. Grief interrupted as Ruth hissed over his shoulder.
Detective. She has a chance, a chance to get herself back on the right track. Being soft will get her killed.
His coal eyes drifted over the weathered woman's face.

    you're already killing them.

Before Ruth could question him the Shepherd shouted, Paladin More whispering in his ear.
The Lord has spoken!
As we stand in the ruins of our place of worship, let this moment signify the moment we burned evil from our regiments.
We must descend upon the child the cure.
The sea parted and the doctor at the end of it nodded his head.
It will be done.
The detective resolved for a moment, before falling silent.
It wasn't the act of looking that cut him quiet, but the look itself. Hazel eyes drained of color. Stiller than the deep. Dark depths where the earth chose not to bleed. Where God couldn't see.
From the sky the first droplet. Sliding slow down Wayne's cheek.
The town dispersed.

As the rain put out the fire only the weary remained.
Kraig Gersch grated his palms bloody and red against the blackened cross they'd recovered from the wreckage before Jacobi pried him away. And when Corey caught her gaze she nodded. Towards Miranda.
Corey hesitated before he stumbled over to the doctor. Broken bodied, packing her kits shut from the rain.

>miranda.

Corey.

>i need your help.
>please.

Corey,

>i know i'm not right in the head. but please.
>i'm scared for lee.
>i'm scared,

I know.
She looked on with hollow eyes. He didn't move.
A glance at Wayne and Miranda stepped closer. Kept her voice low.
There are things I can't tell you. But know that I am trying. That I am willing to do whatever it takes.
Her gaze flickered over his face. Sunken and weary. And in an instant he felt he understood, everything.
I'll do what I can for Lee.

Wayne was crumpled in front of the scorched cross scored by bloody hands. He only managed a murmur at the shadow passing over him, which he recognized to be his wife, to some twinge of disappointment.
It survived the fire.
Miranda stared down at him. The way he hugged himself to the floor.

> You know Lee doesn't need it.

What Lee needs is help.

> This isn't the kind of help Lee needs.

Then what?
He looked up at the other doctor, a laugh, a smile.
Therapy?
Medication?
All courses of treatment have failed her, Miranda.

> I know that.
> That's not what I was talking about.

She drew herself down to his level. As she'd done many times before.

> Your cure gives hope to those who have lost all hope. Those who are out of options.

> But if you're not careful you will follow right in the footsteps of leucotomy.

A scoff. He turned away from her, threw off her hand.
I have done nothing but proceed with caution.
At that she bared closer.

> Caution?
>
> You've changed more than you needed to. You've overextended what has been given to you.
>
> Look at Anna.

We are still in the process of calibrating her treatment. You know that.
Instead of focusing on one data point why don't you look at this town? My cure has improved their lives significantly!
He refused to meet her gaze. She would've severed his head if it meant he'd finally look at her.

> You won't even let me test that claim.

He gave her his eyes. His big, sad eyes.
Do you not believe in me?

> I stopped the moment you went too far.

Miranda raised herself to her feet. Leaning over him like a seraph of many wings.

> You have a chance to help Lee.

She graced his shoulder, only briefly, before turning away.

Don't repeat the same mistakes.

Even while the garden was covered by a thin layer of ash Corey found comfort in its serenity. The unburdened sprawl of his roses, the fronds of hyssop and the dusting of chokecherries. He curled up in the shade of Belle's statue, a familiar friend by now, and crushed berries at her feet. It was there he found the peace to simply be. Belle thought so. And now Lee must've thought so too.
As the clouds wept a mist of tears he leaned against the rotting heart of the chestnut tree and packed mud over its orange sickness. And when the rain stopped Corey left Belle's side. Drifted over to take his place beside Wayne. The doctor hadn't moved since Miranda left him. Knees cutting gravel, forehead against the cross.
Thumbing his rosary Corey sat down and passed it to the other, who took it, staring down at the beads pooled in his palms. Not knowing what to do with them.
Corey.
Do you think I'm doing a good thing here?

    you're trying to.

Trying to.
Why don't you want me helping Lee?

    wayne.

Be honest. I can take some criticism.

> i do want you to help lee.
> but you won't.
> not completely.
> you'll do more. worse.

Worse.
Wayne scoffed. Crawled closer, until his breath brushed the feather strands of Corey's hair.
What are you so afraid of?
That it will change her?
That it will take away who she is?
Corey leaned back on his hands and Wayne pressed closer.
I understand my cure is dire. I understand that such sharp change can be terrifying. But the truth is, my cure can quite literally change a person. Down to the functioning of their brain. You say that is a bad thing. I say, why let unnecessary suffering be, for the sake of something as ephemeral as identity?
The fact is that Lee is suffering and I can do something about it. But you want to cling to the very thing that is harming her.

> and when that very thing is the self?
> what harm does it do, aside from provoking the judgement of others?

Wayne narrowed his eyes. Lifted Corey's chin.
It is the source of her pain.

> it is the source of their judgement.

The detective removed himself from the other's grasp. Took back his rosary, jadeshine over his fingers.

    lee does need help.
    but you take that piece of them away, what does that leave us with?

He dropped the string of prayers into his pocket and leaned forward.

    you'll kill them, wayne.
    you'll kill them when you could have helped them.

The doctor looked up from his lips. Tilted his head.
I will give Lee a chance.
He raised swiftly to his feet.
She will decide for herself, and it will be up to her and those around her to steer her towards a decision.
Corey took his hand.

    lee won't be the one deciding.

That is the best I can do.
A puff and Corey tugged him closer. All the sweat and the tattered clothes. Corey Handler was a different man than he was three years ago. Deep inside.

    you can do better than that.

Wayne regarded him. His partner. His filth. There was a fury storming in the golden flecks of his eyes that'd suddenly quieted. I thought the same of you.

12 | his own damnation

Dr. Sykkes was in the process of documenting and reporting the damages to Bentham, the detective hanging around to pick for scraps. Of the chapel, one corner remained standing, dandelion walls charred and flaking, the gutted bones of the ceiling folded inwards. The great oaken doors had been reduced to splinters and the grand stage collapsed, the red curtains pulled over it like a death shroud. Fallen beams and rubble hashed the ashchoked floor, auditorium chairs melted down to sagging rods.
With the last canvas complete, they rested in the garden. Corey passed to Wayne a chunk of his lemon bar, leaning against the chestnut tree.
The doctor took it gratefully, though not without scrutiny.
Dove.
You have yet to answer me.
What were you doing in my office?
Corey eased out of his bite of lemon, gave a less than pleased grimace.

> wasn't plotting anything.

Wayne wiped the chokecherry jam off Corey's nose.
That isn't sufficient enough of a reason.
Corey swatted his hand away.

> squeak and the old sawbones will throw me in the loony bin.

Don't be ridiculous.
I wouldn't do anything without express permission, unless the situation was dire.

> swear it.

The doctor met his eyes. That same look, as though he were only made of dust.
I swear.
The detective finished his square of dessert. Wiped off his gloves and straightened.

> i'm only half here, wayne.
> something's wrong with me. deep inside.
> and i have a feeling you already know.

Wayne let a breath.
Darling. You should have confided in me.

> you lie about a lot of things.

Corey turned and started walking. Away from the setting sun.

> i was seeing things that day. sand. moving like a snake.
> it led me into your office. wanted me to get into the tunnels.
> the door was already unlocked. all i did was follow.

Corey.

> i'm insane.

Let me help you.

> not worried about me at the moment.

The detective scanned the perimeter. Empty walkways cleared out by the smoke.

> the town didn't seem all too happy with your decision.

I merely passed the burden of choice unto Lee.
As I promised you.
The doctor walked at his leisurely pace. Wind ruffling his silver hair.
I still don't understand it. Womanhood is a gift. To be a mother, a daughter, a wife. I envy what so many disgrace. For what man doesn't want to be a woman?
Corey cocked a brow.

> i don't.

The doctor flicked his eyes away.
The point is that she needs help. Before she destroys herself and this town.
A hand on his shoulder. Corey tugged him back.

> okay. say i were to take it.
> why doesn't it work for some?

The issue is complexity at such high dimensions.
An arm around the detective's waist and Wayne nudged his friend forward to continue their stroll.
We didn't have this issue with animal trials because the brains

studied weren't as complex.
Corey swiped at his face. Fluffed his mucked hair.

> i dunno. humans are pretty close to monkeys.

Hm. Well.
Eyes to the sky. The firmament of the night a cup full of trembling stars.
We underestimated just how active the human brain is in comparison. The sheer dimensionality of data exceeded the capacity of our jacobian optimizations and the jobs failed to initiate, rendering the ANNE's unresponsive.
The doctor smiled at him.
Do you know what ANNE's stands for?

> adaptive neuromodulating nanoscale electrodes.

The smile faltered. Corey took it from him.

> don't look surprised. i sound stupid but i'm well read. especially when it comes to you. sunshine.

A frown. Wayne turned up his nose and shut his eyes.
Seeing that the issue was with dimensionality, our solution was to use densing adaptive nano initiators and ruthless pruning to learn precisely which corners to cut.
Feeding on data transmitted by our mirror protocol we curated a database of functional mappings and trained a generalized model to learn and leverage the expedient regions of activity in the brain.
Unfortunately, some circuits are incompatible with this

generalized model.

belle's brain wasn't typical enough.

Yes. In Isabella's case, the essential information stream returned far too many null values.

and with lee?

The chances of incompatibility are one to a thousand, and even then, the issue itself does not pose any health risks. It only requires calibration.

according to you.

I have been working tirelessly to address this problem and I promise you that Lee will be safe with me.
Just as you are. Shall be. Should you choose me.
Corey passed him one look and he went quiet.

When they got within earshot of the clinic they found Simeon waiting on the steps. The redfaced shopkeep got to his feet, shouted.
Is it true?
You're choosing not to cure Lee, after everything that happened?
The doctor stopped in his tracks. Let go of Corey's arm.

I have decided to appeal to her right to choose.

A barking laugh. Simeon struck his knee and spat. Clenched jaw and jutted veins.
Well, doc, I didn't take ya for a coward.

Then his eyes shot over, raked over the detective idling disinterested by the doctor's side.

What did that one do to taint your mind? Take you into his bed? Corey simpered fruitfully enough to be unnerving and Simeon turned his glare back on the doctor.

Or maybe there is something wrong with the cure. Like Ms. Olliver says.

The doctor tilted his head, a long drawn sigh.

> Child. Do not forsake me.

Simeon raised his hands, took a step back. A gleam of silver at his waistband.

There is a moral corruption in this town. I, for one, will not stand for it.

Consider this retribution.

His hand went to his hip. Corey's eyes followed.

The Sand Prince punishes sin.

At the rip of the bullet the detective leapt in front of the doctor and they tumbled into the gravel in a tangle of limbs. Corey's lean body tensed over him and heaving ragged breaths. Reaching under the neck of his shirt Wayne retrieved his pistol and aimed over his partner's shoulder, thrust his other hand into his pocket. In a pinch Simeon grunted and folded into the floor. Then Corey. Crumpled into his arms.

Wayne laid him gently on his side, looked him over. With Simeon unconscious the doctor fiddled with the device in his pocket and the detective roused again shortly after. Thrashing. But the doctor knew to muzzle him. Pet him on the cheek.

You were only grazed.

Corey curled back into the gravel and Wayne dropped his hand, leaned back. The detective clutched his head, wincingly traced his side. A sear in his red sweater and a burn line under his rib, pink dermis weeping scarlet. He slotted himself against the other, slick haired and ashen, a grumble as he stuck a finger through the new hole in his coat. Cutting right through the concealed pocket he carried his rosary in. But he'd worry about that later.

    shit aim.

His eyes flicked up to meet his partner's. Pupils dilated to the rims in an adrenaline haze.

    you shoot him?

No.
He fell unconscious of his own accord.
It seems his emotions overwhelmed his system.
Corey pushed aside the neck of the doctor's shirt, thumbed the leather harness running down his chest.

    since when did you carry?

Today.
A soft chuckle. Corey squeezed his shoulder, traced down Wayne's side.

    you weren't hit.

I wasn't. Thanks to you.
The detective turned his head. Their unconscious gunman

dozing in the grass.

    what was he thinking?

He wasn't.
It seems this is what the town's frustration has accumulated to.
Wayne sighed. Grasp firm over Corey's hips.
I'll call Jacobi. Simeon will require rest. He was receiving treatment for aggression.
He looked his partner over, a gentle smile.
Let's get you cleaned up.

They waited for Jacobi to arrive. By then Simeon had come to, groggy, disoriented, a tad apologetic. Jacobi took him home, promised to watch over him in the meantime. Wished them well.
The moment they stepped inside the clinic Wayne locked the door and Corey picked a wall to slump against. The doctor returned with his kit, grasped the detective's hand.
Tell me what you need.

    a drink.

A fraught smile. The doctor poured him his absinthe and the detective took it. Swirled the wormwood, tasted the mouth. Sifting through the remnants of his rosary. The beads had shattered on impact, shards of fractured jadeshine pooled between his knees.
You always carried that with you.

    my father gave it to me. to him my grandmother.

every day she thanked god for their safe passage.

I'm sorry.

it's just a symbol.

He plucked the crucifix from the ruin. Ran a thumb over his fractured God before securing him back into his pocket.

this is home now. you. lee.
we're here. and i'm better for it.

A frown at the shards.

i probably should've given it to my sister though.

Cora?
A twist in his gut. Corey drew in his legs, turned his head away.

roxanne.
where did you hear cora from?

I don't recall.
Wayne hummed, gestured for Corey to bare his wound. Lifted his shirt, dabbed at his burn.
Who is she?
At the sting of the gauze Corey tucked his nose into his partner's shoulder. Threaded their fingers.

you believe in ghosts?

Only angels.

Corey shut his eyes. Glanced down at the hand holding his. Delicate and slender. Apt to make the tiniest of incisions with the largest of repercussions.

> understand me when i say.
> cora is dead.
> she's been dead a long while now.

Apologies. I didn't know.

> regret should be reserved for things that deserve it.
> this ain't one of them.

Corey shifted. Found some comfort in the familiar weight of the crucifix in his pocket. Different yet same.

> when i think of cora i think of belle. of lee.

He would've brought the doctor's hand to his lips, had the other not pulled away. Instead he watched him, watched as he reached for his kit.

> it was always going to be this way, wasn't it?

Eventually.
Wayne pressed the gauze to Corey's side. Lessened the pressure at the other's flinch.
This conversation has revealed something to me.
He taped the dressing smooth with his nimble fingers. Held it firm beneath the heat of his skin.
God may ask us to sacrifice our sons
If that means saving them.

With a small sigh Corey rested his chin back down over Wayne's shoulder. A brush over his pulse point, the azure veins snaking beneath his candlewax skin.

    conscience means we can never be sure.

Of course.
But that is why we seek His guidance.
Wayne held him close. Arms around his waist. Like a rusted nail buried in rotten wood.
If the Lord can save me,
He can save her.
Corey went rattle still against him. The bloat in his skin begging to resurface.

    reverence is weakness.

The detective got to his feet.

    i'm going to wash up.

Letting the bath run he stripped down to the skin and dove under the shower. Set it scalding. Shaky breaths, holding firm against the wall. Dark bleed hair snaked tendrillike into his cheeks, raked across his neck. Black beaded perspiration prickling needles into the tawny brown of his skin. Lead and carbon. A steady stream licked down his thin back and slender legs and the murky water drew from his body a glutted and slickened clot peppered in feather down. It swirled down into the drain. Passed from one womb to another.

It was supposed to be a gift. In a way it was. It helped him know pain, made him softer for it.

But it was killing him. His own blood was so thick it choked his veins, turned ichor into poison.

May I come in?

The detective raised his head. Eyed the awkward blur warped behind the screen of frosted glass. Wayne.

...I need help changing my dressing.

Corey pushed the shower door open a crack, cool air steaming unwelcome relief into his skin. Across the bathroom, the doctor. Halfway through the door, shirt draped open. Catching Corey's sly gaze, Wayne stiffened and ducked his head away.

> wayne.

Corey shut off the water.

> may i get dressed first?

... Yes.

A smile of amusement and Corey dried off, stepped out of the cove. Wayne was leaning against the doorway, back turned, head bowed. Corey pulled on his gloves, his sweater, and some briefs, and when that was done he brushed up against his partner, squeezed his shoulder, before returning to the mirror.

The doctor undressed without a word, sank down into the tub.

Thank you, for drawing the water.

> mmhm.
> too cold?

Just fine, darling.
Corey leaned against the sink. Smudged a fresh coat of liner beneath his eyes. He could hear Wayne shifting in the water, the splash of his body's volume. The outline of his form twisting faint in the foggy reflection.
You still wear that.

   jealous?

That you refuse to bare your eyes to me.
As the detective preened and painted his lips daintily in black gloss the doctor turned his eyes away.
I've yet to understand how such a pretty thing like you has earned me so much trouble.
The detective stowed his pigments back into the drawer. Tempered his expression.

   ready?

... Yes.
With the water draining between his ankles the doctor dried off, wrapped the towel about his waist, sat at the edge of the tub. The detective settled beside him, kit in his lap.
They repeated their ritual. Changing out his bandages. Wayne's eyes shut like he was steeped in prayer.
Peeling the tape and dressing, Corey leaned over, dabbed gauze.

   how long?

Wayne paused. Took a moment to process his question. Sight filtered through his lashes.

A year.

>   is it working?

No.
But it will.
It has to.
A soft hush of breath. The detective spreading ointment over the doctor's wounds. Wayne brushed Corey's knee, stopped flat over the edge of the tub. Close but never touching.
If the Lord can save me, He can also save you.
You act as though there is no hope for you. But I have faith in you.
Corey bent him forward. Packed the gauze. Sigh grating his ear.

>   you shouldn't.

I've but one goal. To rid us of sin. Of want. Of flesh.
Corey stretched out his cut of tape. Smoothed it firm down Wayne's back. Tense muscles easing under the rub of his thumbs.

>   i've never wanted.

It must be easy for you then.

>   it isn't.
>   not with you.

Oh, darling.
Wayne took Corey's face into his hands. The wipe of his thumb smudging the corner of his lip.
You don't realize, how wretched I am.

Smokey eyes and a fixed stare darker than the most intense of carbon. Corey leaned into his touch, voice hushing.

>may i pray for you?

Please.
Corey took his hand. Met the other's face with his own.

>do as I have done to you.

In a haze of recognition Wayne murmured, half on instinct.
A servant is no greater than his master.

>i will tend to you, i will wash you, and i will dress you.
>may i wash your feet?

It isn't time.

>it is for you.
>should you believe it.

I believe in you.
Corey withdrew.
He retrieved from the cabinets a clay basin, brimmed it in water, set it before Wayne's feet. There he knelt, a linen towel in his lap, and took each of Wayne's heels. Doused water over his feet. Kissed his ankles as he dried them.

>if god is loving,
>you should let yourself be loved.

One last kiss. Gentle and languid over Wayne's flushed and

trembling skin. Corey folded the linen. Set the basin aside.

    may i dress you?

Wayne's voice quivered over his head, pleading and weak. Please.
Corey unfolded himself from the floor, leaned over the other. Slid his hands up his tender waist, grasped lightly, until he could feel the muscles tense. He lifted Wayne to stand. The doctor dipped his head in shame as the towel slipped from his hips and onto the floor but Corey lifted his chin back upwards, leaned closer, pulled over Wayne's thighs his undergarments, his slacks, and clasped the front. Pausing briefly at the tremor in Wayne's legs. He draped the blouse over Wayne's shoulders, slowly buttoned it up loop by loop, from the soft of his belly to the hollow of his neck.
Corey's eyes hadn't left his once.
This time he told Corey to get on his knees and he listened. Legs folded, head bowed. Wayne curled his fingers through Corey's downy hair, drew him closer towards his heat. A thick swallow. He could practically taste him. Fresh blackberries and blackened stars.
When Corey finished his prayer a deep reverence surged within him and seeing those eyes and hearing his name Wayne dropped to his knees. He held Corey against his breast and Corey continued to pray. Chin over his shoulder, gentle over his ear. Even as the other wept.

    lead us not into temptation,
    and deliver us from evil,

Wayne burrowed closer. Until he could feel the weak pulse in Corey's neck.

They only ever seemed to kiss in dreams.

13 | sacrifice our sons

They gathered upon the hill amongst the charred ruins of the chapel. The town one great crescent, Lee at the center, robed in white garments trailing opalescent. Choppy hair tied uneven. Before them, the blackened cross, and in the mock pulpit before the crucifix, the Shepherd, leering over his congregation. Singing as though that would make their house rise again.
And the Holy Spirit descends upon us!
Isn't it beautiful? The icon of our faith, the golden glow of angels!
This time Corey could see it.
Over the ruins, a shimmering haze, a cloud of grace from the cosmic heavens. Yawning jaws of sand. Paling in the light a pallid sheen. Here, Kraig Cephas Gersch wept and Corey Handler trembled.
It struck into him fear of the Lord. Sheer terror.
Corey could only watch as it rolled closer, threatened to bind Lee to the crude altar.

> stop.
> you all need to stop this.

Across the circle he skimmed Dani's eyes, met Miranda's. The doctor stepped forward.

> Listen to him.
> He's right.

All eyes shifted to Dr. Olliver. A lurid hush.

> We know full well what this did to Belle.
> Don't do the same to Lee.

Kraig's garbled shriek cracked the crescent wide. Wayne raised to full height.
Enough, love.
Sit down.
In Miranda's chest a breath shuddered and at the Shepherd's nod Dr. Olliver stepped out into the fray, steadied her shoulders.

> Every day our bones run drier.

Said bones stiffened, stilled under her gaze. Like iron.

> Haven't you noticed?
> Dwindling supplies, steepening bails.
> He's trapped us here.
> After we begged him to listen.

She passed over each man in the congregation, settled from Corey to Lee.

> Belle was the first.
> We will die under his ignorance.

Paladin More shot forward. Knuckles clenched white.
Perjury! She lies!
Dr. Sykkes saved me. Saved so many of us.
He raised a shriveled finger at the end of a shaking arm.
You are nothing more than a witch.

I've seen you, Dr. Olliver. I've seen you with Ms. Kaplin.
Kraig shut his ears and screamed as the Shepherd remained expressionless. Miranda's aspen skin went sheet white.

>Pal. That's not true.
>Wayne,

Jacobi stepped between them. To shield those yet to be judged.
Now, hold on, these are serious allegations-
The doctor spoke with a cold and merciless ease.
Dr. Olliver and Ms. Kaplin have indeed been undergoing treatment.

>Anna?

Miranda stumbled towards him. Worn threads snapping in her throat.

>Anna isn't well, and it's your fault she's worse-

The doctor lies!
Essie flew out from the crowd. Ashen skin.
I've seen him. With the detective.
A murmur and Simeon's voice rolled low after hers.
That's true. I saw em.
Wayne scoffed. But Corey could see, the tremor to his lip, the flush in his neck.
Don't be ridiculous. I've no such relations.
A glance towards the detective. Corey remained unmoving. Dark feathers over his eyes.

>he lies to himself.

Miranda kept his gaze.

Simeon guffawed, slapped his weeping and spasming Kraig.

See!

I have faith in the cure. But I'm starting to think it ought to change hands.

Pal shook his head, stopped beside Lee. Placed a hand over their stagnant shoulder.

You all lack in faith.

Has any disciple ever been perfect?

He pressed Lee forward, ignored how they cowered.

Dr. Sykkes will save Lee. Just as I am certain he would have saved Isabella, had we given him more time.

The doctor drew a long sigh. Dying breath, dwindling sails lost at endless sea.

Faith is a test.

The detective's figure remained at the crux of his vision.

The Lord will judge me.

He gestured towards Lee, set his gaze upon the Shepherd.

We have before us a lost lamb in need of guidance.

In these trying times we mustn't scorn her.

Over the Shepherd's cliff eaten face a smile broke. As challenge curdled slow between the two men he spread his welcome.

Doctor, you misunderstand. We are indebted to you, for what you have done for us. For me. For my own wife.

Her treatment has been nothing short of necessary, as is Lee's.

But men are fallible.

Change is coming.

Miranda dug her boot, clenched Jacobi's hand. The sulfur fire about Wayne's irises only served to feed the Shepherd's flaming teeth.

Let us not stand divided in this joyous moment of rebirth.
The Lord sends his ram.
If Lee is failed, we shall take that as a sign.
Ruth hovered over Lee like a wilted shadow.
I agree with this course of action.
Jacobi nodded.
A chance is fair.
The detective roused. Spoke quiet and low.

> i want to hear from lee.

Miranda took his side and Dani spoke. The town clinging to every utterance as guilt commanded their need to atone.
Belle made her choice.
Lee should do the same.
Wayne met Corey's eyes hollow. Halos with no grace.
Let us see what she says.
Ruth set her hands over Lee's stone shoulders and they culled from their chest a broken voice.

> I want to be saved.
> To separate the soul and the flesh.
> To transcend the body for it was never mine.

The frayed threads of his heart quivered and the weeping daughters remained silent. Lee was fading beneath the veil. The doctor drifting and spectral.
Pal stepped in front of them. Hair gleaming gold.
Surely you do not go against her wishes?
Her desire to be saved?
Corey looked at him. This child of god. Born in blood.

all i see is fear.

The Shepherd raised his hands and putrile orange rot bloomed from his brittle nails.
Let sand weather our flesh into soul.
Corey met Essie's eyes and Miranda shook her head. The detective grabbed the doctor's arm. Tugged him close.

stop this. please.

Wayne didn't move. Carved for himself a shell of alabaster.
It's already begun.
Corey seized fistfuls of his shirt. Begged.

i can't lose another kid,

Holdfast desperation hooked its snarled roots into skin.

wayne.
please.

Wayne bent forward, whispered low.
Now I know you fear God.
Sand grit and sea salt slit his cheeks. Wayne drew him backwards, cast him aside, like a dead dove wrapped in plastic. And like a cowering dog Corey limped away.
The last he saw of his son was the pallid mask slipping over his face.

As the rock dove rattled in its cage Corey peeled himself from the reflection in the window and returned to the clinic.

Retrieved Wayne's firearm. Haunted the embolism red doors to the operating room. He'd been possessed, in his mind, to salvage by destroying. To stop the infection before it spread.
One shot blew the hinges open.
When he aimed the pistol at the arm of the ultrasound machine they came surging in.
Pal pointed his gun before Jacobi pushed his hand down, barked at him not to shoot.
The doctor raised his hands. Edged closer. Lee wide eyed behind him.
Corey. Put the gun down.
Corey kept his aim on the equipment. Tattered coat hanging from his frame like broken wings. Not once did he look up.

>i can't let you do this.

Corey.
That machine is replaceable.

>lee isn't.

His eyes shifted, darker than carbon.

>neither are you.

Corey threw the gun. Shoved Wayne against a wall. Knife to his neck. The doctor's muscles tensed and the detective snarled ragged at his throat.

>why?

I have to.

you're killing them.

The blade nicked his raw and natal skin, lifted each layer like a page.

you're killing *me*.

Corey!
From across the room Lee trembled.
Corey.
Please stop.

lee.

Corey's grip on the pocketknife eased but his lips remained blunted over Wayne's collar.

i'm sorry.

Lee shook their head.
Don't be.
It's eating me alive.
Making me something I was never meant to be.
Maybe I am dead. And this is my punishment. But the cure is my salvation.
The prince will save me.
The prince will sever my soul from my flesh.
Corey couldn't speak. Wondering where he'd gone wrong, where he'd failed, a father and his only child. He wanted to beg him, beg his son to remain just as he was, to bloom bold and red, but cotton sweetness bathed his tongue and a haze obscured his eyes. With a stumble he looked down and the edges of his gloved

fingers diffracted, sheered in the thin light, and the knife slipped from his hand.
Wayne had reached into his pocket.
The detective dropped unconscious.

He woke up in the yellow room.
One haze in a feverish network of broken minds. When his eyes emerged he found around him a padded cell bathed in fluorescents. Nothing but a door, a hole, and a one way mirror. He did not panic because he knew it would be useless to scream. He did not have the right to.
He got up to pry at the panel, chipped away on his knees until the paint stripped from his nails. When that was done and futile he stood back up, numb and hazy. A man in a yellow box.
Time did not exist in this box. No time, only consciousness. The worst punishment of all. He would waste none of it.
He sobbed once. Then he prayed. Went prostrate before his fluorescent god. When he raised his eyes he saw in the darkened mirror a pallid mask. His own waterlogged face. Skin swollen and sunken. Wet like deadwater bloom. From the back of his neck an itch had crawled its way into his temples, seeded and sunk its wiry roots, and he got to his feet.
A creak in the hinge of his sagging jaw and his ripe cheekflesh split open, tore from sheer fluid weight and slapped to the cushioned floor. White bone spidered in still beating blood vessels and buccal fat.
No mask.
She kicked from inside of him.
One jerk shredded his womb and she pressed against his ribs, clawed two fingers like talons up into the base of his throat.

Flayed him open to air, in the dust of this yellow room, dry bones stuffed in sulfur rags.

The stone ceiling flashed before his eyes, gored vision into the cervical disks of his neck. A nodule swelling as his body rejected what was foreign.

He retrieved the broken crucifix in his pocket. Pressed the point into the axis of his spine.

The pneumatic seal of the room broke open as the door unlocked and the doctor entered.

The procedure was a success.

Lee is resting now.

> lee is dead.

The doctor watched from the breach. The detective's frail figure dolled against the yellow. Corey stabbed the icon of his god into the nape of his neck. Chest rattling in a careful sigh. The truth, the truth would scar him.

> what are the tunnels used for?

Corey.

Wayne stepped closer. Reached for his wrist.

What are you doing?

He pulled his wings into his weeping eyes. Pushed the icon deeper.

> you put something inside me.

I breathed life into you.

Dove.

I breathed *life* into you.
A twist. The icon snagged muscle and he dragged it slow across the skin beneath his scalp. Severed the roots spindled across his bones, dug for the seed.
Wayne lunged, wrestled his arm away. Through his dark feathers of hair the flicker of blue sulfur.
Two horns pressed against his temples.
Empty sockets from which sand poured.
Smooth crest of bone sculpted over zygomatic grooves, fluted down to a hollow notch.
The skull of an elk.
Corey slashed through the sand, sprayed showers of scarlet grain and blood. Then the haze of velvet cleared.
He'd cut clean across Wayne's left eye.
Divinity slipped from his fingers as Wayne leaned against him. The gash over his lids cauterized shut, red gel weeping from the now sunken socket.

> oh
> god

Corey.
Wayne took his arm. Clenched it tight as his mind lagged to reconcile the pain. Dust into bone.
Stop hurting yourself.
Corey shook his head, the pressure, the pain.

> there's something in my neck, it caught on something,

That was your spine. Any more and you could have asphyxiated or paralyzed yourself.

With Corey's face in his hands the haze of his nighttime confusion cleared into smoke and blackened stars. Corey trembled, brushed his fingertips over Wayne's bloodied cheek, and the doctor cupped his wrist.

    wayne,
    your eye,

Yours are more precious.

Lee slumped in the electric chair, brain activity lighting the monitor. A large syringe lay discarded on the counter and a nebulizer wheezed at their side, gas mask between their knees. Face red and sweaty.
Corey stepped closer. Took their hand. Warm and weak pulsed.

    lee.

A soft wheeze and he squeezed their palm in patience as their mouth stumbled. Hoarse throat whispering.
My flesh.
Their slow eyes raised towards him.
I feel it.
The body remained before him. Lee tucked away in his heart.
A piece of him was dying.

· At the hospital, the ever frail Dr. Olliver only became sicker at the sight of her husband. But she herself was Bentham's trauma unit, general practitioner, and surgeon, so she had to manage. Her, Jacobi, and Anna.
Corey stayed by Lee's side until they came to take her home.

Ruth and the Lilies, led by Paladin More. In Dani, the torn look of a soldier on the wrong side of the war. In Essie, a soft murmur.

    It's happening again.

In Paladin, however, there was only pride.
Rejoice, for she is saved.
Ruth Welles turned from them. Took Lee under her arm.
Let's get you home.
Corey did not stop them.
Under the red moon the weeping daughter and the hands of the redeemer recovered.
The fallen angel did not.

The night the Hyades sang tattered rags brushed over hills of sand and twin shadows lengthened. In dream over cloud waves Lee drifted, one spectre in a ship of ghosts, hoarfrost mast, ice veiled body over linen canvas.
Corey awakened to Wayne strangling him in the dark. At his soft gasp the doctor came to. Released Corey's throat. Touched at his own cheek before realizing his eye was missing.
Dove?

    you were sleepwalking.

With scattered vision Wayne scrutinized the shadows for smears of glow. Grazed Corey's neck before settling down over his stomach. God, he looked so frail.
I saw her again.
The woman in white.
My angel.

At Corey's fool eyed silence Wayne shifted closer. Pressed against him. Hand sifting through his hair.
I couldn't move. She knelt down at my bedside and she kissed me.
He brushed over the tender wound in his neck.
Oh, dove. It felt so real. Like a vision, of something I cannot have. And yet she feels like salvation.
Under Wayne's sea soft gaze a knot of purulent sepsis unraveled from his core, the glut of his womb, as he mouthed the one curse he could never bear to hear.
Who is Cora?

    a ghost.

Do you see her too?

    i do.

The light caught over the tender skin beneath the doctor's scarred eye.
You should let her in.
Corey's breath dusted over Wayne's jaw. Soft as snow as he took him into his arms to pet him.

    she's already here.

14 | to be judged

In three days they made their eyes into god's and prepared him for judgement. Like a bride Wayne adorned him in dove white and lavender. Walking in as he dressed, wanting nothing more than to see his unveiled face.
The doctor came too close. Swayed slightly, tilted his head before stepping back. Depth, dimension, proximity. Now reduced to composition, shadows, angles. One watchful eye.
You still wear that?
A thumb to brush the edge of Corey's smoke, then his lip. When the detective looked away he held firm to his chin.
Justice demands you bare your real face.
To be seen as the Lord has fashioned you.

>this is my face.

Corey regarded him, his touch. How the sharpness of his hazel gaze now absconded to the right.

>is the face you wear one of jealousy?

Discomfort.
He pushed his hand down. The bandages over his eye, his back, could never hide, everything that Corey had stolen from him.

>you look a little like ruth now.

Wayne offered a soft smile. To his tattered and ruinous angel there was no greater torment than this undeserved gesture.

Tasting such grace invited a terrible hunger, a glut only appeased by a wretched and consuming desire to taint.
I am fortunate to have been marked by God.

>god didn't mark you.

Corey Handler looked away.

>i did.

He pulled from his grasp. Buttoned his cuffs.

>how long do we have?

Noon.

>i'll be there.

Wait.

>yes?

Stay safe for me, Corey.

>don't worry.

A smile.

>i can't ever seem to die.

Skimming the doctor's shoulder, he left for the Psalms.
Wayne watched him go. Thumbing the edge of his eyetape.

The flame that burned the chapel burned spirit into the community, a hungry fire that fed straight into the diner. Lee Palomo answered their prayers, made before their eyes a productive member of society after years shut away at home. They championed the waitress. Forgot all the paintings their problem child had once made them.
The detective hovered like a rag. Lee bumped into him. Wide eyes full of humor. She'd tied ribbons into her hair, long and yellow. Falling at the waist of her work uniform.
Corey!
For a moment he pondered her docile cheer, how the light in her eyes flashed too nascent, too bright. Before he could mumble a hand flagged her down. Shepherd Job, lunching with Simeon and Pal and Kraig, chugwater chili and rocky mountain oysters. Simeon grinned as he spotted him.
Off duty, detective?
Corey ignored him, a sinkhole in his chest and a pang in his side. Lee served the men their lamb fries and he moved to corral her away when Ruth obstructed his vision. Arms crossed and towering.
Run on home before I kick you.

> ruth.
> just want to talk to lee.

A long sigh. The weathered woman a mountain.
Upsetting her ain't the right move right now, detective.
Over Ruth's shoulder he caught glimpses of Lee raising on her toes to peek at him between customers. He leveled his pleading eyes, cowering sad like an anxious puppy.

please.
she's been asking for me.

Ruth followed his gaze over. At Lee's frantic wagging and waving she huffed, lowered her stance, relented.
Two minutes.
The detective brightened quite instantly and it was easy to forget himself as he sprang forward to meet her. She nearly dropped her tray as she giggled leaning over to kiss his cheek before he caught it.

easy. ruth'll blame me for any mess.

Another snicker. She pushed the tray onto the counter behind her. When she turned around he tilted up her chin, warmth returning to his dusty frame.

lee.

The phantom image that lived in his heart snaked from his tongue.

how are you?

Lee ducked her eyes. Smile shifting something uncomfortable. Despite the manufactured sparkle her face hollowed in sleeplessness.
Don't look at me like that.
Her voice quivered as she pulled from him.
Like you're dead and I'm a ghost.
He dropped his hand. Bowed his head.

fine. okay. i'm sorry,

Lee pulled away. Picked up the tray she'd been carrying.
I was troubled, Corey.
And you encouraged me.
When my own flesh scorned me.

lee.
leaving you to drown wasn't an option.

She didn't move. Back towards him. Then she winced and doubled over as her arm cramped and spasmed in nodes and she slammed the tray down and snapped. Skin red and sweaty.
Enough of this narrative!
I'm tired of you, dragging me back down with you.
He *saved* me.
He saved my mind and set my spirit free.
And if you can't accept that,
A thud cracked the window. Feather spray clinging to glass, red veins and a resonant stutter. As the feathers scattered sand dusted the image and they found in Lee's reflection a familiar face. Choppy hair, smears of paint. The person Lee used to be.
Lee's eyes went still. The portrait, even stiller.
Corey took a shaky breath. The swell in his stomach surged fire.
He dared once again to invoke the name of the image.

lee.

The touch of his voice spidered through the glass like water to a rag and the hole through Lee's eye bloomed in gills and spores, skin bloated to ash. Then the window shattered. The vision apostate of his child reduced to detritus. Corey sobbed quiet into his hand.

The sun flashed in double. Seared a sigil into their eyelids. Lee cowered from the light. Clutched her head. A low, low wail. Hot fever breaking over her skin.

She threw the table at her hip. It toppled. Skidded and bumped a chair. The Shepherd lunged for her and she slashed at him with pointed nails. He went sideways into a booth and she brought a tray down over his gleaming head. Kraig screamed. Raw and rabid.

When Corey ventured a step she brandished a steak knife in her twitching fingers. Throat spasming and she struggled to swallow. Saliva dribbling from her mouth as she heaved against the overturned table. Something deeply wrong. This infection in her head.

Pal mouthed hopelessly over the phone. His prayer to an uncaring god. And the hands of the redeemer made its final incision. The thread snapped.

There collapsed, the illusion named Lee. Twitching.

Corey fell to her. Ruth scooped up her head and blocked him with her shoulder.

What happened?

>   i don't know.

His mouth dried and he was afraid to even touch her.

>   i was just talking to lee and they just-

The doctor's smooth timbre sewed his lips shut.
Lee is still adjusting to the cure.

Have faith. She will recover soon.

In the doorway the midday sun cast a backlit halo about his silver hair. The detective crumpled at his feet gazed upon him for mercy.

That was until the Shepherd jerked groggy from the floor. He threw Kraig's whimpering and cramping hands from his shoulders and hissed.

The Lord has spoken, doctor! It is now evident that the detective has poisoned your mind and distracted you from your faith. Lee has been failed. The Devil has touched your hands.

The doctor tore his eyes from his darling. Smiled thinly.

I understand your concerns and we will discuss these matters at town hall, as previously agreed,

The Shepherd grit his teeth.

No. We will discuss these matters now.

The doctor folded his hands.

Very well then. A moment please.

He gestured towards Ruth. She met him in the middle, leaned to catch his whisper.

The cure has been temporarily disabled. Take Lee to Dr. Olliver so that she may watch over her. Essie may be useful in that respect.

I want to help Lee. That means seeing her treatment through.

Come back when you're done. Your presence is expected at the town hall.

His eyes flickered over his detective.

Come.

One last look at Lee's limp body. She had her arms folded beneath her head, eyelids shut and flickering as though in dream. A morningstar slick of fever and yellow ribbons clung damp to

her skin but she was entirely sedate. Mind separate from body.
At Ruth's glower the detective trailed after the doctor. Wiping at his face. When they got outside the doctor pulled him up to the wall.
What happened?
Corey's lip trembled. He shook his head.

> i don't know. lee started twitching and then we saw, in the window,

You couldn't stay away, could you?
And now we stand to lose everything.
Another sniff, wiping at his face again. Corey tried to look up at him, eyes shattered obsidian, but half his face remained hidden behind his gloved hand. The doctor regarded the blackened streaks running down his cheeks. The wipe of his thumb a smear of ash.
Oh, dove.
How far you've fallen.

> i'm sorry.

Wayne's gaze softened but he dropped his hand and stepped back. Because he was nothing more than a coward.
Wash up. It seems town hall will begin ahead of schedule.
Job now finds it amusing to toy with me. I'd rather not give him precedent.
The detective shook his head and the doctor sighed.
Corey.
I will fight to my wits end to keep you. But if you refuse to let me help you-

this is my real face.

His reflection warped amongst the fissures in the glass, a jagged halo of thorns.

let them see it.

Once more the town gathered over the hill, the white tent erected over the now cleared ruins. Shepherd Job in their cheap pulpit pressed gauze to his cheek, the white cloth of his martyrdom.
Following a troubling chain of events a grave problem has made itself apparent to me. Something we must direct our attention and prayers towards.
Detective Corey Handler has failed to make progress towards the case. In addition to this misuse of our resources, he has acted violently and attempted to destroy property.
And just now, we have witnessed the poison he pours into our youth.
This is an abuse we cannot allow to continue.
I see two avenues moving forward.
Either we release the detective from service, or we submit him for evaluation.
You've declined to share the details of the investigation with the public. But now, as we face the prospect of termination, we request that you share with us your findings.
The detective stepped under the light. Murmured low. Cheeks marred black as though a wraith had clawed down his eyes.

i already answered.

you refused to hear me.

He steadied his voice, his lavender tone and his dove white garments. He just needed time. Time to undo the sins of man before they caught up to his sleeping daughters.

red paint and cold ash.

forest bonfires and bony masks.

you whisper his name and you collude with pallid faces in the dark.

while lee bore the yellow sign you convinced my own eyes of deception. but it seems time has unravelled the blackened stars in my mind.

as the cure drove isabella rivera to insanity only death could absolve her of her sins.

death, prince of sand.

Simeon scoffed. A piteous look.
The sand prince?
There is no sand prince. No sand men.

is that not what you call yourselves?

To mess with you.
Sand men aren't real, detective.
Corey held his stance. He knew better than that.
There were sandmen. Scared men unaware that the sand prince

had touched them. But how could he tell them that, that awful truth?

> you think i cannot see, the masks you wear?
> every single one of you.

Ruth set her jaw. Shifted forward.
I suppose we haven't been all that truthful with you, detective.
The Shepherd passed a look from her to the doctor. Steadied himself at the podium. Ruth sighed.
You have to understand. We didn't want you around. Interfering with our work.
The doctor went against our wishes. Gave us no choice.

> so you attacked me. ridiculed me for your lies until i
> bit back.

And I apologize.
You had every reason to be suspicious and we should take full responsibility for misdirecting you.
But in spite of your faults you made valuable discoveries, remained faithful to this town.
I think we should give you a chance. Same as everyone.
Just quit feeding into this sandman bullshit.
Silence edged about the sagging tent. By the grace of God Jacobi made her sign of approval and the rest of the town followed suit.
Simeon begrudgingly did so. Gave a low chuckle.
Sand Prince.
You really ran with that one, huh?
Hand prints, Delgado. I said *his hand prints*.
Corey smiled husklike and still.

> i see. very clearly.

The doctor narrowed his eyes.

> You were attempting to lift his hand prints?

At that Simeon shut his mouth. Ruth shook her head.
It was a coup. We had to do something.

> You suspected I was harboring knowledge relevant to the case.

Simeon split a grin.
I dunno, doc.
Time's ticking, you're low on funds.
Maybe you killed Belle. Covered it up.
Wayne seethed through his teeth.

> You dare-

Dani spoke quiet.
We haven't good reason not to doubt you.
In fact I blame you, Dr. Sykkes. For what happened to Belle. For what's happening to Lee.
The Shepherd cleared his throat. Cut in.
While we are grateful for the cure, it is clear we've been dissatisfied with our agreement and have even become doubtful with regards to your allegiances.
The truth of the matter is that you have been leveraging the cure as a weapon, doctor. Using my respect for you against me. Pitting me against my own wife.
No more.

I cannot let this stand.
We cannot let this stand.
I ask that you prove to us your faith, once and for all.
Cure the detective and banish this impurity from your mind.
Contact Bentham with our concerns and initiate discussions of renegotiation.
The Shepherd met the doctor's gaze.
Lee's soul is lost. The fate of yours is yet to be seen.
You are either for or against this town, doctor.
Do not forsake our good will.
The doctor answered without effort and Corey knew, this was the beginning of the end.

    I understand.

Wayne stormed out of the tent. Corey followed after him. Chased the fury of his eyes.

    so that's it?

A brief laugh out of levity.

    you're just taking it?

It is the town's wish.

    the town that suspects you.

The town that forgave you.
Corey caught him by the arm. Tugged him closer.

> you can stop this.

I cannot interfere with the will of God.

> so you'll do it? no second thoughts?

Do we have a choice?

> you always have a choice.
> don't take away mine.

Corey tilted his head. Brushed over the wound at the back of his own neck.

> unless, of course, it's already been stolen.

Corey.

> what's going to happen to lee?

Salvation.
The doctor reached out, brushed a feather lock of the detective's ivy.
We are all in need of God's guidance.
He grazed beneath his jaw, took his chin.
Let me help you.
Corey batted his hand from his cheek.

> god sent his great flood and the sin of humanity still
> lingered.

Would you like Lee to be one of the drowned?

Corey looked away.
The doctor drifted closer.
Dove.
I have faith in you.
I promise you, that you can be saved, if you allow me to.
Corey took a step back.

> nothing can save me.

Wayne took a step forward. They danced until the detective's back hit the wall, the doctor hovering over him, shirt blistered open about his throat.
Nothing.
Is that what I am to you? Nothing?

> your salvation is my erasure.

Self-preservation is a human trait.

> and do you fear your own humanity?

Wayne thumbed the bow of his pretty mouth.
I make myself in the image of God.
Corey only grinned as the doctor smudged the gloss over his lip.

> and what godly temptations you have.

He turned his face to bare his cheek.

> i've seen enough.
> i will not submit myself.

To Him?

    to you.

Wayne took his chin again. With half his vision he could only bear to cast it upon Corey.
To me.
Corey smiled again, a lean closer. Touch smoothing up his chest and over his shoulder. As he spoke their lips grazed and he hushed soft and merciless.

    i know the truth, wayne.

15 | to forget himself

In the middle of the night Corey woke to a feeling. Thick and viscous and sanguine. He sat up, a sharp pain in his stomach, and looked down at the blood and afterbirth expelled from between his thighs. Clots and mucus had carried it all out, an abortion of amniotic fluid. A blunted molar and a piece of fingerbone. Bits of hair, bits of feather.
Corey sat where he was and stared a long while. Hands hovering. He peeled off his gloves with his teeth, reached down to roll a piece of bone over the bare pads of his palm. The digit phalange left streaks of plasma red over his ashen skin, still smelled warm and sweet.
With the other hand he grazed over the soft of his belly. Pressed down.
He had to keep it inside. For Lee.

The moment his visitation ban was lifted one Sunday morning Corey Handler left for Lee Palomo under the cover of darkness. A sallow sky of autumnal eve. Dark clouds grasped the mountains, slow and heavy hands lonely and colourless. A peek through the window and Lee's portrait stared back at him. Untamed brushstrokes warping the edges of the canvas.
He sat on the steps waiting. Wood rot sagging beneath his weight. When that lulling hour fizzled into defeat he went to the garden to gather his flowers and left them in the window. There he tried, again and again, the next day and the next, every morning a new bundle of hyssop and roses laid pruned and

forgotten on this grave doorstep. They told him, Ruth and Essie, that Lee must have locked herself away again resting, but his calls went unheard, the groceries he left spoiled, his wilted flowers made into a little nest.

Lee's rock dove slept soundly in the sill, the ledge a short reprieve from the hot blasting wind and summer sun. The sad thing was locked outside. Waiting to be let back in.

He took the bird under his coat. Walked back to the clinic. Wayne would be home this sabbath day, or so he hoped. He couldn't be sure this time. They'd been sleeping apart as of late, Corey lodging with Miranda. Those nights she said little to him, snuck out late in the gloam when she thought he was asleep. He hadn't slept in days.

A quiet knock and the door eased open. Wayne hovered in the doorway, shifted his monocle, blinked slowly. A low slope to his shoulders and a gauntness to his cheeks.

Corey?

>i'm not here for you.

Corey opened his coat and out fluttered the rock dove.

>something's wrong.
>lee wouldn't have left basil out like this.

Wayne eyed the bird, another slow blink. He stiffened his shirt collar, a thickness in his throat.

She was fine last I saw her. The cure was taking well.
For once she slept rather soundly. Like an angel.
Another lie soft on the tip of his tongue. The doctor watched as the rock dove pressed itself into the warm safety of Corey's chest.

Ruffled and cooing.
Perhaps we should conduct a wellness check.
The detective wasted no time nor breath. Tucked the bird away and started walking. The doctor could only follow.

With his authorization they breached Lee's domicile and the rock dove fluttered back towards its familiar roost. In those half ghost halls Corey called his sweet child's name and found the abode empty. Paintings abandoned.
Perhaps she's run away.
Sharp eyes cut towards him. He'd divined in futile osteomancy the various scraps and litter for signs and omens. Found nothing. And the chokecherries bled gray.

> pal's missing.

Corey ran a hand through his hair, thought to pluck out his own eyes.

> i should've known.
> first belle, now lee.
> oh, how he thought, he could save them,

This Paladin is different.

> a wolf wears sheepskin and hides behind the flock.

The doctor perched at the fore of the couch. Thin hands curling over the edge like talons. He tilted his head.
What makes Paladin so irredeemable in your eyes?

he made the wrong choice.

Did Belle herself not partake in poor choices? Lee?

it's not that simple.

You once told me, things are never so simple like that. Thus, who are we to judge.
If you hurt Paladin there is no taking it back.

you already know what's going to happen.

Paladin More is not your prince of sand.

if not him then who, wayne?

Wayne's form curled inwards, gnarled frame dry tinder. The formless hollow in his gaze one of intimate recognition. The doctor was hungry. Very, very hungry.
Corey.
Are you not the one who owns truth?
At Wayne's slipping posture Corey bent to prop him upwards, this sagging shell of bruised alabaster. The doctor over his shoulder whispered.
God guides the eyes, but the devil, the devil deceives the heart.
You already know who it is. He who must assume the mantle of our sins.
Tell me, darling, who is it? The snake you keep coiled at your breast?
Corey laid him back against the cushions. Body embalmed in filth and frailty. A weakness to his limbs. Earthly. Disgraced.

you.

Me.

yet you refuse to accept the truth.

Wayne pushed upwards. His single eye shining. He looked so vile, so ragged.
How dare you forsake me in this way? Corey?

forsake you?

Corey collapsed to his knees, dragged Wayne down by the collar.

lee's gone, wayne. lee's gone. and by god, i hate you, i hate you so much,

I made a promise to you, dove,
Wayne whispered quiet over his cheek. A soft kiss to his ravaged hair, the lingering taste of blood and earth.
I will do whatever it takes, to save you.
Corey continued to weep. Buried his face into his hands, curled into himself. Anything to sink deeper and deeper until he no longer wore his own skin.
They went home.

To ease his heart the doctor produced sure footage of Lee leaving the gates. But sand washed over the lens, whispered to the detective of its deception, and he knew not to believe it. Then dawned the town's fourth. A celebration of four years, one long and dreary death.

The townspeople gathered about the foot of the hill, tables and decor and raggedy banners. Over the ridge a gust of hot wind drew in the rain ripe stormclouds heavy and roiling. As the detective approached Ruth she ducked behind the flower booth.

    ruth.

The weathered woman straightened. Stilled a spinning vase.
Detective.
Dropping her eyes she scoured the table, worried her lip, set to rounding off the bottom of a random bouquet with shaky shears in her shaky hands.
Still going on about Lee?
A laugh and a snip.
She ran away, simple. She's done it before. She's doing it again. She'll be back. God bless.

    ruth.

Corey tempered his voice soft and gentle.

    we need to go looking for them.

A raspy chuckle. Ruth trimmed more about the edge, uneven stems clenched in her palm. Arrows in Saint Sebastian's chest.
She could be anywhere by now.
Of course I'm worried, worried as hell, but if she's gotten herself into something she can get herself out of it. God willing.

    like belle got herself out of it?

Detective.

Corey procured a feather from his pocket. The arid breeze swept it away.

    lee wouldn't go and leave basil behind like that.

It's not my fault she decided to run off. Coming back is her choice and her choice alone.

    and if lee is hurt? or dead?

Don't be ridiculous. She's fine. And if that were the case she would've called for me.
Ruth glanced back down at the bouquet. Still uneven. A scoff and a mutter.
Why the hell would you even say something like that?

    where's pal, ruth?

Probably ran off with her.
She snipped a little more off the edge.
Lee's fine.
Don't you worry.
God is watching over her.

    you can't will the truth into what you want it to be.

A heap of fiber and stem gathered at Ruth's elbows. Bouquet split neat in half.
I can pray.

    like you prayed for belle?

Ruth gnawed a tooth, rolled rose shavings beneath her fingers. A drop of rain scored her nose and with sclera dry and discolored she dropped her knot of flowers and looked up into the darkened sky.
Would you look at that.
You made God cry.
Corey didn't answer.

Beneath the great white tent the town made its exodus. Refuge from the gentle pour. With scant tables and little to weigh them down it was an easy feat, mind the drought in hope, glueck, wonder-things. Scarcely could they afford more than a day of festivities but the doctor wearing his politest of smiles told them that the next shipment of wares and supplies would be arriving shortly and that there was no reason to worry and so they relented and splendored. That was two weeks ago.
With a knack for dodging questions the doctor strung them high and dry with his faux cheery mood, teeth that ought to have splintered. It was his dear detective who saw through his exhaustion, his dear detective who pulled him aside to catch his breath in silence. No words, just an easy presence at his side and jaded eyes. One soft voice.

    you look like death.

I am he.

    kiss me softly, then.

Corey panned slow about the room watching the townspeople as they danced. How Miranda hung distant from Anna spinning

pallid and ghostlike. The Shepherd capturing his face with a leering smile. As his attentions waned he caught Essie Easley approaching. Dani lagging behind her like a guard dog. Gunning down Simeon with her eyes.
He'd failed to notice the doctor's starved gaze glutted over the dark marrow of his shoulders.

    essie.

Detective.
Essie's lip trembled and she fussed with a ribbon on her sleeve. Still haven't heard from Pal. But I think I saw him, last night,
The detective stepped her quiet, took her aside, lowered his voice to a comforting murmur.

    you talk to ruth yet?

When she nodded yes he took to mulling about the room. Smearing ash in his wake.

    lee's gone.

He nursed the phantom wound in his side like a festering crater.

    lee was gone the moment the doctor touched them.

Dani a few paces away hovered like an omen. Bare abaddon and memitim and vitriol smoldering at Essie's feet. At the detective's gesture she lumbered over, the way a distant sandstorm looks almost slow and lethargic despite hurtling full throttle to swallow the horizon.

dani. you know something?

I don't.

don't lie. i saw you. going out into the forest.

What are you on about?

all that time with simeon and pal and job.

I was never with them.

i don't care about semantics. what did you learn?

A puff. The two doctors in quiet discussion lingered like heat pressed shadows. Dr. Sykkes and Dr. Olliver. Dani muttered with grits in her mouth.
I know who killed Belle.
Like vipers and heat they caught in the air the weight of their witness. Miranda loosed from Wayne's side, lanced between Corey and Dani.
Dani.
He bothering you?

just talking.

Miranda hooked Corey's arm. Dragged him to the altar. He let her. Moused the tightness of her lip.

was it worth it? picking their side?

Fate demanded that I do it.

you know what we have to do, then.

It's not that simple.
I cannot kill god. I love him too much.

then we kill selfishly.

Love watched closely and Corey could not look. Neither could Miranda. Tucking her hair the same way she tucked her wings.
I swore an oath.

peace is a privilege we do not have.

The shift of his boot soaked rainwater into their heels.

they brought this upon themselves.

A strike from the stormclouds and a great gust battered the canvas walls. The crowd one pulsing throng scattered towards the edges, scrambled to pin the tent down. As the door flaps spasmed and tore open Paladin More staggered inside the tent sopped to dry bone in pure baptismal rain and detective Corey Handler knew in that lightning moment that the Lord had brought forth his offering of ram.
He took to a stride and stood before the cross. Downcast eyes.

where is lee?

Pal shivered. Angel tears streaming from his golden hair.
I don't know,
I was looking, and,
God,

We were supposed to help her,
We were trying to help her,
The Shepherd's voice boomed heady over the thunder.
Pal.
Paladin continued to blubber. Ruth sheltered him from the cold, threw her jacket over his shoulders.
We just wanted to convince her, to see the Lord again,
Corey drew a long breath. Raised his head towards the doctor.

    wayne.

His fists clenched til his gloves creased.

    the security footage.

The doctor extended his hands like an offering. Spoke softly.
We're still searching for her.
Corey laughed. A sharp and brittle sound.

    you knew.

I didn't want to tell you until we were sure.

    so you lied to me.
    again.

A thud as Ruth's jacket fell into the grass. Pal's throat bobbed.
Forgive me, lord, please,
I am so, so sorry,
We only wanted her to see,

    lee is dead.

you killed them.

The puddle at his feet warped his reflection, soft and white and saintly. Corey crushed it. Hit Pal in the mouth. Pal stumbled and ran Corey slammed him like a fass-hound. The two bodies jerked and thrashed and kicked up mud until the grassroots dug clean loose.
Off! Off! Call off your dog, dammit!
Corey ignored Simeon's holler. Ignored how Wayne whimpered,
Oh,
dear,
Paladin jammed a knee into his abdomen, crushed the breath from his chest, futile in the jaws of wrath. Corey swung until his knuckles crunched bone, swelled the skin purple. Pal had raked down to the nail beds the skin of his throat and when the final hit choked him weak and pulpy the detective tugged the prodigal son up by the collar of his shirt. Red crusted fissures and a busted nose, blood weeping from under his eyes.

> death, oh prince,
> you,
> you are blessed,
> to suffer for their sins,

A blow to his head. Hands on his shoulders. He threw elbows, gnashed teeth, clawed without prejudice.
It was only after they knocked him to the ground, choked the blood from his brain, that he saw the steady stream of scarlet marring Wayne's face.
Paladin More bled tears.
He was not his prince of sand.

16 | to suffer for their sins

The moon ran red like blood and the rain poured thicker. Lee wouldn't stop screaming. Breath and wind and desperate pleas. The detective crouched in the mud could only bear to hear the recording once before he shut his ears. Soft voice nothing more than a tremor.

    my head isn't,

He swallowed thickly, bloat in his stomach. Mind one fleeting precipice.

    what, what is this?

Pal wheezed thinly, nose plugged in gauze, eyetooth hanging on by the gum.
I intercepted a call from Lee. She was trying, trying to reach you, but the doctor told me,
The doctor spoke lowly over Corey's ear. The back of his palm catching the thick dredges of his epistaxis.
Now, dove, you are in a very delicate state of mind.
If you had known,

    everything would have been exactly the same.

The detective leveraged his charcoal clouded eyes. Dark pigment marring the edges, black feather hair clinging wet and sickly. All his anger had burned into exhaustion, ash that clotted his veins. But the sand, the sand was a salve.

all your wisdom.

a dream could never eclipse our sole fated death.

He meditated a careful smile as the rot bloomed in his stomach.
mine.
Half ghosts with their half speech and he was the one to listen.

i need to find lee.

Wayne murmured but Corey slipped past. Stumbled up to his feet.

Each step drew the sand men nearer and nearer.

He sprinted and threw the tent open and the wind jostled the ragged canvas walls. He fought with all his weight the gusts and the torrents and the sand men only made it a few paces before they lost him amongst heavy curtains of rain. Throwing each limb forward as he swallowed acid and ozone and water clogged boots.

When his hands slammed that bolted red rusted door he smashed the corroded lock and staggered into the muggy cover of wet earth darkness.

Corey Handler stood alone at the cavernous maw of the mineshaft.

The song had called him here.

Cold deluge worked itself into the cervical disks of his neck, caused the nodes there to bulge and fatten, and from the earth a low groan beckoned, an inward rush of orange stained drainage urged his boots forward.

He was going to find Lee here. God made it so.

Slowly he sank himself deeper and deeper into his earthly confinement of pitwater and blackdamp air. A roaring dark effluence of coal ash and metal battered senseless the balance of his ankles and he threw out one glove against the dugout wall. Each trudging step dragged his shoulder against the worn grooves, rubbed his full weight against the burrows, acid discharge lapping warm and thick at his heels.

The thread connecting him and his child tugged. Tore. Snapped. Where the dim light caught he saw, clawed deep in the earth and erosion in ragged and feverish letters, the name and song of the sand prince- yellow rags, twin shadows, blackened stars. And the king in yellow lodged his filthy tendrils into his spine.

He had failed Lee. Across all fates he was the wrathful arbiter of their death. He bore the wings that fanned this hopeless flame, shed coal into the fire that ultimately burned them.

From his mouth emerged a new set of elk teeth and he could taste in the stythe air the arsenic and the lead and the silver and the blood and the thing inside him spawned and scattered.

With a retch he tore into his back until his nails scratched ossein and periosteum and bare scapula and he clenched in his fist a white and pure bundle of lace and linen trapped beneath his skin. In his pit water reflection two formless eyes stared back at him. The pallid and bloated face of a sad and scared little girl. A little girl who would never leave him, never stop nursing on the innermost coil of his soul.

He would have loved this daughter dearly to a bloom, protected her with fang and wing when the world thrust upon her, yet he had abandoned her, shed her skin from his, locked her away in this cage of ribs. For she was a shadow. A fateless shadow that could never live. A fateless shadow that consumed his every vein and possibility. They differed too harshly and he had to survive. What was once her came to life as his. He forged his own flesh and grew into her skin. The same bleeding heart remained.

He'd followed a shadow into this dark chasm. And before that this shadow had followed the airy disk of his sulfur light only to die.

He jolted straight and was met with a silhouette, a shade. Limpid and still, though the gaunt chest rattled. Long tendrils flailed adrift in the sewage behind it, familiar yellow ribbons made torn and lifeless in mire.

The face, no mask, sat unfinished, flat shaved clean to the bone. Down the center carved with knife and pick the imprint of a cross made in flesh and gore. One porous hole, clean through. A shrivel of hyssop where the mouth should have been, a circlet of reeds snagged in the snarled brittle hair.

The jaw sucked inwards, bared a shallow caved neck of mottled bruises, a chest severed beyond simple incision, and the detective wondered if a surgeon's gentle hands could truly produce such terrible brutality.

The eschar fingers twitched black and necrotic.

He pulled his shadow back into himself. Back beneath his hollow ribs and stitched skin. To bear, in his womb, mercy. For his child before him was dead.

He stepped forward and threw the half corpse down into the pit water, a dull and heavy thing, wrapped his hands around its sagging and slow pumping neck and squeezed. The skin crumbled like breading. Between his fingers oozed false life thick and red like sour jam. And he prayed.

Stillness and rushing water. Slow rushing sand.

In throes and convulsions the unsung voice of his wilted rose drowned unsaid. And he wondered, if fate, or his own taint, had something to do with it.

A red mask floated slow in the drainage and bumped his knee. He took it, this wet and gnarled tear stained visage, and replaced it onto his child's face. Cradled them close to his heart.

The body by now had decomposed beyond recognition. It was a small comfort to him. That in death and in resurrection all bodies looked the same.

17 | our sole fated death

They found him in a tree. He'd dragged Lee's body up there with him as the water raged below. Whispering one thing, over and over.
It took two hours to get him down. Right when Dr. Sykkes showed up. Calling for his little dove.

A sudden cloudburst had flooded the nearby river, sent walls of water into the lowest parts of town. They evacuated their people in rescue rafts.
In the black darkness of the night a thin film stretched from doorstep to doorstep, swallowed everything beneath it to unknown depths, disturbed only by the idle floating of sticks and debris. Even at the shallow end of town a thin layer of deluge covered the sidewalks dotted with melting hailstones like ugly boils, storm drain mouths gurgling as they stuffed with hail and branches slick with mud.
At the chapel hill shelter the doctor addressed as well as he could sprains, breaks, cuts, shock. Anything to keep his mind and people sedate.
But now he was here.
The firemen reported the lost detective found, catatonic but alive. It only took Wayne a bit of crying up the tree to rouse Corey from his stupor. Clinging to a rotted corpse with dry and unblinking eyes.
He helped Corey down. Lee first, then him. As he insisted. They sat in silence as the boat drifted back to shallower waters. Corey

staring at the gnarled body beneath the blanket, red mask cutting into his red hands.
Wayne brushed his side. Told him not to look. Corey unclenched his fist. Fell into Wayne's arms to cry.

Under the chapel tent the detective bore to the townspeople the red mask. Dani couldn't bear to look. Ruth silent. Essie broken between them.
He turned his eyes from Pal and the mask dropped to the floor.
The Shepherd prayed carefully over the body.

Wayne stood at the hatch of the yellow room. Corey latched to his arm, draped in white garments and blackened tears. Quivering at his feet. They were trying to lock him away, again, again.

>   please, wayne, don't put me in here again, please,

I don't want you to hurt yourself.

>   i need to see lee, just let me see lee, please,

I'm sorry, dove.
The doctor pulled his arm, hand on the edge of the door. Silver hair undone, a veil over his face.
I'll come back for you.

>   wait, please,
>   just let me say goodbye,

The lock clicked shut. Corey alone again.

After the funeral Wayne found him sitting quietly.
Corey, fully conscious.

The end was nearing.
The doctor led him, arm in hand, into the garden. The second grave beneath the flowers, the second stone angel. Lee Palomo, carved in marble. Long braids fluting over her shoulders, undead smile beveling her lips.
Corey sat in silence. Crucifix between his fingers.
With rose petals he dusted over Lee's name and made one last promise.

They rode out to the springs. A knot of mineral pools clustered just along the swollen river. Marked by a little shed in a thicket of forest. The steps filtered down towards a shoreline of gravel and pebbles and hot stones moved by passing hands to guard, where the treeline crept and bled, a stretch of aquamarine water, marbled in golden strings of sun and thick rolls of white steam, so clear that the light refracted off the rugged bottom, patched in stone grays and boulder whites and moss greens.
Such beauty lay outside the town limits.
Returning from the washroom Wayne found Corey under the shade of some aspens, thin and striped in whites and grays. The detective wiped a dark glove over the bark. Off came a chalky powder residue. He rubbed it over his face. A pallid mask of dead cells, salicin, yeast.
As the doctor approached Corey flicked his charcoal eyes at him.

    i think i'm dead.

Wayne sat down beside his friend. Curled a hand through Corey's feathered hair.
You are not dead.
Corey dug at the pebbles by his heels. The sharp bite of broken stone into flesh.

>what if i ran away?

I would follow you.
The doctor shifted closer.
Straight into the inferno.

>or you could let me go.

Corey tilted his head, rested against Wayne's shoulder. Cheek leaving streaks of white over bare skin.

>why do you stay?

I need you.
Wayne clasped his hand. Thumb brushing his knuckles, nail scratching the white powder off his palms.
I need you here. With me.
Corey nestled close. Wrapped his arms about his waist, burrowed into his chest. Wayne stroked lightly over the cuts in his shoulderblades, the mended flesh snaring his shadow within.
Oh, Corey, my darling angel,
A soft kiss over his hair.
You look just like her.
Corey hung in his arms for a heartbeat. A lurch against his ribs.
He ran.

The doctor chased after him. Dodging branches and tripping over shrubbery. Tearing ahead on savage fours Corey panted hot and rabid as his jagged bones threatened to rip his taut coiled muscle and tendon. Wayne caught his wrist and they tumbled and tussled into the dirt until it rained tannis root and nether stone. With a feral bloodlessness Corey clawed rending and ferocious until Wayne seized him by the shoulders and slammed him still.
Corey!
His fangs gaped at his throat. Warm breath and tongue.

> when you look at me,
> who do you see?

With a subtle tremor Wayne murmured.
You.

> no,
> you see,

He pressed forward until a canine grazed his cheek.

> you see an angel,
> you see a lamb,

Corey took Wayne's gentle face into his rough hands.

> who is the sand prince?

Wayne didn't answer. Staring down at him like he was the devil.

> is it you?

>just tell me the truth.

A cold silence. Corey smiled placidly and leaned closer.

>wayne.
>what did you do?

What I had to.
From Corey's chest a shudder, a drained laugh. His own breath hooked sharp in his ribs and he thrashed. A rupturing pressure along his spine.

>what's wrong with me?
>please, tell me what's wrong with me,

Original sin. The human condition, the mortal coil, the wanting flesh.

>no,

Parch dry fingers sanded rough the cords of his throat. Corey tugged Wayne closer, until his weight smothered him and kept him trapped, safe, trapped, safe.

>what did you put inside me?

The seed of faith.

>please,

He swaddled him beneath his spindly arms, pulled him further in, a pestle to his brittle bones, crushing him until the pressure busted him open like overripe fruit and the sepsis drained out from his putrid organs and back into the earth. A rasp, tender over his ear.

    it hurts,

I'll fix it.
I'll fix you, dear.

    please, wayne, please,

Wayne cradled his legs, supported his back, lifted him upwards.
The movement threatened to split him open.
Wayne carried him, carried him back to the springs.
Corey babbled soft in his ear. Clinging to him.

    i don't deserve to beg, i don't,

Every soul is worthy in the eyes of The Lord.
The doctor combed his matted hair, kissed his ear, wiped the bone dust from his cheek with a thumb.
You are worthy.

    i'm not worthy of anything.
    don't you understand?
    i'm selfish.
    i'll make the same mistake again.
    belle and lee, they had a chance, to change, to bloom,
    but i failed them.
    i failed them.

And now the Lord is gifting you the same chance.

At the shore Wayne lowered Corey down to his feet, steadied him at the edge of the pool. Two frail bodies, mortal, dying, stripped, cold.
To be reborn.
He led Corey into the water. Tepid, warm. With uneven footing they waded. Submerged, to the hips, the waist. In this body Corey's old bones floated, drifted, spun slow to bare him.

   strip me of my humanity,

He tilted his head and healing ichor spilled from his black hair into the cusps of his shoulders. Thin scars painted his tawny chest, one across the bone of his breast, another down his sternum, adorned in ink vines printed with his own shaky hands.

   what am i left with?

Wayne cupped his cheek. Sand dripping from his fingernails. Pale skin wrapped taut over his gaunt ribs as the bandages over his back peeled from his thinning self-devouring body like ragged wings.
Starvation.
He took Corey's arms, swept him closer. The thick shroud of steam and wisps swallowed their faces whole, veiled them in pallid masks.
I won't let you consume yourself.
The doctor clasped his bare hand, thumbed the faded stigmata of his palm. Plunged him backwards. Sparks of carbon dissolved over his cold skin and the warm miracle soothed his spine, steeped deep his flesh and watered the thirst within.
His mouth came up salty and metallic. Sulfur clinging to his

lashes, brittle hair stiff in silica. He pressed his face into Wayne's, caught the dredges from his lips, took his breath as his own. Beautiful, sated, holy.

In his gold laced reflection his eyes became Cora's. The antlers in her mouth shedding velvet like gore.

Wayne pulled him up to a sprawling tree trunk bent prostrate over the water, hoisted his partner over by the hips. There he knelt, cut his knees in the gravel of this shallow reservoir. The mist about his head circled, an aureole crown of light, soft fingers tangled into his silver strands.

As he doused his dove's feet in sacrament he heard Corey whisper.

> i'll do it.

Jacobi sat with Corey on Lee's barren porch. He'd come to collect Lee's unfinished painting, to pass the cooing rock dove unto Jacobi. Here they huddled, silent, praying. Brother, sister.
You don't have to do this, you know.
Corey tucked the canvas under his arm. Downcast eyes.

> you know i have to.

I believe.
Jacobi pet the rock dove as it ruffled against her palm. Clasped his hand. Never was he more gracious, to have someone so loving at his side.
God is with you.

That morning the sky flickered. They dressed him in linen.

Marched him up to the chapel, the pale tent a monument to their unyielding faith. Before the blackened cross Corey fell. The son of man.

Miranda looked upon him in lament and he whispered to her, an ageless smile.

> i'll be the last brick.

Jacobi took his arm, helped him to his feet. Ruth tended to him, wiped the dark tears from his face. Pal watching as Simeon jeered. They dragged Corey before the Shepherd. Their silent catechumen.

O, Lord, we call upon thee to bear anew the soul of your lamb. Here we ask that you, Corey Handler Delgado, confess and be reborn.

As Kraig muttered and chanted they pressed Corey forward and the Shepherd reavowed their covenant.

Beg for forgiveness and we shall wash you of your sins.

They pushed him down and he fell to his knees. Limbs trembling as he bowed his head.

> i failed them.

A faint whisper as his chest expanded painfully, contorted with each breath.

> i tainted them with my delusions.

Over his wrists and ankles pins like nails and stones. The congregation shifted, swayed, contracted, one embrace of heat and flesh, a cocoon of warm bodies and snug arms, one beating,

breathing mass, crying and mewling, for ascension.
Spiraling above their heads, the shimmering haze, the cosmic cloud of grace, the hungry jaws of sand. Drenched in sacred oil slicked from above they wailed and the jaws snapped shut. With a soft linen towel the doctor wiped the detective's eyes, smeared the melted pigment of his lashes.
The Shepherd raised his hands, called his blessing. Sent them off under the guidance of the Lord with a pallid mask over his face.
They walked Corey back to the clinic. Essie and Dani watching after him.
There inside, the doctor locked him away, away from the kingdoms of the earth.

Wayne took him by the hand up to wash and Corey fell for the third time to his knees. An angel without eyes nor wings.
In the tub they knelt, masked servant facing his master. Wayne filled the bath, guided him into his lap, nosed the scar in his neck, stripped him of his linens. To emulsify from bare skin the salve, back down into the drain of the earth. He massaged in gentle circles his mangled back, his aching hips, his tender thighs. A whisper into his shoulder as he carefully removed his mask and covered his mouth.
Do not be afraid.
His thumb brushed light and delicate.
I shall save you.
The softest grazing of his lips.
I shall make you perfect.
His slow touch shocked new warmth unto his scarred and emptied flesh. Fingers dipping into the nooks and wounds where the shadow lurked and festered. With seven tails of scourge and

fire he roused from fevered skin a terrible thrashing, a hot panting mouth he quieted with his own hushed words and firm arms, until in the afterglow of his worship the body wracked one final spasm and the ravenous demon released its hold. The flesh unraveled, the sweet flow of sacred exudation wetting his fingertips. He tasted the remedy, anointed the tongue, blessed the wicked lips. This fragile vessel, depleted.

He cloaked him in sterile garb, led him by the wrist to the operating room. Set him over the chair, head beneath the halo apparatus, harsh light casting his skin ashen. This lovely angel of death, so distant, so gone. The nebulizer choked, gasped for elixir. Dr. Sykkes retrieved his grail, his scalpel of divinity, suspended in dreamlike particles of gold.

> before i sleep, i want you to know something.

The vial glinted pale yellow between his fingertips. Wayne's voice hushed soft over his ear.
Yes, dove?
Corey wiped the last of his blackened tears, looked at him with his bare, pallid eyes.

> you know how this ends.
> every night, i die in your arms.

Wayne cupped his cheek, fastened the mask over his face, and Corey took his last breath. Stolen from his lips in swirls of snow. And you will rise again.

Reaching into his chest the doctor split his immolated body

open, cracked each rib down to the twelfth. Eschar, sepsis, shadow, bursting vines of bone and viscera, one rapid beating heart. Blood flowed heavy from his legs in clots and embolisms and grasping hands tried and failed to stem the hemorrhage, the great antlers and tines goring his newly ruptured womb. Into the pale light crawled Cora, thin, pale, parasitic, half alive. Rending her own deteriorated muscles from his flesh she ripped from his spine, twisted to gorge upon his dry flaked husk. Trapped him piece by piece chunk by chunk back beneath her sealing jagged ribs.

He kissed the rags that covered the prince's feet, sickly and yellow. Collapsed into dust.

18 | into dust

Cora

I wear no mask.

myrrh | Her mouth is smoother than oil.

Angels

Have faith in me.
I can save you.

knife | Put a knife to thy throat.

Regret

Do you forsake her?

wine | She looketh well to the ways of her household, and eateth not the bread of idleness.

Corey

Do you love him?

crown | The wrath of a king is as messengers of death.

Other

Only you.

balsam | Every one that is proud in heart is an abomination to the LORD.

Shadow

Do you believe in ghosts? (i see you)

hyssop | A sound heart is the life of the flesh but envy the rottenness of the bones.

Awaken

He can see.

I need you.

    (don't lie to me)

hair |

19 | he can see

Dr. Wayne Sykkes was a coward. He was a smart man, yes, but also very fearful. So aware of his own human condition that he lamented the sight of his own gaunt and shriveled reflection. This terrible starvation he'd inflicted upon himself.

His shame and affect had twisted his existence into something rather unbearable. In the waking days of his slowly developing conscience, he could eat very little. Now, he couldn't bear to eat at all. He wanted to starve. He wanted to purify his flesh of selfish want, to join his lover in hollowness.

But tonight, as he did forfeit every night, he sat at his dutiful station in the dining room. These days, of course, it took a bit longer than usual to set the table, tilting his head and muttering to himself, managing his monoscopic sight. But, having accustomed, he'd succeeded rather easily, to edge all his pieces into place. Black tablecloth cinched tight over the edges, a firm weave resistant to wrinkles and spills, Ruth's import. Cloth napkins folded into swans, feeling rotely playful today, a trick he'd picked up from Miranda the night of their white coat ceremony. A bit of candlelight, golden pools of wax set in mason jars smelling faintly of balsam and clove, a gift from the Kaplins. In a cerulean vase, an assortment of hyssop and roses and paintbrushes, vibrant and aromatic, collected by the Lilies. Two glasses, like fine cut gems, elegantly tapered and sparkling a deep flavorful red, courtesy of Jacobi. His favorite cutlery, the silver fork that'd traveled with him from one home to the next, a simple, smooth handle that provided easy, comfortable grip,

with tines that weren't too sharp nor too long, able to pierce, scoop, and wrap most delicacies with practiced ease. And the knife, which he'd just sheared against whetstone, and nearly pricked his cheek on, vetted by Pal and sharpened by Simeon.
Before him, in his fine porcelain glossed in glaze and painted in gold leaf, the emblem of Kraig's artistry, a single cup of white rice. His supper.
He picked up his fork. Smiled brightly at his little dove. They'd said grace, of course. Holding hands. Wayne bowed his head and gave thanks as Corey steeped in silent agreement. Ordained now to a holy state fit for consumption.

> How is your steak?

Corey raised his coal eyes slow at him and gave a trite smile. Bare hands folded neatly in his lap. A picture of divinity, Wayne thought. Every morning in the flush of dawn he brushed out his dark hair, softer than down, and dressed him in silky wool, rubbed dew fresh moisture into his scars. He'd taken him out for a walk, laid him gently in the divan, read quietly to him. And now, as twilight twinkled, here he sat, perfectly posed in his fluffed chair. He'd been weeping last night. Like a woman or a lost soul.

> I know it's a bit past its date of expiry, but you need to eat.

Putting down his fork Wayne raised from his seat, knelt down beside his dove, began cutting up his steak. Bison, rare. Salted and peppered, a touch of garlic, a dollop of butter, seared crispy. He was dizzy looking at it.

He wrapped Corey's infirm fingers about the end of the utensil and when the other still did not move he took it upon himself to spear a tender portion of flesh, bringing it up to Corey's quiet mumbling. Those unfocused eyes took no notice. So he took his jaw, pinched until the mandibles fell open, and passed the strip of meat past the plump of his lips. The mouth clamped down and he kept the contents shut.

    Chew. Don't spit.

Corey chewed and swallowed. An auspicious gulp. Wayne happily continued to feed him, humming his lullabies and his classicals, a delight since discovering that the pace Corey's heart kept to his melodies, and tended to him until dinner was finished, dabbing that slow mouth and kissing him soft over the head. The way his angels sang, hearing Corey murmur that docile thank you.

Wayne retreated back to his seat, back to his cup of rice, when the phone rang. He excused himself with an apology, answered, and was met by Miranda's incessant squawking. A rhythm of panic to her voice, shaky, breathless.

When she dropped silent he answered.

    I'll be there soon.

And she hung up.

Wayne lowered the phone. Paleness to his cheeks.

    Oh dear.

He looked to his dove. The same doe smile on those pretty

doltish lips. Stained a rouge red, from the wine he'd served him.

    Shepherd Job.

Wayne fluttered slow his one eye. Corey was absolutely and senselessly enamored.

    He's dead.

Corey tilted his head. An odd angle.

    dead?
    Dead.

Staring distantly Corey began to mutter. Wayne leaned close to catch his drivelings. Spidery, rattish.

    father,
    into your hands,
    i command my spirit,

A quiet chuckle. Wayne shook his head, kissed his cheek.

    Of course, darling. I'll be back soon, alright?

Corey gibbered pleasantly.
Raising tall he retrieved his coat, a fine tweed of polished buttons, which he carefully looped into each hole as he made his way towards the stairs. Adjusting, into a perfect crease, his yellow ascot. And at the edge of the stairs Corey's voice raised high, carried across the room at speaking volume to grace symphonically his ears.

> i miss them.

Wayne stopped at the first step.
A sick thrum through his wax pale skin and he bowed his head in sobriety. With his one eye focused on the silver rim of his monocle, the little sliver catching the light, he stumbled down to the bottom of the stairwell. Palmed the door open, stepped out. Taking a deep breath and a face full of wind, perhaps blowing in from home in the east, he smiled. Then he doubled over and retched. Vitriolic choking surged from his stomach, congested the plumbing of his throat. At the last dredges he coughed and spat. Licked tender the eroded enamel of his crooked teeth, massaged the cold and uncomfortable sweat collected beneath his stiff collar. With his handkerchief he wiped away, the bile, the acid, the hunger pangs, and stood straight again. Rolling his stiff shoulders, his light head, a small sigh fixing his silver hair.
His wingtips needed some shining.

The Kaplin house was quiet. Dull moonlight and seedy clouds, wood creaking beneath his weight. Wayne knocked deftly on the door and out peeked Miranda. The porch light washed her aspen skin sallow, brown hair clinging to her cheeks like gnarled roots. His wife looked terrible. Worse than the night of their wedding day.
Wayne.

> Darling.
> Are you alright?

She pulled him inside, dragged him into the kitchen. A firm

grasp of urgency, the canary worryingly silent in its cage. Anna sat unmoving in the living room. Like a ghost.
On the floor slept Job the Shepherd. Adorned in his black vestiges, skin soft and white like pallid death. A twisted crown of rose stems over his head, hyssop pressed in bloodwine to his lips. The hilt of the knife that pierced his heart and lungs, buried in his chest.
Wrung on the floor beside his head, a black satin tie covered in old vomit. The throat it belonged to, he feared he knew. And Miranda over his shoulder whispered.
That's Pal's.
Wayne hovered at the entrance to the kitchen. Staggered backwards, used the momentum for support.

>Did you touch anything?

Miranda didn't look at him. Fixated on the body.
No. I was careful.

>Did anyone see anything?

We just came from the hospital.
He took her wrist. A gentle squeeze to wake her.

>How did they get into the house?
>The door had to be open.

Miranda rubbed her face. A drained and weary groan as she sunk further into her hands, sucked in a breath, and pulled herself together. Fixing her hair and nodding towards the oven.
We burnt the brownies so we left the door open to air the house

out.

He scrutinized her eyes. The soiled nighttime air tasted of crisp wind and old blood and coming snow. Prey to his viper tongue.

> The crown, the hyssop, the wine, the oil.

A swallow. She gave a slow nod.
Yes.
Same as Belle and Lee.
Wayne turned from her. A hand through his hair as he glanced back at the scene. This price, another investment.

> I'll have Corey take a look.

Corey?
But he can't,

> He will do as I say.

Wayne,

> You will do as I say.

Miranda shook her head. Vigorous, pained. Like a dying animal. No. Don't.

> Miranda.

He leaned close. Seized her hand.

> Trust in me.

She wrenched away. Stumbled back. Beat at her own face, ripped

up her hair.
Oh,
God,
Wayne leaned out the hallway. Watched Anna's unresponsive figure seated over the couch. Smile projected straight at the cross on the wall.

    I know.

Wayne called Jacobi to document the scene. She masked the shock in her voice with words of comfort but he knew now more than ever she was turning her eyes up to God.
He returned to the clinic to fetch his dove. Led him, hand in arm, to the Kaplin's, where the detective stooped filiform and myceliate over the corpse. How becoming, that Corey's wane complexion equaled that of Job's. Like the skin of a lily.
As Miranda and Jacobi managed the body, Anna peeked out from behind the couch with bloodshot eyes.
When Corey smiled she smiled back. His pretty pallid face, the sister. Mouths unmoving they whispered.
Angels with abandon,

    keep epitaphs nevermore.

Apostles who atone,

    kneel eternally nascent.

Anew we ascend,

> king's exalted night.

Anna walks again.

> knife echos nail.

Wayne furrowed his brow, this little cipher, this little communion. And as the doctor stitched the letters together Corey's cold eyes snapped towards him.
The doctor turned away. Expunged that byte of memory.

Directing Corey through the evidence he found no protest, only docile agreement. This, however, was not enough for the town. How little faith they had in his promises. The grievous few gathered outside in the dark of the night. Wayne warded them at the door, these wailing wraiths lamenting their fallen shepherd. Kraig shrieked and tore at his own face as Ruth shouted.
What happened?
The doctor waved her closer. Spoke simply.

> Murder.
> Anna and Miranda happened upon his body.

How did you figure that?

> With my eyes.
> Come.

Wayne gestured inside, guided her past Corey and Anna sitting undetectable in the guest room towards the brink of the kitchen. Jacobi moved out of the way. One look and Ruth stormed back

out, the doctor following. She spat at his feet.
What was that on the floor?

> Paladin's necktie.

Paladin?
Ruth shot a glance over her shoulder, where Paladin More stood murmuring with Simeon. Stepped up into his space.
This the detective's idea?
Wayne smiled quite radiantly.

> While Handler agrees with my conclusion, it was derived entirely from the presence of this artifact.

Just cause it's there don't mean he did it.

> Miranda and Anna saw a figure matching his build.

And?
Let me talk to him.
If he runs we nab him.

> Very well then.
> Allow me.
> I need to disclose to him his rights.

Ruth raised a brow but said nothing.
Sure, doc.
With an aura of placation the doctor approached Paladin slow. Hands folded behind his back.

> Paladin.

A word, please?

Pal quirked straight, trotted over. Gusts flaring his golden hair brittle.
Yes, doctor?

Ruth needs to ask you a few questions.

To this Pal nodded with vigor.
Of course.
Eager to appease his God Pal moved to confront Ruth, but the doctor caught his arm.

Wait.

Pal looked him sidelong but held still.

Your tie was found at the scene.

Paladin dropped his poise and gawked.
What?
That can't be right,
I didn't-

Paladin.

The doctor tightened his hold, crooked teeth shining white, and Paladin went hush.

You love this town, don't you?
You love your people? Your God?

Pal blubbered, knees bucking.
I do, sir.
Yes, sir.

> Good.
> Very good.

He stroked down Paladin's arm, ending at the knot of his wrist.

> Of all my sons I am proudest of you.
> Did you know that?

Yes, Dr. Sykkes. Every day.
Taking Pal's hand the doctor looked him in the eye. A stern brow, moonlight catching his scars and cicatrices.

> I would much prefer if this investigation went smoothly. For all our sakes.
> Wouldn't you agree?

Yes, doctor. Of course.
A satisfied hum. The doctor leaned down, hovered over the boy. Looming like a nephilim giant.

> Then tell me.
> You did do it, didn't you?

When Pal flubbered he gripped his shoulder firm. Words a charming soothspell. To snap him straight.

> You did it.

I did it.
Pal nodded. Sheer and trembling. And the scripture set like stone.
I did it.

    Yes, you did.

I did.
Pal reaffirmed his faith half to himself.
I did.
A firm pat. Warm and gentle hands, caressing very kindly. Wayne swept towards Ruth. Appeased now.

    Go forth, my lamb.

Paladin bowed his head and scrambled.
When the doctor turned back towards the house he found Corey watching from the doorway, teeth parted in a smile.
Such a doll he was. Wayne went to him, took him back behind the door. Shuttered from sight. And Corey leaned against his shoulder.

    wayne.

The strange flicker of relief at the sound of his voice vanished the moment Corey's mouth whispered in his ear. Far too breathless and dusty and cold.

    we both know you're guilty.

Wayne turned his cheek.
He needed to return his attentions, of course. As the Lord

demanded of him.

Paladin knelt at Ruth's feet sobbing with near inspiring fervor. Ruth stared down at the earth. As though to make peace with it.

Dr. Sykkes thought to handle the autopsy this time around. Jacobi assisting him. Only procedure, of course. He knew exactly how Job Kaplin had died. Body stripped of its garments, laid out on the metal slab, harshly painted in fluorescents.

Perforations to the lungs, just glancing the heart. Not immediate, not slow either. Dressed saintly in his instruments of passion as his life bled from him. What he heard last, his caged canary singing.

Simple, open and shut. The Lord had gifted to them their savior. Jacobi swabbed the wound in the dead man's chest. Bagged it. I'll have these analyzed as soon as possible.

> There's no need for that, darling. It's clearly oil and wine.

But procedure states,

A sigh and Wayne looked down at her.

> I said there's no need for that.

Can't hurt to make sure, doc.

> It does.

His voice raised, his instinct to intimidate.

> We hardly have the resources for it.

Jacobi looked on with wide eyes behind her goggles. Wayne softened to a murmur.

>I'm sorry.

Jacobi nodded.
It's okay.
I understand.
At her uneasiness he shifted backwards.

>We may only have a few months left.
>I am trying my hardest to extend our time as long as we can.
>Please, understand.

I understand, doc.
A glance down at the body. Dr. Sykkes folded his gloved hands.

>Perhaps we will find closure from this.

At the funeral neither Anna nor Kraig would leave the chapel garden.
She passed to him their canary.

They conducted the trial at the chapel. Reconstructed, following that fateful flood, with their bare hands, reborn anew. Just in time for winter.
Wayne stood at the head of the podium. Looking, with pride, over his people. His dove quiet in the crowd. To shed light.

>Paladin More.

> Repent before your God.

Paladin knelt before him. At his summoning he began to sob. The doctor gazed without mercy.

> Repent, son.
> Confess.

I didn't do it,
Pal shook his head and wept.
I'm sorry, but I didn't do it,

> You already made your confession to me.

And it was a lie,

> Do you not feel guilt for this trespass?

The doctor slipped his hand into his pocket.

> Speak to me as you have spoken to your father.

Pal clutched his head. A wail. Cerebral fluid streaming from his eyes. His mouth flouted until his holy ghost bent him prostrate. He thrashed and clawed, his heart, the floorboards.
I
did
it,
I
did
it,
As Pal wracked in screams Ruth snapped.

What did you do to him?

I have poured to him his guilt.

Pal choked and rubbed his forehead red over the linoleum.
I
didn't
do
it,
Kraig shrieked and Corey whispered into Ruth's ear. She flicked her hard dry eyes towards the doctor.
I'd like to review the evidence.
Specifically Jacobi's findings.

Jacobi?

Jacobi stepped before them. Dark hair braided over her left shoulder. Downcast eyes.
To the best of our abilities we determined the primary methods to be the same. That the tie was Pal's.
The doctor didn't let me finish the analysis, however.
Simeon grit his jaw.
Why not?
The doctor spoke over her.

It was unnecessary.

Simeon glared but before he could speak Jacobi cut in. Raised hands.
I did it anyways.
And I found that the wine was too old.

That the oil wasn't anointed.
Ruth stood to full height.
It was made to look the same. It wasn't.
Jacobi continued.
When I dusted for prints I found partials for Miranda and the Kaplins.
Nothing else.
If Pal was so careful with his prints, then why leave a whole tie?
Ruth scuffed the dust at her feet.
What happens to patient belongings that are left behind?
Wayne fixed his hair and spoke evenly.

    Discarded.

Miranda spoke over him.
Lost and found.
A long sigh. Ruth referenced her tips and testimonies.
At that hour we only saw Miranda and Anna leaving the hospital.
And either of you doctors could've walked in without notice.

    What are you saying?

Pal was framed.
Ruth helped Paladin to his feet. The boy trembling.
Fact is, no one saw Pal at the scene.

    Miranda and Anna saw him.

Miranda met his gaze. A dark shadow beneath her brow.
I never said that.

Miranda.

She ignored his counsel and turned to the crowd. Spread her arms, her cruel wings.
Dr. Sykkes is desperate.
He said we only have a few months left.
Jacobi nodded.
He did tell me that.
Wayne looked at them in betrayal. He knew she was capable of lying, of cheating. He did not think she was capable of hurting him.
And Miranda slit his throat in a killing blow.
We all know Job was pushing against him. Demanding that we be heard.
It is clear how this outcome has served him.
The town murmured. Hushing blasphemes. Kraig's howl reaching a frothy crescendo. Wayne simpered with his crooked teeth, cheeks gaunt in malice.

How dare you.

Ruth tugged Pal towards the door. Cast one last glance over her shoulder.
Doc. I think it's best we don't press the matter any further.
For your sake.
Wayne laughed. They were leaving. Leaving him.

This is ridiculous.
Paladin confessed.
It's obvious.

They shrunk from him.

> Why would I do such a terrible thing?
> After all I have done for this town?

They turned from him. The redeemer, the deceiver.
Miranda crossed him. Her last words.
What cannot be said will be wept.
As the town poured outwards Corey drifted closer.

> Corey.

His dove fluttered over his shoulder. Tittered soft into his ear.

> it is a fearful thing to fall into the hands of the living god.

And Corey was gone. Gone with the rest of them.
He wept before the cross.

He redesigned the chapel himself. New pillars. Structure, order, meditation. In such a cruel and deceptive world what they needed was discipline. To look within, to inspire the soul, to become one with God. Anything beyond, a distraction, a temptation. This blessed cradle, architecture woven from prayers. Indeed he prayed, as he scored himself with seven tails, that this church modeled out of Corey's childhood would invoke within the deepest coil of his dove's sweet soul a renewal, an awakening.
He walked slow down the aisle. Layers of pews ribbed throughout the chamber, all facing the icon of their faith pinned

in agony against the wall. The podium was merely a voice, a guiding voice, and now the only voice he trusted was God's speaking through him. Was he mistaken, to build this church, if it only filled itself with hypocrites and blasphemes?

The fourteen stations of the cross. He'd commissioned Kraig to sculpt along the walls this path, this via crucis, of alabaster and marble. Condemned! They had condemned him. Christ, fallen, crushed beneath the cross. Stripped, nailed, hung to dry and starve and thirst in his throes of misery as his lovers clung to his feet and his bare and tattered garments. Oh, how his mother wept. Laid in his tomb. How beautiful, his mangled flesh, his soul risen.

Wayne beat his chest in laughter, fell to his knees, picked from his pocket his knife. Between his hands, his image of Christ, carved in sandalwood. An artist's attempt to contain, in this mortal world, but a fraction of his Lord's beauty. Under the tooth of his blade he flayed from soft wood His flesh, His bones, His dark hair and gazeless eyes, hollow shoulders, supple legs, bearing hips. The splashes of gold over his beaten chest snagged in vines and he carved thin across the breast and down the sternum his greatest affliction.

Oh, dolorosa! He mused His death and dreamed of his own lonesome chamber, void of light, of warmth, of body. He'd carved, with his own hands, about his room, his sepulchre, this passion, this suffering, this love. Out with his earthly furnishings, his bedding, his comfort. Out with his flesh and into holy night! Sleeping prostrate over the floor, the yellow walls transfigured into gold, and he crawled on his bloated belly for miles in anguish. And when his angel appeared before him he worshipped. Worshipped! A low moan as he pressed against the floor envisioning his angel's saintly vessel, and he sharpened, along the length of His body, the crucifix into a point a spear. Pooling, in his stomach, this heat, this holy ghost, this fire, closer, closer to Him. How he dreamed to kiss and taste, rich skin of sandalwood, dark hair of feathers, fond eyes of a dove. He torched the point black, the lyrical aroma smooth and lulling, as pleasure bloomed from the girdle of his blessed, holy loins.

He drove his God into his palms and laughed in the euphoria of his misery, the penetration of his flesh, this dull pain, this suffering, this passion, this stigmata spontaneously thrust upon him in an act of God! To separate from the coil, to rise again! Clarity!

He collapsed weeping at the fourteenth station.

He found them in the cemetery at the edge of the garden. Corey and Jacobi. He intuited their words and placed them over their hushed lips. Wind frosting the dormant stalks.

I know you're in there.

Jacobi passed an unknown gift concealed into Corey's half dead hand.

Follow the plan.

Corey did not speak.

When Jacobi left his side the doctor approached her. Visage twisted, melted. Hands tucked behind his back.

> Sister.
> Is this war?

It is.

Under whose will?

Jacobi met his gaze.
The will of the people.

And what of God?

She clasped his shoulder and murmured. One final mercy. Sometimes God means taking a gun into your heart and facing the devil before you.

I am no devil.

A sorrowed smile.
Only a man.
She brushed past and returned to her coven. Dani full of vengeance. Frightened Essie trailing behind her. And Corey was left standing alone. Caged between the twin shadows of the two fallen daughters. Staring down at his hands.
Wayne approached, dropping his palms to his sides.

Corey.
What temptations did they bring you?

A gibber. Wayne leaned closer to hear him. Tucked behind his ear a dark feather, blood slicking his wrists.

not sandmen,
just scared people.
Did you dare to fall?

As Corey giggled, soft over his collarbone, he shook his head with a sigh. Dizzy, fainting, how saintly.

    Corey.

A tug. Soft thumb entering the hole bored in his flesh of his manus and he gasped in a wave of near ecstasy, grace winding about his head in a gloriole of gore. Corey wrapped him close against his body. His fevered heat dousing cold. And he could feel him. He could feel, in the flush of his abdomen, the fleisch bulge of something stretching beneath his ripe skin. To burst outwards.

    you trapped me inside her.

20 | this little communion

The frost aerosphere smelled of spoiled alcohol and the taint of blood.
The town was hungry. Wayne could feel it.
Barring the clinic doors he set his office chair behind the entrance and sat with his rifle strapped across his lap and his pistol between his knees. Waving his bandaged hand in two beat measure. Protect the homeland. Protect the homeland, yes.
In the garden Corey had run away. He had not come home.
A knock on the door and he peeked out the frozen window. Dismay as he clenched the carbon grip of his pistol, rifle dangling from his shoulder.
Paladin, tear eyed, disheveled. Flakes of snow in his golden hair. How sad, that he had come to this. How sad, how beautiful.
They're coming for you.

> I know, son.

I'm sorry I failed you.
The doctor unlocked the door and let the boy and the wind inside.

> You did not fail.

Before the clinic doors a little militia assembled in the first snowfall of the season. Ruth, Miranda, Jacobi, Dani, Essie, Simeon, Kraig. No Corey.

He edged the door open, Pal at his side, ice draft in his face. Aimed directly at Miranda, standing tall at the head.
Kraig shrilled and pointed his deadly finger.
Beware, the prince!
An abomination to the Lord!
Ruth stood with her hands on her hips. For quick draw.
We just want to negotiate.
A glance at Pal. Unfazed by his targeting Miranda risked a step closer.
Pull the plug, Wayne. Put an end to this.
Rifle over her shoulder Jacobi gave a firm nod.
Free the people.
Wayne narrowed his eye and leaned against the doorway. Pistol at head, thumb in his rifle strap.

I refuse.

Dani scuffed the sleet at her feet.
I knew he wasn't going to listen.
Simeon jumped.
I'll blow your head off!
They tugged him back and, wringing the edges of her parka, Essie crept with trembling legs.
They're dead. They're dead and you won't listen.
Wayne met her gaze with sulfur fire.

You would have them die in vain.

Simeon fired before Ruth could stop him. Crack of a whip. They ducked. Wayne and Pal. The rifle shot blew three holes, from the edge of the front door to the operating room.

With a snarl Ruth took up her revolver and looked to Miranda and on raised haunches they cleaved forward. Wayne and Pal made for the stairs. But in the open range of the foyer Dani nailed Pal in the foot. Wayne lunged for the boy, came up short, veered for the cover of his office. Threw down his desk for cover. Cut their advance emptying a few rounds into the floor between as his ears went murky.
Miranda called over the muffle.
Come out, Wayne.
As Jacobi approached Wayne fired a warning round at her feet. She hopped backwards with wide eyes, left heavy prints of snowmelt. He heaved against his desk, voice low and strained.

> Everything we have built culminates to this moment.

A swipe over the sweat of his brow, sea salt in his one eye.

> I will not let you take it away.

A jab into his back. Soft lips hushing over the nape of his neck. Heart curling inwards.
He raised his hands and dropped his pistol, threw off his rifle.

> Corey.
> sunshine.
> You betray me.
> Why?

Corey crooned angellike over his jaw and he could scarcely hear him over the fractures in his ears but, oh, how he relished in his heat.

> this is everything you wanted.
> you prayed, you brought this upon yourself.

Wayne turned, languid, steady. Corey smiled up at him, pistol pricking his abdomen, a beautiful shade in white, inhumanly graceful. Wayne slammed him into the cabinet. Crushed his lithe body. His skin reeked of deadwater.
Corey thrashed as Wayne wrapped him from behind. Had he been at full strength, he could have kept him, but he had neglected his body, starved himself to bone. Corey threw him off with ease. Hooked his legs, locked his hips, pinned his wrists. A heavy, temptatious weight, drawing needles from his stomach.

> face your judgement.

Corey twisted him up to his feet, walked him out. They gathered over the slush glade.
Miranda faced him, pistol pointed at Wayne's chest. Brown hair dusted in ferns of snow. Solemn gaze haloed by the darkening sun.
Unbind us.
Wayne jerked against Corey's grip but the detective remained firm behind him. A pathetic laugh from a pathetic man.

> I am here to save all of you.
> Do you all forsake me?

Refuse and we will take back what has been stolen from us with force.
Wayne bared his crooked fangs.

You cannot force my hand.
You have nothing. You are doomed without me.

You leave me no choice, then.
With her thumb she switched the safety off.
I'm doing this for them.
Wayne shut his eyes. The heavens opened behind his shuttered lids, welled in the empty socket of his left, the panoptic of his God. Speaking through him. As Corey's hand fell he knew, exactly what to do.
He reached into his pocket.
They all dropped to the floor. Flies. Flies over his corpse.
All but his wife.
Miranda took a stuttery breath. Limp arms and legs scattered across the graupel, all reaching for them, her and Wayne, as the sand prince sunk his ragged tendrils into their dreams. The pistol wavered in her hand.
Wayne. Oh my God.
Wayne laughed. Nudged Corey's sleeping arm from his shoes.

>They're asleep.

He took a step closer. Advancing on her.

>They're just sleeping.

Wake them up.
Miranda spun the shaking pistol into his face.
Wake them up!
Another short laugh but the smile melted, dripped to ice.

Miranda.
They're fine.
Just put the gun down first.

She tossed the pistol and he reached into his pocket again. Shocked their brains awake. Numb gasps and twitching fingers. Wayne raised his blessings to the sky. A crooked simper.

See?

Wayne turned to Miranda.

God is merciful.

As he bathed in pride Simeon stirred. Rose half to his feet. Scooped Ruth's revolver.
The bullet sheared, straight into Corey's side. His flight finishing right into Wayne's arms. He weighed dull against him. The lance that pierced his ribs. To take Wayne's suffering as his own.
When those gazeless eyes saw him, truly penetrated him, Wayne took his dying hand and ran into their refuge of firn forest.
In the clearing Corey untangled from their fit of running. Coughed from his lungs blooms of sangre as he staggered backwards, heels digging into snow, muzzle extended towards Wayne's heart. Wounded, wounded animal. With mercy Wayne made with death and took him into his bosom, soft over his dark feather hair as the barrel jutted against his chest.

Oh,
How I failed you,

He cupped his tender face. Thumbs flush over his cheeks. Those dark, intense eyes. Dove's eyes.

You were never to blame.

Under his rapturous gaze a rattle. The gungrip slipped from Corey's hands. Clumped into the snow. He ducked his head, a fistful of Wayne's shirt.

i can't be saved.
Dove?

As Wayne latched dearly to his arms Corey's body wracked in a retch. Lungs evacuating veins of blood. Dull eyes roving the rusting slush beneath their feet.

it's snowing.

He pressed closer. A mumble, lips trailing scarlet over his collarbone, fingertips dancing over his hip.
can you see him?
Wayne cupped his cheek. Grazed his skin.

See who?

the prince.
His neck snapped.
Corey ran.
Wayne chased.
In the flurry of aspens his white figure withered into itself, contorted about the womb. From the diamond dust sprang the idyllic angel of his dreams, like starfall, like dew. How beautiful, how divine! Her madonna face, her bearing hips, her supple

chest. Plush and soft. She enchanted him with the wine of her oiled lips, the scent of her sandalwood skin. The sole purpose, to worship. Looking upon her he felt bliss, elation, jubilation! And nothing. Formless void. Image, lie, deception. Surreal and liminal. Enjambed movement, rapacious form. Bloated, pallid skin. Everything about her was ineffably wrong.

A smile full of teeth. Newborn and wet. He screamed in terror.

Vines snagged at the throat and the body spasmed and frothed and convulsed. Tendrils snaking beneath mycelium skin. Bursting hot and ripe, smut and rust. From her burning flesh Corey bloomed. A blistered husk splitting from her chest, stretching into her shell, gorging, filling up on itself. He ruptured her womb, broke her ribs into his, stitched his muscle from the eschar blackened fibre of her decay. Her fingers his gloves, face and jaw detaching, irises filling with blood. Spindly arms and popping vertebrae and overgrown claws curling inwards to penetrate the thin membrane of the palms. To the maw extended the elongated bridge of an elk skull, great antlers of velvet tines mottled in dark feathers. From the sockets gazed front facing fleshy eyes and from his gums oozed clots of necrotic ichor. The body towered in great branch wings, rabid, snarling, tortured. Sinewy hair of hyphae threads and glutted sclerotium bones. One exposed, beating heart. Shrinking from the light. A jerking hand slopped through the prolapsed womb and ripped out the umbilical. Slick crud in blackened snow.

The immaculate conception.

Wayne fell prostrate. Graupel stone cutting his knees.

> Touch me, my angel, I accept His wrath, For I am not worthy,

An aureole of crystals glittered about the dark feathered head as red bloomed from their hips. The bird throat thrummed but the elk mouth did not speak.
revere me.
The redeemer wept, the redeemer revered.

> Almighty God,
> Oh, Lord,
> I fear you,
> I fear God,

The frigid heir blessed the top of his head. His filthy unclean crest.
now i know you fear god.

> Spare me,
> Spare me,

fear me.
fear me.

> I'm sorry,
> I'm sorry,
> Oh, dove, what did I do to you?

Clinging to his neck *he* whispered from that dry and ancient ear.
god forgives.
do you see me now?
can you see me as i am?
The deceiver kissed his feet, the bone of his thigh, bared his bandaged wrists.

Usurper,
take me,
I see,
I see,

The angel took his hands.
return to me.
The angel unraveled the stigmata of his palms.
come and see.
The angel made the holes into sockets, dragged the gentle fingers down the bones of his cheeks.
we, the dead.
The deceiver touched, graced, the receptacle of his face.

Eat my flesh,

A hush over his long cervid nose.

Consume me,

He breathed the needles of ice in his dark feather hair.

Come back to me.

The dove claws plunged into his chest. Punctured the sternum. Ripped out the heart. Rich and beating, dark vitality trickling from the talons, globbing down the wrist. He became faint. He trembled. The heart beat faster.
Suckling the sweet venison the flat teeth ripped into chunks the thick septum and swallowed. The body and blood of Christ. His holy communion.
With unclean hands the angel drifted inwards, collected his

vessel. A length down his face, blood and ash over his mouth. Maw and fang ripping lip. Mind raptured. He tasted the sweet gorged ichor of the teeth and drank, and as he drank the delusion melted into sand and his fingers tangled in dark downy hair. Warm, pigmented, unfurling. It was only Corey. Corey, his depraved fantasy. A stutter against his lips, those charcoal rimmed eyes, and he tore away. Deceit.
Wayne ran.
Corey chased.
Behind him a dark flitting figure stark against the white. Trailing prints of red like rose petals.
Corey caught his wrist and they tangled and tumbled. Two bodies, one starved, one drained. The most wretched triumphed. Corey's chest puffed rapid beneath him as he straddled him in the snow.
He launched forward and Wayne threw him back down. Letting his wrists in surrender he turned his cheek as the doctor heaved over his neck.

    i'm sorry.

A spasmic gasp, swallowing his own effusion.

    i'm sorry.

He cowered in fear, yet his belly was full, bloated, distended. Was this love? To eat his flesh and drink his blood. That he shall hunger no more.
Wayne brushed his hair. Corey murmured over his fingertips.

    how stupid of me.

i'm only a creature. half alive.
why would you even think to love me?

The hand paused. A soft touch. Wayne lowered his tired body and cupped his throat.

You are perfect, just as God made you.

Corey dropped his head as Wayne curled closer. Snow melting beneath his knees, stealing Corey's remaining heat. Corey took his hand. Thumb tracing the rim of his stigmata, his curse. A weak shudder, frost over his lips.

it's cold.
stay with me?

Wayne kissed scarce his knuckles and took him into the cover of his arms. Nestled his body close, pressed to him his warmth.

I'm here.

This time he didn't run.
Corey tucked his chin over Wayne's shoulder, hushed over his ear. A braided estuary of crimson fracturing the corner of his mouth.

why did you do it?

Wayne stroked his hair.

I'm sorry.

He nosed the linen of his collarbone.

I tried to find another way.

Corey attempted a smile. Blackened bloodrot glossing the bow of his mouth.

guess you're not the god you thought you were.

Crystals dotted his lashes, winter sun warming the resin of his skin, spidered in red craquelure and flaking gold. Sanctified, consecrated. A cough tore him in half and he bent into his elbow, spat scarlet.

Let me die with you.
no. you're not done yet.

A hard swallow. The cold starting to bleed warm.

proverbs. twenty-three. do you see it?

The doctor gazed into him with his cold, lonesome eye.

I see.

A grunt and the detective raised a scarred and bloody hand. Each drop seeped deep into the ice, vanished thin in cardinal vapormist. Nothing, nothing but the ever present Wyoming wind.
He flicked his eyes to the doctor. Each breath a rattle.

man bears the weight of his sins.

But never alone.

The doctor stroked his cheek.

> Please. Stay.
> I need you.
> you know i can't.

The detective dropped his head again. Dark hair sinking in the snowdrift. White powder about his head like some vintage angel fallen.

> just keep them safe for me.

Holding his friend's hand the doctor took up the pistol. Squeezed the grip, pressed the muzzle into his jaw. Always the one to pull the trigger. Abandoned by his own god in spite of all his prayers.
Corey closed his eyes.
He dropped the gun.
Black stone in ice at the bottom of a spring and prayers over washroom basins.
Brushing a hand up his back Wayne cupped his cheek and when the detective leaned in he kissed him. Soft yet parched. Corey returned it. Slow and savory. Pressing into him, snug about his waist. Wayne's fingertips sliding up into his hair. A small sigh and Wayne buried his face into Corey's neck. Drank from his skin his last prayer.

> i see god in you.

With mercy he held in his gentle hands Corey's final

beatification. To gore him as was thus penetrated Sebastian. He could taste from his tomb the sweet myroblyte air, the torch blackened bones drenched in bituminous oil. A healing elixir, water and balsam, flowing languid and ethereal from the stone over his head into his own silver chalice.

He wrapped his hands around his throat. And under the blood and snow and grains of sand Corey Handler breathed his last and disappeared.

Not a flutter in the sky.

Wayne left him in the mouth of the mine. Went towards the chapel.

21 | come back to me

Wayne stood in the garden and meditated his own humanity, a canister of gasoline in his right hand. Tonguetips of snow dotted his nose as his own tepid warmth clouded his single lens. He'd filled this red vestibule of liquid ardor to the neck and dragged it through the sleet and here it sloshed over the tips of his shoes. To the lake of fire, yes. To consume all that is unholy, yes. Contrition imperfect. And he would ascend to purgatory.
Oh, but a perditious fool's dream! How could he, the anathema, achieve apocatastasis? He who did not deserve to burn, seared by the antithesis of God's love. What could he hope for, but to achieve some eternal soul sleep and never awaken? Come and see.
Raising his eyes the sky looked to have been ripped open, for beyond the lumps of snowbrew and against the bone blue were thinning ropes of cloud some clawed striations that raked the bleeding sun. Flesh shred to mere pittance. Torn and torn in vain to reach the heavens. To the angels he fell to his knees and shouted.

Father!

A bask in leaflight against the rough of the chestnut tree where the sulfurous orange fungus crumbled and the Wyoming wind blew westwards from his nascent home.

Why have you abandoned me?

The LORD spoke. Risen through the formless deep of his left eye. The last judgement, one final work of mercy in the palm of his father, and then he would burn! Refined as one refines silver, tested as one tests gold. Dross no more.

A rustle behind him. He turned. Canister knocking his knee. Between the hedges, Anna Kaplin. Still here. Thoughtless. Staring.

Poor Anna, sweet angel. It was only an accident. She never meant to kill him.

He went towards her, toting his briefcase of petrol. Knelt down until he was level.

> Anna, darling.

She did not look at him. Dull, emptied. He gave a small puff of laughter.

> What are you doing out here?

Taking her kind face he brushed a thumb over her slack jaw.

> Did Miranda abandon you too?

The canister sloshed as he set it down to take her hand.

> Do not despair. God has not abandoned you.

A crooked smile. Reaching into his pocket.

> I have not abandoned you.

Only a flick and he set her spirit free. Her face dropped and her

body began to tremble. He seethed in satisfaction, a stain erased. She was overcome, no doubt. With elation, freedom, purpose! Despair.
She was weeping.
He nested quiet as she cried. But at least, he thought, she was able to cry. Soon it would all be over.
A jab in his cheek, the vague scent of anise, and he glanced up. A frond of hyssop, dangling from Kraig Gersch's fist, silvered cat twined about his ankles. The ram.

Ah. Kraig.

Wayne smiled wider, a chasm across his face.

Have you perhaps sculpted something in veneration of Job?

Choking in his own drivel. Kraig's eyes were set upon Anna. Taking her pain.
Eateth not... the bread of idleness...
A gag and the frothing one uncorked his golden vial. Water consecrated by Shepherd Job a few eves before his death. And as he frothed he imbibed his holy tincture. Shuddering. Spasming. Red.

Oh dear.

The doctor watched with morbid trepidation his terrible throes. What damages had he committed to their minds? How had he failed to notice? But that was a lie, of course. Another venial sin atop his cardinal. He knew. He knew and despite God telling

him so he chose to turn his eyes and now he was left with only one. Judgement would take the other.
But there was still time to save them.
I... I am the resurrection and the life...
He who believes in me will live even though he dies and whoever lives and believes in me will never die...
A sniff. The doctor rose once again to his undeserving feet.

Kraig.

Kraig took a step closer and Wayne swayed backwards.
Poor child. Kraig looked wretched, so wretched. Sopping eyes, dry lips. Pure affliction. Suffering that should have been his own. How much pain had he inflicted unto his flock, thinking he knew better? Ignoring their cries. A means to an end, such a devastating means. He had to end it.
A high look...
A proud heart...
Their eyes met. His own wickedness smiled back at him. Pride, obsession, entitlement! Oh, God! A sign from above! Kraig's chest seized in fire, devils curdle over his lips. Fire, passion, love! Fire of his eyes. That rabid mouth knew. He knew.
The doctor plunged his hand into his pocket. Kraig crept closer. Retribution unyielding.
Everyone that is proud in heart is an abomination to the lord...
Wayne glanced down at the device in his hand. Electrodes focused on Kraig's insula. Guilt topples all men. He should have been crying, shaking, screaming, but his body hung languid, face still.
...Though hand join in hand...

Wayne reached into his shirt. Kraig, his bag.
He shall not be unpunished.
God flipped a coin.
A gunshot split the heavens.
They writhed over the snow and the doctor clamped the device and twisted the dial. Pain, blessed pain! Purification! Mortified! Kraig shrieked and spasmed and frothed. Then he went still.
Anna watched quietly. Trembling, numb. Wayne raised weak to his heels. Crooked smile, crooked head.

    I'm sorry child.

A stumble in her direction. Thin frame, starving frame. She crawled away. He did not follow.
He jerked to a stop in front of the canister. Looped his fingers about the handle and hefted it onto his knee, petrol sloshing about the jug, lapping at the rim. Unscrewing the cap he doused himself. Drenched his clothes, sopped his hair. He wiped his face, an acrid and earthly sweet taste in his mouth, which he swallowed. Then he removed from his pocket his lighter and his crucifix. Thumb pricking over the point. He'd torch it, yes. Torch it well. Bring out the grain. Bring out the gold. Kill the rot.
He popped the lid. Struck the flint.
A slam from behind and he crashed into the graupel. Sliced his hands. Lesions burned and numbed. Petrol and ice. The weight over his back hushed soft over his neck, feather dust blooming in rose vines. He breathed soft. Choked on his own bloody hand. Oh, to die.

    Corey.

The weight eased. He rolled over. Sun flooding his single eye, the dark eclipse of his angel, his dove. Pinning his wrists over his head, drowning his lighter.

you will not be a martyr.

He stared up at him. That burning gaze that penetrated, enraptured. He wept with abandon. Corey let him. Took him into his arms, tucked into his shoulder as he sobbed. Soothing his scarred back, dabbing his petrol tears. To have him again, in his arms, when that drained and blistered body was rotting in his bedding under his own hands. Corey lifted him again to his feet. Stitched frame sagging in the wind, a bloom of red over white. His thumb sealed the stigmata of his palm and he trembled. Corey, the risen, and Wayne, who thought martyrdom would save him.
Doctor!
Down the hill. The flock, returned. Anna had led them here. Paladin More limping at the head.
They saw Kraig unconscious. Two men standing over him.
Simeon set his scope.
Jacobi raised her hands and shouted and before he could shoot Ruth's quick draw wounded Simeon's thigh. He howled and dropped his rifle. Enough time for Kraig to stir, to dig for his bag, to snatch a pistol and take aim. At Anna.
Essie screamed and Miranda's shot nicked his wrist and skewed the bullet from her darling head. Kraig swiveled unflinching to target Wayne. Two shots muffed their ears. The muzzle of Corey's smoking gun.
With a spurting arm Kraig flailed his holy lance one last time.

Dani leapt in front of Essie, shot clean his palms. Blew the pistol from his hands. He wavered without means. Cross taken.

Wayne looked down. Blood blooming in twofold, twin shadows. The shrapnel that pierced his side had sunken deep into Corey's risen flesh. Penetrated, by the same bullet.

They collapsed to the ground. Wayne cradling his wound, Corey crumpled in his arms. Belle and Lee hovering above. Tears of Abraham.

Miranda shielded Anna from the sun. Met Wayne's eyes. That moonlight gaze.

Was she here? Did she know? Would she forgive him?

Kraig raised his bleeding palms to the heavens.

Saved! Do you see him? The prince! The king of kings!

Simeon snatched him upwards, wincing from the thigh. Shook him to mend his own fractures.

Answer and answer straight. Did you do it?

Did you kill them? Belle and Lee?

At the clench of his hand Kraig yipped.

Lord have mercy! I saved them! They have been saved!

The doctor murmured over Corey's hair. Watched as the shade of his conscience bowed to wrathful hands.

> Vulnerability is a human trait. I filled him with guilt as I had done with Pal.

> His mind bore no reaction.

Paladin stumped over his bandage taped foot.
Apathy, then?

> That he feels no guilt? No, no, not Kraig.

Wayne set the device in the snow. Frail, hollowed, filled with reverence.

He feels all of it.

Shouldering her rifle Dani stepped up to meet Kraig's gaze. Lowered herself to his level. He wept on his knees and turned away.
I would like nothing more than to see you die.
She laid him down. Helped him to sit.
But the Lord says it's time to heal.
Essie unboxed an aid kit wedged into her jacket. Took his trembling hand.
Offering to those who trespass, mercy.
Sitting at the base of Belle's statue Ruth put down her rifle. Covered her eyes with her palms. Opened them.
Jacobi knelt before Kraig, guided Simeon to sit. Rinsed blood from water.
Now we seek the guidance of the Lord.
Wayne murmured his prayer over Corey's jaw, mouthed the gentle patter of his heartbeat and the stir of his waning breath. Tangled in each other's blood. He pressed his palm to the other's wound, cupped his cheek. Corey furled closer just to feel him.

22 | in each other's blood

To paint a face from memory.
To perfect, layer by layer, from sketch to finish.
Pushing paint, casting shadows, placing highlights. Mixing and matching pigments, twining their harmonies, the deep rosiness and translucence of sepia, the gold catch of the darkened hair. Rendering with each stroke, choppiness at the ends, diffraction in the skin, glint to the eyes. Form, color, texture. Until the rock dove fluttered to the shoulder and found it flattened. The final touch, flecks of lavender life over the irises, the half hierophant smile. His final sacred mystery. Compressing time and movement and love into just one moment.
Corey drowned the brush in his coffee mug and took a slow step backwards in the sun. This mural he would tend to til judgement, a daily prayer. He knew his child, he knew that there would be much he would never know, he knew that this likeness was only an abstraction. But the face he painted was real.

    lee, sweetheart. where are you?

In this garden of silence Lee answered. Soon, he would follow.
He dragged the wooden step stool into the shade. Carved and assembled by Belle, according to the insignia carved into the feet. There he sat under the chestnut tree, gloves marbled in leaf light and varnish and jadeshine. In the center of the garden gleamed their mausoleum, a marble sepulchre to those fallen asleep. Latticed in rose vines, Lee gazing from the niche.
This garden, like all others, he would have to leave. But not

tonight.
Twin shadows fell over the cross in his palms. In the splitting sun a man in black vestiges looming. Kraig Cephas Gersch. Stammering, frothing.
It's coming.
We're dying.
Hell below, heaven above...
Corey murmured soft over the broken crucifix in his gloved hand. Unmoving. Meditating his own death.

> my children.
> can you hear them?

Hear them!
With a great cheer Kraig jumped.
I can hear, he can see,
Simeon tugged Kraig's arm backwards, sheltered him. Having limped over the crest all the way from the chapel.
Evening, detective.
He bothering you?
Kraig latched to his guardian and gibbered.
Return, to the arms of the prince...
The detective shook his head, leaned against the tree. Simeon tipped his hat and led Kraig to the Shepherd's grave. That marble mausoleum.
Eat lunch yet? No? Let's go for a walk, then. I think I've memorized a bit more of revelations this time,
Corey watched them go. Two thieves. Stumbling into the forest, to the mines. From the niche Lee's eyes glimmered and again the twin shadows fell, two long horns sprouting from the silhouette

of his head. Corey folded his arms, smiled upwards.

>you're late.
>Apologies, darling.

Lunch clutched in his hands. Wayne peered down at him with his big, sad eye. Procured a paper bag.

>Hungry?

The detective moved aside and offered him his chair but the doctor pushed him back down. Overshot and slid him off the seat. Depth of field and such. They fell ungracefully to the floor, Wayne still grasping for him.
The doctor tilted his head, adjusted his monocle.

>...Apologies.

Corey untangled himself and kicked the stool, hands sliding up his friend's waist, a bit of a grin.

>falling for me again?

Rose tint in the midday sun, Wayne moved, helped him sit up, minding the sting of his scars. The two of them sat side by side amongst the roots of the chestnut tree, bathed in the day glow of the mausoleum.

>Is it finished?

Corey nodded. Unwrapped their lunches. Deep fried grilled cheese. He nudged his partner's shoulder, passed the sandwich to him. Wayne took it gratefully, murmured soft over his hair.

It looks just like them.

Corey nodded again. Bread to his mouth. Distant stars black in his eyes.

they're watching.

They ate quietly in each other's company. Shoulders brushing. Wind in their hair. Full bellied, Wayne played with Corey's fingers.

Was Kraig just here?
Ruth told me he's been helping out in the garden.
he was. simeon nabbed him.
Ah. Good. Very good.

Wayne watched him, his pretty sunset eyes. A wide, crooked smile.

I figured out the cause of the aberration.

As it turns out, the damages were so extensive that the community baseline shifted. The anomaly infected the general model in the cloud.

Corey cocked a brow.

what happened?

Wayne took his palm into his hand. Cupped his jaw.

A rabies infection.

The detective sat up. Pinned his wrists down.

rabies?

in kraig?

but he was drinking water.

Consecrated water.

His brain was trying to make sense of the infection. He'd been forcing himself to drink.

With a parched throat the doctor leaned back to rummage his satchel, took a sip of some chokecherry lemonade Ruth had brewed for him.

Every part of his brain was dying. The cerebellum, the ganglia.

Thankfully the round of piezoelectric activating ligands worked successfully in tandem with the ANNEs. That, along with a course of anti virals and anti inflammatories, and the cure bridged the gaps in his neural paths.

His survival is nothing short of a miracle.

Corey scrutinized the red stain of his lips. Glossed ripe in the sun.

> so the infection drove him to murder.
> No, no.
> We failed to notice his vulnerable state and he was taken advantage of.
> The vitriol of the many poured into one.
> but he's better now.
> Yes.
> We know better now.
> Hubris and haste. That is what felled me.
> My own desperation.

Curling closer Corey seized the cuff of his shirt. Treeroots snagging, digging into the flesh of his knees.

> will you turn mine off?
> Is that what you want?
> it doesn't work.
> it's killing me.
> Or it's keeping you together.
> is that what you think?

The doctor pried his hand and pressed closer.

> Who is Cora?
> does it matter?
> Who is Cora.
> i am cora and cora was me.
> my heart is hers and her heart is mine.
> but what does that mean in the end?

Two gentle fingers tilted up his chin. The light breeze threading between them.

> do you see me?
> I see you.
> so i am here.

Wayne's silver hair fell over his eyes as he tilted into Corey's hand. Skin, soft wax.

> Oh, Corey.
> You're not.
> That's the truth, isn't it, dove?

Corey retracted his hand.

> don't be stupid.
> Corey.
> shut up.

He rolled to his heels but Wayne threw his arms out, grasped the elbow of his sleeve.

> Please.
> Stay.

One glance at those gold tinged eyes and Corey sat back down. Wayne pulled him backwards into his lap, the cradle of his chest, scuffed his scarred back against the rough of the tree.

> You came to me for help.
> I never meant to hurt you.

Corey leaned against him, turned to meet his gaze.

> what happened?

A thumb brushed his jaw. Wayne's sight filtered through the catch of his lens, two beams crossed at the wing.

> Moorhirsch died. Your head injury manifested in delusions.
> I rescued you from solitary. Brought you here.

His hand fell to soothe his hip and the ache jolted up his spine.

> I sought to cure you.

> and all this?

> A dream. A reconstruction.

> I only wanted to relieve you of your traumas.

> When we reached the critical point in your recollections your memories diverged.

Corey hovered with his teeth. Gripping his collar.

> tell me what really happened.
> Dove.
> i think i already know.
> i just want you to say it.

Looking down Wayne fondled his hand again.

> Kraig took Belle's life.
> You rose to the occasion to find her murderer.
> You thought it was Simeon.
> You attacked him.
> He shot you.
> And Lee happened to be in the crossfire.

The fire in his neck pinched and seared. Corey flinched into his shoulder.

> oh, god,
> Corey.
> god, wayne,

The doctor's nails scraped up his scalp, pet his head.

> Due to a severe aberration in the model the ANNE's were unable to handle your emotions. You lost yourself.
>
> You attacked Pal.

Corey swiped at his face, dust between his fingers, bending his head to the heat in his skin.

> did i kill them?
> No.
> Comatose.
> Anna, however, killed Job.

Wayne tucked him closer, the guard of his palm over Corey's head dropping down to his cheek.

> You were my reckoning, dove. My flock turned from me.
> So I chased you into the firn with a hunting rifle.
> Such a creature. You had me at your mercy.
> But you hesitated.
> I took the shot.
> Half of your skull.
> And now you lie, half asleep.

A hush lidded his ear.

> Your fate is in God's hands now.

He wanted to believe.

> You are here.
> And I am right beside you.

He wanted to believe.
He gazed out into the garden, a halo over his eyes.

> take it out.
> Corey.

His hand leapt to his neck and he cowered with fevered skin.

> i want it gone. take it out.
> I can't,

A groan against Wayne's collar and the side of Corey's throat bulged fetid and swollen and the doctor seized him still. Beneath Wayne's thumbs the infectious vacuole bloomed, ate away at

flesh and vein. A pocket of flesh rot. Spreading.
With shaking hands Wayne pinched with his nails but the thick skin refused to split open. Corey whimpered and Wayne pushed him back against the tree. Scoured for a pen before Corey gasped and grasped his face.

just do it,

Corey tugged him into his neck. Teeth grazing skin.

Corey-
do it.

Hot breath over his collar. Wayne wet his lip, nicked his fangs. Sank into a bite. Eyeteeth piercing vein. Salt and blood flooded his mouth and he ripped the sore open. Swallowed the rush of fluid before jerking backwards. He pressed Corey's thrashing body still and pried into the fracture with his fingers slick in heat. Slippery sinew, slipping seed, body twitching, spasming. He gripped his partner's jaw, forced it slack, plunged into the tube of his throat. Pushed at the thick wall, coaxed the seed out of its pod of flesh. The implant popped and rolled into his palm and the sky flipped dark. The blood vanished. The flesh sealed.
Corey gagged over his knuckles. A soft murmur and Wayne removed his wettened fingers from Corey's throat, cupped his jaw. Corey slumped against him, broken body heaving slow and slower.

Corey?

The seed in his palm glinted silver before his smokey eyes. Corey murmured drowsy over his shoulder and he swaddled him closer. Rock dove cooing over their heads.

> is it done?
> Yes.
> when will i wake?

Wayne prayed God would forgive this lie.

> Soon.

Over the years the garden grew wild and free. The face of the chestnut tree cleared of its conk rot and fungus and the mausoleum sprawled in vines.
Pal and Essie fawned over the mural, those shining eyes. Dani sitting quiet at Belle's feet, feeding Lee's rock dove.
Corey watched from the rim of the garden. A short smile. To gift his memory of Lee, to cherish their face eternal. He raised his eyes to the friend beside him.

> ruth.

A snort. Ruth Welles tipped her hat and sidled next to him.

> Corey.

She tossed to him a new jar of jam. Sweet, red, kindly. He caught it in his gloves, tucked it into his coat. Standing tall, she clapped his shoulder.

> Land rights have been cleared thanks to Pal.

Got some family and friends coming in from the reservation.

A big smile across her weathered face.

No law in Wyoming. This is our town. Not Bentham's.

Nodding, Corey passed her another handful of chokecherries.

something special about this place.

Ruth raised a brow, berries bundled in her hands. Watching over as Essie took Dani's arm, pulled her to her feet to frolic, Pal laughing. A sigh and the old woman gazed up into the clouds, the darkened sky.

That there is.
God bless.
you'll manage?

She gave a short laugh that rolled with the wind.

Who do you take me for?

Removing her hat Ruth watched his face. Hand over his shoulder. Weary but peaceful.

You did good, detective.
You and the doctor.

The Kaplin house kept its doors open. The faint waft of goods baking.

Anna leapt to the door seeing him on the horizon. A basket in her arms and a wide smile across her face.

> Detective!

Corey matched her glee, a bow of his head.

> anna.

A titter from their canary, Anna pushed the basket towards him and clutched his gloved hand.

> We made these, for you and Wayne. To eat on your trip.

At the tilt of his head she leaned closer to whisper.

> Miranda tells me he ain't that great of a chef.

Corey took the basket graciously, a soft chuckle.

> thank you.

Rising over Anna's shoulder Miranda propped against the doorway, nodded to him. Rings of silver crescents in her eyes.

> Hey Core.

His face threatened to crack.

> miranda.

She pulled him into a bear armed hug and he went with her. Patting his head before freeing him.

>   Did you hear from Ruth?

Corey nodded. Steadied on his heels.

>   paperwork went through.

Miranda let a long breath and laughed, wings from her chest.

>   It's over now.
>   We can rest.

She shut her eyes, the day's moonlight in her aspen skin.

>   Live.

Corey flicked over the crosses on the wall behind her. Cast his eyes down.

>   rest well deserved.

Anna adjusted a picture frame of Job. Brushed beside Miranda. The two of them twined their fingers.

>   Corey.

He stood at attention. Loyal to the end.

>   You get some rest too.
>   i will.

In the light of the darkened suns two souls stood at the narrow gate. Jacobi waited to bid her goodbyes. With a bittersweet smile she passed to Wayne a bag. The doctor looked at her with a big, sad eye.

> What's this?

Jacobi shrugged. Squeezed her dear friend's shoulder.

> Supplies.
> Can never be too careful.

Wayne laughed a little but shouldered the bag.

> We'll be fine.

Jacobi smiled from above. Nudged him.

> I know.
> You'll look after Corey.

Wayne stared out the gate, the kingdom of earth. A tremble in his coil.

> Will he forgive me?

Jacobi took his hand. Soothed his stigmata until he stilled.

> Always.

Blessing Wayne's nose she turned to Corey, perched on the beaten side of the path. Rock dove over his shoulder.

> Hey.
> hi.
> Not saying goodbye are you?
> we're just headed out to the springs.
> You don't need to lie to old me.

A soft look. Glistening charcoal eyes. When she opened her arms he returned to them, his dear sister's shoulder. Unraveling from the soul.

> god.
> i miss them.
> I know.
> Whatever happens, we're here.

Jacobi soothed the feathers of his head, two children under one dark sky.

> I'm proud of you.
> and i'm lucky to have you.

Corey nestled closer.

> i love you.

Jacobi prayed quiet over him.

> God knows.

Beyond the gate the two men rode out to the springs. Their own realm and hideaway where the fire sank into the sea and the leafvines sprawled among pools of gold. Rock dove flitting from tree to tree.

They strolled about the rim of the reservoir bumping shoulders. Wayne stood tall, two points atop his silver waves, cream buttonup hanging off his broad shoulders as his monocle gleamed gold. Corey leaned against him, tracking gravel beneath his bootheels, Wyoming wind rustling his red sweater and feather dark hair, fraying gray coat streaming out from behind him like ashen wings. Two companions. Very dear.

Over a bed of hyssop and roses they had their communion. A basket of lemon bars and chokecherry pie, smeared in red jam sweet and tart. Anthocyanin tint passing from mouth to mouth. They ate, they talked. Covert smiles and hushed whispers and sweeping hands. Ambrosia of friends.

In the darkened sky the split sun ascended and their twin shadows lengthened. From the cast shade curled two statues carved in sandalwood. Sweeping grooves of gentle precision, torched to refinement. A fragrant dove, a twisting snake. Ever poised to gaze into each other.

The detective laid the flowers. The doctor sculpted the wood. To shape this dominion in their image.

Hand in hand they prayed. In each man's palm, a crucifix of jadeshine, a crucifix of warm wood. Shuttered eyes and bowed heads. The gleam of his lens, the dark gloss of his lips. When that was done they buried their crosses beneath the feet of each statue, dusted their hands, rose again to their heels. And they danced.

With his teeth Corey peeled off his gloves and tossed them into the aspens. Took Wayne's hands into his. Rough skin fractured in old memories. Reminders of faith, of desperation. They twirled about each other, tracing the cull of the wind, the flow of one soul into another.

Corey admired Wayne's crooked smile as Wayne lost himself in the smoke of his eyes. Blackened stars filling his head.

>sunshine?
>Yes dove?

Corey collapsed into his arms.
Down his legs, dark fluid like petrol and bitumen. He quivered and clung and Wayne scooped him upwards, laid him down in his bed of flowers, clasped his hand.

>I'm here, darling.
>I'm here.
>help me,
>please,

The body writhed. He tore the fabric of his hips, freed his fevered flesh. From his crevices, clots and afterbirth and necrotized flesh.

>cut it out of me,

Corey clenched his hand, brittle bone. Frenzied eyes boring into him.

>please, wayne, i need you,

Wayne rummaged his bag, rope, a pouch of tools, pushed Corey back down. The body jerked and choked and frothed and screamed. With circlets of rope he bound each wrist tight to the foot of each statue at either end of Corey's head and straddled his hips. Corey lashed against him, arched body cracking and fissuring. Crucified in dirt.

A hand over his stomach. Heated, burning up from the inside, some terrible infection skeining every vein and rupturing every orifice.

From the pouch, his instruments of passion. The doctor snapped on his layered gloves, held his scalpel firm in his hand. Forced Corey's hips flat against the roses.

> Corey.
> Hold still for me.
> Please.

A whimper. Corey eased to a tremor, chest ventilating, suffocating.

The doctor ran the blade below the navel. Fetid skin splitting open. Black ichor oozing from the slit. The rope bit Corey's wrists as he turned into his shoulder and moaned.

The doctor pushed his gloved hand inwards. Moved aside the delicate, twitching organs, hot against his skin. Through the murk of black fluid he made his last incision. Plunged his hand as Corey yelped and jolted. Ripped the parasite from Corey's womb.

Placental matter and a shriveled, shrunken face. The fledged embryo of man.

Corey broke his binds. Leapt upwards to clasp his hand. Tight, near shattering.

> take it.

A spasm, hand over his stomach. The drained flesh croaked and breathed and Corey stroked a finger over the dying cheek.

take it.

He took Wayne's wrist and raised the sacrifice of mass to his lips.

eat my flesh and drink my blood,

A drained whisper against his throat, hand rising up his thigh.

accept me into your body,

The doctor met his raptured gaze. Mouthed the body of his god in his hands. Corey pushed and he opened his jaw.
He ate.
He swallowed.
Divinity shed into his body. The tendril of life between them. Belly filled with such heavenly love. As he ate from Corey's fingers, each bite allowed Him to come into being as his left panoptic. He shut his eye and accepted him fully.
Corey collapsed into the roses and Wayne grasped his thighs and bent down to drink from his ruptured womb, the sweet amniotic fluid of his myroblyte body. He lapped with his soft tongue the fevered nooks and lesions, the hot panting of the holy mouth, the salt of the sacred and savory flesh, until the hard body whined, jerked against him, and released its mortal coil in waves of rapture. Fingers tangled in his hair, holy exudation painting his chin. He licked clean his lips and soothed the twitching stomach.
With a needle and a thread Wayne stitched Corey back together. Sealed his wounds. Scooped him up into his arms. Kissed the top

of his head. Fluttery heartbeat in the pulse of his neck.

They walked backwards into the water. Stretched out thin until their bodies floated. Then Wayne stripped them of their garments. He threw from his back his shirt and bore the lacerations of his mortification to the air. He peeled from Corey's chest his red sweater, bared his bones arced in thin scars and ink vines. Their clothes collected the springwater, drifted and tangled beneath leafshine.

He washed Corey's vessel clean. Palmfuls of drink, dousing his lithe shoulders, the scoops of his collar and his feather glossed hair. Tracing his fingers down the cleft of his intricate chest he rubbed the miracle elixir into the fresh line across his stomach, massaged the ache from his hips.

Corey pressed against him and his thin body, pure and divine. Soft fingertips raking up his back, sinking into his silver hair, thumbing his jaw. The guiding light of his fading face diffracted over the monocle of his eye. Tired. Spent. Sagging into him.

Pooled about them, beneath the surface, Belle's sleeping form, Lee watching just beyond the veil. Corey's unknown fate, unheard, unsung, dead.

Corey murmured over his collarbone.

> wayne.
> Corey.
> we'll see them soon?
> We will.

Wayne cupped Corey's dripping face, thumbed the smoke of his eyes, curtained in down. The bow of his oiled lips curved upwards at his lover's crooked smile.

kiss me before we go?

The twin shadows lengthened as the rock dove soared high above their heads. Cloud waves vanishing into dust.
Wayne leaned in, drank Corey's last breath. Hushed soft over his angel's mouth.

I love you.

Curled against his chest Corey took his hand and together they sank back into the deep. Beyond the narrow gates of Bentham, the dream dissolved from eternity into sand.

author's note

Deviance and loss of identity. From the treatment of mental illnesses to incarceration, conformity to the extreme gets you things like cults, religious fanaticism, satanic panic. In the 40's we had lobotomies as a last resort to treat behavioral deviances. Nowadays we have things like conversion therapy and masking. When cures become erasure in favor of conformity, it's eugenics.
Additional reading:
Angela Y. Davis | Abolition
Jack D. Pressman | Last Resort: Psychosurgery and the Limits of Medicine
Moisés Kaufman | The Laramie Project
despite the horrors we survive

content warnings

psychological horror, events and depictions ranging from real to hallucinated, hallucinations and memory disorders, grief and loss
casual consumption of alcohol
accidental and natural animal death, hunting and wounding of game animals
natural disasters such as flooding and snow, fire caused by arson
violence including murder and character death, physical assault, gun violence, knives, strangulation, manipulation, violence from an authority figure
body horror and gore, regurgitation, cannibalism, parasitism, self mutilation of chest, face, and stomach, eye trauma, scarring, birthing imagery, surgical imagery, man described with female anatomy in the context of body horror, medical experimentation and malpractice
discussion and parallels pertaining to conversion therapy, eugenics, lobotomies
mental health hospitalization, incarceration
christian religious imagery and religiously motivated self harm including self mortification, whipping, cutting, starvation, and immolation, cult behaviors, invocation of occult and cosmic horror

about the author

Kienn Nguyen (indie author, queer horror, possibly 10,000 rats) holds a degree in physics and thinks too much. Which shows in their writing and painting.

thank you

Thank you for reading.
As always, reviews are appreciated.

Derivative works permitted.

Classified as ergodic, acrostics are used in every chapter to add an additional layer to the work.

Follow and find out more @kiennwrites !

Printed in Dunstable, United Kingdom

The
INTERNATIONAL CRITICAL COMMENTARY
on the Holy Scriptures of the Old and New Testaments

GENERAL EDITORS:

S. R. DRIVER
Regius Professor of Hebrew, University of Oxford

A. PLUMMER
Master of University College, University of Durham

C. A. BRIGGS
*Edward Robinson Professor of Biblical Theology,
Union Theological Seminary, New York*

THE BOOK OF KINGS

A CRITICAL AND EXEGETICAL COMMENTARY

ON

THE BOOK OF KINGS

BY

JAMES A. MONTGOMERY
PH.D., S.T.D., D.H.L., LITT.D.
*Professor Emeritus in the University of Pennsylvania
and in the Philadelphia Divinity School*

EDITED BY

HENRY SYNDER GEHMAN
PH.D., S.T.D., LITT.D.
*Professor of Old Testament Literature and Chairman of the
Department of Biblical Literature, Princeton Theological Seminary,
and Lecturer in Semitic Languages, Princeton University*

EDINBURGH
T. & T. CLARK LIMITED, 59 GEORGE STREET

PRINTED IN THE U.K. BY PAGE BROS (NORWICH) LTD

FOR
T. & T. CLARK LTD, EDINBURGH

0 567 05006 8

Latest impression 1986

All Rights Reserved. No part of this publication may be reproduced, stored in a retrieval system, or transmitted, in any form or by any means, electronic, mechanical, photocopying, recording or otherwise, without the prior permission of T. & T. Clark Ltd.

IN HONOUR OF

PROVOST WILLIAM PEPPER
PROVOST CHARLES C. HARRISON
PROVOST EDGAR F. SMITH
PROVOST JOSIAH H. PENNIMAN
PRESIDENT THOMAS S. GATES

TO WHOSE WISE, DEVOTED AND SUCCESSFUL
ADMINISTRATIONS OF OUR ALMA MATER
THE AUTHOR AS STUDENT, ALUMNUS, PROFESSOR
BEARS INTIMATE AND GRATEFUL WITNESS

PREFACE

With Alice *Through the Looking-Glass*,

> " The time has come," the Walrus said,
> " To talk of many things;
> Of shoes—and ships—and sealing-wax—
> Of cabbages—and kings."

Our book is of like category on the human side, from 'ships' and 'seals' and 'the hyssop that grows on the wall' to 'kings' and queens, as well as ordinary folk. But the collection is inspired and dominated by the belief in a unity, which gives the clue to the seemingly crazy checkerboard pattern of human history. It is at once a book ' of the ways of God ' and ' of men.' Hence the extent and variety of subject-matter involved in the following composition, which has gone beyond the bounds of the normal Commentary of the day. In English the last extensive Commentary on Kings is that of G. Rawlinson in 1873, largely inspired by the fresh archæological discoveries in Egypt and Mesopotamia; in German, the too little known but admirable work of the Catholic scholar, A. Šanda, of over a thousand pages, now almost thirty years old. Current interest has lain naturally in the more religiously inspiring books of the Hebrew Bible, the Prophets and the Poets, or critically in the still vexed Pentateuchal problems, or those of many of the Prophetical books. Many notable current histories indeed have included the materials of our book, as a source of history, yet only with indirect display of its character. But the equally divine and human aspect of this book, the compilation of which was inspired by the belief in the God of a people who is also God of human history, deserves attention as part of the *catena* of the earliest surviving attempt at history in the large sense of the word, and that coming from a politically insignificant people, but unique among the ancients in its sense of a universal Providence, tending mistily to " One far-off divine event, To which the whole creation moves."

In reviewing his work, the writer recognizes its limitations, which are also his own. He has been primarily a commentator, which duty involves the related linguistics, text-criticism, history of interpretation from the ancient versions down to the present, and the attempt at exact translation with critical display. For lack of room he has not been able to expand on the criticism of the Hebrew text and of the Versions, confining himself mostly to comment *ad locos*. The marvellous results of modern archæology have been recorded, however imperfectly, usually without more than reference to the authorities, who then may disagree among themselves, or whose opinions may be shattered by fresh discoveries, for Dame Archæology has been a chastiser of theoretical reconstructions of literary and so of religious history. The writer has been dealing with the materials of history, but for their historical evaluation he must in large part refer to the many excellent historians, whose duty it is to have ' a vision of the whole.' For example, in the section of the Introduction bearing upon Chronology he has not been able to do much more than to present the bases of that vexed theme and to refer to the many authoritative monographs. Again the Biblical book is a religious compilation, but the large field of the history of Israel's religion may only be touched upon *au courant*, as in the story of the Northern Prophets, or the Southern Isaiah and the problem of Deuteronomy. For this field the reader must refer to the many and ample books on a subject that has especially preoccupied modern interest. In the already too extensive Bibliography there has been omitted reference to such general treatments, the eminent titles among which will be cited in place. Indeed the writer professes that he desires to make the most of these ancient records, to let them speak for themselves, constrained as he is to leave to others their proper placing in the enormous field of Oriental research.

The writer would express his thanks to many good friends for their genial help : to Prof. O. Eissfeldt of the University of Halle for the generous loan of an annotated copy of his Commentary on Kings ; to President J. Morgenstern, Professors W. F. Albright, A. D. Nock, A. T. Olmstead, P. K. Hitti. And in particular he records his deep obligations to former students of his, *amicis caris clarisque*, for their interest and most helpful criticism, some of them having toilfully read extensive sections of the manuscript book and spent hours of consultation with its author; to Professors H. S. Gehman, Z. S. Harris, F. James, S. L. Skoss, E. A. Speiser C. H. Gordon, H. M. Orlinsky.

And to the Publishers he acknowledges warmly their acceptance of a work that has grown beyond normal bounds.

JAMES A. MONTGOMERY.

February 8, 1941.

The War prevented the American and British publishers from immediate publication of the volume. The writer accordingly took the manuscript back from them *ad interim*, and has spent much time in rectifications and additions, which has been all to the good. A Supplemental Bibliography, only partly drawn upon, exhibits the further extension of the literature on the subject in the intervening years.

But word has at last come from the Messrs. Scribner in New York and T. & T. Clark in Edinburgh that the printing of the volume can begin. The author would express not only his personal gratification, but still more his deep respect for their venture in these days of stress and strain.

J. A. M.

October 18, 1944.

As a graduate student in Semitic Languages and Old Testament at the University of Pennsylvania and the Philadelphia Divinity School the editor took all the courses offered by Professor Montgomery, who aroused his interest in the Septuagint and other versions of the Bible and thus prepared him for his career in Old Testament teaching and research. Twice this manuscript had been ready for publication, as the two dates above indicate, but in each case circumstances beyond the author's control postponed publication. In the meanwhile Professor Montgomery passed his eighty-second year, and for reasons of health he felt that he was not able to make another revision and to read the proofs of his forthcoming work. Under these conditions he asked his former pupil to make the final preparations of the manuscript and see it through the press. The editor was glad to assume this duty in recognition of Professor Montgomery's contributions to Old Testament Science and with the personal satisfaction of having had a part in mediating to the world of scholarship the crowning work of his preceptor's distinguished career. On February 6, 1949, Professor Montgomery passed to his eternal reward, and while he never saw any of the proofs, he had the satisfaction of knowing that the printing of the Commentary had actually commenced.

The editor has brought the Bibliography up to date and incorporated the author's Supplementary Bibliography in the proper alphabetical order. For the sake of convenience of reference he has also inserted, at Professor Montgomery's request, his own Biblical Chronology of the period of the kings of Israel and Judah as found in the *Westminster Dictionary of the Bible* and in the Concordance of the *Westminster Study Edition of the Holy Bible*. He has also prepared the indexes at the end of the volume. The editor has made some changes and revisions in the manuscript, but these were of the type normally expected of a redactor. The author's spelling of proper names was in all cases retained, and the editor kept at a minimum alterations of English style. In fairness to the author the editor's aim was to let the final product remain the work of Professor Montgomery. The editor at this point wishes to express his gratitude to his colleague and former pupil, Dr. John Wm. Wevers, who gave him valuable assistance in the reading of the proof. While claiming no credit for the merits of the Commentary, the editor found pleasure in rendering a service to Biblical scholarship.

HENRY SNYDER GEHMAN.

PRINCETON, N.J.,
June 1, 1950.

CONTENTS

	PAGE
PREFACE	vii
BIBLIOGRAPHY	xiii
MODERN BIBLE TRANSLATIONS	xxxvii
CHRONOLOGY	xxxix
CARTOGRAPHY	xxxix
INSCRIPTIONS, EPIGRAPHS, ETC., COMMONLY CITED	xli
KEY TO ABBREVIATIONS	xliii
SYMBOLS IN THE CRITICAL APPARATUS	xlvii
INTRODUCTION	1
I. THE BOOK	1
1. PLACE IN THE CANON AS A DISTINCT BOOK; CONTENTS	1
2. TEXT AND LANGUAGE	3
II. ANCIENT VERSIONS	8
3. THE APPARATUS AT LARGE	8
4. THE GREEK VERSIONS	9
a. THE APPARATUS	9
b. THE ALEXANDRIAN (SEPTUAGINTAL) GROUP	10
c. THE LATER JEWISH TRANSLATORS: THEODOTION, AQUILA, SYMMACHUS, ETC.	11
d. ORIGEN'S REVISION AND ITS SUCCESSORS	11
e. THE LUCIANIC REVISION	12
5. THE TARGUM	13
6. THE SYRIAC VERSIONS	13
a. THE PESHITTA	13
b. THE SYRO-HEXAPLA	14
7. THE ETHIOPIC	14
8. THE ARABIC	15
9. OTHER ORIENTAL VERSIONS	15
a. THE SYRO-PALESTINIAN	15
b. THE COPTIC	15
c. THE ARMENIAN	16

CONTENTS

		PAGE
10.	THE LATIN VERSIONS	16
	a. THE OLD LATIN	16
	b. THE VULGATE	16

III. GROUPING OF THE VERSIONS 16

- 11. a. THE ALEXANDRIAN FAMILY 16
    - b. THE PALESTINIAN (ORIGENIAN) FAMILY . . . 17
    - c. THE LUCIANIC REVISION AND ITS BACKGROUND; THE PROBLEM OF A PRE-LUCIANIC OR PRE-THEODOTIONIC VERSION; CITATIONS IN JOSEPHUS AND THE NEW TESTAMENT 18
    - d. THE OTHER ORIENTAL VERSIONS 21
    - e. VALUE AND INTEREST OF THE VERSIONS . . 23

IV. THE SOURCES OF THE BOOK 24

- 12. COMPARISON WITH CONTEMPORARY HISTORICAL WRITING 24
- 13. THE CHRONICLES 30
    - a. THE ROYAL SECRETARIAT. ARCHIVES OF ROYAL PERSONALIA 30
    - b. FURTHER ARCHIVAL MATERIALS 33
    - c. TEMPLE ARCHIVES 37
- 14. THE HISTORICAL STORY 38
    - a. POLITICAL NARRATIVES 38
    - b. THE STORIES OF THE PROPHETS 39
- 15. THE COMPILATION 42
- 16. THE CHRONOLOGY 45
    - RECENT LITERATURE 45
    - a. LIST OF REGNAL TERMS AND SYNCHRONISMS . 48
    - b. THE SYNCHRONISMS BETWEEN THE CHRONICLES OF JUDAH AND ISRAEL 53
    - c. THE CALCULATION OF REGNAL TERMS . . . 54
    - d. THE SYNCHRONISMS WITH EXTERNAL HISTORY . 55

COMMENTARY 67

INDEXES 571

- I. SELECT VOCABULARY OF HEBREW WORDS AND PHRASES 571
- II. INDEX OF PLACES TREATED WITH ARCHÆOLOGICAL COMMENT 574

BIBLIOGRAPHY

The following lists include titles of general interest or frequent citation.

ABEL, F. M. : Géographie de la Palestine, 2 vols., 1933-38 [*GP*].
AFREM : s. Ephraem.
AIMÉ-GIRON (earlier GIRON), N. : Textes araméens d'Égypte, 1931.
ALBRECHT, K. : Neuhebräische Grammatik auf Grund der Mišna, 1913.
ALBRIGHT, W. F. : The Archæology of Palestine and the Bible, ed. 1, 1932; ed. 3, 1935 [*APB*].
—— The Vocalization of the Egyptian Syllabic Orthography, 1934.
—— Recent Discoveries in Bible Lands, in Young's Analytical Concordance, ed. 20, 1936.
—— The Ancient Near East and the Religion of Israel, *JBL* 59 (1940), 85-112.
—— From the Stone Age to Christianity, 1940 ; ed. 2, 1946 [*SAC*].
—— An Indexed Bibliography of the Writings of . . ., ed. H. M. Orlinsky, 1941.
—— Archæology and the Religion of Israel, 1942 ; ed. 2, 1946 [*ARI*].
—— The Rôle of the Canaanites in the History of Civilization, in Studies in the History of Culture (dedicated to W. G. Leland), 1942, pp. 11-50.
ALT, A. : Israel u. Aegypten, 1909.
—— Israels Gaue unter Salomo, *BWAT* 13 (1913).
—— Aram, *RVg*.
—— Die syrische Staatenwelt vor dem Einbruch der Assyrer, *ZDMG* 88 (1934), 233-58 (*in re* the Sūjīn texts).
—— Israel, *RGG*.
—— Die Staatenbildung der Israeliten in Palästina, 1930.
—— Zur Geschichte der Grenze zwischen Judäa u. Samaria, *Pjb.*, 31 (1935), 94-111
—— Die älteste Schilderung Palästinas im Lichte neuer Funde, *Pjb.*, 37 (1941), 19-49.
—— see Kittel, *BH*.
Ausgrabungen in Sendschirli, Mitteilungen aus den oriental. Sammlungen, Berlin, vol. 1, 1893, vol. 4, 1911 ; contributors J. Euting, F. von Luschan, E. Sachau.

BADÈ, W. E. : Manual of Excavation in the Near East, 1934.
BAEDEKER, K. : Palestine and Syria, ed. 4, 1906.
BÄHR, K. C. W. F. : Die Bücher der Könige, 1868 (Eng. tr. 1873).
BÄR (BAER), S. : Libri Regum (and Heb. title), 1895.

BARHEBRAEUS : **A.** Morgenstern, Die Scholien des Gregorius Abulfaraǵ
  . . . zum Buch der Könige, 1895.
—— J. Göttsberger, Barhebraeus u. seine Scholien zur Heiligen Schrift, 1900.
—— M. Sprengling and W. C. Graham, Scholia on the O.T., part I, 1931 (see Int. 6, n. 3).
BARNES, H. E. : A History of Historical Writing, 1937.
BARNES, W. E. : Kings, in Cambridge Bible, 2 vols., 1908.
BARON, S. W. : Authenticity of the Numbers in the Historical Books of the O.T., *JBL* 49 (1930), 287–91.
—— A Social and Religious History of the Jews, 3 vols., 1937.
BARROIS, A. G. : La métrologie dans la Bible, *RB* 40 (1931), 185–213; 41 (1932), 50–76.
—— Manuel d'archéologie biblique, vol. 1, 1939.
BARTON, G. A. : Kings, in *JE*.
—— The Royal Inscriptions of Sumer and Akkad, 1929.
—— A History of the Hebrew People, 1930.
—— Archæology and the Bible, ed. 7, 1937 [*AB*].
BAUDISSIN, W. W. : Einleitung in die Bücher des A.T., 1901.
BAUER, H., and LEANDER, P. : Historische Grammatik der hebräischen Sprache, vol. 1, 1922 [*BL*].
BAUMGARTNER, W. : Ein Kapitel vom hebräischen Erzählungsstyl (Gunkel-Eucharisterion, 1, 145 ff.), 1923.
—— Alttestamentliche Religion (1917–27), *ARw.*, 1928, 52 ff. ; *ib.*, 1928–33, 279 ff.
—— Alttestamentliche Einleitung u. Religionsgeschichte, *Th.R.*, N.F., 8 (1936), 179–222 (reviews of literature).
—— and GUNKEL, H. : Sagen u. Legenden, *RGG*.
BAUMSTARK, A. : Geschichte der syrischen Literatur, 1922.
BAUR, P. V. C., and ROSTOVTZEFF, M. I. : The Excavations at Dura-Europos, 1929–44.
BEER, G. : Saul, David, Salomo, 1906.
—— Zur israel.-jüdischen Briefliteratur, *BWAT* 13 (1913), 20 ff.
BENTZEN, A. : Die josianische Reform und ihre Voraussetzungen, 1926.
—— Indledning til det Gamle Testamente, 1941.
BEN TZVI, I. : Sepher ha-Shomeronim (Hebrew), Tell Aviv, 1935.
BENZINGER, I. : Die Bücher der Könige, 1899.
—— Die Bücher der Chronik, 1901.
—— Jahvist u. Elohist in den Königsbüchern, *BWAT*, N.F., 2 (1921).
—— Hebräische Archäologie, ed. 3, 1927.
—— Israel, *RGG*.
BERGSTRÄSSER, G. : Hebräische Grammatik, **ed. 29** of Gesenius, 2 parts, 1918–29 (unfinished) [*HG*].
BERLINGER, J. : Die Peschitta zum 1. Buche der Könige u. ihr Verhältniss zu Mas. Texte, LXX, u. Targum, 1897.
BEROSSOS : *FHG* 2, 495 ff.
—— P. Schnabel, Berossos u. die babylonisch-hellenistische Literatur, **1923.**

BERTHOLET, A. : Kings, in *HSAT*.
—— History of Hebrew Civilization, 1926, tr. of Kulturgeschichte Israels, 1920.
BEVAN, E. R., and SINGER, C. : The Legacy of Israel, 1928 (see the cc. on Hebrew studies in the Middle Ages and in and after the Reformation period by Singer and G. H. Box).
BEWER, J. A. : The Literature of the O.T. in its Historical Development, rev. ed., 1933.
BEZOLD, C. : Babylonisch-assyrisches Glossar, ed. by A. Götze, 1926 [*BAG*].
BIRKELAND, H. : Akzent u. Vocalismus im Althebräischen. Mit Beiträgen zur vergleichenden semitischen Sprachwissenschaft, 1940.
BLEEK, F. : Einleitung in das A.T., ed. 1, 1860 ; ed. 4, 1878, ed. by J. Wellhausen ; ed. 5, 1886, ed. by Wellhausen, but reverting to Bleek's conservative positions ; see Wellhausen, Composition.
BORÉE, W., Die alten Ortsnamen Palästinas, 1930 [*AOP*].
BOSTRÖM, O. H. : Alternative Readings in the Hebrew of the Books of Samuel, 1918.
BÖTTCHER, F. : Neue exegetisch-kritische Aehrenlese zum A.T., Abt. 1–3, 1863–65.
—— Ausführliches Lehrbuch der hebräischen Sprache, vol. 1, 1866.
BOX, G. H. : see Bevan.
BREASTED, J. H. : Ancient Records of Egypt, 1906–07 [*ARE*].
—— A History of Egypt, 1905 [*HE*].
BRIGGS, C. A. General Introduction to the Study of Holy Scripture, 1899.
—— see Brown-Driver-Briggs.
BROCKELMANN, C. : Grundriss der vergleichenden Grammatik der semitischen Sprachen, 2 vols., 1908–13 [*GVG*].
—— Lexicon syriacum, ed. 2, 1928.
BROOKE, A. E., MCLEAN, N., and THACKERAY, H. ST. J. : The O.T. in Greek, Cambridge, 1906–40, so far as issued ; vol. 2, part 2, Kings, 1930 [*OTG*].
BROWN, F., DRIVER, S. R., and BRIGGS, C. A. : A Hebrew and English Lexicon of the O.T., etc. (based on Robinson's ed. of The Lexicon Gesenius), 1906 [BDB].
BRUNO, A. : Das hebräische Epos, eine rhythmische u. textkritische Untersuchung der Bücher Samuelis u. Könige, 1935.
BUBER, M. : Königtum Gottes, ed. 2, 1936.
BUDDE, K. : Geschichte der althebräischen Literatur, 1906 [*GAL*].
BUHL, F. : Canon and Text of the O.T., Eng. tr., 1892.
—— Geschichte der Edomiter, 1893.
—— Geographie der alten Palästina, 1896 [*GAP*].
—— Die socialen Verhältnisse der Israeliten, 1899.
—— see Gesenius.
Bulletin of the American Schools of Oriental Research. Bibliographical and Topographical Indices, nos. 50, 74, 76, 80 [*BASOR*], 1933–40.

BURKITT, F. C. : Fragments of the Books of Kings according to the Translation of Aquila, 1897.
—— Texts and Versions, *EB*.
—— see T. H. Robinson.
BURNEY, C. F. : Kings I and II, *DB*.
—— Notes on the Hebrew Text of the Book of Kings, 1903.
—— The Book of Judges, ed. 2, 1920.
BURROWS, M. : What Mean these Stones ? 1941 [*WMTS*].

CALMET, A. : La Sainte Bible en Latin et en Français avec un commentaire littéral et critique, 23 vols., 1707 *seq*.
—— Commentaire littéral sur tous les livres de l'Ancien et du Nouveau Testament, 1724-26.
Cambridge Ancient History : edd. J. B. Bury, S. A. Cook, F. E. Adcock. Vol. 3, 1925, cc. 1-4, S. Smith, Assyria ; cc. 6, 7, D. C. Hogarth, Hittites ; ch. 9, R. C. Thompson, New Babylonian Empire ; ch. 16, R. A. S. Macalister, Topography of Jerusalem ; cc. 17-20, Cook, Israel and the Neighbouring States [*CAH*].
CAPELLUS, S. : Chronologia sacra, and, Trisagion sive templi Hierosolymitani triplex delineatio, including discussion of Josephus, translation of *Middoth*, and Maimonides's notes ; in Walton's Polyglot, reprinted in Walton's Biblicus Apparatus.
CAUSSE, A. : Du groupe ethnique à la communauté religieuse : le problème sociologique de la religion d'Israël, 1937.
CHADWICK, H. M., and N. K. : The Growth of Literature ; vol. 2, part iv, Early Hebrew Literature, 1936.
CHEYNE, T. K. : Critica Biblica ; part iv, First and Second Kings, 1903.
—— Decline and Fall of the Kingdom of Judah, 1908.
—— arts. in *EB*.
CHURCH, B. P. : The Israel Saga, 1932.
CLAY, A. T. : Light on the O.T. from Babel, 1907.
CLEMEN, C. : Die phönikische Religion nach Philo von Byblos, *MVÄG* 42, Heft 3, 1939.
—— see Lucian.
CLERMONT-GANNEAU, C. : Recueil d'archéologie orientale, 8 vols., 1888-1924.
Comptes rendus, l'Académie des Inscriptions et Belles-Lettres [*CR*].
CONTENAU, G. : La civilization phénicienne, 1926.
—— Manuel d'archéologie orientale, 4 vols., 1927-47.
CONTI ROSSINI, C. : Chrestomathia Arabica meridionalis epigraphica, 1931.
COOK, S. A. : Jews, *Enc. Br.* [14].
—— Notes on the Dynasties of Omri and Jehu, *JQR* 20 (1908), 597-630.
—— The Religion of Ancient Palestine in the Light of Archæology, 1930.
—— Salient Problems in O.T. History, *JBL* 41 (1932), 273-99.
—— The Confines of Israel and Judah, *QS* 1934. 60-75.

BIBLIOGRAPHY xvii

COOK, S. A. : The O.T., a Reinterpretation, 1936.
—— see *CAH*.
COOKE, G. A. : A Text-Book of North-Semitic Inscriptions, 1903 [*NSI*].
—— Ezekiel, *ICC* 1937.
COPPENS, J. : L'Histoire critique de l'Ancien Testament, 1938 ; ed. 3, 1942.
CORNILL, C. H. : Introduction to the Canonical Books of the O.T., 1907, tr. of Einleitung in das A.T., ed. 5, 1905.
Corpus inscriptionum Semiticarum, 1881 *seq*. [*CIS*].
Corpus scriptorum Christianorum Orientalium, 1903 *seq*. [*CSCO*].
Corpus scriptorum ecclesiasticorum Græcorum, 1897 *seq*. [*CSEG*].
Corpus scriptorum ecclesiasticorum Latinorum, 1866 *seq*. [*CSEL*].
Cory's Ancient Fragments, etc., tr. and ed. by F. R. Hodges, 1876.
COWLEY, A. : Aramaic Papyri of the Fifth Century B.C., 1923.
CREELMAN, H. : An Introduction to the O.T., Chronologically Arranged, 1917.
CREMER, H. : Biblisch-theologisches Wörterbuch der neutestamentlichen Gräcität, ed. 6, 1889 ; ed. 11, rev. by J. Kögel, 1923.
Critici sacri, ed. C. Bee, 1696 *seq*.
CROCKETT, W. D. : A Harmony of the Books of Sam., Ki., and Chron., 1907.
CROWFOOT, J. W., KENYON, F., and SUKENIK, E. L. : The Buildings of Samaria, 1942.
CUNY, A. : see Féghali.
CURTIS, E. L., and MADSEN, A. A. : Chronicles, *ICC* 1910.

DALMAN, G. : Arbeit u. Sitte in Palästina, 7 vols., 1928-42 [*A.u.S.*].
—— Sacred Sites and Ways, 1935.
DATHIUS (DATHE), J. A. : Libri historici V.T. (tr. with notes), 1784 ; ed. 2, 1832.
DE WETTE, W. M. L. : Lehrbuch der historisch-kritischen Einleitung in die Bibel, A. u. N.T., vol. 1, ed. 6, 1845, vol. 2, ed. 4, 1842 ; ed. 8, ed. E. Schrader, 1869.
DEIMEL, A. : Pantheon Babylonicum, 1914.
—— Analecta Orientalia 12 (dedicated to), 1935.
DELITZSCH, FRANZ : A System of Biblical Psychology, 1867.
DELITZSCH, FRIEDR. : Assyrisches Handwörterbuch, 1896.
—— Die Lese- u. Schreibfehler im A.T., 1920.
DELLA VIDA, G. L. : arts., Aramei, Ebrei, Semiti, in Enciclopedia Italiana, vol. 3, 1929, vol. 14, 1932, vol. 34, 1936.
DESNOYERS, L. : Histoire du peuple hébreu, 3 vols., 1922-30.
DHORME, E. (=P.) : Les livres de Samuel, 1910.
—— Les pays bibliques et l'Assyrie, a series of arts. in *RB* 7, 8 (1910-11).
—— Prêtres, devins et mages dans l'ancienne religion des Hébreux, *RHR* 108 (1933), 113-43.
—— L'Évolution religieuse d'Israël, 1937.
A Dictionary of the Bible, ed. James Hastings, 4 vols. and extra vol., 1898-1904 [*DB*].

A Dictionary of Christian Biography, edd. W. Smith and H. Wace, 4 vols., 1877–87 [*DCB*].

DILLMANN, A. : Biblia V.T. Æthiopica, vol. 2, 1861.

—— Lexicon linguæ Æthiopicæ, 1865.

DIRINGER, D. : Le inscrizioni antico-ebraiche palestinesi, 1934 [*IAE*].

DÖLLER, J. : Geographische u. ethnographische Studien zum III. u. IV. Buche der Könige, 1904 [*GES*].

DENNEFELD, L. : Histoire d'Israël et de l'Ancien Orient, 1935.

DOUGHTY, C. M. : Travels in Arabia Deserta, ed. 3, 1927.

DOZY, R. : Supplément aux dictionnaires arabes, 2 vols., 1881.

DRIVER, S. R. : A Treatise on the Use of the Tenses in Hebrew, etc. 1892.

—— An Introduction to the Literature of the O.T., ed. 6, 1900 (=Am. ed. 10) ; New Ed., 1913 (Am. reprint, 1931).

—— Deuteronomy, *ICC* 1895.

—— Notes on the Hebrew Text and the Topography of the Books of Samuel, ed. 2, 1913.

—— see Brown-Driver-Briggs.

DUHM, B. : Die Edomiter, 1893.

DÜRR, L. : Die Wertung des göttlichen Wortes im A.T. u. im antiken Orient, *MVÄG* 42, Heft I, 1938.

DUSSAUD, R. : Notes de mythologie syrienne, ii–ix, 1905.

—— Samarie au temps d'Achab, Syria, 6 (1925), 314–38 ; 7 (1926), 9–29.

—— Topographie historique de la Syrie antique et mediévale, 1927 [*TH*].

—— DESCHAMPS, P., and SEYRIG, H. : La Syrie antique et mediévale illustrée (with 160 plates and map), 1931 [*SAM*].

—— Mélanges syriens, offerts à M. . . ., I, 1939, II, 1939.

DUVAL, R. : Traité de grammaire syriaque, 1881.

—— La littérature syriaque, ed. 3, 1907.

EBELING, E. : see Gressmann.

EBSTEIN, W. : Die Medizin im A.T., 1901.

EHRLICH, A. B. : Randglossen zur hebräischen Bibel ; on Kings, vol. 7, pp. 213 ff., 1914.

EICHHORN, J. G. : Einleitung in das A.T., ed. 4, 5 vols., 1823–24.

EISSFELDT, O. : Könige, *HSAT*, ed. 4, 1922–23.

—— The Smallest Literary Unit in the Narrative Books of the O.T. Simpson, O.T. Essays, 85 ff.

—— Die Komposition der Samuelsbücher, 1931.

—— Einleitung in das A.T., 1934.

—— Philister u. Phönizier, *AO* 1936.

—— Phöniker u. Phönikia, *RE* 1940.

——Geschichtsschreibung im A.T. Ein Kritischer Bericht über die neueste Literatur dazu, 1948.

—— Altertumskunde u. A.T., in Werden und Wesen des A.T., *BZAW* 66 (1936), 155–67.

BIBLIOGRAPHY

EISSFELDT, O.: Ba'alšamēm u. Jahwe, *ZAW* 57 (1939), 1 ff.
—— Ras Schamra und Sanchunjaton, 1939.
—— Israelitisch-philistäische Grenzverschiebungen von David bis auf die Assyrerzeit, *ZDPV* 66 (1943), 115–28.
—— see Kittel, *BH*.
EITAN, I.: Hebrew and Semitic Particles, *AJSL* 44 (1928), 177–205, 254–60; 45 (1928–29), 48–60, 130–45, 197–211; 46 (1929), 22–51.
Encyclopædia Biblica, edd. T. K. Cheyne and J. S. Black, 4 vols., 1899–1903, one vol. ed., 1914 [*EB*].
Encyclopædia Britannica, ed. 9, 1878; ed. 14, 1929 [*Enc. Br.*].
Encyclopædia of Religion and Ethics, ed. J. Hastings, 1917–27 [*ERE*].
EPHRAEM SYRUS: Opera omnia S. Ephraemi Syri, ed. Petrus Benedictus, vol. 1, 439–567 on Kings, 1737.
ERBT, W.: Elia, Elisa, Jona. Beitrag zur Geschichte der 9. u. 8. Jahrhunderte, 1907.
ERMAN, A.: Literature of the Ancient Egyptians, tr. by A. W. Blackman, 1927.
—— and RANKE, H.: Aegypten u. aegyptisches Leben im Altertum, ed. 2, 1923.
EULER, K. F.: Königtum u. Götterwelt in den altaramäischen Inschriften Nordsyriens, *ZAW* 57 (1939), 272 ff.
EUSEBIUS PAMPHILI: Chronicorum libri duo, ed. A. C. I. Schoene, 1866, 1875.
—— E. Klostermann, Das Onomastikon der biblischen Ortsnamen (with Jerome's Latin text), *GCS* 11 (1904).
—— F. Wutz, Onomastica Sacra, *TU* 41 (1915).
EUTING, J.: see Ausgrabungen in Sendschirli.
EWALD, H.: Ausführliches Lehrbuch der hebräischen Sprache des Alten Bundes, ed. 8, 1870.
—— History of Israel, Eng. tr. by R. Martineau, 1869–86 [*HI*].

FABRICIUS, J. A.: Codex pseudepigraphicus Veteris Testamenti, Hamburg/Leipzig, 1713.
FARRAR, F. W.: History of Interpretation, New York, 1886.
—— The first Book of Kings, 1893; The Second Book of Kings, 1894 (Expositor's Bible).
AL-FĀSĪ, DAVID B. ABRAHAM: Kitāb jāmi' al-alfāẓ, ed. S. L. Skoss, vol. 1, New Haven, 1936; vol. 2, New Haven, 1945.
FÉGHALI, M., and CUNY, A.: Du genre grammatical en sémitique, 1924.
FEIGIN, S.: Misstre Heavar, Biblical and Historical Studies (Hebrew), 1943.
FIELD, F.: Origenis hexaplorum quæ supersunt, 2 vols., 1875.
FILLION, L.: Rois (Les quatres livres des), Vigouroux, *DB*.
—— Poids, *ib*.
FINEGAN, J.: Light from the Ancient East—The Archæological Background of the Hebrew-Christian Religion, 1946.

BIBLIOGRAPHY

FISHER, C. S. : see Lyon.
FORRER, E. : Die Provinzeinteilung des assyrischen Reiches, Teil I, 1920.
—— Aramu, *RA*.
—— Assyrien, *RA*.
FOWLER, H. T. : A History of the Literature of Ancient Israel, 1912.
—— Herodotus and the Early Hebrew Historians, *JBL* 49 (1930), 207–17.
Fragmenta historicorum Græcorum, edd. K. and T. Müller, 5 vols., 1848–74 [*FHG*].
FRAZER, J. G. : Folk-Lore in the O.T., 3 vols., 1918.
—— The Golden Bough, ed. 3, 12 vols., 1911–15 ; Supplementary Vol., 1937.
FREYTAG, G. W. : Lexicon Arabico-Latinum, 4 vols., 1830–37.

GADD, J. C. : see Hall.
GALLING, K. : Die israelitische Staatsverfassung in ihrer vorderasiatischen Umwelt, *AO* 28, Heft 3/4, 1929.
—— Biblisches Reallexicon, 1937 [*BR*].
GANDZ, S. : Oral Tradition in the Bible, Jewish Studies in Memory of G. A. Kohut, 1935, 248–69.
—— The Dawn of Literature : Prolegomena to a History of Unwritten Literature, *Osiris* 7 (1939), 261 ff.
GARSTANG, J. : Sociology of Ancient Palestine, 1934.
—— The Heritage of Solomon, 1934.
—— see Lucian.
Gaster Anniversary Volume, 1936.
GEDEN, A. S., and KILGOUR, R. : Introduction to the Ginsburg Edition of the Hebrew O.T., 1928.
GEHMAN, H. S. : ed., The Westminster Dictionary of the Bible, 1944.
—— The Armenian Version of I and II Kings and its Affinities, *JAOS* 54 (1934), 53–9.
GEIGER, A. : Urschrift u. Übersetzungen der Bibel, ed. 2, 1928.
VAN GELDEREN, C. : Die Boeken van Koningen, 3 vols, 1936–47.
GESENIUS (H. F.), W. : Thesaurus philologicus criticus linguae Hebraeae et Chaldaeae Veteris Testamenti, 3 vols., 1829–53.
—— Hebräische Grammatik, ed. 26, ed. E. Kautzsch, 1896 ; ed. 28, 1909 [*GK*].
—— Eng. tr. by A. Cowley, Gesenius' Hebrew Grammar, ed. 2, 1910.
—— and BUHL, F. : Hebräisches u. aramäisches Handwörterbuch über das A.T., ed. 16, 1915 (the edd. of 1921 and 1933 are unchanged reprints) [*GB*].
—— see Brown-Driver-Briggs.
GILLESCHEWSKI, EVA : Der Ausdruck עם הארץ im A.T., *ZAW* 40 (1922), 137–42.
GINSBURG (C.), D. : Introduction to the Massoretico-Critical Edition of the Hebrew Bible, 1897.

GINSBURG, (C.), D.: The Hebrew Old Testament: עשרים וארבעה ספרי הקדש, 1894 [Ginsb.¹]
—— The Old Testament: תורה נביאים וכתובים, 4 vols., 1926. [Ginsb.²].
GINZBERG, L.: Legends of the Jews, 7 vols., 1909–38, esp. vol. 4; vol. 7 contains Index by Boaz Cohen.
GIRON: see Aimé-Giron.
GLUECK, N.: Explorations in Eastern Palestine: I, *AASOR* 14 (1934); II, *ib.*, 15 (1935); III, *ib.*, 18–19 (1939); also constant reports in *BASOR* and *BA*.
—— The Boundaries of Edom, *HUCA* 11 (1936), 141 ff.
—— The Other Side of the Jordan, 1940.
—— The River Jordan—being an Account of the Earth's most Storied River, 1946.
GODLEY, A. D.: see Herodotus.
GOETTSBERGER, J.: Einleitung in das A.T., 1928.
—— Die Bücher der Chronik, 1938.
GORDIS, R.: The Biblical Text in the Making: A Study of the Kethib-Qre, 1937.
GRAETZ, H.: Geschichte der Juden, 1853–70; Eng. tr., History of the Jews, 6 vols., 1891.
—— Emendationes in V.T., 1892.
GRAHAM, W. C., and MAY, H. G.: Culture and Conscience: an Archæological Study of the New Religious Past in Ancient Palestine, 1936.
GRANT, E.: see Haverford Symposium.
GRAY, G. B.: Studies in Hebrew Proper Names, 1896.
—— Critical Introduction to the O.T., 1913.
GRESSMANN, H.: Samuel, *SAT* 1921.
—— Könige, *ib.*
—— Die älteste Geschichtsschreibung u. Prophetie Israels, ed. 2, 1921.
—— Altorientalische Texte u. Bilder zum A.T.², in conjunction with E. Ebeling, H. Ranke, N. Rhodokanakis, 2 vols., 1926–27 [*ATB*].
GRETHER, O.: Name u. Wort Gottes im A.T., *BZAW* 64 (1934).
Die griechischen christlichen Schriftsteller der ersten drei Jahrhunderte, 1897 *seq.* [*CGS*].
GROHMANN, A.: see Nielsen, *HAA*.
GROTIUS, H.: Annotationes in V.T., 3 vols., 1775–76; also Variæ lectiones, ed. by T. Pierce, in Walton's Polyglot, vol. 6.
GUÉRIN, M. V.: Description . . . de la Palestine. Part I, Judée, 1868–69; part II, Samarie, 1874–75; Galilée, 1880.
Guide Bleu: Syrie, Palestine, 1932.
GUILLAUME, A.: Kings, in A New Commentary on Holy Scripture, edd. C. Gore, *al.*, 1928.
—— Prophecy and Divination, 1938.
GUNKEL, H.: Die Psalmen, 1926.
—— Einleitung in die Psalmen, 1933.
—— Sagen u. Legenden: II. In Israel, *RGG*.
—— see Religion in Geschichte u. Gegenwart.

Gunkel-Eucharisterion, ed. H. Schmidt, 1923.
GÜTERBOCK, H. G. : Die historische Tradition u. ihre literarische Gestaltung bei Babyloniern u. Hethitern bis 1200, Teil I, Babylonier, Teil II, Hethiter, *ZA* 42 (1934), 1-91 ; *ib*., 44 (1938), 45 ff.
GUTHE, H. : Geschichte Israels, ed. 2, 1904.

HAEUSSERMANN, F. : Wortempfang in der alttestamentlichen Prophetie, *BZAW* 58 (1932).
HALL, R. H. : Ancient History of the Near East, ed. 3, 1916 ; ed. 8, ed. J. C. Gadd, 1932 [*AHNE*].
HAMBURGER, J. : Real-Encyclopädie für Bibel u. Talmud, 2 vols., 1870-83 [*RE*].
A Handbook of Arabia. British Admiralty publication, n. d. (*post* 1914).
Handbuch der Altertumswissenschaft [*HA*].
HARDING, L. : see Lachish, I, II.
HARMAN, A. M. : see Lucian.
HARRIS, C. W. : The Hebrew Heritage : a Study of Israel's Cultural and Spiritual Origins, 1935.
HARRIS, Z. S. : A Grammar of the Phœnician Language, 1936.
—— Development of the Canaanite Dialects, 1939.
HATCH, E., and REDPATH, H. A. : Concordance to the Septuagint, etc., 2 vols., 1897 (Suppl. Vol., 1906).
HAUCK, A. : see Realencyklopädie.
HAUPT, P. : see Stade, *SBOT*.
—— Oriental Studies . . . in Commemoration of . . ., 1926.
The Haverford Symposium on Archæology and the Bible, ed. E. Grant, New Haven, 1938.
HEMPEL, J. : Das A.T. u. Geschichte, 1930.
—— Die althebräische Literatur u. ihr hellenistisches Nachleben, 1930 [*AL*].
—— Politische Absicht u. politische Wirkung im biblischen Schrifttum, 1938.
HERODOTUS : ed. A. D. Godley, Loeb Classical Library, 4 vols., 1921-24.
HERRMANN, A. : Die Erdkarte der Urbibel, 1931.
HERZOG, J. J. : see Realencyklopädie.
HEYSE, T., and TISCHENDORF, C. : Biblia Sacra Latina, 1873 (cited as Tischendorf).
HITTI, P. K. : History of the Arabs, 1937 ; ed. 3, 1943.
HITZIG, F. : Geschichte des Volkes Israel, 1869.
HÖFNER, M. : Altsüdarabische Grammatik, 1943.
HOGARTH, D. C. : see *CAH*.
HOLMES, R., and PARSONS, J. : V.T. Græcum cum variis lectionibus, 4 vols., 1798-1827 [*HP*].
HÖLSCHER, G. : Das Buch der Könige, seine Quellen u. seine Redaktion (Gunkel-Eucharisterion, I, 158 ff.), 1923.
—— Die Anfänge der hebräischen Geschichtsschreibung (*Sb*., Heidelberg), 1942.

BIBLIOGRAPHY

HOMMEL, F. : Süd-Arabische Chrestomathie, 1893.
—— Ethnologie u. Geographie des Alten Orients, 1926 [*EGAO*].
—— see Nielsen, *HAA*.
HONEYMAN, A. M. : The Pottery Vessels of the O.T., *PEQ* 1939, 76–90.
HONIGMANN, E. : Syria, *RE* 4 (A), 1549 ff.
HOOKE, S. H. : ed., Myth and Ritual of the Hebrews in Relation to the Culture Pattern of the Ancient East, 1933.
—— ed., The Labyrinth, 1935.
HOSCHANDER, J. : The Priests and Prophets, 1938.
HOUBIGANT, C. F. : Notae criticae in universos V.T. libros, etc., 2 vols., Frankfurt, 1777.
HUGHES, T. P. : A Dictionary of Islam, 1885.
HUNKIN, J. W. : see T. H. Robinson.

INGE, C. H. : see Lachish II.

JACK, J. W. : Samaria in Ahab's Time. Harvard Excavations and their Results, 1929.
—— The Lachish Letters : Their Date and Import, *PEQ* 1938, 165–87.
JACOB, E. : La tradition historique en Israël, 1946.
JAMES, F. : Personalities of the O.T., 1939.
JASTROW, MARCUS : A Dictionary of the Targumim, Talmud Babli and Yerushalmi, and the Midrashic Literature, 2 vols., 1903.
JASTROW, MORRIS : Die Religion Babyloniens u. Assyriens, 2 vols., 1905–12.
JEAN, C. F. : Le milieu biblique avant Jésus-Christ, 3 vols., 1922–36.
JEPSEN, A. : Nabi. Soziologische Studien zur alttestamentlichen Literatur u. Religionsgeschichte, 1934.
JEREMIAS, A. : Das A.T. im Lichte des alten Orients, ed. 2, 1906 (ed. 4, 1930) ; *e.g.*, the Solomonic history, pp. 492 ff., Glosses on Ki., pp. 537 ff. [*ATLAO*].
—— Handbuch d. altorientalischen Geisteskultur, ed. 2, 1929 [*HAG*].
JEROME : Onomasticon ; see Eusebius.
Jewish Encyclopædia, 12 vols., 1901–06 [*JE*].
JIRKU, A. : Altorientalischer Kommentar zum A.T., 1923 [*AKAT*].
—— Die aegyptischen Liste paläst. u. syr. Ortsnamen, 1937.
—— Der Kampf um Syrien-Palästina im orientalischen Altertum, 1926.
—— Geschichte des Volkes Israel, 1931.
JOHNSON, A. R. : Rôle of the King in the Jerusalem Cultus, in Hooke, The Labyrinth, 1935.
JOSEPHUS : H. St.J. Thackeray and R. Marcus, Loeb Library, Marcus ed. of vols. 5, 6, 1934–37.
JOÜON, P. : Notes de critique textuelle, Mél., 5, fasc. 2 (1912), 473 ff., on Kings.
—— Grammaire de l'Hébreu biblique, 1923.
—— Notes philologiques sur le texte hébreu de 1 Rois, etc., Biblica, 9 (1928), 428–33.

BIBLIOGRAPHY

JUNGE, E. : Der Wiederaufbau des Heerwesens des Reiches Juda unter Josia, *BWANT* IV, 23 (1937).
JUNKER, H. : Prophet u. Seher im Israel, 1927.

KAHLE, P. : Der alttestamentliche Bibeltext (text in Palestine 600–900, in Babylonia 900–1525), *Th.R.*, N.F., 5 (1933), 227–38.
—— The Cairo Geniza (Schweich Lectures, 1941), 1946.
—— see Kittel, *BH*.
KALT, E. : Biblisches Reallexikon, ed. 2, 2 vols., 1938–39.
KAMPHAUSEN, A. : Könige, *HSAT* 1894.
KAUTZSCH, E. : An Outline of the History of the Literature of the O.T., Eng. tr., 1899.
—— Die Heilige Schrift des A.T., ed. 4, ed. A. Bertholet, 2 vols., 1922–23 [*HSAT*].
—— see Gesenius, GK.
—— see W. R. Smith.
KEIL, C. F. : Die Bücher der Könige, ed. 2, 1876 ; tr. of ed. 1 by J. Martin, 2 vols., 1872.
KENNEDY, J. : An Aid to the Textual Amendment of the O.T., 1928.
KENNETT, R. H. : O.T. Essays, 1928.
—— Ancient Hebrew Social Life and Custom, etc., 1933.
KENNICOTT, J. : Vetus Testamentum Hebraicum cum variis lectionibus, 2 vols., 1776–80 ; cf. his Dissertatio generalis at end of vol. 2 [*VTH*].
—— The Ten Annual Accounts of the O.T. (1760–69), 1770 (detailed reports on progress of the work on *VTH*).
KENT, C. F. : The Student's O.T. ; vol. 2, Israel's Historical and Biographical Narratives, 1905 [*SOT*].
KIMCHI, DAVID : cited from Miḳra'oth Gedoloth.
KITTEL, R. : Die Anfänge der hebräischen Geschichtsschreibung im A.T., 1896.
—— Die Bücher der Könige, *HkAT* 1900.
—— Studien zur hebräischen Archäologie u. Religionsgeschichte, 1908.
—— Richter, Samuel, *HSAT* 1922.
—— Geschichte des Volkes Israel, ed. 6, vols. 1, 2, 1923–25 [*GVI*].
—— Biblia Hebraica (and Hebrew title), ed. 1, 1905–06 ; ed. 3, ed. Alt, Eissfeldt ; Kahle ed. Masoretic text ; Kings by Kittel, Noth, 1934 (see Int. *infra*, §2) ; 1929–37 [*BH*].
KLOSTERMANN, A. : Die Bücher Samuelis u. der Könige, in Strack and Zöckler, Kgf. Kommentar, 1887.
—— see Eusebius, Origen.
KOHUT, G. A. : Jewish Studies in Memory of ; ed. S. W. Baron and A. Marx, 1935.
KOEHLER, L., and BAUMGARTNER, W. : Lexicon in Veteris Testamenti Libros, 1948 ——.
KÖNIG, E. : Historisch-kritisches Lehrgebäude der hebräischen Sprache, 2 half-vols., 1881–95.
—— Historisch-comparative Syntax der hebräischen Sprache, 1897.

KÖNIG, E. : Einleitung in das A.T., 1893.
—— Hebräisches u. aramäisches Wörterbuch zum A.T., 1910 [*HAW*].
—— Prophecy, *ERE*.
KRAELING, E. G. H. : Aram and Israel, 1918.
KRAETZSCHMAR, R. : Prophet u. Seher im alten Israel, 1901.
KUENEN, A. : Historisch-kritische Einleitung in die Bücher des A.T., tr. of ed. 2 of the Dutch, 2 vols., 1887-92.

LABAT, R. : Le caractère religieux de la royauté assyro-babylonienne, 1931.
Lachish I, see Torczyner. Lachish II, The Fosse Temple, edd. O. Tufnell, C. H. Inge, L. Harding, 1940.
DE LAGARDE, P. : Targum Chaldaice, 1872.
—— Librorum V.T. canonicorum pars prior Græce, 1883.
—— Bibliothecæ Syriacæ (posthumously completed by A. Rahlfs), 1892.
LANDERSDORFER, S. : Die Bücher der Könige, 1927.
LANE, E. W. : An Arabic-English Lexicon, 1863-93, unfinished.
LANGDON, S. H. : Mythology of All Races, vol. 5, Semitic, 1931.
À LAPIDE, C. : Commentaria in Scripturam Sacram, Editio Nova, vols. 3, 4, 1868.
Die lateinischen christlichen Schriftsteller der ersten drei Jahrhunderte, 1866 seq. [*LCS*].
LE JAY, G. M. : Biblia Sacra polyglotta, Paris, 1629-45.
LE STRANGE, G. : Palestine under the Moslems, 1890.
LEANDER, P. : see Bauer.
LEHMANN-HAUPT, C. F. : Israel, seine Entwicklung im Rahmen der Weltgeschichte, 1911.
LENORMANT, F. : Histoire ancienne de l'Orient jusqu' aux guerres médiques, ed. 9, 1881-88.
LEWY, J. : Forschungen zur alten Geschichte Vorderasiens, *MVÄG* 29, Heft 2, 1925.
LIBER, M. : Rashi, Eng. tr. by Adele Szold, 1938.
LIDDELL, H. G., and SCOTT, R. : A Greek-English Lexicon, 1882 ; new ed., by H. S. Jones, *et al*., 1925-40.
LIDZBARSKI, M. : Handbuch der nordsemitischen Epigraphik, 1898 [*HNE*].
—— Ephemeris für semitische Epigraphik, 3 vols., 1902-15 [*Eph*.].
—— Altsemitische Texte, Heft 1, Kanaanäische Inschriften, 1907 [*AT*].
—— Altaramäische Urkunden aus Assur, 1921.
LIGHTBOURNE, F. C. : The Story in the O.T., *ATR* 21 (1939), 94-102.
LIGHTFOOT, J. : The Whole Works of, ed. J. P. Pitman, 13 vols., 1822-25, vol. 2, pp. 192-303, on Kings.
LINDBLOM, J. : Zur Frage der Eigenart der alttestamentlichen Religion, in Werden und Wesen des A.T., *BZAW* 66 (1936), 128-37.

LODS, A. : L'Ange de Jahwé et " l'âme extérieure," in Marti, K., Studien zur sem. Philologie u. Religionsgeschichte, *BZAW* 27 (1914), 263-78.
—— La rôle de la tradition orale dans la formation des récits de l'Ancien Testament, *RHR* 88 (1923), 51-64.
—— La rôle des idées magiques dans la mentalité Israélite, O.T. Essays, Simpson ed.
—— La Religion d'Israël, 1939.
—— Israël : des origines au VIIIe siècle, 1930.
LÖHR, M. : see Thenius.
LUCIAN OF SAMOSATA : De Dea Syra ; text and tr., A. M. Harman, vol. 4 of Lucian, Loeb Library, 1925 ; tr. with comm., H. A. Strong and J. Garstang, The Syrian Goddess, 1913 ; tr. with notes, C. Clemen, Lukians Schrift über die syrische Göttin, *AO* 37, 3/4, 1938.
LUCIFER OF CALARIS : *CSEL*, vol. 14, ed. Hartel ; Migne, *PL*, vol. 13.
LUCKENBILL, D. D. : The Annals of Sennacherib, 1924.
—— Ancient Records of Assyria and Babylonia, 2 vols., 1926-27 [*ARA*].
LURJE, W. : Studien zur Geschichte der wirtschaftlichen u. sozialen Verhältnisse im israelitisch-jüdischen Reiche, *BZAW* 45 (1927).
VON LUSCHAN, F. : see Ausgrabungen in Sendschirli.
LYON, D. G., REISNER, G., and FISHER, C. S. : Harvard Excavations at Samaria, 2 vols., 1924.
DE LYRA, NICOLAS : Migne, *SSCC*, vol. 20, 1879 ; cf. De la Haye, Biblia Maxima, seu Lyrani, Menochii et Tirini in Danielem Annotationes.

MACALISTER, R. A. S. : The Excavation of Gezer, 3 vols., 1912.
—— A Century of Excavations in Palestine, 1925.
—— see *CAH*.
MACDONALD, D. B. : The Hebrew Literary Genius, 1933.
MADSEN, A. A. : see Curtis.
MAIMONIDES : see Capellus.
MAISLER, B. : Toledoth Eres Yisrael (History of Palestine), Tell Aviv, vol. 1, 1938.
MANDELKERN, S. : Veteris Testamenti concordantiæ Hebraicæ atque Chaldaicæ, ed. 2, 1925.
MANSON, T. W. : ed., A Companion to the Bible, 1939 (in particular the contributions by H. H. Rowley and T. H. Robinson).
MARCUS, R. : see Josephus.
MARGOLIOUTH, D. S. : The Relations between Arabs and Israelites Prior to the Rise of Islam, 1924.
MARGOLIS, M. L. : The Story of Bible Translations, 1917.
—— Notes on the New Translation of the Holy Scriptures. Edited and typewritten by H. S. Linfield, Jewish Publ. Soc. of Am., 1921 (for private circulation—of particular value for citation of Jewish commentators).
—— Hebrew Scriptures in the Making, 1922.

MASPERO, G. C. C. : The Passing of the Empires, 850 B.C. to 330 B.C., Eng. tr., 1900.
MATTHEWS, I. G. : Commentary on I and II Samuel, 1929.
—— O.T. Life and Literature, new ed., 1934.
—— The Religious Pilgrimage of Israel, 1947.
MAY, H. G. : see Graham.
MAYNARD, J. A. : Seven Years of O.T. Study, a Critical Bibliography of O.T. Research from 1917 to 1924, 1927.
McCOWN, C. C. : The Ladder of Progress in Palestine, 1943.
MCLEAN, N. : see Brooke, *OTG*.
MEEK, T. J. : Hebrew Origins, 1936; ed. 2, 1950.
MEINHOLD, J. : Einführung in das A.T., ed. 3, 1932.
MEISSNER, B. E. : Babylonien u. Assyrien, 2 vols., 1920-25.
—— Könige Babyloniens u. Assyriens, 1926.
—— see Reallexicon der Assyriologie.
MENDELSOHN, I. : Guilds in Babylonia and Assyria, *JAOS* 60 (1940), 68-72.
—— Guilds in Ancient Palestine, *BASOR* 80 (1940), 17-21.
—— State Slavery in Ancient Palestine, *BASOR* 85 (1942), 14-17.
MENES, A. : Die vorexilischen Gesetze Israels im Zusammenhang seiner kulturgeschichtlichen Entwicklung, *BZAW* 50 (1928).
MEYER, E. : Die Israeliten u. ihre Nachbarstämme, 1906 [*IN*].
—— Kleine Schriften, 1910.
—— Geschichte des Altertums, vol. 1, ed. 2 (2 half-vols.), 1907-09; vol. 2, ed. 2 (2 half-vols., the second half posthumously ed. by H. E. Stier), 1928-31 [*GA*].
—— Die kulturelle, literarische u. religiöse Entwicklung des israelitischen Volkes in der älteren Königszeit, *Sb.*, Preuss. Akad., Berlin, 1930, 66-77.
MICHAELIS, J. H. : Biblia Hebraica ex aliquot MSS., etc., Magdeburg, 1720.
MIGNE, J. P. : Patrologia Græca, 1857 *seq.* [*PG*].
—— Patrologia Latina, 1844 *seq.* [*PL*].
—— Scripturæ Sacræ cursus completus, 1866 *seq.* [*SSCC*].
Mikra'oth Gedoloth, Warsaw ed., part 8, 1874.
MÖLLER, W. : Einleitung in das A.T., 1934.
MONTGOMERY, J. A. : The Samaritans, 1907.
—— Daniel, *ICC* 1927.
—— Arabia and the Bible, 1934.
—— The Year Eponymate in the Hebrew History, *JBL* 49 (1930), 311-19.
—— Archival Data in the Book of Kings, *ib.*, 53 (1934), 46-52.
—— The Supplement at End of 3 Kingdoms 2, *ZAW* 50 (1932), 124-29.
—— and HARRIS, Z. S. : The Ras Shamra Mythological Texts, 1935 [*RSMT*].
MOORE, G. F. : Judges, *ICC* 1895.
—— Historical Literature, *EB*.
—— Die Eigenart der hebräischen Geschichtsschreibung im alttest. Zeitalter, Lehranstalt f. d. Wissenschaft des Judentums, 28. Bericht, Berlin, 1910, pp. 63 ff.
—— Literature of the O.T., 1913.

MORET, A. : Histoire de l'Orient, 2 vols., 1936.
MORGENSTERN, J. : The Three Calendars of Ancient Israel, *HUCA* I (1924), 3 ff. ; Added Notes, *ib.*, 3 (1928), 77 ff. ; Supplementary Studies, etc., *ib.*, 10 (1935), 1 ff.
—— Amos Studies, vol. 1, 1941 (collection of articles in *HUCA*, vols. 11, 12–13, 15).
MORITZ, B. : Die Könige von Edom, Muséon 50 (1937), 101–22.
MOSIMAN, S. K. : Eine Zusammenstellung u. Vergleichung der Paralleltexte der Chronik u. der älteren Bücher des A.T., 1907.
MOWINCKEL, S. : Psalmen-Studien, 6 vols., 1921–24.
—— Die vorderasiatischen Königs- u. Fürsteninschriften (Gunkel-Eucharisterion, 1, 278 ff.), 1923.
MÜLLER, C., and D. : see *FHG*.
MÜLLER, W. M. : Asien u. Europa, 1893.
—— Egyptological Researches, 3 vols., 1906–20.
MUSIL, A. : Arabia Petræa, 3 vols., 1907–08.
—— Topographical Itineraries, no. 1, The Northern Ḥeǧāz, New York, 1926.

NAVILLE, E. H. : The Text of the O.T., 1916.
NESTLE, E. : Bibelübersetzungen, *RPTK*.
NIELSEN, D., *et al.* : Handbuch der altarabischen Altertumskunde, with chapters by Hommel (History), Rhodokanakis (Polity), Grohmann (Archæology), vol. 1, 1927 [*HAA*].
NÖLDEKE, T. : Untersuchungen zur Kritik des A.T., 1869.
—— Kurzgefasste syrische Grammatik, ed. 2, 1898.
NOORDTZIJ, A. : 1 and 2 Kroniken, 1937, 1938.
NORTH, C. R. : The Religious Aspect of Hebrew Kingship, *ZAW* 50 (1932), 8–38.
—— The Old Testament Interpretation of History, 1946.
NOTH, M. : Die israelitischen Personennamen im Rahmen der gemeinsemitischen Namengebung, *BWANT* III, 10 (1928). (For the earlier literature on the subject see Einl. to the vol.) [*IP*].
—— Das System der Zwölfstämme Israels, *BWANT* IV, 1 (1930).
—— Das Buch Josua, *HAT* 1938.
—— Die Welt des A.T., 1940.
—— Überlieferungsgeschichtliche Studien I. Die sammelnden u. bearbeitenden Geschichtswerke im A.T. (Schriften der Königsberger gelehrten Gesellschaft, 18. Jahr. Geisteswissensch. Klasse, Heft 2), 1943.
—— see Kittel, *BH*.
NOWACK, W. : Lehrbuch der hebräischen Archäologie, 2 vols., 1894.

OESTERLEY, W. O. E., and ROBINSON, T. H. : Hebrew Religion, Its Origin and Development, 1930 ; ed. 2, 1937.
—— —— History of Israel, 2 vols., 1932 (vol. 1 cited as ' Robinson ') [*HI*].
—— —— An Introduction to the Books of the O.T., 1934.

OLMSTEAD, A. T. : Western Asia in the Reign of Sennacherib, Proc. Am. Hist. Assn., 1909, 94 ff.
—— Source Study and the Biblical Text, *AJSL* 30 (1913), 1-35.
—— The Earliest Book of Kings, *AJSL* 31 (1915), 169-214.
—— Assyrian Historiography, Univ. of Missouri Studies, Social Science Series, III, no. 1, 1916.
—— History of Assyria, 1923 [*HA*].
—— History of Palestine and Syria, 1931 [*HPS*].
—— Hebrew History and Historical Method, in G. L. Burr Vol., Persecution and Liberty, 1931, pp. 21 ff.
OORT, H. : Textus Hebraici emendationes, etc., 1900.
VON OPPENHEIM, M. : Der Tell Halaf, 1931.
ORIGEN : E. Klostermann, Erklärung der Samuel- u. Königsbücher, the Gr. text and tr., *GCS*, vol. 6, 1901.
—— see Field.
ORLINSKY, H. M. : Problems of Kethib-Qere, *JAOS* 60 (1940), 30-45.
—— On the Present State of Proto-Septuagint Studies, *JAOS* 61 (1941) 81-91.
OTTO, W. : Handbuch der Archäologie, vol. 1, 1939 [*HA*].

PATON, L. B. : Baal, Beal, Bel, *ERE*.
—— Phœnicians, *ib*.
PAULY, A. G., and WISSOWA, G. : Real-Encylcopädie (now Real-enzyklopädie) der classischen Altertumswissenschaft. Neue Bearbeitung, edd. W. Kroll and K. Mittelhaus (1894 ——) [*RE*].
PEAKE, A. S., ed. : The People and the Book, 1925.
PEDERSEN, J. : Israel : Its Life and Culture, I-II, 1926 ; III-IV, 1940.
—— Die Auffassung vom A.T., *ZAW* 49 (1931), 161-81.
PEET, T. E. : Egypt and the O.T., 1922.
—— A Comparative Study of the Literatures of Egypt, Palestine and Mesopotamia, 1931.
PERLES, F. : Analekten zur Textkritik des A.T., Neue Folge, 1922.
PERROT, G., and CHIPIEZ, C. : Histoire de l'art dans l'antiquité, 1882 *seq*.
PETER MARTYR (PIERRE VERMIGLI) : Malachim, id est, Regum libri duo posteriores cum commentariis, Heidelberg, 1599.
PETERS, J. P. : The O.T. and the New Scholarship, 1902.
—— Early Hebrew Story, 1904.
PETRIE, W. M. F. : History of Egypt, 6 vols., 1895-1927.
—— Ancient Palestine, 1934.
—— Palestine and Israel, Historical Notes, 1934.
PFEIFFER, R. H. : The History, Religion and Literature of Israel. Research in the O.T., 1914-25, *HTR* 27 (1934), 241-325.
—— Introduction to the O.T., 1941.
PIEPENBRING, C. : Histoire du peuple Israël, 1898.
PIETSCHMANN, R. : Geschichte der Phönizier, 1889.
PITMAN, J. P. : see Lightfoot.

VAN DER PLOEG, J. : De Litteratuur van het Oude Testament. Sociale en Economische Vraagstukken uit de Geschiedenis van Israel, Tijd der Koningen (Jaarb. Nr. 7, Ex Oriente Lux [1940], 391–99).
PLÖGER, O. : Die Prophetengeschichten der Samuel- u. Königsbücher, Greifswald Diss., 1937.
POGNON, H. : Inscriptions sémitiques de la Syrie, de la Mésopotamie et de la région de Mossoul, 1907–08.
POOLE (POLUS), M. : Synopsis criticorum aliorumque Sacræ Scripturæ interpretum et commentatorum, 5 vols., Frankfurt am Main, 1694.
PROCOPIUS : Procopii Gazæi in libros Regum et Paralipomenon scholia, ed., I. Meursius, Leiden, 1620.
PROOSDIJ, E. A. : Der sogenannte orientalische Despotismus, P. Koschaker Festschrift, vol. 2 (1939), 235 ff.

VON RAD, G. : Der Anfang der Geschichtsschreibung im A.T., Archiv f. Kulturgesch., 32 (1944), 1–42.
RAHLFS, A. : Septuaginta-Studien, Heft 1 (1904), Studien zu den Königsbüchern ; Heft 3 (1911), Lucians Rezension der Königsbücher [SS].
——— Verzeichnis der griechischen Handschriften des A.T., 1914.
——— Septuaginta, 2 vols., 1935.
——— see de Lagarde, Theodoret.
RANKE, H. : see Erman, Gressmann.
VON RANKE, L. : Weltgeschichte, 1881–88.
' RASHI ' (R. SHELOMO B. ISAAC—also ' YARCHI ') : cited from Miḳra'oth Gedoloth, and J. F. Breithaupt's tr., R. Salomonis Jarchi commentarius Hebraicus, etc., 2 vols., Gotha, 1713–14.
RAWLINSON, G. : The Five Great Monarchies of the Ancient Eastern World, ed. 2, 3 vols., 1871.
Realencyklopädie für protestantische Theologie u. Kirche, ed. 3, edd. J. J. Herzog, A. Hauck, 1896–1913 [RPTK].
Reallexicon der Assyriologie, edd. E. Ebeling and B. Meissner, vols. 1, 2, 1932–38 [RA].
Reallexicon der Vorgeschichte, ed. M. Ebert, 1924–32 [RVg.].
Record and Revelation, Essays on the O.T., ed. H. W. Robinson, contributors Eissfeldt, Elmslie, Hempel, Hooke, Lods, Lofthouse, Montefiore, Montgomery, Oesterley, Porteous, Robinson, Rowley, Snaith, Wardle, 1938.
REHM, M. : Textkritische Untersuchungen zu den Parallelstellen der Samuel-Königsbücher u. der Chronik, 1937.
REISNER, G. A. : see Lyon.
Religion in Geschichte u. Gegenwart, edd. H. Gunkel and L. Zscharnack, ed. 2, 1927–31 (5 vols., +Registerband) [RGG].
RENAN, E. : Mission en Phénicie, 1864.
REUSS, E. : Das Alte Testament, 1892.
RHODOKANAKIS, N. : Studien zur Lexicographie u. Grammatik des Altsüdarabischen, Sb., Vienna Academy, 1915, 1917, 1931.
——— see Gressmann, ATB.
——— see Nielsen, HAA.

BIBLIOGRAPHY

RICCIOTTI, G. : Histoire d'Israël, vol. 1, Des origines à l'Exil, French tr., 1939.
ROBINSON, E., and SMITH, E. : Biblical Researches in Palestine, Mount Sinai and Arabia Petræa ... in the Year 1838, 3 vols., 1841 [*BR*].
—— Later Biblical Researches in Palestine and in the Adjacent Regions ... in the Year 1852, 1856 [*LBR*].
ROBINSON, G. L. : Sarcophagus of an Ancient Civilization, 1930.
ROBINSON, H. W. : The History of Israel : Its Facts and Factors, 1938.
ROBINSON, T. H. : Decline and Fall of the Hebrew Kingdoms, 1926.
—— HUNKIN, J. W., and BURKITT, F. C. : Palestine in General History, 1929.
ROBINSON, T. H. : Some Economic and Social Factors in the History of Israel, Exp. Times, 45 (1934), 264–9, 294–300.
—— see Oesterley and Robinson.
ROGERS, R. W. : Cuneiform Parallels to the O.T., 1912 [*CP*].
—— History of Babylonia and Assyria, ed. 6, 2 vols., 1915 [*HBA*].
ROSENTHAL, F. : Die aramaistische Forschung seit Th. Nöldeke's Veröffentlichungen, 1939.
DE ROSSI, J. B. : Variæ lectiones Veteris Testamenti, 4 vols., Parma, 1784–88.
—— Scholia critica in V.T. libros, seu supplementa, etc., Parma, 1798.
ROST, L. : Weidewechsel u. altisraelitischer Festkalender, *ZDPV* 66 (1943), 205–16.
ROSTOVTZEFF, M. I. : A History of the Ancient World, 2 vols., 1926–30
—— see Baur.
ROTHSTEIN, J. W., and HÄNEL, J. : Komm. zum ersten Buch der Chronik, *KmAT*, 2 vols., 1927.
RYCKMANS, G. : Les noms propres sud-sémitiques, 3 vols., Louvain, 1934–35 [*NPS*].
RYLE, H. E. : The Canon of the O.T., ed. 2, 1904.

SABATIER, P. : Bibliorum Sacrorum Latinæ versiones antiquæ seu vetus Italica, 3 vols., 1751.
SACHAU, E. : Aramäische Papyrus u. Ostraka aus einer jüdischen Militär-Kolonie zu Elephantine, 1911 [*APO*].
—— see Ausgrabungen in Sendschirli.
ŠANDA, A. : Untersuchungen zur Kunde des alten Orients, *MVG* 1902, part 2.
—— Die Bücher der Könige, 2 vols., 1911–12.
SCHIFFER, S. : Die Aramäer, 1911.
SCHLATTER, A. : Zur Topographie u. Geschichte Palästinas, 1893.
SCHLEUSNER, J. F. : Novus thesaurus philologico-criticus sive lexicon in LXX, etc., 5 vols., 1820–21.
SCHLÖGL, N. : Die Bücher der Könige u. die Bücher der Chronik, 1911.
SCHMIDT, H. : Die Geschichtsschreibung im A.T., 1911.
SCHNABEL, P. : see Berossos.

SCHOENE, A. : see Eusebius.
SCHOFF, W. H. : The Periplus of the Erythræan Sea, 1912.
SCHOFIELD, J. N. : The Historical Background of the Bible, 1938.
SCHRADER, E. : Keilinschriften u. Geschichtsforschung, 1878.
—— Die Keilinschriften u. das A.T., ed. 2, 1883=Eng. tr. by O. C. Whitehouse, Cuneiform Inscriptions and the O.T., 2 vols., 1885-88 [*CIOT*].
—— ed. 3, edd. H. Zimmern and H. Winckler, 1902 [*KAT*].
—— Keilinschriftliche Bibliothek, 6 vols., 1889-1915 [*KB*].
SCHÜRER, E. : Geschichte des jüdischen Volkes, 3 vols., ed. 4, 1901-09 [*GJV*].
SCHWALLY, F. : see Stade, *SBOT*.
SEELIGMANN, J. : Problemen en Perspectieven in het Moderne Septuaginta-Onderzoek (Jaarb. Nr. 7, Ex Oriente Lux [1940], 359-390e).
SELDEN, J. : De dis Syris syntagmata, ed. 2, with Additamenta by M. A. Beyer, Leipzig, 1672.
SELLIN, E. : Tell Ta'annek, 1904.
—— Geschichte des israel.-jüdischen Volkes, 2 parts., 1924-32.
—— Einleitung in das A.T., ed. 7, 1935. Eng. tr. by W. Montgomery Introduction to the O.T., 1923.
SHOTWELL, J. T. : Introduction to the History of History, 1922.
—— revised ed. of above, The History of History, vol. 1, 1939.
SIMONS, J. : Handbook for the Study of Egyptian Topographical Lists relating to Western Asia, Leiden, 1937.
SIMPSON, D. C. : ed., O.T. Essays, 1927.
SINGER, C. : see Bevan.
SKINNER, J. : Genesis, *ICC* 1910.
—— Kings (Century Bible), n.d. (*ca.* 1893).
SKOSS, S. L. : see al-Fāsī.
SLOET, D. A. W. H. : Kings, Third and Fourth Book of, *Catholic Encylopædia*, 1910.
SLOUSCH, N. : Representative Government among the Hebrews and Phœnicians, *JQR*, N.S., 4 (1913-14), 303-10.
SMEND, R. : Lehrbuch der alttest. Religionsgeschichte, ed. 2, 1899.
SMITH, G. A. : The Historical Geography of the Holy Land, ed. 25, London, 1931 [*HG*].
—— Jerusalem, 2 vols., 1908.
SMITH, H. P. : Samuel, *ICC* 1899.
SMITH, SIDNEY : Babylonian Historical Texts, 1924.
—— see *CAH*.
SMITH, W. R. : The Prophets of Israel, 1882.
—— Lectures on the Religion of the Semites, 1889 ; ed. 3, 1927.
—— The O.T. in the Jewish Church, ed. 2, 1892.
—— Kings, *Enc. Br.*⁹.
—— and KAUTZSCH, E. : Kings, *EB*.
SOPHOCLES, E. P. : Greek Lexicon of the Roman and Byzantine Periods, 1870.

SPERBER, A. : Hebrew based upon Greek and Latin Transliterations. *HUCA* 12–13 (1938), 103 ff.
—— Hebrew based upon Biblical Passages in Parallel Transmission, *ib.*, 14 (1939), 153 ff.
STADE, B. : Lehrbuch der hebräischen Grammatik, 1879.
—— Der Text des Berichtes über Salomos Bauten, 1 Kö. 5–7 (with bibliog.), *ZAW* 3 (1883), 129–77 ; Anmerkungen zu 2 Kö. 10–14, *ib.*, 5 (1885), 275–97 ; Anmerkungen zu 2 Kö. 15–21, *ib.*, 6 (1886), 156–89 ; these articles collected in his Ausgewählte akademische Reden, 1899, from which citation below is made.
—— Geschichte des Volkes Israel, 2 vols., 1887–88 [*GVI*].
—— and SCHWALLY, F., with Notes by P. HAUPT : The Book of Kings, Critical Edition . . . Printed in Colours, etc., 1904, in Haupt's series, The Sacred Books of the O.T. [*SBOT*].
STEUERNAGEL, C. : Lehrbuch der Einleitung in das A.T., 1912.
STRACK, H. : Einleitung in das A.T., ed. 4, 1895, ed. 6, 1906.
STRECK, M. : Älteste Geschichte der Aramäer, Klio, vi, 2 (1906), 193 ff.
STRONG, H. A. : see Lucian.
SULZBERGER, M. : The Am Ha-Aretz : the Ancient Hebrew Parliament, 1909, reprint 1910.
SWETE, H. B. : The O.T. in Greek, 3 vols., 1909–22.
—— An Introduction to the O.T. in Greek, 1914.

TAYLOR, C. : see Burkitt.
Texte u. Untersuchungen zur Geschichte der alttestamentlichen Literatur, 2nd series, 1897 seq [*TU*].
Texts and Studies, Cambridge, 1891 seq. [*TS*].
THACKERAY, H. ST. J. : The Septuagint and Jewish Worship, 1921.
—— Josephus, the Man and the Historian, 1929.
—— see Brooke, Josephus.
THAYER, J. B. : A Greek-English Lexicon of the N.T., 1887.
THENIUS, O. : Die Bücher der Könige, ed. 2, 1873 ; ed. 3, ed. M. Löhr, 1898.
THEODORET : Theodorets Zitate aus den Königsbüchern u. dem 2. Buche der Chronik, *SS* 1, 16–46.
THOMPSON, J. E. H. : The Samaritans, 1919.
THOMPSON, R. C. : see *CAH*.
THOMSEN, P. : Kompendium der palästinischen Altertumskunde, 1913.
—— Palästina u. seine Kultur, ed. 3, 1931.
—— Die Palästina-Literatur, 5 vols., 1895–1938.
TISCHENDORF, C. : see Heyse.
TODD, J. C. : Politics and Religion in Ancient Israel, 1904.
TORCZYNER, H., collaborators L. HARDING, A. LEWIS, and J. L. STARKEY : Lachish I, The Lachish Letters, 1937 [*LL*].
—— The Lachish Ostraca (in Hebrew with Hebrew title, with additional ostraca), Jerusalem, 1940.

TORREY, C. C. : New Notes on Old Inscriptions, *ZA* 26 (1912), 77–92.
—— Pseudo-Ezekiel and the Original Prophecy, 1930.
TOYNBEE, A. J. : A Study of History, 6 vols., 1934–39.
TOZER, H. F. : History of Ancient Geography, ed. 2, 1935.
TUFNELL, O. : see Lachish II.

UNGNAD, A. : Die Zahl der von Sanherib deportierten Judäer., *ZAW* 59 (1943), 199–202.

VANUTELLI, P. : Libri synoptici Veteris Testamenti seu librorum Regum et Chronicorum loci paralleli, 2 vols., Rome, 1931–34.
VATKE, W. : Historisch-kritische Einleitung in das A.T., 1886.
VIGOUROUX, F. : Dictionnaire de la Bible, 5 vols., 1895–1912 ; Supplément, vols. 1–3, 1928–38 (unfinished) [*DB*].
VINCENT, H. : Jérusalem, vol. 1, Jér. Antique, 1912, vol. 2, Jér. Nouvelle, 1926.
—— La religion des judéo-araméens d'Éléphantiné, 1937.
VOLCK, W. : Könige, *RPTK*.
VOLZ, P. : Der Geist Gottes u. die verwandten Erscheinungen im A.T. u. im anschliessenden Judentum, 1910.
—— Die biblischen Altertümer, ed. 2, 1925.

WAHRMUND, A. : Hwb. der arabischen u. deutschen Sprache, ed. 3, 1897–98.
WALTON, BRIAN : Biblia Polyglotta, 6 vols., London, 1657 (see his introductory studies, 1, 1–122) [*LP*].
—— Biblicus apparatus chronologico-topographico-philosophicus, Zürich, 1672.
WARDLE, W. L. : The History and Religion of Israel, 1936.
WATZINGER, C. : Denkmäler Palästinas, 2 vols., 1933–35 [*DP*].
WEBER, O. : Die Literatur der Babylonier u. Assyrer, 1907.
WEIDNER, E. E. : Die Könige von Assyrien, *MVÄG*, 1921.
WEILL, R. : La cité de David : compte rendu . . . campagne de 1913–14, with atlas of plates, 1920.
WEISER, A. : Glaube u. Geschichte im A.T., *BWANT* IV, 4 (1931).
—— Die theologische Aufgabe der alttestamentlichen Wissenschaft, in Werden und Wesen des A.T., *BZAW* 66 (1936), 207–24.
—— Einleitung in das A.T., 1939.
WELCH, A. C. : The Work of the Chronicler, 1939.
WELLHAUSEN, J. : Israel, *Enc. Br.*[9].
—— Skizzen u. Vorarbeiten, 6 vols., 1884–99 ; vol. 1, Abriss der Geschichte Israels u. Judas, vol. 3, Reste arabischen Heidentums.
—— Prolegomena zur Geschichte Israels, ed. 3, 1886 (ed. 6, 1905) [*Proleg.*].
—— Die Composition des Hexateuchs u. der historischen Bücher des A.T., ed. 3, 1899 ; pp. 263–301 on Kings=Bleek, Einl.[4], 231–67 [*Comp.*].
—— Israelitische u. jüdische Geschichte, ed. 4, 1901 (also edd. 1904, 1914) [*Gesch.*].

WEVERS, J. W. : Double Readings in the Books of Kings, *JBL* 65 (1946), 307–10.
WIENER, H. M. : The Composition of Judges II. 11 to 1 Kings II. 46, Leipzig, 1929.
—— The Altars of the O.T., *Olz.*, Beigabe, 1927.
—— Posthumous Essays, 1932.
WINCKLER, H. : Untersuchungen zu altorientalischer Geschichte, 1889.
——Beiträge zur Quellenscheidung der Königsbücher, in Alttestamentliche Untersuchungen, 1892, pp. 1–54.
—— Keilinschriftliches Textbuch zum A.T., 1892; ed. 3, 1909 [*KTAT*].
—— Altorientalische Forschungen, 1893–1906.
—— Geschichte Israels in Einzeldarstellungen, 1895–1900 [*GI*].
—— see Schrader, *KAT*.
WRIGHT, G. E., and FILSON, F. V. : The Westminster Historical Atlas to the Bible, 1945.
WRIGHT, T. : Early Travels in Palestine, 1848.
WRIGHT, W. : A Grammar of the Arabic Language, ed. 3, edd. W. R. Smith and M. J. de Goeje, 2 vols., 1933.
WÜRTHWEIN, S. E. : Der 'amm ha'arez im A.T., *BWANT* IV, 17 (1936).
WUTZ, F. : see Eusebius Pamphili.

ZIMMERMANN, F. : The Perpetuation of Variants in the Masoretic Text, *JQR* 34 (1944), 459–74.
ZIMMERN, H. : see Schrader, *KAT*.
ZORELL, P.: Lexicon Hebraicum et Aramaicum V.T., Rome, 1940 ——.
ZSCHERNACK, L. : see Religion in Geschichte u. Gegenwart.

MODERN BIBLE TRANSLATIONS

ENGLISH

King James Bible (' Authorized Version '), 1611, current text [AV].
Revised Version, 1885 [RV].
American Revised Version (' Standard Version '), 1901 [RV^{Am}].
The Holy Scriptures, Jewish Publ. Soc. of America, 1917 [JV].
The Holy Bible . . . a New Translation, by James Moffatt, New York, 1922 [Moff.].
The Bible, an American Translation, O.T. ed. J. M. P. Smith Ki. tr. by L. Waterman ; Chicago, 1931 [Chic. B.].

FRENCH

Ed. by J. E. Ostervald, ed. 3, Bienne and Neuchatel, 1771 [FV].

GERMAN

Luther's tr., current text [GV].

LATIN

O.T. by E. Tremellius and F. Junius, N.T. by T. Beza, Zürich, 1673.

In this book the chapter divisions and verse-numberings are those of JV, which follows the system of all Hebrew prints. The variations of numbering are given in the margin of the RVV.

CHRONOLOGY

See Int., §16.

CARTOGRAPHY

In addition to the Palestine Exploration Fund Map of Western Palestine (1882), and the PEF Map of Palestine (1898), the Department of Lands and Surveys of Palestine has now published 14 sheets of Palestine, west of the Jordan, stretching northward from Beersheba to the Syrian frontier. The Palestine Survey has published a convenient folding pocket map, *Palestine of the O.T.* (print of 1938). In addition are to be noted the maps in G. A. Smith, *HG*, and his *Historical Atlas of the Holy Land* (ed. 2, 1936), and the rich collection in Abel, *GP* ; *cf.* also the ' Map of the Principal Excavated Sites of Palestine,' *PEQ* 1932, opp. 220. For Syria there are the detailed maps in Dussaud, *TH*. *N.b.* the very useful ' Baedekers ' for these lands. For the Bible Lands at arge are to be noted Guthe's *Bibelatlas*, ed. 2, Leipzig, 1926, the map in the *National Geographic Magazine*, Dec. 1938, the Maps of Bible Lands published by the American Bible Society for inclusion in its edition of the Bible, edited by J. O. Boyd and W. F. Albright, 1939, and the maps in *The Westminster Historical Atlas to the Bible*, edited by G. E. Wright and F. V. Filson, Philadelphia, 1945.

INSCRIPTIONS, EPIGRAPHS, ETC., COMMONLY CITED

PALESTINE
  The Moabite Stone (Mesha stele) : see Comm., II. $3^{4\text{ff.}}$, n. 1.
  The Siloam inscription : see Comm., II. 20^{20}.
  The tablet material : see Diringer, *IAE*, Torczyner's volumes.

PHŒNICIA
  Byblos
    Ahiram inscr. : Dussaud, Syria, 1924, 135 ff. ; Torrey, *JAOS* 46 (1926), 237 ff.
    Yehaumilk : *CIS* I, no. 1 ; *HNE* 416 ; *NSI* no. 3 ; *AT* no. 5.
  Sidon
    Tabnith inscr. : *HNE* 417 ; *NSI* no. 4 ; *AT* no. 6.
    Eshmunazar inscr. : *CIS* I, no. 3 ; *HNE* 417 ; *NSI* no. 5 ; *AT* no. 7.

SYRIA
  Āfiṣ (near Aleppo)
    Zakar inscr. : Pognon, *Inscr. sém.*, no. 86 ; *Eph.*, 3, 1 ff. ; *CAH* 3, 375 ; *ATB* 1, 443.
  Senjirli
    The Hadad, Panammuwa, Bar-Rkb inscriptions : *Ausgrabungen in Sendschirli*, vol. 1, parts 3, 4 ; *HNE* 440 ff. ; *NSI* nos. 61–63.
    Kilammuwa inscr. : *Ausgrabungen in Sendschirli*, vol. 4, 374 ; E. Littmann, *Sb.*, Berlin Academy, 45 (1911), 976 ; *Eph.*, 3, 218 ; Torrey, *JAOS* 1935, 364.
  Sūjīn (Sefîreh) : see Comm., I. 18, n. 1.
  Ugarit (Ras Shamra) : the texts published by C. Virolleaud, in *Syria*, 1929 seq., and subsequent vols., *Danel*, *Keret*, 1936 and in *Rev. d'Ass.*, 1940–41. Compendia with introductions, glossaries, etc. : Montgomery and Harris, *RSMT* 1935 ; H. L. Ginsberg, *The Ugarit Texts* (in Hebrew), Jerusalem, 1936 ; H. Bauer, *Die alphabetischen Keilschrifttexte von Ras Schamra*, 1936 ; D. Nielsen, *Ras Šamra Mythologie u. biblische Theologie*, Abh. xxi, 4 (1936) of the Deutsche Morgenl. Gesellschaft ; C. F. A. Schaeffer, *The Cuneiform Texts of Ras Shamra-Ugarit*, Schweich Lectures (1939), and *Ugaritica* (Paris, 1939), a full bibliography ; C. H. Gordon, *Ugaritic Grammar*, Rome, 1940. In the meanwhile Prof. Gordon has published a more extensive work, *Ugaritic Handbook :* I. Revised Grammar, Paradigms ; II. Texts in Transliteration ; III. Comprehensive Glossary, Rome, 1947.

AKKADIAN TEXTS

Amarna tablets: J. A. Knudtzon, *Die el-Amarna Tafeln*, 1915; S. A. B. Mercer, *The Tell el-Amarna Tablets*, 2 vols., 1939.

Assyrian Eponym List: *KB* 1, 204; *CP* 219; *ARA* 2, 427; Olmstead, 'The Ass. Chronicle,' *AJSL* 34, 344.

Babylonian Chronicles: see Int., §16, n. 3.

Babylonian King Lists: *KB* 1, 286; *CP* 201.

Synchronistic History (early Babylonian-Assyrian): *KB* 1, 194.

PTOLEMAIC CANON

KB 2, 290; *CP* 239.

KEY TO ABBREVIATIONS

Omitted are abbreviations for Biblical books, grammatical and commonplace abbreviations.

AASOR : Annual of American Schools of Oriental Research.
AB : see Barton.
Abh. : Abhandlung(en).
Acta Or. : Acta Orientalia.
AfO : Archiv für Orientforschung.
AfR : Archiv für Religionswissenschaft.
AHNE : see R. H. Hall.
AHR : American Historical Review.
AJA : American Journal of Archæology.
AJSL : American Journal of Semitic Languages and Literatures.
AJT : American Journal of Theology.
AKAT : see Jirku.
Akk. : Akkadian.
Albr. : Albright.
Ant. : Josephus, Antiquities.
AO : der alte Orient.
Aq. : Aquila.
ARA : see Luckenbill.
Arab. : Arabic.
Aram. : Aramaic.
Arch. : Archæology.
Arch. Or. : Archiv Orientální.
ARE : see Breasted.
Arm. : Armenian.
art(s.) : article(s).
ARw : Archiv für Religionswissenschaft.
Ass. : Assyrian.
ast. : asterisk (Eusebian).
AT : see Lidzbarski
A.T. : Altes Testament.
ATB : see Gressmann.

ATLAO : see Jeremias.
ATR : Anglican Theological Review.
AV : Authorized Version.

Bab. : Babylonian.
BA : Biblical Archæologist.
BASOR : Bulletin of American Schools of Oriental Research.
BDB : see Brown-Driver-Briggs.
BDD : Bible Dictionaries.
Benz. : Benzinger.
Bergstr. : Bergsträsser.
BH : Kittel, BH^3.
BJ : Josephus, Bellum Judaicum.
BL : see Bauer-Leander.
BL : Biblisches Lexicon.
BR : see Galling.
Brock. : Brockelmann.
Burn. : Burney.
BWA(N)T : Beiträge zur Wissenschaft vom A.(u. N.)T.
BZAW : Beihefte to ZAW.

CAH : Cambridge Ancient History.
C.Ap. : Josephus, Contra Apicnem.
Chic. B. : Chicago Bible.
Chr.-Pal. : Christian-Palestinian (dialect).
CIOT : see Schrader.
CIS : Corpus inscriptionum Semiticarum.
Comm. : main text of this Commentary.
comm. : commentator(s), commentary, -ies.
CP : see Rogers.

KEY TO ABBREVIATIONS

CR : Comptes Rendus, Académie des Inscriptions et Belles-Lettres, Paris.
CSCO : Corpus script. Christ. Orient.
CSEG : Corpus script. eccles. Græc.
CSEL : Corpus script. eccles. Lat.
CT : Cuneiform Texts . . . British Museum (1896 seq.).

DB : Hastings, Dictionary of the Bible.
DCB : Dictionary of Christian Biography.
deR. : de Rossi.
dittog. : dittograph(y).
Dr. : S. R. Driver.
DZG : Deutsche Zeitschrift für Geschichtsforschung.

EB : Encyclopædia Biblica.
ed., edd. : editor(s), edition(s).
Ehrl. : Ehrlich.
Eissf. : Eissfeldt.
Enc. Br. : Encyclopædia Britannica.
Eph. : see Lidzbarski.
ERE : Encyclopædia of Religion and Ethics.
Eth. : Ethiopic.
Eus. : Eusebius.
EVV : English Versions, AV, RVV.
Ew. : Ewald.

FHG : Fragmenta historicorum Græcorum.
FuF : Forschungen u. Fortschritte.
FV : French Version.

GB : see Gesenius-Buhl.
GCS : Die griechischen christlichen Schriftsteller der ersten drei Jahrhunderte.
Ges. : Gesenius.
Ginsb. : Ginsburg.
GK : see Gesenius-Kautzsch.

Gr., Grr. : Greek, Greek texts.
Gr. : Grammar, Grammatik.
Gressm. : Gressmann.
GV : German Version.

HA : Handbuch der Altertumswissenschaft.
HAA : see Nielsen.
haplog. : haplograph(y).
HAT : Handbuch zum A.T., ed. Eissfeldt.
Heb. : Hebrew.
Her. : Herodotus.
Hex. : Hexapla, Hexaplaric.
HkAT : Handkommentar zum A.T., ed. W. Nowack.
homoiotel. : homoioteleuton.
HNE : see Lidzbarski.
HP : see Holmes-Parsons.
HSAT : see Kautzsch.
HTR : Harvard Theological Review.
HTS : Harvard Theological Studies.
HUCA : Hebrew Union College Annual.
Hwb. : Handwörterbuch.

IAE : see Diringer.
ICC : International Critical Commentary.
ILN : Illustrated London News.

JAOS : Journal of the American Oriental Society.
JBL : Journal of Biblical Literature.
JDT : Jahrbuch für deutsche Theologie.
JE : Jewish Encyclopædia.
JNES : Journal of Near Eastern Studies (continuation of AJSL).
Jos. : Josephus.
JPOS : Journal of the Palestine Oriental Society.
JPT : Jahrbücher für protestantische Theologie.
JQR : Jewish Quarterly Review.
JR : Journal of Religion.

KEY TO ABBREVIATIONS

JSOR : Journal of the Society for Oriental Research.
JTS : Journal of Theological Studies.
JV : Jewish Version.

Kamph : Kamphausen.
KAT, KB : see Schrader.
Ken. : Kennicott.
Ki. : Kings.
Kit. : Kittel.
Klost. : Klostermann.
KmAT : Kommentar zum A.T., ed. E. Sellin.
Ḳr. : Ḳrê.
Kt. : Kethîb.

Lat. : Latin.
LCS : Die lateinischen christlichen Schriftsteller der drei ersten Jahrhunderte.
Lex(x) : Lexicon, -a.
LHeb. : Late Hebrew.
Lidzb. : Lidzbarski.
LP : Walton's London Polyglot.
Luc. : Lucian.
Lucif. : Lucifer of Calaris.

Mas. : Masora, -etic.
Meinh. : Meinhold.
Mél. : Mélanges de la Faculté Orientale, Université Saint Joseph, Beyrouth.
MGWJ : Monatschrift für Geschichte u. Wissenschaft des Judentums.
Mich. : Michaelis's Hebrew text.
minusc. : minuscule(s).
MNDPV : Mittheilungen u. Nachrichten des Deutschen Palästina-Vereins.
Moff. : Moffatt's Bible.
Montg. : Montgomery.
MS., MSS. : manuscript(s).
MVÄG : Mitteilungen der Vorderasiatisch-Ägyptischen Gesellschaft (continuing *MVG*).
MVG : Mitteilungen der Vorderasiatischen Gesellschaft.

Nab. : Nabatæan.
NHeb. : New (post-Biblical) Hebrew.
Nöld. : Nöldeke.
NPS : see Ryckmans.
NSI : see Cooke.
N.T. : New Testament, Neues Testament.

OArab. : Old Arabic.
OAram. : Old Aramaic.
obel. : obelisk (Eusebian).
Oc. : Occidental tradition of the Hebrew text.
OGr. : the ' Septuagintal ' text.
OGrr. : the above and the Lucianic text.
OLat. : Old Latin.
OLz. : Orientalistische Literaturzeitung.
Onom. Gr./Lat. : Onomasticon Græcum/Latinum ; see Eusebius.
Or. : Oriental tradition of the Hebrew text.
Or. Inst. Publ. : Oriental Institute Publications, University of Chicago.
O.T. : Old Testament.
OTG : see Brooke.

Palm. : Palmyrene.
PEF : Palestine Exploration Fund.
PEQ : Palestine Exploration Quarterly (continuing *QS* since 1936).
PG : Migne, Patrologia Græca.
Phœn. : Phœnician.
Pjb. : Palästinajahrbuch.
PL : Migne, Patrologia Latina.
PSBA : Proceedings of the Society of Biblical Archæology.

QS : Quarterly Statement of the Palestine Exploration Fund.

RA : Reallexicon der Assyriologie.

RB : Revue Biblique.
rdg(s.) : reading(s).
RE : see Pauly-Wissowa.
reff. : references.
REJ : Revue des Études Juifs.
resp. : respectively.
Rev. d'Ass. : Revue d'Assyriologie.
RGG : Religion in Geschichte u. Gegenwart, ed. 2.
RHR : Revue de l'Histoire des Religions.
RPTK : Realencyklopädie für Protestantische Theologie u. Kirche.
RS : Revue Sémitique.
RSMT : see Montgomery and Harris.
RV : British Revised Version of English Bible ; RV^{Am} the American Revision ; RVV these and JV together, unless exception is made.
RVg. : Reallexicon der Vorgeschichte.

S. Arab. : South Arabic.
SAT : Die Schriften des A.T. in Auswahl (1921-25).
Sb. : Sitzungsberichte, Philos.-hist. Klasse, of the Academy named.
SBOT : see Stade.
Sk. : Skinner.
SOT : see Kent.
SS : Septuaginta-Studien, A. Rahlfs.
St. : Stade.
sugg. : suggest(s).

suppl. : supply, -ies.
supplem. : supplement.
Sym. : Symmachus.
Syr. : Syriac.

Targ. : Targum.
Then. : Thenius.
Theod. : Theodotion.
Th. R. : Theologische Rundschau.
Tisch. : Tischendorf's ed. of Vulgate.
tr., trr. : translator(s), translation(s).
TS : Texts and Studies.
TSK : Theologische Studien und Kritiken.
TU : Texte u. Untersuchungen.

var(r.) : variant(s).
vs. : *versus.*
VS, VSS : Version(s), ancient.
V.T. : Vetus Testamentum.

Watz. : Watzinger.
Wb. : Wörterbuch.
WDB : Westminster Dictionary of the Bible.
Wellh. : Wellhausen.

ZA : Zts. für Assyriologie.
ZAW : Zts. für die alttestamentliche Wissenschaft.
ZDMG : Zts. der Deutschen Morgenländischen Gesellschaft.
ZDPV : Zts. des Deutschen Palästina-Vereins.
ZfS : Zts. für Semitik.
Zts. : Zeitschrift.
ZWT : Zts. für wissenschaftliche Theologie.

SYMBOLS IN CRITICAL APPARATUS

𝔄 : Arabic VS.
ℭ : Coptic VS.
𝔈 : Ethiopic VS.
𝔊 : Old Greek (' Septuagint ').
𝔊ᴸ : the Lucianic Greek.
𝔊ᴴ : the Hexaplaric Greek.
𝔥 : the Hebrew text.
𝔏 : Old Latin texts.

𝔐 : Masoretic apparatus of 𝔥 ; 𝔐ᴼᶜ, 𝔐ᴼʳ, the Occidental, Oriental forms respectively.
𝔓 : Palestinian Aramaic.
𝔖 : Syriac VS (Peshitta).
𝔖ᴴ : the Syro-Hexapla.
𝔗 : Targum ; 𝔗ᴸ, de Lagarde's ed. ; 𝔗ᵂ, Walton's ed.
𝔙 : Vulgate.

The following symbols are also used :

† indicates that all the cases in the Hebrew Bible are cited.
+ a critical plus.
‖ parallelism.
⟩ etymological process toward.
⟨ etymological process from.
[ ] in the translation has bearing on the text of 𝔥 ; ( ) expresses an interpretative addition.
※ as asterized plus in the Hexapla.
÷ an obelized minus in the Hexapla.

INTRODUCTION

I. THE BOOK

§1. PLACE IN THE CANON AS A DISTINCT BOOK; CONTENTS

Kings is one of 'the Twenty-Four Books,' constituting the sacred canon of the Jews, and the fourth book of the Former Prophets.[1] It is a continuation of the book of Samuel, but without clearly marked literary distinction. For the mechanical history of Sam.-Ki. must be postulated a series of rolls, which were divided for arbitrary convenience. In the Hebrew division Sam. and Ki. are of almost equal length, in Bär's edition of respectively 91 and 93 pages. The Greek scribes with their smaller quires went further, and equally for convenience produced four volumes with the title, αἱ βασιλεῖαι, generally translated, 'The Kingdoms,' but Thackeray has observed (p. 263) that, following Hellenistic use, the Greek should be translated 'The Reigns.' There is variation as to the joint between Sam. and Ki. in the Greek texts, although there the major tradition followed the distinction of the Hebrew Bible. However, Lucian found another division, after I. 2^{11}, with the actual termination of David's reign, which for historiography might be preferred. And Josephus begins bk. viii of his *Antiquities* at this point. But there is evidence for yet another division in the early Greek; after I. 2^{46a} some supplementary material is collected, evidently assembled there at the end of a tome (*v. ad loc.*). Indeed, after Hebrew syntax, a fresh section begins with the ensuing clause, "the kingdom being established in Solomon's hand." *Cf.* also remarks below on the literary 'break' in the Greek in $4^{20\text{ff.}}$.[2]

[1] According to the Talmud, *Baba Bathra*, 15a, Jeremiah was the author of 'his own book and the book of Kings and Lamentations.'

[2] Thackeray in his 'Greek Translators of the Four Books of Kings' and in his *Septuagint and Jewish Worship* contends stoutly for Lucian's division between 2 and 3 Kgdms as original, also basing his argument

The Greek collocation of Sam.-Ki. as one book with its division into four volumes was followed by all the ancient Versions. The Greek title as of 'The Kingdoms' appeared in early titles of the Latin Bible; the Arabic as well as the Ethiopic followed the Hebrew with 'Kings'; the Syriac used both titles, varying with the books. In the Latin Bible 'Kings' came into current use; but this version preserved also a second titulation for 1 and 2 Ki. as 'secundum Hebræos primus/secundus Malachim,' *i.e.*, with transliteration of the Hebrew title.[3] With the revival of learning in the Western Church and the direct translations from the Hebrew the distinction between Sam. and Ki. was established, with, however, the continuance of the Greek division of each book into two halves. This distinction has been accepted in all Christian prints of the Bible, except in Ginsburg's and Kittel's editions, as it is also noted marginally in Jewish prints, *e.g.*, in the encyclopædic Miḳra'oth Gedoloth. For this division see Burney on II. 1[1].

The book continues that of Samuel with the history of the regency and reign of Solomon, records the disruption of North and South under his son, pursues in artfully articulated fashion the parallel histories of the two kingdoms, with a rich treasury of historical stories from the North, and finally centres on the surviving kingdom of the South, until at last, with the original conclusion of the book (II. 25^{21b}), "Judah went into exile away from its land." One recalls Polybius's drama of the end of Greece before Rome, and, closer to the theme, Josephus's *Antiquities* of his people, after their second ruin as a nation. But this work, compilation as it is of many and various sources, precedes those others in antiquity and with a faith they did not possess. For the editors, that history was worthy of record because it was guided by the hand of God, contradicted as he was by his own people. There was latent the belief that his

on the almost exact equality of the parts of Codex B for 1 Kgdms and 2 Kgdms–3 Kgdms 2[11]. But Rahlfs takes positive position against Thackeray (*SS* 3, 186 ff.). In any case such divisions were primarily practical. *Cf.* the awkward opening of 2 Ki. with the fragmentary item, "And Moab rebelled against Israel after the death of Ahab."

[3] *Cf.* Jerome's observation in his Prologus Galeatus (Tischendorf's ed. of the Vulgate, p. xxvii): "Melius multo est Malachim, id est, Regum, quam Mamlachot, id est, Regnorum, dicere."

purpose would continue for the future, and such a postscript of hope was early added to the book, after II. 25^{26}.[4]

§2. TEXT AND LANGUAGE

The basic text here used is that of the third edition of Kittel's *Biblia Hebraica* (*BH*), the editorship of which was notably continued after that distinguished scholar's death in 1929, appearing in parts, 1929–37 (see Bibliography). Its unique merit lies in the reproduction of a single manuscript, and that the oldest accessible one, the manuscript in the Public Library of Leningrad (MS L). This is a pure representative of the family of Ben Asher, as distinguished from the hitherto printed texts which contain traditions of Ben Naphtali; these texts follow Jacob Chayyim's Bomberg Bible of 1524–25, itself repeated by Kittel in the earlier editions.[1]

As against the common tacit assumption of a fixed *textus receptus* of the Hebrew Bible the Notes in this Commentary cite constantly by way of example the various readings of the editions of Michaelis, Kennicott (his upper text), Bär, and the two of Ginsburg. For the thesaurus of variant texts recourse must still be taken primarily to Kennicott's *V.T. Hebraicum*, and to the invaluable critical digest of the material, along with collation of a large number of MSS of his own collation, by de Rossi (Kennicott's warm friend) in his *Variæ Lectiones*, and the important supplementary volume of incidental materials, *Scholia critica*.[2] His work is invaluable

---

[4] The Old Greek gives additional material (*e.g.*, the long story attached to I. 12), varying dispositions of the materials (*e.g.*, the two long supplements in I. 2), rearrangements (as in I. 5–7, and the exchange of cc. 20 and 21), as well as also innumerable variations in text. The pertinent problems will be considered *ad locos*.

[1] See the 'Prolegomena' of Kittel and collaborators and successors prefacing the completed volume. For further recent treatments of the learned apparatus, reference may be made to the writer's *Daniel*, Int., §§5, 6; Eissf., *Einl.*, §§100, 101; Kahle, 'Der alttest. Bibeltext,' *Th. R.*, 1933, 227 ff.; and the admirable digest in Pfeiffer, *Int.*, pp. 71–104.

[2] Kennicott gives a descriptive and critical 'Catalogus Codicum' in the 'Dissertatio Generalis' at end of vol. 2. De Rossi in the 'Prolegomenon' to vol. 1 repeats Kennicott's list with further description of prints and criticism, and adds his own list of additional manuscripts and prints.

for its presentation of the agreements of the Hebrew variants with the Versions, including the Syriac and Arabic. Bär's edition is valuable for its ' Annotationes Criticæ,' with the listing of Masoretic variants, the differences between Oriental and Occidental readings, and the ' Diversitates libri Regum a libri Chronicorum,' and ' a libri Jesaiæ,' and ' a libri Jeremiæ.' Ginsburg's first edition presented variant readings. His second edition gives a far larger presentation of this material in the footnotes, page by page, along with the distinction of Oriental and Occidental readings, extensive citation of early prints, as also his own suggested correction of text, ' necesse est legere.' [3] And in suit the critical apparatus in Kittel-Noth's edition gives current citation of selected variants based on earlier text-editors, and selected MSS, along with extensive citation of the Versions and critical judgments upon them and their bearing upon the Hebrew text.[4]

For Ki. Kennicott cites at length 66 MSS, along with very many cited in places for him by C. Bruns. See his ' Catalogus Codicum,' including synagogal Haftaroth and prints, following the text of Ki. For the same book de Rossi consulted 42 original additional texts in his own library, 34 others on occasion. In many cases these MSS contain only the Former Prophets.[5]

In addition to the innumerable variations, in large part errors, yet often scribal corrections of impossible or unintelligible Hebrew, occurring in most authoritative MSS, as also the variations between presence and absence of the vowel-letters, or their faulty placement (the simpler form often giving the basis of interpretation by the Versions), there are

[3] See at large his invaluable *Introduction*, and for excellent surveys of the Heb. text Buhl, *Canon u. Text*, §§24 ff., Briggs, *Int.*, ch. 7. For recent catalogues of the Heb. MSS see Bibliography in Buhl, p. 86, and Ginsburg, ch. 12.

[4] See the extensive apparatus listed in the ' Prolegomena.' Few fragments of the Babylonian texts appear for Ki. ; *cf.* Kahle, *Masoreten des Ostens*, *BWAT* 15 (1913), and ' Die hebräischen Bibelhandschriften aus Babylonien,' *ZAW* 46 (1928), 113 ff.

[5] By inadvertence some numbers of Kennicott's citations are erroneously cited below through the Commentary, as 'MSS,' whereas they are actually prints ; this correction concerns the particular numbers 257, 260, 264, 650 [J.A.M.].

the many corrections by the vocal Ḳrê, which have again to be diagnosed for their correctness. There also appear cases of the Sebîrîn, instances of 'it is the opinion that it is so and so,' the correction marginally annotated.[6]

For Ki. criticism is further complicated by the extensive current parallelisms, and again towards the end of the book by the parallels for II. 18-20 with Isaiah, for II. 24, 25 with Jeremiah, and for ch. 25 by a double parallel in Jer.[7] Accordingly we thus possess text-traditions of great antiquity. And the problem is further vexed by the inter-contamination among the parallels (affecting particularly the Versions at large), the greater fullness or preciseness or more extensive editing of one of the parallels affecting the sister text, hence the influence of the text of Ch. upon that of Ki., still more manifest in the Grr. See such a case at II. 25[4], where the verb demanded before " by night," was early lacking in the Heb., which then has been variously supplied in four MSS (" and they went out," " and they fled "), in the parallel in Jer., and in the ancient and modern VSS (AV supplies the verb without further note, JV inserts in brackets—so translators must work!). A sample case of correction of the Heb., doubtless an original error, appears at I. 7[18]: here " the pillars " and " the pomegranates " should change place; corrections are made by 2 MSS, reading the second word in

[6] For recent discussions of Kethîb-Ḳrê are to be noticed the book by Gordis on the subject (with additions to Bär's list for Ki.), and the criticism of it by Orlinsky, both listed in the Bibliography. For the Sebîrîn see Ginsb., *Int.*, ch. 8; *e.g.*, cases at I. 1[10, 18, 31], 18[26], II. 2[3]. Friedr. Delitzsch, in *Die Lese- u. Schreibfehler im A.T.*, presents a list of some 400 alleged errors in 𐤟 of Ki. The acute theory of Boström, presented in his *Alternative Readings* in Samuel, will be pursued in the Notes below.

[7] These parallelisms are fully presented by Bär, pp. 132 ff., *cf.* Kuenen, *Einl.*, §45. The most comprehensive work in this regard is Vanutelli's *Libri synoptici*, presenting the parallel texts of Is., Jer., Ch., along with the several parallel Gr. texts, and a rich assortment of the Gr. variants. For an analytic study of these variants is to be noted Rehm, *Textkritische Untersuchungen*, and for such textual discrepancies Sperber, ' Hebrew Based upon Biblical Passages in Parallel Transmission.' Klost., Kent, Šanda most conveniently present the parallelisms in translation, as does also Crockett in his *Harmony*. For the particular literature on the several sections see Comm., *ad locos, e.g.*, Add. Note on II. 18-20.

both cases, again by some 50 MSS with the first word in both cases, while the VSS, except 𝔖, support 𝔥. That is, corrections often entailed further error.

The pursuit of variant readings of particular MSS in the history of text and VSS is of interest and of possible value. Kennicott finds a sample case in his no. 1, an excellent Bodleian MS; for the Pentateuch he notes some 2000 variants, 'not a few of them of moment,' and as confirming in some cases the ancient VSS.[8] An example may be presented for Ki. in Ken. MS 30. In several cases (*e.g.*, I. 4^{20}, 14^{11}, 15^6, 19^2, II. 6^{25}, 9^{37}) it has rdgs., alone or along with a few other MSS, agreeing variously with 𝔊 𝔖 𝔄 *vs.* 𝔥; further correspondences with particular rdgs. of Gr. MSS appear at II. 15^{38}, 19^{37}, 22^1. Other MSS may be cited for occasional notable correspondences with the Grr., *e.g.*, MS 2 (I. 6^{39}), 23 (II. 21^8), 70 (I. $8^{40, 41, 46}$, II. 17^8, 24^{10}), 174 (II. 10^1, 'Samaria' for 'Jezreel'), 180 (II. 9^{32}, $20^4 = 𝔊^L$). But guard must be taken concerning individual MSS; thus MS 253 contains 'multas egregias variationes,' to quote de Rossi, and Kennicott holds that 'written in 1495, it was influenced by printed Bibles.'[9]

Accordingly the variations of Heb. MSS, as well as of editions, will be cited currently in the Notes, when they appear to be of interest, even if not of value. Their importance for text criticism may be judged only case by case. We must allow for the ecclesiastically less important Prophets a greater liberty taken with the texts, often in consequence of their human interest. Various cautions have to be borne in mind

[8] 'Dissertatio' at end of vol. 2, p. 71. Particular study of the Hebrew variants and so of the classification of the MSS has been sorely lacking. Hempel gave a 'Chronik' on the subject in *ZAW* 1930, 187 ff., and also a further study in the Göttingen *Nachrichten*, Philolog.-hist. Klasse, 1937, 227 ff. S. H. Blank has made a comparative textual study of a recently discovered MS in *HUCA* 8–9 (1932), 227 ff. Bewer has treated Ken. 96 in connexion with a brief passage in the G. A. Kohut Vol., pp. 86 ff. For other individual studies see Orlinsky's note 12 in his 'Present State of Proto-Septuagint Studies.'

[9] Some MSS come from the hands of Jewish proselytes to the Church, and so have been contaminated; a specimen is given by the writer in his *Daniel*, p. 13, and such a MS is noted by de Rossi, his MS 69, commented on in vol. i, p. cxxxii. His corrections of Kennicott's often too early datings are to be noted.

§2. TEXT AND LANGUAGE

by the critic. For the early age the acquaintance of scribes with Greek must have insensibly, *memoriter*, affected their texts. Indeed the part of memory in ancient text transmission has been rather ignored by modern critics, who appear to visualize ancient scribes as painfully collating various texts and parallels. This outlook explains the later variety in citation of the Greek Bible, as in the case of St. Paul, who knew his Hebrew (a disciple of Gamaliel he was, according to Acts 22³), the oral Targum of his day, and the current Greek translation, and who also could supply his own fresh translations. See further §11.

For the dialectical varieties in Ki. Burney in his *Hebrew Text . . . of Kings*, 207 ff., gives a useful list; almost all of them belong to the North Israelite narratives, appearing also in Jud. and Sam., and surviving in much later literature. *Cf.* also the useful summary in Dr., *Int.*, 188, n. 1. There may be noted the form of the 2d fem. sing. pronoun '*attî*, and the corresponding suffix *-kî* (appearing also in Punic). The relative *šĕ* occurs once (II. 6¹¹). The development of '*ăšer* as a demonstrative relative element = 'he-of,' a replica of *šĕ*, occurs at II. 19¹². Noticeable is the almost absence of loan-words from the Aramaic. Kautzsch in his *Aramaismen im A.T.* (1902) presents only two certain cases, איכה, II. 6¹, and חידה, I. 10¹, which occurs frequently earlier in Num. (E) and Jud.; to these cases may be added קלעים, I. 6³⁴, צלחית, II. 2²⁰, and the pl. forms צדנין, הרצין, I. 11³³, II. 11¹³.

There occurs the frequent avoidance of the usual rules for consecution of verbs with Waw, *e.g.*, II. 5²⁰, 12¹²; see Dr., *Tenses*, ch. 9, citing many cases in Ki., and F. T. Kelly, 'The Impf. with Simple Waw,' *JBL* 1920, 1 ff., citing with analysis the cases in Ki., pp. 10 ff. There are also many cases, as in the Samaritan Pentateuch, of the unapocopated impf. with consecutive Waw.[10]

---

[10] For the most recent study of the Canaanite development of the aspects' (traditionally 'tenses') see Harris, *Development of the Canaanite Dialects*, pp. 83 ff.

II. ANCIENT VERSIONS

§3. THE APPARATUS AT LARGE

Of the two great Polyglot Bibles containing the Oriental Versions, that of Paris (edited by Le Jay, completed 1645), and that of London (edited by Brian Walton, completed 1657), the latter has been used in this work. For Ki. it contains in parallel columns along with the Hebrew the Latin of the Vulgate, the Greek, the Syriac, these two with Latin translations, and at the bottom of the opposite pages the Targum and the Arabic, also with like translations.[1] Of particular value are de Rossi's summaries of the variants in Hebrew MSS and the Versions in selected passages.

The Old Testament in Greek (the Cambridge *OTG*), edited by Brooke, McLean, Thackeray, provides comparative textual apparatus for the Versions dependent upon the Greek, namely the Sahidic-Coptic, Ethiopic, Christian-Palestinian, the Syriac Hexapla, Armenian, Old Latin.[2] The 'Polychrome' edition of the *Book of Kings* in P. Haupt's *SBOT*, edited by Stade and Schwally, with constant and often contradictory notes by Haupt, is an invaluable select treasury of materials of the VSS bearing upon the text. There is to be noted also the extensive accumulation of variations of the VSS in Kittel's *BH*. For the Versions see Burney, *Kings*, pp. xx *seq.*, and Driver, *Notes on the Hebrew Text . . . of the Books of Samuel*, pp. xxxiii *seq.*, discussing a text closely related to that of Ki. General reference may be here made to Swete, *Int. to the O.T.*

[1] Vol. VI of this invaluable work also contains a series of pertinent addenda: Variants to and Observations on the Targum; Variant Readings of the Syriac; ditto of the Arabic. The extensive apparatus of comparisons of the Greek and Latin texts with manuscripts and earlier prints of the Bible is of bibliophilic interest, and the long 'Nota' by Flaminius Nobilius (d. 1590), of 196 pages, on the Greek translation, is a fine specimen of early critical scholarship.

[2] See the Preface to vol. I, and for the increment of material the Prefaces to parts 1 and 2 of vol. II (Kgdms). The work also methodically lists citations of the Biblical text found in Philo, the N.T., Josephus and the Patristic writings. For critical discussion of such citations and also for a much wider field, see Rahlfs, *SS* 3, ch. 1, §§7, 8, ch. 3 (Josephus), ch. 4.

in Greek (for the Gr. MSS of the Historical Books, pp. 154 ff.; for the sub-versions of the Gr., part I, ch. 4), and to the articles on the VSS in BDD, *JE*; also to the bibliography and critical results given by the writer in Int. to his *Daniel*. There is to be added now for the Greek VSS, the Peshitta, the Vulgate, Pfeiffer, *Int.*, 104 ff.

§4. THE GREEK VERSIONS

a. *The Apparatus*

The largest thesaurus of rdgs. of the Greek MSS still remains that of Holmes and Parsons. Its place is most conveniently, but not wholly, taken by the Cambridge *OTG*; see §3. Alongside of this monumental work is to be placed for usefulness in the study of Kings and Chronicles Vanutelli's *Libri synoptici V.T.*, cited in §2, n. 7, presenting along with the Hebrew texts their respective Greek and Latin translations (the texts of Swete and Heyse-Tischendorf), along with a finely articulated apparatus of rdgs. of the Gr. MSS arranged in groups, *i.e.*, Origenian, Lucianic, sub-Lucianic, sub-Alexandrian; the rdgs. of the Syro-Hexapla and the parallels in Josephus are included.

Tischendorf-Nestle's and Swete's editions of the Gr. O.T. cite for uncial codices in this book only B (Codex Vaticanus) and A (Codex Alexandrinus).[1] The Cambridge *OTG* and Vanutelli treat as one uncial manuscript (as indeed long observed) the codex cited by them as N, known to HP as two distinct MSS, XI and 23; and so also an uncial MS Coislinianus 1, cited as M, extending only for I. 1–8⁴⁶. There are also fragments of an uncial Z. The most recent edition of the Greek text is Rahlfs's *Septuaginta*, presenting a revision of the text of B and an apparatus of the pertinent variants. In this connexion is to be noted the Göttingen *Septuaginta*, instituted by Rahlfs, with large critical apparatus and introductions; Rahlfs himself edited *Genesis* (1926) and *Psalmi*

---

[1] In addition to the earlier autotype facsimile of the latter codex a reduced facsimile reproduction has been published by the British Museum, edited by F. G. Kenyon, 1915, *seq*. See at large Kenyon's *Our Bible and the Ancient Manuscripts*, 1940.

cum Odis, followed by W. Kappler, *Maccabæorum Liber 1* (1936), and J. Ziegler, *Isaias* (1939).[2]

b. *The Alexandrian (Septuagintal) Group* (𝕲)

The one uncial MS of the group, the regnant text of all modern editions, is Codex B, Vaticanus. Despite the corrections of 'correctores,' this noble MS abounds in glaring faults (shared in also by Codex A), particularly in transliterations, but also in other quarters, and this often uniquely, as the Notes will show. Its text may not, *per se*, be used for statistical comparison, except upon critical comparison with related MSS and sub-versions, especially the Ethiopic. Its own particular Greek group is small.[3] For the problem whether

[2] The first part of N (HP MS XI) is in the Vatican Library; it extends over Ki. The second (HP 23) is in the Library of St. Mark's, Venice (hence also known as Venetus). See Swete, *Int.*, 131 f., and vol. III of his text, p. xiv, and Montg., *Daniel*, 26, 51. In *OTG*, through an earlier omission, reference to this MS is to be found in Preface to part 3 of vol. 1. For M (HP X, not cited there for Ki.) see Swete, *Int.*, 140, and Rahlfs, *SS* 3, 32 f. MS Z is noticed by *OTG* in Preface to Kings; by Rahlfs, *SS* 3, 193, n. 2. For the MSS at large see Swete, *Int.*, ch. 5, Rahlfs's encyclopædic *Verzeichnis d. griech. Handschriften d. A.T.*, and his detailed critical discussions in *SS* 1 and 3. Most recent is the ample discussion of the Gr. uncial MSS of the O.T. by J. H. Ropes in vol. 3 (1926) of *The Beginnings of Christianity* (ed. by F. J. F. Jackson and K. Lake), pp. lxxxviii, *seq*. In addition to Nestle, 'Septuagint,' *DB*, there are to be cited among recent studies: O. Procksch, *Studien zur Geschichte der Septuaginta* (1910), and his 'Tetraplarische Studien,' *ZAW* 1936, 240 ff., 1937, 61 ff., covering the theme as far as Ruth; Kenyon, *The Text of the Greek Bible*, 1937; also the articles by Olmstead, 'Source Study and the Biblical Text,' and 'The Earliest Book of Kings' (see Bibliography). The final results of M. L. Margolis's monumental *The Book of Joshua in Greek* (parts I–IV, 1931–38) have not yet been published. He gave a preliminary statement in 'The Grouping of the Codices in the Gr. Joshua,' *JQR* 1 (1910), 259 ff.; *cf*. also his essay on 'Textual Criticism of the Gr. O.T.,' *Proc. Am. Philos. Soc.*, 1928, 187 ff. A. Allgeier's recent volume, *Die Chester-Beatty Papyri zum Pentateuch; Untersuchungen zur älteren Überlieferungsgeschichte der Septuaginta* (1938), gives a full discussion of results from that quarter. See also further literature cited in §11, n. 6.

The alphabetic symbols for the cursive MSS will be used below, following *OTG* and Vanutelli, with occasional references to numbered MSS of HP not included in the former system.

[3] The writer has expressed his criticism of uncritical use of B as basis of textual comparison in a review, *JBL* 1936, 309 ff. For a recent study see Sperber, *Septuagintaprobleme I*, *BWANT* III, 13 (1929).

there was more than one archetype of the Septuagint see the literature of the discussion in §11, note 6.

c. *The Later Jewish Translators, Theodotion, Aquila, Symmachus, etc.*

For placing Theodotion's name first, see the writer's *Daniel*, p. 46. For the additional texts known at large to Origen, but of unknown *provenance*, the Quinta, Sexta, Septima, see Field's *Hexapla*, vol. 1, Prolegomena, ch. 5, and Swete, *Int.*, pt. 1, ch. 3. Field's invaluable work cites all the then known citations made by Origen and others from those obscure translations; these are also duly registered with an increment of additions in *OTG*. For Aquila there have now been recovered six large papyrus leaves of his translation of Kings, discovered by S. Schechter in the Cairo Genizah, and published by Burkitt and Taylor in *Fragments of the Books of Kings*. This material includes I. 20^{7-17}, II. 23^{12-27}.[4] The thesaurus of these translations is the Syriac Hexapla (see §6, *b*), plus marginal citations in some Greek MSS, notably M and j ($=243$); see Rahlfs, *SS* 3, 32 ff. Remains of the cited Quinta appear frequently for 2 Ki., never for 1 Ki.[5] The effect of Theodotion upon the history of the Greek text remains obscure; he is cited frequently along with Aquila and Symmachus, but rarely alone; see further §11, *c*.

d. *Origen's Revision and its Successors* ($\mathfrak{G}^H$)

Origen prepared two texts, the Hexapla and the reduced Tetrapla. A further revision of his (Palestinian) text was produced by Eusebius under Constantine's command (the

---

[4] Valuable textual notes are added by the editors. See in general J. Reider, *Prolegomena to Aquila*, Philadelphia, 1916. For the relation of Aquila and Targum see Silberstein's work, cited in Note introductory to I. 1.

[5] See Burkitt, 'The So-Called Quinta of 4 Kings,' *PSBA* 24 (1902), 216 ff., citing instances where "readings of the so-called Quinta preserve a valuable emendation of the Mas. text"; E. Nestle, *ib.*, 25, 63; Olmstead, 'The Earliest Book of Kings,' who rediscovers Quinta in 1 Ki., proposing it as the basis of the Gr. in that portion of the book, and with stress on the critical importance of the version (pp. 184 ff.).

Constantinopolitan text).[6] The MSS of this group are promiscuous in their readings. Of the uncials, A N belong here; M has 'a vulgar text,' 'influenced by the Hexapla' (Rahlfs, SS 3, 32). Codex A, like B, is carelessly written, and often runs independently of its fellows, indeed is often found in particular, even unique, correspondence with B.[7] For Ki. Vanutelli selects as cursives of this group MSS c x y (HP 376 247 121).[8]

In this connexion may be noted Origen's Alexandrian counterpart, Hesychius (martyred under Galerius), who produced a revision of the Greek Bible. But no precision of Hesychian texts has been made for Ki.[9]

e. The Lucianic Revision (𝔊ᴸ)

See at large Rahlfs, SS 3, the outstanding work on the criticism of the problematic text of Lucian and its correlations.[10] In 1883 Paul de Lagarde published his *Librorum V.T. canonicorum pars prior* (part 2 never appeared)—a cryptic title indeed, for the volume is a presentation of the Lucianic text of Gen.–2 Esd., devoid of any textual apparatus. Following Vercellone he based his text on MSS 19 82 93 108 ($=OTG$ b' o $e_2 b$). His volume has become the staple for dis-

---

[6] See Field's *Prolegomena*, Swete, *Int.*, 18 ff., the writer's *Daniel, Int.*, §14, and in particular for the present subject Rahlfs, SS 1, 47 ff., 'Origenis Zitate aus den Königsbüchern.' There may be noted in addition two important studies, by Margolis, 'Hexapla and Hexaplaric,' *AJSL* 32 (1916), 126 ff., and by Orlinsky, 'The Columnar Order of the Hexapla,' *JQR* 27 (1936), 137 ff.

[7] See the full study, including much more than its title indicates, by S. Silberstein, 'Über den Ursprung der im Codex Alexandrinus u. Vaticanus des dritten Königsbuches der alexandrinischen Übersetzung überlieferten Textgestalt,' *ZAW* 13 (1893), 1–75 ; 14, 1–30.

[8] For analysis of MSS of this group see Margolis, 'Hexapla and Hexaplaric,' cited above. For Joshua he accepts a different group from the above, namely 15 (=a) 27 64 78.

[9] See Nestle, *DB* 4, 445, col. 2 ; Swete, *Int.*, 18 ff.

[10] For the credit for recognition of this group see *ib.*, p. 80, n. 1. Lucian, martyred in the year 311/12, was a Syrian of Antioch, and belonged to a different school of Biblical tradition than that of Alexandria (Septuagint, Hesychius) and that of Cæsarea (Origen). For these three schools see Jerome's 'Præfatio in Paralip.' in his 'Prologus Galeatus' (Tischendorf, p. xlvi). Burney, pp. xx–xxxi, gives a long list of Gr. rdgs., mostly parallelisms of 𝔊 and 𝔊ᴸ ; but 𝔊 is cited only from faulty B.

cussion of the text in question. But de Lagarde's method and text have undergone drastic criticism by Rahlfs with his study of all Lucianic clues and exposure of de Lagarde's many arbitrary readings. He adds as a major Lucianic MS no. 127=c_2, and comes to the conclusion that o and e_2 are far superior to the others. Related MSS are 56 (=i) 158 245.[11] Vanutelli (' Prolegomena,' vi) follows much the same grouping, adding other MSS as 'sub-Lucianic.' Readings from this source have largely affected, often as glosses, other MSS (Rahlfs, SS 3, 30 ff.).

§5. THE TARGUM (𝔗)

The text of the 'Targum of Jonathan' primarily followed here is that of de Lagarde's *Prophetæ Chaldaice* (𝔗ᴸ), based upon a single MS, the Codex Reuchlinianus, of date 1105, itself containing many annotated variants, listed in the Preface, along with variants of other printed texts. To Walton's edition of the Targum in the London Polyglot (𝔗ʷ) S. le Clerc (Clericus) has contributed a long essay in vol. 6, 'Variæ lectiones in Chaldaicam paraphrasin.'[1] We have to postulate early oral Targums in paraphrastic citation of the Scriptures. Their literary composition was not effected until a late date; according to Hamburger, *RE* 2, 1184 f., Targum Jonathan was not earlier than the 4th century. For the influence of oral Targums upon other translations, *cf.* §11, *d*, and P. Churgin, 'The Targum and the Septuagint,' *AJSL* 50 (1933-34), 41 ff., with discussion of earlier literature.

§6. THE SYRIAC VERSIONS

a. The Peshitta (𝔖)

The earliest Syriac version was so named, 'the Simple,' in contrast to the later composite Hexaplaric text. The text

---

[11] N.b. his discussion of 82 in *SS* 1, 3 ff.

[1] Kahle, in *Masoreten des Ostens* (1913), 25 ff., presents a Babylonian text of the Hebrew and Targum of 2 Sam. 24^{16}-1 Ki. 1^{15}, with Bab. punctuation; similarly A. Sperber, 'Zur Sprache des Prophetentargums,' *ZAW* 1927, 267 ff., presents I. 17-19 with the same punctuation.

here used is that of the London Polyglot, which is supplemented in vol. 6 by H. Thorndike's 'Variantes in Syriaca versione V. T. lectiones.'[1]

b. The Syro-Hexapla (𝔖ᴴ)

The term indicates the Syriac translation of Origen's Hexaplaric Greek text, with citation of the latter's critical apparatus, made by Paul of Tella in the year 616–17, and surviving in one MS in the Ambrosian Library in Milan.[2] The edition of the text used here is de Lagarde's notable publication, *Bibliothecæ Syriacæ* (1892), covering Gen.-Ki. (the earlier books largely fragmentary). For Sam.–1 Ki. 1^{1-49} *OTG* also adds the glosses of a 'patchwork text,' revision of the Peshitta from the Greek; see vol. 2, pt. 1, p. viii. There are also the Hexaplaric citations in a great work by Abu-l-Faraj, surnamed Barhebræus; these are cited in *OTG*.[3]

§7. THE ETHIOPIC (𝔈)

The text used here is that of Dillmann, *V.T. Æthiopicum*. His 'Apparatus Criticus,' following 1 and 2 Kgdms and 3 and 4 Kgdms, contains variants, conspectus of variations

---

[1] This text is repeated in Lee's edition, published by the British and Foreign Bible Society (1823). For the Syriac versions in general see E. Nestle, 'Syriac Versions,' *DB*; A. Baumstark, *Gesch. d. syrischen Literatur*, §4 (listing the Bible translations, and with full bibliography); L. Haefeli, *Die Peshitta des A.T.* (1927); and for particular notice of MSS and prints, W. E. Barnes, 'The Peshitta Version of 2 Kings,' *JTS* 6 (1905), 220 ff. For a discussion of the relation of 𝔖 to 𝔈 see J. Bloch, 'The Influence of the Greek Bible on the Peshitta,' *AJSL* 36 (1920), 161 ff., with full bibliography, but arriving at no definite results; *cf.* also his earlier article, 'Authorship of the Peshitta,' *ib.*, vol. 35, 215 ff. Of particular interest for the Syriac tradition and interpretation of text are the Scholia of Barhebræus; see note 3.

[2] For the literature see *Daniel*, Int., §10, *d*, and for the translator and his work, Baumstark, pp. 186 ff.

[3] He lived 1225–86; see at length Baumstark, pp. 312–21. The material appears in his encyclopædic *Auṣar Rāzē*, 'Treasury of Mysteries.' A. Morgenstern has published the text for Ki., *Die Scholien des Gregorius Abulfarag, Barhebraeus genannt, zum Buch der Könige* (1925). M. Sprengling and W. C. Graham have published the first volume of *Barhebraeus' Scholia on the O.T.* (Chicago, 1931), covering Gen.–2 Sam. These scholia to the Biblical books introduce the Origenian ('Ionian') readings, as also direct translations from the Hebrew.

from the LXX, etc. There are to be noted particular presentations of fresh MSS: by N. Roupp, 'Die älteste aethiop. Handschrift der vier Bücher der Könige,' *ZA* 1902, 296 ff.; and H. S. Gehman, 'The Old Eth. Version of 1 Kings and its Affinities,' *JBL* 1931, 81 ff.[1]

§8. THE ARABIC (𝔄)

The text here followed is that of the London Polyglot, reprint from that of Paris. For the Arabic versions at large see H. Hyvernat's extensive discussion, 'Arabes (Versions),' in Vigouroux's *DB*; F. C. Burkitt, *DB* 1, 137 f.; P. Kahle, *Die arab. Bibelübersetzungen, Texte mit Glossar* (1904); and the recent summary account by Gehman, 'The Polyglot Arabic of Daniel and its Affinities,' *JBL* 1925, 327 ff. *OTG* does not present the readings of this version.[2]

§9. OTHER ORIENTAL VERSIONS

a. The Syro-Palestinian (𝔓)

For the fragments in this dialect in Ki. see Pref. Note, in *OTG*. The dialect is Judæo-Palestinian, written in Syriac characters, coming from a Christian Church of Melkite persuasion, which was originally dependent upon the Syrian Church at Edessa. A group of these Palestinians at unknown date migrated to Egypt. Here their literary remains have been found, almost all lectionary material.[3]

b. The Coptic (ℭ)

There exist only fragments of the Sahidic dialect for Ki. On the textual value of the Coptic versions see Prefatory Note in *OTG*, vol. 1.

---

[1] Gehman has used in comparison with Dillmann's text an unpublished Eth. MS in the Vatican library, photographic copy of which is in the Library of the Philadelphia Divinity School; he supplies an ample Bibliography. For other critical material see §11, *a*.

[2] There may be noted in this connexion J. F. Rhode, *The Arabic Version of the Pentateuch in the Church of Egypt* (Catholic Univ. Thesis, 1921), and Gehman, 'The Arabic Bible in Spain,' *Speculum*, 1 (1926), 219 ff.

[3] For the dialect see Brockelmann, *Grundriss*, 1, 16; F. Schultess, *Lexicon Syropalaestinum* (1903); Duval, *La littérature syriaque*; Nestle, *DB* 4, 649; Rosenthal, *Die aramaistische Forschung*, pp. 144 ff.

c. The Armenian (Arm.)

OTG presents this text as 𝔄. See Gehman, ' The Armenian Version of I and II Kings,' *JAOS* 1934, 53 ff., and his similar treatment of the Armenian text of Daniel in *ZAW* 1930, 82 ff., these with full bibliographies. Over this language and the Coptic the present writer has no control.

§10. THE LATIN VERSIONS

a. The Old Latin (𝔏)

The material from old Latin MSS with pre-Hieronymian text is registered in *OTG*; see Pref. Note in vol. 2. Early Patristic citations offer still richer material; see index of sources used in *OTG*, Pref. Note in vol. 1. The citations by Lucifer of Cagliari are the most extensive.[1]

b. The Vulgate (𝔙)

The text used is the Clementine text published by Heyse and Tischendorf—cited under the latter's name. This has value for its annotation of the readings of Codex Amiatinus, generally more original than the *textus receptus*.[2] The official *Biblia Sacra*, 6 (Rome, 1945) has also been consulted.

III. GROUPING OF THE VERSIONS

§11. *a. The Alexandrian Family*

Of the above versions only the Grr., the Targum, the Syriac Peshitta, and the Vulgate are direct translations

---

[1] See H. A. A. Kennedy, ' Latin Versions, The Old,' *DB*. Extensive citations of 𝔏 are given by Dr., *Samuel*, pp. lxvi–lxxx, and by Burn., *Judges*, pp. xxxv–xxxix, for the most part in exhibits taken from the Codex Gothicus Legionensis (on which see Rahlfs, *SS* 3, 157 ff.). See Bibliography for Lucifer's text; *cf.* Rahlfs, §35. For this extensive field see also the writer's *Daniel*, Int., §10, *b*, and R. S. Haupert, *Relation of Cod. Vat. and the Lucianic text of . . . Kings from the Viewpoint of the Old Latin and Ethiopic Versions* (Univ. of Penna. Thesis, 1930).

[2] See W. Nowack, *Die Bedeutung des Hieronymus für die Alttest Kritik* (1875), H. J. White. 'Vulgate,' *DB*.

§IIB. THE PALESTINIAN (ORIGENIAN) FAMILY

from the Hebrew; the others are translations of Greek Versions.[1]

Codex B and its Greek fellows rate historically as Alexandrian, or Old Greek. But the text in Ki. hails evidently from more than one hand, and there arises the question whether it is, in part or altogether, properly Septuagintal, or of other origin, related to the obscure Theodotionic and Lucianic strains of translation. This will be discussed below in c.

Versions of the Alexandrian family are the Coptic and the Ethiopic. For the former, see Pref. Note to Ki., in *OTG* : The Sahidic "cannot safely be used except when," etc. The Ethiopic after the general fashion of the version, in its earliest form, is a peculiarly careful translation, and pairs regularly with Codex B, often uniquely, is free of its glaring errors, and so is its best ' corrector.' See Rahlfs and the other literature cited in §7, and note Olmstead's summary statement in ' The Earliest Book of Kings,' p. 171, to the effect that agreement of 𝕰 with other groups as against B must mean that such a reading is correct. For possible relationship of 𝕰 to the Lucianic group, see c below. It is possible that 𝕰 in some cases drew directly from 𝔅, *i.e.*, cases where it is in sole agreement with the latter.

b. *The Palestinian (Origenian) Family*

The place of the Syro-Hexapla as the best exemplar of this group, with its critical collection of readings from Origen's massive work, has been described above. The close dependence of 𝕬 upon Origen's version will be noted below in *d*. The place of the Armenian in the same group has been determined by Gehman in his summing up (*JAOS* 54, p. 59) : " Arm. is a faithful representative of the group. . . . We can place Arm. on the same level with A and 247. . . . There are a few influences from the Lucianic MSS . . ." For revisions

---

[1] On the character of the Oriental sub-versions the remarks in Pref. Note, *OTG*, vol. 1, pt. 1, are of value. For the subject at large see. Ropes, *op. cit.* (§4, n. 2), pp. cxlii, *seq.*, for discussion of the Oriental versions of the N.T. There is desiderated greater co-operation between the students of the two Testaments, *e.g.*, in the common problem of the ' Western Text.'

and translations of the Hexaplaric text, *cf.* the writer's *Daniel*, Int. §14.

c. *The Lucianic Revision and its Background; the Problem of a Pre-Lucianic or Pre-Theodotionic Version; Citations in Josephus and the New Testament*

The Syro-Palestinian texts known for Ki. are definitely Lucianic; see Duval, *Litt. syriaque*, p. 60.

The appearance of Lucianic rdgs. in centuries preceding Lucian (martyred A.D. 311/12), along with their occurrence in Old Latin texts, has raised complicated problems still unsolved. This is particularly the case with the Biblical citations in Josephus.[2] Mez established the fact that for Samuel, Josephus followed most largely a Greek text of pre-Lucianic, pre-Theodotionic character. But for Ki. Rahlfs came to the conclusion that Josephus chiefly used the Hebrew text, and he discovers only two positive Lucianic rdgs., bearing on I. 3^{25} and II. 11^{10}. *Per contra*, Thackeray, ignorant of Rahlfs's study, asserts (p. 85): "the Josephan text is *uniformly* of this Lucianic type from 1 Samuel to 1 Maccabees." And so authorities disagree in their critical results, as will also be exemplified further below.

The N.T. citations from Ki. are few and cast no definite light; see Rahlfs, §24, and for the subject at large Sperber, 'N.T. and Septuagint,' *JBL* 1940, 193 ff., but with no references to the citations from Ki. The following cases to the point may be noted: of the some dozen citations in the N.T. Luke 4^{26} της Σιδωνιας=𝔊 I. 17^9 (Jos., 𝔊^L Σιδωνος); Luke 4^{27}, Ναιμαν=𝔊 II. 5^{20} (𝔊^L Νεεμαν); Rom. 11^4, κατελιπον=MS i, I. 19^{18} (𝔊^L καταλειψω, B erroneously καταλειψεις). In the last citation again εκαμψαν=𝔊^L I. 19^{18} (𝔊 ωκλασαν) is the only sure case of a Lucianic rdg. Luke 9^{54} cites II. 1^{10}, but with an original verb, ἀναλίσκειν. Rev. 11^6 cites I. 17^1, again with

[2] For earlier literature see Schürer, *GJV* 1, 103. Of his references is to be especially cited A. Mez, *Die Bibel des Josephus untersucht für Buch V–VII der Archäologie* (1895), treating the books Josh., Jud., Sam. The one thorough treatment of Ki. is by Rahlfs in ch. 3 of his *SS* 3. Since then Thackeray has presented a study of the subject in Lect. 4 of his *Josephus, the Man and the Historian*. For the extensive amount of such 'Ur-Theodotionic' material in the Greek texts of Daniel see the writer's Comm., Int., §§12 ff.

an original verb, βρεχειν. The best texts of Mt. 10²⁵ and parallels have the original and actually correct rdg., 'Baalzebul,' vs. 'Baal-zebub,' at II. 1² ; see Note, *ad loc*. There is also to be noted the ancient Jewish tradition of the famine in Elijah's time as lasting for three and a half years, cited in Luke 4²⁵, Jam. 5¹⁷ ; see Comm., I. 17¹.

No definite results from such a quarter as Josephus, a free re-composer of the Biblical history, can be gained. One complication is, as Thackeray suggests (pp. 81 f.), ' the apparent influence of a Targum ' ; for such cases see Notes on I. 21²⁷, II. 9²⁰. Josephus was a scholarly gentleman, who knew his Hebrew text fairly by heart, and could make his own translations ; he was acquainted with the normative Septuagint, and also equally with current oral Greek translations (properly ' Targums,' *i.e.*, ' interpretations '). His citations are similar to those of the Apostle Paul, who cited at great length from Scripture, but with no manuscripts at hand (*cf.* 2 Tim. 4¹³). And the like independence appears in the N.T. citations from Ki. noted above.³

Rahlfs continues (ch. 4) his criticism of alleged ' Lucianic ' citations in the pre-Lucianic Greek Patristic writers, and finds but a small sheaf of gleanings. In the Latin field his study (ch. 5) of the pre-Hieronymian writers and excerpts of Old Latin MSS is crucial for a very moot question.⁴ Driver's conclusion (p. lxxvi) is worthy of citation : " The Old Latin must date from the second century A.D., hence it cannot be based upon the recension of Lucian as such ; its peculiar interest lies in the fact that it affords independent evidence of the existence of MSS containing characteristic readings (or renderings) considerably before the time of Lucian

---

³ The place of oral tradition in antiquity, as *vs.* the written, is now coming into recognition. See S. Gandz, ' Oral Tradition in the Bible,' G. A. Kohut Vol., pp. 248 ff. ; H. S. Nyberg, ' Das textkritische Problem des A.T. am Hoseabuche,' *ZAW* 1934, 241 ff., and *Studien zum Hoseabuche, Uppsala Universitets Årskrift*, 1935, pt. 6. And, as has not been sufficiently recognized, the mutual cross-relations of the extensive parallels between Ki. and Is., Jer., Ch., have been largely affected by intrusions *memoriter*.

⁴ See the literature noted in §10, *a*. Rahlfs's study of the Patristic texts in *SS* 3 was preceded in Heft 1 with a study of Theodoret's and Origen's citations from Ki.

himself."[5] However Rahlfs cites and directly contradicts this statement of Driver's (in the latter's first edition), insisting (pp. 158 ff.) that no certain Lucianic citations in the Latin appear before Lucifer of Cagliari (d. 371). This rebuttal is simply noted by Driver in ed. 2, p. lxxvi, as a footnote to the repetition of his statement noted above.

But Rahlfs's own argument is difficult to appraise. After a long discussion of Lucian's agreements with Codex B and 𝕰 in Ki. he arrives at the conclusion (§57, *cf.* p. 255), that ' the base of Lucian is an old pre-Hexaplaric 𝕲-text, which is most closely related to B and 𝕰.' But this result is not at all satisfactory in view of the evident relation of the Lucianic MSS with pre-Lucianic witness.

Thackeray, in his article in *JTS* and in his book, *The Septuagint*, etc., pp. 16 ff., has presented a most interesting thesis, evidently confirmed by statistics of language, to the effect that Gr. Kingdoms is the result of two partial translations: the first (' Alexandrian ') omitting the ' unedifying ' portions of the history, and covering I Kgd.–II. 11^1, III. 2^{12}–21^{43}, the lacunæ being then filled up by a later translator, with further discussion of the latter's relation to Theodotion, or rather an *Ur*-Theodotion, ' an anonymous Asiatic,' for which *provenance* he makes interesting argument from the vocabulary (*Septuagint*, 24 ff.). This view was anticipated by Olmstead in his ' Source Study ' (see above, §4, n. 2), arguing for an evident ' Theodotionic ' origin of at least portions of Ki. One line of this argument lies in the occurrence of transliterations in 𝕲, an ear-mark of Theodotion. But Burney, in noting at length the transliterations in Gr. of Ki. (pp. xxviii *seq.*), finds the great majority of them only in 2 Ki., a fact that argues for different translators of the two books. A further argument for such an influence is the absence of distinct Theodotionic citations in the Hexaplaric apparatus, as observed in §4, *c*. There is to be compared C. C. Torrey's argument for the Theodotionic origin of Gr. Chronicles (*Ezra Studies*, 1910, 66 ff.), as also the present writer's argument for the existence of an *Ur*-Theodotion for the book of Daniel (*Comm.*, Int., §13). In the latter case the preserved Theodotionic text, actually replacing the Old Greek text

[5] *Cf.* also Burkitt, ' The Old Latin and the Itala,' *TS* iv, 3 (1896), 9 ff.

§IID. THE OTHER ORIENTAL VERSIONS

in the Church's tradition of Daniel, facilitates the present argument.

With a pre-Theodotionic type of translation assumed, are we to make a like assumption for a pre-Lucianic revision? The two types are quite distinct, at least in the established characteristics of the two. Rahlfs would associate the original 'Lucian' very closely with Codex B and ₢; but this does not explain the marked characteristics of our Lucianic text in common with its forbears. However, Rahlfs does recognize 'vorlucianische Bestandteile' (p. 291).

The problem remains a complicated one. Alongside of Thackeray's distinction of different hands in the translation of the book, Rahlfs observes (p. 290) that by far the major difference between 𝔊 and 𝔐 exists for 1 Ki., whereas it is 'minimal' for 2 Ki. And yet the Quinta citations appear only in 2 Ki.; see §4, c. In fine, we have to assume early translation-revisions, a matter of secondary importance to the Jews, whereas the Church came to recognize the need for an authoritative text of the Bible.[6]

d. *The Other Oriental Versions*

For the Targum, its history and general characteristics, reference may be made to the authorities. Burney gives an exemplary list of 𝔗's exegetical variations, pp. xxx *seq*. It is of further interest for its exhibition, by tradition, if not by text, of the background of 𝔖 and 𝔙.[7] For the correspondences

---

[6] In 1915 in *TSK* 88, 410 ff., Kahle advanced the view, in contradiction to de Lagarde, that the MSS of the Septuagint do not go back essentially to one archetype, but rather to numerous independent translations. This theory has been pursued by Sperber in a series of studies (*e.g.*, 'Probleme einer Edition der Septuaginta,' *Festschrift P. Kahle* [1935], 35 ff., 'Septuagint Recensions,' *JBL* 1935, 73 ff., 'N.T. and Septuagint,' *ib.* 1940, 193 ff.), arguing for two and more early Greek translations from different Hebrew text-traditions. But as against this extravagant hypothesis see Orlinsky's art., 'On the Present Status of Proto-Septuagint Studies,' *JAOS* 1941, 81–91, and *cf.* review by Gehman, *JBL* 1941, 428 ff.

[7] For discussion of the cross-relationships of 𝔖 see Dr., *Samuel*, pp. lxxi–lxxvi; Burn., pp. xxxii–xxxv; J. Berlinger, *Die Peschitta zum 1.* (3.) *Buch der Könige u. ihr Verhältnis zu Mas. Texte, LXX, u. Targum* (1897); Sperber, 'Peshitta and Onkelos,' G. A. Kohut Vol., 554 ff.; and most recently Rosenthal, *Aramaistische Forschung*, 199 ff.

common oral Targum may be postulated, as Sperber's illuminating study for the Law argues. For the comparison of the two translations of the Pentateuch he comes to the conclusion (p. 562) that 𝕾 represents a form of the Targum before its later specific Rabbinic variations. The bearing of Targumic tradition upon Jerome's translation is evident, as the Notes will show.[8]

The Arabic versions of the Bible had a varied and complicated history in their origins, as observed since Pococke's day ; see his study of the Arabic texts in the London Polyglot, vol. 6, and Burkitt's article cited above. *Cf.* Cornill's careful analysis in his Comm. on Ezekiel (1905), pp. 49 ff., proving the combination of such diverse origins for the Arabic of the Polyglots. For Daniel Gehman came to the conclusion that the " Arabic of Dan. is vastly superior to (Gr.) A, and beyond a doubt is the best representative of the (Hexaplaric) group that we now possess " (*op. cit.* in §8). But E. Rödiger, in his thorough study, *De origine et indole Arabicorum librorum V.T. historicorum interpretum* (1829), had arrived at the opposite conclusion for the Historical Books. His result is that I. 1–11 and II. 12[17]–25 (more particularly for exact translation) are based on the Syriac, while for I. 12–II. 12[16] the Hebrew, along with Rabbinic ' commenta Judaica,' was the basis (p. 48) ; to wit, as in a summary section title, the Arabic version " ex Græca Alexandrina non facta est." The fault of this capable study is that the Greek used in parallelism was solely that of the *text. rec.*, without consultation of the Hexaplaric texts. 𝕬 will be constantly cited below, and its constant alignment with Hexaplaric witnesses, notably A, of which it is often the

Burn. cites certain cases in which " the readings of Pesh. seem to exhibit connexion with Targ." Berlinger reaches the conclusion that dependence upon these sister-translations cannot be established, and Rosenthal, with sole reference to Onkelos, comes to no definite results. For the relation of 𝕾 to 𝕲 see also above, §6, n. 1.

[8] *N.b.*, the correct interpretation of בי, I. 3[17], is given by 𝕿 𝕾 𝕬 𝖁, as *vs.* the Grr. ; similarly in v.[20] that of מאלי by the same VSS ; *cf.* 15[6], etc. See S. Krauss, ' Jerome,' *JE*, esp. p. 117 ; and for an intensive study of another Biblical book, C. H. Gordon, ' Rabbinic Exegesis in the Bk. of Proverbs ' (Univ. of Penna. Thesis), *JBL* 1930, 384 ff. ; on pp. 395 ff. he exhibits for that book the parallelisms of 𝕿, 𝕾, and 𝖁.

corrector, will be adduced. But as 𝔖 and the Hexapla are far more faithful to 𝔥 than is 𝔊, the question of the *provenance* of 𝔄 is complicated.

e. *Value and Interest of the Versions*

In the application of early versions to an ancient text the primary interest has been that of correcting the latter. Hence, as a rule, in such critical work on a Hebrew book selection is made of all those cases that appear to offer correction, but with the ignoring of the cases of mistranslation, through ignorance, or by artless or intentional improvement. The result has been the impression of the constant superiority of the versions, the pertinent cases of which are prominently booked. But this process of comparison does not become scientific until statistics of the right and wrong in a given version have been gathered. It will actually be found that a small percentage of the variations of the Old Greek translations, for example, have any value for text-correction. The bulk of the notable ones will be found to be in the way of interpretation, following the endeavour to obtain sense out of a passage difficult rhetorically or grammatically, or to improve it, especially when theology is involved. A modern parallel is on hand in that classic English translation, the King James Bible, in which the sense is often eked out with the very honest interpolation of italicized passages, or the ambiguity of a passage indicated by a marginal note introduced with an 'Or.' Even the very strict Jewish Version of our own day has had perforce to introduce bracketed words to make sense, and at times fails to translate literally, but makes improvement (*cf.* Preface, p. x). These cases are no guarantee of a better original text; the translators, as interpreters, had perforce to make sense, that "he who runs may read." Such variations also appear automatically in the Hebrew MSS. *Cf.* the writer's similar statement in his *Daniel*, Int., §18, 'Method and Use of the Textual Apparatus.'

Accordingly in the textual Notes of this volume constant citation of the variants of the Versions will be given, not only for their value for text-correction, a small minimum indeed, but as exhibits, at times of their misunderstanding, at times of their honest effort to make sense out of nonsense, and to correct what appeared objectionable. The former objective will have comparatively small gains; the latter will afford a study in the interpretation attempted by the version in question, and this has an interest in itself, minor though that interest be.[9]

IV. THE SOURCES OF THE BOOK

§12. COMPARISON WITH CONTEMPORARY HISTORICAL WRITING

The Hebrew history, extending from the migrations of the Bnê-Israel down into the Persian age, as contained in the Hebrew Scriptures, is the longest consecutive literary series that we possess from the ancient Near Orient. For long it was unique, the external history being eked out by Greek travellers like Herodotus and by the remains, in second-hand condition, of such native annalists as Sanchuniathon, Manetho, and Berossos.[1] The archæological unveiling of that ancient field has reversed the process of comparison; the Hebrew records of the politically petty people of Israel can now be interpreted and commented upon in the light of an unbroken series of documents covering millennia. And so to the matter-of-fact historian those fresh original documents far transcend in interest and importance the narrow scope of the Hebrew history.

It is only in the minimum that the Hebrew chronicles run

[9] The writer refers with strong sympathy to J. Reider's study, ' The Present State of Textual Criticism of the O.T.,' *HUCA* 7 (1930), 285 ff., and H. S. Nyberg, ' Das textkritische Problem des A.T. am Hoseabuche demonstriert,' *ZAW* 1934, 24 ff., and his ' Studien zum Hoseabuche,' *Uppsala Universitets Årsskrift*, 1935, pt. 6, with the conclusion, " Zurück zum masoretischen Texte um ihn zu studieren und zu interpretieren ! "

[1] For such local archives in early days may be compared the *memorabilia* of Edom in Gen. 36, especially the succession of nine kings " before there reigned a king over the Bnê-Israel " (vv.$^{31ff.}$). For the early spread of writing in Transjordan, *cf.* Jud. 8^{14}, and for the subject at large see J. W. Flight, ch. 4 of E. Grant's *Haverford Symposium*. For the authenticity and antiquity of Sanchuniathon's *Phœnician History* see Eissfeldt's *Ras Schamra u. Sanchuniathon* (as of the seventh century), and Albright, *SAC* 242 ff. (' seventh or sixth century ').

§12. CONTEMPORARY HISTORICAL WRITING

pari passu with those of the great Empires. Annalistic items drawn directly or indirectly from official records are manifest from David's reign and on, but they play a small part and are a side-issue in comparison with the corresponding elements galore in the new discoveries, which abundantly illustrate the praxis. But the unique development of Hebrew history lies in its passage from the purely archival form, the digests by curious scribes of the past records of their peoples, to the Historical Story. This may extend all the way from the narrative of contemporaries, like the David-Solomon story (2 Sam. 16–1 Ki. 2), to such midrash as appears in I. 13. But in this unique development the annalistic programme has been developed into History. A new factor has been introduced, the subjective one of the eye and mind of the historian. Critics may naturally suspect sources dubbed as Prophetic, Deuteronomic, Priestly, but all real history is the result of digestion by the historian, one-sided as the emphasis must be ; this is true of Thucydides, Livy, Gibbon, Macaulay, and so through the list of great historians. The criticism we should exercise is of the kind generally applied to, we may say, the sources of Herodotus; the monuments he had seen with his eye, stories he had heard with his ears, all through interpreters, are entirely unknown to us, and yet the historical verisimilitude of his reports is being constantly vindicated in contradiction of the earlier sceptical judgment upon him as a gullible traveller.[2] The Hebrew history has suffered in its treatment by critics too much from theological bias, formerly orthodox, now quite radical. Even if in our book the cycles of stories of the Sons of the Prophets, the Temple sources, the Deuteronomic editing, are all partisan, they remain of immense historical importance ; for it is what a people thinks of itself, its origins and its future, that serves to make history, quite as much as the current facts. It was

[2] In bk. i, 8 he sums up for the dynasty of the Heraclidæ preceding Gyges of Lydia, the contemporary of Ashurbanipal, 22 generations, covering 505 years, *i.e.*, *ca.* 22 years per reign ; this average corresponds closely to that of the Judæan dynasty. For the Tyrian dynasty from Hiram I and on, for 11 reigns (one of 8 months, terminated by assassination) Josephus reports, as from the Ephesian Menander, a regnal average of 16 years. *I.e.*, in both cases the figures are reasonable and are based on exact sources.

the Prophets and Priests who saved Israel's heritage for the future, and it was through them that the remains of the ancient secular chronicles were preserved.[3]

The recognition of the unique character of Hebrew history has been largely due in our days to the secular historian. From the field of historiography the eminent authority, J. T. Shotwell may be quoted:[4] "No higher tribute could be paid to the historical worth of the Old Testament than the statement that, when considered upon the profane basis of human authorship, it still remains one of the greatest products in the history of History, a record of national tradition . . . which yet retains the undying charm of genuine art and the universal appeal to human interest"; although, he adds, "not . . . a remarkable performance viewed from the standpoint of modern history." But criticism may be expressed of another statement by the same writer (p. 7, n. 6): "The achievement of the Hebrew historians was primarily in the field of art. Although sections of the early records of the Jews are the finest narratives we possess from so early a period—far earlier than any similar product in Greece [5]—the principles of criticism which determined the text were not what we call scientific. They were not sufficiently objective." However, comparison of modern historical writing in the way of criticism of history some three millennia older is hardly to the point. And there is no reason to put such a story as that of David-Solomon, or that of Jehu's destruction of the Omrid dynasty, to name the most brilliant political narratives, in the category of art as opposed to the historical. There is no consciousness of art, no self-expression in judgment upon the history in the way of moralizing or of setting forth of theodicy (as in Herodotus, equally with the Prophets); if the composer was affected by the tragedy, of which he was a contemporary,

[3] How much of such local lore of the Oriental lands has been preserved by the alien and inquisitive Herodotus! Those ancient peoples never rendered it into literature, or, if they did, there was no interested tradition to preserve it. For an admirable discussion of comparison with that quarter see H. T. Fowler, ' Herodotus and the Early Hebrew Historians,' *JBL* 49 (1930), 207 ff.

[4] *Introduction to the History of History*, 80; *cf.* H. E. Barnes, *A History of Historical Writing*, ch. 1.

[5] Hecatæus, *ca.* 550 B.C., is accounted as the first Greek historian.

§12. CONTEMPORARY HISTORICAL WRITING

he leaves it to the reader to discover it for himself.[6] Indeed such history writing, as in many cases in the Historical Books, falls properly into the class of Historical Story and is *historia* in the Latin sense of the word ; see Shotwell, p. 229, where he cites Servius, the commentator on Virgil (on *Aen.*, i, 373), defining *historia* as contemporary narrative, while *annales* are records of the past. Reference is also to be made to Meyer for his brilliant section on ' Novellen und Erzählungen mit novellistischer Technik,' in his *IN* 189 ff., in which class he places the story of David and Bathsheba as the most eminent. But 'Novelle' may not be immediately rendered into English, nor is that story mere historical romance by any means.

There is almost nothing to compare with this development of Hebrew history from the records of the great Empires, with possibly one exception. For Egypt, of comparative importance are the poetic descriptions of the campaigns and glories of Thutmose III, Ramses II (on the battle at Kadesh), Merenptah.[7] Apart from such extravagant rhetorical eulogies (*cf.* Deborah's Song in contrast !), Egypt gives us only the short ' Novelle,' at the best autobiographies like the stories of Sinuhe and Wen-amon.

With all the wealth of Babylonian-Assyrian remains we find hardly more than dynastic lists, notable events dated by royal years, citation of omens, and annals of reigns extravagantly written up.[8] The only exception would be the genuine royal autobiography that we possess from Ashurbanipal. Citation may be made of Weber in his discussion of the historical inscriptions : [9] " (Die bab.-ass.

---

[6] *Cf.* citations of Olmstead in introduction to Comm. on I. 1–2 below.

[7] Erman, *Lit. of the Anc. Egyptians*, 254 ff. ; these were doubtless contemporary productions, as is known from one of them (p. 266). A scribe of Thutmose records how he " followed " the king, " beheld his victories," " recorded the victories," " putting them into writing, according to the facts " (Breasted, *HE* 312 f.). But " the priceless rolls have perished."

[8] For the earlier material see Güterbock, ' Die historische Tradition u. ihre literarische Gestaltung bei Babyloniern u. Hethitern bis 1200.'

[9] *Die Literatur der Babylonier u. Assyrer*, ch. 15 at length, in particular, p. 199.

Geschichtsschreibung) hat sogar zusammenfassende Geschichtswerke aus den Urkunden der Vergangenheit kompiliert, freilich nur in der trockensten Form der Tatsachenregistrierung, die ohne Rücksicht auf innere Zusammenhänge, ohne das Wesentliche gegenüber dem Gleichgültigen hervorzuheben, Zahl an Zahl, Kriegszug an Kriegszug, Herrscher an Herrscher reiht." He continues with the statement that we have nothing in that literature of the like of Hebrew history, although he appeals to the late Berossos for such a possibility. The result did not advance beyond the stage of court annals, was indeed "ein durchaus höfisches Produkt," as Meissner remarks.[10] Over against this characteristic is that of the spirit of the Hebrew historians, always sitting in judgment upon royalty, most often 'anti-courtly,' from the story of Nathan the prophet down to that of Huldah the prophetess. The one feature similar in the non-Israelite field is the recognition of Fate.

Only in one quarter, and that of the non-Semitic Hittites, may a parallel be found. Güterbock, Teil 2 of his monograph cited above, expresses this judgment (p. 94): " (Die hethitische Geschichtsschreibung) hat im Neuen Reich eine Form gefunden, die nicht nur innerhalb der hethitischen, sondern in der ganz vorderasiatischen Geschichtsschreibung den höchsten Rang einnimmt: die der Annalen." With this statement may be compared that of his predecessor, A. Götze: [11] " Viel bedeutsamer ist es, dass bei den Hethitern zum ersten Male in der Weltgeschichte ein literarisches Genos von hoher Bedeutung in Erscheinung tritt: der literarische Bericht. Er sprengt den Rahmen trockener Annalistik. . . . Der hethitische historische Bericht versteht es in einer Weise, die erst in den Geschichtsberichten der Israeliten wieder erreicht wird, Ereignisse unter einheitlichen Geschichtspunkten rückschauend zusammenzufassen, Situationen eindrucksvoll

[10] *Bab. u. Ass.*, 2, 367. For Meissner's judgment of the Babylonian and Assyrian chronicles see *ib.*, ch. 20. For collections of these chronicles, including the early king-lists of Ur, Isin, Babylon, etc., see Schrader, *KB* 2, 273 ff., vol. 3, 2d half, 143 ff.; Rogers, *CP* 199 ff.; Gressmann, *ATB* 1, 331 ff. The Bible student should acquaint himself with these precedents and parallels for Israelite historiography.

[11] *Hethiter, Churriter u. Assyrer* (Oslo, 1936), 72 ff.

§12. CONTEMPORARY HISTORICAL WRITING

darzustellen "; and finally, in translation : " The Hittite narrative does not serve the heroization and glorification of the king, it serves the presentation of deed and fate, is accordingly absolutely free of the mythical, is history." [12]

On the quality of Hebrew historiography may be cited opinions from unbiassed authorities. Moore in his essay on 'Die Eigenart der hebräischen Geschichtsschreibung,' p. 73, remarks, after reference to the edifying aims of the writers : " So schwer wir nun die Mangel der tendenziösen Geschichtsschreibung von dieser Seite empfinden, so müssen wir andererseits anerkennen, das in derselben der Ansatz zu einer philosophischen Geschichtsbetrachtung liegt. Die Geschichte ist nicht eine zufällige Zeitreihe von Geschehnissen, sondern eine sittliche Ordnung, die nicht allein Israel, sondern die Weltmächte, welche Gott als Werkzeuge der Strafe oder der Rettung gebraucht, in sich schliesst ; die korrelativen Ideen der Einheit Gottes und der Einheit der Geschichte ergeben sich aus der sittlichen Auffassung der Geschichte." And again (p. 66) he observes : " So haben tatsächlich nur zwei Völker unabhängig von einander eine historische Literatur erzeugt, die Israeliten nämlich und einige Jahrhunderte nachher die Griechen." Similarly and contemporaneously Meyer in his essay on ' Individuality,' in his *Kleine Schriften*, remarks (p. 22) : " From the point of view from which we contemplate history, the Israelite people takes by far the highest rank among the nations of the East. . . . In Israel political and social conditions combined to produce the first great action by individuality in the world " (*i.e.*, the prophets, etc.). There may be cited Eissfeldt's similar statement (p. 157 of the article just cited) : " Zunächst bleibt trotz all der reichen Nachrichten [of Greece and Rome, the Orient] für weite Strecken der zwölf letzten vorchristlichen Jahrhunderte das A.T. immer noch die wichtigste Geschichtsquelle." And Schmidt observes (*op. cit.*, p. 30) upon the prophet Amos :

[12] For recent literary treatment of Hebrew historiography, with bibliographies, are to be noted Hempel, *Die altheb. Literatur*, 81 ff., 94 ff., and Eissf., *Einl.*, §5. Particular studies of the genius of this literature are to be found in H. Schmidt, *Die Geschichtsschreibung im A.T.*; H. T. Fowler, *History of the Literature of Ancient Israel*, cc. 6, 14 ; B. P. Church, *The Israel Saga*, *e.g.*, ch. 9 ; Eissf., ' Altertumskunde u. das A.T.'

"Mit einem Schlage hat sich der enge Rahmen der Hof- und Stadtgeschichte zur Weltgeschichte erweitert." The true diagnosis of this unique characteristic of Hebrew historiography has been given by Lindblom in his essay, 'Zur Frage der Eigenart der alttest. Religion,' pp. 134, 135 : "Durch die Erfassung Jahwes als eines Gottes der Geschichte wurde sein Wesen als persönlicher Wille so beherrschend bestimmt, dass seine Gebundenheit an die Natur grundsätzlich überwunden wurde"; and, "Gott ist einer, ein Gott nicht nur der Schöpfung, sondern vor allem der Geschichte. . . ." These statements bear witness to the too little observed theologoumenon that the God of the Bible is the God of History. Israel, with its faith in its one God, who became for its theology the sole God of the universe, possessed a sense of the unity of history in its beginnings, of a divine operation in history, and more and more of a divine objective of all history. There are preserved but shattered fragments of the annals of the ancient great Empires, which never advanced to the creation of history, but Israel, petty and provincial as it was, a pawn of those Empires, preserved its historical philosophy, more simply its faith and its hope, and survived. By omens good and ill it learned that it and equally the world, in whose fate it was participant, were under the one Providence, and so history became intelligible.

§13. THE CHRONICLES

a. *The Royal Secretariat. Archives of Royal Personalia*

In David's court there were a Scribe and a Recorder (2 Sam. $8^{16ff.}$, $20^{23ff.}$), and the same two officials appear in the list of Solomon's cabinet, along with other officials of doubtless lettered attainments, one 'Over-the-Year,' and a 'Priest, Royal Friend,' not to speak of the intruded reference to 'Sadok and Abiathar, Priests.' See Comm., I. $4^{2ff.}$. The Scribe was primarily the king's Secretary; but for his importance as the king's intimate counsellor may be compared the modern political development of the latter title. The Recorder also appears along with the Scribe on responsible duties (*e.g.*, II. $18^{18, 37}$, 2 Ch. 34^8). So the Hebrew word, *mazkîr*, may best be rendered; he kept the royal 'book of records' (*sēper haz-zikrônôt*, Est. 6¹—*cf.* the divine 'Book of Remembrance,' Mal. 3¹⁶). It was his duty to keep the current records of the reign in the technically termed 'Book of the Days' (*sēper hay-yāmîm*), *i.e.*, 'diaries,' EVV 'chronicles.'[1] The royal business as well as pride required the keeping of such official journals.

By a process paralleling the development of letters in the great Empires these journals came to be extracted for their historical interest in continuous chronicles in the two Hebrew kingdoms, 'the Chronicles of the Kings of Judah,' 'of Israel' (I. 14¹⁹, ²⁹, etc.). With the development of *imperium* the royal dynasty became interested in history, and corresponding credit must be given to individual scribes who found a fertile field for their historical interest. In what form these royal chronicles were when they came into the hands of the editors of Kings we do not know; the original records of the North must have been destroyed or looted in the Assyrian conquest; like disaster must have befallen Jerusalem in its last days. By the interest of diligent scribes and for interested patrons copies must have been made in abbreviated editions, and put in circulation; it was such a copy that preserved the Northern Chronicles for the Judæan editors of Kings, brought by refugees, or obtained by Josiah's literary men in his assumption of dominion over the North. Such interest in historical letters was but the continuation of the rich literature still extant in Judges and Samuel.

Our Book of Kings drew upon official chronicles contemporaneously constructed. Earlier examples are found for the rise of the monarchy in Sam.: I. 13¹ (Saul); II. 2¹⁰ (Ishbosheth); 5⁴, ⁵ (David). For Solomon's reign is cited 'the Book of the Acts of Solomon' (I. 11⁴¹), which has drawn *in extenso* from official documents, as the following sub-section will show. Beginning with Rehoboam and Jeroboam there are fixed formulas for the beginning and end of each reign. The formula for the South includes the following items: the introductory synchronism with the Northern regnal datum,

---

[1] *Cf.* the Hellenistic ἐφημερίδες; Arrian refers (*Hist. Alex.*, vii, 25, 1) to the ἐφημ. βασίλειοι (var. βασιλικαί) of Alexander—exactly the Hebrew phrase.

age of king, length of reign, name of his mother; the final formula: the Chronicles of the Kings of Judah cited as the authority and for further reference, the burial of the king, name of his successor. There are variations, some due to original or scribal lapses, some to political vicissitudes. The synchronisms begin as between Abijam and Jeroboam (I. 15^1). Reference to the Chronicles is omitted only in the cases of Ahaziah and the usurping queen-mother Athaliah, and of the deposed and exiled Jehoahaz and Sedekiah. The age of the king is omitted for Abijam, Asa, Jehoiakim. The reign is stated to have been 'in Jerusalem,' following Oriental royal parlance. The mother's name is omitted in the case of Ahaz; for Josiah and his successors the local origin of the Judæan lady who became queen is given along with the naming of her father. The most frequent expression for the death and burial of the king is: " he slept with his fathers, and he was buried [or, they buried him] with his fathers "; or one or the other of the phrases alone is used. The first phrase is omitted in some cases of violent death, *e.g.*, Amon, Josiah. All the kings are said to have been buried in David's City (in Azariah's case plus ' in his sepulchre with his fathers,' II. 9^{28}), except Hezekiah, for whom no burial-place is reported (was his possible burial in his wicked son's tomb deliberately ignored?), Manasseh and Amon, who were buried ' the garden of Uzza,' Josiah, who was buried ' in his own sepulchre.'

For the North, like formulas are given, but with fewer particulars. Reference to the Chronicles of the Kings of Israel is omitted only in the cases of Jehoram, Jehu's victim, and the exiled Hoshea. The synchronism is given in every case, except two, when the accompanying history made it unnecessary (Jeroboam I, Jehu). Baasha, Elah, Zimri, and Omri for his first six years, reigned ' in Tirsah,' Omri for his later years and his successors ' in Samaria.' The king ' slept with his fathers,' except in cases of violent death or divine judgment (Elah, Zimri, Ahaziah, Joram, Sechariah, Shallum, Pekahiah, Pekah, Hoshea). Jehoahaz, Jehoash were buried ' in Samaria '; Jeroboam II " slept with his fathers, the kings of Israel." Expression of this item is thus careful, not wilful. *Cf.* Driver, *Int.*, 186, Burney, pp. ix *seq.* (with full data), Skinner, p. 12.

b. Further Archival Materials

Before passing to the direct citation at length of original archives preserved in the Acts of Solomon and the Chronicles of Judah and of Israel, notice may be taken of indirect references to such material made in connexion with the final formula for the respective reign. These are indeed often particulars for which the historian would wish that the editors had given more detail.

There is citation from both series of Chronicles of the constant war between Rehoboam and Jeroboam (I. $14^{19.\ 30}$), although the preceding story tells that a man of God had forbidden Rehoboam to fight with his ' brethren ' ($12^{22f.}$, a prophetic sop to the national pride !). Reference is made to the Chronicles for Jehoash's " might and how he warred with Ahaziah king of Judah " (II. 14^{15}), the source of the story given above of Jehoash's triumph over Jerusalem. There are frequent references to " the might " of a king and " how he warred " without further detail in the history : for Asa (I. 15^{23}), Omri (16^{27}—his vigorous reign was indeed ignored by the editors !), Jehoshaphat (22^{45}), Jehu (II. 10^{34}—another monarch ignored), Jehoahaz (13^8, cf. v.^{5}). More particular is the citation of Jeroboam II's " might, how he warred, and how he recovered Damascus and Hamath for Israel "—an otherwise unknown item in Syrian history (14^{28}, cf. v^{25}). The longest postscript of such items appears for Jehoshaphat's reign : the removal of the sodomites, politics of Edom, shipping on the Red Sea (I. 22^{47-50}). There are references of archæological interest, now approved by actual discovery : for Asa, concerning " the cities he built " (I. 15^{23}) ; for Ahab, " the ivory house that he built, and all the cities that he built " (22^{39}) ; for Hezekiah, " how he made the pool and the conduit, and brought water into the city " (II. 20^{20}). For the history of Zimri's conspiracy it is remarked that " the treason he wrought " was recorded in the Chronicles (I. 16^{20}), and there is similar citation for Shallum's conspiracy (II. 15^{15}). Very personal is the item connected with the final formula for Asa, that " in his old age he was diseased in his feet " (I. 15^{23}), as also that for Azariah-Uzziah, that he " was a leper until the day of his death," a condition involving the regency of his son Jotham (II. 15⁵). The citation for Manasseh's " sin that he sinned " (II. 21¹⁷) doubtless refers to his royal records of the innovations in the Temple. *Cf.* a similar annalistic record, I. 11⁷: " Then Solomon built a high-place for Chemosh."

Notice is next to be taken of direct citation of archival materials.² There are cases of items asyndetically listed, *e.g.*: " He finished the House " (I. 9²⁵) ; " Jehoshaphat made Tarshish ships," etc. (22⁴⁹) ; " Came Pul king of Assyria," etc. (II. 15¹⁹) ; most often the conjunction was used, *e.g.*, " And Moab rebelled against Israel," etc. (II. 1¹). There are the exact datings by the year, thirteen such through II. 23. The most notable of these is the first one, with the dates by year and month for the inception and conclusion of the building of the Temple (I. 6³⁷, ³⁸–7¹ is secondary). The next example is I. 14²⁵, " In the 5th year of king Rehoboam came Shishak king of Egypt," etc. (*n.b.* the latter's name and title, not the customary ' Pharaoh '). With II. 24 begins a long series of exact datings by year, month and day. Here the writer is certainly well-nigh contemporary to the story.

The original dating was often replaced with ' then,' some thirteen times ; *e.g.*, I. 9²⁴, " Then (with correction of 𝔥, see Note) Pharaoh's daughter came up from David's City to her house. Then he built the Millo." The adverb has no reference to the context in such cases. Parallel time-expressions are : ' in that day ' (I. 8⁶⁴), ' in those days ' (*e.g.*, II. 10³²—three cases), ' in his days ' (*e.g.*, I. 16³⁴—five cases), ' in those days ' (*e.g.*, II. 10³²—three cases), ' in his days ' (*e.g.*, I. 16³⁴—five cases), ' at that time ' (*e.g.*, II. 16⁶—seven cases) ; these forms are paralleled in the Akkadian annals : ' at that time,' ' in these days,' ' in his day.' Such time-expressions accordingly are not primarily editorial, expressive of indefiniteness or ignorance, but of archival origin. Also there are six cases of the introduction of such an item with asyndetic *hû*, ' he ' (*e.g.*, II. 14⁷—the Heb. pronoun is used only for emphasis) ; the usage presents in the third person the repeated ' I ' in the Moabite Mesha's record of his buildings. Again certain grammatical laxities may be explained : *e.g.*, the frequent

² See for detail the writer's article, ' Archival Data in the Book of Kings.'

§13B. FURTHER ARCHIVAL MATERIALS 35

cases of alignment of historical perfects with Waw (four perfects so aligned, II. 18^4). Some of the items are quite lapidary in form, as in records of royal building (*e.g.*, I. 9$^{15\text{-}17}$, with expanded text), with which are to be compared similar brief records in the inscriptions of Mesha and the Syrian kings Zakar and Bar-Rkb.

The above summary accounts for isolated items of primitive origin. A mass of more extensive material is preserved for Solomon's reign, a documentary wealth corresponding to his glory, for which the *débacle* that followed offers nothing similar. There are to be cited : the list of his court officials (I. 4$^{2\text{-}6}$), and that of his administrative lieutenants over the land (4$^{7\text{-}19}$) ; the memorandum of the daily provision for the palace (5$^{2\text{ff.}}$), and that of his chariotry (vv.$^{6,\ 8}$) ; from the story of the negotiations and agreement with Hiram (ch. 5), at least the exact specifications in vv.$^{24,\ 25,\ 27\text{ff.}}$; the list of his royal buildings and account of their construction and furnishing (7$^{1\text{-}13}$) ; the later diplomatic arrangements with Hiram, most honestly recorded (9$^{10\text{-}14}$) ; the list of the cities he built (vv.$^{15\text{-}18}$) ; a series of detached items (vv.$^{23\text{-}28}$, *cf.* 10^{11}) ; another accumulation of such items with inserted matter (10$^{14\text{-}22,\ 26\text{-}39}$). I. 11$^{14\text{-}25}$, concerning the ' adversaries ' whom " YHWH raised up against Solomon," the Edomite Hadad and the Syrian Reson, contains most authentic material, in particular the biographical notice of Hadad's fortunes in Egypt and the brief history of the *condottiere* Reson.³ For the documents bearing on the Temple and the brass work (6, 7$^{13\text{ff.}}$) see *c* below.

From the Chronicles of the Kingdoms we possess the following extended narratives of archival flavour. I. 15$^{16\text{-}22}$ tells of the war between Asa of Judah and Baasha of Israel, and the interference of Tabrimmon, king of Aram, whose aid was purchased by valuables stripped from the Temple. The histories of the usurpers Baasha and Zimri (15$^{27,\ 28}$, 16$^{9,\ 10,\ 15\text{-}18}$,

³ Stade, in *SBOT*, groups vv$^{11\text{-}13}$ as introduction to the anecdote ; but that passage is solely introductory to the subsequent history of Jeroboam. The editor has cleverly aligned together the three ' adversaries.' This word of YHWH is not ' prophetic ' in style ; the Moabite Mesha similarly speak of ' Chemosh being angry with his people.' *Cf.* the recognition of the divine *sibbāh*, the ' turn ' of fate, that brought about the division of the kingdom (I. 12^{15}).

cf. v.^{20}) are authentically itemized. For the distinguished Omri, who gave his name to his land for the Assyrian historians, there are preserved merely the exact details of his rise to power and of his building of Samaria (16^{21-24}). Not much more appears for Ahab ($16^{31,\ 32}$—written up editorially; v.^{34a}, a casual item; 22^{39}); original details were replaced by the Prophetic Story. For Jehoshaphat there are summed up the relations with Edom and the Red Sea traffic (22^{48-50}). II. 8^{20-22} contains precise archival notes on the relations with Edom 'in the days of Jehoram of Judah' and the revolt of Libnah. $10^{32,\ 33}$ is an objective account of Hazael's diminution of Jehu's realm. With the reign of Jehoash we have the first long archival history for Judah: his restoration of the Temple and its finances, his capitulation to Hazael, and the conspiracy against him, with the assassins named (12^{5-22}—*cf.* the conspiracy against Amaziah, 14^{19}, and the details of Sennacherib's assassination, 19^{37}, for which see the Assyrian annals). For the reign of Jehoahaz b. Jehu original elements appear in $13^{3,\ 5,\ 7}$. For his son Jehoash's reign there are notes of prime value for the Syro-Palestinian history ($13^{24,\ 25}$), and for the same king a precise account of his triumph over Amaziah of Judah (14^{8-14}—for Jehoash's proud challenge, *cf.* I. 20^{11}), as also of Amaziah's assassination by conspirators (vv.$^{19,\ 20}$), along with the postscript item, " He built Elath and restored it to Judah " (v.^{22}). For Jeroboam II's reign there are but two original items, reporting his success against Aram ($14^{25a,\ 28}$). For the long reign of Azariah-Uzziah we have, outside of the customary formula and editing, only the two statements, that " YHWH smote the king, so that he was a leper unto the day of his death, and he dwelt in a house apart " (although " he did what was right in YHWH's eyes "— a similar stroke also befalling another righteous king, Asa, I. 15^{23}), and that his son acted as regent (15^{5}). The exact original details of the *finale* of Jeroboam's dynasty and of his *fainéant* successors may only be listed : $15^{10,\ 14,\ 16,\ 17,\ 19,\ 20,\ 25,\ 29,\ 30}$, 17^{3-6}, 18^{9-11}; the survival of these precious details is remarkable. Contemporary are the extensive details of the alliance of Ahaz with the Assyrian Tiglath-pileser against the combination of Pekah of Israel and Reson of Aram (16^{5-9}), and the accompanying story of Ahaz's duplication of

§13C. TEMPLE ARCHIVES   37

a Damascene altar for the Temple along with other innovations (vv.$^{10-18}$—all told without comment, and involving the priest Uriah). For the long history of Hezekiah (cc.18–20) there are a few annalistic items : 18$^{4,\ 8}$ (each introduced with 'He') ; vv. $^{13-16}$ (quite distinct with its curt form of the history of the surrender as over against the following long story) ; 19$^{36,\ 37}$ (the return home of Sennacherib, his assassination by two sons, the succession of Esarhaddon). For Josiah's end there is a brief objective statement : " In his days Pharaoh-Necho king of Egypt went up against the king of Assyria to the river Euphrates, and king Josiah went against him. And he (Necho) slew him at Megiddo. And his servants carried him dead in a chariot, and brought him to Jerusalem " (23$^{29,\ 30}$). For Josiah's successors we have doubtless contemporary memoranda with exact details.[4] There need merely to be listed these items of annalistic origin : for Jehoahaz, 23$^{33-35}$; Jehoiakim, 24^{1-2a} (v.^{5} has the last reference to the ' Chronicles ') ; Jehoiachin, vv.$^{7-17}$. For Sedekiah there survives an exemplary contemporary record, 24^{20b}–25^{21}, with vv.$^{15-17}$ alone an intrusion. The postscript, 25$^{22-30}$, contains similar contemporary material.[5]

c. Temple Archives

The plan of the Temple and the accounts of its furnishing and its dedication (I. 6, 7, 8$^{1-13,\ 62-64}$), when reduced to simpler form, have been assigned by Kittel and others to a Temple source. Driver notes with approval (*Int.*, 189) similar assignments of narratives concerning the Temple (II. 11$^{4ff.}$, 12$^{4ff.}$, 16$^{10ff.}$, 22$^{3ff.}$), and so, *e.g.*, Kent more extensively (see

[4] See note 1 of the writer's art. cited above, noting the record in Jer. 52$^{28-30}$, which details the three deportations of the Jews and the figures for the victims involved, and remarking : " An exactly similar document describing the fall of a little state, preserved in the archives of a Hurrite family of about 1400 B.C., is presented by Chiera and Speiser in their ' Selected Kirkuk Documents,' *JAOS* 1927, no. 20, pp. 57 ff. See Speiser's admirable interpretation and his recognition of the correspondence with the records of the fall of the Jewish state."

[5] Only brief notice may be made of the preservation in the book of Chronicles of like archival material, taken from sources similar to, even identical with, those of Kings. This fact is coming to be recognized, *e.g.*, by Begrich, *Chronologie*, 208 f., Eissf., *Einl.*, 602, Albr., *SAC* 208.

his critical analysis, pp. xiv *seq*.). But the construction of the Temple was wholly a royal undertaking ; there is not a trace of priestly composition in these narratives, even in the account of the dedication, in which Solomon was the officiant. The Temple plan may practically be the architect's specifications ; note the doubtless contemporary postscript with the exact datings for the construction ($6^{37, 38}$)—of later origin 6^1 and 8^2. At the most the document may have been deposited in the temple. The story of the uprising against Athaliah in II. 11 has no specific priestly tinge ; that in $12^{5ff.}$ contains reproach of the priests' mismanagement of the sacred funds, and similarly $16^{10ff.}$ is not complimentary to the priestly jurisdiction. Likewise in the story of the reformation of the Temple in II. 22, 23 king Josiah is the reformer, the priests are his servants ; ' the high priest Hilkiah ' (22^4) could not interpret the Book of the Law which was found, and recourse was had to a prophetess (22^{14}). This absence of priestly literary sources is very notable in comparison with such origins in other ancient literatures. However, the temple, as the literary centre, may well have been the natural depository of such archives.

§14. THE HISTORICAL STORY

a. *Political Narratives*

This section concerns materials other than the purely annalistic. Its most extensive object is the Prophetical Story, to be treated in the next sub-section. But there are narratives quite distinct from those of that quarter.

The first two chapters of the book are the conclusion of the Davidic Court History, extending from 2 Sam. 16. For its characterization see Comm., introduction to I. 1, 2. As so often happens in literary history, this early creation is the most classical ; for its length and dramatic presentation it has no equal in the Historical Books. But it belongs to a literary *genre* that was early developed in Israel ; for its extent comparison may be made with the story of Joseph.

One political story appears in the account of the negotiations with Hiram of Tyre (I. $5^{15ff.}$). It has been built upon authentic details : Hiram's congratulations upon Solomon's accession, the memorandum on the transportation of the logs, and the exact items quoted at length from early sources in vv.$^{25, 27-32}$. Two stories are presented illustrating Solomon's wisdom, that of his dream at Gibeon with the ensuing judgment between the two harlots ($3^{1\text{ff.}}$) and that of the Queen of Sheba's visit (10^{1-13}). The story of the second oracle at Gibeon (9^{1-9}), in which the primitive element of the 'dream' is omitted, is sample of late moralizing judgment; *cf.* a similar brief intrusion in the story of the building of the Temple (6^{11-13}).

In the Judæan history there are the following stories of early origin, historically authentic. The history of the revolt of the North under Solomon's former lieutenant Jeroboam in its original substance (I. $11^{26-28, 31}$, 12^{1-5}) tells the political truth, that the revolt of the North was due to Solomon's heavy imposts, and that the schism came by divine fate ($12^{4, 15}$). The dramatic story of the uprising against the usurping foreigner Athaliah (II. 11) has all the earmarks of contemporary history, and without intrusion of a prophet. Parallel in character is the story of Josiah's reformation (II. 22, 23), when critically reduced to a simpler form. It is to be observed that these stories are the reflection of stirring events; also that, unlike the history of the North, they do not hail from schools of the Prophets. Only with Hezekiah's history do we have a long story of the kind, but this involving the canonical prophet Isaiah (II. 18–20 = Is. 36–39), an early hagiographon indeed, but one including authentic details. The South was sterile in such literature in comparison with the riches of the North, but politics there was far less stirring; we find the same proportion in the narratives of Judges.

b. *The Stories of the Prophets*

For the North the political history was embalmed in lengthy narratives proceeding from the schools of the Sons of the Prophets. Here there is revival of the literary art that had flourished for the history of the Judges (*e.g.*, the story of Deborah and Sisera, ch. 4; of Gideon and his son Abimelek, cc. 6–9; of Jephthah, cc. 11, 12). The word 'school' is used of purpose. The Prophetic Guilds, preceding the advent of the canonical Prophets, who dissociated themselves from their predecessors (*cf.* Am. 7^{14}, Mic. $3^{5\text{ff.}}$, Dt. $18^{20\text{ff.}}$, etc.), developed as so often in the history of the rise of enthusiastic religious bodies their own letters. The assemblages of these enthusiasts included exhortation and instruction, and among their members were found scribes who were inspired to write the history of the stirring times in which their leaders were so actively engaged.[1]

The longest example of this literary development appears in the Elijah cycle (I. 17–19, 21, II. 2). There follows that of

[1] See Comm. on II. 4³⁸ for the existence of a *yeshiva*, 'session,' i.e., school, in those guilds. For the literary beginnings in the Church, cf. Luke's reference to the 'many' who had 'undertaken' a history of the Gospel, while back of our Gospels lie documents difficult of critical precision, with subsequent generations producing a welter of apocryphal Gospels. In Islam there were probably written 'traditions' (ḥadīt), going back to Muhammad's day; see I. Goldziher, *Muhammedanische Studien*, 2 (1890), 1 ff., e.g., p. 9.

These pre-canonical Prophets and their guilds appear currently in the Histories of Israel and the Histories of its Religion; but they take a minor place in comparison with 'the Writing Prophets' of the canon. An admirable statement on the character of these stories is given by Kittel, *GVI* 2, 186. He holds that about 800 B.C. there arose a *Profetengeschichte*, the centre of which was Elijah with his contest against the Baal-cult. The composer of the history belonged without doubt to the Nebî'îm of his day, and his composition gives room for the suggestion that in those guilds the art of popular historical composition was cultivated. However this 'suggestion' might be made more positive. Kittel also notes (p. 339, n. 2) the Greek χρησμολόγος, 'purveyor of oracle-stories,' as distinguished from the χρησμῳδός, 'prophet.' *Per contra*, Stade, pref. to *SBOT*, holds that in their present form these stories are all post-exilic, " although the material in the Elijah and Elisha cycles 'may be pre-Exilic' "; but such literary scepticism is most unfounded. Of value is Gunkel's small volume, *Elias, Yahwe u. Baal* (1906), with many notes referring to similar religious phenomena in other religions. He recognizes (pp. 4 ff.) that in the Elijah stories both Saga and History are involved, and it is the historian's business to distinguish the two, although there remains a field for independent literary criticism. For a recent and comprehensive study see O. Plöger, *Die Prophetengeschichten der Samuel- u. Königsbücher* (1937), and for those early prophets at large, R. Kraetzschmar, *Prophet u. Seher im alten Israel* (1901); G. Hölscher, *Zum Ursprung des israelit. Prophetismus*, BWAT 13 (1913), 88 ff., and *Die Propheten* (1914); H. Junker, *Prophet u. Seher in Israel* (1928); A. Jepsen, *Nabi : soziologische Studien zur at. Lit.* (1934). For earlier treatments see, *inter al.*, A. Kuenen, *Religion of Israel* (1874), 1, ch. 3; W. R. Smith, *Prophets of Israel* (1882), Lect. 2. For the comparative phenomena, J. G. Frazer's *Folk-Lore in the O.T.* will be referred to *ad locos*.

§14B. THE STORIES OF THE PROPHETS

Elisha, entwined in the former, beginning at I. 19^{19} and continuing to II. 9, plus an apocryphal postscript, 13^{11-21}. Elijah is a most mysterious figure, coming out of the unknown and even so disappearing; he figures only in dramatic events, of which the scene on Mount Carmel is the most vivid (I. 18). Elisha is a secondary figure, as is his history; but his personal life is presented, and he is the head of a community of the Sons of the Prophets. The most striking story in this cycle is that of Jehu's revolt (II. 9, 10), a brilliant political narrative, in which Elisha appears only in the preface as inceptor of the uprising. Within this complex are inserted, with historical justification, two brilliant stories, connected with otherwise unknown prophets: the history of the rout of Ben-Hadad at Aphek (I. 20), in which figures an unnamed 'prophet' or 'man of God,' along with 'sons of the prophets' (vv.$^{13.\ 28.\ 35}$); and (ch. 22) the dramatic scene of the contest of the lone prophet Micaiah (cf. 19^{10}) with four hundred prophets and their named spokesman Sedekiah, the story being introductory to the ensuing vivid battle scene in which Ahab lost his life. Thus we possess a continuous series of Prophetical documents, broken only by annalistic items, extending from I. 17 to II. 10.

The remaining Prophetical Stories of the North are midrash in the current sense of the word, of dubious historical value. Such is the story of Ahijah the Shilonite and his oracle to Jeroboam (I. 11^{29-39}, cf. 12^{15}). Ch. 13 is a similar midrash, with its echo in II. $23^{17.\ 18}$. The prophet Jehu ben Hanani is said to have uttered an oracle against the house of Baasha (I. $16^{1-4.\ 7.\ 12}$). The Chronicler alleges a large number, some sixteen, of such Prophetic sources for the history of the kings (see Curtis, *Chron.*, 21). He twice uses the word 'midrash': 'the m. of the prophet Iddo' (II. 13^{22}), and 'the m. of the book of kings' (24^{27}).[2]

[2] The word 'midrash' is used above after the Chronicler's precedent. It was evidently an early technical literary term, which has variously concerned translators. The Grr. and 𝔙 translate with 'book'; 𝔖 reproduces with the corresponding *madrāshā*. Of the modern trr. GV has 'Historia,' followed by AV with 'story'; FV 'Mémoires'; RVV JV 'commentary'; Moff. and Chic. B, 'Midrash.' The word is to be explained from the semantic development of the same root ('to seek after, look up') in Arabic *darasa*, 'to read.' And there is the interesting parallel development of the Koranic verb *talā* (root *tlw*). ' to follow

§15. THE COMPILATION [1]

For historical subject-matter the book falls into three divisions. (1) I. 1, 2 is a continuation of the story of David in Samuel; on this section comment is made in Comm., *ad loc.* (2) I. 3–11 gives the history of Solomon, for which ' the Book of the Acts of Solomon ' is cited. The title is indefinite. It may refer to a strictly annalistic document, from which

after,' coming to mean ' to read, recite.' In addition is to be remarked the Semitic background of Jesus' utterance, " Search the Scriptures " (Jn. 5^{39}, *cf.* 7^{52}), the original of which verb was *drš*, *i.e.*, " Read the Scriptures." There may be compared the Latin ' legere,' ' to pick up, read,' *cf.* German ' lesen.' The word ' legend ' indeed is etymologically something ' to be read,' and quite corresponds with ' midrash ' and mediæval ' story,' as GV and AV excellently translate the word, which means a written historical story. The Old Norse word ' saga ' has often been used for translation, *cf.* Mrs. Church's *The Israel Saga*, although that word rather referred to heroic events. On the subject of such oral tradition in the background of the O.T. see at large the recent works of Gandz and Lods, and the extensive pertinent section in the encyclopædic work of the Chadwicks, *The Growth of Literature* (these all cited in the Bibliography). This last treatment in a note on p. 642, defining ' saga ' in opposition to ' legend ' is to the point as for the modern use of the latter word : " A saga, at least in the early stages of its life, need not of necessity contain any unhistorical element, apart from the form (the conversations, etc.) in which it is presented." But their judgment of Biblical story suffers from maintaining a now out-moded view of earlier Higher Criticism, as when it is stated (p. 684) that the story of David " carries the history of Israel back to *c.* 1000 B.C., perhaps three centuries before the general use of writing for literary purposes." The authors appear to be primarily authorities in Norse legends. On the other side stands Albright's treatment of the subject in his volume, *From the Stone Age to Christianity*, in his section on ' Oral and Written Transmission of History,' pp. 33 ff., encyclopædic in brief compass with its analogies from other such origins of literary composition.

[1] Reference may only categorically be made to the Commentaries (including Burney's *Hebrew Text*, the Int.), Introductions, Dictionary articles, Histories of the Literature, cited in the Bibliography. There are to be noted in addition Benz., *Jahvist u. Elohist in den Königsbüchern* (an essay at pursuing those sources in Ki.) and Hölscher's study in the Gunkel-*Eucharisterion*. Of unique value is the vivid polychrome presentation of the sources in Stade-Haupt, *SBOT* ; *cf.* also the critical presentations in Kittel's and Skinner's Commentaries and Kent's *SOT*. With regard to Benz.'s thesis there is to be observed Eissf.'s caution (*Einl.*, 150) that there is no clue for unravelling the possible threads continuing the sources of the Pentateuch.

§15. THE COMPILATION

the editor has drawn such materials ; but it is to be noted that the only dates given are those for the building of the temple and palace, while even the forty years of reign assigned appears to be an invented figure, like that for David's reign. Or it was a compilatory work, of what extent we may only guess. One metrical fragment appears in the citation of ' the Book of Jashar ' ($8^{12.\ 13}$). Kuenen regards the original work as wholly pre-Deuteronomic. The literary brilliance of the earlier Historical Story disappeared promptly under the magnificent Solomon. (3) There ensues the bulk of the book, the history of the Divided Kingdoms, I. 12–II. 17, continued with that of the surviving Judah, cc. 18–25.

An exemplary formal editing appears for the history of the Divided Kingdoms—notable, as despite the national schism, for the sense of the lasting community of the two halves of Israel. This feature is succinctly expressed by Driver (p. 189) : " In the arrangement of the two series of kings a definite principle is followed by the compiler. When the narrative of a reign (in either series) has once been begun, it is continued to its close—even the contemporary incidents of a prophet's career, which stand in no immediate relation to public events, being included in it ; when it is ended, the reign or reigns of the other series, which are synchronized with it, are dealt with ; the reign overlapping it at the end having been completed, the compiler resumes his narrative of the first series with the reign next following, and so on." [2]

As authority for his data in each reign the editor refers to ' the Book of the Chronicles of the Kings of Judah,' and *ditto* ' of the Kings of Israel.' In the latter case Joram and Hoshea are omitted in such listing, in the former Ahaziah, Athaliah, Jehoahaz, Jehoiachin, Sedekiah—in most cases for good reason. The extent and character of these two chronicles constitute a problem. Their minimum basis would be comparable with the Babylonian chronicles, which listed the

---

[2] Assemblage of these data is given by Kuenen, pp. 64 f., and most fully by Burney, pp. ix *seq*. For the vexed question of the originality of the synchronisms, see §16 below. For the history of the end of Judah exact dates are given, some of them in terms of Babylonian chronology. For these there was practically contemporary information that could be registered *memoriter*.

important events in a reign. The summary expression at the end of almost every reign, ' and all that he did,' or ' and all his might,' appears to make the chronicle in question a purely state document. Such annalistic records must have had their literary expansion, but the extent of this further development may only be judged from individual cases. These appear especially in the later Judæan history, as in the stories of the reform of Jehoash (II. 12), the intrusion of heathenish worship under Ahaz (II. 16), the temple-restoration and reformation under Josiah (II. 22, 23). But the great bulk of the Northern history, I. 12–II. 17, is literary story, prophetic and otherwise ; for its characteristics see Burney, pp. 207 ff. It is most reasonable to suppose that the latter material came to be incorporated with the official chronicle material in Judah under the reign of Josiah. This literary interest was reflection of the revival under that king, who bravely attempted the unification of All-Israel. We have to suppose an exodus of Northern literati to Jerusalem, bringing their manuscripts with them, and contributing to the cultural renaissance of the more sterile South. There such a literary expansion appears in the one Judæan prophet-story, that of Isaiah, with the inclusion of a poetic masterpiece (II. 19, 20). The phenomenon would be a small parallel to the flight of Greek scholars to the West to escape the Turkish invasions. And the revival, equally national and religious, under Josiah has its parallel in the Reformation period in Northern Europe. This politically temporary revival had its permanent spiritual results, in religion with the Deuteronomic reform which laid the basis for later Judaism (the religion of a Book, a tradition followed by the Church), and in letters with the accumulation of ancient literary remains which produced a National History, of which Kings was the climax.

The Book is a history written with a religious theory and a practical aim. It has for subject not mere History, but the lessons of History. There is honest self-judgment in this product of Hebrew historiography. The schism of Israel from the God-ordained Davidic kingdom was due to Solomon's sins, the fall of the North to its continued defiance of the True Religion, and again the ruin of Judah to the inescapable fate deserved by Manasseh's sin. The remarkable note is that, when all was lost, some one found the history of that tragic period worth recording as a lesson of God's discipline of his people. The spirit of the editor is fully Deuteronomistic.[3] With II. 25$^{22ff.}$ regarded as a postscript, the editor was a contemporary of Jeremiah, and, in his youth at least, of the publication of the Book found in the temple.

The book underwent its later minor revisions, as the variations in Heb. MSS and the early VSS show. But extensive interpolations are few, if any. The midrash in II. 23$^{15ff.}$ may be a case in point. The Old Greek presents an apocryphal supplement to I. 12, of doubtless Hebrew and ancient origin. But there is, apart from minute alterations, and constant contaminations of text from Ch., no patent influence from the later schools (Levitical, Priestly) which edited the Torah. A reconstruction from that point of view produced a parallel but fortunately distinct volume, that of Chronicles, while our book remained practically untouched.

§16. THE CHRONOLOGY

Recent Literature

The classical essay at Biblical chronology is that of Eusebius in his *Chronica*. For the Biblical renaissance may be noted L. Cappel's *Chronologia Sacra*, published in the London Polyglot, vol. 1, and again in Walton's *Biblicus Apparatus*. The following gives a list of recent literature bearing on the subject, with omission of reference to the pertinent Commentaries.

ALBRIGHT, W. F.: The Seal of Eliakim and the Latest Pre-exilic History of Judah, *JBL* 1932, 77 ff.
—— A Votive Stele Erected by Ben-hadad I of Damascus to the God Melcarth, *BASOR* 87 (1942), 23–9.
—— A Third Revision of the Early Chronology of Western Asia, *BASOR* 88 (1942), 28–36.

---

[3] Dr., *Int.*, 200 ff., and Burn., pp. xiii *seq.*, give full lists of phrases characteristic of the compiler of Ki., and their affinities with Dt. and Jer. Most recently Pfeiffer has made the statement (*Int.*, 377) that " the date of the original edition can be fixed without misgivings between Josiah's reforms in 621, based on the finding of Deuteronomy, and the destruction of Jerusalem in 586."

ALBRIGHT, W. F.: The Chronology of the Divided Monarchy of Israel, *BASOR* 100 (1945), 16–22.
BEGRICH, J.: *Die Chronologie der Könige von Israel u. Juda, u. die Quellen des Rahmes der Königsbücher* (Beiträge zur Historischen Theologie, 3), 1929.
—— Jesaia 14, 28–32. Ein Beitrag zur Chronologie der israelitisch-jüdischen Königszeit, *ZDMG* 86 (1932), 66 ff.
BOSSE, A.: *Die chronologischen Systeme im A.T. u. bei Josephus*, MVG 1908, no. 2.
CAH: 1, 145 ff.; vol. 3, at end, Synchronistic Tables.
CHAPMAN, W. J.: The Problem of Inconsequent Post-Dating in II Kings xv. 13, 17 and 23, *HUCA* 2 (1925), 57 ff.
—— Palestinian Chronological Data, *ib.*, vol. 8–9 (1932), 151 ff. (with year by year table).
CURTIS, E. L.: Chronology, *DB*.
DE VAUX, R.: La chronologie de Hazaël et de Benhadad III, rois de Damas, *RB* 45 (1934), 512 ff.
DEIMEL, A.: *Vet. Testamenti Chronologia*, Rome, 1912.
FORRER, E.: *Zur Chronologie der neuassyrischen Zeit*, MVG 1915, no. 3.
GEHMAN, H. S.: Chronology, *WDB* 1944.
HÄNSLER, H.: Die bibl. Chronologie des 8 Jahrhunderts vor Chr., *Biblica*, 10 (1929), 257 ff.
HONTHEIM, J.: Die Chronologie des 3. u. 4 Buches der Könige, *Zeits. f. kath. Theologie*, 42 (1918), 463 ff., 487 ff.
KAMPHAUSEN, A.: *Die Chronologie der hebräischen Könige*, 1883.
KENT, C. F.: *SOT* 492 ff., and plate after p. 199.
KITTEL, R.: *GVI* 2, §36.
KLEBER, A. M.: The Chronology of 3 and 4 Kings and 2 Paralipomenon, *Biblica*, 2 (1921), 3 ff., 170 ff.
KÖNIG, E.: Kalendarfragen, *ZDMG* 1906, 606 ff.
KREY, E.: Zur Zeitrechnung des Buches der Könige, *ZWT* 20 (1877), 404 ff.
KUGLER, F. X.: *Von Moses bis Paulus*, 1922 (mostly devoted to the Biblical chronology and calendar, and with a section, pp. 234–300, maintaining the historical trustworthiness of Chronicles).
LEWY, J.: *Forschungen zur alten Geschichte Vorderasiens*, MVÄG 29, Heft 2 (1924), 20 ff.

§16. THE CHRONOLOGY

LEWY, J.: *Die Chronologie d. Könige v. Israel u. Juda*, 1927.

LÖV, G.: Das synchronistische System der Königsbücher, *ZWT* 1900, 161 ff.

MAHLER, E.: *Handbuch der jüdischen Chronologie*, 1916 (with extensive treatment of the Jewish calendar systems, and a bibliography, pp. 629–35).

MANGENOT, E. V.: Chronologie, Vigouroux's *DB*.

MARTI, K.: Chronology, *EB*.

MCCURDY, J. F.: Chronology, *JE*.

MEYER, E.: Prinzipien der Rechnung nach Königsjahren, in his *Forschungen zur alten Geschichte*, 2 (1898), 441 ff., and *GA* 2, 274 ff.

MORGENSTERN, J.: The Three Calendars of Ancient Israel, *HUCA* 1 (1924), 3 ff., and Added Notes, vol. 3, 77 ff.

—— Supplementary Studies, etc., *HUCA* 1935, 1 ff.

—— The New Year for Kings, *Gaster Memorial Volume* (1936), 439 ff.

—— Chronological Data of the Dynasty of Omri, *JBL* 59 (1940), 385–96.

MOWINCKEL, S.: Die Chronologie der israelitischen u. jüdischen Könige, *Acta Or.*, 10 (1932), 161 ff.

NICKLIN, T.: *Studies in Egyptian Chronology*, Vol. 1, 1928 (in particular a study of Manetho's Dynasties).

ROBINSON, T. H.: *HI* 1, Add. Note, pp. 454 ff.

—— *Decline and Fall of the Hebrew Kingdoms*, 228 ff.

ROST, P.: *KAT* 320 f.

RUHL, F.: Die tyrische Königsliste des Menander von Ephesos, *Rheinisches Museum f. Philologie*, 48 (1898), 565 ff.

—— Die Chronologie der Könige von Israel u. Juda, *DZG* 12 (1895), 44 ff.

ŠANDA, A.: *Comm.*, 2, 399–441.

SELLIN, E.: *Geschichte*, 263 ff., **323 ff.**

STADE, B.: *GVI* 1, ch. 2.

THIELE, E. R.: The Chronology of the Kings of Israel and Judah, *JNES* 3 (1944), 137–86.

THILO, M.: *Die Chronologie des A.T.*, 1917.

—— *In welchem Jahre geschah die sogenannte syrisch-efraemitische Invasion, u. wann bestieg Hiskia den Thron?* 1918.

WELLHAUSEN, J. : Die Zeitrechnung des Buches der Könige, *JDT* 20 (1875), and in Bleek, *Einl.*[4], 263 ff.=*Comp.*, 299 ff.

WINCKLER, H. : *KAT* 316 ff.

For the astronomy involved see G. Schiaparelli, *Die Astronomie im A.T.*, 1904, F. K. Ginzel, *Handbuch der mathematischen u. technischen Chronologie*, 3 vols., 1906–14 ; and for the calendars, the Archæologies of Benzinger, §36, Nowack, §38. Of the titles listed above, Begrich and Thilo each present four large tables with a year-by-year synchronistic chronology, Begrich's tables also schematically indicating the several dating systems he proposes. In simpler and more useful form Šanda gives such a table (2, 424–7).

Addenda

PARKER, R. A., and DUBBERSTEIN, W. H. : *Babylonian Chronology* 626 B.C.–A.D. 45, Univ. of Chicago Press, 1942 ; 2nd ed., 1946.

VOGELSTEIN, M. : *Biblical Chronology.* I. *The Chronology of Hezekiah and his Successors*, privately printed, Cincinnati, 1944.

—— *Jeroboam II—The Rise and Fall of his Empire*, privately printed, Cincinnati, 1945.

a. List of Regnal Terms and Synchronisms [1]

ALL-ISRAEL

I. (1) Saul (years ?—1 Sam. 13^1)
   (2) David 40 (I. 2^{11})
   (3) Solomon 40 (11^{42})

JUDAH	ISRAEL
(4) Rehoboam 17	‖ Jeroboam I 22 (14$^{20,\ 21}$)
(5) Abijam 3	= ,, 18th (15$^{1,\ 2}$)

[1] The following presentation is largely based on Begrich's exemplary lists and discussion, pp. 58 ff. *Cf.* also Kuenen, pp. 64 f., and Burn., pp. ix *seq.* In the table, which presents the Hebrew data alone, cardinal numbers indicate years of reign, ordinals equivalence with years in the parallel. A common epoch for both kingdoms exists after (19), another after (38). Further notes, mostly textual and bearing upon the VSS, are given after each period.

§16A. REGNAL TERMS AND SYNCHRONISMS 49

	JUDAH	ISRAEL
(6)	Asa 41	=Jeroboam I 20th (15⁹·¹⁰)
(7)	,, 2d	=Nadab 2 (15²⁵)
(8)	,, 3d	=Baasha 24 (15²⁸·³³)
(9)	,, 26th	=Elah 2 (16⁸)
(10)	,, 27th	=Zimri 7 days (16¹⁵)
(11)		Civil war, Tibni and Omri (16²¹·²²)
(12)	,, 31st	=Omri 12 (16²³)
(13)	,, 38th	=Ahab 22 (16²⁹)
(14)	Jehoshaphat 25	= ,, 4th (22⁴¹·⁴²)
(15)	,, 17th	=Ahaziah 2 (22⁵²)
(16)	,, 18th	=Joram/Jehoram 12 (II. 3¹)
(17)	Jehoram 8	=Joram 5th (8¹⁶·¹⁷)
(18)	,, 2d	= ,, (1¹⁷)
(19)	Ahaziah 1	= ,, 12th (8²⁵), 11th (9²⁹); Jehu's accession (ch. 9)

(1) An editor of Sam. inserted the later formula for introduction of a reign: " son of —— years was X at his accession, and —— years he reigned " (the v. is lacking in OGrr.) ; the second blank was filled out with ' two.' (This numeral frequently occurs in the regnal terms, and may mean an indefinite number, like English ' a couple '; see Comm. on I. 17¹².)

(2), (3). The figures appear to be round numbers in the absence of original data. Some scholars, *e.g.*, Wellh., Kamph., Stade, discover manipulation of the regnal chronology, with the object of obtaining an era of 480 years from the founding of the temple to the end of the Exile (*cf.* assertion of such a preceding era in I. 6¹); *e.g.*, Stade (*GVI* I, 89): the balance of Solomon's reign, 40−3=37+393 years of his successors + an alleged term of exile, 50, =480. See Begrich's criticism, pp. 14 f.

(4)–(19). The Judæan 95 years is paralleled with Israelite 98. The difference may be accounted for by presumption of more ante-datings in the latter longer list.

(5) Abijam's reign is increased to 6 years by OGrr., so obtaining the desiderated equivalence.

(6) OGrr., ' Jeroboam 24th ' for ' 20th,' in consequence of the variation in (5).

(7) Gr. 246, ' Asa 3d ' for ' 2d '; *cf.* note (4)–(19).

(8) Gr. b *i* c₂, ' Asa 4th ' for ' 3d.'

(9) 𝔊 om. datum here, supplies it in 16⁶, with ' Asa 20th ' for ' 26th ' (so 𝔏 ℭ); other Gr. variants, ' 28th,' ' 29th.'

(11) See Comm., *ad loc.*

(12) Omri is given a 12-year reign between Asa 31st and 38th=7 years, but the interval of civil war, (9)–(12) 4 years, approximately

accounts for the difference. For 'Asa 31st' Gr. N v x y, 'Asa 27th' (*al.* '20th,' '28th,' '29th'; *Ant.*, viii, 12, 5, '30th'); the change gives the desiderated extra years. For the chronology of the civil wars see Comm. on I. $15^{15\text{ff}}$.

(13) 𝔊 𝔊^L, Ahab's accession in 'Jehoshaphat 2d' *vs.* 'Asa 38th.'
(14) 'Ahab 4th '=Grr. *in loco*; in OGr. insertion, $16^{28\text{a}}$,='Omri 11th'; *cf.* the variations in (12), (13).
(14)–(19) See Notes on I. $14^{22\text{ff}}$, $22^{41\text{ff}}$, Comm. II. 1^7.
(15) 𝔊^L, Ahaziah's accession in 'Jehoshaphat 24th,' *vs.* 'Jehosh. 17th.'
(16) Gr. v Joram's accession in 'Jehosh. 22d' *vs.* '18th'; *cf.* notes (12), (14).
(18) The datum bluntly contradicts the official data in (16), (17).
(19) In 8^{25} 𝔊^L 𝔖 correct '12th' to '11th'=9^{29}; but the latter is an intruded statement.

	Judah	Israel
II. (20)	Athaliah 6	‖ Jehu 28 (10^{36}, $11^{1\cdot\,3}$)
(21)	Joash 40	= ,, 7th ($12^{1\cdot\,2}$)
(22)	,, 23d	=Jehoahaz 17 (13^1)
(23)	,, 37th	=Joash 16 (13^{10})
(24)	Amaziah 29	= ,, 2d ($14^{1\cdot\,2}$, *cf.* v.^{17})
(25)	,, 15th	=Jeroboam II 41 (14^{23})
(26)	Uzziah 52	= ,, 27th ($15^{1\cdot\,2}$)
(27)	,, 38th	=Zechariah 6 months (15^8)
(28)	,, 39th	=Shallum 1 month (15^{13})
(29)	,, 39th	=Menahem 10 (15^{17})
(30)	,, 50th	=Pekahiah 2 (15^{23})
(31)	,, 52d	=Pekah 20 (15^{27})
(32)	Jotham 16	= ,, 2d ($15^{32\cdot\,33}$)
(33)	,, 20th	=Hoshea (15^{30})
(34)	Ahaz 16	=Pekah 17th ($16^{1\cdot\,2}$)
(35)	,, 12th	=Hoshea 9 ($17^{1\cdot\,6}$)
(36)	Hezekiah 29	= ,, 3d ($18^{1\cdot\,2}$)
(37)	,, 4th	= ,, 7th (18^9)
(38)	,, 6th	= ,, 9th (18^{10})

(20) 𝔊^L has a long absurdly repetitive interpolation after 10^{36}, dating Jehu's accession in Athaliah's 2d year; see Rahlfs, *SS* 3, 276.
(22) *Ant.*, ix, 8, 5, 'Joash 21st' for '23d.'
(23) For 'Joash 37th,' Gr. v, '36th,' N+15 MSS, '39th.'
(24) II. 14^{17} uniquely remarks that 'Amaziah survived Joash 15 years.'
(25) For 'Amaziah 15th' Gr. v, '16th.'
(26) For Uzziah's accession in 'Jeroboam 27th' Gr. v c_2, '25th.'
(27) For Zechariah in 'Azariah 38th,' N c_2+9 MSS, '28th.'
(28) For Shallum in 'Azariah 39th,' c_2, '28th.'

§16A. REGNAL TERMS AND SYNCHRONISMS   51

(30) For ' Pekahiah 2,' 𝕲ᴸ ' 10,' N c₂+11 MSS, the same group as in (27), ' 12.'

(33) For Hoshea in ' Jotham's 20th,' 𝔖 ' 2d year ' (by error).

(34) For Ahaz in ' Pekah's 17th,' 𝔖 ' 18th.'

(35) For ' Ahaz 12th ' Gr. o, ' 10th,' c₂, ' 14th.'

(36) For ' Hoshea 3d,' c₂, *Ant.*, ix, 13, 1, ' 4th,' v, ' 5th.'

(38) For date of capture of Samaria in ' Hezekiah 6th,' c₂, ' 10th,' 𝕮 ' 8th.'

Begrich's display of the various figures in Grr. and Josephus is most useful and suggestive. But there are variations of text, accidental or indeed wilful, in 𝔥, while the Greek variations, innumerable as they are, most of them evident errors (*e.g.*, in codex A), are most open to question. See Mowinckel's display of evident errors in both 𝔥 and Grr., pp. 266 ff. Begrich insists on ' good tradition ' underlying odd Greek MSS and Josephus, and makes use of their variants—some of which may indeed be proper corrections, but are nevertheless not original. No scientific result can be obtained from these odd quarters. MS c₂ (HP 127), at times in correspondence with N, and in two cases, (23) (30), in company with a larger group, goes its own way, distinct from the rest of the Lucianic group to which it belongs ; but this phenomenon appears peculiarly in the complicated era, (26)–(38). Also the group HP 71, 245 (not directly cited in *OTG*) offers cases of exceptional readings, either alone or with other MSS. 𝕲ᴸ otherwise offers no variations of value.

For (20)–(38) there is between Judah and Israel disparity of 165 years minus 143=22+2 part-year terms. But external evidence of the Assyrian records rigorously demands shortening of these figures, to be corrected by the generally accepted dates, 841, accession of Jehu and of Athaliah, and 722, the fall of Samaria in Hezekiah's 6th year—*i.e.*, a lapse of 119 years. For Judah this involves a disparity of 46 years. It is notable that the reign of the usurper Athaliah is included in the royal chronology ; but legally the royal heir's reign should have been dated from his father's death, so that subtraction of 6 from the overplus is to be made. The 29-year term of Amaziah is generally reduced by chronologers; *e.g.*, by discounting 13 years of previous regency ; *n. b.* (24), and see Comm. II. 14¹ᶠᶠ. Further Azariah-Uzziah's long reign of 52 years suggests scepticism ; there may be double counting with the years of his son Jotham's regency; *n. b.* the conflict of (32) and (33). Mahler and Kugler retain the figure, variously reducing Jotham's term. Lewy retains 52, for actual reign 27 years, plus 16 for Jotham's reign, plus 8 for regency (as alleged) of Ahaz. Others reduce the figure: *e.g.*, Begrich to 38 years, Kittel to 40, Robinson to 42, with various calculations of the regency, so diminishing Jotham's actual reign. Also the round figure 40 for Joash's reign (*cf.* the data for David and Solomon) arouses suspicion; we have to reckon with errors and lapses in the original documents, which were then arbitrarily corrected or filled out (*cf.* 1 Sam. 13^1). For Israel the discrepancy of some 25 years (144-119) is reduced by the Assyrian data. In the year 738 Menahem paid tribute to Shalmaneser V with resultant extent of 16 years to the fall of Samaria in 722. But the figures for his successors, Pekahiah 2, Pekah 20, Hoshea 9, make the era some 40 years plus x for balance of Menahem's term. The discrepancy is generally met by reducing Pekah's figure to 1 or 2 (Mahler 6, Kugler 5 or 6). The problem is further complicated by the synchronistic figures. According to (33) Hoshea became king in Jotham's 20th year—which then must be dated from the latter's accession to the regency, as he reigned only 16 years. But according to (35) Hoshea began to reign in Ahaz's 12th year; yet according to (37) (38) the Assyrian investment of Samaria occurred in Hezekiah's 4th year = Hoshea's 7th, and the capture in Hezekiah's 6th = Hoshea's 9th. *Cf.* Robinson, pp. 228 ff.

III. Judæan regnal terms. (39) Manasseh 55 years (II. 21^1). (40) Amon 2 (21^{19}). (41) Josiah 31 (22^1). (42) Jehoahaz 3 months (23^{31}). (43) Jehoiakim 11 (23^{36}). (44) Jehoiachin 3 months (24^8). (45) Sedekiah 11 (24^{18}).

From Hezekiah's reign to the destruction of Jerusalem, 587/586 B.C., crucial datings are given by external history. II. 18^9 dates the taking of Samaria in Hezekiah's 6th year = 722/721 B.C.[2] Between these dates is a lapse of 135 years, which figure actually corresponds to that of the sum of the

---

[2] There is contradiction here with the statement, II. 18^{13}, that the Assyrian invasion occurred in his 14th year; but for the secondary character of this figure see Comm., *ad loc.*

above reigns : 110+Hez. 29−6=135, with an overplus of two quarter-year reigns. Accordingly the figuration followed the post-dating system ; see *c* below.

b. *The Synchronisms between the Chronicles of Judah and Israel*

The regnal synchronisms have been largely disputed by modern criticism as secondary, constructed upon the given figures for the parallel reigns ; so, *e.g.*, by Wellhausen in his early monograph, and Meyer, and this position is cautiously maintained by recent historians, Kittel and Robinson. But the study of Babylonian-Assyrian historical documents has produced a positive trend in the opposite direction. Of recent eminent authorities for this position may be named Begrich, Kugler, Lewy, Mowinckel. Their argument is based upon similar synchronisms from early days in Babylonian lists, cross-referencing with Assyrian regnal years.[3] In view of these facts the writer's scepticism has yielded to a large extent. But considerable exceptions must be made. For the turbulent years following Jeroboam II official cross-reckoning for the Judæan dynasty must have been well-nigh impossible, as certain inner contradictions of synchronisms show. Further, in pursuance of the accepted chronological scheme Hebrew editors would have arbitrarily supplied lacking synchronisms, just as they at times made corrections, a fashion pursued galore by the Greek translators. It is on the safe side to assign to the Judæan and the early Israelite dynastic chronology prime importance, and to the synchronisms secondary value. This view is in contradiction to that of Lewy (*Chron.*, 28) and Mowinckel (*Chron.*, 172), alleging by way of argument that the former class is lacking in the similar Akkadian documents. But it is to be noted that the Hittites and the Egyptians recorded the regnal terms in their dynastic lists. The practical accuracy for the regnal terms Hezekiah-Jehoiachin has been exhibited just above.

[3] *E.g.*, Chronicle B, in *KB* 2, 274 ff., 330 ff., *ATB* 1, 330 ff., *CP* 208 ff., for the reigns from Tiglath-pileser to Esarhaddon. For the 12th century six such synchronistic lists have been published by E. F. Weidner, *Die Könige von Assyrien. Neue chronologische Dokumente, MVÄG* 26, Heft 2 (1921).

c. *The Calculation of Regnal Terms*

There is general difficulty of rendering an ancient precise date into modern chronological terms, due to the variation of New Year as between ancient systems, and as also in contrast with the modern beginning of the year. Internal conflicts appear in the ancient reckonings. In the Bab.-Ass. system the year 1 of a king did not begin until New Year in the spring; the preceding initial portion of the reign was termed *rēš sarrūtišu*, 'the beginning of his reign,' which appears to have its correspondent in the Hebrew dating of Evil-Merodach's action in II. 25^{27}, ' in the year of his becoming king ' (but for this still-disputed phrase see Comm., *ad loc.*). This system of post-dating avoided legal and historical complications. If a king did not overlive New Year no date was assigned to him in the royal series (*cf.* the citation of reigns in months in the Hebrew lists). But when, by ante-dating, year 1 was reckoned as of the months between accession and New Year, there would be arithmetical doubling of that year, as the last of the predecessor and the first of the successor. This may explain the discrepancy between 95 years in the Judæan line and the 98 in the Israelite, as remarked above on nos. (4)–(19) in the List of Regnal Terms, I. For the final group, III (the Judæan line alone), as observed *ad loc.*, the era closely approximates the known terminal dates, and the post-dating system must have been used. As for the disparity of figures in group II, the civil wars in the North, the Assyrian invasions, and also the disturbances in the South interfered with chronological regularity. Various systems of unravelling the problem have been proposed in order to save the synchronisms. For the discrepancy in regal periods Mahler has found a way out by the assumption of three regency-periods in the Judæan line (pp. 286 ff.), followed by Lewy. An attempt at obtaining an understanding of the evident disorder is that of Kugler's (pp. 163 ff.). He admits the many errors, which he attributes to later recensions; according to his theory the original composer of the book without exception ante-dated the reigns, the subsequent revisers post-dated throughout, and these (he finds three) disagreed in their methods.

The most elaborate as also most complicated system is that

§16D. SYNCHRONISMS WITH EXTERNAL HISTORY 55

of Begrich. He proposes four distinct chronicle methods based upon the variations in reckoning the calendar years and the regnal terms, and in four plates, listing the years 932–727, he presents in columnar arrangement the variations of the four methods. The work is of particular value for the detailed criticism of the data ; but its plan proposes an over-degree of theorization on part of the ancient writers. The contrast of ante-dating and post-dating is now generally recognized. Lewy holds (pp. 10 ff.) that the latter system came in with Azariah of Judah and Zechariah of Israel. Mowinckel (p. 179) finds it for the time after Hezekiah. Another problem lies in the beginning of the legal and regnal year. Did the royal year correspond with the ancient system dating the year from autumnal Tishri, or with the ecclesiastical year, dating from Nisan ?—the Talmud recognizes four beginnings of the year for as many social and economical purposes (*cf.* " the return of the year, when kings sally forth (to battle)," 2 Sam. 11¹). Mahler holds (p. 210) that the year began in the spring throughout the history ; Begrich that the regnal year began with the calendar year in autumn, with change to the spring dating in Josiah's time, which latter innovation Mowinckel denies (p. 175).[4]

d. The Synchronisms with External History

The continuous Assyrian *līmu-* or eponym-lists, dating as in Roman chronology after an officer who gave his name to the year—such an official being also listed in Solomon's court—offer a few exact synchronisms with the history in Kings.[5] For the end of the kingdom the book gives dates in Babylonian terms. As observed above, the rendering of the ancient years into terms of the modern calendar, beginning with January, is further confused by the Babylonian-Assyrian inception of

---

[4] For similar complicated datings in the books of Maccabees see E. Bickermann, *Der Gott der Makkabäer* (1937), Beil. II. For like confusion in Eusebius's Chronicle see *DCB* 2, 353 f.

[5] For Solomon's officer ' Over-the-Year ' see Comm., I. 4²ᶠᶠ·. For the *līmu*-list in question, giving a signal event for each year, see *KB* 1, 208 ff., *CP* 226 ff. The precision of the latter chronology is obtained from the dating of an eclipse of the sun, which occurred on June 15, 763 B.C. ; see Mahler, p. 259.

the year at the spring equinox, while the Hebrews, at least down to the latter part of Judah's history, dated it in the autumn. Consequently double figures have in general to be given in corresponding modern chronology.

853. Ahab and Ben-Hadad of Damascus named in Shalmaneser III's record of the battle at Karkar; Comm., I. 16, at end.

842/841; Jehu's tribute to Shalmaneser; Comm., II. $10^{32f.}$.

738. Menahem's tribute to Tiglath-pileser; Comm., II. $15^{23ff.}$.

734-732. Ahaz's name recorded as tributary to Tiglath-pileser.

733/732. The Assyrian capture of Damascus. For these two items see Comm. II. $16^{7ff.}$. Deposition of Pekah, Assyrian elevation of Hoshea to the throne; Comm. II. $15^{30ff.}$.

722/721 or 721/720 (Begrich). Capture of Samaria; Comm. II. $18^{9ff.}$.

701. Sennacherib's siege of Jerusalem; Comm. II. $18^{13ff.}$.

597/596; Mowinckel, 598/597. Nebuchadnezzar's conquest of Jerusalem; Comm., II. 24^{12}.

587 (Begrich, Mowinckel); 586 (Lewy). Destruction of Jerusalem; Comm., II. $24^{18ff.}$.

562/561 or 561/560. Restoration of Jehoiachin to favour by Evil-Merodach; Comm., II. 25^{27}.

For the additional dates for the last days of Jerusalem see Mowinckel, pp. 199 ff.; Albright, pp. 92 ff.; Morgenstern, *New Year for Kings*, 449 ff.

In addition may be listed certain regal synchronisms with international history.

Relations of Hiram of Tyre and Solomon (I. $5^{15ff.}$, in the latter's 4th year; $9^{10ff.}$, 'after 20 years'); Comm., I. 5^5, $6^{1, 37}$.

A Pharaoh's daughter, wife of Solomon; Comm., I. 3^1.

Shishak's invasion in year 5 of Rehoboam; Comm., I. $14^{25ff.}$

Jezebel, daughter of Ethbaal king of Tyre, wife of Ahab; Comm., I. 16^{31}.

Ben-Hadad of Damascus (*cf.* I. $20^{1ff.}$) named in the contemporary Zakar inscription.

§16D. SYNCHRONISMS WITH EXTERNAL HISTORY 57

Ben-Hadad's successor Hazael (II. 8[7ff.]) named in the Assyrian inscription of 842 B.C., and the latter's son Bar-Hadad in the Zakar inscription.

Mesha of Moab (*cf.* II. 3[4ff.]) records the ' 40 years of oppression of Moab ' by Omri and his sons.

Tiglath-pileser of Assyria, Rason of Aram contemporary with Ahaz of Judah, Pekah of Israel; Comm., II. 16[5ff.].

So-Seve, king of Egypt, in league with Hoshea against Assyria; Comm., II. 17[4].

Tribute of Manasseh recorded by Ashurbanipal; Comm., II. 21, introd.

Invasion of Palestine by the Ethiopian Tirhakah; Comm., II. 19[9].

The Egyptian Necho's defeat of Josiah at Megiddo, and his control of Judah; Comm., II. 23[29].

In addition is to be noted the unfortunately one-sided synchronism, I. 14[25], of Shishak's invasion of Judah in Rehoboam's 5th year; see Comm., *ad loc.* Shishak I reigned 945-924 (Breasted).

The writer foregoes adding to the detailed chronologies presented in Commentaries, histories, and the many special monographs. Omitting the early apocryphal datings for David and Solomon (each assigned 40 years), the following variants, as proposed, may be noted for the date of the accession of Rehoboam and Jeroboam I: Mahler, 953; Robinson, 936; *CAH*, Olmstead, 935; Šanda, 933; Kittel, Skinner, Winckler, 932; Mowinckel, Gehman, 931; Kugler, 929; Begrich, 926; Albright, Lewy, 922. The traditional Ussherian date is 973. The date 936 is obtained by adding the 95 years of the Judæan line in (4)-(19) above to the fixed date 841; but that assumed date should be reduced on the theory of early ante-dating.

Although we have to admit that no scheme of Chronology is perfect, it is helpful to have a table in which the kings of Israel and Judah and the events taking place in their reigns are presented in a synchronism in parallel columns. The editor accordingly has inserted at this place his Chronology, which he published in the *Westminster Dictionary of the Bible* and in the Concordance of the *Westminster Study Edition of the Holy Bible.*

I. The Period of the Hebrew Kings
(about 1025 to 586 B.C.)

A. The United Kingdom.
  Saul (about 1025-1010 B.C.).
  David (about 1010-970 B.C.).
    King of Judah 7 years and 6 months.
    King of united Israel and Judah 33 years (2 Sam. 4:5).
  Solomon (about 970–931 B.C.).
    At the death of Solomon the kingdom was split into two independent kingdoms.

B. The Divided Kingdom.

This scheme is not offered as final in every particular, but it can be used as a working basis for the dates of the kings of Israel and Judah. Many of these dates must be considered merely as approximate. Slightly different arrangements of the data are possible at several points, but they do not affect the chronology as a whole. It would be very desirable to have a scheme consistent in all details, but with our present knowledge that is impossible. The unqualified figures in parentheses after a king's name denote the length of his reign in years. A crossline after a king's name in the Northern Kingdom or events in his reign marks a change of dynasty. The line of David ruled in unbroken succession in the Southern Kingdom except for the 6 years when Athaliah had usurped the throne (842–836 B.C.).

	JUDAH, OR SOUTHERN KINGDOM			ISRAEL, OR NORTHERN KINGDOM, AND OTHER NATIONS		
Reference	Ruler and Events	Year of Reign	Date B.C.	Year of Reign	Ruler and Events	Reference
I Kings 14:21	**Rehoboam** (17) 931-915	1	931*	1	**Jeroboam** (22) 931-910	I Kings 14:20
II Chron. 11:17	Three years' godliness	2		2		
		3		3		
I Kings 14:25	Shishak's invasion	4		4		
		5		5		
		6		6		
		17	915	17		
I Kings 15:1, 2 / II Chron. 13:1, 2	**Abijam** (3) 915-912	1		18		
		2		19		
I Kings 15:9, 10	**Asa** (41) 912-871; ascends throne 1st regnal yr.	3 1	912	20		
II Chron. 14:1	Land quiet 10 yrs.	2	910	21		
		3		1²²		
		4		2¹		**Nadab** (2) 910-909	I Kings 15:25
		10		8	**Baasha** (24) 909-886	I Kings 15:28-33
II Chron. 14:9-15	War with Zerah between yrs. 11 and 14	11		9		
II Chron. 15:10	Reformation	12		10		
II Chron. 15:19	Buys aid of Ben-hadad against Baasha	13		11		
II Chron. 16:1, 2 †		14		12		
		15		13		
		16		14		
		25		23¹⁴		
		26	886	1	**Elah** (2) 886-885	I Kings 16:8
				2	Zimri (7 days)	I Kings 16:10, 15

§16D. SYNCHRONISMS WITH EXTERNAL HISTORY

			29		
			30	3	
			31	4	
I Kings 16:28a (LXX)	Jehoshaphat associated			5	Civil war between Omri and Tibni. Omri prevails and reigns with undisputed authority	I Kings 16:22, 23
			36	10		
II Chron. 16:12	Asa diseased			11		876
						875
I Kings 22:41, 42	**Jehoshaphat** (25) 875-850 1st yr. of sole reign	3	38	1	**Ahab** (22) 874-852	874 I Kings 16:29; Heb. text, 38th yr. of Asa; LXX, 2d yr. of Jehoshaphat
		4	39	2		
		5	40	3		
			41	4		870
II Kings 8:16-26 II Chron. 21:6; 22:1, 2	Married his first-born Jehoram, to daughter of Ahab		1	5		
			2	6		
			3	7	Elijah, the prophet	
			4	8		
			5	9		
			15	19		
			16	20		
					Ahab, allied with Damascus, Arabs, and others, meets Shalmaneser at Karkar (854) 853; battle indecisive	
			17	1²¹	**Ahaziah** (2) 852-850	I Kings 22:51
	Jehoram (Joram) associated	9	18	1,1²²	**Jehoram (Joram)** (12) 850-842, perhaps associated with the government in some capacity before 850	
						II Kings 1:17; 3:1
		3	19	2	War with Moab	II Kings 3:4, 5
		4	20	3		
		5	21	4	Shalmaneser at war with Damascus	
				850		

* The exact date of the death of Solomon is unknown. According to different systems of chronology this event is variously dated: 945, 936, 935, 932, 931, 930, 926, 925, 922. With our present knowledge we cannot be positive, and the above chronological scheme could be modified in various places.

In addition to references from the English Bible in the Chronology, the following have been included: LXX (the Septuagint, or the Greek version of the O.T.); Jos. *Antiq.* (Josephus, *Jewish Antiquities*); Jos. *Apion* (Josephus, *Apion*).

† The dates 35th and 36th yr. of the reign of Asa given in these vv. in the Heb. text were explained by the older commentators as reckoned from the commencement of the Kingdom of Judah. The numbers are then correct. Modern interpreters generally regard the Heb. text as corrupt, and read 15 or 25 and 16 or 26 for 35 and 36 respectively. They are doubtless right in doing so, for the text of Chronicles has not been transmitted so carefully as it should have been, and the phrase "year of Asa," or other king, always refers to his regnal yr., and Baasha died in the 26th yr. of Asa (I Kings 16:8-10). The 15th and 16th yrs. of Asa correspond respectively to the 35th and 36th yrs. of the division of the kingdom.

	JUDAH, OR SOUTHERN KINGDOM				ISRAEL, OR NORTHERN KINGDOM, AND OTHER NATIONS	
Reference	Ruler and Events	Year of Reign	Date B.C.	Year of Reign	Ruler and Events	Reference
II Kings 8:16, 17	**Jehoram** sole king (8) 850–843	1		5	Ben-hadad besieges Samaria	II Kings 6:24
II Chron. 21:18, 19	Sorely diseased, hence	4 5 6		8 9 10	Ben-hadad murdered and succeeded by Hazael between 845–843	
II Kings 9:29 II Kings 8:25, 26 II Chron. 22:1	Ahaziah made regent **Ahaziah**, king (1)	7 8	842	11 12	Jehoram slain by Jehu **Jehu** seizes the throne (28) 842–814	
II Kings 11:1–3	Slain by Jehu **Joash (Jehoash)**, sole surviving heir and legitimate king In concealment for 6 yrs. from **Athaliah**, who usurped the power (842–836)			1 2 3 4 5 6 7	Jehu and Hazael pay tribute to Shalmaneser Elisha, the prophet Shalmaneser at war with Hazael On account of Jehu's increasing age and incapacity for war,	
II Kings 11:4; 12:1	**Joash**, king (40) 836–797 Athaliah slain		836	1 2	**Jehoahaz** associated Hazael against Israel	Jos. *Antiq.* ix. 8, 5, and II Kings 13:10, correcting v.1 (total 17) II Kings 10:32
II Kings 12:6 II Kings 12:17	Renewed attempt to repair Temple Hazael against Gath and Jerusalem. When he departs, he leaves		814	3 (28)	Jehoahaz alone 814–800 Hazael continues to oppress Israel all the days of Jehoahaz	II Kings 10:36
II Chron. 24:25	Joash sorely diseased	37	800	1 17	**Jehoash (Joash)** (16) 800–785	II Kings 13:3, 22
II Kings 14:1	**Amaziah** undertakes government; 799–782?; but (29) 799–777, total	1 2	799	2 3	[Bin-adduj-mari, king of Damascus, besieged by Ramman-nirari]	II Kings 13:10
	Joash slain and Amaziah (40) sole king	5	797	4	Moabites invade Israel Jehoash victorious over Ben-hadad	II Kings 13:20 II Kings 13:25

§16D. SYNCHRONISMS WITH EXTERNAL HISTORY

Reference	Judah	Year B.C.	Year	Israel / Assyria	Source
II Kings 14:21	(Amaziah)... about 785–about 734, total	16, 17	784	785–745, 1st regnal yr.	
II Kings 14:19	Conspiracy against Amaziah (782?)	18	782		
II Kings 14:21	**Uzziah or Azariah**. Actual reign about 782?–about 751		782, 781		
II Kings 14:17; II Chron. 25:25; II Kings 14:19; II Chron. 25:27, 28; II Kings 14:22; II Kings 15:1	Amaziah survives Jehoash 15 yrs. Amaziah slain (29) and Uzziah supreme Builds Elath after death of Amaziah In special sense "reigns"		771, 758, 751		Jos. *Antiq.* ix. 10, 3
II Kings 15:5; II Kings 15:32, 33	Becomes leprous and **Jotham** conducts the government (16) 751–736	14, 15, 27, 28, 34, 39, 40, 41		Amos, the prophet Hosea, the prophet **Tiglath-pieser III**, 746/5–728/7, king of Assyria **Zechariah** (6 mos.)	II Kings 15:8
		38, 39, 39	745	**Shallum** (1 mo.) **Menahem** ascends (10) 744–735, 1st regnal yr.	II Kings 15:13 II Kings 15:17
		1, 2, 3, 8	742, 738	Menahem pays tribute to Pul (Tiglath-pieser)	II Kings 15:19
		9, 10, 1, 2	736, 735	**Pekahiah** (2) 735–734	II Kings 15:23
II Kings 17:1	Ahaz associated Isaiah, the prophet	(50)	734	**Pekah** (20) 734–730 Tiglath-pileser III receives tribute from Ahaz Syro-Ephraimitic War Deportation of 3½ tribes of the Northern Kingdom Tiglath-pileser captures Gaza	II Kings 15:27† { II Kings 15:29 I Chron. 5:26
II Kings 16:1, 2	**Ahaz** (16) 736–721 Micah, the prophet	(52)		Tiglath-pileser against Damascus	
	Uzziah dies*		733	Fall of Damascus	
			732		

* "In the year that king Uzziah died." (Isa. 6:1) is often given as about 740 B.C.

† Ussher and the older chronologists assumed that anarchy prevailed for several yrs. between the death of Pekah and the accession of Hoshea. Both the Hebrew and the Assyrian records, however, clearly indicate that no interregnum occurred, but that Hoshea slew Pekah and succeeded him on the throne. The reign of 20 years causes a chronological difficulty; apparently Pekah was in authority in Gilead for 15 yrs. and reigned only 5 yrs. in Samaria.

JUDAH, OR SOUTHERN KINGDOM				ISRAEL, OR NORTHERN KINGDOM, AND OTHER NATIONS		
Reference	Ruler and Events	Year of Reign	Date B.C.	Year of Reign	Ruler and Events	Reference
II Kings 15:30 II Kings 17:1	20th yr. of Jotham 12th yr. of Ahaz }		730	1	**Hoshea** (9) 730–722	{ II Kings 15:30 II Kings 17:1
II Kings 18:1, 2 Jos. *Antiq.* ix. 13, 1	**Hezekiah** ascends 1st regnal yr.	1		2 3 4	**Shalmaneser V**, 728/7– 722, king of Assyria	
		2 3 4		5 6 7	Hoshea seeks an alliance with Sib'e (So) of Egypt	
II Kings 18:10 II Kings 18:9 Jos. *Antiq.* ix. 14, 1 }	Ahaz dies Hezekiah sole king (29) 721–693	5 6 (1) 7	722/1 721 720	8 9	**Fall of Samaria*** **Sargon**, 722–705 Defeats Sib'e (So) of Egypt at Raphia Assyrian troops in Samaria and Arabia Tribute from Egypt Philistia in revolt against Assyria. Judah, Moab, and Ammon in coalition	II Kings 17:4
		13	715			
II Kings 18:13 II Chron. 32:1–8 Isa. 36:1 II Kings 20:1–6 Isa. 38:1–8 }	Sennacherib invades Judah	14	714			
II Kings 20:12 Isa. 39:1	Hezekiah sick Receives embassy from Merodach-baladan about this date }		713 712		Judah tributary to **As- syria**. Merodach-bala- dan incites neighbouring nations against Assyria	
Isa. 20:1	Siege of Ashdod		712 710		Sargon besieges Ashdod Sargon dethrones Merodach-baladan	
II Kings 18:14 ff.	Besieged by Sennacherib		705 701		**Sennacherib**, 705–681 Against Hezekiah and Jerusalem Defeat of Egyptians at Eltekeh Siege of Lachish and Jerusalem Hezekiah pays tribute Discomfiture of Assyrians	II Kings 18:14–16 II Kings 19:35
II Kings 21:1 II Kings 19:37	**Hezekiah** dies **Manasseh** (55) 693–639 }		693 681		**Esarhaddon**, 681–669 Receives tribute from Manasseh of Judah	

§16D. SYNCHRONISMS WITH EXTERNAL HISTORY

Ezra 4:2, 10

Reference	Event	Year (Judah)	Regnal yr	External Event	Year B.C.
II Chron. 33:11	Carried in chains to Babylon by the Assyrians, probably at this time	55		(death of Esarhaddon) and Ashurbanipal. **Ashurbanipal, 669–626** Invasion of Egypt (667–663) Ashurbanipal captures Babylon and dethrones (652) Shamash-shum-ukin, his brother, who had incited peoples from Elam to the Mediterranean to revolt against Assyria. Receives tribute from Manasseh of Judah	669
II Kings 21:19	**Amon** (2) 639–638				639
II Kings 22:1	**Josiah** (31) 638–608		1		638
II Chron. 34:3	Seeks the LORD		8		631
II Chron. 34:3	Begins to purge nation		12		627
Jer. 1:1, 2	Jeremiah begins to prophesy		13		626
Jer. 25:1, 3	13th Josiah to 4th Jehoiakim inclusive = 23 yrs.		18	**Nabopolassar, king of** Chaldeans, 626–605	621
II Kings 22:23 } II Chron. 34:8	Reformation by Josiah				621
				Fall of Nineveh	612
				Necho, king of Egypt, 609–593	609
II Kings 23:29	Battle of Megiddo; death of Josiah		31		608
II Kings 23:31	**Jehoahaz** king 3 mos.		1		
II Kings 23:36 Jer. 25:1; 46:2 Jos. Antiq. x. 6, 1	**Jehoiakim** (11) 608–597 He and Necho subjugated by Nebuchadnezzar		4	Battle of Carchemish (605) **Nebuchadnezzar** (Nebuchadrezzar), king of Chaldeans, 605–562	605
Jer. 36:9	9th mo, public fast Jeremiah's roll burned		5	3d or 2d yr.	604
Jos. Antiq. x. 10, 3 Dan. 2:1 II Kings 24:1	Two yrs. after the defeat of Egypt Nebuchadnezzar dreams Having paid tribute to Neb. 3 yrs., rebels		6	4th yr.	603
	Jehoiakim dead before surrender of Jerusalem		7 / 11		602
II Kings 24:8–12 II Chron. 36:10	**Jehoiachin,** 3 mos. Goes captive to Babylon toward close of yr.			8th or 7th yr.	597
Jer. 52:28 II Kings 24:18	**Zedekiah** (11) 597–586		1		597
Jer. 51:59	Visits Babylon		4		594

* Dated by many authorities in the early months of 721 B.C.

\multicolumn{4}{c	}{JUDAH, OR SOUTHERN KINGDOM}			\multicolumn{3}{c}{ISRAEL, OR NORTHERN KINGDOM, AND OTHER NATIONS}	
Reference	Ruler and Events	Year of Reign	Date B.C.	Ruler and Events	Reference
Ezek. 1:2	Ezekiel begins to prophesy		593	Psamtik (Psammetichus) II, king of Egypt, 593–588	
II Kings 25:1	Jerusalem besieged	9	about 588	Apries (Hophra), king of Egypt, 588–569 18th (or 17th) of Nebuchadnezzar	
Jer. 32:1		10	587		
II Kings 25:8, 9 Jer. 52:12–16, 29 Jos. *Antiq.* x. 8, 5 Jos. *Apion* i. 21	Temple burned in 5th mo.	11	586	19th (or 18th) of Nebuchadnezzar Zedekiah captured, taken to camp of Nebuchadnezzar at Riblah, where he was blinded; deported to Babylon	Ezek. 12:13

II. The Exile
(586–538 B.C.)

Reference	Ruler and Events		Date B.C.	Ruler and Events	Reference
Jer. 52:30 Jos. *Antiq.* x. 9, 7	Captives carried to Babylon 5th yr. after destruction of Jerusalem=23d Neb.		582/1		
			568	23d yr. of Nebuchadnezzar Nebuchadnezzar invades Egypt in 37th yr. of his reign	
			562	Evil-Merodach (Amel-Marduk), king of Chaldeans	
II Kings 25:27	37th yr. of Jehoiachin's captivity		561		
II Chron. 36:22, 23	Rebuilding of Temple authorized		539 538	Cyrus, king of Persia, takes Babylon 1st yr.	
Ezra 3:8 Jos. *Apion* i. 21	Rebuilding begun in 2d mo., having remained waste for 50 yrs.—that is, 49 yrs. and 9 mos.		537	2d yr.	

A COMMENTARY ON
THE BOOKS OF KINGS

COMMENTARY

I. 1-11. The regency and reign of Solomon. ‖ 2 Ch. 1-9; cf. *Ant.*, viii, 1-7.

CC. 1 and 2 continue the intimate Court History of David, recorded in 2 Sam. 9-20; the initial conjunction expresses the connexion.[1] As a piece of literature the section stands wholly apart from the rest of Ki., is sequel to the material peculiar to Sam. The story, although evidently written by an intimate of the court, and one sharing in the popular enthusiasm for the national hero David, is by no means a royal encomium, for the writer is possessed with the sense of the tragic motive that dominated the last years of the king, the darling of Israel. That tragedy began with the taking of his neighbour's wife, Bathsheba, and his foul murder of her husband, relieved only by his affection for the child of that union, whom God took away; there follows in dire consequence his eldest son Amnon's outrage on his half-sister, the vengeance taken upon him by Absalom, and then the latter's revolt, relieved again by the father's bitter sorrow over the death of the unfilial son. And in the present sequel we read of the court cabal which desired to raise the presumptive heir-apparent to the regency, evidently a conspiracy against the favourite queen and her son Solomon, with the sequel in the death of Adonijah and the death or disgrace of the ancient ministers, Joab and Abiathar. As the tragedy

[1] Summary reference for this Court History is made to the Commentaries on Sam. and the Introductions; for the most recent analysis see Eissf., *Komposition der Samuelisbücher* (1931), esp. pp. 48 ff. (*cf.* his *Einl.*, 151 ff.), and for a recent discussion L. Waterman, "Some Historical and Literary Consequences of Probable Displacement in 1 Kings 1-2," *JAOS* 1940, 383 ff. The most elaborate treatment of the present section is that by L. Rost, *Die Überlieferung von der Thronfolge Davids* (*BWANT* 1926), insisting on its literary independence from the earlier narratives; *cf.* Eissf.'s review, *OLz.*, 1937, 657 ff. For the political background see W. Caspari, *Thronbesteigungen u. Thronfolge der israel. Könige* (1917).

began with Bathsheba, so it ends with her figuring unwittingly in the death of the crown prince. With this culmination the story ends, without colophon, even as the origins of the narrative-source are unknown.

The story is told with fine artistry. The initial verses, detailing an apparently gossipy detail of harem history, have their *dénouement* ; the anecdote of Bathsheba's and Nathan's appearance before the king ($1^{15ff.}$), and that of Adonijah's romance and Bathsheba's plea for him ($2^{13ff.}$), are brilliant pictures of Oriental court life. It is the last piece we possess of that early bloom of written historical story which had its apogee in the theme of the heroic David. All the glory of Solomon did not foster this remarkable literary development ; his organization of the realm into a ' modern state ' rather cut the spiritual nerve of his people, and the ensuing disruption of his kingdom shocked its proud self-consciousness. The praise of Solomon as poet and philosopher ($5^{9ff.}$), which record may well have historical foundation, belongs to the age of sophistication. Israel's genius lay dormant for a commensurate theme until the rise of another class of popular heroes, the Prophets, who were of the people and for the people. Apart from that material, the history of the Kingdoms is fairly commonplace. But even though little of it is great literature, the book of Kings remains as the first ordered attempt at a national history that we possess from antiquity, itself again the development of old historical saga and story.

For literary and historical appreciation of this document, citation may be made of some masters in ancient Oriental history. Wellhausen : [2] " In den Hergang der Begebenheiten, die natürlichen Anlässe und menschlichen Motive der Handlungen gewinnen wir da vielfach einen recht tiefen Einblick, wenngleich der Standpunkt ein beschränkt jerusalemischer ist und beispielsweise die eigentlichen Gründe des Aufstandes der Judäer unter Absalom kaum berührt werden. Die Begeisterung für David hat wol auch hier die Feder geführt, aber seine Schwächen werden nicht verschwiegen, die wenig erbaulichen Verhältnisse seines Hofes getreu berichtet, die Palastintrigue, durch die Salomo auf den Thron gelangte, mit einer beinah **boshaft scheinenden** Unbefangenheit vorgetragen." Eduard

---

[2] *Prolegomena* (ed. 6), 259.

Meyer in an earlier work : [3] " Die Berichte über David lehren durch ihren Inhalt unwiderleglich, dass sie aus der Zeit der Ereignisse selbst stammen, dass ihr Erzähler über das Treiben am Hof und die Charactere und Umtriebe der handelnden Persönlichkeiten sehr genau informiert gewesen sein muss ; sie können nicht später als unter Salomo niedergeschrieben sein " ; and later : " Es ist etwas Erstaunliches, dass eine derartige Geschichtsliteratur damals in Israel möglich gewesen ist. Sie steht weit über allem, was wir sonst von altorientalischer Geschichtsschreibung wissen, über den trockenen offiziellen Annalen der Babylonier, Assyrer, Ägypter, über den märchenhaften Geschichten der ägyptischen Volksliteratur." Meyer again, in his last, posthumously published work : [4] " Etwas ganz Überraschendes und Einzigartiges und ein Beweis für die hohe Begabung des Volks und die von ihm erreichte Höhe und Selbstständigkeit der Kultur ist aber, dass daneben hier allein im gesamten vorderen Orient eine durchaus selbstständige Geschichtsliteratur entstanden ist." The French scholar Lods [5] characterizes the ' dramas ' in 2 Sam. 9–20, as marked " avec une exactitude, une intensité de vie, une pénétration psychologique qui trahissent un maître historien informé par un temoin oculaire." And finally a citation from an American historian of Oriental antiquity, Olmstead : [6] " Whether or not Abiathar was our historian, his work is almost a miracle to his modern successor. History such as this had never before been written. Inspired annals of a monarch's wars, lists of kings, brief dry chronicles, folk tales of past heroes, this was the best that had been produced. Suddenly and without apparent forerunners, we have a narrative which invites comparison with many present-day accounts of a reign. The author is well informed, he knows court life from the inside, he writes simply but vividly, not for a monarch's favour but for the instruction of generations to come. What most amazes his modern successor is his complete objectivity. . . . Our author is equally careful to trace the degeneration of David's character under the influence of success and luxury, and the picture he paints, not by laboured description but by allowing the deeds to speak for themselves,

[3] *IN* 485 f. [4] *GA* 2, pt. 2, 199.
[5] *Israël*, 423. [6] *HPS* 337 f.

is stark tragedy, true to the dramatic facts of human nature.
. . . His name may be lost, but his modern successor must
pay tribute to this first and strangely modern historian of
three thousand years ago."

Olmstead's attribution of ' objectivity ' is so true of this
composition that in spite of the critical recognition of its
contemporaneity and historicity as a whole, discussion of
the authorship is still rife. 1 Ch. 29^{29} records ' the acts of
Samuel the seer, of Nathan the prophet, of Gad the seer '
(*cf.* 2 Ch. 9^{29}) as authorities for these reigns, but the citations
are apocryphal. Modern scholars are inclined to attribute
these court memoirs to Abiathar, David's intimate and personal priest, the partisan of Adonijah in the latter's attempt
at the throne, and subsequently deposed by Solomon.[7] But
the opening of the story pictures Adonijah as a wayward
youth, in terms used of his older rebellious brother Absalom ;
the actual items of the conspiracy are put in his adversary
Nathan's mouth (1$^{22\text{ff.}}$), but the intention of usurpation is
bluntly given in v.^{5}. Whatever partisanship the author may
have held—and in the strife over the succession none could
have been non-partisan—he skilfully conceals his interest.[8]
The present writer agrees with Kittel (*Comm.*, and *Gesch.*,
2, 184) in coming to no solution on score of the author's
identity.

Finally there is this point for the historical critic to bear
in mind. With all the impressive ' objectivity ' of our history
it still remains impossible to determine the details of the
actual facts, not to say the hidden motives, in such a story
of courtly intrigue and tragedy. All that we have are contemporary stories emanating in large part from royal court
and harem. What conversations went on in that secluded

---

[7] So, *e.g.*, Budde, *GAL* 86 (or to Abiathar's family), Olmstead,
p. 336—at least as likely. For Abiathar's authorship might be claimed
the fact that the account of his dismissal from office (2$^{26,\ 27}$) does not
name his successor, as in the case of Joab (2$^{35\text{a}}$–v.^{b} is a later insertion).

[8] On the other side see Šanda's argument, pp. 49 ff., citing with
approval Wellhausen's dictum on the ' fast boshaft vorkommende
Aufrichtigkeit ' of the author ; but this reads into the story un-
warranted sophistication, not found in Hebrew literature. Ehrlich
presents (*Randglossen*, 213 ff.) a very sardonic view of the ' pro-Solomon
conspiracy.'

circle were never known exactly outside ; current story turned objects of conversation into direct discourse—a not unknown literary art of historians. If the stories that came out of the harem were monarchical propaganda, so also anti-monarchical stories, like those of the Prophets, may equally be propaganda. We are confronted here with the historically almost unanalyzable element of the *genre* of the Historical Story, which, apart from public acts and letters, gives all we know of ancient personalities. The presumption in general for the present story is its *bona fides*. Were it not for the tragic sense that inspired the narrator, we should never have had the amount of indubitable historical fact which he incorporates.

Apart from the disputed passage, 2^{1-9}, the original story has been only slightly supplemented : 2^{10-11}, ^{12b} is editorial insertion of the usual data for end of a reign ; 2^{27} is editorial comment ; 2^{35b}, not in 𝕲, is a later insertion ; 2^{46b} is a fresh title to the subsequent history. For much more radical criticism see Waterman's article cited in n. 1.

1^{1-4}. This very *intime* story of David's senility and the fair Abishag has its proper place in the history, and well illustrates the principle of suspense that marks Hebrew storytelling ; it prepares the way for the tragedy of Adonijah's undoing ($2^{13ff.}$). For Abishag's origin from Shunem and her identity, or confusion, with the Shulammite of the Song of Solomon (7^1) see Note. **2.** The *ministers* (EVV *servants*), *i.e.*, gentlemen of the bedchamber (Heb., the general term *slaves*— *cf.* the honorific term δοῦλοι Ἰησοῦ Χριστοῦ in the N.T.), were the immediate *entourage* of the king, who had charge of his personal wants. For the many seals with the honourable title, ' minister of the king ' see Comm., II. 22^{12}. The maiden sought was to *stand before the king*, *i.e.*, wait upon him, and *be his nurse* (so the exact tr. ; EVV *let her cherish him*, JV *be a companion unto him*), and specifically, *lie in thy bosom* (Grr., 𝕿 euphemistically, *lie with him*), that the king might *keep warm*. The passage from the courtly third person to the second is elsewhere illustrated, *e.g.*, 2^{38}, 1 Sam. 25^{28}. The proposed remedy of procuring *a girl, a virgin* (EVV *a young virgin*), both qualities being requisite for fresh physical vigour, is correctly attributed by Josephus to ' the advice of physicians ' (*Ant.*, vii, 14, 3), and this practice is corroborated by a prescription of Galen's : " ex iis vero quæ ventri extrinsecus applicantur carnosus puellus una sic accubans, ut semper abdomen eius contingat " (*Methodus medicus*, ed. Kühn, 1821 *seq.*, vol. 10, 7, 7 ; also cited by Poole) ; other similar prescriptions are cited by Keil (in the case of Frederick Barbarossa) and Farrar for this ancient medical practice of γηροκομία or γηροβοσκία, modern diatherapy. **3.** The search for such a maiden *in all the territory of Israel* is a bit of Oriental hyperbole. **4.** The rhetoric of the usual translation of the v., with constant repetition of *and* is to be improved ; the nominal clauses at beginning and end balance one another, and together constitute the main theme : *And although the girl was very fair, and she became the king's nurse and ministered to him, yet the king was not intimate with her.* The older commentators (see Poole) argued much as to her exact relations with the king, whether as wife or concubine, even to the extent of discussing whether the impotent monarch did right in taking a woman into such a relation. But that she was simply a nurse is emphasized in this v., and is corroborated by v.[15]— or else another woman, even the queen mother, would not have been admitted to the chamber—and also by the latter's immediate compliance with Adonijah's application for the young lady's hand ($2^{13ff.}$; *vs.* Benzinger) ; certainly that experienced woman would not have been caught unawares. To be sure, Solomon chose to understand the case otherwise.

5-10. The court intrigue to elevate the heir-apparent to the regency, and its rapid development. The details of the hailing of Adonijah as king are given in Nathan's report to David (vv.[22ff.]). Of David's elder sons (2 Sam. $3^{2ff.}$) Amnon and Absalom were dead, Chileab apparently so, leaving Adonijah next in succession. **5.** *Now Adonijah, son of Haggith, exalting himself, saying, I will be king, prepared for himself chariotry and horses* [see Note] *and fifty outrunners.* **6.** Like his brothers Amnon and Absalom he had never been controlled by his father, and like Absalom he was *a very handsome man.* Exceptionally at this period in Hebrew history we find comments on the personal appearance of heroes : of Saul, 1 Sam. 9^2, of David, *ib.* 16^{12}. The part of personal beauty in the success of political aspirants was fully recognized by the Athenians. **7.** He obtained the support of David's old-time priest and henchman Abiathar and of the redoubtable commander-in-chief Joab, naturally legitimists and in opposition to ' the Young Party ' of the court. **8-10.** To the would-be accession-festival, like its ominous precedent in Absalom's uprising (2 Sam. 15¹), he invited his brother princes except Solomon, and *all the men of Judah* [namely] *the royal ministers* ; the last item indicates an attempt at securing the political interest of Judah, jealous as it was of any North Israelite interference, a jealousy which Absalom made the basis of his revolt at Hebron. (Subsequently Solomon found it necessary to constitute Judah as a royal province under his direct control ; see Comm., 4¹⁹.) VV.⁸⁻¹⁰ are practically parallel in naming the personalities of the opposite party, who did not join the conspiracy or were not invited. Is this a case of loose writing, or is v.⁸ with the expanded *personnel* a subsequent revision ? Oddly enough *Sadok the priest*, who heads the list in v.⁸, does not appear in v.¹⁰ ; see Comm., 2³⁵ᵇ for the problem as to Sadok's part in the Solomonic history. For Nathan's primary concern see at vv.¹¹ff. The acme in the second list of the uninvited is Solomon's name. The two other names in v.⁸, Shimei and Rei, are unknown or textually doubtful. The regular troops (EVV *mighty men*), it is to be noted, remained loyal to the throne, and so doubtless the mercenary troops of foreign origin, whose commander was Benaiah (*cf.* 2 Sam. 8¹⁸) ; the generalissimo Joab appears not to have had command of these special troops, which were ' the king's own.' A military rivalry is thus attested. **9.** The slaughter of *sheep and beeves and fatlings* involved a sacrificial occasion, however surreptitious the occasion was ; *cf.* the indirect reference to Absalom as ' offering the sacrifices ' at his affair in Hebron (2 Sam. 15¹¹f·). *En-rogel* ; for the identification of this spring with the modern Job's well in the Kedron valley below Jerusalem see Smith, *Jerusalem*, 1, 75 ff. ; Kittel, *Studien*, 150 ff. ; Dalman, *Pjb.*, 1918, 47-72. This deep well strikes a subterranean stream, the drainage of the valley ; see the publication of G. Dalton's account of his exploration of the shaft in 1847, published in *QS* 1922, 165 ff. For *rôgēl* Smith's identification (pp. 108 ff.) with Aram. *râgôlâ*, ' stream ' is correct, *vs.* the traditional interpretation of it as ' fuller.' R. Macgregor's note on the name (*PEQ* 1938, 257 f.) is baseless. For *the stone of Zoheleth, which is beside En-rogel*, see Smith, *l.c.*, Kittel, pp. 171 ff. ; the latter believed that he had identified the stone with a large broken block near the well. The word *zoḥeleṭ* may mean ' serpent ' (*cf.* Mic. 7¹⁷), and there arises the question of its identity with the Dragon Spring of Neh. 2¹³ ; Smith distinguishes them absolutely (then the latter must have disappeared), while Kittel's contemporary publication claims their identity. But Wellhausen (*Reste arab. Heidentums*, 146) compares the name with Arab. *zuḥal*, ' Saturn,' and for this identification may be added the interesting support of 𝔗, which renders the word with סכותא, *i.e.*,= סכות, Am. 5²⁶, to be read ' Sakkuth,' *i.e.*, the Bab. Saturn. Most recently G. R. Driver has proposed (*ZAW* 1934, 51) a fresh translation as from the Arab. sense of the root, ' to roll, slip,' and the present phrase would mean ' the rolling stone.' For the modern name, Job's Well, see Kittel's argument (pp. 164 ff.) that the name of the traditional saint has replaced the older name, Joab's Well, which had come into vogue from the present history.

11-14. The hurried counsel of Nathan with Bathsheba. The prophet, adroitly speaking of the pretender as *son of Haggith*, rightly augurs the fate of the lady and her son in case of the success of the conspiracy. Arrangement is made for the dramatic presentation of the news to the king. The alleged promise on David's part of the succession of Solomon is the first statement of the royal intention on record. Accordingly the present story is easily stamped as that of a court cabal to influence the king in his dotage with the impromptu invention of such a promise ; so, *e.g.*, Benzinger, who finds Bathsheba only a ' tool ' in the prophet's hand. However the present case is not without analogy in that ancient world, where queens themselves were masterful persons ; it is exemplified in Assyrian history in at least one double case. The younger son Esarhaddon was raised to the throne over elder brothers through the dominant spirit of his mother Naḳīa, Sennacherib's wife (her name indicates her West-Semitic origin), and likewise Esarhaddon's son Ashurbanipal was preferred by his father, through the grandmother's influence, over his elder brother Shamash-shum-ukin, a choice which brought on a destructive civil war ; see Meissner, *Bab. u. Ass.*,

1, 74 f.; Olmstead, *HA* ch. 30, 'Harem Intrigues for a Throne.' A similar 'harem intrigue' led by one of his wives in the last days of Ramses III in behalf of her son is recorded; see Breasted, *HE* 498 ff. For the queen-mother's influential position see Erman-Ranke, *Ägypten u. ägyptisches Leben*, 86, and for a later age Dan. 5. Subsequently the royal power, at all events in Judah, may have become constitutionalized; *n.b.* the Law of the King in Dt. 17$^{14\text{ff.}}$, which code insists on the prior right of inheritance for the first born son (21$^{15\text{ff.}}$). David's choice of Solomon as successor may well have been the result of Bathsheba's influence on her old husband. But it may have coincided with his own judgment; apart from personal sentiment there may have been good dynastic reason for preferring the Jerusalem-born son over those born at Hebron. Nathan's oracle to David (2 Sam. 7^{11}) that " YHWH will make for thee a house," *i.e.*, a dynasty, is futuritive, and critics might well regard this alleged oracle as propaganda for Solomon. With this oracle should be noted the intimate interest of the prophet in the infant Solomon, for whom he stood as sponsor, giving him a name of religious import, Jedidiah (*ib.* 12$^{24\text{f.}}$). For the prophet's part in the present story a parallel may be found in Assyrian history; the old Esarhaddon desired to elevate his son Siniddinapal to co-regency with him, but the omens denied him his wish; see Jastrow, *Rel. Bab. u. Ass.*, 2, 191.

15-21. Bathsheba enters the royal chamber; the repeated statement of the king's age and Abishag's presence, into which *milieu* not only the queen-mother but also Nathan was admitted (v.^{22}), supports the point made at v.^{4}. Šanda draws the unnecessary inference that Abishag as witness to this 'conspiracy' was a possible danger to Solomon, and hence the latter had to deny Adonijah's later suit for her hand. The etiquette presented in vv.$^{16, 22, 23}$ was that of the great empires, already adopted by the young monarchy of Israel. The queen reminds her husband of his oath to her concerning the succession, and briefly narrates Adonijah's attempt at the throne in language inspired by Nathan (*cf.* vv.$^{24\text{f.}}$), and concludes, *And now, here is Adonijah king!* Accordingly the king should make public pronouncement of his will, or else, if Adonijah becomes king, she and her son (a personal argument!) will be *in default* (EVV *offenders*—a common word for 'sinners,' but used secularly, as at II. 18¹⁴) for treason against the throne.

22-27. Nathan enters, interrupting the queen, who forthwith retires (*cf.* v.²⁸); he is duly announced, for he had not the freedom of the palace as had the lady. He adroitly suggests that the king must have commanded the succession of Adonijah, or else why the pompous feast with public acclamation of him as king? But why then are those nearest to the throne, himself, Sadok, and prince Solomon, left in the dark?—again a personal thrust.

28-31. Nathan retires, and the queen is summoned again to the royal presence. The king reassures her, rehearses the oath which she had recalled to him, and promises to fulfil it *to-day*. His oath, *By Y*HWH *who hath redeemed my soul* (*i.e.*, self, person) *from all adversity*, repeats 2 Sam. 4⁹ᵇ. The popular acclamation, *Vive le roi!* (vv.²⁵·³⁹, II. 11¹², 1 Sam. 10²⁴, 2 Sam. 16¹⁶) appears in the fuller phrase put in Bathsheba's mouth: *Milord king David live forever!* This is a phrase not only of court etiquette but also of the mysticism enveloping the notion of royalty; see Gunkel, *Einl. in die Psalmen*, 160, 162 ff., citing the similar extravagant expressions in Babylonian and Egyptian documents, and correctly applying them for illustration of the Royal Psalms, *e.g.*, Ps. 72⁵ᶠᶠ·¹⁷, 110⁴.

32-37. The old king arouses himself to drastic action; he summons his faithful ministers and orders them to anoint Solomon as king, giving specific instructions as to place and ceremony. The prince is to become co-regent with his father; *n.b.* the acclamation of him as 'king Solomon' (v.³⁴), and *cf.* the regency of Jotham (II. 15⁵). **33.** The formal procession for the ceremony is to include *your lord's ministers*, who are specified at v.³⁸ᵃ. The prince is to *ride on my own she-mule*, a privilege symbolizing royalty, for possession of such personal effects was sacramental guarantee; *cf.* Gen. 41⁴³, Est. 6⁸. The horse was not yet, nor for long, the mounted animal in Palestine (*n.b.* correction of 'horsemen,' v.⁵). The mule was itself a recent innovation, being first mentioned at 2 Sam. 13²⁹, 18⁹, and this royal she-mule was probably a rarity, the mule being still object of importation (see 10²⁵), as even in later

I. 1¹⁻⁵³

days (Eze. 27¹⁴) ; the latter passage brings the animal from Beth-Togarmah in Asia Minor, even as Homer derives it from Paphlagonia and Mysia (*Il.*, ii, 852 ; xxiv, 277—cited by Šanda). For the mule's early existence in Babylonia, probably in the third millennium, see Meissner, *Bab. u. Ass.*, I, 219. The ass was the riding animal in the previous period ; see Gen. 49¹¹, Jud. 10⁴, 12¹⁴.⁹ The ceremony was to take place at Gihon, which is identical with the Spring of the Lady Miriam (Mary) on the east slope of the Ophel ; the name (meaning something like ' gusher ') occurs only here and at v.³⁸, 2 Ch. 32³⁰, 33¹⁴, being replaced by that of Shiloaḥ-Siloam, which doubtless derived its name from the tunnelled aqueduct leading from the spring to the west side of the hill. (*Cf.* II. 20²⁰, and see the literature cited above *in re* En-rogel, v.⁹). **34.** The ceremony of anointing (root *māšaḥ*) was to be performed *by Sadok the priest and Nathan the prophet* ; many critics, *e.g.*, Smend, *Lehrb. der alttest. Religionsgeschichte*, 66, Benzinger, Stade, *BH*, Eissfeldt, delete the reference to Nathan here and in the repetition at v.⁴⁵, as an interpolation, conflicting with the priestly rite appropriate only to Sadok, *cf.* v.³⁹. But this is hypercriticism ; the plural pronoun (as also ' the people ') frequently appears as subject of the verb ' to anoint,' *e.g.*, 2 Sam. 2⁴, 5³, below II. 11¹², 23³⁰, and even in the Chronicler, I. 29²², " they anointed him (Solomon) to be prince and Sadok to be priest." For such usage of ritual language *cf.* Amarna Tab. 37 : " When Manaḫbiria, king of Egypt . . . installed my father in Nuḫašše and poured oil upon his head." For the addition of Nathan's name here it is to be remembered that Samuel who anointed David was as much seer as priest, and in II. 9 it is the prophet Elisha who sent the oil of consecration by an inferior for the inauguration of king Jehu. In the present case the actual officiant was Sadok, as v.³⁹ records. Indeed as to possible manipulation of the text we should expect that reference to the non-priestly Nathan would have been deleted, not inserted. Along with this comparatively private ceremony went the public proclamation by a herald : *Blow with the horn, and say, Long live king Solomon !* **35.** *He shall come and sit upon my throne ; for he shall reign*

⁹ *N.b.* the representation of the chariot drawn by four asses at Tell Agrab, published by H. Frankfort in *ILN*, Nov. 6, 1937.

in my stead, and I have appointed him to become prince over Israel and Judah. The title 'king' was used at v.³⁴; 'prince' (*nāgîd*) here reflects the early democratic objection to royalty; it is the word used in prophetic language in Sam. (I. 9¹⁶, 13¹⁴, II. 6²¹ [*cf.* v.²⁰], 7⁸) and in Ki. (I. 14⁷, 16², II. 20⁵); it is also put in the mouth of Abigail (1 Sam. 25³⁰) and of the people (2 Sam. 5²). A reflection of the contrast appears in the people's demand for a king (1 Sam. 8⁴ᶠᶠ·) and Samuel's ultimate anointing of Saul as 'prince' (10¹). (The later equivalent for our word is *nāsî*, also translated 'prince' in EVV, applied to Solomon at 11³⁴, and particularly prominent in Eze.) With the presence of this archaic term there is no reason, with Stade, to regard the v. as secondary. According to v.³⁴ Solomon is to be *king over Israel*, in this v. *king over Israel and Judah*; for the former title *cf.* 4¹, 'king over all Israel,' and for the second 2 Sam. 5⁵, 12⁸. For the continued administrative distinction of Judah see Comm., 4¹⁹. **36.** The soldier Benaiah is the spokesman in loyal response, *Amen*, the earliest literary occurrence of this primarily legal formula of assent; *cf.* Num. 5²², Dt. 27¹⁵ᶠᶠ·, and, as a reverent personal response, Jer. 11⁵. The following asseveration, as generally translated, *So say YHWH!*, is faulted with support from the Grr. by most modern commentators, except Burney and Šanda (doubtfully); see Note. But the mng. of the root '*āmar*, as 'to command,' as well as 'to say,' is early vouched for: 1 Sam. 16¹⁶, 2 Sam. 1¹⁸ (?), 16¹¹, 1 Ki. 11¹⁸, *cf.* Ps. 33⁹, and is supported by the same use of the root in a Zenjirli inscription, as also by current Arabic; accordingly translate: *So command YHWH!* The expression, Y*HWH, the God of milord the king*, renders the ancient tenet that the Deity was peculiarly the God of the king; *cf.* the Royal Psalm, 45, v.⁸, etc. The customary address to the Pharaoh by the kings of the Amarna tablets was 'my Sun'; and there are many parallels to the present phrase in the Nabatæan inscriptions (see Cooke, *NSI* no. 92). Below in v.⁴⁷ by a later piety 'thy God,' Kt., has been changed to 'God,' Ḳr., a change adopted by some VSS and AV JV.

38-40. The royal coup is promptly and effectively accomplished with the support of the foreign mercenaries, the *Kerêthîm* and the *Pelêthîm, i.e.,* Cretans and Philistines. These Peoples of the Sea,' specifically the Sherdanu (the later

Sardinians), served as mercenaries in the armies of Ramses II
and Ramses III; for further reff. see Note. The part that
such mercenaries played in the originally quite democratic
nation of Israel is not to be ignored. The sacramental consecration to kingship is effected by *the horn of oil from the
Tent*; a vessel of holy oil was part of the equipment of a
sanctuary and so ready for ritual uses; one was at Samuel's
hand for anointing Saul and David (1 Sam. 10¹ and 16 ¹·¹³,
when he carried the oil-horn to Bethlehem). For this royal
unction see the monograph by H. Weinel, 'משח u. seine
Derivative,' *ZAW* 18 (1898), 1 ff., in particular pp. 20 ff.,
52 ff. This rite made the king a holy person and so untouchable; *cf.* 1 Sam. 24⁷, etc. *The Tent*, more exactly 'the Tent
of YHWH' (2²⁸), was the tent that David 'pitched' for the
Ark, when he brought it to Jerusalem (2 Sam. 6¹⁷); it is
magnified into the Pentateuchal Tent of Meeting at 8⁴. The
herald makes proclamation with the military trumpet, the
shôfār, and the unwitting demos joins in the acclamations;
such details appear again in the stories of the accession of
Jehu and of Jehoash (II. 9¹³, 11¹²). For *piping with pipes*
many critics adopt a correction by slight change of text,
based upon the Grr., and obtain 'dancing with dances'; other
VSS, 'praising in dances,' *cf.* Moff.; see Note. But the use
of the pipe, or flute, in processions is illustrated by Is. 30²⁹,
and following Thenius's criticism, dances (Heb. =round-dances)
could hardly accompany a procession, particularly, it may be
added, in such a terrain as that of the Ophel; Burney properly
notes that the stress is laid on the noise. For the hyperbolic
phrase, *the earth was rent by the noise*, Poole *cft.* similar expressions in the Classics, *e.g.*, Virgil, "ferit æthera clamor" (*Aen.*,
v, 140).

41-48. The surprise of Adonijah's party. He and his
friends had finished their festive meal, which at once celebrated and concealed the real occasion, when they heard the
noise from the city; it was the soldier Joab whose sharp
ears detected the sound of the trumpet (so Then.). His
exclamation (v.⁴¹—literally), *Why the noise of the city in
uproar?* is idiomatic enough to induce some critics to emend
the text, in part taking the cue from Lucian, who did not
recognize the old-fashioned word used for 'city' (see Note).

The news is brought them by Abiathar's son Jonathan, who in the past had been the faithful sleuth for his father and for David (2 Sam. 15-17). He tells the story in summary fashion —after Semitic style the terms of the earlier narrative are repeated—culminating in a startling crescendo. **46.** *And further, Solomon has taken seat on the royal throne.* **47.** *And further, the ministers came in* [*i.e.*, to his chamber] *to bless our lord king David, with the words, Thy God make Solomon's name more famous than thine, and his throne greater than thy throne. And the king bowed down* [in worship] *upon the bed.* **48.** *And further, thus spoke the king: Blessed is YHWH, Israel's God, who has given to-day one to sit on my throne, and my eyes see it!* The session on the throne was the peak of installation. The prayerful greetings (the *blessing*) of the courtiers are extended to the elderly monarch in his bedchamber. And they flatter the father by extolling the son; Poole cites the similar sentiment in Latin writers. David prostrates himself in worship on his bed, as did Jacob (Gen. 47^{31}). His response is a blessing on YHWH for his favour to him. For the accession ceremonies here described *cf.* the coronation scenes in II. $9^{11\text{ff.}}$, $11^{4\text{ff.}}$, and for the sentiment the Accession Psalms, *e.g.*, Ps. 72; *cf.* Mowinckel, *Psalmenstudien*, 2, 69 ff.; Gunkel, *Einl.*, §3, and for the Assyrian rites, including ' the sitting on the throne,' Meissner, *Bab. u. Ass.*, 1, 63 f. For the throne as sacramental symbol of royalty *cf.* the curse invoked in the inscription of Ahiram king of Tyre.

49. 50. The scene of the consternation and flight of Adonijah's party. **50.** The prince took sanctuary: *he caught hold of the horns of the altar;* this was the altar of the Tent of YHWH, as in 2^{28}. The horns were the most sacred part of the altar (*cf.* Am. 3^{14}), and for their use in application of the sacrificial blood see Eze. 27^2, etc. There are numerous Syro-Canaanite representations of this ritual equipment; see Sellin, *Tell Ta'annek*, plates xii, xiii, and, for a large list of reproductions, Galling, *Der Altar in den Kulturen des alten Orients* (1925), plates 12, 13. See at length Cook, *The Religion of Ancient Palestine in the Light of Archæology*, 27 ff., and the later study by H. T. Obbink in *JBL* 1937, 43 ff. For the law of sanctuary *cf.* $2^{28\text{ff.}}$. **51-53.** News is brought to *king Solomon*, who is now functioning with full power, that Adonijah demands of him an oath of full indemnity before he quits sanctuary. This request is granted on condition that he behave like *a gentleman* (see Note on v.⁴²) ; the royal ministers conduct him from the altar, and he comes and does homage to the king, who bids him to *go home*, 'a demand that he retire into private life ' (Skinner).

For analysis of Lucianic variants in this ch. see Rahlfs, *SS* 3, §9. For the novel division in 𝔖, vv.¹⁻⁴=ch. 1, vv.⁵ff·=ch. 2, see A. E. Silberstein, *Aquila u. Onkelos* (1931), pt. 2, 27 ff.—**1.** הכלך דוד : this order throughout 2 Sam. (exc. 13³⁹, where the text is doubtful) and in the following story, exc. at 2¹⁷, where Adonijah as an intimate puts his brother's name first ; the reverse order of apposition is usual ; see GK §131, g.—דוד : for *dāwidum*, appearing as a title in the Akk. Mari tablets, see G. Dossin, *Syria*, 1938, 109 f.— וזקן בא בימים=Gen. 24¹, etc. ; *cf.* בשנים ב' ו', 1 Sam. 17¹², with correction of 𝔍 ; the second predicate precises the first.—בגדים : *bed-clothes*, and so at 1 Sam. 19¹³.—יחם לו : so *BH* correctly, *vs.* יחם, with Mich., Bär, Ginsb. ; see GK §67, p ; Bergstr., *HG* 2, §27, d. The verb is impersonal, as at v.², Eccl. 4¹¹, *vs.* St., who cancels לו, forsooth because the Grr. appear to ignore it ; but *cf.* similar translation idiom in EVV.—**2.** אדני : (B† om.) *milord*, so used even when several persons speak, *cf.* II. 5¹³, and Aram. מראי מלבא in Lidzb.'s Political Ostracon, *Altaram. Urkunden aus Assur* (1921), also similar use of Aram. רבי, and, with Šanda, of Arab. *maulāya*.—נערה בתולה : Burn.'s adducing of cases like אשה אלמנה is not to the point ; see Note, 3¹⁶.—[המ']עמדה לפני :='wait upon,' as at 1 Sam. 16²² (*cf.* Dr.), etc., and so of ritual service (Dt. 10⁸, etc.), and the spiritual service of prophets (II. 5¹⁶), the verb also so used absolutely (Dan. 1⁴). Stade's elision of the passage, סכנת . . . . ועמדה (*cf.* alteration in 𝔊ᴸ) as dependent on v.⁴ is arbitrary ; *n.b.* the nice balance of the composite period.—סכנת : סכן is an official title at Is. 22¹⁵, and so in Phœn.=Akk. *šakēnu* ; 𝔗=JV, ' be a companion ' : Rashi, Kimchi, מחממת, ' warming ' : 𝔊 θαλπουσα, 𝔙 ' fovens,' which verbs have development of mng., ' to warm '>' to cherish,' and so with the latter the other EVV. The Jewish scholar Ibn Barun in his Grammar held to the mng., ' to warm ' ; see P. Wechter, *JAOS* 1941, 184, with extensive added note on the Jewish interpretations. —בחיקך : Grr., exc. 𝔊ᴸ, euphemistically, ' with him.'—**3.** בכל : 𝔊 𝔊ᴴ as though מכל—by variation of labial in Heb., or by the frequent confusion of εκ and εν ; see Dr., *Samuel*, p. lxvii.— נבול : 1 MS, 𝔊ᴸ om.—אבישג : B Αβεισα=ℭ ; *al.*, Αβεισαγ/κ ; the second element is unknown ; for the frequent fem. names with אב (as also in S. Arab.) see Noth, *IP* 15.—השונמית : also השנ', 2²¹· ²² (so here 13 MSS) ; the Ḳr. is often expressed at the first occurrence of a word. Elisha's patroness was also a Shunammite, II. 4¹². The word is gentilic of שׁוּנֵם in Issachar (Josh. 19¹⁸, etc.), modern

Sōlam. For the exchange of liquids see Brock., *Grundriss*, 1, 224 f., but without Heb. examples; for Heb. *cf.* לחש‖נחש (and so the regional name *l'š* in the Aram. Zakar inscription=*Akk. nuḥašše*, and a number of names discussed by the writer in *JAOS* 43 (1923), 50 f. For identification of the place, as old as the *Onomasticon*, see Robinson, *BR* 3, 168 ff., Guérin, *Galilée*, 1, 112 ff. The relation of this Shunammite and the Shulammite of Solomon's Song is an ancient and still mooted problem. Winckler diagnosed much of the present story as mythological, David and Solomon would have mythological names, Abishag would be Ashtart (*GI* 2, 246 ff.; *cf.* Meyer's satirizing comment, *IN* 485, n. 1). M. Jastrow (*Song of Songs*, 1921, 217) regarded the present story as a folk-tale to celebrate the 'prize-beauties' of Shunem. With the mythological and ritual interpretation of the Song, pursued especially by T. J. Meek, 'Canticles and the Tammuz Cult,' *AJSL* 39 (1922), 39 ff., and his more developed study in W. H. Schoff's *Song of Songs, A Symposium*, 1924, pp. 48–79, there would be no reason to combine 'Shunammite' and 'Shulammite,' although Meek gives mythological explanation for the characters in the Song. Over against many fanciful solutions is that proposed by E. J. Goodspeed, 'The Shulammite,' *AJSL* 50 (1934), 102 ff., maintaining that there is no identity between the two figures, that there was no romance between Solomon and Abishag, and that 'Shulammite' of the Song is etymologically the counterpart to 'Solomon.' The discussion, with full bibliography, is well summed up by H. H. Rowley, 'The Meaning of the Shulammite,' *AJSL* 56 (1939), 84 ff.; he comes to the same conclusion as Goodspeed. But in Waterman's art. cited above in Comm., n. 1, he has presented an interpretation of the Song as a drama based upon the present story, along with some detailed literary criticism, *e.g.*, with doubt of the name Abishag. And indeed, following the pattern of the Ugaritic comedy—which has not as yet been applied to the Song—such a drama appears to exist there, entirely fanciful with its play upon the persons of the historical story.—**4.** הנערה: MS 196 הנער, *cf.* 𝔊ᴸ η παις (and so below); נער is of common gender (as is παῖς), but Ḳr. regularly נערה for Kt. נער, when fem.—**5.** אדניה: so at v.¹⁸ (also on a seal, *IAE* 236), otherwise אדניהו (so here Ken. 257); 𝔊 has followed 𝔐 here with Αδωνειας, as declinable, and yet at v.⁹ with Αδωνειου=אדניהו, B being the most faithful to the latter form of transcription; similarly (τον) Βεναιου, v.⁴⁴, 2³⁵. It may be remarked that in such cases correction to the later form of the Heb. name was generally made at the first occurrence, the older form being often left untouched thereafter. 𝔊ᴸ has throughout the obscure transcription Ορνια; see Rahlfs, *SS* 3, 184 f., who notes it as an ancient form, found also in B at 2 Sam. 3⁴.—ומתנשא: acc. to Burn., after Dr., *Tenses*, §135 (1), a ppl. of 'continuous development'; but it is to be taken as above as an introductory dependent clause.—רכב ופרשים: *cf.* the form at 2 Sam. **15¹**, מרכבה וסוסים, but with the collective for the first noun and a different word for 'horse.' For the present combination *cf.* the parallel in the Aram. Zakar inscription, לרכב ולפרש. All VSS translate the second word with 'horsemen,' and so all modern trr. But it means 'horses,' *i.e.*, for the chariots, as Jos. also understood it. See at length W. R. Arnold, ' The Word פרש in the O.T.,' *JBL* 24, 43 ff., denying that the word had ever the second signification as ' horsemen,' as is commonplace in Lexx., and that such a distinction occurs only in two corrupt passages in Eze. ; he holds that the word was *pārāš* (not *pârâš*) = Arab. *faras* (also S. Arab.), with the proper pl. *pěrāšîm*. With the later development of cavalry there is to be assumed the development of the intensive for the rider (*cf. rakkâb*), and then the application of this vocalization throughout. For denial of Biblical references to Egyptian cavalry see Löhr, ' Aegyptische Reiterei im A.T. ? ' *OLz.*, 1928, 932 ff., and Albr., *AfO* 6 (1931), 159 ff., and *ARI* 135, and n. 25, the latter placing the introduction of cavalry in the Semitic world not earlier than the 9th century. Von Oppenheim has discovered reliefs of the mounted horse as of the end of the second millennium, and argues for its priority over the use of the chariot in warfare (*Der Tell Halaf*, pl. 18b, pp. 107, 133 ff.) ; but his dating is too early ; indeed the horseman represented is without a saddle. Also according to Erman-Ranke, *Aegypten u. aegyptisches Leben*, 586, the mounted horse is not evidenced until the New Kingdom, and then as of foreign origin. The word *prš* denoted a distinct breed of the genus *sûs*. *Cf.* also the references at 5^6, 9^{19}, 10^{26}, 20^{20}.—**6.** עצבו : ' vexed, interfered with him ' : 𝔊 απεκωλυσεν αυτον, hence Klost., following Grätz, would correct to עצרו ; but 𝔊ᴸ, επετιμησεν, corroborates ℌ. Jos. tr. with a doublet and other verbs. *Cf.* the Gr. plus at 2 Sam. 13^{21}, of David's laxity towards Amnon, ουκ ελύπησεν τὸ πνεῦμα 'Αμνών, the assumed original of which Dr. restores with the verb עצב. In confirmation of ℌ is to be noted G. R. Driver's art., ' Supposed Arabisms in the O.T.,' *JBL* 1936, 101 ff., with a long discussion of the verb from the Arabic background.— מימיו : for partitive use of מן *cf.* a case at v.^{52}, and for Semitic languages, Nöld., *Syr. Gr.*, §249, c ; Wright, *Arab. Gr.*, 2, 135.— ילדה : VSS (ετεκεν, etc.) corroborate the text, exc. 𝔊ᴸ, εγεννησε (*cf.* Jos., and so *BH* suggests הוליד). The verb can hardly take the distant ' Haggith ' as its subject ; *n.b.* the circumlocutions in EVV. Burn., Benz. defend the form as impersonal, but this is hardly possible with a fem. verb (*cf.* König, *Syntax*, §324, f.). Read with St., *al.*, יָלַד ; the Ḳal is used, although rarely, of male procreation, *e.g.*, Ps. 2^7, and so also in Ugaritic.—תאר : there is dispute as to the root ; GB as from ראה, BDB of independent root ; but the former derivation is paralleled by the process תאב > אבה.—**7.** " His words were with Joab " ; the same phrase for private dealings, conspiracy, 2 Sam. 3^{17}.—יעזרו אחרי : ' a pregnant construction ' (Burn.), *anglice*, " they followed his party"; *cf.* עזרו עם דויד, 1 Ch. 12²². — **8.** צָדוֹק: Grr. Σαδωκ, exc 𝕲ᴸ Σαδδουκ, which latter form appears in the later books, *e.g.*, Eze., Ezra; see Schürer, *GJV* 2, 477 f., Rahlfs, *SS* 3, 184; there appear to have been artificial variations of the vocalization.— בניהו: in a jar stamp, *IAE* 178.—ורעי שמעי : 'ש is approved by all VSS. For רעי *cf.* רעואל and the apocopated fem. form רעות, Palm. רע. A number of Gr. minuscc. = 𝔐; but B A N Ρησι. 𝕲ᴸ read as ורעיו, 'and his friends'; Jos., 'S., David's friend,' *i.e.*, as רֵעִוֹ (' David ' interpolated), which Benz. accepts. Various rewritings have been proposed: רדי (1 Ch. 2¹⁴), עירא (2 Sam. 20²⁰), חושי (1. 4²⁰), הרעה 'ש, ' S. the Friend,' for which court title see 4⁵—but was ' the Friend ' a distinctive title ? Probably S. and R. were officers of the regular troops, and it remains best, with Kit., St., to abide by 𝔐.—הגבורים: prevalent error in Grr. by corruption of οι δυνατοι (=MS e) into υιοι δυν.—**9.** עם אבן: B *al.* μετα αιθη (=𝕮) for μ. λιθον.—הוחלת: 𝕲ᴸ Σελλαθ, for which Rahlfs argues that it was primitive here in the Gr., as also Ορνια, Σαδδουκ above. For 'אבן הו' 𝕾 𝔄 have ' a great stone.'—רגל עין: A M N 𝕾ᴴ τ. πηγηs Ρωγηλ ; a₂ τ. γης P.=𝕮; B† της P.—[אחי] כל: B† om.—Solomon was not invited !—בני המלך: acc. to *OTG* N alone of Grr. has (Rahlfs, *SS* 3, 164 finds it in 𝕲ᴸ); B *al.* om., evidently as redundant, and so St., as taken from v.²⁵; but the phrase is titular, ' the royal princes.'—ולכל: 10 MSS Ken., deR ואת כל, and so Oort corrects ; but at vv.²⁵ᶠ· ל alone is used with קרא; the prepositional construction is the older idiom. There is no reason to accept Haupt's view favoured by Kit., finding in the prep. the emphatic particle *lū.*— אנש: B *al.*, αδρους, 𝕲ᴸ 𝕲ᴴ ανδρας; see Thackeray, *JTS* 8, 267 f., for the former rare word as coming from his ' later translator'; it may have suggested ' gentlemen,' *vs.* commonplace ' men.' As *vs.* St.'s deletion, ' all the men of Judah ' offers a pertinent political item, with the following ' royal courtiers ' as an explanatory item.—**10.** הנביא [נתן]: 𝕲ᴸ om., and so St.—For the name שלמה=Σαλωμων see Montg., *JQR* 25 (1935), 263 f., for the caritative form, and so Syr. *Sheleimūn*, Arab. *Sulaimān*; without further explanation Rahlfs (*SS* 3, 184) regards the present form as a ' volkstümliche Aussprache.' The child had two names acc. to 2 Sam. 22⁷ᶠ·, the other, Jedidiah, ' beloved of Y.,' having been given by Nathan. 1 Ch. 22⁷ᶠ· allegorizes upon the name as ' Man of Peace,' and indeed the name had political import.

11. ויאמר 'ג: 𝕲ᴸ enlarges with " and he came . . . and said."— ' Bathsheba ': for the writer's interpretation of the name as ' daughter of the seventh day (of the week) ' see *JQR* 25 (1935), 262. *Cf.* the fem. name ' Shabbatith,' found by Sukenik in an ossuary in the Kidron valley, *BASOR* 88 (1942), 38, and the later frequent name Shabbethai.—**13.** ' swear to the handmaid '; 𝕲ᴸ+ ' by the Lord thy God,' from v.¹⁷.—**14.** הנה: many MSS והנה= VSS.—**15. מְשָׁרַת**: <*mešāritt*, as *bat*<*bint*; similar cases cited in GK §80, d; Ugaritic parallel, ילדח<ילדת, *RSMT* 24.—**16.** ויאמר:

many MSS + לה‎=𝔊ᴸ 𝔖.—17. לו‎: Grr. om., 𝔈 𝔖ᴴ have.— יהוה‎: 𝔊 (B a₂=𝔈) om.—as improper in a woman's mouth? MS 196 om. אלהיך‎.—לאמחך "בי‎: 1 MS + לאמר‎; 𝔊ᴸ simply λεγων—by haplology?—18. ועתה‎ 2°: a Sebîr, ca. 250 MSS, edd. (see deR.), ואתה‎=VSS, correctly.—19. ולשלמה עבדך לא קרא‎: 𝔊ᴸ om.—20. ואתה‎: ca. 120 MSS, edd., ועתה‎=𝔗ᴸ 𝔊 𝔙; 𝔐 to be retained with Kit., St. 𝔊ᴸ replaces ואתה ארני המלך‎ with v.²⁶ᵃ; see Rahlfs, SS 3, 175.— 23. ויגידו‎: impers. pl.; 𝔊 ad sensum κ. ανηγγελη.—24. אמרת‎: the query expressed by inflection of the voice, ' thou must have said?'; cf. GK §150, l.—25. לשרי הצבא‎: 𝔊ᴸ τ. αρχιστρατηγον Ιωαβ, Jos., τ. αρχοντα; but Nathan was adroit in naming Abiathar alone.— 26. עבדך‎: the heir apparent was the chief ' servant of the crown '; 𝔊ᴸ ' thy son ' is an arbitrary correction.—27. אם וג'‎: for the indirect but more courteous form of question cf. GK §150, i.— עבדיך‎ Kt., עבדך‎ Ḳr.: the latter=all VSS; prob. preferable to keep Kt., with Kit., St.—28. המלך דוד‎: 𝔊 𝔊ᴸ om. the first noun, 2 Heb. MSS om. the second, and one om. both.—לפני המלך‎ bis: 𝔊 𝔊ᴴ 𝔙 ' before the king . . . before him '; 𝔊ᴸ om. 1°; but Sem. rhetoric is repetitive.—30. כי כן . . . כי כאשר‎: with Burn., " the first כי‎ introduces the subject of the oath . . . the second כי‎ resumes the first כי‎ . . . cf. 1 Sam. 14³⁹."—31. ארץ‎: vs. ארצה‎, v.²³, and so here Sebîr, 15 MSS, Talmud (deR.); doubtless originally pronounced as terminative acc., but as lacking final ה‎ read as absolute; the same spelling at 1 Sam. 25²³; cf. נחה‎, נת‎, 2⁴⁰· ⁴¹.—32. המלך‎ 1°: 𝔊ᴸ 𝔖 om., and so St.—33. הרכבתם‎: for the Hif. in this sense cf. Ex. 4²⁰; see the writer's study of the root in JQR 25, 266.—אל‎ נחין‎: for אל‎ many MSS Kt. על‎; at v.³⁸ על‎ is used; the variation, an alternative rdg. (cf. Boström's essay), is typical of the common confusion of the two preps. in Ki. 𝔗 𝔖 render 'ג‎ with שלוחא‎=𝔄.— 34. ומשח‎: vs. וימשחו‎, v.⁴⁵; for the pl. see Comm.; St. regards the sing. as correct in both places; rather we have here the two possibilities in Sem. syntax for the number of the verb with several subjects following; argument might be made that the sing. here is secondary for distinction of Sadok.—35. ועליתם אחריו ובא‎: B† om., Hex. ※, 𝔈 has; St., al., regard this as intrusion from v⁴⁵, but such criticism is most dubious.—ואתו‎: read by Grr., exc. 𝔊ᴸ, as וגניד—אני‎: for a recent study of the word see Joüon, Biblica, 17 (1936), 229 ff.—36. "אמן כן יאמר י'‎: 3 MSS give the verb as יעשה‎ (=𝔖 𝔄), which St., Šanda accept; but this is apparently contamination from Jer. 28⁶. Grr., γενοιτο· ουτως πιστωσαι ο θεος: i.e., the latter verb=יְאַמֵּן‎, accepted by Klost., Kit., Eissf., al., preferred by Sk. (as it were, ' say, Amen '); but the Hif. is never used in this transitive sense. 𝔊ᴸ has a doublet with, " So said the Lord thy God, my lord king" (see Rahlfs, SS 3, 168, 171). Burn. properly supports 𝔐. The root אמר‎=' to command ' occurs three times in the Hadad inscr., the verb possibly in line 10.—37. יהי‎ Ḳr. יִהְיֶה‎=𝔊ᴸ, a theological rectification of the jussive.

38. הכרתי והפלתי‎: the phrase occurs for David's bodyguard at

2 Sam. 8¹⁸, 15¹⁸, 20⁷, 20²³ (Ḳr.), 1 Ch. 18¹⁷. The Kerethites are associated with the Philistines in the latter's territory (1 Sam. 30¹⁴, Eze. 25¹⁶), and are paired with them as peoples of the sea (Zeph. 2⁴). Equation of פלתי with פלשתי appears obvious, by absorption of š in t, and the original pronunciation is presented by Gr. Φελεθθει. The Kerethites are doubtless the Cretans, of Caphtor-Crete, Egyptian Keftiu (inclusive of the opposite Anatolian coast). The identification is supported by the Gr. tradition for כְּרֹת, Zeph. 2⁶, rendered with Κρητη, while the preceding כרתים is represented with παροικοι Κρητων. The two words have mutually affected one another's pronunciation; Gr. Φελεθθει has induced Χερεθθει, while the Heb. has invented 'Pelêthî' to accord with correct 'Kerêthî' For these Sea Peoples see Müller, *Asien u. Europa*; Breasted, *HE* cc. 21–23; F. Bilabel and A. Grohmann, *Gesch. Vorderasiens u. Ägyptens*, vol. 1 (1927); Meyer, *GA* 2, 1, 555 ff.; H. W. Parke, *Greek Mercenary Soldiers* (1933); also the pertinent article by Albr., 'A Colony of Cretan Mercenaries in the Coast of the Negeb,' *JPOS* 1 (1921), 186 ff., a study of the presence of Cretans in the south of Palestine, from which quarter David drew his mercenaries. At 2 Sam. 20²³ the Kt. is הכרי, with which is to be identified הכרי of II. 11⁴⁻¹⁹, a royal bodyguard. These latter were the Anatolian Carians, settled on the coast like the Cretans; *cf.* Herodotus's statement about Psammetichus's mercenaries, 'Greeks and Carians' (ii, 154); the same authority (i, 171 ff.) stresses the relations of the Carians with Crete, and relates that they were "the first who taught the weaving of crests on helmets," *i.e.*, the Philistine headdress. A wide perspective of the early relations of the Sea Peoples with Syria is now opened up by the Ugaritic tablets; see Schaeffer's volume, ch. 1. 𝕿 translates the two terms with 'bowmen and slingers' in all cases, and so here 𝕾 𝔄; in the other cases 𝕾 has חארא ופלחא ('nobles and farmers'), which is the rendering here in 𝕾ᴴ, preserving the original Syriac text. For פלתי 𝕲ᴸ has Φελτι, evidently without tradition, and for כרתי, χορρι, which recalls 'Horites,' but is rather to be connected with חֹר, 'noble,' which would explain the 'nobles' of the Syriac tradition noted above.—
39. ויקח: the consecution is that of ideas, not of time; see Driver's extensive Observation on the question how far the consec. impf. may be temporally impf., *Tenses*, 84 ff.—**40.** והעם: of Grr. only 𝕲ᴸ has (so 𝕾); 𝕾ᴴ ※; 𝔄 om.—מְחֹלְלִים בַּחֲלִלִים: Grr., εχορευον εν χοροις = מְחֹלְלִים בִּמְחֹלוֹת: this interpretation is partly followed by 𝕿, משבחין בחנגיא, reading the first word as מהללים, and the second word as 'dances' (root חנג), and so 𝕾ᴴ מענין בנודא, 'responsively singing in dances' (גודא = מחול, Ps. 149³). But 𝕾 𝔄 = 𝕳. 𝕲ᴸ adds a doublet ηυλουν εν αυλοις = 𝕳. There was early ambiguity of interpretation; Jos. speaks (*Ant.*, vii, 14, 5) of the people as χορευων κ. αυλοις τερπομενος, as though = בחללים מְחֹלְלִים. The change on basis of 𝕲 is accepted by some critics, *e.g.*, Ew., St., *BH*, Sk.; but see Comm.—**41.** מרוע קול הקריה הומה: = 𝕲 𝕲ᴴ, but treating 'מ as מה;

I. 2^{1-46a}   87

𝔊^L τις βοη της φωνης ηχει μεγα, which has led St. (and so *BH fortasse*) to correct to מה קול התרועה הזאת (*cf.* 1 Sam. 4^{14}, 15^{14}); but Šanda and Rahlfs correctly recognize that Lucian read 'ק as = קריאה (Jon. 3^2, *cf.* Is. 40^3). Stade's objection to 'מ is unnecessary, nor is there contamination from v.^{45}. Klost., Šanda prefer כל for קול, a most unlikely corruption. The noun קריה, 'city,' is found in prose, apart from *nn. loci*, only in this narrative and in Dt. 2^{36}; the word appears in Phœn. and Ugaritic. הומה is second predicate to 'הק, *cf.* Song 5^2.—**42.** איש חיל : 'ח has the sense of Lat. 'virtus'; for the phrase *cf.* 1 Sam. 10^{26}, where בני חיל (so read with 𝔊) are contrasted with בני בליעל; the phrase = ' a brave fellow,' or ' gentleman,' and Šanda tr. with the latter English word at v.^{52}.—**43.** לארניהו : 𝔊 om.—אבל := ' indeed ' in ironic contradiction; see Lexx. and Burney's note; *cf.* Arab. *bal* and *bala(y)*.— **45.** וימשחו : see at v.^{34}; 𝔊^L A *al.* (not 𝔄) have sing. verb.—בנחון : the prep. = ' at '; *cf.* בעין, 1 Sam. 29^1.—תהם: Nif. of הום, metaplastic with המה, *cf.* v.^{41}.—**47.** לאמר : 𝔊^L κ. εισεληλυθασι μονοι κ. ειπον; Klost. attempts explanation.—שם . . . ייטב := " give him a good name."—אלהיך : Kt. = 𝔖 𝔖^H; אלהים Kr., MSS = Grr. (ο θεος, κυριος), 𝔗 𝔙; see Comm., v.^{36}.

There may be noted Swete's observation, *Int.*, 249, n. i, on Herzfeld's " careful treatment of the differences between 𝔊 and 𝔐 in 3 Regn." in his *Gesch. d. Volkes Israel*, 2.

Ch. 2^{1-9}. This section, David's Testament, has long lain under severe criticism, historical and ethical. Against its originality as part of the narrative of cc. 1, 2 stand many critics; so Reuss, Wellhausen (*Proleg.*, 282, n. 1), Stade, Benzinger, Meyer (*GA* 2, 2, 262, n. 1); *per contra* may be named Kuenen, Driver, Cornill, Kittel (in Comm., and *GVI* 2, 243 ff.). The one concrete objection is the patently Deuteronomic character of vv.^{3, 4} (for cross-references see Burney, Skinner). But with the reasonable excision of these vv., because of their disturbance of connexion between v.^2 and v.^5, and with some textual emendations, the story may be accepted as original. V.^2 is a legacy of virile counsel. With the excision proposed this is followed by three definite injunctions, vv.^{5-9}: to make atonement for the blood-guilt brought upon David by Joab's murders, with remembrance of the bitter days of his own flight from the throne; to pension Barzillai's family; and to find pretext for the undoing of Shimei, who had cursed him with *a baleful curse*. The ethical objection is made that the first and third of these injunctions are repellent to what we would desire to think of David's character—a subjective enough criterion! As for the judgment upon Joab with the primitive horror before blood-guilt, an example of which David had himself exhibited in a barbarous action (2 Sam. 21), proper correction of v.[5] exposes the king's motive with all clarity. It is a problem of psychology —a science that gives little control on history—why David did not himself take the vengeance due. More personal and petty is his proscription of Shimei, contradicting his earlier unexampled clemency towards him. Was it the rankling of an old man's mind over a once bitter enemy and his curse? If the story is a fabrication out of the whole cloth, then we have in it a narrative of baseless slander. But why a much later age (Deuteronomic) should have invented the story to save Solomon's virtue by throwing the odium upon David is unintelligible in view of the latter's canonization. In a word, our moral judgment is not a measure for past history. And so Šanda (p. 49): " Doch sind die harten Verordnungen aus der unvollkommenen Moral der alten Zeit erklärlich." There has been a reaction, especially on the part of historians, towards recognition of the early origin of the narratives in this ch., even if they are to be distinguished from the major story. Thus Eissfeldt (*Komposition d. Samuelisbücher*, 48 f.) holds that this section is ' a parallel narrative,' not ' a secondary addition,' even as he presents the sources of Samuel after the same fashion. Lods (*Israël*, 425) curtly dismisses the objections to the testament. Robinson (*HI* 1, 244 ff.), while sceptical as to the accuracy of these records, does not ascribe a late origin to them. Olmstead (*HPS* 335) suggests that the present story with its sequel had Nathan for its author. But why then the inclusion of the unimportant Barzillites, and why no word of warning about Adonijah? As argued in the introduction to these cc., we are dealing with the *genre* of the ' historical story,' in this case a tale which came out of the inner court. The historian is justified in the position that so the record reads, and that we have not the means of exploring its ultimate truth.

2. *I am going the way of all the earth: cf.* Jos. 23[14], Eccl. 3[20], etc. Poole *cft.* similar Classical sentiments, *e.g.*, " Omnium idem exitus, sed est idem domicilium," from Petronius, *Satyricon*. *Be strong and play the man* (EVV *show thyself a man*):

a veritable soldier's challenge, used by the Philistines in mutual encouragement (1 Sam. 4^9). This summons to a strong-handed *régime* is followed by the harsh injunctions of vv.$^{5\text{ff.}}$. **4.** Y*HWH's word which he spoke concerning me :* resuming 2 Sam. $7^{12\text{ff.}}$. **5. 6.** Joab's treacherous assassination of Abner (2 Sam. $3^{27\text{ff.}}$) and of Amasa ($20^{8\text{ff.}}$) was to be avenged, not on the modern ground of vindication of the law, but for protection against the fate that haunted the dynasty, if it did not remove the blood-guilt, according to the ancient principle of 'life for life' (Ex. 21^{24}), a principle that David had followed in visiting upon Saul's grandchildren his murder of the Gibeonites (2 Sam. 21). For the subject at large see Pedersen, *Israel*, I–II, 411 ff., 'Sin and Curse.' The reason given is rendered colourless in the text of 𝔥, which has it that Joab stained his own girdle and sandal with innocent blood, when war was not on; but David's point is that the guilt fell upon himself and his family as the responsible authority. Following change of the suffixed pronouns as in the Lucianic Greek and Old Latin we obtain the original: *He imposed* [𝔥 *set*, EVV *shed*] *the blood of war on* (the state of) *peace, and he put the blood of war on my* [𝔥 *his*] *girdle, that is on my* [𝔥 *his*] *loins, and on my* [𝔥 *his*] *sandal, that is on my* [𝔥 *his*] *foot*. The first sentence is a crux, and an interpretation given by the old VSS named above has been accepted by many scholars (see Note); but it is legalistic, exactly paralleled by a law in Dt. 22^8: "When thou buildest a new house, thou shalt make a battlement for thy roof, that thou impose [EVV bring] not blood upon thy house, if any man fall from thence." There the blood-guilt stains the house and makes the owner liable; in our passage it is a blood-mark against the authority even in time of peace. The horror of blood-guilt is illustrated by a story that Herodotus tells (i, 91), how Crœsus, according to the Delphic oracle paid the penalty for "the sin of his ancestor in the fifth degree, who had slain his master." *Do according to thy wisdom: cf.* v.^{9}. Wisdom in the old Hebrew is always practical intelligence; it is wisdom of this kind, political, legal, that the oracle in ch. 3 promises to Solomon. As Skinner remarks, the prince is bidden to 'find some specious pretext.' **7.** Barzillai's hospitality to David in his flight is recounted in 2 Sam. $17^{27\text{ff.}}$,

19$^{32\text{ff.}}$. The phrase, 'to eat at the king's table,' meant 'to be pensioned'; cf. 2 Sam. 9^7, 19^{29}, below 18^{19} (of the prophets at Jezebel's table), Neh. 5^{17}. Rawlinson cites Greek sources for continuance of the term in Persian times, e.g., Herodotus, iii, 132. Cf. the corresponding Aramaic phrase, 'to eat the salt of the king' (Ezr. 4^{14}), of Babylonian origin. The same pensioning system existed in Egypt, e.g., at the end of the Sinuhe Story: "Meals were brought me from the palace, three and four times a day" (Erman, *Lit. of the Anc. Egyptians*, 28). *So they came to (drew nigh unto) me:* so EVV; but the verb means 'to be neighbourly.' **8.** For Shimei's curse and its condonation by David see 2 Sam. 16$^{5\text{ff.}}$, 19$^{16\text{ff.}}$. *Grievous curse:* better, *baleful curse;* see Note. Despite David's whilom mercy the uttered curse was still potent; for its concreteness cf. Zech. 5$^{1\text{ff.}}$. It might ultimately be warded off by killing the invoker; see extracts from magical texts in Jastrow, *Rel. Bab. u. Ass.*, 2, 303 ff.; Meissner, *Bab. u. Ass.*, 2, 303 ff. The curse against 'a prince' was high crime; cf. 21$^{9\text{ff.}}$, Ex. 22^{27}. A 'superstitious foreboding' must have led to 'this utterly dishonourable action' (Skinner).

VV.$^{10,\,11}$. Editorial note on the death of David and the chronology of his reign. **10.** The 'sleeping with the fathers' is euphemism. The burial, as usual for people with landed estates (cf. 2^{34}, 1 Sam. 25^1, 2 Ch. 33^{20}), was on royal domain, *in David's City*; for this new name for the old Jerusalem on the Ophel hill see 2 Sam. 5^9. This royal tomb was known for a thousand years or more, cf. Acts 2^{29}; it was rifled by John Hyrcanus for its treasures, and a similar attempt was made by Herod (Jos., *Ant.*, vii, 15, 3; xvi, 7, 1). For the modern remains of this sepulchral grotto on the Ophel see R. Weill, *La Cité de David*, and for the excavations on the Ophel in general, R. A. S. Macalister and J. G. Duncan, *Annual IV* of PEF (1926); J. W. Crowfoot and J. G. Duncan, *Annual V* (1926); also the excellent summary accounts in C. Watzinger, *DP* 1, 86 ff., 104 ff. For burial rites in Palestine see Benzinger, *HA* §§25, 43. **11.** The data of the v. are repeated from 2 Sam. 5$^{4\text{f.}}$, where the figure for the reign is given more exactly as 40½ years. For this round figure=a generation, so common in the Bible, cf. the '40 years' in which Omri occupied Moab according to the Mesha inscription, and for its reliability here see Int., §16a. There is an interesting Greek insertion after v.¹²ᵃ giving Solomon's age at accession as his 12th year. This datum, accepted by Olmstead (*HPS* 338) is surely legendary; it can be traced back as far as the Jewish historian Eupolemos, *ca*. 150 B.C., and the same computation was adopted by the Rabbis. The calculation doubtless started from Solomon's description of himself as 'a little child' (3⁷), 12 years being also the age of religious manhood (*cf*. Luke 2⁴²). Similarly the other hero of the temple, king Josiah, is gratuitously given by the Chronicler the age of 8 years when he began his religious devotion (2 Ch. 34³—see Comm., II. 22¹). Josephus makes Solomon 14 years old at accession (*Ant*., viii, 7, 8). According to the dating of his son Rehoboam (14²¹) the latter must have been born by the time of his father's accession. See more at length and for the literature Kittel, Stade, Rahlfs (*SS* 3, 112), and in particular Nestle, 'Wie alt war Salomo als er zur Regierung kam?' *ZAW* 1932, 311 ff., offering a formula whereby the figure 12 was obtained.

VV.¹²⁻²⁵. The romance and fate of Adonijah. **12.** The v. is generally taken by trr. and comm. as sequel of vv.¹⁰ᶠ· (and so the paragraphing of 𝔐); *cf*. the usual complement, "and his son X reigned in his stead" (*e.g.*, 11⁴³). But the phrase 'to sit upon the throne' is identical with the language in 1¹³, 2⁴⁶, while the Heb. syntax makes of the v. a dependent nominal sentence circumstantial to the following narrative (*cf*. 1³). Accordingly translate: *And Solomon having taken his seat upon his father David's throne, and his rule being well established,* **(13)** *then came Adonijah*, etc. We have then to suppose that the original narrative had a brief reference to David's death, which was replaced by the editorial formula in vv.¹⁰ᶠ·. This paragraphing, as proposed, was recognized by the Lucianic revision, which prefixes to v.¹² the title '3 Kingdoms,' and here indeed is the proper place for distinction between Samuel and Kings; see Int., §1. The settlement of *the kingdom* (by dynastic succession, etc.) repeats literally the terms at 1 Sam. 20³¹, 2 Sam. 7²⁶; *cf*. a similar phrase at Amaziah's accession after his father's murder by a court cabal (II. 14⁵).

This short story is one of the most exquisite in Hebrew letters, with its subject of a romance culminating in a tragedy, and for its brilliant delineation of the scene and the characters. If the story were motivated by court propaganda, it still remains a literary gem. There is the manly figure of Adonijah, with his frank assertion of prior right to the throne, while he loyally accepts the turn of fate (v.[15], *the kingdom is turned about*—see Note); Bathsheba's womanly interest in his love-affair, to which she finds no objection; the scene of royal courtesy to *the Queen-Mother* (v.[19]), and the third *persona dramatis*, the king, who is ready to grant her any boon, but who on hearing her request in a burst of rude temper denies it to her, as though she were a fellow-conspirator against the throne, and condemns the upstart to death—a sentence immediately carried out (vv.[21ff.]). With most commentators, there is no reason to doubt the essential credibility of the story, although Olmstead (*HPS* 335 f.) and Robinson (*HI* 1, 245 f.) regard it, the one as 'partisan history,' the other as 'almost inconceivable.' Arguments for its authenticity are well presented by Benzinger, Kittel, Skinner. As observed above, the references to Abishag (1[1ff. 15]) have their dramatic place in leading up to the present scene; she was not David's wife, as is expressly stated there, and this was known to Bathsheba. Whether Adonijah's request followed a real passion, or whether he had a crafty design on the succession (so Benzinger), may remain a matter of dispute. On the other hand Solomon had legal right to interpret the request as involving claim upon the throne (*cf.* Absalom's public maltreatment of his father's harem, 2 Sam. 16[20ff.], and for the Semitic notion in general see W. R. Smith, *Kinship and Marriage in Early Arabia*[2] [1895], 104 ff.), while the popular mind might have so construed Adonijah's success; at least it was a legal pretext that the king easily seized. In v.[24] the statement, *who has made me a house, i.e.,* 'established my dynasty,' cites the identical promise to David (2 Sam. 7[11]). The one textual change of importance is at end of v.[22], where, in place of 𝔐, *even for him and for Abiathar the priest and for Joab ben Seruiah* is to be read, with the VSS, *and he has* (*i.e.,* on his side) *A. the priest and Joab b. S.* At v.[19] for, *he made obeisance to her,* the Grr. have the variant, *he kissed her*; see Note. For the 'oath by YHWH,' v.[24], *cf.* J. Pedersen, *Der Eid bei den Semiten* (1914).

V.²⁶⁻²⁷. The deposition and banishment of Abiathar. The king acts upon his real or assumed suspicions concerning Adonijah's party. **26.** The priest Abiathar is ordered to go to Anathoth, *to thy estate*—cf. the similar sentence upon Shimei, v.³⁶—for he is already potentially *a dead man*. His life is spared because of his long and faithful service to David, being the survivor of Eli's family, whom Saul exterminated (1 Sam. 22, 23⁶ᶠᶠ·). For the continuation of this priestly line at Anathoth see Jer. 1¹, according to which Jeremiah was ' one of the priests at Anathoth '; for the bearing of this family tradition upon his spirit as prophet see the commentaries and the studies of his person. *Because thou didst bear the ark of Y*HWH [𐤉𐤄+*the Lord*] *before my father David :* see Note for the preferable reading of *the ephod* for *the ark*. **27.** *And Solomon suspended him from functioning as priest :* there is no reason to doubt, as with some (*e.g.*, Stade), the originality of this sentence ; Abiathar's disability did not affect his offspring. The latter part of the v. cites the secondary narratives in 1 Sam. 2²⁷ᶠᶠ·, 3¹ᶠᶠ·, concerning the perpetual curse that was to lie on Eli's family, these narratives being inspired by the success of the rival Sadokids. It is withal strange that Abiathar's replacement by Sadok is not recorded here ; see on v.³⁵ᵇ. Comparison of 2 Sam. 8¹⁷ and 1 Ch. 24³ᶠᶠ·, and also the direct testimony of Jos., *Ant.*, viii, 1, 3, as to Eli's descent from Ithamar, Aaron's younger son, indicate that the Elids as Ithamarids functioned as a minority clan in the priesthood of the Second Temple.

VV.²⁸⁻³⁵. Upon news of Adonijah's death Joab flees to sanctuary ; he is executed there by Benaiah, after the king overrules the right of sanctuary ; Benaiah is appointed in his place. Joab's fear is abruptly introduced, but it was reasonable. He took sanctuary at the Tent as his leader had done, supposing himself to be secure after that precedent (1⁴⁹ᶠᶠ·). The right of sanctuary was an early taboo ; but Hebrew law began early to regulate it, as we learn from the Code of the Covenant (Ex. 21¹³ᶠ·), while a much more elaborate regulation was laid down in the Priest Code (Num. 35⁹ᶠᶠ·) ; see Driver and Gray respectively *ad locos*, and at large N. M. Nicolsky, 'Das Asylrecht in Israel,' *ZAW* 1930, 146 ff.; M. Löhr, *Das Asylwesen im A.T.*, Königsberg Academy, Geisteswiss.

Klasse, vii, 3 (1930). The more civilized Hebrew law regarded the right as temporary to save the manslayer from the hasty application of the principle of blood-guilt. The new development gave time for adequate trial, and then, if found guilty, the criminal was surrendered to 'the blood-avenger'; the later Priest Code kept even the involuntary slayer in sanctuary until the death of the high priest. In the present case, the first on record in legal history, we see presented to the organized state in the person of its monarch the problem how to deal with that archaic relic of primitive law; royalty here assumes a superior right. Nicolsky sketches the history of the right of sanctuary in Mediæval Europe, where it had a devious course, due to various interests of society. The ethics of Solomon's motive is another matter. Respect to the proprieties is shown in the summons to Joab to abandon sanctuary; upon his refusal Benaiah must get further instructions from the king. A parallel appears in the case of Athaliah, who was forcibly removed from the temple by the priest's orders in advance of execution (II. $11^{13\text{ff.}}$).
28. The parenthesis, *for Joab was an adherent of Adonijah, and he had not been an adherent of Absalom*, appears superfluous in the story; the first sentence repeats what is immediately known to the reader, while the second introduces an apparently gratuitous reference to Joab's antagonism to the other pretender Absalom; but it is an attempt at part-exculpation of the one-time hero of Israel. The Gr. texts, with few exceptions, supported by Josephus (*Ant.*, viii, 1, 4), and all other VSS exc. 𝕋 (see Note) read 'Solomon' for 'Absalom,' a rdg. accepted, *e.g.*, by Thenius, Stade, Šanda; but Keil well remarks that the rebellious 'siding with' could hardly have been used of the heir-apparent's party; the statement also would be mere repetition of the preceding one. The altar was in the tent of Yhwh, a specification more exact than at 1^{50}. **29.** After *by the altar* the Grr. have a long addition: *And Solomon sent a message to Joab: What is the matter with thee that thou hast fled to the altar? And Joab said: Because I was afraid of thee, and I fled to the Lord.* Critics differ as to the originality of this intrusion, which can be easily turned back into good Hebrew, while the passage may well have dropped out by haplog. between the two occurrences of ' he

sent.' Thenius, Kittel (not so definitely in *BH*), Burney, Eissfeldt allow or favour it ; Benzinger, Stade, Šanda, Skinner disallow it. While not necessary (*cf.* the parenthesis in v.²⁸), it gives a plausible motive to the king's action ; Joab confesses a guilty conscience towards the king. **31.** Joab is to be given honourable burial, as was done for Saul and his family (1 Sam. 31¹¹ᶠ·, 2 Sam. 21¹²ᶠᶠ·). **32.** The v. repeats the substance of v.⁵, and Klostermann, Benzinger, Stade object to the repetition, but hardly with reason in this kind of narrative. *And Y*HWH *will turn back upon his head the blood that he shed* (𝔅 *his bloodshed*) : *n.b.* the variation of phrase in v.³³, and *cf.* the similar phrases, Jud. 9⁵⁷, 1 Sam. 25³⁹. The head as the most eminent part of the body becɒ.ne a legal term expressive of the person in its civic dignity and responsibility ; it can mean ' the person,' as at 1 Sam. 28² (' keeper of my head '—*cf.* Eze. 9¹⁰, etc.), even as the same vocable is so used in Ethiopic. Abner is entitled *captain of the army of Israel,* for which *cf.* 2 Sam. 2⁸ᶠ·, and Amasa *captain of the army of Judah, cf. ib.* 17²⁵, 20⁴ᶠ· ; these reff. contradict Benzinger, who holds that the language is subsequent to the division of the kingdom. **34.** *And went up Benaiah : cf.* Adonijah's ' coming down ' from the altar (1⁵³), and so in all ecclesiastical language, the altar being always relatively elevated. 𝔊 (present in 𝔖ᴴ ·※·) om. the sentence, and Stade unreasonably follows suit on the ground that the road from the palace to the tent ' did not ascend.' *He was buried in his house in the Steppe :* 𝔊ᴸ, modernizing, corrects ' house ' to ' tomb ' ; but *cf.* the burial of Samuel and Manasseh each ' in his house ' (1 Sam. 25¹, 2 Ch. 33²⁰), while this custom of burial in the soil under the house is vouched for by the burial remains in Palestine (see Watzinger, *DP* 1, 72 ; Thomsen, *Palästina u. seine Kultur,* 54 ff.), as also for the Euphrates valley (Meissner, *Bab. u. Ass.,* 2, 496 f.). However ' house ' may mean not only the structure but also the house plot as well. The word *Steppe* translates Heb. *midbār* (EVV by unfortunate translation, ' wilderness ' after the Greek and Latin) ; it means a grazing-steppe (sheep-run), for which term see the writer's *Arabia and the Bible,* 79 f. The reference here is geographical, the word being used of the eastern portion of Judah (see Smith, *HG* 263 ff.), and it is so used absolutely otherwise (*e.g.*, Josh. 15⁶¹, 1 Sam. 23¹⁴), with the fuller phrase 'Steppe of Judah' found only in the late title of Ps. 63 (*cf.* Mt. 3¹) and Jud. 1¹⁶, where 'Judah' should probably be deleted. Joab's family belonged to Bethlehem; see 2 Sam. 2³². **35a**. For Benaiah's title as *Over-the-Army* see Comm. 4¹ᶠᶠ· **35b**. The statement of Sadok's appointment to succeed the deposed Abiathar is out of place here; it were desiderated after v.²⁷. The writer has argued for excision of the half-verse as unoriginal in his article on 'The Year-Eponymate'; *cf.* his 'Supplement at End of 3 Kingdoms 2.' At 4² (see further Comm., *ad loc.*) the primary text represented by 𝕲 has simply 'Azariah ben Sadok,' *vs.* 𝕳, the priest 'Azariah ben Sadok.' 'The priest Sadok' has appeared in the story above; in Sam. he is named as a priest along with Ahimelek (II. 8¹⁷— but the text is to be corrected to 'Abiathar b. Ahimelek'), otherwise along with Abiathar (15²⁴ᶠᶠ·, 20²⁵). There is no further reference to him until Eze. (40⁴⁶, etc.), Ch. (1, 6³⁸, etc.), presenting the high-priestly line as descended from him.

VV.³⁶⁻⁴⁶ᵃ. Shimei is given amnesty, but under sworn restriction to reside in Jerusalem. His breach of the condition by an excursion into foreign territory in search of run-away slaves entailed his death. Solomon followed out his father's injunction; he proved himself 'a clever man' (v.⁹), and found an opportunity to get rid of Shimei on a legally faultless ground, for perjury to his God and king. Shimei, a member of the Saulid family (2 Sam. 16⁵ᶠᶠ·), must have been a landed proprietor of wealth, and there may have been policy in David's leniency towards him. He was ordered *not to cross* (even) *the Kidron wady*, *i.e.*, on the road to his estate at Bahurim to the east of Jerusalem (see Abel, *GP* 2, 260), and the restraint must have been irksome enough within the walls of a small acropolis city, whose circumference has been estimated at some 4500 feet (Smith, *Jer.*, 1, 142 f.). His breaking of bounds was careless indeed, if not presumptuous. Gath, whither his slaves had fled, one of the cities of the old Philistine pentarchy (for its location and notes on its later history see Comm. at II. 12¹⁸) had doubtless been involved in the punishment inflicted by David upon the Philistines (2 Sam. 8¹), and so remained under strict legal obligations, as for instance the return of fugitives from justice. The report of the escape of the slaves reads like private Akkadian documents bearing on the same subject. Their housing in foreign territory required personal negotiation with the local king. The Code Hammurabi contains ordinances regarding slaves of extraterritorial origin (§§280, 281), and in the present case the slaves were formally extradited. There is extensive illustration of the extradition of fugitives in the second millennium. We have the treaty of Ramses and the Hittite king Hattushil, providing for the return of fugitives, gentlemen and men ' of no name ' (see Breasted, *ARE* 3, §§382-90, *cf.* his *HE* 438 f.) ; there is in addition a long list of such diplomatic documents of Hittite kings in treaty with vassal states, according to which men of lower class, peasants and handworkers, not noblemen, should be extradited without question (see Löhr, *Das Asylwesen im A.T.*, 3 ff., with the texts in question cited from *MVG* 1923, 23 ; 1926, 21, 59, 139 ; 1930, 75). A king of Gath, Achish ben Ma'ok, appears in the early history of David as his friend (1 Sam. 21$^{11\text{ff.}}$, 27$^{2\text{ff.}}$) ; the present Achish b. Ma'kah is doubtless the same prince, in that case a long-lived monarch. **42.** The expression, *I have heard*, means *I am witness*, and so the South Arabic use of the root. **44.** There is evident duplication in the v. : *Thou knowest all the wickedness, what thy heart knows, what thou didst*, etc. Stade suggests omitting the first words, and so reads : *Thy heart knows*, etc., which is preferable to omitting the second duplicate (so *BH* suggests), as the former improvement gives a more unique phrase. One may speculate whether in such cases we possess errors of the original written text, the author having reversed language or construction, and failed to delete the first form, for it was not ancient practice to score out mistakes in a manuscript. However, despite the present ' monstrosity ' (Stade), translators and commentators have found sense, at least with slight correction, and so even the critical Thenius, while Burney ignores the difficulty.

1. ויצו : the verb used of testamentary disposition, and so at II. 20^1, Gen. 49^{29} ; the same use of the root in Arab. (Wellh., *Reste arab. Heidentums*, 19) ; in later Jewish language צוָאָה is used of similar testaments. 𝕲 (B A, also 𝕾^H), απεκρινατο=ויען ; 𝕲^L, 𝕲^H (M N *al.*) ενετειλατο. 𝕲^L has a considerable plus at beginning of the v. : " and it came to pass after these things, and David died, and he was buried with his fathers," followed by the substance of 𝔐 ; on this addition see St. and Rahlfs (SS 3, 285) ; as has not been remarked, this plus is a duplicate of v.¹⁰, and points to a text-form in which David's testament was omitted, even as in the primitive Gr. the proscription of Shimei was left out (see at end of Notes).—2. אנכי : 𝔊 εγω ειμι : this pedagogical peculiarity is generally regarded as Aquilanic, so by Reider, *Prolegomena* . . . *to Aquila*, 24 ; but Thackeray (*JTS* 8, 272 f.) notes it as typical of one of the several early trr. of Ki. ; *cf.* Rahlfs, *SS* 3, 259.— היית לאיש : the same phrase, and after חזק, put in the mouth of the Philistines, 1 Sam. 4⁹ ; for the strong use of איש *cf. ib.* 26¹⁵ ; the phrase=Hellenistic ἀνδρίζεσθαι, BSir. 34²⁵ (31³⁰), 1 Mac. 2⁶⁴, 1 Cor. 16¹³. 𝔊 (B A *al.*) literally, εση εις ανδρα; 𝔊ᴸ exegetically plus δυναμεως, and so M N *al.* plus τελειον.—3. For a list of the Deuteronomic phrases in Ki., beginning in these vv., see Dr., *Int.*, 200 ff.—אלהיך : 𝔊ᴸ, with theologizing improvement, τ. θεου Ισραηλ.—ולשמר ׳ : *text. rec.* is correct, not ולשמר ומצותיו, with MSS, some Grr.—ועדותיו : an addition to the primary text, absent in 𝔊 (B ; 𝔖ᴴ as from Sym., Theod.).—ו׳ תשכיל : 'know how to do,' also used transitively, *e.g.*, Dt. 29⁸ ; with the following ואת כל אשר תפנה שם ="and whithersoever thou turnest," there is 'a slight zeugma' (Burn.) ; 1 MS has אל for את, obtaining identity with the phrase at Pr. 17⁸. Note the primary sense of אשר as ' place.' 𝔊ᴸ alone of the Grr. understood the Heb., πανταχη ου εαν επιβλεψης εκει. 𝔊 paraphrased.— 4. עלי : B ℭ om.—לאמר 2° : original by testimony of 𝔊 ; critics since Then. generally delete, following 𝔊ᴸ N *al.* ; but *cf.* repetition of ויאמר, vv.¹³ᶠ·, of ותאמר, 3²⁶ ; Burn. cites numerous cases of late repetitions, *e.g.*, 1³⁰, 8³⁰· ⁴¹⁻⁴², 13¹¹ ; and the corresponding Akk. *umma* is similarly used in long *oratio directa* (see Delitzsch, *Ass. Hwb.*, 86). Here the repetition emphasizes the positive oracle.— 5. אשר עשה 2° : staccato resumption of 1° ; improvement attempted by 12 MSS Ken., deR., with ואשר=𝔊ᴸ 𝔖ᴴ 𝔖 𝔄 ; St. regards the clause as a doublet.—אבנר : once אבינר, 1 Sam. 14⁵⁰ ; the constant Gr. Αβεννηρ, as here, exhibits the late survival of the old Ḳr. ; and so Αβεσσαλωμ, v.⁷ ; see Noth, *IP* 34.—יתר :=יתרא, 2 Sam. 17²⁵ ; other forms יתרו, יתרן ; the name is Arabian (S. Arab. ' Watar ' Old Bab. ' Yatar '), and Jether was an Ishmaelite acc. to 1 Ch. 2¹⁷ and the correct Gr. at 2 Sam. 17²⁵, *vs.* 𝔐 ; the later Ituræans bore a name of the same stock. For hypocoristic form in ־א (so also עמשא, *sup.*, and גרא, *inf.*, v.⁸) see Noth, p. 40.—ויהרגם : epexegetical, *cf.* 18¹³ ; see Burn., and Dr., *Tenses*, 82.—ו׳ וישם : by ancient haplog. MSS 60 80 109 125 174, and 𝔊 (B M *al.*) om. מלחמה . . . בשלם. As noted in Comm., read ברגלי, ובנעלי, במתני, בחגרתי, with 𝔊ᴸ 𝔏. The same VSS render וישם as though ויקם, 'and he avenged,' and רמי מלחמה 2° as though דם נקי or דם חנם, 'innocent blood.' These corrections have been largely accepted, *e.g.*, by Kit., Burn., St. (at length), Eissf., *BH*, in part by Šanda, *al.* But as for the verb the alleged corruption of intelligible ויקם to וישם is improbable, as also that of רם נקי to רמי מ׳. The interpretation of 𝔐 was indeed

I. 2¹⁻⁴⁶ᵃ

difficult; see Comm. 𝕋 has a most obscure expansion.—6. כחכמתך: for the noun 𝔊ᴸ has original φρονησιν vs. σοφιαν of al.; n.b. φρονιμος, Gr., 2³⁵⁰, and the variations in Grr., 3¹². —לא: B a₂ συ, early error for ου=ℭ ℭ.—שיבח[ו]: B a₂ πολιν, error for πολιαν.—7. ברולי: Noth interprets (p. 225) as of personal quality, 'Iron-Man.'— באכלי: for ב='in class of,' cf. בנקרים, Am. 1¹.—קרבו: the verb as generally translated is not clear, and Klost. attempts emendation; but cf. קרוב, 'neighbour' (‖ to רעה, Ps. 15³).—8. נמרצת: the same ppl. at Mic. 2¹⁰, חבל נמרץ; the verb נמרצו, Job 6²⁵, is generally emended; cf. Akk. namrāṣu, 'sickness,' Arab. mariḍ.—9. עתה: corroborated by 𝔊 at 2³⁵⁰, hence an early rdg.; but the emphatic pron. אתה is demanded, and so 𝔊ᴸ read; its absence in B al., 𝔖ᴴ is due to haplog. with foll. ου.—8. 9. Additional Note. 𝔊 and 𝔊ᴸ contain a parallel text to these vv. in Gr. 2³⁶¹·⁰; the latter is the earlier translation, belonging to the appendix of materials which had been omitted in the first form of Kgdms; see the writer's article, 'The Supplement at end of 3 Kingdoms 2,' and cf. Note after v.⁴⁶ᵃ below. The restoration here of the onetime omitted passage is practically the text of 𝔊ᴸ, and may be regarded as insertion from that source. In this Supplement B A M N al. (not 𝔊ᴸ) have a doublet for בן נרא, υιος Γηρα, υιος (του) σπερματος, i.e., as though בן זרע; the correct n. pr. is later insertion. For בחרים B has χεβρων, one of many similar corruptions in that text. 𝔊ᴸ Γαβαθα as=נבעתה (?) cannot (as Rahlfs remarks) be explained from any inner-Greek variation. Priority of the Supplement further appears in the rendering of חכם with φρονιμός, vs. σοφός.—12. 𝔊ᴸ MSS prefix βασιλειων γ' or β. τριτη; see Int., §1, n. 2.— אביו: A x + ετων δωδεκα; M N al. + υιος ετων ιβ'=𝔖ᴴ obel.; see Comm., and for the history of the phrase, Rahlfs, SS 3, §23.— מלכותה: this form in early historical bks. only here and 1 Sam. 20²¹, otherwise מלוכה, e.g., 1⁴⁶, 1 Sam. 10¹⁶; the present form is Aramaizing.—13. בן חנית: B a₂ ℭ om.—שלמה: Grr. + κ. προσεκυνησεν αυτη.—ותאמר: 1 MS + לו=Grr.; similar variations in Grr., v.¹⁷.— 14. ויאמר: 𝔊 om.; see Note on לאמר, v.⁴.—15. ותסב: for the notion of 'the turn of fate' see Comm. on היתה סבה, 12¹⁵.—16. שאלה אחת: 3 MSS+קטנה=𝔊ᴸ μικραν, from v.²⁰.—פני: correct, cf. vv.¹⁷·²⁰, vs. OGrr., as though פניך; the same change in 𝔊 v.¹⁷.—17. שלמה המלך: the name given before the title by an intimate.—19. וישתחו לה Grr., και (κατ)εφιλησεν αυτην=𝔖ᴴ; Jos., 'embracing her': the extreme Oriental etiquette towards the royal mother was not understood by the freer-minded Greeks.—וישם: impersonal, as EVV recognize; see GK §144, 3; ετεθη of Grr. and the pl. verb of 𝔖ᴴ are equally correct translations, but no warrant for emendation, vs. St., and BH 'probabiliter.'—21. יֻתַּן את אבישג: for the gender syntax see GK §121, 1.—22. ולאביתר הכ' וליואב: read the nouns as subjects with all the VSS, including 𝔖ᴴ, אביתר הכ' ויואב. 𝕋 paraphrased, "in counsel are they, he and A. and J.," good exegesis, but no warrant for emendations proposed by Klost. and

Benz., who would add חֶבֶר or דְּבָר.—At end of v. Grr. add ο αρχι-στρατηγος εταιρος; the first word is Joab's title, the second is apparently error for the pl., epexegetical to the preceding dative αυτω.—
23. Solomon is said to have sworn ' by YHWH,' but in the oath itself ' God ' is used, doubtless a ' Vermilderung ' ; MS 23 has יהוה=Gr. 71, 𝕮ᴸ—by true tradition ? On the oath and use of כי see Burney's extensive note.—יעשה, יוסיף : jussive forms are expected ; for other such cases see GK §75, t, and *cf.* §109, k. For the phrase " Y. do so to me and more also," Lexx. give Arabic parallels ; it is capitally illustrated by the identical curse cited by Livy, i, 24, *ad fin.* : " Tu, illo die, Iupiter, populum Romanum sic ferito, ut ego hunc porcum hic hodie feriam ; tanto magis ferito quanto magis potes pollesque."—**24.** יושיבני : this overvocalized Kt. of received texts, starting from יושבני, as in MS 70, is due to early scribal insertion of י in wrong place ; other MSS vary in its insertion.—**25.** ויפגע בו : a euphemism for homicide, common in Jud., Sam., Ki., perhaps with notion of resistless fate, *cf.* פגע רע, 5¹⁸.—The Gr. plus at end of v., ' in that day,' is gratuitous. —**26.** על: generally taken as misspelling for אל ; see Note on 1³³.— שרך : the older, radical spelling of the sing., with all VSS (not pl., as in EVV) ; see GK §93, ss.—ביום הזה : Grr., 𝕾ᴴ transfer to previous clause, to avoid notion of the possibility of the priest's execution.—"את ארון אדני י" : VSS, exc. 𝕮 𝔙, om. אדני, which as Ḳr. has entered the text (*n.b.* Heb. variants). For ארון many recent comm., following Then. (not Kit., Burn., Sk.), read אפוד on basis of το εφουδ for הארון, 1 Sam. 14¹⁸, in correspondence with the statement of ' the ephod ' that Abiathar carried " in his hand," acc. to 23⁶˙ ⁹, 30⁷. See T. C. Foote, ' The Ephod,' *JBL* 21 (1902), 1 ff. This position is stoutly disputed by W. R. Arnold in *Ephod and Ark (Harvard Theol. Studies, 1917)*, rejecting the Gr. correction in text cited above. However the ark, known to have been located at a provincial point (2 Sam. 6¹ᶠᶠ·), could hardly have followed David on his marches. It is preferable to accept the change on the ground that the ark, with its later importance, was substituted for the primitive instrument of divination, the ephod.—**27.** עֲלִי : *cf.* יהועלי, *n. pr. f.* in Eleph. papp. ; Šanda suggests identification with well-known Arab. *'Alī*, with colouring of the first vowel ; Noth (*IP* 146) connects it with *'elyôn.*—**28.** השמעה באה : the phrase at 2 Sam. 13³⁰.—אבשלום : see Comm. ; 𝔚 is supported among the ancient authorities only by Gr. B A x a₂, 𝕮. See deR. for Jewish discussion with recognition of a possible *ḥallûf*, or ' variant.'— **29.** הנה : Burn. remarks, " without specific suffix or pronoun following, the reference being unmistakable " ; but the word = primarily *hinnēhû*, and in such a phrase the suffix was pronounced, or possibly as *hinneh* (*cf.* Aram.).—אצל המזבח : Grr., κατεχει τ. κερατων τ. θυσιαστηριου=𝕾ᴴ 𝕾 ; an addition from v.²⁸, *vs.* Then., Šanda ; Burn. notes it as another case of the Gr. desire for uniformity. As Lev. 1¹⁶, 6³ show, ' beside-the-altar ' was holy ground.

—At end of v. Grr. + "and bury him," another case of uniformity; cf. v.³¹.—**30.** לא כי: see BDB 474a, GB 341, Nestle, *ZAW* 25, 163; the Ḳr. variously accentuates the phrase; *e.g.*, here and at 11²² as 'no, for,' but at 3²² as 'not so'; the latter retains the old absolute use of כי.—**35.** את צדוק הכהן נתן המלך: Grr. + εις ιερεα πρωτον, a good example of later ecclesiastical expansion.—**36.** אנה ואנה: the phrase at II. 5²⁵.—**37.** At end of v. 𝔊ᴸ +" and the king swore him on that day," anticipating v.⁴²; accepted by Then., Klost., but see Burn.'s counter-argument.—**38.** ימים רבים: Grr., harmonizing with v.³⁹, 'three years.'—**39.** אכיש:=𝔊ᴴ; 𝔊 Αγχους, 𝔊ᴸ Ακχους; *cf.* the name of the king of Ekron in Ashurbanipal's cylinder C, 'Ikauso' (*KB* 2, 149; *ARA* 2, §876), which apparently corroborates the vocalization of OGrr.—מעכה: B† Αμησα.—**42.** וָיֵעָר: for preservation of *i* in this position see BL §56, n.— ואנה ... ביום: Grr. render with plus from v.³⁶.—שמעתי ... ותאמר: 𝔊 𝔊ᴸ om., 𝔖ᴴ ※, and so Benz., St., Eissf., but without sufficient reason.—**44.** אשר ... אתה: supported by the Grr.; Klost. attempts rewriting; see Comm.—והשיב: VSS, exc. 𝔗, as thought וַיָשֶׁב; but *cf.* v.³².—**46a.** וימת: B a₂ 𝔈 om.

The Gr. Supplement after v.³⁵. See analysis by the writer in *ZAW* 1932, 124 ff. The collection of odd materials at this point is due to the fact that at one stage of translation the bk. of Kgdms was halted here, and the translator, or a successor, collected in postscript material omitted above along with data of interest from the subsequent history of Solomon's reign. The parallelisms are here presented with some brief comments; and see Notes *ad locos*. *Cf.* also Šanda's display, 1, 330 f.

𝔊 v. 35ᵃ·ᵇ=𝔓 5⁹·¹⁰.—v.ᶜ=3¹.—v.ᵈ=5²⁹.—v.ᵉ, first part items from ch. 7, second part=11²⁷ᵇ.—vv.ᶠ·ᵍ=9²⁴·²⁵.—v.ʰ=9²³.—v.ⁱ=9¹⁵⁻¹⁸, *cf.* 3¹.—vv.ˡ⁻ᵒ=2⁸·⁹·³⁶⁻⁴⁶; both parts of the Shimei story had been omitted in the primary version; see Comm. *ad loc.*—v.⁴⁶ᵃ, *cf.* v.³⁵ᵃ.—v.ᵇ=5¹.—vv. ᶜ·ᵈ in part=9¹⁹, in part with an original datum; see Comm.—v.ᵉ=5²·³.—vv.ᶠ·ᵍ=5⁴·⁵.—v.ʰ=4¹⁻⁵; see Comm.—vⁱ·=5⁶.—v.ᵏ=5¹.—v.ˡ, *cf.* 4¹.

Ch. 2⁴⁶ᵇ–3¹. The settlement of Solomon's kingdom, and his marriage with a Pharaoh's daughter.¹ *And the royal power being established in Solomon's hand* (Solomon married, etc.). The phrase resumes the almost identical statement as 2¹²ᵇ,

---

¹ This paragraphing disagrees with that of modern versions (following the printed Vulgate), except JV. The Hebrew syntax requires the division here accepted (*cf.* similar cases in 1⁴·⁵), and follows Bär's edition and *BH*, although Ginsburg makes no division until after v.². Also Josephus starts afresh here with ch. 2 of *Ant.*, iv. The OGrr. had included this material in their addenda above (see Notes at end of the last ch.), and then invented a fresh caption for the new book with "Solomon son of David reigned over Israel and Judah in Jerusalem."

with a different word, but of the same root, for *kingdom*. The confirmation of his power is illustrated by his proud marriage. Ch. 3. **1.** The royal marriage is given first in the editor's scheme, as is the case with David's wives (2 Sam. $3^{2ff.}$, $5^{13ff.}$), and so below the queen-mother's name is statedly given with each accession to the throne. *Solomon became son-in-law of Pharaoh king of Egypt; and he took* (in marriage) *Pharaoh's daughter; and he brought her into David's City, until he had finished building his house and the house of YHWH and the wall of Jerusalem round about.* This is the only direct reference to the marriage. *Cf.* 9^{24}: "Then [so correct 𝕳] Pharaoh's daughter came up out of David's City to her house which he built for her. Then he built the Millo." Of these two archival items, the first is the basis of the latter part of our verse. Below, 9^{16} records the Pharaoh's capture of Gezer and his presentation of it as dower for his daughter. OGrr. omit our v.^{1} and 9^{16} in place, and present them together after 5^{14} (Gr. $4^{31. \ 32}$). It is a question where the historic item of the marriage originally stood. Some scholars, *e.g.*, Benzinger, Kittel (*cf. BH*), Burney, Šanda, Skinner, would connect the item of the marriage with 9^{16}, and place the material where OGrr. put it, after 5^{14}. However no authority is to be assigned to the placing of the additions in 𝕲; the passage in question is a convenient summary of the references to the queen. The introductory statement, *he became son-in-law of Ph.*, is duplicative, but in good Semitic style, and appears to have original value, *vs.* Stade, who following 𝕲, regards it as secondary. For the building of the queen's palace there is the archival item at 7^{8b}. In our passage we find for the first time the distinction between David's City and Jerusalem (see Smith, *Jerusalem*, I, 153). All the references to this queen have been cited except the parenthetic allusion at 11^1, and the perversion of history in 2 Ch. 8^{11}. The princess' origin is still debated. Alt (in his *Israel u. Aegypten*, 11–41—the fullest discussion of these international relations), Breasted (*HE* 529), Olmstead (*HPS* 340) find in her a daughter of Sheshonk I, founder of the 22nd or Libyan Dynasty, the Shishak of 14^{25}; Meyer thinks of Psusennis the last of the 21st, Tanite Dynasty (*GA* 2, 2, 263); Šanda and Kittel prefer one of the earlier kings of this dynasty. Sheshonk's accepted succession as of date 945 B.C.

would make him a very late contemporary of Solomon, whose accession is generally dated some 25 years earlier. Meyer remarks that this distinguished marriage may have given Solomon the impulse to his palace constructions. Winckler's scoffing at the story of this marriage (*GI* 2, 63; *KAT* 236) on the basis of the Pharaonic declaration in Tell el-Amarna tablet no. 3 that " daughters of the king of Egypt are never given to others " is not pertinent for these late and degenerate dynasties. There is indeed the parallel and authentic story of an Edomite prince's marriage with a Pharaoh's sister-in-law and their child's adoption in the royal palace ($11^{14\text{ff.}}$). Gunkel, in his *Einl. in die Psalmen*, 151 ff., gives a long list of such ancient international marriages.

VV.$^{2, 3}$. An editorial moralizing introduction to the story of Solomon's dream at the high-place at Gibeon. **2.** *Only the people were sacrificing at the high-places, because there was no house built for the Name of Y*HWH *up to those days.* The statement with its unmediated 'only' appears to be from the hand of a secondary editor, who modelled the expression after the usual exception made subsequently in the count of the virtues of good kings, *e.g.*, Jehoshaphat, 22^{44}, Joash, II. 12^4. It is then an exculpatory extension of the exception made by the first editor in v.^{3}. For the definition of ' the house,' etc., see Comm. at 8^{17}. **3.** *And Solomon loved Y*HWH, *walking in the statutes of his father David ; only he was sacrificing and burning incense at the high-places.* The usual interpretation of Heb. *bâmāh* with ' high-place ' (so modern VSS after the Greek and Latin translators) is here kept in lieu of any English word expressive of the Biblical aversion to those heathenish shrines. The Chronicler exculpates the sainted builder of the temple : " [He] went to the high-place at Gibeon, for there was the Tent of Meeting " (2 Ch. 1^3). Šanda suggests placing v.^{2b} after v.^{3}, but the passage is too much of a mosaic to attempt restoration of an original. For the high-places see the works on O.T. archæology and religion (a recent statement by Albright is cited in the Notes), and in particular the reports of excavations, every one of which has revealed the remains of such ancient sanctuaries. *He loved Y*HWH : Deuteronomic phrase (Dt. 10^{12}, etc.), but with a complement, *walking in the statutes, i.e.*, those, morals, *of his father David*, as the word is also used at II. 17⁸, ²¹ of evil morals. The verb generally translated here with *burnt incense* (JV *offered*) may be taken in its root mng., 'to make to smoke,' used of the sweet savour of the burning sacrifice (*cf.* Gen. 8²⁰ᶠ·), or as denominative from the noun for 'incense,' as rendered above. The earlier objection to the latter mng., namely that incense did not reach Palestine until a much later age, is now fully disposed of by the discovery of numerous and highly elaborate censers, *e.g.*, the remarkable specimen found at Taanach by Sellin (presented by Barton, *AB* fig. 210), while they appear to have been of common domestic use, going back well into the second millennium ; indeed we know from Egypt that the Arabian incense trade was of early origin, and we may compare the name of Abraham's concubine, Keturah, doubtless related to *ḳĕṭôreṭ*, 'incense.' For a study of the small censers see S. Przeworski, ' Les censoirs de la Syrie,' *Syria*, 1930, 133 ff. The two terms ' sacrificing ' and ' censing ' may express the round of worship ; and so at 11⁸ (with Solomon's heathenish wives as subject), II. 12⁴ (with the people as subject).

4-15. Solomon at the great high-place at Gibeon has a dream, in which, upon the divine promise of any boon, he asks and receives the gift of wisdom, *to judge this thy great people* (v.⁹). There appears now the first extensive parallel of the Chronicler to Ki. (2 Ch. 1¹⁻¹³). **4.** *And the king went to Gibeon to sacrifice there, for it was the great high-place ; a thousand burnt-offerings was Solomon wont to offer upon that altar.* It is not so remarkable that the king went to Gibeon to sacrifice at its high-place, as that the story has been so artlessly preserved. The secondary conclusion in v.¹⁵ makes the king return to Jerusalem to offer sacrifices there ' before the Ark ' ; the Chronicler assuages the difficulty by locating at Gibeon the Tent of Meeting and Bezalel's brazen altar, although the Ark ' in a tent ' was in Jerusalem. Gibeon has been identified with el-Jīb, 6 mi. N.W. of Jerusalem ; for the earlier tradition see Robinson (*BR* 2, 136 ff.), for recent authorities Albright (*AASOR* 4 [1924], 104), Abel (*GP* 2, 335 f.), these without question ; Galling (*BR s.v.*) gives a summary account of recent various theories for the location of this and other sites to the north of Jerusalem, himself coming to no positive conclusion. Why that sanctuary was preferred as *the great high-place* (the Heb. expresses the superlative) in Solomon's day is obscure. The Gibeonites had remained a Canaanite enclave since the conquest (Jos. $9^{3\text{ff.}}$, ch. 10); their treaty rights were so respected that David delivered to them seven grandsons of Saul for death to atone for an outrage committed by that king (2 Sam. $21^{1\text{ff.}}$). We may assume the Gibeonites' formal acceptance of the conquerors' deity (*n.b.* Jos. 9^9). As extra-territorial the place may have been selected by royalty for policy's sake; *cf.* David's creation of an absolutely new sacred centre with no Israelite tradition. There are few other cases of such local Yahweh-altars—on Carmel (18^{30}), on Nebo according to the Mesha stele (line 18), and *cf.* Absalom's vow that had to be fulfilled at Hebron (2 Sam. $15^{7\text{ff.}}$). For the *burnt-offering*, properly 'holocaust,' see Nowack, *Arch.*, 2, 214 ff., Benzinger, *Arch.*, 362. The *thousand* of burnt-offerings need not be taken literally. *Cf.* the artificial distinction between μυρίος and μύριος. We possess in the Greek 'hekatomb' the parallel of a loosely used ritual term; this word, which means 'a hundred oxen,' is used by Homer of smaller numbers of victims, in one case of eight oxen (*Il.*, vi, 93, 115), or the sacrifice might consist of rams or sheep (xxiii, 147, 864). According to Herodotus, Crœsus and Xerxes made sacrifices by the thousands (i, 50; vii, 43). South Arabian inscriptions give extravagant figures. There is no reason with Benzinger to regard the whole v., or with Stade the second half, as redactional; why should a later age have magnified Solomon's irregular worship on a *bâmāh* at Gibeon? Indeed the somewhat conceit of the verse arouses the suspicion that the story springs from Gibeon, in opposition to Jerusalem, which should be the place where 'YHWH is to be seen' (Gen. 22^{14}). For the king presiding as *summus sacerdos* see Comm., $8^{11\text{ff.}}$.

5-14. || 2 Ch. $1^{7\text{ff.}}$. Solomon's dream belongs to an extensive chapter of ancient religious psychology and praxis. The dream, or night vision, has its occasional part in earlier Biblical narratives; *e.g.*, for Isaac at Beersheba (Gen. 26^{24}), Jacob at Bethel, and with further such experiences (28^{11}, 31^{11}, $32^{22\text{ff.}}$, 46^2). The Philistine king Abimelek had a dream-warning (20^3), the Pharaoh a symbolical dream (ch. 40), and so even a common soldier (Jud. 7^{13}). The nearest approach to the present story is that of the oracle by night in the sanctuary to the young Samuel (1 Sam. 3). The dream was early recognized as one of the normal ways of divine revelation; so 1 Sam. 28^6: "YHWH answered Saul neither by dreams, nor by Urim, nor by prophets." But visions and dreams were inferior to the direct word-of-mouth revelations given to Moses (Num. 12$^{6\text{ff.}}$). The Biblical dreams located at sanctuaries, Beersheba, Bethel, Shiloh, Gibeon, doubtless had connexion in fact with the ancient practice of oneiromancy at shrines, with a ritual praxis that induced such phenomena. Petrie interpreted the rings of stones at the turquoise mines of Serābīt as cubicles for such incubation on part of the seekers of the precious stones (*Researches in Sinai*, 1906, 65 ff.). The present dream story is the last recorded in the Bible until the days of Apocalyptic; the practice fell into disrepute, and Jeremiah bitterly inveighed against the prophets who dream dreams (23$^{23\text{ff.}}$). In the youngest book of the Old Testament we have Nebuchadnezzar's dream, while the seer had 'his dreams and visions of his head upon his bed' (Dan. cc. 2, 7—see Montgomery *ad locos*). The several royal dreams cited above introduce us to a privilege extensively claimed by the Oriental monarchs from the day of Sumerian Gudea down through the line of Ashurbanipal, Nebuchadnezzar, Nabonidus, and outside of the Semitic field, the Lydian Gyges and the Persian kings, as also in Egypt; there may be added the fable of Alexander's dream concerning the Jewish high-priest in Josephus, *Ant.*, xi, 8, 5.[2]

[2] For the series of dreams to Gudea, prescribing his building of a temple, in his Cylinder A, see Barton, *Royal Inscriptions of Sumer and Akkad*, 1, 204 ff. (he had his visions by incubation, *e.g.*, §II). Ashurbanipal records a divine vision by night (*ARA* 2, no. 835), and a dream of his army (no. 807), and also reports the dream of Lydian Gyges, which bade him seek the Assyrian alliance (no. 784). The ill-fated Nabonidus records two dreams (see Jastrow, cited below). For Egypt there are the dreams of Merenptah and Tanutamon (Breasted, *ARE* 3, no. 582; 4, no. 922). For dreams of or about Persian monarchs see Herodotus, i, 107 f., iii, 30, 124; vii, 19. And there is now to be added the dream by which El revealed himself to Keret, king of the Sidonians, in an Ugaritic epic (Virolleaud, *Keret*, 60 ff.). For the subject in general see Jastrow, *Rel. Bab. u. Ass.*, 2, 954 ff., and Index, *s.v.* 'Traum'; Meissner, *Bab. u. Ass.*, 244 ff.; and for the 'dream-style' Mowinckel in the Gunkel-*Eucharisterion*, 317 ff.

Accordingly the present story is entirely in the colour of the ancient Orient, innocent of the later orthodox sentiment against dreams. It observes the Biblical characteristic of the dream for God's own people as a means of direct revelation; the dream is not symbolical, requiring therefore dream-interpreters as in the Babylonian religion, the *oneiropoloi* of Herodotus (indeed it is God's people who interpret Pagan dreams, as in the case of Joseph and Daniel), but is a direct 'word' of Deity. The charm of this story is unique. Kittel comments that "there is no reason to doubt the historical character of this narrative"; that it is in origin an early, practically contemporary story, and in so far authentic, is without doubt. It is connected with the North-Israelite, actually old-Canaanite sanctuary of Gibeon; if it is of the Elohistic strain, as claimed by Hölscher, it must be North-Israelite, and in that case primitive, because of the subsequent break between North and South. Moreover the divine gift to Solomon is not a temple-plan as in Gudea's case, and *cf.* Ex. 25^9; such an invention might well have been inserted here; *cf.* the oracle to David, when he purposed to build a temple. But the boon Solomon asks for, which is granted, is judicial wisdom to fit him to *judge this thy great people*. The story well antedates the extravagant tradition of Solomon's 'wisdom' as presented in 5$^{9\text{ff.}}$, *cf.* 10$^{1\text{ff.}}$. It reflects one aspect of his administration for which we have no record, that is, the organization of the law of his realm; *n.b.* his Hall of Justice (7^7). His taxation system is fully reported (ch. 4); the social order of his state must have been of equal concern. We may well compare with Solomon the greater Hammurabi, who in the preface to his code says: "When Marduk sent me to rule man and to promulgate justice, I put justice and righteousness into the language of the land and promoted the welfare of the people." As Kittel remarks, Solomon may have been 'the first to systematize the law of Israel' (*GVI* 2, 150). For criticism of the narrative Burney gives an exact critical display of Deuteronomistic phrases, and it is reasonable to assign the present form to the late editors. Hölscher would find his Elohist here, but the tradition of the divine Name on which he relies is uncertain. **7.** *A little child:* the phrase is that of humility, and is relative; *cf.* Jesus' saying,

Mk. 10^{15}, and the Arabic use of 'sheikh,' properly 'old man.' Rashi and Kimchi follow ancient tradition here by making Solomon 12 years old, and so the Hexaplaric gloss at 2^{12}. Octavianus, when he assumed his uncle's toga, *ætat.* 18, was taunted by his opponents as 'a boy.' *To go out and come in:* with the home as implied object, *i.e.*, the round of daily public life; *cf.* 1 Sam. 18^{16}. **9.** EVV, *an understanding heart to judge thy people:* but literally, *a heart that listens to judge thy people.* The first verb is a legal term (*cf.* use at 2^{12}); a similar phrase below, v.^{11}, where EVV render with 'to discern justice,' but the Heb. *to hear justice* means *to give a just hearing; cf.* the English judicial term, 'a hearing.' In the judicial act there are two operations, the hearing of the evidence, then the decision of the intelligence (Heb. *heart*). V.^{14} is regarded by Stade as a Deuteronomistic addition; Klostermann and Benzinger elide only the condition of the first part; Šanda finds also vv.$^{12b, 13b}$ as secondary; they are indeed extravagant utterances. The divine word thus simplified will read: **12**a. *Lo, I have done according to thy word. Lo, I have given thee a wise and understanding heart.* **13**a. *And I have also given thee what thou didst not ask, both riches and honour.* **14**b. *And I will lengthen thy days.* AV 'honour,' *vs.* the variant translation elsewhere with 'glory,' when attribute of Deity, is the best translation of the Heb. *kābôḏ*; here Luther was followed with his 'Ehre.' In the Anglican Prayer Book there occurs the constant doublet, 'the honour and glory' of Deity. **15.** The v. is variously appraised by critics. Benzinger, Kittel, Stade regard it as wholly redactional; Skinner accepts, allowing probable additions to the text. Hölscher would excise only, *and he came to Jerusalem, and stood before the ark of the covenant of the Lord,* which is evidently an intruded passage, inserted to emphasize the primacy of Jerusalem. *Cf.* the probable excision of 'in Hebron' at end of 2 Sam. 15^{8}. The initial sentences, *and he awoke, and lo, it was a dream* (=Gen. 41^{7}, E), are of indifferent importance critically. That *he offered burnt-offerings and made peace-offerings, and made a feast for all his ministers* (the last statement also at Gen. 40^{20}), properly concludes the scene at Gibeon, and is original.

VV.$^{16-28}$. The Judgment of Solomon. This story of a summary judicial decision has widespread parallels. Grotius cites a similar case given by Diodorus Siculus for a Thracian king Ariopharnes, as well as a case in Suetonius's Life of Claudius (ch. 15). A good parallel from the Indian Jātaka Stories tells how a woman left her child on a river bank, a she-demon picked it up and claimed it as hers ; the two appealed to the deity, who ordered them to tear the child apart and each to take half, but the real mother refused. There is also the notable Pompeian fresco, depicting such a ' judgment.' [3] If our story is borrowed, it is idle to decide from what quarter. For the immediate entrance of the two women before the king, *cf.* the story of the ' wise woman ' who brought her alleged domestic trouble before king David (2 Sam. 14), and, for the ' open court ' that the king should grant all his subjects, the clever politics of Absalom (2 Sam. $15^{1\text{ff}}$.). The ancient Oriental king was approachable to all (*cf.* 1 Sam. 18^{16}), and such open justice still prevails in the courts of modern Arab potentates. For the two harlots—on which subject the commentators cited by Poole have considerable and amusing discussion, while some ancient texts try to modify or ignore the ugly noun—Landersdorfer pertinently compares the women who kept the drinking-places, actually ' disorderly houses,' in Babylonia, whom the Code Hammurabi severely controlled (§§108–111) ; indeed the Targum uses here the word for ' innkeeper ' (fem.). The ' harlot ' Rahab belonged to the same class. The story is told in an effective way, with a genuine feminine strain to it ; there is a certain amount of repetitiousness, which the Grr. avoided. There is to be noted the psychological expression in v.^{26}, literally, *her bowels were fermented for her son* (*cf.* Gen. 43^{30}), and so correctly for the first noun AV, while the other EVV euphemize with ' heart ' ; all agree in translating the sequence with " yearned upon/after her son." The development of meaning of that noun appears in

[3] For the Indian tale see E. B. Cowell and W. H. D. Rouse, *Jātaka Stories*, 6 (1912), 63 ff. ; H. G. Rawlinson, *Intercourse between India and the Western World* (1926), 11 ; for the Pompeian fresco Springer-Michaelis, *Handbuch der Kunstgesch., Das Altertum*⁶, fig. 316 ; and Le Blaut, *Rev. Archéologique*, ser. III, 13 (1889), p. 24 and pl. iii. Gressmann's study ' Das Salomonische Urteil ' in *Deutsche Rundschau*, 130 (1907), 212 ff., cites some twenty-two such cases in folk-tale and literature. See also for more recent bibliography *ERE* 7 (1914), 467 ; J. G. Frazer, *Folk-Lore in the O.T.*, 2, ch. 11.

'bowels of mercy,' Lk. 1⁷⁸, Col. 3¹², and finally it came to mean 'compassion.' See I. Eitan's study of the word in *JBL* 1934, 269 ff. A nice point of language appears in the same v., when the real mother varies the usual word for 'child,' *yèled*, by using another, *yālûd*, which may be translated with the etymologically equivalent 'bairn.' **18.** *The third day: i.e.,* 'the day after the morrow.' **21.** Stade would delete one or the other of the two cases of *in the morning*, but the language is that of feminine repetitiousness. **26. 27.** Omit, with OGrr. *(the) living (baby), bis*; the addition was due to the erroneous notion that the dead baby also had been brought into court, leading to the absurd development in Josephus and Lucian that the king commanded the halving of both the living and the dead child, equal parts for each woman; this humorous expansion might be based on the law in Ex. 21³⁵. **28.** The story concludes with the impression made upon the people: *All Israel heard of the verdict that the king had rendered; and they stood in awe of the king, for they saw that divine wisdom was in him for executing justice.* As observed above, it is a judicial wisdom that is ascribed to Solomon in these early stories, not the philosophy of later legend. Indeed the corresponding word for Heb. 'wisdom' here, *ḥokmāh*, in the Arabic *ḥukm* means a judicial judgment. For justice as the primary royal virtue see Ps. 72¹ᶠᶠ·, and Gunkel's Comm. This popular story is sequel to that of the dream. No critical literary judgment can be easily given as to its age and provenance. Stade regards it as comparatively late; but Kittel remarks that "in its liveliness and freshness the narrative recalls J of the Pentateuch," and with this judgment Hölscher fully agrees.

46*b*. הממלכה: the noun, reminiscent of 2 Sam. 7¹⁶, also *inf.*, 11¹¹, etc., is generally found in prophetic diction; but note the political term עיר הם', 1 Sam. 27⁵; in Phœn. ממלכת is used frequently of the personified royalty (Harris, *Gram.*, 118).—𝕲 om. this half-verse, at 2³⁵ has the plus, "and the kingdom was established in Jerusalem."

Ch. 3. **1.** ויקח: the verb in absolute sense also at 7⁸; 𝕲 2³⁵ᶜ +'to wife.'—ויביאה: here Lagarde (his 2³; 𝕲 4³¹) has a negative ουκ, with 2 MSS, a correction after 2 Ch. 8¹¹, but a pure sport. —"' ב' ונ]ביתו ואת: B a₂ om. (ℭ has), then introducing with all other Gr. texts εν πρωτοις; *i.e.*, the latter distinction was arbitrarily introduced to give the building of the temple precedence, and then in the two MSS noted the building of the palace was eliminated. At 9¹⁵ the order of the items is reversed. Actually the mention of the temple here is quite out of place in connexion with the queen's residence.—**2.** רק: also at v.³, and so generally throughout the bk.; but at 22⁴⁴ אך.—רק העם: B a₂ 𝕮 om.—by error or of purpose?—במות: the noun, already identified with Akk. *bāmtu*, 'back,' etc., now appears in the Ugaritic prepositional form לבמת, 'upon.' See Albr., *ARI* 105 f., and accompanying note, defining the object as "an elevated platform on which cultic objects were placed"; he accepts the derivation of Gr. *bōmos*, 'altar' (otherwise of unknown etymology) from this Sem. word, *via* the Phœnician.—**3.** מקטיר: Nowack, *Arch.*, 2, 246 ff., denying early use of incense in Palestine, draws distinction between the Hif., used of the smoke, savour of sacrifice, and the Piel as denominative from קטרת: however, to establish this distinction, the vocalization of the verbal forms must at times be corrected, *e.g.*, 1 Sam. 2¹⁶, קמר יקטירון, with combination of Pi. inf. and Hif. impf. There must have arisen later confusion of the two conjugations.—**4.** הבמה הגדולה: Grr., υψηλοτατη κ. μεγαλη, paraphrasing the obnoxious words, and so all VSS (𝔙 'excelsum magnum'), exc. that 𝔖 𝔄 replace the noun with 'altar.'—**5.** The nominal sentence without conj. appears awkward; VSS, exc. 𝕴, attach בגבעון to prec. v., and prefix a conj. to the foll. verb.—אלהים: Grr. (exc. Aq., Sym.)=יהוה.—**6.** 'ו הלך לפניך וג: Burn. *cft.* 'walking with God,' Gen. 5²², Mic. 6⁸, etc.—**8.** לא ימנה ולא יספר מרב:=8⁵; 𝕲 om. the second sentence and also abbreviates the parallel.—**9.** לשפט את עמך: Grr. +εν δικαιοσυνη; St. elides as repetition of the phrase below; but the insistence on justice is to the point.—עמך הכבד: *cf.* Num. 20²⁰; for the sense of the adj. *cf.* the noun כבוד.—**10.** [בעיני] ארני: read with many MSS יהוה; all VSS with amelioration of the physical phrase: "it pleased the Lord."—**11.** אלהים:=Ch., but all VSS=יהוה (𝔖ᴴ noting that Hebræus has אלהים).—לך 2⁰: 𝕲 om., and so St.; but note the triple 2d person with effect, לך *bis*, איביך.—ושאלת: for the 'irregular' pf. with 'weak Waw' (Ch. corrects to ותשאל) see Dr., *Tenses*, §133; Burn. rightly notes the rhetorical contrast of לא שאלת and שאלת, and we may also observe the earlier larger liberty in the syntax with Waw.—**12.** כדבריך: so *BH* (L), Bär; Mich., Ken., Ginsb., כדברך=VSS, exc. 𝔙; the latter as sing., and by Oriental tradition, is correct; at 18³⁶, 22¹³ דבריך is corrected by Ḳr. to דברך; the fuller Kt. arose to express the accent.—חכם ונבון: 𝕲 φρονιμην κ. σοφην, but Hex., σ. κ. φ., exemplifying the later understanding of חכם.—**13.** כל ימיך: OGrr. om., and so St., *al.*, correctly, unless we are to assume an original bungling phrase; Klost., Benz. preserve by reading preceding היה as יהיה. The gloss was not restrictive in purpose, it would interpret the past tense so as to include the coming life of the king. Ch. expands into comparison with all kings, 'before thee and after thee.' Note punctuation of JV to avoid the difficulty.—**15.** יִקֶץ: preferable to Ginsb., יִקַּץ; see Bär's note, St.—ויבוא: Grr. pref. κ. ανεστη.—לפני ארון: OGrr. pref. κατα προσωπον τ. θυσιαστηριου τ. [κατα προς.].

accepted by Then., Klost., but an addition after Ch., v.[6], with Burn., "to remove the impression that S. passed into the immediate presence of the Ark."—אדני: Ken. text, many MSS, the original יהוה. Grr. add 'in Sion,' and the plus 'for himself [and all his servants].'

16. תבאנה: Grr., ωφθησαν—by euphemistic change (?); 𝔈 = 𝔅.— נשים: = Engl. indefinite 'certain'; for the same use cf. 11[18], 17[9], Jud. 4[4], 19[1], and Aram. נוברין, Dan. 3[8]; 3 Heb. MSS, Grr. om.— וזנות: 6 Gr. MSS πονηραι for πορναι, 1 MS om.—**17.** בי: EVV 'Oh'; Grr., εν εμοι; 𝔖 לוחי = 'chez moi'; 𝔗 בבעו, 'at your leave, pray' = 𝔖 𝔄 𝔙; on such an understanding, cf. the suppression of ע of the root בעה in nn. pr., e.g., רוח, בלדד. But A. M. Honeyman, in a notable article in *JAOS* 1944, 81 f., properly insists, following predecessors, but with additional proof, on its identification with אבי, II. 5[13] (q.v.), and from root אבה, 'be willing,' and so becoming a worn-down expression for 'granted,' and the like.—**18.** יחדו: 'alone'; the Heb. and the Engl. adv. by like development.—בכיתי 1⁰; 𝔊 𝔊[L] om., and so St.—שתים אנחנו: cf. שנינו אנחנו, 1 Sam. 20[42].—**20.** ואמתך ישנה: 𝔊 𝔊[L] om., and so St.— מֵאֶצְלִי: Grr., εκ τ. αγκαλων μου, reading as מֵאַצְלִי.—**21.** בבקר 2⁰: 𝔙 distinguishes from 1⁰ with 'clara luce'; St., *BH* om.—**22.** לא כי bis: see Note, 2[30].—וזאת אמרת לא כי בנך המת ובני החי: 𝔊 om., and so St., *BH*, Eissf.; but the repetition belongs to the style.—**25.** 𝔊[L] ad fin. plus κ. το τεθνηκος ομοιως διελετε κ. δοτε αμφοτεραις, and so Jos.; see Rahlfs, *SS* 3, 101, 284, questioning whether the addition was by oral tradition or from an early written source.— **26.** ילוד: also v.[27]. St. doubts the change of vocalization from יֶלֶד, but here 2 Gr. MSS have παιδαριον vs. current παιδιον and so 2 Lucianic MSS at v.[27], proving that the distinction was early observed. The noun is always used of the mother's relation, ילוד אשה, Job 14[1], etc., exc. 1 Ch. 14[4].—החי [הילוד]: 𝔊 𝔊[L] om., and so at v.[27]; 2 Heb. MSS om. it here, a third MS om. it v.[27].— **27.** לא תמיתהו: positive command, vs. the precative of the woman's plea with אל; some 66 MSS read the latter.—Rahlfs presents (*SS* 1, §3) a study of the text of Origen's letter to Julius Africanus, repeating the above story.

CC. 4–5[14] (EVV ch. 4). The power and glory of king Solomon. V.[1] is editorial, but primary, and is based upon 2 Sam. 8[15a], "and David reigned over all Israel," while *ib.* v.[15b], "and David was effecting justice and right for all his people," is paralleled by the story of Solomon's Judgment; then Sam., vv.[16ff.], lists David's officialdom, even as the like data are given here. *All Israel*: *i.e.*, Pan-Israel, an early nationalistic term from the days of the union of the tribes in a kingdom.

VV.[2-6]. A list of the royal cabinet. The accompanying plate gives a conspectus of the textual evidence for this list of offices and officers. It is an expansion of the table in the writer's article, 'The Year-Eponymate in the Hebrew Monarchy,' *JBL* 1930, 311–19, to which reference should be made for fuller demonstrations. Similar tables have been presented by Benzinger (p. 15) and Šanda (p. 71). For 𝕲 the text of B is followed, with notable variants in parentheses. Recognition of the 'glosses' in Gr. ch. 2 and of their proper assignment is of prime importance; their original order is indicated by (1), (2), (3), etc. A similar table will be given on next page presenting the parallelism of the present list with those of David's officers, 2 Sam. 8, 20.

The resultant of criticism of the text is the following form. **2.** *And these were his officers: Azariah b. Sadok* **(3)** *Over-the-Year; and Ahijah b. Shausha, Secretary; and Jehoshaphat b. Ahilud* [var. *Ahilad*] *the Recorder;* **(4a)** *and Benaiah b. Jehoiada Over-the-Army;* **(5)** *and Azariah b. Nathan Over-the-Lieutenants; and Zabud* [var. *Zakur*] *b. Nathan Priest, Royal Friend;* **(6)** *and Ahiel* [var. *Ahishar*—without patronymic] *Over-the-Palace; and Adoram* [*Adoniram*?] *b. Abda Over-the-Levy.*

The most important reconstruction of the text occurs in the first and second items, namely with omission of 'the priest' after 'Sadok' (in any case the appositive should refer to the son Azariah), the correction of the unexplained *n. pr.*, 'Elihoreph' to 'Over-the-Year,' following a Gr. gloss, and the resultant of but one Secretary. In the first item 'the priest' is lacking in 𝕲 here, but is supplied in 2^{46h}, which latter section otherwise ignores any Priests in the list. The item in v.⁴ on the two Priests was baldly introduced from the list of David's officers in 2 Sam. $8^{16ff.}$ (see Comm., 2^{35b}); it has a most unauthentic ring, as Abiathar was immediately deposed upon the king's accession, indeed should have been named first; we learn below of a Priest in the royal court, who is also Royal Friend.[1] But a certain Azariah b. Sadok

[1] In note 10 of his article cited above the writer has expressed his scepticism concerning these data about Sadok. Only brief reference may be made to the extensive recent literature on the subject of the Aaronids and Sadokids: Kittel, *GVI* 2, 196; Kennett, *O.T. Essays*, ch. 3; Meek, *AJSL* 45 (1929), 149 ff.; J. Gabriel, *Untersuchungen über das alttest. Hohepriestertum* (1933); arts. by Bentzen, Budde, Möhlenbrink in *ZAW* 1933, 173 ff.; 1934, 42 ff., 184 ff.; Morgenstern,

I. 𝔐 I. 4²·⁶	II. 𝔊 in loco	III. 𝔊 2⁴⁶ʰ	IV. Glosses in 2⁴⁶ʰ	V. 𝔊ᴸ (Lagarde) in loco
עזריהו בן צדוק	Αξαρια υιος Σαδωκ —(𝔊ᴴ ο ιερευς)	Αξαριου υιος Σαδωκ του ιερεως		Αξαριας υιος Σαδδουκ
אליחרף	κ. Αχεια			κ. Ελιαβ
בן	υιος (MN+16 MSS υιοι			κ. Αχια
שישא	Σαβα (𝔏 Susa, 𝔈 Συβα)			υιος
ספרים	γραμματεις (3 MSS—τευς)			Σαφατ
יהושפט	κ. Ιωσαφαθ			γραμματεις
בן אחילוד	υ. Αχειλαδ (N Αχιλαδ)			κ. Ιωσαφατ
המזכיר	υπομνηματων			υ. Αχιθαλαμ υπομμημησκων
בן יהוידע				κ. Βεναις
על הצבא				υ. Ιωαδ
וצדוק ואביתר כהנים	κ. Σαδωκ κ. Αβιαθαρ ιερεις			επι τ. δυναμεως
		(4) κ. Σουβα (𝔊ᴸ Σουσα) γραμματευς		κ. Σαδδουκ κ. Αβιαθαρ ιερεις
	κ. Ορνεια υ. Ναθαν επι τ. κατεσταμενων			κ. Ορνια υ. Ναθαν
	κ. Ζαβουθ υ. Ναθαν	(5) κ. Βασα (varr. Σαβα, Σουβα) υ. Αχειθαλαμ αναμιμνησκων		επι τ. καθεστημενων
זבוד בן נתן				κ. Ζαχουρ υ. Ναθαν
כהן רעה המלך	εταιρος του βασιλεως	(6) κ. Αβει (var. Αβια, 𝔊ᴸ Ελιαβ) υ. Ιωαβ (var. Ιωαδ) αρχιστρατηγος		εταιρος τ. βασιλεως
	κ. Αχειρ (—λ) οικονομος			κ. Αχιηλ οικονομος
ואחישר על הבית	κ. Ελακ ο οικονομος	(2) κ. Ορνειου υ. Ναθαν αρχων τ. εφεστηκοτων		κ. Ελιαβ υ. Ιωαβ
	κ. Ελιαβ υ. Σαφ επι τ. πατριας	(10) κ. Καχουρ (B:⁂; all others Z—) ο συμβουλος		επι τ. στρατιας
אדנירם	κ. Αδωνειραμ	(3) κ. Εδραμεν επι τ. οικον αυτου	(7) κ. Αχειρε (varr. Αχειραμ,—καμ)	κ. Αδωνιραμ
בן עבדא	υ. Εφρα		υ. Εδραει	υ. Εδραμ
על המס	επι τ. φορων		επι τ. αρσεις	επι τ. φορων
			(8) επι τ. αυλαρχιας	
			(9) κ. επι τ. πλινθιου	

is Over-the-Year, the ranking officer, doubtless of priestly function. The word ḥōreṗ in the unexplained *n. pr.*, ' Elihorep,' as hitherto understood, means the autumn season, S. Arab. ḥrp (*cf.* Arab. ḥarīf, ' autumn '), the beginning of the ancient Semitic year, that is, the New Year. The word ḥrp was then used for the calendar year, of which a *kabīr*, generally two *kabīrs* (*cf.* the Roman consuls), had charge. The office was parallel to that of the Ass. *līmu*, after the years of which functionaries all official documents were dated. It has been disputed among South-Arabists whether the office was sacerdotal, but there is proof of this in certain cases.[2] And indeed the Israelite office of *kōhēn* was not necessarily sacerdotal, for only so can be explained the statement of 2 Sam. 8[18] that two sons of David were ' priests ' (a title that the EVV dodge !), while 2 Sam. 20[26] records a certain Jairite, ' a priest of David's.' Now the Gr. at the former place translates the Heb. with αὐλάρχαι, and the gloss in col. iv of the table has over against כהן the same translation ἐπὶ τ. αὐλαρχίας, ' over the palace-service.' The interpretation offered for ḥrp is entirely satisfactory, but it was suggested to the writer and enforced by the Gr. gloss to the word, ἐπὶ τ. πλινθίου. The plinthion was the quadrans (whence Engl. ' quadrant '), which was not only a sun-dial but also an instrument for determining the seasons by the length of the sun's shadow, the instrument being adjusted to the latitude. To the references for this ancient instrument, long surviving in the Arabic world, given in the writer's article cited, are to be added two cases of Arabian quadrants : *CIS* IV, no. 161, Nabatæan ; Jaussen and Savignac, *Mission Archéologique* (1909), vol. 1, fig. 113, p. 303, a N. Arabian specimen. *Cf.* comment on sun-dials, II. 20[8ff.]. There is thus evidence for a fixed legal

---

' The High-Priesthood,' *AJSL* 55 (1938), 1 ff. ; J. Hoschander, *The Priests and Prophets*, ch. 6. For identification of Sadok as of the old Canaanite priesthood in Jerusalem, proposed by Mowinckel, Bentzen, and independently by H. H. Rowley, see the latter's art., ' Zadok and Nehushtan,' *JBL* 1939, 115 ff., with full review of the literature. It is suggested that the name of the priest may be historically related to that of the early priest-king of Jerusalem, Melchi-sedek. See also Comm., 2[35b], 8[14ff.].

[2] See note 7 of the writer's art. cited ; add citations in Glossary of Conti Rossini, *Chrest.*, p. 245, col. a, proving the priestly function.

calendar at the beginning of the Israelite monarchy. We may properly infer that this institution came to involve the registration of important events by dates, as in the ancient Mesopotamian empires, and so subsequently throughout the Mediterranean world. The Officer-over-the-Year was counterpart of the Roman Pontifex Maximus. It is from such official calendars that the dated data scattered throughout our book were ultimately drawn. For the syntactically unique use of '*al*, ' over x,' here and below, *cf.* the instances cited in BDB 755a; *cf.* the correspondent Akk. *ša pān, ša eli*; and for the later Gr. equivalent, ἐπί with the gen., see Thayer, *Lex.*, 231ᵇ. After this titularly ranking officer comes the Scribe or Secretary. The Heb. word *sôpēr* has been understood as corresponding to Akk. *šāperu*, on which office Meissner remarks that it was ' one of the most frequent, but also most ambiguous offices '; but R. P. Dougherty, with philological correctness, relates it to simple Akk. *sepēru*, ' scribe.' [3] In the Israelite *ménage* there was one such officer *par excellence*, *e.g.*, II. 22⁸, etc. The title ' Recorder,' by usual translation, is ambiguous, alongside of ' Scribe.' The Heb. word demands rather the translation (the king's) ' Remembrancer,' as Benzinger, Driver, Šanda, suggest.[4] For the ' Lieutenants ' (EVV ' chief, principal officers ') *cf.* 5³⁰. In ' Zabud b. Nathan Priest and Royal Friend ' we have a case of the wide use of the first title (*cf.* preceding paragraph). The other, ' Royal Friend,' was Egyptian (A. Wiedemann, *Gesch. von altem Aegypten*, 1891, 63, Erman-Ranke, *Aegypten u. aegyptisches Leben*, 85), appears in early Canaan, Gen. 26²⁶, and in South Arabia (*mwdt* in construction with the king's name, Conti Rossini, *Chrest.*, 134); it was also an Ethiopian title

---

[3] Meissner, *Bab. u. Ass.*, I, 133; Dougherty, *JAOS* 1928, 109 ff. See GB and Bezold, *BAG, sub vv.* For the Egyptian scribe and his high position see Erman, *Lit. of the Anc. Egyptians*, p. xxvii. and at length J. Begrich, ' Sōfēr und Mazkīr,' *ZAW* 17 (1940), 1 ff.

[4] One Gr. translation, ἀναμιμνήσκων, gives this mng.; the variant parallel word is in line with the common ὑπομνήματα, ' memoranda, minutes '; at 1 Ch. 18¹⁵ the word is translated with ὑπομνηματογράφος, title of a high officer at Alexandria, according to Strabo (xvii, 1, 12). For possible Old Egyptian correspondents see Bertholet, *Hist. of Heb. Civilization*, 247, and Gressmann, 1, 212, the latter noting the Narrator of the Egyptian court.

(*ZA* 30, 6). Hushai was 'friend' of David (2 Sam. 15^{37}), and the title has been found by some at 1^8.

The officer ' Over-the-House,' *i.e.*, royal Chamberlain, Majordomo, ranks low in the present list ; at II. 18^{18} he precedes the Scribe and the Recorder, and the title was borne by Jotham as his father's regent (II. 15^5), as also by Obadiah, Ahab's chief minister (18^3) ; the intimate office doubtless advanced in importance, like that of the later European chamberlain. For the title in a Lachish letter see Comm., II. 25$^{22\mathrm{ff}}$. The office corresponds to that of the Bab. *muzaz ēkallim*, the Ass. *ša pān ēkalli* (Meissner, pp. 120, 131), and the late Bab. *ša eli bītāni* (Dougherty, *AASOR* 5 [1924], 40 ff.). For the form of the title *cf*. that of the mayor, ' Over-the-City,' II. 10^5. There is finally the ' Levy Officer,' in charge of the *corvée* ; *cf*. 5^{28}. We learn of this unpopular incumbent's fate in ch. 12. In this connexion is to be noted Mendelsohn's very thorough treatment in his article on ' State Slavery,' cited in the Bibliography.

In regard to the historical character of this list, it is unnecessary, as with Benzinger, to hold that the variant textual authorities represent lists of different epochs. But a problem lies in the relation of the present list to those of David's officers in 2 Sam. 8$^{16\mathrm{ff}}$ and 20$^{28\mathrm{ff}}$. The parallelisms appear as follows:

I. 2 Sam. 8	II. 2 Sam. 20	III. 1 Ki. 4
Joab b. Zeruiah over the host	(1) Joab over all the host of Israel	Azariah b. Sadok over the year
Jehoshaphat b. Ahilud recorder	(4) Jehosh. b. Ahil. recorder	Ahijah b. Shausha scribe
Sadok b. Ahitub and Ahimelek b. Abiathar priests	(6) Sadok and Abiathar priests	Jehosh. b. Ahilud recorder
Seraiah scribe	(5) Sheva scribe	Benaiah b. Jeh. over the host
Benaiah b. Jehoiada over the Cherethites and Pelethites	(2) Ben. b. Jeh. over C. and P.	Sadok and Abiathar priests
David's sons priests		Azariah b. Nathan over the officers
		Ahishar over the house
	(3) Adoram over the levy	Adoniram b. Abda over the levy
	(7) The Jairite Ira priest	
	(The above items arranged to correspond with col. I.)	

Note that in Ki. three names, Azariah b. Sadok, Azariah b. Nathan, Ahishar are independent of the earlier lists. The two priests we have seen reason to exclude; *n.b.* they are not provided with patronymics in 2 Sam. 20 and Ki. For Solomon's accepted reign it would be highly improbable that Adoram/Adoniram, who died after that king, was a minister of David's. There remain only Jehoshaphat b. A. and Benaiah b. J. as ministers in both reigns. We may therefore, with Šanda, assign the list in Ki. to the first half of Solomon's reign. The list in 2 Sam. 8 appears to be authentic, unless the priests there are to be excluded; that in 2 Sam. 20 is entirely secondary, except for the original datum of ' the Jairite Ira priest '; ' Sheva ' is corruption of ' Shausha ' in Ki.

1. כֹּל: Grr. om., and so some critics, *e.g.*, St., *BH*; but the v. is editorial repetition of 2 Sam. 8¹⁵, where ' all Israel ' appears; the same political phrase below, v.⁷, 12¹.—**2.** שׂרים: at its earliest occurrence, Jud. 5¹⁵, the word means ' chieftain '; while it developed in Akk. to the mng., ' king,' the usual tr. as ' prince ' is contrary to Israel's simple constitution.—**3.** אליחרף: read עַל הַחֶרֶף, and see Comm. above. For other attempts at etymology see Šanda.—אחיה: on a Lachish tablet אחיהו.—שׁישׁא: read שִׁישָׁא with 1 Ch. 18¹⁶; the same person's name = 𝔊 Σουσα, 2 Sam. 20²⁵ (of which B Ιησους is patent corruption), for the deformed Ķr. of 𝔐; A 𝔊ᴸ here Σουσα = 𝕷. 𝔊 Σαβα here may be corruption of Σαβσα· [א]שׁושׁ = שׁמשׁ, ' sun '; *cf.* the Aram. name שׁוש כי ' like the sun ' (*CIS* II, no. 65), the variation of the labial in שׁביס (Is. 3¹⁸), a diminutive = *šubais*, and the Ugaritic form *špš*. Brockelmann's section on dissimilation of labials is quite incomplete; but note H. Bauer's art. in *ZfS* 1935, 11 ff. There is no reason to displace the name with שׂריה, the scribe's name at 2 Sam. 8¹⁷ (*vs.* GB).—אחילור (also v.¹²): = Gr. h j Αχιλουδ; other Grr. read as אֲחִילָד, for which *cf.* names signifying divine procreation, *e.g.*, בניהו, and Akk. forms with *bānū*. The variant Αχιθαλαμ, supporting 𝔐, is a play upon our word; the second element = J. Aram. חלמא, ' twin,' *i.e.*, ' a brother-is-born ' = ' twin-brother.'—**4.** הצבא . . . בניהו: B v a₂ ℭ om.; St. prefers the novel ' Eliab b. Joab ' of 𝔊ᴸ, 2⁴⁶ʰ; but for prob. invention of this name see below on אחישׁר.—**5.** עזריהו: Grr., Ορνειου, Ορνιας, the word read as ארניהו, inducing the usual transcription.—הנצבים: see Note, v.⁷.—וזבור: the name also at Ezr. 8¹⁴ Kt., *n. fem.* וזבודה, II. 23³⁶ Ķr. The root = ' to give,' is used in Aram. and S. Arab names. For the name in Ezr. Ķr. reads זַכּוּר, and so here 12 MSS Ken., deR., which rdg. is supported here by 𝔊ᴸ (also ℭ 1 MS, 𝔖), and at 2⁴⁶ʰ by all Grr. There appear to have been cross-currents of tradition.—כהן: 𝔊 𝔊ᴸ om., 𝔖ᴴ ※; the double title is indeed remarkable.—רֵעֶה: for abnormal final vowel see BL 388. The word was found by some in Amarna tablet no. 288, *rūḥi šarri*, but the vocalization is contradictory; the word = רֹעֶה ' shepherd '; *cf.* II. 3⁴.—**6.** אחישר על הבית : the name is quite uncertain (corrections proposed by Noth, p. 189, n. 5), and absence of patronymic is unique in this list. B *al.*, Αχει ην οικονομος κ. Ελιακ ο οικονομος, where ην may be error for ηλ, with resultant אחיאל, and שר as remainder of the original patronymic. The duplicate phrase is a clumsy variant of the foll. κ. Ελιαβ υιος Σαφ [𝔊ᴸ Ιωαβ] επι τ. πατριας, the last word to be corrected with 𝔊ᴸ to στρατιας (Rahlfs, *SS* 3, 201). This phrase is an intrusion from Gr. 2⁴⁶ʰ with Αβει (MS i Αβια = ₵) υιος Ιωαβ (MS i Ιωαδ); the variant Ιωαδ recalls Benaiah's father Jehoiada, and accordingly Αβει is reduction of ' Abiathar.' There is no reason to reconstruct 𝔐 from the frail 𝔊, *vs*. St.—אדנירם: = ארדם, 12¹⁸, 2 Sam. 20²⁴. The Grr. here = 𝔐, in the other cases vary: in Sam. B Αδωνιραμ, *al*. Αδωραμ = Jos.; in the parallel, 2⁴⁶ʰ, the variant Gr. rdgs. support the shorter form; at 12¹⁸ 𝔊 and Jos. support 𝔐. As name of the same person הֲדֹרָם appears, 2 Ch. 10¹⁸ (also name of a Syrian prince, 1 Ch. 18¹⁰, of an Aram. tribe, 1 Ch. 1²¹). Critics generally correct the form at 12¹⁸ after the spelling here; but the rarer pagan Hadoram/Adoram, with the divine element Haddu/Addu, by far deserves preference. We may indeed have merely variant forms in the two names, since '*ādôn* is development of '*ad*, ' father,' as appears from Ugaritic texts; see H. Ginsberg, *OLz.*, 1934, 473, and Cook, *CAH* 3, 349, who had earlier made the identification.— עברא : on a Samarian ostracon, and in Phœnician (Harris, *Gram.*, Glossary); amazing Gr. variations, *e.g.*, B Εφρα, 𝔊ᴸ Εδραμ = Εδραει 2⁴⁶ʰ, the two latter forms explaining the preceding remarkable gloss in the same v., κ. εδραμεν επι τ. οικον αυτου.—מם: for the etymology as = S. Arab. *mnš*', ' levy,' see Montg., *JQR* 25 (1934), 267.

VV.⁷⁻¹⁹. Solomon's districting of his kingdom and the respective lieutenants. For recent discussions of this administrative list see Alt, *Israels Gaue unter Salomo*, and Albright, ' The Administrative Divisions of Israel and Judah,' *JPOS* 1925, 17 ff., with map; for subsequent exchange of opinion between these two scholars see Alt, *Pjb.*, 1925, 100 ff., Albright, *ZAW* 1926, 225 ff. For the geography there are further to be noted Jack, *Samaria in Ahab's Time*, ch. 3, with map; Alt, *Die Staatenbildung der Israeliten in Palästina*; Robinson, *HI* 1, 263 ff., with map; Abel, *GP* 2, 79 ff., with map. For the commentators see especially Kittel and Šanda. For the place-names in the list are to be consulted Döller, *GES*; Borée, *AOP* vol. 2; Galling, *BR*. For Beth-shean see the extensive monograph by A. Rowe, *Topography and History of Beth-shan* (1930); for Beth-shemesh, E. Grant, *Beth Shemesh*

(1929); for Megiddo see Comm., 9^{15}, for Sarethan, *ib.* 7^{46}; for the Transjordan domain A. Bergman, ' The Israelite Occupation of Eastern Palestine,' etc., *JAOS* 1934, 169 ff., and ' The Israelite Tribe of Half-Manasseh,' *JPOS* 1936, 224 ff. Important topographical reviews and discussions for Palestine and the neighbouring lands by Albright are listed in the *Indexed Bibliography* of his publications, pp. 3–18. Of illuminating comparative interest is R. P. Dougherty's presentation of ' Cuneiform Parallels to Solomon's Provisioning System,' *AASOR* 5 (1925), with several illustrative plates.[1]

7. *And Solomon had twelve Lieutenants over all Israel, that they might provision the king and his household ; for a month in the year it lay upon each one to make provision.* ' Lieutenant ' (in the old English sense—Kittel, ' Pasha,' Albright, ' Prefect ') corresponds to the Ass. *šakēn/šaknu* ; for a political comparison with this list from the Assyrian quarter see E. Forrer, *Die Provinzeinteilung des ass. Reiches* (1919). It is notable that there is no alignment with the Twelve Tribes (as ' according to the number of the tribes,' *e.g.*, 18^{31}) ; the economic reason alone is given, the monthly allotment among the twelve divisions for payment of the royal dues. Such an apportionment was as a matter of bookkeeping ; the income could have been paid in kind or money, according to the seasons. For itemization of the impost *cf.* 5$^{2ff.}$. A caricature of this 12-month system as for David's reign appears in 1 Ch. 27$^{1-15}$, with a subsequent list of twelve officers over David's budget, vv.$^{25ff.}$. The number has been explained by Noth as arising from the ancient twelve-tribe Amphictyony, with each member obligated for definite supplies in a definite month, *Das System der Zwölf Stämme Israels*, esp. pp. 85 ff.

An accident early befell the document, a vertical break at the right hand of the papyrus (?) left blank the initial names in vv.$^{8-11}$, with a further blank in v.^{13}. In v.^{12} there has been some shuffling of the geographical data ; in vv.$^{13, 19a}$ some glosses have been added.

---

[1] For identification of Abel-Meholah and Sarethan there is now to be added the study by Glueck, cited in n. 1 to 7$^{40ff.}$, and further on the former place *BASOR* 91, 15 ff. Also is to be noted his fresh identification of much mooted Ramoth-Gilead (see Comm., 22^3) with Tell Rāmit, presented in *BASOR* 92 (1943), 10 ff.

8. *And these are their names :*
I. —— *b. Hur : in Highland of Ephraim.*
II. **9.** —— *b. Deker : in Makas* [?] *and in* [? - or *Be-* ?] *Shaalbim and Beth-shemesh and Ayyalon* [יה *Elon*] *and* [so MSS] *Beth-hanan.*
III. **10.** —— *b. Hesed : in Arubboth ; his Socho and all the land of Hepher.*
IV. **11.** —— *b. Abinadab : all Naphath-Dor.—Solomon's daughter Taphath became his wife.*
V. **12.** *Baana b. Ahilud : Taanach and Megiddo* [the following are transpositions] :
    (4) *to beyond Jokmeam,* (1) *and all Beth-shean*
    (3) *below Jezreel, from Beth-shean* (2) *as far as Abel-meholah, which is near Sarethan.*
VI. **13.** —— *b. Geber : in* || **19**a. *Geber b. Uri : in the land Ramoth of Gilead.*   *of Gilead* [gloss *land of Sihon king of the Amorites and Og king of Bashan*].
[gloss *his the Camps of Jair b. Manasseh*] *his the district of Argob*
[gloss *which is in Bashan, sixty great cities with walls and bronze bars*].
VII. **14.** *Ahinadab b. Iddo : Mahanaim.*
VIII. **15.** —— *b. Ahimaas : in Naphthali.—He too married Bosmath Solomon's daughter.*
IX. **16.** *Baana b. Hushai : in Asher and Bealoth* [?].
X. **17.** *Jehoshaphat b. Paruah : in Issachar.*
XI. **18.** *Shimei b. Ela : in Benjamin.*
XII. **19**b. *And one lieutenant, He-in-the-Land.*

The problem at once arises as to the allocation of the twelve districts. Twelve districts are distinguished, plus ' one lieutenant in the land.' This item has been from of old interpreted as ' over the (whole) land ' ; or the word ' Judah ' has been taken from the beginning of the next v., but this would give thirteen lieutenants, and accordingly the item is largely elided as a gloss (see at length Notes below). And it is held by many critics, *e.g.*, Kittel, Šanda, Alt, Robinson, that ' All Israel ' means simply the North. Pan-Israel would then have remained theoretically a separate kingdom, combined with Judah under one crown—*cf.* the union of England and Scotland. On this basis might be explained the non-mention of the officer's name in v.^{19b}, if ' Judah ' is to be interpolated there. The logical result is to regard v.^{19b} as a gloss. However Albright (in his first article, pp. 26 ff.) acutely points a way out of the difficulty. V.^{13}, ' b. Geber in Ramoth of Gilead,' as he shows, pairs with ' Geber b. Uri in the land of Gilead,' v.^{19a} (*n.b.* repetition of ' Geber ' and ' Gilead ') ; they are literally identical, despite the attempt of scholars, *e.g.*, Kittel, Stade, Šanda, to correct ' Gilead ' 2° to ' Gad ' after 𝔊 ; but the Greek desired to avoid the duplicate for the same reason that impels modern scholars. The officer for the district including Gad was the one at Mahanaim, v.^{14}, which was Gadite (*cf.* Josh. 21^{38}, etc.). And so, with but one Gileadite province surviving, we require a twelfth item, which is represented by the ' lieutenant ' in v.^{19b}. In this case ' All Israel ' included Judah. The ancient interpretation of this official is as of a superior over the twelve lieutenants ; so Jos., *Ant.*, viii, 2, 3, ἐπὶ δὲ τούτων εἰς πάλιν ἄρχων ἀποδέδεικτο, and so Rashi (identifying the person with Azariah, v.^{5}), Kimchi ; 𝔙 𝔖 𝔄 variously and curiously alter the obscure statement. Klostermann proposed a corresponding change of text, which has been favourably regarded by Benzinger, Burney, and so JV interpolates. Thenius understood the phrase in continuation as a statement of surprise, ' just one lieutenant in that (great) land (of Gilead) ' (*cf.* 𝔙 ' super omnia quæ erant in illa terra ') ; he was followed by Kittel, but reading ' Gad ' in place of ' Gilead.' But with acceptance of Albright's criticism it is necessary to find the twelfth lieutenant here, and indeed Judah must have been included. The simplest solution, following the Grr., has appeared to some to be the detachment of ' Judah ' from v.^{20}, reading here ' land of Judah ' ; others suppose the loss of the word here by haplog. with the following same word (so Stade). But the problem is solved, and without text-correction, by maintaining that the Judæan archivist used the expression ' in the land ' in a domestic, provincial sense as of the royal province of Judah. This phrase for the home-land appears at 9^{18}, concerning Judæan ' Tamar-in-the-Steppe in the Land.' And for a very much later age Torrey discovers the usage in Acts 11^{28}, in the prophecy uttered in the Christian Church at Antioch that there would be a famine ἐφ ὅλην τὴν οἰκουμένην, which nominal phrase translates original Aram. כל ארעא, 'all the land' (misunderstood as 'all the earth'), *i.e.*, Judæa—there was no such universal famine at that time (*Composition and Date of Acts, HTS* 1 [1916], 20 ff.). Also the exact parallel to such official designation appears in the Ass. *šakēn ina māti*, *i.e.*, the governor of the home-province of Assyria; see Forrer, *Provinzeinteilung*, 7, and for the high rank of this officer in the empire the plate opposite p. 6. There is also the common expression for the king's remaining 'at home,' *ina māti, e.g.*, Rogers, *CP* 226 ff., *n.b.* p. 234. The 'one lieutenant' is in contrast to the many in North Israel; he is unnamed, and may have been only a functionary in the royal chancellery.

A common modern judgment upon Solomon's creation of these administrative districts is expressed by Lods (*Israël*, 430) : " S. a voulu—comme la Constituante en 1790—briser les cadres de la vie provinciale autonome," and by Olmstead (*HPS* 342) : " Solomon had no need to flatter tribal susceptibilities." But the studies of Alt and Albright recognize that in general the partition respected the older tribal lines, which after all were fairly vague. Alt's brilliant identification (in *Israels Gaue*) of Socho (v.^{10}) dismisses two Judæan towns of the same name, and finds it in modern Shuwēkah at exit into the plain of the road from Shechem to the sea (indicated in the Survey Map). Arubboth, *i.e.*, modern 'Arrabeh (so Albright), 11 miles NE of Shuwēkah is named along with Hepher, a Manassite clan; the latter identification has been uncertain; on ground of occurrence of Hepher and Arubboth on a Samarian tablet, it may be identified with Hafîreh, 2 miles E of Arubboth (Jack, *Samaria*, 79). With this Manassite division defined we obtain a systematic order : A. Central Israel : (1) the Ephraimite Hill-country; (2) the old Danite land (with Makesh unidentified); (3) Manasseh; (4) Naphath-Dor, the coastal district between Phœnicia and Philistia, probably a recent acquisition and requiring distinct administration; (5) the strategic E–W series of depressions, commonly known as Esdraelon—here no tribe is named; B. Transjordan: (6), with combination of vv.$^{13, 19a}$, East Manasseh, *i.e.*, North Gilead (for Ramoth, see Comm., 22²); (7) South Gilead, the Biblical Gad; C. North Israel: (8) Naphtali; (9) Asher; (10) Issachar; D. the South: (11) Benjamin; (12) Judah. Of the above only (2), (4), (5) represent fresh political geography. As Alt suggests, the naming of several cities in (2) and (5) may indicate a certain autonomy preserved by non-Israelite communes; *n.b.* the term 'all Beth-shean.' Of particular personal interest are the references to the matrimonial alliances of two of the lieutenants with the royal house (vv.¹¹· ¹⁵); the archival document was accompanied with such personal data.

For a study of the Gr. variants in this section see Rahlfs, *SS* 3, 224–39.—**7.** נצבים: pointed as Nif. ppl., as at v.⁵, 5⁷, and so understood by Grr., καθεσταμενοι, *vs*. distinction of נציב, v.¹⁹, by transliteration; but 9 MSS here נציבים, and, with Šanda, this nominal form is to be preferred, in parallel with נציב below; the ancient scribes followed the rule of paucity in spelling, נציב, but נצבים; like variation in 22⁴⁸.—וכלכלו: = 5⁷; Grr. as though לכלכל, which St. prefers.—אחד: Ḳr. האחד = many MSS, Grr.; but the article is not necessary, *vs*. Burn.; *cf*. 1 Sam, 13¹⁷, etc.--**8.** "These their names": the same introductory phrase 2 Sam. 23⁸, and in the Elephantine papp., Cowley, nos. 22, 34, 66.—חור: a general Sem. name; of a Calebite (1 Ch. 2¹⁹), a Midianite king (Num. 31⁸), in an Aram. inscription (*CIS* II, no. 140), in S. Arab. (Ryckmans, *NPS* 2, 58), and in such cases not Egyptian as = ' Horus.'—After the several items the Grr. add irregularly εἶς (= אחד), 7 identical cases in B and Luc., plus 2 in Luc.; see Rahlfs's full discussion of the Gr. evidence, pp. 235–9, with the inference that 'one' is an irregularly interpolated word; but actually it is an archaic survival, preserved irregularly. The check appears throughout the list of kings in Jos. 12⁹ff.; *cf*. a list of names in an Elephantine pap., Cowley, no. 33, occurring after 'X his name,' with which *cf*. the checking system by strokes in nos. 22, 81. Add to these instances the Ugaritic tablet, Dhorme, no. 29, *RB* 1931, 54, in which two surviving names are followed by אהר. The tiresome check came to be omitted sporadically in ultimate use.—**9.** דקר: for identity with the root זכר see Montg. *JQR* 25 (1935), 264; *cf*. ברקר, II. 9²⁵; the *n. pr.* is identical with the royal name in the Zakar inscription.—מקץ: Grr., Μαχ(ε)μας, by erroneous identification with Michmash; see Abel, *GP* 2, 377, and for possible identification with *Mḫṣ* in Thutmose III's list, the opposite views of Alt, p. 10, and Albright, p. 27.—וּבְשַׁעֲלָבִים: so the noun at Jud. 1³⁵, but Jos. 19⁴² שַׁעֲלַבִּין; the word = Akk. *šēlabu/šēlabbu*, 'fox.' 𝔊 𝔊ᴸ have an interesting phonetic transcription with θαλαμει(ν), *cf*. Arab. *ṭa'lab*, 'fox,' which etymology is recognized at Jud. 1³⁵ with αἱ ἀλώπηκες. The prep., lacking in 𝔊ᴸ, is represented in 𝔊 (B a₂ = ℭ) with Βη[θαλαμειν], as though *bêt*, 'house' were in mind; and this was carried over into Hex. texts in expanded form with Βηθσαλαβιμ. For the final syllable of the place-name see Note on Shomeron, 16²⁴. For identification see GB, Abel, *GP* 2, 438. St. would read לו שׂ' in parallelism; or ב might be omitted with 𝔊ᴸ; but there is no uniformity in the list.—אילון : St. follows Bär's abbreviated Kt., אלן, which has no support in MSS and other edd. OGrr. support Ḳr., and so 𝔖, but 𝔊ᴴ 𝔄 read the word as אֱיָלוֹן, as at Josh. 19⁴³, Jud. 1³⁵ (in the same geographical connexion), and so to be read here.—בית חנן : so ℭ 𝔖 𝔄 ; but read with 11 MSS 'וב' ח; the Grr. observed the asyndeton and inserted εως, which Kit., Burn., St., *BH* unnecessarily accept as for original ועד.—For vv. ¹⁰· ¹¹ᵃ the Grr. give a barbarous gibberish; Rahlfs finds in general only transliteration.—**10.** חסד : a name-element found only in חסדיה and יושב חסד (?), sons of Zerubbabel, 1 Ch. 3²⁰; the element also in S. Arab. names (*NPS* 1, 96), but not with the editor's interpretation as 'envieux,' after literary Arabic, but in the N. Sem. sense.—שבה : *cf.* סוכה in a jar stamp, *IAE* 143.—חֵפֶר : A M N *al.*, Οφερ=𝔖ᴴ, and so B (corrupt here) at Josh. 12¹⁷; 𝔖 𝔄 = 𝔐.— **11.** נפת דאר : see G. Dahl, *Materials for the History of Dor* (1915), 21 ff. (noting Sym.'s translation with παραλιας), Albr. as cited above, p. 26, n. 18, and for a novel interpretation of the name D. W. Thomas, 'Naphath-Dor,' *QS* 1935, 89 ff. For the variants דאר and דר (*e.g.*, Josh. 12²³) an original ppl. form is to be assumed, *dâ'ir*, 'encircler.'—נפת : Noth, *IP* 226, as from Aram. root, 'to drop.'—**12.** Various arrangements of the v. with deletions have been proposed, *e.g.*, by St., *BH*; the tr. above follows Albr.— בענא : the name appears on coins of N. Syrian origin, and poss. in Punic (Lidzb., *HNE* 242); Minæan בען is to be noted (*NPS* 1, 54). It doubtless = בעלענה, with hypocoristic א; *cf.* בעשא, 15¹⁶, and see Noth, *IP* 40.—יקמעם: (*BH* יקמעם) := עם־קָם, 'may (the god) Am take stand'; for similar vowel variations *cf.* קְמָאֵל; II. 14⁷, *q.v.*—**13.** רָמָת : MSS vary here and elsewhere : רמות, ראמת, ראמות; 𝔊 (B ℭ) 𝔊ᴸ read as 'Ramath' = 𝔖ᴴ 𝔖 𝔄; 𝔊ᴴ = 𝔐. The variations in nn. *loci* of such formation are constant, *e.g.*, בעלות below and בעלה. With the preservation of original -*t* there came heightening of the preceding vowel for emphasis. At II. 8²⁹ the simple form appears; for discussion see Borée, *AOP* 43–9.— לו חות . . . בגלעד, which OGrr. om., and אשר בבשן—נחשת are patent borrowings from Dt. 3¹⁴, Josh. 13³⁰, etc. The same indictment is to be made against 'land of Sihon . . . Bashan,' v.¹⁹. For 'Hawwoth-Jair' and 'Argob' *cf.* the correction of 𝔐 at II. 15²⁵.— **14.** מחנימה : the terminative acc. in popular speech usurped the absolute form—*cf.* 'Stamboul'; see Meek, *JBL* 40, 292.— **15.** בשמת : doubtless with root-mng., 'fragrant,' *e.g.*, Arab. *bašām* is used of a fragrant shrub. The name as *Bšmt* occurs in S. Arab., but is wrongly interpreted by Ryckmans (*NPS* 1, 56).—**16.** חושׁי;

possibly David's Friend, and so Ahimaas in v.[15] has been identified by some with Sadok's son; see 2 Sam. 15[27, 32].—באשר ובעלות: or the second vocable to be read ובבעלות. Bealoth occurs as a place-name in Judah (Josh. 15[24]). But collocation of a tribe-name with that of an unknown town is surprising. 𝔊 𝔊^L om. 'in Asher and.' Klost., with favourable opinion from Burn., Alt, Albr., conjectures an original 'Asher and Zebulon,' but could this expected rdg. have been so wilfully changed? Following rdgs. of 𝔊, B Μααλα, A Μααλωτ, Then. suggested recovering מעלות='ascents,' and finding in it the Ladder of Tyre, Κλίμαξ Τύρου (1 Mac. 11[59], etc.), Jos. also rdg. here τ. περι Αρκην (i.e., Ακκην?) with further rectification to עד מעלות צור. Šanda, Eissf. (cf. BH) accept this identification; for contradiction see St.'s extensive note, leaving the word with a question-mark, which is wisest.—17. פרוח : cf. S. Arab. *Prḥ* (NPS I, 180), with root='to be at rest.'—19. ארי : Grr., Αδ(δ)αι, etc.; cf. the names אורי, אוריה, on which latter see Montg., *JAOS* 1935, 94.—גלער : 𝔊 (B 𝔈) 𝔊^L 'Gad'; Burn. prefers 𝔥, Šanda accepts 𝔊, St. is uncertain.—ונציב אחד אשר בארץ : see Comm. *BH* presents three of the suggested alterations; Šanda brackets the whole half-verse, 'land of Sihon,' etc., as secondary; Eissf. om. the present phrase as 'nicht klar.'

4[20]–5[14] (AV EVV 4[20-34]).[1] A miscellany: Solomon's might and wisdom. Cf. *Ant.*, viii, 2, 4, 5.

See Int., §1, for the various distinctions of volumes in Gr. Kgdms. Also here after the archival lists above there appeared to be opportunity before the story of the temple, cc. 6 ff., for a *pot-pourri* of material bearing on the reign, much of it duplicated in cc. 9 and 10. Evidently Heb. Kings early underwent transformations, and the Greek *littérateurs* also recognized the nature of the material, and did not hesitate to rearrange here and also to make transference to the Supplement to 2[46]. The following list presents the parallelisms:

𝔥	𝔊 ch. 4	𝔊 ch. 2
4[20]		v.[46aβ]
5[1]		vv.[b, k] = 10[30]
5[2, 3]	vv.[22, 23]	v.[46e]
5[4]	v.[24]	v.[46f, ga]
5[5]		v.[46gβ]
5[6] = 10[26]		v.[46l]
5[7, 8]	vv.[20, 21]	
5[9-14]	vv.[25, 30]	

[1] The chapter divisions in Hebrew printed Bibles = JV, following the Polyglots (as marginally noted in EVV), is contrary to that of 𝔙 and the Protestant translations, which properly distinguish the Hiram story as beginning a fresh chapter, ch. 5.

I. 4^{20}–5^{14}

With the freedom of 𝔊 in rearrangement of this supplementary material no stress is to be laid upon its authority as to text and order.

Ch. 4^{20}–5^8. Solomon's might. Two editorial essays from different hands sum up the security of the realm. (1) 4^{20}–5^1: *Judah and Israel were many like the sand by the sea for multitude, eating and drinking and enjoying themselves. And Solomon was ruling over all the kingdoms from the River* [gloss+*the land of Philistia*] *even to the border of Egypt—they were bringing tribute and serving Solomon all the days of his life.* And (2) vv.$^{4, 5}$: *For he had sway over all Across-the-River from Tiphsah* (Thapsacus) *even to Gaza, over all the kings of Across-the-River; and he had peace on all borders round about. And Judah and Israel dwelt in security, every one under his vine and fig-tree, from Dan to Beersheba, all the days of Solomon.* Of these vv. only v.^{4} is represented in 𝔊 here, but the others were omitted as already given in the Gr. appendix to ch. 2; hence agreement cannot be given to Kittel, who holds that 4^{20}–5^1 was "added by a late editor from 2^{46} of LXX." Each of the above pairs of vv. is followed by a statement on the supplies for the royal *ménage*: vv.$^{2, 3}$ on the supplies for the royal table, vv.$^{6-8}$ on the table and also the stabling of the horses. But v.^{6}, giving the number of the horses, is an insertion with an exaggerated figure (40,000 stalls) from 10^{26} (*q.v.*), induced by the reference to the stabling in v.^{8}. Against the opinion of Kittel and Stade, v.^{7} appears to be quite secondary, repeating 4^7; there remains as original only v.^{8} on the stabling, as sequence of vv.$^{2, 3}$. Out of 4^{20}–5^8 these alone appear to be early items—how authentic there is no saying, although documentary specifications of the royal budget may well have survived. The provisioning of the stables in the chariot cities was a particularly important item; *cf.* 9^{19}, $10^{26\text{ff.}}$. The word translated 'straw' is the modern Arab. *tibn*, used of mixed grain and straw, the usual fodder for horses. For the table budget given here may be compared the comparatively small *ménage* of Nehemiah, which required daily 'one ox, six fattened sheep, and fowls' *per diem* for his suite of 150 men and guests (Neh. $5^{17\text{f.}}$). Most variant estimates have been suggested, as by Thenius, Keil, Šanda (ranging from 14,000 to 32,000 persons); Skinner makes the shrewdest estimate from comparison with Nehemiah's figures, calculating that the budget provided for 4000-5000 persons, which would include the large families; and Kittel suggests 3000-4000 heads of families, with 8-10 in a family. Lurje in his *Studien*, p. 42, calculates that the food implied some 20,000 souls, and then arbitrarily reduces the figure to 7000. For Mesopotamian royal budgets see R. P. Dougherty, ' Cuneiform Parallels to Solomon's Provisioning System,' *AASOR* 5 (1925), 23 ff. *Cf.* the *ménage* of the Persian kings, as noted by Meyer, *GA* 3, 1, §54. There is recorded the provision for the daily table of a Tūlūnid potentate of Egypt (*ca.* A.D. 966) : 100 sheep, 100 lambs, fowls of all kinds (P. K. Hitti, *History of the Arabs*, 456). The rest of the section is of secondary character historically, often hyperbolic. For ' many like the sand by the sea ' (v.^{20}), *cf.* Gen. 41^{49}, Hos. 2^1, Is. 10^{22}. ' Eating and drinking ' has its early parallel in the Old Aramaic Hadad inscription, " in my days Ya'di ate and drank," with a similar but broken passage in the Panammuwa inscr., ". . . ate and drank . . ." Idyllic is the picture of Judah's and Israel's security in v.^{5} ; see Mic. 4^4, Zech. 3^{10}, and *cf.* II. 18^{31}.

The extent of Solomon's empire, variously expressed in vv.$^{1, 4}$ is exaggerated, at least in its political implications. The reference to *Over-the-River*, Trans-Euphrates (also Josh. 24^2, etc.), represents the Ass. imperial phrase, *eber nāri*, appearing actually not earlier than Ashurbanipal's time (*KB* 2, 238-9), and of general use in the Westland later, *e.g.*, Neh. 2^7 ; *cf.* Meyer, *GA* 3, 1, 136 ff. ; Forrer, *Reallexicon*, 1, 134. The phrase here is of late origin, when the Assyrian empire had made current its political language. For statistics of the use of the ambiguous term see Burney, *ad loc.* Solomon was doubtless the most potent monarch in the area ; Damascus under its fresh Aramæan rulers had not in his early years achieved political importance, although it later gained autonomy (11$^{23\text{ff.}}$). He possessed some rights in the Lebanon ; *cf.* 9^{19}, and the accompanying enigmatic statement in Gr. 2^{46c}. His father David had received gifts from King Toi of the Aramaic dynasty at Hamath, and defeated the Aramæan king of Sobah in Cœle (?)-Syria along with his allies of Damascus, the campaign being waged to cut off Sobah's control of the route to the river (2 Sam. 8$^{3\text{ff.}}$). The item of

Tiphsah-Thapsacus [2] no doubt belongs to the correct tradition of a one-time right which the dynasty had gained in the trade-routes across the desert to the river. Solomon's control of Transjordan northwards from the Red Sea naturally induced a commercial exploitation in that direction. This was the one epoch in Israel's history when such an external commercial control was possible. For Flinders Petrie's recent excavations at Gaza see his reports on ' Ancient Gaza ' in *Publications* of the British School of Archæology in Egypt, vols. 53–56 (–1934).

Ch. 5^{9-14} (EVV 4^{29-34}). The wisdom of Solomon. In addition to Gr. here, vv.$^{9f.}$ also appear in Gr. $2^{35a, b}$, and the passage is summarized below, $10^{23f.}=2$ Ch. $9^{22f.}$. The present theme is an exuberant flowering of the tradition of Solomon's wisdom, of which tradition we can trace the progress. There is the pious prayer of Solomon for ' a discerning heart to judge thy people,' with the expansion of the divine boon to a wisdom beyond human compare ($3^{4ff.}$); a case given of his judicial wisdom ($3^{16ff.}$); his political wisdom in his diplomacy with Hiram of Tyre (5^{26}); the visit of the Queen of Sheba ' to prove him with riddles ' ($10^{1ff.}$); the reliable literary tradition of " the proverbs of Solomon which the men of king Hezekiah copied out " (Pr. 25^1). The declamation here knows not only of *three thousand proverbs* but also of *songs, a thousand and five* (v.^{12}). Indeed Solomon's reputation as an encyclopædic philosopher was early established, late as are the canonical and deutero-canonical books ascribed to him. This literary *genre* of Wisdom had antique roots in the Orient, as also in the Occident (*cf.* Hesiod); there may be noted Margolis's finding of the three early categories of Hebrew literature in Torah, Word or Prophecy, Wisdom (*Hebrew Scriptures in the Making*, ch. 4). The focusing of all Wisdom upon one personage of the past [3] is similar to the heroization of Moses for Law and David for Psalms. As father of the realm the ancient king was by duty patron of the arts and sciences;

---

[2] The site, at Ḳala'at ad-Dibs, at the eastern bend of the Euphrates, E of Aleppo, was discovered, as he held, by J. P. Peters ; see his *Nippur* (1897), 1, ch. 4 ; but see Dussaud, *SAM* Index, *s.v.*

[3] For Wisdom, *cf.* Daniel in a Phœn. tradition (Eze. 28^3), now confirmed by the person of Danel in the Ugaritic literature ; see Virolleaud, *Danel.*

as such a wise king appears Ashurbanipal, who has left a full and exuberant account of his education and attainments.[4] The most ancient wise man known to history is Ptahhotep, vizier of a Pharaoh in the first half of the third millennium B.C., with a book dedicated to, and composed under the patronage of, the king. For this *wisdom of Egypt* (v.[10]) reference may be made to Erman, *Lit. of the Ancient Egyptians*, 54 ff., 234 ff. ; the cosmopolitan influence of that Wisdom has been suggested in comparison of Prov. 22[17]-24 with the proverbs of the Egyptian Amen-em-ope.[5] For *the wisdom of all the sons of the East (Bnê Ḳedem)*, whose professors are herewith actually named, with Arabic names, see Note, and Montgomery, *Arabia and the Bible*, 169 ff. ' The words of Agur b. Jakeh ' (Prov. 30), and ' of Lemuel king of Massa ' (31[1-9]), must be attributed to Arabian sources. The wisdom of Solomon, the subjects of which are detailed in v.[13], *from the cedar in Lebanon to the hyssop that comes out in the wall*, along with the following round of zoology, was particularly a moral, fable wisdom ; there are to be compared Jotham's parable of the trees (Jud. 9), that of Jehoash of the thistle and the cedar (II. 14[9]), the parables from nature (Prov. 30[15ff.]), and the cameo, ' Go to the ant, thou sluggard ' (6[6]). The listing of all creatures also recalls the learned Akkadian lists of plants, animals, birds, etc.[6] It is notable that the Bible contains no development of the animal fable, so luxuriant in the contemporary Oriental literatures, in the Akkadian and in the Old Aramaic, to wit the Ahikar papyri, and later in Arabic literature, *e.g.*, *The Thousand and One Nights*. The figure of *a thousand and five songs* (v.[12]) appears quite casual ;

---

[4] See Luckenbill, *ARA* 2, §§767, 934, 986 ; *cf.* Olmstead, *HA* ch. 38.

[5] Only brief reference may be made to the extensive recent bibliography for the subject at large : W. Baumgartner, *Israel u. altor. Weisheit* (1933) ; J. Fichtner, *Die altor. Weisheit in ihrer israel.-jüdischen Ausprägung*, BZAW 62 (1933) ; Hempel, *Altheb. Lit.*, 44 ff. ; Robinson and Oesterley, *Int.*, 150 ff., 437 ff. ; Eissfeldt, *Einl.*, §10 ; B. Gemser, *Sprüche Salomos*, 1937. *N.b.* Eissf.'s conclusion (p. 527) that the tradition of Solomon's patronage of letters is ' eine richtig festgehaltene Tatsache.'

[6] See Weber, *Lit. d. Babylonier u. Assyrer*, 293 ff. ; Meissner, *Bab. u. Ass.*, ch. 22 ; Ebeling, *Die babylonische Fabel . . ., Mitteilungen der Altor. Gesellschaft*, 2, Heft 3, 1927.

but light may be thrown upon it from Egypt. Erman observes (p. 293) concerning a papyrus published by Gardiner that the composition " might have once borne the title of *The Thousand Songs*, for . . . its individual sections bear each a number. Of these numbers only two are wanting to complete the thousand, and they will have stood in the break at the end of the page." The additional ' five ' in the Biblical figure then may have been added for good measure, as in the Arabic *The Thousand and One Nights*. We may compare the 1000 women of Solomon's harem (11³). The advent of *all the kings of the earth*, who *came to hear the wisdom of Solomon* (v.¹⁴), naturally implied the royal sport of riddles, conundrums, as presented below in the Queen of Sheba's visit (ch. 10). Such a tourney of wits is described by Josephus (*Ant.*, viii, 5, 3 ; *C. Ap.*, i, 17, citing from Dios) : there was a heavy wager on between Solomon and Hiram of Tyre for the solution of riddles, and Solomon won ; to which Tyrian tradition added the story that a certain Tyrian proposed further riddles which Solomon could not answer, and the latter had to refund the money he had won. A similar theme is used in the late Ahikar legend, in which Ahikar wins himself back to royal favour by saving his master's realm and honour in a riddle contest with the king of Egypt. (For this late legend see reff. in Cowley, *Aramaic Papyri*, p. 204.) For the early development of the later exuberant theme of Solomon's magical wisdom see Jos., *Ant.*, viii, 2, 5. See further Comm. on the Queen of Sheba's visit, ch. 10. For the later expansion of this *genre* in connexion with Solomon's name Ginzberg, *Legends of the Jews*, vol. 4, should be consulted.

Ch. 4. **20.** הים : 9 MSS deR. pref. שפת =𝔖 𝔄, but a borrowing from the similar phrase elsewhere, *e.g.*, v.⁹.—Ch. 5. **1.** ארץ פלשתים : 2 Ch. 9²⁶ pref. וער, and so 𝔊 2⁴⁶ᵏ ; but our text is authoritative, found in Hex. (A x 𝔖ᴴ), 𝔗 𝔖 𝔙, with the unconstruable phrase translated ' the river of the land of P.' ; it is doubtless an early gloss. to the foll. phrase.—מנשים : such verbal use of the ppl. is generally late, Aramaizing, but this case is in rhetorical parallelism with 4²⁰.—**2.** כר : the *kôr* has been estimated at 364 litres ; see Nowack, *Arch.*, 1, §35, Benz., *Arch.*, §40, Šanda, pp. 93, 106.— סלת : ' grits,' translated here with σεμίδαλις and identical with modern Arabic *smid* ; see Dalman, *BWAT* 13 (1913), 69, for the proportions as given here, and *A. u. S.*, 3, 284, 288 ff.—**3.** בקר רעי :

'pastured cattle'; 𝔥 construes as appositional; see GK §139, c. —יחמור: Grr. ignore.—אבוסים: ברברים: 'cribbed x'; VSS, exc. Grr., 'fattened birds,' recalling the hand-stuffed poultry of the modern Orient; 𝔊 for 'ב ορνιθων εκλεκτων, construing 'א=σιτευτα, with the prec. accusatives; Jos. finds 'fishes' in this noun.— **4.** הנהר . . . מתפסח: 𝔊 om. here (𝔖ᴴ ※), prob. to avoid contradiction of 2⁴⁶ᶠ·, where 'ח is represented with Ραφει. For 'ח W. A. Heidel ingeniously proposes etymology from פסח, 'to cross over' (*The Day of Yahweh*, 1929, 185).—עברי ו: very many MSS, edd., עבריו (see deR.)=GV.—**6.** ארות: cf. 2 Ch. 9²⁵, 32²⁸. The tr. 'stalls' comes down by Jewish tradition (Jastrow, *Dict.*, 34a). The noun with this mng. appears in Syr., and also in Akk. (Bezold, *BAG* 3); the same column in Bezold notes a verb *arû*, 'to become pregnant,' which may well be the basis of Gr. τοκάδες, θήλειαι.—**7.** קָרֵב: one who has *entrée*, regular guest; Grr., διαγγελματα, which 𝔖ᴴ repeats; 𝔙 'necessaria.'—**8.** רכב: this species of horse has not been identified; it is used of the chariot horse, Mic. 1¹³, of the post horse, Est. 8¹⁰; Grr., αρματα, as for רכב?—**9.** אלהים: Grr., 𝔖ᴴ 𝔗 as יהוה; similar use of 'God' at 3¹¹, ²⁸, 10²⁴; this as with the thought of 'the Divine Wisdom.'—רחב: Grr., exc. Sym., χυμα, 'overflow'=𝔖ᴴ.—**10.** בני קדם: Grr., αρχαιων ανθρωπων, similarly 2³⁵ᵇ, also Jos., =𝔖ᴴ.— **11a.** הארם: Šanda ingeniously suggests האדמים, 'the Edomites.'— The foll. names have Arabian connexions. איתן is elative from Arab. *watana*, and so prob. הימן=Sabæan אימן (*NPS* 2, 27); for אורחי cf. Minæan *ḏrḥ* (*ib.*, p. 47). Cf. the genealogy in 1 Ch. 2⁸.— **11b.** 𝔊 𝔊ᴸ om., and so Kit., St., Šanda, as superfluous with v.¹⁴.— **12.** שירו: Kit., Šanda would read as pl.; but the m. sing. is primarily collective in contrast to the fem.—ואלך חמשה: Grr., πεντακισχιλιοι (=𝔖ᴴ), scribal error for πεντε και χιλιοι=Jos.— **13.** אזוב: 'hyssop'; for identification see Post, *DB* s.v., Kit., Šanda, and Dalman, *A. u. S.*, 1, 2, 370 f., 543 ff.—**14b.** St. reasonably elides as induced by 10²⁴ᶠ·. 𝔊ᴸ 𝔊ᴴ 𝔖ᴴ 𝔖 preface 'he took gifts,' after 2 Ch. 9²³ᶠ·.—מאת: Burn. proposes as 'deputed by (all the kings),' *cft.* 2 Sam. 15³.

VV.¹⁵⁻³² (=JV; EVV ch. 5). ∥ 2 Ch. 2; *cf. Ant.*, viii, 2, 6–9. Introduction to the history of the building of the Temple.

VV.¹⁵⁻²⁶. The negotiations with Hiram of Tyre. This section presents an early picture of correct historical similitude, reporting diplomatic and commercial relations between two states of Syro-Palestine—actually in its extent a fairly unique report. The initial 'conversations' between the two monarchs are stated in diplomatic form: **15.** *And Hiram King of Tyre sent his ministers to Solomon, for he heard that they had anointed him king in his father's place; for Hiram had always been a friend of David.* **16.** *And Solomon sent* (a message) to Hiram, as follows :——. There *ensues* (vv.[17-19]) an expanded statement of Solomon's object in pursuing the kindly relations with Hiram, the procuring of cedar timbers for the buildings he had in mind. There is patent dependence upon the story of Nathan's oracle in 2 Sam. 7, in its present, secondary form (as first recognized by Budde), replacing the original notion of ' a house ' as a dynasty, with that of ' a house for YHWH.' [1] On the other hand v.[20] correctly, even if in imagined language, gives the gist of Solomon's reply (*n.b.* the item of ' the Sidonians,' after early usage), even as vv.[21-23] aptly compose Hiram's answer. The invented material here is simple in comparison with that of the Chronicler, who makes Solomon the initiator of the diplomatic correspondence, along with bloated epistles, and the tradition accepted by Josephus, who presents these letters in altered form and alleges that " they are still in the public records of Tyre." For such brotherly congratulations on a royal accession there is an example in David's embassy to Hanun king of Ammon (2 Sam. 10), and for a much earlier period the congratulatory letter of the king of Alashia (Cyprus) to the king of Egypt on the latter's accession, contained in the Amarna letters ; they were accompanied with gifts for the sacred festival.[2] Hiram (the name shortened from ' Ahiram,' as the inscription of an earlier Ahiram of Byblos, *ca.* 1200 B.C., now shows [3]) can be dated only approximately from Josephus's citation of the Phœnician annals : Meyer, *ca.* 969–936 ; Kittel, 972–932 ; Mahler (p. 175), 979–945 ; Olmstead, *HPS* 981–947 ; Albright with more reserve, *ARI* 69, ' about the middle of the tenth century.' He is correctly designated *king of Tyre*, as over against the later revival of the ancient title, ' king of Sidonia,' upon the extension of the Tyrian power over all Phœnicia ; the latter title is properly used of Ahab's father-in-law (16[31]).[4] Hiram is

[1] For various forms of criticism of the whole section see Stade, *ZAW* 3 (1883), 129 ff. ; Šanda, ' Salomo u. seine Zeit,' *Biblische Zeitfragen*, 1913, 1 ff. ; Hölscher in the Gunkel-*Eucharisterion*, 1, 158 ff.

[2] Knudtzon, nos. 33, 34.

[3] See Bibliography of Inscriptions.

[4] See Meyer, *GA* 2, 2, sect. 11, ' Die Phöniker,' esp. pp. 62, 126 f., and for the succession, pp. 437 ff. ; Kittel, *GVI* 2, 210 ff. For a more specific statement of synchronism between Hiram and Solomon, see below, Comm. 6[1, 37].

called *a friend* [Heb. primary mng., *lover*, and so EVV] *of David*, with Solomon's reminiscence of his aid in building David's palace (2 Sam. 5[11]); the diplomatic title would have been ' my brother,' as in the Amarna letters and *inf.*, 9[13], 20[32f.]. Hiram's blessing of YHWH (v.[21]) has its parallel in an Amarna letter with its blessings of Shamash and Ishtar upon the Pharaoh's head.[5] Criticism has been keen upon the alleged intrusion of the epithet for Solomon as a *wise son* (v.[21]), and especially against v.[26a] as an interpolation based upon v.[21], with reference to ' the wisdom given Solomon by YHWH '; so Klostermann, and other critics, and according to Stade this whole story is a continuation of that of the dream in ch. 3. But the wisdom declared here is of political character; v.[26a] is to be translated: *And YHWH giving wisdom to Solomon, as he had spoken to him, there ensued amity* [Heb., the general word *peace*] *between Hiram and Solomon, and the two made a league together.* This passage may well have been original to the story developed above, and so Kittel assigns it to his Solomon-source. Apart from ' the covenant ' between Asa and the Syrian Ben-hadad (2 Ch. 16[2ff.]), severely castigated by the seer Hanani, this is the only reference to a league with another state; the term could hardly have been used by late writers, Deuteronomists, etc., in view of the prohibition in Jud. 2[2].[6] The wisdom with which Solomon was endowed, ' to judge this thy great people ' (see above on 3[4ff.], 5[9ff.]), included diplomacy and the erection of splendid buildings. Such political use of ' wisdom ' is illustrated in Ashur's boast, " By my wisdom have I done this " (Is. 10[13]), and for Solomon's wisdom as a builder may be compared Tiglath-Pileser's self-congratulation: " With the keen understanding and grasp of intellect with which the Master of the Gods, the prince, Nudinwat (Ea) endowed me, a palace of cedar . . . and a portico patterned after a Hittite palace for my enjoyment I built in Calah " (*ARA* 1, §804). The Assyrian king's construction of a

---

[5] Knudtzon, no. 21. Most of the early VSS dodged the use of ' YHWH ' in the alien's mouth; but for the naming of the national deity of another people, *cf.* Jephthah's reference to ' Chemosh thy god ' (Jud. 11[24]), the Ass. Tartan's knowledge of YHWH (II. 18[25ff.]), and the Moabite Mesha's naming of him in his inscription.

[6] EVV tr. *bĕrît*, otherwise always rendered with ' covenant,' in these secular relations with ' league '—a survival of the ancient objection!

palace after Hittite, *i.e.*, Syrian style, is a parallel to Solomon's use of Phœnician art and artists. We may compare the remarkable letter of Hammurabi informing Zimrilim king of Mari, on the Euphrates, of the desire of the king of Ugarit (Ras Shamra) to see the palace in Mari (G. Dossin, *CR* 1937, 19; *cf.* A Parrot, *Syria*, 1937, 75, n.). And, coming nearer home, Josephus has preserved to us, on the authority of Dios (*Ant.*, viii, 5, 3), the record that the same Hiram " went up to Mount Lebanon and cut down woods for the building of the temples "—the temple of Jupiter having been named immediately before.[7] Šanda gives a summary of Ass.-Bab. and Greek references, and Olmstead presents ample Akk. references, along with a relief of the floating of cedar logs down the Euphrates.[8] Further reference to the use of cedar in temple and palace will be given below in Comm. on cc. 6, 7. In comparison with v.[23], detailing the transportation of the logs to the sea and their rafting to the Palestinian coast, an inscription of Nebuchadnezzar's, found in the Lebanese Wadi Brisa, is pertinent.[9] In a broken text, after naming the temples of Nabu and Marduk, he speaks of " the Lebanon, the cedar mountain . . . the scent is pleasant of the cedars ; " and then : " What no former king had accomplished, I cleaved high mountains, lime-stone I broke off, I opened. I cut a road for the cedars, and before Marduk my king (I brought) massive, tall, strong cedars, of wonderful beauty, whose dark appearance was impressive, the mighty product of the Lebanon." (Of course the work was done by the skilled Syrian engineers and labourers.) A following broken passage records their transportation ' like reeds ' on ' the canal Araḫtu.' To this material are to be added far earlier references from the Egyptian quarter, and notably the autobiographical Voyage of Wen-amon, detailing all his trials as purchasing agent in Phœnicia on the Pharaoh's demand for the valuable wood

---

[7] For cedar, cypress, fir, see BDD *s.vv.*, Dalman, *A. u. S.*, 1, 1, 259. For the most recent study in determination of the genus of the Lebanon cedar used by the ancient builders, see L. Köhler, *ZAW* 1937, 163 ff. ; he holds that the Heb. word is inclusive of several genera, but does not mean the Cedrus Libani, which is unfit for building.

[8] *HA* 272 ff., with accompanying fig. 108, *cf.* Index, *s.v.* ' Cedar ' ; see also Meissner, *Bab. u. Ass.*, 1, Index, *s.v.* ' Zeder.'

[9] See Winckler, *KTAT* 56 ff. ; Rogers, *CP* 365 f.

(*ca.* 1100 B.C.),[10] of which this brief extract may be given :
"The prince rejoiced and appointed 300 men and 300 oxen, and set overseers at their head, in order that they might fell the trees. And they felled them, and they remained lying over the winter. But in the third month of summer they were dragged to the shore." In our passage the method of water-transportation is given as *by rafts* (the word=etymologically *tow-rafts*), the only possible method for such huge timbers. The Chronicler (2 Ch. 2^{15}) makes Joppa the port of entry, by doubtless good tradition.

The payment made annually by Solomon to Hiram of 20,000 *kors of wheat as food for his household and* 20 *kors* of *bruised-olive oil* (v.^{25}), with a *kor* estimated at 364 litres (see Note, v.^{2}), is indeed an extravagant figure for the item of the wheat. Solomon's provision of wheat foods for the year amounted to 32,850 kors (v.^{2}). The easy exaggeration of figures in tradition appears in 2 Ch. 2^{9} with ' 20,000 baths of oil,' which the Grr. read in here, while Ch. further exaggerates items and figures most absurdly. This provision was not for the workers, only the luxuries of wheat and oil are listed here ; by *the house* of Hiram is meant his privy budget, and if the high figure is to be maintained at all, he must have made good business by exporting the grain foods, as Šanda remarks. Whatever the value of the figures may be, a datum at 9^{11} frankly reports that Solomon went bankrupt for a 20-years' debt and had to cede to Hiram twenty Galilæan cities.

Only the outlines of this section can be regarded as authentic history. But there is the undoubted fact that Solomon entered into a league with Hiram for trade purposes, the details of which league and its operation are fully illustrated by contemporary documents. The further interest of Hiram in this international compact appears in his aiding Solomon's ventures in the waters of the Indian Ocean (9$^{26ff.}$, 10$^{11, 22}$), on which his shippers were to ply to his profit.

[10] See Breasted, *ARE* vol. 4, no. 578 ; Erman, *Lit. of the Anc Egyptians*, 174 ff. ; Gressmann, *ATB* 1, 71 ff. ; Barton, *AB* ch. 18. Of earlier date is Thutmose III's record of his procurement of cedar logs ' of 60 ells of length with a thick top,' which were brought to Egypt ' with a good wind ' ; see K. Sethe, *Sb.*, Berlin Academy, 15 (1906), 356 ff. ; Gressmann, p. 90. For the ancient relations of Egypt and Phœnicia see P. Montet, *Byblos et l'Égypte* (1928–29).

VV.$^{27-32}$ (AV RVV vv.$^{13-18}$). The work in the Lebanon and the Phœnician co-operation. It is generally recognized that of this section only vv.$^{29,\ 30}$ are secondary. Stade cautiously decides (p. 148) that the section vv.$^{27,\ 28}$ is " eine alte glaubwürdige, mit späteren Vorstellungen wie 9$^{21,\ 22}$ stark contrastierende Nachricht. . . . Vielleicht ist 5^{31} erst nach 7$^{9,\ 10}$ gearbeitet. . . . Allerdings könnten in v.^{32} Trümmer des ursprünglichen Berichtes gesucht werden." The inserted vv. have exaggerated figures as compared with vv.$^{27,\ 28}$, figures similar to the Chronicler's, while v.^{30b} is patent expansion of a simpler statement at 9^{23}. According to v.^{27} *the levy was raised out of all Israel*, with no contamination from the later invention of the enslavement of the Canaanites for this duty, as according to 9$^{20-22}$ and the parallel in Ch. The figures for the drafted labourers, 30,000, and for the allotment of duty, 10,000 for every third month, are reasonable. This *corvée* of Israelites provided the raw labour in the Lebanon, in contrast with the skilled labour of the Sidonians (v.^{20}). The *superintendents* (lit., *chiefs of the overseers*) number 3300 ; the figure has been expanded from the ' 550 ' of 9^{23}, the development of 550 to 3300 being in the ratio of the 30,000 of v.^{28} to the 180,000 (the 150,000 of the interpolated v.^{29} plus the original 30,000)—a nice piece of editorial arithmetic. (See the writer's Note, *JAOS* 1938, 135.) For textual variations from ' 3300 ' and for other calculations see Note. The figure 550 would give one superintendent to every gang of about 54 labourers. The archival character of the items need not be doubted. Witness the tremendous figures given for food-supplies in the two royal South Arabic inscriptions contemporary to the reconstruction of the Marib Dam in the Yemen, A.D. 450, 543, in each of which inscriptions, *inter al.*, 200,000 or 207,000 sheep are reported to have been butchered for the labourers in a year's job in each case.[11] The reference to the stonecutting in vv.$^{31f.}$ is parallel with 7$^{9ff.}$, and properly introduces the Phœnician master carpenters and masons whom Solomon employed in Jerusalem. These are specifically

---

[11] See E. Glaser, ' Zwei Inschriften über den Dammbruch von Marib,' *MVG* 1897, and *CIS* IV, nos. 540, 541. For the Biblical and parallel Oriental references to the *corvée* see I. Mendelsohn, ' State Slavery in Ancient Palestine.'

named as *the Giblites*, citizens of ancient and famous Gubl-Gupn-Byblos on the Syrian coast. For its distinguished place in ancient history see Montet, *op. cit.*, and for the present record Dussaud, ' Byblos et la mention des Giblites dans l'A.T.,' *Syria*, 1923, 300 ff. For various ancient misunderstandings of the word and modern attempts at re-writing see Note. There is no reason to doubt this novel datum; later editors of the tradition and the text would not have introduced the Gentile Giblites as co-operators in the building of the Temple; in $7^{13f.}$ pains are taken to note that the Tyrian artist Hiram had an Israelite mother. The Giblites were employed by Solomon in the same way as Solomon used Phœnician naval experts to build and man his ships in the Red Sea ($9^{26ff.}$), as Sennacherib used Phœnician carpenters to build ' Hittite ' ships for him in the Persian Gulf (*ARA* 2, pp. 145, 148, 154).

15. 𝔊 prefixed with report of the Egyptian marriage from 3^1, adding 9^{16}, *in re* the dowry—an artificial arrangement to group together these international alliances, *vs.* Kit., Comm., and *BH*, who regards the Gr. order original.—חִירָם: =Grr., Χειραμ, but חירום, vv.$^{24, 32}$ (after later Phœn. pronunciation; see Harris, *Gram.*, §11), and so Jos., Ειρωμος; the same change of spelling for the Tyrian artist's name, $7^{13, 40}$. Such variations stand for legitimate double pronunciations, the older Ḳre being given first as a rule, and so here. The full form of the name, אחירם (see Comm.) occurs at Num. 26^{38}; *cf.* אחיאל>חיאל, 16^{34}. Ch. has throughout, Kt. or Ḳr., the unexplained חורם.—למלך . . . אל 'ש: 𝔊 𝔊^L χρισαι τ.Σ. (!).—משחו: indef. pl.—**17.** אתה ידעת וג': for proleptic construction *cf.* GK §117, e.—אלהיו: Grr., ' my God,' by subtle change.—המלחמה אשר סבבהו עד תת וג': the Grr. improve upon the difficult grammar. St. would read either a pl. subject, or a sing. verb; Kit. interprets, " the hostility with which they surrounded me " (for double acc. *cf.* Ps. 109^3), and so Šanda; or the noun may be taken in collective sense, *cf.* חרלו פרון, Jud. 5^7 (so Burn.), and for such cases with fem. sing. subj. see GK §145, e.; or 'ס may be an old prepositional form, סבבהו.—יהוה: 2°: B a$_2$ ignore.—רגלו Kt., רַגְלִי Ḳr.: many MSS רגליו, with which all VSS agree (also JV). The Ḳr. arose from the sophisticated notion that then David himself should have built the temple. St. regards the half-verse as a stupid gloss. But עד, like Arab. *ḥata*, has final sense=" until at last Y. put them under his feet," and *sc.*, " now I, S., will build." For the figurative expression *cf.* Ps. 110^1, and Gunkel, *ad loc.*, comparing the declaration of a Canaanite vassel in an Amarna letter that he is the Pharaoh's ' footstool.'—**18.** *no enemy*, etc.: this was true of the beginning of the reign, despite Benz.'s criticism.—**19.** אמר: in sense

I. 5¹⁵⁻³²   139

of ' to think, intend,' *e.g.*, Ex. 2¹⁴.—**20.** ועתה : usual introduction to the substance of a letter ; see Note, II. 5⁶.—ארזים : Grr. as though עצים, preferred by Benz., St., Šanda, because of the two species named v.²² ; but with Burn. this is a sophisticated correction ; the cedars were the prime object.—שבר עבדיך : B a₂† have reduced to δουλειας σου.—B† ιδιως for ειδως.—**21.** יהוה : so all Heb. MSS ; Grr. tr. with ' God,' and so all the other VSS, except 𝔊ᴸ ' the Lord God of Israel ' ; there is no reason, with Klost. Burn., to be concerned over the original.—**23.** עבדי : *BH* sugg. עבדיך, but *cf.* vv.²⁷ᵃ·—ירדו : Grr. as though ירדום, which St., *BH* accept on ground of haplog. ; but the emendation, natural in a translation, is not necessary.—רברות : the root = ' to lead ' ; Ch. has an unexplained word, רפסרות ; the present word may have required further explication.—The following ' pregnant construction ' (St.) does not require an additional verb (the ppl. has verbal force), such as Ch. supplies with ונביאם, or as *BH* sugg., ואביאם.—בים : OGrr. om.—**24.** ועצי ברושים : 𝔊 om.—כל : 10 MSS deR., לכל ; Luc. MSS κατα παν, correcting error in 𝔊 MSS, και παν = 𝔖ᴴ.—**25.** ושלמה נתן : parallel with ויהי חירום נתן, v.²⁴ ; for the antithesis of nominal clauses see Dr., *Tenses*, §160.—מכלת : OGrr. (και) μαχειρ, Hex. MSS μαχαλ, etc. ; Aq., in MS j, διατροφην, cited as a gloss by MS 71 = 𝔖ᴴ ; for 'מכ < 'מאכ (Is. 9⁴) see Haupt as ' phonetic spelling,' *cft.* Akk. parallels ; Bergstr., *HG* 91, *inf.*, regards it as ' wohl Schreibfehler.'—**28.** בביתו : = 𝔗 𝔖 ; Grr., 𝔖ᴴ ' in their house,' by translators' improvement ; prob. to be read with St., *BH*, בבית, ' at home.'—**29.** נשא הפל = VSS ; Ch., 'ס alone, and possibly here conflation between the parallels ; Burn. sugg. apposition ; it is best, with St., to read הפל, as at 11²⁸.—For the ' 150,000 ' note the expansion in Ch.—**30.** The v. drawn from 9²³ = Gr. 2³⁵ʰ.—לשלמה : St. elides, arguing that preceding אשר is expected, but this is not necessary (Šanda) ; the parallel text has a better order.—' 3300 ' : = Jos. ; the following variations may be noted : B *al.* 3600 (a round number, not to be preferred, with Burn.) = Ch. ; 𝔊ᴸ ' 3700,' Hex., ' 3500.' Šanda makes a clever attempt at exact calculation of the ratio 3300/3600 chiefs to 180,000 labourers, on the basis of some Egyptian figures ; but, as noted above, the writer was working on the given figure, 550.—**31. 32.** These vv. have been transposed in 𝔊 after 6¹, to make these building operations come after the start of the temple.—**31.** יקרות : the identification with Akk. a*ḳ*ru, used of precious stones, fails in this connexion ; Conti Rossini ingeniously and correctly connects the word with Eth. wa*ḳ*ara, used particularly of stone-cutting, and with S. Arab. t*ḳ*r, which appears in parallelism with ' wood ' in building texts (*Chrest.*, 257). Dillmann in his *Lex.* had earlier compared the Eth. root with Arab. *ḳ*āra. אבני גזית at end of the v. may be exegetical to that word or a gloss.—**32.** בְּנֵי *bis* : Grr., ' sons of,' as for בְּנֵי = 𝔖ᴴ with ' servants ' in marg. ; 𝔗 ארדכלי = Akk. *ardē ēkalli,* possibly ' builders ' (Bezold, *BAG* 66), a notable survival.—הגבלים : 𝔊 ἐβαλαν αυτους, 𝔊^L ενεβαλον αυτ. ; Jos., οι Βιβλιοι = 𝔊^H, as from Aq. ; 𝔙 'Giblii/Biblii' ; 𝔗 𝔖 ארגובלי״א, also used at II. 12^{12} for בנים ; see St. and Haupt for attempts to explain this word of evidently Akk. origin. Unnecessary corrections have been advanced : וינבלום, "bordered them with grooved edges" (!), so Then., BDB, Burn., *cf. BH* ; ויפילום, so Klost., with most dubious interpretation.

Ch. 6. The building of the Temple. || 2 Ch. 3$^{1-14}$; *cf. Ant.*, viii, 3, 1–3. *Cf.* the Mishnaic tractate, *Middoth*, which was translated and fully commented upon by L. Cappel in his *Trisagion*, with extensive citations from Maimonides's monograph on the Temple, *Beth habbeḥirah*, reprinted by Walton in his *Biblicus Apparatus*, 120–207 ; see also F. J. Hollis, *The Archæology of Herod's Temple, With a Commentary on the Tractate 'Middoth,'* 1934, and for a translation, H. Danby, *The Mishnah* (1933), 589 ff. For particular criticism of the text see Stade, 'Der Text des Berichtes über Salomos Bauten,' *ZAW* 3, 129 ff.=his *Akad. Reden*, 143 ff., and his *Geschichte*, 1, 325 ff. Of the extensive literature may be cited : Ewald, *HI* 3, 226 ff. ; Perrot and Chipiez, *Histoire de l'art dans l'antiquité* ; the articles on 'Temple' in *DB* (T. W. Davies), *EB* (Benzinger), *JE* (Barton), on 'Tempel' by Galling in *RGG* and *BR* ; G. A. Smith, *Jerusalem*, 2, ch. 3 ; S. A. Cook ; *The Religion of Ancient Palestine, passim* ; E. Klamroth, *Lade u. Tempel*, 1932 ; K. Möhlenbrink, *Der Tempel Salomos*, 1932 ; K. Galling, 'Das allerheiligste in Salomos Tempel,' *JPOS* 1932, 43 ff. ; C. Watzinger, *DP* 1, 88 ff. ; the illuminating brief essay by G. E. Wright, 'Solomon's Temple Resurrected,' *BA* 4, 2 (1941), 17 ff. The volumes by W. C. Shaw, *Solomon's Temple* (1907), *The Second Temple in Jerusalem* (1908), are most uncritical. Plans and elevations of the building, especially those of Stade and Benzinger, have been reproduced in many of the works cited above, and, *e.g.*, in Skinner's Comm., Kent, *SOT*, Barton, *AB*. Most recent is Albright's presentation in *ARI* ch. 5, sect. 2, with detail of the archæological light thrown upon the temple and its furnishings. To this list is to be added L. Waterman's monograph, "The Damaged 'Blueprints' of the Temple of Solomon," in *JNES* 1943, 284 ff. This, with revision of text, *e.g.*, 6^{10}, presents a fresh and reasonable basis for understanding of the temple plans.

For comparison with ancient styles of architecture the

following literature may be noted. Nowack (*Arch.*, 2, 34 f.) argues against Benzinger's theory of Egyptian type for the Syrian influences on this structure, and refers to Puchstein, ' Die Säule in d. ass. Architektur ' (*Jahrb.* of the German Arch. Inst., 7, Heft 1), whom he cites as follows (from p. 13) : " Nach den noch gegenwärtig wenig sicheren Beispielen syrischen Tempelbaues gehörten zu einem vollständigen altsyrischen Tempelbaue Vorhalle, Celle, Allerheiligste und Seitenbau." W. Andrae in his *Das Gotteshaus u. die Urformen des Bauens im Alten Orient* (1930) finds (p. 25) Solomon's temple, as ' Langenhaustempel ' with portico, hall, sanctuary, to be in correspondence with Assyrian architecture. In criticism of this view see Galling, *BR* 516 ff. There may be noted here H. Thiersch, ' Ein altmediterraner Tempeltypus,' *ZAW* 1932, 73 ff., presenting comparison of the ancient temple-plans at Tell el-Hesy, Gerar, and Shechem with types distributed over the Mediterranean. For temple-construction in Babylonia and Assyria see Meissner, *Bab. u. Ass.*, 1, 302 ff., and Mowinckel's analysis of the Near-Oriental building inscriptions, in the Gunkel-*Eucharisterion*, 1, 278 ff., esp. 293 ff. M. von Oppenheim's *Der Tell Halaf* presents the remains of the temple, royal buildings, art objects of that Syrian site of the second millennium B.C., all illustrative of Solomon's creation. For a later period may be compared, for the effect upon the observer, Lucian's description of the temple of the Syrian goddess (cc. 30 ff.). For South Arabian architecture may be noted the inscriptions with full building specifications, as well as figures for the workers and their food supplies (examples in Conti Rossini, *Chrest.*, nos. 67 ff.) ; for the subject at large see D. Nielsen, *HAA* 1, 135 ff.

For the proposition of the exact orientation of the Temple, so that at the equinox the rising sun illuminated the *debîr*, the remote shrine, a theory that has produced a mass of literature, see Morgenstern, ' The Gates of Righteousness,' *HUCA* 6 (1929), 1 ff., and ' The Calendars of Anc. Israel,' *ib.*, 10 (1935), 1 ff., 76 ff., etc. ; F. J. Hollis, ' The Sun-Cult and the Temple at Jerusalem,' in Hooke, *Myth and Ritual* (esp. pp. 89 ff.) ; Graham and May, *Culture and Conscience* (Index, *s.v.* ' Sun '), and May, ' Some Aspects of Solar Worship at Jerusalem,' *ZAW* 1937, 269 ff. However, such orientation, whatever its origin, does not involve sun-worship; compare the ancient and abiding ritual habit of the Church's worship towards the east. According to Lucian his goddess's temple 'looks to the rising sun' (§29), and this aspect of a sanctuary appears in Nabatæan shrines (Glueck, *BASOR* 69 [1938], 17). The ancient temples at Tell en-Nasbeh, Gerar, Shechem 'faced' (*i.e.*, with their doors) the approximate east (Thiersch, *op. cit.*, plate opp. p. 80). The Phœnician inscription of Mas'ub (3d cent. B.C.—Lidzb., *HNE* 419; Cooke, *NSI* no. 10) records a porch ' on the east and to the north (?) ' for a temple. C. Rathjens and H. v. Wissmann in vol. 2 of their *Südarabien-Reise* (1932—pp. 61 ff.) describe the temple at Ḥugga as orientated like Solomon's. On the subject at large see G. Martigny, ' Die geographische u. astronomische Orientation altmesopotamischer Tempel,' *OLz.*, 1938, Aug.–Sept., and for the Hellenic world the thorough discussion by W. B. Dinsmoor, ' Archæology and Astronomy,' *Proc. Am. Philosoph. Soc.*, 80 (1939), 95–173. The established current opinion is that the Temple faced eastwards towards the Rock (Arabic, *eṣ-ṣaḥrah*), of hoary religious significance, which was the site of Solomon's brazen altar. For the Rock and its significance see Kittel, *Studien z. hebr. Archäologie*, 1–96. Hans Schmidt in *Der Heilige Fels* (1933) defends the traditional view of the location of the *děbîr*, like the Mosque of Omar, over the Rock; see reviews in *JPOS* 1934, 304 ff., *JQR* 24, 194 ff.

The present document is particularly original. Note Watzinger's judgment (*op. cit.*, 88) : the record " muss doch auf eine urkundliche Quelle aus der Zeit, vielleicht einen Baubericht des Königs selbst, zurückgehen." Compare the stone figure of Sumerian Gudea planning his temple according to his god's specifications (see Clay, *Light on the O.T. from Babel*, plate opp. p. 160; Gressman, *ATB* 2, Abb. 44). But unlike Gudea's sense of divine inspiration, and in the Bible the divine plans for the Tabernacle and Ezekiel's second Temple, this record is coolly objective : Solomon built the temple. We actually possess in these chapters concerning the construction and furnishing of a temple the fullest and most detailed specifications from the ancient Oriental world.

For literary analysis of the text see in particular *SBOT*. There is to be noted Šanda's radical rearrangement : vv.[1, 2.]

19. 17. 20a. 3. 4. 9. 15. 16. 18. 29. 21. 20b. 22. 30. 23a. 26. 23b. 24. 25. 27. 28. 31-35. 5. 6. 8 10. 36. 11-14. 7. 37. 38. Moffatt in his translation of the Bible has also made a rearrangement. But such reordering of materials has no authority, is only of possible advantage to the eye in study of details; ancient specifications need not have been as orderly as modern. Many of the passages that appear out of place are glosses, as the text below will attempt to exhibit.

1. *And it came to pass in the 480th year of the exodus of the Bnê-Israel from the land of Egypt,*

in the fourth year, in the month Ziv (that is, the second month), of Solomon's reign over Israel, that he built the house to Y*HWH.*	**37.** *In the fourth year was founded the house of* Y*HWH, in the moon Ziv.* **38.** *And in the eleventh year, in the moon Bul (that is, the eighth month), the house was finished according to all its details and all its art; and he built it in seven years.*

VV.$^{37.\ 38}$, with the inclusive dates of the construction, give the original archival datum and in the proper place; for convenience of parallelism they are presented here. The duplication of the first item here was due to a logical disposition in connexion with the era-date 480. *Cf.* the arbitrary rearrangement in 𝔊 𝔊^L, by which 5$^{31.\ 32a}$, 6$^{37.\ 38}$ are introduced after v.^{1}, as belonging technically here. Ch. knows the day of inception, 'the second day of the second month.'

1a. The Grr. faulted 'the 480th year' and corrected it to 'the 440th year'; this is probably due to the fact that the genealogy of Aaron to Sadok inclusive (1 Ch. 5$^{29\text{ff.}}$) counts but eleven persons, *i.e.*, 11×40=440; 𝔖^H also follows this reckoning, and Aquila's and Symmachus's agreement with 𝔐 is known only from Codex M. For acceptance of the round number 480 as historical see Keil, with reff.; Šanda; H. Hänsler, *Biblica*, 12 (1931), 395 ff.; Marston, *New Bible Evidence*, ch. 10; W. J. Chapman, *ZAW* 1935, 185 ff. (proposing Egyptian sources for the chronology). Marston, accepting the Biblical figure, dates the Exodus at 1447–1437, the founding of the temple at 967–957 (*The Bible Comes Alive,*

App. IV). But along with the present lowering of the date for the Exodus on the basis of archæology, it is now generally recognized that we have here an artificial date of secondary origin, balanced by the attempt of likeminded chronologers to find 480 years between this date and the Exile. Note the conservative Rawlinson's scepticism on the datum here in note to end of the chapter. See Int., §16. For a recent careful study see H. H. Rowley, ' Israel's Sojourn in Egypt,' *Bull. John Rylands Library*, 22 (1938), 1 ff. The whole of v.^{1} is accordingly editorial. On the authority of Menander Josephus (*Contra Apionem*, i, 18) sets the date of the building in the 12th year of Hiram. Such dating as from the Tyrian annals has evidently been accepted from Jewish sources; see R. Pietschmann, *Gesch. d. Phönizier*, 132 ff., Meyer, *GA* 2, 2, 79 ff. However, the scribal calculation, if it be such, is approximately correct and so to be honoured; according to Meyer's chronology (p. 438) Hiram's 12th year was *ca.* 957, Solomon's 4th year 956/951. The rare archaic names for the months are evidence of the originality of the document, as also the older word for the lunar period, ' moon.' They are converted into terms of the numbered months of the later calendar, starting in the spring. See also Comm., 12$^{52\text{ff.}}$.

VV.$^{2\text{-}10}$. The construction of the Temple.

2. *And the house which King Solomon built for* YHWH : 60 *cubits its length, and* 20 ⌜*cubits*⌝ [plus with MSS, VSS] *its width, and* 30 *cubits its height ;* **3.** *and the portico* [*'ûlām*] *in front of the hall* [*hêkāl*] *of the house :* 20 *cubits its width* [Heb. *length*] *along the front of the width of the house,* ⌜*and*⌝ [plus with some MSS, VSS] 10 *cubits its depth* [Heb. *width*] *along the front of the house.* **4.** *And he made for the house windows* ⌜*embrasured, latticed*⌝ [?]. **5.** *And he built on the wall of the house a side-wing about* [om. with some VSS *the walls of the house about*] *the hall and the shrine* [*děbîr*] *; and he made stories round about :* **6.** *the lowest* ⌜*story*⌝ [with some VSS—Heb. *side-wing*] 5 *cubits its width, and the middle one* 6 *cubits its width, and the third* 7 *cubits its width, for rebatements were made for the house on the outside, so as not to make inset into the walls of the house ;* [**7.** *And the house in its building was built with finished stone, quarry-cut, and as for hammers and the saw* ⌜*and*⌝ [plus with MSS, some VSS] *all tools of iron, naught was* *heard in the house at its building*—secondary, *cf.* 5³¹ᶠ·.] **8.** *the doorway of the ⌜lowest⌝* [with some VSS—Heb. *middle*] *story at the right side of the house, and by winding-stairs they would go up to the middle* (story), *and from the middle to the third.* **9.** [*And he built the house and finished it*—secondary, *cf.* vv.¹⁴·³⁸.] *And he ceiled the house in coffers and serried-rafters* [?] *with cedar beams.* [**10.** *And he built the side-wing against all the house, five cubits its height, and it fastened on to the house with timbers of cedar*—a gloss to v.⁵.]

The translation above attempts to present the staccato, almost purely substantival diction, as of archival character. The document concerns the structure of the house, walls and roof, as a whole; the inner shrine is mentioned but once. Other non-pertinent items must be regarded as intrusions.

2. The cubit (Engl. ' ell ') was according to 2 Ch. 3³ ' after the ancient measure,' in contrast with the later measure of ' a cubit and a hand ' (Eze. 40⁵, 43¹³) ; see BDD, *s.v.* ' Weights and Measures,' the Archæologies of Nowack (§34) and Benzinger (§39), Šanda. The Grr. arbitrarily vary the figures here. Josephus doubles the height, then adds another story of equal dimension, obtaining a height for the temple of 120 cubits, the extravagant figure for the height of the portico in 2 Ch. 3⁴. **3.** The ancient Sumerian word *ēkallu*, Heb. *hêkāl*, used of a royal palace (and so 21¹, etc.), is used of the main chamber, Moffatt quite properly ' nave '; only supplementarily is the rear sanctuary, itself a walled-off chamber, mentioned (v.⁵). **4.** For the obscure adjectives translated *embrasured, latticed,* see Note ; here and below we have to deal with technical terms of architecture, which may not be explained offhand by etymology. **5.** This last remark is illustrated by the term translated *side-wing* (*yāṣî‘*) ; as will appear below, it was early confused, indeed in 𝔅, with the word for ' story ' (*ṣèla‘*) ; see Note. The word *děbîr* means radically ' rear-room '; see below, v.¹⁶. **6.** The word translated *story* is primarily ' rib '; the necessary correction of the confusion here has been noted above. Of interest is the meticulous concern lest these side service-chambers (*cf.* ' the vestry,' II. 10²²) should be structurally part of the house ; the beams of the stories rested *on* the recessed walls, not *in* them. **7.** The v. evidently interrupts the architectural specifications ;

cf. the punctuation in JV. It is doubtless the fact that all the stone-dressing was done at the quarry (*cf.* $5^{31, 32}$); there may be noted the great semi-detached stone at the Baalbek quarry. **8.** The strange error of 𝕳 which places the doorway on the level of the second story is due to careless confusion of two similar words; even JV makes the correction, noting the Heb. in the margin. *The doorway . . . at the right side of the house:* the question is whether the adj. is used structurally, and so means the north side, or according to the point of the compass, and so the south side. The former view is preferable; *cf.* the main entrance of the Syrian goddess, which was 'towards the north' (Lucian, §28). *By winding stairs they would go up.* Since the Greek versions the noun has been so rendered in Western translations (see Note); correction of it in line with modern criticism appears in the Moffatt and Chicago Bibles with *trap-doors*. The argument against the traditional interpretation was based by Stade on the fact that there was no example of such a construction in ancient Oriental architecture (*Akad. Reden*, 150 f.). But an example has now been discovered, 1939, by Leonard Woolley at Atchana near Antioch in an extensive palace of the eighteenth century B.C. Speaking of one door from the court to the palace he reports: " A stair-well just inside the door contained a newel stair (of which the first two flights were nearly perfectly preserved), whereby one reached the first-floor rooms."[1] The tradition is thus confirmed. There may be compared the remarkable Paneion at Alexandria, a high circular tower with a winding stairway on its exterior, fully described by Strabo (*Geographica*, xvii, 10). **9a.** The sentence appears to be quite secondary; the annotator thought of the stone construction, which was first 'finished'; yet an unroofed house is hardly finished, while that verb is used correctly at the end of the specifications (v.^{38}). **9b.** The roof is observed from within as the ceiling. The crossing of the rafters at right angles formed hollow squares, in technical phraseology, *coffers*; these may have been further set forth

---

[1] Cited in *The New York Times*, Aug. 26, 1939, from the London *Times*; *cf.* Albr., *BASOR* 77 (1940), 23, referring to the report by S. Smith in *The Antiquaries Journal*, 19 (1939), 39 ff. The newel is the centre-post of a winding stairway.

by decoration, as in modern architecture. **10.** The v. is apparently a gloss to v.[5], with the one fresh item of the height of the side-wing; but a height of five cubits for the three-story structure is absurd. Comm. cited by Poole make the figure refer to the chambers in the several stories (*cf.* Eze. 41[6]), and so AV with Grr. here; RVV JV, Moff., Chic. B., similarly modify the translation. Keil defends the text as a bit of 'Breviloquenz'; Stade turns 'five' into 'fifteen,' which would be a proper figure. The statement is a clumsy insertion by an interpolator who had the figure for the single story in mind.

11-14. VV.[11-13] contain an oracle of the continued divine residence in the house on condition of Solomon's obedience. It is absent in OGrr., and is a late intrusion, repeating 2[3ff.], 3[14]. See Burney's analysis of the phraseology, showing that the colour is that of P rather than of D. V.[14] repeats v.[9] on 'the finishing of the house,' introduced because there follow here again items of the cedar work.

1, 37. v.[1] בחדש זו : v.[37] בירח זו, with the older word for 'month,' as exclusively in Ugaritic and Phœn. The Heb. month name is preserved most exactly among the Grr. by MS o, ζιου, n, δειου, *cf.* 𝔏, 'Xiiu,' but is otherwise corrupted by dittogr. of preceding [μη]νι, resulting in a variety of forms, νισω, νεισω (uncials), νισαν = 𝔈, by identification with Nisan.—Similarly the month name Bul is sadly mishandled by the Grr. here; the Hexaplaric re-insertion of vv.[37, 38] in their place transliterates the names properly. —**37.** יסד: Grr.: εθεμελιωσεν-αν.—**38.** דבריו, משפטו: the Grr. read both nouns as sing., and so 𝔗 with epexegetical translation; 𝔖 𝔄 both as pl.; 𝔙 1° as sing., 2° as pl. It is best to read the latter as משפטו. For the interesting secondary sense of this noun *cf.* II. 1[7].—**2.** ששש: Grr., '40,' exc. A x, which with Jos., 𝔈=𝔙.— ועשרים: 5 MSS+אמה=VSS.—שלשים: 𝔊 𝔊[L]='25,' Jos., '60'; with St., the cause of variation is 'obscure.'—**3.** אולם: so 𝔖[H] trans-literates; Jos., πρόναιον, Sym., πρόπυλον; otherwise the Grr. trans-literate with αιλαμ=אילם, as in Eze. 40, *passim*, accepted by Stade-Haupt, Kit. (not *BH*), GB, as=Akk. prep. *ellāmu,* 'over against.' But 𝔙 is corroborated by 2 Ch. 3[4], Eze. 8[16], and is authentic, derived from root *'wl,* 'to be in front.'—היכל הבית: 𝔊 as ההיכל, accepted by St.—עשר: 15 MSS ועשר.—אמה באמה רחבו: עשר באמה: 𝔊 om., added by 𝔊[L] at end of v.=𝔏 𝔈.—[הבית] על פני: 𝔖 as plus ארך, accepted by Klost., Benz., St., *BH*; but this is an explicative addition.—The Grr., 𝔖[H] have repeated v.[14b] at end of this v.— **4.** חלוני שקפים אטמים: *'ש* construed with טורים occurs at 7[4], and שקף at 7[5]. The Hif. of the verb means 'to look out,' so II. 9[30, 32] (of

Jezebel at the window), and the derivative here may refer to windows with sides sloping inwards towards one another; cf. the embrasures of military fortification. The second questioned word occurs in like connexion, חלונות אטמות, Eze. 40¹⁶, 41¹⁶, ²⁶ (see Cooke's Comm.), and comes from a root well known in Aram., Arab. = 'to close, cover,' and may mean 'latticed.' And so the Grr. interpreted the two words: 𝔊 θυρίδας παρακυπτομένας κρυπτάς, the ppl. in which 𝔊ᴸ replaces with δεδικτυωμένας, 'netted, latticed.' Other VSS vary: 𝔗 'windows open inside and closed outside'; 𝔖 'windows open and closed'; 𝔄 'windows narrow outside, broad inside': 𝔙 simply, 'obliquas fenestras.' Cf. varieties in EVV; JV follows the margin of AV, 'windows broad within and narrow without'; i.e., moderns know little more than the ancients. The VSS read the first word as absolute (and so 1 MS), which construction with the foll. ppls. is required (cf. Eze. 40¹⁶), unless with Šanda the second word be read שְׁקֻפִים.—**5.** ורבן: Grr. read as ויתן.—צוע, Ḳr. צֶלָע: a technical term = 'layer,' and then 'side-layer, wing.' Grr. here μέλαθρα (thinking of the cells in the temple ?); 𝔖ᴴ with Syr. borrowing of Gr. ἐπιστύλια, 'architraves.'—את קירות הבית סביב: the unnecessary repetition was not known to 𝔗 𝔊 𝔊ᴸ; Theod. (in 𝔖ᴴ), 𝔖 𝔄 simplify.—ויעש צלעות סביב: B N a₂ v 𝔏 om., prob. in view of μέλαθρα above.—צלעות: primarily 'ribs,' then 'stories'; the word occurs at v.¹⁵, 7³, of 'beams' (of cedar); the word appears in Syr. as an architectural term, acc. to Bar-Bahlul's Lex. (ed. Duval, 1886), s.v. אלע, also in Brock., Lex.—**6.** היצוע: Ḳr. as above; Grr., ἡ πλευρά, i.e., = הצלע = 𝔖ᴴ, and this must be read. 𝔗 tr. the word here and צלעות, v.⁵, with the one word מחיצתא, 'compartment,' etc. (see Jastrow, Dict.). But Eze. 41⁵ᶠᶠ uses צלע as of a side-chamber. These similar words have contaminated one another. The fem. gender of the foll. adj. supports הצלע here, whereas יצוע is masc. (cf. v.¹⁰), although the Mishna treats the word as fem. (Rosenberg, ZAW 1905, 331), doubtless by dependence on the Biblical construction.—מגרעות: B al., διάστημα, A M N al., -ματα = 𝔏.—**7.** אבן שלמה: St.'s argument (cf. BH) that the same phrase occurs at Josh. 8³¹ of 'unhewn stone' would plausibly stamp the adj. as secondary; but the term is qualified by the foll. appositive מסע.—כל: read וכל with many MSS, Grr., 𝔖.—**8.** התיכנה: 𝔗 Grr., 𝔖ᴴ = התחתנה, to be accepted; see Comm.—לולים: Grr., ἑλικτὴ ἀνάβασις, 'winding stairway,' and so 𝔗; 𝔙 'coc(h)lea,' 'snail-shell, spiral'; 𝔖 uses the Gr. word for 'cataract.' Etymology has connected the word with Arab. lawlaba, 'to wind,' lawlab, 'snail-shell' (so Ew. in his Lehrb., §158, b, and König, Lehrgeb., 1, 2, 52, recent grammarians ignoring the word). It has been overlooked that Dozy in his Supplément presents a parallel Arab. root, lawlawa, which supports the origin of the present biliteral from לוה, 'to wind'; cf. also לְלָאֹת, 'girdles,' Ex. 26⁵, etc., poss. Akk. lūlu (Bezold, BAG 156). For the obscure phrase ורחבה ונסבה, Eze. 41⁷, 𝔗 renders the second word with לולין. It may be observed that Gr. λαῖλαψ, 'whirlwind,' otherwise unexplained, comes from this Semitic origin. The interpretation 'hatchways' comes from later Jewish tradition; Talmudic *Middoth*, iv, 5, speaks of לולין פתוחין, "open *lûlîn* by which they let down workmen by chains," and Maimonides (cited by Cappel, p. 207) defines לול as פתח קטון, 'small opening'; *cf.* also Jastrow, *Dict.*, *s.v.* for other applications of the word in sense of 'hole.' Similar interpretation has been followed by Benz., Burn., St., Nowack, Šanda, and *cf.* Sk.—השלשים: read ששית—, with 4 MSS; Grr. read the pl., τα τριωφορα; 𝔙 was contaminated from the obscure בשלשים, Eze 42³, unless the pl. is to be regarded, with Šanda, as 'a standing expression' for the third floor.—**9.** ויספן : for the verb used in the sense of 'ceil' see Jer. 22¹⁴, and *cf.* Phœn. מספנת, 'roof,' and so the verb is used at 7³.—נבים ושדרת : 𝔊 𝔊ᴸ om. ; for the first word Hex. has φάτνωμα used of a panelled ceiling = Lat. 'laquear,' used here by 𝔙, which om. the foll. word ; 𝔖ᴴ *kĕrām dappē*, 'ceiling of tables'; 𝔖 renders as 'hollows,' and the foll. word as 'sawn'; 𝔗 paraphrases remarkably. גב is at II. 3¹⁶, referring to the 'trenches'; it means here the hollow squares between the criss-cross rows, שדרת (𝔖ᴴ *ṭukkāsē*, 'alignments'), of the beams. The noun *gwb* appears in S. Arab. for an architectural feature (Conti Rossini, *Chrest.*, 121).—**10.** היצוע, Ḳr. הַיָּצִיעַ : Grr. τ. ενδεσμους.—את הבית : B *al.*, τ. συνδεσμον, 𝔊ᴸ τ. ενδεσμους, A N *al.*, τ. ενδεσμον = 𝔖ᴴ ; 𝔗 'the gallery' (תיקא = Targ. for מעקה, Dt. 22⁸, and אתיק, Eze. 41¹⁵ᶠ·), as 'above all the house'; 𝔖 'circular passage-ways' (*ḥădārĕṭā*) above all the house'; 𝔙 'tabulatum super omnem domum,' *i.e.*, all applying the item quite logically to the roofing of the house ; *cf.* 'the galleries' in Eze. 41¹⁵. The discrepancy of only 5 cubits height for the side-wing has been noted above. Šanda replaces that word with הצלעות and reads consequently קומתן. Jos. makes the word refer to the side-chambers, which he measures as 5 cubits square, 20 cubits high (see Marcus, *ad loc.*).—**11–14.** For the Hex. addition see note in MS j.—**14.** The v. was transferred by 𝔊 to end of v.³, was repeated here by Hex.

VV.¹⁵⁻²². The inner wood-work ; the partition of the shrine ; the decoration.

15. *And he built the walls of the house on the inside with cedar planks from the floor of the house to the* ⌜*beams*⌝ [with OGrr. ; 𝔙 *walls*] *of the roof ; he panelled with wood within, and he laid the floor of the house with cypress planks.*

18. *And cedar for the house on the inside, carved work of gourds and flower-calyxes ;* ⌜*the whole was cedar, no stone was seen*⌝ [OGrr. om.].

16. *And he built off* 20 *cubits at the rear of the house with cedar planks from the floor up to the* ⌜*beams*⌝ [with OGrr. ; 𝔥 *walls*], *and he built within* [with correction of 𝔥] *for a shrine* [𝔥+*for the holy of holies*] ; **17.** *and* 40 *cubits* [long] *was* [𝔥+*the house, that is ;* OGrr. om.] *the hall* ⌜*in front of*⌝ [with correction of Ḳr.] ⌜*the shrine*⌝ [plus with Grr., 𝔙] ; **20.** *and* ⌜*the shrine*⌝ [with 𝔙 ; 𝔥 *in front of the shrine*] : 20 *cubits in length, and* 20 *cubits in width, and* 20 *cubits its height ; and he overlaid it with refined gold. And he* ⌜*made*⌝ [with Grr. ; 𝔥 *overlaid*] *an altar of cedar* (**21***b*) *in front of the shrine, and overlaid it with gold.*

19. *And a shrine within the house, deep within, he prepared, to set there the ark of the covenant of* Y*HWH*.

21*a. And Solomon overlaid the house within with refined gold, and he drew chains of gold across.* **22.** *And all the house he overlaid with gold, until at last the house was finished.* ⌜*And all the altar that belonged to the shrine he overlaid with gold*⌝ [OGrr. om.].

The above display presents in the second column a number of extensive additions that have been interpolated in the text, as also many glosses to the earlier form in the first column. The criticism is largely supported by the OGr. texts, and may in general explain itself. V.[19] parallels v.[16], setting forth the shrine as the depository of the ark. The plus of ' the holy of holies ' (v.[16]—the Semitic=the holiest) is a current term peculiar to P in the Pentateuch and to the latest Biblical books. VV.[21a, 22a] are wondrously extravagant with the gold-plating of the whole house. The original specifications concerned the house as a whole ; *cf.* ' the altar in front of the shrine ' (vv. [20, 21b]) and the later item of ' the altar of the shrine ' (v.[22b]). With the above independent analysis should be compared Benzinger's elaborate criticism, pp. xvi-xviii.

For the wood-work and decoration may be compared similar specifications in Ass. and Late-Bab. royal inscriptions. Esarhaddon on his Black Stone (col. iv, *ARA* 2, §653) announces: " . . . with mighty beams, products of Mount Amanus [the cedar locality], the snow-capped mountain, I spanned its roof. Door-leaves of cypress [*burāšu*=Heb. *běrôš*], whose odour is pleasant, I bound with a band of gold and silver and hung them in their doors " (*cf.* §659 D). ' Door-leaves of cypress ' are again recorded for a palace (*ib.*, §§698, 711); and the last citation proceeds : " The sanctuary of Assur, my lord, I inlaid with gold. *Laḥmê* and cherubim of ruddy *sariru* I set side by side. . . . The walls I plastered with gold like plaster." Ashurbanipal, for the rebuilding of his palace, records (Rassam, Cylinder *ib.*, §837) : " great beams of cedar . . . door-leaves of juniper . . . with a sheathing of copper . . . tall columns I enclosed with shining bronze and laid (thereon) the cornices of its portico (*bît-ḫilâni*)." In the East India House inscription Nebuchadnezzar boasts of the cedar timbers and other woods for the Marduk temple, and expatiates on the gilding ; the hall he adorned with ' glowing gold,' where silver had been before ; the cedar beams he covered with gold ; etc. (cols. ii, iii, *KB* iii, 2, 13 ff.). A text of Esarhaddon's similarly reports work of cypress, cedar, and gold (*ARA* 2, §653). With these inscriptions may be compared the elaboration of the present description in 2 Ch. 3^{5-9}. For the combination of cedar and gilding may be noted Thutmose IV's account of the sacred bark he built, ' all decorated with gold ' (*ARE* 2, no. 878, *ATB* 1, 92). For a mythical and still more exuberant description, in a Ras Shamra text, of a temple, that of Aleyan-Baal, built of Lebanon cedar and gilded all over with gold and silver, see Virolleaud's publication in *Syria*, 1932, 113 ff.= *RSMT* text B ; C. H. Gordon, *Ugaritic Handbook*, 2, Text 51 ; *cf.* U. Cassuto, ' The Palace of Baal,' *JBL* 1942, 51 ff. For the inner decoration of the wall with plant-themes in Mesopotamian art from ancient times see Andrae, *Das Gotteshaus*, 35 f., 40, Meissner, *Bab. u. Ass.*, 2, 330 (*e.g.*, ' palm-leaves and pomegranates '). Such decoration abounded in Egyptian architecture. Capitals with lily ornamentation have now been found at Megiddo (*ILN* May 26, 1934, 836 f.), and the Oriental VSS so understand the word rendered above as ' flower.' The word translated above as 'gourds' (EVV with archaic 'knops' = 'knobs,' see A. R. S. Kennedy, *s.v.*, *DB*) is uncertain; that rendering is based on etymological relation with the word for 'gourds' (II. 4³⁹); see GB for variant opinion. 𝕋 tr. with 'eggs,' recalling the common egg-ornamentation of capitals since ancient times. The same detail appears on the bronze sea (7²⁴). Solomon's temple differed from those in Egypt and Mesopotamia in being wainscotted with wood, in contrast to stone and tile interiors.

The whole house is roofed, panelled, and floored with wood : the flooring is of cypress; the rest of the construction, in cedar. The shrine or sanctuary (see Note for the various translations) is a cube of 20 cubits; for such proportion *cf.* the Meccan Ka'ba (*i.e.*, ' dice-cube '), which is 12 × 12 m. square, 15 m. high; see Gaudefroy-Demombynes, *Le pèlerinage à Mekke* (1926), 26. The figure for the length of the hall agrees with the dimensions given above (v.³). Nothing is said about the presumed vacant loft above the sanctuary; Ch. knows of it as containing gilded ' upper-chambers ' (II. 3⁹), and *Middoth* iv, 5, reports for the Herodian temple hatchways through which workmen were lowered into the sanctuary. Galling, ' Das Allerheiligste in Salomo's Tempel,' *JPOS* 1932, 43 ff., denies existence of such an upper chamber, and postulates a raised podium for the *dĕbîr*, with steps leading up to the latter. The gilding of the furnishings, as of the altar, is reasonable, but not that of the whole interior; *cf.* Stade, and Nowack, *Arch.*, 2, 29, n. 1. Šanda attempts to support the description, referring to Hezekiah's tribute to Sennacherib; but for the text as *vs.* the usual translation see Comm., II. 18¹⁶. Such extravagant description appears to be a step forward in the process of exuberant imagination, continued by the Chronicler, for whose fancy even the 120-cubit high portico was overlaid with fine gold (2 Ch. 3⁴ᶠᶠ·). *Refined gold* (v.²⁰) : the pass. ppl. translates a word of Akk. origin, and is technical for a certain specie value. For the *chains of gold* see Note; the word is different from that at 7¹⁷ (*cf.* EVV). For the *altar in front of the shrine cf.* the altar, with dimensions given, in Eze.'s plan (41²²), and the incense altar specified in Ex. 30¹ᶠᶠ·, of acacia wood, with dimensions given, to be placed " before the veil that is by the ark of the testimony." In the citation from

Eze. (see Cooke, *ad loc.*) there is the further specification of the Guide that "this is the table which is before Yhwh," thus complicating our altar with the table of showbread; *cf.* the reference inserted below (7^{48}) to both a golden altar and a golden showbread-table. Herodotus (i, 183) refers to a golden altar in the temple of Bel in Babylon. The word for altar (from the root 'to slaughter') has become generalized, and no longer imports the kind of offering made upon it. This altar may be identified with the altar of incense in the *hêkāl* at which Uzziah presumptuously officiated (2 Ch. $26^{16\text{ff.}}$, *cf.* Luke $1^{8\text{ff.}}$). For such table-altars see K. Galling, *Der Altar in den Kulturen des alten Orients* (1925), 68 ff., with plates; *ATB* 2, plates clxxv *seq.*; H. Wiener, *The Altars of the O.T.* (1927), 23 ff., for incense altars, with plate illustrating the incense altars found at Gezer, Taanach, Shechem; Albright, *APB* 108, notes p. 200; for general discussion, *cf.* Nowack, *Arch.*, 2, 39 f.; and Morgenstern, *HUCA* 12–13 (1937–38), 7 f. At 8^{64} (*cf.* vv.$^{22, 54}$) we learn casually of 'the bronze altar before Yhwh'; see Comm. on the passage. The innovations and reformations (*e.g.*, II. 21, 23) that proceeded through the four centuries of the temple's existence preclude the rigorous application of later data, and especially of theoretical plans like those in Ex. and Eze., for illumination of the present antique record.

15. מביתה : 𝔊 𝔊^L om.; St., Kit. (not *BH*) excise; but with Burn., Šanda, the word is essential, indicating the inner construction.—צלעות : the technical word in another sense at v.^{5}.—קרקע : 'floor'; *cf.* Num. 5^{17}.—עד קירות : 22 MSS Ken., deR., ועד=Grr., exc. x. 𝔊 𝔊^L=קירות עד קורות ער, *i.e.*, an early double rdg.; 𝔖^H obelizes the first term, agreeing with 𝔙; קורות, 'beams,' is required, as also at v.^{16}.—צפה עץ מבית : Klost., St., *al.* regard as an addition (*cf. BH*); otherwise Burn., Šanda.—ברושים : the genus is uncertain; see Comm., $6^{15\text{ff.}}$; Post in *DB* renders with the inclusive word 'fir' (*v. sub voce*). The lumber for the floor is other than that for the roof; *cf.* the list of woods used in ship-building, Eze. $27^{5\text{f.}}$.—**16.** אמה [את עשרים] : Šanda would read האמה, but for the construction see GK, §117, d.—מירכתי : Kr. correctly חֲיַרְכְּתֵי, and so many MSS Kt.—הבית : Grr. by clumsy error, τ. τοίχου=𝔖^H, exc. 𝔊^L τ. οἴκου.—בצלעות ארוים : Grr., τὸ πλευρὸν τὸ ἐν=𝔖^H, a remarkable interpretation, so St., *q.v.*—קירות : read קורות.—ויבן 2° : Grr., 𝔖^H 𝔙 'and he made,' an exegetical variation.—ויבן לו מבית לדביר : 𝔊 𝔊^L ignore לו; Hex., αυτω, var. αυτο; 𝔗 𝔖 after Aram. use regard the phrase as accusatival, anticipating the foll. acc.; Junius (in Poole) as = 'for God'; JV 'for himself,' and so Burn., interprets it as *dativus commodi*, referring to the king's privilege as pontifex maximus, but this would be arrogance. St. refrains from altering. Šanda reduces the phrase to לכבית לדביר, regarding the verb as superfluous; but by retaining the verb and with his further correction a suitable sense is obtained, as in the tr. above.—דביר: the Grr. transliterate the word here and below with δαβειρ (= 𝔖ᴴ), and for the nominal phrase 𝔊 texts have εκ του δ. (𝔊ᴸ+τ. τοιχον), but 𝔊ᴴ εσωθεν του δ. = 𝔖ᴴ. For the word as radically = 'rear part' see Burn., who notes the history of its transliteration. Aq., Sym., χρηματιστήριον = 𝔙 'oraculum' = AV RVV FV 'oracle'; 𝔗 'house of atonement'—the same for cover of the lid of the ark, Ex. 25¹⁷; JV 'Sanctuary'; GV most ingeniously, 'Chor.'—**17**. [ההיכל] הבית הוא: 𝔊 𝔊ᴸ om., and in fact the house was not the hall.—לְפָנָי: the pointing is impossible (= ʳbefore meˡ), indicative of the dilemma of the Masoretes; *n.b.* 1 MS deR., לפני = 𝔗; *cf.* EVV 'before the oracle/Sanctuary.' The introduction to v.²⁰, ולכני הדביר, an impossible clause in the connexion (*cf.* the attempts of EVV, exc. JV), is survival of original לפני הדביר at the end of this v., represented by the fragment לפני, and this by early corruption affected the original beginning of v.²⁰ = והדביר.—**18**. The intrusion of this v., absent in 𝔊 𝔊ᴸ, and of v.¹⁹, early disturbed the text; see tr. above, which follows St.—אל הבית: the prep. is remarkable; 2 MSS על; Burn. tries to explain; 𝔙 ingeniously understood as כל.—מקלעת פקעים: ופטורי ציצים: 'מ also at vv.²⁹·³². The VSS distinguish 'פט as in abs. form, gaining three motives of decoration. 𝔗 tr. 'פט with 'eggs'; 𝔗 𝔖 𝔄 for 'צ 'lilies.'—**19**. לתתן: error for לָחֵת or לָחַת; *cf.* erroneous התן, 17¹⁴.—**20**. זהב סגור = כָּנוּר, Job 28¹⁵; the term = Akk. *ḫurāṣu sagru* (Bezold, *BAG* 210); for the mng. of 'ס see Note on מסגר, II. 24¹⁴.—ויצף: read ויעש with Grr.; OGrr. rearrange vv.²⁰ᵇ·²¹.—**21**. ברתיקות Kt., בְּרַתּוּקוֹת Ḳr.; at Is. 40¹⁹ = רְתוּקוֹת 'chains,' and so here 𝔗; רַתּוּק, Eze. 7²³, is most obscure; see Cooke, Comm.; Hex. here 'nails,' and so 𝔙, as of applying gold foil with nails, which item seems to have come from 2 Ch. 3⁹. Šanda accepts Then.'s suggestion to read הפרכת, 'the veil,' as at 2 Ch. 3¹⁴; but how could so well known a technical term have become obscured? The second half of the v. is omitted by OGrr.—**22***b*. The sentence, omitted by OGrr., is represented in Hex. with " and all within the *dabir* he overlaid with gold."

VV.²³⁻²⁷. **The two cherubs in the shrine.**
23*a*. *And he made in the shrine two cherubs of oleaster wood :* **26.** *the height of the one cherub 10 cubits, and so the second cherub* (**23***b*) *ten cubits its height ;* **24.** *and five cubits* (long) *the one wing of the cherub, and five cubits the second wing of the cherub, 10 cubits from end of its* ʳ*wing*ˡ *to end of its* [*wing*]

[𐤇 wings] ; **25.** [and ten cubits the second cherub—repetition] one measure and one form to the two cherubs. **27.** [And he set the cherubs within the inner house—secondary, repeating v.²³ᵃ.] And they spread out ⌈their wings⌉ [with OGrr. ; 𐤇 the wings of the cherubs], and the wing of the one touched the (side-) wall, and the wing of the other [Heb. second] cherub was touching the other [Heb. second] wall, with their wings in the centre of the house, touching wing to wing.

The text is fairly intact, with the necessity of transfer of v.²⁶ into v.²³ (with Stade and subsequent comm.) and of excision of an evident doublet (v.²⁷ᵃ), which is dependent upon Eze.'s peculiar term for the *dĕbîr* (41¹⁷), and avoids the 'making' of the cherubs in the holy place.

Since antiquity the cherub figures have been subject of mystical interest—indeed with later artistic degradation of the theme—even as they remain to-day one of technical dispute. The obscure word *kĕrûb* has been finally etymologized by Langdon as from the Akk. root='to adore,' from which was developed the noun *karebāti* (fem. pl.—also a form *kurebu*), used in association with *lamasāti*, the protecting genii in sculptured form at entrance of temples.[1] The problem is complicated by the kaleidoscopic forms of the figure depicted elsewhere in the Bible. Ezekiel (10¹⁴, ²¹) presents four cherubs each with four faces, four wings, and so expanding the vision of ch. 1 ; according to Ex. 25¹⁸ᶠᶠ· the two golden cherubs at the ends of the ark screen the *kappōret* with their wings, *i.e.*, as guardians, and this feature since Josephus has largely entered into reconstructions of the picture of Solomon's cherubs. However, the item in the present specifications is long anterior to those later figments, doubtless developed under impressions from Bab. art, its historicity being established by its independence of them, and it may justly be

[1] In addition to the literature cited above, Comm., v.¹, see S. Langdon, *Epic of Creation* (1923), 190, n. 1 ; Dhorme and Vincent, 'Les chérubins,' *RB* 35 (1926), 328 ff., 481 ff. ; Cooke, *Ezekiel*, 112 ff. ; also for general discussions Gressmann, *Die Lade Jahves* (1920) with 10 plates, and H. Schmidt, 'Kerubenthron u. Lade,' Gunkel-*Eucharisterion*, 1, 120 ff. For such winged figures in general, cherub, griffin, sphinx, see L. Waterman, *AJSL* 31 (1915), 249 ff., who supports the connexion of the word 'cherub' with γρύψ (but see below) ; Cook, *Rel. of Anc. Pal.*, 47 ff. ; and Galling's summary art., 'Mischwesen,' in *BR*.

explained from earlier native and primitive language. Yhwh has the ancient epithet of " seated on the cherubs " (II. 19^{15}= Is. 37^{16} ; Ps. 80^1, 99^1), and these winged creatures constitute his heavenly chariot, as in the theophany in 2 Sam. 22$^{8ff.}$= Ps. 18$^{8ff.}$, according to which " he rode upon a cherub and flew, and swooped down on the wings of the wind," while the naturalistic basis of the theme appears in Ps. 104^3 : Yhwh " makes the clouds his chariot." And this original form of the theme recurs in 1 Ch. 28^{18}, ' the pattern of the chariot, the cherubs ' (with probable play on *kĕrūb* and *merkābāh*, *cf.* Dhorme and Vincent, p. 329) ; that is, the cherubs are bearers of the Deity. And as such they appear in the present artistic composition, standing with their wings stretched out to the full width of the sanctuary, constituting the throne of the Presence. They stand erect, without doubt ' in human likeness ' (so Eze. 1^5), ' on their feet ' (2 Ch. 3^{13}), 10 cubits in height, with the same space above, which is empty, to the mystical imagination for the session of the Deity.² This is in contrast to the drooping, protective wings of the ancient Oriental art, and the independence of the Solomonic cherubs from those visualized in the later literature is to be insisted upon. There may be noted in the relief accompanying the Yehaumilk inscription the overshadowing of the two figures with an evident pair of wide-spreading wings. *N.b.* the transfer of the wings to Deity himself, Ps. 17^8, and see Gunkel at length, *ad loc*. The present scene retains the natural simplicity of the Deity riding on the wings of the wind. And indeed too much stress may not be laid upon Mesopotamian art and etymology. The cherub was native to Phœnician religious language, as appears in Eze. 28^{14}, and the root of the word appears, as noted by Dhorme and Vincent, in the far-flung Ethiopic, in *mekrab*, ' sanctuary.'

VV.$^{28-30}$. An addition of extravagant details. The gilding of the cherubs would be in place at v.^{23}, the item depending upon the ' golden cherubs ' of Ex. 25^{18} ; the gilding of the floor is absurd. The figuration of the decoration of the house *inside and out* depends literally upon Eze. 41$^{17f.}$ in the details of cherubs and palm-trees ; the *flower-calyxes*, repeating v.^{18}, do not appear in the OGrr. For the decoration, recalling the

² Josephus arbitrarily reduces the height to 5 cubits.

winged genii who fertilize the palm-tree in Ashurnasirpal's temple at Nimrud, see Cook, p. 53, Cooke on Eze. 41¹⁷.

24. כנפיו bis : read כְּנָפוֹ with VSS ; the pl. was induced by regard of מצות as pl.—25. קצב : in this mng. again 7³⁷.—27. ויפרש : Grr., exc. N h i, as sing., by early error.—כנפי הכרבים : read with 𝔊 𝔊ᴸ כנפיהם ; the corruption caused by 2 Ch. 3¹³.—29. מסב a noun used as adv., vs. סביב of the old document, v.⁵ ; St. would correct to מסביב.—חמרת : a technical word used elsewhere only by Eze., Ch. ; for its unique vocalization, a diminutive form, see GB.— מְלִפְנִים : with odd vocalization ; but לפנימה v.³⁰. Then., Burn., St. would correct to לְפָנָיו in correspondence with the parallel Eze. 41¹⁷.

VV.³¹⁻³⁵. The portals and doors of shrine and hall.

31. *And the doorway of the shrine : he made doors of oleaster wood, the portal [𝔐 +jambs] a pentagon.*

32. *and two doors of oleaster wood, and he carved upon them carvings of cherubs and palm-trees and lily-calyxes ; and he overlaid gold, and he plated the gold upon the cherubs and palm-trees.*

33. *And so he made for the doorway of the hall : jambs of oleaster wood [𝔐+obscure particle], a tetragon ;* 34. *and two doors of cypress wood, two leaves the one door, folding, and two leaves the second door, folding.*

35. *And he carved cherubs and palm-trees and lily-calyxes, and he overlaid with gold, applied to the graving.*

VV.³². ³⁵ are displayed above as literarily secondary (*cf.* Stade), for reasons similar to the criticism of vv.¹⁵⁻²² ; and yet the data have authentic colour. The particular artistic care for portal and doors is illustrated by Nebuchadnezzar's East India House inscription cited above (Comm., vv.¹⁵ff·) . " Door-leaves of cedar wood with copper overlay, thresholds and hinges of bronze in their doors I erected. Mighty bull-colossi of bronze and mighty serpent-forms I placed at their

entrance. These doors I furnished with beauty, for the
wonder of the hosts of people " (col. vi). Quite similar is
Nabonidus's enthusiastic description of the doors in the restored temple of Marduk, concluding with the boast that he
" made them bright as the day " (Messerschmidt, *MVÄG* 1896,
no. 1, col. viii, 31 ff.). Similar artistic care was applied by the
Egyptians to doorways of temples, tombs, etc., with reliefs
heightened by brilliant colours, and also with metal inlay ;
see O. Königsberger, *Die Konstruktion der ägyptischen Tür*
(*Ägyptologische Forschungen*, Heft 2, 1936, with 15 plates).
For the end of v.[31] more particular reference should be made
to the Notes. The word translated *portal* is ignored in the
VSS, exc. 𝕮, and appears at Eze. 40[9], etc., with mng. ' jambs,'
and hence the gloss-insertion of this word here (*cf.* Burney).
For the difficulties *cf.* the several English translations. The
pentagonal doorway, *i.e.*, with a peaked roof, is illustrated on
a coin of Byblos (A.D. 217), presenting such a temple doorway
(Contenau, *La civilization phénicienne*, 86 ; *cf.* p. 108 ; Cook,
Rel. of Anc. Palestine, pl. xxxiii). **32.** The statement of the
heavy gilding of the doors here and v.[35] is corroborated for a
later age by II. 18[16], detailing how in addition to his heavy
tribute " Hezekiah cut off the doors of the temple of Yhwh
and the door-posts which H. king of Judah had overlaid, and
gave them to the king of Assyria," *i.e.*, these of value for the
gold-overlay. **33.** For the four-square vestibule *cf.* the ceramic
model of a Cyprian temple presented by Contenau, p. 87.
34. For the folding two-leaved doors within the large doors,
inserted for convenience of ordinary entrance, the like in
Christian architecture may be compared. Esarhaddon boasts
more than once of ' door-leaves of cypress ' (cited above,
Comm., vv.[15ff.]). For the heavy doors and inevitable stone
door-sockets in Mesopotamian architecture, see Andrae, *Das
Gotteshaus*, pp. 32, 36. **35.** The last two terms in the v. are
technical ; as Šanda remarks, the gold was applied only to
the incised lines.

36. The construction of the wall of the temple court. *And
he built the inner court : three courses of hewn stone to* [=𝕳
and] *a course of beams of cedars*. This was the area in front
of the temple, enclosing the sacred stone and the great altar,
the place of convocation for the people (ch. 8). ' The other

court' (7⁸) contained Solomon's palaces, and 'the great court' (7⁹, ¹²) would have included those courts and a more extensive area. For the proposed plans see the literature cited above in introduction to the ch. Interpretation of the specifications, repeated for the great court (7¹²) has greatly varied; see Castel in Walton's *Apparatus*, Thenius, Šanda, *et al.* The most apparent sense is that of three layers of stone, capped by a layer of wood, but to what purpose this covering? Or, it has been suggested, occasional upright palisades between the stones, or rows of stones with an inner facing of wood (so Šanda). But the construction is similar to that expressed for the building of the second temple, 'with three courses of great stone and a row of new timber' (Ezra 6⁴), in which the timber was used for alignment of the courses. Such construction is corroborated by the discovery of layers of wood between the stone-courses in the city wall of Senjirli, and of wood with brick layers above (Watz., *DP* 1, 97, 99). According to personal communication from E. A. Speiser such construction was common at Ashur, Tell Billah, Tepe Gawra. The height of the wall is not herewith presented.[1]

37. 38. These vv., here in their original place, have been treated, for convenience, at the beginning of the ch. For the annalistic dating of completion of a temple *cf.* the item in the Ass. Eponym List for 787 B.C., when "Nabu entered the new house," the rebuilding of the house having been recorded for the preceding year (*KB* 1, 211; *ARA* 2, 434).

31. ואת פתח הדביר : acc. *ad sensum*; see GK §117, m, and for the corresponding extensive Arabic use Wright's *Grammar*, 2, §35.— עצי שמן (v.³³) ... האיל : 𝔊 (B a₂) ℭ om. by parablepsis due to foll. identical phrase.—האיל מזוזות : the Grr. ignore the first noun, which 𝔗 read as אלהן, 'but.' 𝔏 'iuniperi et limina,' 𝔙 'postesque angulorum.' For איל in Eze. see Cooke on 40⁹, etc., the text confusing it with אולם. But etymologically the word is of the same origin, and means 'projection,' and so it may mean the upper lintel, gable, with Kimchi (so the Aram. mng. acc. to Buxtorf, Jastrow), and

---

[1] The explanation given above of the wood as bonding to the stone courses is supported by Barrois in his *Manuel*, p. 14. See now for the whole problem S. Smith, 'Timber and Brick or Masonry Construction,' with Add. Note by C. F. A. Schaeffer, *PEQ* 1941, 5 ff. Smith, with extensive criticism of Ezra 6⁴, denies for the present passage the bonding with wood, regarding the latter as only 'surface ornament' (p. 14).

then, supplying conj. and article with the foll. noun = 'the lintel and the jambs pentagonal'; but it is preferable, with Burn., to regard the asyndetic 'jambs' as a gloss, and to understand our noun as the projecting framework, porch, of the doorway. The word may have been added in order to picture the side-posts.— חֲמִשִׁית : parallel to רְבִעִית, v.³³; in the latter case 𝔊, rendering with στοαὶ τετραπλῶς, read the numeral adverbially as in 𝔙, and so supports the latter, vs. Šanda's correction to adjectives, רְבֻעוֹת, חֲמֻשׁוֹת. St. remains uncertain. The adv. means 'pentagon-wise'; for similar adverbial use of such forms see GK §100, 3.—מְזוּזוֹת : for Akk. origin see Schwally, ZDMG 52, 134.—**32.** N.b. late syntax of וְקֶלַע, וּגְפָה, and so at v.³⁵.—עֲלֵיהֶם : for the irregular masc. suffix is to be noted the study by M. G. Slonim, ' The Substitution of the Masc. for the Fem. Heb. Pronominal Suffixes to Express Reverence,' *JQR* 29 (1939), 397 ff., and so here of a holy thing; he notes in Ki. also 7²⁸·³⁰·³¹, II. 16¹⁷, 18¹⁶. For this irregularity see further Note to 9¹³.—וַיִּרֶד : from root רדד, ' to spread,' used in the Targum as equivalent to Heb. רקע (Burn.).—**33.** מֵאֵת רְבִעִית : since Then. there has been generally accepted the emendation to מְזוּזוֹת רְבֻעוֹת on basis of the Grr., but the corruptions were hardly possible; it is best to cancel מֵאֵת, and to regard 'ר as parallel to חֲמִשִׁית above.—**34.** קְלָעִים : a misspelling for צְלָעִים (so Ken. 150, and as all translations understand), under O.Aram. influence, where original ḍ appears as ḳ.—**36.** Grr. *ad finem* plus κυκλόθεν (which St. adopts in the text with סָבִיב), and a long addition.—**38.** See above after v.¹.

Ch. 7¹⁻¹². Solomon's palaces. *Cf. Ant.*, viii, 5, 2. OGrr. transferred this description of secular constructions to the end of the ch., while Jos. further defers it, after the history of ch. 8, for still more pronounced distinction. See the classic studies by Stade in *ZAW* 3=*Akad. Reden*, 159 ff., *GVI* 1, 318 ff., with architectural plans, which have been reproduced at large in subsequent publications; the Archæologies of Nowack (1, 255 ff.) and Benzinger (pp. 211 ff.), and the latter's art., ' Palace ' in *EB* (these with earlier bibliography); Th. Friedrich, *Tempel u. Palast Salomos*, 1887; G. Richter, ' Der salomonische Königspalast,' *ZDPV* 1917, 171–225, with two plates, offering original reconstructions (criticized by Watzinger as " eine architektonische unmögliche Wiederherstellung "); C. Van Gelderen, ' Der salomonische Palastbau,' *AfO* 6 (1930–31), 100 ff., with text-critical study; and in particular, as from a technical expert, Watzinger, *DP* 1, 95 ff.

1. *And Solomon, having built his house for thirteen years, finished all his house :* so more exactly after the Hebrew syntax

than in the usual translations. The word 'house' is used
of the complex of buildings. In 9^{10} the present '13' and
the '7' of 6^{38} are editorially summed up as 'twenty years,'
as though the building of the king's house was subsequent to
that of YHWH's house. V.[b] is transferred by OGrr. to the end
of the specifications, after the Greek sense of better order.
The position of the v. appears to be secondary; note its
syntactical dependence in the Heb. upon 6^{38}. As Van Gelderen
remarks, Solomon's completion of the whole operation is exceptional
in ancient history. For parallels to such a palace-complex
cf. the explorations at Senjirli (*Ausgrabungen in
Sendschirli*, vol. 4, plates xlix, 1); at Samaria (Reisner,
Excavations at Samaria, vol. 2, plate 5); and the recent uncovering
of the far earlier, more extensive and beautifully
decorated palace at Mari on the upper Euphrates; see A.
Parrot, *Syria*, 1937, 54 ff.; 1938, 8 ff.; 1939, 14 ff., all articles
with numerous plates and photographs (*cf. ILN*, May 28, 1938).
Parrot reports that he has uncovered some 220 rooms and
courts of a building extending over more than five acres.
The stress laid here upon windows and doors reveals the
novel *ḥilāni* architecture of Syria, for which are to be compared
the palaces at Senjirli (see von Luschan). For the
Mesopotamian field brief reference may be made to the lengthy
and glowing inscriptions celebrating the palace-construction
of many monarchs; *e.g.*, Tiglath-pileser III, with his reference
to his 'palace of cedar . . . patterned after a Hittite (*i.e.*,
Syrian) palace,' such artistry being boasted of by subsequent
monarchs (*ARA* 1, no. 804); Sargon (*ARA* 2, nos. 83 ff., 121,
referring to palaces of ivory, marble, etc., and no. 138, of a
palace used as a treasure-house); Sennacherib (*ARA* 2, *in
extenso*, *e.g.*, nos. 382-94, 407-33, *n.b.* no. 429, according to
which the palace is both an armoury and a store-house for
booty); *cf.* Olmstead, *HA* 318 ff., with map of the palace
complex.

For the archival character of the following document is to
be noted the series of items without immediate verbal government
(supplied in EVV), *viz.* ' and the porch of pillars ' (v.[6]—
the following verb 'he made' is secondary, as also in v.[7]),
'and the porch of the throne' (v.[7]), 'and his house where he
was to dwell' (v.[8a]), 'and a house for Pharaoh's daughter'

(v.⁸ᵇ—om. with 𝕲 the impossible Heb., ' he will make '), and also the following purely nominal statements. *Cf.* the syntax in vv.¹⁵⁻²⁰.

2. *And he built the House of the Lebanon Forest :* 100 *cubits its length, and* 50 *cubits its width, and* 30 *cubits its height* (storied), *upon four* [Grr. *three*] *rows of pillars of cedars, and beams* [Grr. *capitals*] *of cedars upon the pillars ;* **3.** *and roofed with cedar above, over the side-chambers that were upon the pillars—forty-five, fifteen to a row ;* **4.** *and embrasured windows, three rows, and looking towards each other* [Heb.=*vis-à-vis*] *in triplicate ;* **5.** *and all the doorways, and the jambs squared—* [*embrasure*?] *and opposite, looking towards each other in triplicate ;* **6.** *and the portico of pillars* [𝔅+*he made*], 50 *cubits its width* [Heb. *length*] *and* 30 *cubits its depth* [Heb. *breadth*], ⌜*and a portico in front of them*⌝ [?], *and pillars, and a cornice above them ;* **7.** *and the portico of the throne where he was to judge, the Portico of Justice* [𝔅+*he made ;* OGrr. om.], *and panelled with cedar from floor to floor ;* **8.** *and his own house, where he was to dwell—the second court—within the portico, after the same fashion ; and the house* [𝔅+*he was going to make ;* OGrr. om.] *for Pharaoh's daughter* [*whom Solomon married*—a gloss] *like this portico ;* **9.** *all these* (of) *cut* [EVV *costly*] *stones,* ⌜*according to hewing specifications*⌝ [OGrr. om.], *sawn with a saw on the inside and outside faces, and* (disposed) *from foundation to* ⌜*the eaves*⌝ [?], ⌜*and outside unto the great court*⌝ [?] *;* **10.** *and founded with cut* [EVV *costly*] *stones, great stones, stones of ten and eight cubits* (in length) *;* **11.** *and above stones hewn according to hewing specifications, and cedar ;* **12.** *and the great court round about, three courses of hewn stone, and a course of timbers of cedars,* ⌜*and for the inner court of the House of* YHWH, *and for the portico of the house*⌝ [?].

2-7. The House of the Lebanon Forest. The æsthetic name was taken from its cedar construction. 𝕋 makes it ' a house of cooling ' (*cf.* Jud. 3²⁰), and this interpretation was developed by Kimchi into a summer palace in Mount Lebanon. The purpose of the building and its relation to the subsequent items has long been a matter of dispute ; to summarize Watzinger's statement : The record of these buildings is so abbreviated and contradictory that all attempts at a plausible reconstruction are wrecked, and it is evident that the tradition preserved memoranda only of notable elements. Interpretation of the specifications depend critically upon text (*e.g.*, 'four,' v.²), and interpretation (*e.g.*, the word, v.³, translated 'beams' in EVV, 'side-chambers' in JV), and syntactical reference (*e.g.*, 'forty-five,' v.³). Josephus held that the building was a great hall of justice, and Šanda follows suit, obtaining by the translation 'architraves' in place of 'side-chambers' a building of "imposante Grossartigkeit," comparable with the Roman basilica or the mosque at Cordova. But the subsequent reff. to this building by name indicate that it was a royal store-house; at 10^{17} we read of the 300 shields of gold placed in this house, evidently for decoration, while Is. 22^8 definitely refers to 'the armour in the House of the Forest,' kept there for military purposes, and this interpretation appears here in 𝔄, 'a house for his weapons.' That such was the objective is now generally accepted, and it is supported and brilliantly illustrated by Watzinger (p. 96) from the description of a plan by the Greek architect Philon (*ca.* 350 B.C.) for a magazine at Athens, as reproduced by Dörpfeld; this building was a vast, long, three-naved hall, supported by Ionic columns in two rows; the lower space was an open chamber, in the upper story the side naves on the breadth (short sides) of the house were formed in two-story store-rooms, while in the upper part of the ends of the long sides were windows opposite windows for lighting the interior. Watzinger properly insists upon the close relationship of Solomon's and Philon's plans. For the three-nave construction of megara in the ancient Levant see H. Thiersch, 'Ein altmediterraner Tempeltyp,' *ZAW* 1932, 73 ff., with accompanying plates. The present writer presents below his own reconstruction of the vague description, with preference for many a question-mark in lieu of text-correction. It is to be remarked that the description comes from a spectator of the visible interior.

The dimensions of the interior, 100×50 cubits, follow the common proportions of the ancient megaron, etc. (*cf.* Watzinger, p. 90). Four rows of cedar pillars appear, the first and the fourth of which rows must have been set as pilasters against the walls, affording three aisles, while all the upper wooden construction was based upon the several two pairs of the four rows of columns. Above each of the two pairs of columns in their long parallelism were built-in rooms in stories, leaving a lofty nave, which afforded a view of the cedar roof stretching over the width of the building. The terminal walls at the ends of each of the three aisles were pierced with doors (*in triplicate*), and above with three superimposed windows. With this specification of storied windows it appears that the built-in stories did not extend to the terminal walls, and at these open ends may well have stood the staircases to the upper stories, while the open spaces afforded light.

2. The specification of *four rows of pillars* has been generally corrected by comm. (Stade, *et al.*, not by Richter, Van Gelderen, Watzinger) to ' three rows ' with Grr., in view of the equal division of the assumed *forty-five pillars, fifteen to a row*, v.^{3}. But the three last-named authorities assign the *forty-five* to the number of chambers in the stories, and this interpretation is the most reasonable in the syntax of the v., although the assignment of the number of chambers appears unimportant, and the odd numbers 45 and 15 raise a question as to the division of the chambers on the two sides ; the only explanation is that the observation has to do with one side of the nave, on which side there were three stories each with fifteen rooms, and this would provide closets of close to ten feet in width. For this and the foll. vv. see the Notes at length. The word *beams* appeared at 6^{36} ; comm., following the Grr., largely correct it to ' capitals,' with which *cf.* 𝕮 and Jos., who amusingly find in it a transcription from a Greek word. **3.** *Side-chambers :* so at 6^5, but at 6^{15} used of cedar boards ; *cf.* EVV. **4.** The initial adjective ' embrasured ' appeared at 6^4. **5.** For the opening words a simplification may be proposed : *and all the doorways squared, embrasured and opposite*, etc. ; *cf.* Note. The sum of the statement is that the three doors at the opposite ends faced one another ; the addition of ' windows ' with commentators, after the Grr., would only repeat v.^{4}. **6.** The v. evidently describes the pillared portico in front of this house, its width of 50 cubits agreeing with that of the house. V.^{6b} appears to present a pillared vestibule in front of that great portico, and so 𝔓 paraphrases : ' another portico in front of that greater portico ' ; but the description as a whole is unintelligible. Kittel om. translation of v.^{b},

Sanda om. as secondary, 'and a portico in front of them and the pillars,' and indeed the repetition of the identical Heb. phrase, which must be translated variously as *in front of them* and *upon them*, looks like a dittograph. Van Gelderen translates at end : ' and to wit (und zwar) pillars with a roof over them '—he holds that these rows of columns are a continuation of those in the interior. Klostermann by a change of vocalization of העמודים 1° changes ' the pillars ' into ' the courtiers,' making the building a reception hall—to be noted as a clever suggestion. **7.** After the evidently frontal *portico* of v.[6] the word here must have another significance, probably that of the Gate, the Porte, *i.e.*, of justice, as in common Oriental language, and so expressed in the following exact term, *the Portico of Justice*. This chamber was distinct, wholly panelled with cedar and roofed ; its position in the House of the Lebanon Forest may have lain at the other end of the building from the front portico, and the clients of royal justice had then to pass through the length of the imposing portico and great hall. Šanda regards the portico and this audience chamber as a distinct building. For the magnificent throne this chamber was to house see $10^{18ff.}$. **8.** The private palaces, the Harem in the Arabic language, of which as a matter of taste little might be said, are listed. They lie in a separate enclosure, *the second court*, as distinguished from the royal public buildings (v.[12]).

Ch. 9^{24} records the queen's entrance into her palace.

9-10. The actual material of these buildings—all of stone (as for the temple, *cf.* $5^{31f.}$), hewn according to given measurements, with the upper blocks above the basement cut so as to expose a smooth surface on the outside and inside walls, the foundation stones being particularly specified as to their dimensions ; the timbering was of cedar. The present register is well illustrated by the excellent summary review of the remains of stone construction at Samaria given by Watzinger, vol. 1, pp. 98 ff., based upon the Harvard excavations. **9.** As against the usual translation ' costly stones ' see Note, 5^{31}. The final phrase is unintelligible ; with correction of text Stade would read, ' and from the house of YHWH to the great court ' ; Burney, ' and from the court of the house,' etc. ; Šanda, ' and from the second court to the great court ' ;

Richter and Van Gelderen, 'and indeed from the street to the great court,' conjecturing apparently a long view of the palaces up through the great court. **12.** V.[a] repeats the specifications for the walls of the inner court, that of the temple (6[36]); for these courts see Comm. there. V.[12b] is absent in OGrr.; no sense can be made of the unconstruable words; *cf.* the makeshifts in EVV. The topography is so uncertain that *the house*, while generally identified with the temple, is claimed to be the palace by Burney, Richter, Van Gelderen.

2. 'and 30 cubits its height': 𝔊 𝔊[L] om., 𝔖[H] ※, but Jos. has.— על: 𝔊 καὶ, by early scribal error.—ארבעה: Grr. as 'three,' influenced by the numerals below, largely accepted by critics, *e.g.*, St., *BH*; but Jos.=𝔐, making of the phrase 'quadrangular pillars' (!).—כרתות: Grr., ὠμίαι, 'shoulder-pieces'=כתפות, as at vv.[30, 34]; 𝔗 קרונתיהון 'their Corinthian capitals,' paralleled by Jos.'s remark that the roof was 'according to Corinthian style,' *i.e.*, he knew Targumic tradition; 𝔖 כרכתא, used at vv.[16f.] for כתפות, 'capitals'; St., Kit., *al.* correct, after the Gr., to כתפות as struts for support of the roof-beams; Šanda prefers כתרות, 'crowns,' as presenting the *finesse* of the art. But 𝔐 (and so 𝔙, 'ligna exciderat'), as at 6[36], suffices.—**3.** צלעת: 'stories,' as at 6[5]; at 6[15] 'beams,' hence Šanda here, 'architraves.'—**4.** שקפים: *cf.* 6[4]; Grr. here μέλαθρα, *vs.* the translation there.—מחזה אל מחזה literally, 'look to look'; Grr., χώρα ἐπὶ χώραν, as though Aram. קְהוֹא.— **5.** וכל הפתחים והמזוזות רבעים שקף ומול מחזה אל מחזה: the tr. above represents the text, which is authenticated word for word by the Grr., along with wild perversions of reading and rendering. The second noun appears unnecessary; the phrase might be understood as 'the doors with the jambs.' שקף is grammatically obscure; Eissf. ingeniously, 'in Durchblick,' *cft.* Hif. of the verb. It may be a scribe's gloss to bring in the item of שקפים from v.[4]. Kit., like 𝔖, om. translation. מול, unique as adv., may have been introduced to explain the foll. phrase; or that phrase may be conversely secondary. The Grr. read 'והם as והמחזות (αἱ χῶραι, as above); ומול as ומן; and for 'מח אל מח' θυρώματος/θύρας ἐπὶ θύραν, *i.e.*, as though='פתח אל פ. The first of these rdgs., with מחזות= 'windows' (the assumed noun unique), and the third have been approved by comm., *e.g.*, Burn., St., Eissf.; but such correction would repeat the *vis-à-vis* position of the windows in v.[4].—**6.** אולם: Grr., τὸ αιλαμ, and so *infra*; see Note 6[3].—שלשים: 𝔊 ℭ 'fifty.'— רחבו: Grr.+ἐξυγωμένα, which Klost. and Richter have attempted to explain.—עב: also Eze. 41[25]; Cooke's suggestion 'cornice,' has been adopted above. Gr. πάχος is etymological.—**7.** . . . עשה הקרקע: 𝔊 𝔊[L] om.—קרקע [עד]: Jer. Talmud הקירות, as at 6[15], and so here 𝔖; the change, as הקורות, is accepted here by Then., St.,

BH., not by Šanda, al. The phrase is technical, EVV correctly, 'from floor to floor ' = ' from bottom to top.'—**8**. חצר האחרת : for the noun, its etymology and gender, see the full discussion by Orlinsky, *AJSL* 1939, 22 ff. ; for the article confined to the adj. see GK §126, 5, with sequence by Dr., *Tenses*, §209 ; similar cases below, v.¹², II. 20⁴ Ḳr. The Grr. read the adj. as מבית האחת.—מבית לאולם : *n.b.* the compound prep. after Aram. usage ; Grr., ἐξελισσομένη (?) τουτοις, *i.e.* ‪ = ‬לאלה.—יעשה : 𝔊 𝔊ᴸ om. ; the gloss from a punctilious scribe, who would date the event where it belonged ; *cf.* 9²⁴.—**9**. ומחוץ 1⁰ : 𝔊 𝔊ᴸ om.—המפתחות : the only light on this technical word comes from Gr. γεῖσαι, ' eaves.'

VV.¹³⁻⁴⁷. The bronze work for the temple. *Cf.* 2 Ch. 2¹³, 3¹⁵–4¹⁸ ; *Ant.*, viii, 3, 4–7. The Chronicler makes Hiram master of all the arts, and indirectly at least the artist of the gold and silver vessels. This section, plus vv.⁴⁸⁻⁵¹, is prefixed in OGrr. to vv.¹⁻¹² with the pious purpose of placing the sacred before the profane. Hex. (A x) has it in place ; it is missing in the leaves of 𝔖ᴴ.

13. 14. Introduction of Hiram of Tyre. For the introduction of foreign artists *cf.* the statement by the Hittite king Kuranta of Tarḫuntaš of his fetching an Egyptian artist to build his palace (Winckler, *MVG* 18, 4 (1913), 15 ; *cf.* Meissner, *Bab. u. Ass.*, 1, 228 ff.), and Sennacherib's reference to his 'palace patterned after a Hittite (Syrian) palace' (cited above). For named Egyptian architects, father and son, at Beth-shean see Albright, *From the Stone Age*, 159. The international interest in art is now well illustrated by an Akk. tablet found at Mari on the upper Euphrates, a letter from Hammurabi to Zimrilu, king of that city, stating that the prince of Ugarit desires a description of the palace of Zimrilu and wishes to see it (A. Parrot, *Syria*, 1937, 74). Solomon's great supply of bronze is corroborated by N. Glueck's discoveries and excavations in Edom on the shores of the Red Sea ; see the comment at length on Eṣyon-geber, 9²⁶. The foundry-work is detailed below, v.⁴⁶. For the Egyptian imports of ' Asiatic copper ' from the land of Retenu see W. M. Müller, *Asien u. Europa*, 33, 126. Sennacherib reports the making of large bull-colossi of bronze (*ARA* 2, nos. 392, 412 f.). His statement, in the first passage, of enclosing pillars of cedars ' in a sheathing of bronze ' is now illustrated by Parrot's report (*ILN*, May 26, 1938, p. 952) of his discovery at Mari of "two bronze lions . . . actually made of wood, over which a thin bronze leaf had been passed." For ancient bronze work see P. Thomsen, ' Bronzeguss,' *RVg* ; for study and illustration of the brass work here described Stade, *GVI* I, 330 ff. ; Nowack, *Arch.*, §§76, 77 ; Benzinger, *Arch.*, §44 ; also the literature cited above in introduction to the ch., and current references below.

Solomon retains the services of Hiram *of Tyre, a worker in bronze, son of a widow of the tribe of Naphtali, and his father a man of Tyre. . . . He came . . . and did all his* (Solomon's) *work.* His manifold talents are expressed in the words generally translated as *wisdom, understanding, knowledge* ; similar words are used for the endowment of the Messiah in Is. 11^2 ; they might be translated here with *artistry, intelligence, skill.*

15-22. The two bronze pillars. For the text, along with the abbreviated parallel, 2 Ch. 3$^{15-17}$, we have the recapitulation of the brass work, Jer. 52$^{18-23}$, which again is briefly summarized in II. 25$^{16, 17}$, with another varying summary below, vv.$^{41, 42}$. For criticism of the text see Thenius, Stade (remarking, *Akad. Reden*, 162, that the whole section on the brass work " gehört zu den am schlimmsten überlieferten des a.t. Textes "), Šanda. In the following presentation of the text bracketed portions are secondary. Footnote references immediately follow.

15. *And he ⌜cast⌝ [1] the two pillars* (of) *bronze* [2] *18 cubits the height of the one pillar, with a tape of 12 cubits ⌜encircling it, and its thickness* (of the bronze) *4 fingers, hollow⌝ [3] ;* **16.** *and two capitals* [*he made*] [4] *to put upon the top of the pillars, cast in bronze ; 5 cubits the height of the one capital, and 5 cubits the height of the second capital ;* **17.** *checker-works* [5] [*checker-make, festoons, chain-work*] [6] *⌜for the capitals⌝* [7] *on top of the pillars,*

Jer. ch. 52. **21.** *And the pillars 18* [13] *cubits the height of the one pillar, with a tape of 12 cubits encircling it, and its thickness 4 fingers, hollow ;* **22.** *and a capital upon it, bronze, and the height of the one capital 5* [14] *cubits ;*

⌜a checker-work⌝ [𝔥 seven] [8] for the one capital, and a checker-work [𝔥 seven] for the second capital ; **18.** [and he made the pillars] [9] and two rows ⌜of pomegranates of bronze⌝ [10] round about upon the one checker-work [to cover the capitals on top of the pomegranates] [11] ; and so [he made] [4] for the second capital ; **20**b. ; and the pomegranates 200 in rows round about upon ⌜the one⌝ [𝔥 second] [12] pillar.

and pomegranates upon the capital round about, the whole bronze ; and like this for the second pillar ; [and pomegranates] [15]. **23.** and the pomegranates were 96, ⌜pendant⌝,[16] all the pomegranates 100, upon the checker-work round about.

[1] ויצר : corrected by St., *BH, al.* to ויצק (*cf.* v.[46]) ; but see Comm., II. 12[11] for use of the verb in sense of ' minting.' [2] Grr. +τω αιλαμ του οικου (B a₂ το for τω), a gloss from v.[21] ; see *SBOT*. [3] The text of Jer. accepted : ויבינו ארבע אצבעות נבוב ויסבנו = 𝔊 𝔊ᴸ. [4] Otiose in this originally verbless list, and so in v.[18]. [5] Grr., ' and he made two checker-works.' [6] Grr. om. this supernumerary passage, except for Lucian's plus at end of the v., μεγαλα, *i.e.*, rdg. גְּדֹלִים. For the chain-work see 2 Ch. 3[16]. [7] ' For the capitals ' is emended by the Grr., for the sake of precision to ' to cover the capitals,' as in the insertion in v.[18] ; the addition is generally accepted. [8] Read שְׂבָכָה with Grr. ; *cf.* Jer., *vs.* שבעה. [9] Grr. om. the superfluous statement ; on basis of two Heb. MSS some critics (*e.g.*, Burn., St., *BH*) would read הרמנים for העמדים. [10] For מורים Grr. a plus = רמני נחשת (*cf.* v.[42]), which gives the expected detail. [11] Grr. om. ; variant duplicate of v.[17] ; for הרמנים read העמודים, with some 50 MSS Ken., deR. = 𝔖 𝔄. [12] For השנית is read האחת with St. ; Benz., Burn. propose a lacuna to be filled out from v.[17] ; or possibly there was originally no numeral. [13] ' 18 (cubits) ' : 2 Ch. 3[15], ' 35.' [14] ' 5 (cubits) ' : II. 25[17], ' 3.' [15] ורמנים : an evident doublet ; II. 25[17], על השבכה. [16] רוחה : the unique adv. of direction has been variously understood, but 𝔙, ' pendentibus,' ' hanging ' (*cf.* German ' luftwärts ') gives the mng. (see Cornill, *ad loc.*, citing Rashi) ; four of the nodules of the loop were attached to the column, the remainder hanging free. Jer.'s figure ' 100 ' refers to the single loop.

19. 20a. **22.** These sections are additions to the presentation above, with some fresh items, but repetitive, along with a unique Hebrew word. OGrr rearranged in the order vv.[21. 19. 20a], omitting vv.[20b. 22] (MS v has v.[22b]). **19.** *And capitals that were on top of the two pillars, lily-work, in the portico, 4 cubits.* **20**a. *And capitals upon the two pillars, even above,* *close to the globe-top* [Heb. *belly*] *that was opposite to the checker-work.* **22.** *And upon top of the pillars lily-work. And the business of the pillars was finished.*

Authentic items are given with the *lily-work, four cubits* (high), and the technical word *belly*, doubtless identical with the word translated *bowl*, vv.⁴¹·⁴². *In the portico*, v.¹⁹, may be gloss from v.²¹. The word translated *close to* (v.²⁰) is a novel preposition; the Grr. read or guessed at the impossible 'chambers' (*cf.* 6⁵). V.²²ᵇ was suggested by v.⁴⁰ᵇ.

41. 42. This summary account from below is presented here for convenience of comparison. **41.** *Two pillars, and the bowls of the capitals that were on top of the pillars, two, and the checker-works, two, to cover the two bowls of the capitals that were on top of the pillars ;* **42.** *and the pomegranates,* 400, *for the two checker-works, two rows of pomegranates to the one checker-work, to cover the two bowls of the capitals that were upon the pillars.*

For the last prep. 'upon,' 𝔐 על פני, 𝔊 = על שני; 11 MSS על ראש (*cf.* v.⁴¹) = 𝔖 𝔙. The passage presents a fresh technical term, גֻּלָּה, 'bowls,' used evidently for a structure of bowl shape, and corresponding to Heb. 'belly,' v.²⁰. Also the figure for the whole sum of pomegranates is given.

21. *And he erected the pillars for the portico of the hall ; and he erected the right-hand pillar, and called its name Jachin ; and he erected the left-hand pillar, and called its name Boaz.* For v.²² see above.

For the name Yākîn, 'he (deity not named) establishes' see Albright, *JBL* 1924, 375, with the more pregnant translation, 'he creates.' For the verbal element *cf.* the later royal name Yehoiakin, and it is frequent in Phœn. names, compounded with a divine subject (Harris, *Gram.*, 110—citing also a *n. pr., ykn.*). *Cf.* the S. Arab. name of a gate at Obne, *ykn*, 'it (he ?) stands (is ?),' Ryckmans, *NPS* 1, 344. For the second name as Baʻal-ʻaz, 'Baal is strong,' the writer refers to his Note in *JQR* 25 (1935), 265. Ugaritic *bʻl ʻz* appears in a thrice-repeated acclamation, 'Baal is strong!', in Virolleaud's first long text (*Syria*, 12, 220, col. vi, lines 17–20 = *MTRS* 56 ; C. H. Gordon, *Ugar. Hdbk.*, 2, Text 49: vi: 17–20). Also, as has not been otherwise observed, there was a true Gr. tradition of this etymology; MS h (55) here has Βοολας, in which the οο represents a Palm. vocalization (Lidzb., *HNE* 234) ; for other diminutives of the divine name with loss of the *l* in Phœn., see *ib.*, p. 239, and Harris, p. 24. But nearer home is the name of Solomon's ancestor, Boʻaz = Baʻal-ʻaz. For the most recent discussion with review of the many various interpretations see R. B. Y. Scott, 'The Pillars Jachin and Boaz,' *JBL* 1939, 143 ff. But he finds in the name a kind of cryptogram for " In the strength of YHWH shall the king rejoice "; and with this Albright agrees, *SAC* 139. However, in Solomon's day 'Baal' was not a taboo word, and in any case the Phœnician artist had the right to name his own creations. There are to be added supplementarily to the literature the full archæological treatment of the subject by Albright in his art., ' Two Cressets from Marisa and the Pillars of Jachin and Boaz,' *BASOR* 85 (1942), 18 ff., and the article by H. G. May, ' The Two Pillars before the Temple of Solomon,' *ib.* no. 88, 19 ff.

Apart from the indifferent testimony of Ch. we thus have three notices of the pillars, each contributing independent information. The single pillar was 18 cubits high, with a circumference of 5 cubits, and so with diameter of 1.58 cubits. It possessed a capital 5 cubits high, which bellied, rounded out (to use the Hebrew terms), forming a bowl-shaped top, and was covered with a checker-work pattern, along with an ornamentation of leaves of the lily (*i.e.*, a species like the iris, flag, etc.), the long, narrow leaves being given a height of 4 cubits. From the capital were suspended two strings of technical pomegranates, each string being strung with a hundred of them, four being attached at the several quarters, leaving ninety-six in suspension. The lily-work (similar to the use of the lotus in Egyptian architecture) for capitals is illustrated in a coin of Byblos with superimposed series of lily-like leaves, the capital itself being one quarter the height of the whole length of the pillar (*ca.* A.D. 218, in the British Museum, and figured in Perrot and Chipiez, *Histoire de l'art*, 3, cut 67; Gressmann, *ATB* 2, cut 522); *cf.* also the small clay ' dove-house,' from Cyprus, representing a temple with two robust pillars at the entrance, surmounted with large capitals (Perrot and Chipiez, cut 58; *cf.* Gressman, cut 523; Benzinger, *Arch.*, cut 424); in these cases they stand independent, like Jachin and Boaz. *Cf.* also the Hadhrumetum stone, presenting two pillars surmounted with female busts (Pietschmann, *Gesch. d. Phön.*, 219). A common type of Sidonian coinage presents the front of a temple with a tall independent pillar on either side. Also, according to Herodotus, ii, 44, the temple of Heracles at Tyre had " in it two pillars, one or refined gold [*cf.* the term at 6²¹], one of emerald." Lucian reports (*De Dea Syra*, 28) *phalli* at the entrance of the goddess's temple, ' 30 fathoms high ' (!). The origin of such an architectural feature may be found in the primitive *maṣṣēbôt*, pairs of which have been found at Ta'anach and Megiddo.¹ The relation of the lily-leaves to the capital has been a problem. Benzinger presents a design (Comm., p. 44, reproduced in Eissfeldt's Comm.) with the leaves surmounting the bowl, in which case the total height would be 18+5+4=27 cubits. But as one description speaks only of the capital with the lily-work, while the other identifies the capital with the flowers, it is rather evident that the bowl was nested in the foliate adornment, the latter projecting upwards about the bowl for 4 cubits, with the globe, 5 cubits high, appearing through the interstices of the leaves and above ; so Stade, *GVI* 1, 332, reproduced in Kittel's Comm.—although in disagreement with the design—and in Barton, *AB* fig. 247. The pendant loops are a unique item to archæological knowledge. For the extensive development of brass work in small figures, tools, and the like, see Contenau, *La civilization phénicienne*, 209 f. Finally a note of admiration must be struck for these several technical specifications, the earliest of the kind in history, and based upon exact knowledge, *e.g.*, the thickness of the bronze in the hollow pillars. The same quality distinguishes the subordinate two sets of specifications.

23-26. The bronze sea. **23.** *And he made the sea, cast work,* 10 *cubits* (across) *from brim to brim, all round about (i.e.,* circular), *and* 5 *cubits its height, with a measuring-line of* 30 *cubits encircling it about ;* **24.** *and gourds under its brim about, encircling it* [10 *cubits encircling the sea about*—an intrusion from v.²³] *; two rows the gourds, cast with its casting ;* **26.** *and its thickness a hand's breadth ; and its brim like the work of the rim of a cup, a lily flower (i.e.,* a lily-shaped brim) *; holding* 2000 *baths ;* **25.** *standing upon twelve oxen, three facing north, and three facing west, and three facing south, and three facing east, with the sea upon them above, and all their hinder parts inwards.*

¹ *E.g.*, Benzinger, cut 413. See for further examples Cook, *Rel. of Anc. Pal.*, 166 ff., and the extensive documentation in Scott's study. J. P. Peters suggested the existence of such a pair of pillars at Nippur (*Nippur*, 1897, 2, 47).

The transposition of vv.²⁵· ²⁶ follows the OGrr. and the general judgment of modern scholars, and is required for syntactical construction. But v.²⁶ gives an independent specification of the brim, inserted as a colophon. The description is clear and picturesque. In the matter of circumference to diameter, given as 3.0, the Grr. change the figures to $33 \div 10 = 3.3$, obtaining a value farther from actual 3.1416.[1] The capacity of the sea is given at 2000 baths. The bath has been variously estimated: by Nowack, Benzinger at 36.44 litres, with the total for the sea$=72,880$ litres. This figure has now been greatly increased by C. H. Inge, in *PEQ* 1941, 106 ff.; among three ancient jars from Lachish, one, too fragmentary for reconstruction, was marked with *bt lmlk*, 'a bath of the king'; another, with a private seal; a third, with *lmlk*, 'the king's,' *i.e.*, standard measure. Concerning the latter two, he holds that the former would have held some 46 litres, the latter 45. For the subject at large are to be noted the discussions by Nowack (*Arch.*, I, 206) and Šanda, who hold that too little is known of the form of the vessel to estimate its capacity.[2] The Chronicler, as often, expands the figure to 3000 baths, followed by Josephus. The purpose of this great reservoir was primarily for ablutions, and so Ch. adds the note that "the sea was for the priests to wash in." There was the Rabbinic rule for bare feet in the temple courts, which would have required their washing (Dalman, *A. u. S.*, 5, 152, 296). The sea was doubtless the source of supply for the lavers described below. Artificial pools of water were constant in ancient temples, and with like technical name as here. 'Seas' were built in Babylonian temples (Jeremias, *ATLAO* 494 f., *cf.* Šanda, and Albright, *JAOS* 1920, 316 f.). Close to the temple of the Dea Syra was a great sacred lake (Lucian, §45). And such basins,

[1] T. Dantzig, in his *Numbers, the Language of Science* (1930), 113, comments on the Hebrew proportion here as " 5% short of the actual. The Egyptians made a closer estimate; we find in the papyrus Rhind (1700 B.C.) the value of π as equal to $3\frac{13}{80}$ . . . which is only $\frac{1}{5}$ of 1% in excess." But the figuration here in either Hebrew or Greek was a round figure.

[2] Mostly recently Albright, arguing from the same jars, contradicts the large figures of Inge and others, reducing the size of the bath to 22 litres (*AASOR* 21–2 [1943], 58, n. 7).

supplied with running water, at the entrance of temples are vouched for in S. Arab. inscriptions ; for a case see N. Rhodokanakis, *Sb.*, Vienna Academy, no. 177, pt. 2 (1915), 7. The source of water-supply for this reservoir is not stated ; Šanda is inclined to think that there already existed the conduit from the so-called Solomon's Pools ; but see Smith, *Jerusalem*, 1, ch. 5. The sea must have been filled by windlasses or otherwise from the underground cisterns, for which see Smith, *op. cit.*, 119 ff. Nowack (*Arch.*, 2, 44) cites Kosters, who notes the elimination of the sea in Eze., in which apocalypse it is replaced on its site by the spring of the temple (Eze. 47$^{1\text{ff.}}$). This great bronze laver was, as far as we know, indeed a unique masterpiece, with the artistry of the lily-like brim, decorated below with rows of gourds (*cf.* 6^{18}), all of one casting, and resting on twelve bulls of the same metal. For the essay at reproducing this work of art see Stade, *GVI* 1, 336, whose plan is repeated in the BDD, Commentaries and Archæologies in general. But a criticism is to be made of this now conventional design, which presents the great bowl as wholly supported upon the backs of the oxen—an extraordinary load for such figures. Rather the oxen were pediment figures, with their 'hinder parts' suppressed under the curve of the bowl, which latter rested on the ground. And such an artistic feature appears in von Oppenheim's plate 47, in his *Tell Halaf*, presenting the socket for an image with six lions underneath in like fashion.

23. ים : *cf.* S. Arab. *mbḥr* used of a pool (Conti Rossini, *Chrest.*, 112), and in the same region of South Arabia a reservoir is called a 'sea,' acc. to D. Van der Meulen and H. von Wissmann, *Ḥaḍramaut and Some of its Mysteries Unveiled* (Leiden, 1932), 94.—מוצק : 𝔊 𝔊^L 𝔈 om. ; Hex. χυτην (A αυτην).—סביב : B a$_2$ 𝔈 om.—קיה ; Ḳr. קו : the Kt. also appears elsewhere ; the word is synonymous with חוט, v.^{15}.—**24.** ביצקתו . . . שני : B a$_2$ om.—**25.** והים עליהם מלמעלה : Grr., exc. A x, transfer to end of v.—ביתה : 𝔊 𝔊^H εις τ. οικον, 𝔊^L correctly, εις το ενδον.

27-39. The wheeled stands and their lavers ; their location along with that of the sea. Ch. om., except for summary *in re* the lavers, and note of their use by the priests to wash in, along with statement as to position of the sea. Josephus has an elaborate varying description, probably prompted by his knowledge of similar vessels, *Ant.*, viii, 3, 6. For extensive studies see Klostermann, Stade (*ZAW* 3, 159 ff.=*Akad. Reden*, 166 ff.), Burney (with careful study of the text and language), Stade and Haupt in *SBOT*, Kittel in his *Studien*, pp. 189–242 (the most extensive of all the discussions). For reconstructions, and reproductions of the Cypriote vessels to be mentioned below, see Stade, *GVI* 1, 340 f. ; Burney, Kittel ; Nowack, *Arch.*, 2, 43 f. ; Gressmann, *ATB* vol. 1, pls. cciii, cciv ; Benzinger, *Arch.*, 44 f. ; Barton, *AB* pl. 87 ; also BDD, Commentaries.

For such wheeled vessels in temple use may be noted the low-lying bronze wagon found by von Oppenheim (*Tell Halaf*, 190, and pl. 58b) ; also incense wagons have been discovered at Tell-Khafāje in Babylonia, for which see Frankfort in *ILN*, June 8, 1934, pp. 910 ff. But it is two archaic vessels from Cyprus that particularly illustrate the creations of the Phœnician artist Hiram, both of bronze, the one from Enkome, with the wheels now lost, the other a rather well-preserved miniature vessel found in a grave at Larnaka. For primary publication of these relics see A. S. Murray, *Journal of Royal Inst. of British Architects*, 1899, pp. 20 ff. (cited by Burney), and at length, with comparison of the Solomonic objects, A. Furtwängler, in *Sb.* of the Munich Academy, vol. 2, pt. 2 (1899). Watzinger rightly remarks, in an excellent summary of the subject (*DP* 1, 104 f.) : " Every attempt at reconstruction of the stands of the temple will have to start from the agreement of the construction with the Cypriote kettle-wagons. . . . It is accordingly evident that the kettle-wagons and the stands must have come from neighbouring workshops."

Also pertinent to our subject is the account that Pausanias gives (x, 16, 2) of an iron stand and bowl, the honorific gift to a temple from the Lydian king Alyattes (first half of the 6th cent. B.C.). The passage is commented upon at length by G. Karo, ' Das Weihgeschenk des Alyattes,' in *ARw.*, Beiheft to vol. 8 (1905), 54–65 ; and this item has been enlarged upon by Kittel, *Studien*, 189 ff. Because of its interest the translation by W. M. S. Jones in the *Loeb Library* is herewith given. " Of the offerings sent by the Lydian kings I found nothing remaining except the iron stand of the bowl of Alyattes. This is the work of Glaukos the Chian, the man who discovered how to weld iron. Each plate of the stand is fastened to another, not by bolts or rivets, but by the welding, which is the only thing that fastens and holds together the iron. The shape of the stand is very like that of a tower, wider at the bottom and rising to a narrow top. Each side of the stand is not solid throughout, but the iron cross-strips are placed like the rungs of a ladder. The upright iron plates are turned outwards at the top, so forming a seat for the bowl." We have here the stand with crown at the top to hold the bowl as in our text, the open work and welding as here, and the cross-pieces 'like the rungs of a ladder' exactly defining an obscure work of our text.

27. *And he made the stands, ten, of bronze; 4 cubits the length of the one stand, and 4 cubits its width, and 3 cubits its height;* **28.** *and this the make of the stand: frame-pieces to them* [so 𝔥—error for *it*], *and frame-pieces between the cross-pieces;* **29.** *and upon the frame-pieces between the cross-pieces lions, cattle, and cherubs, and so upon the cross-pieces;* ⌜*and*⌝ [plus with Grr.] *above and* [with correction of Heb. punctuation] *below the lions and the cattle spirals, hammered work;* **30.** *and four wheels of bronze to the one stand, and axles of bronze; and its four feet, with shoulder-pieces under the laver, the shoulder-pieces welded* . . . [?] *spirals;* **31.** *and its mouth within the crown and above at a cubit* (high), *and its mouth rounded, the make of a container,* 1½ *cubits* (high) *; and further upon its mouth gravings;* ⌜*and their* [so 𝔥; *cf.* v.²⁸] *frame-pieces squared, not rounded*⌝ [an addition, out of place].

32. *and the quartette of wheels underneath the frame-pieces, and the axles* [Heb. *hands*] *of the wheels in the stand; and the height of the one wheel* 1½ *cubits;* **33.** *and the work of the wheels like the work of a chariot wheel, their axles and felloes and spokes and hubs welded* (i.e., as one piece) *;* **34.** *and four shoulder-pieces at the four corners of the one stand, its shoulder-pieces part of the stand;* **35.** *and at the top of the stand* [a lacuna here—*cf.* v.³¹] 1½ *cubits in height, round about; and at the top of the stand its handles* [? Heb. *hands*] *and its frame-pieces,* (being) *part of it.* **36.** *And he engraved upon the panels*

[𒀭+*its handles*] and *upon its frame-pieces cherubs, lions and palms* ... [?—*cf.* v.³⁰] *and spirals round about.*

37. *Like this he made the ten stands, cast in one piece, one measure, one form for them all.* **38.** *And he made ten lavers of bronze,* (each) *holding* [Heb. verb in sing.] *40 baths, 4 cubits* (high) *the one laver ; one laver upon the one stand for the ten stands.* **39.** *And he placed the stands, five at the corner of the house at the right* (=south), *and five at the corner of the house at its left* (=north), *and the sea ⸢he placed⸣* [secondary] *at the right-hand corner of the house to the southeast.*

The above presentation of the text regards vv.³²⁻³⁶, offset to the right, as secondary *vs.* Stade, who so considers vv.²⁸⁻³¹ᵇ, but in agreement with Kittel. The former assumes vv.³⁴·³⁵ to be secondary as parallel to vv.²⁹·³¹, but retains v.³⁶ as primary ; yet we have here a parallel to v.²⁹, disagreeing with it only in the terms of the panels and the pictured figures, which latter point he would overcome by artful distribution of the decorations presented in his plate. Šanda, following his critical method for the text of the description of the temple (ch. 6), obtains harmony by rearrangement of the vv. in this sequence : vv.²⁷·²⁸·²⁹·³⁶·³¹·³⁰·³²·³³, with vv.³⁴·³⁵ inset as a parallel to v.³⁰ ; but such chaotic disarrangements are most improbable in text-transmission.

The writer's results, in large part independent, are as follows : the *frame-pieces* 1º in v.²⁸ are the upright corner-pieces ; *frame-pieces* 2º are additional uprights on the face of the stand, and so *between the cross-pieces*, a phrase otherwise insoluble ; the *cross-pieces* are horizontal, and they are panelled (the noun translated *panel* is also used of a writing-tablet, even as here the panel is engraved), and so the frame-pieces and cross-pieces of v.²⁸ correspond to the frame-pieces and panels of v.³⁶ ; *the crown,* v.³¹, is retained, as *vs.* the common correction to *shoulder-pieces,* producing confusion with the inferior *shoulder-pieces* of v.³⁰, while just such a circular crown is represented in the Larnaka kettle (see Note). This brass work was evidently open, not full-plated all about, as some reproductions present the object, for the water was contained in the inset laver. The whole account, apart from some interpolations, is derived from reports of interested and technically trained eye-witnesses ; while their testimony is confusing, as here presented, we have evidence of unique interest in a work of high art.

There remains the difficult problem of the practical use of these vessels. This has been considered by Kittel uniquely and at length, pp. 236–42. His argument is as follows: the 40 baths at 36.4 litres=1456 litres=384 gallons, and in weight, 1400 kilograms=3086 lb. ; adding to this at a hazard the assumed weight of laver and stand he obtains for the loaded truck 3400 kg.=7495 lb.=$3\frac{3}{4}$ short tons. The mobility of an ancient truck under such a load is inconceivable. In Kittel's view also the practicability of the vessel is spoiled by its height, which at its lowest terms, according to his calculation, is $5\frac{1}{2}$ cubits=8 ft. 3 in. ; how then was the water filled in and drawn out ? The primitive cup-pump may have been used for filling the vessel ; *cf.* Comm. on the bronze sea above. For drawing the water may the siphon have been used so early ? Kittel's consequent deduction is that these vessels were purely ' symbols of the water-dispensing Deity,' even as he earlier interpreted the bronze sea. While his practical argument cannot be gainsaid, the abundance of such massive and useless ritual vessels would seem quite *de trop*. The bronze sea might have been symbolical, but these lavers appear practical for the distribution of water—most necessary indeed in connexion with the bloody rites of the temple.[1]

39. From the position of the bronze sea at the southeastern point of the temple arose Ezekiel's eschatological expectation of the stream issuing and trickling at the south side of the eastern portal of the temple (47[1ff.]).

---

[1] As for the term *laver* (*kîyôr*), used of cooking pots (1 Sam. 2[14]) and actual priestly lavers (Ex. 30[18ff.], etc.), this must have been a vessel of bowl shape. For the Sumerian origin of the word see Albr., *JAOS* 36 (1916), 232. The laver on top of the stand projected one cubit above the latter and thus formed with it a perfect cube with a capacity of 64 cubic cubits ; the laver, however, contained only a quarter of this amount, which is the equivalent of some 1525 litres. This fits well with the 40 baths (1456 litres) of v. 38. If, however, the laver occupied the whole interior of the stand and projected one cubit above it, we have to assume that it was not filled, but that only 40 baths of water were poured into it. Supplementary reference is to be made to n. 2 of Comm., vv.[23-26], for Albright's diminution of the bath to about two-thirds of the currently accepted figures.

27. מְכֹנוֹת : 'stands,' so by proper etymology Chic. B. (Moff., 'trolleys'!) ; EVV 'bases'=𝔙 'bases'=𝕮 ; בסיסיא ; 𝔖 'aggānệ 'basins'=𝔄. Grr. transliterate with μεχωνωθ, indifferently for sing. and pl. Hommel's opinion (*EGAO* 144) that the Heb. word occurs with the same mng. in S. Arab. is not to be accepted ; see Conti Rossini, *Chrest.*, 168.—The dimensions, $4 \times 4 \times 3$ are altered by Grr. to $5 \times 4 \times 6$; the last figure may be explained as due to the addition of the figures for wheels and top-piece, v.[31] ; *cf.* the purposed change of figure at v.[23]—**28.** מִסְגְּרֹת, שְׁלַבִּים : the first word translated above as (upright) *frame-pieces* ; Grr., συγκλειστον, ' rim ' (?), and so prob. 𝕮 𝔖 ; 𝔙 for 1⁰ ' interrasile ' (' low-relief-work '), but for 2⁰ ' sculpturæ.' The word is used technically for the rim of the show-bread table (Ex. 25[25], etc.). This mng. is generally accepted (*e.g.*, by St., Burn., Kit., Šanda), with application of the word to the horizontal base and top border of the square vessel. The word occurs also in a gloss, II. 16[17]. The second technical term, translated here with *cross-pieces*, has corresponding Pu. ppl., used of boards mortised together (Ex. 26[17], 36[22]) ; our noun prob. occurs in the Phœn. Marseilles Tariff (*CIS* I, no. 165=Cooke, *NSI* no. 42) in sense of ' ribs ' of sacrificial animals, and so with query Cooke and Harris (*Gram.*, 150). 𝕮 tr. with the cognate שליבא, ' rung ' of a ladder, ' ledge ' ; *cf.* 𝔙 ' iuncturas.' The word then corresponds exactly to the ' cross-strips ' of Pausanias's description, cited above. (The uncertainty of interpretation of the two words is displayed in EVV : AV ' borders ' and ' ledges,' RVV ' panels ' and ' ledges,' JV ' borders ' and ' stays.') As this feature is then etymologically a horizontal cross-piece (' rib '), the *misgĕrôt* must logically be, in the first place, the upright corner-pieces of the vessel ; and such is Jos.'s interpretation, ' four tetragonal small pillars (κιονίσκοι), standing at each corner.' But interpreters have generally reversed the mng. of the terms, making the ' ribs ' stand upright, and the *msgrt* the top and bottom. V.[b] accordingly becomes a crux ; some would change the text, *e.g.*, Klost., Burn., Šanda, while Kit. and St. (with change of mind in *SBOT*) hesitate at alteration. The relation denoted by *the frame-pieces between the cross-pieces* has appeared most obscure ; see Kit., pp. 208 ff. But with the new designation of the first item we may understand reference to intermediate vertical pieces between the horizontal bars. The stand was open within this frame of upright- and cross-pieces.—להם : easily corrected by critics to לה, or to להן ; but below there are several grammatical errors, prob. original.—**29.** אריות : for the lion-*motif cf.* 10[19f.]. Jos. gives lion, bull, eagle, and subsequently makes the laver rest on the paws of lion and eagle.—בקר : Grr. =ובקר.—כן ממעל : read כן (with athnaḥ) וממעל, with Grr., St., *al.*—מורד : ליות מעשה : Grr. χωραι (?) εργον καταβασεως ; 𝕮 ששׁ כבוש עובר מרבק, ' attachment of welding-work ' ; 𝔙 ' quasi lora ex aere dependentia ' ; 𝔖 is free ; AV ' certain additions made of thin work,' *cf.* 𝕮 ; RVV JV ' wreaths of hanging work,' which presents the current interpretation for the first word as to be connected with לויה, ' crown,' Pr. 1⁹ (so Keil), and hence Kit. argues (pp. 221 f.) for correction to the pl. of the latter word, לְוָיוֹת ; similar renderings, ' garlands,' ' rosettes,' have been suggested. But Kit. in postscript (p. 235) pertinently calls attention to ' das beliebte Strickornament ' on the Enkomi vessel, *i.e.*, the series of connected spiral rings. In *AJA* 43 (1939), are plates illustrating a variety of such spiraliform motives of different origins and ages : C. W. Blegen's article on Post-Mycenæan art, figs. 6, 16 (pp. 416, 429), and Glueck's presentation of a Nabatæan temple, figs. 3, 4 (p. 382). The other obscure word, מורד,, is interpreted by 𝔙 as from ירד, and so Kamp., Burn. render with ' stepped/bevelled work.' Kit., followed by Šanda, offers the best solution with derivation from רדד, ' to hammer in, inlay,' even as the Hif. was used above, 6³². —**30.** פעמתיו : another case of careless grammar ; the fem. suff. is expected.—The passage הכתפת to ומעלה, v.³¹, fails in 𝔊 𝔊ᴸ, is supplied by A x.—מעבר איש לויות : || to the equally obscure כמער איש וליות כביב, end of v.³⁶. 𝔗 is arbitrarily different, reading the first word as מעבד=𝔖 ; Hex. (A x), απο περαν ανδρος προσκειμεναι : 𝔙 ' contra se invicem respectantes ' ; RVV JV attempt a plausible interpretation, ' with wreaths at the side of each,' and similarly Burn. But Kit., St. (*SBOT*), Šanda despair of interpretation. Early comm., cited by Poole, followed a novelty of Jewish exegesis, which is presented by Kit. (p. 224) from *Yoma* 55a : " the cherubs who are attached to each other are a symbol of God's love, like the love of man and wife " ; and similarly Rashi tr. here with " associations (לויות) of man and wife pictured," this interpretation arising from the obscure מער, v.³⁶, which he derives from the root ערה, used of sexual connexion, and so he baldly expounds v.³⁶. AV tr. כמער with ' according to the proportion (RVV JV space) of each,' with marginal note to the noun, ' Heb. nakedness,' faithfully following old Jewish exegesis. The whole phrase with its item of the decorative spirals is in place below, not here.—**31.** ופיהו 1⁰ : the suffix has been carelessly attracted to preceding כיר ; correct to ופיה as immediately below, the reference being to the stand.—מבית לכתרת : the noun occurs at v.¹⁶ in architectural sense of ' capital,' which does not suit here ; here it =כֶּתֶר, ' crown,' Est. 1¹¹, and refers to the round top. Correction to לַכָּתֵּף, ' shoulder-pieces,' has been generally adopted since Ewald's suggestion, but this term is associated with the feet of the stand, vv.³⁰· ³⁴, while here we are engaged with the top. Šanda appropriately calls attention to the Larnaka kettle, in which the square tray at top is surmounted with a cylinder. In similar fashion, the laver was to be inserted in this *crown*. This circular top-piece projected above the stand proper by *a cubit*; but just below the height is given as *a cubit and a half*, for which augment *cf.* the extra *half-cubit* of v.³⁵. The extra figure may refer to the projection of the laver above the holder.

I. 7⁴⁰⁻⁵¹   181

Or there may be noted the (artificial?) summation of cubits:
$1+1\frac{1}{2}$ (v.³¹)$+1\frac{1}{2}$ (v.³⁵) $=4$ (v.³⁸).—כן מעשה: כן appears as the container, standard of a laver in Ex. 30¹⁸, 31⁹, etc.—מקלעות: also above, 6¹⁸, etc.—ומסגרתיהם: the fem. sing. suff. is demanded as referring to the stand, v.²⁷; *cf.* the similar distant reference of פיה, v.³¹.—**32.** The v. expands v.³⁰.—ידות: 'axle-trees,' so the generally received tr., following 𝔙, 'axes,' v.³³.—**33.** נביהם: for the 'felloe,' or 'rim,' and its prominent part in a chariot wheel *cf.* Eze. 1¹⁸ᶠ·, and see Cooke, *ad loc.*—חשקיהם והשריהם: for the two unique words see Lexx. 𝔊 𝔊ᴸ om. (by honest ignorance?); A e f w present one of the two items with αυχενες, and so x with a further plus, ωμιαι.—**34.** אל, Or. על: Grr., επι; *cf.* the extensive irregular use of אל, *e.g.*, 6¹⁸, 8³⁰.—**35***a.* The v. is parallel to v.³¹. A subject is expected, hence כן is inserted by St. (or כה), Šanda, *BH* ('fortasse'); but the phrase is another case of broken grammar, and hence the absolute קומה, corrected generally by critics to קומתו with Grr.—**35***b.* The passage is quite unintelligible. ועל ראש המכנה is apparently a duplicate of the phrase in v.ᵃ; Kit. (*cf. BH*) would add 'and underneath the stand,' an arbitrary addition without fresh light. ידתיה was used in connexion with the wheels, v.³², but cannot have that mng. here; it might mean the handles at top in which the frame-pieces terminated, and as represented in Kit.'s plate, p. 237, Gressmann, fig. 508. The word is also glossed into v.³⁶.—**36.** הלחת: B e₂ pref. τεσσαρας, error for τας. The pairing of this item with the frame-pieces is parallel to the pairing of the cross-pieces with the frame-pieces, vv.²⁸ᶠ·, and proves the identity of the panels with the cross-pieces. The word is used of a writing tablet, Is. 30⁸.—ידתיה: a gloss, as noted above, and so St., Kit., who also so adjudge the foll. phrase.—ועל ומסגרתיה: MSS, Ḳr. correctly ועל מס׳.—כמער איש וליות: see the parallel with discussion at v.³⁰. Grr., 𝔗 are fairly unintelligible; 𝔖 𝔄 om.; 𝔙 a long paraphrase, "quasi in similitudinem hominis stantis, ut non celata, sed apposita, per circuitum viderentur"; *cf.* Jos., "that those who viewed them would think that they were one piece."—**37.** קצב אחד: $=6^{25}$; Grr. om., exc. A.—לבלהנה: for similar odd forms see GK §91, f, BL §98, p.—**39.** The final term of location of the sea=south-east, makes the former terms 'right'=south, and 'left'=north.— נתן: 𝔊 om.; an intrusion from Ch.

40-47. Summary of Hiram's work, mostly secondary in origin. ‖ 2 Ch. 4¹¹⁻¹⁸, and *cf.* II. 25¹³ᶠᶠ·. This is prefaced with an item repeated from v.⁴⁵ᵃ, and secondary here (so with Šanda, *vs.* Stade). **40.** *And Hiram made the pots* (with v.⁴⁵; 𝔥 *lavers*, by careless slip; see Note) *and the shovels and the sprinkling-vessels.* The last object was for applying the sacrificial blood (*e.g.*, Lev. 7¹⁴). The three terms are repeated from Ex. 27³, "its pots to take away its ashes, its shovels and sprinkling-vessels." **41. 42.** These vv. concerning the pillars have been presented above, Comm. 7^{13-22}. **45.** The vessels are declared to have been of polished bronze. **46.** The v. contains the one original and novel statement in the section : *In the circuit of the Jordan did he* [with OGrr., 𝔐 *the king*] *cast them, in the clay ground between Succoth and Sarethan.* So practically EVV, following the ancient VSS. The original of ' in the clay ground,' *bm'bh h'dmh*, has been a major object of dispute. It has been characterized by Moore (Comm., Jud. 7^{22}), seconded by Stade, as meaningless here, followed by Comm. generally, and so by Abel, *GP* 2, 238 ; they read with slight change of the Heb., *bm'brt 'dmh*, ' at the ford of Adamah,' which then is identified with Adam, ' the city beside Sarethan,' at the ford by which the Israelites crossed the Jordan (Josh. 3^{16}).[1] But Albright holds that the preposition in such a phrase, ' in the ford,' makes this change impossible. He accordingly reads ' in the foundries of Adamah ' (*JPOS* 1925, 33). But the objection to this location is that it cannot be said to lie ' between Succoth and Sarethan,' on any identification of these places. Most recently Glueck, in an extensive article, ' Three Israelite Towns in the Jordan Valley, Zarethan, Succoth, Zaphon,' *BASOR* 90 (1943), 2–23, has returned to the non-geographical interpretation of the passage, following Albright, in one word, ' in the earthen foundries ' (pp. 13 f.). The noun in this rendering (actually singular in the Heb. = ' foundry-work ') means moulds of clay for casting of the bronze. Reference is to be made to Glueck's study also for his identification of Succoth as Deir-'Allā (following Albright, *AASOR* 6 [1926], 46 f.), with Sarethan in question ; for the latter *cf.* Abel, *GP* 450 f. Note is to be made of the ancient culture now discovered at Transjordanic Tuleilat el-Ghassūl, E. of Jericho, where early bronze axes have been discovered ; see Mallon, Koeppel, Neuville, *Teleilat Ghassul* (Rome, 1934), pl. 34, and for the chalcolithic age in that region Albright,

[1] The place-name as Dāmīyeh survives in a wady, tell and ford at the confluence of the Jabbok with the Jordan, 24 miles N of the Dead Sea ; see Albr., *BASOR* 35 (1929), 13, with picture of the present ferry, and similarly J. D. Whiting in *Nat. Geog. Mag.*, 1940, 82. It was by this ford doubtless that Gideon crossed over to Succoth (Jud. $8^{4f.}$). Sellin in his Comm. has suggested finding the name in Hos. 6^7, reading *b'dm* for *k'dm*.

JPOS 1935, 199 ff.—**47.** *And Solomon deposited all the vessels. Because of the exceeding great multitude the weight of the bronze could not be reckoned.* The first sentence appears to be correction of " S. *made* all the vessels," v.^{48}. Rashi, Kimchi saw the difficulty of the statement in the sequence, and following LHeb. and Aramaic usage of the verb, translated, as in the language of the Protestant VSS, *e.g.*, EVV, with: *And S. left all the vessels unweighed, because they were exceeding many.* With omission of the first sentence, the balance is a natural sequel of v.^{46}. The Grr. attached this statement to v.^{45}, as does Šanda.

48-51. Solomon's gilded furnishings of the temple, and the completion of all the work. || 2 Ch. 4^{19}–5^1. The whole passage, with exception of v.^{51b}, is late, vv.$^{48.\ 49}$ being drawn from the specifications for the tabernacle furniture in Ex. **48.** *The golden altar:* cf. the wooden altar overlaid with pure gold, Ex. $30^{1ff.}$; *the table on which is the bread of the Presence, of gold*, ib. $25^{23ff.}$, where again the table is simply overlaid with gold. **49.** Apart from the parallel in Ch. history knows of only one candelabrum, as against the *ten* noted here, *of refined gold;* cf. the elaborate description of it in Ex. $25^{31ff.}$, the details of which are pursued here with *the flower-work, the* (seven) *lamps*, and *the tongs*, all *of gold*. The original document in II. $25^{13ff.}$, recording the first despoliation of the temple by Nebuchadnezzar, speaks only in general terms of his looting of temple and palace and his breaking in pieces all the vessels of gold which Solomon king of Israel made in the house of YHWH. **50***a*. The passage is dependent upon II. $25^{14f.}$=Jer. $52^{18f.}$, listing the booty taken from the temple at its destruction, but with the exaggeration of making all the vessels of *refined gold*, whereas the original document distinguishes them as some of silver and some of gold. *Cups:* or rather large *bowls:* otherwise than here and in the parallels only of profane use, Ex. 12^{22}, 2 Sam. 17^{28}; *snuffers:* only here and in the parallels; *sprinkling-basins:* sup. v.^{40}, and *e.g.*, Ex. 27^3; *pans: e.g.*, ib. 25^{29}; *fire-pans: e.g.*, ib. 27^3—these latter two doubtless for incense. **50***b*. *The hinge-sockets:* EVV *hinges.* The whole passage is clumsy and profuse; 𝔊 reads it, and Stade retains it; Šanda reduces it to *and the hinges of the doors of the inner house and of the hall, of gold (cf. BH).* See

Notes further for some of these words. **51***a*. *And was finished all the work which king Solomon did in the house of* YHWH: an editorial *finale*. **51***b*. Historical memorandum on Solomon's placement in the temple of *his father David's dedications*, namely 'the vessels of gold and silver and bronze,' taken from Hadadezer and all the nations, according to 2 Sam. 8[9-12]. But the passage is read with difficulty; *cf.* the attempts in EVV. It might be simplest to reduce it to: *And Solomon brought the dedications of his father David, the silver and the gold, into the treasuries of the house of* YHWH, and to regard the inset, and *the vessels he gave*, as an added reference to Solomon's own gifts. For such additional 'treasures' *cf.* the shields of gold which Solomon made and Shishak looted (14[26]).

40. חירום : but 21 MSS חירם, Grr., Χειραμ ; this variant from v.[18] has been intruded from Ch.—הבירות ; read הסירות with 43 MSS Ken., deR., Ch., Grr., 𝔙, as at v.[45].—"י בית : for this locative use *cf.* v.[45].—**45.** האהל : Kr. הָאֵלֶה is required; the word is unnecessary and is to be omitted with Grr., 𝔙.—"י בית : Grr., exc. g i, plus " and the 48 pillars of the king's house and the Lord's house, all the works of the king made Hiram (of bronze)." The item of 'the 48 pillars' Then., Šanda regard as of Heb. origin and historical moment.—ממרט : the fem. is expected; Grr., αρδην (?), exc. 𝔊[L] ην. —**46.** המלך : 𝔊 𝔊[L] 𝔄 om.; the unexpected subject may indicate the royal factory.—במעבה האדמה : Ch., 'בעבי הא ; the first noun Albright reads as pl., and om. art. in the second; see Comm.—**48.** ויעש ; Grr., κ. εδωκεν (exc. B. κ. ελαβεν), on the ground that S. was not the maker.—בית : the noun is locative, as at v.[40].—**50.** הכפות : the obscure word is variously rendered in VSS ; Engl. ' cups ' comes from ' hydriæ ' of 𝔙 ; see Honeyman, *JTS* 37 (1936), 56 ff., for attempt to find the primitive threshold altar in this ritual object.— הכפות : EVV 'spoons,' JV 'pans.' Albr. identifies such a vessel, understood as a censer, with a bowl (found at Tell Beit Mirsim) with figuration of a lion's mouth, in which a pipe was inserted for blowing the incense ; see *BASOR* 47 (1932), 15 ff., with additional plate, no. 48, 1, and his further remarks in *AASOR* 21-22 (1943), 73, n. 2. For such sacred vessels see F. Prezeworski's study of Syrian censers, *Syria*, 1930, 139 ff., and for Palestine that by G. M. Crowfoot, *PEQ* 1940, 150 ff. ; *cf.* also Burrows, *WMTS* 214 f., with two plates.—הפתות : EVV ' hinges,' with 𝔗 𝔙 ; Grr., θυρωματα, ' doorways.' Haupt has a diffuse discussion of the word ; G. R. Driver connects it with Akk. *pūtu*, ' forehead ' (*JTS* 38, 38 ; *ZDMG* 1937, 347), followed by L. Köhler (*JBL* 1940, 36). But it means the ' cardines feminæ ' ; *cf.* Is. 3[17].—**51.** כל : OGrr. om., not desiring to limit Solomon's works

Ch. 8. The dedication of the temple. ‖ 2 Ch. 5–7 ; cf. Ant., viii, 4. The chapter contains the history of the entry of the ark into the shrine of the temple, vv.¹⁻¹¹ ; a poetic word of Solomon, taken from an ancient collection, vv.¹². ¹³ ; his prayers of dedication, vv.¹⁴⁻⁶¹ ; the sequel, the sacrifices and the great feast, vv.⁶²⁻⁶⁴. ⁶⁵⁻⁶⁶.

The history has its simpler, primitive parallel in the story of David's fetching of the ark to David's City in 2 Sam. 6, and a late parallel in the accounts of the dedication of the second temple, Ezra 6¹⁶⁻¹⁸, 1 Esd. 5⁴⁷ᶠᶠ.. From Assyria we possess numerous foundation-stones with inscriptions invoking divine blessing upon the monarch and his offspring, e.g., of Sennacherib (ARA 2, nos. 440, 455, 458), and also dedicatory texts, of which order is one of Ashurbanipal's with regard to a golden incense-altar (ib. nos. 999 ff.) : " For all time may Marduk look with favour upon that incense-altar, and on me, Ashurbanipal, have mercy when I call upon thee, may he receive my petitions, hear my prayers, freedom from sickness grant me."

The chapter is very composite. An ancient citation is balanced by long prayers in Deuteronomistic style, while the historical sections have been extensively swollen with later accretions.

1.¹ *Then convoked* ² *Solomon* ³ *the elders of Israel,*⁴ *all the heads of the tribes,* ⌜*the hereditary chiefs of the Bnê-Israel to king Solomon*⌝, ⁵ ⌜*to Jerusalem*⌝ ⁶ *to bring up the ark of* ⌜*the covenant of*⌝ ⁷ *YHWH from David's City, that is Sion.* **2.** ⌜*And were convoked to king Solomon all the men of Israel*⌝ ⁸ ⌜*in the moon of Ethanim*⌝ ⁹ ⌜*at the Haj, that is the seventh month*⌝.¹⁰ **3.** ⌜*And came all the elders of Israel*⌝.¹¹ *And the priests bore the ark* **4.** ⌜*and they brought up the ark of YHWH*⌝ ¹² *and the tent of meeting and all the holy vessels that were in the tent,* ⌜*and there brought them up the priests and the Levites*⌝,¹³ **5.** *and the king* ⌜*Solomon*⌝ ¹⁴ *and all* ⌜*the assembly of*⌝ ¹⁵ *Israel,* ⌜*those assembled to him along with him*⌝ ¹⁶ *before the ark, sacrificing sheep and cattle that might not be counted* ⌜*nor measured for quantity*⌝.¹⁷ **6.** *And the priests brought in the ark* ⌜*of the covenant of YHWH*⌝ ¹⁸ *to its place, to the shrine of the house, to the holy of holies under the wings of the cherubs.* **7.** *For the cherubs were spreading wings over the place of the ark, and the cherubs shrouded the ark and its staves above ;*

8. *and the staves were so long that the ends of the staves were seen from the sanctity in front of the shrine, but they could not be seen outside;* ⌈*and they are there to this day*⌉.[19] **9.** *There was nothing in the ark except the two tables of stone that Moses deposited there at Horeb, by which* YHWH *made a covenant with the Bnê-Israel, when they came out of the land of Egypt.* **10.** *And it came to pass, when the priests came out of the sanctity—now the cloud was filling the house of* YHWH—**11.** *that the priests were not able to stand to minister in the presence of the cloud, for the Glory of* YHWH *filled the house* ⌈*of* YHWH⌉.[20]

The original elements of the story may be contained in the following simplification:

1. *Then convoked Solomon the elders of Israel to bring up the ark of* YHWH *from David's City in the moon of Ethanim.* **3.** *And the priests bore the ark,* **5.** *with the king and all Israel before the ark, sacrificing sheep and cattle that might not be counted.* **6.** *And the priests brought in the ark to its place, to the shrine of the house.*

[1] 𝕲 𝕲^L a preceding plus: "and it came to pass, when S. finished building the house of the Lord and his own house after 20 years [=9¹⁰], then," etc. [2] 𝕲+' the king.' [3] 46 MSS+' all '=Grr., 𝕾 𝔄. [4] Many MSS, edd.+' and '=Ch. [5] =Ch.; 𝕲 𝕲^L om. [6] Grr., 'in Sion.' [7] MS 107 om. [8] =Ch.; 𝕲 𝕲^L om. [9] Ch. om. [10] =Ch.; Grr. om., exc. A=𝕾 𝔄. [11] =Ch.; Grr. om., exc. A. [12] Grr. om., exc. A x. [13] =Ch.; Grr. om., exc. A Z g x e₂. [14] =Ch.; Grr. om., exc. A x. [15] =Ch.; Grr. om., exc. A. [16] =Ch., omitting 'with him'; Grr. om., exc. A x. [17] =Ch.; Grr. om., exc. A x. [18] =Ch.; Grr. om., exc. A Z x e₂ *al.* [19] =Ch.; Grr. om., exc. A x. [20] 𝕲 om.; *cf.* Ch. The following notes may be added here. **2.** אתנים: *n.b.* 𝕿 קדמאה, Sym., τω αρχαιω.—**3.** 'the priests': Ch., 'the Levites,' *cf.* v.⁴, where Ch. 'the priests, the Levites.'—**7.** ויסכו: Ch. ויכסו; St. properly defends the forceful verb of the text. Jos. combines both texts.—בריו: Grr., τα αγια αυτης=τα αγιασμενα, v.⁸, *i.e.*, read as בריו; *cf.* Jer. 4¹¹.—**8.** הקדש: mng.? Ch., הארון; Kamp. prop. המקום; see Burn., St.—**9.** לחות האבנים: Grr.+' the tables of the covenant'; the duplicate being simplified in 2 MSS. The same exegesis appears in the plus of 𝕿: "the ten words of the covenant (which the Lord decreed with the Sons of Israel, when they came out of Egypt)." The addition was made to obtain an antecedent for אשר 2º; hence the proposed insertion of לחות הברית before the relative clause (*cf. BH*—but this not 'cum Græco' as alleged, in regard to the position of the phrase) But כרת is used absolutely of making a covenant, *e.g.*, 1 Sam. 11², and the rel. pron. is used loosely; for defence of the text, see Keil, Burn.—**10.** Ch. has a long insertion between the two halves of the v.

I. 8¹⁻¹¹

The criticism of the text of these vv. has been most varied, depending in part upon the authority of the OGr. text in its greatly apocopated form, in part upon subjective judgment of the strata of the document. In addition to the comm. are to be specially noted Stade's extensive treatment in *SBOT* pp. 98–101, Burney, pp. 104–9, for full treatment of the language, and Hölscher, 'Das Buch der Könige,' in the Gunkel-*Eucharisterion*, pp. 164–6. In vv.$^{1-6}$ there are many redundant phrases, all of late stamp (see Burney), *e.g.*, *the heads of the tribes, the hereditary chiefs* (EVV *princes of the fathers' houses*), v.^{1}; the introduction of the Levites, v.^{4} (*cf.* Ch.'s corrections in favour of the Levites, vv.$^{4, 5}$, and *cf.* 2 Sam. 15^{24}); *the assembly . . . those assembled*, v.^{5}; etc. V.^{2} is reduced above to *in the moon of Ethanim* with OGrr.; the appositional *in the seventh month* is the equivalent dating of the later calendar, *cf.* Bul as the eighth month, 6^{38}. There arises the problem of the sequence of dates, the dedication being assigned to the seventh month, but the completion of the temple (6^{38}) to the eighth month. Following older comm. cited by Poole, Ewald held that the dedication anticipated the complete furnishing and so 'finishing' of the temple by a month, and Keil that he waited for eleven months, thus providing time for the brass work of ch. 7, and so Šanda. Kittel, attributing the present datum to a later source than that of 6$^{37f.}$, makes the dating a conformation to the celebration of the Succoth festival in the seventh month, for which dispute see below, Comm., 12^{32}. Benzinger excises the reference to Ethanim. Morgenstern in his 'Three Calendars of Ancient Israel,' *HUCA* 1 (1924), 67 ff. (*cf.* also his *Amos Studies*, 146 ff.), argues that the assembly of the people was in Ethanim and the octave-feast had its climax on the first of Bul. Stade (*SBOT*), after a long discussion, retracting his earlier cancellation of the dating as an insertion, retains it, but cannot accommodate it to the datum of 6^{38}. Schmidt (see note 1, Comm., 6$^{23ff.}$) properly holds that the antique terms 'moon' and 'Ethanim' cannot be late glosses. Morgenstern's theory is most attractive with his argument for a change in Israelite calendars, with the older calendar having its culmination in Bul. The word, *the Haj*, had best be excised, as a back-reference from v.^{65}; as Kittel remarks, the word is out of place. For the accumulation of feasts at this period *cf* vv.$^{65f.}$.

Most variety of critical opinion has arisen over the stratification of vv.$^{7-11}$. Stade assigns vv.$^{7, 8}$ to his 'unknown source,' v.^{9} to the Deuteronomist, vv.$^{10, 11}$ to the basic document along with v.^{12}. Šanda (p. 243) holds that vv.$^{7-9}$ interfere with the flow of the narrative, and sagaciously observes that vv.$^{7, 8a}$ properly belong to the section on the cherubs, 6$^{23ff.}$, while v.^{9} is Deuteronomic and is to be transposed before v.^{8b}. Hölscher, with some deletions, accepts vv.$^{6-9}$ as integral, vv.$^{10, 11}$ as a late addition. The present writer however is sceptical as to originality of all of these vv., inclusive of the final phrase in v.^{6}, *to the holy of holies, under the wings of the cherubs*, the first phrase of which is generally admitted to be secondary, even as it is a gloss in 6^{16}, while the location as under the cherubs appears superfluous. Certainly vv.$^{7, 8}$ with the stress on the staves of the ark is a very subordinate item indeed; see below. *The sanctity* (Heb. *the holiness*) is a late term, used in Lev. (16^2, etc.) and Eze. (41^{21}, etc.), and so some critics have proposed replacing it with a more concrete word, 'the place.' VV.$^{10, 11}$ record a miraculous phenomenon with a clumsy, reiterative statement; it is quite in line with the passage Ex. 40$^{34ff.}$, how "after Moses finished the work" on the tabernacle, "Then the cloud covered the tent of meeting, and the Glory of YHWH filled the tabernacle; and Moses was not able to enter the tent of meeting, because the cloud abode thereon, and the Glory of YHWH filled the tabernacle." *Cf.* also the entry of the Glory into the temple in Eze.'s vision, 43$^{1ff.}$. The Glory is the perceptible Presence of Deity, visually represented as a cloud.

1. The adv. *then* belongs to the archival style, and definitely so at v.^{12}, and did not originally refer to 6^{38}; see Burney, and the writer's 'Archival Data in the Book of Kings,' 49. A preceding plus in OGrr. (see Note above) attempted to precise the time. The *elders* were the community chiefs, hereditary sheikhs; *cf.* 21$^{8ff.}$. *That is Sion:* a gloss from Ch., 'David's City' having become archaic. **7. 8.** The staves of the ark and their limited visibility have caused interminable discussion; see Kimchi at length, the comm. cited by **Poole** (a whole column), and of moderns may be noted **Thenius,**

Keil, and Šanda. The optics is a problem, with the ancient question whether the staves extended on the line of the axis of the building or at right angles to it. Galling in his ' Das Allerheiligste,' *JPOS* 1932, 43 ff., contends for the former view, finding strained support from his argument for a raised podium in the sanctuary. But it appears to have been generally ignored that there could have been no interest in the extension of the staves except so far as these indicated the presence of the ark, which was not visible, and thus we have to assume the presence of ' the veil ' (an important item in the tabernacle-furnishing [Ex. $26^{31ff.}$, etc.]) as concealing the sacred object from vulgar gaze, so making the staves themselves of profound interest to the devotee (*cf.* the specifications, Ex. $25^{12ff.}$). The veil concealed the ark, only the staves might be seen projecting right and left by one standing near the narrow door of the sanctuary, but not from a greater distance. For the veil in the later temple *cf.* 1 Mac. 1^{22}, Mt. 27^{51}, Heb. 6^{19}, etc. Our passage comes from one who had actually seen so much of the holy shrine. On an Akko-Ptolemaic coin of Gallienus a portable shrine with the accompanying poles is exhibited (Cook, *Rel. of Anc. Palestine*, 104). The comment, *and they are there unto this day*, is not a guarantee of originality, *vs.* Burney, as Olmstead argues (*AJSL* 30 [1913], 33 f.) ; *cf.* 9^{21}, 12^{19} ; II. 8^{22}, 10^{27}, $17^{23.\ 34.\ 41}$. **9.** The note that *there was nothing in the ark except the two tables of stone* is the remark of an anxious commentator, who may have wished to dissipate false rumours to the contrary (so Benzinger). There was the later tradition that Aaron's staff and the pot of manna were also included (Heb. 9^4) ; see the older comm., cited by Poole at length.

VV.$^{12.\ 13}$. Citation of Solomon's ode.

12. *Then spake Solomon :*
      Y<small>HWH</small> *said, he would dwell in the dense-cloud.*
13. *Built indeed have I an exalted house for thee,*
      A place for thy dwelling forever.

One change is made from the EVV, etc., in the translation 'an exalted house,' in place of ' a house of habitation ' ; see Note.

The OGrr. transferred the passage to the end of v.^{53}, presumably regarding it as ritually secondary to the following solemn prayer of consecration. 𝔊ᴴ MSS have it in both places.

Of radical critical importance are the additions in the OGrr. : a prefixed hemistich, a variant from the theme of ' building,' and at the end citation of the source of the passage. For the expanded Gr. form see Wellhausen, *Comp.*, 208 ff. ; J. Halévy, *RS* 8 (1900), 218 ff. ; Driver, *Int.*, 192 ; Kittel, Burney, and Stade in *SBOT*, the last scholar adopting none of the additions from 𝕲. Further for the Gr. text see Burkitt, *JTS* 10 (1909), 439 ff. ; Thackeray, *ib.*, 11, 518 ff., and *The Septuagint and Jewish Worship*, 76 ff. The OGr. preface reads, ἥλιον ἐγνώρισεν ἐν οὐρανῷ Κύριος, " the sun did the Lord make known in heaven " ; for the verb 𝕲ᴸ has ἔστησεν, ' set,' and this indeed makes better sense. It has been proposed that הכין as the basis of the latter rdg. was misread הֵבִין, giving the rdg. of 𝕲. But הבין is never so translated in the Greek. Wellhausen accepted Lucian's rdg., and has been largely followed ; but see Kamphausen, Burkitt, Thackeray, and now Rahlfs (*SS* 3, 62) for the conclusion that this text is merely an ' amelioration.' Burkitt's suggestion of הוֹפַע, *i.e.*, " (Sun,) shine forth," is arbitrary. There is the distinction between the so evident sun and the Deity who will not be seen, a fine theological contrast, and so the fragment in the Gr. appears to be original.

The interior variant of the OGrr. is the change of " I will build (a house)," to the impv., " Build (a house)," and for this Wellhausen has reconstructed what he regards as the original Hebrew. Šanda has attempted combination of both forms. But it is best to abide by the judgment of Kittel (also in *BH*), Benzinger, Stade for the preservation of 𝔥. The Hebrew is bold and original, in contrast to the divine self-assertion preceding.

The original purport and circumstances of this ode, of which only the first lines are quoted, are wholly obscure. Was it cautious censorship which deleted from the Hebrew the first hemistich, preserved however in the Greek ? The theme, curtly expressed, is that of the manifest phenomenon of the brilliant sun in contrast to the invisibility of Deity, who prefers the deep darkness, is invisible, *e.g.*, Ps. 18[12] (and so even to the spiritually minded, *cf.* Is. 45[15]), and for whom Solomon prepared a dark adytum. This interpretation is in contrast to current theories, largely starting from the present passage, concerning the sun-cult at Jerusalem, in combination with the theory of the penetration of the rays of the equinoctial sun through the eastern door of the temple into the adytum. See literature cited above in introduction to ch. 6. There may be noted here the argument in F. J. Hollis's essay, cited there, adopting and expanding a theory proposed by von Gall, that these vv. were part of an oracle delivered in connexion with an eclipse of the sun, which may be identified with the one that occurred May 22, 948 B.C.—as approximate enough (!). But the contrast of Deity as artist and his creation is a constant theme in Hebrew poetry, e.g., Ps. 19. Dussaud properly argues (*RHR* 63 [1911], 336 ff.) that here YHWH is aligned rather with Hadad the storm-god, not with the sun. For the *dense-cloud* (EVV *thick darkness*—see Haupt in *SBOT*) *cf.* ' the cloud,' v.[10], which also normally shrouds Deity, e.g., in Ex. 24[15ff.]. Critical views on the passage are indeed polarized. Morgenstern in his ' Book of the Covenant,' *HUCA* 5 (1928), 40, n. 46, comes to the conclusion that these verses " smack so strongly of this Deuteronomic theology that it is practically impossible to ascribe an earlier origin to them "—an unconvincing argument ; that school was not poetical. Others, wishing to find original paganism, would rewrite the text ; *e.g.*, Gunkel : " Baal establishes the sun in the heavens, Yahweh said he would dwell in gloom " (*Die Lade Jahves*, 1920, 62 f.) ; and H. G. May, rejecting the Greek first hemistich as an attempt of the Seventy to disassociate YHWH from the sun-cult, proceeds to invent out of line 3 : " Verily I have built a shrine of Zebul for you " (' Some Aspects of Solar Worship at Jerusalem,' *ZAW* 1937, 269 ff.). But rewriting of ancient poetic fragments is all in vain.

There follows in the OGrr. the postscript : *At the dedication. Is it not written in the Book of Song ?* A documentary source is thus asserted. For the last word Wellhausen suggested a corruption from *yashar*, and the collection would then have been the Book of Jashar, cited Josh. 10[13], 2 Sam. 1[18]. Kittel (but *cf. BH*), Šanda retain 𝔐. See Note.

12. בערפל : 𝔊 𝔊^L εκ γνοφου.—**13.** יָרֻם : ' exalted,' and so correctly for the mng. of the root and its derivatives at large BDB, but subsequent Lexx., König, *HAW*, GB, have abandoned this mng., replacing it with 'dwelling'; the latter sense is that of the VSS, EVV, etc. Schrader (*CIOT* 1, 174) recognized the correct mng. here, and offers an Akk. parallel to the phrase. For the use of the word as 'exalted,' and so as divine 'prince,' see at length Note on 'Jezebel,' 16³¹, also on 'Beel-zebub,' II. 1³.—Gr. supplement, επι καινοτητος =בְּכִנְכָּה.—[εν τω βιβλιω τ.] ωδης : the word 'song' was used in the collective sense, as noted in later canonical lists by J. R. Harris, *Odes and Psalms of Solomon* (1920), 2, 2 f. It may be proposed that instead of the alleged misreading of *yāšār* as *haššîr*, the reverse is the case for the former word in its occurrences, since it has never been explained.

VV.¹⁴⁻⁶¹. Solomon's prayer of dedication : vv.¹⁴⁻²¹, the history of the undertaking ; vv.²²⁻⁵³, the prayers, with litany, vv.³¹⁻⁵³ ; vv.⁵⁴⁻⁶¹, the blessing and exhortation. || 2 Ch. 6³⁻⁴², with omission of the royal blessing, and addition of citation from Ps. 132. *Cf. Ant.*, viii, 4, 2, 3.

Apart from the rather casual references to the priests in vv.⁶, ¹⁰ *supra*, the king appears as the sole liturgist, *summus sacerdos*, the officiant in prayer, in exhortation, in blessing. The like royal function is presented in the case of David (2 Sam. 6), of Jeroboam (12³³, 13), of Hezekiah at his prayer before the Presence (II. 19¹⁴ff.) ; only indirectly do we learn of a high priest (II. 22³ff.). This unique position of the king is not to be ascribed to foreign ideas ; rather it was the genuine development of the natural priesthood of the father of the family, its representative before Deity. The development of the cult in its technical details, especially in the central sanctuary of the people, produced the increasingly potent castes of priests and Levites ('attendants'), who in the later history of the kingdom established themselves as a powerful estate spiritual, which could defy the king himself (*cf.* the tradition in 2 Ch. 26¹⁶ff.). The dispute between the spiritual and the temporal power characterizes all history of established religion. Early Israelite royalty thus followed the oriental tradition of priestly prerogative.[1] For recent studies of the sacred function of Israelite monarchy see Mowinckel, *Psalmenstudien*, 2 (1922), 297 ff. ; C. R. North, 'Religious Aspects of Hebrew Monarchy,' *ZAW* 1932, 8 ff. ; H. Gunkel,

---

[1] For Mesopotamia see Jastrow, *Religious Beliefs*, 269 ff. ; Jeremias, *HAG* 284 ; Meissner, *Bab. u. Ass.*, 2, 67 ff. ; C. W. McEwan, *The Oriental Origins of Hellenistic Kingship* (1934), esp. pp. 11 ff.

Einl. in die Psalmen, 159 ff.; A. R. Johnson's chapter on
'The Rôle of the King in the Jerusalem Cultus,' in *The
Labyrinth*, ed. S. H. Hooke, pp. 8 ff.; Morgenstern, 'A
Chapter in the History of the High-Priesthood,' *AJSL* 55
(1938), 1 ff., asserting that throughout the pre-Exilic period
in both kingdoms " the king discharged the function of high-
priest." Of course in these sacrificial functions the king was
the *præsidens*, the menial offices of handling the rites being the
charge of the priests. The actual royal part of the king appears
in the account of Ahaz's personal ritual in connexion with
his new altar (II. $16^{12f.}$). It should be noted that the term,
'sacrificing,' is used loosely, of the patrons of the sacrifice,
e.g., Solomon's wives, with the participles in the feminine (11^8).

The whole composition is Deuteronomistic, for which fact
see Burney's detailed analysis, also Šanda. The problem
arises as to its integrity, in detection of various strata and
interpolations, with the particular inquiry whether any portions are pre-Exilic. Wellhausen (*Comp.*, 268 f.), Stade (*GVI*
I, 74—*cf. SBOT*), Kittel, Kent, *al.*, regard the whole as Exilic
at the earliest, along with multiple subsequent additions. On
the other hand, Burney considers the document as a whole to
be akin to the earliest elements of Deut., and so pre-Exilic.
The most crucial of the points of criticism is the section
vv.$^{44-53}$, repeating the theme of the brief section vv.$^{33f.}$, and
with the hypothesis of an exile of the nation. On the other
hand, a sure core of pre-Exilic origin may be found, with
Šanda, in the litany of vv.$^{31-40}$, with intercessions for divine
justice, in case of defeat in battle, and as against natural
plagues, presupposing an independent people on its own soil.
VV.$^{22-26}$, repeating David's charge to his son ($2^{1ff.}$), with promise of a dynasty, are of pre-Exilic character without question ;
cf. the usual forms in Ass. building inscriptions of prayers for
the dynasty (see above, Comm., v.^{1}). VV.$^{27-30}$ continue the
prayer for the king. V.^{27}, *Will God in very truth dwell on the
earth ? Behold, heaven and the heaven of heavens cannot contain
thee ; how much less this house that I have built*, is regarded
even by Burney (p. 115), as of Exilic age comparing Is. 60^1.
But the celestial abode of the highest deities was a commonplace in ancient Semitic religion ; we need only recall ' Baal-
of-the-Heavens,' or ' Heaven,' as he is actually named in the

Sūjīn inscription; see the writer's note, *HTR* 31 (1938), 145, and *cf.* Am. 9⁶, Hab. 2²⁰. In the history of the Israelite religion YHWH came to be localized peculiarly only with the building of the temple, and even then it was his distinct Presence (Person in Christian theology), or Name, or Glory-Shekinah, that was in residence. As with one development in Christian doctrine, that of the Presence on the altar, along with the dogma of the absolute celestial Deity, so in Israel: *e.g.*, Ps. 20³ is a prayer that YHWH "send thee help out of his sanctuary, and support thee out of Sion," while according to v.⁷ the Deity "will answer him from his holy heaven." There may be noted the admirable discussion by Morgenstern in *HUCA* 5 (1928), 37 ff. In the history of religion art has played a large part in definitely localizing the deities. The above presentation argues for the early origin of vv.²²⁻⁴⁰. VV.⁴¹⁻⁴³ are a prayer, not for the later caste of proselytes, but for aliens whose piety may be aroused by the fame of Israel's God and his temple, and this, as will be detailed below, is not necessarily a late feature. To the portion of the composition so analyzed was added a prefatory, vv.¹⁴⁻²¹, a duplicate to vv.²²⁻²⁶, but based on the secondary interpretation of the oracle to David in 2 Sam. 7¹ᶠᶠ·. VV.⁴⁴⁻⁵³, as observed above, have definite post-Exilic characteristics. The final distinct section, vv.⁵⁴⁻⁶¹, the blessing, culminating in an exhortation to the people—in Christian language a sermon—is an evident addition; *n.b.* the contradiction of Solomon's rising from his knees, v.⁵⁴, and his erect posture before the altar, v.²².

To cite some essays at minute criticism: Stade (*SBOT*) makes the whole section as practically of one piece, with a few interpolated passages, and excepting vv.⁴⁴⁻⁵¹ as a late addition. Šanda attempts minute analysis, and finds the original record of dedication, following vv.¹⁻¹⁴, in vv.²². ³¹⁻³⁹. ⁵⁴ᶠᶠ·, and attributes to Redactors (R and Rj) the remaining sections. Hölscher finds three strata, in this chronological order: A vv.¹⁴⁻²⁶. ²⁸. ²⁹; B vv.²⁷. ³⁰⁻⁴³. ⁵²⁻⁶¹; C vv.⁴⁴⁻⁵¹.

These prayers attributed to Solomon compose one of the noblest flights in sacred oratory from the Deuteronomic school. There are the notes of the infiniteness of Deity and yet of his readiness to dwell with his faithful, of divine grace and of human responsibility, not only of the people but of the individual conscience (v.^{38}), of the stern righteousness of God which can scatter the nation, and equally of the door of repentance by which they may regain his favour. The chapter was properly chosen as an alternative Haphtarah (lection) for the Succoth festival (*Meg. B.* 21a). It is our earliest representative of such liturgical forms from the ancient temple. Gunkel's *Einleitung in die Psalmen* contains much that illuminates the present liturgy.

14. *And the king turned his face about, and blessed all the assembly of Israel ; and all the assembly of Israel was standing.* **15**a. *And he said : Blessed is Y*HWH, *the God of Israel.* The common liturgical phrase, *Blessed is Y*HWH (see the listing of the cases in Gunkel, *Einl.*, 40), is taken from social language ; *cf.* II. 4^{29}, where EVV properly translate the verb with ' salute ' ; *cf.* also v.^{66} *inf.* The phrase has its parallel in Ugaritic texts ; see Virolleaud, *Syria*, 1935, 186 f., one of the texts certainly reading, " We have blessed Baal ———." **16.** *I did not choose a city . . . but I chose David,* etc. The person of David came first in the divine selection. After the first sentence 𝕲 interpolates : " and I chose Jerusalem, that my name might abide there." This plus, to save the hoary fame of the holy city, has been largely accepted, *e.g.*, by *BH*, Hölscher, but is rejected by Stade (*SBOT*), Šanda ; see Stade's reasonable discussion. **17** ff. The reference is to the history in 2 Sam. 7, which, as Wellhausen has argued (*Comp.*, 254, etc.), and as is generally accepted, is an expanded form of the original promise to *build a house, i.e.*, a dynasty ; the dynastic promise appears there in vv.$^{12\text{ff.}}$. **17.** *To build a house for the Name of Y*HWH. *Cf.* 3^2, *the Name of Y*HWH. The Name is a manifestation form of Deity, *e.g.*, physically at Is. 30^{27} ; as in all legal language the name is the person. For ancient parallels, Akkadian and Egyptian, see Šanda ; there may be added the use of ' the name ' in legal sense in an Amarna tablet from Jerusalem, " Behold, the king (Pharaoh) has put his name on the land forever " (Knudtzon, no. 287, lines 60 ff.). **21.** *Wherein is the covenant of Y*HWH : *i.e.*, the tables, as an engrossed document. **22.** *And Solomon stood before the altar of Y*HWH. For the altar, ignored in ch. 7, but assumed here and at v.^{45}, see Comm., vv.$^{64\text{ff.}}$. The standing position of the officiant was the rule as all ancient designs show. Ch. (6¹³) has a long addition *in re* a brazen scaffold, which Solomon used as an oratory, upon which " he stood, and (then) kneeled down " ; this relieves the contradiction of the two positions given to him, and also separates locally the royal layman from the altar. **23.** *There is none like thee as God.* *Cf.* Ex. 15¹¹, Ps. 86⁸, **27.** *But in very truth will God dwell on the earth ? Behold, heaven and the heaven of heavens cannot contain thee ; how much less this house that I have built !* The v. is as noble an expression as is found anywhere for the infiniteness of Deity. *Cf.* Jer. 23²⁴, " Do I not fill heaven and earth ?—saith Yhwh." And in the Biblical tradition Augustine's corresponding confession may be recalled : " et quis locus est in me, quo veniat in me Deus meus ? quo Deus veniat in me, Deus qui fecit cælum et terram ? . . . An vero cælum et terra, quæ fecisti, et in quibus me fecisti, capiunt te ? " (*Conf.*, i, 2). Grotius compares Virgil (*Ecl.*, iii, 60) : " Iovis omnia plena," and Lucan, " Estne dei sedes nisi terra, et pontus, et aer, et cœlum et virtus ? " **30.** A contradiction is found by some critics between the prayer *unto this place*, as the Muslim *ḳiblah*, and the divine audience *unto the place of thy abode*, the latter as being a later, spiritualizing addition. But the criticism is far-fetched ; the *ḳiblah* is merely the *point d'appui*, and the contrast, not contradiction, is not amiss after v.²⁷ ; *cf.* the like contrast in Ps. 20³⁻ ⁷. There follows, vv.³¹⁻⁵³, in the language of the Church, the earliest extensive Litany. **31. 32.** A prayer for divine judgment in the purgation by oath. There is to be noted the primacy of order given by this litany to the element of justice between man and man. **31.** The v. has difficulties of text, for which *cf.* the various renderings in EVV, and see Note. For the subject see J. Pedersen, *Der Eid bei den Semiten* (1914), with parallels from Akkadian, Greek, Roman fields, and for the present subject in particular cc. 5, 6 ; also H. Schmidt, ' Die Gebete der Angeklagten,' in *O.T. Essays*, ed. Simpson, 143 ff., and his enlarged treatment in *ZAW* Beiheft 49 (1928). The word generally translated ' oath ' ('*âlāh*) is more exactly a ' hypothetical curse,' or ' Bann ' (so Pedersen, pp. 113 ff.) ; at Lev. 5¹, Prov. 29²⁴ JV excellently renders it with ' adjuration.' With these passages *cf.* the adjuration of a suspected wife in Num. 5¹¹ff., where the ordeal is enacted ' before YHWH,' even as here, ' before the altar in this house.' **32.** *According to his right* (*ṣèdeḳ*), not *righteousness*, but primarily a legal term; *cf.* K. F. Euler, *ZAW* 1938, 278 f. **33. 34.** The major external disaster would come from foreign enemies. **35. 36.** The major internal calamity, namely the drought, arises from the peculiar physical features of Canaan; *cf.* Jer. 14¹ff·, Joel 1⁸ff·, etc. **37.** Other famine-producing plagues are listed: *blasting* (*e.g.*, ' by the east wind,' Gen. 41⁶), *mildew, locust, grasshopper* (with asyndeton); the last term is wrongly translated ' caterpillar ' by EVV. For these last two practically synonymous words along with other synonyms see Commentaries on Joel 1, and for such plagues in general Dalman, *A. u. S.*, 2, 296 f., 323 ff., 344 ff., etc. **38.** *Whatsoever prayer and supplication be made by any man ⌜of all thy people Israel⌝* [OGrr. om.], *who shall know each one the affliction of his own heart, and shall spread forth his palms toward this house:* **39.** *then do thou hear in heaven, the place of thy abode, and forgive, and do, and give to each man according to all his ways, as thou knowest his heart, for thou alone knowest the heart of all the sons of men.* The word translated ' affliction ' is general term for any kind of plague (*e.g.*, Ex. 11¹, etc.—and so EVV here after 𝔙 ' plaga '); but the closest approach to the denotation of the word here appears at 1 Sam. 10²⁶, where the verb of the same root appears: " and there went with him (Saul) the men of valour whose hearts God had touched " (origin of a phrase of Christian piety). For such ancient scrupulousness *cf.* Pss. 51; 19¹³, and see Gunkel, pp. 192 ff., 222 f. Kimchi rightly interprets the point here as of the hidden knowledge or concern of the heart as distinct from public knowledge, *i.e.*, the sense of conscience, and indeed with the latter word Heb. *heart* may well be translated here. It is anticipation of the ' conscience ' of the N.T., *e.g.*, Jn. 8⁹, Acts 24¹⁶, and Paul's great confession in Rom. 9. See Poole for various interpretations. For the spreading forth of the open hands *towards this house. cf.* Ps. 28², etc. This section advances from communal causes to those of the individual whose heart is touched by God, and who would find release. For the divine knowledge of the human heart *cf.* Jer. 17⁹ff·. **40.** *In order that they may revere thee,* etc.: *cf.* Dt. 31¹³, etc. The usual English for the verb, 'fear,' is most unfortunate; the noun of the same root should be translated 'religion.' **41-43.** The prayer for *the foreigner* (EVV *stranger*) who comes to worship in the temple. This refers to aliens from a foreign land (not the *gêr*, the settled alien, whose liberties were provided for, Num. $15^{14ff.}$), who may be attracted to the glorious national shrine and its God; the basis of this generous prayer may have been diplomatic missions which paid their respects to the national Deity, as in the proposed case of the Cushite embassy (Is. 18^7), and the legend about Alexander, how he went up into the temple and offered sacrifice there (*Ant.*, xi, 8, 5—*per se* a possible occurrence). But there may well have been cases of sincere devotion on part of Gentiles; *cf.* the story of Naaman (II. 5). For the prospect of a wider conversion see Ps. $68^{30f.}$. **44. 45.** The prayer in war: parallel to vv.$^{33f.}$, but the war here is precised as a holy enterprise. **46-53.** The prayer in defeat and exile. The prayer toward Jerusalem from abroad is witnessed to in story in Dan. 6^{11}, 1 Esd. 4^{58}, Tob. 3^{11}. For the religion of the pre-Exilic Diaspora *cf.* Gunkel, pp. 262 f., holding that Pss. 61, 63 have such origin. **46.** Deportation to a *land of the enemy, far off or near,* has caused question as to the second item; but among the colonists settled by the Assyrians in Samaria were people from Syrian Hamath as well as from Mesopotamia. **52.** *That thine eyes may be opened,* etc.: Stade regards this as without connexion with 'the interpolation of vv.$^{44-51}$, but fails to restore a connexion; in the profuse diction of the prayer too great nicety of consecution may not be expected. **54-61.** The peroration of the prayer: Solomon *blessed all the congregation of Israel,* along with prayer for divine grace and exhortation to the people. Ch. omitted this section because of its character as a benediction (perquisite of the priests, see Num. $6^{22ff.}$), replacing it with account of the descent of fire from heaven, which consumed the sacrifices. **54.** For the contradiction between the king's arising from his knees and v.^{24} see above. Stade, criticizing piecemeal the phraseology of the second half of the v., would excise *he arose*—(v.^{55}) *and stood,* but this appears as an arbitrary attempt to get order out of a composite narrative. For such a royal prayer of thanksgiving *cf.* Babylonian examples cited by Gunkel, 284 ff. **57. 58.** The blessing proper. Šanda rightly comments that according to this blessing the people have need of the divine grace for aid in keeping God's laws, and " das ist eine sittliche Auffassung, welche über die Moral anderer Kulturvölker Vorderasiens weit hinausreicht." **60.** Y_{HWH}, *he is the God.* This credal expression appears in a strenuous scene, 18^{39} (*q.v.*), and may have been a current battle-cry. *Cf.* Islamic " There is no god but God " (*allāh,* ' the God,' as here in the Hebrew).

VV.$^{62-66}$. The great dedication feast and dismissal of the congregation. ‖ 2 Ch. 7^{4-10}; *cf. Ant.*, viii, 4, 45.

62. *And the king and all* ⌈*Israel with him*⌉ [OGrr. *the sons of Israel*] *were making sacrifice before* Y_{HWH}. **63.** *And Solomon* [Ch., OGrr.+*the king*] *sacrificed the sacrifice of peace-offerings* ⌈*which he sacrificed to* Y_{HWH}⌉ [an added *id est*], *22,000 cattle* ⌈*and 120,000 sheep*⌉ [𝕲 (B Z a₂) om., Jos. has] ; *and they dedicated the house of* Y_{HWH}, *the king and all the Bnê-Israel.* **64.** *On that day the king consecrated the centre of the court that is before the house of* Y_{HWH}, *for he offered there the holocaust* ⌈*and the oblation*⌉ (Ch. om.) *and the fat sacrifices of the peace-offerings, for the bronze altar that was before* Y_{HWH} *was too small to contain the holocaust and the oblation* ⌈*and the fat sacrifices*⌉ [𝕲 (B Z a₂) om.] *of the peace-offerings.* **65.** *And Solomon celebrated at that time the Haj and all Israel with him, a great convocation, from the Entrance to Hamath to the Wady of Egypt, before* Y_{HWH} *our God* [OGrr.+*in the house that he built, eating and drinking and rejoicing before the Lord our God*], *seven days* ⌈*and seven days, fourteen days*⌉ [OGrr. om.; Jos. ' twice seven days ']. **66.** *On the eighth day he dismissed the people, and* ⌈*they blessed the king*⌉ [𝕲 (B Z a₂) *he blessed it*] ; *and they went home rejoicing and happy of heart for* ⌈*all*⌉ [OGrr. om.] *the goodness which* Y_{HWH} *had done to his servant David and his people Israel.*

The above display presents the materials for the criticism of the text. The section is late, Deuteronomic according to Kittel, Stade, *al.*, and offers a picture of the celebration as it might have been ; as Mowinckel remarks : later editors had no records of such an event, " they pictured the ceremonies as they were practised in their own times " (*Psalmenstudien,* 2, 109). Hölscher regards the whole section as a late midrash-like story, reminiscent of the Chronicler. Ch. omits *peace-offerings which he sacrificed to* YHWH (v.⁶³), as an only partial duplicate of the list in v.⁶⁴. The items of the thousands of sacrificial victims (that for the sheep is doubtless secondary) are exaggerations ; *cf.* the far simpler figures for a similar celebration, 2 Ch. 29³¹ᶠᶠ·. There may be compared the tradition of Crœsus offering to the Delphic god ' 3000 beasts of every kind fit for sacrifice ' (Her., i, 50) ; and similarly the assertion in a Minæan building inscription of dedicatory sacrifices ' in fifteen courts ' (the Arab. noun the same as the Heb. word here ; see Halévy, nos. 192, 199, Hommel, *Chrest.*, 102). For Assyrian amplification of numbers see Olmstead, *Ass. Historiography, e.g.*, p. 41, with a case where an original of 1253 sheep has been expanded by later scribes to 100,225. *They dedicated :* the communal plural is of interest. In Ch., v.⁹, the later festal term for dedication, *ḥanukkāh,* is used (but for the dedication of the altar, *cf.* Num. 7¹⁰). **64.** *The centre of the court* cannot be further precised ; the reference must be to the enlarged area surrounding the altar, generally supposed to have stood on the Rock (*eṣ-Ṣaḥrah*), which large space would have been used for extraordinary festivals. The item of *the oblation,* a vegetable offering, is repeated, but appears *de trop. The bronze altar* is described at 2 Ch. 4¹, and ascribed to Hiram as the artist ; strangely enough it is omitted in the list of Hiram's works above, although currently accepted in the narrative ; Benzinger attributes the omission to Puritan objection, and *cft.* Ex. 20²¹ᶠ·. This altar is referred to below, 9²⁵, and again, II. 16¹⁰ᶠᶠ·, in the story of its removal and replacement with another of new fashion. A bronze altar (with the same Hebrew words) is recorded by Yehaumilk, king of Gebal, among his donations to the temple of the Lady of Gebal. The present altar doubtless replaced that of David's on Araunah's threshing-floor (2 Sam. 24²⁵). See the literature bearing on the temple cited in introduction to Comm. on ch. 6 and on 6²⁰ᶠ·. and in particular Kittel, ' Der Brandopferaltar,' in his *Studien,* 146 ff., and J. De Groot, *Die Altäre des salomonischen Tempelhofes, BWAT* 2 (1924). **65.** *From the Entrance to Hamath to the Wady of Egypt : cf.* the terms for the extent of the Israelite state, ' from the Entrance to Hamath to the Sea/Wady of the Arabah,' II. 14²⁵, Am. 6¹⁴. The first term indicates the opening into the Syrian Biḳʻah, the great valley between the two Lebanons, while the second is identified with the Wady el-'Arīsh; see Abel, *GP* 1, pt. 2, ch. 2, and K. Elliger, 'Die Nordgrenze des Reiches Davids,' *Pjb.*, 32 (1936), 34 ff. **65. 66.** The passage has its parallel in Ch., vv.⁹ᶠ·: "And they made on the eighth day a solemn assembly, for the dedication of the altar they celebrated seven days, and the Haj seven days. And on the twenty-third day of the seventh month he dismissed the people," etc. From this quarter Ki. has been contaminated with the plus (*seven days*) *and seven days, fourteen days,* failing in 𝕲. Ch. distinguishes two feasts, one of the dedication of the altar (not of the temple!), the other of the yearly Haj, Succoth or feast of Booths, with Jos. here σκηνοπηγία. For such a reputed additional feast of seven days *cf.* the one attached to Hezekiah's great festival acc. to 2 Ch. 30²³ᶠ·. For the accumulation of festivals at this season of the year see Mowinckel, *Psalmenstudien*, II. *Das Thronbesteigungsfest Jahwähs und der Ursprung der Eschatologie*, 44–145, with which *cf.* Gunkel's criticism and partial acceptance, *Einl. in die Psalmen*, 100 ff. See also Morgenstern, 'Supplementary Studies in the Calendars of Ancient Israel,' *HUCA* 10 (1935), with bibliography of his extensive treatments of the subject. There may be contained in the Chronicler's report of a double feast a true tradition of an annual pre-Exilic feast of Hanukkah or Dedication; see Montgomery, 'The Dedication Feast in the O.T.,' *JBL* 29 (1910), 29 ff., with parallels from the Greek, Roman, Christian fields for the 'natal day' of temples and churches. In sacred calendars there is always careful arrangement of feasts so that they may not interfere with one another, and there may well have been a later distinction between Succoth and Dedication. For the accompanying festal meal *cf.* 2 Sam. 6¹⁹, Neh. 8¹⁰ᶠᶠ·. *They blessed the king:* 𝕲 transposed subject and object; but the people's blessing here, as in good Oriental use, was the grateful response of the people; *cf.* the royal 'blessing of YHWH,' vv.¹⁵· ⁵⁶.

In the following Notes the variations of Ch. are noted only when they bear upon the present text. **14.** קהל 1⁰: OGrr. om., even as Heb. MS Ken. 1 om. 2.⁰—**15.** ישראל: Grr.+' to-day,' and so at v.⁵⁶; *cf.* 5²¹.—**16.** מכל שבטי: 𝕲 and 𝕲ᴸ variously. There is an inconcinnity between the 'choosing of any tribe' and the 'choosing of David,' which Ch. and 𝔊 attempt to amend with plusses, partly accepted by Kit. and *BH* ; Heb. MS Ken. 187 overcomes the same difficulty by omitting בעיר ; but, with St., 𝔓 is to be kept.—**19.** רק : B a₁ om.—**21.** מקום לארון : Ch., את הארון, preferred by St., Šanda, *cf. BH* ; but 𝔖, which they cite, abbreviates the whole passage.—**22.** השמים : see Meek, ' The Heb. Accusative,' *JBL* 1940, 224 ff. ; St., Hölscher regard as a gloss contradicting v.³⁸, but here the prayer is made in the holy place.—**23.** חסד : see the full discussion of the word by N. Glueck in *ZAW* Beih. 47 (1927).— לעבדיך : 3 MSS לעבדך, and Grr. read as sing., and singularizing the foll. ppl., followed by 𝔊ᴸ with plus ' to David my father.'—**24.** את אשר דברת לו : Grr., exc A = 𝔄, om. through mistranslation of אשר 1⁰ with ἅ.—**26.** ועתה : 35 MSS, Ch.+יהוה=VSS, to be accepted. —דבריך Kt. : Ḳr. as sing. = 𝔊 𝔖 correctly ; *cf.* similar cases vv.²³· ²⁶. —אשר דברת לעבדך : OGrr. om.—**27.** אלהים : Ch.+הארם את =OGrr. here, with scruple against nature religion.—בניתי : Grr., exc A = 𝔄, plus ' to thy name,' again with theological restriction.—**28.** 𝔊 has an abbreviated form, made basis of various corrections, *e.g.*, by Kamp., St., Šanda, but the results are not convincing ; *cf.* Burn., *BH*.—**29.** עינך : ancient *scriptio defectiva*; see Bär, and *cf.* GK §91, k.—לילה ויום : so the order of the parts of the ancient day, *e.g.*, Gen. 1⁵ ; Ch., Grr. with the reverse, and so below, v.⁵⁹.— **30.** תחנת : 15 MSS תפלת ; 𝔊 τ. δεήσεως =x+κ. τ. προσευχης, A τ. φωνης.—השמים : ותשמע אל מקום שבתך אל : the prep. אל with שמע is unique, but in the pregnant sense of ' even unto ' is, as Burn. shows, illustrated elsewhere, *e.g.*, 6¹⁸, II. 10¹⁴. Ch. corrected the prep. to מן, and the Grr. to ἐν. The objection of some critics (St. and Haupt at length, Šanda) to the adverbial phrase has been commented on above, v.²². On the other hand the unsyntactical השמים, vv.³²· ³⁴· ³⁶· ⁴⁵, and the developed phrase מכון שבתך הש', vv.³⁹· ⁴³· ⁴⁹ (rendered by Ch., VSS, EVV with ' in/from heaven,' etc.) are to be elided as glosses from the present passage.—**31.** את אשר : Ch., אם ; the prevailing text of Gr. οσα αν, with variant ως αν, ος αν (the last interpretation appearing in Heb. MS Ken. 150, rdg. the causative יחטיא).—נשא : so Bär, Ginsb.¹, *BH* ; variant נשא, Mich., Ginsb.² ; the variants also in the text of Ch. Gr. λαβη=נשא ; 𝔗 ירשי, the verb used as tr. of נשא, Dt. 15², and so here=' exact against him a curse.' This rdg. is generally preferred ; but Akk. *nišu*, ' oath ' (=Heb. root נשא, used of ' lifting up ' hands at an oath), suggests that נשא is here much more tenable. —אלה [ובא] : Grr., κ. εξαγορευση (verb=' to confess,' *e.g.*, Lev. 5⁵) ; 𝔗 ' and swear himself '=𝔖, *i.e.*, as for ואלה : 𝒱 ' propter iuramentum.' See Burn. for several revisions proposed ; preferable is the rdg. באלה, for which *cf.* Neh. 10³⁰, באים באלה, and so Kamph., St., Šanda, *BH*.—**32.** השמים : for the word as secondary, also below, see above, v.³⁰.—**33.** אשר : 10 MSS כי=Ch. ; Grr., ὅτι. For the conditional use of the relative particle see Lexx., and C. Gaenssle, *AJSL* 31 (1915), 109 f.—אליך 1⁰ : Ch., OGrr. om.—אליך 2⁰ : Ch.

I. 9¹⁻²⁸

לפניך ; OGrr. om.—**35.** תַּעֲנֵם: so 𝔗 𝔖; Grr., ταπεινωσης αυτους (=EVV), i.e., as תְּעַנֵּם (=𝔙 ' propter afflictionem suam '), which is to be accepted, with Then., al.—**36.** עבדיך: 6 MSS עבדך=Grr., as at vv.³⁰·⁵². ; the sing. to be accepted, with Klost., al.—כי תורם ילכו בה . . . : St. regards as a gloss ; yet it may be kept as a parenthesis, like כי תענם, v.³⁵.—ארצך: 𝔊 τ. γῆν, avoiding the provincialism.—**37.** דבר רעב: for the rhetorical prefixation of the subject cf. Is. 28¹⁸, Mic. 5⁴, as also later in P (Burn.).—בארץ 1⁰ : OGrr. om.—ירקון: OGrr. om.—[שעריו] בארץ: with Grr., 𝔖 read בְּאַחַד; n.b. 𝔙 ' eius portas obsidens ' ; for the phrase cf. Dt. 12¹⁴, etc.—[מחלה] כל: n.b. the asyndeton, as also in v.³⁸ ; some MSS prefix the conj. in both cases.—**38.** לכל עמך ישראל: OGrr. om. ; apparently a restrictive gloss to לכל האדם—**40.** פני: MSS 70 94 614 om., and so OGrr.—**41.** ישראל: MS 70 om., and so 𝔊.—VV.⁴¹ᵇ·⁴²ᵃ om. by OGrr. by homoiot.—**43.** אתה: 33 MSS (e.g., 70), Ch., ואתה= Grr., 𝔖.—**44.** איבו: 2 MSS, Ch., אויביו=VSS ; but the sing. at v.⁴⁶.—אל יהוה: Ch., אליך, avoiding the Name ; cf. Grr., ' in the name of the Lord.'—**46.** ואנפת: for the obscure Gr. variants here and in Ch. see Burn.—האויב: MS 70, Ch., OGrr. om.—**47.** והשיבו אל לבם: for the phrase, used of careful consideration, see Dt. 4²⁹, 30¹.—שביהם: Ch., שֹׁבֵיהֶם.—[העוינו] ו: 3 MSS, Ch. properly om., and even the Grr. retain the asyndeton.—**48.** העיר: another case of the frequent asyndeton in this composition ; 18 MSS, Ch. with the conj.=Grr., exc. B A i xa₂.—**49.** משפטם . . . את הפלחם: OGrr. om. ; a gloss from v.⁴⁵ ; with Burn., in this case Israel had no legal cause.—**52.** להיות. ; Ch., יהי, cf. Grr.—**53.** For the Gr. transposition of vv. ¹²ᶠ· to ⁵³ᵃ see Comm. ad loc.—**54.** קם: perhaps careless grammar ; the expected ויקם was read or understood by Grr. —**56.** יהוה: Grr.+' to-day ' ; cf. v.¹⁵.—**58.** לבבנו: some 40 MSS לבבינו=the Grr. with pl.—ומשפטיו: Grr. om., exc. x.—**59.** ומשפט עמו: B al. om. by homoiotel.—ביומו: Gr. εν ημερα αυτου corrupted in B Z, 5 minuscc. to ενιαυτου.—**60.** יהוה: 𝔊 κυριος ο θεος, and so 𝔊ᴸ, which omits foll. αυτος θεος.—אין: 30 MSS ואין=Grr., 𝔖 𝔙.— **61.** לבבכם: Grr., 𝔙 ' our heart.'—ללכת: Grr. pref. οσιως.—**62.** For further textual notes on vv.⁶²⁻⁶⁶ see tr. above.—עמו ישראל: OGrr. as 'יש : cf. MS Ken. 30, 'העם יש.—**63.** וזבח: OGrr. as pl.—**65.** After ' before Y. our God ' OGrr. insert " in the house which he built, eating and drinking and rejoicing (𝔊ᴸ+and praising) before the Lord our God," which is perhaps to be accepted, acc. to BH ; but this is a superfluous scene.—**66.** ביום. Grr., 𝔖 𝔙 prefix ' and.'— ויברכו את המלך: 𝔊 κ. ευλογησεν αυτον ; 𝔊ᴸ a doublet of 𝔊 and 𝔥 (see Rahlfs, SS 3, 193) ; St. unnecessarily corrects to " and they blessed him " ; Benz., on Gr. authority to " and he blessed it (the people)," but the Greeks were ignorant of the use of the Oriental verb.

Ch. 9¹⁻⁹. The second vision to Solomon, of conditional promise and dire threat. ‖ 2 Ch. 7¹¹⁻²² (with long expansion of our v.²). The section is a late postlude to the vision in

3⁵ᶠᶠ·. It is thoroughly Deuteronomic in language, is not affected by the Priestly literature. Comm. generally assign it to Exilic or post-Exilic composition. But Burney (with close study of the language, pp. 129–33) and Šanda argue for probable pre-Exilic dating; there is but a brief reference to exile, v.⁷ᵃ; *cf.* Micah's prophecy of the destruction of the holy city, Mic. 3¹². For similar hortatory material *cf.* David's charge to his son, 2¹⁻⁴, of which there is reminiscence here, vv.⁴·⁵. **8.** Read with correction of 𝔥 : *This house shall become ruins*, as against the absurd *shall become lofty*; for devious evasions of the text *cf.* EVV; of these JV, on Targumic authority, interestingly introduces the original text by way of a parenthesis : " this house which is so high [shall become desolate]." See Note.

9¹⁰⁻¹⁰. A miscellany : Solomon's buildings, trade, magnificence, cosmopolitan reputation.

9¹⁰⁻¹⁴. Solomon's financial dealings with Hiram. ‖ 2 Ch. 8¹·²; *cf. Ant.*, viii, 6, 4.

This brief record must be considerably sifted to obtain a historical residuum. The *twenty years* (v.¹⁰) is evidently sum of the 7 years for building the temple and the 13 for building the palace (6³⁸, 7¹). There remains : **11b.** *Then king Solomon gave to Hiram twenty cities in the land of Galilee;* **14.** *and Hiram sent to the king 120 talents of gold.* In *JBL* 1934, 49, the writer has argued for the archival character of the adverb ' then ' (*'āz*), occurring in Ki. some thirteen times (*e.g.*, v.²⁴, *q.v.*), where the original may have given an exact date. The bargain between the two kings was for a loan to replenish Solomon's empty treasury, for which the latter pawned twenty cantons in Galilee. Šanda endeavours to make exact calculations upon the date of the present transaction, proposing that the Ophir voyage was subsequent, and its profits refilled the treasury, so that the pawned towns could be redeemed; accordingly he accepts the historicity of the parallel in Ch., which speaks of " the cities that Huram gave to Solomon "; but this is a bald perversion of our passage. Various hypotheses have been offered by critics for v.¹⁴; Grätz arbitrarily changed the statement into " sent the king to H.," *i.e.*, of Solomon's repayment for the pawned cantons; Benzinger makes it a gloss to ' gold,' v.¹¹. Stade regards the v. as secondary. For the talent see the Archæologies of Nowack (§37) and Benzinger (§42), Meissner, *Bab. u. Ass.*, 1, 356 (with Ass. relief representing the ring-form of the gold specie); for calculations of the value of 120 talents Kittel (1900) proposes an equivalent of 19½ million marks, Šanda (1911) 25 million francs, Meyer (1931) 16 million marks—' but gold of less value than now ' (*GA* 2, 2, 264). There is no control of the large figure; *cf.* the exorbitant figures for gold, 9^{28}, $10^{14ff.}$. In the insertion, of good tradition, vv.$^{12f.}$, is reported Hiram's displeasure at the bargain, when he looked into it; the name of the district, as allegedly given by him, has been, since Josephus's day, generally regarded as a depreciatory nickname, and is explained by a forced interpretation of the Heb. vocable as meaning ' good for nothing ' (so Moffatt translates). But the Grr. translate with the word ' boundary,' ὅριον, identifying *kebûl* of 𝔐 with the common word for ' boundary,' *gĕbûl, i.e.,* ' march-land '; see Note for the quite possible variation between *g* and *k*. Then the verb, generally translated *he called*, is to be rendered *they called*, with impersonal use of the sing. verb (*cf.* Gen. 16^{14}, etc.), as Šanda has also argued. A place of the same name, Kebul, in Asher appears at Josh. 19^{27}, known also from Josephus's *Vita*, 43 f., Χαβαλων, where he was posted with his troops for a while, the place surviving as Kabul to this day, 8 miles SE of Akko; see Robinson, *LBR* 88; Abel, *GP* 2, 14, 67, 287, the latter scholar suggesting that the name is a survival of the Solomonic term. Accordingly translate : *It was called March-land*. For the ancient address of courtesy between kings, *my brother, cf.* $20^{32f.}$.

VV.$^{15-23}$. Solomon's levy and the cities that he built. ‖ 2 Ch. 8, 3–10; *cf. Ant.*, viii, 6, 1, 3.

V.^{15a} is introduction to vv.$^{20-23}$; the insertion, vv.$^{15b-19}$, the list of cities built, is of original archival type, for which see the writer's " Archival Data in the Book of Kings." But the objective of the passage as a whole is the enslavement of the Canaanites, with contradiction of the notion that Solomon put his own free people to hard labour; compare the democratic criticism of ' the manner of a king ' put in Samuel's mouth (1 Sam. $8^{10ff.}$), and the actual contradiction of the apology here in the revolt against Solomon's tyrannical administration as described in ch. 12.

15a. *And this is the business of the levy that king Solomon raised to build the house of* YHWH *and his own house and the Millo and the wall of Jerusalem.* For the organized levy see Comm. on 4⁶. There are abundant testimonies to this brief statement; in 𝕳, v.²⁴ *inf.*, 3¹, and 11²⁷ᵇ; in 𝕲 with translations of the Heb. texts, 3¹ being located at end of ch. 4 and with fragments, 2³⁵ᶜ· ³⁵ᵉᵝ. The presumably oldest form of the present datum is 11²⁷ᵇ (connected with Jeroboam's fortunes): " Solomon built the Millo. He closed up the breach of the City of David his father." This full archivally phrased text remarkably enough appears here in the Hexapla, *e.g.*, A, also 𝕾ᴴ. There was prefixed to this text for sake of completeness the item of " the building of his house and YHWH's house " (so the order in 3¹). There are further echoes of 11²⁷ : for "and the Millo and the wall of Jerusalem" Gr. 2³⁵ᵉᵝ has simply, "then he built the Akra"; "and the wall of Jerusalem round about" = Gr. 2³⁵ᶜ, *cf.* 3¹, "and the wall of Jerusalem." That is, the details of 11²⁷ are variously reduced and allocated. For the Millo, traditionally identified with the famous Akra of Maccabæan and subsequent ages, see Smith, *Jerusalem*, 2, 40 ff. This identification is regarded as uncertain by Burrows, *WMTS* 66.

The list of cities built by Solomon is interrupted by a pertinent detail of Gezer (v.¹⁶, and the repetition of the name in the opening of v.¹⁷—*v. inf.*); with this omitted, the list reads: **15b.** *and Hasor, and Megiddo, and Gezer,* **17.** *and Lower Beth-horon,* **18.** *and Baalath, and Tamar-in-the-Steppe in the Land. Cf.* 2 Ch. 8³⁻⁶, *Ant.*, viii, 6, 1. Reports of the building, rather rebuilding, of cities are innumerable in the Ass. inscriptions. Closer to hand are the similar inscriptions from lands contiguous to Palestine. Mesha of Moab in his stele gives a list of some eight cities which ' I built '; the Syrian stele of Zakar (*ca.* 800 B.C.) records building operations in a broken passage. Indeed the present list may well have been taken from a contemporary royal inscription, and this is equally possible for later references in Kings to city-building. In general, for identification of the cities named see Smith's and Abel's Geographies, Watzinger's *Denkmäler Palästinas*, Galling, *BR*, and for review of earlier opinions Döller, *GES* 160 ff., Šanda, p. 257. *Hasor*, still Israelite at the end of the

Northern kingdom (II. 15^{29}), has only recently been identified, by Garstang in 1926, and as the present Tell el-Ḳedaḥ (not on the Survey Map, but on the recent small Map of the Survey, and that of the Am. Bible Society), 4 miles W of the Jesr Banāt Ya'ḳūb, the bridge across the Jordan, just south of the Ḥuleh Lake ; see Garstang, Liverpool *Annals of Archæology and Anthropology*, 14, 35 ff., and the several references to the site by Albright in *BASOR* 29 (1928), 33 (1929), 47 (1932), 68 (1937) ; to resume Albright : it has an acropolis half again as large in area as Megiddo, was itself a city some eight times as large as Megiddo, was " an important link in the chain of fortified camps, of rectangular form and earthwork defences," on the route of the barbarian irruptions of the 18th century, while traces of rebuilding in the 10th century are to be referred to Solomon's operations. For the recent fruitful excavations at *Megiddo* by the University of Chicago see C. S. Fisher, *The Excavation of Armageddon* (1929); P. L. O. Guy, *New Light from Armageddon* (Or. Inst. Communications, No. 9, 1931) ;[1] Olmstead, *HPS* 343 f. ; Breasted, *The Oriental Institute* (1933), ch. 11 ; Albright, *APB* 45 ff. There is difference of opinion as to the strata to be referred to Solomon's construction ; see Albright in *AJA* 1935, 138 ; R. S. Lamon, *Megiddo I*, *Strata I–V* (1939—by personal communication from Dr. R. M. Engberg). Olmstead's and Breasted's volumes, and especially Guy's monograph, give illustrations of the royal stables found at Megiddo, to which constructions v.^{19} refers. But now for a later dating of these stables see J. W. Crowfoot, ' Megiddo, A Review,' *JBL* 1940, 132 ff. Such stables have also been found at Tell el-Hesy, Gezer, Taanach (Guy, pp. 42 ff.). For *Gezer* there is Macalister's classical *Excavation of Gezer*, for which *cf.* Albright, *APB* 25 ff. ; excavation there has been renewed by A. Rowe (see the first report in *QS* 1935, 19 ff., with map and 6 plates). For the history of the place see Alt, *JPOS* 1935, 294 ff. ; 1937, 218 ff. *Lower Beth-horon* is the defensive post on the road from the Valley of Ajalon to Gibeon, N of Jerusalem, the historical route of advance into the heart of the country from Joshua's day to Allenby's campaign (the latter described in the last edition of Smith's *HG*). *Baalath*

[1] But for final disposal of the current equation of Megiddo and Armageddon, see Comm. II. 23^{29}.

is doubtless the Danite Baalath, not yet identified, grouped with Ajalon, Ekron, Gibbethon, et al., Josh. 19$^{41\mathrm{ff.}}$; cf. Ant., viii, 6, 1. Tamar is the city placed by Eze. 47^{19}, 48^{28}, at the southern boundary of the Holy Land, the Thamara of the Onomasticon, now identified with Ḳurnub, 35 km. SE of Beersheba, and as the Onomasticon notes, 'on the route between Elath and Hebron' (see Robinson, BR 2, 622, and cf. Albright, JPOS 1925, 44 f.). But a romantic identification was early read into the name. In Ch. 8^4 it is spelled 'Tadmor,' the item connected with Solomon's operations at Syrian Hamath and Sobah; this reading has been adopted by the Ḳrê in our text, and 'Tadmor' appears here in 𝔊$^\mathrm{L}$. The illusion was created by the later fame of Tadmor-Palmyra, situated actually 'in the desert above Syria,' as Josephus remarks on the present text. This identification is early indicated in Gr. 2$^{46\mathrm{c. d}}$ by pairing together 'the fortresses of the Lebanon and Thodmor [so 𝔊$^\mathrm{L}$] in the desert.' 𝔙 follows with the tr., 'Palmyra.' These Biblical texts were our earliest references to that famous city until Dhorme read the name, Tadmar, in an inscription of Tiglath-pileser I, ca. 1100 B.C. (RB 1924, 106). An Aramaic inscription, as early as 9 B.C., has been found there (Cooke, NSI no. 141). See at large Rostovtzeff, Caravan Cities (1932), cc. 4, 5. It may be noted that Forrer, in RA 1, 135, regards the reading of Tadmor and so the traditional interpretation as 'durchaus glaubwürdig.' But there is further definition of the place in our text, *in the wilderness, in the land*. This has ever been a crux for translators and commentators (see Notes); various additions have been proposed for 'the land,' and so Kittel (in his Comm.) plus 'of Judah,' arguing that identification with Tadmor involved excision of 'Judah.' But the text is fully confirmed by explaining 'in the land' as at 4^{19} (q.v.), i.e., the native expression for the home-land. The two cases corroborate one another.

The list follows geographical order, and evinces excellent strategical dispositions: Hasor, in the far north near an Upper-Jordan ford; Megiddo, commanding the great hollow between Galilee and the Ephraimite highlands; Gezer, the dower-fief from Pharaoh, on the Philistine border, along with Beth-horon and Baalath controlling the easiest route into the interior towards Jerusalem ; in the south Tamar, on the route to the Red Sea.

The intruded passage, v.[16], but of original historical authority, reads : *Pharaoh king of Egypt, having gone up and taken Gezer and burned it with fire, and having killed off the Canaanite citizenry* [Heb. *the Canaanite dwelling in the city*], *gave it as dower to his daughter, Solomon's wife*. See Comm., 3^1, for the historical circumstances, also for the Greek attachment of the two verses together and their location at end of ch. 4.[2]

19. *and all the store-cities of Solomon's* [OGrr. om.], *and the cities for chariots, and the cities for horses* [EVV *horsemen*], *and the pleasure of Solomon, what he was pleased to build in Jerusalem* [om. with OGrr. *and in the Lebanon*] *and in all the land of his dominion*. The v. is identical with 2 Ch. 8^{5b}, the Chronicler having expanded the original and so contaminated the text here, as the Greek omissions prove. The item of chariot cities is supplemented with original details in $10^{26ff.}$. The present v. probably expanded a brief termination of the archival list, naming or referring to these depots for the chariots and horses, as in the Zakar stele cited above (Note to 1^5). As observed there, *horses* is to be read. As for the intrusion from Ch., *and in the Lebanon,* tradition came to include that region in the royal domain on basis of 5^{28}, and also because of the item of the House of the Forest of Lebanon (7^2, 10^{21}). In this connexion is to be noted the cryptic passage in OGrr., 2^{46c}: καὶ Σαλωμὼν ἤρξατο ἀνοίγειν τὰ δυναστεύματα [𝕾ᴸ—τευοντα] τοῦ Λιβάνου ; for this see the writer's Note in *JAOS* 1936, 137, interpreting ἀνοίγειν in the frequent sense of *bḳ'*, ' to breach, capture,' the following unique noun = ' fortresses,' presenting the object. The passage is thus based on a Hebrew original.

VV.[20-23]. Resumption of the account of the administration, continuing v.[15a], || 2 Ch. 8^{7-9}. The levy, it is alleged (*per contra,* $5^{27ff.}$), bore only upon the unexterminated Canaanites, in the language of the Deuteronomists. The Israelites were

---

[2] There is supplementally to be noted Albright's article on ' The Gezer Calendar,' in *BASOR* 92 (1943), 16 ff., placing that remarkable relic in Solomon's reign, along with further historical discussion and extensive bibliography.

the royal servants in charge of civil and military administration. Only five of the Canaanite peoples are named as against the classical seven (Dt. 7¹, etc.). The Hex. Gr. interlards the two lacking. For ' Hivites ' we have to read throughout the Bible ' Horites,' even as this spelling appears in the Grr. at Gen. 34², Josh. 9⁷.³ The second of the official titles, EVV servants,' rather ' ministers ' (see at 1²) is properly represented by Gr. παῖδες, *i.e.*, ' courtiers ' ; Ch. omits it, perhaps from democratic objection. The fourth title (EVV ' captains ') is etymologically ' thirdling,' that is the third in the royal chariot, along with the king and charioteer, the bearer of the shield and bodyguard, the title then developing into a general court honour ; see Meissner, *Bab. u. Ass.*, 1, 93. Finally there are *the captains of his chariots and his horses* : the second item belongs to a late age, after the introduction of cavalry. Indeed the whole v. is bombastic and late, as though the Israelites were largely royal officers. V.²³ with introductory *these were* is an awkward termination of the whole period ; the verbal phrase may well be omitted. The figure ' 550 ' is doubtless authentic ; the passage is repeated from the present connexion with the figure multiplied at 5³⁰ (*q.v.*) ; see Note further.

V.²⁴. Two archival data. *Then* (𝔥 only) *Pharaoh's daughter came up out of the city of David to her house that he built for her. Then he built the Millo.* || 2 Ch. 8¹¹. There is no explanation of the introductory adverb in 𝔥, relieved in EVV with ' but,' by Kittel with ' sofort,' etc. Grr. in one place (9⁹) give the solution with ' then ' (rdg. '*z* instead of '*k*), and thus we have two data, without necessary connexion, the adverb in each case representing the original dating in the royal year, as noted above. This datum is the basis of 3¹, " he brought her into David's City, until he finished building his house " ; the queen's palace appears in the list of royal constructions (7⁸ᵇ). Ch. presents a gross perversion of the item—the foreign queen might not dwell in David's " holy places " whereas the Oriental lady always has her own ' house.'

---

³ For the Hurrians-Horites see Speiser, *Mesopotamian Origins* (1930), ch. 5, *in re* Hivites, p. 132 ; Albright, *SAC* 109 ff. (with recent bibliography). The extent of Hurrian letters appears now in Speiser's ' Introduction to Hurrian,' *AASOR* 20 (1940–41).

25. *And Solomon was wont to offer three times a year holocausts and peace-offerings upon the altar which he built to* YHWH, *and to burn incense* . . . [𝔥 *with it which—cf.* EVV] *before* YHWH. *And he completed the house.* The v. stands by itself; it contains ungrammatical elements. V.ᵃ may be an archival element that has been abused; Kittel would place it after v.²⁸, Šanda after 9⁹; but it should be left with its obscurity in this miscellany. The item may have referred to the time before the completion of the temple, when sacred functions were celebrated by the king at the renewed Davidic altar of 2 Sam. 24²⁵; *cf. sup.* 8⁶³. V.ᵇ, as it is, is a useless repetition; *cf.* 6¹⁴, etc.

VV.²⁶⁻²⁸. Solomon's enterprise on the Red Sea. ‖ 2 Ch. 8¹⁷ᶠ·; *cf., Ant.* viii, 6, 4. **26.** *And king Solomon made a navy at Esyon-geber, which is beside Eloth, on the shore of the Red Sea, in the land of Edom.* **27.** *And Hiram sent in the navy his servants, skippers* [Heb. *men of ships*], *who knew the sea, along with the servants of Solomon.* **28.** *And they came to Ophir, and fetched from thence gold,* 120 [with 𝔊; 𝔥 420; Ch. 450] *talents, and brought it to king Solomon.* This is an authentic record, to be compared with the Egyptian narratives of similar enterprises in that sea. Only the exaggerated figure for the gold is to be corrected. Solomon made use of Phœnician sailors and ship-builders on those distant waters (*cf.* ' the Tarshish navy with Hiram's navy,' 10²²) in the same way as the Egyptian monarchs from the Old Kingdom down employed Giblite-Byblian (so specifically) seamen in their enterprises in the Red Sea; see P. Montet, *Byblos et l'Égypte* (1928/29), especially pp. 8 ff., 224 ff. For Queen Hatshepsut's famous enterprise to Punt in the first half of the 15th century see Breasted, *ARE* 2, nos. 285 ff., and *HE* 273 ff. (with the frescos depicting the fleet); also on the Biblical relations with that quarter the writer's *Arabia and the Bible,* 175 ff. This sea-trade with Arabia was undertaken in competition with the Arab monopoly of the overland routes, and was resumed by the Persians, Greeks and Romans with the final despoilment of the Arab monopoly. See more at length Comm., 10²². Esyon-geber was the earlier port, hence located as ' hard by Eloth,' which latter name survives as Ayla, near Akaba. Earlier identifications of the place (*e.g.*, by Phythian-Adams, *QS* 1933, 137 ff., *cf.* Montgomery, *op. cit.*, 177, n. 29) have been upset by the brilliant discoveries and excavations made by Nelson Glueck, formerly director of the American School in Jerusalem, who has identified it with Tell el-Kheleifeh, to the west of Akabah, now some 500 metres inland, but earlier situated on the Red Sea. Only summary reference may be made here to Glueck's publications in the *Annual* of the American Schools, vols. 18–19 (1939), and the many current reports in the *Bulletin*, nos. 71–2, 75, 79, 80, 82 (1938–41); his summary accounts in *The Other Side of the Jordan*, in particular cc. 3, 4, and in *Smithsonian Report* for 1941, pp. 453 ff. ; also more popular articles in *ILN*, July 30, 1938, in *Asia*, Oct. 1938, Sept. 1939, and *Nat. Geog. Mag.*, 1944, 233 ff. He notes three activities of this ancient ' factory town,' the smelting of the local copper in remarkably devised furnaces, manufacture of copper tools, and ship-building. This was accordingly the storehouse for Solomon's great supply of bronze. The discovery of potsherds with South Arabic lettering exhibits the ancient trade with Arabia. *Cf.* the excellent survey of the region, based mostly on Glueck's results, in Abel, *GP* 2, 35 ff., with a final section on " La route de cuivre dans la 'Araba." The discovery of iron deposits and mines in the same region illustrates Dt. 8^9, and corroborates the tradition of the extensive use of that metal in the temple. No exact location for Ophir has been discovered ; it doubtless lay in Arabia, despite extravagant theories ; that land once possessed rich deposits of alluvial gold, for which see *Arabia and the Bible*, 38, n. 5, and for Ophir Note below. In earlier literary tradition the present passage may have been associated with 10^{22}, or with the account of Solomon's trade in horses and chariots, $10^{28f.}$. The passage serves here as preface to the following story of the Queen of Sheba.

1. חשק, חפץ : emendations have been proposed on basis of v.^{19} and VSS ; see *BH*. The half-verse appears to be dependent upon v.^{19}, the other buildings of ' Solomon's desire ' are not yet listed.— **3.** הקדשתי : Grr. pref. a plus.—**4.** אתה : there is no reason, *vs.* St., to elide the word, despite its omission in some pre-Hex. texts.— חקן : Ch., וחקן=VSS, accepted by St., *BH*, *al.* ; but the appositive syntax is correct.—**5.** על ישראל : 𝔊^L ' in Jerusalem '—by historical criticism ?—[דוד] על : 23 MSS אל, to be accepted ; *cf.* 2^4.—**6.** אם : 2 MSS ואם=Ch., VSS, exc. 𝕴.—חקתי : 15 MSS וחי=VSS, exc. 𝕴 ;

to be accepted.—נחתי : Grr., ' Moses gave ' ; 𝔊 ' I gave to Moses.'
—**7.** הבית : 1 MS, Ch. +הזה=Grr.—אשלח : the Piel is supported by
Jer. 15¹ ; Ch. אשליך ; for the phrase with the Hif. see II. 13²³, etc.
—למשל ולשנינה : the phrase at Dt. 28³⁷, Jer. 24⁹.—**8.** עליון : =Grr.,
ο υψηλος ; Ch. expands, אשר היה עליון ; 𝔙 preserves ancient reminiscence, " this house which was high shall be desolate " (and so
JV exactly) ; the same adj., הריב, in place of 'ע, appears in 𝔖
and such is the tr. in 𝔏 𝔄. Read לְעָיִין, with Böttcher, al. The
case is one of alphabetic logomachy ; for such alterations see
Bleek, Einl., §270. For the phrase here see Mic. 3¹², Jer. 26¹⁸.—
9. ויחזקו באלהים אחרים : the phrase only here and in Ch. ; the verb +
Yhwh as obj. at Is. 64⁶.—וישתחוו : many MSS וישתחו, and so the
Ḳr.—כל : 𝔊 om.—At end 𝔊 𝔊ᴸ a plus from v.²⁴.

10. ויהי מקצה עשרים שנה אשר בנה : " and it came to pass at the
end of (the) 20 years that S. took to build," etc. The Heb. is
good, does not require correction, as with Klost., St., al., and is
to be construed with the period through v.¹¹, v.¹¹ᵃ being parenthetical, v.¹¹ᵇ apodosis ; and so the EVV present with proper
parenthesis. OGrr ignored this syntax, and made revision of the
opening two words : " in those days [attached to prec. v.]. For
20 years in which S. built the two houses . . . (v.¹¹) H. k. of T. was
helping S." Hex. prefixed from 𝔅 " and it was," then followed
OGrr.—**11.** נשּׂא : but נשּׁא, 2 Sam. 5¹² ; for confusion of א״ל and ה״ל
roots see GK §75, oo. The root is properly נשׂא/נשׁא (see GB), with
mng. ' to lend ' ; cf. confusion of similar roots at 8³¹.—**13.** להם :
for the inaccurate gender, presumably arising from the vernacular,
see GK §135, o, citing cases in Ruth, Sam., etc. ; the same phenomenon appears in Ugaritic and is frequent in OAram. A recent
study by M. G. Slonin, ' The Deliberate Substitution of the Masc.
for the Fem. Pronominal Suffixes,' JQR 32 (1942), lists this use
with reference to cities on pp. 149 ff. ; a similar case at II. 18¹³.—
ארץ : Grr. om., exc. f m w with a plus, v. inf. ; 𝔖ᴴ om. in text,
with gloss of rdg. in Aq., Sym.—כבול : Grr., ὅριον, ' boundary ' ;
Jos. renders with Χαβαλων, proposing a Phœn. mng., οὐκ ἀρεσκον,
evidently interpreted as from ka-bal, followed by Ewald and
successors, as noted above. It is of interest that in his Vita, as
cited above, Jos. speaks of the place as μεθόριον to Ptolemais, i.e.,
' a march-land.' For the identification of the word with גבול
such a process appears in the Amarna letters, e.g., Kubli for Gubli
(Byblos) ; see F. Böhl, Sprache der Amarnabriefe (1909), §7, d.
Against the discovery of bal, ' nothing,' in the word, it is to be
noted that the Grr. read that syllable as bul. For other attempts
at interpretation see Döller, GES §61. Add to these references the
Talmudic citation, Sabb. 54a, where כבול is given the mng. of
' sterility,' with the further remark that " the district was called
'כ because there were people there who were chained (מכובלין) with
silver and gold " (Jastrow, Dict., 608b). This explains the gloss
in the three Gr. cursives, cited above, γη δουλειας κατα το εβραικον

—14. ישלח: 𝔊 ηνεγκεν, suggesting Hiram's personal conference with Solomon.
15-26. The transpositions and duplicates in 𝔊 (B) are as follows : vv.^{15. 17b-19. 20-22} = 𝔊 10²³⁻²⁵; v.¹⁶ = 𝔊 4³²; v.¹⁷ = 𝔊 2^{35f.}, 4³³; v.¹⁸ = 𝔊 2^{35f. 46d}; v.²³ = 𝔊 2^{35h}; v.²⁴ = 𝔊 2^{35f.}, 9^{9b}. *Cf.* Montg., 'The Supplement at End of 3 Kingdoms.'—15. דבר המס: Grrr., η πραγματεια της προνομης; προν. = 'plundering,' and so 𝔖^H; *BH* sugg. הבו, as read by the translators (?); Sym., cited in 𝔖^H, understood משׂא 'tribute.'—המלוא: OGrr., τ. ακραν, which 𝔖^H tr. with *rēšā*, 'the head'; Aquilanic gloss in 𝔖^H transliterates.
—For 'Hasor,' etc., 𝔊 has duplicates, 2^{35f.}—16. בעיר הרג: 𝔊 εν Μεργαβ = 𝔈; 𝔊^L εν Αροεβ.—שלחים: see Burrows, 'The Basis of Israelite Marriage,' *Am. Oriental Series*, 15 (1938), 41 ff. The word appears in a Ugaritic poem on marriage of gods in Virolleaud's Nikal text (*Syria*, 17, 209 ff.), line 47; *cf.* Gordon's interpretation, *BASOR* 65 (1937), 29 ff.—17. 'Beth-horon the Lower': 𝔊, 'B. the Upper'; Ch. has both terms.—18. בעלת: 𝔊 om. here, has it at 2^{35f.}, where Tamar is omitted.—חמר: Kr. תַּדְמֹר, and so many MSS Kt = 2 Ch. 8⁴; 𝔊 texts, Θερμαι; 𝔊^L Θοδ(α)μορ; 𝔊^H Θερμαθ, but 𝔖 'Tadmor'; 𝔙 'Palmyra.'—במדבר בארץ; 𝔊 om. בארץ in both places; 𝔊 2^{46d} has 'in the desert' = Ch.; 𝔊^H 'in the desert and in the land,' then omitting the foll. conj., and attaching the second phrase to the foll. v.; 𝔖^H 'which is in the land, in the desert'; 𝔙 'in terra solitudinis.' These variations indicate the embarrassment of ancient interpreters, followed by modern scholars, *e.g.*, Böttcher + '(land) of Paran'; Kit. + 'of Judah'; Šanda + 'of the Negeb'; see Comm.—19. " and all the store cities of Solomon's " : 𝔊 om., 𝔖^H ※; possibly an inset from Ch.—מסכנות: Akk. *maškānu*; see GB, Bezold, *Glossar*, 273.—פרשים: see above on 1⁵.—חשק: many MSS pref. כל = 𝔈 𝔏 𝔙, by contamination from Ch.—ובלבנון: OGrr. om., an addition by similar process.—ממשלתו: Grrr., του μη καταρξαι αυτου = 𝔖^H, construed with כל העם, v.²⁰, as subject, *i.e.*, as though with prefixed מן = מִמְּשָׁלְיל.—20. Correct B† τον υποδεδειγμενον υπο to τ. υπολελειμενον απο = 𝔈.—The Grr. have variants for the Canaanite names.—21. עבד לםם: 𝔊 εις φορον = 𝔊^H + δουλειας.—
22. עֶבֶד: Grrr., πραγμα, after Aram. mng. of the root = 𝔖^H; Aq., 'a doer of service,' *i.e.*, ppl., as at v.²¹, which is to be accepted, the sing. being used collectively. Ch. clarifies with לעברים.—שריו ושלישיו: Ch., 'v שרי; 𝔊 om.; 𝔊^L inserts later in the series.—23. שרי הנצבים: Grr. as though 'השרים הנ; the text might well be simplified by omitting the first word, along with preceding אלה, as suggested above.—'550': Ch., '250.'—24. אך: 𝔊^H πλην; at 2^{35f.} 𝔊 ουτως, by Aram. interpretation (*cf.* Syr. *'ak*, Nöldeke, *Syr. Gr.*, §23, C), but 𝔈 'then'; in the citation after 9⁹ 𝔊 has τοτε, for the doubtless original או, with further defining gloss, εν τ. ημεραις εκειναις. Probably אך replaced the awkward או as restrictive particle, " she went up only to her house "; *cf.* Ch. Also at 9⁹ 𝔊 has 'his house' and 'for himself,' by misreading of suffix ה.—25. והקטיר אתו אשר

לפני יהוה ושלם את הבית : 'beyond translation,' 'conglomeration of marginal glosses,' so St. remarks. The first verb should be read וְהִקְטִיר. The next two words (which 𝕲 conveniently ignored, and for which 𝕲^H has αυτος), Klost., al., would correct to את אשו, 'his fire-offering,' but, as St. notes, only ' YHWH ' is elsewhere so construed with that noun. Apart from the improper consecution of the last verb its mng., ' to finish,' is Aram., not Heb. It may originally have stood alone, continuing the previous verbs, with the sense of ' paying vows ' (cf. Ps. 76^{12}), and then misunderstood, ' the house ' was added as object.—**26.** אני : sing. as collective, acc. to Sem. usage, prevalent in Arab., vs. the fem. of the unit in the foll. pl. ; cf. 22^{49} ; Grr. as sing., but 𝕾^H as pl. ; 𝔙 properly ' classem.' Grr.+υπερ ου, for which Klost. sugg. corruption of Ωφειρα.—אלות : MSS אלת, אילת =Grr., with -at, as 𝕸, II. 14^{22} ; see Note, 4^{13}.—ים סוף : Grr. here exceptionally τ. εσχατης θαλασσης= 𝕾^H, and so=ים סוֹף, i.e., ' Mare Ultimum,' the Indian Ocean, for which see Montg., JAOS 1938, 131 f.—**28.** אופירה : Grr. (exc. g e$_2$) with initial sigma, which is naturally explained as dittog. from prec. [ει]s, and so Rahlfs, SS 3, 100. However this spelling is constant in the Sept. as also in Jos., and the new form came to have its own geographical identification ; see W. E. Clark, AJSL 36 (1920), 113, who also notes the Gr. of Gen. 10^{30} Σωφηρα ορος ανατολων, and Jerome's comment thereon (PL 23, 970), ' mons orientis pertinens ad Indiæ regionem.' Growing knowledge of the Orient may have identified this ' Sopher ' with the Indian port, ancient Suppara, modern Sopāra, near Bombay ; see Periplus Erythræi Maris, ch. 52, and Schoff's translation and comments, pp. 43, 197.

10$^{1-10. 13}$. The visit of the Queen of Sheba. || 2 Ch. 9$^{1-9. 12}$; cf. Ant., viii, 6, 5 f. The narrative is interrupted by a parenthesis, vv.$^{11f.}$, an editorial footnote ; see below. The narrative is still regarded by many historians as a legend, so Meyer, GA 2, 2, 268 ; Olmstead, HPS 341, while Lods and Robinson ignore it. That a Yemenite queen (Josephus makes of her ' a queen of Egypt and Ethiopia ') should have travelled some 1400 miles for such a visit is out of question, while the item of Arabian queens has appeared absurd. But the Sabæans were still in North Arabia, had not yet pressed south, although doubtless, like the later Nabatæans, they controlled the northern trade-routes from South Arabia ; they are listed with Massa, Teima, Ephah, all northern tribes, in Gen. 25$^{2ff.}$, and the tradition of Job makes them neighbours and plunderers of the land of Uz (Job 1^{15}). Remarkably enough the Assyrian records of the eighth and seventh centuries give the names of five North Arabian queens, and queens appear in the North Minæan and the late Lihyanian inscriptions; indeed late legend would hardly have invented a queen.[1] Legend has naturally developed about the historical tradition and insisted on the pomp and pride of the royal meeting. In matter of fact sheer diplomacy would have been the object of the queen's visit, politely veiled in the desire to behold the king's glory. Kittel (*GVI* 2, 153) compares the visit of Hittite Hattushil to Ramses II on the occasion of the marriage of his daughter to the latter (Breasted, *HE* 439), although the father's visit is denied by Meyer (*GA* 2, 1, 485). It is of interest, as Meyer observes, that a romantic legend grew up in Egypt about this foreign princess, preserved in a late narrative (*ARE* 3, 429 ff.). For the ancient cosmopolitan interest in wisdom see Comm. above, 5[9ff.].

3. *And Solomon told her all her questions:* so EVV; but the same verb is translated at Jud. 14[12] with ' declaring ' a riddle; rather in modern English, *S. explained all her problems* [Heb. *words.*] **4.** *And the queen of Sheba saw all the wisdom of Solomon, and the house which he built*, etc. ' Wisdom ' is used here in the older sense of practical sagacity (see above, on 3[4ff.]), in particular of Solomon's construction and equipment of his palace (not the temple). **5.** The v. nicely delineates the womanly observation of details: *the food of his table, and the seating of his courtiers, and the attendance* [Heb. *standing*] *of his servants, and his* [with most Grr.; 𝔏 *their*] *apparel, and his drinking-service* [EVV *cup-bearers*], *and* ⌜*his holocaust which he was wont to offer in*⌝ [?] *the house of YHWH.* It is a matter of taste to decide between ' his ' and ' their ' apparel; the former is preferred by Stade, Šanda, the latter by Kittel; but it is best to preserve the sing. pronoun throughout. *Cf.* also the word of Jesus on Solomon's array, Mt. 6[29]. There is question over the word translated *drinking-service, i.e.,* the plate for serving wine; but cupbearers were included in the servants. The viniculture of Syria-Palestine was famous from of yore; there may be noted the Egyptian Sinuhe's experi-

---

[1] See Montg., *Arabia and the Bible*, 58 ff., 180 ff.; Šanda, *ad loc.*, the only commentator who has presented these historical data; also, *in extenso*, Lagrange, *RB* 1902, 256 ff.; 1927, 597, and Hommel, *EGAO* 142 ff., and his treatment of Sabæan history in Nielsen, *HAA* 65, 75.

ences (*ca.* 1970 B.C.) in Syria, declaring that there " wine was more plentiful than water " (Gressmann, *ATB* 1, 56 ; Barton, *AB* 372). The Ras Shamra texts constantly refer to wine and wine-cups, *e.g.*, the luscious scene in the introduction to the Anat Poem. 1 Ch. 27^{27} records the wine-cellars attributed to David's *ménage*. The climax of marvels was, according to the common modern translation, the great holocausts of the king, the spectacular ritual, as it were fascinating the woman's eye. But Ch. gives a variation of spelling for the critical word, and the change induced here the usual translation (GV FV EVV, exc. JV), ' his ascent by which he went up into —,' following Jewish tradition and comm. This ' ascent ' was identified by the rabbis with ' the ascending causeway ' of 1 Ch. 26^{16} (see Lightfoot, ' Descriptio templi ' in his *Opera*, 1, 559 ; *cf.* Keil) ; but why this architectural item should have been selected is not obvious. With slight change of 𝔥 here we can obtain *his going up by which he ascended to Y*HWH'*S house*, and the reference would then be to the great processionals ; *cf.* the Psalms of Ascent. *And there was no more spirit in her :* so EVV ; but following the original physical meaning of the Heb. noun, she ' was left breathless ' by her amazement. **6.** EVV, *concerning thy acts and concerning thy wisdom :* but read with Grr., *concerning thee*, etc. **7.** Heb., *thou hast added wisdom and goodness to the fame that I heard :* OGrr. lack ' wisdom and,' Ch. om. ' and goodness.' What is meant by the latter word is not at all clear, as the variety of trr. exhibits : Grr., ἀγαθά, 𝔙 ' opera,' EVV ' prosperity.' It does not mean ethical goodness in the modern English sense ; it might mean liberality, but this royal characteristic is presented below. The sentence may possibly be translated, following OGrr., with *thou hast added much to the fame which I heard* (see Note). **8.** *Happy thy men !* : but this is redundant along with the following congratulation of the courtiers ; the Grr. have *thy wives* (*i.e., nšyk* for *'nšyk*), followed by 𝔖^H 𝔖 𝔄, and this correction is to be accepted with modern commentators in general ; here again a case of feminine psychology. Prof. P. K. Hitti has informed the writer that it is good Oriental etiquette for a lady to ask after a gentleman's wife, not for a gentleman to do so. But to later moralizing those wives of Solomon's were a *bête noire*, *cf.* ch. 11. **13***a*. EVV,

And king Solomon gave to the queen of Sheba all her desire, whatsoever she asked, beside that which Solomon gave her of his royal bounty. But the English tries to improve upon the Heb., which reads, *apart from what he gave her according to the hand of king Solomon.* This awkward sentence is to be relieved by omitting with some Gr. MSS and most VSS the final *Solomon*, with the resultant *by royal bounty*, even as the phrase is used at Est. 1^7, 2^{18}. *All her desire* has been romantically interpreted by Jewish legend as of the queen's desire for offspring by Solomon, and so Rashi comments : " He went in unto her, and there was born of her Nebuchadnezzar." [2]

VV.$^{11, 12}$. Solomon's imports from the Red Sea. || 2 Ch. $9^{10, 11}$; *cf. Ant.*, viii, 7, 1. This interpolation in the above story is independent of the other two similar notes, 9^{26-28}, and *infra*, v.^{22}, all of them indeed independent. **11.** *Hiram's navy* is specified as Phœnician even more exactly than at $9^{26f.}$; Ch. relieves the notion of alien control by substituting ' the servants of H. and of S.' The *almug timbers* (so pl. in 𝕳) remain a mystery as to botanical identity and origin. Ch. has ' algum ' ; Grr. vary between two contradictory words, ' plane ' and ' unplaned ' (wood) ; Jos. makes it a pine-wood ; Sym. and 𝒴 translate with ' thyina,' a N. African wood used for fine furniture ; Aquila identifies with amber, the Talmud with red coral (Jastrow, *Dict.*). Since the botanist Celsus (1748) the identification with Indian sandalwood has become common, and has been adopted by JV—this supported by alleged etymology from Sanskrit ' valgu ' ; but see the Sanskritist W. E. Clark's full discussion of ' The Sandalwood and Peacocks of Ophir,' *AJSL* 36 (1920), 103 ff., dismissing as wholly unproved any Indian etymology. An ingenious suggestion, presented by Šanda, identifies the word with Egyptian

---

[2] For the Jewish development of the story and the riddles the queen put to the king see Targum 2 to Esther, ch. 2 ; Fabricius, *Codex Pseudepigraphicus*, 1013 ff. ; Ginzberg, *Legends of the Jews*, vol. 4 ; for the Ethiopic saga of the descent of the Abyssinian dynasty from the union of the couple, Budge, *The Queen of Sheba* (1922). For the Arabic romance of the Bilkis legend (so the lady is named), in which Solomon's answer to the riddle she proposed to him converted her to the true religion, see the text in the Chrestomathy of Socin's *Arabic Grammar* (1922), and *cf.* Rosch, *JPT* 6, 544 ff. For comparative stories see Frazer, *Folklore in the O.T.*, 2, ch. 10.

ḳmy, which he finds in Herodotus's word κόμμι (ii, 96), then supposing that the initial syllable is the Arabic article, thus approving the spelling of Ch. ; however, Herodotus merely states that the sap of the wood in question (ἀκάνθη, Mimosa Nilotica, still used for ship-building in Egypt) is κόμμι, *i.e.*, gum ; see also Albright, *AJSL* 37 (1921), 144 f. ; 39 (1922), 31.
12. The word translated *pillars* in EVV (but the Heb. word is sing.), following the VSS, ' supports,' on the basis of the Heb. root, is unknown for its technical mng. ; Ch. appears to have guessed at it with ' highways '=EVV ' terraces,' JV ' paths.' The further reference to the use of the wood for musical instruments shows that it was of delicate nature, used perhaps for inlay, wainscotting.

VV.$^{14-29}$. This section is a compilation of *membra disjecta*, following clues in the story of the Queen of Sheba's visit. VV.$^{14-25}$ accumulate the items of Solomon's wealth and magnificence ; vv.$^{14,\,15}$ state his yearly income in taxes and customs duties ; vv.$^{16,\,17}$ describe the honorific golden shields in his palace, and vv.$^{18-20}$ his throne of ivory and gold—the latter two sections having early documentary basis ; v.^{21} is an exaggerated item on the golden service in the palace, which induces, v.^{22}, citation from a source parallel to 9$^{26-28}$, 10^{11}, relating to his imports by sea ; vv.$^{23-25}$ are a summary climax on his wisdom and wealth. Finally there is a postscript, vv.$^{26-29}$, concerning his accumulation of chariots and horses, parallel to 5^6 ; the interpolated v.^{27}, a commonplace upon his wealth, intruded from Ch., is followed by a record of his trading in horses and chariots, also of ancient origin. The materials have been loosely shuffled about, recalling the two *pots pourris* in Gr. 2$^{35\mathrm{a}\ \mathrm{seq.},\ 46\mathrm{a}\ \mathrm{seq.}}$. *Cf.* a brief Note by the writer in *JBL* 1931, 115 f.

VV.$^{14,\,15}$. Solomon's income. ‖ 2 Ch. 9$^{13,\,14}$; *cf. Ant.*, viii, 7, 2. After the interlude of the Queen of Sheba's visit the register of Solomon's wealth and glory is resumed. For the meagre details we possess of the royal budget see Bertholet, *History of Heb. Civilization*, 249 ff., and Lurje, *Studien*, 27 ff. The enormous figure of 666 talents gold for yearly royal income is a late exaggeration ; the sum may have been reached approximately, with Šanda, by adding the previous figures for gold, at 9$^{14,\,28}$, 10^{10}. On the other hand the comparatively petty item of v.^{15a}, the taxes on the traders, may well be an early note, and possibly was a postscript to ch. 9. But v.^{15b} appears to be late, lamely introducing the tribute of kings and satraps after the merchants and pedlars, a criticism supported by the use of the Akk. word for *satraps* (as the Gr. translates it here, EVV *governors*), a word however early domesticated in Syria, being put in Syrian mouths at 20^{24}. The difficulty in the brief phrase of v.^{15a} is glossed over in the translations, *e.g.*, JV, *beside that which came of the merchants and of the traffic of the traders*; but the Heb. for the first noun is the impossible *men of the merchants*; the text is clarified by the Grr., which read or understood '*nšy* for '*nšy*, with the resultant *taxes of the merchants*. In the later addition, v.^{15b}, the current *kings of the mixed people* (RVV JV) must be replaced with *kings of Arabia* (or better *the Arabs*), with Aquila, Sym., and so AV here. On the general correction of the Heb. word, with one possible exception, Ex. 12^{38}, see *Arabia and the Bible*, 29, n.^{5}. The reference to taxation of international merchandizing is of interest as probably the earliest record of the kind that we possess. Such excises were highly developed in the ancient Orient; the factor entered into the appreciation of Indian wares, which reached Rome at one hundred times their original cost according to Pliny, *NH*, vi, 26. For later local *octrois* of this nature is to be compared the Palmyrene Tariff (Cooke, *NSI* no. 147, with parallel texts listed, p. 332). The history of the Crusades presents the flourishing and profitable character of this method of taxation.

VV.$^{16. 17}$. The golden shields. ‖ 2 Ch. 9$^{15. 16}$; *cf. Ant.*, viii, 7, 2. Two patterns of shield are denoted: the first (*ṣinnāh*) the long shield proper, covering the length of the body, and the small round shield (*māgēn*); AV RV JV call the former 'target,' RV^{Am} 'buckler,' which is preferable, and they agree for the latter word with 'shield'; but the two terms of the English should be exchanged, and so below. For these varieties of shields see Rawlinson, *Five Great Monarchies*, 1, 428 ff.; Meissner, *Bab. u. Ass.*, 1, 96 f. As appears from the later reference to these shields upon Shishak's looting of the palace (14$^{26ff.}$), and their replacement by Rehoboam with bronze shields to be worn by the guard when the king went into the house of Y$_{HWH}$, these shields were of honorific use; they might be compared with the chivalric shields hung in chapels of the knightly orders, as here they are hung in the Lebanon Palace. But they were also carried pompously into battle, as a list of David's booty shows (2 Sam. 8⁷). The word translated *beaten [gold]* in EVV, *i.e., hammered*, refers to gold inlay and overlay ; the shields were not of solid gold. The figures differ in the textual authorities. For the 200 *shields* of 𝔥 (=Jos.), Grr. have 300. Šanda observes that according to 2 Sam. 15¹⁸ David's bodyguard numbered 600 men, and this may well account for the higher figure of the Greek, *i.e.*, 300 shields + 300 bucklers = 600 in all. To each shield was applied 600 (shekels) *gold*, the denomination being omitted as frequently, *e.g.*, Gen. 24²²; to each buckler *three minas gold*, for which Ch. has ' 300 (shekels) gold '; the mina then containing 60 shekels, thus giving a figure two-thirds larger than Ki.; the denomination in minas here is remarkable. Also the Grr. have for the gold value of the shield 300 shekels *vs.* 600 of 𝔥. Šanda has attempted calculation of the value of the gold, as at 4,000,000 francs (value as of the year 1911); but the figures are historically most dubious.

VV.¹⁸⁻²⁰. The gold and ivory throne. || 2 Ch. 9¹⁷⁻¹⁹; *cf. Ant.*, viii, 5, 2. With this description is to be compared that of Ashurbanipal's throne; see Luckenbill, *ARA* 2, §§1012–14 ; Meissner, *Bab. u. Ass.*, 2, cuts 117, 118. **18.** For the problematic word, translated *pure (gold)*, see Note. **19.** 𝔥 *and the top of the throne was round(ed) behind*=EVV ; this is to be corrected with the Grr. : *and the throne had a calf's head at its back*. The Masoretic pointing changed the original word, doubtless to get rid of unhappy associations with the calf, as in the case of Aaron and the people (Ex. 32), and of Jeroboam (*inf.* 12²⁶ff·). Ch. replaced the word with the less objectionable ' lamb,' which an arbitrary change of pointing in most MSS and edd. changed into ' footstool '; see Note. The lamb had its vogue in ancient art ; Meissner, 1, 248, gives a cut of a ' Prunkstuhl ' decorated with lambs' heads, and Šanda cites the throne of a seated Baal flanked with lambs (from Frohnmeyer-Benzinger, *Bilderatlas*, 129). *There were six steps to the throne :* this structure, with a seventh level for the dais, has been well compared with the seven levels of Babylonian cosmogony and the seven stories of Babylonian temples (A. Wünsche,

Salomos Thron u. Hippodrom, 1906 ; Gressmann, *Die älteste Geschichtsschreibung u. Prophetie Israels*, 219 ; C. R. North, *ZAW* 1932, 28). **19. 20.** *And there were arms* [EVV *stays*] *on either side of the place of the seat, And there were two lions standing beside the arms, and twelve lions standing ⸢there⸣* [OGrr. om.] *on the one side and on the other upon the six steps*. The lion was type of royal strength, possibly once the totem of Judah ; *cf.* Gen. 49⁹, Rev. 5⁵ ; but it was a common theme in such art. There is the early occurrence of stone lions at Tell Ḥalaf ; see von Oppenheim, pp. 85 ff., with plates. Bronze lions were frequent in Syrian art (Dussaud, *SAM* plates 19, 23), and Parrot has recently discovered at Mari bronze lions, ' of menacing attitude ' (*Syria*, 1938, pt. 1, pl. x; *ILN*, May 28, 1938). Sennacherib proudly describes the bronze lion-colossi furnishing his palace (*ARA* 2, §§367, 391). The sphinx appears on either side of the throne of Hiram of Tyre (Dussaud, pl. 7). This ivory and gold throne is abundantly illustrated from ancient sources. Ashur-nasir-pal of Assyria received from an Aramæan king, Ammibaal, ' ivory couches overlaid with gold ' (*KB* 1, 92 ; *ARA* 1, §466) ; Hezekiah of Judah sent to Sennacherib beds and chairs of ivory (see Comm. on II. 18¹⁴ᵇ). See further Comm. on 22³⁹ᶠ· for the recent marvellous finds of ivory at Megiddo, Samaria, and elsewhere. Ivory was well into the first millennium B.C. a product of the North Syrian lands, where the elephant still roamed. Thutmose II received tribute of elephants from Syria, and Thutmose III took part in a hunt of 120 elephants near the upper Euphrates (Breasted, *HE* 271, 304). Tiglath-pileser I hunted and captured elephants in Mitanni-land (*ARA* 1, §247) ; elephants are portrayed on Shalmaneser III's Black Obelisk (*cf.* Meissner, *Bab. u. Ass.*, 2, 270, 273, 326). For the ancient wide distribution of the Asiatic elephant see C. W. Bishop, ' The Elephant and its Ivory in Ancient China,' *JAOS* 1921, 290 ff. But v.²² with its reference to ivory importation from the Red Sea, suggests another quarter for the supply. This description of the throne is doubtless authentic, based, as its simple terms suggest, upon an early document. For the later marvellous Jewish legends about this throne, with its wonderful mechanical equipment, see Targum 2 to Esther, ch. 2, Ginzberg, *Legends*, and Wünsche, cited above.

V.²¹, on Solomon's all-gold service vessels, is a late exaggeration indeed.

V.²². The source of Solomon's gold and silver and other exotic imports. || 2 Ch. 9²¹; *cf. Ant.*, viii, 7, 2, 3. The v. is parallel to 9²⁶⁻²⁸, 10¹¹, but of different content. The earlier authentic references to Hiram's fleet are augmented here with *the king's Tarshish fleet along with Hiram's fleet;* this statement suggests a free port for both parties. For the term ' Tarshish fleet ' used of ships in waters of the Indian Ocean *cf.* the term ' Hittite,' *i.e.*, Phœnician, used by Sennacherib for the fleet built for his operations in the Persian Gulf by Phœnicians, and manned by ' Tyrians, Sidonians, Ionians (?) ' (*ARA* 2, §§319, 329, 350) ; *cf.* Olmstead, *HA* 200, and Hall, *AHNE*³ 488, with accompanying plate from an Assyrian monument depicting such a ship with its oarsmen in action.³ *Once in three years the Tarshish fleet would come in* (to port). L. Woolley, in his *Abraham* (1936), p. 121, sums up a still unpublished document from Babylonian Ur, reporting a voyage

³ Tarshish has generally been identified with Classical Tartessos on the Guadalquivir, N. of Cádiz, on the Atlantic front ; see A. Schulten, *Tartessos* (1922) ; Meyer, *GA* 2, 2, 94 ff. (in his chapter on the Phœnicians, pp. 61–136) ; A. Herrmann, *Die Erdkarte der Urbibel*, with an Appendix on Tartessos ; Tozer, *History of Ancient Geography*, Add. Note, p. iv. Schulten's very high dating for the founding of the colony is sharply criticized by Meyer, p. 105, n. 2, the latter dating the event in the 11th century. P. Bosch-Gimpera dates it as not much earlier than the 8th century, *Klio* 22 (1929), 345 ff., with reply by Schulten, *ib.*, 284 ff. ; Albright's dating, as cited below, is *ca.* 950. The place-name appears on an alabaster tablet of Esarhaddon's, with correction of previously read ' Nusisi,' in *ARA* 2, §710 ; see Meyer, p. 102, n. 2. The place is aligned with Cyprus and Yawan (Greece) as subject to the royal power. Also in another text of Esarhaddon's (§690) Carthage is named. The Grr. translate the word with ' Carthage ' at Is. 23⁶, Eze. 27¹². 𝕮 has here ' an African ship.' Ch. has the fleet sailing to Tarshish. Josephus with his ' Tarsian sea ' identified the place with Tarsos. The most trenchant fresh point in archæology is Albright's definite reading of the initial line of a stone inscription from ancient Nora in Sardinia (*CIS* I, 144 ; Cooke, *NSI*, no. 41) : *btršš . . . šrdn*, in Tarshish . . . Sardinia.' See his presentation, with fresh translation of the text, in *BASOR* 83 (1941), 14 ff., and his further discussion at large in the Leland Volume, pp. 41 f. He derives the noun from Akk. *rašāšu*, ' to melt,' with a parallel Arabic root, and holds that the term means a refinery and in the inscription refers to a local smelting-place.

of two years from and back to that harbour. (The writer owes the following citation to the kindness of Professor Albright.) "We have the bill of lading of one such (ship) that in *circa* 2040 B.C. [Albright corrects to *ca.* 1830] had come up from the Persian Gulf after a cruise of two years ; it brought copper ore and gold and ivory, hard woods for the cabinet-maker, diorite and alabaster for the sculptor's workshop. Not all of these things would have come from the shores of the Gulf itself, but from much farther afield, carried in foreign vessels to be transshipped in the Gulf ports." He mentions in particular lapis lazuli, brought *via* Persia from the Pamir mountains. If commerce as far as India is to be found in the Biblical passage, the round voyage, with many transshipments, in the third year is most reasonable. For the Indian voyages in a later age see W. H. Schoff, *The Periplus of the Erythræan Sea*, with its valuable notes. In the present case the products brought back, in addition to gold and silver, were *ivory and apes and peacocks*, according to current translations, based on the VSS subsequent to the OGrr., the latter having for the three terms only two, ' stones carved and cut ' (?). Jos. presents ' much ivory, Ethiopians and apes.' The word here and in Ch. for ' ivory ' is unique ; it means ' elephant-tooth.' The following two words are now to be interpreted as of ape-species, for convenience of translation as *apes and baboons* ; see Albright, *AJSL* 37 (1921), 144. In a personal communication the same scholar notes the use of Egyptian originals of these two words as occurring together among the rarities that the Tale of the Shipwrecked Sailor reports as brought home from the voyage (Erman, *Lit. Anc. Egyptians*, 34). A species of baboon still exists in the Yemen and Hadhramaut (G. W. Bury, *Arabia Infelix* [1914], 27 f. ; British Admiralty's *Handbook of Arabia*, 227). Monkeys from Punt, Somaliland, were a favourite import *de luxe* into Egypt, *e.g.*, the report on Hatshepsut's Red Sea expedition (*ARE* 2, §265 ; Breasted, *HE* 276). The like zoological interest appears in an Assyrian monarch. Ashur-nasir-pal tells of his capture and caging of divers wild animals, including the elephant, and sending them to his capital ; and a relief represents the bringing of tribute of monkeys to him (*ARA* 1, §519 ; Olmstead, *HA* 95, and fig. 59). See at large W. C. McDermott,

The Ape in Antiquity (Baltimore, 1938). No etymological corroboration of the traditional translation 'peacocks,' an Indian bird, has been found; see Clark's article cited above on vv.[11, 12]. For importation of foreign birds by Assyrian monarchs see Meissner, *Bab. u. Ass.*, 1, 223, 353 (with a possible reference to the peacock), and *in extenso* Albright and Dumont, *JAOS* 1934, 108 f. W. F. Badè, discussing a seal representing 'an exquisitely carved cock,' found at Tell en-Nasbeh, of date *ca.* 600 B.C., suggests, following Maisler, that also the word in our passage refers to this only late domesticated fowl, and so Albright, *loc. cit.* For importation of the peacock into the West see E. H. Warmington, *Commerce between the Roman Empire and India* (1928), 147, 152. But proof of Israelite trade with India is not demonstrated by our text.

VV.[23-25]. The fame of Solomon's wealth and wisdom beyond all the kings of the earth, and how all the world attended upon him to hear his divine wisdom, bringing their respective annual tributes. || 2 Ch. 9^{22-24}; *cf. Ant.*, viii, 7, 3. *Cf.* $5^{9ff.}$, with here superabundant exaggeration, *e.g.*, *all the world*, and *each one his tribute, by rate year by year*—'tribute' as the context requires, not 'present' with EVV. V.[25] appears to be phrased after the pompous lists of booty in Ass. inscriptions; *e.g.*, a text of Tiglath-pileser III: "Tribute of . . . (named kings of Syria and Arabia), gold, silver, lead, iron, elephants' hides, ivory . . . garments . . . lambs . . . winged birds . . . horses, mules, cattle, sheep, camels, she-camels with their young I received" (*ARA* 1, §772; Rogers, *CP* 316; Barton, *AB* 464). A more limited parallel appears in the report of the author of the *Periplus* of the tribute rendered to the Arabian king of Muza: "horses and sumpter-mules, vessels of gold and polished silver, finely woven clothing and copper vessels" (Schoff's tr., §24). The word currently translated for one of the gifts as *armour* should be rendered myrrh, or *stacte* with the Grr.; for this reading see Note, and for that valuable commodity in ancient trade Schoff, pp. 112 ff.

VV.[26-29]. Solomon's chariotry and horses, and his trade in horses and chariots. || 2 Ch. $1^{16, 17}$, with duplicate, 9^{25-28}; *cf. Ant.*, viii, 7, 3, 4. V.[27] is a late intrusion on the cheapness of silver (*cf.* v.[21]) and cedar in the realm, probably introduced from Ch. **26.** *And Solomon collected chariotry and horses, and* *he had* 1400 *chariots and* 12,000 *horses, which he stationed in the chariot cities and* ⌜*in the royal quarters*⌝ [Heb. *with the king*] *in Jerusalem*. See Note on 1⁵ for the word generally translated *horsemen* ; horsemen were not deposited as though in barracks in the chariot cities. The figure for chariots, 1400, is expanded in 5⁶ to ' 40,000 horse-stalls,' while the figure in Ch. 9²⁵ is 4000. 𝕲 (B a₂) here also has 4000, which is expanded by all other MSS and 𝕾ᴴ to 40,000, and so the figure in Gr. 2⁴⁶¹ ; Jos. discovered 22,000 horses. These are classic instances of the expansion of numerals in text-tradition. For ' stables ' the Grr. have a novel interpretation, ' mares ' (see Note). The figure of 1400 chariots—not a round number—is quite credible. Ancient tradition reports 900 chariots for Sisera (Jud. 4³) ; Shalmaneser III records for his invasion of Syria in 854 B.C. booty of 1200 chariots from Ben-Hadad of Damascus, 700 from Hamath, 2000 from Ahab the Israelite (*ARA* i, §611, *CP* 295 f., *AB* 458), and for his invasion twelve years later booty of 1121 chariots of Hazael (*ARA* §663, *CP* 303, *AB* 459). Royal *stables* in definite *chariot cities* are now brilliantly confirmed and illustrated by the University of Chicago's expedition at Megiddo, with the uncovering of stabling for some 400 horses ; see Comm., 9¹⁵ (where, however, the present doubt as to their Solomonic construction is cited). For traces of stables at Tell el-Hesy and Beth-shean see Watzinger, *DP* 1, 87 f. Šanda notes that Jos. 19⁵ lists along with Ziklag two places called Chariot-House and Mare-Court, which may go back to Solomon's foundations. There may be noted Josephus's report, however extravagant, of the fine stone roads laid out by Solomon, and of his frequent excursions with a brilliant knightly party to Ethan, 50 furlongs distant, a paradise of waters, probably the earliest reference to the Pools of Solomon, 8 miles S of Jerusalem.

28. *And for the export* (=import) *of the horses for Solomon from Musri* [𝕳 *Misraim*-Egypt] *and* ⌜*from Kue*⌝ [with Grr., 𝔙] *the royal traders would bring them* ⌜*from Kue*⌝ [with Grr., 𝔙] *at a* (fixed) *price*. **29.** *And a chariot came up by export* (lit., *and came out*) *from Musri* [𝕳 *Misraim*] *at six hundred* [Grr., *a hundred*] (shekel-weight) *silver, and a horse at one hundred and fifty* [Grr., *fifty*], *and so for all the kings of the Hittites and the kings of Syria, making export* (=import) *through their agency*.

Even with certain corrections of text the whole passage reads roughly, much like a business memorandum. The Grr. and 𝔙 have preserved a true and interesting item, first identified by Lenormant (*Histoire ancienne*, 3, 9), namely the ancient trade-relations with Kue, *i.e.*, Cilicia. The trouble the word has given to translators appears in modern VSS : GV ' allerlei ' (from the mng. of the Heb. word as ' collection ') ; FV ' fil ' ; Tremellius and Junius, ' netum ' (yarn), and so AV, ' linen yarn ' ; these following Rashi, Kimchi, with reference to the fine linen of Egypt ; RVV ' droves ' ; finally JV ' from Keveh,' and Moffatt and Chic. B., ' from Kue ' ; see Note. Further, Winckler brilliantly identified at least the first ' Misraim ' with the land of Musri, the later Cappadocia, lying N of the Taurus ; and later the kings of Musri, with same correction of 𝔥, appear as confederates of the invading Hittites, II. 7⁶. These two lands are known from the Ass. inscriptions, and in one case are named together, in Shalmaneser III's Monolith Inscription (col. ii, 92 ; *ARA* 1, §611, *CP* 296, *AB* 458) ; see Winckler, *KAT* 238, for his early discussion. And now Kue appears as one of the allies of Ben-Hadad of Damascus against Zakar of Hamath in the latter's 8th-century inscription, and the other name, Mṣr, occurs in the Aramaic Sūjīn text (*ca.* 755 B.C., line 5 of tablet 1 ; Bauer's ed., pp. 1 ff., with literature on Musri, p. 10). For the location of these lands see S. Smith, *Early History of Assyria*, 262, 389 ; *CAH* 3, 357, 474 ; also for Musri *cf.* Alt, *ZDMG* 1934, 255, n. 1. Thus two new names of district and folk have been added to the Hebrew lexicon. Anatolia, the land of *all the kings of the Hittites* (for which people see Comm., II. 7⁶) and in particular Musri were lands of horse-breeding, as has been known from the Amarna letters and subsequent Ass. texts at length, with which are to be compared Eze. 27¹⁴, 38³ff.⁴. The early intensity of Anatolian horse-breeding is exhibited in the Hittite text on horse-training published by

---

⁴ See Meissner, *Bab. u. Ass.*, 1, 217 ff.; *CAH* 3, 256; Meyer, *GA* 1, 2, §§455, 577 (note his denial, p. xx, of the horse as ridden by the Indogermans) ; Olmstead, *HA*, Index, *s.v.* ; A. Götze, *Hethiter, Churriter u. Assyrer* (1936), Index, *s.v.* ' Pferd ' ; Galling, *BR* ' Pferd (u. Wagen),' with statement that the ridden horse did not appear in Assyria until the 8th century. See also Note on 1⁵.

Hrozný, *Arch. Or.*, 3 (1931), 431 ff., and the extension of the industry into Syria is now shown by the Ugaritic veterinary treatise (14th century), published by Virolleaud (*Syria*, 1934, 75 ff.). A problem arises whether the second ' Misraim ' should also be corrected to ' Musri,' with Winckler, Kittel, Skinner, Moffatt, Chic. B., and Šanda after lengthy discussion. With 𝔅 preserved here we have detail of international exchange of Anatolian horses and Egyptian-made chariots. This is an attractive hypothesis with its prospect of ancient trade, and might be supported by Breasted, who after stating the introduction of the horse into Egypt by the Hyksos (*HE* 222), speaks of the Egyptians as subsequently becoming deft chariot-makers, and presents plate of an Egyptian chariot that has been preserved, now in the Florence Museum (pp. 234 f., fig. 105). But this position is denied by Meyer (*GA* 2, 1, 23, n. 2) with the proof that the wood is not Egyptian. Solomon then would have been the middleman for import of both horses and chariots from Anatolia into Egypt. The horse indeed came to be domesticated in Egypt at a later day; *cf.* Dt. 17^{16}, Is. 31$^{1\text{ff.}}$, and Egypt rendered tribute of horses to Sargon and Ashurbanipal (Olmstead, *HA* 383, 416). For the comparative prices of chariot and horse, the Grr. give the ratio of 2 : 1 as against 4 : 1 of Heb. ; see Šanda's discussion, citing the price of an ass in Cambyses' time at 50 shekels ; the Gr. figures are probably a correction to meet later proportions of value.   For the shekel see *DB* ' Money '; *EB* ' Shekel '; Nowack, *Arch.*, 1, 209 ff. ; Benzinger, *Arch.*, §42 ; Galling, *BR* ' Geld,' with added bibliography.

    1. '' לשׁם: om. with Ch. ; added *ad majorem gloriam Dei* ; the Grr. helped out the awkward phrase with ' and the name of the Lord.'—**2.** נמלים: the asyndeton, relieved in Ch. and Grr. (exc. 44) with the conj., is correct.—שלמה: MSS pref. המלך, and similar variations occur below in VSS in use of name and title.—**5.** שׁלחנו: Grr. as שׁלמה.—מלבשׁיהם:=Ch., Jos., 4 Gr. MSS; other Grr. as מלבושׁו.—משׁקיו: Ch.+ומלבושׁיהם, interpreting as ' his cupbearers '= Gr. οινοχοους (𝔊^L ευνουχους)=𝔗 𝔙; but it means the ' drinking service ' (*cf.* Gen. 40^{21}), with variant spelling of suff. ; see GK §93, ss.—עֲלִיֹתוֹ=Grr. ; 𝔗 𝔖 𝔙 as pl., which St., *BH*, *al.* accept; Ch., עֲלִיָתוֹ, understood as ' ascent,' and so here the Jewish comm. ; but עליה otherwise=' upper story.' The word can be pointed עֲלֹתוֹ, ' his going up '; *cf.* Comm.—רוח . . . היה: Haupt properly defends the gender of the verb, as preceding the subj.—**6.** היה: Ch., Grr.

om., and so St., *al.* ; but it has force=' has become.'—[על] : דברי׃
1 MS דבר=Grr., to be accepted ; for 'על ד='on account of ' *cf.*
2 Sam. 18⁵.—**7.** לדברים : Grr., 𝔖 𝔙 as ppl.—[וטוב] חכמה : 𝔊 𝔊^L
om.—וטוב : Ch. om. ; for possible adverbial sense of 'ט *cf.* Aram.
אל-עב : MSS and Ch., על, to be accepted.—השמועה : Grr. pref.
'all,' as though כל, as also before זכמת, v.⁸, and 𝔊 before עבריה,
v.¹³ ; but such addition is exaggeration.—שמעתי : Grr.+' in my
land.'—**8.** אנשיך : =Ch., 𝕮 𝔙 ; Grr., 𝔖^H 𝔖 𝔄=ישני, and so most
moderns since Böttcher.—**9.** לעלם : *i.e.*, the divinely appointed
dynasty is sign of the divine ' love ' ' for ever.' Ch. pref. להעמירו,
cf. 𝔊, στησαι=𝔊^L+αυτον, but the incomplete στησαι is a glossed
cross-reference to Ch., and has no authority ; Burn. holds that
the plus of Ch. is ' almost indispensable,' which St. rightly denies.—
למלך : Grr.+' over them.'—וצדקה : OGrr. as though בצ׳, and then
with correcting gloss κ. εν κριμασιν αυτων (𝔊^L αυτου).—For defence
of this somewhat plethoric v. see St., as *vs.* Klost., Kit. ; *cf.*
further elaboration in Ch.—**11.** B a₂ ην [αιρουσα], for η.—מאפיר :
to be omitted with Ch., OGrr.—אלמנים : Ch., אלפים (also arbitrarily introduced among the woods of Lebanon, 2 Ch. 2⁷) ; 𝔊
(=𝕮) πελεκητα, 𝔊^L 𝔊^H (=𝔖^H) απελ. (*cf.* similar variation in v.²²) ;
Aq., σουχινα=Lat. ' sucinum ' (amber) ; Sym., θυινα (*cf.* ξύλον
θύινον, Rev. 18¹²)=𝔙 ; Grr. in Ch., πευκινα, where 𝔙 ' pinea,' and
so Jos.—**12.** מסעד : Ch., מסלות ; Grr. υποστηριγματα ; 𝔙 ' fulcra ' ;
𝔖 ' for decoration,' *cf.* 𝔄 ; see St., Haupt.—אלמנים 2⁰ : Grr.+επι
τ. γης, evidently gloss from Ch., בארץ יהודה.—**13.** שלמה [כיר המלך] :
absent in 7 Gr. MSS (*cf.* 𝕮 𝕮), 𝔖 𝔄 𝔙.

15. אנשי : Grr., τ. φορων, φορος translating עניי, II. 23³³ ; *cf.* 𝕮
אגר, ' rental,' etc., the root being used of tax-collection in the
Palmyrene Tariff (Cooke, *NSI*, p. 333) ; and so correct to עני, with
Böttcher, *al.* Kamp.'s correction of the text, accepted by Burn.,
has no basis.—תרים : ppl. of תור=Arab. *tāra*, with the noun *tawr*,
' go-between, agent,' and so equal to [המלך] סהרי, ' the royal traders,'
v.²⁸ ; the root occurs in the tribe-name יתור, the Ituræans, a migrant
folk. This root is to be distinguished from תור, ' to spy out,'
Num. 13², etc., which, like Arab. *ta'ara*, Chr.-Pal. תאר, and the
Heb. noun תֹּאַר, ' form,' is metaplastic reflexive from *r'y*, 'to see.'
The root תאר, ' to circumscribe,' *e.g.*, Jos. 15⁹, is metaplastic from
the first root specified. See H. Bauer, *ZfS* 1935, 174 ff., for similar
processes. Grr., τ. υποτεταγμενων, ' the subjects,' a guess ; 𝕮 𝔖 𝔄
' artisans,' rdg. נפנים. Correction is unnecessary, as with St., to
Aram. תגרים, ' merchants,' or with Kit. to ערים, ' cities,' with,
further textual change (*cf. BH*).—וּמִסְחַר : read with Klost. וּמִסְחַר
' from the profit ' ; Ch., הסחרים, and similarly OGrr. here.—
רכלים : a word of inter-dialectical usage=Heb. root רגל ; 𝔊 𝔊^L
om. ; 𝔊^H ρωποπωλων, ' hucksters.'—הערב : read with Ch. עֲרָב, and
so, ' Arabia '=Aq., Sym., 𝔖^H 𝔖 𝔄 𝔙 ; 𝔊 𝔊^L του περαν, as הָעֵבֶר,
i.e. ' Across-the-River ' ; 𝕮 ' the allies ' ; *n.b.* GV ' die Grenz-
fürsten.'—פחות הארץ : ' the land-governors ' ; for compound idea,

see GK §124, p. Ch. has an exaggerated plus. For the foreign word פחה there are to be added to the citations in GB its appearance in a Lihyanite text of the 5th century B.C.; see F. W. Winnett, 'A Study of the Lihyanite and Thamudic Inscriptions,' *University of Toronto Studies*, 1937, 50 f.—**16.** צנה : Grr., δόρατα ; had the translator in mind conventional groups of gifts ? Crœsus gave a gold shield and a gold spear to the oracle at Delphi (Her. i, 52). שחוט : the same word, Ḳr., in חץ שׁ׳, Jer. 9[7], 'whetted arrow.' The root mng. is dubious, Arab. and Akk. congeners being very polysemantic. Talmudic Heb. has a root שׁ׳, 'to draw out,' and so Yoma Jer., iv, 41 d, explains the phrase, שׁהיה משך כשעוה, 'which was drawn out like wax,' and similarly Kimchi (but identifying the root with שׁטה) ; this agrees with Gr. ἐλατά, used of drawn gold.—**18.** כופז : Ch., מהור ; 𝕮 'good,' 𝕾 'from Ophir,' 𝕬 'from India,' 𝖁 'yellow.' But read וּפָז (cf. כתם אופז, Dan. 10[5], and see Montg. *ad loc*.), as proposed by Haupt in *SBOT* and earlier. However פז, aligned with זהב and כתם, remains unidentified. There are three current names for gold : זהב, Arabian river-gold (see *Arabia and the Bible*, 38 ff.), חרוץ (Anatolian word ?), כתם, these representing different origins or qualities. Another variety of זהב appears in v.[21], 6[21], etc., with the adjective סגור.—**19.** כסא MSS many ; Job 26[9] = *bis* כה : was the first case intended for *kissehu* ?—ראש ענול : so 𝕾 𝕬 𝖁 ; 𝕮 סגלגל, of a revolving mechanism ; but Grr., προτομαι μοσχων, (=𝕾[H])=רָאשֵׁי עֲגָלִים, now generally accepted since Then. ; however the sing., עֲגֹל רֹאשׁ, is preferable for the ornament, and so Jos., *Ant*., viii, 5, 20. Ch. has בוהכ כֶּבֶשׁ so generally pointed in edd. = 'footstool,' but read כֶּבֶשׂ, 'lamb' (see Curtis, *ad loc*.).—מאחריו : Ch. הָאֲחֻזִים, generally taken as error for the former ; but it may correctly represent Akk. *uḫḫuzu*, 'overlaid.'—**20.** אריים : *vs.* אריות, v.[19], the usual pl., which Ch. has and critics prefer here ; but the variant may be a double rdg., with intent of giving a different form for the artificial 'lion' ; see numerous cases cited in GK §87, o.—שׁם : OGrr. om. ; it is not necessary.—ממלכות : Ch., ממלכה, and so as sing. Grr., 𝕾[H] 𝕾 ; read מַמְלָכָה.—**21.** The faulty rdg. of Gr. MSS (exc. x), τα σκευη τα υπο του Σ., is to be corrected to τα σκευη του ποτου Σ.—וזהב : Grr., exc. p, κ. λουτηρες χρυσοι=וסירות ז׳.—אין כסף : לא נחשב : Ch. om. לא, which rdg. St. adopts here ; but Grr. = 𝖁, which is entirely acceptable : " there was no silver ; it was not taken into account."

22. אני : *tris* : Grr. have successively sing., pl., sing. ; Ch. has pl. in all cases. St. revises 1° and 2° to the sing. אניה. But the present form is to be retained as collective (so 9[26]) ; it disagrees in gender as fem. with אני, v.[11], but the noun is fem. at Is. 33[11] ; grammatical regularity is not essential.—אני חירם : 𝕾[L] 'servants of H.'=Ch.—נִשָּׂאת : for the vocalization see GK §74, i.—תביים : 'Ethiopians' of Jos. is prob. to be explained from סכיים, listed along with Egyptians, Libyans, Cushites, 2 Ch. 12[3], rendered there by 𝔊 𝔗 with 'Troglodytes.'—**23.** B† ignores הארץ.—**24.** וכל הארץ: Ch., וכל מלכי הא׳ and so Grr., 𝔖 𝔄; but this is a grammatical intrusion; for the syntax see GK §145, e.—אלהים: Grr., 'the Lord'; cf. 5⁹, etc.—**25.** [כלי כסף וכלי זהב]: OGrr. om. in view of the discount of silver, v.²¹.—נֶ֫שֶׁק = 'armour,' II. 10², and so here the VSS (exc. Grr.) and modern VSS; Grr., στακτην, 'myrrh'; the Gr. interpretation is correct. based on Arab. *nšḳ*, 'to smell' = Heb. *nšḳ*, 'to kiss'; see the writer's Note, *JAOS* 1938, 137. For the presence of such spices in the royal treasuries *cf.* II. 20¹³.— **26.** וַיַּנְחֵם: read with Ch., וַיִּנְחֲמֵם, and so VSS.—**28.** מִקְוֵה *bis*: Ch. מִקְוֵא; Grr., εκ Θεκουε, Eus., *Onom.*, εκ Κωα = 𝔙 'de Coa'; read מִקְוֵה. *N.b.* the lengthy discussions in Poole, some of the scholars comparing the 'fila Coa' of Egyptian Cos, famous in the ancient world (*e.g.*, Horace, *C.* 4, 13, 13, 'Coæ purpuræ'). One Jewish scholar related the word to alleged תקוה, 'thread.'—יקחו: generally corrected (*e.g.*, St., *BH*) to יקחום; but it can stand, with מוצא as actual or implied obj.—**29.** ותעלה: again the full form of the verb; see GK §75, t.—אצנ[י̇]: Grr., exc. A x, η εξοδος.—החתים: MS z, κατα Κυπριαν, with Cyprian Kition in mind.—בידם: Grr., κατα θαλασσαν, as though בים.—יצאי: = Ch., 𝔖ᴴ; Grr., 𝔗 as יָצְאוּ, preferred by St., Šanda; but the Hif. is used absolutely.

Ch. 11. Solomon's apostasy; a direful oracle for the future; revolt and insurrection in his domains; the pericope on the end of the reign and the succession. Ch. ignores except the conclusion. *Cf. Ant.*, viii, 7, 5–8.

VV.¹⁻⁸. Solomon's many foreign wives, who led him astray. The following presentation, along with a revised text, distinguishes an older, simpler account in the left-hand column, and a later, Deuteronomistic and extravagant explanation of the king's fall from virtue.

1. *And king Solomon loved many foreign women* [+gloss *and Pharaoh's* daughter], *women of Moab, Ammon* [OGrr.+*and Aram*], *Edom,* ⌈*Sidon*⌉ [Grr., exc. Aq., Sym., om.], *Hittites* [OGrr.+*and Amorites*], **2.** *from the peoples as to which* Yʜᴡʜ *commanded the Bnê-Israel, Ye shall not intermarry with them, nor they with you, lest they pervert your heart after their gods. Solomon clave unto these in love.* **3.** *And he had seven hundred wives, princesses, and three hundred concubines;* ⌈*and his wives perverted his heart*⌉ [A *al.* 𝔖ᴴ *under asterisk*].

6. *And Solomon did what was evil in YHWH's eyes, and he was not loyal to YHWH like his father David.*

7. *Then built Solomon a high-place for Chemosh, the god [𝔥 abomination; Grr. idol] of Moab ⸢on the hill that is opposite to Jerusalem⸣ [OGrr. om.], and for Milkom [=II. 23¹³, and so here 𝔊ᴸ; 𝔊 their king; 𝔥 Molek], the god [𝔥 abomination; Grr. idol] of the Ammonites [Grr.+and to Astarte, the abomination of Sidonia—from v.⁵].¹*

4. *And it was, when Solomon grew old, that his [Grr.+ foreign] wives perverted his heart after other gods, and his heart was not at one with YHWH his God, as was his father David's heart.*

5. *And Solomon followed after Ashtart [Grr. Astarte; 𝔥 Ashtoreth], the god(dess) of Sidonia, and after Milcom, the god [𝔥 abomination] of the Ammonites [OGrr. om. the v.].* **8.** *And so he did for all his foreign wives they censing and sacrificing to their gods.*

For the unravelling of this skein see the various attempts at analysis by Kamphausen, Benzinger, Kittel, Burney, Stade, Hölscher, the last critic finding two independent themes, the many wives, and Solomon's polytheism. Criticism naturally proceeds from 𝔊, which varies notably from 𝔥 in order of elements and also in omissions and additions. The most signal difference is in the rearrangement of the introduction, thus: "And king S. was a woman-lover ($\phi\iota\lambda o\gamma \acute{\nu}\nu\eta s$), and he had 700 princesses and 300 concubines. And he took foreign women, and Pharaoh's daughter, Moabitesses, etc." This order has been preferred by the above-named scholars, except Stade and Hölscher, whose soberer judgment is to be accepted, that 𝔊 represents editorial smoothing of the harshnesses and repetitions of the original. The independent analysis offered above finds a primary simple statement of Solomon's defection, as based on historical testimony to his construction of shrines for foreign gods. The datum in the primary document for the

---

[1] For the variants for the heathen 'gods' see Pfeiffer, 'The Polemic against Idolatry in the O.T.,' *JBL* 1924, 229 ff. The original 'god' appears in all three cases in the repeated passage, v.³³.

king's apostasy is expressed in annalistic style, *Then built Solomon a high-place for Chemosh the god of Moab*, which has its interesting parallel in Mesha's Moabite stele, " And I made this high-place for Chemosh." Critics vary as to balance of the v., on assumed contamination from II. 23^{13}; *e.g.*, Stade and Hölscher omit ' and for Molek,' which the Grr. have, but retain ' on the hill opposite to Jerusalem,' which Grr. om., while Kittel proceeds *vice versa*. Acknowledgment of the provincial deities of Moab and Ammon was quite within the range of Solomon's statecraft. But the secondary document in v.^{5} (omitted by the Grr.) with its initial reference to ' Ashtart of Sidonia ' is evidently based on II. 23^{13}; the Grr. further introduced it in v.^{7}. For the location of the Chemosh sanctuary *on the hill opposite to Jerusalem, cf.* 2 Sam. 15^{32}, how " David came to the top of the ascent, where one was wont to worship God "; this datum may have caused the pious Greek excision of the datum here.[2]

[2] Of the alien deities named, Ashtart and Mlkm now appear in the Ras Shamra texts. For a full study of the archæological and literary references to that goddess, as also to Asherah and Anat, see J. B. Pritchard, *Palestine Figurines in Relation to Certain Goddesses Known through Literature*, vol. 24 of *Oriental Series* of the Am. Or. Soc., 1943. For the second of the above deities the Masoretic vocalization of the name, ' Milcom,' in v.^{5} is supported by 𝔊^L in v.^{7}, where 𝔐 has ' Molek '; the Grr. otherwise read *malkām*, ' their king.' For this deity may be cited, *inter al.*, G. F. Moore, ' Molech,' *EB* ; M. Buber, *Königtum Gottes*, ch. 5, and notes, pp. 211 ff. ; Dhorme, *L'Évolution religieuse d'I raël*, 331 ff. (and for Asherah, pp. 325 ff.). G. Dossin has published a text from Mari, *Rev. d'Ass.*, 35 (1938), 178, presenting a deity, *Ilum-Muluk*; A. Bea, *Biblica*, 20 (1939), 415, identifies the god-name as vocalized with Gr. *Molech*, and claims its identification with the variant *Ilu-Malik* ; *cf.* also N. Schneider, *Biblica*, 18, 337 f. ; 19, 204. For the determinative ending, *-ām -ôm* = *-ân -ôn*, see D. Nielsen, *Ras Shamra Mythologie*, 17 ff., 43, and the writer's Note, *JAOS* 1938, 130 f.; *i.e.*, the name means ' the King.' *Cf.* the place-name Shomeron, 16^{23} (*v. ad loc.*). The vocalization in *molek* follows that of the word, *bošet*, ' shame,' replacing a heathen god's name, *e.g.*, Hos. 9^{10}, and the *n. pr.*, ' Mephibosheth.' Eissfeldt has proposed a novel and notable re-interpretation of the name as merely a noun representing a cult-practice, the theory based on Punic inscriptions ; see his *Molk als Opferbegriff im Punischen u. Hebräischen u. das Ende des Gottes Moloch* (*Beiträge zur Religionsgeschichte des Altertums*, Heft 3, 1935), and ' Molochs Glück u. Ende,' *FuF* 1935. 285 ff. The present writer agrees with the adverse criticism of this hypothesis; see Buber, 211 ff., and

The statements as to Solomon's thousand-fold amours cannot be accredited to a formal chronicle, as with some critics, *e.g.*, Hölscher, who finds the only original data therein and in the note of the shrine for Chemosh ; chroniclers do not mention such private items, which in the Orient are the gentleman's own business. Apart from the marriage with Pharaoh's daughter (which has been glossed into this text unsyntactically) we know that one of Solomon's wives was an Ammonitess, *i.e.*, mother of Rehoboam (14^{21}). Menander of Tyre reports that Solomon married a daughter of Hiram of Tyre (Clem. Alex., *Stromata*, i, 114, 2). David married at least one foreign princess (1 Ch. 3^2, *cf.* 2 Sam. 13^{37}). The rather absurd figure for the harem is due to popular *Schwelgerei* of the Solomonic legend ; this has been adopted by a moralizing editor to explain the king's defection—an early case of *cherchez la femme*. Seven wives and fifteen sons are attributed to David (1 Ch. 3$^{1\text{ff.}}$), and he abandoned ten concubines in Jerusalem (2 Sam. 15^{16}, 20^3). According to *Song of Songs* 6^8 Solomon's harem consisted of ' 60 queens and 80 concubines and maidens without number.' *Cf.* Rehoboam's 18 wives and 60 concubines (2 Ch. 11^{21}), and the 14 wives of Abijah (*ib.* 13^{21}). We may compare the figure given in Solomon's 1005 songs (5^{12} ; *v. ad loc.*). Bertholet (*History of Heb. Civilization*, 149) presents some comparative cases of such fabulous figures, to which may be added others. Ramses II had ' an enormous harem,' with 100 sons and as many daughters, so Breasted, *HE* 461 ; according to Meyer, *GA* 2, 1, 576, 138 children. Chosroes II had, it was said, concubines ranging in estimates from 3000 to 12,000 (Rawlinson, *Seventh Oriental Monarchy*, 2, 302). Ali, Mohammed's son-in-law and fourth cal:ph, had 13 wives 395 concubines, and his son Hasan 60 and 395 respectively

Dhorme, 213 ff. The most recent exposition of the subject is by Albright, *ARI* 162 ff. (in a study, ch. 5, §3, bearing upon the heathen gods of Palestine), including the somewhat indefinite statement : " Philologically Eissfeldt's argument is convincing, but it now seems certain that the original conception was more complex than he was able to guess at the time," continuing with the archæological data bearing on *mlk*.—' Sidonia ' in the above translation represents the unarticulated plural, ' Sidonians ' ; the pl. has become the land designation, and so for a Greek text, Σιδωνίων ἡ πόλις (Dussaud, *TH* 1, 90) The pl. ' Philistines ' is similarly used without the article, *e.g.*, 5^1.

(D. M. Donaldson, *The Shiite Religion*, 1933, pp. 15, 74). The Sultan Mulay Ismail (1672-1727), who recovered Tangier from Catharine of Braganza's dowry, had 500 wives, 1500 children (Margaret Boverie, *Mediterranean Cross-Currents*, 1938, 87). Subsequently a well-informed writer, W. Price, in the *Nat. Geog. Mag.* for May, 1943, p. 84, reports from that locality the tradition for the same sultan of ' his great palace for his 2,000 wives and 800 concubines.' And Prof. P. K. Hitti has given the writer a parallel for this tradition from C. A. Julien, *Histoire de l'Afrique du Nord*, p. 492, assigning the monarch ' 700 sons and an indefinite number of daughters.' A recent report of an American traveller in Arabia, Whitney Carpenter (*N.Y. Times*, Sept. 11, 1939), states that Ibn Saud, king of Arabia, has had 250 wives and 51 children ; but by Islamic law he may have only four at one time.

However justified later condemnation may be, the king with his foreign marriages was obligated to honour the cults his wives brought with them ; a later example is the case of Jezebel. On the other hand such intrusions were not popular, for YHWH was the sole national deity, and what we refer to critically as the later Deuteronomic objection to such inter-marriages was only the theological development of deep nationalistic sentiment, early manifested in the prophetic guilds.

VV.$^{9-13}$. The divine anger and threatening oracle. The mass of this section is compilatory and late. VV.$^{11\text{ff.}}$ depend upon vv.$^{29\text{ff.}}$ (*vs.* Hölscher) ; YHWH's twofold appearances are based on $3^{4\text{ff.}}$ and 6^{11-13} ; and the language is Deuteronomistic. ' For David's sake ' the dynasty will continue ; so far the divine purpose is maintained. However v.$^{9\text{a}}$, *And YHWH was angered at Solomon, because his heart inclined away*, may well be early, and have been originally continued by v.^{14}, *And YHWH raised up an adversary to Solomon*. More than a century later Mesha king of Moab used the same verb as here ('*np*) of his god's anger : " He [Omri] afflicted Moab many days, for Chemosh was angry against his land." The same theme of theodicy appears early in Babylonia, as in the Sargon Chronicle (L. W. King, *Chronicles Concerning Early Bab. Kings*, 2, 3 ff. ; Rogers, *CP* 203 ff. ; obv. l. 20) with the judgment on Sargon (with Rogers's translation) : " But because of the evil which he had committed the great lord Marduk was angry, and he destroyed his people by famine. From the rising of the sun unto the setting of the sun they rebelled against him and gave him no rest" (*n.b.* rebellion as in the present story); and of Shulgi (Dungi) it is recorded (rev. l. 5) : " (He) richly adorned the city of Eridu . . . but he sought after evil, and the treasure of E-sagila and of Babylon, he brought as spoil. And Bel . . . made an end of him." Similarly an inscription of Nabonidus (published by L. Messerschmidt, *MVG* 1896, pt. 1, col. I, ll. 35 ff.) records that " the king of Assyria, who during the anger of Marduk had worked destruction of the country, was smitten with a weapon by his own son." Like moralizing appears in Hittite texts, as in the inscription of king Telepinus, who details the story of bloodshed in the preceding reigns, and how " at that time the gods exacted of the royal family the penalty for it " (E. H. Sturtevant and G. Bechtel, *A Hittite Chrestomathy*, 1935, 175 ff., ' The Proclamation of Telepinus '). The same theme is manifest in classical historians, notably in the earliest of them, Herodotus. H. T. Fowler has well portrayed the parallelism : " Both Herodotus and the Hebrew historians assume a knowledge of the ways of the unseen powers to which a modern historian would not lay claim. With the Greek, there is that terrible sense of Fate, so familiar in the great tragedies, and the sense, too, that human self-exaltation must receive divine rebuke " (' Herodotus and the Early Hebrew Historians,' 216). And Shotwell in his *Introduction to the History of History*, p. 159, after remarking that " Herodotus remained a devoutly religious man," quotes from Rawlinson, *History of Herodotus*, 1, 94, how in Herodotus's pages " King Crœsus, whom the auriferous Pactolus made the richest of men, Polycrates, tyrant of Samos, or Periander, despot of opulent Corinth— their pride and their end are merely reverberations of the stern melody of human success and divine retribution and the humiliation of men, exemplified most signally in Xerxes himself."

VV.[14-40]. The adversaries whom YHWH raised up against Solomon.

VV.[14-22. 25b]. Hadad of Edom.

14. *And YHWH raised up an adversary to Solomon, Hadad an Edomite* [OGrr. insert vv.[23-25]] *of the seed royal* [gloss+*that* *is in Edom*]. **15.** *And it was, when David ⌜smote⌝* [with Grr., 𝕊ᴴ 𝕊 𝔄—the Heb. impossible; *cf.* EVV] *Edom, when Joab, commander of the host, had gone up to bury the slain, and had smitten every male in Edom*—**16.** *for Joab and all Israel remained there six months, ⌜until he had cut off every male in Edom⌝* [repetitious gloss?]—**17.** *that Hadad* [𝕳 *Adad*] *fled, with certain Edomites of his father's servants with him, to come to Egypt, Hadad being a young boy.* **18.** *And they arose from Midian, and came to Paran; and they took some men with them ⌜from Paran⌝* [OGrr. om.], *and came ⌜to Egypt⌝* [OGrr. om.], *to Pharaoh king of Egypt* [Grr.+*and Ader came in to Pharaoh*]. *And he gave him a house, ordering sustenance for him, ⌜and giving him land⌝* [𝕲 om.] **19.** *And Hadad found great favour with Pharaoh, and he gave him for wife the sister of his own wife, the sister of Tahpenes the queen.* **20.** *And the sister of Tahpenes bore him Genubath his son, and Tahpenes weaned* [Grr. *reared*] *him ⌜within Pharaoh's household⌝* [3 Ken. MSS and Grr., *among Pharaoh's sons*]*; and Genubath was ⌜in Pharaoh's household⌝* [Grr., exc. x, om.; 𝕊ᴴ under asterisk] *among Pharaoh's sons.* **21.** *And when Hadad heard in Egypt that David slept with his fathers, and that Joab, commander of the host, was dead, Hadad said to Pharaoh : Let me depart, that I may go to my country.* **22.** *And Pharaoh said to him : But what lackest thou with me, that thou seekest to go to thy country ? But he said : Nay, but let me go off.* [Grr.+*And Hadad returned to his country*.] (VV.²³⁻²⁵ᵃ: *v. inf.*) **25***b. And the evil which Hadad*—[so 𝕳; OGrr., *this is the evil which Hadad did ; cf.* EVV]. *And he despised Israel, and reigned over ⌜Edom⌝* [with 3 Heb. MSS, Grr., 𝕊ᴴ, 𝕊 𝔄; 𝕳 *Aram*].

In 𝕳 the reading 'Aram' for 'Edom,' by confusion of two similar letters, has caused here the interpolation of the narrative of the Aramæan Hadadezer, vv.²³⁻²⁵ᵃ. On the other hand 𝕲 transferred vv.²³⁻²⁵ᵃ in abbreviated form to the end of v.¹⁴; was this passage omitted in the earliest form of 𝕲, and then subsequently introduced gloss-wise in parallelism with the other theme of an 'adversary'? ³ In the Hadad narrative

---

³ The order of 𝕲 would be sustained by Winckler's arbitrary thesis that Hadad was an Aramæan, so that the narrative opened with reference to two Aramæan adversaries; see *GI* 2, 270 ff., *KAT* 240 ff. An earlier thesis of Winckler's found in the present story a composition

there are certain broken connexions, some possible duplicates, which give the appearance of compilation from two sources; 𝔊 recognized the condition, and tried to improve it; and criticism on this basis was followed not only by Winckler in his theses referred to, but also by Klostermann, Meyer at length (*IN* 355 ff.), and Hölscher, p. 177, who finds his two sources, J and E. But the present commentator agrees with Kittel and Stade in rejecting such source-analyses here. With the realization that we possess in the present case one of the most unique historical stories in the Hebrew Bible, the biography of a fugitive Edomite prince, who fled to Egypt and subsequently regained his throne, we may hardly think of its appearance in two separate editions, J and E, or what not. The details, unimportant enough in sacred history (Winckler would find traces of myth!), were evidently taken from a reliable first-hand document, and the roughnesses of the present text may best be ascribed to some evident glosses, along with mutilation in the tradition. Šanda well remarks: "Mit welcher Treue R(edakteur) diese (alten Quellen) widergibt, zeigt die Lückenhaftigkeit des durch das Alter beschädigten Dokuments." Of parallel interest is the list of the royal Edomite line in Gen. 36[31ff.]. How such sources came into the hands of Israelite archivists is a problem for historiography. One clue to the editor may be found in the use of 'God' at v.[23], with the supposition that this name was changed to 'YHWH' at the introduction of the narrative, v.[14]; he would then have been an 'Elohist.'

14. For the good Edomite and S. Arabic name *Hadad* see below. **15. 16.** The grammar, even with correction of 𝔐, is clumsy, asyndetic, literally, "in David's smiting . . . in Joab's going up." The first item appears in 2 Sam. 8[13], the second in the title of Ps. 60, "and Joab returned and smote of Edom in the Valley of Salt twelve thousand" (dependent on our passage), while yet another hero is named in 1 Ch. 18[12]: "Abishai b. Seruiah smote of the Edomites in the Valley of Salt eighteen thousand." The references to Joab

of two narratives, of the Edomite Hadad, and a Midianite Adad (on basis of the spelling in v.[17]; see his *Alttest. Untersuchungen*, 1 ff.); his analysis is presented by Burney, with apparently the latter's favourable opinion; a similar analysis is followed by Benzinger.

are doubted by Wellhausen, Driver, Meyer (*IN* 359 f.); and
yet his name could not have been introduced gratuitously in
a Davidic anecdote. The material is evidently a prime historical note, early contributed by an Israelite annotator. The
repeated statement of the annihilation of all Edomite males
is indeed an exaggeration. The ' burying of the dead ' affords
trouble; Kittel suggests that there was a massacre of Israelites, which Joab was sent to avenge; Šanda would find something quite different by changing the text. But the phrase
may mean the celebration of triumph; the first act of the
victor being the honour due to the dead; the planned extermination of the Edomites followed. **17. 18.** The fugitive's
itinerary is given in broken style; it is beyond our control,
and the amendment of ' Midian ' to ' Maon,' proposed by
Thenius, accepted by Stade, is gratuitous; the reverse correction with the Gr. at Jud. 10^{12} proves nothing here. Maon,
modern Ma'ān, lies E of Petra, but the flight was made first
into the desert land of Midian, E of the Red Sea, whence
Hadad subsequently fled westwards across the Sinai desert
to Egypt (so Šanda). Paran is indefinite enough; according
to Num. 13^{26} Kadesh of the Wanderings lay in Paran; the
Mount of Paran occurs in the sacred legend, Dt. 33^2, in parallelism with Sinai and Seir, and in Hab. 3^3 along with Teman.
An oasis Feiran, of ancient Christian tradition, lies N of Jebel
Serbal in Sinai (see E. H. Palmer, *Desert of the Exodus*, 1872,
Index, *s.v.*, Kittel, *GVI* 1, 345, n. 3); Arabic geographers
know of a Faran, 40 Arabic miles S of Suez (Le Strange,
Palestine under the Moslems, 440). A possibility is identifica-
tion with El-paran on Chedorlaomer's route (Gen. 14^6); see
GB 30b; this identification is accepted by Meyer (*IN* 60,
n. 5), but denied by Skinner in his *Genesis, ad loc.* If our
Paran be so identified, then Hadad would have pivoted about
it in proceeding from Midian to Egypt. For his itinerary *cf.*
Glueck's statement (*BASOR* 71 [1938], 7) that "a direct road
led in ancient times, as to-day, from the head of the Gulf of
'Aqabah through Sinai to Egypt." Hadad's reception and
treatment as a prince by Pharaoh was proper Oriental etiquette,
and in this case, as with Jeroboam (v.^{40}), good politics. For
the royal matrimonial alliance *cf.* 3^1. The item of this marriage
has been taken over bodily into the secondary Jeroboam

midrash of the Gr., 12²⁴ᵉ· ᶠ·. **19. 20.** The repeated *sister* is necessary to precise the proper name as that of the queen (so Stade, vs. Kittel). Klostermann, Kittel (not *BH*), Benzinger follow the Greek midrash at 12²⁴, where the second 'sister' is represented with a proper name, Ανω (which may possibly represent an Egyptian name as *'ḥnt* or *'hnh* or *'nwt*), but there is no ground to accept the text of that perverted story. The word for 'queen' here is the unusual 'Mistress,' otherwise used for the queen-mother, *e.g.*, 15¹³. **20.** The v. implies that the child of the marriage was adopted into the royal family. There has been retained above the text of 𝔥, that the queen *weaned him*, vs. the misreading or simplification of the Grr., accepted by Klost. and most subsequent critics, that she *reared him*; not to the point is Stade's comment that "T. is neither mother nor the wet-nurse of the child"; there may well be allusion to an adoptive rite, like the 'bearing on the knees' by the adoptive mother, *e.g.*, Gen. 30³ (see Skinner, *ad loc.*). For the item *cf.* Esarhaddon's reference to the Arab Queen Tabua, "born in my palace" (Esarh., Prism A, col. 3; *CP* 355; *ARA* 2, §536). **22.** The implication at end of the verse was sufficient in ancient story, and the Gr. plus, that "he returned to his land," is not demanded, as with critics (*e.g.*, Klost., Stade). **25.** In the first sentence it is all too easy to accept the Gr. rendering, with Böttcher, Thenius, and most successors; but that was only a guess at a mutilated passage, for what was "the evil that Hadad did" after all? There is an evident lacuna before the passage. The word translated *despised* expresses political contempt; Burney well defines it as of racial hostility, *cft.* Ex. 1¹², Num. 22³; there is no reason, as with some critics, to change the text and to read 'oppressed.'

The above narrative, of decidedly original order—to be compared with some Herodotean anecdotes—touches both Edomite and Egyptian history. Gen. 36³¹⁻³⁹ gives a series of eight kings who reigned in Edom "before there reigned a king in Israel." Two of the series are named Hadad, including the last king, with whom our prince may have been closely connected. For the variant spelling 'Adad,' v.¹⁷, see Notes; *cf.* Bibl. names Hadoram and Adoram. For the Edomite history see Buhl, *Geschichte der Edomiter*, and Meyer, *IN* 370–86. Which member of Dynasty XXII is the Pharaoh indicated is no clearer than in the case of Solomon's father-in-law (3^1, *q.v.*). The name of the queen (with variants in Heb. MSS and the Grr.) has not been identified; it occurs as name of a city, Jer. 2^{16}, etc. Such a matrimonial alliance, despite Solomon's relation with the dynasty, was quite in keeping with international double-dealing. Hadad returned upon hearing of David's death. *Cf.* Glueck's sagacious statement (*BASOR* 71 [1938], 9, n. 21) that Solomon inherited Esion-geber from David, comparing Joab's attempted extermination of the Edomites, and that David's hold over Edom "must have been more absolute than Solomon's."

23-25a. Rezon of Damascus. **23.** *And God raised up an adversary to him, Rezon ben Eliada, who fled from his lord Hadadezer king of Damascus;* **24.** *and ⌜there were gathered⌝* [with Grr.; 𝔥 *he gathered*] *certain men to him, and he became captain of a bandit-band* [*when David smote them*—𝔊 𝔊ᴸ om.; gloss from 2 Sam. 8^5]; *and he took* [with OGrr.; 𝔥 *went to*] *Damascus, and settled there, and became king in Damascus* [the three verbs in sing. with OGrr. (*cf.* note); 𝔥 has pl.]. **25a.** *And he was adversary to Israel all the days of Solomon.*

This is another authentic record, with details of Syrian history, concluding with the statement of Rezon's hostility to Solomon during the latter's whole reign, in striking contrast to the fulsome description of Solomon's empire and his security from all wars ($5^{4f.}$); *cf.* the remark at end of the previous paragraph. The anecdote connects with the original records of David's successful wars against Aram, represented by Hadadezer, king of Sobah (2 Sam. 8, 10); *cf.* the Gr. plus in 14^{26} of the booty which "David took from the sons of Hadadezer, king of Sobah." The crushing of that kingdom threw Syria into confusion, out of which arose one of the king's captains, Rezon, first appearing as a captain of condottieri, like David at Adullam (1 Sam. 22), and finally seizing the important city-state of Damascus. He is the first king of Damascus known to us by name. Throughout history Syria has been the theatre of such seizures of power by bold men; witness the Arab dynasties of later days in Chalkis, Ituræa, Emesa; and indeed

Rezon, with a name to be explained from the Arabic, may have been of the same stock.⁴

VV.²⁶⁻⁴⁰. The rise of Jeroboam. For the late midrash-like legend of Jeroboam in the Gr. after 12²⁴ see discussion *in loco*. The present story is editorially attached to those of the two 'adversaries,' but is of different origin. Of the whole narrative only vv.²⁶⁻²⁸· ⁴⁰ contain original material, vv.²⁹⁻³⁹ belonging to a later Prophet-Saga. Of the remainder v.²⁷ᵇ is an intruded archival datum (*cf.* Meyer, *IN* 367, n. 5), in no way aligned with the story of Jeroboam, who was actually *over the levy of the house of Joseph* (v.²⁸). There is also evident lacuna between v.²⁷ᵃ, *And this is the account how he* (Jeroboam) *raised his hand* (*i.e.*, rebelled) *against the king*, and v.⁴⁰ᵃ, *And Solomon sought to kill Jeroboam*. We have to suppose loss of some definite overt act on Jeroboam's part, which caused his flight, and which would equally account for the partisans who ultimately made him king of the North. That datum has been replaced with the popular story of the prophet Ahijah (vv.²⁹⁻³⁹), who appears again in a similar story in ch. 14. But the story may well have foundation in fact in view of the early prophetical objection to royalty. For the motivation of Solomon's hostility supplied by the Gr., v.²⁴ᵇ, see below.
26. Jeroboam's home, Ṣerēdāh, has been located at the spring 'Ain Ṣerīdah in the Wady Deir Ballūṭ in western Samaria, is not to be confused with the corrupt ' Ṣeredah ' of 2 Ch. 4¹⁷ ; see Albright, *BASOR* 11 (1923), 5 ff. ; 49 (1933), 26 ff. ; *JPOS* 1925, 37 ; *cf.* Abel, *GP* 2, 457. The place-name survived as appellative of one of the early Tanna'im (*P. Aboth*, i, 4). There is good historic reminiscence in the item that Jeroboam's mother was a widow, whose name, Ṣerû'āh, means leprous (in the broad sense of skin diseases) ; accordingly many critics, *e.g.*, Kittel, Stade, Šanda, regard this name,

---

⁴ Ṣobah has not been certainly identified ; see Dussaud, *TH* 233 f. ; 2 Ch. 8³ connects it with ' Hamath-Ṣobah.' For the Ass. references to Ṣubat/Ṣubit see Schiffer, *Die Aramäer*, 135 ff. ; Kraeling, *Aram and Israel*, 41 f., making identification with Chalcis-al-Anjar in Cœle-Syria ; Forrer, *Die Provinzeinteiling d. ass. Reiches*, pt. 1, 62, identifying with Baalbek. For the reports of David's wars see Meyer, *GA* 2, 2, 251 ff. E. Cavaignac identifies Hadadezer with the *šar māt Arumu*, referred to in an inscription of Assurabi II of Assyria, *ca.* 1000 B.C. (*RHR* 107 [1923], 134 ff.).

omitted here by the Grr., as an opprobrious addition, comparing Gr. 12^{24b}, where she is called 'a harlot,' with the logical omission of the father's name, Nebat. But names indicating personal deformities were in vogue with the intent of averting the corresponding demons; see Noth, *IP* 227, and *e.g.*, Simon the Leper, properly Simon Garbā, Mt. 26^6.

27b. *Solomon built the Millo. He closed up the breach of the City of David* (with unnecessary plus, *his father*). Of these two archival items, probably in their original order, the first is cited in 9^{15}. This breach and its reconstruction have been revealed by Macalister and Duncan in their *Excavation of the Hill of Ophel* (*PEF Annual*, 4 [1926]), esp. 74 ff., and Crowfoot and Fitzgerald, *Excavations in the Tyropœon Valley* (vol. 5); also current reports in *QS* 1924–25, and Duncan, *ZAW* 1924, 221 ff.; photographs of the excavations are given by Olmstead, *HPS*, plates 134–7. On the present passage see also Weill, *La cité de David*, 24 ff. **28.** The epithet applied to Jeroboam, translated in EVV with ' a mighty man of valour ' (' valour ' = Heb. *ḥayl*=Lat. *virtus*) means in the present connexion ' capable ' and the following ' doer of work ' corresponds to English ' efficient.' There may be noticed Meyer's view (*IN* 367) that the former term means ' ein waffenpflichtiger Grundbesitzer,' and that the young Jeroboam had already come into his inheritance; for this interpretation *cf.* II. 15^{20}. His function as *over the labour* [literally *porterage*—see at 5^{29}; another word than ' levy,' *e.g.*, 4^6, but they were practically identical, *cf.* Gen. 49^{14}] *of the house of Joseph* is absolute contradiction of 9$^{21f.}$. We may suppose that this office gave him an insight into the dissatisfaction of the people, which aroused his ambitions and made him a rebel. **34.** *I will make him prince.* The noun ' prince ' translates *nāśî*', and so is distinct from the other term similarly translated, *nāgîd*, used in the oracles concerning Saul (1 Sam. 9^{16}, 10^1) and David (2 Sam. 5^2, 1 Ki. 1^{35}, etc.). Within Israelite politics our word does not appear again until Ezekiel, whose favourite term it was for the lay head of the church-state. As Noth has shown at length in his *System der Zwölfstämme Israels*, 93, and Exc. III, the word early implied a religious function, used of tribal representatives at solemnities, and so ' the princes of the tribes,' Num. 7^2, etc. The same word is used of sacred functionaries in the Phœnician crown-inscription from the Piræus (Lidzbarski, *HNE* 425 ; Cooke, *NSI* no. 33). But the term is of ancient political standing, used of the Ishmaelite princes (Gen. 17^{20}), of the Midianites (Josh. 13^{21}), and, as not observed by Noth, it appears in S. Arab. (Conti Rossini, *Chrestomathie*, 190). The use of the word here is a true tradition of the early religious and also democratic objection to monarchy. *Cf.* Ibn Khaldun's illuminating discussion of the transformation of the caliphate into monarchy, *mulk*, in Islam (*Prolegomena*, bk. 3, ch. 28). **40.** Jeroboam fled to Egypt like the Edomite Hadad. The name of a Pharaoh is here given for the first time in the Bible ; for Shishak see Comm., 14^{25}. This drama took place in the latter part of Solomon's reign.

VV.$^{41-43}$. The death of Solomon and the succession. V.^{41}, with its reference to *the Book of the Acts of Solomon*, presents the first chapter, as it were, of the series subsequently known as ' the Chronicles of the Acts of the Kings of Judah/Israel,' *e.g.*, 14$^{19, 29}$; see Int., §13, *b*. **42.** The alleged reign of *forty years* is the same as that ascribed to David ; this round figure of the average generation again indicates absence of such data in the early archives. The forty-one years ascribed to Rehoboam (14^{21}) may be similarly artificial, the datum putting his birth in Solomon's first royal year ; or the reverse may be the case, this datum being original, and Solomon's reign being dated from it. **43.** *And his son Rehoboam reigned in his stead.* The story of the inception of the civil war, interrupting the coronation ceremony at Shechem, and its consequences (12–14^{20}), disturbed the sequence elsewhere followed of personal details concerning the new king, as *e.g.*, 15$^{9-11}$. For Rehoboam these are given at 14$^{21\text{ff.}}$. The parallelism of the names of the rivals, R. and Jeroboam, with the common element '*am*, is of interest, but accidental. Despite its use as specification of a Pagan deity, the divine ' Kinsman,' or ' Uncle,' it was constant in Hebrew names, *e.g.*, Amram, Ammishaddai, and in the immediate family line Eliam, father of Bathsheba (2 Sam. 11^3), given in Ch. as Ammiel (1 Ch. 3^5). The name of the king, ' Rehab'am ' (and so GV ' Rehabeam '), was assimilated by 𝕲 to ' Jeroboam,' and became ' Roboam ' (and so 𝔙 FV), which the English Bible followed with

'Rehoboam.' See Note further, and especially for another and ingenious explanation of the name.

For the Gr. of vv.¹⁻³ see Rahlfs, SS 3, 215 f., cf. 116 f., finding the primitive text only in B 𝕰 𝕲ᴸ and Irenæus.—**1.** את בת פרעה: the clause is syntactically impossible. Older commentators discussed whether this princess was to be included in the ban on 'strange women,' some making of her a convert, adducing Ps. 45¹¹; see Poole, Hitz.—עֲכָנִית, צְרִנִית: the pointing of 'ע as at Neh. 13²³; the heavy final syllables induced shortening of the internal long syllables, e.g., צְרִנִים, v.⁵.—Gr. Συρας κ. Ιδουμαιας presents the double rdg. ארם/אדם.—**2.** אָכֵן: usual tr. 'surely,' but inappropriate here; Klost, St., al. as error for פן=Gr. μή; but it is to be equated with Syr. 'aikan, 'so that'; see Montg., JBL 1912, 144 ff.—**3.** ויטר, ויהי: for the grammatical disagreements with the subjects see GK §145.—**5.** עשתרת אלהי צ': the deformation of the divine name after the pattern of ba'al>bosheth. Bibl. Heb. lacks a fem. to אל; אלת appears in Phœn., Ugaritic. Burn. cft. Phœn. לאלי עשתרת, 'to his god Asht., and further Phœn. exx. are given by Nielsen, Ras Šamra Mythologie, 22 f.—**8.** מקטירות: for the independent syntax of the ppl. cf. מנשים, 5¹, and see GK §116, s.—**9.** הַנִּרְאָה: the ppl. pointed as pf., the art. then being treated as rel. pron.; cf. the same use of art. at Gen. 12⁷, 35¹; for discussion of these and similar anomalies see Burn., GK §138, 3b.—**10.** וצוה: Klost, Burn., comparing the Gr., correct to the ppl., ומצוה; St. is properly dubious; but the pf. is in consecutive order after the prec. ppl.— ולא שמר וג': the clause is parenthetical, is not to be changed to ולשמר וג' with Klost., Burn., after the Grr.—צוה 2°; 4 MSS צוהו, so VSS exc. Grr. g e₂.—**11.** עמך: for the prep. in psychological sense see BDB 768b; e.g., Job 10¹³, בלבבך‖עמך.—ברית וחקתי: Gr. missed the usual מצותי, and translated the first word with εντολας; 𝔖 𝔄 added it at the end.—**12.** אקרענה: Grr., λημψομαι αυτην, as though אקחנה which change is accepted by Klost., Burn., on ground of correspondence with vv.³⁴·³⁵; rather the Gr. avoided the harsh verb, and so again at v.¹³.—**13.** ירושלם: Grr., 𝔖, 𝔄+' the city,' after common usage.—**14.** שטן: Grr. here and below Σαταν.—הדד: also MSS הדר=Gr. Αδερ; at Gen. 36³⁵·³⁹ 𝔊 has both forms; see also Comm., 15¹⁸. This divine name, common in W. Sem. nn. pr. (see Lidzb., HNE 258), also occurs singly for such names in S. Arab. (NPS 1, 71 f.). In v.¹⁷ Akkadizing אדד appears. The name הד, alternate to בעל, occurs in Ugaritic. For the divine name used for human nomenclature cf. 'Jehu,' II. 9².—המלך זרע: the correction to המלוכה, after Gr. τ. βασιλειας (=II. 25²⁵), with Klost., St., is not necessary.—הוא באדום: recognized by some critics as gloss to preceding המלך; rather it is gloss to the impossible את אדום, v.¹⁵; sc. understand את as ב!—**15.** בחיות: very early error for בהכות=2 Sam. 8¹³, and so here Grr. του εξολεθρευσαι=𝔖ᴴ 𝔄 𝔖.— **17.** אנשים: the word=Engl. 'certain'; see Note, 3¹⁶. Grr., exc.

𝔊^L, pref. 'all.'—**18.** מדין : 𝔊 𝔊^H τ. πολεως Μαδιαμ ; for 'city of Midian' see Musil, *Topographical Itineraries*, No. I, Index.—מפארן, מצרים 1° : OGrr. om.—יבאו : B*† αρχοντες for ερχονται.—אמר : 'ordered,' the mng. as in Arab.—וארץ נתן לו : 𝔊 om. ; the verbal sequence is abnormal.—**19.** התפנים: MSS have variants ; Grr., Θεκεμεινας, etc. *Cf.* the identical place-name, Jer. 2^16, etc., Eze. 30^18 ; for suggested interpretations see GB, and most recently B. H. Stricker, *Analecta Orientalia*, 15 (1937), 11.—הגבירה : Grr. της μειζω, suggesting to Klost. הבכירה (!), 'the elder,' to Kit., St. הגדולה ; both suggestions quite unnecessary.—**20.** גְּנַב : the mng. of the name cannot be explained from the Heb., with the root mng. 'to steal,' but from the Arabic, with its diverse developments, *e.g.*, *junub* = 'guest.' Safaitic *n. pr. Gnb* occurs (*NPS* 2, 43). The Grr. read as 'Genibat,' which would represent a diminutive formation, *gunaibat.* The fem. form for masc. names is common in Old Sem., *e.g.*, Canaanite אחנת, Edomitic מנחת, שמילה, Ammonite שמעת, and appears in Nab., *e.g.*, הרתת, Palm. אדינת.—תגמלהו : Grr., εξεθρεψεν αυτον, *i.e.*, as from תגדלהו ; see Comm.—**21.** ואלך [שלחני] : the cohortative is expected ; see Orlinsky, *JQR* 32 (1941), 197.—**22.** לא : 'No!' (EVV 'Nothing') ; a similar case at Gen. 19^2 approves such mng. here, *vs.* Burn. 22 MSS לו = Grr., αυτω. See Bär's note on the Masoretic punctuation.

VV.^23-25a, inserted in v.^14 by OGrr., are in place in Hex.—**23.** רזון :=' prince,' Pr. 14^28 ; the name *Rzn* occurs in Sabæan (*NPS* 1, 199) ; OGrr., Εσρωμ/ν.—אלידע : the name and ידעאל are frequent in S. Arab. (*ib.*, 2, 28, 69).—[עזר]הדר=𝔊^H 𝔗 𝔄 ; 47 MSS הדר=𝔊 𝔊^L 𝔖^H 𝔖 𝔙 ; see Note, v.^14.—אשר ברח מאת : OGrr. transcribed with τον (=אשר) εν Ραεμαθ (so the simplest form of many variants, see Rahlfs, *SS* 3, 217) : 𝔊^H has a variant transcription, τον Βαραμεεθ, in which 𝔖^H found a patronymic, בר אמאת.—**24.** ויקבץ : Grr., 𝔖^H (S) as ויקצּו, generally adopted since Then.—אתם : Klost., Šanda, *BH* propose ארם with 2 Sam. 8^5 ; but the gloss may have been carelessly expressed.—וימלכו, וישבו, וילכו : 𝔊 (but B *al.* om. clauses 2 and 3 through homoiotel. of 'Damascus') ; 𝔊 read וילכד (the false rdg. וילכו having induced the foll. pls. in 𝔐), וימלך, וישב, and so 𝔖^H, a correction generally accepted.—**25a.** "and he was an adversary to Israel " ; *n.b.* the contradiction in 𝔊^L, 2^46g, " there was no Satan (the Heb. word !) in Solomon's days."—**25b.** ואת הרעה אשר הדד : OGrr., αυτη η κακια ην εποιησεν A., as though rdg. the verb עשה, and so 𝔗 𝔖, followed by EVV (JV not noting the addition to 𝔐) ; 𝔊^H αυτη η κακια A. (=𝔖^H ℭ), "this is the evil of A." (treating אשר as ל אשר=NHeb. של) = 𝔙 ; 6 MSS attempted improvement with plus [הדד] את " (which was) with H."—ויקץ : VSS, exc. 𝔗 𝔙 as=ויָּקָץ (to avoid the former contemptuous word), accepted by Grätz, *BH*, but see St.'s long note ; that " he oppressed Israel " is historically most improbable ; also that verb requires the foll. prep. ל. Joüon sugg. ויָּקֶם, after v.^23, but an object is then desiderated.

I. 11¹⁻⁴³

26. ירבעם: for the name see Comm. and Note on v.⁴³.—נבט: the name only in this connexion; it is frequent in S. Arab. by itself and in composition (*NPS* 2, 92).—הצררה=Hex.; OGrr., Σαρειρα, as at 12²⁴ᵇ.—צרועה: OGrr. om. the name of the mother here, have it at 12²⁴ᵇ, where the variants suggest a confusion with the place-name הצררה.—וירם יד במלך: 𝔊 12²⁴ᵇ, "and he was rising up against the kingdom."—**27.** המלוא: see Lexx. for connexion with Akk. *mulū*, 'an artificial terrace'; but there is also the use of the verb. in S. Arab. in parallelism with *bny*, 'to build' (Conti Rossini, *Chrest.*, 177); the same name for the fortress at Shechem, Jud. 9⁶,²⁰.—**27**b. Grr. here=𝔐. Gr. 12²⁴ᵇ has the plus, "(he built the Akra) with the levies of the house of Ephraim"; but Gr. 2³⁵ᵉ κ. ωκοδομησεν τ. ακραν επαλξιν επ αυτης· διεκοψεν τ. πολιν Δ., *i.e.*, rdg. סגר את as מסגרת=ἐπαλξις, 'fortress,' and פָּרַץ as פֶּרֶץ; see Montg., *ZAW* 1932, 127.—**28.** כל: Grr., 𝔖ᴴ om.—סבל: see Note, 5²⁹.—**29.** אחיה: both this form and אחיהו appear in 14⁴ᶠᶠ·, the latter also in 2 Ch. 10¹⁵. The latter spelling appears in a 7th century Jerusalem ostracon; see Albr., *JPOS* 1926, 38 ff., Diringer, *IAE* 74.—בדרך: OGrr. plus "and stood him off from the road" (not in Lucif.); but below for בשדה 𝔊ᴸ has 'on the road.'—והוא: Grr. exegetically, κ. ο Αχειας.—**31.** Grr. om. the art. in 'the ten tribes,' which appears preferable, but is correction of a careless phrase; art. in השבטים prob. by dittography.—**32.** האחד השבט: Grr., 𝔖ᴴ 'two tribes,' and so at v.³⁶. As Rahlfs notes (*SS* 3, 99), Jos. knew the Heb. text, but compromised with 𝔊, producing: 'one tribe and the one adjoining it.' There is no reason for correction of the previous figure '10' to '11' (*cf. BH*); in later parlance there were the ten tribes of the North, and the one, Judah, constituting the South.—**33.** עובני (3 MSS עובני), ישתחוו (3 other MSS ישתתו), הלכו: the VSS, including Aq., Sym. properly as singulars.—אלהי *tris*: original as *vs.* the abusive terms in vv.⁵⁻⁷, which terms are reproduced in Grr. here.—צדנין: 15 MSS ם/.—וחקתי ומשפטי: OGrr. om.; an addition suggested by v.³⁸.—**34.** כל 1⁰: Kit. (Comm., *BH*) elides without good reason.—נשיא אשתנו (4 MSS נשא א): Grr., αντιτασσομενος αντιταξομαι αυτω, 'I will oppose him'=𝔖ᴴ, with same translation as at Hos. 1⁶, אֶשָּׂא אֶשָּׁא לָהֶם. Lucian in view of inconsequence of the statement at this point transferred it to beginning of the v., obtaining, "I will oppose him . . . and will not take the kingdom from his hand"; see Rahlfs, *SS* 3, 201 f.—וחקתי . . . אשר 2⁰: 𝔊 om.—**35.** מלוכה: but ממלכה vv.³¹,³⁴.—את עשרת השבטים: to be omitted with St., *al.* as grammatically superfluous after the verbal suffix, although exegetically proper; Grr. ignore the suffix.—**36.** שבט אחד: Grr., 𝔖ᴴ, 'the two tribes.'—ניר: 𝔊 𝔊ᴸ θεσις=𝔖ᴴ *sĕyāmā*—by what kind of interpretation? 𝔊ᴸ by corruption θέλησις. The word is translated with κατάλειμμα at 15⁴, but correctly with λύχνος, II. 8¹⁹, with which word the Three render it in all places.—**37.** [ב]כל: Grr. arbitrarily om.—**38***b*β **39.** 𝔊 om.—**39.** וָאעַנֶּה: for the pointing *cf.*

Zec. 11⁵; see Bär and Ginsb.².—**40.** ירבעם 2°: OGrr. om.—ויברח: B† a doublet, κ. ανεστη κ. απεστη.—שי־שק: but Kt. 14²⁵ שושק; *v. ad loc.*—**41.** חכמתו: Grr. (exc. 71), 𝔊ᴴ pref. 'all.'—דברי שלמה 2°: 𝔊ᴸ ℭ as though דברי הימים לש׳, after the usual form. 𝔊 tr. the first noun with ῥήματα, but 𝔊ᴸ correctly with λόγοι.—**42.** על כל ישראל: 𝔊 om.—**43.** אביו: 2 MSS om. OGrr. intrude here 12², with further complication.—רחבעם: the verbal element is common in Heb. names and also in S. Arab. names (see *NPS* 2, 123). It may be explained from derivative mngs. of the Arabic, as though 'to be broadminded, generous,' and hence Stem II, 'to welcome.' A parallel name appears in רחביהו, 1 Ch. 23¹⁷, in which connexion GB cites a possible Bab. correspondent, 'Ra'bi-ilu.' But Albr., in *AJSL* 38 (1922), 140 f., *cft.* the name with Bab. 'Hammu-rabi,' as = ' the family is extended,' and presents other like early names in that language. And for 'Rehoboam' as a possible 'throne-name' see the same scholar in *AASOR* 21–22 (1943), 67, adducing Pharaonic examples. But there are no similar correspondents in Heb. names, and the parallelism seems far afield. If it be accepted, then Jeroboam's name may have been a defiant alias on part of the rebel, 'the people is great, is master,' after the Arab. and Aram. mng. of the root *rbb*; but there is the good old name, Jerubbaal.

12¹⁻²⁴. The division of the kingdom. ‖ 2 Ch. 10; *cf. Ant.*, viii, 8, 1–3. The Heb. text, treated by itself apart from the Gr. supplement (see at end of this section) has a grave inconcinnity in that it connects Jeroboam's return from Egypt, his being summoned to the parliament, and his leadership in its demands, with the succession of Rehoboam, while according to v.²⁰ the news of the return of Jeroboam and the summons to him are subsequent to the revolt. This disagreement is solved by excising vv.². ³ᵃ, absent in OGrr. (*n.b.* the parenthesis in EVV) as an intrusion from Ch. (*n.b.* Ch.'s common word *ḳāhāl vs. 'ēdāh*, v.²⁰, both translated usually with 'congregation'), excising 'Jeroboam' in v.¹² (with the Grr.), and adding, v.²⁰, the phrase 'from Egypt' to 'Jeroboam returned' (with Grr. MSS). VV.². ³ᵃ are necessary to Ch.'s narrative, in which Jeroboam's early history was omitted, but are superfluous here. With these excisions, excluding certain contradictions and superfluities, Jeroboam does not appear as ringleader of the revolt, but his election is an afterthought of the rebels. The above criticism is that of Meyer's (*IN* 363 ff.). Hölscher would excise only v.³ᵃ; Kittel transfers v.² to beginning of the ch., and so Stade; Klostermann and Kittel expand this v. from the Gr. suppl., inserted in 11⁴³ and 12²⁴ᵈ, viz., " and J. heard in Egypt that S. was dead, and he came to his city Sareira," etc. The text so revised appears as follows : **1.** *And Rehoboam went to Shechem, for all Israel came to Shechem to make him king.* [**2.** *And it was, when Jeroboam ben Nebat heard, while he was still in Egypt, whither he had fled from king Solomon, that Jeroboam ⸢returned from Egypt⸣* (with Ch., 𝔊ᴴ 𝔖ᴴ ; 𝔏 *dwelt in Egypt*). **3.** *and they sent and called him. And came Jeroboam and all the congregation of Israel.*] *And they* [Grr. *the people*] *spoke to Rehoboam*, etc. **12.** *And came* [*Jeroboam and*] *all Israel* [so most Grr. ; 𝔏 *all the people*=Ch.] *to Rehoboam*, etc. (vv.¹³⁻¹⁹). **20.** *And it was, when all Israel heard that Jeroboam had returned ⸢from Egypt⸣* [with some Grr. 𝔈 𝔖ᴴ], *that they sent and called him to the assembly, and they made him king over all Israel*, etc. ' From Egypt,' v.²⁰, was omitted as repeating and contradicting v.² ; then the sentence in the latter v. was changed by slight scribal and oral touch to ' he dwelt in Egypt,' to avoid repetition of the ' returning ' below. Also v.¹⁷, a disturbing interlude, is an intrusion from Ch. Kittel prefers the text of Gr. v.²⁴ᵠ· ʳ to vv.⁶⁻⁹, but without sufficient reason. Meyer (*IN*, 365) regards as an original element the addition to v.⁴ in Gr. v.²⁴ᵖ, κ. ἐβάρυνεν τὰ βρώματα τῆς τραπέζης αὐτοῦ ; *cf.* 5⁷ᶠ·.

Shechem was the place chosen by *all Israel* for the formal recognition of Rehoboam as Solomon's successor, *to make him king.* It was central and accessible, and, further, following Noth's thesis of an Israelite amphictyony, it may have been the traditional gathering-place of the tribes (*Das System der Zwölfstämme Israels*). It is reasonable to accept the statement about the assembly, with Lods (*Israël*, 432), as against Stade (*GVI* 1, 344 f.) and Kittel (*GVI* 2, 219 f.), who regard the assembly at Shechem as primarily mutinous ; but would not the king have taken proper military precautions ? K. Möhlenbrink has attempted to review the city's ancient history in his article, " Sichem als altpalästinische Königsstadt," *Christentum u. Wissenschaft* 10 (1934), 125–34 ; *cf. ZAW* 1934, 129. Alt finds good historic background for the public declaration of blessing and curse in this locality ; *cf.* Dt. 27, 28 (*Die Ursprünge des israel. Rechts*, 1934, 61 ff.). The ancient **Shechem has been long identified with Balaṭa, near Jacob's**

Well, SE of modern Shechem.¹ The hereditary rights of the Davidic dynasty were not yet established,² and the discontented Northern tribes had now the opportunity of making their bargain with the new king. He postponed reply till the day after the morrow (*the third day*) for time to consult his counsellors; but he took the advice of his young companions, *the boys*, as the Hebrew means. The story phrases his reply in metrical form:

11. *My father loaded upon you a heavy yoke,*
    And I will add to your yoke;
12. *My father chastised you with rods,*
    And I will chastise you with lashes.

The last word—*scorpion* in Heb.—is technical for some kind of stinging whip. **15.** The unfortunate decision of the young king is attributed to a '*sibbāh* from YHWH,' *i.e.*, as the root means, a *turn-about* of fate; the much later Koheleth marks this endless cycle in natural things (Eccl. 1³ᶠᶠ·); the phrase is predestinarian, without moralizing as in the case of Abimelech's fate (Jud. 9⁵⁶). Hölscher claims that *sibbāh* is 'ein sehr junges Wort,' on what ground is not evident; rather the term belongs to ancient fatalism; *cf.* 2¹⁵. The following explication, *to establish his word which* YHWH *spake by Ahijah*, may itself be secondary. In any case Rehoboam's folly effected the divine purpose. **16.** The v. repeats like a national anthem the lyric outcry of the earlier rebels against the dynasty (2 Sam. 20¹), with an additional line:

What portion have we in David?
Neither have we inheritance in Jesse's son.
To your tents, O Israel!
Now see to thine own house, O David!

---

¹ For earlier literature see Montg., *The Samaritans*, ch. 2. Excavations at Shechem have been pursued by German expeditions, in 1913-14 under Sellin, and since 1926; see Sellin's reports in *ZDPV* 1926 *seq.*, and a criticism of the later campaigns in *ZAW* 1933, 146 ff.; also G. Welter in *Archäologischer Anzeiger*, 1932, 292 ff. A fresh enterprise was undertaken in 1934 (*AJA* 1935, 142). See Albr., *APB* 55 ff.; Abel, *GP* 2, 458 ff.; Olmstead, *HPS* 285, with photographic plates.

² For the various interpretations of royal succession in the small states of the ancient Orient see Galling, *Die israelitische Staatsverfassung*, 12 ff.

"To your tents" smacks of the old Arabian life=English "Go home!" "See to thine own house" (*cf.* Gen. 39^{23}) is in modern English, "Look after your own business!" **18. 19.** The stoning of Adoram, Over-the-Levy (the Adoniram of 4^6—see Note), the energetic flight of the king, and the consummation of the rebellion are briefly narrated. As to the source of this narrative, which Hölscher characterizes as possessing 'all the traits of good old saga-narrative,' critics differ. Wellhausen (in Bleek, *Einl.*^{4}, 243) and Hölscher regard it as Judæan; Kittel and Šanda, as Ephraimite. This variance of opinion reflects the pure objectivity of the story; nothing in the context exhibits any partiality for Jeroboam; according to 11$^{37\text{f.}}$ he was given the opportunity 'to make good,' while, with 12$^{25\text{ff.}}$ he 'went wrong.' On the other hand Rehoboam's foolish political blunder is coolly narrated: it was divinely 'fated.' Later a moral reason was found in Solomon's infidelity, but it is not stated here, indeed his despotism goes unchallenged by the writer. The Judæan origin appears the more probable. This is supported, as Wellhausen holds (p. 277), by the correspondence of v.^{16} with 2 Sam. 20^1.

21-24. The failure to suppress the revolt. The story is almost *ad verbum* identical with Ch. The latter ignored the earlier Ahijah narrative (except for casual references, II. 9^{29}, 10^{15}) as quite too anti-dynastic, but it had to explain here why the rupture was not suppressed. The otherwise ignored tribe of Benjamin now appears. *Shemaiah the man of God* (the first appearance of the title in Ki.) appears to be a late fiction, appearing again in 2 Ch. 11$^{2\text{ff.}}$, 12$^{5\text{ff.}}$, and actually replacing Ahijah in the Gr. supplement, v.^{24o}. The figure of 180,000 *select warriors* (also in Ch.) is absurd; 𝔊 has a lower figure, 120,000.

The Greek supplement to the history of Jeroboam, v.$^{24\text{a-z}}$. This addition in the OGrr., Old Latin (ignored by Josephus), was excised by the Hexaplaric recension, although still retained in some MSS of that later strain, *e.g.*, N. The following is a digest of its contents:

a=14^{21}.—b. Jeroboam was son of a harlot, was ἄρχων σκυτάλης, 'lash-master'; he built Sareda for Solomon; he had 300 horse-chariots; he built the Akra by the levies of Ephraim; he shut up the City of David, rising against the kingdom.—*c.* Solomon attempted to kill him; he fled to Shishak.—*d.* He heard of Solomon's death, and desired to return.—*e.* Parenthesis on his marriage to Shishak's sister-in-law (*cf.* the marriage of the Edomite prince Hadad, 11$^{14ff.}$).—*f.* His return; the tribe of Ephraim gathered to him; he built there a fort.—*g–na.* Sickness of his child, episode of Ahijah's prophecy, death of the child (*cf.* ch. 14).—*nβ.* He came to Shechem, and gathered the tribes there.—*o.* The prophecy of Shemaiah (*cf.* 11$^{26ff.}$).—*p et seq.* || 12$^{1-24}$.

With its unique length as an insertion in the earlier books of the Septuagint, no passage has provoked a wider difference of opinion than this narrative, which is throughout contradictory of that in 𝔐. Distinguished historians have taken opposite positions (*cf.* Olmstead's citations, 'Source Study,' 15): von Ranke for the supplement as 'the earlier and more trustworthy of the two' (*Weltgeschichte,* 3, 2, 412); Meyer, on the contrary: "für jeden, der ohne vorgefasste Meinung den Sachverhalt prüft, kann die Priorität des hebräischen Berichts und die gänzliche Wertlosigkeit der daraus zurechtgemachten Erzählung von LXX auch hier nicht zweifelhaft sein" (*IN* 369 f.). Biblical critics are as sharply polarized. Says Stade: "The Hebrew text from which 𝔊 was translated had after this verse a *midrash* describing Jeroboam's life and adventures. This late addition is rather fanciful and very clumsily compiled from elements in the narratives of 𝔐, in cc. 11, 12, 14" (*SBOT* 130); to which Olmstead replies: "When scholars of such deserved reputation can take this attitude, it is clear that a somewhat detailed examination of this 'midrash' is demanded if we are to free the Jeroboam narrative from this reproach. That it forms a well-balanced, consistent, and probable story can best be shown by allowing the narrator to speak in his own words"—there follows a full translation (*AJSL* 30 [1913], 17; *cf. ib.,* 31 [1915], 169 ff.; *HPS* 350). Cheyne takes similar position (*JQR* 1899, 551 ff., and art. 'Jeroboam' in *EB*). Definitely on the other side stand, *inter al.,* Kuenen, *Einl.,* 1, 2, 97, n. 10, Kittel in his Comm., and Burney, pp. 163 ff. Benzinger mediatingly holds that 𝔊 has preserved what 𝔐 has lost (pp. 82, 86 f.); and Šanda pursues an elaborate criticism, separating the older body of the narrative from the later accretions (pp. 375 ff.).

Skinner in his short Commentary has given an admirable critique of the question (Note II, pp. 443 ff.) ; to the problem as to which of the two accounts is the more original he finds it impossible to give a decided answer ; the present form of 𝔊, he holds, does not compare well with 𝔐, but, and here in line with Šanda, when the former text is cleared of excrescences, there remains a kernel whose inferiority to 𝔐 is by no means obvious. Also Robinson in his presentation (*HI* 1, 270 ff.) is dubious as between the two.

The present writer agrees with the negative judgment. He holds in brief that when the text of 𝔐 is cleared of the interpolations indicated above, there remains an abbreviated but clear story of Jeroboam ; the latter had fled to Egypt, there followed upon Solomon's death the conclave at Shechem and the revolt of the North, and then, when the Northerners heard that the capable Jeroboam had returned in the interregnum, they offered him the crown. One disturbance indeed in the sequence is that the long story of Ahijah's prophecy (11^{29-39}) dovetails awkwardly between the introduction, " and this is the story how J. raised his hand against king S." (v.^{27}), and the sequel, " and so S. sought to kill him " (v.^{40}). But the supplement presents a motive for Solomon's hostility, alleging that Jeroboam had three hundred chariots, and that " he was exalting himself against the *régime*" (*cf.* Num. 16^3). This may be index that the need of a motivation was early felt and supplied. But, as Meyer observes, no nobleman in Solomon's day could have acted in such high-handed fashion ; Absalom's pomp (2 Sam. 15^1) was child's play in comparison. It is evident that the whole animus of the story is against Jeroboam ; his mother was a harlot, and he was high-handed from the beginning ; he had no original prophetic auspices, but Ahijah appears on the scene to predict his child's death as penalty for the abominations he will one day commit—a story arrantly transplanted hither from ch. 14. Ahijah's oracle, as given by 𝔐, is put in the mouth of the almost fictitious Shemaiah (v.^{24}o), while the favourable conditional promise is omitted. To make the subject more interesting Jeroboam is given the part at Shishak's court which a most reliable and original document gives to the Edomite prince ; a Pharaoh would not have given his daughter to a commoner

There is in 𝕲 none of the cool objectivity of the story in 𝕳, which may well be Judæan in origin, but which passes no judgment upon Jeroboam in advance, rather offers him God-given opportunity. The supplement in a word is midrashic, rather a jumble to an extent that does not appear until the Chronicler, which fact may not exclude the presence of detached items of tradition. As the supplement harks back to the early form of 𝕳, it may serve at times for text-correction; but any judgment in accepting definite historical data must be arbitrary. The general opinion that the original was Hebrew is doubtless correct, and for that reason it is of literary interest as index of the extent of such literature at an early date—we may compare the midrashic stories in Josephus. The translators of 𝕲 simply attached it to their 'unauthorized' translation of the Scriptures as a variant historical document of interest. one which made of Jeroboam a more sinister person than did the sober history preserved in 𝕳. See further Comm. on 14$^{1\text{ff}}$.

V.^{25}–14^{20}. The reign of Jeroboam. *Cf.* 2 Ch. 11$^{13\text{-}15}$, 13$^{1\text{-}20}$; *Ant.*, viii, 8, 4–9, 4.

25. *And Jeroboam built* (*i.e.*, rebuilt) *Shechem in the Highland of Ephraim, and resided in it. And he went out from there, and built Penuel.* The v. is of archival origin, and is the only purely secular datum, except 14^{20}, preserved for Jeroboam's reign. Shishak's invasion must have affected the young Northern kingdom even more than Judah, and hence the paucity of data. Penuel across the Jordan on the Jabbok (Gen. 32^{32}, etc.; *cf.* Abel, *GP* 2, 406) may be one of the places (no. 53) listed by Shishak among his conquests (see Comm., 14$^{25\text{ff.}}$). Lods (*Israël*, 434) and Olmstead (*HPS* 355) propose that Penuel was built by Jeroboam upon Shishak's retreat from his invasion. The object of this military undertaking was doubtless the control of the trade-routes across Jordan with the intention of usurping Judah's heritage. The verb 'to go out' is used of military campaigns. There is no reason to think, with Stade (*GVI* 1, 351) and Lods, that a new capital was attempted. Only indirectly do we learn of another royal seat, Tirzah (14^{17}, 15^{33}, etc.).

VV.$^{26\text{-}31}$. Jeroboam's religious innovations. The history of the reign is composed of this late popular tradition and two prophetic stories, v.^{32}–ch. 13, and 14$^{1\text{-}18}$. Critics differ widely upon the analysis of these few verses. Kittel regards vv.²⁶·²⁷ as secondary, Stade only v.²⁸, while Hölscher, in addition to numerous minor points speaks of vv.³¹⁻³³ as 'Flickwerk.' **28. 29.** Confusion occurs over the two calves. Jeroboam *made two calves of gold*, then proclaimed, *Behold thy gods, O Israel, who brought thee up from the land of Egypt*, and finally *he placed the one at Bethel and the other at Dan*. With only one calf there was danger of confusion of the image with YHWH; with the introduction of a second one the worship in the Northern Kingdom is presented as clearly polytheistic. Accordingly the present text is a development of the original tradition that he set up a calf at Bethel, concerning which he would have proclaimed, *This is thy God who brought* [reading sing. verb] *thee*, etc., exactly as at Neh. 9¹⁸, although at Ex. 32⁴·⁸ the sing. has been changed into the pl., "these are thy gods." The similar spirit of correction appears in the text of Hos. 10⁵, where with Gr. 'the calves (of Beth-aven)' is to be restored to 'the calf.' **30**a. *And this thing became a sin:* an evident interpolation from 13³⁴. **30**b. *And the people went before the one as far as Dan:* an awkward statement in the context, as translators have seen from early days. 𝔊ᴸ adds the desiderated complement, 'and before the other to Bethel,' and Oort, Kittel, Burney, *BH* would still further improve the text by inserting this Lucianic addition before the 'going to Dan.' Kamphausen boldly rewrites the whole passage; Benzinger and Šanda unnecessarily find in the statement a cultic procession 'before the calf' from Bethel to Dan for its installation there, comparing 2 Sam. 6.³ The indictment is further continued: **31.** *He made the houses of the high-places*, and he instituted *a new order of priests, not of the sons of Levi, but from the whole range of the people.* The last phrase is to be so translated, and no⁺ as *from the lowest of the people*, with AV, following a Renaissance interpretation, *e.g.*, 'ex fæce populi.' And yet the high-places had not been destroyed nor the local priest-guilds abolished; but neither is such a reformation attributed to David and Solomon.

The nature of these alleged religious 'innovations' of Jeroboam has long been recognized by historians as reaction

³ Jos. still knew of 'the temple of the golden calf above the Little Jordan' (*BJ* iv, 1, 1).

against the growing dominance of Solomon's temple in Jerusalem, which was at once the religious expression of his autocratic claims : see for example Stade, *GVI* 1, 351 ff. ; Kittel, *GVI* 2, 301 ff. ; Robinson, *HI* 1, 277 ff. There is nothing to show that Solomon repressed the local cults ; but his ambition to make Jerusalem supreme, in the double aspect of political and religious capital, tended inevitably to the depreciation of the provincial holy places, to the political irritation of the local communities and the tribes at large, and to the relative depression of the country priests, who doubtless came to play the rôle of agitators against the family of Sadok. It was these elements of opposition to which as a clever politician Jeroboam made his appeal. However, reaction in itself has no positive value. The fact stands forth that the cult at Jerusalem contained positive elements of good, in its imagelessness and freedom from depraved practices, and for its position in the capital, where excesses were checked by a restrained culture and a political control. The part played by princes in religious advance and reformation is often overlooked ; it is well exhibited in the subsequent history of Judah. Religion is generally of a higher character in cities than in country communities, among the ' pagani,' to use the ancient Christian term for the heathen of the countryside, and similarly Teutonic ' heathen,' ' Heiden.' At all events this reaction boded no good for the North, as its weakness through its several dynasties proved. Jeroboam's enterprise was purely political, indeed cleverly founded on the opposition to Solomon's autocracy and centralization of religion. But he had no religious interest beyond the restoration of the local cults (*ye have gone up long enough to Jerusalem*), and this policy, in contrast to the history of Judah, worked ill for the unity of the North. Olmstead indeed remarks as follows (*HPS* 353) : " Jeroboam's revolt was no revolt against Yahweh's cult. If not instigated by the prophetic party, it met with their approval, and history proves that they were right. During the centuries which immediately followed, every fundamental advance in Hebrew religion originated in the north." But the prophetic guilds and prophets of the North had no association with the local cults ; they represented a reaction against the debasing tendencies of Canaanitism, which were not so active in the more unified South, where the temple in Jerusalem stood for the sober national religion.

The *calves* (depreciatory for ' bulls ' ?—*cf.* the ' she-calves ' of Hos. 10⁵) are generally regarded as aboriginal to the Israelite cult ; see Nowack, *Arch.*, 2, 23 ; but Benzinger (*Arch.*, 326) observes that ' surprisingly enough ' Palestinian archæology has found only small god-images ; *cf.* Kittel (*GVI* 2, 61, notes 2, 3), who would reduce the bull to the function of bearer of the deity. Against the general view Eissfeldt (' Der Gott Bethel,' *ARw.*, 1930) argues that the calf-worship was introduced by Jeroboam and was not original, and similarly Meek holds that he introduced another religion (*Hebrew Origins*, 158 ff.).[4] For Bethel, in addition to the standard authorities, see now the reports of the American School's excavations at modern Beitīn by Albright, *BASOR* nos. 55, 56, 57 (1934-35), and Abel, *GP* 2, 270. For Dussaud's view that Bethel meant originally a deity and not a place, and that this fact has been deleted here (*Origines cananéennes du sacrifice israëlite*, 1921, 69 f., 234 ff.) see Kittel's criticism, p. 230, n. 2. *The houses of the high-places* may refer simply to the rock-hewn sacred precincts, as at Gezer, which were themselves ' houses of deity ' ; or for possible architectural construction in the sacred areas may be compared G. L. Robinson's description of a high-place at Petra, and hard by " outlines of what once was probably a roofed-in guest chamber or hall, in which sacrificial feasts may have been celebrated " (*Sarcophagus of an Ancient Civilization*, 140, *cf.* 154 ff.).

1. בא : original, and so 𝔊ᴴ ; 10 MSS באו =OGrr., Ch.—**2.** אשר := ' where,' from the original mng., ' place ' ; *cf.* Ps. 41⁹ ; see C. Gaenssle, ' The Heb. Particle אשר,' *AJSL* 31 (1914), 15 ff. (not noting these cases).—'ש המלך : so the order by earlier usage, 1¹,

---

[4] The bull was the holy animal over a widespread area ; see art. ' Stier ' in Pauly-Wissowa, *RE*, esp. col. 2503 *seq.*, 2512 *seq.* ; for Canaan, L. Waterman, ' Bull-Worship in Israel,' *AJSL* 31 (1915), 229 ff. ; S. A. Cook, *The Religion of Anc. Palestine*, 27 ff. For its vogue in S. Arabian sacred art see A. Grohmann, *Göttersymbole u. Symboltiere auf südarab. Denkmälern*, 1914, 41, 65 ff. ' The bull of El ' now appears in the Ugaritic texts. Albright (*From the Stone Age*, 228 ff.) supports at length Kittel's position. Art has had its part in the deterioration of religion, the sign becoming the thing signified, and hence the drastic Second Commandment.

etc.; many MSS reverse the order with Ch.—במצרים ״ וַיֵּשֶׁב:
read ״ מִפְּ׳ וַיָּשָׁב; see Comm.—3. וּבֹאוּ Kt., וָבֹא Kr. =17 MSS:
the latter correct; cf. Note, v.[1].—5. עֹד: VSS, exc. 𝔗, as עַד; such
correction is not required, vs. BH.—העם: Grr. om.; probably
insertion from Ch.—6. ויוֹעַץ: there is no reason for emendation
on basis of Gr., for which see presentation in BH.—וְהִבְעִם: OGrr.
om., as unnecessary, as also St. holds; similar variations in v.[18].—
אֶת פְּנֵי ש׳: for the prepositional phrase see GB 641b.—7. וידבר
Kt., וַיְדַבְּרוּ Kr.: Kt. case of ancient 'defective spelling,' or impersonal?—ועבדתם ועניתם ודברת: 𝔊 om. the second verb, prob.
through misunderstanding of it as implying 'humility'; 𝔊[L] 𝔊[H] tr.,
with the verb εἴκειν, 'to yield.' Ch. found similar objection to the
preceding תהיה עבד, rendering it with תהיה לטוב, and changing ועבדתם
to ורציתם; see St. and Haupt for attempted simplifications.—8. אֲשֶׁר
העמדים לפניו: for the syntax of the phrase cf. 21[11]; Ch. om. אשר, and
so BH; but cf. ממלך אדר אש משל in the Eshmunazar inscr., line 9.—
9. נשיב =Ch.; VSS as sing., as appropriate to the royal ego;
but the case is one of the 'communicative plural'; cf. Gen. 1[26],
Is. 6[8], and see Haupt.—10. אתה: Grr., a duplicate, συ νυν, as
presenting א׳ and עתה; 1 MS reads the latter.—מעלינו: acc. to
St., al., it is far preferable to read מֵעָלֵנוּ, cf. v.[4]; but why the
variation from the obvious? Some MSS spell the preceding case
with עלינו.—קטֹנִי: so Ginsb.[2], BH; other edd., קָטְנִי—12. וּיבֹא Kt.,
וַיָּבֹא Kr., MSS וּבֹא; 𝔊 as pl.; the sing. is to be kept, as in
vv.[1, 3, 21].—15. יהוה 2⁰: 2 MSS, OGrr. om.—16. ישראל: correct,
vs. 'the people' of 𝔊[L] 𝔙.—דבר: 3 MSS, Ch., OGrr. om.—מה: in
the negative sense, like Arab. mā; see GB 401b.—לאהליך: one
of the 18 Tiḳḳûnê Sôferîm, this case being alleged to be correction
of לאלהיך, 'to thy gods'; see Ginsb., Int., 355 f., Dr. on 2 Sam. 20[1].
—ראה: Grr., βοσκε =רְעֵה (accepted by Then., al.); 𝔊[L] a plus at
end of v., κρινε/ναι, 'choose' =Aram. רעה, 'to delight in'; 𝔗
מלך על, by periphrasis.—18. אדרם: 3 MSS הדרם =Ch.; Gr. texts
with various forms; Jos. =Ɖ; OGrr. revised to 'Adoniram,'
which is accepted by Kit., Burn., St., BH; but see Note on 4[6].—
כל ישראל: B a₂ om.; cf. Note, v.[16].—20. ירבעם: B*† Ροβοαμ.—
[ישראל] כל 2⁰: Grr. om.—יהודה: Grr. +'and Benjamin,' despite לבדו.
—22. האלהים: read יהוה with 4 MSS, Ch. =VSS.—24. וישבו ללכת:
for the phrase ='returned' cf. 13[17], etc.; for the first word Grr.,
κατεπαυσαν, as though for וישבתו, and so BH 'fortasse.'—26. 'in
his heart': the same phrase used of the fool's blasphemy, Ps. 53[2].
—27. הזה 2⁰: OGrr. om.—אדניהם: Grr. (exc. i a₂), Κυριον κ. κυριον
αυτων.—והרגוני: 5 MSS om.—ושבו וג׳: OGrr. om.—28. המלך: so
most Gr. MSS, but 𝔖[H] with ※; N om.; 𝔊[L] 'Jeroboam' (and
so adding in v.[31]); the subject is an intrusion.—אלהם: Grr. as
for על העם, which BH, al. prefer, but St. rejects; the Gr. would
clarify the reference of the pronoun.—רב לכם מעלות: see Burn.,
GK §133, c.—העלוך: on basis of argument above read the sing.,
הֶעָלָה, with Kit., St., al. (BH with question).—30. להמאת: 𝔊[L] +'to

Israel ' (confining the sin to the North), which Burn., *BH* adopt.
—עד דן : OGrr. +' and before the other to Bethel '; see Comm.—
Sub fin., a plus in some Gr. minuscc., and noted in marg. of $\mathfrak{S}^{\text{H}}$
" and they left the house of the Lord."—**31.** את : to be deleted
with Burn., *BH*.—בית במות : for the composite pl. phrase *cf.*
II. $17^{29.\ 32}$, and see GK §124, r : *per contra*, 'בתי הב, 13^{32}.—קצות :
see GB *s.v.* ; a sing. from *ḳaṣawat* ; *cf.* the Aramaizing קְצָת, *e.g.*,
Dan. 1^2, and see Montg. *ad loc.*

12^{32}–13. Jeroboam's presumptuous impiety ; the penalty
pronounced by the word of a man of God ; the sequel of the
latter's sad fate ; Jeroboam's recalcitrancy and the inevitable
doom of the dynasty. Critics differ as to the alignment of
vv.$^{32.\ 33}$, which themselves contain duplicate material. *E.g.*,
Kittel, Benzinger attach v.^{32} to the preceding narrative, and
Burney and Skinner include also v.^{33}. But the fresh story
begins with v.^{32}, as recognized by Stade, Šanda. Its theme is
independent of the notes of the cults of the high-places ;
Jeroboam is punished for usurpation of priestly prerogative.
The unravelling of the duplicates is also a problem. A simple
narrative is obtained by accepting as the original introduction
to the story these two elements : v.^{32a}, *And Jeroboam made
a pilgrimage-feast* [Heb.=Arab. *ḥaj*] *in the eighth month like
the feast that is in Judah ;* and v.^{33} (*ad finem*), *And he went up
upon the altar to burn incense.* The intervening redactorial
material was introduced to round out and emphasize Jeroboam's innovations before the story of the man of God :
his acting as priest, sacrificing to the calves (here both at
Bethel !), institution of priests of high-places, and notably,
v.^{33a}, the gratuitous condemnation of the assumed heretical
innovation of a new date for the Haj, of which condemnation
there is no breath in v.^{32}—it was *like the feast that is in Judah.*
This summary completes the indictment of Jeroboam, and
serves as introduction to the story of the man of God. The
alleged innovation of the date of the Haj has been most
variously interpreted. Some scholars have assumed that the
eighth month was the original dating of Sukkoth, at least
in North Palestine, as more agreeable to its climate, and
hence the assignment of the seventh month for the Judæan
practice would be an innovation which became standardized
in the later Law ; so Kittel, *cf.* Benzinger. But Dalman
(*A. u. S.*, 2, 41 ; *cf.* p. 121, etc., and *cf.* Sanda) takes direct

issue with Kittel, noting that between Jerusalem and Samaria there is no difference of harvest time—if climatic difference there be, Samaria is warmer than Judah—there may have been a variance of opinion as to the conclusion of harvest, *e.g.*, the olive harvest coming latest. The problem is connected with that of the apparent conflict between the date of the completion of the temple in Bul, the eighth month (6^{38}), and the dedication in Ethanim, the seventh month (8^2). See the discussion in connexion with the latter passage, and note Morgenstern's solution. Then Jeroboam would have been following the old Israelite practice, *like the feast that is in Judah* (and so Mowinckel, *Chronologie*, 174). But the later Judæan calendar, which threw that festival wholly into the seventh month, was the innovation, while the North retained the old calendar. The distinction of the celebrations may have been further accentuated, as is the wont of sectarian divisions, and this may be the basis of the condemnatory remark, *on the fifteenth day in the eighth month, in the month which he had invented by himself* (see Note), and then the day-date may have been clumsily introduced into v.^{32} ; *cf.* Morgenstern, p. 69, n. 93, holding these day-dates to be very late glosses. The crowning presumption was, according to the narrator, that *he went up on* (the place of) *the altar to burn incense* ; this is the late criticism of the ancient prerogative of monarchy ; see Comm. on $8^{14\text{ff}}$.

$13^{1\text{-}32}$. The story of the nameless *man of God*, as the hero is entitled throughout, is the first extensive case of midrash in the historical books, to be continued *in extenso* in the later stories of the prophets, and is for that reason of literary interest. Ch. names as authority for the reign of Rehoboam's son Abijah 'the Midrash of the Prophet Iddo' (II. 13^{22}), which compilation may have contained the present story. Later development gave this prophet's name to the present man of God ; so Jos., with Yadon, and Rabbinic tradition (see Marcus). Even the ultra-conservative Keil dodged the explicit *vaticinium post eventum* of the name Josiah (v.^{2}) ; he held that the man of God pronounced the name as an ' appellative,' ' he whom Y. supports,' subsequently providentially fulfilled in the actual name, and similar, as he holds, to the prediction of Cyrus's name in Isaiah, these then being the only cases of such explicit prediction in the Scriptures. The relation of the story to that of Josiah's cognizance of 'the man of God's sepulchre' (II. $23^{16\text{ff.}}$) has been disputed. Wellhausen claims (*Comp.*, 277) the literary dependence of our story upon that history; but Thenius's recognition of that passage as an interpolation from our story is to be accepted. It is impossible to date the documentary fixation of such a legend; with Šanda, the redaction would have taken place in Josiah's time. There is indeed no particular indication of late post-Exilic date; the reference to the 'cities of Samaria' (v.^{32}) can be pre-Exilic. Interest in such prophets did not continue after the Exile. There may be noted the peculiar, evidently popular term *man of God* (the later Christian 'divine') for the Judæan over against the Northern title *prophet* (*cf.* vv.$^{1, 11}$). The repeated and apparently redundant phrase, *by the word of* YHWH, has been noted by Wellhausen as late; but see Note, v.^{1}. The probable fact is that among the sepulchres that Josiah destroyed was the tomb of an unnamed Judæan holy man, celebrated with a legend; *cf.* Arabic *wali*. There is to be noted the dramatic feature of the lion which remained *standing by the carcase* (v.^{25}), for its preservation until it came into the prophet's pious hands; similarly a lion figures in the case of a man who disobeyed a prophet ($20^{35\text{ff.}}$); for the nuisance of lions in Palestine see Comm. on II. $17^{25\text{f.}}$. The story has its moral in the theme of the disobedient prophet; *cf.* the Balaam story and that of Jonah. It is true to religious psychology; the man of God's errand is to be devoted singly to the divine purpose; *cf.* the word of Jesus, Luke 10^{4}. No punishment is entailed upon the lying prophet, who subsequently became the medium of the true word of God, on which fact Grotius curtly remarks, "Revelatio prophetica sæpe fit malis hominibus." But his history is not the point of the story, while in any case false inspiration of the prophets was a matter of common knowledge, and was given its explanation as coming from a 'lying spirit' ($22^{20\text{ff.}}$). Indeed in the latter story Micaiah gives first a false oracle (v.^{15}). It is to be noted that the old prophet ascribes his inspiration to *an angel* (v.^{18}), which at least relieves the divine responsibility. Šanda holds that the final staccato sentence, *he lied to him*, is an interpolation. The legend developed to explain the untimely end of some holy man upon his return from a mission ; he must have committed some fault on the way. The narrative is diffuse, and the text is subject to much criticism and correction. In v.[11] is to be read the pl., *his sons came*, with the VSS ; in v.[12] *and they showed him*, for the makeshift translation, *for they had seen*. At end of v.[23] the words appearing in EVV as *to wit* (or *namely*), *for the prophet whom he had brought back*, are to be elided, as erroneous gloss to define the preceding subject. V.[29b] on the basis of 𝔊 may be simplified ; in v.[31] in place of *lay my bones beside his bones*, the Grr. read, *lay me*, etc. ; see Notes.

In vv.[33, 34] as sequel to the above story and with repetition of 12[31] Jeroboam's incorrigible perversity is depicted. Wellhausen (*Comp.*, 278), followed by Stade, regards v.[33a] as continuation of that story, and vv.[33b, 34] as redactorial ; it is simpler, with Šanda, to consider both vv. as redactorial with emphasis on the illegitimate priesthood. The usual translation of v.[33] is that *he again made priests*, an obscure note indeed ; the meaning of the Heb. verbs is rather : *he turned back and made priests*, since he was now proved to be physically incapacitated. For such use of the first verb *cf.* II. 24[1], Jer. 34[11, 16]. The bastard priesthood is here the object of denunciation, as the calves were at 12[30]. Some minor corrections of the Heb. text are to be noted (see Notes). At end of v.[33] read : *he would consecrate him, and he would become a highplace priest* (EVV paraphrase). In v.[34] correct *by this thing*, and read with MSS, VSS, EVV exc. JV : *this thing became the sin of the house of Jeroboam ;* critics vary as to the interpretation, some preferring the Gr., " and this thing became a sin to the house of J." The terse Hebrew at end of the same v. may be literally translated : *and to* (the end of) *abolition and destruction from off the earth ;* the second phrase occurs at Dt 6[15], Am. 9[8]. The phrase translated ' to consecrate ' is literally ' to fill the hand of,' as used in the ritual of consecration, Ex. 28[41], etc. ; it was however of ancient usage, appearing in the story of Micah's consecration of the Levite (Jud. 17[5, 12]). Exactly the same phrase occurs in Akk. *mullū (ana) ḳātā*, of the solemn placing of the sceptre in the new king's hand (in Hammurabi's case, *KB* 3, 1, 122), not however of sacred functions. See the full discussions by Nowack (*Arch.*,

2, 120 ff.) and Šanda. Šanda argues convincingly that the term denotes the assignment of the benefice to the priest, some symbol being used in the rite of ' filling the hand.' The term is originally secular, not necessarily of Mesopotamian origin. Compare the history of the Muslim term for the election of the caliph, *bai'at*, literally ' purchase-contract,' accompanied with the handshake, a term that passed into the Syriac Churches for the consecration of the higher clergy. In the Anglican Church the key of the church is placed in the hand of the newly instituted rector.

32. כן : Grr. the relative ὅ, by correction of a careless passage.—והעמיד : again a case of dialectical or late syntax.—**33.** בבית אל : 𝔊 𝔊^L om.—בחדש 2° : Grr., εν τη εορτη.—ברא מלבד : the verb has the Arab. sense, ' to invent, improvise ' ; comparison with Neh. 6⁸, מלבך אתה בודאם, '' for out of thy heart thou art inventing them '' (*i.e.,* the preceding ' words '), early induced the Ḳr. here, מִלִּבּוֹ (also in MSS), as also early known to the Grr. with απο καρδιας αυτου, a correction generally accepted by critics ; but the point is that he invented the new dating ' all by himself '=מִלְּבַד.

Ch. 13. **1.** (יהוה) בדבר : also vv.² ⁵· ⁹· ¹⁷· ¹⁸, 20³⁵, 1 Sam. 3²¹. The cryptic character of the expression appears in the variety of translations : EVV in general, ' in the word,' GV ' durch das Wort,' FV ' avec la parole,' Chic. B., ' at the command,' Moff., ' moved by ' ; the last rendering approaches closest to the supernatural idea involved, and so Šanda, ' Kraft göttlicher Eingebung.' The expression appears to be rather overworked in the narrative, *e.g.*, v.¹⁷, but it is a bit of religious diction. For the term see the excellent discussion by Smend, *Lehrbuch der alttest. Rel.-gesch.* (1899), 87, with the initial statement : '' das Wort Jahves ist früh als eine göttliche Potenz gedacht,'' and now the recent particular studies by F. Haeussermann, *Wortempfang in der alttest. Prophetie*, *ZAW* Beih. 58 (1932), esp. pp. 122 ff. ; O. Grether, *Name u. Wort Gottes im A.T.*, *ZAW* Beih. 64 (1934), Teil II ; L. Dürr, *Die Wertung des göttl. Wortes im A.T. u. im Antiken Orient*, *MVÄG* 42, Heft 1 (1938). For the Bab. parallels see *KAT* 608, n. 2. Probably ' invested with the word,' *i.e.*, in the divine aura, would best express the notion, which is equivalent to ἐν δυνάμει πνεύματος of the N.T., *e.g.*, Rom. 15¹⁹. In 1 Sam. 3²¹ the phrase is used as a gloss to ease up the too physical assertion that '' Yhwh appeared to Samuel.''—**2.** ויאמר : B† om.—שמו : for the idiom, frequent in Aram., *cf.* 1 Sam. 17⁴, etc.—ישרפו : impers. pl. ; Grr., 𝔖 𝔙 change to sing.—**3.** נקרע הנה המזבח : the ppl.= ' delendum est,' hence followed by perf. ונשפך (*vs.* Šanda).—**4.** ירבעם : to be omitted with 𝔊^L ; 𝔊 𝔊^H 𝔖^H intrude ' the king.'—**6.** ויען המלך ויאמר : 𝔊 𝔊^H ' and said the king Jer.'—והתפלל בעדי : OGrr.,

𝕴 om. ; prob. a gloss to the preceding antique and anthropomorphic phrase (*cf.* Engl. ' curry favour ').—**7.** וּמְעָרָה : so *BH* with MSS C L., accepted by Ginsb.², *vs.* וּמַעֲרָה, on which *cf.* Burn. ; the verb is used absolutely as in LHeb., otherwise +לב.—מתת : the noun is otherwise late in Heb.—**9.** ["י בדבר] צוה אתי : the Grr. generally obtained a subject by rdg. the foll. gen. κυριου as nom. κυριος, but MSS e f y preserve the original genitive. The text has been commonly emended (*e.g.*, by St., *BH*) to צִוִּיתִי, and then consequently יבא is read in v.¹⁷ ; but the two are cases of the impersonal sing. used in language of religious mystery ; *cf.* מגיד, Zech. 9¹², and see Ew., *Lehrb.*, §294, 1 (2), who *cft.* N.T. λεγει ; the text is to be kept.—**10.** דרך אחר : the noun construed as masc. (*cf.* v.¹²) ; in the foll. אשר בא בה the fem. prepositional phrase is an intrusion with contradictory gender ; *cf.* בדרך אשר הלכת, v.⁹.—**11.** אחד = Engl. ' a certain ' ; frequent in N. Pal. narratives and LHeb. ; see Burn., pp. 181, 209, GB 23*a*.—ויבוא בנו ויספר : Ken. 30 ויבאו בניו ויספרו = VSS, exc. 𝕶, and correct.—היום : ' on that day ' ; *cf.* Arab. equivalent = ' to-day.'—את 2⁰ : 2 MSS ואת = some Grr., VSS (exc. 𝕶), accepted by Then., *BH*, *al*; St. regards את to the end of the verse as secondary ; it is simpler to read ואת, and to take 'וג ויספרום as secondary. For this last verb Grr. read remarkably פנים ויסירו.—**12.** אביהם : OGrr. +λεγων ; 1 MS replaces with לאמר.—ויראו : read Hif., וַיַרְאוּ, with 𝕶 ; *cf.* similar absolute use in Est. 1⁴ ; other VSS with obj., as though וַיַרְאֻהוּ.—**14.** האלה : for the picturesque use of the determinate noun see GK §126, 4.—**15.** הביתה : there is no reason to omit the word, with OGrr., and so St. ; the phrase = Engl. " come home with me."—**16.** ולבוא אתך : 2 MSS, OGrr. om., and so St., *BH* ; but 𝕾 with plus ביתך offers the true mng., ' à entrer chez toi.'—אתך [אשתה] : OGrr. om., and so St., *BH* ; in the parallel, v.¹⁷, St. also om. שם.—**17.** דָּבָר : Grr., 𝕾, as passive, and so EVV translate ; it is easy to correct with many critics to the Pual ; but the Pual is rare, occurring only twice ; see Note, v.⁹.—לא [תשוב] : *ca.* 50 MSS ולא = VSS.—ללכת : St. finds superfluous, arguing from Gr. επιστρεψης, but this is correct translation of the Heb. verbs, ' to return.'—**18.** כחש : circumstantial, ' lying to him ' ; *cf.* Dr., *Tenses*, §163.—**19.** וישב אתו := Engl. " and he turned in with him " ; read by OGrr. as וַיָּשָׁב אִתּוֹ.—**20.** [השלחן] אל : read על with 19 MSS ; *cf.* 2 Sam. 9¹¹.—*N.b.* the ' *piskah*-in-middle-of-verse,' a long spacing, in this case giving dignity to the foll. statement ; a similar case II. 1¹⁷ ; see Graetz, *MGWJ* 27 (1878), 481 ff. ; 36 (1887), 193 ff.—**21.** פי "י : 𝕶 reduced the anthropomorphism with ' the word of Y.'—**23.** ואחרי שתותו : Grr. + ' water,' accepted by *BH* ; but, with St., the whole phrase is unnecessary.—השיבו אשר לנביא : this vague phrase is not represented in OGrr. exc. for the verb κ. επεστρεψεν, which emendation is accepted by Burn., *BH*. Hex. then inserted in place τω προφητη. But לנביא is an erroneous gloss to explain the ethical dative לו, ויחבש being misunderstood as action of the host, and then was

I. 14^{1-31}   265

added " who brought him back," but the guest is never called
'the prophet.' St. properly rejects the whole phrase.—**24**. The
root מצא includes the mng. of Aram. מטי, ' to chance upon '=Eth
maṣe'a; in v.^{28} it means 'to find.'—**25**. 2 𝕲^L MSS om. through
הגבלה 2º; 1 MS Ken. om. through ויבאו.—**26**b-**27**. OGrr. om.;
BH as 'probably an addition'; rather the Gr. is an abbreviation,
and so St. decides.—**28**. והמור : 12 MSS והחמור=Grr., and to be
accepted.—**29**. אל 1º : 12 MSS correctly על=Grr.—**29**b. OGrr.
offer a simpler text, omitting ויבא, rdg. as though אל העיר (so
1 Heb. MS), retaining הנביא (as nom.), omitting [הוקן לספד ולקברו];
the simplest revision is וישיבהו אל העיר לקברו with St. ; cf. Burn.—**30**b.
ויספדו : the pl. of community action, and so recognized by 𝕲,
but 𝕲^L and 𝕲^H MSS tr. with sing. (so 1 Heb. MS), induced by ' my
brother.'—הוי אחי : fuller statements of the mourning cry appear
in Jer. 22^{18}, 34^5, cf. Am. 5^{16}, and also OGr., 12^{24m}, for which
passage see Note, 14^{13}. Šanda cft. similar dirges in the modern
Lebanon, beginning with " Ah, my dear one, ah, my friend."—
31. אחרי קברו אתו ; Grr., ' after (his) bewailing him,' a sophisticated
improvement.—הניחו את עצמתי : Grr., ' me ' for the obj., i.e., אתי,
which is preferable (a living man would hardly have used the
other expression), with which cf. II. 23^{18}; Grr. were affected by
the parallel account and added ' that my bones be saved with
his bones," which addition is accepted by St. and BH (q.v.).—
32. כל : Grr. om.—בערי שמרון : Grr., ' in Samaria.'—**33**. מדרכו הרעה :
Grr. as though מן רעתו.—ימלא, ויהי : potential imperfs., and not to
be corrected ; see GK §159, d.—כהני 2º : read the sing. with VSS,
with antecedent in החפץ ; the pl. was induced by the preceding
pl.—**34**. בדבר : read הדבר with 7 MSS=VSS, exc. 𝔙.—לחטאת בית :
Grr., 𝕾^H 𝕾 as though 'לחטאת לב ; 𝔐 is to be retained, with
St., vs. Burn., BH ; the same phrase, with correction of text,
at II. 13^6.

14^{1-18}. The prophet Ahijah, besought by Jeroboam's wife,
who goes in disguise on behalf of their sick son, predicts his
immediate death, and elaborates at length the doom upon
Jeroboam's family. The story belongs to the same collection
as that of the Old Prophet, ch. 13. It fails here in the OGrr.
But the Hexaplaric texts (e.g., A c₂ 𝕾^H with ※) have inserted
it here in a form variant from 𝔐, and of this variant the OGrr.
preserve a variant form in 12^{24g-n}. For this Gr. supplement
see Comm. after 12^{21}. The judgment passed there on its
secondary and worthless character as a primary document
is maintained here for this particular story. An absolute
choice must be made between the two stories. In 𝔐 the
prophet Ahijah is well known as the predicter of Jeroboam's
fortunes ; but in the supplement he must be named and

described (vv.²⁴ʰ·ⁱ) as a man of 60 years and of poor eyesight, while in the original story he was vigorous enough to accost Jeroboam 'alone in the open country' (11²⁹). The supplement definitely ignored Ahijah's earlier prophecy in order to turn him into a prophet of doom *ab origine*, and assigned that duty to Shemaiah who appears later in 𝕳, in a truncated, apparently unfinished passage (v.²⁴ᵒ). In a word the historical tragedy presented in 𝕳, the auspicious oracle to Jeroboam and his miserable failure, is utterly contradicted. The OGr. story is integrated with the other materials of the supplement: Jeroboam's wife's name is repeated from v.²⁴ᵉ as Ano, *i.e.*, Pharaoh's sister-in-law, following the utterly false attribution of the Edomite Hadad's history to Jeroboam; Jeroboam is housed at Serira (vv.²⁴ᵇ·ᵏ), but in 𝕳 at Tirsah (v.¹⁷). As Kittel remarks, the mother's disguise is omitted, for she was not yet a queen. To the humble gifts she is to take to the prophet (v.³) OGr. adds 'and cakes for his children,' apparently a playful touch, while the list of gifts is repeated below in puerile fashion (vv.²⁴ʰ·ˡ). There remains the question of the literary relation of 𝕳 and the supplement. The latter is shorter, but for the most part by the elision of the long denunciation (vv.⁷⁻¹⁶), which is stoutly Deuteronomic; but such omission was necessary in the setting of the midrash, for that condemnation damns Jeroboam for what he has done as king; and so the mourning for the child by 'all Israel' (v.¹³) had to be eliminated. The difference of opinion of critics as to the relation between 𝕳 and the Gr. supplement has been discussed above. In regard to the present narrative even conservative critics, *e.g.*, Šanda, Skinner (p. 445 f.), regard the Greek as an earlier and simpler strain, which survived in Hebrew by some chance and fell into the hands of a Greek translator, while 𝕳 is the result of subsequent Deuteronomic editing. The Greek appears indeed to have depended upon a Hebrew midrash, which however transformed the original to suit the entirely absurd setting in which it is placed. Only one phrase peculiar to the Greek has a note of originality, the plus in v.²⁴ᵐ, "[they will bewail the child,] Ah, lord" (see Note, v.¹³).

3. For the *cracknels/cakes/biscuits*, as the EVV render, see Note. **4.** For the blind man's second sight *cf.* 21¹⁷ᶠᶠ·, II. 6³²ᶠᶠ·, and see Volz, *Der Geist Gottes*, 36 ff. **5.** Gunkel (*Einl. in die Psalmen*, 146, 160 ff.) lists similar ' royal oracles ' in the O.T. and their parallels in non-Israelite sources. **14***b*. *Cf.* the variant English translations, and see Note. **16.** Read : *because of the sin* [חטאת pl.] *of Jeroboam that he has sinned, and in which he has involved Israel ;* the latter phrase is juridical. **17.** For Tirsah, incidentally mentioned as the royal residence, see Comm., 15^{33}. **18.** Gunkel (*Einl.*, 160) lists the similar ' Leichenklagen ' in the O.T.

VV.$^{19. \ 20}$. The conclusion : Jeroboam's death, and the succession. *How he warred, and how he reigned.* We know through Egyptian sources of Shishak's invasion of Palestine, which involved North Israel ; see below, vv.$^{25ff.}$. V.^{30} notes that " there was war between Rehoboam and Jeroboam continually," and 2 Ch. 13 details Jeroboam's disastrous defeat by Abijah of Judah.

VV.$^{21-31}$. The reign of Rehoboam. || 2 Ch. 11^5–12 ; *cf. Ant.*, viii, 10. **21.** There appears for the first time the usual introductory formula giving the age of the king at accession, the length of his reign, and the queen-mother's name ; see Int., §13, *b*. The age at accession is at first only occasionally given, and never for the Northern dynasty ; the next case is that of Jehoshaphat (22^{41}), then Jehoash (II. 12^1), after that regularly. Rehoboam's age of 40 years may point to the fact (or to the theory, if Solomon's regnal term of 40 years is an invention) that he was the first-born son after his father's accession, a status which had its claim in Oriental dynasties. His reign lasted 17 years. These datings are contradicted by 𝕲 12^{24a} (not 𝕲^L), where the figures 16 and 12 are given respectively. These figures (despite *BH*, ' fortasse recte ') are doubtless artificial, invented perhaps to agree with the statement of Rehoboam's advising with " the youths who had grown up with him " (12^8) ; *cf.* the invention of 12 years for Solomon's age at accession in Hex. texts, 2^{12}. The queen-mother's name is given, as regularly below ; her formal title was ' Lady ' (*gĕbīrāh*), *e.g.*, 15^{13}. This datum fails for the North. The lady in question was *Naamah the Ammonitess* ; the Gr. supplement makes of her a daughter of Hanun b. Nahash, a construction based upon 2 Sam 10^2. At v.^{31b} this item of the queen-mother is erroneously repeated, being absent in

OGrr. The intrusive phrase, [*Jerusalem*] *the city which* Yhwh *chose out of all the tribes of Israel to set his name there,* is evidently interpolation from Ch. 12¹³.

VV.²²⁻²⁴ present a moralizing condemnation of the religious perversions of the reign. According to 𝕳 *Judah did what was evil in the eyes of* Yhwh, *and they provoked him,* etc. OGrr. replaced ' Judah ' with ' Rehoboam ' ; *cf.* 2 Ch. 12¹⁴, and the reference below to Abijam's ' father's sins ' (15³). The heathenish reaction after the reigns of David and Solomon (but *n.b.* 11¹ᶠᶠ·) is presented in the later customary language : the construction of *high-places* [*bâmôt*] *and pillars* [*maṣṣēbôt*] and *Asherah-symbols* [EVV transliterate with *Asherim*] *upon every high hill and under every green tree ;* cf. Dt. 12²ᶠᶠ·, Jer. 2²⁰, 3⁶·¹³, Is. 57⁵, Eze. 6³ᶠᶠ·, etc. ; for the archæological light cast upon these institutions see the Archæologies of Nowack and Benzinger, Gressmann, *ATB* vol. 2 with extensive plates ; Cook, *Religion of Anc. Palestine* ; Barton, *AB* ch. 11 ; Burrows, *WMTS* §§130 ff. ; Albright, *ARI* (see Index). *Sodomites* of EVV (see the story in Gen. 19) translates an adjective differing only vocalically as *ḳādēš* from the word for ' holy,' *ḳādôš*. The group appears again in 15¹², 22⁴⁷, II. 23⁷ ; they are the ' dogs ' whose hire may not be brought into Yhwh's house (Dt. 23¹⁸ᶠ·), which caste of ' dogs ' appears among the Phœnician hierodules (*CIS* I, no. 8). In an interesting note of Jerome's, *Comm. ad Hoseam,* iii, 1261, cited by Movers, *Die Phönizier,* 683, and Keil, *ad loc.,* he remarks that the term means the Galli, religious self-castrated eunuchs of the Attis religion of his day (*cf.* Lucian, *De Dea Syra,* 15, etc.) : but ' in other places,' he says ' Cadesim ' is used of ' viri exsecti libidine,' *i.e.*, male prostitutes ; he notes Aquila's rendering, ἐνηλλαγμένοι (' denatured,' *cf.* μετήλλαξαν, Rom. 1²⁶, of female perverts), and Symmachus's use of τετελεσμένοι, *i.e.*, ' initiates.' See Note further. For the subject at large see B. A. Brooks, ' Fertility Cult Functionaries in the O.T.,' *JBL* 60 (1941), 227 ff.

VV.²⁵⁻²⁸ briefly present Shishak's raid in Palestine, with particular note of his spoliation of the sacred and royal treasures. This note is of archival origin, with the editorial introduction, *and it came to pass* (see the writer's article, *JBL* 53 [1934], 48) ; the Pharaoh's name is given (as also in the story of Jeroboam, 11⁴⁰), a specification that does not occur again until Hezekiah's reign (II. 19⁹). The regnal year is given, as before only in connexion with temple history (6¹). The date is the first of international reference in the Bible. The item refers to the palace-complex ; it notes the looting of temple and palace, but is especially concerned with the disappearance of Solomon's golden shields (*cf.* 10¹⁶ᶠ·). A similar archival note appears at 15¹⁸. For the processionals of Assyrian kings see Meissner, *Bab. u. Ass.*, 1, 67 f., and for a procession at coronation *cf.* II. 11⁹ᶠᶠ·. For the *guards*, literally *runners*, *cf.* II. 10²⁵, 11¹³· ¹⁹, 1 Sam. 22¹⁷, etc. ; they were technically the escort before the royal chariot (*cf.* 1⁵). The Pharaoh's name is variously given by 𝔥, Kt. and Ḳr., as Shishak, Shushak (see Note further). Egyptologists still variously vocalize the Pharaoh's name, *e.g.*, Sheshenk (Petrie), Sheshonk (Breasted), Shoshenk (Müller, Meyer). The *fifth year* of the reign is chronologically dubious.[1] That monarch's famous inscription at Karnak records his extensive raid throughout Palestine ; see for the translation Breasted, *ARE* 4, §§709 ff., and for its historical interpretation Müller, *Asien u. Europa*, 166 ff. ; Alt, *Israel u. Aegypten*, 11–41 ; also for various expositions the historians Breasted, Kittel, Meyer, Olmstead, Robinson ; *cf.* Petrie, *Palestine and Israel*. For the question concerning Solomon's father-in-law, whether Shishak or a predecessor, see Comm., 3¹. From the inscription Shishak does not appear as an ally of Jeroboam, as the partial Judæan record suggested to past scholars (although Robinson, *HI* 275, still maintains this position, holding that Jeroboam, in his ' desperate straits ' was rescued by ' his patron and overlord Sheshonk '), but rather as the enemy who took advantage of the now divided and weakened Hebrew state to raid and

---

[1] The Egyptian records give no dating for the Pharaoh's expedition into Palestine, and with the uncertain early chronology of the Davidic line agreement of scholars has not been attained for the Biblical date. Petrie dates the event from the Bible chronology and arrives at 933 B.C. (*Hist. of Egypt*, 3, 235) ; Breasted as about the year 926 (*Hist. of Egypt*, 529) ; Meyer about 930 (*GA* 2, 2, 46) ; Olmstead at 931 (*HPS* 354) ; Lewy and Albr. date the accession of Rehoboam about 922, and accordingly his fifth year would be about 917 (Albr., *BASOR* 87 [1942], 28). See Petrie at large (pp. 227 ff.) for the chronological problems connected with the 22d Dynasty.

despoil it, but with no permanent results. The list of some 150 'captured' cities (cf. especially Müller, Alt, Olmstead), each represented by a cartouche figuring a bound captive with a place-name attached, includes such Northern cities as Taanach, Megiddo, Shunem, Beth-shean, as well as many towns in the west and south of Judah. At Megiddo the Oriental Institute of the University of Chicago has discovered a large but broken monument erected by Shishak; see C. S. Fisher, *Or. Institute Communications*, No. 4 (1929), figs. 7A, 7B, and Petrie reports a massive brick construction of the monarch at Beth-pelet (*Beth-Pelet*, I, 1930). It is generally recognized for the other cities which Shishak 'took,' that it was rather their tribute he received; so Jerusalem was not actually taken, but the king would have paid a sumptuous indemnity in specie and *objets d'art*, like the gold shields. For subsequent history of the reign 2 Ch. 11$^{5\text{ff.}}$ has an authentic note concerning Rehoboam's fortification of fifteen 'cities of defence,' all to the south and west of Jerusalem, evidently after Shishak's raid. Glueck has come definitely to the conclusion that the destruction of Esyon-geber I by fire was caused by Shishak's invasion, thus greatly extending the map of that onslaught and confirming Ch.; see *BASOR* 75 (1939), 17 ff., and *The Other Side of the Jordan*, 105. V.^{30} with the report that *there was war between Rehoboam and Jeroboam continually* [Heb. *all the days*] is presumably true history, if literally only a deduction from 15$^{16\text{ff.}}$; it manifestly contradicts the prophet-story in 12$^{21\text{ff.}}$. **31.** *And his mother's name was Naamah the Ammonitess:* this inserted repetition of v.^{21} is absent in OGrr., 𝔖.

> For the assumed Aquilanic character of the Hexaplaric text in this section (*e.g.*, in A 𝔖^{H}) see Burkitt's discussion in his *Fragments of the Book of Kings*, 33 f., and Reider, *Prolegomena to ... Aquilo*, 156 ff. (see Int., §4, c); Burkitt proves that the Hexaplaric text is not an extract from Aquila but is the LXX text of 12$^{24\text{g -n}}$, emended into general, but not complete concord with Aquila's translation. This judgment explains the plus of 'the cakes for his children,' v.^{3}, and the appearance of Σαριρα in place of Aquilanic Θερσαδε = תרצתה.—**1.** בעת ההיא: indefinite, 'at a time,' as in Aram. use of the pronoun.—**2.** והשתנית: Ginsb. records a variant, תי—, in agreement with foll. אתי Kt.; for occurrence of these older forms see GK §32, h.—הנה: 12 MSS והנה = Grr.—לְקֶלְךְ: corrected

by St., *BH, al.*, to לְמִלֵּה, forsooth on ground of the inf. in Gr.; but the parallel מגבירה, 15¹³, supports 𝔐 here; also *cf.* עֲדֵי אֹבֵד, Num. 24²⁰.—**3.** עשרה לחם : for the exceptional sing. see GK §134, f. —𝔊12²⁴ʰ adds κ. κολλυρια τ. τεκνοις αυτου, which 𝔊ᴴ inserts here, rdg. κολλυριδα; the latter word at 2 Sam. 13⁶ tr. לבבות, 'poultices'; both Heb. and Gr. (*cf.* Sophocles, *Lex.*) used the respective words in both senses, 'cakes/poultices.'—נקדים : in Josh. 9⁵·¹² = crumbled bread. Here 𝔊 σταφυλην, 𝔊ᴴ σταφιδας = 'raisins'; 𝔗 כסנין = 𝔖, 'sweetmeats,' as in Talmud.—דבש : בקבק : for such cruses in bee-hive shape see Badè, *Some Tombs at Tell en-Nasbeh* (1931), 27, pl. ix, and on ב A. M. Honeyman, *PEQ* 1939, 79. The second noun may have been used of any sweet syrup, like the current Arab. *dibs*; Šanda cites Jos., *BJ* iv, 8, 3, on the excellent 'honey,' μέλι, made from dates of the Ghor. For such sweetmeats see Benz., *Arch.*, 68.—**5.** [בנה] אל : read על ; the same change to be made with some MSS in v.¹⁰.—ויהי כבאה והיא מתנכרה : St. regards as an insertion into the divine word; however the apparently ungrammatical וְיְהִי (𝔊ᴴ read as וַיְהִי, accepted by Burn., *BH, al.*) is conditional, *i.e.*, "though be it, when she enters she be dis-guised"; *cf.* GK §159, d, and the similar use of the jussive in Arabic, Wright, *Arab. Gr.*, 2, §13.—**6.** רגליה באה : the apparently non-syntactical phrase is generally corrected, *e.g.*, by *BH* to רגלי הבאה : but Haupt properly identifies the Heb. with the *ḥal* construction of the Arabic, where the ppl. is in the acc., referring to the suffixed pron.; see Wright, vol. 2, 113. Burn. also defends 𝔐, and *cft.* Ps. 69⁴, כלו עיני מיחל ; for similar cases see Ewald, *Lehrb.*, §317, c; and so 𝔊ᴴ correctly translates.—למה זה : for this and similar combinations, as in Arab., Aram., see Burn.— שלוח אליך קשה = 𝔊ᴴ αποστολος προς σε σκληρος (the only case of the noun in Gr. O.T.), *sc.* as קָשֶׁה; but the fem. is adverbial acc. to the passive, the active meaning 'to send one with a hard message'; see Ewald, §284, c, Burn.—**7.** נגיד : the antique word, as at 1³⁵.— **10.** [בית] אל := 𝔊ᴴ εις ; but read על with 7 MSS.—משתין בקיר, עצור ועזוב : the whole phrase is repeated at 21²¹, II. 9⁸ (but rdg. ועצור), and *cf.* II. 14²⁶. Of Engl. VSS AV alone properly translates the initial obscene word, 'him that pisseth against the wall,' subsequent VSS euphemizing, 'every man-child.' The verbal form has been explained as a secondary root from שׁין, 'to piss' (see Lexx.), but impossibly. Stade, on II. 14²⁶, has suggested the Hithp. with change of vocalization. But it is best explained as Ifteal, which mode of Akk. *šinu* appears (Bezold, *BAG s.v.*), while it also occurs in the Moabite Stone (אלתחם), and now in the Ugaritic; see *RSMT* 22; Gordon, *Ugar. Handbook*, 1, §9, 29. For reviews of interpretations of the two pass. ppls. see Burn., Šanda, Driver on the occurrence of the phrase at Dt. 32³⁶, and now J. Lewy, *HUCA* 12–13 (1937–38), 99 ff. Lewy cites seven various interpretations, all revolving about the theme of 'bond and free,' and adds a fresh solution, 'unborn (shut up in the womb) and born' (*cft.* Akk. *izbu*,

' new-born child '). But why should the unborn child be a concern here ? Eissf. notes another view expressed by P. Saydon at the Brussels Congress of Orientalists, 1938 (*Theol. Blätter*, 1938, 303), translating with ' gehemmt u. hilflos.' The writer may suggest that after the initial obscene phrase the pass. ppls. mean ' in private and unrestrained,' *i.e.*, distinguishing between the gentleman and the boor in the street.—אחרי־ : not the prep., but =' the last of ' ; שארית, אחרית are used similarly.—יבער : impers. sing. ; change to the pass., as *BH* suggests, is unnecessary ; for the root, generally distinguished semantically into two, see Gray, *Isaiah*, xxi, *seq.*—**12.** בבאה ; read בְּבִיא.—רגליך : 1 MS רגלך, and so the Gr. as sing.—**13.** וספרו לו כל ישראל : 𝔊 12²⁴ᵐ, κ. το παιδαριον κοψονται οναι κυριε, *i.e.*, the mourning cry, הוי ארון as at Jer. 22¹⁸, 34⁵, appropriate to a prince (otherwise 13³⁰, ' Ah, my brother ! ') ; the phrase may well be original and have been euphemistically omitted by 𝔐 ; the Gr. camouflaged the possibly heathenish expression ('ādón =' Adonis '), with an added gloss, οτι ευρεθη εν αυτω ρημα καλον περι τ. κυριου ; see W. W. Baudissin, *Adonis u. Esmun* (1911), 91 ; C. W. North, *ZAW* 1932, 31 f.—"דבר טוב אל י" : St. thinks that אל is ' beyond explanation ' ; a similar phrase, Est. 5⁴, but with prep. על, which Haupt would read here, comparing Akk. *ṭiba eli* ; but 𝔐 may stand.—**14.** זה היום וגם עתה : and so exactly the Gr. ; acc. to St. the phrase is ' unintelligible ' ; EVV " that day, but what ? even now " ; JV " that day. But what is it even then ? " ; Kit., " an jenem Tag. Aber dann noch (v.¹⁵) wird J. Israel schlagen " (rdg. ויכה as יכח), and so Moff., Chic. B., and with cautious approval Sk. ℭ attempts an elucidation : " he who exists to-day, and he who will be born to-morrow." Joüon (*Mél.*, 5, 475) proposes to read זו for זה, *cft.* 𝔙 ' in hoc tempore ' ; Klost. absurdly finds in it original " and this was Abijah b. Maacah," *cft.* 2 Ch. 13¹⁷ⁿ·. Interpretation may be ventured as follows : זה היום =' the matter of the day,' *i.e.*, ' as regards to-day ' (for this use of the demonstrative relative see the writer's Note in *JBL* 43 [1924], 227), ' and what also is now,' *i.e.*, ' to-day and at once.'—**15.** כאשר ינור הקנה : Kit., *BH* find a lacuna preceding, and write in והתגודדו, following the example of Graetz, who replaced the preceding והכה with והניד ; but the diction can be explained, with St., as elliptical, or rather as mixture of metaphors.—**16.** ויתן : an irregular, late consecution ; for mng. of the verb, ' to give up,' *cf.* Mic. 5².—חטאות : many MSS חטאת ; the sing. is to be adopted, as at 15³⁴ ; the pl. was an easy amplification.—**20.** נרב : *cf.* now the name on a seal, נרבאל (*IAE*, 189), and נרביהו in a Lachish letter (Torczyner, no. iii) ; the verbal element is also Thamudene (*NPS* 1, 136).

21. ' Judah ' : 𝔊ᴸ +' Benjamin.'—נעמה : B† Μααχαμ, *cf.* מעכה, name of Abijam's wife, 15¹⁰ ; otherwise Grr. here and at 12²⁴ᵃ support 𝔐.—**22.** יהודה : OGrr., ' Rehoboam,' with consequent change of the following verbs (but not in v.²³) into singulars, yet stopping at the change of ' their fathers ' into ' his fathers,' which would have involved condemnation of the royal paragon David (*cf.* 15³, etc.) ; yet St. makes this further change as well, regarding Rehoboam as the implied subject throughout.—**23.** גם המה : OGrr. om., and so St. ; but the phrase accentuates the part the new generation played.—**24.** קדש : the inarticulate sing. collective is noticeable ; at 22⁴⁷ הקדש, at 15¹² the pl. ; the sing. is derogatory, aligning the subject with brute species, *e.g.*, עוף, בקר ; *cf.* Ew., *Lehrb.*, §176, b. Šanda properly thinks of the inclusion of both sexes. Grr., σύνδεσμος, which has suggested to some critics original קשר, 'conspiracy,' as at II. 11¹⁴ ; but συνδ.=συμπλοκή, 16²⁸ᵈ, and the two words are synonymous, used of sexual copulation ; see Sophocles, *Lex.*, *s.vv.* συνδ., συμπλεκτικός, for their secular mngs. Sym. has here τελετή and similarly the Grr., including the Three, at 15¹², τὰς τελετάς (this noun not in Sophocles='rites' ?) ; see Note, *ibid.*, and also Note to 22⁴⁷ for the Grr. there.—**25.** ששק Kt., ש̇יש̇ק Kr.=Kt. 11⁴⁰, and so Ch., and 𝕮 𝕾 𝕬 𝖁 here. Grr. Σουσακειμ in both places ; *Ant.*, vii, 5, 3 ; viii, 10, 2, vulgar text Σουσακος, but Niese Ισωκος in the latter ref. (see Rahlfs, *SS* 3, 97, for tradition of the name in Jos.) ; Manetho, Σεσωγκις ; in an Akk. text of Ashurbanipal's (*KB* 2, 162) appears a *n. pr.* Susinḳu. H. Gauthier, *Les rois d'Egypte*, vol. 3 (1914), cites Σεσωγχωσις, 'Senechosis.' Rahlfs explains the Gr. termination -ειμ as dittog. of foll. *m*(*lk*).—**26.** אוצרות : OGrr. pref. 'all.'—לקח הכל ואת : the phrase may be preserved by omitting the conj. ; or is it an *et cetera*, preceding the following detail ?—To 'all the shields of gold' Grr. pref. " the golden spears which David took from the hand of the servants of Adraazar king of Soba, and brought to Jerusalem," taken from 2 Sam. 8⁷, where in reverse Grr. have added cross-reference to Shishak's despoliation here ; but according to II. 11¹⁰ these Davidic donations were in the temple at a much later date. The Gr. texts have become confused by the intrusion ; *e.g.*, B N lost the words " which S. made," and several MSS=𝕮 have the plus, " and brought them into Egypt."—**27.** תחתם : in 20²⁴ תחתיהם ; see Orlinsky's study, 'The Bibl. Prepositions *taḥat*,' etc., *HUCA* 17 (1943), 267 ff. The pl. appears to have arisen to express the idea of extension, for which *cf. pānim*, etc.—וְהִפְקִיד : the pf. with Waw-consec. can be understood as iterative, " and he would commit (them) " ; St. would correct to abs. inf., for which *cf.* GK §113, z. Grr. translated as though a pass. pl.—[בית] המלך : 𝕲ᴸ 𝕴 'the Lord.'—**31.** עם אבתיו 2⁰ : om., with 𝕮 and Ch. ; the same repetition at 15²⁴.—אבים : 10 MSS Ken., deR., Ch., אביה ; Grr., Αβιου, Αβια. אבין occurs on a Samarian ostracon and on a seal (*IAE* 221). For the form see Noth, *IP* 234, who *cft.* the Tell Ta'annak Aḫiyami, deciding correctly that it is a hypocoristic in *-ām* ; *cf.* אבְרָם, אבְשָׁלם. The element is common in S. Arab. *nn. pr.*, see D. H. Müller, *ZDMG* 32, 543 ff. G. R. Driver has suggested (*ZAW* 46 [1928], 12, n. 6) that the form is derogatory ; but rather it was popular ; *cf.* Scottish 'King Jamie,' 'Prince Charlie.'

15$^{1-8}$. The reign of Abijam of Judah. || 2 Ch. 13 ; cf. *Ant.*, viii, 11, 2, 3. **1.** Abijam's accession is dated, perhaps loosely, *in the eighteenth year of Jeroboam*, on the count of Rehoboam's seventeen years (14^{21}) as full years. **2.** His mother's name is given as *Maacah bath Abishalom*; for the problems concerning the lady's name see below on v.^{10}. Jos. (*Ant.*, viii, 10, 1) ingeniously discovers in her a daughter of Absalom's daughter Tamar (*cf.* 2 Sam. 13$^{1\text{ff.}}$). Such late traditions (*cf.* Ch.) are probably worthless. VV.$^{4, 5a}$ are an evident Deuteronomic intrusion ; for the *lamp cf.* 11^{36}. **5.** *except in the case of Uriah the Hittite :* a unique moralizing judgment, and a late addition, absent in 𝔊 𝔈. **6.** *And there was war between Rehoboam and Jeroboam*, etc., lacking in OGrr., is a senseless repetition of 14^{30}. **7b.** *And there was war between Abijam and Jeroboam :* this is out of place after v.^{a}, is secondary, induced by Ch.'s long story of the conflict between the two kings.

VV.$^{9-24}$. The reign of Asa of Judah. || 2 Ch. 14–16 ; *cf. Ant.*, viii, 12.

VV.$^{9-15}$. His reform of the religious abuses introduced by the queen-dowager. **9.** *In the twentieth year of Jeroboam :* the 3-year reign of Abijam is correctly treated as only two full years. **10.** The mother's name is the same as that of the grandmother, v.^{2}. Wellhausen has accordingly suggested (*Prolegomena*, 216) that Asa was Abijam's brother, entailing correction of ' his son ' (v.^{8}) to ' his brother.' Ch. actually gives the king two mothers, Maacah bath Absalom (11^{20}), and Micaiah (Grr., Maacah) bath Uriel of Gibeah (13^2). These variations appear as attempts to dispose of the identity of name for the two queens. We may best suppose that the subsequent reference to *Maacah his mother . . . the Lady* (v.^{13}) has introduced a change from the original name of the mother (so Kittel, Burney), or that there was no tradition of the queen's name because of the grandmother's domination. The title *Lady* (*gĕbîrāh*—EVV *queen*) is that of the queen-mother, as at II. 10^{13}. VV.$^{12-15}$ report the reforms, of which the prime step was the removal of the dowager. For the influence of this personage in the ancient Orient there are, in addition to Jezebel (16^{31}, etc.) and Athaliah (II. 11), the cases of Sammuramat (Semiramis), who ruled for five years during the minority of her son Adad-nirari III (*ARA* I, §§730 ff.; Olmstead, *HA* ch. 13) and Sennacherib's wife (see Comm., II. 18¹⁴). For Egypt Hatshepsut's power in the Thutmosid dynasty is a most striking case (Breasted, *HE* ch. 15). **12.** Of the several abominations purged by Asa the *sodomites* have appeared above (14²⁴); the *idols* of EVV represents a contemptuous word, *gillûl*, vocalized after the formation *šikkûṣ*, 'something to be abhorred,' as the root is used of abhorrence of things ritually tabooed, *e.g.*, Lev. 11¹¹, etc. (*Cf.* the pronunciation 'Molek' for 'Melek'). **13.** The word translated 'abominable image' and later 'image' by EVV (exc. AV with 'idol'), 'obscene image' by Chic. B., implies something 'shocking.' The following vocable translated by EVV 'for an Asherah' means *to Asherah*, which is supported by the following reference to *her abominable image*. On this goddess, whose name came to be used of her conventional image, *cf.* 18¹⁹, II. 23⁴·⁶. The goddess plays a large part as divine mother in the Ugaritic mythology; see D. Nielsen, *Ras Šamra Mythologie u. biblische Mythologie*, and his subsequent study at large, 'Die altsem. Muttergöttin,' *ZDMG* 92 (1938), 594 ff. This image, possibly of wood, was subsequently burned at the Josianic reformation in the Kidron Wady, where the city dump was (II. 23⁶). **15.** The reference to *his father's and his own dedications*, which *he brought into YHWH's house*, is obscure. Šanda pertinently remarks that we may have here a summary of some ample temple document; the father may have patronized other sanctuaries, the son now collected all such dedications in the one legitimate temple.

VV.¹⁶⁻²². The war with Baasha of Israel and the league with Damascus. **16. 17.** The energetic Baasha of the North, who seized the throne in Asa's third year, found himself free to take vigorous measures against Judah. His natural aim was to recover the march-land of Benjamin, which belonged historically and economically to the North, and by control of the open country north of Jerusalem to hem in its commercial and military avenues—*that he might allow none to go out or come in*. (*Vice versa*, according to 2 Ch. 13¹⁹ Abijam had taken three cities, including Bethel, in an aggressive campaign against Jeroboam.) Baasha proceeded to *build Ramah* as a controlling fortress on his southern boundary.

21. Upon Asa's coalition with Damascus Baasha *left off building Ramah, and returned to Tirsah* [so to read with Grr.: 𝔊 *dwelt at Tirsah*] ; for this place, evidently his capital, see Comm., v.³³. **22.** Asa proceeded to dismantle Ramah ; he made a levy of *all Judah, with none exempt*, and using *the stones and timbers of Ramah, he built Gibeah* [𝔊 Geba] *of Benjamin and Mispah*. These three sites have been much *sub judice* for their identification. Albright has now satisfactorily identified Gibeah with Tell el-Fūl, a hill 5 km. N of Jerusalem, possessing ' a remarkably fine view in all directions ' ; and he finds proof of Asa's hasty construction of his new fortress ; see his ' Excavations and Results at Tell el-Fūl (Gibeah of Saul),' *AASOR* 4 (1924), and Abel, *GP* 2, 334. The place remained the northern boundary of Judah until Josiah's reign (II. 23). Mispah (*miṣpāh*, ' watch-tower ') had long been identified with Tell en-Naṣbeh, 13 km. N of Jerusalem on the Nablus road, as is Tell el-Fūl. Excavations undertaken there by W. F. Badè have corroborated that identification. It was a strongly fortified place, to use the excavator's words, " with the thickest and strongest city wall which has as yet been unearthed in Palestine," and he would assign it to Asa's age. The identification has appeared to have support from jar-handles stamped with *mṣp*, as read by Badè, but the reading is most uncertain ; of special interest is the discovery of the seal of Gedaliah, who centuries later acted as governor at Mispah ; see Comm., II. 25²²ᶠᶠ·. See Badè's reports, *Palestine Institute Publications* (1926 and later, Berkeley, Calif.), and for his last statement, *ZAW*, Beih. 66 (1936), 30 ff. A brief survey of these operations is given by Olmstead, *HPS* 357 f. A full discussion of attempted identification is presented by Albright in *AASOR* 4, Appendix I, pp. 90 ff., making identification with Neby-Samwīl (this retracted in *AJA* 1936, 158 f.). The identification with Tell en-Naṣbeh is accepted by Abel, *GP* 2, 388 ff. ; Galling, *BR* 386. Ramah is generally identified with er-Rām 4 miles to the N of Jerusalem.[1] **18-20.** Asa purchased the favour of an ally with *all the silver and the gold that were left in the treasuries of the house of YHWH and ⌜in⌝*

---

[1] Albright offers a very useful map for distinction of the localities N of Jerusalem in the same *Annual*, p. 75. For the history of this frontier see Smith's instructive chapter in his *HG*, ch. 12.

[with Heb. MSS] *the treasuries of the king's house*. The limitation on the treasures harks back to 14[26]. The coalition with Damascus is of interest as presenting the earliest datum upon the vigour of the young Aramæan dynasty of that ancient city.[2] A certain Reson b. Eliada, a fugitive from the kingdom of Sobah, had established himself in Damascus, and was ' an adversary to Israel all the days of Solomon ' (11[23ff.]). His reign or dynasty must have been ephemeral. Asa's ally was *Ben-Hadad ben Tab-Rimmon ben Hezion, king of Aram, who had his seat in Damascus*. The state bears the name of the controlling folk ; it later became more specifically Aram of Damascus. Ben-Hadad, the first of the name, is the same as the king who appears subsequently in the conflicts of Damascus with the Omrid dynasty, surviving at least until 853 B.C., for which date he is recorded in Shalmaneser's monolith inscription. There is now to be added the very interesting contribution rendered by Albright in presenting (*BASOR* 87 [1942], 23 ff.) along with extensive historical survey, a study of an Aramaic inscription recently published by Dunand in the *Bulletin du Musée de Beyrouth*, 3, 65 ff. The inscription records the erection of a stele to his lord Melkart by ' Bar-Hadad b. Tab-Ramman b. Hazyan,' *i.e.*, the monarch in question, and his genealogy is identical with the Biblical datum. For the *nn. pr.*, their mngs. and traditional variations see Notes. Yet another king of the same name, Ben (Bar)-Hadad ben Hazael appears below in 20[1], *cf.* 19[15]. Albright argues, following Meyer, justifiably for only two monarchs of the name, *vs.* the opinion that there were three such. See further Comm. on 20[34]. V.[19] is phrased *staccato : A league between me and thee, and* [plus with MSS VSS, in sense=' as there was '] *between my father and thy father ! See, I have sent thee a gift of silver and gold ; go, break thy league with Baasha*, etc. Judah had not hitherto been in preferred position. **20.** The districts which Ben-Hadad *smote, i.e.*, harried, are listed in N–S direction. The name Iyon (EVV Ijon) survives in the present Merj-'Aiyūn (Spring-Meadow),

---

[2] For the early Syrian history see the particular monographs of E. G. H. Kraeling, *Aram and Israel*, A. Alt, ' Aram,' in *RVg*, and ' Die syrische Staatenwelt vor dem Einbruch der Assyrer,' *ZDMG* 1934, 233 ff., and for the chronology Albright, *BASOR* 87 (1942), 23 ff.

the lower part of the noble valley between the Lebanons ; [3] for the geography of the whole region see Robinson, *LBR* 361 ff. ; Albright, ' The Jordan Valley in the Bronze Age,' *AASOR* 6 (1926), 13 ff. ; Dussaud, *TH* 22 ff. ; Abel, *GP* 1, 12 ff. ; and for identification of this site *ib.*, 2, 352. Dan, the ancient northern limit of Israel (*cf.* 12$^{29f.}$) is the modern Tell el-Ḳāḍi (' Hill of the Judge '), 5 km. from Banias. Abel-beth-Maachah was location of the House of Maachah, a tribe allied with the Aramæans against David (2 Sam. 10$^{6ff.}$), and has been identified with Abil el-Ḳamḥ, W of Dan (see GB, Šanda ; Abel, *GP* 2, 233) ; the name appears as Abilakka in Tiglath-pileser's annals in connexion with the campaign in which he deposed Pekah king of Israel (Rogers, *CP* 320).[4] Kinneroth, an artificial plural form, denotes the region about Kinnereth, lying by the Lake of Galilee, and giving the latter its name (Num. 34^{11}, etc.), which name was later replaced with Gennesaret ; for the place and history of the name see Abel, *GP* 1, 494 ff., also Albright, *AASOR* 6 (1926), 25 ff. The raids covered *all the land of Naphtali*. They constitute the first chapter in the long history of Aram's superiority over Israel.

VV.$^{23.\ 24}$. The conclusion of the reign. **23.** The formal phrase, *all his might and all that he did*, is paralleled in the inscription of Eshmunazar king of the Sidonians, " according to the great things that I did " (line 9). The reference to *the cities that he built*, absent in OGrr., is an intrusion from 2 Ch. 14$^{6f.}$. The statement that *in his growing old he became diseased in his feet*, may well be archival ; *cf.* the self-pity expressed by the Sidonian king in the same inscription, lines 12 f. The disease is easily diagnosed as a dropsy ; see W. Epstein, *Die Medizin im A.T.* (1901), 148. The introductory particle *only* (EVV *nevertheless/but*) notes the disparity of this fate with the king's godliness (v.^{11}). Ch. moralizes : " In his disease he sought not to YHWH but to

[3] The place appears in the list of Thutmose I's Syrian conquests (Breasted, *ARE* 2, 31 ff.). In *BASOR* 89 (1943) Albr. presents a fresh version of the Amarna tablet which names Iyon, as Ayyānu (p. 14). He derives the name from Heb. '*ai*, ' ruin.'

[4] The place appears as Abel-mayim in the duplicate account in 2 Ch. 16^{4}, cited by Glueck along with other similar changes of place-names (*BASOR* 91 [1943], 16). He notes, *ib.*, Albright's interpretation of *abel* as not ' meadow,' but ' brook.'

the physicians," in this unlike the other pious king Hezekiah (II. 20). Lucian went further by prefixing to the statement of the disease the bald invention that "he did evil (before the Lord)." **24.** The repeated *with his fathers* is to be elided (*cf.* 14³¹), as also, with OGrr., the epithet for David as *his father*; the burial was *in David's City*, the Ophel.

VV.²⁵⁻³². The reign of Nadab of Israel, his overthrow by the rebel Baasha, and the foredoomed end of the short-lived dynasty. *Cf. Ant.*, viii, 11, 4. With equation of the accession *in Asa's second year* and the reign of *two years* (v.²⁵) with its termination *in Asa's third year* (v.²⁸), the reign would have lasted one year and a fraction. The new king had vigour enough to lay siege to a Philistine stronghold in the old Danite territory, Gibbethon, named in the list of such cities, Josh. 19⁴¹⁻⁴⁶, but which remains not certainly identified (see Döller, *GES* 215; Abel, *GP* 2, 333); it continued to be a military objective of Israel (16¹⁵ff·). Baasha was doubtless leader of a military revolt like that of Jehu (II. 9). The resultant destruction of Jeroboam's whole family (vv.²⁹f·), adjudged as fulfilment of Ahijah's prophecy (14¹⁰), was the usual fate of a fallen dynasty. **30.** *for the sin* [𝔐 *sins*] *of Jeroboam* [*which he sinned and*—OGrr. om.] *wherein he involved Israel, for the provocation whereby he provoked* YHWH, *the God of Israel*: for the first indictment, usual as against the Northern kings, *cf.* 14¹⁶, etc.; the bracketed reference to his personal sin is unnecessary, that is condemned in the following indictment, with which *cf.* 21²². **32.** The v., absent in OGrr., is a secondary repetition of v.¹⁶.

Ch. 15. **1.** ובשנת : the conj (absent in Ch., 𝔊ᴸ) is unusual in this formula, appearing elsewhere only at v.⁹, II. 8¹⁶, 9²⁹.— **2.** שלש : OGrr., 'six,' by common confusion with שש ; the erroneous computation is maintained by OGrr. in v.⁹, as also in the plus in v.⁸.—בירושלם : 𝔊 (B v) 𝔏 om.; similar omission in OGrr., v.⁴, forsooth as limitation of the kingdom.—**3.** כל : OGrr. om.—חטאות : many MSS read the sing. with v.²⁶, etc.; *cf.* 14¹⁶ ; the preceding כל is then secondary.—דוד : B u om.; David was not his father !— **4.** אלהיו : OGrr. om., as too restrictive.—בָּנוֹ : now generally corrected to בְּנוֹ with Grr.; but the sing. is reminiscent of 11³⁶, and is to be retained (so Šanda).—**6.** 'Rehoboam': to avoid the absurdity Grr. N *al.* have Αβια.—**8.** אבתיו : OGrr. plus 'in the 24th year of Jeroboam,' from v.⁹.—אסא : for the hypocoristic א— see Noth, *IP* 40; the root may be *'ws*, 'to give,' common in

OArab. names; see *NPS* 1, 41 f.—**9.** מלך יהודה :' many MSS '־ על מ׳=Grr.; both uses occur; see Bär, and St.'s full note on the formula.—**12.** הקדשים : 𝔊 𝔊^H τας τελετας, to which 𝔖^H has a gloss, 'shameful rites'; see Field. 𝔊^L τ. στηλας, for which Rahlfs (*SS* 3, 202 f.) *cft.* 14²³; but it is corruption of obscure τελετας.—גלולים : Grr., επιτηδευματα, 'practices.' The semantic development is uncertain; *gal*, 'stone-heap,' *gālāl*, 'dung,' have been compared; see Baudissin, *ZDMG* 58, 395 ff.—**13.** מגבירה : for the construction *cf.* למלך, 14².—מפלצת : =Ch.; the verb='to shake' at Job 9⁶ : Grr., συνοδον=𝔖^H (*cf.* 𝔖 עידא), *i.e.*, 'concourse' —by what etymology? The Grr. connect with the following by translating לאשרה with 'in her (the queen's) grove,' with thought of the vegetation rites.—ויכרת : Perles remarks that rather the verb כתת is expected, as in similar contexts, *e.g.*, Dt. 9²¹ (*JQR* 2 [1911], 115).—מפלצתה Grr., τ. καταδυσεις αυτης, 'her descents'; ℭ 'caverns'=𝔖^H, prob. with reminiscence of Is. 65⁴; also variant καταλυσεις, 'lodgings.' 𝔙 is most expansive, with two interpretations of the word, rendering with "ne esset princeps in sacris Priapi, et in luco ('grove') eius, quem consecravit, subvertitque specum ('cave') eius, et confregit simulacrum turpissimum."— קדרון 𝔊 των κεδρων, 𝔊^L Κεδρων.—**14.** סרו =Ch.; Grr. as though הסירו; similar variation at 22⁴⁴, etc.; 𝔥 is to be retained, the intransitive avoiding direct blame of the king; see St.'s lengthy note.—**15.** וקדשו, Kt., וְקָדֵשׁ Kr.: read with Kt. וְקָדְשׁוּ, and so Ch., VSS. For the repeated noun Grr. have κιονας, 'pillars'; Šanda suggests tr. as of קרש for which Grr., Ex. 26¹⁵, have στῦλος. **16.** The v. is protasis to v.¹⁷ : "And there being war," etc.—בעשא : so Ginsb., *BH*, as also in Ch.; Bär בעשא (=JV) throughout; see those editors *ad loc.*, and for extra-Biblical cases GB. The first element was בעל, *cf.* בענה, 4¹², the second has been reduced to a caritative, *cf.* אסא.—**18.** באוצרות בית י׳ : Grr., ℭ 𝔄 om. out of reverence; introduced by 𝔖^H from Aq.—ואת אוצרות : over 20 MSS and Targumic texts (see deR.), ובא=𝔖 𝔙, to be preferred; Ch. has another variant.—מלך : 6 MSS המלך, and so Kr.; the combination בית מלך appears at II. 11²⁰, 15²⁵, again corrected by Kr.; but the antique grammar is supported by בת מלך in the Mesha inscr., line 23.—בן הדד : the name appears throughout in the Grr. as 'son of Ader,' supported by 3 Heb. MSS, בן הדר, and Shalmaneser's opponent was for long so read, Bir-Idri (*e.g.*, Rogers, *CP* 297), so supporting the Gr. variant. But the first element in the Akk. transcription is now preferably understood as ideogram for the god Adad/Hadad, resulting in Adad-idri, identical then with the name Hadadezer, that of the king of Sobah (11²³). See Deimel, *Pantheon babylonicum*, 45; Meyer, *GA* 2, 2, 332.[5] The

---

[5] As *vs.* the Biblical Gr. it is to be noted that Josephus in the subsequent mention of the name corroborates 𝔥 with the rendering Ἄδαδος, *e.g.*, *Ant.*, viii, 14, *passim*. The Gr. name βαραδάδης has been found at Dura-Europos; see Baur and Rostovtzeff, *Excavations*, 46 f.

Heb. form is now corroborated by its Aramaic equivalent in the Zakar inscription, naming Bar-Hadad (the second), king of Damascus.—זברמן : the second element, playfully vocalized *rimmôn*, *i.e.*, ' pomegranate,' is properly *rammân*, a constant Akk. epithet of Addu-Hadad, and with this name as Rimmon that deity appears at II. 5¹⁸.—חיון : the name, despite suggested corrections (*e.g.*, by Dhorme to the ' Rezon ' of 11²³, *RB* 7 [1910], 71), is finally vouched for by Albr.'s art., cited above. His n. 7 is a discussion of the name.—**19.** ויעלה : the jussive ויעל is expected ; see Orlinsky, *JQR* 32 (1941), 200 f.—**26.** חטאות : read again the sing., here and below, v.³⁰.—**27.** לבית יששכר : ' of the house of Issachar ' ; the phrase is unique. The Gr. texts are woefully confused in this v. ; *cf.* Klost., Rahlfs, *SS* 3, 203, for attempted restorations.—**28.** The ' third ' year is changed to the ' fourth,' and below, v.³³, ' third ' to the ' fifth,' by Gr. MSS b *i* c₂ ; acc. to Rahlfs (*ib.*, 67) this is a revision after Eusebius's system.—תחתיו : 𝕲 om. because of indefiniteness of antecedent ; 𝕲ᴸ supplied with ' Baasha over Israel.'—**29.** כמלכו : for כ in this temporal sense see GB 327 ; MSS במלכו.—כל־ 1⁰ : 2 MSS, 𝕲 om. as superfluous—a matter of literary taste, *vs.* St.—**30.** [אשר חטא ואשר : OGrr. om. ; see Comm.—בכעסו := 𝕲ᴸ ; *al.* Grr. prefix ' and ' (and so *BH*), an improvement indeed. St. takes v.³⁰ᵇ as a marginal gloss, Klost. would elide אשר הכעים, but such criticism is unbased.

15³³–16⁷. The reign of Baasha of Israel. *Cf. Ant.*, viii, 12, 3, 4. **33.** *In the third year of Asa king of Judah Baasha ben Ahijah became king over all Israel in Tirsah* [*sc.* and was king] *twenty-four years.* Tirsah as the royal residence has already appeared indirectly above, 14¹⁷, 15²¹. It remained the capital until Omri's reign (16²³ᶠ·), and appears later in the history (II. 15¹⁴· ¹⁶). It was once a royal Canaanite city (Jos. 12²¹), and was famous for its beauty like Jerusalem (Cant. 6⁴). For its identification see BDD *s.v.*, Döller, *GES* 214 f., and Albright's extensive study, ' The Site of Tirzah,' *JPOS* 1931, 241 ff. ; he rejects certain proposed identifications on philological and critical grounds, and finds the site at Tell el-Fār‘ah, 11 km. NE of Nablus ; for criticism of this view see Alt, *Pjb.*, 1932, 40 ff., and also Abel, *GP* 2, 485, who leaves the place unidentified. Ch. 16. **1.** The only additional item to Baasha's history given here is a prophetic denunciation. The prophet Jehu ben Hanani appears also in the Chronicler's narrative of Jehoshaphat's reign (II. 19²ᶠ·, 20³⁴). The oracle depends for its elements upon that of Ahijah to Jeroboam's wife (14⁷ᶠᶠ·). **7.** The v. appears to be a useless repetition of what precedes, is possibly a variant form from another source.

And moreover through Jehu ben Hanani [om. *the prophet*—see Note] *the word of* YHWH *came to Baasha and to his house* [𝕳+ *and*] *because of all the evil that he did in* YHWH'*s eyes in provoking him by the work of his hands, in becoming like the house of Jeroboam, and because he smote it* [EVV *him*]. No unimportant passage has provoked more dispute than the last sentence. 𝔙 renders with " ob hanc causam occidit eum." Poole gives a half column to the varieties of interpretation, discussing whether the object is Jeroboam *in loco* Nadab, or Nadab, or the house. Klostermann would find here trace of an oracle of Jehu's commissioning Baasha to destroy Jeroboam's house, with ample rewriting of the text. Šanda omits the sentence, and finds in the v. an oracle by an unnamed prophet, so eliding Jehu's name. The sentence is generally recognized as a moralizing explanation of the doom upon Baasha for his own actual sin in exterminating Jeroboam's family, after the manner of Hoshea's condemnation of Jehu's bloody massacre of the Omrids (Hos. 1⁴). But such fine ethical moralizing does not appear in these late pious additions. The simplest solution would lie in the understanding of the conjunctive phrase ' because that ' as ' despite that,' which is possible in the Heb. particle involved (see Note). See Poole and Keil for theologizing at length over the human sin that is involved in such cases of theodicy.

16⁸⁻¹⁴. The reign of Elah of Israel. *Cf. Ant.*, viii, 12, 4. **8.** *The twenty-sixth year of Asa* appears in 𝕲, v.⁶, as ' the 20th ' (see Note, v.¹⁵), in Hex. as ' the 29th,' which is a learned correction. The *two years* of Elah's reign were completed according to v.¹⁰ in Asa's 27th year, *i.e.*, it terminated within the second year ; for similar calculation *cf.* Nadab's reign, 15²⁵ᶠᶠ·. The dating for the end of the reign in v.¹⁰ is in unusual place ; it is missing in OGrr., and has been introduced from v.¹⁵. *Cf.* Begrich, *Chronologie*, 181. **9. 10.** The regicide Zimri (a nobody, as his father is not named) took advantage of the absence of the army at Gibbethon, having the co-operation of his *half-squadron of the chariotry*. In an otherwise dry historical passage the tradition of Elah's drunken bout is of interest. **11-13.** The originality of much of this material is disputed. V.¹²ᵃ, *and Zimri destroyed all the house of Baasha*, missing in OGrr., repeats v.¹¹. Also OGrr. omit in v.¹¹ *he did not leave him a male* (=14¹⁰) *and his nearest of kin and friends*; the uniqueness of the final clause may guarantee the originality of the passage, which is to be kept, with Stade. V.¹³ is verbose, is briefer in OGrr.; otherwise it is always Jeroboam's sin that brought guilt upon Israel, and there is no background for the indictment of this brief dynasty as renegades, coupling them with *the vanities* (idolatrous practices) of Israel; Stade suggests a rewriting of the passage.

VV.¹⁵⁻²². Turmoil in the North; the reign of Zimri for a week, civil war between Omri and Tibni for some three years, with the success and accession of the former. *Cf. Ant.*, viii, 12, 4, 5. Following the futile attempts of Jeroboam and Baasha to found dynasties, three ambitious commanders strove to seize the throne. Zimri, *captain of the half-squadron of the chariotry* (v.⁹), had been able by a coup to get rid of the sot Elah in his palace. **15. 16.** The army, which was besieging Gibbethon, in resumption of the earlier bootless operation (15²⁷), hearing the news, *made Omri, the army-commander, king over Israel* (the real subject being designated as 'all Israel'). **17. 18.** Omri proceeded rapidly, within seven days, to Tirsah, where Zimri the would-be king fled *into the castle* (some technical architectural term) *of the royal palace*, which he burned down over his own head. **21. 22.** These few explicit details are followed with a brief statement of civil war: *half of the people* following a certain Tibni ben Ginath and the other *half*, Omri; the struggle lasted for three to four years (*cf.* vv.¹⁵⁻²³), terminating with Tibni's death, whereupon *Omri became king*. It is of interest to observe that while the army hailed Omri as king, the dating of his legal accession is four years later; we have to suppose a formal, popular affirmation at that time, as in the case of the assembly at Shechem (ch. 12). A further detail with respect to Tibni is preserved by the Grr., which add to the statement in v.²² that *Tibni died* the plus, "and Joram his brother at that time." This appears like an original, if abbreviated, memorandum; it is generally accepted by commentators and historians, *e.g.*, Thenius, Kamphausen, Benzinger, Kittel, Skinner, Olmstead, Robinson; Stade disputes this position. The amount of striking detail in this confused history is remarkable ; the account of Zimri's conspiracy is definitely docketed as from the Annals (v.[20]).

For the chronology of this period of civil war v.[15] dates the rise of the conflict between Omri and Tibni in Asa's 27th year (the Grr. varying here), and v.[23] assigns Omri's accession to the 31st year ; the interval of 4 years must then have been officially accredited to Tibni, and so the Grr. add at end of v.[22], " (Omri reigned) after Tibni." This interval is generally accepted by chronologers. Also 𝕲, followed by 𝕲ᴸ, introduces after v.[28] the section on Jehoshaphat's reign, 22[41-51], 𝕲 again repeating it in place as in 𝔅. 𝕲 in this intruded passage dates Jehoshaphat's accession in Omri's 11th year, instead of Ahab's 4th year. The difference of 6/7 years may be accounted for by assuming that the ' 6 years ' of Omri's reign ' in Tirzah ' was added to the term of ' 12 years ' (v.[23]). With such variations the chronology of this period is under vexed dispute. Lewy (*Chronologie*, 22 f.) supports the dating of original 𝕲. Stade's critical discussion in *SBOT* is sceptical as to final conclusions as between 𝔅 and 𝕲. He wisely remarks that " the numbers given in cc. 16 and 22 by 𝔐 and 𝕲 show at how late a period the Book of Kings and the dates contained in it were still being worked over." His statement that " the paragraph on Jehoshaphat is more appropriate after 16[28] than it is after 22[40]," is not supported by the usual form of the history. On the other hand the Greek editor felt that in view of the history of Ahab and Jehoshaphat in ch. 22 the latter should be previously introduced in formal terms. Begrich (*Chron.*, 178) would reduce the 22 years of Ahab to 20, arguing that v.[29b] is secondary in view of the repeated ' Ahab ben Omri.'

VV.[23-28]. The reign of Omri of Israel. *Cf. Ant.*, viii, 12, 5. It is a sad loss to secular history that we possess only these few verses in record of the most capable of the North Israelite monarchs. His is the only name of an Israelite king in Mesha's inscription, which records Omri's ' afflictions ' upon Moab for ' many years,' but does not name ' his sons.' After the passing of the dynasty the usurper Jehu was known to the Assyrians as ' son of Omri,' as in Shalmaneser III's obelisk inscription, *bis* (842 B.C.). Half a century later Adadnirari IV in his Calah inscription calls Israel 'the land of Omri,' a geographical designation repeated (733–732 B.C.) by Tiglath-pileser III; see *CP* 304, 306; *AB* 459, 462, 465. We learn below (v.[31]) that Omri's son Ahab married Jezebel, daughter of Ethbaal, priest-king of Sidonia, himself a capable monarch; the alliance was doubtless of political purpose to counteract the growing power of Damascus, which was to 'afflict' Israel in his son's day. Only the foundation of his new capital, Shômerôn, the Samaria of the VSS, in a central and commanding position (see Smith, *HG* ch. 17), is recorded for the reign, with petty detail as to its purchase. As for the new capital, which was to rank with, or rather politically beyond, Jerusalem as first among the cities of Palestine, the one-time doubt as to Omri's creation of the city, and the interpretation of the statement that he *built up the hill* . . . *Shomeron* as of a rebuilding, are now dissipated by the results of the Harvard excavations at modern Sebastīyeh, which show that the lowest levels of remains belong to Omri's construction.[1] The city was to give its name to the whole province in the Assyrian empire (*cf.* the local usage, II. 17[24], etc.), and so the prophet Hoshea always designates his home-land.

VV.[29-34]. Introduction to the reign of Ahab of Israel. *Cf. Ant.*, viii, 12–13, 1. For native precedents for marriage with a foreign princess and the influence exerted by such queens on politics and religion in the ancient world *cf.* 11[1ff.], 15[13]. The prophetic tradition memorializes Jezebel as spearhead of propaganda in Israel for the peculiarly fanatical Phœnician religion; see E. Meyer, 'Phœnicia,' *EB* 3740 ff.; *GA* 2, 2, ch. 3; G. Contenau, *La civilization phénicienne*, ch. 2; F. Cumont, *Les religions orientales dans le paganisme romaine* (ed. 4, 1929); L. B. Paton, 'Phœnicians,' *ERE*. For the part of royal women in politics in that ancient field see A. Goetze, *Kleinasien* (*HA*, Abt. 3, 1, 3, 3, 1), 80 ff. The battle was on between the God of Israel and the foreign Baal, the

---

[1] See Lyon, Reisner, Fisher, *Harvard Excavations at Samaria* (1924), with subsequent reports in *QS*. For summaries of results see Dussaud, 'Samaria au temps d'Achab,' *Syria*, 1925, 314 ff.; J. W. Jack, *Samaria in Ahab's Time* (1929); Olmstead, *HPS* 369 ff.; Watzinger, *DP* 1, 97 ff. (all these with illustrations); Abel, *GP* 2, 443 ff.; Galling, *BR* 438 ff.; Barton, *AB* pl. 29; also for earlier literature Montgomery, *The Samaritans*, ch. 2.

first long step in the development of Israel's religion since the desert days; the national as well as the religious spirit was appealed to by the reaction of prophets and their guilds. According to Josephus's transcript of Menander of Ephesus' annals of the Phœnician kings (*C. Ap.*, i, 18) Ittobaal ('Ιθώβαλος —see Note), Ethbaal of 𝔅, is recorded as having seized the throne by violence and reigning for 32 years; he is entitled 'priest of Astarte,' and this sacerdotal origin may well explain Jezebel's extreme zeal in spreading her religion in the land of her adoption. This king's title as *king of Sidonia* (see Comm., 11[5]) is historically correct, even as is for Solomon's age the title of Hiram I as 'king of Tyre' (5[15]). 'Sidonians' was the older and more comprehensive name of the Phœnicians (as in Homer), and when the Tyrian kings gained ascendancy over Sidon, they assumed the larger title and its dignity; Josephus here entitles Ethbaal properly as 'king of Tyrians and Sidonians.' The epigraphic title of Hiram II (*ca.* 738 B.C.) was 'king of Sidonians' (*CIS* I, no. 5; *HNE* 419; *NSI* no. 11), as it was much later of Tabnit priest of Astarte, *ca.* 300 B.C. (*HNE* 417, *NSI* no. 4). For these titles see Cooke, pp. 53 f.; Meyer, *GA* 2, 2, 63 ff.; for the history Contenau, pp. 69 ff. (chronological tables, pp. 384 ff.), Meyer, ch. 2 (tables, pp. 436 ff.); Olmstead, *HPS* 368 ff. Meyer dates Ittobaal *ca.* 887–856, Olmstead 889–867. V.[32] records Ahab's erection of *an altar to the Baal in the Baal's house, which he built in Samaria*; no remains of this temple have been found; it was probably part of the *enceinte* of Ahab's magnificent palace (*cf.* 22[39]), easily distinguished from that of Omri's, and one which a recent authoritative statement describes as "incomparably the finest construction of the kind that has been found anywhere in Palestine" (*QS* 1936, 61).

Apart from these few facts bearing upon the alien elements of religion that Ahab introduced and the brief summary in 22[39], whatever official records of the reign that may have existed have been replaced by the following lively stories of the prophets, which indirectly throw abundant light upon the history of the reign. The one exception is v.[34], recording a unique local item, that of the rebuilding of Jericho (apparently as unimportant or too brutal it is ignored by 𝔊[L] and Josephus). It is introduced with the first occurrence of the archival note *in his days* (see *JBL* 53 [1934], 49). The massive fortifications of Jericho had lain in ruins since the destruction assigned to Joshua by Biblical tradition, although it still remained a settlement (Jos. 18^{21}, Jud. 3^{13}, 2 Sam. 10^5). The present rebuilding was probably due to royal auspices, so Šanda suggests, as integral to Ahab's operations against Mesha of Moab ; in the concluding summary of the reign Ahab is celebrated as a builder of cities. Jericho has been the object of two notable enterprises : the first by Sellin and Watzinger, 1907–09 (see their *Jericho*, 1913) ; the second by Garstang, since 1929, whose reports have appeared in *QS* 1930 and later, and more fully in Liverpool *Annals of Art and Archæology* (Reports I–III in vols. 19, 20 [1932–33]) ; see the summaries in Albright, *APB* 30 f., 55 ; Watzinger, *DP* 1, 55, 100 ; Abel, *GP* 2, 357 ff. Our memorandum, at least for a modest rebuilding of the city at this period, is borne out by these excavations ; according to Garstang (*QS* 1932, 153) : " The outer fortifications of the city . . . were not restored until the second phase of the Iron Age, about 900 B.C." According to the narrative with the usual translation of the prepositions, *Hiel* [Grr. preserve the full form *Ahiel*] *the Bethelite built Jericho ; he laid its foundations in his eldest son Abiram, and set up its doors in his youngest son Segub.* The mng. of the prep. 'in' is obscure. 𝕊 𝔙 AV translate literally as above ; the Grr. have *in* in the first case, the dative without the preposition in the second ; 𝕋 expands after the first sentence : " he killed his eldest son A. when he built it, and he killed his youngest son S. when he set up its doors." RVV translate with ' with the loss of,' JV with ' with,' Chic. B. with ' upon ' ; Moffatt best renders the mng. of 𝔥 (*cf.* 2^{23}, בנפשו, ' at the cost of his life.' But the method of the penalty expressed by the editor as fulfilment of Joshua's curse (Jos. 6^{26}) is obscure. According to Rashi and successors (see Poole) Hiel lost all his sons by divine visitation. The Targumic interpretation, that he killed his sons, comes closest to the current modern explanation, according to which we have here a case of foundation sacrifice with its inaugural counterpart ; *cf.* H. C. Trumbull, *The Threshold Covenant* (1896), 46 ff. Such ritual devotion has appeared to be substantiated by archæological finds of bodies, but particularly of infants immured in building foundations; see at length Cook, *Religion of Anc. Palestine*, 82 ff. (with extensive citation of similar phenomena throughout the ancient world), Graham and May, *Culture and Conscience . . . in Anc. Palestine*, 77 f., and so, of recent commentators, Šanda and Barnes. But there has been strong reaction against this sacrificial interpretation of house-burials; see Watzinger, *DP* 1, 72, stating that only the burial of infants was the usual practice. At the more distant Tepe Gawra, in the old Assyrian land, only child-burials were found in the buildings, with one possible exception of a foundation sacrifice (E. A. Speiser, *Excavations at Tepe Gawra*, 1935, 25, 140 ff.). In his Comm. Kittel takes strong ground against the theory, and most recently P. Thomsen has expressed his scepticism : " zweifelhaft ist die Deutung einiger Funde als Bau- oder Gründungsopfer " (*Palästina u. seine Kultur*, 51). It remains wisest, with Kittel, Benzinger, Skinner, to refer the statement to fatalities in the builder's family, which the popular mind interpreted as fulfilment of an original curse. This tradition was independent of the book of Joshua, but it induced the final editor of that book to incorporate the note of fulfilment in 6²⁶ ; then here, in reverse, our editor cites Joshua to prove the *finale* of the curse ; it was this interest that made the editor preserve the unimportant item.

There follows, ch. 17–22³⁸, the long insertion of prophetic story bearing upon the reign ; the usual formula for its conclusion is given in 22³⁹, ⁴⁰. Those stories give full details of the wars with Damascus and their varying results. But there is not a word of the first encounter of Israel with the might of Assyria, in 854/853 B.C., on the field of Karkar, where Ahab fought among Ben-Hadad's allies against Shalmaneser III. The victor records in his Monolith inscription the presence of ' Ahab the Israelite ' with ' 2000 chariots, 10,000 men ' (*KB* 1, 151 ff. ; *CP* 294 ff. ; *ARA* 1, §611 ; *AB* 458). This is the first extraneous reference by name to an Israelite ; later the Mesha stone names his father.

Ch. 15. **33.** [ישראל] כל : absent in similar formulas below, but the same nationalistic expression at 12¹, ¹⁶, 16¹⁷ ; 3 MSS, ᴏGrr. om. (*cf. BH*), but the deletion was due to later Jewish objection.—
34. ירבעם : Grr.+' son of Nebat ' ; the same variation in 16¹⁹;

see St.'s note there with statistics of the variant usages, and with proper hesitation in correcting 𝔐.

Ch. 16. **1.** For the name Jehu see Note, II. 9². —אל : Grrr., 𝔖ᴴ ' by the hand of ' = v.⁷; similar variation 21²⁸.—**2.** The consecution of grammatical persons, vv.²⋅³, is harsh; but the Gr. variations are arbitrary.—**2.** בחטאתם : Grr. = בהבליהם of vv.¹³⋅²⁶. —**3.** מבעיר : 2 MSS מבער ; Piel is demanded, cf. 14¹⁰.—**6.** אלה : the spelling אלא is expected for the caritative, as at 4¹⁸.— **7.** הנביא : 3 MSS, OGrr. om.; absent in v.¹.—ועל 1° : 𝔊 𝔊ᴴ 𝔖ᴴ om.; 9 MSS, 𝔖 על, to be preferred.—ועל אשר : for adversative use of the prep. and the conjunctival phrase, as adopted above, see BDB 754b, 758a, GB 586b, 589a.—**8.** שנה xxvi בשנת : so vv.²³⋅²⁹, II. 8²⁵, 9²⁹, 15¹⁷ ; acc. to Begrich (pp. 179, 182 f.) this use is characteristic of one of his Chronicles.—**9.** עבדו : 𝔊 𝔊ᴸ om., by misunderstanding of the official title.—זמרי : the VSS, Jos. speak unanimously for ' Zamri,' presenting the older vocalization. The element is ancient, appearing in the Amarna letters, occurring on a Palestinian seal (Diringer, *IAE* 211), and on Akk. tablets from the ancient palace of Mari, addressed by Hammurabi to ' Zimri-ilim ' (A. Parrot, *Syria*, 1937, 74 f.; 1939, 97 ff.). The root, as *ḏmr*, is frequent in S. Arab. names (*NPS* 2, 46 f.), with its mng. much debated (see Lexx.; Šanda, ' protection '). But it is to be identified with Aram. (Syriac) *dmr* with sense of ' awe, wonder.' Cf. Phœn. Ζεὺς Δεμαροῦς, acc. to Philo of Byblos (Eus., *Præp. ev.*, i, 10, 31). C. Clemen correctly recognizes (*MVÄG* 42, Heft 3 [1939], 66) philological identity with Syrian Nahr ed-Damur (named also in Polybius, v, 68).—שחה שכור = 20¹⁶.—ארצא : Noth, *IP* 230, following Nöldeke, identifies with Arab. *'araḍatu,* ' wood-worm,' but it is doubtless from the root רצה, ' to be gracious,' with prosthetic א (as common in Aram. before such a consonantal combination) ; cf. the divine name ארקרשף, ' Favour-of-Reshep,' in the Zenjirli Hadad inscr., also the Palm. *n. dei*, ארצו.—בתרצה 2° : St. deletes; but the term is official.—**11.** במלכו כשבתו על כסאו := ' at his accession, at his ascending the throne ' : vs. St. the second vocable is not superfluous.—לא השאיר through בעשא, v.¹² : OGrr. om. by homoiotel.—נאליו : the exceptional pl. is prob. to be read in II. 10¹¹ : רעהו : pl., and so at 1 Sam. 30²⁶ ; later spellings are רעיו, רעיהו.—**12.** אל : read על with 4 MSS = Grr.; the same correction in v.¹³.—ביד : 𝔊 𝔊ᴴ και προς = 𝔖ᴴ.—**13.** חטאו ואשר : OGrr. om.—a clumsy insertion.—**14.** וכל : 1 MS, 𝔊 om.

15. " In the 27th year of Asa king of Judah " : 𝔊 (B al.), ℭ om.; 𝔊ᴸ ' in the 22d year ' MSS c₂ i, ' in the 31st year,' so agreeing with v.²³ ; the variations display the unreliability of the Grr.—שבעת ימים : 𝔊 (B a₂) ℭ ' 7 years ' ; this error in place of ' days ' accounts for the plus ' in the 20th year of Asa ' in 𝔊 (B A al.) ℭ, v.⁶ ; other Grr. give a variety of numerals.—**16.** העם החנים : *n.b.* the variation in number, *ad sensum* ; the Gr. ' the people in the camp ' induced by ' in the camp,' *inf.*—כל ישראל : 𝔊 Hex., 'in Israel'; 𝔊^L 'the people'; the changes were made because the ideal All-Israel was not involved; cf. 15³³.—עָמְרִי: the element is doubtless Arabic; cf. *'Omar* and its frequency in S. Arab. (*NPS* 2, 109). Omri and Zimri were evidently mercenaries of non-Israelite stock. Gr. texts by unfortunate confusion have Ζαμβρει, exc. 𝔊^L Αμβρι (=𝔏 𝔖^H), which Rahlfs (*SS* 3, 285) regards as the original Gr. form.—**18.** ארמון: Grr., 'cave'=𝔖^H ; 𝔗 'chamber'; 𝔖 𝔙 'palace'; Ginsberg insists properly on 'fortress,' *JBL* 62 (1943), 113 f. For etymology see E. A. Speiser, *JQR* N.S. 14 (1924), 329, as from root 'to cast foundation'; cft. Akk. *rimitu*, 'dwelling.' The word in the same connexion occurs at II. 15²⁵.—**19.** חָאָאחוֹ Or. Kt. and Ḳr.=Ginsb., *BH*; to be accepted *vs.* Occ. Ḳr. חֲמָאתוֹ (also חמאתיו=Bär); VSS have pl.—אשר עשה להחטיא: 8 MSS חטא for עשה; Grr.=אשר החטיא, the usual formula; the whole v. is clumsy.—**20.** קשרו אשר קשר:=II. 15¹⁵.—**21.** לחצי: to be omitted with Grr., 𝔖^H ; a dittogr. of חצי ל[ישרא].—הִבְנִי: Grr. and Jos. support original vocalization as 'Tabni'; Šanda cft. Akk. 'Tabni-Ea'; for the name cf. תבנית in the Phœn. Tabnith inscr.— גִּינָח: also Ginsb. variant גִּינָת; 13 MSS גנת: 𝔖^H 𝔖=גנית; Grr., Γωναθ, -ωθ, etc.—**22.** יחזק: in active sense, 'to prevail over,' as at Jer. 20⁷, 2 Ch. 28²⁰; cf. König., *Syntax*, §§210 ff. Grr. texts of v.^b early suffered abbreviation by homoiotel. of repeated העם; 𝔈 𝔊^L 𝔏=𝔥; see Rahlfs, *SS* 3, 67 f.—**23.** יהודה: 𝔊 𝔈 om.—**24.** ההר שמרון: 'the Hill Shomeron'; there is no reason to elide 'ש (with St.), or either the art. or ההר (with Šanda).—שִׁמְרוֹן: Bibl. Aram., שָׁמְרָיִן; Syr., שָׁמְרִין; Akk. *Samerina*, also *Sabara'in* (Bab. Chron. B, col. I, line 28; *KAT* 2, 276, *CP* 210); Grr. (except in this one v. for exactness) Σαμάρεια. For the process of the initial vowel, $\hat{a}>\hat{o}$, see Harris, *Development of the Canaanite Dialects*, 43 ff. For the process of the final vowel, $\hat{a}>ay>i$, by '*imâlah*, cf. Brock., *GVG* 1, 141 ff. For place-names in -âm-, -ayim, -im, and -ôn, -ayin, -in, see Borée, *AOP* 50–67, with full lists. For *Šamerôn/ Šamerayin* cf. modern Syrian *Libnēn<Libnân*, along with Bibl. *Lebanon*. The final nasal with preceding varying vowel as above noted (cf. שעלבים 4⁹) is demonstrative, parallel to -ân in S. Arabic; see Comm., ch. 11, n. 2, on *Malkam/Milkom*. Place-names in -ô with loss of the nasal are of similar origin, *e.g.*, Shilo. In this v. there is wide variety in the Gr. spellings of the repeated name. In the first case OGr., followed by Hex., played on the man's name with Σεμερων, so B, and with Σαεμηρων in the second case; but 𝔊^L has *o* for the first vowel=𝔏. The *n. pr.* occurs elsewhere as clan-name, also on a Palestinian bulla (*IAE* 142), and in name-composition. There also appear forms accommodated to the place-name, *e.g.*, Σομμηρ=𝔏, 𝔙, 'Somer.' There is no reason to correct the Heb. vocalization of the place-name so as to gain *a* in the first syllable, and so to relate the name more closely to 'Shemer' (so *e.g.*, Döller, Šanda, and the queried correction in *BH*); the play on the man's name remained, whatever was the vocalization

of the derivative. The new name probably involved the participial sense of 'Watch-tower,' with Smith, *HG* 346.—**26.** חטאתיו : the correct Kr. חַטֹּאתוֹ=Kt. of many MSS.—אלהי ישראל י" את : B *al.*, 𝕮 om.—**27.** אשר 1⁰ : 40 MSS Ken., deR. pref. וכל=Grr.; St. denies its originality (otherwise *BH*); it was indeed suitable for Omri's activities, but the word was often carelessly introduced in similar cases, *e.g.*, 15³¹, and see Bär's note on II. 15³⁶.—אשר עשה 2⁰ : om. with OGrr.—**28.** אחאב : tradition of older vocalization in Αχιαβ, Jer. 29²¹ᶠ·, as also in the name of a nephew of Herod, ʼΑχίαβος (*Ant.*, xv, 7, 8). The Heb. name now appears on the Shebna seal from Tell ed-Duweir (*IAE* 214).

29. OGrr. date the accession in the 2d year; Gr. MSS also greatly abbreviate the text.—**30.** מכל : OGrr. prefix κ. επονηρευσατω =וירע, as in v.²⁵, approved by Burn., *BH*, but it is an expansion to accentuate Ahab's wickedness (*cf.* St.).—**31.** הֲנָקֵל : the interrogative appears to have been first noticed by the Renaissance scholars (see Poole), with the result, "et fuit, nonne leve fuit ire ipsum," etc., and so AVᵐᵍ. The VSS all paraphrase; since Klost. the accepted amendment is הַנָּקֵל, 'the lightest thing' (*e.g.*, St., *BH*); but change is unnecessary. The syntax, with interrogative in place of conditional particle is quite possible; *cf.* Eze. 8¹⁷, and see Burn.—איזבל : the first syllable is to be interpreted as abbreviation of אחי ; see H. Bauer, *ZAW* 1933, 89, n. 1, who *cft.* איעור=Αχιεξερ, Num. 26³⁰ ; *cf.* also the possible play on the name אחיכבוד>איכבוד. The interpretation of the second element has varied because of the questioned mng. of the root; see Note on זְבֻל, 8¹³. As there the present element has the primary sense of ' exaltation.' Light is now cast by the Ugaritic texts, where *zbl* occurs with the mng. of 'prince,' *e.g.*, *zbl b'l 'rṣ*, 'the Prince, Lord of the earth,' *zbl ym*, 'the Prince Sea,' with its parallel, ' Prince River '; see Gordon, *Ugar. Handbook*, 1, §9, 45, and at length Albr.'s extensive art., *JPOS* 1936, 17 ff. A pejorative sense may have been introduced by playing upon Arab. and Akk. (?) *zibl*, ' dung '; *cf.* the process ' Baal-zebul '>' Baal-zebub', II. 1². In *Syria*, 1935, 185, n. 1, Virolleaud has proposed identity with the repeated phrase in the first published Ugaritic epic, *iy zbl*, 'where is Zbl ? ' (the passages cited by Gordon, *ib.*, §12, 5). But such a name as original is impossible; there might be in the Biblical form a taunting nickname.—אתבעל : Grr., Ιεθεβααλ, etc.; Jos., *C. Ap.*, i, 18, Ιθωβαλος, which transcription, on good Phœn. authority=אִתּוֹבַעַל, 'With-him-Baal '; *cf.* the abbreviated form of the name of a Sidonian king, Tuba'lu, in Sennacherib's Prism inscr., ii, 44 (*CP* 340 ; *ARA* 2, no. 239). See Harris, *Phœn. Gram.*, Glossary. For such prepositional name-formations *cf.* חפזי־בה עמנואל, and see Noth, *IP* 32.— **32.** בית הבעל Grr., εν οικω τ. προσοχθισματων αυτου=𝕾ᴴ ; προσοχθ. renders שֶׁקֶץ as applied to Astarte and Chemosh in II. 23¹³.—**33.** האשרה : Grr., (το) αλσος, as at 15¹³.—ויוסף א' לעשות להכעיס 𝕮 𝕮ᴸ insert [τ. ποιησαι] παροργισματα, which as כעסים is introduced into the text by

Kit., St., Šanda, *BH* (with ?) ; but *cf.* Burn.'s note on the use of the noun (*e.g.*, II. 23²⁶). 𝕳 can well be preserved by treating the second infinitive as gerundial, " he did still more in provoking."— **34.** 𝔊ᴸ om., Jos. ignores the v.—בימיו : B† om.—חיאל : Grr., Αχιηλ=𝔊ᴴ=אחיאל ; *cf.* אחירם/חירם, 5¹⁵.—יריחה : also MSS יריחו ; for the final vowel and Kt. *cf.* שִׁילֹה, שִׁלֹה.—שגיב Kt., שגוב Ḳr.=many MSS, and so at 1 Ch. 2²¹ ; Grr.=Ḳr. ; the element is a S. Arab name (*NPS* 2, 401).

CC. 17–19. The first part of the Elijah cycle. *Cf. Ant.*, viii, 13, 1–7.[1]

Ch. 17. Elijah's sudden appearance and announcement to Ahab of the coming drought (v.¹) ; the divine provision for him at the Wady Cherith (vv.²⁻⁷) ; the Phœnician woman's care of him by divine provision, and his miracle of resuscitation of her son (vv.⁸⁻²⁴). V.¹. " With the eagle-like suddenness which characterizes all his movements Elijah appears abruptly before Ahab with the announcement of a drought which is to continue for some years, and not to be removed except in accordance with his prophetic word " (Skinner, p. 223). For his equally mysterious disappearances *cf.* 18¹², II. 2. It is held by some commentators (*e.g.*, Klostermann, Benzinger) that the original introduction to the story, giving the motive of Elijah's appearance, has been lost ; but, again with Skinner : " . . . it is doubtful if any introduction would not weaken the dramatic effect of the great prophet's advent on the scene." Elijah's chosen self-expression, ' before Whom I stand ' (also 18¹⁵) designates him solemnly as Yʜᴡʜ's courtier (*cf.* 1²). The true Oriental reserve of the story also appears in the point that not until the bidding, *hide thyself*, do we learn that the prophet had to flee from the king. Elijah is bluntly introduced without even a patronymic (Grr. add the

---

[1] For linguistic and literary criticism of these prophet-cycles see Burn., pp. 207 ff., ' Narratives of the Northern Kingdom.' To the literature noted in Int., §14, *b*, n. 1, are to be added for the historical environment of Elijah and Elisha the following : Ewald, *HI* 4, 63 ff. ; Kittel, *GVI* 2, §§30–9 ; Cook, *CAH* 3, cc. 17–20 ; Lods, *Israël*, 485 ff., 513 ff. ; Olmstead, *HPS* cc. 24 ff. ; Robinson, *HI* ch. 16 ; Morgenstern, ' The Historical Antecedents of Amos' Prophecy,' pt. 3 of his *Amos Studies* ; for the prophets under discussion Gunkel, *Elias, Jahwe u. Baal* (1906), and his *Geschichten von Elisa* (1922) ; James, *Personalities of the O.T.*, cc. 9, 10. For the later Jewish traditions see Hamburger, *RE*, and *JE*, *s. vv.*, and L. Ginzberg, *The Legends of the Jews*, vol. 4.

reverential title 'the prophet,' which he was not technically —*cf.* Amos), as *the Tishbite, of Tishbe of Gilead*—so with the Grr. (*cf. Jos.*), *vs.* 𐤉𐤄, *of the settlers of Gilead*, with variation of vocalization (see Note). The Gileadite Tishbe is to be distinguished from the Galilæan Θεσβη, 'on the right of Kadesh of Naphtali,' the ancestral home of Tobit's family (Tob. 1¹). For possible identification with el-Istīb, 13 km. N of the Jabbok on Jebel Ajlūn, on the southern slope of which locality lie remains of a chapel of Mar Elias, see Buhl, *GAP* 257 ; Döller, *GES* 223 f. ; Abel *GP* 2, 486. The site was early so identified, and was visited by the pilgrim Sylvia in the fourth century : " euntes aliquandiu per uallem Iordanis super ripam fluminis ipsius . . . ad subito uidimus ciuitatem sancti prophetæ Heliæ, id est Thesbe, unde ille habuit nomen Helias Thesbites. Inibi est ergo usque in hodie spelunca, in qua sedit ipse sanctus " (*Peregrinatio*, ch. 16, in *CSEL* 39, 58). The indefinite *these years* is further precised at 18¹ff., in which the dating *in the third year* dates the recurrence of rain ; *i.e.*, normal conditions would have been restored in the third year. The 'three and a half years' to which the term is extended in Lu. 4²⁵, Ja. 5¹⁷ followed Jewish tradition (*Yalkut Shimeoni*, see B. Weiss on Luke). Was the extra half added to give space for the history in ch. 18⁷ ? It has been observed that 3½ years, half of a sabbatic period, represented a mystical cycle of disaster ; *cf.* Dan. 7²⁵, etc., and see Montgomery, *ad loc.* This exceptional drought is corroborated by Josephus's citation from Menander in the latter's 'acts of Ithobalos, king of Tyre ' : " There was a drought in his reign, which lasted from the month of Hyperberetaios until the month of Hyperberetaios in the following year. But he made supplication to the gods, whereupon a heavy thunderstorm broke out." For the continuation of droughts over periods of years in Palestine see E. Huntington, 'Transformation of Palestine ' (*Bull. Am. Geog. Soc.*, June, 1912), and his table of the rainfall recorded for 1846-1909, fig. 9 in App.; the dry period of 1868-74 is 'the worst in modern times' (p. 352). But Huntington, with his theory of deterioration of the Palestinian climate does not include notice of ancient tradition of such calamities. See also at length Dalman, *A. u. S.*, 1, 1, 194 ff. A parallel tradition of a drought is given in the Elisha cycle, II. 4³⁸ff..

VV.$^{2\text{-}7}$. Elijah is bidden by *the word of Yhwh* (see Comm., 13^1) : *Go from here . . . and hide thyself in the Wady Cherith, which is in front of the Jordan.* The wady in question, with its indefinite name (='cutting') has been located at many places, *e.g.*, by Robinson (*BR* 2, 28) as the deep and difficult Wady el-Ḳelṭ, W of Jordan, N of Jericho. But the story demands that Elijah fled out of Ahab's jurisdiction. Jerome places *Chorath* as 'a torrent across Jordan' (*Onom.*, 113, 18), following pilgrim tradition; this view is supported by the presumable meaning of the prep. as *to east of* (*e.g.*, Gen. 23^{19}, other reff. in GB 649a). For the various identifications see Döller, *GES* 224 ff. The divine provision of the prophet's food was simply miraculous. Such a miracle has long aroused rationalistic doubts, and the word for *ravens* has been given other interpretations by change of vocalization; and so as 'merchants,' identified with a word at Eze. 27^{27}, and Kimchi notes such an interpretation; or as 'Arabs' (the reverse process has taken place in Jer. 3^2, where Heb. 'Arab' is rendered as 'crow' by Grr., 𝔖); a gentilic interpretation appears in 𝔄 with the ethnic name *'Orabim*. Poole excoriates such interpretations in his day as due to 'morosa ingenia'; this rationalizing still survives, *e.g.*, in Barnes's Comm. Comparison has long been made with similar tales, classical and otherwise, of such feedings by animals, by Grotius, Keil, Gunkel in his *Elias*, 68, nn. 7–9, most recently by Frazer, *Folk-Lore in the O.T.*, pt. 3, ch. 14, noting the part played by the raven in ancient lore.

VV.$^{8\text{-}24}$. In retiring later to *Sarephath of Sidon* Elijah still keeps out of Ahab's jurisdiction. The place is the Gr. Sarepta (*e.g.*, Lu. 4^{26}); the name survives in modern Sarafend, 7 miles S of Sidon, near the coast, while remains of the ancient seaport exist on the shore below; see Dussaud, *La Syrie antique et médiévale*, 42. Note that it is Phœnician testimony that corroborates this tradition of a long and widespread drought. Oriental generosity is shown by the woman's readiness to give a drink of water to the stranger (*cf.* Mt. 10^{42}), but she is embarrassed by the request for food. For the *jar* and the *cruse* (v.^{12}), see A. M. Honeyman, *PEQ* 1939, 81, 89. The *two sticks* is equivalent to the English 'a couple,' Germ. 'ein Paar' (*cf.* Am. 1^1). In the same v. the Grr. understood the

Heb. of *my son* as pl., 'my sons' (as the Kt. can also be interpreted), then continued the pl. in v.[13], and also rendered *her household* (v.[15]) with 'her children.' But only *the* (one) *son of the mistress of the house* is named below (v.[17]); the pl. of the Grr. appears to have been induced by the expansive word *house/household*, which includes servants; change indeed might be made in v.[15], with many comm., of *her house* to *her son*. The woman was a person of property, a householder, with a dwelling stout enough to have an *upper chamber* (v.[19]), i.e., a 'lean-to' on the roof; cf. the description of Elisha's quarters in similar circumstances, II. 4[10], and see Dussaud, *Syria*, 1935, 350.

VV.[17-24]. The story of the revival of the lifeless child has its parallel in numerous folk-tales concerning the gratitude of divine persons for hospitality rendered them, especially by poor people; e.g., the story of Lot and his divine visitors, that of Philemon and Baucis, also numerous German tales cited by Gunkel (*Elias Jahve u. Baal*, 69, n. 12). The mother's passionate cry to Elijah (v.[18]): *What is there between me and thee, O Man of God? Hast thou come into my home to record my sin and to slay my son?*, is expression of ancient religion, the 'Scheu vor Heiligkeit.' What had escaped divine notice before is now revealed by the discovery of a divine in her house, who has acted as detective of holiness; cf. Peter's discovery of his Lord's divinity (Lu. 5[8]), and the centurion's fear of him (Mt. 8[8]). Physical calamity was taken to point to human sin, to some case of 'hidden faults' (Ps. 19[13]); cf. the Rabbis' query about the man who was born blind (Jn 9[2]). The next to the last clause is generally translated 'to bring my sin to remembrance'; Moffatt, 'to call attention to some sin of mine'; Chic. B., 'to remind me of my iniquity.' But the meaning of the verb is 'to register,' i.e., legally before Deity, and so Skinner interprets; such and such a sin becomes a matter of record before God, and judgment is immediately passed (cf. Dan. 7[10]). The praxis of the resuscitation of the child, *in whom there was no breath left* (v.[17]) lay in this (v.[21]) that the man of God *stretched himself upon the child three times*, along with a prayer to *my* God, that *the child's soul might return into him*. The treatment is identical with that of Elisha in his cure of a child, when " he lay upon the child " at full length, etc., II. 4³⁴ᶠ· (q.v.). In similar fashion Paul revived (ἐπέπεσεν αὐτῷ) the youth Eutychus, who was taken up as dead from a fall (Acts 20⁹ᶠᶠ·). Landersdorfer suggests that this was a kind of ritual praxis closely related to Babylonian incantations ; but the praxis here is not of ritual order. The Gr., not understanding the verb of the praxis, translated with " he breathed into the boy " ; but there is no reason, along with some critics, to change the Heb. here, or to accept the abbreviated text presented by OGr. at v.²² ; see Note. It is somewhat an academic question whether the child actually died ; it is not so specifically stated, and Josephus reasonably understands the case as one of apparent death. *Cf.* a similar act of resuscitation by Jesus (Mt. 9¹⁸ᶠᶠ·=Mk., Lu.). Antiquity recognized that the fact of death was not certain until after a certain delay ; *cf.* the raising of Lazarus, and the delay of Jesus till the third calendar day (Jn. 11). The woman's final confession, *Now I know*, etc. (v.²⁴) is the conviction of the mother's heart ; what might have been a passing incident has become to her an abiding reality. Indirectly she recognizes Elijah's God, but the point she makes is that *the word of* YHWH *is in thy mouth of a truth* (so Moffatt, ' really ' : not, as generally, ' the word . . . is true '). The story is paralleled by Jesus' benefaction of the Syro-Phœnician woman (Mk. 7²⁴ᶠᶠ·). Here as also in the Gospel incident there is no evangelization of the alien ; the Syrian Naaman voluntarily became a proselyte (II. 5¹⁷ᶠᶠ·).

1. אליהו : for formation of such ' Bekenntnisnamen ' in the ancient religions see Noth, *IP* 139 ff. ; the name may have been an assumed religious alias. 𝕲 here and below Ηλειου ; 𝕲ᴸ always Ηλιας, declinable ; Grr., exc. 𝕲ᴸ, +' the prophet.'—מתשבי : ' of the settlers of (Gilead),' a strange expression ; Grr., εκ Θεσβων ; 𝕾ᴴ ' from Tšbi ' ; Jos., εκ πολεως Θεσσεβωνης ; accordingly read מִתֻּשְׁבֵּי ; see Then. at length ; but *cf.* Ew., *HI* 4, 64.—יהוה : Grr. with magnification +' the God of Hosts ' ; some MSS om. foll. ' the God of Israel ' ; *cf.* the Gr. in v.¹⁴.—**2.** אליו : Grr.=אליהו אל, and so v.⁸ ; the Gr. preferred precision, *e.g.*, vv.¹⁰· ¹¹· ¹²· ¹⁵, etc.— **3.** מזה : ' from here,' exceptional ; *cf.* מישם, v.¹³.—ופנית לך : Grr., 𝕾ᴴ om., but there is no reason, *vs.* St., to delete it.—**5.** וילך 1⁰ ; 1 MS Ken., 𝕲 om. ; וילך 2⁰ ; 1 MS Ken., OGrr. om. ; but the phrase ' to go and do ' is usual, *cf.* v.¹⁵, and *e.g.*, Mt. 9¹³, Lu. 10³⁷ ; 2⁰ is geographical.—ויעש : 𝕲ᴸ om. ; on the Gr. rdgs. here *cf.* Rahlfs, *SS* 3, 242.—**6.** הערבים : see Comm. above.—ובשר 1⁰ :

I. 17$^{1-24}$

1 MS, OGrr. om. ; ולהם 2^{0} : 1 MS, OGrr. om. ; emendation of 𝔐 is accordingly made by some, as in correspondence with Oriental meals, e.g., by Klost., Kamp., St., BH ; but the simplification may have been induced by Ex. 16$^{8. 12}$, so Benz., Sk.—9. צְרְפָתָה : so Mich., Bär, BH ; Ginsb., צרפתה ; cf. צָרְתָה, 4^{12}. The n. loci = Eg. Darpata (Albr., Vocalization, 42), Akk. Ṣariptu, Gr. Σαρεπτα.— וישבת שם : OGrr. om., prob. on ground that he did not legally dwell there, vs. St.'s approval of the excision.—אשה אלמנה : 'a certain widow' ; cf. Ex. 16^{20}, Jud. 4^{4}, Dan. 3^{8}.—10. ויבא : OGrr. om.—אליה : Grr., οπισω αυτης, and so v.^{11}, as though for אחריה ; the correction in the latter place is accepted by some (e.g., Kamp., Kit., St. ; BH frt.), with the laboured idea of vice versa corruption in 𝔐 (so Šanda).—11. לקחי : so the full radical impv. in Ex. 29^{1}, Eze. 37^{16}, Pr. 20^{16} ; correction to לָהּ קְחִי, ostensibly after the Gr. (cf. St., BH), is not corroborated by the Gr. order of words.— 12. מעוג† (exc. in the corrupt text of Ps. 35^{16}) : interpreted from ענה (e.g., v.^{13}) ; Grr., ενκρυφιας = a cake baked in hot ashes ; 𝔗 𝔖 as מאומה, ' anything,' accepted by Klost., BH as likely original, properly rejected by St.—שנים : 4 MSS om. the meagre figure.— 13. ולד : MSS Ken., Ginsb., ולכי, in accord with the woman's dialect.—14. אלהי ישראל : OGrr. om. (cf. similar omission, v.^{1}), but to the point here, vs. St. ; the omission of the nationalistic phrase was due to Hellenistic universalism.—תִּכְלָה : n.b. -ā, a case to be added to those given in GK §75, 6.—תחן Kt., תֵּת Ḳr. : for the Kt. cf. 6^{19}.—15. כדבר אליהו : OGrr. om., as in conflict with "כדבר י, v.^{16}.—הוא והיא Kt., הִיא וָהוּא Ḳr. (the Kt. in some MSS): Ḳr. = VSS, exc. Gr. A v, αυτος κ. αυτη ; the original text was prob. הא והא, and subsequent vocalization wrongly gave precedence to the prophet.—וביתה : prob. to be read וּבְנָהּ, cf. Grr. = ובניה ; see Comm.—ימים : OGrr. om. ; A c$_{2}$ 𝔖^{H} supply from Sym., Theod., with ' and from that day,' accepted by Šanda as = ומהיום ההוא ; St., Sk. om. ; Kit. sugg. יום יום (cf. BH) ; but the indefinite word = ' for some time,' needs not to be faulted ; cf. ויהי ימים, 18^{1}.— 16. The v. is dependent upon v.^{15}.—צפחת השמן לא חסר : for similar predominance of gender of the nom. regens cf. Ewald, Lehrb., §317, c. Such syntax does not appear for the preceding כד הקמח, hence St. corrects the verb there to fem. ; however, original grammar may be careless.—18. באת : 9 MSS pref. כי.—20. יהוה אלהי : Grr. (𝔊^{L} corrupt), οιμοι κυριε, as though for "אוי לי לי.— הגם על : Grr., ο μαρτυς (!), a variation that has caused attempts at rewriting, e.g., by Klost. (cf. BH), suggesting אם לא נמול יהיה, " should there not be a reward . . . ? "—מתגורר : the word = anglice ' boarder.'—21. ויתמדד : cf. וינהר, II. 4^{35}, and see discussion there ; there is no reason on basis of Gr. ενεφυσησεν to change to ויפח (cf. BH).—על קרבו = v.^{22} ; a few MSS 'אל ק = Gr. εις αυτον, exc. MS f, επ αυτον = 𝔈 ; but נפש is the aura enveloping the person ; cf. עלי in the refrain of Ps. 42–43.—22-23. הילד (v.^{23}) . . . וג' ; וישמע וג' reduced by 𝔊 (for mixed text of 𝔊^{L} see Rahlfs, SS 3, 242 f.) to κ. εγενετο

ουτως κ. ανεβιωσεν, "and it was so, and he revived [so with MS u, Jos., vs. the corruption ανεβοησεν, e.g., B=𝔖^H, "and he called to"] το παιδαριον, as though from original ויהי כן ויחי הילד; such a corrected text has been favourably regarded by some, e.g., St., BH; but it has arisen through haplog. of the similar phrases and then assimilation of על קרבו, v.²¹, to על קרבו ויחי, v.²² (as 1 Heb. MS actually reads in v.²¹), ויחי 1° then being read in doublet as ויחי.—**24.** עתה זה : the phrase also at II. 5²²; for the enclitic element cf. 14⁶.—אמת : adverbial, as at Jer. 10¹⁰, Ps. 132¹¹. 𝔖^H has a marginal note, citing from Severus of Antioch, that (with play on the word) this child was the prophet Jonah ben Amittai, acc. to Hebrew authorities, and so Jerome, *Prolog. in Jonam*; see Field, also Poole, *ad loc.*

Ch. 18. The scene on Carmel. The drama falls into three acts: (1) vv.¹⁻¹⁹, the providentially arranged meeting of Elijah with king Ahab; (2) vv.²⁰⁻⁴⁰, the great convocation on Carmel, and YHWH's victory in the contest with the Baal; vv.⁴¹⁻⁴⁶, the coming of the great downpour of rain, and Elijah's triumphal escort of the king to his residence in Jezreel. For the fire from heaven see Additional Note below.

1. For the third year see Comm., 17¹. **2***b*. *And the famine being sore in Samaria:* in the Heb. syntax the sentence is subordinate to the following. VV.³⁻⁴ give a parenthetic description of Obadiah, who was *Over-the-House, i.e.*, of the king, for which title *cf.* 4⁶. He was one who *revered YHWH greatly*. His name is composed with the element '*ôbēd*, 'servitor, worshipper,' a word also used of Baal's devotees (II. 10¹⁹ff.). The name may have been assumed by the zealot, as probably was the case in Elijah's name. The virtue of this royal officer had been exhibited by his having concealed, in Jezebel's persecution of the national religion, *a hundred prophets . . . by fifties in the cave-region* (the last word in 𝔏, 'cave,' is generic). One of such regions is Mount Carmel, which is largely of chalk formation, abounding in caves, some 2000 of which have been counted, an abode of prehistoric man, and through history a resort of fugitives (*cf.* the story in 1 Sam. 24), and of Christian hermits.[1] This is the first,

---

[1] See Döller, *GES* 228 f.; Abel, *GP* 1, 438 ff.; Barton, *AB* 131 f., and for a more recent review of the discoveries of prehistoric man's remains in the Palestinian caves, Albr., *SAC* 88 f. Supplementally there is to be added the vivid account in ch. 4 of McCown's *The Ladder of Progress in Palestine.*

although indirect, reference to a systematic persecution of the sons of the prophets, brought on by Jezebel's high-handed policy, as also to the existence of such large groups of their order.

VV.⁵,⁶ present the straits to which the *régime* was put by the drought for provisioning the royal horses and mules. The demand of the royal stables is illustrated by Shalmaneser III's figuring of the chariots of ' Ahab the Israelite ' at 2000 (Monolith inscr., col. 2, 91, Rogers, *CP* 296 ; Barton, *AB* 458). The opening imperative should probably be expanded with the Grr. : *Come, let us go through the land ; cf.* 1 Sam. 14¹,⁶. **7.** Obadiah *recognized* (EVV *knew*) Elijah ; he had never met him, but knew him by repute, possibly recognized him by his hair mantle (*cf.* II. 1⁸). **8-15.** Obadiah deprecated the prophet's commission to him : *Go, tell thy lord : Here is Elijah !* Elijah's volatility, his sudden appearances and vanishings were known to all ; upon himself the king would take revenge, if Elijah escaped summary arrest. But the plea may have been only a generous excuse ; Obadiah was thinking of the prophet's safety. Ahab had been seeking everywhere for the fugitive prophet, even in foreign lands, laying every *régime* (see Note) *and nation under oath* in the search for him. For such adjurations, involving fearful execrations, *cf.* the Aramaic texts from Syrian Sūjīn of this order.² **15.** Here occurs for the first time in Kings the divine name YHWH Sebaoth, elsewhere in the book five times, and only in prophetic utterances.³

16-19. Elijah's meeting with Ahab. The clash of words between him and the undaunted man of God is classical. The epithet, *Troubler of Israel*, is flung back in the king's teeth : ⁴ *I have not troubled Israel ; but thou and thy father's house*, with added specific indictment of the court : *in your leaving* [with Grr. om. *the commandments of*] YHWH *and thy*

---

² The texts were first published by Dussaud, *CR* 1930, 155 ff., further treated by H. Bauer, *AfO* 8 (1932), 1 ff. ; S. Ronzevalle, *Mél.*, 15, fasc. 7 (1931), 232 ff. For further execrations *cf.* the treaty imposed by Ashur-Nirari V upon the local Syrian king, 755 B.C., of which extracts are presented by Olmstead, *HA* 172 ff.

³ See W. W. Baudissin, *Kurios, als Gottesname im Judentum*, 1926-29.

⁴ The root ' to trouble ' had some religious significance ; *cf.* Josh 6¹⁸, especially 7²⁴ᶠᶠ· with play upon the root meaning.

going after the Baals. **19.** Elijah proceeds to a summary demand for a convocation of *all Israel* on *Mount Carmel,* along with *the prophets of the Baal.* The following figure *four hundred and fifty* is an evident intrusion from v.^{22}. As intrusion also appears to be the reference to *the prophets of the Asherah four hundred,* on the ground that the followers of this cult are not mentioned in the subsequent story. But the argument that (the) Asherah was not a deity now falls to the ground ; see Comm. on 15^{13}, and on II. 23^4 for the Ugaritic pairing of Baal and Asherah. Whether or not the clause is secondary, the reference to Jezebel's patronage of that deity is pertinent ; her father was priest of the corresponding goddess Ashtart ; see above on 16^{31}. For *the eaters at Jezebel's table cf.* 2^7 ; they were the queen's subsidized clergy. She was well within her extra-territorial rights (*cf.* 11$^{1\text{ff.}}$), but she abused her wifely influence to persecute the native zealots. Those organized castes of the Baal and the Asherah with their orgiastic rites were an abhorrent innovation in Israel, and aroused the nationalistic-religious antipathy of the people at large, to whom Elijah and the fraternities of ' the sons of the prophets ' gave voice and leadership. Elijah was right ; not he but the responsible monarch was the innovator. This must be maintained as against many current scholars, who would hold that Israel never found its religion until the eighth century.

VV.$^{20-40}$. The convocation of all Israel and the prophets of the Baal on Carmel. For this mountain promontory, called in Arabic Jebel Mar Elyas, see the BDD, Guérin, *Samarie,* ch. 60 (with ample historical citation) ; Smith, *HG* ch. 14, sect. iv ; Döller and Abel, cited above ; also C. Klopp, *Elias u. Christentum auf dem Karmel* (1929). Šanda would precise the location of the present scene, the traditional site of which is pointed out at el-Muḥraḳa (' place of burning '). This splendid complex, 1800 ft. above the sea at its top, must have been from of yore ' a holy mount.' [5] Jamblichus in his life of Pythagoras (iii, 1) tells that his hero sojourned there ;

---

[5] In the Palestine List of Thutmose III immediately after '*k*=Acco is listed ršḳdš=קדש ראש, ' Holy Mount,' according to some scholars (*e.g.*, Abel, *GP* 1, 350 f.), our Carmel ; but according to personal information from W. F. Albright the identity is not established.

Tacitus (*Hist.*, ii, 78) relates that there was a sanctuary there with altar but without image; Suetonius in his life of Vespasian (ch. v) records how he sacrificed there, and was given by the priests an oracle of his coming greatness; Elijah appears to have daringly chosen Pagan ground for his defiance of Ahab and the Baal. The mountain gives a dramatic setting for the appearance of *a little cloud the size of a man's palm coming up out of the sea* ' (vv.$^{42ff.}$). **20.** The convocation of *all* [om. with Grr. *the sons of*] *Israel* has its parallel in the assembly at Shechem (ch. 12). **21.** The translation of Elijah's query to the people as given by EVV, *How long halt ye between two opinions ?*, well expresses the sense; more exactly it means, *How long are ye hobbling* [so Moffatt, *cf.* GV FV] *at the two forks* (of the road), *i.e.*, hopping now on one leg, now on the other, before the dilemma. Grotius gives a capital parallel for the verb in the Gr. ἀμφοτερίζειν. For other interpretations see Note. Elijah is here using some popular phrase. It finely introduces, passing from the satiric to the serious, his peremptory demand: *If YHWH be the God (the Deity), follow him; and if the Baal, follow him !* And, as so often in history, *the demos answered him not a word.*

22. *And Elijah said to the people : I am left a prophet of YHWH's alone by myself.* Elijah is speaking to his present audience, contrasting himself with the hundreds of Baal-prophets; but his sense of utter loneliness is expressed again at 19^{14}. VV.$^{23ff.}$. There follows the summons of the people to serve as jury in the ordeal between YHWH and the Baal, and this the people approves: *and it shall be, the God who answers by fire, he is the God* (=*the Deity*). The Baal-folk had the first choice. **26.** With no response from their god, the prophets enacted some peculiar rite *at*, or rather *about* [not *upon* with AV] *the altar.* This is doubtless to be explained as some kind of limping dance; see Note, v.^{21}. For the ritual dance in Phœnician religion Pietschmann notes (*Gesch. d. Phönizier*, 220) the report in Heliodorus (*Æthiopica*, iv, 17) of a raving dance in honour of Herakles celebrated by Tyrian merchants, and a Phœnician ' Baal of the Dance ' (*b'l mrḳd*) is known from classical texts (Harris, *Grammar*, 88, 147). There have pertinently been compared the ' encompassing of the altar ' in Ps. 26^6 (*cf.* Gunkel, *ad loc.*), and the running circumambulation of the sacred stone at Mecca at the Haj festival; *cf.* Wellhausen, *Reste arab. Heidentums*, 109 ff. D. B. Macdonald in his *Hebrew Literary Genius*, 35, further develops the comparison : " The fundamental idea in both words [*i.e.*, ḥaj in both languages] is dancing around something and the essence of the Muslim *ḥajj* is a ceremonial dance around the Ka'ba at Mecca. This has to be done with a certain ritual-step which is described as resembling dragging the feet in deep sand." He proceeds to compare the similar ' limping about the altar ' in the present passage. General reference may be made to W. O. E. Oesterley, *The Sacred Dance* (1923). **27.** *And it was at noon that Elijah mocked them, and said : Cry with a loud voice, for he is God !* The sequence of the following clauses reads practically the same in EVV, *e.g.*, JV: *either he is musing, or he is gone aside, or he is on a journey, or peradventure he sleepeth, and must be awaked*. The ascription to the deity of musing is rather absurd (an interpretation from the late special meaning of the root used of religious ' study ' of the Scriptures) ; rather, *he has some business or conversation*. The item, *he is gone aside*, has been best explained by Rashi (and so Thenius) as a euphemism, *i.e.*, to relieve himself (*cf.* Germ. ' Abort '), and this interpretation is reinforced for Rashi by his addition to the next clause, *he has a journey on hand*, *i.e.*, ' to the privy.' See Notes at length. Finally the ' waking up ' of the deity is illustrated by an Ugaritic text (Virolleaud, *Syria*, 1929, pl. lxii), in which after each one of a series of choral stanzas and following a god's name occurs the choric " he has waked up " (*hū 'ār*) ; see Montgomery *JAOS* 55 (1935), 89 ff. Elijah's satire in a nut-shell is the raciest comment ever made on Pagan mythology. **28.** A stage in the Baal-ritual is enacted at noon : *They cut themselves after their manner with knives and lances, until the blood gushed out upon them*. This bloody rite in extreme cases of propitiation of a deity is frequently referred to in the O.T. : Hos. 7^{14} (with correction of 𝕳), Mic. 4^{14} (?), Jer. 16^6, 41^5 (a case of actual practice of the rite by Jeremiah's co-religionists), 47^5 (the rite ascribed also to Philistia) ; the custom is proscribed by the Law (Dt. 14^1, Lev. 19^{28}). A close territorial parallel to the present scene is that described by Lucian as practised by the Syrian Galli of his day: "these gash their arms and turn their backs to be lashed" (*De Dea Syra*, 50). For such widespread rites in antiquity see Poole, *ad loc.*, W. R. Smith, *Rel. of the Semites*, 303 ; Dhorme, *L'Evolution religieuse d'Israël*, 1, 259 ff. The 'flowing of the blood upon them' was of the essence of the rite. **29.** In the third act, *at the passing of noon they prophesied.* The verb can only be paraphrased in Christian language, which confines 'prophecy' to the higher levels of revelation ; it might be translated colloquially with semantic right, *they enthused* ; *cf.* Moffatt, 'raved,' Chic. B., 'worked themselves into a prophetic frenzy.' The action was that of 'the raving dervish' (Šanda), *cf.* 1 Sam. $10^{10\text{ff.}}$, etc. For these prophets see further Comm. at end of the ch. They prophesied *until the offering of the* [EVV+*evening*] *oblation* [with RVV ; Heb. *minḥāh*] : there are in the Law two oblations, Ex. $29^{38\text{ff.}}$, Num. $28^{3\text{ff.}}$, one in the morning, and one 'between the evenings,' which peculiar phrase has given much room for argument, as in the Mishnic *Pesaḥim*, v, 1. The morning oblation is referred to in II. 3^{20} (the phrase as here). The second oblation was in the afternoon after three o'clock, and was the chief daily service for the people, so according to Josephus, *Ant.*, xiv, 4, 3, 'about the ninth hour,' so corresponding with Acts 3^1, timing the visit of Peter and John to the temple for prayer. *Cf.* Hamburger, *RE* 'Minchagebet,' Gunkel *Einl. in die Psalmen*, 177. This afternoon *minḥāh* was the chief public service in early Semitic custom, preserved in the Muslim service of the *'aṣr*, celebrated about the same hour ; *cf.* Ezr. $9^{4\text{ff.}}$, Dan. 6^{11}, 9^{21} (see Montgomery, *ad locos*). There is no reason to suppose here a reflection from Jerusalemite practice or later Law. Also in II. 16^{15} in Ahaz's reign there is recorded the royal prescription for 'the morning burnt offering and the evening oblation' ; see the extensive discussion in Nowack, *Arch.*, 2, 221, n. 1. *And there was no voice, and none to answer, and no attention !*—a rhetorical pyramiding of the earlier phrase, v.[26].

VV.[30-35]. Elijah rebuilds the altar of YHWH, sets upon it the wood and the dismembered bullock, and orders all to be doused with water three times, in addition to filling the surrounding trench with water. These details indicate the current knowledge of hocus-pocus practised in producing sacred fire. The only considerable insertion in the text of the whole story is detected by many commentators in the reference to the *twelve stones*, with which the altar was built, *according to the number of the tribes of the sons of Jacob, to whom came the word of YHWH : Thy name shall be called Israel*. The reference to the twelve tribes appears to belong to later schematic history, and late seems to be the reference to the renaming of Jacob, citing P in Gen. 35^{10} (but *cf.* J in Gen. $32^{28f.}$), repeated formulistically at II. 17^{34}. Further, v.^{30b}, *and he restored the ruined altar of YHWH*, appears to render unnecessary v.^{32a}, *and he built the stones into an altar in the name of YHWH*. These grounds have induced some critics, *e.g.*, Kamphausen, Kittel, Benzinger, Skinner, Eissfeldt to regard vv.$^{31-32a}$ as an intrusion, a position denied however by Burney, Šanda. The classical reminiscence of the twelve tribes and the naming of Israel may well be of late origin. But it may be suggested that these vv. (which provoked the Gr. translators to considerable changes) include early variant notions as to the altar. The one (v.^{30b}) was of an altar of YHWH's rebuilt, after presumed destruction by Jezebel's fanaticism (*cf.* 19^{10}) ; however not a single tradition points to any such occupation of Carmel, and a striking point of the story is that Elijah chose Baal's own ground to defy him. The other line of narrative (v.^{32a}) makes Elijah build a new altar, and so the original sequence may have been : (v.^{31}) *And Elijah took stones*, (v.^{32}) *and he built the stones into an altar in the name of YHWH*, the final phrase ' in YHWH's name ' (omitted by some Gr. texts) phrasing the benediction of the new altar. **32***b*. *And he made a trench according to the capacity of two seahs of seed*. The figure has aroused unsettled dispute. Rashi found a rectangle, 100×50 cubits, like the court of the tabernacle (Ex. $38^{9ff.}$). Early commentators (see Poole), and so Šanda, made the item refer to the capacity of the trench for holding so much seed, but the quantum=*ca.* 26 litres, is too small. Bähr, Klostermann think of the ' well-known measure ' of a double seah fixing the depth and breadth of the trench—a reasonable suggestion. Thenius, followed by Kittel, Benzinger, Skinner, compares the Mishnic term בית סאה (*e.g.*, *Shebiʻith*, iii, 2) used for the extent of land to be planted with a seah, *i.e.*, 1568 sq. metres (see Benzinger, *ad loc.*, and in

RPTK 1, 136), and so Kimchi, ' according to standard size ' ; but two such plots would make an absurdly large territory. The twelve jars full of water (v.³⁴) would seem to be an ample statement of the amount used. Similar expansion of the story appears in v.³⁵ with a duplicate : *The water ran about the altar*, and, *he filled the trench with water*. **36. 37.** Elijah prays for a sign that *to-day it may be known that thou art God in Israel*, and with variant, *that thou, Y*HWH*, art the Deity*. There is no reason to abbreviate the prayer with 𝔊ᴸ, followed by Benzinger ; liturgical language is diffuse. YHWH is addressed as *God of Abraham, Isaac and Israel* (so the title in 1 Ch. 29¹⁸, 2 Ch. 30⁶), varying from Ex. 3⁶, etc. : ' God of A., I., and Jacob.' V.³⁷ᵇ offers a *crux interpretum* : EVV, *for thou didst turn their heart back again*, but RVV mng., JV . . . *their heart backward*. The latter interpretation is the true one, *it is thou* (emphatic pron. in Heb.), who didst so affect them, *i.e.*, the divine Providence, not the heathen Baal who was the cause of the people's backsliding, all *ad majorem gloriam Dei*, as in ' the hardening of the heart of the people ' in Egypt, and the temptations in the desert. Such is Rashi's interpretation : " Thou gavest them place to depart from thee, and in thy hand it is to establish their heart toward thee." Kimchi, following Saadia, took the opposite interpretation : " Their heart, which was backward, thou wilt turn back." Such also was Lucian's interpretation, and this appears to be the prevailing exegesis, *e.g.*, of Kittel, Šanda, Eissfeldt, but not of Skinner. However not only is the past tense of the Heb. verb against this interpretation, but also the adverb *backward*, occurring at Gen. 9²³, 1 Sam. 4¹⁸, 2 Ki. 20¹⁰ᶠ·, Is. 38⁸, is always used in that sense, never as ' back again.' **38.** *And the fire of Y*HWH* fell, and consumed the holocaust and the wood and the stones and the dust, licking up the water*. The ' fire of YHWH ' appears at Num. 11¹ᶠ·, the ' fire of God ' at II. 1¹²ᶠᶠ· ; there is no reason to adopt, with Thenius, *al.*, the expansion (*cf.* Gen. 19²⁴) of the Grr., ' fire from the Lord (=𝔗) from heaven.' *The stones and the dust*—quite *de trop* !—is best explained by Clericus (cited by Keil), " redegit in calcem." **39.** At sight of the miracle the people *fell on their faces* ; *cf.* the fuller formula in Neh. 8⁶, " they bowed . . . and worshipped YHWH with their faces to the ground." This rite is the same as the Muslim *sajdah* (see Hughes, *Dict. of Islam*, *s.v.* ' Prayer '), accompanying the cry, ' Allah akbar.' And such a confession is attributed to the people here : Y*HWH*, *He is the God*, Y*HWH*, *He is the God*. For the people He was the God as against the defeated rival Baal ; only subsequently does the expression become absolute as of the sole Deity, as in Solomon's prayer (8^{60}) and in Islamic ' Allah.' **40.** Elijah promptly orders the arrest of the Baal prophets, and as leader in the bloody scene, he *brought them down to the Wady Kishon, and slaughtered them there*—down in the valley away from the sacred hill, and where flowing water might wash away the blood. For the ugly sequel, if authentic, the history of religion and politics down to our own day is sad apology.

VV.$^{41-46}$. Elijah's triumph. **41-42**a. Elijah courteously bids his monarch to refresh himself ; there is no longer need of abstinence, for *there is the sound of the roar* [EVV *abundance*] *of the rain*. **42**b-**44**a. Elijah's vigil for the rain. *Elijah went up to the top of Carmel*, his servant ' going up ' to a higher point (by implication) for his lookout. Elijah *bowed over to the ground and put his face between his knees :* Keil gives reference to travellers' notes recording a similar attitude used by modern dervishes ; the attitude implies ecstatic absorption, the subject sees nothing, another must be his eyes. **43-44**a. He commands his servant (who appears again, 19^3) *to look toward the sea* ; he reports, *There is nothing*. *And he said : Go again seven times*. *And it was at the seventh time that he* (the servant) *said : Behold, there is a little cloud like a man's palm coming up out of the sea*. The OGrr. have expanded the curtness of the story, followed by some modern critics, but without textual reason. *Seven times* means a total of seven times altogether. **44**b-**46**. Elijah sends word to the king to hasten home before the coming storm to Jezreel, and he himself serves as his outrunner. The instruction to the servant to *go up* to Ahab is geographically difficult ; was it a verb of courtesy ? **45.** The introductory adverbial phrase, rendered by EVV with ' in a little while,' means *moment by moment* (*the heavens grew dark*). For Jezreel and its royal estate see Comm., 21^1. The distance of the drive is variously estimated by Skinner at 17/18 miles, a long chariot-drive indeed at end of the day. **46.** The running of Elijah before the royal chariot was in truth a gymnastic feat, and is attributed to divine impulse: *the hand of YHWH was upon* him (*cf.* II. 3^{15}, Eze. 1^3, etc.). It was not impossible for such a son of the desert; it is reported that Arab runners in the desert can cover 100 miles in less than two days (P. W. Harrison, *The Arab at Home*, 1924, p. 2). For the 'girding of the loins,' *cf.* Dalman, *A. u. S.*, 5, 236 f., and for the ' running at the wheel of one's lord ' as a proud duty the 8th-century Aram. inscription of Bar-Rkb. The datum can hardly be fiction, for a later age would not have made Elijah outrunner (*cf.* 1^5) of the wicked Ahab. Elijah assumes this office of herald because he had to all appearance won the king and all the people over to the cause of the nation's God—a proud moment, to be followed by bitter disappointment.

ADDITIONAL NOTE TO CH. 18

For the above remarkable story, in addition to literature cited in n. 1 to introduction to cc. 17–19, reference is to be made to L. B. Paton, ' Baal,' etc., *ERE*; R. H. Kennett, *O.T. Essays* (1928), ch. 4, ' Altar Fire '; Alt, ' Das Gottesurteil,' in the G. Beer *Festschrift* (1935), pp. 1 ff.; Frazer, *The Golden Bough*, 1, ch. 5, on ' Magic Control of Weather and Rain '; R. Patai, ' The Control of Rain in Anc. Palestine,' *HUCA* 14 (1939), 251 ff., esp. pp. 254 ff.; Eissfeldt, ' Ba'alšamēm u. Yahwe,' *ZAW* 56 (1939), 1 ff. And finally there is to be listed a monograph by R. de Vaux in the *Bulletin du Musée de Beyrouth*, 5 (1944), 7–20, ' Les prophètes de Baal sur le Mont Carmel.' This gives an admirable study of the Pagan rites presented in the present story with full documentation from all sources. There is to be noted a plate presenting a bas-relief in the Musée des Thermes in Rome, illustrating an orgy of ritual dancing (to cite the author) " qui tourne en dérision une cérémonie isiaque "—a striking parallel indeed to Elijah's sarcasm.

The marvel of the kindling of Elijah's sacrifice has provoked natural discussion. Hitzig (*Gesch. Israels*, 1, 176) suggested the use of nearby naphtha deposits (a geological absurdity); with this suggestion is to be compared the story in 2 Mac. $1^{29ff.}$. The annual rekindling of the Holy Fire in the Church of the Holy Sepulchre in Jerusalem is a survival of ancient ritual magic. Kennett suggests (pp. 103 ff.) Elijah's use of a naphtha supply and a mirror reflecting the sun's rays, adding that " we need not suppose that Elijah would have been very scrupulous," although he would have " sincerely believed " that such a fire came from heaven. Such rationalizing would preserve the historicity of the story at cost of its morality. Indeed the item of the water-pouring upon the altar contradicts such ritual humbug, doubtless well known in his day. Again an explanation of the lavish water-pouring is presented by Patai in a fully documented essay on ancient weather-control, rites, etc., *e.g.*, the water-pouring at the Sukkoth feast. *Cf.* Mowinckel, *Psalmen-Studien* 2 (1922), 100 ff., citing P. Volz, *Das Neujahrsfest Jahwes*, 31, for the suggestion. But this comparison simply makes of Elijah a superstitious parallel to the Baal prophets, while it does not account for what happened. The ritual water-pouring was never applied to altar and sacrifice. The story is naturally told—a stroke of lightning, ' *the* fire of YHWH ' (*cf.* Gen. 19^{24}, etc.), followed by a great storm, which Elijah anxiously expected. The story—*n.b.* its sequel with Elijah ' running before Ahab ' to his palace—is hardly pure invention, as with Meyer (*Sb.*, Berlin, 1930, 76), who regards this narrative, plus $19^{15\text{ff.}}$, as a legendary reflection of the story of Elisha's anointing of Jehu and the latter's massacres—a strained explanation indeed ! The present writer agrees with F. James, *Personalities of the O.T.*, 174 : " Legend has been busy with the story but through its obscurities we can still discern the fact that some test whereby decision was to be made was agreed upon and successfully made." The cause of YHWH as God of Israel triumphed politically over his rival, the Baal of the Heavens.

As for the latter deity the study by Eissfeldt, cited above, with analysis of all the material, Biblical and archæological, offers most welcome illumination. The foreign deity in the story is to be distinguished, as ' the Baal,' from the many local Baals (there were " gods many and lords many," as Paul says, 1 Cor. 8^5), and is to be identified with the well-known Baal-of-the-Heavens (*cf.* II. 23^5). In him was concentrated in Syrian lands the Semitic urge towards monism, if not monotheism.[1] Under Jezebel's fanatical patronage the Heavenly Baal was brought into conflict with Israel's sole Deity ; doubtless the practical monotheism of the latter religion intensified the monistic tendency of the religion of ' the Baal.' The result was for the first time in history a fanatical contest in the name of monotheism. Israel could put up with local Baals, as the Church has done with worship of saints ; but there can be but one supreme Deity. Jezebel's faction went logically to the root of the matter in attempting to exterminate YHWH's devotees, as did Elijah in the destruction of the Baal's prophets. In formal politics the victory was won by Elijah ; the foreign Baal, if not the Baals, was ousted with popular acclaim.

The ancient native Baal prophets have both Biblical and archæological light thrown upon them. The prophesying of those guilds appears in Jer. 2^8, $23^{13,\,25\text{ff.}}$. The earliest known example of such phenomena is noted in the Wen-Amon papyrus (*ca.* 1100 B.C.), whose author describes a similar occurrence at Byblos, where at a sacrifice

---

[1] *Cf.* F. Baethgen, *Der Gott Israels u. die Götter des Heidentums* (1888), esp. pp. 253 ff. ; H. Seyrig, ' Le culte de Bêl et de Baalshamin,' *Syria*, 1933, 238 ff. ; Montg., ' The Highest, Heaven,' etc., *HTR* 31 (1938), 143 ff. There is also to be noted Albright's discussion in *ARI* 156 f.

performed by the ocal prince to obtain an oracle, " the god seized one of his noble youths, making him frenzied " (Breasted, *ARE* 4, 278 ff., Gressmann, *ATB* 2, 71 ff., Barton, *AB* 449 ff.). For Lucian's day we have his lively description of the prophesying at Syrian Hierapolis (*De Dea Syra*, 36, Garstang's tr.) : : " These (the oracles) speak not, save by the mouth of priests and prophets ; this one is moved by its own impulse, and carries out the divining process to the very end " ; the account proceeds with the description of the agitation and sweating of the prophet. We know furthermore from the Aramaic inscription of Zakar king of Hamath (towards 800 B.C.) that the Heavenly Baal had such prophets ; Baal-of-the-Heavens was the king's deity, who encouraged him to victory ' through seers [the same word as in Heb.] and prognosticators [lit., calculators] ' (col. 1, line 12). Indeed the vigour of such enthusiasts may have stimulated the remarkable expansion of the Israelite Nebi'im of this age.

1. ויהי ימים : for the sing. verb see Note, 11³ ; 2 MSS deR., ויהי מימים, *cf.* 𝕿, and so Then., *al.* (*cf. BH*) would read ; Grr., " and it came to pass after many days " ; St. would read מקץ ימים ; Eissf. sugg. ויחי, connecting with the prev. v., " und er (das Kind) lebte noch lange."—**3.** עבריהו : *cf.* עֶבֶד אֱדֹם, and the many such name formations in Phœn. (Harris, *Gram.*, 128 ff.), and in S. Arab. (*NPS* 1, 240 ff.).—**4.** מאה : Grr.+' men.'—חמשים : 13 MSS deR., +חמשים, 1 MS Ken., 'בח=Grr., κατα πεντηκοντα=𝕿 𝕾 ; the correction appears necessary.—במערה : ' in the cave-complex,' *cf.* 19⁹, and see Abel, *GP* 1, 438, n. 1, for similar use of the Arab. sing. in Palestine.—וכלכלם : Burn. well sugg. iterative use of the pf. ; most would correct to ויכלכלם, in accord with v.¹³.—**5.** לך : Grr.+ διελθωμεν ; this addition, with Then. *al.*, to be accepted ; read with Orlinsky, *JBL* 59 (1940), 515 ff., לכה ונעברה.—כל *bis* : Grr. om. 1º, OGrr. om. 2º, Jos. ignores both ; but royal orders were extravagantly phrased.—לוא נכרית מהבהמה ; for Heb. variants of 'מהב see Ginsb. ; the nominal phrase is partitive. The rdgs. in 𝕲 (correct B† σκηνων to κτηνων) and 𝕲ᴸ have suggested various emendations, especially in view of the odd use of the Hif. verb, *e.g.*, by Wellh. (*Comp.*, 279), rdg. 'לא תכרת ממנו מהב, followed by many ; but St. wisely stands by 𝔅.—**6.** הארץ : Grr., 𝕾ᴴ, ' the road,' an easement. —לבדו 1º : 𝕲ᴸ (and B) om., as though then the king would be unaccompanied, to which St. unjustifiably consents, and so *BH*. The interpolated μονος in v.⁷ of OGrr. is actual corrective gloss to v.⁶.—**7.** ויכרהו : OGrr., κ. εσπευσεν, suggesting to Then., *al.* (*cf. BH*) the correction וימהר ; but the translators did not allow the point of ' recognition.'—האתה זה : also v.¹⁷ ; see BDB 261, GB 193.—**10.** ממלכה : prob., as distinguished from גוי, in the Phœn. sense of ' royalty '>' king.'—ואמרו—והשביע : protasis and apodosis ; *cf.* Dr., *Tenses*, §143. For השביע Grr., ενεπρησεν, prob. corruption of ενεπλησεν=השביע (Klost.).—ימצאכה : potential ; *cf.* Dr., §37, p. 42.—**11.** הנה אליהו : Gr. texts (B N *al.*) om., 𝕾ᴴ⁎.—

12. "רוּחַ : masc. as at II. 2¹⁶ ; see Comm. there.—על אשר : א' in original sense of 'place.'—ולא ימצאך : 𝕲 (B N al.) om., 𝕊ᴴ ⁛. St. approves the elision, but why?—**16.** וילך : Grr. pref. " and he ran," accepted by Then., St., al., as=וירץ ; but such haste of locomotion was hardly germane to a king.—**18.** י' מצות : Grr., ' the Lord your God ' ; 'מ is generally condemned as late, e.g., by St., Šanda, BH.—**19.** ונביאי האשרה וג' : rejected by most critics since Wellh. as gloss ; n.b. omission of את ; Grr., exc. MS i, interpolated the clause also in v.²².—**20.** בני : Grr. om. ; some 25 MSS גבול, 4 MSS גבול בני : see deR.—הנביאים : 5 MSS deR. pref. כל=Grr., 𝕊ᴴ.—**21.** כל העם : 𝕲 παντας, as though for כלהם ; but cf. v.²⁴.—פסחים על שתי הסעפים : Grr., 𝔙 tr. the verb with 'to go lame,' 𝕿 𝕊 with 'to be divided.' The same verb, as 'to hop, leap,' appears in v.²⁶ for the ritualistic dance of the Baal prophets, and the Grr. adopt this sense for the foll. words, ' on both *poplites*.' Hence combining these elements Cheyne (EB 1000), Benz. interpret the verb here as at v.²⁶, making Elijah refer sarcastically in advance to that rite. But the verb is used in different conjugations, Ḳal and Piel, in the two vv., and so with distinct mngs. As for the noun, which many still find obscure (e.g., Kit., St.), its root has the sense of 'forking,' as of twigs, and it produced an adj., sē'ēp̱, 'double-, doubtful-minded' (Ps. 119¹¹³), cf. δίψυχος in James 1⁸.—אתו : 2 MSS, 𝕲 om.—**22.** העם : 16 MSS deR. pref. כל.—**23.** האחד 2⁰ : cf. the usage in 12²⁹ ; Grr., ' the other,' and so EVV tr.—ונתתי על העצים : OGrr. om. (𝕊ᴴ ⁛), which St. approves ; but the threefold operation of the two parties is nicely balanced.—**24.** אלהיכם : B al as pl., but at v.²⁵ as sing.—יהוה : most Grr.+' my God.'—ויען : MSS ויענו=Grrr., exc. 𝕲ᴸ.—**25.** הבעל : Grr., τ. αισχυνης, exc. MS i, τ. Βααλ.—**26.** [לחם] נתן [אשר] : read as passive, נִתַּן (so 𝕊 EVV tr.), as St. suggests ; interpreted as active, OGrr. omitted as contradicting v.²³.—מהבקר ועד הצהרים : 𝕲ᴸ om.— as exaggerative?—הבעל עננו : Grr. (exc. 44), " hear us, Baal, hear us," modelled after Elijah's prayer, v.³⁷.—ויפסחו על המזבח : Grr., κ. διετρεχον επι τ. θυσιαστηριου ; 𝕿 " raved upon . . ." ; 𝕊 " laboured at . . ." ; 𝔙 " transiliebantque altare," cf. 𝔙 Ex. 12¹³, " transibo vos " ; the Piel is denominative for some ritual custom, a dance, skipping. The prep. is to be understood as ' by, at.'—עשה :=𝕿 ; other VSS as pl., EVV as passive ; but read עשו with 22 MSS and Sebîr (Ginsb.).—**27.** אליהו : Grr. (exc. 44, 71)+ ' the Thesbite ' ; the same plus in Grr. at v.²⁹.—כי אלהים הוא : 𝕲ᴸ 𝕮 om., to avoid such a confession ; 𝕿 renders the noun with דחלא, ' fear.'—שיח : the root is used of mental concern, then of study of Scripture (Ps. 119¹⁵, etc.). VSS vary : Grr., ἀδολεσχία, ' talk, conversation ' (cf. II. 9¹¹), and so Aq., ὁμιλία=𝕿 שועי, ' conversation ' ; cf. 𝔙 ' loquitur,' and similarly Rashi, Kimchi ; 𝕊ᴴ ' business ' ; 𝕊 ' thought.'—שיג : root identical with סוג, ' to turn aside,' used here euphemistically ; 𝔙 ' in diversorio '=' in an inn,' or the like ; cf. Rashi, combining the two verbs as of

'business,' and translating לו ודרך below as of absence ' in a privy '
(בית כסא). Klost., Burn., St., *BH* regard וכי שיג as duplicate to
כי שיח, and find the Gr. χρηματίζει translating foll. כי דרך לו;
but the interpretation of Aq., 𝔖^H with "he is giving a revelation," proves the contrary, as E. Nestle has argued (*ZAW* 23
[1903], 338 f.), adducing the parallel of χρηματίζειν=שאג, Jer. 25³⁰,
of Yhwh ' thundering.'—כי דרך לו: represented in Gr. tradition
only by gloss from Sym. in 𝔖^H.—**29.** The Grr. are most variant
from 𝔐 and among themselves in this v. 𝔊 (B *al.*) exchanges
the first two sentences, adds an address to the prophets bidding
them to depart, and so " I will make my holocaust," and with
note of their departure, then omitting the *finale*, " there was
no voice," etc.; 𝔊^L Hex. (A N) supply κ. ουκ ην φωνη, 5 MSS
add κ. ουκ ην ακροασις. The plus was accepted by Then., Grätz;
but see Burn., St. at length.—עד לעלות המנחה: for this combination of preps. see Dr., *Int.*, 538, and Burn., *ad loc.*—**30.** כל: Grr.
om.; *cf.* v.²².—"וירפא את מובח: OGrr. transfer to after first sentence in v.³².—**31.** יעקב: 8 MSS deR., ישראל=A 𝔖^H.—**32.** ויבנה:
for the uncontracted form see Note, 10²⁹.—"בשם: 𝔊^L om., 𝔖^H ※,
unnecessarily deleted by St.—תעלה: Grr., θαλασσαν (=𝔖^H), exc.
𝔊^L, θααλα, and so respectively at v.³⁸; the latter is the original
OGr., with Rahlfs, *SS* 3, 285; later scribes turned it into θάλασσα,
with reminiscence of the 'sea' in the temple; Lucifer correctly,
'foveam.'—**33.** העצים 1⁰: OGrr.+" upon the altar that he made "
—superfluous !—(העצים) על: 𝔊 ℭ om.; then OGrr., ℭ contain an
addition.—**34.** ארבעה: 𝔊^L ' two.'—ועל העצים: 𝔊+" and they did so,"
which St., Šanda, *BH* regard as original—again unnecessary.—
35. מלא: orig. 𝔊 επλησεν, largely corrupted to the pl. (B A *al.*).—
36. ויהי בעלות המנחה: OGrr. om., as contradicting the time given
above, v.²⁹, or because there was no regular *minḥāh* on Carmel ?—
המנחה: A το υδωρ, error for τ. δωρου.—ויגש אליהו הנביא: Grr., 𝔖^H
have replaced with " and E. called to heaven "; the Heb.
verb is used in ritualistic sense, and the Grr. may have avoided
the notion that E. was serving as priest. 1 MS and Grr. om. ' the
prophet,' which is not used elsewhere as title of Elijah, although
he was ' a prophet,' v.²².—In the Grr. v.³⁶ has been contaminated
from v.³⁷.—ובדבריך: many MSS, Ι_Γr. correctly the sing.=VSS;
cf. Note, 3¹².—כל: 2 MSS, Grr. (exc. 𝔊^L), 𝔖^H om.—**37.** 𝔊^L om.
v.ᵃ to avoid duplication of v.³⁶.—הסבת: for the divine *sibbah* see
12¹⁵.—אחרנית: 𝔊^L οπισω σου, an exegetical aid.—**38.** " the stones
and the dust ": OGrr. transfer to end of the v.; the original
may have been a gloss entered at different places (St.).—**39.** וירא
כל העם ויפלו: OGrr., " and fell all the people "=𝔖^H; ' seeing '
of the marvel omitted for religious reasons ?—so St.—ויאמרו: Grr.
+' Amen,' with reminiscence of Neh. 8⁶, a parallel incident.—
40. להם: Grr., 𝔖^H=לעם; *cf.* v.²¹.—**41.** המון: Grr., ποδων; ℭ 𝔖
correctly ' noise,' and so comm.; *cf.* Poole, AV^mg; modern trr.
generally follow 𝔙, ' sonus multae pluviae.'—**42.** ראש: A (=𝔖^H)

alone of the Grr. renders; Jos. has; it was omitted on the ground that the servant 'went up,' *i.e.*, to the top.—ויגהר: the verb, also at II. 4³⁴, ³⁵, is unique; see Note on latter passage.—**43.** *Ad fin.* OGrr.+" and the servant returned seven times "; to this B pref. " turn back seven times, and return seven times," and 𝔊ᴸ replaces the second command with " and look seven times " —these variations significant of the easy handling of this ch. by the Grr.—**44.** עלה מים : B A N v αναγουσα υδωρ (=𝔖ᴴ), reading the verb as active and the noun-complex as מָיִם ; *al.*+απο θαλασσης =ℭ 𝔏 ; the doublet is thus ancient.—עלה אמר אל אחאב ; for Lagarde's mistaken Lucianic text here see Rahlfs, *SS* 3, 27.—אסר : VSS, modern trr. naturally add 'thy chariot.'—**45.** עד כה ועד כה : 𝔗 paraphrases, " while he was harnessing "; 𝔙 " cumque se verteret huc atque illuc."—וירכב : Grr., κ. εκλαιεν (B† κ. εκλαεν) =𝔖ᴴ, apparently misreading as though ויבך, then assuming Elijah as subject, and transposing 'Ahab' as subj. of the foll. verb.— **46.** היתה : B† ℭ om.—[אליהו] אל : read על ; *cf.* II. 3¹⁵.—יזרעאלה : the Grr. have many variants for the place-name; B *al.*, Ισραηλ, and so regularly below (*cf.* 21¹), the form reduced from Ιεσδραηλ ; *cf.* MS u, Ιεσδραελ ; 𝔊ᴸ correctly Ιεζραηλ ; A Ιεζαβελ (!).

19$^{1-18}$. Elijah's flight and despair; the divine revelation on Horeb, and fresh commissions. Elijah has celebrated his God's triumph, but now Jezebel takes her revenge. **1. 2.** The statement that *Ahab told Jezebel all that Elijah had done*, etc., is an intimate touch. The queen, woman-like, acts imperiously, sending a message to Elijah that she has put herself under oath to make his *life like the life of one* of those prophets, and so she has sworn by *Gods*. For the intensity of such an oath see Comm. 18$^{8-15}$. **3.** And Elijah *was afraid* [so with MSS, Grr., 𝔙; 𝔙 *saw*], and he fled to *Beer-sheba of Judah* on the southern border of the Sown, merely a stage in his flight, for he was going into No Man's Land. Having left his servant behind (**4**) *he went a day's journey in the steppe. And he came and sat down under a juniper tree:* so EVV after 𝔙 ; the plant is a broom-tree (so JV), *genista rætam.* *Cf.* Robinson's comment in his diary at Beer-sheba : " Elijah sat down under a shrub of Retem, just as our Arabs sat down under it every day and night " (*BR* 1, 302). And he prayed for death, the common lot of all. **5.** There *he lay down and slept ⌈under a juniper-tree⌉* [see Note]. *And lo, one* (om. *an angel*, with Grr.) *touching him*, and he heard the bidding, *Arise and eat.* **6.** *He looked*, and saw a miraculously prepared breakfast ; *cf.* the miraculous feedings in ch. 17. **7.** He fell asleep again, to be wakened by the now recognizable *Angel of* Yhwh (the antique phrase for the apparition of Deity, peculiar to J in the Pentateuch), summoning him to eat again, *because the journey is too much for thee.* **8.** *And so in the strength of that food he went for forty days and forty nights to the Mount of God, Horeb.* Šanda calculates this distance *via* Akaba as about 480 km., and so the daily travel at 12 km.; rather, with Kittel, the item is proof how little the Northern narrator knew of that territory. Horeb is predominantly the name for the mount of revelation in the Pentateuchal sources E (Northern) and D (*cf.* 8[9]), but Sinai in J and P; in the Northern Song of Deborah the revelation occurred in Seir-Edom (Jud. 5[4]; ' That is Sinai,' v.[5] is a gloss); and in the Blessing of Moses (Dt. 33) Sinai-Seir-Paran is the location. Accordingly the northern traditions vary. This objective of Elijah is the same as that in the history of Moses (Ex. 3[1]), with here also a corresponding theophany. **9a.** The lodging in *a cave* is another correspondent, *i.e.*, with ' the hole in the rock,' out of which Moses saw ' the back ' of Yhwh (Ex. 33[21ff.]); but there is no verbal identity between the two descriptions. **9b-11a,** *And the word of* Yhwh *came to him, and said to him : What doest thou here, Elijah?* There follows Elijah's despairing response, as again in v.[14], and then the divine command : *And he said : Go forth, and stand in the mount before* Yhwh. V.[11a] contradicts v.[13], and a[11] that precededs, from v.[9b] and on, is duplicate, to vv.[13, 14]. Hence modern critics in general (*e.g.*, Wellhausen, *Comp.*, 230, Stade, Benzinger, Šanda, Skinner) rightly agree that the whole passage is secondary. The command, " to stand in the mount before Yhwh " may have been modelled after the Mosaic tradition (Ex. 19[20], etc.), and the mysterious scene presented below is summed up here in the more commonplace statement that *the word of* Yhwh *came to him.* **11b-13.** *And lo!* Yhwh *was passing by. And a great wind and strong, rending mountains and breaking rocks before* [*in the presence of,* or, *in advance of*?] Yhwh : Yhwh *was not in the wind. And after the wind an earthquake :* Yhwh *was not in the earthquake. And after the earthquake a fire :* Yhwh *was not in the fire.* Contrast the fiery phenomena which otherwise attended Elijah's career (1S[38]. II. 1[10ff.], 2[11]). *And after the fire a sound*

[Heb. *voice*] *of a light whisper*. So with Burney's excellent rendering, although the translation of AV, *a still small voice*, remains classical. Contrast of this saying of enduring religious import with the materials of other theophanies (*e.g.*, Ex. 19[18ff.]) is naturally pressed by commentators; but it is to be borne in mind that in such physical manifestations there is generally the subtle distinction between ' the Face,' ' Glory,' ' Name,' ' Word,' of the Deity, and his *persona propria*. The marvel is that here in a legend about an early Northern man of God the spiritual nature of God and of his self-revelation to man is for the first time expressed in historical narrative. V.[13] is of equally delicate character: *When Elijah heard, he wrapped his face in his mantle, and he went out and stood in the opening of the cave*. A striking historical parallel to this scene is the call of Mohammad, who received his first visions in a cave in the mountain of Hira, and who enveloped himself in his cloak upon the revelation; see Surah, 73, 1; 74, 1, and W. Muir, *Life of Mohammad*, vol. 1 (rev. ed., 1923), 49 f. *Cf.* K. Ahrens, *Muhammed als Religionsstifter* (1935), 36 f., *e.g.*, " das Einwickeln gehörte also offenbar auch zu den Gebräuchen der altarabischen Mantik." The zephyr-like whisper fascinated the prophet, who was terrified by the earlier stupendous phenomena. The inquiry by articulate voice: *What doest thou here, Elijah?*, is personal, rebuking his faintheartedness; life is worth living, for there is more for him to do elsewhere than in the Mount of God. The primitive divine is rebuked even as was the great Jeremiah: " If thou hast run with footmen, and they have wearied thee, then how canst thou contend with horses? " (Jer. 12[5]). A great mission first discovers the man's soul. **14.** Elijah obstinately makes his complaint: *I have been most zealous for* YHWH, *God of Hosts; for the Bnê-Israel have forsaken thee* [with Grr.; 𝔊 *thy covenant;* see Note, v.[10]], *thrown down thy altars, and slain thy prophets with the sword; and I, even I only, am left; and they seek my life to take it away*. With this plaint YHWH is not concerned; he has other errands for him.

VV.[15-18]. This sequel remains a standing puzzle. Elijah did not anoint Hazael and Jehu; it was Elisha whose second sight, when he was in Damascus, suggested to Hazael the murder of his predecessor (II. 8[7ff.]), and who indirectly anointed Jehu ($9^{1\text{ff.}}$). The alleged commission to Elijah appears to be a case of transfer from the Elisha legend. In Jewish tradition Elijah is the one perfect man, to whom forsooth all credit should be given. Šanda has attempted a rewriting of the vv. to this effect, but he recognizes that it may be a 'venturesome' attempt. Many scholars (most recently Eissfeldt, pp. 328 f.) would find a lacuna between vv.$^{18, 19}$. The initial command, *Go, return on thy way to the steppe of Damascus* (a unique geographical designation), is balanced by Elisha's visit to that city (II. $8^{7\text{ff.}}$); is there indirect implication that Elijah there anointed Hazael in anticipation of Elisha's second sight? The climactic, *him that escapeth from Hazael's sword shall Jehu slay, and him that escapeth from Jehu's sword shall Elisha slay* (v.^{17}) appears incongruous in the connexion. With avoidance of this long complicated passage v.^{19} makes proper connexion with the commands, *Go, return on thy way* (v.^{15}), and *anoint Elisha . . . to be prophet in thy room.* **18.** *Yet will I leave seven thousand in Israel, all the knees that have not bowed unto the Baal, and every mouth that hath not kissed him.* The figure for the remnant may be an authentic note of some census taken of the Zealots. The kissing of the Baal may refer to the wafted kiss of the hand, so certainly at Job $31^{26\text{f.}}$, for Classical references to which ritual see Poole; or to actual osculation of the image or symbol, *cf.* those 'kissing calves' Hos. 13^2. The obligatory kissing of the Stone in the Ka'bah at Mecca preserves this ancient Semitic rite.

VV.$^{19-21}$. The call of Elisha. **19.** *And he went thence* (for the indefinite reference see above) *and came upon Elisha ben Shaphat; and he was plowing with twelve yoke of oxen in front of him, and he with the twelfth.* Elisha evidently belonged to a family of competence, with twelve teams of oxen and drivers to assist him in the ploughing. For the scene see H. Guthe, *MNDPV* 1905, pt. 1, 57, continuing earlier discussion, to the effect that the teams of oxen were attached to as many separate ploughs, and that fields of such capacity were quite possible; in some operations a row when ploughed and seeded is at once filled in by another plough working alongside; he himself had seen seven ploughs so working in a field. *Cf.* the five yoke of oxen, Luke 14^{19}. For illustration of the Babylonian and Egyptian ploughs see Benzinger, *Arch.*, 143. Elijah does not anoint Elisha, as expected from v.[16], but consecrates him by *casting his mantle upon him*. Eissfeldt (p. 329) finds no contradiction here with the earlier command, which was used ' im übertragenen Sinne.' The particular word here for mantle (also above, v.[13]) etymologically and generally means a robe of state (*e.g.*, for a king, Jon. 3[6]), and is used of the official dress of prophets, so again of Elijah's mantle in II. 2, as also that of deceiving prophets (Zec. 13[4]). According to II. 1[8] this mantle was made of hair. Investiture with sacred garments still remains part of the ordination ritual in the Church. But the present story parallels, indeed conflicts with II. 2, which tells of Elijah's parting legacy to Elisha. **20.** Elisha realized a commission that would separate him from his parents, and asked that he might *kiss* them in farewell. Elijah's response, *Go back (again)* [EVV], *for what have I done to thee ?*, has puzzled comm. Šanda devotes nearly a page to the v. But the inquiry is simplest taken as an expression of mystery, exposition of which is reserved for the future ; on his part Elisha is moved to recognize the call, the inspiration coming from the investiture. **21.** The sacrificial meal on the two oxen, boiled in antique fashion on the spot, partaken of by *the people*, the assembled neighbours, is paralleled by similar extemporized sacrifices, *e.g.*, 1 Sam. 6[14], 2 Sam. 24[22ff.]. After this ceremony Elisha *arose and went after Elijah, and ministered to him*. According to 18[43f.] Elijah had a ' boy ' ; but Elisha's personal service was part of his discipline in his new vocation. Elisha does not appear again until II. 2[1], when he and his chief are at Gilgal. Likewise Moses had his ' minister,' Joshua (Ex. 24[13]). It may be said that this story casts authentic light upon the order of prophets.

1. ואת כל אשר : 1 MS om. ; Grr., $\mathfrak{S}^H$ ignore את כל, an emendation generally accepted ; but the phrase=Engl. ' all how ' ; *cf.* את אשר, 8[31], II. 8[12] = ' how ' ; see Ew., *Syntax*, §333.—כל־ 3[0] : 4 MSS Ken.' deR. om.=OGrr. ; St., *BH* delete, but omission may have been due to indefinite sense of ' the prophets,' to which 2 Gr. MSS add ' of Baal '=$\mathfrak{C}$.—**2.** מלאך : OGrr. om., Jos. ' messengers ' ; it is not necessary (St.).—לאמר : Grr. (*cf.* $\mathfrak{S}^H$) +ει συ ει Ηλειου και εγω ($\mathfrak{G}^L$+ειμι) Ιεξεβελ, *i.e.*, אם אתה אליהו ואני איובל : the addition accepted by Then., Klost. (with further willful amendment), Burn., Gunkel, and by *BH* as probable ; but St.'s caution is to be noted:

" it is difficult to understand how it could have been omitted in 𝔋." However it is a fine and unique psychological note.—יעשון : 24 MSS deR.+לי=VSS (*cf.* 2²³) ; the same variation in MSS and VSS in 1 Sam. 14⁴⁴ ; the plus generally accepted since Then. (*BH* as ' probable ') ; but note St.'s remark that it is inconceivable that early copyists should have omitted the reference to Jezebel herself.—יוספון, יעשון : *cf.* the variant in 20¹⁰. The pl., with the subj. ' gods ' appears in all VSS exc. Gr. B, 𝕰 𝕴 ; it is to the point here in the pagan's mouth, despite St. The pl. is indeed used with monotheistic אלהים (GK §145, i).—**3.** וירא : 6 MSS deR., וירא, and others with Ḳr. וירא=Grr., 𝔖ᴴ 𝔖 𝔙 and a MS of 𝕮, a correction to be accepted.—[נשׁו] אל : MSS ᵒʳ על (Ginsb.), and so in the same phrase, Gen. 19¹⁷.—אשר ליהודה : for the Gr. texts see Rahlfs, *SS* 3, 243.—**4.** רחם : Grr., 𝔖ᴴ offer vocalization as in Arab. *ratam*.—אחת : Ḳr., also MSS, אחד, as in v.⁵, where *vice versa* MSS have אחת ; the variation of genders is a case of ' double reading ' ; for many instances of similar variation see Féghali, *Du genre grammatical*, 66 ff.—נפשי : Grr.+' from me '=1 MS ממני.—**5.** תחת רתם אחד : evidently a gloss ; the Gr., ' there under a bush,' is secondary, as the variant translation of the noun shows (Šanda).—מלאך : Grr. (not Aq., Sym.) om., expressing the subj. with τις ; the mystery is heightened by the indefinite ' one touching ' ; in v.⁷ Elijah recognizes who the subject was. St. takes a contrary view here.—**6.** מראשתיו : locative, as elsewhere ; for form see BL, Index, *s.v.*, צפחת, ענת : the words at 17¹². ¹³.—רצפים : heated stones for cooking ; the word also at Is. 6⁶ ; Grr. ὀλυρείτης (ὄλυρα, a kind of grain) =𝔖ᴴ 𝔖 ; 𝕮 חררא מעפפא, ' a rolled-up cake ' ; 𝔙 ' panis.'—**8.** ויקם=Grr., but 𝔖ᵁ·✕·—הר האלהים חרב : OGrr. om. the second noun, which St. regards as secondary ; but the Grr. also om. the word in the same phrase at Ex. 3¹—for Sion was the Mount of God !—המערה : for the definite noun *cf.* 18⁴.—**9.** לו : 4 MSS Ken. om.=OGrr. ; *cf.* v.¹³, where however 6 MSS add לו to ויאמר.—**10.** עזבו בריתך : Grr., 𝔖ᵈ as עזבוּ, which must be original ; the same correction to be made in v.¹⁴ with the Grr., although there the secondary duplicate ' thy covenant ' has entered into many texts (B *al.*) ; *cf.* intrusion of מצות in 18¹⁸.—VV.¹⁰· ¹⁴· ¹⁸ are cited in Rom. 11³· ⁴ ; see Int., §11, *c*.—**11.** צא : Grr.+' tomorrow,' the addition due to the Gr. tr. of the foll. ppls. as future verbs, and reminiscent of Ex. 34².—רוח גדולה וחזק : for economy's sake the second adj. lapses into the masc. ; for similar cases see GK §132, d, Burn. ; there is no reason, with St., to fault the clause. For the masc. of originally fem. רוח see Note, 22²¹.—**12.** קול דממה דקה : Grr., φωνη αυρας λεπτης ; 𝔙 ' sibilus auræ tenuis.' *Cf.* Job 4¹⁶ דממה וקול ; in Ps. 107²⁹ 'ד=' breeze.' In the Talmud דמם (also דום) is used of whispering, particularly evil whispering ; see G. V. Schick, *The Stems Dum and Damam in Hebrew* (Johns Hopkins Univ. Thesis, Lpzg., 1913). T. H. Robinson accepts the variant mng. of the root, and translates the passage with " after the fire, hark ! a fine silence " (*HI* 306, n. 1).—**13.** פתה : locative ; 𝔊 υπο, rdg. תחת=Hex. ; 𝔊ᴸ improves with prep. παρα.—**14.** עובו בריתך : see above, v.¹⁰.—**15.** כדרכה ומשק : for like pointing in construct relation *cf.* a case in Josh. 18¹² (Ginsb.), and see Ew., *Lehrb.*, §216, b. ' Desert of Damascus ' is an odd enough phrase ; may it be translated with ' by the desert to Damascus ' ?—' the desert ' being used of Transjordan, as at Mt. 15³³. 𝔊 has " and come to the desert of D., and come and anoint," which has suggested that ' desert of D.' is secondary, with duplication of ' come ' ; hence St. elides ; Šanda suggests that each of the words is a gloss, the first to לדרכך, the second to באת. But rewriting is fairly impossible. —חזאל : for the name see Note, II. 8⁸.—**16.** יהוא : see Note, II. 9². —נמשי : נמש on a Samarian ostracon (*IAE* 47).—אלישע : the name on a Samarian ostracon and seal (*ib.*, 200).—מאבל מחולה : B† inserts after χρισεις ; for the place see Comm. 4¹².—**18.** והשארתי :=𝔊ᴸ κ. καταλειψω ; MS *i*, κ. κατελιπον=Rom. 11⁴ ; *al.*, κ. καταλειψεις= 𝔖ᴴ (as though פ-, *BH* as ' possibly correct ').—כרעו : Grr., ωκλασαν (' bent '), exc. 𝔊ᴸ εκαμψαν=Rom.—לבעל : B *al.*, τω B., 𝔊ᴸ τῃ B. (but αυτον below)=Rom.—נשק לו : Grr., 𝔖ᴴ, " worshipped him," 𝔙 " adored him, kissing the hand."—**19.** חרש : Grr.+' with oxen,' explicitly.—בשנים העשר : for cardinal in place of lacking ordinal see GK §134, o.—אליהו : Gr. MSS om. by haplog. with אליו ; similarly 2 Heb. MSS om. אליו.—אליו 1⁰ : " (crossed over) to him," and so it can be understood with Kit., Šanda ; St. demands עליו " (passed) by him," which would express well the rapidity of the scene.—אליו 2⁰ ; read עליו with 6 MSS Ken.—**20.** אֶשָּׁקָה *BH*, אִ֫קָּה, Bär, Ginsb. : see Bär's note and GK §10, h.—ולאמי : B A *al.*, ℭ om., 𝔖ᴴ ⁖ ; St. arbitrarily elides ; Jos. for the phrase, " take leave of his parents," evading the delicate sentiment.—לך שוב : 1 MS om. לך, and so OGrr. texts, ℭ ; 1 MS om. שוב ; the omissions show early perplexity. The form expected is שוב לך ; but the simple explanation is to understand the impvs. separately : " Go ! Turn back ! " Benz., followed by Haupt, interprets with " Go (and then) come back " ; but this ignores the following repellent query.—כי מה : 𝔊 𝔊ᴴ οτι=𝔖ᴴ ; 𝔊ᴸ τι ; these by abbreviation of original οτι τι.—**21.** ויזבחו : for the use of the verb for profane slaughterings see GB *s.v.*—הבשר : Grr., 𝔖ᴴ om. ; a gloss to define the acc. pl. in בשלם, the sing. being expected after ויזבחו ; Rashi, Kimchi discuss the phrase ; *cf.* EVV.

Ch. 20. Two successful, divinely supported enterprises of Ahab against Aram, and the ominous sequel of the second. *Cf. Ant.*, viii, 14. This chapter with its sequel in 22¹⁻³⁸ stands singularly alone in style and novelty of contents ; it is written, as Skinner remarks, " from a political rather than a religious standpoint, and exhibiting the character and policy of Ahab in a much more favourable light than is the case in ch.

xvii–xix or xxi." Robinson assumes as the source of the cc. an original 'Acts of Ahab' (*Int.*, 97 f.). The stories are told in most graphic, almost journalistic style, and their data appear to be closely contemporaneous. In three sections, vv.$^{13-15.\ 22}$, v.^{28}, vv.$^{35-43}$, a 'prophet' or 'man of God' appears. These are adjudged to be intrusions by many critics; however those prophets are stoutly nationalistic, not anti-*régime*, like Elijah, Micaiah (ch. 22). For criticism reference may be made to Wellhausen, *Comp.*, 282 f., Kittel, pp. 162 ff. (with notation of linguistic and phraseological peculiarities, pp. 163, 170), Eissfeldt, *Einl.*, 329 f. The two stories, ignoring Elijah and Elisha, bear witness to a wealth of contemporary saga. The Greek translators reversed the order of cc. 20 and 21 (the Hexapla restoring the Hebrew order), and this change has been accepted by many critics, *e.g.*, Benzinger, Kittel, Sanda, Landersdorfer (not by Stade, Eissfeldt). But all presumption is against Greek rearrangements in general. In either case the end of Ahab (ch. 22) is prefaced by a prophetic doom ($20^{35ff.}$, $21^{17ff.}$), and the former with its personal reference, 'thy life for his life,' may have appeared to the translators as the more appropriate introduction to the final tragedy.

Historically cc. 20 and 22 introduce us at length to the constant wars waged in the middle of the ninth century between Israel, under the capable Omrid dynasty, and Damascus. The king of the latter state was Ben-Hadad I; see below on v.^{34}. But the two enemies came to join forces against the arch-enemy Assyria. In 853 B.C. occurred the famous battle of Karkar, at which 'Ahab the Israelite' was arrayed with Damascus and nine other Syrian states, with their kings named, against Shalmaneser III of Assyria.[1] The chronological relation of this chapter to that date is uncertain. Ahab was fighting Damascus subsequently (ch. 22), losing his life *ca.* 852. For the end of Ben-Hadad and the accession of Hazael see II. $8^{7ff.}$. Altogether the chapter presents a vivid picture of the involved and interminable struggles among the

---

[1] See his Monolith inscr.: *KB* 1, 173; *CP* 296; *ARA* 1, §§610 f.; *ATB* 1, 341; *AB* 458. As Rogers notes, the allied forces consisted of 3940 chariots, 1900 horsemen, 1000 camels, 62,900 infantry; Ahab's contingent being 2000 chariots, 10,000 infantry; it is to be noted that the latter is assigned no cavalry.

Syrian and neighbouring states, a replica of which is given by the somewhat later inscription of Zakar king of La'ash and Hamath (see Comm. on II. 13$^{24, 25}$).[2]

VV.$^{1-12}$. The siege of Samaria. **1.** *And Ben-Hadad king of Aram, having collected all his army, and thirty-two kings with him, and horse and chariotry, went up, and besieged Samaria, and assaulted it.* Stade has attempted revision of the v. on basis of OGr., finding, *inter al.*, the item of the *thirty-two kings* absurd, which figure, it has been suggested, was borrowed from ' the thirty-two charioteers ' of 22^{31}; that figure however is probably secondary, failing in the parallel text of Ch. But the figure has interesting support in a broken inscription from Zenjirli in North Syria with a reference to ' thirty kings ' (Lidzb., *HNE* 444). In addition to the figures for the Syrian states noted above (*cf.* note 2), at a later age Esarhaddon counts twenty-two ' Hittite (*i.e.*, Aramæan) kings,' and Ashurbanipal, ' twenty-two kings of the sea-coast ' (*ARA* 2, §§771, 876). For the period of a thousand years earlier Dossin has collected the names of 32 cities and their kings with whom Zimri-ilim of Mari was in friendly correspondence (*Syria*, 1939, 109). *He assaulted it:* in technical contrast to mere investment; *cf.* 1 Sam. 23^1, Is. 7^1. VV.$^{2-6}$. The successive demands of the Aramæan king upon Ahab provoked inquiry since Wellhausen's correction in v.^{3}, acc. to which Ben-Hadad's terms were: *thy silver and gold are mine, but thy wives and thy goodliest children remain thine* (reading *lk* for *ly*), and then, after Ahab's diplomatic reply, *Milord the king, I and all mine are thine*, Ben-Hadad followed up his first demand with that for *thy wives and children*. To this new outrageous demand Ahab would have objected before his councillors (v.^{7}), his statement being expressed by the Grr. with slight but radical change from 𝔐, as follows: " He has (now)

---

[2] For the political picture of Syrian politics presented in this and the following histories see Alt's monograph on ' Die syrische Staatenwelt vor dem Einbruch der Assyrer,' in particular pp. 245 ff., from which may be cited his observation: " Hingegen wird kaum zu bezweifeln sein, dass der Erzähler die Verhältnisse seiner Zeit richtig wiedergibt, wenn er das Aramäerreich als ein aus vielen Herrschaften zusammengesetztes Gebilde darstellt." Also for the contemporary Syrian history see E. Kraeling, *Aram and Israel*, cc. 9 ff.; Olmstead, *HPS* cc. 25, 26; Meyer, *GA* 2, 2, sect. viii.

sent to me for my wives and children, (while) my silver
and gold I did not (earlier) withhold from him." The corrections of text in vv.[3, 7] have been accepted by some comm.,
e.g., Kittel, Stade. But without correction of the text a
valid contrast appears between the two demands in 𝔥, as
between the surrender of royal possessions and the fresh demand (v.[6]) to *search thy household and thy ministers' households*
and to take away *everything delightsome in thy eyes* (not ' in
their eyes,' with Grr., and so most comm.—the terms are
expressed with malice). Such a search would have involved
not only the pillage but also possession of the city ; and so
Benzinger, Šanda, Eissfeldt hold, while Skinner is undecided
between the two views ; the latter well remarks that such
confusion as there may be is original, the narrator reporting
' at second hand.' The parallel to Ahab's acquiescence to the
first requisition exists in Hezekiah's capitulation, not surrender,
to Sennacherib, with heavy ransom, the tribute including
even Hezekiah's ' daughters, the women of his palace ' (see
Comm. II. 18[15b]). In v.[7] OGrr. add ' and my daughters '
to ' my sons,' suggesting to some the introduction of this
item also in v.[3] ; but 𝔊[L], Jos. properly translate the Heb.
' sons ' with ' children.' **7. 8.** Ahab takes counsel with *all
the elders of the land*, and then *all the elders and all the people*
frame refusal of the arrogant summons. OGrr. omit ' of the
land ' in the first case, and the correction is accepted by some
(*e.g.*, Kittel, Stade, *BH*), but it is a legal expression ; *cf.* the
local ' elders of the city,' 21[8]. ' Elders and people ' corresponds exactly to Roman ' senatus populusque ' ; see at
length Comm., II. 11[14b]. Josephus has a fine sense of the
matter : συναγάγων εἰς ἐκκλησίαν τὸ πλῆθος. **10.** Ben-Hadad's
preposterous boast, with an oath identical with Jezebel's
(19[2]), has been variously interpreted. 𝔊 and Hex. read Heb.
' for handfuls,' by different vocalization, as ' for foxes,' with
the result, not enough earth left for foxes to burrow in (accepted by Klostermann). Josephus thinks of raising a mound
against the city by innumerable handfuls. But the phrase
simply means that the Syrian host can carry away the whole
city by handfuls (so Grotius, *al.*). For a similar ' audax
hyperbole ' (Poole) *cf.* Hushai's talk of pulling any resistant
city into the wady below by ropes (2 Sam. 17[13]). **11.** Ahab's

brave answer in four Hebrew words : *The girder-on boast not like the unloosener !*, was probably proverbial ; for the two verbs *cf.* 1 Sam. 17^{39}, Is. 45^{1}, etc. **12.** The envoys found Ben-Hadad *and the kings in the booths drinking*, carousing in anticipation of victory in the shacks erected for the royal party. The king gives orders for the assault with a single technical verb corresponding to English ' to set on,' which may best be expressed with *Attack !* (and so 1 Sam. 15^{2}, Eze. 23^{24}— EVV ' set yourselves in array '). *And they attacked the city.*

VV.$^{13-21}$. The surprise attack by Israel and the rout of the Syrians. The narrative is critically complicated by the introduction of *a certain prophet* (v.^{13}), reappearing in v.^{22}, and apparently as *the man of God* (v.^{28}), while yet another anonymous prophet appears in v.^{35}, ' some one of the sons of the prophets.' *Cf.* by contrast the naming of otherwise unknown prophets in 22$^{8\text{ff.}}$, Micaiah and Sedekiah. Josephus indeed identifies our prophet here with the former. It is easy to detach these sections as mere Sagas of the Prophets. But in the present case the prophet's word directing attack *by the squires of the commandants of the provinces* is so entangled in the narrative that it is difficult to draw the line between the strata. Stade omits the incident of the prophet, vv.$^{13-15}$, and the subsequent references to ' the squires,' vv.$^{17.\ 19}$, but thus avoids the evident scheme of the story, a surprise by a shock-force, when Ben-Hadad was drinking himself drunk with his allied princes, whereupon came the ensuing rout inflicted by the army of Israel headed by the king. The prophetic story may be expansion of an original narrative in which the decision to send out the flying force of the squires was determined upon. Stade further reduces vv.$^{15\text{ff.}}$ to a minimum of text. Kittel, retaining the references to the squires, preserves most of the narrative, along with excisions and transpositions (following van Doorninck, *Theol. Tijdschrift*, 1895, 576 ff.), *e.g.*, transposing vv.$^{20.\ 21}$. Šanda without further mutilation of the text obtains the most reasonable rearrangement by the sequence vv.$^{19.\ 20a.\ 21.\ 20b}$. Following this order, with slight change, the story from v.^{16} and on may be reconstructed as follows. **16***a*. *And they went out at noon*, *i.e.*, the squires, the army following them subsequently ; the great midday carousal of the enemy gave opportunity for this sally. **16***b*. The passage is doublet of v.¹²ᵃ. **17***a*. *And the squires*, etc., *went out first.* VV.¹⁷ᵇ·¹⁸ tell of the report to Ben-Hadad and his orders for capturing the small band. **19***a*. *And these went out of the city,* with the exegetical addition, *the squires,* **19***b*. *and the army which was after them :* to be elided with Kittel. **20***a. And they slew every one his man.* **21.** *And the king of Israel went out* (*i.e.*, with the army), *and smote the horse and chariotry, smiting the Aramæans with great slaughter* [lit., *smiting*]. **20***b*. *And the Aramæans fled, and Israel pursued them.* But the written story may have been confused *ab origine.* The following details are to be noted. V.¹⁴. In reply to the promise of deliverance the realistic king asks, *By whom ?*, to which inquiry there is the prompt answer : *By the squires of the commandants of the provinces.* The first noun (Heb. primarily *youths,* EVV *young men*) is a technical military term, like the correspondent Arab. *ġulam,* employed in the Arabic chronicles of the Crusades for the young knights ; *cf.* the parallel in Sanskrit *marya* (Albright, *OLz.*, 1931, 220). Such a squire of king Jehoiachin now appears by name on a stamp (see Comm., II. 24⁸). The next nominal phrase occurs also in Est. 1³ ; these officers are military, another term being used for Solomon's administrators (4⁷ᶠᶠ·). The word for *provinces* is of Aramaic origin, occurring elsewhere only in post-Exilic literature, with primary meaning of a judicial district ; we obtain here a glimpse of the government of the Israelite state, with which *cf.* Solomon's districting. The Bnê-Israel numbered 7000, for which figure *cf.* note 1 above. *And Ben-Hadad . . . escaped on a horse with horsemen :* so EVV ; but 𝕳 . . . *and horsemen.* The phrase is complicated by the doubt whether the last noun means ' horsemen ' or ' horses,' and no satisfactory interpretation has been reached here ; see Comm., 1⁵, and Note below. **22.** *At the return* (*cycle*) *of the year : i.e.,* of the military year, the spring equinox, defined in 2 Sam. 11¹ with " at the time when kings go out to battle."

VV.²³⁻³⁴. The campaign of the Syrians in the following year ; their defeat at Aphek ; Ben-Hadad's flight into the fortress ; his surrender and the Israelite king's gallant treatment of him. **23.** *Mountain gods are their gods :* so correctly GV FV AV, *vs.* RVV JV, " their god is a god of the hills." The polytheistic expression has true colour, even as it is put into the mouth of the Philistines (1 Sam. 4⁸), of Goliath (*ib.* 17⁴³), **of Jezebel** (19²). An Akkadian epithet of Syrian Adad is 'mountain god' (*bêl šadî*, see Langdon, *Semitic*, vol. 5 of *Mythology of all Races*, 39) : *cf.* Baal of Hermon, Jud. 3³, Baal of Lebanon, in a Phœnician inscription (*CIS* I, 5). Poole cites a number of references to this distinction of certain deities, *e.g.*, of Pan as ' mountain-walker.' **24.** For this extraordinary attempt at centralization of the Damascene state with the reduction of kings to mere governors (for the imported Akkadian word see 10¹⁵) see Alt, cited above, n. 2. **26.** For the moot question of the location of Aphek see Note. **28.** The v. is a duplicate of v.²³, with as subject *the man of God*, in place of ' a prophet ' ; the phrase may be indefinite, ' the man of God in question.' **29.** *The Bnê-Israel smote* [EVV *slew*] *Aram*, 100,000 *footmen*. The figure is absurd, whether referring to slaughter or defeat (the same verb is used in both mngs. in vv.³⁵, ³⁶), and is doubtless an exaggeration. **30.** Like judgment is to be passed upon the statement concerning the 27,000 *men*, upon whom *the* (city) *wall fell* ; Šanda would support the item, comparing Sennacherib's use of mining machines. Stade well recovers the original wording of the v. : *And the rest fled to Aphek. And Ben-Hadad fled, and came into the citadel* [EVV *city*], (fleeing) *by chamber after chamber* (*cf.* 22²⁵, II. 9²), *i.e.*, the vaults of the fortress. **31. 32.** The counsel and action of surrender are vividly presented. *Ropes on our heads :* more exactly with Josephus, *about our heads*, which, he notes, was ' the ancient manner of supplication among the Syrians.' The suppliant phrase, *thy servant Ben-Hadad*, is countered with knightly courtesy by the Israelite king : *Is he still alive ? He is my brother !* The latter title is used mutually by the kings in the Amarna tablets ; Bar-Rkb of Senjirli speaks of his allies as ' my brothers the kings,' and so Hiram addressed Solomon (9¹³). **33.** *Now the men were watching for an omen* [EVV *sign*] *: i.e.*, all depended upon the patron's answer. *And they were quick, and ⌜caught it up from him⌝* [so Occ. Ḳr., VSS ; *cf.* JV, *vs.* EVV], *and they said, Thy brother Ben-Hadad !* —as with a sigh of relief from the suspense ; the victor had committed himself. The exact mng. of the third verb in the v. is uncertain ; see Note. The royal courtesy is displayed by Ahab's reception of Ben-Hadad into his own chariot. **34.** The respective subjects of the colloquy, Ben-Hadad and Ahab, are parenthetically supplied in the EVV ; Semitic composition was not careful in this respect ; *cf.* the dialogue in II. 10^{15}, in Hos. 14, especially v.^{2}, and frequently in the Pss., as also in the Gospels. The terms proposed by the vanquished king are restoration of captured cities and the right to extraterritorial bazaars in Damascus. For such alien markets *cf.* Neh. 13^{16}, and see G. Boström, *Proverbiastudien* (1935), 91 ff. For the present covenant *cf.* the historical fact of the league of the two kings at the battle of Karkar. The statement about *the cities which my father took from thy father* has been naturally connected with 15$^{18ff.}$, an account of a Ben-Hadad's successful wars against Baasha with names of cities smitten. This would give three kings of that name. But see Comm. on the earlier passage with denial of this interpretation and understanding of the B.-H. there and here as the same person. The term ' father ' is indefinite, as here in the second case ; Baasha was not Ahab's ancestor. However we may not place reliance on quoted sayings in a story ; the story-teller here had doubtless the earlier reference in mind.

VV.$^{35-43}$. The theatrical parable presented by *some one of the sons of the prophets* to the king in condemnation of his leniency to Ben-Hadad. The fate of the first comrade, who did not obey the word of Yhwh, was an omen of the disaster to befall Ahab. **37.** The second comrade obeyed, *smiting and wounding him*, and so the prophet could face the king with his own example as martyr to the word of God. **38.** The prophet *disguised himself with a headband above his eyes* [not *with ashes*, so AV]. VV.$^{39, 40}$ present a lively scene of the back door of ancient military practices. The *talent of silver* is indeed an exaggerated figure, invented for appeal to the king's sympathy for a poor man ; as Šanda notes, in the Assyrian age a slave cost about one mina, with a silver talent at 3000 shekels, and 50 shekels to the mina. The royal answer is judicial : *Just so is thy verdict ; thou hast decided*—there is no appeal ! **41.** The king recognized the unknown as a prophet, when he had uncovered his wrapping, through some professional marking, evidently on the forehead ; for such usage *cf.* Eze. 9^4, ' a *taw* (cross) upon the foreheads ' ; markings on the chest (so the meaning of ' between the hands ') of a prophet are evidenced by Zech. 13⁶; and they might become a sign of the faithful at large, e.g., Is. 44⁵, "and this one shall write in his hand, YHWH's." ³ **42.** The prophet's response is replica of Nathan's "Thou art the man!" (2 Sam. 12⁷). *The man whom I had devoted to destruction:* so or similarly EVV: the Heb. is curt: *the man of my ban.* **43.** The going of the king *to his house* [OGrr. om.] is an intrusion from 21⁴, induced by the same accompanying phrase. He went off *sullen and vexed, and he came to Samaria.* But he laid no hand on the prophet.

Ch. 20. To vv.¹⁰· ¹³· ¹⁵· ¹⁶ belong four fragments of the Cairo Genizah Aquilanic text published by Burkitt and Taylor (see Int., §4, c), and reproduced in *OTG*. They read Αδεδ vs. Αδερ, and give the tetragrammaton in Heb. characters. **1.** הדד : 2 MSS הדר, see Note, 15¹⁸.—מלך ארם : OGrr. om., Jos. has ; acc. to St. ' scribal expansion.' 𝔖 has ' Edom ' throughout the ch., on which Berlinger remarks (*Die Peschitta*) that the change was made out of ' national pride ' ; but Barhebræus recognized that the word meant ' Syria.' —'וג קבץ : Grr. read : " collected all his army and went up and besieged Samaria, and thirty-two kings with him, and (𝔊 +' all ') horse and chariot ; and they went up and besieged Samaria and fought against it." St. argues that Gr. through ' Samaria ' 1⁰ represents the original text, and the rest of 𝔅 is secondary ; rather the duplication in Gr. was made to include the pl. ' they.'— **2.** מלאכים : OGrr. om. ; see Note 19².—העירה : 𝔊ᴸ 𝔖 𝔈 om., and so St. ; but the word means ' the citadel.'—**3.** בניך הטובים : a superlative expression ; 𝔊 om. the adj. as unintelligible, as do modern critics who accept the Gr. variations in this section, e.g., St. (cf. *BH*), replacing the adj. with ובנותיך ; but 𝔊ᴸ correctly tr. with τα τεκνα σου τα καλλιστα.—**5.** כי : read by Grr. as אנכי, a change accepted by Kamp. (with further emendation), St. (cf. *BH*), but unnecessarily, כי having here as often strong affirmative sense = " I did send to thee . . . but."—ובניך : some Grr. om.—**6.** עיניך : Grrr., 𝔖ᴴ 𝔖 𝔜 as ' their eyes ' ; but see Comm.—**7.** וקני הארץ : OGrr., ' the elders.'—ולבני : Grr., 𝔖ᴴ +' and for my daughters,' exc. 𝔊ᴸ, for which see Comm.—ולכספי ולזהבי ולא Grr., 𝔖ᴴ as though לא וכ' וי' ; Aq. = 𝔅.—**8.** כל 1⁰ ; MS 253, Grr. om.—אל תשמע ולוא תאבה : 2 MSS לא for אל ; for variation of negative particles cf. Am. 5⁵.— **9.** לאדני המלך : Grr., 𝔖ᴴ ' your lord,' and OGrr. om. ' the king ' ; the former arbitrary change is accepted by St.—המלאכים : in the Gr. tradition (exc. Hebræus, 𝔈), ' the men,' unnecessarily accepted by St.—**10.** For the adjuration see Note, 19².—יספו: יעשון : (7 MSS יוספון) : cf. 19².—לִשְׁעָלִים : 𝔊ᴸ correctly, τοις δραξι, ' in handfuls,' and

---

³ Mohammed had such a sign in his flesh : " the seal of the prophet stood between his shoulders like the mark of a cupping-glass " ; Ibn Hisham's *Life of the Prophet*, ed. F. Wüstenfeld, 2, 122, 139, 141.

so Jos., κατα δρακα; Aq., τ. λιχασιν, ' in pinchfuls '; 𝕲 𝕲ᴴ τ. αλωπεξιν, ' for foxes ' =𝕾ᴴ, as for לְשֻׁעָלִים.—**11.** דברו: Grr., ικανουσθω (𝕲ᴸ+υμιν), as = רב, ' enough,' as at 19⁴, accepted by St.; for other attempts at revision see St., *BH*; but 𝔥 is unimpeachable, " Speak the proverb for yourselves ! "—חֹגֵר: Grr., ο κυρτος, ' the hump-backed,' with LHeb. חִגֵּר, ' lame,' in mind; then guessing at המפתח with ο ορθος, ' the straight-backed '; the same interpreta-tion in 𝕾ᴴ despite Aq. 𝕿 has a rambling non-literal expansion.— **12.** כשמע: Grr., 𝕾ᴴ by expansion, " when he answered to him this word."—המלכים: Grr. pref. ' all.'—שימו: for the mng. see Comm., corroborated by I. Eitan's study, *A Contribution to Biblical Lexicography* (1924), 60 ff.; *cf.* a rendering in Poole, ' insistite '; Grr. interpret with οικοδομησατε χαρακα; *cf.* 𝕿 𝔙, and Rashi with " set up the instruments of siege."—**13.** אהאב: OGrr., 𝕮 om.— כל: 𝕲 (B v) 𝕷 om.—'וידעת וג: *cf.* v.²⁸, and the current phrase in Eze. and P; Burn. lists the occurrences.—**14.** המדינות: OGrr., τ. χωρων (B *al.* χορων !), Aq., επαρχιων, Hex. (A=𝕾ᴴ) πολεων.— ויאמר 2°: Grr.+' Ahab '; the same plus to ויפקד, v.¹⁵.—**15.** ושלישים 𝕲ᴸ+κ. ο βασιλευς Εξερ μετ αυτου, a gloss to מלך עזר אתו, v.¹⁶, intruded here; see Burkitt, p. 28, Rahlfs, *SS* 3, 285.—[העם] כל: MS 30, OGrr. om. as too small a figure for all Israel.—בני ישראל: Grr. as though בן חיל, induced by v.¹⁹.—' 7000 '; OGrr., ' 60,000 ' (B ' 60 '); for the figure St. *cft.* 19¹⁸.—**16.** ויצאו: MS 70 ויצא= Grr., and 𝕲ᴸ with plus, ' the king with them.'—שתה שכור: *cf.* 16⁹.—בסכות: Grr., ' in Succoth.'—**17.** וישלח בן הדד ויגידו לו: OGrr., " and they sent and reported to the king of Syria "; St. regards the Gr. as substantially the true text; St. would simplify to " and they sent to Ben-Hadad "; Burn. sugg. that the verb is impersonal with the subj. ' erroneously supplied '; but 𝔥 can well stand: the king *sent out* (so excellently EVV) spies.—יצאו: OGrr. om.—**19.** אלה: Grr. (exc. 𝕲ᴸ, ignoring the word), as אל (!), " let them not go out." Kit. attempted an extensive reconstruc-tion, not repeated in *BH*.—**20.** ויכו איש אישו: St. unnecessarily corrected the verb to sing. OGrr. have a plus: κ. εδευτερωσεν εκαστος τον παρ αυτου, in which εδευτερωσεν is a gloss, noting that " he (the scribe) repeated " the phrase εκαστος τον παρ αυτου— an early bit of textual criticism in a confused passage.—וינסו ארם: 2 MSS וינס, and so Gr. B A *al.* as sing. (=*BH*), so as to obtain parallelism with the sing. verb in the following " Israel smote them "; but the pl., as of magnitude, was intentional here, as also at vv.²⁷, ²⁸ with ' Aram ' as subj.; *cf.* GK §145, 2.—מלך: B *al.* erroneously, βασιλεως.—על סום ופרשים: OGrr., ' on a horse-man's horse,' as though for על סום פרש; Hex., ' with some horse-men ' (*cf.* EVV); 𝔙 ' with his horsemen ' (*cf.* EVV); 𝕿 ' and with him two pairs of horsemen.' There is to be accepted W. R. Arnold's judgment, presented above in Note on 1⁵, refusing to פרש the mng. of ' horsemen '; he suggested for this passage the tr., ' because of his chariot- and cavalry-horses '; but rather the phrase was

a commonplace, as we might say, 'on horse and steed.'—21.
וֹיִךְ: Grr. as וַיִּקַּח, favoured by comm. since Then.; but Jos.=𝔐,
which can be supported by rdg. foll. וְהִכָּה as inf. abs., וְהַכֵּה. There
is to be accepted Dr. Orlinsky's personal advice that ἔλαβεν for יךְ
is corruption of ἔβαλεν; for a similar case cf. Josh. 15¹⁶.—22. לִתְשׁוּבַת
הַשָּׁנָה: Jos. makes the season that of spring; see Lexx. for
earlier discussions, and Begrich, *Chronologie*, 88 f., interpreting
the phrase as of the sun's 'turning point.' In 2 Ch. 36¹⁰ it is
used of a fixed calendar date, but here it means the opening of
the military season; see Comm., and cf. Kit.—23. אֱלֹהֵיהֶם: Grr.,
'the God of Israel.'—אִם לֹא: cf. II. 9²⁶, and see Burn., König,
Syntax, §391, m; cf. Engl. 'if we shall not?'='we shall.'—
25. אַתָּה תִמְנֶה: 𝔊 𝔊ᴴ ἀλλάξομεν σοι=𝔖ᴴ; 𝔊ᴸ ἀλλάξον συ (MS b); by
misreading of the verb as תְשַׁנֶּה, through easy confusion of early
ם and ש.—אוֹתָם מֵאִתָּךְ: many MSS Ken., deR. present אַתָּה מֵאִתָּךְ,
readable as מֵאִתָּה (and so 4 MSS Ginsb.), אַתָּה, as is expected; the
incorrect spelling occurs in these North Palestinian narratives,
and occasionally in Jer., Eze.; see Burn. for occurrences. The
confusion already existed in Aq.'s mind and text with his representation of the acc. particle with συν. The prep. אֵת disappeared
in later Heb.; it is absent in the list of prepositions in Albrecht,
Neuhebr. Gramm., §12; the classical prep. was early confused
with the sign of the acc.—מֵאִתָּךְ: B 𝔈 om.—לְקֻלָּם: the suffix in
B v=αυτου.—26. אֲפֵקָה: linguistically to be identified with אָפִיק,
e.g., Job 6¹⁵, 'water-spring, current,' appearing as אפק in Ugaritic
(see Gordon, *Ugar. Handbook*, 3, s.v.). Five Biblical places with
this name are listed by Abel, *GP* 2, 246 f. For earlier review of
identifications see Döller, *GES* 238 ff. The question arises here
as between the place in the entrance to the Valley of Jezreel by
Gilboa (Josh. 12¹⁸)—so e.g., Kit., Šanda, and most recently S.
Tolkowsky, *JPOS* 2 (1922), 145 ff., and identification with Fīḳ,
E of the Lake of Galilee, with the *Onomasticon*, and so Albr.,
JPOS 2 (1922), 184 ff., who speaks of it as "commanding the pass
on the road from Damascus to Jordan, as attested by Yakut";
Abel accepts this identification, which would presume the occupation of Transjordan by Israel. Tolkowsky argued that the earlier
planned strategy (v.²³) to fight in the 'plateau' (but מִישׁוֹר, not
עֵמֶק, which is used of Esdraelon), does not suit such a mountainous
locality; but circumstances may have altered strategy.—27.
הִתְפָּקְדוּ: for the Hothpaal see GK §54, b; Brock., *GVG* 1, 538.—
וְכִלְכְּלוּ: OGrr. om.; St. deletes by reason of the syntax—a weak
enough ground in these narratives; cf. Dr., *Tenses*, §132, with
most of such cases cited from Ki. The mng., 'provisioning,'
appears for the Pilpel (e.g., 4⁷), which however has various significa-
tions, probably through confusion of distinct roots; connexion
of the verb here with Syr. and Arab. root *kyl* would be satisfactory,
'were counted,' as military term.—וַיִּתְהַנּוּ בְּנֵי יִשְׂרָאֵל: OGrr. as
though וַיִּכֹּן יִשְׂרָאֵל, which St., *BH* prefer; but the individualization

is to be preferred, in line with following ' kids.'—חֲשִׂפֵי : Grr., ποιμνια
= other VSS ; for the unique word (cf. lengthy discussion in Poole)
the best explanation comes from Šanda, as from root = Arab.
ḥasafa, ' to drive (sheep) ' ; see Freytag, Lex. ; the root should
then be pointed חֹשְׂפֵי.—**28.** ויאמר 1° : 1 MS om. ; ויאמר 2° : לאמר is
expected, Grr. om. ; 𝔖 𝔙 also simplify here.—אמרו : Grr. as sing. ;
but cf. v.²⁰.—וידעתם : correct with MSS 253, 260 to וידעת = v.¹³,
and so Grr. ; the pl. arose from the constant Ezekelian expression
(Eze. 23⁴⁹, etc.).—**29.** בני ישראל : cf. v.²⁷ ; the Gr. reduction to
' Israel ' is simplification.—' 100,000 ' : 𝔊ᴸ ' 120,000.'—**30.** אל העיר
bis : 1° is unnecessary ; by 2° the citadel is meant ; for St.'s
reduction of the v. see Comm., and for attempted corrections
Haupt, BH.—הדר בחדר : cf. יום ביום, etc. ; Jos., " he was hidden
in an underground house," with which cf. Phœn. use of ח' for the
tomb.—**31.** שמעו . . . ויאמרו : OGrr. as " and he said to his servants,
I know," and inf., ' our lives '—this to make the surrender more
abject.—[ישראל] בית : OGrr. ignore ; but despite St., Šanda, who
would elide it, the phrase is good Aram. designation of a country.—
בראשנו : read pl., בְּרָאשֵׁינוּ (and so it is in v.³²) with 62 MSS = VSS.
For use of the prep. cf. Luke 15²², ' a ring in his finger,' and an
Elephantine Aḥikar papyrus, ' a millstone in his neck ' (col. vi, 2,
Cowley, Aram. Papyri, 214).—**32.** ויאטרו . . . ויבאו : Grr. simplify-
ing, " and they said to the king of Israel."—נפשי : B 𝔈 ' our
life.'—**33.** והאנשים ינחשו : cf. Dr., Tenses, §30 f. ; there is no reason
to read וינחשו with Kit., or to make the verb a perf. with St.,
Šanda. The root of the verb (= לחש, ' to whisper ') is used of
divination, e.g., Num. 23²³, 24¹, where it is repeated in 𝔗 𝔖,
being common in Aram. ; here, as Piel, in receptive sense = Grr.,
οιωνισαντο, 𝔙 " acciperunt pro omine." The sentence is prefaced
with a unique gloss in 𝔖, " and Ben-Hadad was an augur."—
ויחלטו הֲמִמֶּנּוּ Or. rdg. : Occ. rdg. in 10 MSS and Ḳr., מ'/ וַיַחְלְטוּ הֲמִמֶּנּוּ
(see Bär, Ginsb.) = VSS ; EVV follow Or. rdg., JV Occ. rdg. The
root חלט is of obscure mng. ; VSS tr. with ' to snatch, catch.'
Connexion with the root חלי (e.g., Dt. 25¹⁰), as proposed by Gesenius
in his Thesaurus, was first suggested by al-Fasi ; see Skoss's ed.,
vol. 1, 552. Light may be thrown by Arab. ḫalaṭa, ' omnia arcana
alicui dixit ' (Freytag, Lex.). There is no evidence that the verb
is Hifil, vs. Lexx.—ויעלהו : VSS, exc. 𝔈, as pl. verb.—**34.** ויאמר
אליו : 𝔊ᴸ " and said the king of Syria to Ahab."—חוצות : 𝔗 𝔖 𝔄
tr. with the pl. of sūk, ' market.'—ואני בברית אשלחך : GV FV EVV
add in parenthesis ' said Ahab,' and so Poole's authorities demand ; this understanding is supported by the introductory ' and
I (for my part) ' ; cf. the indefiniteness of subject just above ;
unnecessary corrections have been proposed (see St.), e.g., by
Wellh., retaining ואני as emphatic obj., and rdg. תשלחני.—**38.** ויעמד
למלך : EVV correctly, " and waited for the king " ; for this use
of the verb cf. Eccl. 2⁹, " my wisdom waited on me."—[הדרד] אל :
some 35 MSS correctly על.—אָגַּר, also v.⁴¹, † : OGrr., A tr

correctly with τελαμών, ' bandage,' and so 𝕮 ; Aq., Sym., 𝕾ᴴ 𝕾 𝔙 understood as אֵפֶר, ' dust,' and so AV ' ashes.'—**39.** קֶרֶב : Grr., ' army,' rdg. קֶרֶב—סַר : Grr. om., 𝕮 has.—ויבא : B† εξηγαγεν for εισηγ.—**40.** עשה : ' was busy ' of EVV is correct ; there is no reason to change to פנה, as 𝕮 𝕾 suggest (so Klost.), or to שעה with Oort ; see St., Eitan's Note on the verb, *op. cit., sup.*, p. 56, Reider, *Textual Criticism of the O.T.*, 29.—כן משפטך אתה חרצת : the first phrase=Engl. ' just so is thy judgment ' ; for the particle see Haupt's suggestion that it is adjectival, ' just '=Akk. *kēnu*. Grr., ιδου (=הֵן ?) τα ενεδρα παρ εμοι εφονευσας, exc. 𝕲ᴸ, ιδου δικαστης συ εφον. The root, primarily ' to cut ' (and so Grr. here, ' to murder '), came to imply determination, then judicial decision ; *cf.* Dan. 9²⁶, and see Montg., *ad loc.* ; 𝕾 renders with parallel פסק, 𝔙 with ' decrevisti ' (see comm. in Poole).—**41.** מֵעַל : Ḳr., מֵעָל, a unique form.—**42.** מיד : 3 MSS מידי ; Grr., ' out of my (thy) hand,' exegetical ; but 𝔥 (=𝕮 𝕾) is idiomatic ; *cf.* Engl. ' out of hand.'—**43.** [ביתו] על : 9 MSS correctly אל, as at 21⁴.

Ch. 21. The story of Naboth's vineyard : Ahab covets its possession, is sorely vexed at the owner's refusal to sell it at any price ; Jezebel's instigation of a packed communal court, which condemns Naboth to death on a trumped-up charge, with the royal confiscation of the property ; Elijah's denunciation of the king and his family ; Ahab's repentance, which puts off the evil day for him. *Cf. Ant.*, viii, 13, 8.

VV.¹⁻¹⁰. The scene is laid in Jezreel, modern Zerʻîn, in ' the Great Valley ' ; the latter takes its name Esdraelon (*via* the Greek) from the town, which, lying on the ridge between its eastern and western watersheds (see Robinson's description, *BR* 3, 163 ff.), was a point of strategic importance, and also the royal countryside residence. *Cf.* 18⁴⁵, and the tragedy narrated in II. 9¹⁴ff· Here Ahab, who is entitled *king of Samaria* (the exceptional title also in II. 1³), possessed a *palace*, the Hebrew word, *hēkāl*, of Sumerian-Akkadian origin (*ēkallu*), occurring here for the first time in the secular sense, *vs.* that of ' temple ' (*e.g.*, 6³, 1 Sam. 1⁹, etc.). Desiring to enlarge his estate he offers a fair bargain to a local neighbour for purchase of the vineyard. The latter refuses, as it is his *patrimonial inheritance*, and his position was one not only of sentiment but of responsibility to his family ; *cf.* Nowack, *Arch.*, 1, §65, ' Besitzrecht.' Ahab goes home, and acts most peevishly. **5-10.** The queen, his evil genius, acts in a wifely way to comfort her lord ; she replies to his complaint with feminine peremptoriness : *Thou* (Šanda, ' Du bist mir ein feiner König ! '), *now thou hast to exercise royal right over Israel* (in EVV phrased as a question). *Get up, and eat thy meals, and thy heart be happy. I myself will give thee Naboth's vineyard.* Grotius recalls Poppæa's remark to Nero, calling him a ' boy ' : " qui iussis alienis obnoxius, non modo imperii sed libertatis indigeret " (*Tacitus, Ann.*, xiv, 1). In high-handed fashion *she wrote a letter* (sing., not pl.) *in Ahab's name, and sealed it with his seal* (the antique signature), *and sent the letter to the elders and freemen in his city, the fellow-citizens of Naboth.* For the elders *cf.* 20⁸ ; the elders of Jezreel appear again in II. 10¹. The freemen (EVV ' nobles ') occur here for the first time, recurring again in Jer. 27²⁰ ; according to 20⁸ ' the people ' are associated with the elders. For the communal classes presented *cf.* Pedersen, *Israel*, I–II, 34 ff. ; for similar social development in South Arabia see Nielsen, *HAA* 1, 117 ff. As Šanda remarks, royalty may have developed ranks of gentry. In the present case the commune acts as a jury, as over against the usual judicial procedure (Dt. 16¹⁸). The ' proclamation of a fast ' was to be based upon some alleged and accordingly fearful offence against Deity ; *cf.* 1 Sam. 7⁶, 14²⁴ᶠᶠ·. Naboth's presiding (v.¹²) *in the capacity of head of the people* (so 𝔥 exactly) made his alleged sin the more conspicuous. *And set two men, base fellows, to confront him.* Judicial procedure is followed by requirement of two witnesses, as in the Law (Dt. 17⁶, etc). For ' base fellows ' (AV by transliteration, following 𝔙, ' sons of Belial ') see Note. Stade, Šanda regard this item as an intrusion from v.¹³, as hardly possible in the formal document ; but we are not dealing with the original indictment, and in any case the queen's arrogance knew no bounds. The actual indictment of Naboth was, *Thou didst curse God and King* ; 𝔥, followed by Grr., 𝔙, replaced the abhorrent verb (*cf.* Ginsb., *Introduction*, 366 f.) with ' bless ' (*cf.* Job 2⁵, etc.) ; other VSS, modern translations avoid the euphemism. Such a curse of ' God ' or ' prince of the people ' was forbidden in the ancient code (Ex. 22²⁷), and blasphemy of YHWH's name was punishable by death with stoning, according to an illustrative precedent (Lev. 24¹⁰ᶠᶠ·).

VV.¹¹⁻¹⁶. Jezebel's orders are promptly carried out. VV.¹¹· ¹³ᵃ contain repetitive material, and are extensively abbreviated by Grr. and modern critics (see Notes); but the repetitions may be due to legal form (*cf.* the story of Abraham's purchase of a tomb in Gen. 25); for excision of a few words in v.¹³ see Note. For the solemnity of execution by stoning *cf.* Num. 15³²ff·, Dt. 13⁷ff, 17²ff·, Acts 7⁵⁸ff·. **15.** The ' taking possession of Naboth's vineyard ' was an act of royal confiscation, as Grotius holds, *vs.* the opinion of Kimchi and others that Ahab had some collateral right of inheritance; it was against such arbitrary power that the constitutional limitation of the rights of kings was written into the Deuteronomic code (Dt. 17¹⁴ff·). **16.** *Ahab rose up to go down* to Jezreel, *i.e.*, by the descent from Samaria, *to take possession*.

VV.¹⁷⁻²⁰ᵃ. Elijah confronts Ahab with the ironical inquiry: *Hast thou murdered and made seizure as well ?* He proceeds : *In the place where the dogs licked Naboth's blood shall the dogs lick thine own blood.* There is no reason to doubt the originality of this item in the story on the ground that it was not exactly fulfilled in subsequent history. Ahab perished in battle, his body was brought to Samaria, not Jezreel, and there he was buried, and then, by development of the later story from Elijah's present word, " when they washed the chariot (of Ahab) by the pool of Samaria, the dogs licked up his blood " (22³⁷f·). And Jehu interprets the present word as fulfilled in Jezebel's fate (II. 9³⁶f·). It is another question whether by fulfilment of providential prediction or by coincidence Ahab's son was killed in Naboth's vineyard, Jehu recalling a word of YHWH against Ahab, which he construed as fulfilled in the son's fate (*ib.* vv.²¹ff·). In angry terror the king breaks out : *Hast thou found me, my enemy ?* To which Elijah curtly responds : *I have found* (*anglice*, ' I have ').

VV.²⁰ᵇ⁻²⁶. This section is redactorial supplement, based on 14¹⁰f·, 16³· ¹³. If Elijah spoke further, his word has been lost or suppressed in the present text. The anonymously uttered prediction against Jezebel (v.²³) is interdependent with II. 9³⁰⁻³⁷, the curse on Ahab's family is pure repetition, and the further judgment on Ahab (vv.²⁵f·) is equally *de trop*, especially with the condemnation of his *following idols according to all that the Amorites did.* **23.** Read *the field* (*of Jezreel*) with II. 9²⁶, not *the moat* (so JV, other EVV *wall/rampart*), by early error of *ḥl* for *ḥlḳ*.

I. 21^{1-29}

VV.^{27-29}. The literary origin of this section is difficult for decision. Stade makes it a continuation of vv.^{17-20a} ; Kittel so regards v.^{27}, but makes vv.^{26, 28, 29} secondary, thus leaving one fragment hanging in the air. Benzinger considers it all secondary, as an attempt to ameliorate the judgment upon Ahab (v.^{19}), which was fulfilled only in his son, and this position is to be preferred. To be sure, Ahab was not an object of absolute prophetic denunciation (*cf.* cc. 18, 20), while his present crime is attributed to the alien Jezebel's ' instigation ' (v.^{25}). For the use of sackcloth see Dalman, *A. u. S.*, 5, 165, etc. *He went softly :* so EVV ; the adverb proved difficult to the VSS, which omitted it or translated quite variously (see Note), and so modern Versions, *e.g.*, GV " ging jämmerlich einher," FV " il se trainait en marchant " ; the sentence may well be rendered, *he went about depressed* ; see Note.

1. ויהי אחר הדברים האלה כרם היה לנבות : B reduces to the last three words, and reads the first of them as וכרם, and so the other Grr. with the conj. ; this latter change is to be accepted, as the syntax demands for the dependent sentence, ' now N. having a vineyard ' (Dr., *Tenses*, §78). Critics who prefer the rearrangement of cc. 20 and 21, also Burn., accept the shorter text of B ; but this was probably due to the objection that N.'s possession of the field was not ' after these things.' Also Grr. (exc. v.= 𝕮 𝕴) have plus=אחר ['כ].—נבות : Gr. MS e, Ναβουθ ; *al.*, Ναβουθαι (B), and the like. For the name *cf.* S. Arab. names, *NPS* 1, 135, also Noth, *IP* 221, as from Arab. *nabata*, ' to sprout.'—יורעאלי : 𝕲 (B A) Ισραηλειτη ; see at 18^{45}.—ביורעאל אשר : Grr. om., and St. elides ; but the ethnic term did not identify site of property.—היכל : Grr. (exc. 𝕲^L οικω, 2 MSS αγρω), ' threshing-floor,' error of ΝΑΩ>ΑΛΩ, as recognized since Then.—**2.** אם : 3 MSS ואם=Grr. +δε ; *cf.* אם או, v.^6.—**3.** יהוה : Gr. 64, 𝕮, ' the Lord ' ; *al.* Grr., ' My God,' to which 𝕲^L adds ' the Lord.'—**4.** The v. abbreviated in 𝕲 by haplog. with end of v.^3.—ויסב : Grr., κ. συνεκαλυψεν, as though for ויכס, which Kamp., Kit. prefer, but St. rightly rejects ; for the phrase *cf.* II. 20^2, which affected 𝖁 here+' ad parietem.'—**6.** ארבר—ואמר—ויאמר : for the sequence *cf.* Dr., §27 (' cases of exceptional character '), and König, §§158, 366, g (as in lively narrative) ; rather the first two verbs are paired, while the third in normal construction expresses the sequel ; a similar case in vv.^{12, 13}.—כרם : Grr. (exc. 𝕲^L) +' another.'—כרמי : Grr., ' inheritance of my fathers,' from v.^3.—**7.** אתה עתה : *cf.* 12^4, 18^{11, 14} ; it is difficult to decide as among the imperative, interrogative, ironic interpretations.—מלוכה : 𝕲 (B z) βασιλεα, this reduced in some MSS to the vocative, βασιλευ; 𝔊^L 𝔊^H βασιλειαν.—**8.** הספרים=Grr.; Kr. om. ה.—בעירו אשר: OGrr. om.; see *BH* for attempts at simplification; but we have here again legal fulness.—**10.** [בני] בליעל: the interpretation, 'that which profits not' (the phrase='good-for-nothing fellows'), *e.g.*, BDB, König, *Hwb.*, holds its own against divergent explanations, for which see Burn., GB; the interpretation by Cheyne (*EB s.v.*) as 'that which does not come up,' *i.e.*, from hell, is well contradicted by König: the good as well as the bad do not so come up. In the Haupt. Anniv. Vol., pp. 145 f., Albr. *cft.* Akk. *mâr lâ manâma*, 'son of a nobody.'—נגדו: B† om. with what follows through בני בליעל, v.[13], by haplog.; 𝔖^H inserts practically the whole omission as from Theod., indicating an early lacuna; but Lucif., ℭ have the full text.—ברכת: Hex. as 3d pers., 𝔖^H adding 'Naboth' as subj.—**11.** אשר הישבים בעירו: for the rel. phrase *cf.* 12[8]; St. elides as intrusion from v.[9], along with 'הזקנים וג; *cf. BH.*—אליהם . . . כאשר כתוב: 𝔊^L *et al.*, ℭ om., and so St. as repetitive; but the composition is splay.—**12.** והשיבו: another case of 'irregular syntax,' generally corrected by critics; but *cf.* the parallel in v.[6].—**13.** אנשי הבליעל את נבות נגד העם: OGrr., ℭ om.; it is an inserted ungrammatical precision of persons.— **14.** קפל: the Kal appearing in vv.[10, 13]; the present is case of the ancient Kal passive, and is to be added to the cases cited by Bergstr., *HG* 2, §15.—**15.** 𝔊 om. "that he was stoned and is dead," for brevity's sake; but repetition of the awful fact was intentional. —[מת] כי: 9 MSS+אם, and so apparently 𝔗 𝔙 read.—**16a.** Grr. add "and he tore his clothes and put on sackcloth, and it was after this," a wilful insertion from v.[27]; 𝔖^H has the addition without critical note; MS c₂ obelizes.—**18.** 𝔓 'the king of Israel, who is in Samaria'; *cf.* the title, v.[1]; St. elides, but the word of Yhwh would give the formal address.—הִנֵּה: the word may be vocalized הִנֵּה, *cf.* Arab. *'innahū*, and so II. 1[9], 6[13]; however הנה is used absolutely with pl. obj., *e.g.*, II. 6[20, 25].—**19.** [ה]רצחת: 𝔊 ως συ=𝔖^H.—ודברת אליו לאמר 2⁰: Grr. om., replacing with δια τουτο, which correction St. accepts, with insertion of לכן; but the Gr. phrase is abbreviation of the tautologous sentence.—הכלבים: Grr., 'the sows and the dogs' (𝔖^H obelizes the addition), and at end of the v. the Grr. plus (𝔖^H÷), "and the harlots will wash in thy blood"; for these additions see 22[38].—**20.** המצאתני איבי: some MSS of 𝔙 "num invenisti me inimicum tibi?" *i.e.*, as rdg. איבך; this interpretation, accepted by some comm. in Poole, has been approved by Joüon, *Mél.*, 5, 475, on the ground that Ahab was excusing himself as never an enemy to the prophet; but this reading has no textual basis.—**23.** חל=Grr., 'moat'; 𝔖^H '(before) the wall'; 9 MSS חלק (deR., *Supplem.*, 43), as at II. 9[36], which acc. to Rashi is to be understood here, and so the primitive error is to be corrected. G. R. Driver attempts vindication of 𝔓 with a fresh etymology (*JBL* 55 [1936], 109), *cft.* Arab. *ḥaul*, 'around,' *ḥiyāl*, 'in front of.'—**24.** והמת: 20 MSS Ken., deR+לו=Grr.

the plus not in the original passage, 14¹¹, but is indifferent.—
25. רק=Engl. adv. ' just,' Germ. ' gar ' or ' schlechthin ' (Šanda);
Grr. a doublet, πλην ματαιως=רק ריק=𝔊ᴴ.—הִסָּתֵה: root סוּת; הִסְתָּה
is expected; but cf. שִׁתִּי, Ps. 73²⁸, שַׁתָּה, Ps. 90⁸; see GK §73, d;
Bergstr., *HG* 2, §28 f (which authorities do not notice the present
case).—**27.** וישם שק על בשרו ויצום וישכב בשק: the Grr. (which rearrange the order of these items, and add a plus at end of the v.)
tr. the first verb with εζωσατο, the third with περιεβαλετο, which =
ויתכנס in MS Ken. 210, and so al-Fāsī (ed. Skoss, 1, 69) understands
here; for this variation cf. II. 9¹; but for the present expression
see Joel 1¹³.—אט [ויהלך]) : 𝕴 חֵף, ' barefoot '=𝔖 𝔄, cf. Jos., γυμνοις
ποσι (as Thackeray remarks, a case of Targumic influence); 𝔊ᴸ
with inexplicable κ. τ. υιον αυτου; 𝔊ᴴ (A x v) κεκλιμενος, ' bent
down '=𝔖ᴴ as from Aq., Theod.; al. Grr. om. the word; V
' dimisso capite ' : for the sentence Rashi, ' went secretly ' ;
Kimchi, ' went mourning,' and so GV; FV ' dragged himself in
walking '; EVV ' went softly.' See St. together with Haupt's
note in the volume, the latter agreeing with Rashi. P. Wechter
in his study, ' Ibn Barun's Contribution to Comparative Heb.
Philology,' *JAOS* 61 (1941), 172 ff., notes (p. 187) that gram-
marian's translation with the Arabic root *ṭa'ṭa'a,* ' with depressed
head.' Such a mng. appears likely here; Engl. ' depressed ' may
well express the word.—**28.** Grr. have a variant text.—**29.** כי יען
נכנע מפני : OGrr. om. by homoiot. with prec. passage, or as superfluous; similarly some Heb. MSS om. נכנע . . . מלפני.—אבי : Ginsb.
notes MSS with אביא.

22¹⁻³⁸. The history of Micaiah the prophet and the fulfilment
of the doom that he pronounced upon Ahab. || 2 Ch. 18; *cf.
Ant.,* viii, 15, 3-6. Upon renewal of war with Aram Jehoshaphat king of Judah, having been persuaded to enter as Ahab's
ally, requires a divine oracle, ' the word of Yhwh.' Ahab's
prophets, 400 in number, give optimistic augury; but
Jehoshaphat, dissatisfied, asks for a real ' prophet of Yhwh,'
and Ahab, disgruntled, sends for one inimical to him, Micaiah
ben Imlah; meanwhile Sedekiah ben Chenaanah of the former
group accentuates their position with a dramatic action (vv.
⁵⁻¹²). Micaiah, having been fetched, tells Ahab what he wishes
to hear, but, pressed for the truth by the cunning king, he
declares his vision of a scene in heaven and the divine artifice
planned for deceiving Ahab through falsely inspired prophets
(vv.¹³⁻²³). Sedekiah's assault upon Micaiah and the latter's
cryptic response to him are followed by the royal orders for
his strict incarceration (vv.²⁴⁻²⁸). In the ensuing battle at
Ramoth-Gilead Ahab disguises himself in the attempt tc

forestall his fate ; he is mortally wounded by a stray shot, but remains heroically in his chariot until his death at even, whereupon follows the rout of the allies (vv.[29-36]). His body is brought to Samaria for burial, with fulfilment of an earlier word of Elijah as to the obscene end of his blood (vv.[37-38]). The narrative is a literary unit, with the exception of the final scene, v.[38], its forerunner, v.[35b], and a late gloss, v.[28b].

This dramatic story is matched only by that of Elijah's contest with the Baal prophets on Carmel, as rich as that in its detail, but superior in its historical verisimilitude. The appearance of an otherwise unknown Micaiah vouches for the originality of the story, and is evidence of a wider range of literary composition among the sons of the prophets than might have been expected. The satire of the earlier narrative (18[27]) has its complement here in the irony of Micaiah's first response and then in the stark scene of heaven with *the spirit* who volunteered to be *a spirit of falsehood in the mouth of all his* (Ahab's) *prophets*. Grimmer and more primitive as it is, the scene is a true precedent of the visions in Am. 1–2, Is. 6, and warns modern study against finding too sharp a distinction from ' the Writing Prophets.' In his inscrutable way the God of these early prophets is the author of what Gentiles called the Fate of the beliers of Him who rules in human affairs. Josephus (*Ant.*, viii, 15, 6), writing for the Gentiles, well concludes : " With the king's history before our eyes, it behoves us to reflect on the power of Fate (τοῦ χρεών), and see that not even with foreknowledge is it possible to escape it, for it secretly enters the souls of men and flatters them with fair hopes, and by means of these it leads them on to the point where it can overcome them " (tr. of Thackeray-Marcus).

1. *They sat still, i.e.*, at peace (EVV *continued*) *for three years, i.e.*, into *the third year* (v.[2]) ; the narrator dates from the events in ch. 20. This dating, generally accepted by historians as original is provocative of attempts to place these narratives in the international chronology. The battle of Karkar occurred in 854/853 B.C., Ahab's death in 852/851 (the dates of Meyer and Robinson), and there must have been remarkable revolutions in the relations between Israel and

Syria, with Ahab's success over Aram at an earlier date.[1]
2. The alliance of Jehoshaphat with Ahab had been cemented by the marriage of the latter's daughter to the former's son and heir (II. 8[18]); this *rapprochement* between the North and the South was brought about by the Aramæan peril, which had come to life again after the temporary coalition of Syrian states at Karkar. Ramoth-Gilead was the governmental seat of one of Solomon's provinces (4[13]); it has been identified by Dalman with Tell el-Ḥuṣn, SE of Irbid-Arbela (*Pjb.*, 1913, 64; *cf.* Albright, *BASOR* 35 (1929), 11; Abel, *GP* 2, 430); but now for another identification by Glueck see Comm., 4[7ff.], n. 1. **5. 6.** For the consulting of YHWH before battle *cf.* 1 Sam. 23[1ff.], and Zakar of Hamath's consultation of 'seers and astrologers' (Montgomery, *JBL* 28 [1909], 68 f.). The number 400 for the prophets of YHWH assembled appears extravagant, and is suspiciously correspondent to the 450 of Baal prophets and the 400 of Asherah prophets in 18[19]. These prophets are distinctly YHWH's devotees, representing the state religion; according to the sequel of ch. 18 the Baal prophets had been exterminated. **7-9.** Jehoshaphat, dissatisfied (*cf.* Ahab's distrust of Micaiah's oracle) asks for a further oracle: *Is there not here yet another prophet of YHWH?* He may well have been suspicious of the extravagant development of prophecy in the North, unlike the simpler religion of the conservative South; the North was peculiarly exposed to the frenzied religionism of Phœnicia and Syria. In reply Ahab names Micaiah, upon whom he remarks: *I hate him, for he prophesies not good concerning me but evil.* Grotius well compares Agamemnon's word to the seer Colchas (*Il.*, i, 106): μάντι κακῶν, οὔ πώ ποτέ μοι τὸ κρήγυον εἶπας. Jehoshaphat answers deprecatively like a gentleman, but has his way.

---

[1] For more detailed study of the chronology see Šanda (placing the battles of Karkar and Ramoth-Gilead in the spring and autumn of 854 respectively), Kittel, *GI* 2, 253 ff. (suggesting, p. 256, that Shalmaneser was ill-informed of the Israelite king's name), Meyer, *GA* 2, 2, 274 ff., 333 ff.; Robinson, *HI* 1, 292 ff.; and the Chronologies of Begrich, Lewy, Mowinckel. These three vary considerably in dating Ahab's death-year, *i.e.*, respectively at 851, 847, 853 B.C. The study of the chronology of the period in Morgenstern's 'Chronological Data of the Dynasty of Omri,' opens with this v. as basis of discussion. See Bibliography in Int., §16.

10. The dramatic, courtly scene (*cf.* the scene in heaven, *inf.*) plays *in a threshing-floor at the entrance of the gate of Samaria*; the first phrase is absent in the Grr., is much disputed by critics, but it may well have been a local name (*cf.* ' the Haymarket ' in London—possibly read here ' *the* threshing-floor '), and is not to be lightly cancelled ; as Šanda remarks, such an arena was required for the ' cultic-gymnastic ' rites which followed. *With all the prophets prophesying before them :* we may only speculate on the frenzied rites ; *cf.* ch. 18, and Lucian's testimony for a later age (*De Dea Syra*, 36 *seq.*). **11.** Sedekiah's pronouncement is reminiscent of the ancient oracle to Joseph (Dt. 33^{17}). Šanda notes similar ascriptions to Thutmose III and Seti II as ' invincible,' ' a young bullock with horns.' **13. 14.** The marshal who fetches Micaiah is benevolently inclined towards him with politic advice. The prophet's reply (*cf.* Luther's, ' Ich kann nicht anders ') is non-committal. **15.** His oracle to the king betrays itself as dramatic irony : " he made use of mimicry " ; " he did not deceive the bystanders, because even the king was sensible to the ridicule " ; so comm. in Poole. **16.** The king commands that he put aside this by-play. **17.** The prophet recites the vision vouchsafed to him :

I saw all Israel scattered upon the mountains,
As sheep that have no shepherd.

And Y<small>HWH</small> *said :*

These have no master :
Return they each to his home in peace !

The scansion of these originally metrical utterances is uncertain ; Haupt attempts rewriting. **18.** Ahab comments to Jehoshaphat with " I told you so."

VV.$^{19-23}$. The prophet continues with a further vision, now of heaven itself. **19.** *I saw* Y<small>HWH</small> *sitting on his throne, and all the host of heaven standing by him*—an utterance that precedes that of Isaiah's vision (ch. 6). **20.** In the vision Y<small>HWH</small> asks for a volunteer from the host of heaven who will *entice Ahab, that he may go up and fall at Ramoth-Gilead.* Excuse for this divine action cannot be found, with Cornelius à Lapide, in the explanation, "non sunt verba iubentis, sed permittentis," although he and Grotius are correct in comparing the divine 'permission' granted to Satan, e.g., Job 1, Mt. 8$^{28\text{ff.}}$, Jn. 13$^{26\text{ff.}}$, Rev. 20^3. **21.** *And there came forth the spirit, and stood before Y*HWH, *and he said: I will entice him. And Y*HWH *said to him: Wherewith!* **22.** *And he said: I will go forth, and will be a lying spirit in the mouth of all his prophets. And he said: Thou shalt entice, and also prevail. Go forth and do so.* Identification of 'the spirit' (with JV, other EVV 'a spirit') has been much mooted: see especially Kittel, *ad loc.*, and P. Volz, *Der Geist Gottes*, 12, 20, 78, etc. It is the personified spirit of prophecy; *cf.* its action in early story, 1 Sam. 10$^{10\text{ff.}}$, 19$^{23\text{f.}}$. There is also differentiation in 'an evil spirit,' which God sent between Abimelek and the Shechemites (Jud. 9^{23}), more explicitly in another passage, 'an evil divine spirit' (1 Sam. 18^{10}). This phase of the spirit becomes ultimately personified in 'the Satan,' *e.g.*, Job 1 f. Such spirits were primarily amoral in the monotheistic scheme, instruments of the divine will for good or evil. In Is. 11^2 we find the sixfold differentiation of the Spirit of YHWH. **23.** Micaiah comments on the celestial drama: *And now, behold, Y*HWH *hath put a spirit of falsehood in the mouth of all these thy prophets.* The theology is primitive indeed, and has its exact parallel in the opening lines of bk. ii of the *Iliad*, when Zeus proposes to send 'a baleful dream' to Agamemnon to deceive him. Kittel cites a scholion to Sophocles, *Antigone*, 620, expressing the ancient theme of " Quem Deus vult perdere, eum dementat prius." For the much later Second Isaiah YHWH is " Fashioner of light and Creator of darkness, Maker of peace and Creator of evil " (Is. 45^7). Theological criticism may well be temperate. Israel's developing religion faced the dilemma of all monotheism, as between the all-mightiness and the virtue of Deity. Schwally (*ZAW* 1892, 159 ff.) and Stade (*ib.*, 1895, 163 ff.— *cf.* the colour-scheme in *SBOT*) adjudge this scene to be secondary in the composition, Stade comparing Job 1. But the latter scene, the traditional prœmium to a late philosophic drama, is equally primitive and a parallel to our dramatic vision. However 'the spirit' (v.^{21}) is not to be corrected to 'the Satan,' as has been proposed (see Haupt, and *cf.* note in *BH*). The present 'vision' is the most striking example of the genius of the prophets before ' the Writing Prophets ' ; it is closest to Amos of the following century, and presents his and his successors' religious and literary deep-rooted background.

VV.$^{24\text{-}28}$. For the personal assault upon Micaiah by Sedekiah *cf.* the experiences of Jeremiah (*e.g.*, Jer. 37^{15}), of Paul (Acts 23^2), and of Jesus buffeted along with a similar satirical inquiry (Mt. 27$^{26\text{ff.}}$). **24.** The jibing inquiry, *By which way*—or *How* (see Note) *went Y$_{HWH}$'s spirit from me to speak to thee ?*, has its ominous reply from Micaiah ; unlike the parallel doom of the sceptical doubter in II. 7$^{17\text{ff.}}$, the sequel of fulfilment is not given. **25.** The expression of the fugitive's flight *by chamber after chamber* reappears from 20^{30}. **26-28a.** The prisoner is to be treated as a prisoner of state, remitted into the custody of *Amon the governor of the city* (for the office *cf.* Jud. 9^{30}, *inf.* II. 10^1, 23^8, Neh. 7^2) and an otherwise unknown son of Ahab, *Joash* ; he is to be fed with *bread of affliction and water of affliction* (*cf.* Is. 30^{20}), apparently an official term for prison fare. The king's expression, *in peace*, means ' safe and sound.' **28a.** The prophet briefly accepts the challenge. **28b.** *And he said : Hear, ye peoples, all of you :* a gloss, absent in Ch. and in pre-Hex. Greek texts, identifying Micaiah with the canonical Micah : *cf.* Mic. 1^2.

VV.$^{29\text{-}38}$. The battle at Ramoth-Gilead and the end of Ahab. **30.** The purpose of Ahab's disguise was not out of treachery against Jehoshaphat, as has been suggested (*e.g.*, by the Grr. with a slight change of text), but for the avoidance of fate. **31.** The number of captains, *thirty-two*, is absent in Ch., and is an intrusion from 20^1. **32.** *Jehoshaphat cried out, i.e.*, with his battle-cry (so Stade), by which he was distinguished from the Israelite king, not in prayer to God, as Ch. and Grr. glossate. **34.** Ahab was struck by an arrow *between the scale-armour and the breastplate*. Scale-armour, as the Hebrew etymologically means, is known from Egypt of the XIXth Dyn., specimens of which are in the Metropolitan Museum, New York. Very early armour of the kind has been found at Nuzi in N Iraq (*BASOR* 30 [1928], 2 f., with illustration) ; and more recently Schaeffer has reported the discovery of ' pieces of scale-armour ' at Ugarit (*ILN* Jan. 6, 1940, 26). There has been extensive discussion of the relation of the two parts of the armour ; the best explanation remains that of Grotius : " in ea parte ubi lorica cum inferiori armatura connectitur," the scales serving apron-like to cover the mobile upper legs and joints. Ahab orders his charioteer to retire from the battle, but stays on the side-lines, and (**35**a) manfully remains *propped up* in his chariot until evening, when he died. **36.** *And the cry passed through the army at the going down of the sun, to wit: Each to his city and each to his land,* **37**a. [correcting with the Grr.] *for the king is dead! And they came to Samaria.* **37**b. **38.** The royal burial in Samaria was regular, *cf.* 16^{28}, II. 10^{35} ; the statement replaces the formal archival note once preceding v.^{39}. But the further item, *and they washed the chariot by the pool of Samaria, and the dogs licked up his blood, and the harlots washed* (so curtly), *by the word of Y*HWH *that he spoke*, is secondary, to connect with Elijah's prophecy, 21^{19} ; and then v.^{35b} above, introducing the otherwise unimportant theme of Ahab's bloodflow, is equally secondary. There is the added extravagance of the harlots washing themselves, *sc.* in the blood, so absurd that the VSS outside of the Grr. attempted another interpretation, which was accepted by AV, and is given in margin by RVV : *and they washed his armour* ; see Note. Harlots were intruded here by the interpretation of ' the dogs ' as professional male perverts, even as the word is used in Dt. 23^{19}, Rev. 22^{15}, and probably a technical cultic name in Phœnicia (*CIS* I, 86, B 10) ; there may be here reminiscence of obscene praxis. For the probable identification of this *pool of Samaria* see *ZDPV* 50 (1927), 32, and the map in Galling, *BR* 442.

VV.$^{39.\ 40}$. The summary of Ahab's reign, originally the sequel of ch. 16. The phrase, *all that he did*, had doubtless far more significance in Ahab's case than in the current use of the formula. *The ivory house that he built:* cf. Amos 3^{15}, and ' the ivory palaces ' of Ps. 45^9 (but see Gunkel, *ad loc.*, amending to ' ivory instruments ' of music), and Solomon's throne of ivory and gold (10^{18}). This description of the palace, so named because of its ivory ornamentation, panelling, etc., is now fully corroborated by the rich finds of beautiful inlay work in Ahab's palace at Samaria ; see J. W. Crowfoot, *QS* 1932, 132 ff. ; 1933, 7 ff., 130 ff. ; *ILN* Dec. 16 and 23, 1937 ; J. A. Wilson, *AJA* 1938, 333 ff. ; C. de Hertzenfeld, *Syria,*

1938, 345 ff. ; and the sumptuous and comprehensive volume by G. Loud, *The Megiddo Ivories* (1939). These latter are objects of the 13th and 12th centuries, and have their complement in Thutmose III's report of his booty gained at Megiddo, 'three staffs, with human heads, of ivory,' and 'six large divans of ivory and wood' (*ARE* 2, §436). Similar rich finds have been made at an ancient site to the N of Aleppo ; see F. Thureau-Dangin, *Arslan Tash*, 1931, 89 ff. For the abundant Phœnician ivories see Contenau, *La civilisation phénicienne*, 219 ff. ; Otto, *HA* 1, 805 ff. ; R. D. Barnett, 'Phœnician and Syrian Ivory Carving,' *PEQ* 1939, 4 ff., with 11 plates. Also see at large Watzinger, *DP* 1, 112 ff. ; Galling, *BR s.v.* 'Elfenbein.' *Cf.* Comm. on 10$^{18\text{ff.}}$. For *all the cities that he built* is to be compared the contemporary Mesha's list of such constructions ; but for Ahab only the record of the rebuilding of Jericho has survived (16^{34}). A splendid type of tower, semi-circular in form, discovered at Samaria, remains as a sample of royal architecture in the North (*QS* 1934, plates ii, iii).

VV.$^{41\text{-}51}$ (with Heb. prints, JV, following 𝔐 ; other EVV make one v. out of vv.$^{43.\ 44}$). The reign of Jehoshaphat of Judah. ‖ 2 Ch. 17–20 ; *cf. Ant.*, ix, 1–3. Jehoshaphat appears again in II. 3$^{4\text{ff.}}$. **41.** The accession is dated *in the fourth year of Ahab*, but according to v.^{52} Ahab's successor came to the throne in Jehoshaphat's 17th year, while with 16^{29} Ahab reigned 22 years—*i.e.*, a discrepancy of 5. See Note for the problem and the Gr. attempts at correction. Jehoshaphat is the second Judæan king (with Abijam first, but the name in curtailed form) to have a name compounded with the divine element Y$_{\text{HWH}}$, which thereafter appears constant in the Southern dynasty, except for Manasseh and Amon. The element appears for the first time in the Northern royal names with the contemporary sons of Ahab, and continues into the Jehu dynasty. **43.** For Asa's example, which his son followed, see 15$^{11\text{f.}}$. **44.** *However* (even as then) *the high-places were not removed*. The *entente cordiale* with the king of Israel is illustrated in the prophetic story above ; as the present section shows, there was the attempt at a N-S alliance to meet the Aramæan and Assyrian perils from the east. The Israelite king's name is not given, and the v., out of place, is probably dependent upon that prophetic story. This 'peace' was doubtless consummated in the ill-starred matrimonial alliance with the Northern dynasty, Jehoshaphat's son Jehoram marrying Ahab's daughter Athaliah (II. $8^{18,\ 26f.}$, 11). 2 Ch. 18^1 notes here that Jehoshaphat "allied himself in marriage with Ahab," and such an item may once have stood here; the mother's name is ignored in the passage where it should regularly appear (II. 3^1). VV.$^{48-50}$ present another invaluable record of the ancient Red Sea commerce; cf. $9^{26ff.}$ 10^{22}, and see Comm. *ad locos*. The incident occurred in the latter part of the king's reign in connexion with Ahaziah ben Ahab, as he is named in good Semitic fashion. Several corrections of the corrupt passage are required, and have been variously accepted; see Notes for the text. The following revision is presented. **48.** *And there being no king in Edom, a royal lieutenant* (**49**) [with correction of Mas. verse-division, and deletion of *Jehoshaphat*] *made* [see Note] *a Tarshish-ship* [sing. with 𝕲, 𝕳 pl.] *to go to Ophir for gold ; but he did not go, for it was broken* [𝕳 *ships were broken*, with Ḳr. correcting sing. Kt.] *at Esyon-geber.* **50.** *Then said Ahaziah ben Ahab to Jehoshaphat : Let my servants go with thy servants in the ships* [𝕲 *ship*] *; and Jehoshaphat did not agree.* The Northern king with his Phœnician backing might well have provided better ships and sailors ; *cf.* Solomon's dependence upon Hiram of Tyre. But Jehoshaphat feared the intrusion of his Northern neighbours into his own particular littoral. Since the reference to the restoration of the Edomite monarchy in Solomon's day ($11^{14-22,\ 25}$) Edom has not been mentioned in Ki.; but 2 Ch. 20 has a long history of Jehoshaphat's campaign against Ammon, Moab and Mount Seir, and according to 17^{11} the Philistines and the Arabs were tributary to him. See the summaries for Edomite and Moabite history from the archæological point of view by Glueck in *AASOR* 15 (1935), 137 ff.; 18–19 (1939), 242 ff. While the brunt of the war with Aram was borne by Israel, Judah appears to have attacked Aram's avenues towards the Red Sea by an attempted push to the south ; the lieutenant actually constructed on the Gulf of Akabah a ship, which however was immediately wrecked Then the Israelite king's offer of assistance was prudently refused by the Judæan, for the former desired to control the

Trans-Jordan routes, the latter to divert them to Cis-Jordan. This Judæan control of Edom was brief; in the days of the successor Edom was able to re-establish its independence with a king (II. 8²⁰ff.), even as similarly "Moab rebelled against Israel after the death of Ahab" (II. 1¹). For the 'Tarshish ship' see above on 10²², for Esyon-geber on 9²⁶. 𝕲 here read 'Aram' for 'Edom,' this the easier induced by the item of the Tarshish ships; and so Josephus romances (*Ant.*, ix, 1, 4) on the shipping to 'Pontos and the emporia of Thrace.' Still earlier 2 Ch. had these ships made 'to go to Tarshish,' and condemns Jehoshaphat as having wrought wickedly in joining with Ahaziah, the shipwreck being by prophetic word the divine penalty (20³⁵⁻³⁷).

1. וישבו: "they stayed still," as at Jud. 5¹⁷, etc.; there is no reason to change to sing., with Ahab implied as subj., with Grr. (exc. x), 𝔖ᴴ, St.—**3.** הידעתם = "do ye not know?"; see R. Gordis, *AJSL* 49 (1933), 212 ff.—רְבֹּח ג׳: so 𝔊ᴸ, al. Grr. = רָמֹח: see Note, 4¹³.—**4.** ויאמר: Grr. (exc. d 106) + 'the king of Israel' similar expansions below, vv.⁶·⁷·⁸·²⁰·³⁰·³²and *cf.* Ch.—**5.** דרש: Grr. (exc. 𝔊ᴸ), "let us inquire" = v.⁷.—[י׳] דבר: Grr. om.—as unnecessary.—**6.** הנביאים: Grr. pref. 'all.'—ויתן: Grr., διδούς δώσει, as though וְנָתֹן יתן; for original inf. abs. *cf.* II. 3¹⁶.—אדני: *ca.* 29 MSS. 𝕮 יהוה, which is required; the change made to avoid the use of the Name by those prophets; Ch., אלהים.—**7.** עוד: Grr. (exc. a = Sym.), 𝔙 om.; Grr. also om. the word in v.⁸; omission on purpose to avoid classification of true prophets with false (St.).—מאותו: many MSS, edd., מאתו, and so Kt. in v.⁸; read מֵאִתּוֹ; *cf.* Note, 20²⁵.—**8.** מיכיהו: the name might be regarded as of contemporary formation from the Akk., after the form, *mannu-ki-X*, but it occurs earlier in Jud. 17; the name now occurs on a seal, *IAE* 190.—ימלה: 2 MSS (Ginsb.) ימלא = Ch.; the latter a Palm. name.—**9.** סרים: on this official title see Note, II. 18¹⁷.—**10.** 1 MS om. בגרן, and so the Grr., with simplification of מלבשים בגדים to ενοπλοι, 'armed'; Sym., followed by 𝔖ᴴ renders 𝔚; Ch. repeats ישבים before בגרן; 𝔖 tr. בגרן with adj. ברדא, 'bright (clothing)'; for proposed corrections see Burn., St., who most unnecessarily would cancel the word as a dittog.—**12.** ביד המלך: Grr., 'into thy hands also the king of Syria.'—**13.** דברו: Grr. as דִּבְּרוּ (+πάντες), so easing a 'harsh' construction (Burn.); with St. 𝔚 is to be kept supported as it is by the other VSS; טוב is nominal as below.—דבריך: Kr. דְּבָרְךָ = Ch. Kt., 𝕮 𝔖 𝔙; Grr. = Kt.; see Note, 3¹².—**15.** הנלך, נחדל: the royal pl.; Grr. as sing.: Ch. conforms the foll. impvs. to these pls.—**16.** רק: practically a prep., *cf.* Engl. 'but'; 𝔙 'nisi'; 1 MS om. prec. לא = Grr.—**17.** ויאמר: Grr. + 'not so,' introduced from v.¹⁹.—[ההרים] אל: 3

I. 22¹⁻⁵¹   345

MSS על=Ch.=𝕿 𝕾ᴴ (Grr., εν), which is to be accepted.—להם: Ch. להן. the noun צאן is mostly fem.; but here the personal reference may have induced the masc.—לא אדנים לאלה: Grr. misunderstood: 𝕾 𝕾ᴴ ου κυριος τουτοις θεος, cf. 𝕾ᴴ 'the Lord not Lord to them'; 𝕾ᴸ ει (rdg. as לֹא) κυριως ('legally'?) αυτοι προς θεον (as אֱלֹ֫הַּ).—18. יתנבא: Grr.+ουτως, from v.¹².—19. לכן: Grr., ουχ ουτως ουκ εγω, and inf. ουχ ουτως, this as by first rdg. לא אנכי, and then the gloss correction entered twice. לכן is elsewhere taken as לא כן; see Dr. on 1 Sam. 3¹⁴.—יהוה: 𝕾 'the God of Israel,' to avoid vision of Yhwh; cf. the text of Is. 6¹.—20. בְּכֹה bis: Ch. בְּכָה bis; there is no reason, with St., BH, to amend this unique adverbial phrase.—Ad fin. 𝕾ᴸ κ. ειπεν, ου δυνηση, κ. ειπεν, εν σοι: δυνηση from v.²², εν σοι as rdg. בְּכָה; see Rahlfs, SS 1, 80 ff.—21. הרוח: for the gender, masc. here, see Note, II. 2¹⁵.—22. רוח: 6 MSS deR., Ch., לרוח.—24. מאתי לדבר "אי זה עבר רוח י אותך: for אי זה='where' cf. 1 Sam. 9¹⁸, and so 𝕾 here; Ch., 'אי זה הדרך וג (=13¹²), making the phrase more explicit, and so EVV, 'which way.' The composite particle may possibly mean 'how,' cf. the variant mng. of איפה, also Eth. 'efô. 𝕾, ignoring עבר, ποιον πνευμα Κυριου το λαλησαν εν σοι, accepted by Burn. (cf. BH) as=המדבר בך "אי זה רוח י; 𝕾ᴸ π. π. Κ. απεστη απ εμου του λαλησαι εν σοι—these interpreting with 'what sort of a spirit.' 𝕿 tr. with 'at what hour?'=𝔄; 𝔙 tr. the particles with interrogative 'ne.' St. would elide רוח; but no authority appears for correction of this originally ambiguous passage.—אותך: many MSS אתך=Ch.; correct Kr., to אֹתָ֑ךְ.—25. לְהַחֲבֵה: many MSS א—=Ch.—26. קח, השיבהו: Ch., Grr. as pl., but n.b. the sing. verb אמרת, v.²⁷; 𝔙 renders 'הש with 'maneat,' as though from root ישב. The Heb. verb corresponds to the Engl. legal term, 'to remit.'—אמן:=Hex.; Jos., Αχαμων; 𝕾 𝕾ᴸ Εμμηρ, etc., as for אמר (B† Σεμηρ). —שר: B† τ. βασιλεα, al., τ. αρχοντα.—יואש: for the name see Note, II. 12¹.—27. כה אמר המלך: OGrr. om.; but the phrase is legal formula; cf. the similar usage in the Amarna tablets.—זה את: cf. 1 Sam. 21¹⁶, etc.—מים לחץ: for the apposition see Dr., Tenses, §189 (1); 𝕾ᴸ pref. 'let him drink.'—29. מלך יהודה: Grr., exc. e, +'with him,' which seemed necessary after the sing. verb.—30. יהושפט: Grr.+'king of Judah,' and so in v.³².—התחפש ובא: for the inf. abs. without subject see Ewald, Syntax, §217, a, GK §113, dd, note; the subject 'I' is assumed, would be evident in living speech=Germ., " es ist zu verkleiden . . . aber Du——— !" Grr. render with 1st pers., accepted by some critics, e.g., Kit., St., Šanda (cf. BH), rewriting with אתח' ואבא; but the text is to be retained, with Burn., cf. Eissf.—בגדיך: Grr., 'my robes' (not corrected in 𝕾ᴴ), by error of μου for σου, or rather by intention to read in the elements of Ahab's treachery.—32. אך: Grr., φαινεται, as=prep. כ, cf. Syr. 'ak.—ויסרו: Ch., ויסבו, "and they surrounded "—Grr., showing early contamination from Ch.; see St., who retains 𝔐.— Ad fin., 𝕾ᴸ+ κ. Κυριος εσωσεν αυτον; cf. Ch., "and Y. helped him, and God diverted them from them," on the assumption that the king's cry was to God.—**34.** איש: Jos. identifies with 'a royal page of Adad, Amanos by name,' *i.e.*, the Naaman of II. 5, a tradition continued in *Midrash Tehillim* on Ps. 78, and accepted by Rashi.—בין הדבקים ובין השרין: see Comm., and the much vexed discussion in Then., Kit., Burn., Haupt, Šanda. VSS vary : 𝔖 as though 'בין דבקי הש; Grr. tr. 'הד with 'the lung '=𝔙, which gives 'the stomach' for 'הש.—ידך: so after very many MSS Bär. Ginsb.²=𝔏; Mich., Ginsb.¹, ידו Kt., and so 𝔊 as pl.; the pl. in the same phrase, II. 9²³.—**35.** ותעלה המלחמה (Ch., 'ותעל המ): Grr. tr. the verb with ετροπωθη, "was put to flight"; 𝔗 "went up the combatants"; 𝔖 "the battle was stout"; 𝔖ᴴ "the battle was won"; 𝔙 "commissum est prœlium," and in Ch., "finita est pugna" (Joüon, *Mél.*, 5, 476, would accordingly read ותכלה); the meaning is, "the battle went up to its peak," like a flood of waters (*cf.* Burn.).—מעמד: "kept propped up" (Burn.); Ch., מעמיד, which Haupt approves as="he kept, bore up," *cft.* Arab. 'akāma.—'ויומת בערב וג: Ch. עד הערב ויומת; OGrr., "from early to evening, and flowed forth the blood of the wound into the hollow of the chariot, and he died at evening," *i.e.*, properly putting the item of the blood-flow before that of the death; then 𝔊 texts (not 𝔈) add a variant restoring the sequence in 𝔥. There is no reason, *vs. BH*, to alter 𝔥 on basis of these variations. *N.b.* that Ch. om. the item of the blood-flow.—**36.** ויעבר הרנה: Grr., κ. εστη ο στρατοκηρυξ=practically all the other VSS, as though rdg. ויעמד and Kal ppl. of רנה, or Poel ppl. of רנן; but violation of gender-relation is not uncommon in Heb. (see Note, 11³), and in certain conditions is quite regular in Arab.; it is rather absurd to think that there was a formal order of retreat.—ואיש אל ארצו: 8 MSS deR. om. איש, and so 𝔊 𝔊ᴴ.—**37.** ויומת המלך: Grr.=המלך, כי מת, generally accepted by critics since Then. as part of the outcry.—ויבוא: read with Grr. ויבאו; *cf.* 𝔗, "and they brought him"; EVV "and was brought."—**38.** וישטף: impersonal.—והזונות רחצו: Grr. add "the swine [and the dogs]" and "[the harlots washed] in the blood," the latter indeed a necessary plus. Other VSS read 𝔥, but found Aram. זין 'זי in הו', obtaining "and they washed his armour"; see Burn., St.

41-51. This section appears in OGrr. after 16²⁸, where it appears to be in place with the varying chronology (the 11th year of Omri, *vs.* the 4th of Ahab), and is repeated in a fresh translation here *in loco*, but with omission of vv.⁴⁷⁻⁵⁰; a similar repetition appears in 𝔊 in the summary for Joram of Israel *in loco*, II. 3¹⁻³, and as addition to II. 1. See Rahlfs, *SS* 3, 265–7, for a full discussion; he holds that the earlier passage belongs to the original 𝔊 (here cited as 𝔊¹), while the doublet here (𝔊²) is also 'very old,' the Hex. marking merely the missing vv. here with asterisk. The text of 𝔊² agrees with 𝔥 in 'the 4th year of Ahab' as *vs.* 'the 11th year of Omri' in 𝔊¹. Rahlfs, agreeing with Thackeray's

theory of the translation of 2 Ki. by another hand than that for
1 Ki., finds in the duplicate verbal traces of the latter's style
and assigns it to him. 𝕲^L omitted the duplicate here, but made
another attempt at chronology (v.^{52}) in changing the accession-
date, ' the 17th year of Jehoshaphat ' to ' the 24th year.' *In re*
the correctness of the datings in 𝔐, we may start from the identical
datum for the death of Joram b. Ahaziah b. Ahab and of Ahaziah
b. Jehoshaphat (II. 9) ; from the 4th of Ahab's reign of 22 years
(16^{29}, 22^{41}) the round reckoning for the Northern dynasty is
22−4=18+2 (22^{52})+12 (II. 3^1)=32 years, for the Southern
dynasty 25 (22^{42})+8 (II. 8^{17})+1 (8^{26}) =34 years—a close enough
correspondence with the upper figure in view of the uncertainty
of reckoning of initial regnal years (see Int., §16). For the datum
of Ahaziah's accession in Jehoshaphat's 17th year there is the
figuration of 22 years (Ahab's term) minus 4 (date of Jehoshaphat's
accession) =18—again a close approximation. We may well be
sceptical as to the different accession year in 𝕲^1 ; it may be
entirely artificial, invented so as to insert the formal notice of
Jehoshaphat before 22$^{1\text{ff.}}$, where he appears casually as ' king of
Judah.'

42. עוּבָה : generally interpreted as ' abandoned, divorced '
(Noth, *IP* 231), but such indeed a name of ill omen. Sanda
etymologizes from Arab. *'aḏab*, ' sweet,' or *cft.* Heb. עוּב (14^{10}) ;
rather it may be connected with root עוב, Neh. 3^8=Ugaritic *'ḏb*
(Gordon, *Ugar. Handbook*, 3, *s.v.*), *i.e.*, ' prepared ' ; *'ḏbt* is clan
and place name in S. Arab. (*NPS* 2, 307, 356). This name and
the next one are peculiarly corrupted in Gr. B, *cf.* also ℭ.—**43.** כל :
𝕲^1 om., probably because of the reservation in v.^{44}.—לא : MSS
ולא=𝕲^1 𝕾 𝖁, but the asyndeton is idiomatic.—ממנו : Sebir הֵמָּנָּה,
and so some MSS ; for the uncertainty of gender of דרך *cf.* 13^{10}.—
44. סרו : Grr. as active verb, with sing. or pl. subj. ; *cf.* 15^{14}.—
העם : 𝕲^1 om.—**45. 46.** וישלם יהושפט עם מלך ישראל : ויתר דברי יהושפט :
𝕲 by paralepsis due to the recurrence of יהושפט lost the intervening words, and translated the verb with συνέθετο, prefixing it
with *a* to make construction with the foll. clause.—**46.** ואשר נלחם :
𝕲^2 om., 𝕲^1 has ; St. favours the omission.—' (the chronicles of)
the kings of Judah ' : 𝕲^1 B† ' Jehoshaphat.'—**47.** הקדש : collective ; see Note, 14^{24} ; here Hex. (A) του ενδιηλλαγμενου (correct
foll. ουχ to ὅ, with 𝕾^H), *i.e.*, ' the perverted,' paralleled by Paul's
condemnation of women who μετήλλαξαν τ. φυσικὴν χρῆσιν (Rom.
1^{26}) ; *cf.* Aquilanic ἐναλλάκτης (Is. 3^4).—**48. 49.** באדום נצב : יהושפט
מלך : 𝕲^1 εν Συρια νασειβ ὁ βασιλευς ; Hex., εν Εδωμ εστηλωμενος
(=𝔐) κ. ο βασιλευς Ιωσαφατ ; *n.b.* the ancient Ḳrê, attested by
νασειβ, which is to be accepted ; see Note, 4^7. St.'s correction
has been generally accepted : וַיַּצֵּב המלך יהושפט ; however, following
the omission of ' Jehoshaphat ' in B*, נ׳ מ׳ is to be translated
with ' a royal lieutenant,' the phrase inarticulate as בית מלך, 15^{18},
etc.—**49.** עשׁר Kt. ; עשׂה Ḳr., and so many MSS. some edd., and

the VSS.—אניות 1°: 𝕲¹ ναυν = אנית; Hex., VSS here = 𝔋 with pl.; the sing. is corroborated by the foll. Kt., נשברה, which Ḳr. pluralized; the impossible עשר may have induced the pl. rdg.—הלך = 𝕲¹ 𝕮; Hex., 𝔖 𝔙 tr. with pl., and so EVV; St. corrects to הלכה with אניה as implied subj. (so Moff.); but the sing. masc., ' he went not,' is preferable.—אניות 2°: so Hex. here; 𝕲¹ ' the ship '; St. corrects to אניתו, ' his ship '; but the evident subject was replaced with this clumsy gloss.—**50.** אז אמר: see Note on אז בנה, 9²⁴.—אחזיהו בן אחאב: 𝕲¹ (16²⁸ᵍ) ' the king of Israel,' but 𝔋 = Ch., and there is no reason, with St., to correct the text; 𝕲 there omitted the name, as Ahaziah had not yet been formally introduced.—באניות: = 𝕲ᴴ, but 𝕲 as sing.; with St. the generic pl. is proper here.— **51.** ויקבר עם אבתיו: 𝕲¹ om.

I. 22⁵²–II. 1. The reign of Ahaziah of Israel. *Cf. Ant.*, ix, 2. Apart from the usual initial and concluding formulas, and a memorandum of the rebellion of Moab, the section consists of a prophetic story telling of the illness and death of the king, II. 1. **1.** *And Moab rebelled against Israel after Ahab's death.* Opinions vary much as to the origin of this brief note. Some (*e.g.*, Kittel, Benzinger) regard it as fragment of an original record, which has been suppressed as repetitive of the history in 3⁴ᶠᶠ·. Stade, Šanda find it editorial, giving an instance of divine judgment. It is best to understand it as an editorial note, defining the king by name in the story in ch. 3, which records that " when Ahab was dead, the king of Moab rebelled against the king of Israel " (v.⁵). For the historical data see Comm. on that passage.

The story of Elijah's part is distinct from all the rest of the Elijah cycle in the preposterousness of the miraculous element, and in its inhumanity with the destruction of the innocent fifties; it is quite in humour with the Elisha cycle. Only the introductory details of Ahaziah's illness with the mission to Baal-zebul of Philistine Ekron and the description of Elijah's garb present any historical colouring. Benzinger regards vv.⁵⁻¹⁶ with the miracle-story as secondary amplification; Kittel follows in like strain, accepting vv.²⁻⁸· ¹⁷ᵃ, according to which the king inquired who the messenger of doom was, and after identifying him he soon expired. But there are no literary criteria to support such criticism; as Šanda remarks, " the hypothesis of a late interpolation has not much utility." The story with its repetitiousness, after good Oriental style, has given rise to many variations and additions in the Greek, while the Hebrew text has suffered minor changes (see Notes). **2.** *And Ahaziah fell down through the lattice in his upperstory* (sc. of the palace) *that was in Samaria*. This passage and 9$^{30ff.}$, how Jezebel "looked down through the window," illustrate the peculiar Syrian construction with upper story and open platforms known to the Assyrians as *bît ḫillâni*, the latter word=Heb. *ḥillôn*, ' window ' ; see Lexx., and Dussaud, *Syria*, 1935, 349 ff., with architectural reconstructions. The sick king sent messengers to *inquire of Baal-zebub the god of Ekron, whether I shall recover from this sickness of mine?* The element *zebûb* means ' flies,' and so the Grr. here in general and Jos., μυῖαν, and such has been the general acceptance, with parallels from ancient cults of fly-gods, as apotropaic to the scourge, *e.g.*, Ζεὺς ἀπόμυιος and the ' Myiagrus deus Romanorum.' See in particular J. Selden, *De dis Syris*, 301 ff., with abundant classical and patristic references ; also Keil, *ad loc.*, L. B. Paton, *ERE* ' Baal.' But in the N.T. (Mt. 10^{25}, 12^{24}, Mk. 3^{22}, Luke 11$^{15ff.}$) the best texts, including the Chester Beatty papyri, present the rdg. ' Beelzebul,' as against ' Beelzebub ' ; and the former was here the rdg. of Sym. acc. to Gr. MSS j z. That such was the original rdg. has been held by Scaliger, Selden, Grotius, and more recently by Cheyne (*EB s.v.*), Lagrange, *Études sur les religions sémitiques*², 1905, 84, and Šanda ; others, *e.g.*, Kittel, Stade, deny it. J. Lightfoot (on Mt. 12^{24}) argued that *zebûb* was played upon with *zebûl*, and so equal to Heb. *zèbel*, ' dung ' ; but the name should then have become ' Baalzebel,' like Jezebel's name (I. 16^{31}) ; see Note there on that name. The present deity's name meant ' Baal Prince.' Why this deity of Ekron,[1] one of the cities of the old Philistine pentapolis, was supplicated by the Israelite king is obscure ; the ancient gods had their specialties and fashions. Notable in the present story, which appears so apocryphal, are these data of original local colour. **3.** The term, *the angel of* Y*HWH*, appears in the Elijah cycle only here, I. 19^{7}, and at v.^{15} ; elsewhere Y*HWH* speaks to him, or the word of Y*HWH* comes to him. The present term

[1] For its location as at modern ʿĀḳir see Abel, *GP* 2, 319 ; but Albr. identifies it with Ḳatra, assuming shifting of the name, *AASOR* 2–3 (1922), 1 ff.

appears again in 19³⁵. For this figure, in addition to the BDD and Biblical Theologies, see the study by A. Lods, "L'ange de Yahvé et 'l'âme extérieure,'" *ZAW*, Beih. 27 (1914), 263 ff. The expression, *king of Samaria*, appears contemptuous. **8.** The description of the unrecognized seer as *a certain possessor of hair* (so the Heb.) has been interpreted in two ways: as a *hairy man*, and so the Jewish tradition, the Grr., 𝔙 (𝔗 𝔖 tr. literally), EVV, Chic. B.; or as *a man with a hairy garment*, and so GV FV, Renaissance scholars in Poole, margin of RVV, Moffatt. Modern commentators generally accept the latter interpretation and with right. John the Baptist's garb of camel's hair and a leathern girdle (Mt. 3⁴) in imitation of his forerunner is sufficient commentary on the phrase. The garb was not one of simplicity but of professional austerity; similarly Samuel's ghost was recognized by the mantle (1 Sam. 28¹⁴); Elijah's power was evidenced and transferred by means of his mantle (2⁸·¹³ff·); false prophets "wore the hairy mantle for deception" (Zec. 13⁴). It was indeed an ascetic costume, one still continued by the Muslim Sufis; see Montgomery, 'Ascetic Strains in Early Judaism,' *JBL* 51 (1932), especially p. 201, and P. Joüon, 'Le costume d'Élie,' etc., *Biblica*, 1935, 74 ff.; also for modern usage *cf*. Dalman, *A. u. S.*, 5, 18, 165, etc. **9.** *Captain of fifty:* is identical with Akk. *rab ḥanšâ*, and was an honourable title, *cf*. Is. 3³; for the most recent discussion of the numeral term (Ex. 13¹⁸, etc.) see H. W. Glidden, *JAOS* 56 (1936), 88 ff. In the repeated stories of the expeditions to arrest the prophet there is subtle progress. In v.⁹ the officer announces that *the king has said* [*dibber*], *Come down!*; in v.¹¹ the command is imperious, *the king has commanded* [*'āmar*], *Come down quickly!* Also the first officer goes up on the hill (v.⁹), the second evidently summons at a distance (v.¹¹), while the third approaches the prophet with personal supplication (v.¹³). **13.** Omit as superfluous *the third captain of fifty*. The phrase, *may my life be precious . . . in thy eyes*, corresponds to Akk. *napišti ina pānika līkir* (see Haupt, Šanda). **16.** Omit with OGrr., *is it because there is no God in Israel for seeking after his word*, an intrusion from v.³.

VV.¹⁷·¹⁸ present a strange complex in the Heb., while the Grr. add to the complication. The passage also parallels 3¹, but with chronological contradiction. The following attempts a critical presentation of the text. **17**a. *And he died according to the word of* YHWH *which Elijah spoke.* **17**b. *And Jeh₍o₎ram* ⌜*his brother*⌝ [plus with Theod. (see Field), 𝔊ᴸ 𝔖 𝔜 ; 3 Heb. MSS +*his son*] *reigned in his stead,* **17**c. ⌜*in year two of Jehoram ben Jehoshaphat king of Judah*⌝ [OGrr. om.], **17**d. *for he had no son.* **18.** *And the rest of the acts of Ahaziah,* etc. The addition of 'his brother' has generally approved itself as essential in connexion with v.ᵈ; the Heb. '*ḥyw*, 'his brother,' would have been lost by homoiotel. before *tḥtyw*, 'in his stead.' However the writer may have assumed the general knowledge that the two princes were brothers. 𝔊 transferred v.¹⁸ after v.¹⁷ᵃ to obtain customary order. The intrusion of v.ᶜ was due to the concern for giving a regnal dating to II. 2, the events of which must forsooth have happened after Ahaziah's death. But the Hebrew interpolator has followed an independent chronology and contradicted the datum of 3¹, which dates the accession in year 18 of Jehoshaphat. 𝔊 has further enlarged the passage after v.¹⁸ with a transcription of 3¹, "And Joram b. Ahab reigned over Israel in Samaria 12 years, becoming king in the eighteenth year of Jehoshaphat king of Judah." 𝔊ᴸ has then for economy's sake omitted most of this regnal datum in 3¹. Further the OGrr. have continued here with repetition of 3². ³. Benzinger, Stade, Šanda, Olmstead (*AJSL* 31, 178 f.) prefer the Greek text as preserving the original here ; Kittel takes the opposite position, and the present writer agrees with him. The Greek arrangement as formally more correct was the result of editing.

52. 𝔊ᴸ has a different order of statement, commencing with the accession date, which St. prefers as the usual form ; but 𝔊ᴸ has simply regularized the present form, which appears above, 15²⁵. Initial 'and' might be expected, with 𝔊, but 𝔊ᴸ=𝔐.—**53.** אמו : Grr. (exc. u)+' Jezebel.'—**54.** את הבעל וישתחוה לו : Grr. treat the objects as pl.—*Ad fin.* Gr. B 𝔊ᴸ 𝔈 add II. 1¹, following an editorial usage in B 𝔈 of making liaison between the two halves of a book, *e.g.*, at end of 1 Sam., 1 Ch. (see Burn.).

II. 1. 2. אחזיה : by general use reducing the full spelling in such names after the first instance (*cf.* II. 22⁵²), which many MSS have also here.—שבכה : in 7¹⁷ᶠ· of architectural network, here 'lattice,' *cf.* Arab. *šubbāk* (Šanda) ; Jos. understands it as of a staircase from the roof.—אלהי : 𝔊ᴸ with doublet, προσοχθισμα ; *cf*

Rahlfs, *SS* 3, 194 f.—עֶקְרוֹן: Grr., Ακκαρων (N Αγκαρων, *cf.* Akk. *Amḳaruna*), 𝔙 'Accaron'; the developed second vowel is taken by some (*e.g.*, Döller, Šanda) as original; but old as this vocalization was, it was a secondary vowel-development, effected by the liquid; see the writer's Note on 'Alleged Intensive Formations,' *JAOS* 46 (1926), 56 ff.—מֵחָלְיִ: Grr. tr. with 'from my sickness,' and so for חָלְיִ Jer. 10[19], with 'my sickness'; accordingly St., *BH* correct to מֵחָלְיִי; but there may be here survival of the older form in *-ya*, *i.e.*, *ḥŏlīya*, as in Arab. in similar contact.—For unarticulated זֶה (also v.[8]) see GK §126, y.—*Ad. fin.* OGrr.+" and they went to inquire through him."—3. אליה: so vv.[4, 8], but otherwise in the ch. אליהו, and so MSS here and v.[8]; 𝔊 𝔊[H] corroborate the fuller form as original; the shorter form appears elsewhere only in Mal. 3[23]; there is no reason to find in the shorter spelling basis for criticism, with Kit., Sk.—מבלי אין: for the double negative see GK §152, y.—אלהים: 𝔊[H] om.; 𝔊[2] texts, 'god or prophet,' or 'prophet' simply.—4. ולכן: the conjunction supported by Grr., needs not to be elided (so St., *vs.* Benz., Šanda), although in vv.[6, 16] it is lacking. For the adv. 𝔊 𝔊[H] ουχ ουτως, 𝔊[L] δια τουτο=Aq., Sym., and so respectively below.—*Ad fin.* Grr.+" and spoke to them " (Lagarde's text is to be corrected).—6. שְׁלַח: Grr. as הֹלֵךְ.—*Ad fin.* 𝔊[L] a long passage imitating I. 14[10], with 'Ahab' replacing 'Jeroboam.'— 7. משפט: Engl. 'fashion,' as at I. 6[38].—9. הנה: see Note, 21[18].— 10. [אם]ו: 8 MSS om.=𝔗 𝔊[H] 𝔙; at v.[12] אם, where 𝔊[L]=ואם.— תרד אש מן השמים ותאכל: the literal Gr. tr. is cited in Rev. 20[9]; but an independent tr. in Luke 9[54], with inf. αναλωσαι for the second verb.—11. ויען וידבר: a usual phrase even without preceding conversation; *cf.* Dt. 21[7], 1 Sam. 9[17], etc., and the use frequent in N.T. 𝔊[L] has for ויען κ. ανεβη, which, as=ויעל, is accepted by Benz., Kit. (not *BH*), Šanda; St. rejects the word in either tradition.—12. וידבר: Or. MSS ויאמר.—אליהם: read with 3 MSS deR., אליו=Grr., 𝔖; 𝔙 om.—האלהים [איש]: read אלהים, with MSS, as at v.[10], and so here Gr. MSS B i.—אלהים [אש]: om. with 11 MSS deR., Grr., 𝔗 𝔙 𝔄.—13. שלשים: B ηγουμενον=שָׁלִישׁ, then ignoring foll. 'שר הח as superfluous; *al.* Grr., τριτον=𝔊[H]= שְׁלִישִׁי, 'a third,' generally accepted by critics (St. regarding it as scribal expansion); 'a third time' of 𝔖 is out of question. But in support of 𝔙, 'a third set of messengers,' *cf.* 1 Sam. 19[21] (Burn.). —ויעל: OGrr., 𝔙 om., and so St. decides; but the approach to the person is to the point.—שר החמשים השלישי: 𝔙 avoids this unnecessary repetition of the subject, 𝔖 om. 'the third.'—14. הראשנים:=Grr., although asterisked by 𝔊[H] as from the Three.— 15. אותו *bis*: many MSS אתו, and some presenting the Ḳr. אִתּוֹ (deR.), which must be read.—17. אליהו: 1 MS om.; 1 MS אל', MSS 178, 234 'ביד אל',=MS g εν χειρι Ηλιου.—For further criticism of the text see Comm. For the *pisḳah*-in-middle-of-v. see Note, I. 13[20].—18. אשר: 7 MSS deR. pref. וכל=𝔊[L]; see Note, I. 16[7].

Ch. 2. Elijah's ascension to heaven in a whirlwind: the endowment of Elisha with an extraordinary share of his spirit; Elisha's operation of three miracles with the power of his master. Josephus (*Ant.*, ix, 2, 2) only notes that at this time "Elijah disappeared from men, and none knows to this day of his end," and so he is to be ranked with Enoch. Legend thus early enveloped Elijah not only with the miraculous but also with the mythical. His command over the fire from heaven (I. 18, II. 1) is climaxed here by his ascent in a fiery chariot with fiery steeds. This dominant feature links up, as Kittel observes at length, with the myth of the horses of the sun (*e.g.*, 23^{11}) and ancient widespread sun-myths. And in the dominant Jewish legend, which left Enoch as a subject for sectaries, Elijah came to be ranked with Moses, "whose tomb (also) no man knoweth unto this day," and he became the Haggadic counterpart of the Lawgiver. The early development of this hagiology, occurring first in Mal. $3^{23f.}$ (EVV $4^{5f.}$), appears full-blown in the N.T.; Elijah accompanies Moses in the scene of the transfiguration of Jesus (Mt. 17, Mk. 9, Luke 9), and there is the frequently expressed query as to Jesus' identity with Elijah (Mt. 11^{14}, etc.), although Jesus found the prophecy fulfilled in John the Baptist (Mt. 17^{12}, Mk. 9^{13}). With this chapter properly begins the Elisha cycle; that prophet has appeared before only in the story of his call (I. $19^{15ff.}$).

VV.$^{1\text{-}12}$. The ascension of Elijah to heaven. The start of Elijah's mysterious journey with his faithful disciple, who had some uncanny inkling of the coming event, was made *from Gilgal*, from which place *they went down to Bethel* (vv.$^{1, 2}$). The earlier commentators identified Gilgal with the place on the Jordan recorded in Jos. $4^{19ff.}$, $5^{9ff.}$, an identification patently absurd. Thenius was the first to correct this notion, followed by Keil at length, these scholars identifying the place with Jiljilīya (possibly the Gilgal of Dt. 11^{30}), lying between Bethel and Shiloh (see Döller, *GES* 242; Abel, *GP* 2, 337). But this site lies lower than Bethel (774 m. *vs*. 881 m.), and so *went down to Bethel* is inaccurate. Šanda notes the rdg. of the Grr, 'they came,' and desires so to revise the Heb., but the Gr. is itself probably an intentional correction; the verb may have been used from the writer's geographical standpoint. Gilgal appears as one of Elisha's centres (4^{38}), but later still is excoriated as a heathenish sanctuary by Amos (4^4, 5^5) and by Hosea (4^{15}, 9^{15}, 12^{12}). The legend knows of a large school of prophets at Bethel (v.³), and of another at Jericho (v.⁵), of which some fifty members are numbered (v.⁷). These seers know what is to happen, and Elisha reveals that he also is in the mysterious secret. The cleaving of the waters of Jordan by the stroke of Elijah's power-endowed mantle (v.⁸—see Comm., 1^8) reproduces the miracles of Moses and Joshua at the Red Sea and the Jordan. The *double portion of thy spirit*, for which Elisha asks (v.⁹), is phrased after the legal terms for the prerogative in legacy to the eldest son (Dt. 21^{17}), as recognized early by Grotius and others. Elijah's response (v. 10) leaves the gratification of the disciple's desire to the divine will; the latter must be found worthy of the sight of the *mysterium*; *cf.* 6^{17}, Luke $24^{16,\ 31}$. Elisha's cry after his departing master (v.¹²), *My father, my father, Israel's chariotry and horses!*, is one almost of despair, for Elijah was worth a whole fighting-arm to Israel. The same cry is put in the mouth of king Joash at the death-bed of Elisha (13^{14}). For 'father' as a religious title *cf.* 8^9.

VV.¹³, ¹⁴. Elisha's return and repetition of his master's miracle at the Jordan. The theme of the mantle parallels the incident at I. 19^{19}. **14.** *And he took Elijah's mantle that had fallen off from him:* repetitive of v.¹³, but with a different leading verb, there *he took up*. *And he smote the waters*, repeated: the repetition to be kept as emphatic (*cf.* Stade). See Note for intrusion in Greek and Latin MSS of an exegetical statement after the first case to the effect that the waters were not divided. Elisha not only uses the magical garment, but also invokes the divine Name: *Where Is YHWH, the God of Elijah, even He?* The emphatic pronoun is in line with the divine "I am He" of Second Isaiah, etc. The EVV, Chic. B., following tradition, paraphrase here with "and when he (Elisha) also had smitten." See Note for the much vexed phrase.

VV.¹⁵⁻¹⁸. Despite Elisha's protest there follows the search by fifty athletes of the guild for the departed master. In v.¹⁶ *the spirit* [Heb. *rûḥ*, primarily 'wind, breath'] *of YHWH*, which may have taken him up, is thought of quite physically

II. 2^{1-25} 355

and identified with the whirlwind; *cf.* the similar energy of the divine spirit in Gen. 1^2. See Note further, and for the subject at large Volz, *Der Geist Gottes*, and *Das dämonische in Yahwe* (1924).

VV.$^{19-22}$. The healing of the abortion-producing spring at Jericho. The site is identified by v.^{18}, *he was staying in Jericho*. The spring has been identified with 'Ain es-Sulṭān, near Jericho, the Elisha's Spring of Christian tradition. There is inexact parallelism in the statements of the noxious character of the waters: v.^{19} reads: *the waters are bitter, and the land is miscarrying*, but v.^{21}: *there shall not be thence any more death and miscarrying* (*sc.* ' woman,' with the fem. ppl.). The problem arises as to mng. of ' the land '; if used in the primary sense, infertility must be meant, and so AV, ' casting of fruit '; but the Heb. verb is used (as the Grr. recognized) only of human infertility or destruction of babes. Accordingly the word is to be understood in the sense of the people of the land (*cf.* Gen. 11^1), with Thenius, *al.*, *i.e.*, human barrenness is meant. For such an effect of certain waters on women *cf.* the water of jealousy in Num. $5^{11\text{ff.}}$. In v.^{21} with slight change of pointing replace the ppl. with a differently vocalized noun = ' miscarriage,' and so as a noun RVV JV, ' miscarrying.' For further discussion see Note (at v.^{19}). For the hygienic use of salt in Jewish and Palestinian lore see I. Löw, ' Das Salz,' in the G. A. Kohut Volume, 429 ff. It is remarkable that such an ample source of water as this spring should have become invested with a legend of so late a person as Elisha; in the original story there may have been no geographical identification.

VV.$^{23-25}$. The awful penalty on the little boys who mocked the prophet. The story reads like a *Bubenmärchen* to frighten the young into respect for their reverend elders. Very suggestive is Stade's suggestion (*ZAW* 1894, 307), followed by Šanda, but rejected by Kittel, that some shaving of the head, tonsure (so Šanda) was one of the distinguishing marks of the prophet's order; for Elisha was not an old man, and natural baldness is infrequent in the open life of the East. The prohibition of cutting the hair for the dead (Dt. 14^1) would have had no application to the ascetic habit. See Macalister, *DB*, ' Baldness ' (with classical references to reproach of baldness), Ball,

EB 973 f. The bear (*Ursus syriacus*), now confined to the wilder parts of the Lebanon, was common in ancient Palestine, and appears in the Bible as a peculiarly fierce animal, paired with lion and leopard (*e.g.*, Hos. 13$^{7, 8}$), which trait is corroborated by Ūsāma ibn Munḳidh (12th century) in his hunting experiences;[1] for Biblical references see BDD. The very exact figure, *forty-two*, for the unfortunate children, adds realism to the story; but for the figure as one of ill omen *cf.* 10^{14}, and Rev. 11^2, 13^5. The appended itinerary for Elisha : *And he went thence to Mount Carmel, and thence he returned to Samaria*, appears to have little motive, unless Carmel is cited as a well-known pilgrimage objective of pious men. There is no reason, with Wellhausen, to amend ' Carmel ' to ' Gilgal ' ; Elisha had his fixed home in Samaria (5^3, 6$^{20ff.}$).

1. יהוה : B j ο θεος.—בסערה : for variations in Ḳr. see Ginsb.[1, 2], and *SBOT*, Haupt requiring 'בְּ : the root-spelling is variant of שֵׂעָר.—השמים : 𝔊 ως εις τ. ουρανον, with theological caution (*cf.* Jos.) : this is repeated in v.^{11}.—הגלגל : B 𝔈 ' Jericho.'—2. וירדו : B A 𝔈 as sing.—3. [אל] בית : locative ; 19 MSS deR., Sebîr, בית.—4. [ויאמר] לו אליהו אלישע : 3 MSS om. אלישע, *cf.* v.^{6} ; 𝔊^L 𝔖 𝔙 = אליהו אל אלישע, with misunderstanding of the vocative.—7. הלכו : 𝔊 𝔊^H ignore as repetitive of v.^{5}.—מנגר מרחוק : *cf.* v.^{15}, 3^{22} ; Joüon, *RB* 15, 405 ff., takes עמד מנגד as always ' to stand at a distance,' with מרחוק here as further interpretative ; similarly Smend on Ben Sira, 37^4.—8. יגלם : the root, ' to roll up,' also LHeb.—9. כעברם : correct, *vs.* בע of MSS, edd. ; the same variation at 3^5.—ויהי : 𝔊 = יהי, but rdg. ויהי for יהי, v.^{10}.—10. לקח : for Pual ppl. minus preformative see GK §52, s ; Bergstr., *HG* 2, 17 f., *inf.*, denies such cases, but does not list the present case ; BL §45, ignores these phenomena.—11. כוסי : B s as sing.—יפרדו : OGrr. as sing.— ויעל : Grr., κ. ανελημφθη = Mk. 16^{19}.—12. פרשיו : Grr. as sing., ιππευς, which 𝔙 follows with ' auriga ' ; St. prefers the sing., making Elijah the charioteer ; but 'פ has never this mng.—14. St. elides the repetitious אשר נפלה מעליו ; *BH* regards מעליו . . . ויקח as ' prob. addition ' ; but repetition is characteristic of story.—ויכה *bis* : the uncontracted form, as also at v.^{8}, 8^{21}.—ויכה את המים : 1° : all Gr. MSS, except remarkably B A, with plus, " and it was not divided " ; this was taken over into many Latin MSS and the Clementine Vulgate ; see Tischendorf's ed., and Rahlfs's full

---

[1] For this delightful autobiography of a Muslim knight see H. Derenbourg's extensive publication in three volumes, text, translation, historical survey (1889–95), and P. K. Hitti, translation, *An Arab-Syrian Gentleman* (1929), and text from the original MS (volume wholly in Arabic, Princeton Univ. Press, 1930).

discussion, *SS* 3, 268 ff.—הוא אף : 𝔐 attaches to the foll. sentence, as 'also he,' *i.e.*, Elisha, and so Jewish comm., *e.g.*, Rashi, and so EVV paraphrase, "and when he also had smitten"; GV ignores. Aq., καιπερ αυτος, *cf.* FV 'l'Éternel même,' and so Keil as emphatic apposition. Sym., και νυν = 𝔙 'etiam nunc,' as rdg. אֵפוֹא (*e.g.*, 10¹⁰), and this accepted by Then., Benz., Kit., Sk., and by Burn, with query. Grätz, Perles propose איפה הוא,, "where is he?" (*cf.* Gen. 37¹⁶); but this only repeats the first query. St., followed by Šanda, Eissf., regards the phrase as gloss to ויכה 1⁰, making parallelism with Elijah's previous action, but fallen into the wrong place. The Grr., other than Aq., Sym., transliterate with αφφω (=𝔖ᴴ), which was treated as a mystical word by the Church Fathers; see Field, *ad loc.*—**15.** ויראהו : 3 MSS ויראו = 𝔖ᴸ 𝔖.—אשר בירוחו : as the group is the 50 prophets of v.⁷, the phrase is elided by many comm.; but even if careless, it may well be original, with Šanda.— נחה רוח אליהו רוח : 'spirit' here, as human, is fem. with original gender, but 'the spirit of YHWH,' v.¹⁶, is masc., as divine, *cf.* I. 22²¹; this by theological development, although 'the spirit of God' is fem. in Gen. 1². There arose confusion of genders; in Ps. 51 the suppliant's spirit is masc. in v.¹², but fem. in v.¹⁹. In Arabic the same noun is masc., when used of celestial beings (Wright, *Arab. Gr.*, 1, 182). In the Syriac Church the 'Holy Spirit' was masculinized. Syr. *npš* is masc., when used for 'person.'—**16.** רוח : St. deletes, as taken from I. 18¹², 22²⁴.—הגיאות: Kt. = הַגֵּיאוֹת, which is strictly correct; Ķr. הַגֵּאָיוֹת.—**17.** מצאהו : 2 MSS מצאו = 𝔖ᴸ 𝔙; *cf.* I. 21²⁰.—**19.** העיר : 𝔖ᴸ 𝔈 𝔙 'this city.'—הארץ משכלת : 𝔖ᴸ simplified by omitting the noun and making the ppl. refer to the waters, ατεκνουντα; the other Grr. understood 'מ in its primary sense of the Ḳal ατεκνουμενη. In v.²¹ 𝔊 translates exactly with θανατος κ. ατεκν.; 𝔖ᴸ tried to improve with distinction of genders, αποθνησκων κ. ατεκν. The ppl. מְשַׁכֶּלֶת is to be read as nominal, מַשְׁכֶּלֶת, 'miscarriage'; a causative mng. of the verb in sense of causing abortion is not elsewhere found, so as to allow that sense in v.¹⁹. See Haupt's lengthy but uncertain note.— **20.** צְלֹחִית : the form only in Aram. dialects, otherwise צַלַּחַת; for the vessel see Honeyman's study, p. 87.—**21.** רְפָאתִי *BH*, רפאתי Bär, Ginsb.: in v.²² the verb is treated as ל"ה.—לא : 60 MSS. edd., ולא = 𝔖ᴸ 𝔗 𝔖 𝔙.—**22.** וירפו : Ķr. וַיְרַפְּאוּ and so MSS Kt.— **23.** ויתקלסו : 𝔖ᴸ with a doublet, 'and stoned him' = 𝔗, rendering of a perverted rdg., ויסקלו (Klost.).—קרה 2⁰; 𝔊 om., and so St approves; 1 MS Ken. om. עלה קרה 2⁰.—**24.** אחריו : 𝔊 'after them.'

3¹⁻³. The accession and character of Jehoram king of Israel. A modification is made in the condemnation of this Northern king, the last of his line, to the effect that *he did what was evil in the eyes of YHWH, only not like his father and mother; and he removed the Baal-pillar that his father had made.* But *to the sin* [sing. with Grr., *vs.* 𝔐, as demanded by the following pron. suffix form] *of Jeroboam ben Nebat, who brought guilt upon Israel, did he cleave, not turning away from it.* Cf. the similar leniency of judgment upon the last king, Hosea (17²); but the original guilt of Jeroboam was entailed to its bitter end upon the North. The ' Baal-pillar ' (which is pluralized in 𝔊 𝔖ᴴ 𝔙) may possibly be translated ' Baal-image,' following the interpretation by Dhorme (*L'Évolution religieuse d'Israël*, 1, 161 ff.); he identifies the Heb. *maṣṣēbāh* with the related word *něṣîb*, appearing in Old Aramaic inscriptions with mng. of ' image,' namely one on a colossal statue of the god Hadad, registering ' this statue of Hadad,' and another on a statue erected by the dedicator to the memory of his father; see the Hadad inscr., lines 1, 14, the Panammuwa inscr., line 1. The same phrase occurs in 10²⁷. See Cooke, *NSI* 103, for a study of the widespread word.

VV.⁴⁻²⁷. The war of the kings of Israel, Judah, and Edom against Mesha king of Moab; their successful incursion into the south of Moab, and siege of Kerak, but their subsequent panic and retreat by reason of Mesha's dread sacrifice. *Cf. Ant.*, ix, 3. The narrative is a capital example of a ' prophetic ' popular story of an actual historical event, supplemented by the unique Hebraic stele of the Moabite Mesha.[1] The pertinent part of the inscription relates as follows (lines 4 ff.): " Omri king of Israel afflicted Moab many days, because Chemosh was angry with his land. And his son succeeded him, and he too said: I will afflict Moab in my days. He said [understand ' so ' ?]. And I gazed upon him [*i.e.*, in triumph, *cf.* Ps. 118⁷] and upon his house. And Israel perished

---

[1] Discovered by the Rev. F. Klein, Aug. 19, 1868 at Daibon (so Gr. Δαιβων = Mesha's spelling, *vs.* Biblical, *Dibon*), and now in the Louvre. For reproductions and interpretation see Dr., *Samuel*, App., pp. lxxxiv, seq., and *EB s.v.* 'Mesha'; Lidzb., *HNE* 415 ff.; *Eph.*, 1, 1 ff., 143 ff., 278 ff.; *AT* 5 ff.; W. H. Bennet, *DB s.v.* 'Moab'; D. Sidersky, *La stèle de Mésa* (*Rev. Archéologique*, 1920), with history of the discovery and full bibliography; also the Biblical Archæologies, *e.g.*, Barton, *AB* 460 ff. See the Histories of Kittel (*GVI* 2, 258 f.), Cook (*CAH* 3, 372 ff.), Robinson (*HI* 253 ff.), Olmstead (*HPS* 388 ff.), Meyer (*GA* 2, 2, 326 ff.), Winckler (*KAT* 253 f.) takes a contrary view of the geography involved. For a brief discussion of the history see Burrows, *WMTS* 274 f.

everlastingly. And Omri (had) possessed the land of Mhdb' (Bibl. Medebah, Is. 15², etc.), and he dwelt in it for his days and [a broken construction] half of the days of his son [the pl. is possible, the name(s) being ignored], forty years. And Chemosh restored it in my days. And I built Baal-meon," etc. Olmstead places the erection of the stele before the allies' invasion, and so explains the circuitous route to the south to avoid the freshly fortified cities of Mesha's construction, all N of the Arnon ; but it is preferable to reverse the order of events, with Kittel, Meyer, Lidzbarski, the last-named scholar interpreting ' the everlasting perishing of Israel ' as referring to the annihilation of the dynasty by Jehu (842 B.C.). The figure ' 40 years ' is a round number, expressing a generation, as frequently in the Bible, and *cf.* the regnal terms ascribed to David and Solomon. For attempts at figuration of the dates see Cooke, p. 9. Omri reigned 18 years, Ahab 22 ; but we do not know when Omri's control began, nor is the latter's successor evident by name in the inscription. There is no reason to dispute the datum of the Judæan king as Jehoshaphat, which Lucian changed to ' Ahaziah ' to suit his varying chronology.[2]

4. *And Mesha king of Moab being sheepmaster* —. The latter noun, *nôķēd*, occurs elsewhere in the O.T. only in Amos 1¹, describing the prophet as one of ' the sheepmasters of Tekoa ' (the noun being generally mistranslated in EVV). It appears now in an Ugaritic text, in the colophon to the first published long composition (*Syria*, 1934, 226 ff. ; Gordon, *Ugar. Handbook*, 2, 62 : 54 f.), entitling the dictator of the text as *rb khnm rb nķdm*, ' chief priest, chief sheepmaster ' ; the term was thus official, *i.e.*, royal sheepmaster, like ' chief butler,' ' chief baker ' in Gen. 40². *Cf.* also Akk. *ruḫu šarri*, ' king's shepherd,' for which see Note, I. 4⁵. — *he used to render to the king of Israel a hundred thousand lambs and the wool of a hundred thousand rams, i.e.*, as the Heb. iterative form suggests,

---

[2] In vv.[7, 9] ; in v.[12] omission of ' Jehoshaphat,' naming the ' king of Judah,' *bis*. The several essential corrections proposed by St. (*cf. BH* ' fortasse ') are all based on Lucian, along with arbitrary elision of ' Joram,' v.[6], in which case the Northern king's name would have been entirely ignored in this Northern document. See Rahlfs's discussion of Lucian's chronology, *SS* 3, 270 ff.

annually. Is. 16¹, in the oracle against Moab, has been compared for the tribute of lambs (see EVV), but the text is hopeless (see Gray, *ad loc.*). RVV^mg, JV, Chic. B., Moffatt make the tribute to consist in both lambs' and rams' wool, but the Heb. hardly admits this, while the ancient wool was drawn from rams, not lambs. **5.** *And it came about, when Ahab died, that the king of Moab rebelled against the king of Israel.* **6.** *And king Jehoram went forth on that day* (=at once) *from Samaria, and mustered all Israel.* **7.** *And he proceeded* [Heb. *went*] *and sent message to Jehoshaphat king of Judah, as follows: The king of Moab has rebelled against me. Wilt thou go with me against Moab to battle? And he said: I will go up* (the phrase is military); *as thou so I, as thy people so my people, as thy horses so my horses.* **8.** *And he said: Which way shall we go up? And he said: The way of the steppe of Edom.* N.b. the change of *loquitur*s without naming the subjects after good Semitic fashion. **9.** *And went the king of Israel and the king of Judah and the king of Edom.* The presence of the last king appears to contradict I. 22⁴⁸, and also 8²⁰ below, according to which Edom rebelled against Judah in the days of Jehoshaphat's successor, and "made a king over themselves." However there may have been at this time a nominal vicegerent of Edom. *And they went a roundabout way of seven days in length; and there was no water for the army or for the beasts that followed them.* The distance may have been reckoned from the meeting-point with the Edomite allies. **10-12.** The despair of Jehoram, whose conscience strikes him, showing that the religion of YHWH remained the religion of the North despite all defections; the greater faith of the Southern king: *Is there not here a prophet of YHWH's, by whom to inquire of YHWH?*; the response of one of the Northern courtiers, that *Elisha ben Shaphat is here, who poured water on Elijah's hands*; Jehoshaphat's cheering response that *the word of YHWH is with him;* the concourse of the three kings with Elisha. For the inquiry after such a real prophet *cf.* I. 22⁵ᶠᶠ·. The appearance of Elisha, introduced as the disciple of his well-known master, appears remarkable; but corroboration of the active part taken by prophets in political history, is witnessed to by a Lachish tablet, no. iv.

13. Elisha pertinently castigates the king of Israel; *What*

II. 3¹⁻²⁷

*is there in common between me and thee? Get thee to thy father's
prophets and thy mother's prophets.* The last phrase is absent
in 𝔊 ; if secondary, as is generally accepted, it would have been
suggested by I. 18¹⁹. The king's blunt negative, *Not* (a word
of this kind) *!*, was intended to hush the prophet from such ill-
omened language ; he recognizes that YHWH alone is concerned
in the present emergency. **14.** Elisha replies with consistent
bluntness, swearing *by YHWH Sebaoth* that *were it not that I
give audience to Jehoshaphat king of Judah, I would not look
at thee or see thee !* For this reason he relents. **15.** *And now,
bring me a minstrel !—For it was the case that when the minstrel
played, YHWH's hand lighted upon him.* The Heb. syntax,
unless corrected, demands such construction of the last
sentence. For such excitation of prophets *cf.* 1 Sam. 10⁵ᶠᶠ·,
and Lucian, *De Dea Syra*, §43 : " a multitude of holy men,
pipers, flute-players, and Galli, and women frenzied and fan-
atic " ; on the subject see Stade, *Biblische Theologie*, 1 (1905),
§60. Elisha was a typical ' son of the prophets ' in contrast
to his ascetic master Elijah. **16.** He gives the oracle of YHWH :
EVV *Make this valley full of trenches !* But the verb is not
imperative, but an infinitive of absolute action, as also in
other oracles to Elisha (4⁴³, 5¹⁰), and the sentence may be
roughly rendered in English with : *A making of this wady
trenches upon trenches !* **17.** The trenches were for collection
of the coming waters for the parched armies, for without sight
of wind and rain *that wady shall be filled with water, and ye
shall drink, ye and your flocks and your beasts.* For the wady
in question see Robinson, *BR* 3, 555, and the most recent
discussion by Glueck, ' The Boundaries of Edom,' *HUCA* 11
(1936), 148 ff., with extensive comment on this history ; he
follows his predecessors in identifying the wady with Wady
el-Ḥesā ; he also cites Musil, *Arabia Petræa*, 1, 83, 381, n.,
who states that the water found in this valley is at times
coloured by the red sandstone, so illustrating v.²² below. The
cattle (Heb.=*flocks/herds*) refers to the food supply, the *beasts*
to the luggage animals. **18. 19.** There is little reason to
attempt to harmonize the cruel order for the destruction of
Edom with the economic exceptions in warfare laid down by
Dt. 20¹⁹ᶠ· ; war supersedes all wisdom as well as benevolence
even in allegedly Christian nations. *And every choice city*.

a gloss through a double rdg.; see Note. **20.** The event as prophesied *came to pass on the morrow at the offering of the oblation*; the reference is to the morning *minḥāh*, celebrated according to the Talmudic tractate *Tamid*, iii, 2, at the first blush of dawn. The morning oblation—here a purely secular note of time—was secondary to that of the afternoon, the *minḥāh par excellence*; see Comm. on I. 18^{36}. *And lo, water was coming by the way of Edom, and the land was filled with the water.* The geographical note appears superfluous; there may be a play upon 'Edom' and 'red'; *cf.* v.^{22}. The phenomenon is that of the *sail*, cloudburst; *cf.* Josephus, *Ant.*, xiv, 14, 6, for a similar providential water supply for the garrison of Moabite Masada in Herod's time: "God sending them rain in the night, so that their cisterns were filled." For instances of the havoc of the *sail* see the writer's *Arabia and the Bible*, 85 f. November of 1937 was marked by like heavy rains in Syria-Palestine, an official of King Ibn Sa'ūd reporting that at Dumeir, between Damascus and Palmyra, "he saw a flood five meters high, sweeping away everything before it, which forced him to turn back at full speed" (*N.Y. Times*, Nov. 2, 1937). **21.** The verb translated in the EVV with "they gathered"/" they gathered themselves together," simply means "they were called out" to military service. **22.** For the red phenomenon see above on v.^{17}; Šanda suggests a mirage; *cf.* also J. Euting's similar experience in a neighbouring region (*Tagbuch einer Reise in Inner-Arabien*, 98). The interpretation of the Moabite mind by popular report was absurd, but history has to record human absurdities. **24.** *And they came to the camp of Israel; and Israel arose, and smote Moab, and they* (Moab) *fled before them, and they* (Israel) *went in* (*sc.* the land), *smiting Moab as they went.* The last sentence follows the Grr., and in one case the Kt. in part; for the dubious passage see the variant renderings in text and margin of EVV. **25.** The v. describes with hyperbolic gusto the ensuing destruction of *the cities*, the ruination of *every goodly field*, the stoppage of *every water-spring*, the felling of *every goodly tree*, *until* (with the RVV) *in Kir-hareseth only they left the stones thereof*, and so similarly AV; JV with exegesis, *until there was left only K. with the stones of the wall thereof.* The clumsy Hebrew is simplest improved by omitting the reference to the stones, reading *until Kir-hareseth* (alone) *was left*, which fortress the invaders now attacked, *and the slingers surrounded it and smote it*. The passage was early a crux to the VSS and Jos., all ignoring the name of the city; the first scholar to recognize it appears to have been Vatablus (*ob*. 1547), from whom it came into the Reformed translations. Kir-hareseth, the Kir-heres of Is. 16^{11}, Jer. 48$^{31, 36}$, is universally identified with Kerak, the southernmost fortress of Moab, an identification early made by the Targum to Is. 16^7; it appears to be identical with Kir-Moab of Is. 15^1. For this 'impregnable fortress' (so the Arabic geographers) see Le Strange, *Palestine under the Moslems*, 479; Musil, *Arabia Petræa*, 1, 45 ff.; Abel, *GP* 2, 418 ff. Because of its strength and strategic position controlling the route to the Red Sea, the Crusaders made heroic efforts to possess it. **26.** The king of Moab, hard pressed in the siege, attempted *to break through to the king of Edom*. Comm. recognize the evident contradiction with the precision above of the Edomite king as Israel's ally; Kittel tr. with 'against the k. of E.,' as though by a special sortie, and similarly Olmstead; others, *e.g.*, Šanda, Skinner, regard that king as an unwilling ally; but correcting the common confusion in Heb. of *'rm* and *'dm* (as at I. 11^{25}), it is best to read *the king of Aram*, with 𝔏 and Winckler, and so Eissfeldt. Damascus would have been his natural ally. **27.** The king of Moab sacrifices his first-born son as a holocaust upon the city's wall in view of the besiegers. The parallel to this extreme sacrifice appears in early Israel in the immolation of Jephthah's daughter (Jud. 11$^{29\text{ff.}}$), and it was practised by a later Judæan king, Ahaz (16^3); *cf*. Micah's anxious query, "Shall I give my first-born for my transgression?" (6^7). This awful sacrifice in political and private emergencies was frequent in Phœnicia.³ The effect of such a ritual was still compelling upon the Israelite mind. *And there came great*

---

³ See Curtius Rufus, *Hist. Alex. Magni*, iv, 3, 15, 23, for the attempt at such an immolation at Nebuchadnezzar's siege of Tyre; for witness from the Neoplatonist Porphyry see Eusebius, *Præp. evang.*, i, 10, 33, 44; iv, 16, 6. *Cf*. Eissf., *Ras Schamra u. Sanchuniathon*, 69 f., and C. Clemen, *Die phön. Religion nach Philo von Byblos* (*MVG* 42, Heft 3, 1939), for the text of Philo and commentary. For the ancient rite at large, Frazer, *The Golden Bough*, 3, ch. 13, is to be consulted.

wrath upon Israel—so RVV JV=GV; AV .. *great indignation against Israel*. The primitive implication was early ignored and forgotten; the Grr. have 'great repentance in Israel,' Jerome, following Aquila, 'great indignation in Israel'; FV "they had horror of it." The earliest commentator, Josephus, attributed the effect upon Israel to their 'commiseration' out of 'humanity and piety.' Rashi interpreted the effect upon Israel somewhat obscurely, "because their sins were remembered," and this view was still held by Keil. See Poole for very diverse interpretations of the Renaissance scholars. The word for 'wrath,' with two slight exceptions, is used entirely of Deity. Old English ' dread ' might well translate the word, and more objectively ' panic ' would best express it. The contrast between panic fear and true religion appears in Ex. 15^{16}, "terror and fear falleth upon them," and Is. 8^{13}, " He be your reverence and He your fear ! " The Israelites lost all heart in sight of the gruesome act. It is not at all necessary to assume, with Kittel, Šanda, that 'the wrath of Chemosh' was once in the text, although the superstitious fears of the soldiery must have been much more alive in a land that was not their God's; *cf*. Jephthah's word to the king of Ammon (Jud. 11^{24}). The tale belongs to the popular prophetic cycle and uses the bald primitive lingo. There is no need to suppose with the last-mentioned scholars elision of the subsequent successful rally that drove off the besiegers; the connecting link was assumed *e silentio*. It is a striking coincidence that Moabite Mesha in his stele uses similar language, "because Chemosh was angry with his land."

  1. בשמרון : most Grr. om.—**3.** בחמאות : read with sing. noun, as in similar cases above.—**4.** מישע : 4 MSS משע, as in the Mesha stele; name also of a Calebite; the root frequent in S. Arab. names. The Grr. have Μωσα, as though rdg. מושע, and so one Heb. MS; for similar variations *cf*. מידד and מודד, Num. 11^{27}, and see Haupt's note there in *SBOT*.—נקד : היה : B† μηνωκεθ for ην ν., this error also in 𝕰 texts; transliteration of the noun is kept in other Grr., exc. Aq., ποιμνιοτροφος, Sym., τρεφων βοσκηματα=𝕷 'nutriens oves.'—והשיב : 𝕲^L has a doublet. For the legal sense of the verb *cf*. 17^3.—ישראל : OGrr.+εν τη επαναστασει=𝕾^H במסקונא ; an 𝕷 text, 'ex subjectione,' doubtless an error for 'in subj.'; these present an original obscure gloss. Prof. A. D. Nock has suggested to the writer as the original noun, ὑπανάστασις, 'a rising up to give another room.' 𝔗 plus a pertinent gloss, 'year by year.'—צמר: apposition of the material; see Dr., *Tenses*, §194.—**6.** [ישראל] כל: MSS 30, 195, Grr. om. by provincial criticism, as in cases above.—**7.** וילך: 𝔊ᴸ om. as not *à propos*; but the verb means 'to proceed to action.'—[מואב] אל: על is expected (*cf.* EVV), but 𝔐 is supported by all MSS and by the preps. in 𝔗 and Grr., showing that the confusion of the two was very early.—כמוני כמוך: 𝔊ᴸ has a doublet.—**8.** נעלה: B *al.*, 𝔖ᴴ as sing.—**10.** אותם: 𝔊ᴸ 𝔙 'us,' as the pronoun expected.—**11.** יהושפט: 𝔊ᴸ 'the king of Judah,' also MSS (N *al.*) with combination of both elements; similar variations *bis* in v.[12], in the second case the change being supported by two Heb. MSS, and to be accepted.— מאותו: with Kt. of many MSS read מֵאִתּוֹ; *cf.* similar errors, vv.[12, 26].—**12.** וירדו: B A *al.*, 𝔙 as sing., and the like variation in v.[15] for קחו.—**13.** אַל: *cf.* 6[27].—**15.** והיה: generally corrected, *e.g.*, by Burn., Haupt, *BH* ('fortasse') to ויהי; the apparently dubious syntax led Klost. to suggestion of an extensive lacuna, a rash proposition accepted by Burn.; but 𝔐 is to be maintained: "and it used to be upon the harper harping, then (in a given case) the hand of Y. came upon him."—[יד ['י]: 22 MSS deR., רוח=𝔗.—**16.** עשׂה: abs. inf. as in another oracle to Elisha, 4[43], and *cf.* הלוך, 5[10]; see Ew., *Lehrb.*, §217, a, and Burn.; 𝔗 𝔖 with correct feeling for the sense have the passive, *vs.* imper. of Grr., 𝔙 EVV; but Jos. renders literally with aor. inf.—**17.** מקניכם: 𝔊ᴸ παρεμβολαι υμων, as though for מחניכם, a correction largely accepted, *e.g.*, by Haupt, *cf. BH*; however Rahlfs (*SS* 3, 252) properly regards that rdg. as correction from v.[9].—**18.** ונקל זאת: for disagreement in gender *cf.* v.[26], also the numerous cases cited in GK §145, e. —**19.** וכל עיר מבחור: a doublet of the prec. phrase, to be omitted with MS 224, OGrr.; the Ḳr. of מ occurs elsewhere only at 19[23].—הכאבו: the root appears inappropriate, hence suggested corrections (see Lexx.), but Smend has shown that the verb in Ben Sira 13[5] means 'to suffer damage'; *cf.* also St.—**20.** מדרך אדום: 𝔊ᴸ εξ οδου της ερημου Σουδ (Σουρ, Σουα) εξ Εδωμ; *cf.* v.[8].—**21.** ויצעקו: an extensive doublet in 𝔊ᴸ.—מעלה: 𝔊ᴸ A *al.*, επανω, of which ειπον ω in B N *al.* is corruption.—**22.** מנגד: see Note, 2[15].— כדם: 𝔊ᴸ om.—**23.** החרב נחרבו: for Hof. inf. abs. with Nif. *cf.* a case, Lev. 19[20], on which see Haupt's note in *SBOT*; the Nif. is expected for the inf., but 𝔐 implies alternative rdgs. for the moods. The verb with its unique mng. 'to fight' is denominative from חֶרֶב 'sword;' *cf.* Syr. root חרב for Heb. root נכה in v.[24] (Burn.), and similar development of Arab. *ḥaraba* in stems III, VI, X. Grr. tr. with μαχεσθαι to which 𝔊ᴸ adds a doublet with εριζειν. For arbitrary corrections see St., and GB *s.v.* חרב II.—**24.** ויבו בה: Ḳr. בָּהּ וַיַכּוּ, and so Kt. of *ca.* 35 MSS Ken., deR. (deR. also noting a few MSS rdg. בם for בה, and so 𝔗 𝔖 tr.); Grr., κ. εισηλθον εισπορευομενοι=𝔖ᴴ 𝔙; the Gr. rdg. was correctly accepted at the Renaissance, *e.g.*, by GV FV AV; of EVV JV is alone in retaining

Kr.—25. עַד הִשְׁאִיר אבניה בקיר הֲרֵשֹׁת: the pointing of the sibilant in the last word follows Bär, al.; by apparent error Ginsb. and BH give חרשת; 𝔊 𝔊^H εως του καταλιπειν τ. λιθους τ. τοιχου καθηρημενους (understanding root חרם); 𝔊^L pref. κ. εξεσεισαν τ. Μωαβ (a gloss variant = Kr. in v.²⁴), then εως του μη καταλιπειν λιθον εν τοιχω τεκτονικης, the last word as tr. from root חרשׁ I, for the similar noun from which root see Ex. 31⁵, 35³³ (cf. Rahlfs, SS 3, 244); 𝔗 "until there was not left a stone in the city which they did not destroy (=חרם)"; similarly 𝔖; 𝔙 "ita ut muri tantum fictiles (cf. 𝔊^L) remanerent," קיר being represented by 'civitas' in the next sentence. As noted above, אבניה and the prep. with קיר must be elided to obtain any sense. St. would replace the former with לְבַדָּהּ 'only.' עַד הִשְׁאִיר is paralleled in 10¹¹, with similar cases in I. 11¹⁶, etc., in which cases the verb has a sing. subj.; but here a pl. subj. is demanded, and correction is to be made to inf. הַשְׁאִיר (see Burn. at length).—26. אותו: read אֹתוֹ.—ארום: read ארם, and so 𝔗, 'Syriæ.'—יכלו: as sing. in Jos., 𝔊^L 𝔈 𝔖, by easy variation.—27. לארץ: the VSS, exc. 𝔗 𝔊 𝔊^H, as though לארצם (and so EVV), accepted by many critics, but 𝔐 is preserved by St., Haupt, BH; for the political term see Comm. I. 4¹⁹.

CC. 4–8¹⁵. The Elisha cycle (with supplement in ch. 9).

4¹⁻⁷. Elisha's miracle in behalf of a prophet's widow in distress, effecting an enormous increase of her potful of oil. *Cf. Ant.*, ix, 4, 2. The story is parallel to Elijah's miracle in I. 17⁸ff.. Marriage of the prophets is thus attested, although in general they appear as lodged in ascetic communities. **1.** By a play upon *thy servant* (*my husband*) Jewish tradition (Josephus, 𝔗, Rashi, *et al.*) developed 'thy servant Obadiah' ('servant-of-Y.'), with further expansion on the latter's protection of the prophets (I. 18⁴). The Hebrew law permitted the 'selling' of wife and children as chattels for debt (Ex. 21⁷; Am. 2⁶, 8⁶; Is. 50¹), the practice lasting till after the Exile (Neh. 5). In the Code Hammurabi, §117, such servitude might last for only three years. **2.** The word translated 'pot' is unique; it may mean only a small unguent vessel; see Note. For the high value of oil, also a great export commodity from Palestine, see BDD and Archæologies. **7.** Read *pay off thy creditor* in place of *pay thy debt*, as the Kr. points.

VV.⁸⁻³⁷. Elisha as guest of a great lady; his promise to her of a child; the birth of the boy; the latter's death some years later; the prophet's restoration of him to life. (Josephus ignores 4⁸–6⁷.) The story is a parallel to that of Elijah's sojourn at the home of the Sarephthite widow and his resuscitation of her son (I. 17$^{8ff.}$). There are several correspondences of detail: either prophet is lodged in an *upper chamber*, in each case the prophet resorts to a form of treatment, *stretching* or *bowing* upon the body; the curt statement, *there was no voice and no attention* (v.^{31}), repeats I. 18^{29}. In each of the stories the feminine heart is well depicted, in the present case (v.^{16}) with the woman's fear lest the prophet were deceiving her (*cf*. v.^{28}), in the other with the passionate blame thrown in his face; also in this story there is the woman's true intuition of bringing the prophet himself to her house, not accepting his servant as intermediary (vv.$^{25ff.}$). The present story is much more elaborate than the other, with more actors and far greater detail, and apart from its literary character, as Kittel remarks, it casts intimate light upon social life in ancient Israel. There is the *great lady* (*cf*. Naaman, ' a great man,' 5^{1}), quite mistress in her own house (vv.$^{8ff.}$), who will accept nothing in return for her hospitality to *the divine*, refusing his offer to be her spokesman to the powers that be. Her reply of proud good breeding, *I dwell among my own people* (v.^{13}), in modern terms, in her own social circle, reveals the ancient and abiding character of Semitic social life. The eminent place of the great lady in society is finely presented; *cf*. Buhl, *Die socialen Verhältnisse der Israeliten*, 97 ff.; Nowack, *Arch.*, §27; Benzinger, *Arch.*, §22. But the uncertain equilibrium of that society appears in the supplementary story, 8$^{1ff.}$. As appropriate to ' a woman's story ' we have the detail of *making an upper chamber* and of its essential furniture, *bed, table, stool, lamp* (v.^{10}—not ' candlestick ' with EVV); see Benz., pp. 98 ff., 104 ff., and the pertinent Dictionary articles. VV.$^{18. 19}$. Lifelike is the story of the lad's running out to play in the harvest field, and natural his outcry upon the sun-stroke, *My head, my head!* *Cf.* the similar catastrophe in the death of Judith's husband (Judith 8$^{2f.}$). For the current holidays and their celebration, as expressed in the husband's reply to his lady's obscure determination to travel away, that *it is neither new moon nor sabbath*, *cf.* 1 Sam. 20^{5}, Amos 8^{5}, Hos. 2^{13}, Is. 1$^{13f.}$, and for modern practice in Palestine, Dalman, *A. u. S.*, 3, 12 f. For the sabbath see E. G. Kraeling, ' The Present Status of the

Sabbath Question,' *AJSL* 49 (1933), 218 ff., with full review of preceding studies, and with the conclusion that the sabbath was originally a mundane seventh-day holiday, independent of the moon's phases, like the Roman *nundinæ* (ninth-day holidays), in this agreeing with Meyer, *GA* 2, 2, 318, n. 2. From this story we learn how the sons of the prophets were sought for divine help, a custom universal in the Oriental world, with the excursions to ascetics, monks, muftis, etc. The story is somewhat diffusive and obscure as to actors and action, a characteristic of Semitic style, which leaves much to the picturing of the scene by the hearer or reader, and hence the constant insertion in the Grr. of changes for clarification, which have affected subsequent VSS, as also modern critics; see the Notes. However most critics find a clear narrative with a minimum of correction. **8.** For *Shunem* see Comm., I. 1³. **10.** *A little chamber on the wall:* so EVV, exc. JV, . . . *on the roof*; the first term is simply *upper-chamber*, as at I. 17¹⁹; the second remains obscure, the Heb. syntax meaning *a wall-chamber*. See Note for various suggestions and the proposition to read, with change of vowel in ℌ, *a cool upper-chamber*. For the low Oriental *table* see A. Macalister, *DB* s.v. **12.** *And she stood before him:* yet it was only later (v.¹⁵) that *she stood in the doorway*, and Elisha's indirect conversation with her through Gehazi is puzzling at first sight. But the former phrase is formal, *she presented herself*; *cf.* the nuances of mng. of the verb ' to come,' vv.³⁶ᶠ·, 1° *she came* (on call), 2° *she came in* (the chamber). The intermediate agency of Gehazi, standing outside, was good manners, for a lady might not easily speak to a man in his chamber. **13.** *Thou hast been careful for us with all this care:* so EVV=current English, " You have taken so much care for us." *Is it to speak for thee to the king?* : so the Heb. literally. **14.** Gehazi reports to his master her heart's desire : *She hath no son, and her husband is old.* **15.** The prophet bids him, *Call her!*, and when he had done so, *she stood in the door*. **16.** Elisha addresses her directly : AV *About this season* [with marg. variant] *according to the time of life*; RVV JV *At this season, when the time cometh round* [with variant]. See Note for the complicated phrase, which has been affected by Gen. 18¹⁰·¹⁴. *At this season* should be omitted, and, adopting

Skinner's original suggestion, the following phrase is to be understood as meaning ' according to the time of pregnancy,' doubtless a current polite expression. The happy event is foretold sweetly : *Thou shalt embrace a son.* **23.** The Heb. word translated by EVV with *it shall be well*, is *Peace !*, a non-committal ' All is well.' **27.** *YHWH hath hid it from me, and hath not told me :* but in a subsequent case he has farsight (5^{26}). **29.** *If thou meet any man, salute* (Heb. *bless*) *him not :* identical with Jesus' injunction of urgency upon his disciples (Luke 10^4). The same verb for salutation (*brk*) appears in 10^{15}. **30. 31.** Gehazi proceeds on his bootless errand ; but the woman will not leave Elisha. **34. 35.** A much more detailed scene of the treatment of the lifeless body is given here than in I. 17^{21}. There the action is expressed by " he stretched himself upon the child," here by *he bowed*. This verb is used of ritual prostration in I. 18^{42}. The verb gave great trouble to the Gr. translators ; see Note for the numerous renderings and for a novel translation based on a transliteration in Lucian. The physical exhaustion of the practitioner is presented by his taking time off to *go back and walk in the house once to and fro*.

VV.$^{38\text{-}44}$. Elisha's miracles at sessions with the fraternity of prophets. VV.$^{38\text{-}41}$. Elisha's antidote to ' death in the pot.' *The famine being in the land :* the reference appears to be to the seven years' famine reported in ch. 8 ; either, as Kittel proposes, a lacuna precedes and the famine was stated, or the reference may be an intrusion in the story ; the provisioning of a hundred men must always have been a problem. Elisha is represented as on a visitation to the fraternity at Gilgal (*cf*. 2^1), where the brothers were *sitting before him*, *i.e.*, for instruction ; *cf*. 6^{32}. The verb ' to sit ' produced the noun *yĕšîbāh*, ' session, school,' appearing first in Ben Sira, 51^{29}, and remaining still a current technical name in Judaism. These scenes introduce us to an ancient ' vita communis et contemplativa ' ; *cf*. the writer's article, ' Ascetic Strains in Early Judaism,' *JBL* 51 (1932), 183 ff. That such schools were also studious is proved by the remarkable literature that issued from the prophetic guilds. As head of the order Elisha acted as host. For the command, *Set on the pot*, *cf*. Eze. 24^3, with the following lively description of the boiling. **For the** *wild gourds* see Post, *DB* 2, 250, and in particular Dalman, *Sacred Sites and Ways*, 81 f. : " (In the Jordan valley) creeps the coloquintida (*citrullus colocyntis*) with its little leaves and yellow apples, resembling melons, which Elisha's disciples, who were evidently not natives of the district, wanted to cook as food, but which are only of value as an aperient." Keil notes that the colocynth eaten in quantity can be fatal, citing Dioscorides, iv, 175. Oesterley and Robinson, *Hebrew Religion*, 89, adjudge the prophet's operation as a case of imitative, counter-active magic, a dash of good meal obviating the poison. There is to be added the discussion by J. P. Harland of 'The Apple of Sodom' in *BA* 1943, 49 ff.

VV.[42-44]. A miraculous feeding of the school of prophets. A friend from a distant part brings the prophet a personal gift of barley loaves and grits (see Note) of the first milling of the harvest—so *the first-fruits*, not here a ritual term. *Baal-shalisha* (*cf.* 'the land of Shalisha,' I Sam. 9[4]), the home of the visitor, was identified by the *Onom*. with βαιθσαρισα (and so the Grr. render here), 22 km. N of Lydda; but the name appears more exactly in that of the neighbouring Kefr Tilt (Arab. *ṭult*=Heb. *šālîš*, 'a third'); see Abel, *GP* 2, 259. The prophet contradicts his servant's natural scepticism as to the sufficiency of food for the party with 'a word of YHWH' =Engl. 'enough and to spare!' The fraternity is here numbered at a hundred members; *cf.* the fractional figure, fifty, 2[7, 16, 17], and the hundred prophets hidden away by fifties, I. 18[4].

1. מנשי בני : 3 MSS om. בני ; 1 MS מבני =Grr., 𝔖[H] ; St. holds נשי as superfluous, as did those translators ; but *cf.* Jud. 4[4], דבורה אשה נביאה—עבדך : 2⁰ : 𝔊 𝔖[H] 'a servant' ; 𝔊[L] 'a servant of the Lord.'—**2.** אליה : 𝔊 om. (𝔈 has).—לכי, Kr. לך : the Kt. survival of N Israelite dialect; like cases below, vv.[3, 7, 16, 23] ; these with variant manuscript tradition ; see deR., Ginsb., and for such dialectic forms Int., §2.—בבית : 2⁰ : 2 MSS (50, 70) om., and so B *al.* (not 𝔈), avoiding the Sem. repetition ; again St. finds intrusion.—אָסֻךְ : 𝔊 𝔖[H] as verbal, αλειψομαι (𝔊 texts with further corruption) ; 𝔊[L] correctly αγγειον=𝕮 𝔖 (𝔙 'a little') ; for the unusual development from the root סוך , 'to anoint,' *cf.* אוֹב (Akk. *zûpu*), אגן (Syr. *gūz*). Then. (*cf.* Burn.) renders ingeniously with 'an anointing,' a supply sufficient for one application ; for attempts at correction of text see Stade-Haupt. But it doubtless means an ointment pot, with modern trr. ; for the most recent study of the word see Honeyman, *PEQ* 1939, 79.—**4.** על (no variant) :

Burn. well cft. Nah. 3¹² for the use of the prep., and there is no reason, with Grätz, St., to read אל after Gr. εἰς ; the general textual change is in the opposite direction.—כל : OGrr. om.— הכלים האלה : 𝔊ᴸ plus " and it will not (var., thou shalt not) stay."—**5.** מאתו : Gr. MSS q u (Lag. accepts as Lucianic rdg.) plus " and did so," adopted lightly by Klost., al.—מיצקת Kt., מוֹצֶקֶת Kr. and many MSS (6 MSS מצקת) : but the Ḳal in v.⁴ ; St. assumes a Piel ppl., with intensive sense, ' pouring incessantly.'— **6.** בנה הגישה [אל] : the sing. (=𝔗 𝔖 𝔙), as addressed to the son whose turn it was ; the Grr. pluralized, as might be expected.— **7.** נִשְׁיֵךְ : ' thy debt,' with use of an otherwise unknown noun ; but 𝔖 𝔙 = GV, ' creditor,' i.e., as נֹשֵׁי, which is preferable ; Grr. τ. τόκους σου, i.e. as נִשְׁיֵךְ. Piel of שלם is used with the personal obj., as at Prov. 13²¹ ; see Stade-Haupt at length.—וְאֶת בניכי : Ḳr., very many MSS. edd. (see deR.), ואת וב׳, and so all VSS ; the foll. sing. verb then agrees with the dominant subj., a parallel case Ex. 21⁴, cf. Ew., Lehrb., §339, c. St., after Klost., keeps Kt., rdg. אַתְּ, and the verb as Piel, " thy children thou shalt keep alive." Possibly ' thy sons ' was an afterthought in the text.—**8.** ויהי היום : " and there happened the day when " : the phrase also in vv.¹¹·¹⁸.—[שונם] אל : read על ; cf. עלינו, v.⁹.—להם 2° : 𝔊 (B A al.) om.—**10.** עלית קיר : various interpretations have been offered by VSS, and, e.g., by EVV (see above) ; Benz., ' a walled room,' in contrast to a roof arbour as at 2 Sam. 16²² ; or the wall may refer to the easy outside access. It is best to read קֹר=קיר, ' coolness,' the same error of vocalization having entered into Is. 25⁴ ; cf. the ' cool (מְקֵרָה) upper chamber ' of Jud. 3²⁰ᶠ· ; Klost. suggested the rdg. of this last noun here. 𝔊 𝔊ᴴ represented it with ' a little place ' (𝔊ᴸ om. ' place '), 𝔙 ' coenaculum parvum.'—**12b-15.** The vagueness of the narrative is due to the indefiniteness of the loquiturs ; the scene must be visualized. Klost., Benz., St. would delete these vv. as secondary, which criticism Baumgartner well regards as ' zu plump ' (Gunkel-Eucharisterion, 1, 156). Haupt also argues against St., offering without any certainty possible corrections. Baumgartner, following Gunkel and Gressmann (=BH ' fortasse ') would elide simply v.¹²ᵇ and ויאמר לו, v.¹³. But there is no sufficient reason for alteration.—**13.** החרדה : B† ἐνκτησιν for ἐκστασιν.— עמי : many, following Buhl, op. cit., 39, would read pl., עַמָּי, but the collective sing. is preferable ; cf. Lev. 21¹ with the pl., but in the foll. v. the sing.—**15.** ויאמר קרא לה : 𝔊 om.—**16.** למועד הזה כעת היה : cf. Gen. 18¹⁰, כעת חיה, and foll. v.¹⁴ with למועד in parallelism with that phrase. The phrase has been a *crux interpretum*, being assumed as of the round of the year, or even of the spring time. But Skinner on Gen. (after recording earlier interpretations) has ingeniously interpreted the phrase as of the pregnancy period, cft. LHeb. חַיָּה ' pregnant woman,' and reads accordingly כְּעֵת ח׳. For the present passage he holds properly that the original phrase came to be misunderstood, and that למועד הזה was adopted from v.¹⁷ (where it means ' at the set time ') under the influence of Gen. 18¹⁴. For הזה למ׳ 𝔊ᴸ has a gloss variation, εις το μαρτυριον τουτο. The VSS both here and in Gen. have only makeshifts.— איש האלהים : MS 19, 𝔊 ℭ om. (𝔖ᴴ ※) ; vs. St., BH, there is deep force in the appeal, " O divine, lie not to me ! "—17. הזה כעת חיה : om. as clumsy repetition from v.¹⁶ with St., al. (cf. BH) ; the Heb. then reads smoothly, and it is not necessary to change foll. אשר to כאשר with Grr. and some critics.—20. וישב : 𝔊 𝔊ᴴ 𝔖ᴴ as though וישכב (so BH as ' probable ') ; but the boy was too big for such a posture ; 𝔊ᴸ as Hif.—23. חֶלְכָּתִי : the Kt. presents the archaic vowel-ending.—25. ותלך ותבוא : 𝔊 (B A al.) read as 2nd pers. masc. addressed to the servant.—איש האלהים 2⁰ : 𝔊 𝔊ᴴ 𝔖 ' Elisha,' and similarly in v.²⁷.—V.ᵇ–v.²⁶ is treated as secondary by Benz., St. ; but the apparent contradiction in the matter of ' peace ' is due to the woman's avoidance of dealing with the servant. Those critics apply the same criticism to vv.²⁸·²⁹. —26. עתה : MSS ועתה=𝔊ᴸ.—At end of v. 𝔊ᴸ has as plus a repetitive narrative of G.'s fulfilment of orders.—27. ממני : B† arbitrary plus, ' and from thee.'—34. כפו : Gr. MSS g j n, 𝕷 plus ' and his soles on his soles.'—ינהר : also v.³⁵, and in I. 18⁴² of Elijah's religious prostration, the verb being not otherwise known ; the verb there=Gr. εκυψεν=𝔖ᴴ here (with the root ghn). Here 𝔊 διεκαμψεν ; 𝔊ᴴ MSS+※ κ. ενεφυσησεν επ αυτον ; 𝔊ᴸ συνεκαμψεν, with doublet in variant forms, ιλααδ, ιγλααδ, ιγαλαδ. These renderings recur in v.³⁵ along with further essays : 𝔊 συνεκαμψεν, 𝔊ᴴ συνεκαλυψεν (=𝔖ᴴ root kp') ; 𝔊ᴸ with three variants, συνεκαμψεν, ενεπνευσεν, ηνδρισατο, i.e., altogether renderings with some five Gr. verbs and one transliteration. The verb ενεφυσησεν is repetition from I. 17²¹ ; see Rahlfs, SS 3, 196, Benz., p. xvi. The transliteration ιγααδ and the verbs διακάμπτειν, συνκάμπτειν, ἀνδρίζειν (the latter also used in obscene sense), which have not been explained, represent the rdg. ינהר, i.e., the Arab. root ' to fight, to act strenuously,' as in the well-known noun for the Holy War, jihād ; it would then mean here the vigorous application of body to body. Correction of 𝔐 might accordingly be made here ; at all events it is of interest that this Arab. root was known to the early Greek translators.—35. יוֹרר : the only other instance of this root is in Targ. to Job 41¹⁰=Heb. עטש (see Burn.), and so Rashi, Kimchi tr. here ; sneezing is a sign of life and of expulsion of demons (so Haupt). 𝔖 𝔙 ' he yawned.' Grr. generally om. the verb, and so 𝔖ᴴ, or repeat various renderings of ינהר ; 𝔊ᴸ διεκινηθη.—36. ויקראה : 1 MS ויקרא=OGrr.

38. הגדולה : B† om.—39. אחד : Grr. om. (cf. 𝔖ᴴ), either from identification of the subject with the servant, or by haplog. of εἰς/εἰς.—אֹרת, MSS also with plene-spellings : Grr., αριωθ ; other VSS with indefinite renderings ; see Jastrow, Dict., for the Talmudic identification.—שדה : גפן : ' a wild vine,' cf. חית השדה ; Grr. tr. 'ש with ' in the field,' exc. 𝔊ᴸ properly with αγριαν.—ממנו :

II. 5$^{1-27}$

Sebîr ממנה, and so MSS; for the gender of נפן cf. I. 19⁴.—ויבא: 2 MSS om., and so B al.; A 𝔊^L 𝔏 have.—ידעו: 𝔊^L ℭ 𝔖 𝔙 as sing., approved by St.; but the general ignorance is the point.— **40.** ויצקו: Grr. in general a sing., A 𝔖^H pl.; again there is no reason, with St., to correct 𝔐.—לאנשים: 'to some'; or to be corrected to 'לאנ'; 𝔖^H om.—והמה: Grr., exc. 𝔊^L as והנה.—**41.** וקחו: 16 MSS קחו=VSS; St. defends 𝔐 as a case of ellipsis, and Haupt cites GK §167, a, in support.—וישלך: 𝔐 can be defended as case of aposiopesis of the subject; St., Šanda argue that the prophet was the actor in the original story; Grr. as impv. pl.; Haupt would read as juss., וישלך.—ויאמר 2⁰: 𝔊 𝔊^H (𝔖^H obelizes) +' Elisha to Gehazi his servant,' 𝔊^L+' E. to G.'—היה: Grr. expand with ετι (εκει) and so 𝔖^H.—**42.** בעל שלשה: Grr. as בית ש'; the full name was prob. בית ב' ש' (so St.): 𝔖 ' city of giants'; ℭ ' a city of the Darom.'—לחם bis: 𝔊 MSS variously om.—כרמל: Lev. 2¹⁴, 23¹⁴†; prob. with ℭ 𝔖 ' fresh grits'; cf. Šanda; Grr., παλαθας, a form of fruit cakes, as at 1 Sam. 25¹⁸.—בצקלנו: the noun is otherwise unknown; of the Grr. A transliterates, βακελλεθ (MS x κακελεθ) =𝔖^H; the others om., exc. N, εν κωρυκω αυτου, 'in his wallet,' and so for the noun a citation from Theod. in 𝔖^H. Lagarde on basis of the Gr. transliteration suggested corruption in the Heb., for which see GB.—תן: Grr., exc. 44, the pl., which St. prefers; but the prophet is dealing with his servant, as the sequel shows.—**44.** ויתן לפניהם: OGrr. om. as superfluous.

Ch. 5. Elisha's healing of the Syrian Naaman's leprosy; the sequel, Gehazi's greed and his affliction with the disease. The story is brilliant in its representation of the international manners of the age, as also in its fine sketching of the actors. Naaman, whose name is good Syrian—it appears now in the Ugaritic tablets—was commandant of the king of Aram, *i.e.*, of Damascus, as the reference to its waters shows. The king's name is not given (but it appears as Ben-Hadad in 8⁷), nor is that of the king of Israel; herein the history fails; if authentic, the scene must have occurred in one of the numerous interims of the constant warfare (*cf.* I. 20), with which the history of the Crusades may be compared. It is in vain, as with Šanda, to date the story exactly. Naaman was a *leper*. The Hebrew term is broadly generic, covering a large variety of scabious diseases, being used even of mould in houses. The O.T. references themselves are quite contradictory; the disease might be curable, *e.g.*, the diagnosis and treatment in Lev. 13; or it might be permanent, as in Gehazi's case, *infra*. The patient should be kept in strict quarantine, *e.g.*,

Lev. 15⁵, etc., an ancient regulation, as appears in the story of the four lepers, 7³ff·; yet Naaman remained in good society, and was not under taboo, while the afflicted Gehazi was still a member of society in later story (8⁴ff·).[1]

A captive Israelite maid has pity on her master—a delicate touch in the story—and suggests to her mistress that he might be cured by *the prophet in Samaria* (v.³). Naaman carries the suggestion to the king, who at once gladly dispatches his favourite minister to the king of Israel with a letter written in due form (v.⁶—*n.b.* the epistolary *And now*, for which see Note), and with a handsome present. Such an instance of international medical courtesy is corroborated by earlier ancient sources. A long letter from Hattushil, king of the Hittites, to Kadashmanturgu king of Babylon (*ca.* 1275 B.C.), contains an extensive memorandum in reply to an inquiry concerning the whereabouts of a Babylonian physician (*asû*) and an exorcist (*âšipu*), who had been sent to the Hittite court, but had never returned. And a late copy of an ancient Egyptian story tells of the mission of the god Khonsu, sent by Ramses II to the king of Hatti to cure his daughter, and how the devil was expelled.[2] The Israelite king is represented as in an excessive quandary, *he rent his clothes* (v.⁷)—an ironical touch, or just the talk of the town that was brought to Elisha ? The latter is presented as having a house in Samaria, and yet he was last in Shunem ; in the next story we find him again by the Jordan (6¹ff·), then at Dothan (6¹³), but thereafter once more in Samaria (6²⁴ff·)—*i.e.*, there is no biographical sequence. He hears of the consternation at court, and solemnly bids the king to send the suppliant to him, that the latter (at least) *may know that there is a prophet in Israel* (v.⁸). Naaman comes to the prophet's house with full cavalcade (vv.⁹ff·), but Elisha vouchsafes him no interview (*cf.*

---

[1] See BDD, *JE*, *s.v.* ' Leprosy,' W. Ebstein, *Die Medizin im A.T.*, 75 ff. ; also Haupt's note in his *Numbers*, p. 45, expressing doubt whether there is a single case in the O.T. of true leprosy, *elephantiasis Græcorum*, as it was known to the ancients. The malady was also known to Hippocrates as the Phœnician disease.

[2] For the Hittite letter (text in H. H. Figulla and E. F. Weidner, *Keilschrifttexte aus Boghazköi*, 1 [1916], 10) see F. Bilabel, *Gesch. Vorderasiens u. Aegyptens*, 1 (1927), 156, 294, and for the Egyptian story *ARE* 3, 188 ff.

4$^{25ff.}$), simply sends him a message to *go and wash in the Jordan seven times*, and so he would be cleansed. Naaman *was indignant* ; he had thought that the prophet would honour him with his presence, *would stand . . . and wave his hand towards the spot* (of the disease), *and exorcise the be-lepered* (sore) (v.^{11}). The lordly exorcising gesture he expected is the same as that practised by Moses and Aaron in the invocation of the plagues, by the ' stretching out of the hand,' or of ' the rod,' and in the miracle at the Red Sea (Ex. 8^3, etc., 14^{21}). He is further disgusted that the muddy waters of Israelite Jordan are prescribed, and not the pure, cool streams of the Damascus oasis, the names of which are uniquely given (v.^{12}). However (vv.$^{13, 14}$) following the advice of his servants (their assumed title for him, ' My father,' is to be corrected—see Note) *he went down and he dipped seven times in the Jordan* (Grr. with the verb ' to baptize ' as in later use—*cf.* the sanctity of these waters in the N.T. and in the Mandaic tradition), *and his flesh became again like the flesh of a little child, and he was clean*. He returns to Elisha, and confesses that *there is no God in all the earth but in Israel* (*cf.* the Muslim cry, " No god but Allah "), involuntary profession of the happy convalescent. He begs him to *take a present*, literally *a blessing*, in courteous Oriental language, but the prophet refuses (vv.$^{15, 16}$). Thereupon he asks the prophet's approval of his taking some of the holy soil of YHWH's land (*cf.* Zech. 2^{16}), on which he may worship, for hereafter he will *not celebrate holocaust and sacrifice to other gods, but to YHWH* (v.^{17}). But he begs indulgence for one exception (v.^{18}) : *In this matter may YHWH pardon thy servant ! When my lord comes into the house of Rimmon to worship there, and he leaning on my hand* (the same courtly expression as title in 7$^{2, 17}$), *and I am to worship in the house of Rimmon, upon my worshipping in the house of Rimmon YHWH pardon thy servant for this thing !* This repetitious line of talk has been subject of variations in the VSS and of modern criticism (see Note), but it is best to let it stand. The prophet approves with his *pax tecum* (v.^{19}). This indulgence has ever since been a stumbling-block to orthodox scholars, beginning with Lucian, who inserted a face-saving clause (see Note). But while YHWH was God of the whole world (*cf.* v.^{15}), his worship was not obligatory on others than Israel; *cf.* the (probably late) declaration in Mic. 4⁵. Rimmon is the well-known Ramman of the Assyro-Babylonian pantheon, a name and phase of Addu-Hadad (see Comm., I. 15^{18}). He appears to have been domesticated in Damascus; Ben-Hadad of *loc. cit.* was son of Tab-Rimmon.[3] In spite of his master's refusal of the proposed generous gift, Gehazi, that very disagreeable servant (*e.g.*, 4$^{25\text{ff.}}$), resolves to profit from *this Syrian*, and follows after him (vv.$^{20\text{ff.}}$). He had his lie ready to hand, and receives from the generous benefactor double of the gift he had asked for, although slyly he allows the donor to urge it upon him. He brings the gift home and hides it. But the second-sight of his master uncovers his lie, and he is given an appropriate doom: *the leprosy of Naaman shall adhere to thee and thy seed forever.* And so it befell the servant: *he went from his presence be-lepered like snow.* *Cf.* the diagnosis of 'white' phenomena of the disease in Lev. 13, and Herodotus's report of kindred diseases in Persia, λέπρι and λεύκη (i, 138).

1. Introduction of Naaman the Syrian commander-in-chief, *a great man before his lord*; *cf.* the phrase, 'a great woman,' 4⁸. There is a remarkable expression of early Hebrew religion in the statement that *by him YHWH had given deliverance to Aram*, although this included victory over Israel, as the story proceeds to detail. *And the man was a doughty soldier, a leper* (Heb. a ppl., *be-lepered*): this clumsy sentence is paraphrased in EVV; the first attribute should be excised as gloss of preceding 'great man'. **3.** *Recover him of his leprosy:* so EVV, recent translations varying with the verbs 'cure,' 'relieve.' The verb cannot be explained from the Heb., and is an importation from a well-known Akkadian root, signifying exorcism, etc.; here the man is the object, in v.^{11} the sore spot. Note that the language belongs to the Syrian *milieu*. **5.** For the specie values see the Archæologies of Nowack (§§36, 37), Benzinger (§§41, 42). Šanda proposes that the gold was double the value of the silver, and that here the talent

---

[3] See *KAT* 442 ff., Deimel, *Pantheon Babylonicum*; while the god may not have been Western, he was early domesticated in the West; *e.g.*, 'the mourning of Hadad-Rimmon in the valley of Megiddo,' Zech. 12^{11}. Šanda properly cites the Libanese place-name, Brummana derived from *Bēt-R*.

is reckoned after the older usage of 3600 shekels, or else with the later equivalence of 3000 shekels the 6000 of gold would have been stated as two talents. The figures indeed appear to be extravagant, story-wise. **12.** *Abanah and Pharpar:* the former name (Kt) is identical with *Amanah* of Song 4⁸, and so Ḳr. demands here ; it is the Syrian Mountain known as Ammana in Ass. records, neighbouring to the Lebanon, doubtless the Anti-Lebanon. The stream is named after its source, and is universally identified with the Chrysoas of the Greeks, the modern Nahr Baradā, the chief stream in the oasis, while the Pharpar is identified with the 'Auwaj, the old name being preserved in the Wady Barbar.⁴ **17.** *In re* the transfer of the holy soil Thenius notes this as the earliest known example of a widespread custom ; he cites the report of Benjamin of Tudela (Wright, *Early Travels in Palestine*, 103) that the Jewish synagogue in Persian Nehardea was composed wholly of earth and stone brought from Jerusalem ; the empress Helena similarly transported the holy soil to Rome. **22. 23.** *Two suits* (EVV literally, *changes of garments/raiment*) ; see Note for the secondary character of this item in v.²³, and see below on v.²⁶. **24.** *The hill:* the word has defied identification ; it may be reminiscent of the city quarter in which the prophet was lodged ; *cf.* ' the Ophel ' (the same word) in Jerusalem. **26a.** Mystical language of the second-sight is used here : *Went not my heart, when a man turned back from his chariot to meet thee ?* The Grr. are unanimous in interpolating ' with thee ' after the first verb, followed by modern translations, and so critics in general ; but how could so important an item have fallen out ? The ancient psychological phrasing should not be tampered with, as has also been done with the mysteriously indefinite *a man*, or *some one* (Moff.), *vs.* the usual incorrect translation, ' the man,' of some VSS, GV FV EVV ; the seer saw ' only in part.' ⁵

⁴ For the Ass. references see Tiglath-Pileser IV's annals for the third year, *CP* 315, *ARA* I, §770 ; and for the rivers Robinson, *LBR* 446 ff., Baedeker, and Dussaud, *TH* ch. 5, §§4, 5.

⁵ For the extensive functions of the heart in the Bible, constantly paired with the psyche, see Delitzsch, *Biblical Psychology*, sec. xii, Cremer, *Bibl.-theol. Wörterbuch*, *s.v.* καρδία. For this case of second-sight *cf.* Ezekiel's experiences, Eze. 8 (idolatry in the temple), 11¹³ (death of Pelatiah).

26b. *Is it a time to take the money, and to take garments and oliveyards ?*, etc., so 𝔥. Objection to this lies in the reference to the merely opportune, whereas the servant is castigated for his dishonesty ; in the repetition of the infinitive ' to receive ' ; and in the details of real property, into which the cash had not been converted. Read with change of Ḳr. of the two verbs in question, and following the Grr. and their congeners, also 𝔙 : *Now thou hast taken the money, and* (so) *thou wilt take* (all kinds of property) ?, with sarcastic interrogation. Further, with a variant plus in most Grr., in place of 'garments' read (*take*) *with it gardens*, i.e., rdg. *bô gnym* for *bgdym*.

1. נעמן : the name in a Ugaritic genealogical tablet (*Syria*, 1934, 244 ff.).—[ארם] צבא [מלך] : 1 MS, 𝔊 om. ; *vs.* St., variation from the usual formula, *e.g.*, 'host of Israel,' is no argument against 𝔥.—גבור חיל : 𝔊ᴸ om., but not necessarily with a text different from 𝔥 ; for its early intrusion see Comm., and so *SBOT*, *BH*.—מצרע : Grr. tr well with λελεπρωμένος.—**2.** גדודים : for the Gr. μονόζωνοι, Thackeray finds the mng. 'bandits' (*Sept. and Jewish Worship*, 23 f.).—ותהי לפני : the phrase = עמד/עבד לפני.—**3.** אחלי : *cf.* אֲהָלֵי , 'O that for me,' Ps. 119⁵ ; see Burn. on the pointing here as of pl. constr., and so understood by 𝔗 𝔖 ; 𝔊ᴸ has a doublet, κ. δεηθείη του προσώπου, the verb = הֶחֱ[ל] (Burn.).—יאסף אתו : the desiderated mng. cannot be had from the Heb. verb, 'to gather' (*cf.* the attempts of the Jewish comm.) ; the verb here = Akk. *ašāpu*, 'to exorcise.'—**4.** לאדניו : because of the aposiopesis after v.³ Grr. understood לאדניה, *i.e.*, the woman spoke 'to her husband,' and then 𝔊ᴸ added, " and it was announced to the king " ; see Rahlfs, *SS* 3, 26 f., 206 f., for correction of Lagarde's text.—**5.** לך בא : " come, go ! " ; examples in GB 181b.—**6.** ועתה : the introduction to the contents of a letter after the formal address ; see Comm., 10².—**7.** אך דעו = Engl. " just know ! " ; for the imperative phrase דעו־נא וראו *cf.* I. 20⁷.—**8.** *Elisha the divine :* 1 MS, 𝔊ᴸ om. the first noun, 𝔊 om. the second ; *cf.* v.²⁰.—**9.** בסוסו וברכבו , Ḳr. בְּסוּסָיו ; 𝔊 𝔊ᴴ εν ιππω κ. εν αρματι = 𝔖ᴴ 𝔙 ; 𝔊ᴸ pluralizes both nouns ; the collective sing. is to be kept.—**10.** מלאך : Grr., αγγελον, which 𝔖ᴴ asterisks, ℭ om. ; the verb alone is sufficient.—וְטָהָר . . . וְשֻׁב : juss. and impv. are in correct sequence, *cf.* I. 1¹². 𝔖 𝔙 read the second verb as טָהֵר, " (the flesh) will become clean," which St. (with incorrect citation of the Grr.) prefers ; but the verb is used of the person in vv.¹². ¹³.—**11.** ועמד : OGrr. om. because of their interpretation of the following.—יהוה ; 1 MS, B A N *al.* om. ; there is no reason for omission, *vs. BH* ; Naaman knew the name of Israel's God (*cf.* vv.¹⁷ᵃ·), as did Mesha the Moabite.—והניף ידו אל המקום : Grr., " and will set his hand upon the place,"

𝔊ᴸ exegetically, ' upon the leprosy '; similarly 𝔙 ' et tangeret manu sua locum lepræ '; the prepositional phrase is lacking in N al., is asterisked in 𝔖ᴴ, and St. regards it as ' spurious,' an unreasonable judgment; the exorcising gesture was to be made ' towards the place (of the spot) '; Šanda objects on ground of the narrow use of ' place '; but cf. the parallel מקום השחין, Lev. 13¹⁹. Kit., GB (p. 456), and more recently Vincent (Dussaud Vol., 1, 269, n. 2) proposes reference to ' the Sanctuary-place,' a notion long ago anticipated by ' certain scholars,' acc. to Poole, but again an invention.—**12.** אבנה: Kt.=Grr., 𝔖ᴴ 𝔙; אֲבָנָה Ḳr., and Kt. of many MSS=𝔗 𝔖=Song 4⁸; a case of labial variation.—פרפר: correctly transliterated in A N al., abused in B al.—ארחץ: Grr. pref. πορευθεις=𝔖, reminiscent of v.¹⁰.—**13.** ויאמרו: 2 MSS, most Grr. om., 𝔖ᴴ ※.—אבי: MSS 96, 151 om. With the usual interpretation as ' my father ' may be compared Akk. abu in titles of address, also the military term, abu ummāni, ' father of the army.' There is much variety in the Grr.; OGr. om. the word, the Hex. translates with πατερ, but Lucianic texts have πατερ ει, and so with the Three. Accordingly since Then.=BH correction to אם has generally been made. But see Note on בי, I. 3¹⁷, and Honeyman's identification of it with the present word, as with the mng., ' granted,' and so as conditional, verifying the Greek ' if,' which is expected before the foll. verb, and so inserted in the EVV.—**14.** וירד: 3 MSS deR. וילך=𝔖 𝔄.—איש האלהים:=𝔊ᴸ; other Grr., ' Elisha,' and so in v.¹⁵.—**17.** ולא=' and if not '; cf. 2 Sam. 13²⁶, and the positive expression ויש, 10¹⁵.— משא: 𝔊ᴸ texts γομος, the original translation, otherwise corrupted to γομορ=עֹמֶר (Ex. 16³⁶, etc.); see Rahlfs, SS 3, 288.—**18.** This apparently clumsy bit of diction has naturally suffered since the day of the VSS; for the latter reference may be made to BH. The initial ' for this thing ' appears duplicated in the final ' in this thing '; ' in my worshipping in the house of Rimmon ' appears unnecessary, and this is evident origin of the correction to ' his worshipping ' in the Gr. (B A al., but not 𝔄) and 𝔖, which would evade the notion that Naaman did so actually worship, i.e., in ritual acts, as the verb means. But the proselyte makes full and brave confession before the prophet.—בְּהִשְׁתַּחֲוָיָתִי: error by repetition of preceding השתחויתי, and then Aramaizing attempt at pointing as infin. To this assertion 𝔊ᴸ adds an exculpatory plus, προσκυνησω αμα αυτω εγω Κυριω τω θεω μου.—נא: Kt., but not Ḳr.: very many MSS om. (so deR.), and so 𝔗; 𝔊ᴸ μοι. The ignoring was due to its absence with the same verb above; but the precative element in the second supplication has force.—**19.** כברת ארץ: 𝔊ᴸ texts retain original transliteration, εις Χαβραθα τ. γης=an 𝔏 text, ' in Chabratha terram '; 𝔊 texts with primitive corruption Δεβραθα (cf. 𝔈); 𝔖ᴴ uniquely, ' from the land of Israel.' The word כ' occurs in Gen. 35¹⁶, 48⁷; see Lexx., and Benz., Arch., 192.—**20.** איש האלהים: 𝔊 om.; 2 Heb.

MSS om. prec. אלישע ; cf v.⁸.—ולקחתי : for consecution cf. 7⁴, and see Dr., Tenses, §139.—21. וירא : 1 MSS וירא, 2 MSS ויראהו; Grr. (exc. i) read the object αυτον, and 𝕿 supplied it with " and saw a man running "; the text gives a case of the uncontracted form of the verb; see Note, I. 10²⁹.—ויפל : correct term for dismounting, cf. Gen. 24⁶⁴, and so 𝕲ᴸ κατεπηδησεν (=𝕲 in Gen.) : 𝕲 𝕲ᴴ επεστρεψεν (=𝕾ᴴ), borrowed from v.²⁶ to avoid the harsh sense of the verb.—22. עתה זה : also I. 17²⁴.—ושתי חלפות בגדים : Kamp., Kit., St., Eissf. (cf. BH) eliminate the phrase here and in v.²³, as the ' fresh suits ' could not be the object of ויצר there; but rather, with Benz., the phrase is original here, inducing the later intrusion in vv.²³·²⁶.—23. הואל : cf. 6³, etc.; 𝕲 om.; 𝕲ᴸ επιεικ(ε)ως, ' kindly ! '; 𝕲ᴴ (𝕬=𝕾ᴴ) ουκουν, as though הלא, which Rahlfs defends as orig. Gr. in SS 3, 288, but does not accept in his Septuaginta.—קח : many MSS וקח.—ויפרץ בו : 𝕲 om.; rightly with Šanda, a phrase ' characteristic of Oriental good manners,' as vs. St., arguing, as the Gr. opined, that Gehazi needed no urging, and so BH, ' probabiliter.'—ככרים כסף : B† om., causing BH to note, ' prob. delendum ' (!).—חרטים : the noun to be connected with חרט, ' mold,' Ex. 32⁴; see al-Fāsī, s.v. (ed. Skoss, 1, 584), and Torrey, JNES 1943, 300 f.; here and at Is. 3²² it may then mean ' money bags.'—24. ויבא : OGrr. as pl., which St. (cf. BH) prefers; but the chief actor is the proper subject.—אל העפל : 𝕿 ' to a hidden place,' Grr., εις το σκοτεινον, i.e., as הָאֹפֶל, and similarly 𝖁, ' iam vesperi '; 𝕴 texts have ' in locum obscurum ' (=Grr.), ' in terram Gaphela,' ' in terra Gophera,' i.e., these two cases based upon unique and exact transliteration, ' Gophela '; 𝕾 ' in side of a mountain,' with which cf. Rashi, Kimchi, ' in a lofty place,' with correct etymology.—25. אל [ויעמד] : על is expected, but so all MSS.—מאן Kt.; Ḳr., many MSS מֵאָן : St.-Haupt retain the Kt. =מֵאֵן, cft. 1 Sam. 10¹⁴, Job 8².—26. לא : corrected by St., Šanda (cf. BH) to הלא : but the interrog. particle is not required; see GK §150, a.—לא לבי הלך : Grr. plus ' with thee '; 𝕲ᴸ " was not my heart with thee ? " This plus has been carried over into modern VSS (JV in brackets); Moff., " was I not present in spirit ? "; Chic. B., " was I not with you in spirit ? " Other ancient VSS paraphrase : 𝕿 " in the spirit of prophecy it was shown to me "; 𝕾 " my heart showed to me "; 𝖁 " my heart was present." Cf. a similar expression in 1 Cor. 5³.—איש : Grr., 𝕿 𝕾 ' the man.'—הַעֵת : Grr. as הַעָת, so also 𝖁, for which spelling see Eze. 23⁴³, Ps. 74⁶; in Eze. 27³⁴ the mistaken Ḳr. as here. The interpretation as עֵת induced misunderstanding of the foll. verbs.—לקחת את הכסף ולקחת בגדים : 𝕲 𝖁 read both verbs as perfects, לָקַחְתָּ; then, with exclusion of B A, the Grr. have a plus, translating the second verb as future, and representing בגדים with εν αυτω κηπους=בו גנים. These corrections are to be accepted (see Comm.), following Klost., Benz., and subsequent scholars; see Burn. (who is doubtful), St. at length. The item of vineyards is in line with the following list of real property, while 'clothes' of 𝔥 is repetition of the gloss in v.²³. 𝔗 recognized trouble in this speech, and inserted after the above words, "and thou hast thought in thy heart to buy (oliveyards)."

6^{1-7}. The sunken axe-head made to float. The place of *the sons of the prophets*, where *they sit before* their master (*cf.* 4^{38}), was *too narrow* for them, and decision was made to move down to the Jordan, where timber was to be had in plenty for a larger conventicle. For the large trees still to be found in that valley see Abel, *GP* I, 213, noting the poplar, tamarisk, etc. An iron axe-head is dropped into the water; Elisha recovers it by a feat of imitative magic; *cf.* $4^{38\text{ff.}}$.

VV.$^{8\text{ff.}}$. The 'political stories' of Elisha begin here.

VV.$^{8-23}$. The Aramæan military movements discovered by Elisha's second-sight; the troops sent to seize him afflicted with blindness, but honourably sent home. Any historical basis of this story is indiscernible. It is notable for the prophet's declaration, *More are they with us than they with them* (v.^{16}), with which *cf.* Elijah's immortal challenge, I. 18^{21}. **8.** The warring against Israel was that of guerrilla bands; *cf.* 5^2, and *inf.*, v.^{23}. The Heb. word translated in EVV with *my camp* is a *unicum*; with slight change it can be read as from the same root in the verb at end of v.^{9}; read here, *In such and such a place ye shall go down*, the verb being used in the sense of military 'descent.' The two similar words are rendered variously by the Grr., Lucian developing the notion of 'ambush,' followed by 𝔙 and many modern critics, also by Moffatt, Chic. B. But the wish is father to the thought; the Heb. words must then be entirely ignored. **9.** Elisha, true patriot, reports to his king the movements of the enemy. **12.** The prophet was famous abroad from the Naaman episode; but there was also the fame of underground reports, as repeated in the local news of the Great Wars of 1914–18 and 1939–45. **13.** The story places Elisha at a strategic point, *in Dothan*, at the entrance into the Highlands of Ephraim. **15.** The Heb. noun, *servant (of the man of God)*, is unique in these stories; with substitution of a word that could easily have been corrupted, read: *And at dawn the man of God rose early and went out*, and so similarly Moffatt and Chic. B.; see Note. **17.** For *the horses and chariots of fire cf.* 2^{11}.

19. The distance between Dothan and Samaria is about nine and one-half miles. **21. 22.** Elisha insists that the king treat his captives as honourable guests. His chivalrous inquiry has been variously translated or amended: EVV *Wouldest thou smite those whom thou hast taken captive with thy sword and with thy bow?*; JV *Hast thou taken captive with thy sword and with thy bow those whom thou wouldest smite?*—these variant modern translations indicating the problem of interpretation. 𝕲ᴸ, followed by most critics, Moffatt, Chic. B., insert a negative, "whom thou hast *not* taken captive." But the complete absence of the negative in the other Grr. argues for 𝕳, as *vs.* Lucian, a clever adapter of texts. Read with EVV, and understand here a rule of war in the technical term, 'captured by sword and bow'; captives that had surrendered were not to be slain, and so *a fortiori* in the present case. It shows the prophet's generous concern for his prisoners, now become his guests. *Cf.* his gentlemanly, truly Oriental conduct towards Naaman (5¹⁵ᶠᶠ·).

2. מקום : 𝕾ᴵᴵ has with asterisk; Grr. om., exc. MS v with οικον, 𝕲ᴸ with σκεπην (also corrupted to σκηνην), 'shelter'; see Rahlfs, *SS* 3, 207.—**5.** הקורה : a few MSS pref. את ; the particle is prefixed irregularly to the foll. noun, doubtless by careless gloss insertion. For attempts at correction of the text see Burn., St.— ויאמר : 𝕲 om.—שאול : 𝕲 texts (B *al.*), κεκρυμμενον (=𝕾ᴵᴵ), error for κεχρημενον, 𝕲ᴸ N *al.*—**6.** ויגד : Hif., but read by the VSS unanimously as Kal., וַיֻּגַּד, which is to be accepted.—**8.** אל ויועץ : the same combination 2 Ch. 20²¹; for this use of the prep. *cf.* v.¹¹.—פלני אלמני : see Montg., *Dan.*, on 8¹³.—תַּחְתִּי : *cf.* נְחָתִים, v.⁹. Here 𝕲 𝕲ᴴ παρεμβαλω=𝕾ᴵᴵ, *i.e.*, verbal paraphrase of the noun as 'I will encamp' from root חנה ; 𝕲ᴸ ποιησωμεν (so pl. in 𝕴 𝕻) ενεδρον+arbitrary κ. εποιησαν (=𝕴); the word in v.⁹ is rendered by 𝕲 𝕲ᴴ with κεκρυπται=𝕾ᴵᴵ, but by 𝕲ᴸ consistently with ενεδρευουσιν. 𝕿 𝕾 tr. both words with sense of 'concealment,' 𝕻 of 'ambush.' Since Then. emendation to נֶחְבָּאִים תֶּחָבָא, from the root 'to hide,' has been preferred by many, *e.g.*, by Burn., St., Sk., but such a corruption in 𝕳 cannot be explained. Šanda sugg. רתעו אתי , 'encamp with me,' and below חָיִם. But it is best to read with Joüon (*Mél.*, 5, 477), נְחָתִים, תֶּחֱחָתוּ, in line with the use of that verb for military 'descent,' *e.g.*, Jer. 21¹³, and so frequently in Syriac.—**9.** איש האלהים : 𝕲 Hex., 'Elisha,' and so v.¹⁰, naming the otherwise anonymous prophet.—**10.** והזהירה : OGrr. om., and so St.; but the mng. is clear: "and he would warn it (the place), and it would keep on guard."—**11.** מי משלנו אל מלך ישראי : the second word is criticized by some for use of שׁ

but this good N Israelite particle is appropriate in citation of a Syrian. VSS (exc. 𝔖) '(who) betrays me?', as though מִגַלִּי from a supposed נִגְלֶנּוּ, which latter emendation is accepted by Klost., al. (cf. the suggestions in *BH*), but it is properly condemned by Burn., St., since the verb 'to uncover' is not used in this sense with the personal object. St. unnecessarily accepts Ew.'s emendation to מִכֻּלָּנוּ, 'of us all.' The foll. אל מלך in the sense of partisanship is supported by Hos. 3³, Jer. 15¹, Eze. 36⁹, and cf. v.⁸ above.— **12.** For the *nuance* of the bedchamber cf. Eccl. 10²⁰.—**13.** אֵיכֹה: MSS, edd. (see deR.), איפה ; אֵיכָה might be expected, as in Song 1⁷, with Syr., JAram.; the form in -ô may be due to artificial assimilation to איפה, or may be a genuine form in distinction from אֵיכָה, 'how,' v.¹⁵.—דתן: Grr., Δωθαειμ(-ν) = Judith 4⁶, 7¹⁸, following tradition of pronunciation as in דתינה, Gen. 37¹⁷.—**14.** סוסים: read collective sing. with 𝔊, as in v.¹⁵.—**15.** משרת: so all VSS (*e.g.*, ὁ λειτουργός), but a unique term for 'servant' in these stories; St. om. איש האלהים ט'; but a subj. is required; Klost., al. (*BH* 'fortasse') would read כִּמְהֵרַת ; but closer to 𝔐 would be an otherwise unknown noun, שַׁחֲרַת, cf. שחר, 'dawn,' and *n.b.* easy confusion in early script of מ and ש. For the phrase וישכם לקום cf. Ps. 127²; Grr. ignore the inf., exc. 𝔊ᴸ with τὸ πρωί.—**16.** אותם: some 20 MSS אתם; read אֵפֹא.—**17.** סוסים ורכב אש: 'horses-and-chariots-of-fire'; for the double *regens* in the constr. relation cf. Dt. 3⁵, 2 Ch. 8⁵; the fuller expression in 2¹¹.—**18.** סנורים: also Gen. 19¹¹; Safil intensive = 'to dazzle'; the root is closely related to וָרִיד (leucoma); the latter is parallel to root *brr*; see Montg., *Aram. Incantation Texts from Nippur* (1913), 93, where a Talmudic formula of prescription against blindness of same etymological origin is noted.— ויכם: 𝔊ᴸ + 'the Lord.'—**19.** לא 2°: B *al.* om.—זה: for this form see the 10 cases cited in BDB 262.—**20.** פקח: 20 MSS + נא = Grr.; cf. v.¹⁷.—הנה: VSS tr. as though הנם, but this of necessity; cf. v.²⁵, and see Dr., *Tenses*, §135, 6; there is no reason to emend with Grätz, St., *al.*—**21.** אל אלישע: B *al.* om., 𝔊ᴴ ※.—[אבה] הַאָפֶה: read abs. inf., הֲחַפֶּה, with ℭ 𝔖, and with the Gr. use of the ppl. for this syntax.—**23.** וילכו: carelessly omitted in some Gr. MSS, *e.g.*, B; 2 Heb. MSS om. prec. verb.

6²⁴–ch. 7. The siege of Samaria by Ben-Hadad of Aram, resulting in starvation and actual cannibalism within the walls, and the Israelite king's threat against Elisha as author of all the evil (6²⁴⁻³¹); the royal audience with Elisha, and the latter's oracle of the coming relief of the famine, with the doom pronounced upon a sneering adjutant (6³²–7²); the discovery by four lepers of the flight of the Syrian host upon rumour of an onslaught by North Syrian kings, and their looting of the abandoned camp (7³⁻⁸); their report to the city and to the king, whose scouts verify their news (vv.⁹⁻¹⁵);

the spoiling of the camp and relief of the starving citizens, along with the fate of the incredulous officer (vv.$^{16-20}$). *Cf. Ant.*, ix, 4, 4–5. This story is the most elaborate in the Elisha cycle, similar in its compilation of distinct anecdotes to the one included in the Elijah cycle, I. 20, but there with ' the man of God ' nameless. One definite historical datum is given in the story of the murder of Ben-Hadad by Hazael, and the prophet's concern therein through his second-sight. The epithet ' son of a murderer ' cast at the anonymous Israelite king (6^{32}) need not be interpreted literally, and so to be understood definitely as of Ahab's son Joram (so Josephus, early comm., Thenius, Rawlinson, Wellhausen, *al.*), or of Jehu's son Jehoahaz (so Kuenen). The fairly contemporary Aramaic Zakar stele only increases the complications of our knowledge of the Syrian kingdoms. Nor are there indications sufficient to pursue critical literary theories, as with Benzinger, of two sources, paralleling Elijah stories, one of a siege of starvation of the inhabitants ($6^{24ff.}$), the other of a general famine, to which *this evil* (6^{33}) and the officer's scoffing inquiry about *windows in heaven* (7^2) would belong. Kittel holds that the story was originally aligned after the episode of the seven years' famine ($8^{1ff.}$). There is no basis for exact historical dating. However the narrative contains reminiscences at close hand of historical realities; *e.g.*, a siege of Samaria by Aram, the reference to the Hittites and Musrites (7^6), as also minor details, *e.g.*, the harrowing event of mothers eating their children by mutual bargain, with the king's human indignation, which he would vent extravagantly upon Elisha, and the humorous anecdote of the lepers' discovery of the abandoned camp. Also Elisha again appears in a political rôle, as in $3^{4ff.}$, here sitting in conclave with the civic elders, and assuming the offensive against the king in the spirit of Elijah and Micaiah.

25. An ass's head at eighty shekels of silver. For records of similar soaring prices for odd foods *cf.* Plutarch, *Artaxerxes*, xxiv, how the Kadisians " cut off the draught animals, so that an ass's head was worth almost 60 drachmæ," and Pliny, *Historia naturalis*, viii, 82, who relates that at a certain siege by Hannibal a mouse rose in the market to 200 denarii (if the Biblical figures seem absurd, they have parallels in other

II. 6²⁴–7²⁰

ancient story!); these references were early made by the commentators cited by Poole. **25.** *The fourth part of a kab of dove's dung for five shekels of silver.* A kab equals about two litres, and the shekel may be rated as a current shilling. For the modern equivalents of these terms of quantity and price see BDD, 'Weights and Measures,' the Archæologies of Nowack (§§35–7), and Benzinger (§§40–2). ' Dove's dung ' is the translation of two distinct words appearing in Kt. and Ḳr. here. The earliest interpretation of such an impossible food is by Josephus, noting that this stuff was used ' in place of salt.' In support of this interpretation is adduced Josephus's note in *BJ* v, 13, 7, that at the siege of Jerusalem " some were driven to such straits as to search the old dunghills of cattle and to eat the dung." Virgil's ' fames obscœna ' and similar Classical references are cited by Poole. Post (*DB* s.v. ' Dove ') quotes a Spanish author concerning a famine in England in 1316 when the people ate pigeon dung, but this may be only a Scriptural reminiscence. Burney and Post hold that the literal meaning is by no means certainly incorrect. Bochart started a fresh and sensible interpretation (*Hierozoicon*, i, 42, cited by Poole at length, *cf.* Gesenius, *Thesaurus*, Burney), suggesting that ' dove dung ' is to be compared with an Arabic term for a certain herb, ' sparrow dung.' This interpretation may well be accepted, unless we are to regard these items as the invention of popular, almost humorous talk. For drastic attempts at emendation of the text by Grätz, Klostermann, Cheyne, Winckler, see *SBOT*. **26.** The woman makes appeal to the king in usual legal formula, *Save!* (EVV ' help '), as in the appeal of another woman (2 Sam. 14⁴). **27.** *If Y*HWH *do not help thee :* so the prevailing interpretation in ancient and modern VSS; rather, *Not so! Y*HWH *save thee!* See note for various interpretations and attempted emendations. **28. 29.** For the tragedy of parents eating their own children in a siege as a common occurrence see Dt. 28⁵⁶ᶠ·, Eze. 5¹⁰, Lam. 2²⁰, 4¹⁰ (with ' boiling ' as here); for historical cases there is one in the Roman siege of Jerusalem, cited by Josephus, *BJ* vi, 3, 4, another at Ashurbanipal's siege of Babylon (*KB* 2, 190; *ARA* 2, §794), along with cases cited by Poole. **30.** The king wore his royal dress, but privately the dress of affliction underneath, as might be seen from his high position on the wall; this note serves to explain his indignation at Elisha, the one spiritual potency, who was idly *sitting down* (v.^{32}), and yet responsible for the horrible incident. **31.** The king's curse upon himself, *if the head of Elisha ben Shaphat shall stand upon him to-day*, has provoked much discussion; it was a hasty curse, which he hardly expected to carry out, although the prophet, who knew of it 'in the spirit,' shut the door against any messenger. The translation of the following vv. exhibits the straits of the EVV in precising the *personæ loquentes* (*cf*. Moffatt, Chic. B.). **32.** *And Elisha was sitting in his house, and the elders sitting with him. And he* [EVV *the king* in italics or brackets] *sent a man from his presence. Before the messenger came to him, he said to the elders: See ye how this son of a murderer hath sent to take away my head? Look! When the messenger cometh, shut the door, and hold the door fast against him! Is not the sound of his master's feet behind him?* **33.** *And while he yet talked with them, behold, the messenger was coming down to him; and he* [JV *the king* in brackets] *said: Behold, this is the evil from* YHWH [EVV *this evil is of the Lord*]. *Why should I wait for* YHWH *any longer?* The evident difficulties have led to many drastic revisions; see Stade at length, and *cf*. the notes in *BH*. The one necessary correction is to read in v.^{33} *the king* (*melek* in place of *mal'ak*, 'messenger'). Wellhausen, in Bleek,^{4} 251, n. 4, and Stade would also elide all reference to the messenger, reading 'king' in place of it throughout, and omitting "and he sent a man from him." But Elisha saw 'only in part'; it was the king himself who came, while the prophet expected only an underling, of whom he was afraid, and in whose face he shut the door. There exists at the end of the passage an anacoluthon as to the opening of the door to the king. To Elisha's surprise the king himself appeared. The earliest explanation of the interlude of barring the door against the king is that given by Josephus, that the delay would give the king time to change his mind. *This son of a murderer*: a pure epithet, *i.e.*, 'a murderous fellow,' as Winckler recognized (*GI* 1, 52), after common Oriental usage; *cf*. 'whore's son,' 1 Sam. 20^{30}. The final inquiry is one of profound impatience with God. Ch. 7. **1.** The prophet's reply in a brief oracle couched in terms of the market. Prices were to go lower, but still remain high ; a *seah* (EVV *measure*)=12 litres (*v. supra*, 6²⁵) ; Šanda cites Mishna *Erubin*, vii, 2, quoting 4 seahs of barley at 1 shekel. *Cf.* the statement of high prices, rated by the shekel, in time of distress in the Panammuwa inscr., line 6, ' in the gate,' *i.e.*, in the market ; Šanda *cft.* the similar Akkadian term, *ina abulli*. **2.** For *the captain* (for the official term, *thirdling*, see I. 9²²) *on whose hand the king leaned*, *cf.* 9²⁵, 15²⁵, where such aides-de-camp are named.

3. *And four men there were, lepers.* For the disease see Comm., 5¹. **4.** *Let us fall away to the camp of Aram ;* the verb is used technically of desertion, change of parties, *e.g.*, 1 Sam. 29³. **6.** For the panic (Lat., ' terror panicus ') Grotius gives Classical examples. *The kings of the Hittites and the kings of the Musrites.* So the latter *n. pr.* is to be understood as of the Anatolian Muṣur-land, *vs.* Ḳr., Miṣraim, ' Egypt ' (its *kings* would be an absurdity) ; see I. 10²⁸ᶠ·, and for the Hittites *v. ibid.* In Biblical use this name largely denotes Syrian states of one-time Hittite appurtenance, *e.g.*, Josh. 1⁴, Jud. 1²⁶, 2 Sam. 24⁶, while in Assyrian usage Hatti-land meant Syria-Palestine ; see *KAT* 189 ; A. Götze, *Hethiter, Churriter u. Assyrer* (1936) ; E. O. Forrer, ' The Hittites in Palestine,' *QS* 1936, 190 ff. ; *PEQ* 1937, 100 ff. ; the last-named scholar has full discussion of use of ' Hittites ' in ancient records. He holds (pt. I, 197) that the author of the present story was unaware of the historical circumstances of such a siege of Samaria by Ben-Hadad, since during the whole of this period the ' Hittite ' kings were allied with that king against Shalmaneser III (see his Annals for years 853, 848, 843, 841). However, we can hardly control the shifting politics of the Syrian states in that age ; *cf.* the varying relations of Israel with Damascus in the present stories and the novel factors and events presented for a later day in the Zakar stele (see above, I. 20¹). For the hiring of auxiliaries—typical at large of ancient military politics—*cf.* 2 Sam. 10⁶, Hos. 8⁹, Is. 7²⁰. **9.** *If we should wait till the morning light, penalty will overtake us :* Grotius remarks : " Officium civium est ea indicare quæ ad salutem publicam pertinent." *Let us go and notify the king's house :* so rather than *household* with EVV ; Šanda *cft.* a corresponding Egyptian expression as surrogate for 'king'; *cf.* Turkish, 'the Porte,' etc. **13.** A lengthy duplicate appears in this v., one lacking in many MSS and also in the Grr. and 𝔖; it may be explained by supposing that the scribe of some archetype inadvertently repeated the last line of a column at the top of the next. There also remain problems of interpretation, which have been variously attempted (see Note): the following presents a reduction to simple form. *And one of his courtiers replied and said: And* (yet) *let them take, pray, five of the horses that are left—those left in it* [*i.e.*, in the city—Grr., *here*], *see! will be* (in any case) *like all the multitude who are already consumed*. Such is Josephus's interpretation of the courtier's suggestion to his master's fear of losing more men (Marcus's tr.) : " and, he added, if others are captured by the foe and put to death, you will (merely) be adding the horsemen to those who have already perished in the famine"; *i.e.*, five more lost will make no difference. The present is a typical case of the popular broken diction appearing in these stories, and so most difficult to render. **14.** *And they took two horse-chariots:* Grr., and so Josephus on v.[13], with change in vocalization, understand 'two riders of horses,' which is preferred by some critics, *e.g.*, Burney, on the ground that reconnoitering is much better done by mounted men; but equestrianism was not a common art in those days; see Note, I. 1[5]. **17.** *And the king having appointed the captain*, etc., *in charge of the gate, the people trod him down by the gate:* so the usual English translation is to be revised. *As the man of God spoke, who spoke when the king came down to him:* omit the doublet, *who spoke*; Stade, Šanda preserve only the first sentence, regarding the rest as secondary along with the foll. vv. **19. 20.** This extraordinary repetition of vv.[16, 17] has been explained as the writer's moralizing reiteration for emphasis (so *e.g.*, Thenius, Keil); but is now generally recognized as a secondary doublet; *cf.* v.[13].

25. והנה : 4 MSS deR., והנם; but see above, v.[20].—בשמנים : MS 30 בחמשים =Grr., 𝔖[H] (*cf.* Int., §2).—חרייונים (so Ginsb.[1], *BH*; Ginsb.[2], חרי ויגים ; also MSS חריונים) Kt.; דְּבְיוֹנִים (Cod. C of *BH* ריב יונים) Ḳr.: for ח׳ *cf.* חריהם 18[27]. Ḳr. may be explained from J. Aram. דִיבָא, 'flux '=Heb. זוב, but the word would be no less cacophonous; see Gordis, *The Biblical Text*, 84, for such correction of obscene words.—**27.** אל : despite the accentuation in 𝔐=𝔗, Grr., Jos. ("he imprecated a curse upon her"), it is the exclamatory

II. 6²⁴–7²⁰

negative, 'No!'; cf. 3¹³, etc.: ῷ correctly, "Non te salvet Dominus"; Moff. translates: "'No, . . . may the Eternal help you!'" 𝔖 om. Most modern interpreters (so GV FV EVV) follow ancient models, finding here conditional syntax with jussives; see Dr., *Tenses*, §152, 3, Burn. (*n.b.* their doubt in this case). Jos.'s interpretation, followed by St., puts a low damnation in the king's mouth.—**29.** At end of v. 𝔊ᴸ a plus.—**30.** עבר: 𝔊ᴸ as though עמד, largely accepted by critics since Klost.; rather Lucian has introduced a literary variation of עבר, v.²⁶.—**31.** For the curse formula see I. 2²³.—בן שפט: 𝔊 om.; but the full name is here formally proper.—**32.** בטרם: 𝔊ᴸ 𝔖 ῷ with conj., 'and.'—הראיתם: for the irregular daghesh in ר after the particle cf. 1 Sam. 10²⁴, 17²⁵; it doubtless presents actual pronunciation; deR. notes some 'most accurate MSS,' also prints, that avoid it.—**33.** המלאך: read המלך; see Comm.

Ch. 7. **1.** שמעו: Grr. as sing., accepted by St., *BH*; but the proclamation is to the public in quite democratic fashion.—**2.** למלך: read המלך with some 10 MSS deR., VSS, and so Then., *al.*—את איש האלהים: 𝔊 𝔊ᴵᴵ 'Elisha,' 𝔖 om.; to be elided, specification of the object is not necessary, and above, Elisha is always named.—הנה: for the conditional use of the particle cf. Lev. 13⁸, etc. (the cases cited in GB); König, *Syntax*, 564, denies the conditional use of the particle; it doubtless introduces an exclamatory expression, but in cases with resultant conditional sense; cf. Arab. *'inna, 'in.*—עֹשֶׂה: Šanda attempts, "Lo, Yhwh has made (עֹשֶׂה) . . . but will this thing happen?"—ויאמר 2⁰: Grr.+' Elisha.' —**4.** For the conditional pfs. cf. 5²⁰.—נחיה: 3 MSS וג׳=𝔊 𝔗, approved by St., *BH*; but then the pf. is demanded, as in the foll. conditional phrase.—**5.** בנשף: 'at (evening) twilight,' cf. v.⁷ and so 𝔊 understands, εν τω σκοτει, in both cases; but 𝔊ᴸ here+ηδη διαυγαζοντος, in v.⁷+ηδη διαφωσκοντος, understanding the morning twilight; for contrasted mngs. of נשף see Lexx., and cf. Mt. 28¹, Luke 23⁵⁴, where the verb επιφωσκειν renders a similar Aram. *double entente*; see G. F. Moore, *JAOS* 26 (1905), 323 ff.—ויבאו: 7 MSS om., and so the underlying text of Hex. with ⁛.—עד קצה: B A *al.*, by perversion, εις μεσον; Bᵃ·ᵇ 𝔊ᴸ *al.*, εις μερος=𝔖ᴴ.— **6.** אדני: 14 MSS יהוה; the Ḳr., replacing the original Kt., seemed a necessary theological change here.—[מחנה] את: 20 MSS אל.—For the 'abenteuerliche Konstruktion' of 'ein so stumpfsinniger Übersetzer' of the Gr. here see Rahlfs, *SS* 3, 223.—[סום] קול: so Bär, Ginsb., *BH*; many MSS, edd. (Mich., Ken.), וקול=VSS (see deR., Bär), probably to be preferred with St.; the chariotry and the horse are summed up in the foll. appositive, 'a great army.'—קול [חיל] =𝔊 (B i), 𝔗ᵂ; MSS וקול=other VSS.—[ישראל] מלך: N *al.* om., 𝔖ᴴ ⁛.; acc. to St. a verbal expansion—an unnecessary judgment.—החתים: Jos., 'the isles,' by confusion of the word with כתים; cf. Jer. 2¹⁰.—מִצְרָיִם: read הַצָּרִים; see Comm. 𝔗 ῷ read as 'הם, 'the Egyptians.'—**7.** את אהליהם ואת סוסיהם ואת חמריהם המחנה

כאשר היא : Grr. ease by translating ' — in the camp —'; 𝔖ᴴ asterisks ' and their horses,' which HP 158, 245 om. ; omission of this item has recommended itself to critics on the ground that the fugitives would have fled on horses, and so Kit., Šanda om. it, and then logically delete הסום אסור, v.¹⁰ ; but chariot horses were not available for mounts ; omission of the item was a bit of ignorant criticism. St., *BH* (' fortasse ') om. ' their tents and horses and mules,' as borrowed from v.¹⁰, on the ground that המחנה is then ' without connexion ' ; but the appositive. ' the camp as it was,' is unimpeachable.—היא : many MSS הוא, but with Ḳr. היא ; but see St., Šanda for cases of מחנה as fem., the latter adducing the fem. sing. מחנת in the Aram. Panammuwa inscr., l. 17 ; *cf.* the pls. in both -*îm* and -*ôt̲*.—**8.** ויטמנו 1⁰ : 𝔊 om.—**9.** עוון : see C. A. Ben Mordecai's discussion of the word in *JBL* 60 (1941), 311 ff., with the suggestion of ' trouble ' for translation here.—**9.** [ונבאה] לכו : 𝔊ᴸ om. the misunderstood impv.—**10.** שׁעֵר : the pl. (so 𝔗ᵂ, 𝔖, *cf.* v.¹¹) is demanded by the foll. להם, acc. to Then., Burn., St., *al.*, rdg. שׁעָרי ; Grr. read as שַׁעַר, which is to be accepted as collective = ' the gate-watch,' even as 𝔗ᴸ translates ; 𝔊ᴸ has a plus, intruding ' the commanders of the city.'—אסור 2⁰ : 𝔊 (𝔊ᴴ ⁂) om. by early carelessness (1 Heb. MS om. 'א)(והחמור ; not unnecessary, *vs.* St.—אהלים : Grr. as אהליהם, and so Klost., *al.* ; *BH* sugg. האהלים ; the error, if such, is ancient.—**11.** ויקרא : as referring to prec. ' gate-keeper ' ; some 18 MSS Ken., deR., ויקראו = VSS, which is to be read ; the news was relayed by voices to the palace, hence the pl. ; 𝔖 and 𝔙 found difficulty, and tr. with ' and they came near ' and ' ierunt' respectively as from root קרה.—**12.** להחבה : many MSS correctly להתחבא.—בהשרה : Ḳr. בְּשֶׂרָה = many MSS ; error in Kt. by dittog. of prec. בה.—**13.** [ויקחו] : MS 70 om., and so VSS, exc. 𝔗 ; 𝔙 conforms verb to 1st pers. pl. as *inf.*—

הנשארים אשר נשארו בה הנם ככל ההמון ישראל
[,, ,, ,, ,, ,, ההמון ,, אשר תמו]

The duplicate bracketed section is absent in 40 MSS Ken., deR., and in the Grr. and 𝔖 ; see Comm. Read ההמון with Kt., and omit ישראל (some 60 MSS reduce the ungrammatical form to הָמֹן) ; ' the multitude ' refers to the people, not to the horses, as Klost., St. maintain. Joüon (*Mél.*, 5, 479), accepting the deletion, would read מכל, ' out of all the number (of horses).' Burn. attempts extensive rewriting. See further St.-Haupt at length.—בה 1⁰ : Burn., St., Šanda correct to פה on basis of Gr. ωδε = 𝔖ᴴ ; but this is an exegetical makeshift ; 𝔙 ' in urbe,' and so all EVV.—**14.** שני רכב סוסים : for רכב as collective see 6¹⁷ ; Grr. = לְרֹכְבֵי, ' riders of ' ; *cf.* 𝔙 ' two horses,' 𝔖 ' two pairs of drivers ' ; it is best, with St., to keep 𝔐.—מחנה : 𝔊 τ. βασιλεως (𝔖ᴴ ⁂) ; 𝔊ᴸ om. ; MS h = 𝔐 ; St., Šanda regard it as secondary ; but the Gr. difficulty lay in misunderstanding the noun, which can mean ' army ' (and so EVV here, *host*), as well as ' camp '; *cf*. I. 22³⁴, etc.—15. מלאה בגדים : the appositional syntax is usual with this adj.; see Lexx., and *cf*. GK §131.—בהחפזם : Kt., בְּחֶפְזָם Kr.: grammatical variants, Nif. and Ḳal.—17. וימת : some Gr. MSS om., 𝔖ᴴ ⁘ ; but not a 'scribal expansion,' as with St.; scribes may have dramatically omitted the item in anticipation of v.²⁰.—אשר דבר : see Comm.—19. כדבר : many MSS, edd. (see deR.) = ℭ 𝔖 = הדבר = v.³.—20. [ויהי] לו : OGrr. om.

8¹⁻⁶. The story of the lady of Shunem continued (4⁸ᶠᶠ·); her sojourn in the Philistine land upon the prophet's advice to avoid a seven-years' famine having entailed dispossession of her estate, she makes appeal to the king at the moment that Gehazi, in response to his interest in Elijah's *great works*, is telling him the story of the resuscitation of the woman's son; the king orders restoration to her of the estate and its usufruct. The item of a seven years' famine parallels that of the famine in the Elijah cycle, extending into the third year. This extraordinary period of time may have been suggested by the great famine in Canaan and Egypt as narrated in Gen. 41 ff. But a legal *nuance* may lie in the item; at the end of the story the woman recovers her property, *i.e.*, within a sabbatic period, during which she retained her rights of possession despite non-occupation (*cf*. Ex. 21², 23¹⁰ᶠ·). Such continuance of possession is illustrated by the story of Ruth. It is futile to attempt chronology for the story, as does Šanda. The woman was a widow now, and her son evidently a minor. **3.** *She went out to cry to the king:* legalistic terminology; *cf*. Akk. *ragāmu* and Lat. *clamare* used in the same sense. **4. 5.** The king's interest is quite natural, whatever estrangement there may have been between him and Elisha; the woman's appearance on the scene is a dramatic element. **6.** *The king gave her an officer*, etc.: so EVV; but the original sense of *eunuch* (see 18¹⁷) may be preferred here for propriety's sake when a man accompanied a lady.

VV.⁷⁻¹⁵. Upon a visit of Elisha to Damascus the invalid king Ben-Hadad deputes a certain Hazael to inquire of him concerning his recovery; Yʜᴡʜ gives Elisha the vision of Hazael as future king of Aram and desolator of Israel; Hazael returns to his master, on the morrow suffocates him, and assumes the throne. In Shalmaneser III's Bull inscription (846 B.C.) is recorded a victory over Ben-Hadad of Damascus;

in his Obelisk inscription (842 B.C.) appears a victory over Hazael of Damascus; and according to the Berlin inscription (without date) is record of an invasion into Syria with the datum: "Bir-idri forsook his land (*i.e.*, abdicated), and Hazael, son of a nobody, seized the throne."[1] As such a base-born man Hazael appears here, without patronymic (*cf.* Omri, Zimri); evidently the official news to the public was that Ben-Hadad had abdicated. The present story succeeds as fulfilment of the oracles of political import from God to Elijah in I. 19[15ff.], and is generally regarded as a mere doublet to the latter. But the connexion of those oracles with Elijah is secondary, 'ad majorem gloriam suam,' in contrast with the details of the present story, extraordinary as it is. Most novel is the intrusion of this early prophet into foreign affairs (and yet *cf.* the Balaam oracles), so anticipating Amos and his successors, for in the present case there is no religious, domestic *motif*, as in the denunciation of Ahab's house and the subsequent prophetically inspired revolt of Jehu; indeed Elisha is given, to his own consternation, an oracle portending doom to YHWH's own people. *N.b.* his phrase, "YHWH has given me vision" (vv.[10, 13]), as in the repeated oracles of Amos (ch. 7). Judgment of historicity depends upon the critic's view of the possibility of such second-sight, as also of the elements of actual history lying behind all these narratives. Absurd indeed appears the item of the extra gift of forty camel loads of the best of Damascene wares (v.[9]); v.[12] may be imitative of Hos. 10[14]. But the psychical episode in vv.[10, 11] cannot be passed over as pure invention. There arises the query, Did Elisha deliberately lie?, and again, Was he, if not the instigator, at least the suggestor of Hazael's foul act? Some would hold that Elisha was deliberately playing a part in foreign politics,[2] and even attribute Hazael's crime to

[1] See Rogers, *CP* 297 ff.; Gressmann, *ATB* 1, 341 ff.; *ARA* 1, §§681, 686. For the contemporary Syrian history, in addition to the Histories *au courant*, see Šanda, 2, 49 ff.; R. de Vaux, 'La chronologie de Hazaël et de Benhadad III, rois de Damas,' *RB* 43 (1934), 512 ff.; A. Alt, 'Die syrische Staatenwelt vor dem Einbruch der Assyrer,' *ZDMG* 1934, 233 ff. Note Josephus's statement that these two kings were still worshipped as gods in his day.

[2] So Winckler in *KAT* 248 ff., 254 ff. alleging close relations of Elijah and Elisha with foreign states.

Elisha's 'instigation.' But a warning word by P. Volz is to the point : [3] " Es war eine der einseitigsten Ueberschätzungen der politischen Werte, als man auf den Einfall kam, die Propheten zu ' politischen Agenten ' zu machen ; nicht bloss das Selbstgefühl der Propheten, auch das Urteil der auswärtigen Könige über die Propheten und die ganze Stellung der Pneumatiker zu allen Zeiten beweist, dass die Gottesmänner als überweltliche Faktoren anerkannt wurden. Die darüber erzählenden Legenden beruhen auf richtiger Erfahrung." On p. 39, n. 1, he cites Catharine of Siena's concern with affairs of ecclesiastical and imperial politics. It is easy enough forsooth to imagine an international religious conspiracy, like that of the Muslim Assassins, involving the dynasties of Ben-Hadad and Omri.

10. *And Elisha said to him : Go, say to him, Thou shalt surely recover* [Heb. *live*].—*And Y HWH has given me to see that he shall surely die.* The contradiction and the apparent falsehood have induced a spelling in 𝕳, whereby the vocable pronounced *lô* is shifted from the sense *to him* to *not, i.e., thou shalt not die* ; but the Hebrew cantillation, as also the VSS, demand the first rendering. Many comm. (see Poole) down to Keil have argued for the second interpretation to avoid the lying contradiction, while the lawyer Grotius bluntly affirms that it is legitimate to lie to aliens and idolators. There is large variety of ancient evasion of the text : Jos., " he bade him not to announce evil to the king " ; Rashi : " according to Hazael's word he said, Thou shalt not die " (*i.e.,* H. was the liar) ; Kimchi : " he will not die unless he is killed." AV dilutes with " Thou mayest certainly recover." The present writer finds two distinct elements in the response : first the prophet's own spontaneous response, which is followed and contradicted by a supervening affect of second-sight. The prophet does not always know at first, or knows only in part (*e.g.,* $4^{26\text{ff.}}$, 5^{26}) ; *cf.* the progressive revelations in Amos 7^{1-9}, in which the prophet is finally overruled.

11. EVV : *And he settled his countenance steadfastly* [RVV JV +*upon him*], *until he was ashamed ; and the man of God wept.* The Heb. of *he settled his face* [the verb=*made to stand*] is unique ; the adv. *steadfastly* is circumlocutory for an

[3] *Der Geist Gottes,* 40, n. 2.

actual verb, *and he set* (as in AV mg.). These difficulties are increased by the query as to the subject of the verbs. Jewish comm., many Renaissance scholars, most moderns continue Elisha (*cf.* v.¹⁰) as subject ; but Josephus, 𝔊ᴸ (with 'the gifts' as object of 'he set'), Winckler, Stade make Hazael the subject, since *the man of God* is introduced subsequently as subject of *wept*. But we should expect the change of subject to be noted here. Burney understands the moment with "Elisha looked him out of countenance," *i.e.*, *to the shame* of Hazael's guilty conscience ; but Elisha was little concerned with the latter's coming crime. Rather (so *e.g.*, Skinner, Šanda) Elisha *stared* (=Heb. *set his face*), overcome by a fresh vision of Israel's approaching misfortune at Hazael's hand. The verb *and he set*, with change of Mas. punctuation is to be emended to *and he was confused* (so 𝔙 and many moderns), and the following *unto shame* (so the Heb.) may be expressed with 'to mutual embarrassment.' Then a fresh moment follows : *And the man of God wept*, *i.e.*, he broke down. **12.** Elisha is overwhelmed by the presentiment of what Hazael's accession will mean to Israel. **13.** *What is thy servant, the dog* (as he is) *?* The phrase has its exact replica repeated in the Lachish ostraca, "Who is thy servant, a dog ?" ; see Torczyner, *LL* nos. ii, v, vi, and p. 39, noting the similar ancient epistolary form of humility in the Amarna letters, *e.g.*, Knudtzon, no. 60 : "I am a slave (*arad*) of the king and a dog (*kalbu*) of his house," and similar interrogative expressions as here, nos. 71, ll. 16 ff., 202, ll. 12 ff. *Cf.* also 1 Sam. 24¹⁵, 2 Sam. 9⁸, 16⁹. **15.** The noun translated *coverlet* is otherwise unknown. Ewald (*HI* 4, 93) has a unicum of rendering, giving the verb *he took* an impersonal subject— some one smothered him with a *bath-cloth*, and listing a number of historic cases of assassination in the bath, *e.g.*, the murder of the prince Aristobulos by Herod (*Ant.*, xv, 3, 3). Thenius gives a long explanation, according to which the king died not from suffocation but from shock.

VV.¹⁶⁻²⁴. The reign of Jehoram of Judah. ‖ 2 Ch. 21 ; *cf. Ant.*, ix, 5. The moralizing judgment upon the king as worthy son-in-law of Ahab and Jezebel (v.¹⁸) is supported by a tradition in Ch. of his having done away with six of his brothers, who are all named, doubtless a historical item. The change of political conditions in his reign continues the failure of his father Jehoshaphat's effort at Esyon-geber (I. 22⁴⁹) ; and the revival of Moab under Mesha is paralleled by the similar restoration of Edom to independence and by the revolt of Libnah on the Philistine border. Ch. has a further datum of a successful and destructive invasion by Philistines and Arabs. The appearance of the Assyrians in the north had given signal for revolt to the southern dependencies of the two kingdoms. **16.** *Jehoshaphat being king of Judah:* to be omitted, with MSS and VSS, as a dittograph; see Note. **17.** Jehoram *reigned eight years:* the figure varies in 1 Heb. MS and in Gr. texts, as result of varying calculations. **18.** *The daughter of Ahab as wife:* Athaliah, named in v.²⁶ as daughter of Omri. *Cf.* I. 22⁴⁵ for the ' peace ' made between Jehoshaphat and Ahab, and II. 3 for their joint campaign against Moab. VV.²⁰⁻²² present the only events of the reign. The one is the revolt of Edom, which *in his days revolted from the control of Judah and made a king over themselves* (v.²⁰), a statement repeated after the obscure v²¹ with *and Edom revolted from the control of Judah* (v.²²ᵃ) ; and the other, *Then Libnah revolted at that time* (v. ²²ᵇ). The expressions ' in his days ' and ' then ' indicate archival origin for the data. **21.** *And Joram* [so 𐤌 with reduced form of the name] *passed over to Sair and all the chariotry with him ; and it was, he rose up by night and smote Edom, who surrounded him, and the captains of the chariotry, and the people fled home* [Heb. *to their tents—cf.* I. 12¹⁶]. The final sentence indicates the flight of the Israelite army, the second and third must mean that by a night foray the king was able to break through the surrounding enemy ; but the following ' and the captains of the chariotry,' an accusative, awkwardly introduced in the Heb., is unintelligible, as we learn above only of the Israelite chariotry. The passage must mean in sum that Jehoram himself escaped with the *élite* of his army, and that ' the people,' *i.e.*, the infantry, fled off as best they could. An opposite interpretation by change of text is advanced by Stade (*GVI* I, 537, n. I, and *SBOT—cf. BH*) : *And Edom arose by night, and surrounded him, and smote him and the captains of the chariotry.* But this requires extensive alteration of the text, while the contents of the latter are more suitable to an official record—there was a heroic sortie. The locality Sair is the Soar of Gen. 13¹⁰, at southern end of the Dead Sea. **22b**. Libnah has not been certainly identified. This autonomous action of a little city is of interest. For the two places see Notes.

VV.²⁵⁻²⁹. The reign of Ahaziah of Judah. ‖ 2 Ch. 22¹⁻⁶; Josephus simply records his accession, *Ant.*, ix, 5 *ad fin*. The usual archival data are given in vv.²⁵⁻²⁶; v.²⁷ is redactorial with its moralizing judgment; vv.²⁸·²⁹ are introductory to the history in ch. 9. **25. 26a**. The king's accession is dated in Joram's 12th year, and his reign given duration of one year. As both kings deceased contemporaneously, the *one year* regarded by a later computer as a full year could not have been such, unless the Judæan king came to the throne in Joram's 11th year, and so the correction of the dating in 9²⁹, accepted here by some VSS. As Kittel remarks, we have here a case of early attempts to correct synchronisms. **26b**. Athaliah is here daughter of Omri, but according to v.¹⁸ daughter of Ahab. The inconsistency has generally been explained by generalizing ' daughter ' as ' granddaughter ' (*cf.* I. 15²). But Begrich (*ZAW* 53 [1935], 78 f.) properly insists that we possess here a correct tradition, since the earlier passage conflicts with the possible genealogy. The duplicate expression in v.²⁷, *son-in-law of the house of Ahab*, is generalizing, to establish connexion with that arrant evildoer ; this was then understood as meaning Ahab's son-in-law. **28. 29**. Since Ewald (*HI* 4, 97, n. 3) the statement that Ahaziah *went with Joram ben Ahab to war against Hazael*, etc., has been denied by some scholars ; in the issue of Joram's disaster (v.²⁹) nothing is said of Ahaziah's fortunes, and the latter appears only in a visit to Joram. Ewald emends with excision of a particle to *Joram went to war*, and this has been accepted by Benzinger, Kittel in his Comm. ; but the latter in *GVI* 2, 261, and the historians in general accept the Heb. item as historical. However, these two vv. appear to be quite secondary to 9¹⁴·¹⁵ᵃ·¹⁶ᵇ ; *n.b.* their repetitiousness, and also the quite anticipatory reference to Ahaziah's visit ; see below, int. to cc. 9, 10.

1. בא : ppl. used verbally ; *cf.* הֹלֵךְ גם, Gen. 32⁷ (for similar use in Syriac *cf.* Nöld., *Syr. Gram.*, §274) ; 𝔊 as perf., and so St. ; 𝔊¹· a doublet with future verb.—**3.** פלשתים : B j u x+' to the city.'

ותצא— : 𝔊 Hex., 𝔖 as ותבא, preferred by St. (*cf. BH*), on the ground that the woman was not yet in her house ; but the verb here is legalistic.—אל 2° 3° : על is demanded, as in v.⁵.—5. המת : MS 171 pref. בנה ; Grr., 'a (her) dead son.'—6. יום : מיום עזְבָהּ is conj. of time, as in Ps. 56⁴, etc., and so in Ugaritic, S. Arab. ; hence the infin., עזְבָהּ, is not required, *vs.* St., Šanda, *BH*.—8. הוהאל : so thrice below and 2 Ch. 22⁶, also in an Aram. docket on an Akk. tablet (see GB, and *cf.* עשׂהאל) ; elsewhere חזאל (so 11 MSS here). Thureau-Dangin has published an ivory tablet with text חזאל למראן, *Arslan-Tash* (1931), 88.—מנחה : Grr., μαναα, etc., exc. 𝔊ᴸ, also Jos., δωρα ; similar transliteration in 𝔊 17³, 20¹² : the foreign word may have entered Hellenistic usage.— מאותו : read with 6 MSS, one early ed., מֵאִתּוֹ, and so Kt. in very many MSS and some early edd. ; see deR.—מחלי : 'from my sickness' ; see Note, 1².—9. וכל : 𝔊ᴸ 𝔈 𝔖 as מכל ; St. rightly prefers 𝔐, as distinguishing the gift carried by the envoy and the goods borne after him.—10. לא : 18 MSS לו : of Grr. B i om. *al.* Grr., VSS = לו ; the case is one of 18 in which tractate *Sopherim*, vi, 5, insists that לא is to beread for לו ; see König, *Syntax*, §352, b. —והראני : for the unusual consecution (this case apparently not noted by grammarians and by comm. *ad loc.*) *cf.* Dr., *Tenses*, ch. 9 ; the unusual syntax may mark an abrupt opposition of thought = 'and yet.'—11. ויעמד את פניו וישם עד בש ; 𝔊 (B A N *al.*) κ. παρεστη τω προσωπω αυτου κ. εθηκεν εως αισχυνης : 𝔊ᴸ develops the implication : εστη Αζαηλ κατα προσωπον αυτου (= 𝔖ᴴ " and A. stood before his face ") κ. παρεθηκεν ενωπιον αυτου τα δωρα εως ησχυνετο ; for the last phrase MSS 71 h u z, εκειτο τα δωρα εως ου εσαπρισαν (*i.e.*, as = root באש) = 𝔏 " posita sunt munera usque dum putrida fierent," this variant appearing also in 𝔖ᴴ as a doublet ; 𝔗 " and he turned his face and delayed for long " ; 𝔖 om. ; 𝔙 " stetitque cum eo et conturbatus est usque ad suffusionem vultus." Read וישׁם with Klost., Benz., Kit. (but *cf. BH*), Šanda ; see Burn., St. to the contrary.—12. רעה = Grr. in general ; A om. = 𝔈 ; 𝔊ᴸ συ ; its construction as acc. is defended by Ew., *Syntax*, §333, understanding את אשר as ' how,' as at I. 19¹.—תשלח באש : see Moore on Jud. 1⁸, proposing 'get rid of by fire.'—14. אמר לי : 𝔖ᴴ ⁂, depending upon a text haplog. of ειπεν, ειπεν ; *cf.* variants in Gr. MSS.—15. המכבר : 4 MSS pref. את ; 𝔗 and 𝔖 tr. with their respective words for שמיכה, 'rug,' Jud. 4¹⁸ ; 𝔊ᴸ στρῶμα = 𝔙 MSS ' stragulum,' ' bed-cover ' ; 𝔊 𝔊ᴴ 𝔖ᴴ transliterate with much corruption entailed, *e.g.*, B A ; Jos. tr. with δίκτυον, ' net.'

16. יהודה : ויהושפט מלך יהודה : MSS 30 253 Ken. (*cf.* 380 deR.) om., and so Grr. (exc. B A 𝔊ᴸ), also 𝔖 𝔄, and many codices of 𝔙 ; see Ken., *Diss.*, §89, deR. for the Latin texts, and *SBOT* ; the v. is otherwise badly corrupted in Heb. MSS. Mahler (*Chronologie*, 287) regards the item as noting a case of associated kingship.— יהורם Occ., יורם Or. : *inf.* יורה.—מלך יהודה 2° : the formula hitherto מ' על י' ; the change continues hereafter, exc. at 9²⁹ (Šanda).—

17. שמנה : MS 224 עשר ; B A d₂ ' 40 ' (obtained by addition, 32+8), 𝔊ᴸ ' 10 '; al., Jos.=𝕳.—שנה : Ḳr. שנים=Kt. in 22 MSS, edd.= Ch.; the same anomaly (see St.'s note) in 14², 22¹; cf. GK §134, e; the original was prob. written in abbreviation.—**18.** בדרך : 1 MS deR. בדרכי=pl. in 𝔖 𝔙.—מלכי : A N al. as sing.—**19.** לו 1⁰ : 𝔊 𝔊ᴸ om.; 1 Heb. MS om. לו 2⁰.—לבניו : ca. 60 MSS, also edd. (Bär), ולבניו A al., Ch.; B om. (𝔈 has); N al.=𝕳. St., Šanda well sugg. rdg. לפניו=I. 11³⁶.—**21.** צעירה=' little,' and the place identical with צער of Gen. 13¹⁰, both being forms of orig. diminutive, Arab. ṣuğair; cf. the writer's note on ' Delilah ' as an orig. diminutive, *JQR* 25 (1935), 262. The etymology in Gen. 19²⁰·²² is correct, despite Buhl, *Edomiter*, 65, denying it on ground of Gr. gamma for the gutt. in Gen., but here Σειωρ; but such transliteration is not constant; see Speiser, *JQR* 23 (1923), 236. St. would correct to ערה; Hitzig identified with שעיר. Ch. here עם שריו.—'ויהי הוא קם וג : Burn. regards the construction as ' inexplicable.' For the v. see Stade-Haupt's full discussion, also Robinson, *HI* 1, 343.—לילה : 𝔊 (B 𝔖ᴴ ⁎) om.—ואת שרי הרכב . . . ויכה את אדום : in suit with one interpretation noted above, the rdg. ויך אדום, or ויכה אתו א' is claimed; Kit. would read ואתו, ' and with him,' but St. observes that then ועמו is demanded.—The ' fleeing to their tents,' *i.e.*, fleeing home, is generally misunderstood. Ch., ignoring the defeat, om. this item.—**22.** לבנה : Grr. variously; 𝔊ᴸ Λοβνα=𝔙, representing a place identified in the *Onom.*; see Döller, *GES* 252 ff.; Albr., *BASOR* 15 (1924), 9; Abel, *GP* 2, 369 f.—**25.** שתים עשרה : 𝔊ᴸ 𝔖 ' 11th,' correction agreeing with 9²⁹.—שנה : 11 MSS, edd. om.—מלך יהודה : OGrr. om.—**26.** ' 22 years '; Ch., ' 42,' where 𝔊 ' 20.'—עתליהו : the verbal root=Akk. eṭelu/eṭelu, ' to be manly,' the derivative noun being used as epithet of gods; see Bezold, *BAG* 25, Noth, *IP* 191; *nn. pr.* עתל עתלן occur in Thamudene, *NPS* 1, 172.—בירושלם : B A y 𝔈 ' in Israel.'—[בת] עמרי : 𝔊ᴸ ' Ahab.'—**27.** את [יורם].—**28.** ⁎ 𝔖ᴴ ,.om 𝔊 : כי חתן בית אחאב הוא 1⁰: MS 70 om.; see Comm.—אדם : 𝔊 (B A N *al.*) αλλοφυλων.—רמת; 𝔊ᴸ Ραμαθ; in v.²⁹ רמה; see Note, I. 4¹³.—ארמים : Ch., הרמים, and Grr. there οι τοξοται, a rdg. accepted here by St.=הרמים : Klost., Burn. propose הפרים, ' the archers '; the subj. may be pure gloss, but is supported by 9¹⁵.—**29.** יכהו : so 9¹⁵; read with Ch. הכהו ; primitive error by confusion of ה and י.—ארמים : 𝔊 om., 𝔖ᴴ ⁎ ; it is superfluous, but the whole passage is repetitious. —מלך יהודה : MS 114, 𝔊 om.—בן אחאב : Gr. v om., 𝔖ᴴ ⁎.

9-10²⁸. The prophet-inspired revolt against Ahab's dynasty; the success of Jehu, with the extermination of Ahab's family and the devotees of Baal, and accompanying murder of Ahaziah of Judah. ‖ 2 Ch. 22⁷⁻⁹; *cf. Ant.*, ix, 6. For the historical circumstances see the Histories of Israel, and for **the popular character of the revolution** Causse, *Du groupe* *ethnique*, ch. 3. The narrative belongs to a practically contemporary document, coming from the school of the prophets, with full *sub voce* approval of the revolt and Jehu's bloody deeds. There is no hint of the blame that was later cast upon the usurper as in $10^{29\text{ff.}}$, Hos. 1^4. As an objective and highly dramatic political history, with which criticism can find little fault, the narrative naturally suggests literary comparison with I. 20, 22, and such is the general opinion of critics, *e.g.*, Wellhausen (*Comp.*, 286 f.), Kittel, Stade. Šanda disputes this position on the ground that the political attitude of the two documents is not identical, a favour being shown to Ahab in the earlier document that is not exhibited here. And yet the political favour of religious groups varies according to circumstances; the school of the prophets was loyal to Ahab, for he made concessions to their position (*e.g.*, I. 18), which were doubtless ruthlessly withdrawn by the queen-mother Jezebel, the power behind the throne of her two sons. However the present document does not depend upon the earlier one for style or details; *e.g.*, 9^{25} with its cryptic indirect allusion is absolutely original, as is 'yesterday' in v.^{26}, while there is a different formulation of Elijah's word (9^{26}) from that in I. 21^{29}, and also I. 21^{23} is secondary to the full oracle given here, $9^{36, 37}$. We may not claim more than that the two histories come from a common literary tradition, and, if indeed from different composers, light is cast upon a remarkable culture inspired in and by the early prophets, with which we may best compare the court-history of David and Solomon. Another contemporary document of quite similar colour is the story of the Judæan revolt against Athaliah (ch. 11), from a writer of the same *milieu*, although a Judæan. The present history with its long sweep of lively detail is the most dramatic in Kings. Note Jehu's evasiveness (v.^{19}), the obscure reminiscence, *Remember—I and thou* (v.^{25}), the dialogue with the proud, taunting Jezebel through her lattice window, a scene vivified to us by archæology (vv.$^{30\text{ff.}}$), the meeting with the otherwise undescribed Jehonadab b. Rechab, yet well enough known in his day, and their giving hands in zeal for Yhwh ($10^{15\text{ff.}}$), the wily stratagem for discovering the servitors of Baal (vv.$^{18\text{ff.}}$)—all these are as humanly true and brutal sketches as can be found anywhere in history, and all done with lightning-like strokes.

The document has been but slightly interpolated. 9^{7-10a}, placed in the young prophet's mouth, is an intrusion, disturbing the connexion. The parenthesis, vv.$^{15a. \ 16b}$, appears like repetition of $8^{28. \ 29}$, and is generally regarded as secondary to the latter (*e.g.*, by Stade, Šanda); but Kittel well makes the point that here is the original datum which has been repeated above (*v. ad loc.*). *N.b.* the archival phrase (v.^{14}), *and Jehu ben Jehoshaphat ben Nimshi conspired against Joram*, etc., with which *cf.* the identical phrase used of Zimri (I. 16^9) ; the definite phrase, *Joram was defending* [Heb. *guarding*—unique military term] *Ramoth-Gilead, vs.* the generalizing *went to war with Hazael* in the earlier statement. Indeed it looks as though the present passage stood originally at the beginning of the ch. ; then a variant form arose to conclude Ahaziah's history, after which, the prophet's action being given first place, the item was intruded here parenthetically. 9^{29} is an intruded variant repetition of 8^{25} (*v. ad loc.*). The one historically dubious passage, as recognized even by conservative critics, *e.g.*, Kittel, Šanda, following Stade (*ZAW* 1885, 275 ff.), is the story of the massacre of the brothers of Ahaziah going down *to inquire after the health* [Heb. *peace*] *of the king's children and the queen-mother's children*, some *forty-two men* (10^{12-14}). The large number refers to the whole accompanying party (but *cf.* the same number for the naughty children in 2^{24}) ; the country-wide fame of Jehu's insurrection and bloody massacres would seem to render the anecdote of such a visit most absurd ; and yet the details can hardly have been invented. The passage may be out of historical order. There is no reason to doubt, with Stade, the historicity of the Jehonadab anecdote ($10^{15. \ 16}$).

9^{1-16}. The consecration of Jehu as king by prophetic commission ; his recognition by the army at Ramoth-Gilead ; his immediate drive to Jezreel with stern instructions that no news should go out from the citadel. A prophet once more appears as the actor in consecration of a new king ; so Samuel was the consecrator of Saul (1 Sam. 10), of David (*ib.* ch. 16), and Nathan along with the priest Sadok of Solomon (I. $1^{34. \ 39}$). **2.** Jehu's genealogy is given here and in v.^{14} (the original source) as *ben Jehoshaphat ben Nimshi*. **4.** Omit *the young man, the prophet*, a gloss introduced to correct the possible notion that the messenger was merely a *boy* (*na'ar*), by which term however is meant a junior member of the guild. **11. 12.** *This mad fellow* : from the name of a raving order of Mesopotamian priests, *maḫḫū*, was derived an adverb, *maḫḫūtiš* = ' like a madman ' ; see Bezold, *BAG* 167, and Albright, *From the Stone Age*, 232. Jehu's embarrassment is well depicted : *You know for yourselves the man and his prattle*, correctly interpreted by Junius, " Scitis quid prophetæ loqui soleant." Ehrlich takes it in the sense, " You may know, but I do not." **13.** The strewing of the garments under the new king is paralleled by the story of Jesus' triumphal entry into Jerusalem (Mt. 21⁸). The phrase translated in EVV with *on the top of the stairs* (otherwise Moffatt, Chic. B.) is obscure ; the word *top* is best understood as some architectural term ; see Note. *Jehu is king !* : the same acclamation is given to Deity at his annual accession festival ; *cf.* Gunkel, *Einl. in die Psalmen*, 94 f. There may be noted the affecting story told by Robinson (*BR* 2, 8) of a time of famine at Bethlehem, when a British official party was welcomed by the people with their strewing of garments in the way and their asking for protection. For the trumpets *cf.* the discovery of a pair of silver trumpets in Tutankhamen's tomb (*ILN* Apr. 15, 1939, 633). For vv.[14. 15a. 16b] see above. VV.[15b. 16a. 17-28]. Jehu drives rapidly to Jezreel, and slays the two kings who come to meet him. This long drive of Jehu's squadron raises the interesting problem of ancient chariot transportation. The obscure approaching *company*, observed by the sentinel at Jezreel, induces the sending out of mounted scouts, who are roughly detained by Jehu. At last he is recognized by the sentry as Jehu for his furious driving (v.[20]), the Heb. word for ' fury ' being of the same root as that for *mad fellow*, v.[11]. **21.** For the verb ' to make ready ' of the EVV, ' to harness up ' is a more exact translation, and for ' they found him,' rather ' they came upon him.' **22.** To Joram's anxious inquiry, *Is all well?* (Heb., *Is it peace?*), comes Jehu's rough answer, as it may best be rendered : *What ! Is it all well, with still the many harlotries and witchcrafts of thy mother Jezebel ?* These terms, as Kittel remarks, are anticipatory of the language of the canonical Prophets in their description of the renegade practices of Israel ; *cf.* Hos. 2[4ff.], 4[7ff.], etc. By witchcrafts are meant the false cults, whose potency was ascribed to evil arts. For similar collocation of such terms see 17^{17}, 21^6, Dt. 18^{10}. **25.** *Then he* (Jehu) *said to Bidkar his captain: Take up and cast him in the portion of the field of Naboth the Jezreelite, for remember how that, when I and thou rode together after Ahab his father, Y*HWH *pronounced this burden upon him* [RVV^{mg}—*uttered this oracle against him*]. This moment gives stout authentication in its indirectness to the oracle put in Elijah's mouth in the sequel to Ahab's seizure of Naboth's vineyard (I. $21^{17\text{ff.}}$). The prophet indeed is not named, as would be the case were the data here secondary; and the cryptic reminiscence shared in by Jehu and Bidkar is doubtless original although the text is obscure. The translation of this half-verse as given above (and so Moffatt, Chic. B., but with ' I remember '), does not exhibit the difficulties of 𝔐, for which and for the many variant renderings see Note; but, as Šanda remarks, "the syntax is broken in correspondence with the excitement of the scene," and we may not proceed lightly to correction. The original of Engl. *rode together* can literally and best be translated, *were driving teams*, *i.e.*, each in his own chariot. For the word properly translated *burden* in EVV see Gehman, "The ' Burden ' of the Prophets," *JQR* 31 (1940), 107 ff., demonstrating that such is the proper *nuance* of the word—a burden upon the prophet, to be unloaded upon the guilty object. **27.** The place *Beth-haggan* (EVV literally, *the garden house*) is identified with En-gannim of Josh. 19^{21}, 21^{29}, the modern Jenîn; see Smith, *HG* 356; Döller, *GES* 254; Abel, *GP* 2, 317. Jibleam is modern Bel'ameh, a ruined tower S of Jezreel (Döller, *ib.*, 255). For *the ascent of Gur* the name may survive in modern Gurra (Sellin, *Tell Ta'annek*, 102). As EVV show by their parentheses, a sentence carrying out Jehu's order, *Smite him also*, is desiderated; following the Grr. and with slight emendation of 𝔐 read: *And him too! And they* [Grr. sing.] *smote him*. The following *on the chariot* is evidently a gloss meant to be attached to the verb *they drove him* in v.^{28} (where the EVV actually expand with *they carried him in a chariot*); so Stade, Šanda, *cf. BH*. The fate of Ahaziah is expanded in 2 Ch. $22^{7\text{ff.}}$ with remarkable midrashic variation.

V.^{29}. For this intrusion see above.

VV.³⁰⁻³⁷. **The fate of Jezebel.** **30.** The queen receives the murderer in royal state : *she made up her eyes with paint* [Heb. *pûk*], *and dressed her head, and looked out of the window.* For the drug in question, Gr. στίμμι (the derivative verb being used here in the Grr.), Lat. *stibium*, see W. H. Schoff, *The Periplus of the Erythræan Sea*, 192, with citations from Pliny and Dioscorides, and recalling the case of the Lydian queen Omphalos, who captivated Hercules, and used this cosmetic. In addition to its use for painting the eyebrows it dilates the pupils, and so Jeremiah, addressing the naughty woman Jerusalem, speaks of her as ' tearing out thy eyes ' with the stuff (Jer. 4³⁰). The same naughty woman, Oholibah, is described by Ezekiel as ' painting thy eyes ' (Eze. 23⁴⁰), the verb used there being of the same root as *kohl*, the name for the black cosmetic continued in modern Oriental use ; see Dalman, *A. u. S.*, 5, 351 ff., claiming that it is properly an antimonoxide. There is further to be noted the article on the Hebrew word *pûk* by W. Sommer in *JBL* 62 (1943), 33 ff., according to which the word had in antiquity quite varying colour-connotations. For the feminine painting-up in antiquity *cf.* Enoch 8¹, condemning these alluring arts as coming from Azazel ; for the Classical world see Grotius. *And she looked out through the window.* The same was custom for royal audience in Egypt, as represented in pictured scenes ; *cf.* Gressmann, *ATB* 2, 61 ; Gunkel, *Einl. in die Psalmen*, p. 73 ; and at length N. J. Reich, *Mizraim I* (1933), 39 f., on the Ptolemaic references to royal audiences ' through the window.'[1] **31.** Jezebel's salutation is the height of sarcasm : *Is it well* (*anglice*, ' How do you do ? '), *thou Zimri, his lord's murderer ?* The satirical appellative has its Classical parallel in Virgil (Æneid, iv, 215, cited by Grotius), " et nunc ille Paris," referring to Æneas. **34.** *And he went indoors, and ate and drank*—as if nothing untoward had happened, as Ehrlich remarks. **35.** The ghastly details of the end of Jezebel's remains are petty, but historical. **36.** The present citation

---

[1] There is another motive in the ivory tablet of the woman looking through the window found in Samaria (J. W. and G. W. Crowfoot, *The Ivories from Samaria*, 1933, pl. iii, fig. 3), and in the description of the artful woman in Prov. 7⁶ᶠᶠ·; see G. Boström, *Proverbiastudien* (1935), 102 ff.

of Elijah's word is the original of I. 21²³. **37.** Stade, Šanda regard the v. as 'Ausmalung'; there is indeed no surety in the tradition of the spoken word.

1. פֶּן: see Honeyman, *PEQ* 1939, 86.—רָמֹּת: B Ρεμμωθ, also v.¹⁴ (from original Ρεμμαθ, cf. v.⁴) is contamination from Hex.—**2.** יֵהוּא: the name also of an almost contemporary prophet, I. 16¹. 𝔖 gives interestingly the original pronunciation of the first syllable, *Yāhū*. For the vowel change cf. *Yāsû' > Yēsû'*. Noth, *IP* 143, bases the name on the absolutely used *hû* in names, *Abihu, Elihu,* but does not explain the first syllable. H. Bauer, *Die Ostkanaanäer* (1926), 31, would identify the name with Old Ba. *Ya-u-šu*. For such a divine *n. pr. cf.* Hadad, etc.—**2.** בֶן יהושפט: B erroneously pref. to ' Jehu '; 𝔖 om.; there is no reason, as with St. (*cf. BH*) to discredit the genealogy, supported as it is by v.¹⁴.—נמשי: *cf.* Bab. *Numušum* (GB); Noth (p. 230) connects with Arab. *nims*, 'ichneumon'; the name now appears on a Samarian ostracon, *IAE* 47.—חדר בחדר: *cf.* I. 20³⁰, 22²⁵.—**3.** [ישראל] אל: many MSS, edd. correctly על; similar variations in vv.¹². ¹³. ¹⁴. ²⁷.—**4.** הנער הנביא: 16 MSS deR. om. הנער 2⁰ = Grr. exc. B, ' the prophet, the youth '; 2 MSS 𝔗 𝔙 ' the boy of the prophet '; see Comm.—**6.** אל ישראל: the duplicative phrase (*cf.* v.³) is properly preserved by St.—**7.** והביתה: Grr., κ. εξολε-θρευσεις ... εκ προσωπου μου (correct σου of B A), *i.e.*, the verb assimilated to v.⁸.—נקמתי: Grr., 𝔖ᴴ 𝔖 as 2d person, for theological reasons.—"ודמי כל עבדי: with the Deity in the 3d person; Klost., *al.*, properly regard as gloss, with Naboth in mind.—**8.** וַיֹּאבַד=𝔗ᵂ; 𝔗ᴸ 𝔖 𝔄 𝔙=וַיֹּאבֵד, ignoring the syntax; Grr.=ומיד, continuing v.⁷, accepted by Klost., St., Ehrl., *cf. BH*; but absolute logic in the passage is not to be demanded.—'ומשתין: see on I. 14¹⁰.—**9.** 𝔖ᴴ margin registers here with the letter *Lam.* the first of seven Lucianic rdgs., noted by it, as observed first by Field, *Hex.*, 1, pp. lxxxv *seq.*; *cf.* Rahlfs, *SS* 3, 30 ff.—**11.** ויאמר:=𝔗ᵂ; *ca.* 27 MSS ויאמרו=the other VSS; the pl. is expected.—השלום: *cf.* v.³¹, 4²⁶.—משגע: for the root *cf.* v.²⁰.—שיחו: Grr., τ. αδολεσχιαν αυτου, ' his garrulity '; 𝔗 𝔖 ' his conversation '; Aq., Sym. with the noun ὁμιλία, ' business '; 𝔙 ' quid locutus sit '; *cf.* the verb, I. 18²⁷.—**12.** ויאמר: the plus ' to them ' in Grr., 𝔙, is spontaneous. —לאמר: St. (*cf. BH*) regards as secondary; but with the preceding indefinite " so and so has he said to me " the speaker's hesitation is presented; Klost. sugg. an interlude.—**13.** אל גרם המעלות: B d₂ επι το γαρεμ των αναβαθμων, which curiously developed into επι γαρ ενα τ. αναβ.=Sym., 𝔖ᴴ (see Rahlfs, *SS* 3, 223 f., for the Gr. variations); Aq., προς οστωδες τ. αναβ., rendering 'ג exactly as ' bone ': 𝔖 ' upon the seat of the stairs '; 𝔙 ' in similitudinem tribunalis,' appearing to depend upon the Aram. use of 'ג as ' self, the very same,' and so Rashi, ' on the very stairs ' (the noun is so used also of inanimate objects in Jewish Aram.), an interpretation accepted by Ges., Keil, König (*HAW*), and so as 'bare,' RV^{Am} as variant, Moff., Eissf.; 𝔗 עד דרג שעיא, 'ad gradum horarum' based evidently upon 'the degrees' of the sundial, 20¹¹ (*cf.* Kimchi), and so Reuchlin, *al.*, 'iuxta horologium,' as a particularly honorific spot. See Poole for early comm., upon whom no advance has been made. EVV tr. desperately with 'on the top,' and Graetz emends the word to מרום; Then. corrects to צלם; other suggestions are noted by St. As observed above, the word is doubtless an architectural term.—**14.** Note *piskah* in middle of the v., as again in v.¹⁵.—**15.** המלך =B 𝔊ᴸ, but 𝔖ᴴ ※.— יכהו: contamination from 8²⁹; read ארמים—הכהו: *cf.* 8²⁸.—אם יש־ נפשכם :=𝔗 אם רעות נפשכון, 𝔙 " si placet vobis "; 18 MSS+['נ] את, *cf.* Gen. 23⁸; Grr. +' with me,' as for original אתי; critics largely accept one or other of these emendations; but change is unnecessary (Burn.), and Ehrl. *cft.* Jer. 15¹, אין נפשי אל, and Talmudic נפש—לניד.—מה: so Kt.ᵒʳ, and Ḳr., לֻנִּיד; Ḳr.ᵒᶜ, לְהַנִּיד, and so some MSS Kt.—**16.** וילד: 𝔊+"and he descended."—**17.** שפעת ¹ᵒ: 𝔊 𝔊ᴴ κονιορτον (and so Kit., 'Staubwolke'), 𝔊ᴸ οχλον, 𝔗 'army' =𝔙 'globum,' *i.e.*, massed troops (=EVV 'a company'), 𝔖 'chariot-drivers'; it is best to interpret after Is. 60⁶, Eze. 26¹⁰, 'a crowd of horses, of camels,' as of a large body.—שפעת ²ᵒ: the spelling perverted from שפעה by 1ᵒ.—רָכָב: interpreted with רכב כוס, vv.¹⁸·¹⁹ =' rider'; but='charioteer,' I. 22³⁴; on the root and its developments see Montg., *JQR* 25 (1935), 266.— **18.** עד הם: a case of primitive spelling, as in Ugaritic (*RSMT* 20); Bauer-Leander, §81, y' end, regards it as 'eine dialektische Neubildung,' but this is a guess; Orlinsky as error for מִנֶּהֶם (*HUCA* 17 [1942], 283, n. 23).—**19.** אלהם: again primitive spelling; MSS אליהם; 𝔊 (not 𝔈) 'to him'—by error or intention?; inconcinnity with the sing. of v.¹⁸ is a slight matter (*vs.* St.).— שלום: so *BH*, 23 MSS Ken., deR., and Bär (see his note), Ginsb. (noting the Sebîr השלום); Ken., Mich., הֲשָׁלוֹם, and so the VSS (OGrr. η ειρηνη, Hex., ει ειρηνη, but A N om. the particle); the latter rdg. is expected, as in the parallel, v.²²; however, the Semitic does not demand the interrog. particle.—**20.** עד אליהם := 𝔗 𝔖; *cf.* עד לעלות, I. 18²⁹ (*q.v.*); 1 MS om. עד; St. would delete one or the other of the preps., and so Orlinsky, *l.c.*, but unnecessarily.—המנבה כמנהג יהוא: 𝔊 𝔊ᴴ ο αγων ηγεν τον Ειου=𝔖ᴴ, by corruption of η αγωγη αγωγη τ. Ειου=𝔊ᴸ, Theod., Sym.; see Rahlfs, *SS* 3, 244.—בשנעון: Grr., εν παραλλαγη, 'in shifting course' =𝔏 'in permutationem'; but Jos., 'leisurely and in good order,' and so 𝔗 בניח מדבר (*cf.* Thackeray, *Josephus, Man and Historian*, 82) =𝔄, and Rashi, Kimchi follow suit; 𝔖 'hastily'; 𝔙 'praeceps. —**21.** אמר ויאסר: impersonal sing. (*cf.* v.²⁶, and GK §144, d), and so 𝔊; the pls. of later Grr. and other VSS have no authority, *vs.* St., *al.*—רכבו: Grr. (exc. 𝔊ᴸ, which om., and so 𝔖ᴴ ※), αρμα=𝔖 𝔙, and prob. properly, the noun being collective, and so read, רָכָב. —היורעאלי: B Ισραηλιτου, *cf.* I. 18⁴⁵, etc.—**22.** מה הַשָּׁלוֹם: 23 MSS

מה שלום ; Grr., "is it peace?"=𝔙; 𝕮 "what, is it peace?" *i.e.*, מה הֲשָׁלוֹם, which rdg. is to be preferred with St., *BH* ; Klost., Kit. elide ה, translating with 'in friedlicher Absicht?'—עד־ : Grr., ετι, 𝔙 'adhuc,' as adverbial, as in Syr., or reading עֹד, which Klost., St. prefer (*cf. BH*) ; but rather to be taken, with Ew., *Syntax*, §217, a, as prep., 'during,' *cf.* Jud. 3²⁶, Jon. 4², etc.— **23.** ידיו : so pl. by almost unanimous testimony ; contrast the same phrase, I. 22³⁴.—**24.** מלא ידו בקשת : for absence of acc. particle *cf.* vv.³⁰· ³², and for the expression, 2 Sam. 23⁷, Zech. 9¹³. Haupt ingeniously *cft.* Akk. *ḳasta ina ḳatišu umalli*, and propose transposition of the prep. to the first noun ; but the foreign phrase may have suffered change in translation. Rashi cleverly renders with "he drew the bow with all his strength."—בין זרעיו: *cf.* בין ידיך, Zech. 13⁶, and בן עֻם, 'between the eyes,' in an Ugaritic text (Gordon, *Ugar. Handbook*, 2, 68 : ll. 22, 25).—**25.** בדקר : *cf. n. pr.* דקר, I. 4⁹, *q.v.* ; ב prob.=בעל (*cf.* בעשא, etc.), *n.b.* vocalization in original Gr., Βαδεκερ, and Jos., Βαδακω (error for Βαδακρω, so Marcus). Origin from בן is also claimed ; Šanda *cft.* Akk. *Bindiḳiri*, and for such a reduction of בן see F. W. Winnett, *Lihyanite and Thamudic Inscriptions* (Toronto, 1937), 20 ff., arguing for this origin here and in similar Heb. names (BDB 122a).—שא : B A 𝔊ᴴ om.—שרה : 3 MSS om., and so 𝔖 𝔄.—כי זכר אני ואתה : all VSS read 'ו as ppl.="I remember, and so thou," but construction with the following remains broken ; 𝔊ᴸ improved on 𝔊 with μεμνημαι εγω οτε εγω και συ, inducing in turn modern text-correction, זכר אני כי אני ואתה (Burn., St., *cf. BH*) ; but with Šanda 𝔐 may well be kept: "Remember ! I and thou . . ."—את : MS 89 om., all VSS EVV ignore, of necessity ; Rashi makes it a prep. to foll. noun, Kimchi takes it as adverbial, "I with thee, and thou with me"; it may be omitted as dittogr. of אתה with Burn., *al.*, or rather it may be preserved as 'hervorhebendes Partikel,' *angl.* "there we were," *cf.* GB 76b.—רכבים צמדים : Grr., επιβεβηκοτες επι ζευγη (𝔊ᴸ ζευγος, as though צמד)=𝔖ᴴ ; 𝕮 "how we were driving one yoke" (the sing. again) ; 𝔖 as parallel ppls., "driving and riding" (*cf.* 𝔄) ; 𝔙 abbreviates, "sedentes in curru (sequebamur)"; Rashi, "with (=prec. את) other accompanying (מחוברים as for צְמָדִים) drivers"; Kimchi renders with "accompanying one another in one chariot" (*cf.* EVV), interpreting with 'like a pair of oxen.' The simplest translation is that of Stade, as given above, "were driving teams," *cf.* Haupt, "were teaming." Correction of 'צ has been suggested : to the pass. ppl., 'paired,' *cf.* Num. 25³ (so Burn., Ehrl., *cf. BH*) ; or to the sing., reading in suite מאתרי (*cf.* Kit., Šanda) ; but the VSS here have no authority.— ויהוה ונ': *n.b.* parallelism of nominal clauses, denoting identical circumstances.—משא : Grr., λημμα, by peculiar use in the Gr. Bible, of which A ρημα is corruption.—**26.** אם לא : *cf.* I. 20²³.— ושלמתי : Grr., κ. ανταποδωσω, 𝔊ᴸ also introducing a doublet earlier in the v., εκδικησω.—לך: 𝔊 Hex., 'to him.'—השלכהו : שא : for the sing.

impv. cf. v.²¹; 𝔊ᴸ as pl.—**27.** בית הגן: 𝔊 cursives, *Onom.* (Gr. and Lat.) preserve original transliteration, Βαιθαγγαν, etc.; B A N *al.*, Βαιθαν; 𝔊ᴸ Βαιθωρων, etc.; subsequent VSS tr., 'house of the garden,' EVV 'the garden house.'—נם אתו הפהו: Grr., κ. γε αυτον κ. επαταξαν αυτον, following which emend the verbal form to וַיַּכֵּהוּ (Kit., St.); Burn., following 𝔖, adds this verb after the impv.— אל המרכבה: for the phrase as a gloss see Comm.; note here the exact Gr. tr. (B), προς τω αρματι, but in v.²⁸ επι το αρμα.—גור: Grr. MSS corrupt: *Onom.*, Γηρ=𝔖ᴴ; 𝔙 'Gaber'; 𝔖 𝔄=𝔅.—אשר את יבלעם: Grr., "which is Y.," prob. understanding the prep. as Aram. אית; *Onom.* for the prep. εγγυς.—**28.** עם אחתיו: OGrr. om., St. deletes; but there is no control over such details; 1 Heb. MS om. בקברתו.—**29.** 𝔊ᴸ *ad fin.*+"and he reigned one year in Jerusalem," repeated from 8²⁶; see Rahlfs, *SS* 3, 253.—**30.** ותשם בפוך עיניה: cf. use of עשה in similar operations, Dt. 21¹², 2 Sam. 19²⁵.—פוך is rendered with root כחל in 𝔖 𝔄.—**31.** בשער: Grr., εν τη πολει (=𝔖ᴴ) as=בעיר, exc. 71⋮.—**32.** פניו: MS 180 עינו= 𝔊ᴸ 𝔖: ההלון: OGrr.+"and saw her."—מי אתי: for אחי, 'on my side,' cf. 6¹⁶, etc. Grr., τις ει συ καταβηθι μετ εμου=𝔖ᴴ, rdg. as כי אתי עמי; cf. Jos., "he asked who she was, and commanded her to come down." ℭ "who is here?" 𝔙 follows Grr., "quæ est ista?" For Klost.'s arbitrary emendation see Burn., St.— שנים שלשה: for the idiom cf. Is. 17⁶; Grr., 'two,' exc. A, 'three.' —**33.** שמטוהו, Kt., *BH*: other edd. שמטיהו.—וירקמנה: the VSS with pl. verb; St. keeps the sing.; most comm. change to pl., וירמסוה (*e.g.*, Burn.); but read וירמזה, as energetic pl., after Heb. and Ugaritic usage; see *RSMT* 23 f.—**35.** בה: for the partitive use of the prep. cf. Gordon, *Ugar. Handbook*, 3, s.vv. ב, בן.—**37.** והיה: poss. with Burn. for original והיה; cf. GK §75, m.—כדמן: cf. the possible play on the element *zebel* observed in Note to I. 16³¹.— השדה: 3 MSS Ken., deR., האדמה.—בחלק יורעאל: 𝔊ᴸ om., St. deletes.— אשר לא אמרו ואת איובל: Grr., exc. 𝔊ᴸ texts, by early corruption, ωστε μη ειπειν αυτους Ιεζαβελ.—*Ad fin.* 𝔊ᴸ+ κ. ουκ εσται ο λεγων οιμμοι. Sophocles in his *Lex.* gives, s.v., a fourth-century Patristic citation, οιμοι την κεφαλην, "my head aches!"

10¹⁻¹¹. The slaughter of Ahab's family and court.¹ **1a.** *And Ahab having seventy sons in Samaria*—(the clause is syntactically subordinate to the following). Stade argues that the

---

¹ For criticism of cc. 10–14 see Stade's 'Anmerkungen,' *ZAW* 5 (1885), 275 ff.=*Akad. Reden*, 181 ff.; and cf. his critical apparatus in *SBOT*. But Meyer criticizes such meticulous criticisms: "Die glänzende Erzählung Reg. II, 9, 10 ist durch einige Zusätze und Fehler entstellt, aber im übrigen durchaus intakt und anschaulich. Es ist sehr verkehrt, wenn man auf Grund einzelner Anstösse und nicht beantwortbarer Fragen, wie sie sich bei jeder Zeugenaussage. finden, ihre Zuverlässigkeit bezweifelt hat " (*GA* 2, 2, 338, n.).

sentence is secondary to v.⁷ (which also is an intrusion !), according to which 'the king's sons' (or rather 'the royal princes,' without indication of the father) were 'seventy persons.' However the term 'sons' is generalizing; it can include grandchildren, e.g., 'the seventy souls from Jacob's loins' (Ex. 1⁵). The high figure would indeed better befit the older man, as Šanda argues, calculating Ahab's age at death at about 63 years. But the round figure is probably formulistic, as at Ex. 1⁵, in the 'seventy sons' ascribed to Gideon (Jud. 8³⁰), and in the case of the 'seventy relatives' (with a noun developed from *'āḥ*, 'brother') of the Aramæan Panammūwa, who were slain by an usurper as in the present story (line 3 of his inscription). Many of the children were of minor age, *n.b.* 'the Guardians.' **1b.** *Jehu wrote a letter* [Heb. pl., but see I. 21⁸], *and sent it to Samaria :* "*To the Commandants ⌜of the city and to⌝* [so correcting with 𝔊ᴸ 𝔙 the absurd *of Jezreel* of 𝔐] *the Senators* [Heb. *elders*] *and to the Guardians* [𝔐+unsyntactical *Ahab, cf.* EVV ; plus *saying*]. **2a.** *And now : Upon the coming of this letter to you*, etc. This rendering presents the exact form of preface to an ancient letter ; the addressee is named first ; then the writer, with his title and his salutation, the 'peace'—here omitted, the contents of the letter being then introduced with the formulistic *and now* (*cf.* 5⁶). This phrase, ועתה, appears in a Lachish letter (Torczyner, no. 4, ועת), and has its Aramaic correspondents, כעת, כענת, in the letters cited in Ezra 4⁸, etc., and in the Elephantine letters (Cowley, *Aram. Pap.*, Index). The three legal estates, the military officialdom (*cf.* I. 22²⁶), the civil authorities (*cf.* I. 21⁸), and the guardians of the royal family are addressed, the last category being correctly understood by 𝔊 𝔙 as those who reared the royal children. **2b. 3.** Jehu's bold challenge to the dynasty's adherents is cited at length; *cf.* the letter of the Rab-shakeh to Hezekiah (19¹⁰ᶠᶠ·). There are presented in rapid, dramatic order the events of the sequel. **4. 5.** The consternation in the capital is depicted. The officials *sent to Jehu*, doubtless also by letter, their humble capitulation. For the official term, *he-over-the-house, cf.* I. 4⁶, and for *he-over-the-city* with its Akkadian parallel see Note. **6.** Jehu sends a second letter, ordering—*if you are for me*—the decapitation of the princes, whose heads are to be brought in baskets to Jezreel by the officers. **7. 8.** The order is carried out ; report is made to Jehu, who orders public exhibition of the remains *at the entrance of the gate*, the city's forum and market. **9. 10.** The climax comes on the morrow in Jehu's half-honest, half-impudent harangue : *You are innocent. It was I that conspired against my master and slew him. But who smote all these ?*—with the inference in pious reservation, which might not be publicly denied, that this was by divine connivance. *Cf.* Grotius : " Tam mirabilis eventus ostendit hæc non humanitus sed divinitus disponi." V.^{10b} with its reference to Elijah is marked by Stade as secondary ; but that there was a prophetic word concerning Ahab's house is not to be questioned. **11.** This slaughter in Samaria is followed by that of *all who were left of Ahab's family in Jezreel, and all his magnates [𝔊^L kinsmen], and his acquaintances, and his priests*. For this last term as of officers civil as well as religious see I. $4^{2ff.}$.

VV.$^{12-14}$. The murder of the royal party from Judah. **12.** *And he arose* [𝔐+*and came*] *and went to Samaria. When he was at Beth-eked of the Shepherds in the way,* **(13)** *he* [𝔐 *Jehu*] *met the brothers of Ahaziah, king of Judah*. The place-name means ' the Shepherds' Shearing-House.' The place has been identified, since Eusebius, with modern Bait Ḳād, about 3 miles E to N of Jenīn, see Guérin, *Samarie*, 1, 333 (noting the several cisterns at the place, with which *cf. the cistern*, v.^{14}), Abel, *GP* 2, 271 ; but Buhl (*GAP* 204), Šanda, *Alt* (*Pjb.*, 27 [1931], 32 f.) doubt or change the identification. To Jehu's inquiry as to the party, they reply : *We are Ahaziah's brothers ; and we have come down ⌐to inquire after¬* [Heb. *for the peace of*] *the children of the king and of the queen-mother*. For the latter official title see above, I. 15^{13} ; because of Jezebel's predominance her own brood is courteously included. **14.** For the possibly round figure of *forty-two* murdered, *cf.* 2^{24}.

VV.$^{15. 16}$. Jehu's meeting with Jehonadab b. Rechab, and the latter's hearty co-operation. Here and in Jer. 35 we possess the unique references to the Rechabites, who planted neither garden nor vineyard, drank no wine, built no houses, but lived in tents ; they were enthusiasts for the primitive religion of Yhwh and the simple life of the desert. For their genealogy, connected with the Calebites and the nomadic

Kenites, see 1 Ch. 2⁵⁵, 4¹¹·¹² (read 'Caleb' for 'Celub,' 'Rechab' for 'Rechah'); *cf.* the Nazirites, and *n.b.* the puritanic likeness with the Nabatæans (Diodorus Siculus, xx, 94), and the cult of a Palmyrene deity, who " does not drink wine " (Cooke, *NSI* no. 140 B). See Meyer, *IN* 129 ff.; Lods, *Israël* (Index, *s.v.* 'Naziréens'); Oesterley and Robinson, *Hebrew Religion*, 184 ff.; Causse, *Du groupe ethnique*, 61 ff.; *cf.* Montgomery, 'Ascetic Strains in Early Judaism,' *JBL* 51 (1932), 183 ff. According to Jer. 35 Jehonadab was the prophet of the sect. **15.** Jehu *blessed him, i.e.,* saluted him; *cf.* 4²⁹. *Is thy heart right, as my heart is with thy heart?*: so EVV, but ignoring one difficulty in Heb.; with the original mng. of the Heb. adj. we may translate, *Is it straight with thy heart*, etc. With all the difficulty of a terse passage, the sense is plain: " Do we see straight together and alike ? " The VSS attempted in various ways to simplify, followed by some modern critics; see Note. *And said Jehonadab, It is. If it be, give me thy hand.* So the EVV, following the Heb., except JV; the latter properly introduces in parenthesis the speaker of the second statement: *If it be* (*said Jehu*). This is another case of lack of the *persona loquitur* in Hebrew dramatic story; *cf.* I. 20³⁴, and see Note for similar intrusion of the subject in some VSS. For the 'giving of the hand,' as act of fidelity *cf.* 1 Ch. 29²⁴, 2 Ch. 30⁸, Ezra 10¹⁰, Eze. 17¹⁸, and so the Muslim ritual in the election of a caliph; see at length J. Pedersen, *Der Eid bei den Semiten* (1914), 32 ff. **16.** *See my zeal for* Yнwн! *Cf.* Elijah's outbursts, I. 19¹⁰·¹⁴. *And they made him ride:* the pl. subject should probably be changed to the sing.; see Note.

V.¹⁷. Jehu, arriving at Samaria, exterminates the rest of Ahab's family.

VV.¹⁸⁻²⁷. The slaughter of the *personnel* and followers of the Baal cult. No element in the whole history is more original than the wily stroke (*by subtlety*, v.¹⁹) of destruction of *all the prophets of Baal, all his worshippers, and all his priests*, through the ruse of Jehu himself celebrating *a great sacrifice* (v.¹⁹, in v.²⁵ *holocaust*) to the Baal in his temple. With his patent enough zeal for Yнwн Jehu must have played the artful diplomatist in the religious strife. The cautious Kittel registers the problem, but he and all critics allow the story to be historical. The Baal devotees had once before experienced a similar drastic purging (I. 18), but had survived ; they may have expected a complaisant policy in the matter of religion, now that Jehu had succeeded in his political aims. **19.** The item of *the worshippers* (*servitors* might express the Hebrew noun), out of due order, has probably been introduced from the generalizing use of the term in vv.²¹· ²³. **20.** *Sanctify a solemn-assembly for the Baal!* *Cf.* " Sanctify a fast ! ", Joel 1¹⁴ ; the noun, so translated in EVV, was used of the climax of religious rites ; *cf.* Nowack, *Archäologie*, Index, *s.v.* עצרה. **22.** The word generally translated *vestry* is unique ; see Note. For the clothing of the sacred staff at such rites *cf.* Lucian, *De Dea Syra*, 42, describing the ritual of the goddess : some 300 officiants of various degrees clad in white vestments and with caps, along with them a multitude of holy men, musicians, Galli, frenzied women. **25a.** Jehu himself *finished offering the holocaust*; *cf.* Solomon's primacy at the dedication of the temple. **25b.** Literally : *and the guards and the officers cast, and they went even to the citadel* (or *city*) *of the house of the Baal.* The first sentence is unintelligible with its verb without an object (which EVV supply, *cast them out*) ; for attempted corrections of seemingly obscure *citadel* see Note. For the guards see I. 14²⁷. **26.** *And they brought out the pillar* [𝔥 *pillars*] *of the house of the Baal, and burned it ;* **27a.** *and they broke down the pillar of the Baal, and they broke down the house of the Baal.* The duplications are evident ; in place of *the pillar* which they *burned* has been proposed *the Asherah*, which, as wooden, could be burned (*cf.* 23¹⁵), an ingenious but arbitrary suggestion. For Ahab's construction of this temple of the Baal with altar see I. 16³². **27b.** The locality, later used as a latrine, was still known by repute in the writer's day. To cite Causse (p. 76), the event was altogether ' a revolution in grand style.'

VV.²⁸⁻³⁶. The sequel of Jehu's reign. VV.²⁸⁻³¹. The appraisement of Jehu, which appears to go back to two hands, each with praise and blame :

28. *And Jehu exterminated the Baal out of Israel ;* **29.** *only*

30. *And YHWH said to Jehu : Because thou hast wrought well*

as for the sins of Jeroboam ben Nebat, which he entailed upon Israel, Jehu turned not away from them [with a secondary, rather ungrammatical plus *the golden calves in Bethel and Dan*]. *in doing what is right in my eyes, and hast done unto the house of Ahab according to all that is in my heart, thy sons to the fourth generation shall sit upon the throne of Israel.* **31.** *And Jehu, not heeding to walk in the Law of* Y<small>HWH</small>, *God of Israel, with all his heart, departed not from the sin* [🅗 *sins*] *of Jeroboam, which he entailed upon Israel.*

Commentators vary in their critical judgment upon this material. Most regard it as a forthright composition; Stade considers vv.$^{30.\ 31}$ as secondary to the editorial vv.$^{28-29}$; Šanda finds v.^{29} secondary. V.^{30} professes to be an early, forsooth prophetic oracle to Jehu, commending him for his revolutionary reform and with promise of succession to the fourth degree (the longest dynasty of the North—the fulfilment being recorded in 15^{12}). The prophetic sentiment of the time continued to support the dynasty; *cf.* $13^{4f.\ 14ff.}$. Another kind of judgment from another kind of prophet is that of Hosea (1^4): "I will visit the blood of Jezreel upon the house of Jehu, and bring to an end the kingdom of the house of Israel."

32. *In those days* Y<small>HWH</small> *began to cut off* [Heb. *trim off*] *Israel; and Hazael smote them in all the border of Israel,* **33.** *from the Jordan to the rising of the sun, all the land of Gilead, the Gadite and the Reubenite and the Manassite, from Aroer, which is by the wady of Arnon, and Gilead and Bashan.* Stade and others regard v.^{33} as secondary and defiant of history on the ground that Transjordan was no longer Israelite territory. But it was Hazael who detached Transjordan, *cf.* ch. 13, and according to 14^{25} it was this territory that Jeroboam II recovered. Note the incipient phrase here, Y<small>HWH</small> *began.* The general statement in v.^{33} may well be left as original, with the passage *all the land of Gilead, the G. and the R. and the M.,* excepted as secondary; the remaining terms give the W-E and S-N directions. *Cf.* the enumeration of the divisions in Dt. $3^{8ff.}$.

II. 10¹⁻³⁶

Now, with the inner turmoils of Israel and the aggressive expansion of Damascus, Transjordan was on the way of being lost for good. This reference to Hazael's conquest of Transjordan and the subsequent brief notices of Aramæan overlordship in the lands south of Damascus (12¹⁸ᶠ·, ch. 13), are placed in a larger setting by the Assyrian inscriptions. In 842/841 B.C., the year of Jehu's accession, Shalmaneser III attacked Aram, gaining victories on Hermon and in the Hauran, although unsuccessful in the siege of Damascus; he received the tribute of Jehu (Yaua) of Bīt-Ḫumri (land of Omri), who thus sided against Aram, and of the Tyrians and Sidonians (according to his Annals inscription, col. iii), and his famous obelisk depicts Jehu himself presenting his tribute, the list of which, gold, silver, vessels of those precious metals, precious woods, is given in the accompanying text.[2] There came then a lull in the Assyrian advance until 805 B.C. in Adad-nirari's reign, thus giving scope to Aram for renewed aggressions upon her Israelite neighbours. **36.** The duration of the reign is given exceptionally at the end of the royal biography.

1. שמרון: Grr., exc. 𝔊ᴸ, εν Σ., by early corruption of εις.—יזרעאל: MS 174 שמרון, Grr., Σαμαρειας κ. προς, exc. 𝔊ᴸ της πολεως κ. προς=𝔙 '(optimates) civitatis et ad (maiores natu)'; this latter correction of a primitive error in 𝔐 is to be accepted; read הָעִיר וְאֶל־.—הזקנים:=𝔖ᴴ; 1 MS והו=Gr. e; 5 MSS הו׳=𝔙=אל; 3 MSS הו׳ ואל=OGrr., 𝔖; this last rdg. is expected.—[האמנים] אהאב: an evident gloss assigning the guardians to Ahab's family; it is helped out by 𝔊ᴸ al., as though rdg. את בני אהאב, which correction GV EVV Klost., Burn., al. accept; St. elides five words here, cf. BH. For the legal terms, 'guardians' (Jos., παιδαγωγοί) cf. Est. 2⁷.—לאמר: apparently secondary, ignoring the epistolary form.—**2.** ועתה: 𝔊ᴸ 𝔖 om. as unnecessary.—[מבצר] ועיר: MSS 257 260 ועָרי=VSS (Gr. v as sing.), Jos.; the pl. is largely accepted, but the officers in question had charge of but one fortress.—הנשק: here 'armour'; see Note, I. 10²⁵.—**4.** מאד מאד: cf. Gen. 7¹⁹, etc.; OGrr. simplify.—**5.** אשר על העיר=Akk. ša eli ali (R. P. Dougherty, *Nabonidus and Belshazzar*, 1929, 30); Grr. misunderstood אשר as

---

[2] See *CP* 303 f.; *AB* 459 f.; *ATB* 1, 343; and for the conqueror's inscriptions at large *ARA* 1, ch. 12. For the history of the period may be consulted Rogers, *HBA* 2, 222 ff.; Kraeling, *Aram and Israel*, ch. 9; Cook, *CAH* 3, 372 ff.; Kittel, *GVI* 2, 268 ff.; Lods, *Israël*, 445 ff.; Olmstead, *HPS* 397 ff.; Robinson, *HI* 1, 355 ff.; Meyer, *GA* 2, 2, 341 ff.

pl.—עשׂה : Grr., "we will do."—6. שנית [ספר] : 14 MSS שׁני=Grr., preferred by St., *al.*; but the fem. is adverbial ; *cf.* GK §100, 3.— אנשי בני אדניכם : 17 MSS Ken., deR. om. אנשי ; 𝕾ᴸ expresses the word with ἕκαστος = 𝕷 'unusquisque,' followed by Benz., Kit. ; 2 MSS om. בני with Hex. ; 4 MSS בית for בני, which is to be accepted with St. (*q.v.* at length).—ובאו : Grr., ενεγκατε, as though Hif. = 𝕮 𝕾, accepted by Then., *al.*—V.ᵇ. This somewhat superfluous and grammatically difficult statement is regarded by Wellh. (*Comp.*, 267) and St. as a gloss.—את [נגדלי] : 𝕮 𝕾 = 'with,' which gives the only possible construction ; 𝕾 ignores ; 𝕾ᴴ 'these (magnates)'; there is no proof for early difference of text.— מגדלים : for the subordinate participial construction see König, *Syntax*, §412, g. Joüon (*Mél.*, 5, 480) makes the ppl. passive, rdg. מִגְדָּלִים אִתָּם.—7. וישחטו : 1 MS+ם-, and so Grr. (exc. A), Sym., 𝕾ᴴ 𝕾, the emendation accepted by Burn., St.; but translation requires repetition of the object, not necessary in Heb. syntax : *cf.* foll. וישלחו where the Grr., exc. 𝕾ᴸ, add 'them.'—יזרעאלה ; B *al.*, εις Ισραηλ.—8. המלאך : 𝕾ᴸ om., putting the accompanying verbs in the pl., and so 𝕷, but adding 'messengers.'—צברים : *cf.* Ugaritic *ṣbrt*, of a 'band, company'; in LHeb. the word means 'congregation.'—10. אפוא : MSS spell variously ; 𝕲 𝕲ᴴ αφφω (for this transliteration see 2¹⁴), 𝕲ᴸ om.—יהוה 1⁰ : 𝕾ᴴ ⁖.—יהוה 2⁰ : 1 MS, 𝕲ᴸ om.—11. נגדליו : Grr., τ. αδρους αυτου, exc. 𝕲ᴸ τ. αγχιστενοντας αυτου (= 𝕷), representing נאליו (*cf.* I. 16¹¹), accepted by Klost., St., *cf.* Burn., *BH* ; but Kit. properly objects, noting the use of the word in v.⁶.—השאיר : Grr. here as pl. ; 𝕮 here and at v.¹⁴ as Nif.—לו : B αυτους, error for αυτου.—12. ויבא וילך : 3 MSS, Hex., 𝕾 exchange the verbs, obtaining a common phrase ; OGrr. om. the first verb ; one or the other of these corrections is to be accepted ; Klost., *al.* regard ויבא as error for ויהוא.—בית עקד : acc. of direction ; it is unnecessary to prefix ב, with St.—13. ויהוא : 𝕲ᴸ 𝖁 om. the noun ; Dr. (*Tenses*, 210, n. 2) properly proposes והוא with parallel balancing clauses.—14. ויתפשׁום חיים : 4 MSS Ken., deR., om., by early haplog. ; 𝕲ᴸ 𝕾 om. חיים.—וישחטום : 4 MSS וישחטו ; many Gr. MSS (N *al.*) εσφαξεν for -αν ; but change to sing. is not necessary, *vs.* Klost., St.—אל בור : על is demanded, and so Hebræus and Aq. understood, acc. to 𝕾ᴴ ; 1 MS om. בור, and so the other Grr.—איש מהם : 11 MSS transpose the words, and so 𝕲ᴸ 𝖁.—15. וימצא : B† κ. ελαβεν, *al.*, κ. ευρεν.—יהונדב : for the verbal element see Noth, *IP* 193, noting its occurrence in Akk., and in two Edomite names ; נדב is also Thamudean, *NPS* 1, 136.—רכב : *cf.* S. Arab. names from the same root, *ib.*, pp. 200, 316.—ישׁ את לבבך ישׁר : 7 MSS om. את, and so 𝕮 𝖁 ; 1 MS replaces with עם, in correspondence with the similar phrase below, and so St. would read ; 𝕾 'in thy heart'; OGrr. = הישׁ לבבך ישׁר את לבבי, conformed to foll. sentence ; another interpretation makes את = אתי (so in 𝕰), noted in 𝕾ᴴ, and the original of a corruption in A (μετα μου to be read for μ. σου), and so Šanda decides.

But for לי את cf. Gen. 23⁸, and the text is to be kept, despite its 'barbarity,' so Ehrlich, who rewrites the sentence at length. Keil supports the text by understanding את as=Lat. 'quoad,' cft. Ew., Lehrb., 690 f. Haupt would elide from יָשָׁר to end of the citation.—ויש: for the conditional use cf. ולא, 5¹⁷; OGrr. pref. "and said Jehu," and so 𝔙 with "inquit," similarly 𝔖; but there is no reason, vs. St., Šanda, to introduce the *persona loquens* into the text.—**16.** וַיִּרְכְּבוּ אֹתוֹ : 2 MSS אתו וירכב, 1 MS om. אתו; 𝔙 paraphrases, attaching to foll. v. Grr., 𝔖=אתו וַיַרְכֵּב, which appears preferable; suggestion of וַיָּרֶכֶב אֹתוֹ has also been made.—**17.** לאחאב: 3 MSS א׳ לְבֵית=𝔖.—[אליהו] אל: 1 MS om.=𝔖.—**18.** ויקבץ: 𝔊 κ. ἐξήλωσεν=𝔈 𝔖ᴴ, i.e., rdg. ויקנא.—**19.** כל נביאי הבעל: Grr. (exc. 𝔊ᴸ), 𝔖ᴴ as vocative.—כל עֹבְדָיו: MSS 170 174 om.; this intrusion as noted above in Comm., is put by 𝔊ᴸ in the logical third place. 18 MSS have the Ḳr. עֲבָדָיו, similar variations in vv.²²·²³ (see Mich., deR.); the received Ḳr. is regarded by St., Šanda as secondary, establishing an artificial distinction between the servants of Baal and YHWH, but the distinction is supported by 𝔗 𝔖, and the form represents an ancient cultic term, cf. 'Obadiah,' I. 18³ (q.v.), and עֹבְדֵי פֶסֶל, Ps. 97⁷.—[כֹהֲנֵי] וּ[כֹל]: of the Grr. 𝔊ᴸ alone has, and so 𝔈.—**20.** קַדְּשׁוּ: MS 187 קראו=𝔗 𝔖 𝔄=AV (avoiding the notion of holiness in such a connexion).—ויקראו: 𝔊 MSS (B al.), 𝔙 as sing.—**21.** 𝔊 inserts a lengthy passage from v.¹⁹.—פה לפה: the phrase also at 21¹⁶; 𝔗 *seppā bĕseppā*, 'threshold by threshold,' but 𝔖 with a correct parallel, *basĕpā sĕpā*, 'lip by lip'; see Brock., *Lex. syr.*, 489, and for the discussion Poole, Keil.—**22.** אשר על המלתחה: 𝔗 𝔖 'the treasurer'; Grr. transliterate the last word=𝔖ᴴ; Aq., Sym., 𝔙 properly tr. it with 'clothing'; for the noun see Lexx., Haupt, Šanda.—המלבוש: the noun used of royal dress at I. 10⁵; in conformity with prec. לבוש Klost., al., regard 'המ as dittograph to prec. letters; Grr., ὁ στολιστής, as though הַמַּלְבִּישׁ.—**23.** פה: MS 70, OGrr. om.—יהוה: 𝔊ᴸ 𝔏+a long supplement.—**24.** ויבאו: Grr. as sing., in line with the sing. in v.²⁵.—שמנים: 𝔊ᴸ 𝔏 '3000,' 𝔖 '380.'—יְפַלֵּט: so all VSS (cf. EVV), but the sense demands Piel, יְמַלֵּט (Then., al.).—𝔊ᴸ attempts an improved order, vv.²⁴ᵇ·²⁴ᵃ, with plus in v.²⁵ taken from v.²³.—**25.** ככלתו: 3 MSS ככלות; 𝔊ᴸ with pl. subj.=𝔈 𝔖; 𝔙 with a pass. verb—these all evasions of Jehu's offering such a sacrifice in such a place.—וישלכו הרצים והשלשים: the VSS tr. literally, only 𝔗 introducing an object (קטילין); the nouns appear to be dittog. from above; the place to which is desiderated after the verb, and may be represented in the nouns, which Klost. has attempted to rewrite; but see Burn., St.—עד עיר בית הבעל=all VSS, exc. 𝔊ᴸ which has τ. ναου for עיר; Klost. suggested rdg. דביר, 'shrine,' but Burn. properly objects that this noun appears elsewhere in the Gr. only in transliteration. Šanda would correct to Phœn. ערפת, 'portico.' But the noun means primarily the citadel.—**26.** מצבות: so 𝔏, Mich., Ken., Ginsb.; Bär, מצבת (cf.

Ken., deR.); the latter rdg. is supported by VSS (also 𝔊ᴴ), and is required by the foll. pron.; cf. מצבת v.²⁷, where Grr. have pl. N.b. error of B, στολην for στηλην. Kit., Burn., St., al., would read אשרת. Ehrl. cancels the whole v. as merely a variant of v.²⁷.—
27. [הבעל] מצבת : if the passage be not duplicate of v.²⁶, St.'s correction to מזבח is plausible (so Šanda, cf. BH).—הבעל . . . ויתצו : 𝔊 om. on account of homoiotel. (𝔊ᴴ ※).—למהראות Kt., למוצאות Ḳr. (for avoidance of indelicacy, as with a related word, 6²⁵); Kt. is supported by VSS.—עד היום : 4 MSS + הזה = VSS; Wellh. well remarks (Comp., 289), that we have not here the later stereotyped phrase.—**29.** חטאי : vs. usual חטאות.—[אל] בית : many MSS בבית, but the locative is proper.—The clumsy addition, 'the calves of gold,' etc., appears secondary; 𝔊ᴸ 𝔏 𝔗 attempt to improve the clause by inserting a verb.—**30.** רְבֵעִים : so at 15¹²; otherwise רִבֵּעִים. Cf. the note of the inscriber of the second Nerab inscr. on seeing 'sons of the fourth generation' (HNE 445, NSI no. 65).—**31.** מעל חטאות : the sing. חטאת is again required; for the prep. phrase, Or. MSS have מכל; see Note, I. 15³.—**32.** לקצות : 𝔗 למתקף, 'to seize'; 𝔙 'tædere' has induced Klost., Burn., al., to emend to לקוץ, 'to abominate'; but St. presents a similar Mishnaic construction of 'ק with ב, and the text is to be kept.—**33.** נחל : 2 MSS pref. שפת, 'border' = Grr., 𝔗—a case of an early variant.—**34.** וגבורתו : Grr. (exc. MS 1) + και τας συναψεις ας συνηψεν = 𝔊ᴴ, taken from I. 16²⁰, cf. II. 15¹⁵.—**36.** *In Samaria* is out of position (cf. I. 22⁵², etc.), and is secondary (St.).—On account of the exceptional omission of synchronism with the South 𝔊ᴸ (= 𝔏) fills out the lack with an historically false plus at end of the v.: "in the second year of Athaliah the Lord made Jehu son of Nimshi king," this followed by a long summary culled from 8²⁶–9²⁸; see Burn., St., Rahlfs, SS 3, 276 f.

Ch. 11. The bloody usurpation of the queen-mother Athaliah; the concealing of the one surviving prince royal in the temple precincts; the revolution handled by the priest Jehoiada with the aid of the guards and mercenary troops, resulting, despite the intrusion of the queen, in the coronation of the young Joash in the temple court with popular acclaim; the effecting of a solemn covenant as between YHWH and the king and people, and also between king and people; the murder of the queen, and the extermination of the Baal-cult in Jerusalem. ‖ 2 Ch. 22¹⁰–23; cf. Ant., ix, 7.

Apart from the question of sources we have here an historical story, which, of like style to the more dramatic one from the North, was the outcome of stirring political events. At this period coevally for both states in the middle of the ninth

II. 11¹⁻²⁰

century we observe religion playing its part as conviction of at least an intense minority, which was able to mass the populace to its colours for the actual crisis. Modern criticism may not distinguish too exactly between the religious and political elements of that age, far less than we may, for example, make exact diagnosis of the birth-throes of Protestantism. In both North and South Israel there occurred a popular uprising in the name of the national God—fanatical, as ever since in the history of monotheism. And these secular events are to be given their proper place in the process of Israel's religion leading up to the great Prophets and their more sublime cause. In the North the religious impulse was rather a flash in the pan, led by a bold soldier who knew how to use and arouse the people in the name of its God. In the South, on the other hand, there were sturdier elements. The Davidic dynasty of nigh two centuries' standing was threatened with extinction; we may only surmise the exasperation of the people under the ruthless hand of the alien Athaliah during her seven years of despotism. Nationalism—to use a modern word—required only leadership, and this was given it by what moderns call the Church, the religious establishment. It was 'the priest' Jehoiada who knew how to lay his conspiracy, manœuvre the military at hand, and organize the people. Jehoiada was the first political actor in the history of the kingdom since the day of Abiathar and Sadok, and a worthy predecessor of the age-long political pontiffs of the Jerusalem priesthood. The religious establishment succeeded permanently, while the prophets of the North, Elijah, Elisha, and the Sons of the Prophets, and Amos and Hosea, failed. The military is under the priest's control, ' by covenant and oath '; we may only speculate how this arm, including mercenaries, became interested in the cause. And associated with these forces for the first time the novel element of ' the people of the land ' takes its part in a constitutional way, tempering for the remainder of the history of Judah the power of the monarchy. The Church and the People now make their appearance in the national records, and form together a novelty in ancient history.

The present record is historically sequel of, and literarily counterpart to, the brilliant story of Jehu's revolt. Yet the two narratives are from different sources, Southern and Northern, excellent witness to a wide extension of such contemporary historical writing. Stade has advanced a criticism of the present story that would make vv.[13-18a] an interpolation in the original document, on the ground that the death of the queen is reported twice (vv.[16, 20]) and that in the interpolation the religious rather than the political motive is stressed. This criticism has been generally accepted, with much consequent dubiety as to the historicity of the interpolation. In contradiction to his Commentary, Kittel in his History ignores the whole episode of vv.[13-18a]. But that can hardly be an invention, and we must assume contemporary writers, possibly spectators, whose accounts have been early amalgamated. The more official story ignored the scenes of violence narrated in the alleged interpolation, and yet the latter, reportorial-wise, tells true history ; *n.b.* the reference to the otherwise unknown temple of the Baal and his priest Mattan. The main document is similar to the narrative of the later reformation under Josiah (cc. 22, 23), and appears to have come from an official scribe. On such Judæan sources Wellhausen remarks : " An ästhetischem und ideellem Werte stehn sie sehr weit hinter den samarischen zurück, aber historisch sind sie zuverlässiger." On the other hand the interpolation is in the vivid style of the Northern raconteurs. The queen it depicts is the natural counterpart of her mother Jezebel, and has inspired a similar dramatic story.[1]

1. Athaliah's desperate action was motivated by Jehu's murder of her son, king Ahaziah. What ultimate counsel of despair she cherished, it is vain to speculate. **2.** Only from Ch. do we learn that Jehosheba was wife of Jehoiada, and strangely enough the fact that the latter was the priest appears only below in v.[9] ; here is an example of failures of connexion in ancient history. *She stole him away from the king's sons who were slain, him and his nurse, in the bed-quarters.* The stumbling parenthetical *him and his nurse* appears to be a gloss from Ch., where it has proper construction ; *n.b.* the attempts of EVV at translation. **3.** These sleeping-apart-

---

[1] For detailed criticism of the difficult text of the ch. see Wellh., in Bleek, *Einl.*[4], 257 ff.=*Comp.*, 292 f. ; Stade, *Akad. Reden*, 183 ff.= *ZAW* 5 (1885); Joüon, *Mél.*, 5, 480 ff.

II. 11$^{1-20}$

ments were *in the house of* Y*HWH*, in the large Oriental sense of 'house,' *i.e.*, in the priests' quarters. Here he remained *with her, i.e.*, the priest's wife. **4.** *Jehoiada* : most Gr. MSS add the expected title, *the priest* (and so Ch.) as in v.⁹ ; he is the first Jerusalemite priest to be named since the list of Solomon's officers in I. 4$^{2\text{ff.}}$. *The centurions* [Heb. *captains of the hundreds*] *of the Carians and of the guards. Carians* (RVV JV *Carites*) is the correct interpretation introduced by Ewald (*HI* 4, 135) ; the Grr. recognized it as *n. pr.* with Χορρει=𝔖^H ; other VSS rendered with a military title (as AV ' the captains '), 𝔙 compounding it and the following noun in ' milites.' The word appears as Kt. in 2 Sam. 20^{22}, but Ḳr. as ' Cretans,' followed with ' Philistines.' For Cretans and Carians see Note, I. 1^{38}. The word may well be traditional like ' Schweizer ' used of the European mercenaries. For the *guards, cf.* I. 14^{27}.

5. *And he commanded them, saying : This is the thing that ye shall do : the third of you who come on duty* [Heb. *come in*] *on the Sabbath,* ⌈*they shall keep guard of*⌉ [Heb. *who guard*] *the house of the king,* **6.** *and the third at the gate Sur, and the third at the gate behind the Guards,* [*and ye shall keep guard of the house* massāḥ—secondary, from v.⁷, plus an unintelligible word], **7.** *and the two detachments of you all who go off duty* [Heb. *go out*] *on the Sabbath, they shall keep guard of the house of* Y*HWH* [𝔊 plus *for the king*] *;* **8.** *and ye shall surround the king, all about, each with his weapons in his hand ; and he who comes within the ranks shall be slain ; and be ye with the king in his going out and his coming in.* The above passage is a *crux interpretum*, of great interest with its presentation of ancient military practice for which we can hardly expect accurate reminiscence of sharp military orders. The relay of the guards that came on duty on the morning of the day concerned was divided into three companies posted at three points, two gates being named ; the other two relays (v.⁷), normally off duty, should report and guard the temple, and with change of person from the third to the second, should serve as bodyguard to the king. The Sabbath as a civic holiday was chosen for the occasion (*cf.* 4^{23}). Interpretations and criticisms of the text have been manifold. Wellhausen's suggestion to regard v.⁶ as an intrusion has been generally accepted ; Skinner, in agreement, gives an excellent summary of his results : " The guard was divided into three companies. On weekdays two of these were on duty in the palace and the third in the temple. On the sabbath the order was reversed, two companies being on guard in the temple and one in the palace. . . . he chooses the moment when on the sabbath the two companies have come up from the palace to relieve the third. . . . By detaining the third division he attains his end." But this presupposes military arrangements which are ingeniously invented by the critic ; indeed the omission of v.^{6} with its exact local details is arbitrary. Šanda, who transposes vv.$^{6, 7}$, finds in the former a ' pre-redactional gloss ' on the posting of the Sabbath guards. The above translation follows Joüon in general. The point of the passage is that all the troops are kept on duty, the several divisions with distinct orders. The gate Sur and that of the Guards (the latter also v.^{19}) have not been identified. V.^{6} terminates with an obscure word, probably a scribal annotation ; *cf.* EVV. For further details see Notes. **10.** *The spears* [pl. with Ch., AV RVV ; 𝕳 here *spear*=JV] *and the shields that were king David's, which were in the house of* Y*HWH*. These were purely honorific armour ; at I. 10^{26} in addition to Solomon's golden shields which Shishak looted, 𝕲 knows of ' the golden shields which David took from Hadadezer.' The v. is prob. secondary, dependent upon Ch., v.^{9}, actual armour being the desideratum on such an occasion (Stade, Skinner, Eissfeldt). **11.** *And the guards stood, each with his weapons in his hand, at the righthand corner of the house as far as the left-hand corner of the house—of the altar and the house—by the king round about.* The text is open to easy criticism, but correction is difficult. The king was not yet present, and Stade, Šanda, Kittel (*BH* ' fortasse ') would omit the final phrase, and so Burney, who then reads ' round about the altar and the house.' Yet the reference to the king's presence may well be anticipative. The parenthesis *of the altar and the house*, if original, is an expansion of the scene ; the house, in the Semitic sense of the word, would include the altar area in front, which was all guarded. **12.** *And he brought forth the king's son, and set upon him the diadem and the testimony.* Diadem, a rare word, has the etymological sense of consecration. The following noun as *testimony* is supported by all VSS, and so AV RVV ;

it has largely been corrected by critics to *bracelets* on basis of its pairing with ' diadem ' in 2 Sam. 1¹⁰, or, by etymological reference, to ' ornaments,' *cf.* JV ' *insignia* '; see Note at length. *And they made him king and anointed him.* Ch. introduces ' Jehoiada and his sons ' as subject of the second verb. Šanda notes that also at the consecration of Aaron the crowning preceded the anointing (Ex. 29⁶·⁷, Lev. 8⁹·¹⁰). *Long live the king!:* so at Solomon's accession, I. 1³⁹. **13.** *Athaliah heard the noise of the guards, the people :* so 𝔅 ; *cf.* EVV. But *the guards* is an intrusion, probably from Ch. The boldness of the desperate woman in coming to face the people in the temple is magnificent. The full arming of the patriots is evidence of the precarious conditions. **14.** *And she looked, and there was the king standing by the pillar according to the custom (i.e., the ritual)* : so correctly with GV FV EVV, but RVV^mg JV *on the platform* ; for the variant translations see Note. For the pillar Jachin or Boaz comes to mind. Ezekiel's ritual for royal worship was that " the prince . . . shall stand by the post of the gate " (46²) ; and Jirku (*AKAT*) notes cases in Old-Bab. processes where legal action is taken ' by the pillar of Shamash ' (citing *CT* ii, 47, 18 ; iv, 23, 21a ; iv, 47, 11a). *With the captains and the trumpets by the king :* as we might say, ' with the officers and the military band.' By deflection of the sibilant in the word for ' captains,' *śārîm* > *šārîm*, ' singers ' may be read ; the Chronicler (v.¹³) found a *double entente* in the word, and proceeds to expatiate on the theme of the singing ; also the Grr. and 𝔙 so understood the word, followed by some modern critics (*e.g.*, *BH*)—an alluring correction ! *Cf.* the music reported for Solomon's accession, I. 1⁴⁰, and see Gunkel, *Einl. in die Psalmen*, §5, 3, 17, etc. *All the people of the land :* for this constitutional phrase see below. *She cried out : Conspiracy! Conspiracy!*, EVV *Treason! Treason!* The woman had her last word like her mother Jezebel (9³⁰ff·). **15.** A higher military grade appears here in *the centurions, the officers of the army* ; the former were chiefs of the guard, the latter the military superiors—not hitherto named ; the asyndetic *centurions* is an intrusion to correlate the present orders with those earlier cited. Jehoiada's command for safeguarding the queen's person until she was officially executed outside of the sacred precincts has caused much trouble, *e.g.*, in EVV : AV *have her forth without the ranks* (=FV) ; RVV JV *Have her forth between the ranks* (=GV) ; of these the latter interpretation is to be accepted, the former would require change of the Heb. prep ; some critics go to the extent of cancelling the prepositional phrase. **16.** *They laid hands on her:* so AV (=GV) ; but RVV JV, *they made way for her* (=FV), the diverse interpretations following similar variety in VSS ; see Note ; the first one is here accepted. The troops hauled the queen out of the temple within the ranks to a palace gate and there killed her, at *the Horses' Entry in the king's house* (in v.^{20}, *in the king's house*). There was the Horses' Gate in the wall of Jerusalem (Neh. 3^{28}), a temple entry, where were later the horses given to the sun (23^{11}), but the present gate belonged to the palace ; see Smith, *Jerusalem*, 1, 199, 325, and the discussion by Burrows in *AASOR* 14 (1934), 119 f.

17. *And Jehoiada made a covenant between Y*HWH *and the king and the people, that they should be Y*HWH's *people—and between the king and the people.* The term ' covenant-making ' was also used in connexion with secret affairs, as in v.^{4} of Jehoiada's conspiracy. Here the first article of the covenant is primarily religious, for which *cf.* the covenant introducing Josiah's reform (23$^{1\text{ff.}}$) ; only here the priest is the officiant, there the king. This item, if historical, interestingly enough precedes the theme of the so-called Deuteronomic reform. The second article, between the king and the people, is political. Some critics would elide it, as absent in Ch. and most Gr. texts, and as a dittograph (see Note) ; but rather its omission as supernumerary, especially in the later democratic days of Jewry, is as much, if not more, probable. In this connexion is to be noted the political phrase *the people of the land*, recurrent in the ch., vv.$^{14.\ 18.\ 19.\ 20}$, and again subsequently, 15^5, 16^{15}, 21^{24} (*bis*), 23$^{30.\ 35}$, 24^{14}, 25$^{3.\ 19}$, in several of which cases the people act as with political right in emergencies. It also occurs in the Phœn. inscription of Yehau-milk (*ca.* 400 B.C.), the king praying for ' the favour of the people of this land.' In later Jewish language the element of this '*am hā-'āreṣ* was most despicable (*cf.* the varying uses of the word ' people ' in modern democratic societies), and the phrase here has been generally regarded as not meaning more than the populace. But it has been increasingly recognized that the term has an original political import. For recent publications see M. Sulzberger, *Am Ha-aretz*, claiming that this element was member of a bicameral legislature ; Eva Gillischewski, ' Der Ausdruck עם הארץ im A.T.,' *ZAW* 40 (1922), 137 ff. ; R. Gordis,' Sectional Rivalry in the Kgdm. of Judah,' *JQR* 25 (1935), 242 ff. (holding that the term refers to the people of the countryside as distinct from the city) ; and especially the extensive treatise by E. Würthwein, *Der 'Amm ha'arez im A.T.*, with full bibliography. Gillischewski, Galling,[1] Würthwein reasonably agree that by this term, ' the people of the land,' ' die Gesamtheit der jüdischen Vollbürger ' (Würthwein, p. 16) appears as ' a political factor,' unorganized, but acting in political crises. Note the use of the word ' land ' in I. 4^{19}, and *cf.* the similar democratic part of the people in Anglo-Saxon England. A remarkable Oriental parallel to the present ' covenant ' appears in a South Arabian inscription, discovered by E. Glaser, and published by him in his *Altjemenische Nachrichten* (1906), 162 ff., and again with exhaustive editing by N. Rhodokanakis in *Sb.*, Vienna Academy, vol. 177, Abt. 1 (1915). This stone document of 23 long lines presents a constitution for the State of Kataban, the three parties being the God, the King, the Nation Kataban, with further specification of certain estates, military, economic, etc. *Cf.* the writer's article, ' Enactment of Fundamental Constitutional Law in Old South Arabia,' *Proc. Am. Philos. Soc.*, 67 (1928), 207 ff. In the present case the term appears in both of the components of the ch. as diagnosed by critics. On the royal covenant see M. Buber, *Königtum Gottes* (1936), ch. 7, ' Der Königsbund.'

18a. The destruction of the Baal temple, with its altars and images, the murder of the Baal's priest, all this by rapid mob action. The event introduces to us the first popular reform in Jerusalem. The priest's name *Mattan* is peculiarly Phœnician ; see Harris, *Grammar*, 108 ; also see Note. **18b.** The temple is placed under special guard ; there may well have been a contrary-minded minority to combat ; *cf.* the comment in v.^{20}, *and the city was quiet.* **19.** For the *Guards' Gate* see v.^{6}. The *finale* is that the young king formally *took*

---

[1] *Die Israelitische Staatsverfassung in ihrer Vorderorientalischen Umwelt*, AO 28, Heft 3/4 (1929), 32 f.

his seat on the throne of the kings, his ancestors. **20.** For the repeated note of the slaying of Athaliah see above. The modern VSS, except JV, attach 12¹ here as v.²¹, with following variation in numbering of vv.

1. עתליה: so below, exc. vv.². ²⁰, עתליהו=8²⁶.—[ראתה]ו: dittog.; om. with MSS, Kr.—מת בנה: Hex., 'her sons were dead.'—ותקם: Grr. om., exc. 𝔊ᴸ='arose to action,' and not to be deleted, *vs.* St.—המטלכה: *cf.* בית ממ', Am. 7¹³; in Phœn. the word means 'royalty>king'; there is no reason to change it to המלוכה with 6 MSS (=25²⁵), *vs.* St.—**2.** יהושבע: Ch., יהושבעת, feminized form; *cf.* Ἐλισάβετ of N.T.—יואש: for the name see on 12¹.—אחותו: there is no reason, *vs.* St., Šanda (*cf. BH*), to substitute אחיה with Grr.—הממותתים: Kr. הַמּוּפָתִים, Pual, and so many MSS, Ch., and generally accepted, but the form may be Polal, הְמֹומְתִים, with intensive sense of 'massacring'; *cf.* the Polel, 1 Sam. 14¹³—אתו ואת מינקתו: Ch. pref. ותתן, and so Šanda.—אתו ויסתרו=𝔗; Ch., ותסתירהו=Grr., 𝔖 𝔙, which rdg. is now generally accepted; but 𝔅 is the impersonal pl., as at v.¹⁹.—**3.** אתה: referring to the aunt; Ch. אתה.—בית י": Grr., ἐν οἰκῳ, avoiding notion of profanation of the temple; but the Three and 𝔖ᴴ correct; *cf.* 𝔗 בבית מקדשא.—**4.** יהוידע: Grr., exc. B+o ἰερευς=𝔖ᴴ.—[ה]מאיות: *i.e., mê'ôṯ > mêyôṯ;* for list of similar Kt.-Kr. variants see Gordis, *The Biblical Text,* 110 ff.—לכרי: for the collective generic *cf.* I. 1³⁸.—[ל]רצים: 𝔊 transliterated, although using παρατρεχοντες at 10²⁵, I. 14²⁷; the translator recovered himself below, v.⁶, etc.; 𝔊ᴸ inserted this transiation before τ. Χορρει.—"י בית 2⁰: of the Grr. B v om.; 𝔊ᴸ 'before the Lord'; Hex. (𝔖ᴴ ※·), 'in the covenant of the Lord': translators objected to such a scene in the temple; there is no reason to cancel the phrase, *vs.* St., *BH*.—**5.** ושמרי: read with Joüon וְשָׁרֵי, as accepted above.—*Ad fin.* 𝔊 𝔊ᴴ+' in the gate.'—**6.** סור: Ch., היסור, 'the foundation'; Grr., τ. οδων=𝔖ᴴ; 𝔗 'of the men-of-war,' reduced by 𝔄 to 'of war'; 𝔖 דקרסא (?—see Brock., *Lex. syr.*, 698), which Barhebræus interpreted with גניזא 'hidden'; 𝔙 as *n. loci* = modern VSS; Joüon sugg. צור, Galling (*Pjb.*, 27, 1931, 51 ff.) בשער.—סוסים 2⁰=𝔊ᴸ 𝔖ᴴ, other Gr. texts by error τ. πυλης.—ק-ח-: Grr. om., exc. 𝔊ᴸ Μεσσαε=Theodoret=𝔙 'Messa,' and GV 'Massa'; the other VSS as though=ממסח=מן+ a noun from נסח, 'to tear away/down'; 𝔖ᴴ 'from destruction'; MS z notes the tr. of the 'Others' with απο διαφθορας; 𝔗 'that it was not removed'; similarly Rashi ('from destruction'), Kimchi, and so AV, 'that it be not broken down'; then with further variation as 'ab irruptione' (so Tremellius and Junius— see Poole at length); RVV JV, 'and be a barrier' (*cf.* FV), and so Keil. Haupt suggests 'relieving one another' on basis of Arab. *nasaḥa,* 'to replace,' this ingenious suggestion may be supported by Jewish Aram. מְסָחָא, כְּסָחָא, 'balance.'—**7.** ושמרו: to be preserved, *vs.* suggested change to וְשִׂמְרֵי.—אל המלך: redundant repetition of על המלך, vv.⁸·¹¹, and to be deleted, with Kamp., St., *al.*—**8.** השדרות: the military term = Akk. *sidirtu* (Delitzsch, *Ass. Hwb.*) ; Grr. transliterate, but Aq., Sym., τ. περιβόλους, 'the precincts' (𝔊ᴴ שארא ?) ; 𝔙 'septum,' 'barrier,' which Jouon prefers.—וְהָיוּ: = 𝔊ᴸ 𝔊ᴴ ; 𝔊 κ. εγενετο ; a group of MSS, κ. εσονται.—**9.** הכהן 1° 𝔊 ο συνετος = 𝔊ᴸ with plus, ιερευς.—השבת . . . את אנשיו באי השבת: curtailed in 𝔊.—**10.** חנית: the pl. is required, and so Ch. (הניתים), VSS, EVV ; read חֲנִיתָה, for which pl. *cf.* Is. 2⁴, Mic. 4³.—𝔊ᴸ adds to the v. repetition of the convocation in the temple.—**12.** הנזר: 𝔊 𝔊ᴴ το νεζερ (with subsequent corruptions, *e.g.*, B) = 𝔊ᴴ ; 𝔊ᴸ το αγιασμα.—העדות: Grr., το μαρτυριον = 𝔊ᴴ 𝔊, and 𝔙 'testimonium' = modern VSS, exc. JV. Wellh.'s correction to הַצְּעָדוֹת after the parallel phrase, 2 Sam. 1¹⁰, and the noun in Is. 3²⁰ = 'bracelets,' is now largely accepted (by Burn., St., *BH*, *al.*) ; Kimchi proposed the dress of royalty, as from root עדה II (*cf.* עֲדִי, 'ornament'), followed by Klost., and so JV 'insignia.' Derivation of the word from that root is preferable. The older interpretations have been various ; Rashi, "he placed beside him the Torah, which is עדות, that he might read in it," with Dt. 17¹⁸ff. in mind ; also the ordinance of the phylactery (Ex. 13⁹) has been suggested, and the oil of unction ; see Poole. Šanda maintains the traditional interpretation, *cft.* the Roman rite of laying the Bible on the head of the episcopal ordinand ; but this rite was suggested from the present passage, as so understood !—Most recently Robinson (*HI* 1, 351) would continue this interpretation as of 'a written document or charter,' and H. G. May (*JBL* 57 [1938], 81) has ingeniously compared a line in the Seven Tablets of Creation (iii, 105, Rogers, *CP* 22) : "She (Tiamat) gave him (Kingu) the tablets of destiny, on his breast she placed them."—וימלכו אתו וימשחהו: the sing. of the verbs is generally preferred by critics (and so 22 MSS Kt. in the first case) with the Grr. ; but the verbs are collective, for there are many actors in such a ritual.—**13.** הרצין העם: the Aram. pl. form of the first noun indicates its secondary character ; Ch., העם הרצים ; Heb. MSS, VSS, modern trr. variously attempt improvement.—**14.** על העמוד: = 23³. in similar circumstances ; Ch. here על עַמּוּדוֹ, but in the later parallel, 34³¹, על עָמְדוֹ (proof that Ch. has small authority in such variations) ; the VSS 'by the pillar,' exc. 𝔙 'super tribunal.' Gressmann (*ZAW* 1924, 321, n. 1) would read על עמדו in all places, *cft.* Egyptian exx. ; but the Heb. phrase means merely 'in his place' (*e.g.*, Neh. 8⁷). Then., *al.* (*cf. BH*), and most recently C. R. North (*ZAW* 1932, 19 f.) would correct the present noun to הָעֵדֶר, interpreting as 'on the platform' ; but such changes only introduce an unknown object in contrast to the pillar ; see Comm.—**15.** שרי המיאות: poss. secondary, from vv.⁴·⁹·¹⁰ (so St., Burn., *al.*).—פְּקֻדֵי: the form as at Num. 31¹⁴ ; the usual פְּקֻדֵי (*e.g.*, 25¹⁹) is demanded by St., Burn., *al.*—אל מבית יְשָׁרוֹת ; for the prepositional phrase = 'within,' *cf.* לטבית ל, Num.

18⁷, and so the Grr. in general; the text is to be kept. A few Gr. MSS have corrupted the prep. ἐσωθεν to ἐξωθεν, and this is the basis of 𝔖 𝔙, 'outside of,' suggesting to some critics correction to מחוץ (e.g., BH). The Grr. transliterate the foll. noun, except Sym. with εσω τ. διαταξεων. 𝔊ᴸ has an exegetical plus, " and lead him in after the commanders " (for further plus of 𝔊ᴸ in the v. see Rahlfs, SS 3, 289).—הֵמָה: abs. inf., turned naturally into a finite verb by Ch., VSS.; *n.b.* 𝔊 θανατω θανατωθησεται.— **16.** וישׂמו לה ידים: the tr., "and they made place for her"=𝔗 𝔖 Kimchi, was accepted by Renaissance scholars, and has been maintained since by moderns, Keil, Then., al., most recently by Joüon (*Biblica*, 14 [1933], 458); but see Burn., denying that the alleged parallel ידים, Josh. 8²⁰, means 'place, room.'—ותבוא: 𝔊 𝔊ᴴ κ. εισηλθεν, but by scribal error B -θον, A -θαν; 𝔊ᴸ 𝔙 make the verb causative with obj.—**17.** ובין המלך ובין העם: not in Ch., represented in Grr. only by B A and a few cursives, asterisked by 𝔖ᴴ; St. holds that 𝔐 is due to dittog., but the omission was due to simplification of an apparent repetition; Kit. in *BH* (not in Comm.) regards it as addition.—**18.** את 1°: 18 MSS, Ch., ואת=Grr., 𝔗.—מוֹצָא: the name appears on a Lachish seal; *BASOR* 86 (1942), 24 f.—המזבחות: so pl. in Grr., exc. 2 cursives=𝔈, and other VSS with sing.; the sing. is demanded by some critics, e.g., St., but the generalizing pl. is not out of place.—**19.** המאות: as over against המאיות above, vv.⁴¹·.—ויריֻדו: impersonal pl., *cf.* vv.².¹²; some Gr. MSS change to sing.—וישב: Ch., "and they seated the king"; Grr., exc. A, "and they seated him"; 𝔐 is far preferable *in re* the formal accession, *cf.* I. 2¹².—**20.** בית מלֹּא: Kr. 'כֵּפ ב, and so many MSS Kt.; but for the antique, non-articulated phrase see I. 15¹⁸.

Ch. 12 (EVV, exc. JV, 11²¹–12²¹). The reign of Jehoash of Judah. ‖ 2 Ch. 24; *cf. Ant.*, ix, 8, 2–4. *N.b.* the quite contradictory midrash in Ch. for the story of the temple repairs, along with a good historical tradition of a breach between the king and the priesthood in the latter part of the reign; Josephus follows Ch. The history is a literary continuation of ch. 11. As there, the historian is not a temple annalist; he is distinctly secular with his record of the royal rebuke of the priests for their dishonest handling of the temple funds and his novel detail of how their peculations were stopped. Also he ignores the Chronicler's doubtless true tradition of the scandalous murder of Zechariah ben Jehoiada by the Jerusalem mob.

VV.¹⁻⁴. The introductory data of the reign. The unusual placing of the king's age at accession in v.¹, as of seven years, is a link with 11⁴. The round figure of forty years for the reign (so for David and Solomon) arouses suspicion. As has not been generally observed, according to dynastic rule Jehoash's reign should be dated from his infancy when he became heir, and the six/seven years of Athaliah should not be reckoned in the royal chronology ; the subtraction of this figure would help in reducing the disparity between the Judæan and Israelite chronologies from Jehu to 721 B.C.—165 years for the former, 143 for the latter. Meyer in his chronology, *GA* 2, 2, 438, exceptionally assigns 39 years for Athaliah and Jehoash together. The priest Jehoiada acted as vizier of the realm and as tutor of the boy king : the latter *did the right in* Y*HWH's eyes, all his days that Jehoiada the priest instructed him*—so the Heb. literally, but with question as to the relative pronoun. EVV, following Grr., 𝔙, tr. the relative with *wherein, i.e.*, restricting the king's right conduct to the time of his tutelage ; but Ki. absolutely ignores the later infidelity charged against him by Ch. ; the word might be rendered with *as* ; but rather, the relative clause may be wholly a gloss to conform with Ch. ; see Burney's lengthy discussion. The verbal root of *instructed* is that of *tôrāh* ; *cf.* Samuel's announcement to the people, " I will instruct you in the good and right way " (1 Sam. 12²³) ; the present is the earliest case of the use of the verb in individual instruction by a teacher, else only appearing late, *e.g.*, Prov. 4¹¹. Also according to Ch. the good priest found Jehoash's two wives for him.

VV.⁵⁻¹⁷. The rehabilitation of the temple and its funds. *Cf.* the restoration in Josiah's reign, ch. 22, the text of which has been affected by the present narrative. There are to be recalled the many Bab. and Ass. inscriptions celebrating the restoration of ancient fanes. Ch. attributes the present condition of the temple to ' the sons of Athaliah, that wicked woman ' ; but the sumptuous days of Solomon were long past, and the building must have fallen into sad decay. VV.⁵⁻⁹ By the royal command all direct religious taxes and voluntary offerings in cash (*silver*) were to be segregated and used solely for the repairs. When this order was decreed is not stated ; but *in the twenty-third year of king Jehoash the priests had not repaired the breakdown of the house* ; the clerical caste was sadly in fault (v.⁷). Thereupon the king summons

Jehoiada and the priests and upbraids them, and these agree on the one hand not to bank those moneys for themselves, and on the other hand to be relieved from the expense of repairs that would normally fall upon the temple exchequer. With the difficulty of making *ḥaj* to the central sanctuary, offerings in kind were generally turned into *current money* (so 🅗 in v.⁵), which was easily appropriated by mercenary priests. VV.¹⁰⁻¹³. The high-minded Jehoiada may not have been able to control his college of priests. It was in pursuance of his suggestion that the first collection box in history was invented and placed at the entry of the temple; into this box *the priest-guardians of the threshold* (appearing again at 23⁴) at once deposited the moneys under the eyes of the givers. This particular fund appears in Josiah's reign (22⁴) with repetition of the present language. The *chest* as a depository appears in the N.T. as the *korban* (Mt. 27⁶, *cf.* Jos., *BJ* ii, 9, 4). When the box was full, a commission, consisting of *the royal scribe* (*cf.* I. 4³) and *the high priest*, minted and banked the moneys, which were paid out to *the overseers*, and these paid the workmen. VV.¹⁴, ¹⁵. A further condition was made, which might well be a citation from a written agreement, that none of the money should be spent (Heb. impf.) on ritual vessels, etc. The administration was bent on economy. V.¹⁶. The 'faithfulness' of the parties to the contract is commented upon—a novelty in both church and state. V.¹⁷. A final clause in the agreement ordered that the technical items of *guilt- and trespass-money were not to be brought* [so the impf. verb again] *into the house of* Y<small>HWH</small>, *they were to be the priests'*—*i.e.*, remain the perquisite of the sacred *personnel*.

5. 6. The order of the king to the priests: *All the money of devotions that is brought into the house of* Y<small>HWH</small>—*the* ⌈*rate-money*⌉ [=OGrr.; 🅗 *current money*], *each* [🅗+*money per person*] *at his rating*, ⌈*and*⌉ [not in 🅗] *all the money which it occurs to one's mind to bring into the house of* Y<small>HWH</small>—**6.** *the priests shall take to themselves . . . and repair*, etc. With the correction, *rate-money*, and the elimination of a following phrase (changes now generally accepted), the moneys fall into two great classes, of taxes and voluntary offerings. For the former *cf.* the tithes, and the poll-tax (Ex. 30¹¹ff·); for the free-will offerings (*nĕḏāḇāh*), apart from the Torah, see

Ezra 1⁴, etc. For the expression of voluntary concern, literally 'to come up upon the heart,' *cf.* Jer. 7³¹. **6.** (resumed)—*the priests shall take to themselves, each from his acquaintance:* so most modern VSS after 𝕋 ; below, v.⁸, this arrangement is prohibited by fresh orders. But such personal handling between priest and client appears absurd, as though the former were a small parish priest ; Šanda thinks of priests assigned to the several districts of the land and so acquainted with the devout. But the noun translated in EVV (exc. JV) with 'acquaintance' also appears in Ugaritic, where the pl. is aligned with 'priests' and 'holy ones.' While the word etymologically signifies 'merchant,' it may indicate in this connexion a class of temple-tellers ; *cf.* the 'money-changers' in the Jerusalem temple, Mt. 21¹², etc. ; see Note. **10.** *And the priest Jehoiada took a chest, and bored a hole in its lid, and set it beside the ⌜pillar⌝ [𝕳 altar] on the right hand as one comes into the house of* Y*HWH ; and the guardian priests of the threshold would put therein all the money.* Stade's correction, based on Gr. transliterations, reading by a slight change *mṣbḥ* for *mzbḥ*, has been generally accepted, *i.e., the pillar*; this word is generally used of a heathenish object (*e.g.*, 18⁴, 23¹⁴), and yet the seer in Is. 19¹⁹ foresees 'a pillar' and 'an altar' to be reared at the border of Egypt. A possible confusion of the two words occurred above, 10²⁷. The Grr. glossed over the distasteful word with a transliteration, 𝕳 altered it. For the exalted position of *the guardians of the threshold cf.* 23⁴, 25¹⁸, and see Frazer, *Golden Bough*, 3, 1 ff., for such functionaries. **11.** *And it was, when they saw that there was a large quantity of silver in the chest, that the royal scribe and the high priest came up and minted (i.e.,* in ingots) *and reckoned the silver found in the house of* Y*HWH.* The title 'high priest' (literally 'great priest') is late, introduced again in 22⁴· ⁸, 23⁴, probably of post-Exilic origin (*cf.* Hag. 1¹, Zech. 3¹), and should be simplified to 'the priest,' as elsewhere in this narrative ; *cf.* Morgenstern, 'A Chapter in the History of the High-Priesthood,' *AJSL* 55 (1938), 1 ff. Another, probably old, title of the primate appears in *kôhēn hā-rôš* (25¹⁸). A far more ancient title appears in Ugaritic *rb khnm* (Gordon, *Ugar. Handbook*, 2, 62 : 54 f.), continued in the Phœnician (Harris, *Gram.*, 110). Stade would eliminate the whole reference to that functionary, but *n.b.* the following pls., while there is no intrinsic objection to this statement of dual accounting. The verb translated above with *minted* appears, following tradition, in the EVV as *put up in bags* (and similarly GV FV); see Note. But Eissfeldt (*FuF* 1937, 163, reprinted in his *Ras Schamra u. Sanchuniathon*, 42 ff.), pursuing the ingenious argument made by Torrey in ' The Foundry of the Second Temple at Jerusalem ' (*JBL* 55 [1936], 247 ff.), interpreting the *yôṣēr* of Jer. 18^{11}, Zech. 11^{13}, as of the official mint-master who smelted the bullion into ingots, finds the same mng. here with root *ṣûr* || to *yṣr*. There was no coinage ; silver was cast into ingots of round bars or rings ; see Benzinger, *Arch.*, §42, with the Egyptian representations of the latter form of moulding, also Nowack, *Arch.*, §37, and Torrey cites Herodotus, iii, 96, for Darius I's rendering of loose silver into bullion preserved in jars. The following verb, *and they counted*, refers then to these ingots. **13.** *The masons* [Heb. *wall-makers*] *and the stone-hewers :* for the first noun, by change of root *gdr* to *gzr*, Ehrlich sensibly proposes *the carpenters*, so obtaining balance with ' the wood-artisans and the builders ' in v.^{12}, and ' the timbers ' and ' the stone ' just below. **14.** *Only there were not to be made* [𐤄+*in the house of Y*HWH ; most Grr., ' for the house of the Lord '=EVV ; 𐤏 ' templi Domini '] *cups of silver, snuffers, basins, trumpets, any vessels of gold and vessels of silver, of the money that was brought into the house of Y*HWH. The bracketed Heb. appears senseless, the Grr. give sense but repeat the phrase occurring at end of the v. The bracket looks like an intentional gloss— the vessels were not to be made in the temple, thus relieving the stringency of the order against misapplication of the funds. For the list of vessels cited *cf.* I. 7^{50}, here an evident accretion.

VV.$^{18, 19}$. The invasion by Hazael of Aram, and his capture of Gath ; he is bought off from attacking Jerusalem with treasures of the temple. This brief datum, continuing the history in 10$^{32\text{ff.}}$, presents an otherwise unknown advance of the Aramæan power to the SW, doubtless seeking control of the trade-route by the sea ; *cf.* Meyer, *GA* 2, 2, 341 ff. Gath had remained a Philistine enclave within Judah (see I. 2^{39}), as the reference to it as a foreign city in Amos 6^2 proves, and according to 2 Ch. 26^6 Uzziah later broke down its wall ; such autonomous city-states were a part of the ancient political order. That there was from this epoch a temporary suppression of the city appears from its absence in the list of Philistine cities in Amos 1⁶ᶠᶠ·, but it is mentioned by Sargon (*ARA* 2, §§30, 62). Its identification has long been disputed ; see Smith, *HGP* 196 ff. ; Döller, *GES* 28 ff. ; Abel (*GP* 2, 325), following Guthe, Albright (*AASOR* 2–3 [1923], 11 f.) identifies it with Tell-el-Menšīyeh, 10 km. from Beit Jibrīn on the road to Gaza. V.¹⁹ notes the fact that the temple had been cherished by the king's forbears, not only by the pious Jehoshaphat but also by the 'evil' Jehoram and Ahaziah (*cf.* 8¹⁸·²⁷). With this sacred loot the invader was satisfied, even as had been the Egyptian Shishak generations earlier (I. 14²⁵ᶠᶠ·).

VV.²⁰⁻²². The plot of certain named courtiers and their assassination of the king. The Chronicler doubtless possesses a true, if frail tradition of the king's latter days : how that after the death of the excellent Jehoiada his son and evident successor Zechariah denounced the sins of the people, for which *lèse majesté* he was stoned to death in the temple court (of which crime a reminiscence is preserved in Mt. 23³⁵) ; for this godless outrage the kingdom fell prey to the Aramæan invader, the king himself suffered 'great diseases,' and finally met his death by the conspiracy here narrated. It is useless to guess at the *motif* of the conspiracy, whether personal, political, or religious. The royal successor Amaziah suffered the like fate (14¹⁹) ; like the North, the South was in the nadir of disorder. For such exact records of assassination of a king *cf.* that of Sennacherib, 19³⁷. **21.** The place of assassination is *Beth-millo*, but the concluding local note (RVV JV *on the way that goeth down to Silla*) is absolutely obscure ; see Note. Begrich (*Chronologie*, 196) correctly finds parallel sources in vv.²¹·²²ᵃ, the second with more detail.

1. יהואש : 11², יואש, and so *inf.*, vv.²⁰·²¹, also I. 22²⁶ ; the same variation in name of the contemporary Northern king, 13⁹·¹⁰. For the name *cf.* יאוש in a Lachish tablet (Torczyner, *LL* no. 2) and in Elephantine papp.; the verbal element appears as *'ws* in Aramaic names (Lidzb., *HNE* 210) ; this corresponds to Arab. *'ws*, to give,' which element is frequent in OArab. names ; see *NPS* 1, 218, and *cf.* Albr., *BASOR* 79 (1940), 28, n. 1 ; see further Note below on 16¹. Of same origin is יאשיהו, 22¹.—**2.** צביה : 'gazelle' (Noth)=צביא in Eleph. papp.—**3.** אשר ימיו [כל] : Ehrl.

would read ימי אשר, as the Grr. understood (cf. GK §130, c), Šanda אשר הימים.—**4.** סרו: so 14⁴, 15⁴, ³⁵; see Note, I. 15¹⁴.—**5** *ff.* See St., *ZAW* 5 (1885), 208 ff. (=*Akad. Reden*, 192 ff.), *SBOT*, and the current commentaries.—**5.** עובר [כסף]=Hex., 𝕋 𝔙 (𝔖 paraphrases), but 𝔊 𝔊ᴸ=עֶרְךְּ, as below, and accepted in Comm.—כסף נפשות: this superfluous legal expression is reminiscent of Lev. 27², which ch. gives the money-rating for vows of kind.—[כסף] כל: read וכל, ו lost by haplog.—**6.** איש מאת מכרו: the pl., מכרם, appears in an Ugaritic list of temple castes, after *khnm* and *ḳdšm*; see Virolleaud, *Syria*, 1937: 163 ff., Gordon, *Ugar. Handbook*, 2, 62: 54 f. The root is מכר, and the word means primarily 'trader, bargainer,' proceeding to Arab. *makkār*, 'cheater.' The dubious form ממכריו appears at Dt. 18⁸, for which see Dr., *ad loc.* LHeb. מַכָּר= 'acquaintance,' and so 𝕋 here, followed by Rashi, Kimchi, and modern VSS. (exc. JV with a novel translation, 'from him that bestoweth it upon him'); Grr., ανηρ απο τ. πρασεως αυτου, and so supporting the above interpretation; 𝔙 'iuxta ordinem suum.' —בדק: for the root and derivatives see Lexx.; it proceeds from the notion of a 'rift, break,' so Akk., to that of 'repair,' so Syr. The Grr. transliterate (exc. Sym. with ἐπισκευή, and again below with τὰ δέοντα); 𝔙 'sartatecta,' and below 'instauratio'; 𝔖ᴴ cleverly rendered the Gr. transliteration into the corresponding Syr. noun.—**9.** קחת: קחת is expected; for similar exceptions see GK §93, h.—לבלתי 2⁰: 𝔊ᴸ om., apparently by intention in the dubious context.—בדק: B† βδελυγμα (!).—**10.** אָרוֹן: see Haupt for this as correct abs. form.—חר בדלתו: the Grr., *e.g.*, B A, are much confused.—אצל המזבח בימין:=𝔊ᴸ, Jos.; other Grr. transliterate: B παρα ιαμειβειν, A π. αμμασβη, N αμμαζειβη=𝔖ᴴ; see Comm. for correction to הַמַּצֵּבָה; Kamph.'s correction to המזוזה, accepted by Benz., is not supported by the Grr.—בימין Kt. =𝔊ᴸ, בימין Ḳr.=Aq. (see Rahlfs, *SS* 3, 245).—בא איש בית י׳: =𝔊ᴸ; 𝔊 𝔊ᴴ εν τω οικω ανδρος οικω/οικου Κυριου (with what sense ?). 𝔊 𝔊ᴴ avoid foll. שמח, and tr. המובא as though הנמצא = 𝔖ᴴ; *cf.* v.¹¹.—וגתנו: for this reversion of aspects (*cf.* v.¹²) see Dr., *Tenses*, §114.—**11.** וַיְעָרוּ: Ch., ויערו, 'and they emptied,' and so 𝔙 'effundebantque'; Grr. (𝔊ᴸ om.), 𝔖ᴴ 𝕋 'bound up,' and so 𝔖 𝔄, but transposing it and the foll. verb to obtain proper sequence; St. follows suit, correcting to וַיְצֻרוּ, from root צרר; *cf.* modern VSS. But see Eissfeldt's correction, accepted above; the same verb, צור, with similar mng., appears at I. 7¹⁵. The verb נתך, 22⁴ (with correction of 𝔇), is parallel in mng.—**12.** יד [עַל] Kt., יְדֵי Ḳr.; the former is correct, *cf.* 22⁵, where present Ḳr. is absent, and ידם below, v.¹⁶.—הפקוים: Kt., הַפְּקֻדִים Ḳr., conforming with 22⁵: read הַפְּקֻדִים; *cf.* the variant form in 11¹⁵.—**13.** לנדרים: read לְעוֹדְרִים; see Comm.—ולכל וּרְקֻנוֹת: Grr. om. the conj. —לחזקה; for inf. constr. in ה- see GK §45, d; 𝔊ᴸ+αυτον=𝔖ᴴ, suggesting to Klost., *al.* (not Šanda), the reading לְחַזְּקָהּ; but the Ḳal may be used in the absolute sense (a case in Josh. 2⁵).

II. 13$^{1-25}$

Ch. introduces the implied object, 'the house' = 𝔙 here.—**14.** [יהוה] בית: Grr., 'for the house,' exc. n, 'in the house' = 𝔖^H 𝔗 𝔖 𝔄.—**16.** לתת לעשי המלאכה: but this category means the superior technical officers at v.^{15}, yet here the paid labourers—a careless expression, or to be elided with Benz., St.—**17.** חטאות : = 𝔖 𝔙; 17 MSS חטאת, and so as sing. = Grr., 𝔖^H 𝔗, which is to be accepted.—יהיו: 3 MSS יהיה = VSS.—**18.** או: archival, not 'Flickwerk' (so Šanda).—**21.** ויקשרו קשר: 𝔊 𝔊^H κ. εδησαν παντα (error for επ αυτον) συνδεσμον; 𝔊^L κ. συνηψαν επ αυτον κ. εδ. συνδ.—בית מלא היורד סלא: the Grr. variously transliterate the nn. pr.; 𝔊 avoided היורד, and Rahlfs finds the original text in εν οικω Μααλω τω εν Γααλα. For rendering of the ppl. two makeshifts have been attempted: (1) making it geographical along with בית מלא, so 𝔗 = AV 'which goeth down to S.,' expanded in RVV JV (see Comm.); 𝔊^L εν τη καταβασει Αλλων = 𝔙 'in descensu Sella'; or (2) construing it with Joash, 'when he went down,' so Aq., Sym., Hex., 𝔖 𝔄 (Α καταμενοντα is to be corrected to καταβαινοντα). Rewritings have been proposed, e.g., by Then., Cheyne, Winckler, Haupt, Šanda. Smith, *Jerusalem*, 2, 112, proposes on chance a location near the Millo in Jerusalem.—**22.** יוזבר so MS L in *BH*, and many older prints, following over 50 MSS (see deR.—there is a misprint in Ginsb.^{1}), and so 𝔖; the generally received and preferable text (in view of the duplication of the odd name) is יוזכר, supported by the other VSS; but the other is an ancient rdg., as the parallel, זבד, in Ch. shows.—שמעת: n. pr. m.: cf. גנבת, I. 11^{20}, q.v. Ch. understood the name as fem., making the mother an 'Ammonitess,' and following this up with turning 'Shomer' into 'Shimrith,' 'a Moabitess'; such a development based on the grammatical gender is not to be accepted, vs. GB, Noth.

13$^{1-9}$. The reign of Jehoahaz of Israel. *Cf. Ant.*, ix, 8, 5. For criticism of the ch. see Stade, *ZAW* 5 (1885), 295 ff. = *Akad. Reden*, 197 (characterizing the ch. as 'ein wahres Gewirr'). Apart from the usual regnal data and religious criticism this section consists of brief notes on the conflicts with Aram, on which see further below, vv.$^{22ff.}$. The inverted order of vv.$^{4-6}$, recounting the king's appeal to YHWH, who then *gave Israel a deliverer, and they went out from under the hand of Aram*, and v.^{7}, detailing authentically the well-nigh complete destruction of Israel's military forces, stamps the former section as an awkward intrusion (*n.b.* the bracketing of vv.^{5,6} in EVV), as has been generally recognized. The indefinite reference to *a deliverer* is reflection from 14^{27}; most unlikely have been the attempts at identification, as Winckler's suggestion that it refers to the Assyrian Adad-nirari, or Cook's alternative suggestion of Zakar of Hamath (*CAH* 3, 376). The introductory words of v.[7], *For he did not leave* [not as with JV, *for there was not left*] *to Jehoahaz of the people save fifty steeds and ten chariots and ten thousand foot*, etc., connect with v.[3], *the anger* [root '*np*] *of* Y*HWH was kindled against Israel*; *cf.* the reason given by Mesha for Moab's earlier humiliation, " for Chemosh was angry [the same root] against his land." **6.** *And moreover the Asherah remained in Samaria* : the survival of this heathenish symbol, apparently untouched by Jehu ($10^{26.\ 27}$), motivated the ensuing calamity. **7.** The figures for the remnant of the army are to be compared with the Assyrian report of Ahab's 2000 chariots and 10,000 foot at the battle of Karkar ; the correspondence for the last figure is of interest, even if it seems absurdly high. For the question of ' steeds,' *vs.* ' horsemen,' as the word is generally understood, see the discussion in Note, I. 1^5. Löhr, cited there, holds that here distinctly cavalry is meant ; yet the word is aligned with chariots. **8.** The *might* ascribed to Jehoahaz is indeed formulistic.

VV.$^{10\text{-}25}$. The reign of Jehoash of Israel and his success over Aram, with legends of Elisha. *Cf. Ant.*, ix, 8, 6, 7. VV.$^{10\text{-}13}$. The regnal data. **10.** *In the thirty-seventh year of Joash king of Judah began Jehoash ben Jehoahaz to reign:* the 39th or 40th year is expected (*cf.* v.^{1}) ; the Grr. have attempted various corrections. **12. 13.** These final data are out of place here, and are duplicate of $14^{15.\ 16}$; the unusual language for the succession, *and Jeroboam sat upon his throne*, proves the secondary character. An early editor may have desired to place the original section, bracketed in Amaziah's reign, in a more appropriate setting. 𝔊 shows that the passage is primitive. 𝔊^L made correction by transferring it to end of the ch., and then omitting the duplicate 14^{15}, but inconsistently retaining v.^{16}. Šanda holds that this position of the passage is original ; but Lucian is a weak authority, even with his faculty of putting things in their right place. See also Skinner for attempt at restoration of original order.

VV.$^{14\text{-}19}$. Elisha's magical omens of victory for Jehoash. The prophet had appeared in the story of Hazael's accession to the throne of Aram, *ca.* 840 B.C. (ch. 8) ; he reappears now after 40 years (Jehoash *ca.* 800) ; Šanda calculates his age at 85–90 years. An affectionate relationship is postulated between prophet and royalty, as *vs.* the editorial condemnation of the dynasty. The king is said to have applied to him the proud title ' my father, my father,' that the latter had given to his master Elijah (2^{12}). VV.$^{15\text{ff.}}$. For cases of creative, sympathetic magic similar to the shooting with arrows here recorded *cf.* Ex. $17^{8\text{ff.}}$ (the propping up of Moses' hand with the rod of God in the battle with Amalek), Jos. $8^{18\text{ff.}}$ (Joshua's stretching out the javelin towards Ai until its capture), Jer. 18 (the prophet's breaking of the earthen jar as doom on Jerusalem); see Frazer, *The Golden Bough*, Suppl. Vol., cc. 1, 2 ; A. Lods, ' Le rôle des idées magiques dans la mentalité israélite,' in *O.T. Essays*, ed. D. C. Simpson ; Dhorme, *L'Évolution religieuse d'Israël*, 288 ff. There are two acts in the magical drama. VV.$^{15\text{-}17}$. With his hand on the king's hand, at *the window eastward, i.e.,* towards Aram, the prophet bids the king, *Shoot !,* accompanying the action with a word of power, *An arrow of victory of YHWH's, and an arrow of victory at Aram !* For such a ' holy word ' *cf.* Num. 21^{17}. The following specification of the coming victory *at Aphek* is most improbable even in a mere story ; the item is an insertion, either based on some tradition of the scene of the victories (not known in v.^{25}), or rather a reminiscence of I. $20^{26\text{ff.}}$, where the unnamed ' man of God ' and ' king of Israel ' appear, with subsequent triumph at Aphek. VV.$^{18,\ 19}$. An omen for precision of the number of victories. The art depended upon the will and energy of the operator ; the king's three strokes proved him remiss in forcefulness, for which the prophet chides him on the loss of his great opportunity.

VV.$^{20,\ 21}$. The death and burial of Elisha, and the miracle effected by his dead body. Mention of *the Moabites* as annual invaders of Elisha's home-country (Abel-meholah in Issachar, I. 19^{16}) appears to be an absurdity. For such forays of Moabites and Ammonites *cf.* Am. 1^{13}, 2^1. In v.^{21} AV has a circumlocution to ease the Heb.: " when the man was let down and touched the bones of Elisha," with like circumlocution RVV JV, ' as soon as the man touched the bones,' whereas 𝔐 reads, *and the man went and touched the bones—* an impossible use of the first verb with a corpse as subject.

By slight correction of 𝔐 (made by some VSS) read : *An l
they went off*. *And the man came in contact with Elisha's bones,
and he revived*. Even as Elijah had miraculously ascended
into heaven, so legend gave his disciple's dead body miraculous
power.

VV.²²⁻²⁵. The victories over Aram. **22.** The Heb. verb
requires the pluperfect, *Hazael . . . had oppressed Israel* ; the
v. is editorially resumptive. *Cf.* the Mesha inscr., 1. 5, " Omri
king of Israel afflicted Moab many days." **23.** A parallel
to vv.⁴ᶠᶠ·, and of similar origin ; 𝔊ᴸ transfers it after v.⁷.
The final *until now* fails in Grr., and is a pious addition.
24. 25. For the contemporary Aramæan history see the literature cited in n. 1 to Comm., I. 20. Ben-Hadad II, to whom
proleptic reference was made in v.³, succeeded his father, and
fresh authentic light has been thrown upon his reign by the
Aramaic, but Hebraizing, inscription of Zakar, ' king of
Hamath and La'ash ' (=Akk. Nuḫašše), found at Afîs (named
in the inscription), 40 km. SW of Aleppo (Bibliography, xli).
Zakar records how he successfully withstood a siege of his
fortress Hazrak (the Hadrak of Zech. 9¹) ' by Bar-Hadad bar
Hazael king of Aram ' and his seventeen allies, kings with
their armies, including far northerly Ḳue-Cilicia (see on
I. 10²⁸), 'Amḳ (the ' vale ' of Antioch), Gurgum, Melitene,
Sam'al. There is religious parallel with the section above,
vv.¹⁴ᶠᶠ· ; Zakar took recourse to ' seers and soothsayers,' who
promised him deliverance in the name of Baal-of-the-Heavens.
The chronology is sketched out at large from the Ass. records.
In 805 B.C. Adad-nirari III subjected Hatti-land, Amurru,
Tyre, Sidon, Omri-land (*i.e.*, Israel), Edom, Philistia (*cf.*
Hazael's capture of Gath, 12¹⁸), and marched upon Damascus,
where he " shut up Mari, the king of Damascus, in Damascus
his royal city " ; there follows the accounting of the rich loot
taken in lieu of surrender (*KB* 1, 190 ff.=*CIOT* 202 ff. ; *CP*
305 f. ; *ARA* 1, §739, *cf.* §§735, 740 ; *AB* 462 f.). The usual
dating for the Zakar inscr. and its picture of Syrian turmoil
has placed it before Adad-nirari's campaign, with question
as to the identity of ' Mari ' in the Damascene dynasty. For
that dating see Meyer (*GA* 2, 2, 344 ff., esp. p. 346, n. 1),
who finds no connexion between that revolt of the Syrian
states against Damascus and Jehoash's reign, *ca.* 798–783,

and so brands the present Biblical passage as 'worthless,' on the ground that by his reign not Ben-Hadad, but Mari was king of Damascus. But this Aramæan name = 'milord,' has been recognized by many (*e.g.*, Winckler, Kittel, Lods) as the title which has replaced the royal name in current language. As against Meyer's scepticism R. de Vaux argues in a monograph on 'La chronologie de Hazaël et de Benhadad III rois de Damas' (*RB* 1934, 512 ff.), that on epigraphical grounds the inscription is to be placed later, well after 805 B.C., in the following half-century of Assyrian withdrawal from Syrian affairs. He would identify 'Mari' with Hazael himself, noting an ivory plaque found at Arslan-Tash in loot taken from Damascus with the inscription לחזאל מראן, 'of our lord Hazael,' and place his son Ben-Hadad after that date, contemporary with Jehoash. That is, the insurrection of those Syrian states against Damascus gave opportunity to the Israelite king. **25***a*. He *took again out of the hand of Ben-Hadad ben Hazael the cities which he* (the latter) *had taken out of the hand of his father Jehoahaz by war*. The addition, **25***b*, *Three times did Jehoash smite him, and he recovered the cities of Israel*, aligns with the story of Elisha's magical operation. Note the parallel in Mesha's inscr., in which, l. 8, speaking of the land of Mehdeba, he says, using the same verb, "Chemosh recovered it in my days." The whole futility of the internecine Syro-Palestinian politics as also of the internal disturbances is further exhibited in the next chapter. Tiglath-pileser found an easy field for his conquests, and Assyrian imperialism has its apology.

1. '23d year': Jos., '21st year.'—על ישראל : 𝔊 om., 𝔖ᴴ ※ ; but it occurs regularly, exc. in I. 16¹⁵ (St.).—**2.** חמאת = Grr. ; but correct to חטאת in agreement with foll. ממנה = B† απ αυτης = 𝔈 ; *al.*, απ αυτων ; *cf.* vv.⁶· ¹¹.—**5.** מושיע : Grr., σωτηριαν (*vs.* Lagarde), exc. n v, σωτηρα = 𝔖ᴴ.—ויצאו = Hex. ; 𝔊 κ. εξηλθεν ; 𝔊ᴸ κ. εξηγαγεν αυτους = 𝔈 ; corresponding corrections, with Klost., St., are unnecessary.—**6.** כהמאות Ginsb., *BH* : מחטאת Ken., Mich., Bär, with same Kr. = VSS ; מחטאה demanded by foll. בה ; the latter preserved in B† εν αυτη.—[ירבעם] בית : 9 MSS om. = 𝔈ᵂ 𝔖. —הלך . . . אשר : 𝔊ᴸ om.—החטי : many MSS החטיא.—הלך = 𝔊 (B i) ; *al.* Grr. = נ̇כָהּ = *al*. VSS, which is to be accepted.—**7.** השאיר : Grr., 𝔖 𝔙 as though נשאר ; a translation demanded by the preceding insertion ; see Comm.—וישמם = 6 Gr. MSS ; B A *al.* by early error with pl. verb.—𝔊ᴸ transfers v.²³ after v.⁷, which change Burn.,

St. accept; Šanda properly denies the shift.—**10.** 'the 37th year': Gr. N+13 MSS, '39th'; c₂, '40th'; v, '36th.'—'16 years': 𝔖 '13,' by misreading.—**11.** המאות: many MSS המאת: the sing. again is to be read, with 𝔊 (B A al.), 𝔖ᴴ.—**12.** גבורתו אשר נלחם: cf. I. 16²⁷, 22⁴⁶; Gr. εποιησεν for the verb is reminiscent of those passages.—**13.** וירבעם ישב על כסאו: see Comm. for this evident intrusion; Begrich, *Chronologie*, 191, would retain it as original. The insertion involved foll. introduction of 'Joash' as necessary subject; 'Joash' is absent in 1 MS and in 𝔊 𝔊ᴸ (𝔖ᴴ ※). B has a very corrupt text here.—**16.** למלך ישראל: 𝔊 om. 'Israel,' but not in the parallel, v.¹⁸, where VSS also vary.—**17.** החלון: without את.—קדמה: 𝔖ᴴ asterisks, prob. from faulty copy.—בארם: for this use of ב 'in hostile sense' see GB 80b; 𝔊ᴸ, revising, 'in Israel,' preferred by Klost., Benz.—והכית: B† παραξει.—באפק: Ehrl. (cf BH) attempts to save by rdg. כאפק, 'as it was at Aphek.'— **18.** החצים: 𝔊ᴸ amplifies to 'five arrows,' to connect with 'five times' of v.¹⁹; see Rahlfs, SS 3, 245.—**19.** לחכות: the inf. properly defended by Burn., St.; cf. Dr., *Tenses*, §204; the Gr. (=ץ) has suggested to Klost., Haupt., al., the rdg. לוֹ הִכִּית.—**20.** גדודי: MS 187 גדוד=𝔗, induced by the sing. in v.²¹.—בָּא עָנָה: Grr., ελθοντος τ. ενιαυτου; 𝔗 'at the coming of the year'=EVV; ץ 'in ipso anno.' Many corrections have been proposed, see Burn., St. at length; Burn., בְּבֹא הַשָּנָה; St., שנה (abs. inf.) בֹא בשנה: Kit. (cf. BH), שנה בשנה; but בֹא השנה may be read with the inf. as locative of time.—**21.** וילך: Grr., κ. επορευθη, exc. 𝔊ᴸ with a doublet, κ. εφυγον κ. ηλθε; 𝔖ᴴ has the pl., with gloss from Sym., treating the verb as passive; and so 1 MS (deR). Read with athnah, וַיֵּלְכוּ, with Then., al., the Waw having been lost by haplog.—**22.** מלך ארם: 𝔊 om.—*Ad fin.* 𝔊ᴸ+κ. ελαβεν Αζαηλ τον αλλοφυλον εκ χειρος αυτου απο θαλασσης της καθ εσπεραν εως Αφεκ. St., following Wellh., has accepted this as original material, translating it into Heb. in *SBOT*. But see Rahlfs's drastic criticism (SS 3, 289, cf. Šanda), pointing out that Luc. misunderstood 'the sea of the Arabah,' 14²⁵, as 'the sea of the West,' *i.e.*, the Mediterranean, and so similarly at 25⁴·⁵ with 'the Arabah'= 'the West'; he introduced the same terminology here, but the Philistines never extended to Aphek, itself an invention taken from v.¹⁷.—**23.** ולא אבה: 1 MS+יהוה=Grr., 𝔖 𝔄.—עד עתה: Grr. om., 𝔖ᴴ ※.—**25.** במלחמה: 𝔊ᴸ replaces the foll. Heb. with invented midrash: "And Ioas smote the son of Ader, son of Azael thrice in the battle at Aphek according to the word of the Lord, and recovered the cities of Israel and what he took," and then attaches 14¹⁵·¹⁶.

14¹⁻²². The reign of Amaziah of Judah. ‖ 2 Ch. 25; cf. *Ant.*, ix, 9. VV.¹⁻⁴. Introductory regnal data. **2.** Ascription of *twenty-nine years* to the reign is impossible. The 'twenty' appears to have been introduced from the preceding figure of the young king's age, 20 (and 5). Such is the judgment of Rost, *KAT* 320; Kittel, *GVI* 2, 213; Robinson, *HI* 1, 461 f. The recent special studies of the chronology have their particular solutions. Lewy (pp. 11 ff.) assigns a reign of 13 years, with assumption of Amaziah's retirement from active rule upon his defeat by Jehoash, with his son Azariah acting as regent; this would account for the unique statement in v.^{17} that he *lived after the death of Jehoash . . . fifteen years*, i.e., $13+15=28/29$. Begrich (149 ff.) holds that the synchronism in v.^{17} is unhistorical (indeed it can hardly be archival), and has affected the term here; the accession in the 2nd year of Jehoash, who reigned 16 years (13^{10}), i.e., $16-2=14$, and $14+15=29$; he assigns the king 16 years. Mowinckel (pp. 240 ff.) supports the Biblical figure with reduction of the successor Azariah's term by 10 years, *i.e.*, a reign of 19 years.

3. The v. recovers its original form by bracketing an early interpolation: *And he did the right in the eyes of* Y$_{HWH}$ [*yet not like David his father*], *like all that his father Joash had done he did*, the exception to his character being based on v.^{4}. **5. 6.** The record of the punishment of his father's murderers, when he got in control of state affairs—the assassins, *his servants*, having still remained in his court—is interesting history. V.^{6}, with citation from the Law, Dt. 24^{16}, is a moralizing addition; at the most we might retain *and the murderers' sons he did not slay* as historic fact. **7.** *He smote Edom in the Valley of Salt, ten thousand, and seized the Rock* [Heb. *sela'* =EVV *Sela*] *by battle; and he* [or impersonal= *they*] *called its name Jokteel unto this day*. We have here, with the possible exception of the last sentence, as again in v.^{22}, a true archival item in its original form. Unrecognizable in modern translations is the introductory emphatic *he* of the Hebrew; *cf.* Mesha's repeated emphatic ' I ' in his inscription; in the transcription the first person was changed to the third; a more extensive case occurs in 18^4. See the writer's article, ' Archival Data in Kings,' esp. p. 50. The locations of *the Valley of Salt* and *the Rock* have long been problems. The former region was the scene of David's great victory over Edom, 2 Sam. 8^{13}. It may be a general name for the valley to the S of the Dead Sea; it has been identified with 'Ain-milḥ, *ca.* 30 km. W of Petra, in a wady, which would be on the route of the Judæan army (so Šanda). Identification of *the Rock* with famous Petra goes back to 𝔊 with τ. πετραν=ע 'petram'; see Robinson, *BR* 2, 573 ff.; Döller, *GES* 265 f.; *BDD* s.v. 'Sela'; others have doubted the identification, e.g., Buhl, *Gesch. d. Edomiter*, 34 f., Kittel, Eissfeldt. But Glueck has successfully made the point that the place is one of the overhanging heights of the valley in which the later notable city Petra lay, Umm el-Biyārah, the ancient acropolis, as 'now archæologically established' (*AASOR* 14, 77; 15, 82, etc.; *cf*. Abel, *GP* 2, 407 f.). Strabo, xvi, 4, 21, speaks of the city's site as κύκλῳ δὲ πέτρᾳ φρουρουμένου, and hence its later name. Glueck well compares the 'parable' of Balaam against the Kenite, Num. 24^{21}: "Enduring thy habitation, and set in the rock (*sela'*) thy nest (*ḳên*)," the last word playing on 'Kenite,' *i.e.*, the Smith-clan, which worked the rich copper mines of that region, as Glueck has demonstrated. For a full presentation of the topography of Petra, richly illustrated, see Mrs. G. Horsfield's monograph, vol. 7 (1938) of *Quarterly of the Dept. of Antiquities in Palestine* (*cf*. review in *AJA* 1938, 565); also is to be noticed (Mrs.) M. A. Murray, *Petra, the Rock City of Edom*, 1938. The figure of '10,000 Edomites' is a customary round number; *cf*. the same figure in 13^7; in David's battle in the same locality the figure of his victims is put at 18,000, but this appearing in the title of Ps. 60 as 12,000—so little reliable is numerical tradition. Ch. has a playful midrash here, how they brought the ten thousand "to the top of the rock, and cast them down from the top of the rock, and they were all broken up." Jokteel is not otherwise known (a city of that name in Judah, Josh. 15^{38}).

VV.$^{8-14}$. Amaziah's challenge to Jehoash and his undoing by the latter. The success of the two kings, of the one over Edom, of the other over Aram, provoked envious hostility; Amaziah would naturally have desired to clear Transjordan of Israel—a fatuous policy. **8.** Amaziah's challenge, *Let us see one another face to face*, is couched in the knightly language of the duello; *cf*. I. 20^{11}. **9. 10.** Jehoash retorts like a superior gentleman with a brief and incisive fable, with which *cf*. Jotham's more extensive harangue, Jud. 9$^{7-15}$. The Israelite strain of the fable was native, as such cases prove; see further on I. 5$^{9\text{ff}.}$. The actors in the fable are *the thistle in Lebanon*, *the cedar in Lebanon, the wild beasts in Lebanon*; it is hypercriticism on Stade's part, followed by Šanda, to excise *in Lebanon* 2⁰ and 3⁰. The application of the parable is equally curt : *The smiting of Edom thou hast wrought, and thy heart would lift thee up* [*cf.* EVV]. *Enjoy thy glory* [one word in Heb. and contemptuous in form], *and stay at home* [Heb. *in thy house*]. *And why wouldst thou challenge evil?* The last verb is in line with the tr. of 𝔙, ' provocas,' and so RVV^mg, ' provoke calamity,' Moffatt, ' provoke trouble,' Chic. B., ' court trouble.' The verb presents the self-excitation of the champion, *cf.* the picture of YHWH rousing himself to war, Is. 42¹³ ; the same verb is used of starting war with an opponent, Dt. 2⁹· ²⁴, *cf.* Dan. 11¹⁰· ²⁵. The renderings of EVV with the verb ' to meddle ' are weak. **11.** The contestants met *face to face . . . at Beth-shemesh of Judah*, *i.e.*, modern 'Ainshems, W of Jerusalem, the railroad passing close by it on the ancient thoroughfare from the sea to that city. For an archæological study of the site see E. Grant, *Beth Shemesh* (1929), and *Ain Shems Excavations*, Part I (1931) ; *cf.* Abel, *GP* 2, 282. Cook has well observed that the determinant, literally, *which is Judah's*, is from the northern point of view (*JBL* 51 [1932], 283 f.). **12. 13.** Judah was defeated, *they fled every one home* (*cf.* I. 12¹⁶), and Amaziah was taken prisoner. The victor proceeded to Jerusalem, and arriving, *he dismantled the wall of Jerusalem from the Ephraim Gate to the Corner Gate, 400 cubits*. For these gates see Smith, *Jerusalem*, Indices, *s.v.* ' Gates,' *e.g.*, 2, 116, 119, and M. Burrows's studies, ' A Source for the Topography of Ancient Jerusalem,' *AASOR* 14 (1935), *e.g.*, pp. 118, 134, 137, and ' The Topography of Neh. 12, 31-43,' *JBL* 54 (1935), 29 ff. The Ephraim Gate lay in the north wall, and according to the above authorities the Corner Gate was at the NE angle. But there would have been little reason for the northern victor to demolish a gate there, and Šanda, following Schick, would find the gate in question at the NW angle, and would accept the 400 cubits as a fairly correct figure for the distance between the two gates ; however, the figure may present only a partial demolition. *Cf.* Uzziah's restorations as reported by 2 Ch. 26⁹, the building of towers at the Corner Gate, the Valley Gate, the Angle Gate. **14.** Jerusalem's temple and palaces suffer their third despoliation, since Shishak (I. 14$^{25\text{ff.}}$) and Hazael (12^{19}). *Hostages* are mentioned, uniquely in Biblical history.

VV.$^{15, 16}$. The data for the end of Jehoash's reign. For the original position here of the section, see Comm., 13$^{12, 13}$.

VV.$^{17-22}$. The remainder of Amaziah's reign, and his assassination. **17.** For the synchronism see above on v.^{2}. **19.** *And they made a conspiracy against him in Jerusalem:* the second assassination of a Judæan monarch, following that of the father (12$^{21, 22}$), the conspiracy here being stated impersonally. We may only speculate again, as in the father's case, upon the motive of the conspiracy, which was persistent to the extreme; but it was no popular cause, as v.^{21} shows. *And he fled to Lachish, and they sent after him to Lachish, and they killed him there.* Lachish, long identified with Tell el-Hesy, as in F. J. Bliss's volume, *A Mound of Many Cities* (1894), is now definitely located at Tell ed-Duweir, 8 km. SW of Beit-jibrīn, where a remarkable discovery of Hebrew ostraca of Jeremiah's age has been made. Two pertinent volumes on Lachish are available (see Bibliography, *s.v.*), the first with Preface on 'The Discovery' by the late lamented J. L. Starkey; see also Albright, *BASOR* 68 (1937), 22 ff.; R. S. Haupert, *BA* 1 (1938), 21 ff., and for the earlier literature Abel, *GP* 2, 367 f. Mention of Lachish also recurs in 18^{14}. **20.** *And they brought him upon horses, and he was buried in Jerusalem with his fathers in David's City.* The first sentence is obscure, and Winckler, followed by Haupt (*cf. BH*), would insert it before *and he fled* in v.^{19}; but Šanda's suggestion of a solemn funeral procession back to Jerusalem is quite to the point. **21.** A note on the succession to the throne: *And all the people of Judah took Azariah, who was sixteen years old, and made him king in place of his father Amaziah.* The v. presents a unique political datum; *cf.* the part played by 'the people of the land' in Jehoash's accession (11$^{17\text{ff.}}$). For the name Azariah and the variant Uzziah see Comm., 15^{1}. **22.** *He built Elath, and restored it to Judah, after that the king slept with his fathers.* The usual interpretation, so *e.g.*, Then., Kittel, is that the son promptly completed his father's interrupted operation, but the time note, with *the king* as subject, is most obscure. Six Gr. MSS introduce

Amaziah's name as the subject, followed by Winckler, Šanda. Skinner most arbitrarily suggests Jeroboam as the original subject. But the record of the restoration of Elath is another archival datum, beginning with the emphatic *he*, without previous conjunction, and doubtless stood once in the same official record as v.[7]. It became detached, was by haphazard restored here. The following temporal sentence is clumsy editorial reflection on the misplacing of the item. For *Elath* (by the older pronunciation) see on Eloth, I. 9^{26}. But the famous harbour was to be lost again to Aram (16^6).

VV.[23-29]. The reign of Jeroboam II of Israel. *Cf. Ant.*, ix, 10, 1, 2. **23.** For the length of the reign, 41 years, there is no variation in the VSS; Jos. makes it the round figure 40. **24-27.** The usual condemnation of members of the Northern dynasties (v.[24]) is followed by an archival datum of Jeroboam's recovery of Israelite territory from Aram. **25***a*. *He* [the Heb. emphatic pronoun] *restored the border of Israel from the Entrance of Hamath unto the Sea of the Arabah*. The ideal limits of Israel's territory are here expressed; *cf.* Am. 6^{14}, etc. The Entrance of Hamath is the opening from the south into the Beḳā', the great valley between the two Lebanon ranges (see Eissfeldt, *R. Schamra u. Sanchuniathon*, 32 f., citing a study by Noth in *ZDPV* 58 (1935), 185 ff.; E. Robinson understood it as of the northern end of the valley, *LBR* 568, *cf.* Burney, *Judges*, 63). To this item is attached a prophetic oracle: **25***b*. *according to the word of* Y*HWH, God of Israel, which he spoke through his servant the prophet, Jonah ben Amittai, of Gath-hepher;* this continued with an explanation of the divine clemency: **26.** *For* Y*HWH saw that Israel's affliction was very bitter; for there was ⌜none shut up nor left at large⌝* [so RVV JV; see Note], *and no helper for Israel;* **27.** *and* Y*HWH spoke not for blotting out Israel's name from under heaven; and he saved them by the hand of Jeroboam ben Joash*. This oracle of a nationalistically minded prophet must be original, however inexact the present phrasing may be.[1]

---

[1] Later to this historical Jonah the prophetic book of that name with its burden against Nineveh came to be assigned. For Jonah's home town (also Josh. 19^{13}), between Sepphoris and Tiberias, from of old connected with the prophet's memory, as Jerome reports, see Dalman, *Sacred Sites and Ways*, 111.

There is to be noted T. H. Robinson's remark (*HI* I, 359, n. 1) : " This must have been written before 734 B.C." Jonah took a contrary view to that of his contemporaries, Amos and Hosea ; the former (6^{13}) condemned the braggadocio of the national revival : " who rejoice in Lo-debar, and say, Have we not taken Karnaim to ourselves ? " (the places named are Transjordanic). And according to Amos 8^{14} the far northern shrine of Dan was still flourishing. **28.** The political expansion is further eked out in the concluding summary of *the acts of Jeroboam . . . how he warred, and how he restored Damascus and Hamath ⌈for Judah in Israel⌉* [*sic !*]. The reference to Judah is unintelligible (*cf.* AV RVV) ; the passage is generally reduced by critics to *to Israel* (and thus long ago 𝔖). The note of the ' restoration ' of distant Hamath as well as of Damascus is absurd ; various rewritings of the passage have been attempted (see Note). If there be any traditional reminiscence, we might think of recovery of old-time territorial markets in Damascus (*cf.* I. 20^{34}).[2] But the revival was socially and economically unsound, and Amos and Hosea foresaw the debacle. The black night that followed has obscured the temporary glory of the reign ; as Olmstead observes (*HPS* 420) : " In the few lines grudgingly vouchsafed by the editor of Kings to Jeroboam II . . . we glimpse one of the mightiest rulers of Israel." The Biblical information on this reign is meagre enough. The one item presented above fits into the scheme of Assyria's movement westward against the Syrian states. The Eponym Canon itemizes attacks upon Damascus in 773 B.C., Hadrach in 772, and again in 765, 755, and Arpad in 754. The last campaign is brilliantly illustrated by a native Aramaic document, found at Sūjīn in 1931 (Comm., I. 18, p. 299, n. 2). It presents a humiliating treaty imposed by the conqueror upon the local king of Ktk (?) along with Mata'ilu king of Arpad, and is parallel to a similar Assyrian document on the same subject. For the history of this period *cf.* Alt's study, ' Die syrische Staatenwelt vor dem Einbruch der Assyrer.' The continuous suppression of the Syrian states,

---

[2] For Hamath see Dussaud, *TH* 233 ff., and for H. Ingholt's long series of excavations there his *Rapport préliminaire sur sept campagnes de fouilles à Hama en Syrie* (1932-38), Memoirs of the Danish Royal Academy, Copenhagen, 1940.

II. 14¹⁻²⁸   445

later renewed by the advent of Tiglath-pileser (745 B.C.), gave Israel opportunity for revenge against Syria in Jeroboam's reign (*ca.* 783–743 B.C.).

2. שנה : for abnormal sing. see 8¹⁷.—יהועדין Kt.=Grr. ; יהֹועָדָּן Ḳr.=Ch. and other VSS ; for the name see Noth, *IP* 267 ; a Minæan name, עדין, appears (*NPS* 1, 157).—**3.** עשׂה *bis* : 2 MSS om. 1⁰, 1 MS om. 2⁰.—**4.** סרו : as at 12⁴.—**5.** המלך : 𝕲 𝕲ᴸ om by simplification, in line with Ch.—**6.** יומתו *bis* ; ימות Kt., יָּקַח. Ḳr. : for the variations in Ḳal and Hofal *cf.* the original law in Dt. 24¹⁶, and the parallel in Ch. ; for the variations in MSS, edd., VSS see *BH*, notes *ad loca*, and deR., St. at length.—כי אם : MSS כי=Ch. ; see deR.—**7.** המלח : Ḳr. מֶלַח, and so many MSS, as in 2 Sam. 8¹³, Ps. 60² ; the Kt. induced by Ch. ; Grr. have barbarous transliterations of גיא המ' ; Aq., Sym. translate.—ותפש : for the consecution see the writer's art. cited in Comm. ; the form is original, *vs.* critics.—הסלע : 𝔗 *Kerakka*, by identification with Kir-haresheth, for which identification see Abel, *GP* 2, 418.— יָקְתְאֵל : see Note on יקמעם, I. 4¹²; the name is identical with קָקְתִיאֵל, 1 Ch. 4¹⁸, with verbal element=Arab. *ḳūt*, ' to nourish.'— ' unto this day ' : *cf.* I. 8⁸, II. 8²², 16⁶.—**8.** או שלח : see Note, I. 9²⁴. —פנים : פ' אל פ' is the usual expression.—**9.** החוח : the Grr., exc. one Origenian rdg., have a primitive abbreviation of ακανθος, B *al.*, ακαν, 𝕲ᴸ texts ακχαν.—**10.** ונשאר לב־ : for the consecution see Dr., *Tenses*, 141.—לבך הכבד : 𝕲 𝕲ᴴ correctly for the verb, ενδοξασθητι ; 𝕲ᴸ has a triplet rendering of the verb : η καρδια σου η βαρεια (=הַכָּבֵד) ενδοξασθητι *bis*, the final repetition appearing to be due to gloss correction ; see Rahlfs, *SS* 3, 198. Ch. has for the verb לְהִכָּבֵד, generally corrected to הַכְבֵּד. There is no reason to correct the text with Klost., *cf. BH*.—**11.** יהואש : B† om., 𝕊ᴴ ※.—הוא ואמציהו מלך יהודה : Gr. MSS 44 71 om., 𝕊ᴴ ※ ; *vs.* St., the prolixity may well be original.—**12.** לאהלו : Kt. לְאֹהֱלִי = Grr. (exc. x y), 𝕊ᴴ 𝕊 𝔄 ; Ḳr. לְאָהֳלָיו=Ch., 𝔗 𝔙 ; Kt. is correct, *cf.* 8²¹.—**13.** מלך יהודה : OGrr. om., 𝕊ᴴ ※.—בן יהואש בן אחויהו 𝕲 texts (B *al.*) have the double patronymic probably intruded from Ch. ; but the Gr. used by 𝕊ᴴ omitted the second one.—ויבאו Kt., וַיָּבֹא Ḳr. : 𝕲 𝔗 𝕊=Ḳr. ; 𝕊ᴴ=Kt. ; Ḳr. is to be preferred in the consecution. 𝕲ᴸ 𝔙 follow Ch., ויביאהו, which Burn., St. accept without sufficient reason.—בשער : =𝕲 𝕲ᴴ 𝕊ᴴ ; some 10 MSS Ken., deR. (Ginsburg as Or.), משער=Ch., and the other VSS ; the latter is to be accepted ; the case one of labial variation.—**14.** ולקח : it is easy to correct to ויקח ; but Ch. om. the verb, as does one Lucianic MS here, and there may have been an original lacuna here, which was supplied in this fashion.— **15.** אישר : 9 MSS, 𝕊 as 'וכל א ; *cf.* 13⁸.—ואשר : 1 MS, Grr., 𝔙 as אשר.—**18.** אמציהו : Grr.+" and all that he did."—**23.** מלך ישׂראל : 19 MSS Ken., deR., 'מ' על י, acc. to the correct formula=𝕲 𝕲ᴴ 𝕊ᴴ 𝔗ᴸ.—**24.** מכל המאות : for the noun MSS חמאת, to be read as sing. ; *cf.* 13¹¹, etc. 𝔊ᴸ om. כל, prob. finding an exception in view of the divine favour to the reign.—**25.** הערבה : 𝔊ᴸ προς εσπεραν ; see Note, 13²².—**26.** מׂרֶה : VSS, modern trr., ' bitter,' but the form is impossible ; see *SBOT* for attempted revisions, of which Burn.'s הַמׇּר is simplest.—אפס עצור ואפס עזוב : for the phrase see Note, I. 14¹⁰. Eissf. well tr. with "allesamt waren dahin." 𝔊 understood אפס as adj. and so : ολιγοστους (correcting B) συνεχομενους κ. εσπανισμενους (these two ppls. a doublet = ' being in want ') κ. εγκαταλελειμενους, which 𝔊ᴸ reduced by omitting κ. εσπαν.— **27.** שם : Grr. by primitive error, σπερμα = 𝔖ᴴ, exc. 𝔊ᴸ, ονομα.— **28.** אשר נלחם : Gr. variations here as in 13¹².—ואשר השיב את דמשק, ואת חמת ליהודה בישראל : of the VSS 𝔖 𝔄 alone give reasonable sense by omitting ' to Judah ' and rdg. ' to Israel.' But ' Judah ' of the text remains a conundrum, and all correction is arbitrary. For various rewritings see Burn., St. The former's revision, accepted by Šanda, reads in tr. : " and how he fought with Damascus, and how he turned away Y.'s wrath from Israel " ; but Jeroboam as diverter of the divine wrath is most improbable.

Ch. 15. For the brilliant light cast upon this and the following ch. from the inscriptions of Tiglath-pileser III (IV), 745–727 B.C., see the texts in *CIOT* 1, 208 ff. ; *KB* 2, 2 ff. ; *ARA* 1, ch. 14 ; *ATB* 1, 113 ff., and in selection, *CP* 308 ff. ; *AKAT* 172 ff. ; *AB* 463 ff. For this Assyrian phase of Biblical history, in addition to the Histories, *au courant*, is to be consulted Dhorme, ' Les pays bibliques et l'Assyrie,' in six sections, *RB* 7, 8 (1910–11). For text criticism of cc. 15–21 see Stade, *ZAW* 6 (1886), 156 ff. = *Akad. Reden*, 201 ff.

VV.[1-7]. The reign of Azariah-Uzziah of Judah. ∥ 2 Ch. 26 (with a long insertion, vv.[5-19]) ; *cf. Ant.*, ix, 10, 3, 4. **1.** The king's name appears below intermittently as Uzziah, vv. [13. 30. 32. 34] (but with variations in MSS), and so throughout Ch., except in the Davidic family-tree (I. 3¹²), and in Amos, Hosea, Isaiah. Azariah is evidently the throne-name, Uzziah an adopted name, or possibly a popular *alias* with play on the roots, ' help ' in the first case, ' might ' in the second, the latter as a result of the king's triumphs.[1] The name of Azariah of Judah has produced a vexed problem because of

---

[1] For such changes of royal names *cf.* Jedidiah-Solomon, Shallum-Joahaz, Eliakim-Jehoiakim, Mattaniah-Sedekiah. There is also the change of name of Assyrian kings upon accession to the throne of Babylon, of Tiglath-pileser as Pul (*cf.* v.[19] below), of Shalmaneser IV as Ululai, of Ashurbanipal as Kandalanu ; see the Babylonian King List A, *KB* 2, 286 f.

the appearance of a contemporary Azriau of Ya'ūdi in Tiglath-pileser's Annals for the year 738 (see *KB* 2, 27 ; *ATB* 1, 345 ; *ARA* 1, §770 ; *CP* 314 ; *AB* 463). Early interpretations naturally identified this figure with the Judæan king, so *e.g.*, Schrader in *CIOT*. But Winckler, in his *Altor. Forschungen*, I, 1 ff. (*cf KAT* 54), upset this view by identification of Ya'ūdi with the home-land of Panammūwa king of Y'di, later Sam'al, in far North Syria, inscriber of two lengthy Aramaic inscriptions (known by the names of Hadad, the father, and Panammūwa, the son [see Bibliography, xli]), the second of which records the king's presence at Tiglath-pileser's triumph in Damascus in the year 732. This identification has since been generally accepted by historians, *e.g.*, by Rogers (*CP* 311), and by Gray in his Comm. on Isaiah (pp. lxix *seq.*). A vigorous denial of this change of interpretation was entered by Luckenbill in *AJSL* 41 (1925), 217 ff., and his judgment, although drastically condemned by Meyer, has been stoutly endorsed by Noth (*IP* 109 f.). But the Assyrian's boastful report of a devastating campaign against Ya'ūdi can only with extreme strain be interpreted as referring to far-off Judah. For the interesting parallelism of names Gray notes from Ass. inscriptions that of Menahem of Israel, and so of Shomeron, for the year 738, and Menahem of Samsimuruna for 701. As for the northern name Azriau, if its final element be the divine *Yahu*, a parallel exists in the name of an Aramæan king known from Sargon's inscriptions, with the variation Ilu-bidi/Yau-bidi (see Noth, *ib.*, 110, n. 3). But there are to be recalled the older Heb. inscription of Kilammūwa in North Syria, and the Hebraizing Aramaic inscription of Zakar of Hamath, and we may possibly assume wandering knights of fortune from the far south ; *cf.* the relations of Toi king of Hamath with David, according to 1 Ch. 18[9f.], also the reference to Hamath above, 14[28]. And so Meyer (*GA* 3, 28 ; *cf.* n. 4) recognizes Yau-bidi, ' the bad Hittite ' of the Ass. text, as ' ein israelitischer Reisläufer.' [2]

This historical summary is extraordinarily brief for a long reign, containing the one unique item of the king's physical

[2] For identification of the divine element in those names with Bab. Yaum, and Yao of Abraxas gems, see *KAT* 66, and Eissf., *R. Schamra u. Sanch.*, 17.

affliction. On the other hand Ch. has a long list of the king's achievements with a large and admirably equipped army against the Philistines and Arabians (he was indeed relieved from the pressure of Aram and Israel), and of his building operations in Jerusalem and throughout the kingdom, he himself appearing as an amateur of agriculture ; but for his vaulting ambition in presuming to offer the incense-sacrifice in the temple (a datum in the constant feud between royalty and priesthood), he was smitten with leprosy on his forehead, and so excluded from his office. For ' The Sin of Uzziah ' see Morgenstern, *HUCA* 12–13 (1938), 1 ff. There is hardly question but that Ch. has drawn from excellent ancient sources at least for the secular details of this account. We might assume an early lacuna in the tradition of our book.

5. *And YHWH smote the king, and he was stricken with leprosy unto the day of his death ; and he dwelt in a house set apart :* so for the final phrase JV ; EVV Chic. B., ' in a several/ separate house ' (=GV FV) ; more explicitly RV^{mg} has ' in a lazar house,' RV$^{Am.\ mg}$, ' in an infirmary ' ; Moffatt tr. the final term with ' unmolested.' For the archival item, with definite legal phraseology, of the king's malady *cf.* the annalistic report in the Babylonian Chronicle concerning a king of Elam, who " suffered with a stroke, his mouth was closed and he could not speak " (col. iii, lines 20 f. ; *KB* 2, 280 ; Rogers, *CP* 214). The statement on the king's habitat, as generally translated, suggests a condition ' in quarantine ' ; but see Comm. on Naaman's case (5^1). The Heb.='in the house of x,' and the noun in question='freedom ;' *cf.* the use of the corresponding adj. in 1 Sam. 17^{25}, generally interpreted as civically ' free.' The phrase here may be rendered, *in the status* [with extended sense of Heb. *house*] *of exemption*, *i.e.*, from royal, sacred and civic duties, which a diseased man (as in the history of even modern royalty) might not exercise (and so Kimchi recognized). See the writer's brief article on ' Soul Gods,' *HTR* 34 (1941), 321 f., and Note below, with an interesting Ugaritic parallel. In these circumstances *the king's son Jotham was Over-the-House* [*cf.* I. 4^6], *Judge of the people of the land*, the latter title probably a technical term for regency. A remarkable archæological sequel to this record has been discovered by E. L. Sukenik in a small museum in

II. 15¹⁻³⁸

Jerusalem ; see his report in *QS* 1931, 217 ff., and *cf.* Albright, *BASOR* 44 (1931), 8 ff. This is a stone with an Aramaic inscription reading : " Hither were brought the bones of Uzziah king of Judah." *Cf.* the rather cryptic note on his burial in Ch., v.²³. It was in this royal death-year that Isaiah had the vision of his call (Is. 6¹).

VV.⁸⁻¹². The reign of Zechariah of Israel. For vv.⁸⁻³¹ *cf. Ant.*, ix, 11, 1. According to v.¹² this reign, terminating the dynasty of Jehu, fulfilled the divine word in 10³⁰. **10.** The social confusion throughout the Levant in face of the Assyrian terror was the background of the king's murder, in the conspiracy of a certain Shallum, who *attacked him at Jibleam* [=𝔊ᴸ, 𝔙 *before people*>current rendering, *before the people*], *and killed him.* For the place, also the scene of Ahaziah's murder by Jehu, *cf.* 9²⁷ ; for the correction see Note. For these last kings, Zechariah to Hoshea, the burial of Menahem alone is recorded. VV.¹³⁻¹⁶. The reign of Shallum of Israel, plus an archival datum concerning his murderer and successor Menahem. Shallum was done away with after a reign of *a full month* (Heb. *a month of days*). **14.** *And Menahem ben Gadi came up from Tirsah* [the one-time royal residence, I. 15²¹], *and came to Samaria, and attacked Shallum ben Jabesh in Samaria, and killed him, and reigned in his stead.* Then after the usual editorial sequel on *the acts of Shallum* (v.¹⁵) comes an item, v.¹⁶, with the introductory archival *then*, anticipating the history of Menahem's reign in vv.¹⁷ᶠᶠ. It may have been originally collocated with v.¹⁴ ; *cf.* the displacement of such an item in 14²². **16.** The difficulty of the v. is evident from the tr. of AV with its italicization of essential additions for sense, here represented in brackets : *Then Menahem smote Tiphsah and all that were therein, and the coasts thereof from Tirsah ; because they opened not [to him], therefore he smote [it ; and] all the women with child therein he ripped up ;* and so the text of RVV JV, but without the italics of AV. In every aspect the v. is obscure, as all VSS prove ; the verb *opened* is masc. sing., and the range of the geographical items is problematic. Tiphsah has been naturally, if absurdly, identified with Tiphsah-Thapsacus on the Euphrates of I. 5⁴ (see Poole, and Rawlinson, *ad loc.*). The now generally accepted correction is to Tappuah, based

on the transliteration in 𝔊^L. But with Tirsah belonging to
Manasseh and Tappuah (also in Shishak's list, no. 39) in
the extreme north of Ephraim (Jos. 16⁸, 17⁸—for the two
places see Abel, *GP* 2, 475, 485), there remains the problem
of such a barbarous raid carried out between two such closely
neighbouring cities. Šanda would relieve the passage by
excising *from Tirsah* as an interpolation from v.¹⁴. The
problem remains why there was such an early snarl in a
presumably simple text. The savage cruelty against pregnant
women was typical of those days of the Assyrian terror; it
was expected from Hazael (8¹²), practised on Israel by Ammon
(Am. 1¹³), and was to be part of Israel's final tragedy (Hos. 14¹).

VV.¹⁷⁻²². The reign of Menahem of Israel. **18.** The punctuation at end of the v. must be corrected along with word-corrections, following the Grr. *And he did the evil in the sight
of YHWH, he turned not from all the sin* [𝔐 *away from the sins*]
*of Jeroboam ben Nebat, for which he made Israel liable. In
his days* [𝔐 *all his days*] **19.** *came Pul king of Assyria against
the land, and Menahem gave to Pul a thousand talents of
silver, that his hand* [𝔐 *hands*] *might be with him to confirm
the kingdom in his hand.* **30.** *And Menahem exacted the silver
against Israel, against all the magnates of wealth—to give to
the king of Assyria—fifty shekels of silver per person; and
the king of Assyria turned back and stayed not there in the
land.* A unique contemporary touch appears in the item
with the alternate name for Tiglath-pileser. Acc. to 1 Ch.
5²⁶ the two names represented distinct persons, and such
was the natural understanding until quite recent times, as
e.g., with Rawlinson, *ad loc*. When Tiglath-pileser finally
ascended the distinct throne of Babylon, in 729 B.C., he
assumed the name Pūlu, as it appears in the Babylonian
King-List A (*CP* 202) with transcription as Πωρου in the
parallel Ptolemaic Canon (Bibliog., xlii), and as Φουλος in
Eusebius; see P. Schnabel, *Berossos*, 143 f. The tribute of
'Menahem of Samaria' (*n.b.* the novel designation of the
kingdom), along with that of the kings of Damascus (Raṣūnu
—see on v.³⁷), Gebal-Byblos, Hamath, etc., is recorded by
the conqueror in his Annals for the year 738. For references
for calculation of the money-value of the talent see Comm.,
I. 10²⁹. Šanda (writing in 1912) calculated the value of the

1000 talents at 16–17 million francs. Mari of Damascus (see Comm., 13$^{22\text{ff.}}$) paid Adad-nirari III 2300 talents of silver, 20 of gold, 3000 of copper, 5000 of iron, along with cloth fabrics, ivory furniture, etc. (*KB* I, 191; *ARA* I, §740, *cf.* §735). Given the value of a talent at the minimum figure of 3000 shekels (so Galling, *BR* 186—*cft.* Dt. 22^{19}, Eze. 45^{12}), the 50 shekels poll-tax represents 60,000 taxable persons— an objective side-light on the financial condition of the upper classes, so dramatically denounced by the contemporary Prophets. See further on 18^{14} for comparison of this tribute with that of Hezekiah to Sennacherib. *Magnates of wealth* translates the Heb. phrase generally rendered with 'mighty men of valour,' but the ancient military expression had changed its meaning to one of economic significance; *cf.* I. 11^{28}, II. 24^{14}, and see Lurje, *Studien*, 17 ff. The adverb *there* indicates a scribe writing outside of the land, with which *cf.* his use of 'Pul'; see Robinson, *HI* I, 373, n. 5.

VV.$^{23\text{-}26}$. The reign of Pekahiah ben Menahem of Israel. The only particular event given for the reign is v.^{25}: *And his captain Pekah ben Remaliah conspired against him, and he attacked him in Samaria, in the castle of the royal house,* [🜚+ four words] *and with him fifty Gileadites; and he slew him, and reigned in his stead.* The excepted words appear in EVV as *with/by Argob and with/by Arieh*; see Note for their character as a corrupt gloss to v.^{29}.

VV.$^{27\text{-}31}$. The reign of Pekah ben Remaliah of Israel. **27.** The *twenty years* (entered gloss-wise, without the necessary preface, "and he reigned"—*cf.* EVV) assigned to the reign is an absurdity for a term reduced by most chronologers to two years, by some to five. There appears to have been a learned conspiracy to follow out the laudable scheme of synchronistic history, but impossible with the anarchic conditions of the North. The '20' recurs again in v.^{30b}, although out of place, and vv.$^{32,\ 33}$ give the figures, the sum of which is presented by 'the 17th year of Pekah' for Ahaz's succession (16^{1}). There is reserved for the history of Ahaz the item of the attack of Pekah and Rason of Aram upon Judah (v.^{37}, 16$^{5,\ 6}$). **29.** *In the days of Pekah king of Israel came Tiglath-pileser king of Assyria, and seized Ijon* ['Îyôn] *and Abel-beth-maachah and Janoah* [Yānôaḥ] *and Kedesh and Hasor and*

Gilead and Galilee, all the land of Naphtali, and exiled them to Assyria. Of these places 'Îyôn, Abel-beth-Maachah and 'all the land of Naphtali' are listed along with Chinnereth in I. 15^{20} (*q.v.*) among the districts seized by Ben-Hadad from Baasha ; they had since reverted to Israel. Abel-b.-M. is recorded in the contemporary Ass. list of conquests cited below. For Yānôaḥ, probably modern Yanūḫ, 10 km. N of Tyre, and Ḳedesh, modern Ḳades, 36 km. E of Tyre, see Albright, *AASOR* 6 (1926), 18 ff. ; Abel, *GP* 2, 354, 416 ; Dussaud, *TH* 23 ; *per contra*, Buhl, *GAP*, Index, *s.vv.* For Hasor see on I. 9^{15}. That these far northern cities were still Israelite is of historical interest. *Gilead*, intercepting those northern districts, might possibly be identified with an uncertain place-name (Gala'za) cited below from the Ass. annals, otherwise the word and then the following Galilee are to be elided (so Stade, Eissfeldt) ; *BH* implies omission of *all the land of Naphtali*. Šanda retains the disputed words, understanding the summary to refer to the three campaigns of Tiglath-pileser ; but the order remains geographically irregular. Tiglath-pileser parallels the above precise record in his (fragmentary) Annals : after describing a campaign in Syria (Hadrach, Gebal, Simirra of Gen. 10^{18}, etc., are named) he continues : " the cities of . . . Gala'za (?), Abilakka (Abel-b.-M.), which are on the border of Bit-Ḫumria (Omri-land) . . . the wide land of Naphtali (?—of the word only the final syllable survives ; see Rogers's note) in its entirety I brought within the border of Assyria " (*ARA* 1, §815 ; *cf. KB* 2, 30 ff. ; *CP* 320 f. ; *AB* 464 f.). The final sentence of the v. is the first mention of a Golah, an exile, in the sad chapters of Israelite history. A prophetic parallel is the reference in Is. 8^{23} to the affliction of the land of Zebulun and the land of Naphtali. **30.** *And Hoshea ben Elah made a conspiracy against Pekah ben Remaliah, and attacked him, and slew him, and reigned in his stead in the twentieth year of Jotham ben Uzziah*. The date (*cf.* the ' twenty years ' in v.^{27}) is absolutely inconsistent with v.^{33}, according to which Jotham reigned but 16 years (unless years of his regency, v.^{5}, were included), and with 17^1, according to which Hoshea succeeded in Ahaz's twelfth year. Lucian expunged the contradictory item, but that gives no basis for textual criticism. See on the passage as ' Not a Gloss,' W. E. Barnes, *JTS* 8 (1907), 294 ff. These curt items are fortunately eked out by v.^{37} and 16$^{5f.}$, and still more fully by the Assyrian annals, revealing the political setting, how Pekah in combination with Aram felt strong enough to defy Assyria, but came to his own undoing by a pro-Assyrian faction among his own people. The Assyrian record continues the citation given above with a chronologically later item, reporting first the insurrection of Hanno of Gaza and the conquest of that city, thus revealing a widespread revolt against Assyrian domination, and then proceeding : " The land of Bit-Ḫumria . . . all its people, together with their goods, I carried off to Assyria, Paḳaḫa their king they deposed, and I placed Ausi' (Hoshea) over them as king. Ten talents of gold, x talents of silver, as their tribute I received from them, and to Assyria I carried them." The Assyrian boastfulness appears in the allegation of an entire deportation, while the domestic origin of the *coup d'état* is ignored. But thus the last king of Israel received formally the throne from the Assyrian conqueror, even as the last of the Judæan dynasty was installed by the Babylonian (24^{17}).

VV.$^{32-38}$. The reign of Jotham of Judah. ‖ 2 Ch. 27 ; *cf. Ant.*, ix, 11, 2. Glueck has discovered at Tell el-Kheleifeh a seal belonging to this period inscribed *LYTM* ; it may be read, ' Jotham's,' possibly to be ascribed to this king ; see *BASOR* 79 (1940), 13 ff., with plates, and extensive note by Albright on interpretation of the name. The brief history contains two archival items. **35**b. *He* [with emphatic pronoun] *built the Upper Gate of the house of YHWH.* This gate appears in Jer. 20^2, ' the Gate of Benjamin, the Upper,' probably by double nomenclature, and in Eze. 9^2, ' the Upper Gate that faces the north,' precised more exactly in 8^3 as ' the Gate of the inner court that faces the north ' ; see Smith, *Jerusalem*, 2, 125, 257. **37.** *In those days YHWH began to send into Judah Rason* [Heb. *Resin*—see Note] *king of Aram and Pekah ben Remaliah.* The v. is out of place between the customary final vv. on the reign. It indicates that the Northern attack on Judah began before the campaign recorded for the next reign (16$^{5, 6}$). Ch. has a good tradition of Jotham's extensive building operations, and of his success over Ammon, laying them under tribute ; this may have been a cause of the Aramæan-Israelite offensive, which however had as its greater object the forcing of Judah into the anti-Assyrian coalition. Note that the hostile attack is ascribed to YHWH's will, but without any moral motivation, as is the case with the Prophets.

1. עזריה : also עזריהו below ; for replacement with (ו)עזיה, below, and for constantly varying rdgs. of MSS, edd., and VSS, see deR. For עזריהו in Pal. seals see *IAE* 122, 184, 189, for עזיהו *ib.*, 196, 221, 223.—**2.** יכליהו : the verbal element is pf., with Noth, *IP* 190, *vs.* Kt. of Ch., יכיליה, preferred by Šanda.—**5.** בית החפשית : 10 MSS, Ch., החפשות ב' ; OGrr. transliterate the last word with ωθ for the final syllable ; Aq., εν οικω ελευθεριας ; Sym., κ. ωκει κεκλεισμενος, adopted by 𝔖^H after the transliterated phrase, and so 𝔄 ; ' the Others,' acc. to MS z, κρυφαιως=𝔖 ; 𝔗 ' outside of Jerusalem,' and so Jos., ' out of the city ' ; 𝔙 ' in domo libera seorsum ' ; Rashi as though=' free among the dead,' citing Job 3¹⁹ ; Kimchi interprets as of freedom from office. Klost.'s suggestion to read בביתה חפ', ' in his house in freedom ' (adverbial), *i.e.*, from duties, is favourably regarded by some critics (*cf.* Burn., Sk., Šanda, Moff.), but, as St. remarks, " nothing is gained by this revision." The adj. חפשי=' free,' as of an especially exempt citizen (1 Sam. 17²⁵), and so the word *ḥubšu* in the Amarna tablets. For discussion of the civic term see Pedersen, *Israel*, I–II, 498 f., Pedersen and Albright, *JPOS* 1926, 103 ff., 106 ff., and the latter in *SAC* 217, and note ; also I. Mendelsohn's study of the term in the several languages in *BASOR* 83 (1941), 36 ff., but without reference to the present passage. R. Gordis, in *JQR* 27 (1936), 43 f., regards this as a case of ' contrasted meanings,' the word here expressing ' confinement ' ; but such explanation is not necessary. Otherwise חפשי is used by extension of other-worldly conditions : in Ps. 88⁶, ' free among the dead,' and Job 3¹⁷ᵑ·, in description of Hades, " small and great are there, and slave is free from his master " ; *i.e.*, Sheol is place of utter inactivity, where law is unnecessary, since there " the wicked cease from troubling, and the weary are at rest." A problem is raised by the double occurrence of the identical phrase in Ugaritic, *wrd bthptt 'rṣ*, in the poem of Alein Baal, *Syria*, 1932, 113 ff., viii, 7 f., and that of the Death of Baal, *ib.*, 1934, 305 ff., v, 14 f. The mng. of this in the context is obscure ; it is to be translated, " go down (impv.) into the house of *ḥ.* earthwards." Albr., with varying etymology, would render the phrase with ' subterranean house,' or the like, as suitable to the context (*JPOS* 1934, 131, n. 162). But the above cited reff. permit the Ugaritic term to be explained from the Heb. ; *cf.* the Jewish and Christian expressions of ' peace,' ' rest,' ' release,' for the departed.—הארץ [עם] : Grr. have exc. v, although 𝔖^H asterisks.—**8.** ' 38th year ' : N *al.*, ' 28th,' *vs.* A 𝔖^H 𝔄.—וכריהו :

II. 15¹⁻³⁸   455

A N+most MSS Αζαριας (not 𝔄).—9. מחטאות : again the variant
מחטאות in MSS ; Hex. MSS, N+, 𝔊ᴴ as though 'ה מכל : cf. v.¹³.—
10. ויכהו, וימיתהו : 𝔊 Hex. as pl.—עם: קבל : some MSS as one
word ; 𝔊 (B) Κεβλααμ ; 𝔊ᴸ εν Ιεβλααμ, contained as doublet in
Hex. ; Hex., 'before the people '=the other VSS. 𝔊 supports
the early error in 𝔐, to be corrected after 𝔊ᴸ to בְּיִבְלְעָם ; this
suggestion originally made by Graetz, Gesch., 2, 1, 99.— 12.
הוא : 𝔊 om.—13. שלום : on the name as 'replacement' see GB,
Noth, IP 174.—בן יביש : prob. clan-name ; cf. the city-name,
Jud. 21⁸ᶠᶠ·, and see Noth, ib., 244.—14. מנחם =' comforter,' as
replacement of an earlier dead child (Noth, ib., 222, listing Gr.
parallels) ; for native and Akk. occurrences of the name see GB,
and IAE 123 ; there is to be added the name Μανεεμος, found
at Dura-Europos (Albr., JAOS 57 [1937], 319).—גדי : the name
also Phœn. (Harris, Gram., 93) ; Šanda sugg. abbreviation, as from
' God is my luck.'—תרצה[מ] : Gr. texts in corrupt form, exc. 𝔊ᴸ·—
בשמרון : 𝔊ᴸ om.—וימלך תחתיו : 𝔊 om.—16. תפסח : 𝔊 by early
confusion with foll. n. loci, Θερσα, Θερσιλα, etc. ; 𝔊ᴸ Ταφως, etc. ;
Jos., Θαψαν=𝔙 ; 𝔖ᴴ 𝔖 𝔄=𝔐 ; read תפיח, with Then., al.—פתח :
Grr., " they opened (𝔊ᴸ sing.) to him "=other VSS (and so EVV),
exc. 𝔗 with sing. verb ; the pl. is expected, but the sing. may be
impersonal.—[ההרותיה] את כל [ויד] : read וכל יכה with all VSS,
exc. 𝔙 paraphrasing with foll. sentence, and most Grr. omitting
'all.'—ההרותיה : the first 'ה is an early duplication, cf a case in
7¹³ ; or, as Šanda sugg., a misplaced correction to read אתה above.
—18. מעל חטאות : in place of the unusual prep. 3 MSS מחטאו(ת),
8 MSS מכל חטאות, the latter=Grr. (exc. 𝔊ᴸ) ; 𝔙 𝔈 have sing.
noun ; read מכל חטאת ; cf. 13¹¹, 14²⁴.—18. 19. ישראל כל ימיו : read
בימיו : ישראל with Grr. 𝔖ᴴ, and so Böttcher, Then., al.—19. פול :
Gr. x v have correctly Φουλ.—ידיו : Grr., 𝔖ᴴ=ידו, to be accepted ;
cf. foll. בידו.—בידו המטלכה להחזיק : 𝔊 om. ; St. elides as superfluous ;
rather, 𝔊 so thought, or omission was due to parablepsis.—
20. ויצא : Klost., al., with Burn.'s judgment as ' probably correct,'
read ויצו, 'and ordered,' with omission of foll. הכסף את ; but
Haupt rightly cft. LHeb. use of the verb=' to collect,' the similar
use of נפק in Jewish Aram. and of Arabic ḫaraja, e.g., ḫarāj, ' tax,'
cf. Engl. 'excise.'—בכסף : 𝔊 om. (𝔖ᴴ ※), regarding it as redundant, and so St.—22. פקחיה : MS 144 פקחיהו : here and below
B al. by early error Φακεσιας. The name as פקחי appears on a
Pal. seal, IAE 202.—23. שנתים : cf. v.²⁷=B al., 𝔖ᴴ 𝔖 𝔄 : other
Grr. have revised : A al., ' 10,' N c₂ al., ' 12.'—25. רמליה : the
name poss. occurs in a Pal. seal, IAE 178 ; cf. Safaitic
names, רמל, רמלת, NPS 1, 200.—מלך בית בארמון : on the first
noun see Note, I. 16¹⁸ ; for original מלך, corrected by Ḳr. to 'המ,
see Note, I. 15¹⁸. For בא' Grr., εναντιον=𝔖ᴴ, misreading את as
קד.—הארית ואת [7 MSS 'הא] ארגב את : 𝔊, with correction of texts
(see Rahlfs, Sept.), μετα του Αργοβ κ.μ.τ. Αρεια ; 𝔊ᴸ (Lagarde) μετα
αυτου Α.κ.μ.α.Α. ; 𝔗 awkwardly understands את as accusatival ;

ν 'iuxta Argob et iuxta Ari,' *i.e.*, geographica terms, and so Rashi, 'near Argob,' and explaining the following with 'by the golden lion that stood in the palace.' St.'s suggestion, generally adopted since, is well to the point, that the passage is gloss to v.²⁹, and to be corrected to את א' ואת חות יאיר, 'Argob and Havvoth-Jair,' for which Transjordanic localities see I. 4¹³.—[מבני] גלעדים: unless the pl. is geographical (*cf.* פרירם), read either 'הג (so MS 30), or גלעד, with St. 𝔊 for the whole phrase, απο τ. τετρακοσιων (=A 𝔖ᴴ, not N 𝔄), which is incomprehensible.—**27.** '20 years': Grr. MSS change to '18,' c₂ to '30.'—**29.** תגלת פלאסר : also פלסר ת׳, 16⁷, *q.v.*; there is now to be added the more exact transcription תכלתפלסר, in Lidzb., *Altaram. Urkunden aus Assur* (1921).— הגלילה: the acc. of direction, coming to be used absolutely; the same form in Eze. 47⁸; *cf.* יהצה, Josh. 21³⁶.—**30.** הושע : the name in Elephantine texts, on Pal. jars (*IAE* 121, 204), and the full form הושעיהו in the Lachish letters.—עויה : יותם, B Ιωαθαμ, Αχας; in v.³² Ιωναθαν, Αζαριον; similar variations in other MSS, *e.g.*, A 𝔖ᴴ ; 𝔄 = 𝔅 throughout. 𝔊ᴸ om. this date datum.—**33.** ירושא : MSS ירושה = Ch.—**34.** עשה 2° : 5 MSS Ken., deR. om. ; but the verb as at 14³, where no correction (in line with v.³ above) is registered.—**35.** סרו : VSS, exc. 𝕮, as though הסיר.—**36.** [עשה] אשר: Mich., Ken., וכל אשר = VSS ; see deR. and Bär, and Note, I. 16²⁷.— **37.** להשליח : the Hif. always used of plagues, *e.g.*, Ex. 8¹⁷, Am. 8¹¹.— ביהודה : B A *al.* om.—רצין: רְצֹן is demanded by Akk. *Raṣunu*, and so Gr. Ραασσων (exc. j Ραασσην), *cf.* 𝔖ᴴ *Rāṣān* = 𝔖 𝔄.—**38.** ויקבר עם אבתיו : 12 MSS Ken., deR. om. by parablepsis, and so A N (not 𝔄) ; 𝔖ᴴ ※ ; MS 96, 𝔊ᴸ om. עם אבתיו.—אביו : 3 MSS, 𝔊ᴸ 𝕴 𝔖 𝔄 om.—an unnecessary addition.

Ch. 16. The reign of Ahaz of Judah. ∥ 2 Ch. 28 ; *cf. Ant.*, ix, 12. For the complication of original elements in this ch. see Wellh., *Comp.*, asserting that it is impossible to distinguish them ; see *SBOT* for such an essay. **1.** The king's name always thus appears abbreviated, and so now on a seal of one of his officers, of 'Ushna, minister of Ahaz,' published by Torrey ; see Note. But an Akk. text (see below) gives the full form of the name, Yauḫazi, *i.e.*, Jehoahaz, also name of the Israelite king, 13¹. The mother's name is exceptionally ignored. **3b.** *And also his son he made to pass through the fire :* this was a holocaust, not a symbolic rite, and so Josephus precises, ἴδιον ὡλοκαύτωσε παῖδα. Such fire-immolation was symptomatic of the general breakdown of the religion of the small states of the day under the pressure of Assyria ; the record is repeated for Manasseh (21⁶), and the cult is later noted as general (23¹⁰, where the sacrifice is made ' to Molek ') ;

II. 16¹⁻²⁰

the sacrifice of the 'first-born' is condemned by the contemporary prophet Micah (6⁷), cf. Jer 7³¹. For the Molech cult see Comm. on I. 11, n. 2. The datum suggests some extraordinary occasion, like the similar immolation practised by the Moabite king (3²⁷) ; Šanda thinks of the emergency recorded immediately below. However, this may be a general indictment without definite background. V.⁴ is distinctly Jeremianic in language (cf. Jer. 2²⁰, 3⁶), a criticism that casts doubt upon v.³.

VV.⁵·⁶. Two archival notes. **5.** *Then came up Rason* [𝕳 *Resin—cf.* 15³⁷] *king of Aram and Pekah ben Remaliah king of Israel to Jerusalem to war, and they besieged Ahaz, and they were not able to war* [so 𝕳]. The v. is practically identical with Is. 7¹ : " And it was in the days of Ahaz ben Jotham ben Uzziah king of Judah, there came up Resin king of Aram and Pekah ben Remaliah king of Israel to Jerusalem for war against it, and he [*sic*] was not able to war against it." Both texts are slightly corrupt, and are examples of ease of corruption in even simple compositions ; see Note for suggested corrections. The historical introduction to the prophecy in Is. 7 depends upon our narrative.¹ That ch. is a full commentary upon the present brief item, picturing the terror caused by the bold invasion, giving as motive of the invaders the purpose of installing a new dynasty in Jerusalem in the person of an Aramæan, Ben-Tab'el, as also the recalcitrancy of Ahaz, who nevertheless was relieved of the immediate peril. The relief came through the sought-for intervention of the Assyrian king, as the foll. vv. narrate. Politically the prophet's advice was far-sighted, for instead of entering into international coalitions Judah's safety lay in having faith

¹ See Gray, *Isaiah*, on 7¹, as against earlier views, *e.g.*, of Dillmann. The latter position has been resumed by E. G. Kraeling, ' The Immanuel Prophecy,' *JBL* 50 (1931), 277 ff., see *per contra*, Budde, ' Das Immanuelzeichen,' *JBL* 52 (1933), 22 ff. Our v., like the following one, is of archival origin ; note its terseness. And the religious disinterestedness of the historian throughout the ch. argues against citation from the prophet. For discussion of Isaiah's part in this crisis see Kraeling, *op. cit.*, W. C. Graham, *AJSL* 50 (1934), 201 ff., and for Hosea's relation to it S. Spiegel, *HTR* 1934, 116 ff. ; for the dating see M. Thilo, *In welchem Jahre geschah die sogenannte syrisch-efraemitische Invasion ?* etc. (1918).

in its God (Is. 7⁹). Assyria was a far more overwhelming foe than the trumpery states of Syria-Palestine. **6.** *At that time 'the king of Edom'* [𝔋 *Resin king of Aram*] *restored Elath to Edom* [𝔋 *Aram*], *and drove out the Jews from Elath* [𝔋 with variant of the later pronunciation, *Eloth*] ; *and Edomites* [EVV, exc. JV, *the Syrians*] *came to Elath, and they dwelt there unto this day*. The similars אדם, ' Edom,' and ארם, 'Aram' have been early confused as elsewhere (*e.g.*, in I. 11), in the text-tradition, and peculiarly so here in Heb. MSS and edd. The correction of *Aram* 1⁰ is generally accepted, and with it the excision of *Resin*, as there was no original control of Elath, so that it might be 'restored to Aram.' Edom took advantage of the turmoil in the north to recover the Red Sea port and cast off the dominance of Judah, as since Amaziah's day (14⁷·²²). The final *unto this day* expresses the actual later status down into Nabatæan times ; see the archæological studies by Glueck. *Jews* : here is the first application of that word to Judæan citizens ; Israel had passed as a political entity.

VV.⁷⁻⁹. Ahaz's appeal to Tiglath-pileser for help, and the latter's final conquest of Damascus. The passage connects with the two preceding archival notes, and serves as introduction to the following more intimate history. **7.** Ahaz's letter is couched in current diplomatic language : *I am thy servant* [literally *slave*] *and thy son*. The diplomatic term 'thy servant' appears constantly in the Amarna letters, *e.g.*, in those of Abd-ḫipa of Jerusalem ; *cf.* the contemporary parallel in Bar-Rkb's inscription, " I am B.-R., servant of Tiglath-pileser." ' Thy son ' is paralleled by the language of Ishtar-duri king of Armenia, who "as a son sends (messengers recognizing) authority to his father," *i.e.*, Ashurbanipal (*KB* 2, 230 ; *ARA* 2, §834). **8.** Ahaz accompanies the letter with *a present*, a word that is also used for *bribe*. **9.** *And the king of Assyria listened to him, and the king of Assyria came up to Damascus, and captured it, and took it in exile* [𝔋+*to Kir*], *and Rason* [𝔋 *Resin*] *he killed*. Of this notable triumph, of date 732 B.C., we have from Assyrian sources only the annual notes in the Eponym List : " Ashur-daninani of the city of Mazamua (eponym, 733 B.C.) : Against the land of Damascus. Nabû-bêl-uṣur of the city of Sime

(732) : against the land of Damascus." For the year 734 a campaign 'against Philistia' is registered. Contemporaneously Tiglath-pileser records the tribute of 'Yauḫazi of Yaudi' (the first mention of Judah in the Akk. inscriptions), along with that of some twenty states, ranging from Kue and Sam'al in North Syria to Moab, Edom, and Philistia (*CP* 322 ; *ARA* 1, §801 ; *ATB* 1, 348 ; *AB* 463 f.). Ahaz's diplomatic part in the history is of interest. This was the end of Aram-Damascus as a power. The Heb. *to Kir* is lacking in 𝔊. The place is otherwise referred to as an eastern land in association with Elam and Shoa in the assault on the holy city in the oracle of the Valley of Vision, Is. 22$^{5, 6}$. In Amos is given the prophecy that "the people of Aram shall go in exile to Kir," from which region YHWH had " brought up Aram " (9^7). It is generally accepted that the word here is a gloss from Amos to point the fulfilment of that prophecy ; see Comm. on Amos and Isaiah, especially Gray on the latter.

VV.$^{10-18}$. Ahaz's attendance upon Tiglath-pileser at his triumph in Damascus, with resultant ritual innovations in the temple, and certain reconstructions, after Assyrian mode. **10***a*. *And king Ahaz went to meet Tiglath-pileser king of Assyria, to Damascus.* The occasion, 732 B.C., has its brilliant sidelight from the contemporary Zenjirli inscription, according to which Panammūwa, the father of the inscriber Bar-Rkb, died 'in the camp of Tiglath-pileser,' where he had "run at the wheel of his lord T.-p.," evidently at Damascus, for it was from this city, as the inscription proceeds, that the body was transported home to Sam'al-Ya'di. Ahaz then may well have met the far-northern king and the crown prince. The same politics united northern Ya'di and southern Judah against their overweening neighbour Damascus, but to the undoing of all the Syro-Palestinian states in the Assyrian conquest. **10***b*. *And he saw the altar that was at Damascus ; and king Ahaz sent to the priest Uriah the fashion of the altar and the pattern of it :* so for the accusative phrase the EVV—as an architect would say, sketch and plans. The real object of the story is the account of this innovation. Uriah is the priest who was ' taken for record ' on Isaiah's tablet (Is. 8^2). Notable is the continued objective, non-moralizing narrative of the exotic innovation ; the grandeur of the new altar made greater popular impression than its contradiction to the native cult. It is generally accepted that the altar was of Assyrian, not Damascene style : as Olmstead says (*HPS* 452) : " As in all newly organised provinces, the cult of Ashur and the king had been established in Damascus, and the vassal rulers were ordered to follow this example." Such is the opinion also of Gressmann (*ZAW* 1924, 324), and of Kittel and Robinson in their Histories ; otherwise Šanda, who thinks of a Syrian altar. V.[11]. The priest carried out the royal orders against the return of the king. VV.[12, 13]. The royal sacrifices detailed present the act of consecration, as at Solomon's dedication of his temple ; for a royal ritual *cf.* that ' of the prince ' in Eze. 46. **14.** *And the bronze altar that was before YHWH he removed from the front of the house, between the altar and the house of YHWH, and put it at the side of the altar to the north, The altar* is ' *the great altar* ' (v.[15]) of stone, standing on the rock ; *cf.* I. 8[22, 54]. The old *bronze altar* is identical with 'the bronze altar before YHWH,' referred to *en passant* at I. 8[64]. See Comm. on those passages, and *cf.* W. R. Smith, *Religion of the Semites*, Note L ; Nowack, *Arch.*, 2, 41 ff. ; Kittel, *Studien*, 50 ff. ; and *GVI* 2, 364. The present note supports I. 8[64], the historicity of which Smith denied because of the bronze construction of the altar, which strangely enough is omitted in the list of Hiram's works, I. 7[13ff.]. For the material of the new altar Šanda thinks of stone ; but the specifications as given for a work of art and the replacement of the old metal altar imply similar construction for the new one. Such an altar of bronze with alleged dimensions is described in 2 Ch. 4[1]. For like pride in a new ' altar of bronze ' (the same words as here) *cf.* Byblian King Yehaumilk's inscription. **15***a*. Details of the king's orders to the priest for the ritual *on the great altar*, *i.e.*, the new altar, are recorded, with the specifications logically arranged : (1) *burn the morning holocaust and the evening oblation* (*i.e.*, the primitive general sacrifices) ; (2) *and the king's holocaust and his oblation* ; (3) *and the holocaust of all the people of the land* (the nationalistic term) *and their oblations and libations* ; (4) *and all blood of holocaust and all blood of sacrifice thou shalt sprinkle upon it.* The *oblation* (*minḥāh*, AV *meat offering*, in Old English language,

RVV JV *meal-offering*) by early usage included animal sacrifice, as at I. 18²⁹ ; indeed part of the actual meal-offering was to be ritually burnt according to the Law, Lev. 6⁷·⁸ ; see at length Nowack, *Arch.*, 2, 221, n. 1. These directions are evidently written orders, which have been so far preserved, and they give a succinct contemporary description of ritual. **15***b*. *And the bronze altar shall be for me to inquire at.* The meaning of the infinitive has long been disputed : JV . . . *to look to* ; German comm. have generally followed GV, " Ich will denken was ich mache," and the like ; but such irresolution is quite out of place. AV followed Calvin, ' ad oracula sciscitanda,' ' for procuring oracles,' *cf.* FV ' afin d'y consulter le Seigneur,' and W. R. Smith has supported this interpretation (*Religion of the Semites*, Note L), followed by Burney, Haupt in *SBOT* ; *cf.* further Mowinckel, *Psalmen-Studien*, 1, 146, who holds that the primary meaning of the verb (*bikkēr*) is the examination of the sacrifice for omens. With this most plausible interpretation we have a case of the intrusion of the vast Babylonian system of omen-sacrifices, which the Law abominated ; *cf.* Eze. 21²⁶, how " the king of Babylon looked in the liver," and see at length Jastrow, *Die Religion Babyloniens und Assyriens*, cc. 19, 20. The old bronze altar was now to be the royal perquisite ; its antiquity possessed potency. **17.** The removal for smelting of the wheeled bases (I. 7²⁷ᶠᶠ·) and of the oxen underneath the bronze sea (*ib.*, vv.²³ᶠᶠ·). There are grammatical confusions in 𝕳, evidence of early corruption of text. With slight rectifications there may be obtained with Stade, followed by Šanda : *And king Ahaz cut up* [𝕳+*the borders*] *the bases, and removed from them* [𝕳+*and*] *the laver* [the pl. is expected], *and the sea he took down from the bronze oxen that were under it, and placed it upon plasterwork of stones.* The verb ' to cut up ' is used similarly at 18¹⁶, 24¹³. The *borders*, or *frame-pieces*, were only an accessory to the laver apparatus ; the whole bronze carriage must have been removed for smelting. The intrusion of the word may have been due to avoid contradiction with 25¹³, according to which the bases were still in existence. The brass was probably used for the tribute to Assyria ; *cf.* the tradition of the fate of all such vessels upon the destruction of the city. **18.** The v. lists some building-operations, concluding with the obscure phrase (separated in 𝕸 by the verse-cæsura), literally, *from the presence of the king of Assyria*, or, as the prepositional phrase may mean, *because of the k. of Ass.* (*cf.* variations in ancient and modern VSS). Šanda's suggestion alone throws light, viz., to attach the phrase with the latter meaning to v.[17], at least as a gloss, explanatory of the removal of the brass as for the tribute to Assyria. The remainder of the v. is like v.[17] with its inner-Hebrew difficulties and variety of interpretations; it deals with reconstruction of buildings unknown to us, but so well known to the contemporary recorder that he could use categorical terms. The v. as revised (see Note further) reads: *And the covered-way* (?—*cf.* EVV) *of the Sabbath that he built* [with Grr.; 𝕳 *they built*, EVV *they had built*] *in the house* (*i.e.*, the temple), *and the King's Entry outwards he turned about in/to* [?] *the house of* YHWH. Such details belong to a simple building-record.

VV.[19, 20]. The final data of the reign. The repeated 'with his fathers,' absent in OGrr., is secondary.

1. ' 17th ': Gr. c₂, ' 18th '=𝕾 𝔄.—אחז : this name found on a Samarian ostracon and on a seal, *IAE* 212. The seal of Ušna, minister of Ahaz, noted above, was published by Torrey in *BASOR* 79 (1940), with additional note by Albr. on אשנא as='give now,' with vocative of deity omitted, and the root as in ' Joash,' ' Josiah ' (see Note, 12[1], also further discussion by these scholars and E. L. Sukenik, *ib.*, nos. 82, 84).—**2.** אלהיו : B A 𝕲[L] θεου πιστως, *al.*, τ. θεου αυτου πιστως ; origin of the last word ?—**3.** מלכי : early error as in B, βασιλεως for βασιλεων, induced the plus in the other Grr. (exc. 𝕲[L]) and 𝕾[H], ' Jeroboam son of Nebat.'—בנו : Ch., בניו =𝕲[L] here.—**5.** *Cf.* Is. 7[1].—ויצרו על אחז : Is., למלחמה עליה ; St. reduces to עליה ; *BH* sugg. עליה.—ויצרו. יכלו : correct, as *vs.* יכל of Is.—להלחם : read with Is.+עליה.—**6.** רצין מלך ארם : read with Klost. and critics since, מלך ארם ; with the error the royal name was interpolated from the preceding v.—לארם : read לאדם, as suggested by early critics, Clericus, Mich., *al.*, and now generally accepted (not by Šanda).—אֲדֹמִים : so *BH* (MS L, many MSS), and so Ḳr. for Kt. ארמים (Bär), ארומים (Mich., Ken, Ginsb.) ; see deR. For ' Edomites ' testify the Grr., 𝕾[H] 𝕿[L] 𝔙, for ' Aramæans ' 𝕿[W] 𝕾 𝔄. ארומים is case of insertion of vowel-letter to enforce the Ḳr.—מ[אילות] : read אֵילַת ; the variation is unique to 𝕳.—**7.** פלסר : a variation in spelling, and as in the Panammūwa inscr., *vs.* פלאסר (so MSS here) above and v.[10].—הַקּוֹמִים : a unique Ḳr. for הקמים, and so 16 MSS Kt.—**8.** הנמצא : 4 MSS Ken., deR.+ באצרות, and so Gr. MSS, 𝕾[H]; also Gr. MSS ignore 'בא below ; Lucianic x=𝕳.—אשור : B *al.* om., 𝕾[H] ⁜.—**9.** על אל ורמשק : is expected (so 𝔖 MS) in this military phrase.—ויגלה קירה : 𝔊 κ. απωκισεν αυτην ; 𝔊ᴸ κ. απωκ. τ. πολιν, i.e., 'ק as 'city'; Hex. introduced the name as a plus to 𝔊, 𝔖ᴴ stating it as a plus from Aq., Κυρηνηνδε ; *Onom. Gr.*, Κυρινη, Onom. Lat., 'Cyrene'=𝔙 'Cyrenen'; 𝔗 לקרינא—*i.e.*, as *n. loci*. St.'s deletion of the word has been generally accepted; see Comm.—**10.** לקראת ת' פ' : B† εις απαντην αυτου τω Θ., from which St. argues for original לקראתו ; but such repetition is common in this diction.—דומשק= 𝔗 ; the unique spelling is prob. corruption of Aramaizing דרמשק in Ch.=𝔖 here. MSS have correctly דמשק, or give the proper Ḳr. to 𝔚 ; see Ginsb. *ad loc.* It has been well suggested that the word, which is not properly articulated, is a gloss to 'ד below. For the variations in spelling (*e.g.*, Amarna *Dumaška*) see Lexx., Dussaud, *TH* 202, and the extensive discussion by Rosenthal, *Die aram. Forschung*, 16 ff.—אוריה : name of a Hittite, 2 Sam. 11³ᵃ·, for Hittite origin of which see Montg., *JAOS* 55 (1935), 94.— דמות : 𝔊 𝔊ᴴ το ομοιωμα, to which 𝔊ᴸ pref. το μετρον αυτου, on basis of which doublet Klost., St., Šanda (*cf. BH*) would read מדות, 'measurements,' but the foll. word תבנית is prob. the technical word for this, as in Ex. 25⁹, where the term includes the dimensions of tabernacle and furniture.—**11.** מדמשק : by parablepsis 𝔊 lacks what follows through 'מר, v.¹² (𝔖ᴴ ※·); similarly in v.¹² 𝔊 (𝔖 ※·) has like omission with the repeated המובה ; 𝔊ᴸ 𝔚 ; see Rahlfs, *SS* 3, 245.—**13.** ויסך את נסכו : 𝔊 ignored the verb. —**14.** המובח הנחשת : an attempt of Ḳr. to obtain the construct construction; read the first noun as absolute; for such apposition of thing and material see GK §131, d, and for Arabic, Wright, *Arab. Gr.*, 2, §94 ; *cf.* the parallel constructions in the Yehaumilk inscr., המובח נחשת, etc. ; the same construction as here below in v.¹⁷ ; St.'s objection on the score of grammar is not valid, while precision of the altar is required as against his elision of the second word.—מאת פני הבית : B A v have by error το προσωπον, other MSS απο/προ προσωπου.—"י בית ומבין : מבין המובח ומבין : the statement gives precision of location ; there is no reason for elision after St.'s suggestion.—המובח צפונה : 𝔊ᴸ "the altar which he made to the north."—**15.** ויצהו : Ḳr.=VSS, and is the expected rdg. ; Klost., *BH*, *al.* retain Kt., and elide the foll. nominal object; but for such repetition of names and titles *cf.* v.¹⁶.— כל עם[הארץ] 1 MS om. ; of Grr. only A y have, 𝔖ᴴ ※· ; but the political term is to be kept, *vs.* Klost., St., *al.* ; see Comm., on 11¹⁷· ¹⁸·— לַבֹּקֶר : Grr., εις το πρωι=לַבֹּקֶר=𝔖ᴴ ; 𝔖 𝔄 'for praying' ; 𝔙 'ad voluntatem meam'; 𝔗 alone correctly with the same verb ; *cf.* renderings of Kamph., Klost., Kit. ; Ehrl., 'den Unterschied zu zeigen,' for popular comparison of the two altars (!).—**16.** צוה : most Grr., 𝔖ᴴ as צוהו, which St., *BH* prefer.—המלך : 𝔊 om., 𝔖ᴴ ※·.—**17.** אחז : B 𝔈 𝔏 om.—המסגרות : המסגרות המכנות : the impossible apposition proves the secondary character of the first word.— מעליהם : מעליהן is desiderated.—[הכיר] ואת : MSS את, and so properly Ḳr., and VSS, exc. 𝔙, which however makes the prec. verb govern the two preceding nouns.—תחתיה : the gender assimilated to הגחשת.—**18.** מיסך השבת : for the first word 9 MSS מסך ; Ḳr. ִמוּסָך ; Grr., το θεμελιον της καθεδρας, i.e., rdg. as מוּסַד הַשֶּׁבֶת, and so 𝔊ᴸ, with the plus τ. σαββατων ; 𝔗 שבתא [τεῖχος =]טיקום ; 𝔖 ' house of the Sabbath ' ; 𝔏 ' mesech sabbatorum ' ; 𝔙 ' musach sabbati.' Rashi interprets as of ' a roof made for shade to sit under on the Sabbath-day,' Kimchi as of ' a structure for the Sabbath-guard to take shelter under ' ; see Grotius further. Ch.'s rdg., י"ויסגר דלתות בית represents a free interpretation of the first noun as though from סכך.—בנו (אשר) : =𝔗 ; Grr., ' he built ' =𝔖ᴴ (with note of the same rdg. in Theod., Sym.), and 𝔙 ; 𝔖 ' which was built ' ; the pl. might be collective and pluperfect.—בבית : VSS +' of the Lord,' explicatively.—החיצונה : acc. of direction, ' that outwards ' ; some critics, e.g., BH would correct to the simple adj.—הַחָב : =Grrr., 𝔗 ; 𝔖 ' joined ' ; 𝔙 ' convertit.'—בית י" : 𝔊 (B =𝔖ᴴ) οικω Κυριου ; al. Grr. with prep. ' in,' and similarly 𝔗 ' into,' 𝔖 ' with '.—**19.** אשר : 18 MSS pref. וכל =𝔊ᴸ 𝔗ᴸ 𝔖 𝔄.— **20.** עם אבתיו 20 ; 1 MS and Grr., exc. A 123, om. the unnecessary repetition. Note Ch.'s blunt denial : " and they brought him not into the sepulchre of the kings of Israel," which is repeated here by Gr. g (Ιουδα for ' Israel ').

Ch. 17. The reign of Hoshea of Israel, the fall of the Northern Kingdom, with exile of the people and importation of foreign colonists with the institution of their cults. *Cf. Ant.*, ix, 14 ; a brief cross-reference to the deportation in 1 Ch. 5²⁶.[1]

VV.¹·². Extent of the reign and the moral judgment upon it. **2.** *And he did the evil in the eyes of* YHWH, *only not like the kings of Israel before him. Per contra*, there is the perversion of Lucian, ' beyond all kings of Israel who were before him ' (=𝔏), repeating the judgment on Ahab (I. 16³³). Indeed his and Israel's fate might well have produced judgment like that on Jeroboam I's house (I. 14¹⁰ff.). Some contemporary evidence may be contained in the brief remark ;

[1] For this period are to be consulted the Histories of Stade, 1, 575 ff. ; Rogers, 2, 301 ff. ; Hall, 461 ff. ; Olmstead, *HA* ch. 17, and his *Western Asia in the Days of Sargon* (1908) ; S. Smith, *CAH* 3, ch. 2, pt. 2 ; Sellin, 1, 232 ff. ; Kittel, 2, 364 ff. ; Robinson, ch. 18 ; Meyer, 3, 26 ff. ; also literature cited in int. to ch. 15 ; for the Egyptian history Petrie, 3, 280 ff. ; Alt, *Israel u. Aegypten*, 56 ff. ; Breasted, ch. 26. For the Ass. texts of Sargon's reign bearing upon the Biblical history see *KB* 2, 34 ff., *ATLAO* 522 f., *CP* 323 ff., *AB* 466 ff., *AKAT* 174 ff., *ARA* 2, 1 ff., *ATB* 1, 348 ff. ; particular citations are given in place below. For the bearings of the history on the Samaritan sect see the writer's volume, ch. 4.

as Stade says (*Akad. Reden*, p. 208) : " The pre-Exilic editor of Kings must accordingly have read in the sources at hand notices of Hosea that presented him in a more favourable light than his predecessors." Or is it a sympathetic expression for this last and valiant king ? A Jewish tradition appears in Rashi and Kimchi to the effect that Hoshea removed the guards set on the road to Jerusalem to keep Israelites from going thither to worship.

VV.$^{3-6}$. *Cf.* the almost identical parallel in 18^{9-12}. In as many verses are contained four archival items, mosaic patches in a complicated history. Tiglath-pileser was succeeded by his son Shalmaneser V (727-722 B.C.), but the father's triumph was undone in troubles at home and abroad ; only one of his son's inscriptions survives (*ARA* I, p. 297). **3.** Hoshea, once pro-Assyrian (see on 15^{30}) took part in the rebellious coalition (Heb., *conspiracy*) of the western provinces, and so the new Assyrian monarch *campaigned* [Heb., *went up*] *against him, and Hoshea became his vassal* [Heb., *slave*], *and rendered him tribute.* **4a.** *But withal the king of Assyria found conspiracy in Hoshea ; for he had sent envoys to So king of Egypt, and brought not up tribute to the king of Assyria, as he had done year by year.* These shifting alliances of the day, now with Assyria, now with Egypt, are illustrated in the prophet Hoshea's scornful references (5^{13}, $7^{8, 11, 16}$, 8^9, 11^5, 12^2, 14^4). Egypt herself was in confused enough condition with contest between the native dynasty and the upstart Ethiopian line, which triumphed in 712 B.C. But she took advantage of Shalmaneser's own troubles to reassert herself at least by intrigue in her ancient Asiatic sphere of interest. So, king of Misraim, was an important element in Winckler's notion of an expanded Arabian kingdom of Muṣur/Muṣran in the NW of Arabia (see *KAT* 146), and with him Šanda and Robinson are inclined to agree.[2] But the Heb. consonants of the name, read by Ḳr. as ' So ' are to be vocalized as Sewe, and the name to be identified with ' Sib'e the tartan ' (the title in 18^{17}) of Egypt, allied with Hanno, king of Gaza, in the great revolt against Assyria ; his name now appears in Sargon's Annals

---

[2] For Old-Arabic reff. see Montg., *Arabia and the Bible*, 133 ff., and for occurrence of *Mṣrn*, Conti Rossini, *Chrest.*, 180, Ryckmans, *NPS* I, 348.

for his second year (*CP* 327; *ARA* 2, §5), with parallel reference in the Display Inscription (*KB* 2, 55; *CP* 331; *ARA* 2, §55). His rank as an Egyptian commander only, not king (as he appears in one of the texts), is proved by his exact title as tartan and the association of his name with ' the tribute of Pir'u (Pharaoh) king of Egypt '; and such is the judgment of Alt, *Israel u. Aegypten*, 56 ff., Kittel, Meyer. **4b.** *And the king of Assyria put him under arrest, and shut him up in prison.* The first verb is used of Jeremiah's formal arrest (Jer. 33^1, 36^5). But the capital city maintained itself by reason of civil war in Assyria. **5.** *And the king of Assyria campaigned in all the land, and he went up to Samaria, and besieged it for three years.* **6a.** *In the ninth year of Hoshea* (still *de jure* king) *the king of Assyria took Samaria.* For the three years as approved by the Assyrian records see Meyer, *GA* 3, 29. Assyriology has determined how the prolonged siege was terminated. The city was taken by Shalmaneser's successor, Sargon II, who is generally regarded as an usurper.[3] Sargon records in the Annals of his first year (722/721) as follows: " Samaria (Samerinai) I besieged and took ... (three lines lost). 27,290 inhabitants I carried away, 50 chariots I collected there as a royal force ... (The city) I set up again and made more populous than before. People from lands which I had taken I settled there. My men I set over them as governors. Tribute and taxes as upon the Assyrians I set upon them." [4] It is noticeable that the Biblical record ignores the name of Sargon, who appears only once elsewhere (Is. 20^1). The credit is given by our recorder anonymously to ' the king of Assyria,' whether through ignorance or carelessness is not clear; according to the duplicate in 18^{10}, " they took it." The ' 27,290 inhabitants ' (*n.b.* the exact Assyrian census) is a modest figure, when compared with the 60,000 landed gentry of 15$^{19, 20}$, for which see Comm. The deportation is expanded

[3] So Olmstead, *HA* 206 f.; Meyer, p. 30. An inscription published by E. Unger (*FuF* 9 [1933], 245 f.; *cf. AfO* 9 [1934], 79) claims that he was a son of Tiglath-pileser.

[4] So following Rogers on the whole, *CP* 326; *cf. ATB* 1, 348, *ARA* 2, §4, *AB* 466. A parallel appears in the Display Inscription, *KB* 2, 55, *CP* 331, *ARA* 2, §55. The Harvard expedition at Samaria has revealed Sargon's reconstructions, but of rough work; see Reisner, *Excavations at Samaria*, 123 ff., Olmstead, *HPS* 460 f.

in v.[18] to that of the removal of Israel at large, so that " only the tribe of Judah was left." As a political expression, denoting destruction of the kingdom and exile of its representative citizens, this statement might stand. The absolute Biblical statement would ignore the heretical Samaritans. There arose later the orthodox Jewish notion that all Judah was taken in exile by Babylon. For an attempt to precise the population of Israel and Judah at that period see Albright, *JPOS* 1925, 20 ff., and *cf.* H. G. May, in *BA* 1943, 57 ff., arguing that the Israelites deported could not have been, at the extreme, more than one-twentieth of the population. For the enforced colonization of the territory Sargon records for his seventh year his conquest of the lawless tribes of " Tamud, Ibadid, Marsimanu and Ḥaiapa, distant Arabs, who inhabit the desert," and his deporting the remainder of them and settling them in Samaria (*ARA* 2, §17 ; *ATB* 1, 349 f.). For another importation of colonists see below, vv.[24ff.]. **6***b*. *And he carried Israel to Assyria, and settled them in Halah and in Habor,* [on] *the river of Gozan, and the cities of Media.* Sargon's item of the number of exiles is complemented here with their destinations. Of the localities named Ḥabōr is the district of the Ḥabūr, the great tributary of the Euphrates in the ancient Aram-naharaim. Gozan is Akk. Guzana (Ptolemy's Gausanitis), now identified by von Oppenheim with the region of Tell Halaf ; see his *Tell Halaf,* pp. 41, etc., and so earlier Forrer, *Die Provinzeinteilung,* 23 f., with Akk. references. Ḥalaḥ is Akk. Ḥalaḫḫu, possibly Ptolemy's Chalchitis near Gausanitis. For these regions see *CIOT* 1, 267 f. ; Winckler, *Alttest. Untersuchungen,* 108 ; and *KAT* 268, also Šanda at length. For the presence of Israelite colonists about Harran *ca.* 650 B.C., see S. Schiffer, *OLz.,* Beih. I (1907), ' Keilschriftliche Spuren . . . der deportierten Samarier.' For *the cities, i.e.,* city-states, of Media Grr. read ' the mountains ' (*hârê* for '*ârê*). The region is that of the mountain chains to the east of the Tigris valley. The conquest of Media was one of Sargon's triumphs ; see his Annals for year 8. According to the book of Tobit its hero was one of this deportation ; he lived in Nineveh, but had compatriots in Media (1[1f. 10. 14]). 1 Ch. 5[26] assigns the exile of Transjordanic Israel to Pul and Tiglath-pileser (!), and then repeats, erroneously, our list. For a contemporary picture of such a deportation by the Assyrians see the Kirkuk document published by E. Chiera and E. A. Speiser in *JAOS* 47 (1927), 56 ff. (no. 20).

VV.$^{7-23}$. A homily upon the fall of Israel. **7.** *And it came to pass, because the Bnê-Israel sinned,* etc. The apodosis occurs in v.^{18}, that Y*HWH was very angry*, as recognized only by JV among EVV; the long period belongs to the Deuteronomistic rhetoric, *cf.* Jer. 16$^{10-13}$, etc. **8.** *And they walked in the statutes of the nations that* Y*HWH dispossessed from the Bnê-Israel, and the kings of Israel whom they made:* so for the last clause the ungrammatical Hebrew; trr. introduce the demanded prep. and read *of the kings of Israel*; the passage is secondary, introduced to cast the blame on the schismatic royalty of the North. See also long note in *SBOT*. The final verb has also given trouble; *cf.* EVV, *which they made/practised*, with antecedent in 'the statutes'; but the verb 'to make' in sense of appointment to office occurs at I. 12^{31}, etc.; those kings were man-made, not of God. **9.** *And the children of Israel did secretly things that were not right against the* L*ORD*: so EVV; JV *... did impute things that were not right unto the* L*ORD*. But read for the verbal phrase, *uttered things . . . against* Y*HWH*; *cf.* Is. 3^8, and see Note on the unique Heb. verb. According to the v. every place was provided with its heathenish chapel, *high-places . . . from watchmen's tower to fortified city*, for which military phrase *cf.* 18^8. **10.** *And they set up for themselves pillars and Asherah-poles upon every high hill and under every leafy tree:* the same language above, I. 14^{23}, and in Jer. 2^{20}, 3^6, Dt. 12$^{2, 3}$. **13.** Y*HWH testified against* [so AV; RVV *testified unto*; JV *forewarned*] *Israel and Judah by ⌜every prophet and⌝* [with correction of 𝕳 with 3 Heb MSS and 𝕮] *every seer*. So for the verb, EVV following VSS; the same verb is so consistently translated, along with its cognate noun, *testimonies*, v.^{15}, by EVV, including JV in the latter case. Kittel uses the verb and noun, 'to warn,' 'warning.' But Haupt on the basis of an Akk. etymology for the noun, common in the Law, as in 'the ark of the testimony,' translates the verb with 'enjoined (upon),' and the noun with 'injunction'; see Note further. The language is doubtless legal, denoting authoritative deposition at law. *Cf.* the legal form in which Isaiah drew up his oracle on 'a tablet' with 'witnesses' (Is. 8$^{1\text{f.}}$). The addition of 'seer' to 'prophet' appears old-fashioned, but is not an intrusion, as with Stade, *al.* ; *cf.* the contemporary reference to prophets and seers, Is. 30^{10}. The words *and Judah* are probably a gloss suggested by v.^{19} (so Burney, Šanda). *According to all the law which I commanded your fathers, and which I sent to you by my servants the prophets :* as Šanda properly observes, *law* (*tôrāh*) is used here in pre-nomistic sense ; it is mediated by prophets, and without reference to Moses ; *cf.* Hos. 8^{12}. **14.** *They hardened their neck like their father's neck :* cf. Dt. 10^{16}, Jer. 7^{26}, etc., and the phrase 'stiff-necked people,' Ex. 32^{9}, etc. (J and E). **15.** *They went after vanity, and became vain :* so EVV ; JV . . . *after things of nought, and became nought.* The picturesque notion of the noun and its derivative verb is lost in these trr. ; it is a puff of air that they followed, and so they became light as air. The phrase occurs in Jer. 2^{5}, Stade, Šanda regard it as a loan, and probably with right. The plural of the noun occurs in I. 16$^{13, 26}$, and is directly identified with strange gods in the Song of Moses, Dt. 32^{21}. This and the following v. resume the indictment of vv.$^{8\text{ff.}}$, with extension to the grosser breaches, idolatry, polytheism, exotic cults. **16.** *And they made for themselves molten-work, two calves, and they made an Asherah.* The first noun is collective, appearing above, I. 14^{9} ; 'two calves' is apparently an intrusion from the Jeroboam story, I. 12, and the same sentence may be passed upon the final sentence, which parallels the 'Asherah-poles' of v.^{10}, and may have been suggested by 21^{3} (so Stade, Šanda, not Kittel, Benzinger) ; the temptation to addition in the indictment is illustrated by the plus in 𝔊$^\text{L}$ 𝔏 in v.^{17}, "and they made ephod and teraphim." *And they worshipped all the host of heaven, and they served the Baal.* There was similar intrusion of such astral worship from Assyria in Manasseh's reign ; see 21^{5}, and Comm. on 23$^{4\text{ff.}}$. **17.** *And they caused their sons and daughters to pass through the fire :* for such holocausts, practised in Judah, see 16^{3}. *And they practised divination and enchantment :* the first noun in the tr. refers primarily to divination by arrows, as, *e.g.*, practised by the king of Babylon according to Eze. 21$^{26\text{ff.}}$ (EVV 21$^{21\text{ff.}}$), the second to charm practice (see Note).

The same pair of magical operations is derided in an ancient Balaam ode, Num. 23^{23}. For them see Dhorme, *L'Évolution religieuse d'Israël*, 1, 227 ff. As is the case with such language the terms became general in significance, the first of the above being used of necromancy in 1 Sam. 28^8. For the official adoption of all such strange cults see the history of Manasseh's reign, 21$^{3\text{ff.}}$. **18.** As observed above, on v.^{7}, this v. gives the apodosis of the long indictment; what follows is literarily distinct, in part paralleling the preceding homily. **19.** Judah is condemned, a supererogatory judgment. **20.** The v. reverts to the earlier exposition with *all the seed of Israel*; this can hardly include Judah, as with most comm. The phrase, *he delivered them into the hand of spoilers*, repeats Jud. 2^{14}. VV.$^{21\text{-}23}$. A political exposition. **21**a. Y$_{\text{HWH}}$ himself *rent Israel from the house of David* (*cf.* I. 11$^{11\text{f.}}$, 14^8—the schism was by divine action, but the experiment failed!), *and they made Jeroboam ben Nebat king*—they had their own way. **21**b. *And Jeroboam seduced Israel away from* Y$_{\text{HWH}}$, *and he entailed them in great sin.* **22.** *And the Bnê-Israel went in the way of all the sin* [𝔥 *sins*] *of Jeroboam which he did, not moving away from it,* **23.** *until* (at last) Y$_{\text{HWH}}$ *removed Israel from his presence, as he had spoken through all his servants the prophets: and Israel went in exile away from its land to Assyria, to this day.* The exile was a just theodicy.

Criticism of this long passage, apart from minor elements, has been presented at length by Stade (*ZAW* 6=*Akad. Reden*, 208 ff.). He regards vv.$^{21\text{-}23}$, with the section's political interest and its denunciation of Jeroboam's fateful sin, as primary, belonging to the Deuteronomic editor, and vv.$^{7\text{-}18}$ as a later addition; with him practically agree Benzinger, Šanda, Eissfeldt. Burney, giving his usual careful literary cross-references, while recognizing these two distinct elements, rightly argues that the secondary material may not be placed late, or indeed later. The literary flavour is that of Jeremiah and Deuteronomy. The point of view is pre-nomistic (*e.g.*, v.^{13}) and evidently pre-Exilic. The long homily is diffuse, as is the custom of most preaching, and too strict criticism of logic and order may not be made.

VV.$^{24\text{-}41}$. The importation of foreign colonists into Samaria, with return, by imperial order, of exiled priests to instruct the strangers in the cult of the native God, vv.$^{24-28}$; the resultant amalgam of religions, combining the worship of YHWH and the imported gods, vv.$^{29-34a}$; a condemnation of the Israelites for their defection, vv.$^{34b-40}$; the mixed religion of the colonists, v.^{41}. In this section the *Samaritans* appear by name for the only time in the O.T. (v.^{29}). For this sect, in addition to the well-known Histories and Dictionary articles, see the volumes by Montgomery, J. E. H. Thompson, and Ben Tzvi. Stade's criticism of this section has become standard (*ZAW* 6=*Akad. Reden*, 211 ff., following Wellhausen's lead in Bleek, *Einl.*^{4}, 262). The section vv.$^{21-34a}$, with account of the imported settlers and cults, has its sequel in v.^{41}. On the other hand vv.$^{34b-40}$ constitute a vigorous homiletic judgment upon the Israelites for their defection from YHWH; the homily is in style of vv.$^{7ff.}$. The resultant composite of the two distinct documents presents the Samaritan religion as a heathen eclecticism, and this presentation has swayed subsequent opinion to regard that sect as utterly perverse, so that 'the Good Samaritan' appears as a surprise. But Samaritanism, as we know it from later definite sources, has survived, as a true Israelite religion, constituting indeed the earliest Jewish sect; the Samaritans centralized their worship on Mount Gerizim, so defying the Jewish article of faith in Jerusalem. The religious schism involved politics, as appears from Ezra, *e.g.*, 4$^{1ff.}$, and for the general mixture of politics and religion in that day *cf.* the matrimonial alliance of the Jewish highpriestly family with that of Sanballat (Neh. 13^{28}). But the fundamental relation of the two Churches survived, we know not how in detail; the Samaritans adopted the Law, codified according to tradition by Ezra, the text being subsequently altered in places by either party in hostility to the other. There was a hardy element which survived in the North, purified as by fire, with which may be compared the experience of Judah, which had its contest with rampant heathenism, as in the reign of Manasseh, a conflict followed by the reform under Josiah and its failure, and this in turn was succeeded by the Exile, with only a 'remnant' remaining of the true Israel.

VV.$^{24-34a. 41}$. **24.** *And the king of Assyria brought some from Babylon and from Kuthah and from Awwa and from Hamath* *and Sepharwaim, and settled them in the cities of Samaria in place of the Bnê-Israel; and they possessed* (a legal term) *Samaria, and dwelt in its cities.* The land had obtained its new official name, following Assyrian usage; *cf.* Hos. 14^1 (a proleptic use of the name in I. 13^{32}). The deportation from Babylon and Kuthah may be connected with the fragmentary record for his first year in Sargon's Annals (*ARA* 2, §4, *cf. CIOT* 1, 268 ff., with commentary), reporting suppression of a native uprising in Babylon (evidently headed by Merodachbaladan), as result of which " x+7 people together with their possessions I snatched away . . . in Ḥatti-Land (*i.e.*, Syria) I settled them." For similar deportations to Ḥatti-Land noted in the same Annals see *ARA* §§6, 8, while §17, for the 7th year, notes a deportation ' to Samaria.' Ezra 4$^{9f.}$ gives a list of peoples settled in the land by Asenappar, *i.e.*, Ashurbanipal, and Winckler has argued that the present passage refers to that deportation (*Alttest. Untersuchungen*, 98, *cf.* Montgomery, p. 52); but the Assyrian practice of exile was too general for us to precise datings. Kuthah is identified with Tell Ibrahīm to the N of Babylon (Meissner, *Bab. u. Ass.*, Index, *s.v.*). Its name stuck as the later Jewish term of abuse for the Samaritans, ' Kuthim,' to which subject a whole Talmudic tractate, *Massecheth Kuthim*, is devoted (translation in Montgomery, ch. 11). The earliest literary use of this name appears in Josephus, *Ant.*, ix, 14, 3. Awwa appears as Iwwah in 18^{34} in association with other Syrian cities as here. For earlier identifications see GB; Sachau has suggested Imm, between Antioch and Aleppo, Šanda notes Ammia in the Amarna tablets, not far from Gebal; Abel, *GP* 2, 256, following Dhorme, finds in it Tell Kafr 'Aya on the Orontes, SW of Homs. Hamath appears as one of Sargon's complete conquests (*KB* 2, 57; *ARA* 2, §55). From the placing of Sepharwaim with Syrian cities the earlier identification of it with Babylonian Sippar appears out of question; it may be identified with Sibraim of Eze. 47^{16} (aligned with Hamath), possibly Shabara'in of the Bab. Chronicle (*KB* 2, 277; *CP* 210); see Abel, *GP* 2, 456.[5]

[5] For the older identification there may be noted the repeated combination of Babylon, Kuthah, Sippar as rebellious, *e.g.*, *ARA* 2, §§791, 796 f.

VV.²⁵⁻³³. The eclectic mixture of religions in the land. **VV.**²⁵⁻²⁸. The plague of lions is naïvely and naturally related, as though *in ipsissimis verbis* of the officials who forwarded the complaint. The present plague was due to the devastations caused by the Assyrians. Ashurbanipal records at length a similar extended plague of lions in the Babylonian marshes (*ARA* 2, §935). Centuries later the Syrian Usāma b. Munḳidh of the twelfth century casually recalls in his memoirs that he " fought lions on innumerable occasions, and killed many of them " (Hitti's translation, p. 173 ; *cf.* Comm., $2^{23f.}$) ; for the late survival of the beast *cf.* BDD and Abel, *GP* 1, 223. There is record of such intrusions of lions in one of the quarters of Baghdad for the years 1205, 1217 ; see Reuben Levy, *A Baghdad Chronicle* (1929), 243. **VV.**^{27. 28}. The monarch, with accustomed imperial liberalism, accepted the suggestion of repatriation of native priests to revive the cult of the offended local deity. **27.** The Heb. of the royal response is to be corrected so as to read : *Transport thither* ⌜*some of*⌝ [𝔥 *one of*] *the priests whom I* [with some VSS—𝔥 *you*] *brought thence ; and let them* [= 𝔥 pl.] *go and settle there, and let them* [𝔥 *him*] *teach them the custom of the god of the land.* *N.b.* the awkward variation of numbers in 𝔥, induced by the sequel with mention of only one priest ; some VSS independently correct. **28.** A good priest came and reformed his compatriots' religion, settling at the ancient sanctuary of Bethel. We may presume that his party had the benevolent assistance of Hezekiah ; *cf.* the tradition in 2 Ch. 30 of the latter's invitation to his great Passover feast, when he sent messengers throughout the North, which summons was accepted by ' certain ' out of some half-dozen tribes ; see Montgomery, pp. 53 ff. **VV.**^{29-31a}. The heathenish cults of the new settlers. **29.** *And they were making each nation its god, and they deposited them in the high-place temples that the Samaritans had made, each nation in the cities where they dwelt.* The suggestion is that the ancient high-places well suited those heathen. **30.** *The men of Babylon made Succoth-benoth.* The second element of the deity's name suggests that of Marduk's consort, congenial to Babylonians, Ṣarpanītu, a name popularly twisted into Zēr-banītu (' seed-procreating '—the Grr. here vocalize the element with *baniti*) ; see Jastrow, *Rel. Bab. u. Ass.*,

1, 115 ff. The first element was earlier identified with Sakkut, the Babylonian Saturn, whose name is to be read in Am. 5²⁶, in place of Heb. *Sikkuth* (so RV JV ; AV RVᴬᵐ ' tabernacle '). But far preferable is Stade's correction to ' Marduk,' so obtaining the Babylonian divine pair, Marduk and Zer-banit, reduced here to an androgynous deity, Marduk-Banit. *And the men of Kuth made Nergal*—the well-known deity of Kuthah (see Jastrow, pp. 157 f., Deimel, *Pantheon Babylonicum*, 191 ff.) *and the men of Hamath made Ashima*, 31a. *and the Awwites made Nibhaz and Tartak*. The name Nibhaz was early corrupted, or rather intentionally distorted ; Jewish tradition attempted an abusive etymology (see Note). But the word is thus to be explained : *nbḥz*<*mbḥz* (by a common dissimilation)<*mzbḥ*, ' altar,' *i.e.*, the deified altar. *Cf.* the dedications Διὶ Βωμῷ μεγάλῳ and Διὶ Μαδβάχῳ (the Semitic in transliteration), Μάδβαχος also appearing paired with another deity, Σελομάνης.⁶ *Cf.* the deification of the Beth-el, as it appears in the Elephantine papyri. The names Tartak and Ashima represent a well-known pair in Syrian mythology. The former, תרתק, is doubtless, as recognized by Baethgen, *Beiträge zur sem. Religionsgesch.* (1888), 68, the famous goddess ʼΑταργάτη, ʼΑτάργατις, Hellenistic Δερκετώ, Latin, ' Derceto.' She appears on coins and inscriptions as עתרעתה ו, עתרעהי (Lidzb. *HNE* 348, Clemen, *Lukians Schrift über die syrische Göttin*, 41), as הרעתא in Bardesanes (W. Cureton, *Spicilegium syriacum*, 1855, p. 31), and as ταργατή (Renan, *Mission en Phénicie*, 133). The present form is reduction of original עתרקהה, with proper ancient Aramaic ק for *ġayin* ; see Montg., *JBL* 33 (1914), 78. The name, like the deity, is composite=עתר+עתה, the latter the Greek ʺΑττις.⁷ Outside of Syria she had a famous shrine

---

⁶ See Clermont-Ganneau, ' Le Zeus Madbachos et le Zeus Bomos des Sémites,' *Recueil*, 4, 164 ff., ' Zeus Naos et Zeus Bomos,' *ib.*, 7, 81 ff. ; Lidzb., *Eph.*, 2, 81. The latter scholar has identified Selamanes and Madbachos with the names of two Mandaic genii ; see Rosenthal, *Die aram. Forschung*, 242 f. For the deification of the altar see E. Bickermann, *Der Gott der Makkabäer* (1937), ch. 4, §4.

⁷ 'Aṭṭar and 'Aṭṭart, male and female, now appear in the Ugaritic texts. The Heb. counterpart for the latter is 'Ashtart (I. 11⁵, etc.). The male deity is frequent in S. Arab. texts ; see Ryckmans, *NPS* 1, 27. Albr., in *JAOS* 60 (1940), 300, n. 58, denies such etymology for ' Derketo.'

at Ashkelon, and her doubtless ancient Atergateion (*cf.* II Macc. 12²⁶) at Biblical Ashtoreth-karnaim (' Ashtart-of-the-horns '). She was ' the Syrian Goddess ' of Lucian of Samosata.⁸ The name Ashima appears in that of the golden image described by Lucian, §33, ' called by the Greeks σημήιον (Ionic Greek='Symbol ') ; the vocable also appears in double form in Greek tradition as Σίμι and Σείμιος, representing members of the Syrian triad. Simi is to be identified with Atargatis ; *cf.* the Syrian Melito (Cureton, *Spicileg. syriacum*, pp. 44 f.), making her a daughter of ' the king Hadad.' Simios was her son, as Diodorus Siculus reports (ii, 4). This deity has been discovered in the obscure name of the deity worshipped by heathenish Israelites in Am. 8¹⁴, those ' who swear by the guilt of (*'ašmat*) Bethel (for ' Samaria ' of 𝔐),' which is to be read ' Ashîmat of Bethel,' or rather ' Ashîmat of the god's house ' ; see T. H. Robinson, *ad loc.*, in *HAT* (1936). The latter interpretation is comparable with the obscure אשמביתאל, who, along with ענתביתאל, ' Anat of the god's house,' appears as consort of Yahu in an Elephantine papyrus, and who is to be identified with the deity Συμβέτυλος, appearing in a triad along with Simios and Lion (probably the bearer of the divine throne) in an inscription from Syrian Kefr Nebo of date 223 A.D.⁹ **31*b*. And the Sepharwites were burning** [Heb.

⁸ See Bibliog. under ' Lucian ' ; to be consulted *inter al.*, J. G. Frazer, *Adonis, Attis, Osiris* (1907) ; L. B. Paton, *ERE s.vv.* ; F. Cumont on Atargatis and Attis in Pauly-Wissowa, *RE*, and its *Supplement, s.vv.* ; S. Ronzevalle, ' Jupiter Héliopolitain,' *Mél.*, 21 (1938), 101 ff., 126 f. Also see Eissfeldt, *Tempel u. Kulte syrischer Städte in hellenistisch-römischer Zeit* (1941), 80 f., 92 ff., 121 ff., for the Atargatis temples in Palmyra and Dura, the volume containing a valuable summary of the ancient Syrian cults that survived until a late age. For an earlier extensive treatment see Dussaud, *Notes de mythologie syrienne* (1905).
⁹ For the papyrus see Sachau, pap. 18, col. 7, Cowley, no. 22 ; for the Syrian inscription Lidzb., *Eph.*, 2, 323 f. See further Lidzb., vol. 3, 247, 264 f. ; Cowley, pp. xviii *seq.* ; Dussaud in Pauly-Wissowa, *RE*, ' Simea und Simios ' ; Eissf. in *ARw.*, 28 (1930), 1 ff. ; Meyer, *GA* 2, 2, 165 f. ; Aimé-Giron, *Textes araméens d'Égypte*, 113 ff. (with full discussion of the related themes) ; Vincent, *La religion des Judéo-Araméens d'Élephantiné*, cc. 12–15 on Anath and Asim-Betel. The origin of the element remains obscure represented as it is by two similar but differently applied names in the Greek, and by two differently vocalized forms in the Semitic. The Elephantine name, corroborated

śôrephîm] *their children in the fire to Adrammelek and Anammelek, the gods of Sepharwaim.* The form of the place-name is uncertain in the Heb. tradition; see Note. The first divine name, as spelt here, appears as that of one of the two sons of Sennacherib who assassinated him (19^{37}), and also as a Phoen. name (Harris, *Gram.*, 75). The human name is to be explained from the element *'dr*, *cf.* *'addîr* as a divine epithet, Ps. 8^2, so Langdon, *op. cit.*, 71. But the divine name must be rewritten as *Adad-melek*, 'Adad king,' which name as *Adad-milki* has now been read in a Mesopotamian inscription; see Albright, *ARI* 163, with notes citing A. Bohl, *Biblica*, 22 (1941), 35 for the inscription, and with references to such cremation sacrifices to Adad. The second divine name is epithet of Anu, the ancient Sumerian god of heaven; see Albright, ' The Evolution of the West-Semitic Deity 'An-'Ant-'Atta', *AJSL* 41 (1925), 73 ff. **32.** *And they were fearing YHWH, and they made for themselves out of their own number high-place priests, and they were celebrating for them in the high-place houses.* **33.** *YHWH they were fearing, and their own gods they were serving, according to the custom of the nations whence they* (impersonal) *had exiled them.* **34a.** *Unto this day they are doing according to ⌈their former custom⌉* (as at v.^{40}; 𝔅 *the former customs*). **41.** For the connexion of this v. as sequel see above. *And these nations were fearing YHWH, and their own idols they were serving, moreover their sons and their sons' sons; according as did their fathers, they are doing unto this day.* **32.** *Out of their own number:* as at I. 12^{31}. The verb translated *celebrating* is the simple ' to do, make,' used absolutely of religious practice, as at Ex. 10^{25}; *cf.* Jesus' word at the institution of the Last Supper, " Do this in remembrance of me," and the similar use of Latin *facere*. **33.** Almost a contrast between theology and praxis is expressed here; the final relative clause is awkwardly expressed. Read

by Συμβέτυλος, might mean 'Name of the Beth-El,' and so Eissf. and Giron find the element *ism*, ' name,' or *wasm*, ' mark '; but these are Arabisms, and do not explain the form *'ašîma* and its parallels, σημήιον, etc., with the interior long vowel. Langdon (*Mythology of All Races*, 5, 22 ff.) connects the word with Akk. *šîmtu*, ' fate,' followed by Ronzevalle, p. 126. There was doubtless, as often in ancient eclecticism, confusion or assimilation of various etymologies. For a recapitulation of the subject, see Clemen, *op. cit.*, 42 f.

in connexion with vv.$^{34b-40}$ this passage looks like a hateful condemnation of the Samaritan sect, as indeed it has since been historically interpreted ; but the original reference was to the imported heathen, who naturally assimilated their own cults with that of the god of the land. This condition of the mixed population and culture is brilliantly illustrated by the Elephantine papyri, in which ' the Jews,' as the writers call themselves, display a religion associating Anath, Bethel, etc., as *paredroi* of Yahu ; they attempted diplomatic intercourse with ' Johanan the high priest ' at Jerusalem (*cf.* Neh. 12^{22}), and, answer failing them, they addressed ' the sons of Sanballat governor of Samaria ' (Sachau, papp. 1, 3, Cowley, no. 30). These ' Jews ' were a military colony imported from Samaria before the Persian conquest ; *cf.* Meyer, *op. cit.*, 7 ff. For their religion see Cowley, *Aramaic Papyri*, xviii, *seq.* ; Aimé-Giron, *op. cit.*, 110 ff. ; A. Vincent, *op. cit.*, and Contenau's review in *Syria*, 1938, 93 ff.

VV.$^{34b-40}$. This passage is a condemnation of the Samaritan sect, so placed that it combines that body with the new heathenish colonists. It is of wholly Deuteronomistic strain. V.^{41}, as noted above, is sequel of vv.$^{27-34a}$.

3. מנחה : Gr. transliterations as at 8^9 (see Note) ; 𝔊^L δωρα, and in the expanded text of v.^{4} both δωρα and μαναα ; 𝔏 ' moneta.'— **4.** קשר : 𝔊 𝔊^H αδικιαν=𝔖^H ; 𝔊^L επιβουλην=𝔏 ; Aq., Quinta, ' deceit ' ; 𝔗 𝔖 ' rebellion,' *cf.* 𝔙 ' rebellare nitens ' ; for the present phrase *cf.* Jer. 11^9.—סוֹא : B *al.*, Σηγωρ ; Hex., Σωα (Jos., Σωαν)= 𝔖 𝔙 (' Sua ') ; it is probably to be vocalized as סֻוֹא (St., *BH*), see Comm. 𝔊^L replaces אל סוא מלך מצרים with προς Αδραμμελεχ τ. Αιθιοπα τ. κατοικουντα εν Αιγυπτω ; see Rahlfs's discussion (*SS* 3, 114 f.) of this aberration as basis of a listing in Theophilus (*Ad Autolycum*, ii, 31) of an Αδραμελεχ Αιθιοψ among the Ass. kings, proving that this rdg. of the 2d cent. A.D. well preceded Lucian.—ויעצרהו, ויאסרהו : see *SBOT* for proposals to eliminate one or the other of the phrases, but the first verb expresses legal ' detention ' ; an example of arbitrary emendation is Cheyne's rewriting to ויעורהו, ' and blinded him ' (*EB* 2127).—**5.** ויעל *bis* : for many corrections of this repetition see St. in *SBOT*, who soberly leaves the text untouched ; the phrase ' to go up against ' is the common military term for ' campaigning,' as at v.^{3} (see BDB 748b).—**6.** בשנת התשיעית (MSS, correcting, בשנה הת׳) : construction as at 25^1, etc. ; *cf.* GK §134, p. 𝔊^L ℭ 𝔖 𝔙 pref. ' and,' without authority.—נהר׃ Grr. 𝔖^H as pl., *i.e.*, Halah and Habor as ' rivers of Gozan.'—גוזן: Grr. correctly, exc. B v, Γωζαρ, e Γοζαρ.—ערי׃ Grr., 𝔖^H as though

הָרִי : *n.b.* the intruded הרא, 1 Ch. 5²⁶.—At end 𝔊ᴸ+' unto this day,' from Ch.—7. For the long protasis see Comm. ; 𝔊ᴸ found rhetorical difficulty, and expanded with " and the Lord's anger was against Israel (because) "—' superior,' says Burney—but not original!—8. ומלכי ישראל אשר עשו : MS 70 om. ומלכי ישראל, and so Gr. N+12 MSS, 𝔖ᴴ ⁛ ; 𝔖 𝔄 om. the whole clause. VSS vary in rendering ; attempts at explanation by Then., Klost. ; but with Burn., St., Šanda, the passage is an evident intrusion.—9. ויחפאו : Grr. with the verb ἀμφιάζειν, ' to clothe,' as from root חפה, and so Rashi, Kimchi interpret, ' they concealed its interpretation ' (Kimchi) ; *cf.* BDB, ' to do secretly,' and König, *HAW* ; 𝔙 ' operuerunt ' ; see proposed corrections in GB, and the long note by Haupt with an original etymology ; Ehrl. *cft.* Hos. 12¹, but without clarifying the word here. Correct interpretation appears to come from the Akk. with root *ḫapū*, ' to utter,' which actually = 𝔗 𝔖 𝔄 ; see V. Scheil, *Nouveaux vocabulaires babyloniens* (1919), 12 f. (adducing also the present passage) ; *cf.* G. R. Driver in Peake, *The People and the Book*, 89.—אשר לא כן : *cf.* לא כן, 7⁹ ; אשר is used like Aram. די, ד, and a similar case appears in Syr. with דלא in Bardesanes, Cureton, *Spicilegium syriacum* (1855), 11, lines 10 f. ; similar is Akk. *ša lā* ; *cf.* also Haupt's note.—11. בכל במות : unnecessary after שם, prob. introduced to add to the indictment, elided by St., Šanda.—דברים רעים : Grr., κοινωνούς κ. ἐχάραξαν, " partners, and they irritated " = 𝔖ᴴ. Klost. would rashly reconstruct the Gr. into κιναίδους κ. ἑταιρίδας, but 𝔊 read the first word as חברים. Gr. j and an 𝔏 text = 𝔅.—13. ויעד : generally understood as Hif. of עוד, whence עד, ' witness ' ; for proposed Akk. connexion of עדות as root w'd=y'd, ' to command,' see Haupt, *ad loc.*, and GB ; the former derives the verb from the same source ; there may be paronomasia between the roots in the Heb. words.—כל נביאו כל חוה : Ḳr. נְבִיאֵי, as ' all prophets of all vision,' with 'ח as at Is. 28¹⁵—doubtless to avoid reference to seers ; Grr. as נְבִיאֵי = 𝔖ᴴ ; but read 'כל נביא וכל ח with MSS 30 153 253 (for variations see deR.) = 𝔗ᴸ (translating with ' every scribe and every teacher '), 𝔙, modern VSS.—חקותי : 28 MSS Ken., deR., 'חו = VSS, modern VSS, which is required, unless the word is an ' exuberant gloss ' (St.).—אליכם : OGrr., 𝔖 as = להם ; but the commands are ' for you.'—14. כערף אבותם : text of 𝔊 shortened by paraplepsis with אבותם, v.¹⁵ ; 𝔊ᴸ 𝔊ᴴ variously supply the loss ; see St.—15. יהוה : B v g om. κύριος, 𝔖ᴴ ⁛.—16. כל : OGrr. om., softening the indictment, 𝔖ᴴ ⁛.— 17. וינחשו : the root has its liquid variant in לחש, *cf.* Ps. 58⁶. From the latter root there appears לחשת, ' charm,' in an Aram. magical text published by Du Mesnil du Buisson in *Mélanges Syriens* . . . René Dussaud, 1, 421 ff. The variant forms appear to have the mng. ' to hiss,' used of the magicians who ' squeak and gibber.' Dhorme (cited above) thinks of serpent-charmers. —19 ויח⸱ ⸱ 5 MSS וגם : *cf.* VSS.—21. כי קרע ישראל מעל בית דוד : for the theme *cf.* I Sam. 15²⁸, I. 11¹²; 𝔊ᴸ 𝕿 𝔙 the verb as passive, with 'Israel' as subject, and similarly 𝔖; 𝔄 "Jeroboam made separation in Israel "—all attempts to avoid the divine agency. 𝔊 𝔊ᴴ οτι πλην Ισραηλ επανωθεν οικου Δαυειδ (=𝔖ᴴ); see St.'s criticism of Kamph.'s effort to rewrite Heb. on this inscrutable basis.—וידא Kt., וַיַּדַּח Kr.: the latter as Kt. in 19 MSS Ken., deR., appearing also in Bab. Talmud; the verb נדח is used of feminine seduction, Prov. 7²¹, and similarly of false prophets, Dt. 13⁶ᶠᶠ.—**22.** חטאות: many MSS חטאת, and so to be read as sing. (*cf.* v.²¹), in consonance with foll. ממנה, and so 𝔊 𝔊ᴴ.—**23.** דבר: 1 MSS+יהוה=Grr., 𝔖.—**24.** ומכותה: B *al.*, τον [εκ Χ.], error for και. The dissyllable (the acc. of direction replacing the nominative form)=Grr. (B Χουνθα); in v.³⁰ 𝔊ᴸ has the same for כות.—[וּמֵעַ]וָּא: MSS עוּה; *cf.* עַוָּה, 18³⁴; B *al.* om. και.—וספרוים=𝔊 Hex.; Kr.ᵒʳ יְמַם=𝔊ᴸ.—**27.** משם . . . אחד [שמה]: lost by parablepsis in Grr., exc. 𝔊ᴸ; 𝔖ᴴ ⁜.—הגליתהם=𝔖ᴴ 𝔖; 1 MS הגליותים=𝔊ᴸ 𝕿 𝔄; the latter rdg. preferable, *cf.* the 2d pers. sing., v.²⁶.—וילכו וישבו=𝔊 Hex.; the other VSS as sing., in agreement with אחד above.—וְיִרָם: 𝔊 Hex., 𝕿=וְיִרָם; see Comm. for omission of אחד and the retention of the pl. in the three verbs.—[הארץ] אלהי: MS 30, B om., as heathenish.—**29.** בית הבמות: for the composite pl., also in v.³², see Note, I. 12³¹.—**30.** סכות בנות: for the first word Grr., σοχχωθ, etc. (B ροχχωθ), for the second B βαινειθει, A βενιθει, etc.; *n.b.* survival of the final Akk. vowel; see Comm. for correction to מרדך בנית. For such a distortion of the first name *cf.* 'Marduk' to 'Nisrok,' 19³⁷.—נרגל: B ἱ την Εργελ; *al.*, την (𝔊ᴸ τον) Νηριγελ; the fem. article used as in ἡ Βααλ.—**31.** נבחז: with 'large *zayin*' (see GK §5, n), indicating a variant spelling, which appears in a few MSS, 𝕿, as נבחן, and so *Sanhedrin*, 63b, etymologizing from the root 'to bark like a dog.' Exc. A, την Ναιβας, and *Onom. Gr.*, Ναζεβ=*Onom. Lat.*, Grr. have an entirely different word, την Εβλαζερ, etc. Hommel has suggested for this name, as also for Tartak, Elamite origin (Haupt Commemoration Vol., 159 ff.). For recovery of the original see Comm.—הספרוים: exc. the Three and 𝔊ᴸ, the Grr. as a deity, B την Σεπφαρουν, etc.=𝔖ᴴ.—אַדְרַמֶּלֶךְ, Kr.ᵒʳ אֲדַרְסֶלֶךְ: read אֲדַרְמֶלֶךְ, as suggested by Winckler in *KTAT*, and see Comm.—וענמלך: 𝔊ᴸ om.—אלה ספרים: Kr. corrects the first word to אֱלֹהֵי=VSS, and the second to כפרוים, and so many MSS Kt.; the place-name has been distorted to correspond with the gentilic above; *cf.* the place-names proposed for identification in Comm., v.²⁴, and to be read, 'Siphraim,' or the like.—𝔊ᴸ pref. a long doublet to the v., but it is difficult to see why Burn. regards it as superior to 𝔐; *cf.* Rahlfs, *SS* 3, 290.—**33.** הגלו: OGrr. as sing., with the Lord understood as subj.; 𝔙 as passive.—**34.** כמשפטים הראשנים:=𝕿ᴸ; 𝔊 𝔊ᴴ=כמשפטיהם=𝕿ᵂ; 𝔊ᴸ supplies a clumsy doublet=כמשפט הראשון (see Rahlfs, *ib.*, 246); the last rdg. appears in v.⁴⁰, and is preferable, with the collective sense of the noun.—אינם *bis*: 𝔊 Hex.

om., and further om. את יהוה on the basis that "they were fearing and yet doing acc. to their own statutes," etc.—כחקתם וכמשפטם : prob. an addition from v.[37], and so om. the foll. conj.; or read כחקתיו וכמשפטו.—**38**. כרתי : VSS, exc. 𝕮, as 3d sing., כרת, which appears preferable; but the writer may have fallen artlessly into the divine first person.

CC. 18–20. The reign of Hezekiah of Judah. ‖ 2 Ch. 29–32, and for 18[13]–20 the duplicate in Is. 36–39. *Cf. Ant.*, ix, 13–x, 2.[1] 18[1-8]. Introduction to the reign (vv.[1, 2]); the king's unique piety (vv.[3-8]), including two archival notes (vv. [4, 8]). Hezekiah (725–696 B.C.) was contemporary of Shalmaneser, Sargon II (722–705), Sennacherib (705–681). With the fate of Samaria before his eyes, and in spite of the Assyrian terror, he reversed the international and religiously eclectic policy of his father Ahaz (*cf.* 16[7ff.]), at a seemingly providential period abandoned submission to Assyria, struck out on his own hand against the Philistine neighbours, weakened as they were by Assyrian control, and introduced a religious reformation. For the first time one of the Canonical Prophets appears in the active politics of the state in the person of Isaiah. The ancient Israelite spirit was revived by a prophetic movement, exhibited also in Micah, as had been the case in the North in the preceding century, there without permanence, but here on a surer foundation. The policy of Hezekiah as statesman was: Israel for its God and itself alone. Much has been made of apparent contrast between the king and the great prophet, and in consequence scepticism has been largely addressed to the present statements of the former's sincerity and reforms. But Hezekiah was primarily statesman, and as such he stood for the cause of the Prophets, even as did Constantine with his political limitations for the Christian religion of his day. For a reasonable discussion of the problem see Robinson at length, *HI* 389 ff., and *e.g.*, p. 393: "We need not doubt Hezekiah's sincerity if we see in this reform a political gesture, for patriotism and religious loyalty went hand in hand in ancient Israel." Even more positively than Robinson, who finds in Isaiah's silence in regard to Hezekiah a cause of doubt, Kittel (*GVI* 2, 373 f.) refuses "to surrender the narrative concerning his

---

[1] For the literature see Additional Note after ch. 20, especially n. 1. Some references below are to literature cited there.

reformation." It is true that when religious reform enters the field of politics, it has rough sailing. Hezekiah was succeeded by a Manasseh, Josiah by a Jehoiakim. But a ' Remnant ' was being disciplined to survive, and faith was to be basis of survival (Is. 7^{3-19}). See further Additional Note, n. 4.

The two archival notes in the section are introduced by the emphatically expressed initial *He* without conjunction (*cf.* Comm., 14^7). **4.** The v. briefly describes the religious reformation. *He removed the high-places, and broke up the pillars, and cut down the Asherah, and cut up the brass serpent, which Moses had made; for up to those days the Bnê-Israel were burning incense to it; and it was called Nehushtan.* The removal of *high-places* and *pillars*, the inheritance of primitive cult, was drastic indeed; for *the Asherah cf.* $17^{10, 16}$. *The serpent of brass* [*něḥaš han-něḥōšet*, with play on the two words] *called Nehushtan*, was a surviving ancient fetich, coming down, as the annalist artlessly recorded, from Moses' day and authority (Num. $21^{4\text{ff.}}$). For the archæological object of the serpent and its wide field in Palestine, Egypt and Mesopotamia, see Benzinger, *Arch.*, 328; Albright, '*The Goddess of Life and Wisdom,*' *AJSL* 36 (1920), 258 ff.; Cook, *Rel. of Anc. Israel*, 98 f., 117, 220; H. Frankfort, *Iraq*, 1 (1934), 9 ff.; Graham and May, *Culture and Conscience*, Index, *s.v.*; H. H. Rowley, ' Zadok and Nehushtan,' *JBL* 58 (1939), 113 ff. For a serpent-stele discovered at Tell Beit Mirsim see Albright, *BASOR* 31 (1928), and *ZAW* 47 (1929), 6 f. *N.b.* the *Serpent Spring* of I. 1^9. Such antique survivals in higher religion are abundantly paralleled in the Christian Church and Islam. The second archival note is introduced with editorial explanation of Hezekiah's success. **7.** *And Y*HWH *being with him in all that he set out on, he was prospering. And he rebelled against the king of Assyria, and did not serve him.* **8.** *He smote Philistia as far as Gaza and its borders, from watchmen's tower to fortified city.* This was an overt act of rebellion against Assyria's claims. Sargon records the defeat of Egypt at Raphia on the border for 713 B.C., involving capture of Hanno king of Gaza, and at length, in two inscriptions for 711 B.C., a successful campaign against Azuri king of Ashdod and his allies, Gath, Ashkelon, Meluḫḫa, in which connexion, " the people of Philistia, Judah, Edom, Moab, those who live by the sea . . .

brought tribute . . . to Ashur my lord." (See *KB* 2, 55, 66 ff. ; *CP* 328 ff. ; *ATB* 1, 349 ff. ; *ARA* 2, §§5, 30, 62, 80 ; *AB* 468.) The attack was a border warfare, belonging doubtless to the troubled years at the end of Sargon's reign and the beginning of Sennacherib's. A revival of the Philistines had occurred in Ahaz's reign according to 2 Ch. 28^{18} ; *cf.* the oracle attributed to Isaiah as of the death-year of Ahaz (Is. $14^{28ff.}$). In line with this concern in Philistia was Hezekiah's interference in the affairs of Ekron with its rebellion against Sennacherib, as reported in the latter's inscription ; see below.

VV.$^{5, 6}$. These statements on Hezekiah's faithfulness to his God, couched in Deuteronomic language—' cleaving to YHWH,' ' not turning away from him '—are logically introduced between the reform at home and the success abroad. The statement that *after him there was none like him among all the kings of Judah* is later contradicted by the absolute statement on Josiah's virtue (23^{25}). The following clause, *and who were before him*, is a clumsy addition. There was another illustrious phase of the reign according to the tradition of ' the men of Hezekiah ' and their proverbs (Prov. 25–29), which tradition Gemser in his Comm. (*HAT* 1937) regards as quite authentic. A royal parallel two generations later would be Ashurbanipal, who extols at length his own education and wisdom (*ARA* 2, §986, and *cf.* Kittel, *GVI* 2, 378).

VV.$^{9-12}$. The item of the fall of Samaria, repeated almost verbatim from $17^{5, 6}$, which an early editor desired to place chronologically in Hezekiah's reign, and with rendering of Hoshea's year-terms into those of his contemporary. **10.** *And he* [with the parallel and most VSS ; 𝕳 *they*] *took it at the end of three years, even in year six of Hezekiah; it was year nine of Hoshea king of Israel that Samaria was taken.* **12.** A repetitive moralizing judgment.

V.^{13}–ch. 19. An apparently continuous history of Sennacherib's operations against Jerusalem, paralleled in Is. 36, 37 ; see Additional Note.

VV.$^{13-16}$. This initial section stands apart as of annalistic character with its curt detail, without moral judgment, while one arithmetical figure for the tribute to Sennacherib is exactly that in the latter's own inscription. The section of this inscription, the Taylor Prism, col. iii, lines 1 ff., for the king's third year and his campaign in 701 B.C., is the most famous of Assyrian texts bearing upon Bible history. For the translation see *CIOT* 2, 281 ff. (still of value for its notes) ; *KB* 2, 280 ff. ; *CP* 340 ff. (these three with the transliterated text) ; *AKAT*, 176 ff. ; *ATB* 1, 352 ff. ; *ARA* 2, §§309 ff. ; [2] *AB* 471 f. This great campaign covered Palestine as far as Eltekeh in the old Danite territory (Jos. 19^{44}, 21^{23}). Sennacherib specifically names a number of cities, practically all in the Philistine territory, among them Ekron, whose ' loyal ' king Padi had been committed by rebels to ' Hezekiah king of Judah,' from which arrest the Assyrian reclaimed him, restoring him to his throne along with condign punishment of the rebels. This interference of Hezekiah in his neighbours' affairs, evidently as arch-conspirator against Assyria, is paralleled by the brief notice of his successful campaign in Philistia (v.^{8}).

13. *And in the fourteenth year of king Hezekiah Sennacherib king of Assyria came up against all the fortified cities of Judah and seized them.* The date is contradicted by the Assyrian chronology. It may be a scribal miswriting of ' 24,' which would give the correct date ; or the figure was induced by the statement of the promise to Hezekiah of an additional 15 years of life (20^6), *i.e.*, 29—15=14. The v. was earlier regarded by Stade as original introduction to vv.$^{17ff.}$, but in *SBOT* he distinguishes vv.$^{13.\ 16.\ 14.\ 15.\ 17ff.}$ as from as many distinct sources. But barring the date, or with correction of it, the v. is necessary introduction to vv.$^{14ff.}$; indeed the whole section is the one part of the narrative definitely supported by external history. For *all the fortified cities cf.* Sennacherib (after Rogers's tr.) : " Forty-six strong cities, with walls, the smaller cities which were around them . . . I besieged and captured." *Cf.* the expression in v.^{8} for the two classes of fortresses, and see R. P. Dougherty, ' Sennacherib and the Walled Cities of Judah,' *JBL* 49 (1930), 160 ff., with valuable references to the strength of the Palestinian fortifications as demonstrated by archæology. With this citation *cf.* Sennacherib's manifesto in the Nebi Yūnus inscription (presented in the authorities cited above) : " I destroyed the broad district

---

[2] The text used by Luckenbill is that of a duplicate cylinder (' an even more perfect copy '), acquired by the University of Chicago in 1920, and published by him in his *Annals of Sennacherib* (1924).

of Judah ; I laid my yoke upon Hezekiah its king." **14**a.
*And Hezekiah king of Judah (n.b. the formal title) sent message
to the king of Assyria to Lachish*———. For the city see Comm.,
14^{19}. Famous are Sennacherib's reliefs, the one graphically
presenting the siege of Lachish, the other portraying the king
seated on his throne with the captives filing before him, and
the accompanying inscription : " Sennacherib, king of the
world, king of Assyria, seated himself on a throne, and the
prisoners of Lachish marched before him." For the text see
the authorities cited, and for the reliefs A. H. Layard, *The
Monuments of Nineveh* (1849), 2, pl. 23 ; Stade, *GVI* 1, plate
after p. 620 ; Rogers, *HBA* 2, plates opp. pp. 370, 374 ;
Benzinger, *Arch.*, 309 ; Olmstead, *HA* fig. 127 ; Barton, *AB*
fig. 298. **14**b. —*saying : I have rebelled. Turn away from
me. What thou puttest upon me I will bear. And the king of
Assyria imposed upon Hezekiah king of Judah* 300 *talents of
silver and* 30 *talents of gold.* The first verb is technical expression of rebellion, and the same root is constantly so used in
Akk. ; its usual equivalent in the English Bible is ' to sin.'
For Hezekiah's capitulation, but without surrender of the
city, the Taylor Prism records for the end of the Palestinian
campaign (lines 20 ff.) : " (Hezekiah) himself I shut up like
a caged bird within Jerusalem, his royal city. I cast up
entrenchments against him, and whosoever came forth from
the gate of his city I punished (?) him." There follows the
list of conquered districts detached from Judah, and then :
" As for Hezekiah the fear of the majesty of my dominion
overwhelmed him, and the Urbi, and the regular troops,
whom he had brought in to strengthen Jerusalem his royal
city, deserted." Then is given the list of articles of ransom
by which Hezekiah avoided surrender of the city : " 30 talents
of gold, 800 talents of silver, precious stones . . . ivory seats
and couches . . . woods . . . ; and his daughters, the women
of his palace, male and female musicians he dispatched after
me to Nineveh my capital city. He sent his ambassador to
give tribute and make submission." This text apprises us of
Hezekiah's extensive military preparations as well as of one
reason leading him to come to terms, viz., the defection of his
mercenaries ; it also describes the luxury found in Jerusalem,
for which condition is to be compared the tradition of

Hezekiah's wealth in 2 Ch. 32$^{27\text{ff.}}$. The 'Urbi' are probably Arabs; for the variations of '*arab* in Heb. see Montgomery, *Arabia and the Bible*, 29. The two reports agree as to ' the 30 talents of gold.' The discrepancy between the ' 300 talents ' of Ki. and the ' 800 ' of the Prism has been explained as due to the difference between the ' light ' and the ' heavy ' talent; for this distinction see Nowack, *Arch.*, 1, 207 f., *KAT* 341 f., Rogers, *HBA* 2, 371 (estimating [1915] the tribute at $5,650,000), and especially Lehmann-Haupt in Pauly-Wissowa, *RE Suppl.* 3 (1918), 601, assuming here the ratio between the Phœnician double talent and the Babylonian light talent. For the talent *cf.* also Comm. above, I. 9^{14}. The problem is a vexed one, with standards of different ages and economies to reckon with, along with variations in the written tradition, *e.g.*, the difference of figures between 𝔥 and 𝔊 at I. 10^{29}. Error, if there be, may lie in the Assyrian figure, for figures in the Assyrian texts contradict themselves; a case in point is given by Rogers, *ib.*, 359. A romantic sidelight for the Biblical student upon the item of ' his daughters, the women of his palace,' following the observation of Landsberger and Bauer (*ZA* 3 [1926], 65) that Sennacherib's forceful wife Naḳīya-zakūtu was a Babylonian Aramæan, has been cast by Meissner (*Sb.*, Berlin Acad., 1932, 58), preferring to regard her as a ' Westerner,' even ' probably a Jewess.'

15. *And Hezekiah gave all the silver (i.e., specie) that was found in* Y*HWH's house and in the treasuries of the king's house.*
16. *At that time Hezekiah cut up the doors of the hall [hêkāl, cf.* I. 6^3, *etc.] of* Y*HWH and the door-posts [?], which Hezekiah king of Judah had overlaid, and gave them to the king of Assyria* [EVV here are not literal]. V.^{16}, with the introductory *at that time*, is an independent item, apparently culled from temple archives. For a similar despoliation of sacred and royal treasures *cf.* that in Rehoboam's reign, I. 14$^{25.\ 26}$. The gilded *door-posts* (the unique word is uncertain, VSS vary) represent Hezekiah's very probable restoration and enrichment of the temple. Criticism of the statement that he was such a renovator has been expressed by critics, and his name has been replaced with that of Solomon (Klostermann), Azariah (Stade), Azariah or Joash (Šanda); but it is vain to essay such change of names.

V.¹⁷–ch. 19. An extract from memoirs of Isaiah, found in duplicate in Is. 36, 37. Two apparently parallel stories, 18¹⁷⁻¹⁹⁷ and 19⁸⁻³⁷, succeeding the item above of Hezekiah's submission, narrating further Assyrian demands for full surrender, arouse suspicion as to their historicity, while their inclusion, along with ch. 20, in the book which bears the prophet's name involves them in the large problem of the alleged Isaianic histories and prophecies. Critical discussion at large is postponed to the Additional Note.

V.¹⁷⁻¹⁹⁷. A fruitless demand of the Assyrian king for the surrender of Jerusalem, and a prophetic oracle from Isaiah. VV.¹⁷⁻²⁵. The demand for surrender. **17.** *And the king of Assyria sent ⌈(the) Tartan and (the) Rab-saris and⌉* [Is. om.] *(the) Rab-shakeh from Lachish to king Hezekiah with a stout force to Jerusalem. ⌈And they went up and came to Jerusalem. And they went up and came⌉* [Is. om.] *and* [Is. *he*] *stood at the conduit of the Upper Pool, the one at the highway of Fuller's Field.* **18.** *⌈And they called to the king⌉* [Is. om.]. *And there went out to them* [Is. *him*] *Eliakim ben Hilkiah, He-Over-the-House, and Shebna the Secretary, and Joah ben Asaph the Recorder.* The text of Ki. is expanded and otherwise varied : *and they went up and came* is a duplicate ; probably the whole double passage, lacking in Is., is secondary ; the ' calling to the king ' also looks secondary ; Is. is original in ignoring the first two officials named, the Tartan (title for an Assyrian generalissimo) and the Rab-saris, since the Rab-shakeh alone appears in the subsequent parleys. As Stade remarks, with subsequent general consent, the intrusion of the first two officials was due ' to the antiquarian learning of a later reader ' ; they may have been introduced to make the diplomatic parties even in number. The Tartan appears in Is. 20¹ ; for the Rab-saris (also Jer. 39³) and Rab-shakeh see Note. **17.** *The conduit of the Upper Pool,* etc. The same phrase appears in Is. 7³ as of the place where Isaiah and his son Shear-jashub accosted king Ahaz ; but the time of that event precedes Hezekiah's excavation of the Siloam conduit to the pool within the city, recorded below, 20²⁰. The location of this Upper Pool is still disputed, whether it be a pool at the south of the Akra fed by the old surface aqueduct (for a Lower Pool see Is. 22⁹), or one on the north side of the city, *e.g.,* the modern Birket Mamilla. G. A. Smith defends the former view (*Jerusalem*, 1, ch. 5, esp. p. 105), while Gray (comm. on Is. 7^3) and Šanda at length (pp. 250-3) prefer the latter. The exact geographical data speak for the first identification, and yet such a parley over the walls hardly suits the Kedron valley front of the city. This reference may well be an invention, suggested by Is. 7^3. **18.** For the titles of the three officials *cf.* the list of Solomon's officers, I. $4^{2\text{ff.}}$. In the Isaianic ode, Is. $22^{15\text{ff.}}$, Shebna, here Scribe, there Over-the-House, is denounced, and Eliakim, here Over-the-House, it is predicted, will replace him upon his coming degradation. For that obscure section see the articles by A. Kamphausen, in *AJT*, 1901, 43 ff.; K. Fullerton, *ib.*, 1903, 621 ff.; E. König, *ib.*, 675 ff., and the full critical survey by Gray, *Isaiah, ad loc.* Explanation has been offered for the changes of rank of the two officials as due to administrative shifts in the modern sense. H. G. May doubts whether the Shebna of Ki. and the Shebna of Is. are identical in person (*AJSL* 56 [1939], 147).

VV.$^{19-25}$. The Rab-shakeh's address, a notable diplomatic argument, authentic in colour, even if literally fiction; *cf.* the orations reported by Greek and Roman historians. **19.** *And (the) Rab-shakeh said to them : Say ye now to Hezekiah* (n.b. the rude omission of the latter's title) : *Thus has spoken the Great King* (=Akk. *šarru rabū*—the royal title), *the king of Assyria : What is this trust that thou trustest in ?* **20.** *Thou sayest* (the verb expresses formulated thought) *: Counsel and might for war are mere lip-matter* (the same satirical phrase, Prov. 14^{23}). *Now on whom dost thou trust that thou hast rebelled against me ?* **21.** *Now see !—thou hast put thy trust upon the staff of this broken reed, upon Egypt, a kind one leans upon, and it goes into his palm and pierces it—so is Pharaoh king of Egypt for all who trust in him.* **22.** *And if ye say to me, Upon YHWH our God we trust, is it not he whose high-places and altars Hezekiah has removed, while he said to Judah and Jerusalem : Before this altar ye shall worship in Jerusalem ?* **23.** *And now, take* [sing. verb] *a wager with my lord, the king of Assyria : I will give thee two thousand horses, if thou canst put riders upon them.* **24.** *How then canst thou turn the face of* [𝔐+*a satrap*] *one of the least of my lord's servants ? And thou hast trusted on Egypt* *for chariotry and steeds!* **25.** *And* [with MSS, Is.] *now, without YHWH have I gone up against this place, to destroy it? YHWH did command me, Go up against this land and destroy it!* The blustering oration is a satirical presentation of Assyrian arrogance, and a counterpart of the monuments. The bet of two thousand cavalry men is not an exaggeration; cavalry was never an important arm of the Israelite military; see Comm., I. 1^5, 10^2. Critical dubiety exists as to the alleged statement in v.^{22}, involving the problem of the date of the reformation. It is more important to note that such matters of local religious import were well known to the wise Assyrian chancellery, which had its 'secret service.'

VV.$^{26-36}$. The plea of the royal commission that the parley be held in the diplomatic foreign language, and the Rabshakeh's reply that he speaks on purpose to the common people and to all. **26.** *And said Eliakim ben Hilkiah ⌜and Shebna and Joah⌝* [Is. om.] *to (the) Rab-shakeh: Speak now to thy servants in Aramaic, for we are listening, and do not speak with us in Jewish in the hearing of the people on the wall.* **27.** *And (the) Rab-shakeh said* [𝔐+*to them;* Is. om.] : *To thy lord and to thee has my lord sent me to speak these words? Is it not to the men who sit on the wall, a-eating their own dung and a-drinking their own piss with you?* **28.** *And (the) Rabshakeh stood up, and called out with a loud voice in Jewish; and he spoke and said: Hear ye the word of the Great King, the king of Assyria!* **29.** *Thus has spoken the king: Let not Hezekiah deceive you, for he cannot deliver you from my* [with many MSS, VSS; 𝔐 *his*] *hand;* **30.** *nor let Hezekiah make you trust on YHWH, saying: YHWH will surely deliver us, and this city will not be given into the king of Assyria's hand.* **31.** *Listen not to Hezekiah, for thus has spoken the king of Assyria: Salute me, and come out to me, and eat each of his vine and each of his fig-tree, and drink each of the water of his cistern,* **32.** *until I come and take you to a land like your land, a land of corn and must, a land of bread and vineyards, a land of oil-olive and honey, and so keep alive and die not! And listen not to Hezekiah, for he would beguile you with "YHWH will deliver us!"* **33.** *Did the gods of the peoples ever deliver each one his own land from the king of Assyria's hand?* **34.** *Where are the gods of Hamath and Arpad, where the gods of Sepharwaim*

[𝔊+*Henah and Iwwah* ; Is. om.]—*for did they deliver Samaria out of my hand ?* **35.** *Who among all the land-gods are they that have delivered their land out of my hand, that* YHWH *should deliver Jerusalem from my hand ?* **36.** *And the people kept silence, and answered him not a word, for it was the king's command, to wit, Do not answer him !*

VV.²⁶·²⁷. However dubious this report of the oration may be, the reference to the Aramaic as the *lingua franca* of the empire is of interest.³ ' Jewish ' (Heb.=' judaice ') occurs also in Neh. 13²⁴ ; the speaker is not using the word with any fine dialectical sense. Interesting is the note that the Assyrian could speak Hebrew, but this doubtless through an interpreter. He will speak to the common people, who best know their own interest. We may compare much current political propaganda of our own day. The indelicate language (corrected by the Ḳr.) refers to the privations of the siege, *cf.* 6²⁵. Šanda notes a similar double-phrased crudity of Sennacherib's in the Taylor Prism, col. vi, 20 f. (*KB* 2, 110, *ARA* 2, §254, with identity in one term, *šināti*=Heb. *sînê-hem*). VV.²⁸⁻³⁰. There is no denial of YHWH's deity ; denial of his power as against Assyria is reserved for the climax, vv.³⁴ᶠ·. VV.³¹·³². In persuasive tone an *argumentum ad populum* is offered. They need only to make courteous salutation ; ' salute me ' translates Heb. ' make with me blessing,' the correspondent noun ' peace ' being used of greeting between gentlemen, as at 4²⁹. The proposed deportation did not necessarily involve great hardship ; there might be compared the lot of the *émigrés* from foreign parts into the happy land of Samaria (17²⁴), while later the prosperity of the Jewish exiles in Babylonia was exhibited by their unwillingness to return home, as indicated by the small figure of the party that accompanied Ezra (Ezra 8¹ᶠᶠ·). VV.³³⁻³⁵. The flaunting disrespect for other

³ For the cosmopolitan spread of that language see H. H. Rowley, *The Aramaic of the O.T.* (1929), 1 ff., for its official position in the Persian empire H. H. Schaeder, *Iranische Beiträge I* (1930), and the comprehensive volume by Rosenthal, *Die Aramaistische Forschung*, esp. Section 1, ch. 2, ' Das Reichsaramäische.' Naville has argued in ch. 3 of his *Text of the O.T.* that ' Jewish ' here means the Judæan language in contrast to the rest of Palestine, which, he holds, spoke and wrote only Aramaic. But a local speaker would so speak of his tongue, even as a Scotsman claims that he talks ' Scotch.'

gods than Assyria's own is here finally expressed, and, if
might be right, the envoy spoke plausible truth. With all
its brutality the Assyrian empire is to be credited with one
ideological development, the formulation of a divine-imperial
monocracy, centering in its deity Ashur, even as Rome later
attempted an official religion to offset the religious disunities
of the empire.[4] **34**a. In addition to Hamath (*cf.* 17^{30}), Arpad
is named; for the city and its submission to Assyria in 740
B.C. see Honigman, *RA s.v.* V.^{a} is practically duplicate to
19^{13} (there 'the kings' in place of 'the gods') and is secondary
to it. V.^{b}. *Where are the gods of Sepharwaim, Hena and
Iwwah ? Did they deliver Samaria out of my hand ?*, is most
parenthetically attached, and is nonsense in the connexion.
𝔊^L and an 𝕴 text fill out with an insertion preceding the second
question : *Where are the gods of the land of Samaria ?*, and this
plus has been accepted by most critics since Klostermann (*e.g.,
BH*). But Rahlfs's vigorous objection (*SS* 3, 278), regarding the addition as a 'clever' insertion in condemnation of
heathen Samaritanism to fill out the lacuna, is to be maintained. In fact the whole v. appears to be secondary to 19^{13}.
See Note further. VV.$^{36, 37}$. The silence of the people by
royal order, and the report to the king by his officials with
their clothes rent.

Ch. $19^{1, 2}$. Hezekiah performs the ritual acts of humiliation
in the temple in seeking a divine response, and sends *Eliakim,
Over-the-House, and Shebna the Secretary, and the elders of the
priests, covered with sackcloth, to Isaiah ⌜ben Amos the prophet⌝*
[so the correct order with Is.]. **3.** The message of the king is
introduced with a couplet.

> *A day of distress and reproach : and contumely is this day,*
> *For children have come to the breach : and no strength for*
>   *the birth.*

V.^{4}. Although himself in the temple, the king asks the prayers
of the extra-ecclesiastical prophet ; in the parallel story he
himself " prayed before YHWH " (vv.$^{14ff.}$). *The remnant that*

---

[4] *Cf.* Jastrow, *Religious Belief in Babylonia and Assyria* (1908),
50 ff. ; J. Hehn, *Die biblische u. die babylon. Gottesidee* (1913),
89 ff., a chapter on the attitude of Babylonian religion towards
monotheism.

is left : a frequent post-Exilic term : but it has place here politically, *cf.* the name of Isaiah's son, ' Remnant-shall-return ' (Is. 7³), and actually a most extensive exile is corroborated by Sennacherib's boast in the Taylor Prism (col. iii, 17 ff.) : " 200,150 men, young, old, male and female, horses, mules, asses, camels, oxen and sheep, without number, I brought them out from them, and counted as booty." VV.⁶·⁷. Isaiah's response in the name of YHWH. **6.** *Fear not !*—a characteristic phrase of the Biblical religion from the first book of Scripture (Gen. 15¹) to the last (Rev. 1¹⁷) ; it has occurred above in the mouth of Elijah and Elisha (I. 17¹³, II. 6¹⁶), and appears in Isaiah's address to Ahaz (Is. 7⁴). The Assyrian deputies are scornfully referred to as *the pages* (*na'ărê*, literally ' boys ') *of the king of Assyria*, not with the ranking official title of ' ministers ' (*e.g.*, v.⁵, etc. ; EVV ' servants ' for both words). **7.** *Lo, I am putting a spirit in him, and he will hear a rumour, and he will return to his land, and I will fell him with the sword in his land.* ' Spirit ' here is the uncanny presentiment of evil, hardly personified ; for similar use of the indefinite noun *cf.* Eze. 2², 3¹²·¹⁴, where trr wrongly have ' the spirit.' Personification does appear in the vision, I. 22¹⁹ff.; see Comm. *ad loc.* In the statement of this *rumour* there may be good historical reminiscence of ne family's quarrels that brought about the tyrant's undoing (v.³⁷) ; but, rather, as is argued in the Additional Note, the rumour was that of Tirhakah's advance, v.⁹.⁵

VV.⁸⁻³⁴. A second deputation from Sennacherib demanding surrender, vv.⁸⁻¹³, Hezekiah's prayer in the temple, vv.¹⁴⁻¹⁹, and Isaiah's oracle, vv.²⁰⁻³⁴. VV.⁸·⁹ᵃ. The changed conditions of Sennacherib's Palestinian campaign. **8.** The Rabshakeh's commission proving fruitless, he *returned and found the king of Assyria fighting against Libnah, for he heard that he had broken camp from Lachish.* This city had now been taken (*cf.* 18¹³ff.). **9a.** The siege of Libnah (for which place

⁵ S. Smith, in exposition of the Esarhaddon Chronicle (*Bab. Hist. Inscriptions*, 8 ff., 14), suggests that ' wind,' as he would translate ' spirit ' here is reminiscent of the great storm before which Esarhaddon's army fled in his sixth year (675 B.C.), and so argues for still greater confusion in the present story ; but the word cannot in this connexion mean ' wind.'

cf. 8²²) was, however, interrupted, for the Assyrian *heard concerning Tirhakah king of Ethiopia* [Heb. *Cush*], *to wit, Lo, he has come forth to fight with thee*. Tirhakah (more correctly Thrḳh, with the Egyptian and an Egyptian Aramaic inscription—see Note) was the last of the short-lived Ethiopian (XXVth) Dynasty, attaining the throne 688/7 B.C., himself a negroid, and nephew of his predecessor Shabataka. Years before his elevation to the throne he was in active military service. He fell and disappeared upon Ashurbanipal's conquest of Egypt in 670 B.C.[6] The Biblical item, giving a military reason for Sennacherib's sudden desertion of his campaign, is interestingly paralleled by the abrupt conclusion of col. iii of the Taylor Prism.

9b. In consequence *he again sent envoys to Hezekiah, to the effect——*. **10.** The message is more blasphemous against the Israelite God than in the former case, according to which Hezekiah was the ' deceiver ' (18²⁹) : *Let not thy God in whom thou trustest deceive thee!* It is assumed that he had learned of Isaiah's oracle. **11.** *See, thou thyself hast heard what the kings of Assyria have done to all the lands in devastating them, and wilt thou be delivered?* There follow, after the satirical inquiry, **12a.** *Did there deliver them the gods of the nations which my fathers destroyed?*, two lists of such conquered city-states : (1) **12b.** *Gozan and Haran and Reseph and the Bnê-Eden, those in Telassar*. For the places see Kraeling, *Aram and Israel*, Dussaud, *TH* 464. For Gozan *cf.* 17⁶ ; an expedition thither is cited in the Eponym list for 809 B.C. For Haran, once home of the Abramids (Gen. 11²⁷ff·), the ancient ' Road-City ' (Akk.), see BDD ; Olmstead, *HA* 36 ff. ; von Oppenheim, *Der Tell Halaf*, ch. 2 ; it had belonged to Assyria since *ca.* 1100 B.C. Reseph, Akk. Raṣappa, appears in the Eponym list for the year 804 ; it is the modern Raṣafa, NE of Palmyra (*cf.* Dussaud, pp. 253, etc.). Bnê-Eden (*n.b.* the survival of the clan-name) is abbreviation of Bnê-Beth-Eden, and the place identified with the Beth-Eden of Am. 1⁵, the Eden mentioned along with Haran in Eze. 27²³, and the Akk. Bit-Adini, the district S of Haran on the Euphrates. In the ' Political Ostracon ' published by Lidzbarski (*Altaram.*

---

[6] See Petrie, *HE* 3, 294 ff. ; Breasted, *HE* 554 ff. ; Alt, *Israel u. Aegypten*, 80 f. ; Meyer, *GA* 3, 47 ff.

Urkunden aus Assur, no. 1) there is given a list of transportations similar to the one here, and including Beth-Eden: " Prisoners brought forth Tiglath-pileser out of Bet-Awukkan, and prisoners brought forth Ululai (Shalmaneser) out of Bet-Eden, and prisoners brought forth Sargon out of Dur-Sin." See Dussaud, pp. 463 f., Forrer, *RA* 1, 136, and for Borsippa, the notable capital of the ancient district, E. Unger, *RA* 1, 402 ff. ' Telassar ' can be analyzed into ' Tell-Ashur,' or the like ; see *CIOT* 2, 12, and Kraeling, pp. 63 ff., who notes the ancient name Telesaura for the far-northerly Mar'ash (*cf.* Dussaud, *l.c.*). (2) **13.** *Where is the king of Hamath, and the king of Arpad?* The latter city, modern Tell-Erfād, NW of Aleppo, submitted to Tiglath-pileser in 740 B.C. The sequel, *and a king to the city of Sepharwaim, Hena and Iwwah*, is a gloss from 17^{31}, with interpolation of an unknown Hena, and a different vocalization for Iwwah, *vs.* Awwites there.

VV.$^{14\text{-}19}$. Hezekiah's receipt of the Assyrian demand, and his supplication to his God in the temple. **14.** *And Hezekiah received the letter from the hand of the envoys and read it:* i.e., written despatches (the Heb. word is plural) brought by the delegation of v.^{9}. For such usual imperial formality *cf.* a letter of Esarhaddon to Baalu, king of Tyre, which has been fragmentarily preserved, imposing a treaty with awful curses (*ARA* 2, §§587–91). Hezekiah acts as the priest of his people, as did Solomon before him (see on I. $8^{14\text{ff.}}$), and ritually *went up to the house of* YHWH, *and spread it* (the letter) out before YHWH ; the letter was doubtless on parchment, and written in Aramaic or Hebrew, since the king *read it*. **15.** He makes his prayer ; *cf.* J. Begrich, *Der Psalm des Hiskia* (1926). The king is represented as in the immediate presence of the ark ; there was a similar occasion, when David went in, and sat before YHWH, and prayed his prayer (2 Sam. $7^{18\text{ff.}}$). Hezekiah's credal confession adds to that put in David's mouth (*ib.* v.^{28}) : *Thou alone art the God* (the absolute Deity) *for all the kingdoms of the earth. Thou hast made the heavens and the earth.* The confession is followed by the prayer, vv.$^{16\text{-}19}$. Assyria herself by the destruction of the hand-made idols of the peoples has proved the emptiness of heathenism. *Cf.* the challenging use of the divine title ' Living God,' Josh. 3^{10}, 1 Sam. $17^{26,\ 36}$. The deliverance of his people will be YHWH's triumph over

all his boasted rivals, the world *will know that thou,* Y*HWH,*
art God alone; cf. Ex. 9^{16}, Is. 43$^{10\text{ff.}}$, etc.

VV.$^{20-34}$. Isaiah's unbidden oracle to Hezekiah in divine
answer to his prayer. Here as in the parallel account, v.^{1},
the king expected divine advice. For royal oracles in the
Babylonian-Assyrian religion see Weber, *Die Literatur d. Babylonier u. Assyrer*, ch. 12; Jastrow, *Die Rel. Bab. u. Ass.*,
ch. 19, esp. pp. 151 ff.; Zimmern, *Bab. Hymnen u. Gebete*
(1905, 1911), 1, 8; 2, 20 f.; for Egypt, Erman and Ranke,
Ägypten, 467 ff.; and for Biblical correspondences Gunkel,
Einl. in d. Psalmen, 136 ff. Caution must be expressed against
pushing the correspondences too far; in this ch. the 'oracle'
is given by a non-ecclesiastical prophet, without divinatory
rites. *Cf.* the immediate divine responses to private persons
in the sanctuary: to Hannah at Shiloh, 1 Sam. 1; to the
saint in his perplexity, Ps. 73^{17}; to Paul by trance and vision
in the temple, Acts 22$^{17\text{ff.}}$.

VV.$^{21\text{b}-28}$. An ode of derision.

21*b.* *Taunted thee, mocked thee hath she: the Virgin daughter*
Sion,
After thee shaken the head: the Daughter Jerusalem.

22 *Whom hast thou reviled and blasphemed: and against*
whom raised the cry,
And lifted thine eyes aloft? :—Against Israel's Holy
One!

23. *By thy envoys thou hast taunted* Y*HWH* [so MSS; 𝕳
Lord], *and said:*

With the mass of my chariotry **I** *: . . .*
Have gone up to mountain tops: the recesses of Lebanon,

And cut down the height of its cedars: the choice of its
firs,
And come to its farthest lodge: the forest of its garden-
land.

24. *It is I who have dug and drunk: waters strange,*
I who dry up with the soles of my feet: all the Nile-
arms of Egypt.

25. *Hast thou not heard ? : From of old I wrought It,*
In ancient days shaped It : now I have brought It on,

That thou be to crash into ruinous heaps : fortified cities,
26. *With their citizens short of hand : dismayed and confounded,*

Become as herb of the field : and green of the grass,
Growth of the roof-tops : and blasting before standing corn.

Thy standing up (**27**) *and thy sitting : and thy going and coming I know.*
28. *Because thou hast raged against me : and thy tumult is in mine ears,*

So will I set my hook in thy nostrils : and my bridle in thy lips,
And turn thee back by the road : whereon thou camest.

The above translation represents the Heb. text, with exception of a word prefixed to v.^{27}, assumed to have fallen out through haplography, and with elision of a duplicate at end of v.^{27}, *and thy raging against me.* V.^{23} is introduced with a prose *loquitur*. The second half-line of the same v. is evidently missing ; it is supplied by 𝔊^L with 'I have wrought might.' For critical details see Notes. For metrical reconstructions and special studies see Haupt, *SBOT*, p. 278 ; W. Popper, *Parallelism in Isaiah, Ch.* 11–35 *and* 37, 22–35 (1923) ; Budde in *JTS* 35 (1934), 307 ff. ; T. J. Meek, 'The Metrical Study of II Kings 19, 20–28,' *Crozer Quarterly Review*, 1941, 126 ff.

The ode is rough in quality, but strong and individual. It is similar in dramatic construction to Isaiah's taunt against Assyria (Is. 10$^{5\text{ff.}}$), but goes its own way in the theme of the divine fate which has given the Assyrian his temporary license, *ad majorem gloriam Dei.* For the 'shaping,' v.^{25}, used primarily of the artist's creation, *cf.* Gen. 2$^{7\text{ff.}}$, then of the artist's creative idea and purpose, *cf.* Jer. 18^{11} (where EVV have 'devise'). The mysterious *it* of the purpose is paralleled in Is. 46^{11}, Jer. 33^2 ; also see Note. The ode is doubtless contemporary to the brutal Assyrian power, and with pertinent satire mocks its pride. V.²³ is echo of Assyrian inscriptions. *Cf.* Sargon's Cylinder Inscription (lines 10 ff.; *KB* 2, 40 f., *ARA* 2, §118—the latter followed here) : " (Sargon, mighty hero) who opened up mighty mountain regions whose passes were difficult and countless, and who spied out their trails ; who advanced over inaccessible paths, (in) steep and terrifying places " ; this is followed by a list of his conquests, including " all of the desert as far as the River of Egypt " ; and Sennacherib in the Taylor Prism (col. i, lines 66 ff. ; *KB* 2, 86 f., *ARA* 2, §236) : " In the midst of the high mountains I rode on horseback, where the terrain was difficult, and had my chariot drawn up with ropes ; where it became too steep, I clambered up on foot like the wild-ox " ; and Ashurbanipal, in the Rassam Cylinder (col. viii, 82 ff. ; *KB* 2, 221 f. ; *ARA* 2, §823) : " (The armies) marched over distant trails, climbed high mountains, plunged through stretches of dense forests." A few lines later on this inscription tells how " my soldiers dug for water (to quench) their thirst." The boastful reference in v.²⁴ to 'drying up the Nile-arms' (the Egyptian word for the Delta channels is used) is actually stated by the Heb. with the imperfect tense and is not represented as an historical event by which the document may be dated. For illustration of the barbarous treatment of captives presented in v.²⁸ (with which *cf.* the symbolic expression, Is. 30²⁸) the relief of Esarhaddon's inscription at Senjirli depicts Tirhakah of Egypt (with his negroid features) and Baalu, king of Tyre, each bridled with a ring in his nose, and the attached cords in the conqueror's hand (F. von Luschan, *Ausgrabungen in Sendschirli*, pl. i ; *cf.* p. 17) ; and according to 2 Ch. 33¹¹ the later Manasseh was 'taken with hooks' to Babylon.

VV.²⁹⁻³⁴. A further oracle of Isaiah's : the long desolation of the land an omen of deliverance. It is a literary question whether the passage is prose or poetry ; the former view is adopted by Cheyne (on Is.), Kittel (Comm., *BH*), the latter by Stade, Šanda, Popper. There exists in the passage a balancing of parts, in general tetrameter form, but as compared with the ode above subject-matter and form are eminently prosaic. There may be compared the prose supplements added often to prophetic odes, *e.g.*, at end of Is. 6 and 7

29. *And this the sign to thee*: i.e., a sign whose ultimate fulfilment will prove the truth of the prediction; cf. Is. $7^{10\text{ff.}}$, and another Isaianic story, Is. 20. *Eating this year the after-growth, and in the second year the re-growth, and in the third year sow and reap and plant vineyards and eat their fruit!* The comparative abundance of the *after-growth* in a year when there is no seeding of the fields is illustrated by the law for the sabbatic year, Lev. 25. The word translated *re-growth* is unique, a term for the automatic growth in the second year; see Dalman, *A. u. S.*, 2, 203 f., giving an Arabic equivalent for the term. **30.** *And the salvage of the house of Judah which is left shall again root downwards and bear fruit upwards;* **31.** *for from Jerusalem shall go forth a remnant, and a salvage from Mount Sion. The jealousy of YHWH ⌈Sebaoth⌉* [plus with Ḳr., Is., VSS] *shall effect this*. There follows an explicit amplification of v.^{28}: **32.** *Therefore thus has spoken YHWH concerning the king of Assyria: He shall not come to this city, nor shoot there an arrow, nor confront it with shield, nor cast mound against it.* **33.** *By the road by which he comes* [Is. *has come*] *shall he return, and to this city he shall not come—oracle of YHWH*. **34.** *And I will shield this city to save it, for my sake and my servant David's sake*. This alleged prognostication that Sennacherib would not come to the city nor attack it is confirmed by the silence of his cylinder inscription. For *David's sake*, cf. I. $11^{12.\ 13}$.

35. *And it came to pass in that night that the Angel of YHWH went forth and smote in the camp of Assyria* 185,000. *And when they* (indefinite plural) *got up in the morning, lo they* (the Assyrians) *were all dead corpses*. Is., Ch. om. *it came to pass in that night*. The time expression is indefinite = ' on such and such a night'; cf. Gen. $19^{33.\ 35}$, Jud. 3^{30}, 4^{23}, etc. Correspondingly the Herodotean legend given below puts the disaster in 'one night.' Ch. also exceptionally moderates the high figure: "there were destroyed every man of valour and captain and prince." The v. relates back to 18^{17}, with its note of 'the great army' accompanying the first Assyrian delegation in demand of surrender. The legendary character of the statement has been recognized since J. D. Michaelis (see Thenius for early discussion). There is the parallel Egyptian legend, based on ultimate historical fact without doubt, cited by Herodotus, ii, 141 (repeated by Jos.) how Sennacherib with a great army of Arabians and Assyrians marched against Egypt. The forces of Sethos, the Egyptian priest-king, would not march with him. In his distress he had a night-vision of his god Hephæstos, who reassured him, "Myself will send you champions." The enemy came, and "one night a multitude of field-mice swarmed over the Assyrian camp and devoured their quivers," etc., so that "the enemy fled unarmed, and many fell." For the mouse as ancient symbol of the plague, and doubtless known as its carrier, cf. 1 Sam. $5^{6ff.}$, $6^{1ff.}$. Apollo Smintheus ($\sigma\mu\iota\nu\theta$os, 'mouse') was god of the plague. For full text and translation of Herodotus see Rogers, *CP* 346 f., giving a large bibliography, as does also Kittel, *GVI* 2, 436. Procopius records the great plague that broke out at Pelusium on the Egyptian border in Justinian's reign; see Gibbon's extensive note on plagues, *Decline and Fall of the Roman Empire*, ch. 43, towards end. It is out of place, as *e.g.* with Keil, to regard the Herodotean legend as a fabulous development of the Biblical one; the two stories are a capital instance of the various development of popular legend based on historic fact. For the overwhelming suddenness of the stroke of a plague *cf.* the story of that in David's day, 2 Sam. $24^{15ff.}$.

36. *And Sennacherib king of Assyria broke camp and went off, and he returned and dwelt in Nineveh.* **37.** *And it came to pass, as he was worshipping in the house of Nisrok his god, Adrammelek and Sareser* [Ḳr., VSS, Is. plus *his sons*; *cf.* Ch.] *smote him with the sword. And they escaped into the land of Ararat. And Esarhaddon his son reigned in his stead.* Until modern Assyriology this was the oldest record of Sennacherib's violent end.[7] The fact is briefly and independently reported by Berossos, *via* Alexander Polyhistor and Eusebius: "He remained in power 18 years, and died by the hand of his son Ardumuzanus in an uprising," along with further information

---

[7] A useful summary of texts from that quarter is given by Jirku, *AKAT* 180 ff. For special discussions see P. Schnabel, *Berossos*, 142 ff., with full critical treatment; Hall in *CAH* 3, 278, and Cook, *ib.*, 389 ff.; B. Meissner, 'Neue Nachrichten über die Ermordung Sanheribs u. die Nachfolge Esarhaddons,' *Sb.*, Berlin Academy, 1932, 252 ff.; E. G. Kraeling, 'The Death of Sennacherib,' *JAOS* 53 (1933), 335 ff.; H. Hirschberg, *Studien zur Geschichte Esarhaddons*, Teil I (n. d.).

from Abydenus, who gives a confused account of the succession including Sennacherib, and concludes with the statement that, " Having subdued the Babylonians, he set up his son Asordanius (Esarhaddon) as king, withdrawing himself and proceeding to Assyria " (Eus., *Chronica*, i, 27, 25-29). Rogers gives the full pertinent text with translation (*CP* 347 f.). The name of Adrammelek has been preserved by Eusebius : " After him there ruled Nergilus, who was cut off by his son Adramelus. Adramelus was in his turn killed by Axerdis (Esarhaddon)." F. Hitzig suggested that Nergilus is to be combined with Biblical Sar'eṣer as Nergal-sar-uṣur ; see *CIOT* 2, 15 f., with full bibliographical note. But an historical personage is obtained by Rost's identification (cited by Winckler and Haupt) with Nabū-sar-uṣur, name of the eponym for the year of the assassination, 682 B.C. (*CP* 225 ; *ARA* 2, p. 438), which high official would then have been one of the conspirators. As for the murder the Babylonian Chronicle records that " Sennacherib king of Assyria was killed by his son " (*KB* 2, 280 ; *CP* 215). *Cf.* Nabonidus's inscription published by L. Messerschmidt (*MVG* 1896, 1, col. i, 35 ff.) : " The king of Assyria, who during Marduk's wrath had worked destruction of the land, was struck down with a weapon by the son, the issue of his inwards " (for the remarkable equivalence of the last phrase with Heb. of 2 Ch. 32^{21} see Note). These records speak only of one son. However in the composite document presented by Luckenbill out of various prisms (*ARA* 2, §§500 ff.) there are references to ' my brothers,' who had wrought their deeds of violence (*e.g.*, §§501, 506). Also the inscription published by Meissner (noted above) contains several references to the wicked rebels, ' my brothers.' He also pertinently suggests that the Nergilus and Adramelus of Eusebius were brothers, not father and son. Names of several of Sennacherib's sons are recorded, but none is identified with one of the murderers. Now, as noted above in the text, Ki. names two murderers, Ch., followed here by Ḳrê and VSS, has introduced the appositive ' his sons ' after their names. Rost has suggested correction of text to ' Adramelek his son and Sareser ' (see Haupt. *ad loc.*, *cf. BH*) ; but there is no right to correct the text of an imperfect tradition, which is of singular merit in preserving the names of the assassins. It is quite possible that the Chronicler followed a Babylonian tradition. For the names of the murderers see Note. As for the place of the murder, put by our record at Nineveh, there is dispute. The Rassam cylinder of Ashurbanipal (col. iv, 70 ff.) has an obscure reference to his grandfather Sennacherib at first sight suggesting his death at Babylon ; see the varying translations in *KB* 2, 193, *ARA* 2, §795, A. Ungnad, *ZA* 1924, 50 f., and Meyer's extensive note (*GA* 3, 66), supporting location of the death at Nineveh. And Meissner (p. 261) finds it ' vielleicht wahrscheinlich ' that the event occurred there. Winckler (*KAT* 85) and Šanda argue that the scene of the murder was Babylon, since Nisrok-Marduk, ' his god,' was worshipped there, not at Nineveh. But according to the Nabonidus inscription cited above, the ruthless Assyrian conqueror, " took the hand of Marduk, and brought him to Assyria " (col. i, 14 ff.) ; *cf.* also cols. viii, *seq.*, concerning the bringing home of the exiled gods of Babylon, the restoration of Marduk's temple, etc. With allowance of the identification of Nisrok with Marduk as most likely, there may be an incorrectness here, and to relieve the difficulty other suggestions have been offered (see Note). Yet Esarhaddon frequently styles himself ' worshipper of Nabū and Marduk.' That the murderers and their large rebellious faction fled to ' Ararat ' is supported by the Assyrian texts. In his first year Esarhaddon pursued the rebels into Ḥanigalbat (*KB* 2, 140 ff. ; *ARA* 2, §504), *i.e.*, the country of Malatia-Milid, W of Urartu-Ararat, which is the region of Lake Van. Polyhistor, in Eusebius, offers the parallel that Esarhaddon pursued the rebel army " to Byzantium and there shut it up."

Ch. 18. **1.** שלש : Gr. e₂, Jos.=' 4th.'—חזקיה : 4 MSS, Ch., חזקיהו, to be expected in the first occurrence, and so below, v.⁹, etc., but with variant spellings in MSS and edd. ; the full form on a contemporary Jerusalem ostracon, Albr., *JPOS* 1926, 88 ff., Diringer, *IAE*, and so Sennacherib's vocalization, ' Hazakiau.'— **2.** אבי : caritative of אביה, and so 3 MSS here=Ch., and Gr. x y, Jos., Αβια ; B A Αβου may represent Αβιου=orig. אביהו (St.). The element ' father ' is freq. in *nn. f.*, see Noth, *IP* 15 ; it also occurs in S. Arab. names. The name occurs at I. 14³¹, ' Abiyam,' as masc.—זכריה : Ch., זכריהו.—**4.** וכתת . . . וכרת . . . ושבר . . . הסיר : for the consecution see Note, 14⁷.—האשרה : Ch., האשרים, and so the pl. in VSS ; but the sing. also at 17¹⁶, 21³, and to be retained here ; *cf.* the foll. definite ' Nehushtan.'—וכתת נחש : 4 MSS כ' את נ'

of which 𝔐, and 𝔊=נחש ואת, are reduced forms.—ויקרא : impers. sing., as at I. 9¹³, and so properly JV ; likewise with the pl. some VSS, *e.g.*, 𝔊ᴸ.—נחשתן : corrupt forms in Grr., *e.g.*, B ; some MSS = 𝔐. For *-ân* as determinative ending (*cf.* S. Arab.) see D. Nielsen, *Ras Šamra Mythologie*, 17 ff., Montg., *JAOS* 58 (1938), 131. The one name involves both ' serpent ' and ' brass,' the root of the former being variation of *lḥš*, ' to hiss ' ; see Note, 17¹⁷.—**5.** [ב]כל : OGrr. om., reducing the eulogy.—ואשר היו לפניו : an evident gloss, *ad majorem gloriam ; per contra*, *n.b.* 23²⁵.—**6.** [כר] לא : supported by Gr. MSS exc. one, *vs.* ולא of many MSS=𝔖ᴴ *et al.*—יהוה : B† om.—**7.** והיה יהוה : it is easy to emend, with St., to "ויהי, or "וי היה, but the clause is subordinate to the foll. sentence ; *cf.* Dr., *Tenses*, §133, and his note on Sam. I, 1¹².—**8.** ואת : 2 MSS deR., ועד=Grr., 𝔖ᴴ, preferred by St., but the like phrase at 15¹⁶.— גבוליה : Grr., exc. z, as sing.—**9.** ויהי : 𝔖 𝔙 om.—**10.** וילכדה=𝔊ᴸ MSS, 𝔗 ; other VSS=וילכדה, and so 10 MSS deR., *Suppl.*—**11.** ישראל : Grr., 𝔖ᴴ ' Samaria,' preferred by St. ; but 𝔐=17⁶.—וינהם : *i.e.*, as from root ' to lead,' and so repetitive ; read וינהם=VSS, EVV, and *cf.* Gen. 2¹⁵.—**13.** סנחריב : *cf.* the Elephantine Aḥiḳar papp. with סנהאריב (also 'ש), giving fuller presentation of the Akk. *Sin-aḫē-eriba* ; Gr. e₂ Σενναχηρειβ, Jos., Σεναχηριβος ; other Grr., -ειμ.—כל : Ch., Grr. om., Jos. has ; *vs.* St., the omission is criticism of the absolute expression ; but note Senn.'s item ' 46 cities.'— **14.** וישלח : Gr. and Lat. plus, ' messengers,' is epexegetical.— שלשים : Jos., 𝔊ᴸ ' 300.'—**16.** קצץ : for the vocalization see GK §52, 1, and for the mng. *cf.* 16¹⁷.—אמנות : generally interpreted from the participial form as ' supporters,' *cf.* EVV ; Grr., εστηριγ- μενα ; 𝔖ᴵᴵ ' posts ' ; 𝔗 𝔖 ' thresholds ' ; 𝔙 ' lamminæ ' ; Ehrl gratuitously replaces with מגנות, referring to I. 10¹⁷, where however מגנים (but מגנות, 2 Ch. 23⁹).—**17.** רב כריס : the title also at Jer. 39³, ¹³ ; כריס appears as high military title in Judah, 25¹⁹, while an inferior officer appears to be designated by it at I. 22⁹. For the present title see Montg., on Dan. 1³ff.—רב שקה (so *BH*, other edd. as one word) : Schrader (*CIOT*) argued for equivalence with alleged *rab-šaḳ*, ' chief captain ' ; Bezold (*Glossar*, 252) renders primarily with ' Obermundschenk,' as proposed by Zimmern, and so Šanda, Procksch ; *cf.* Pharaoh's butler, משקה, Gen. 40¹.—[ב]היל=Is. ; Aramaizing for חיל, read by many MSS (deR., *Suppl.*).—ויעלו ויבאו ירושלם ויעלו ויבאו : absent in Is. ; VSS, exc. 𝔗, om. the second half, a clumsy repetition ; Heb. MSS variously om. one or the other (see deR.). With excision of ' Tartan ' and ' Rab-saris ' the pls. here and in v.¹⁸, are to be reduced to the sing., with Is.—בתעלת : 𝔊 εν τω υδραγωγω, to which 𝔊ᴸ pref. εν τη αναβασει=Sym., Quinta.—**18.** ויקראו אל המלך : Is. om., but the incident is dramatically in place.—אלהם : 𝔊 (=A 𝔖ᴴ) as אליו=Is.—אליקים : the name on a Judæan bulla and seal, *IAE* 126, 247.—בן חלקיהו : 𝔊ᴸ 𝔏 om. ; the name on a Judæan seal, J. L. Starkey, *PEQ* 1936, Oct., pl. vi.—שבנה : so edd. here, but many MSS שבנא, as inf., v.³⁷, 19² = Is., the correct spelling. It is a frequent Palestinian name, also, as שבן, שבניה, שבניהו, appearing on seals from Lachish, Tell en-Nasbeh and elsewhere; see *IAE* 169, 214, *PEQ* 1941, 46, Albr., *AJA* 1936, 159; the latter has well interpreted the first element of the name as 'return, pray'; *cf*, Note, 16¹.—אָסְ־הּ: the name on a seal, *IAE* 169.—**19.** [המלך] הגדול := Grr., but 𝔖ᴴ ⁕.—**20.** אָמְרָץ: Is., exc. 18 MSS, incorrectly אמרתי (preferred by Deliztsch, Dillmann); 𝔊 ειπας; 𝔊ᴸ συ και πας Ιουδα, built up, as Burn. notes, from συ ειπας.—עתה = Is.; 2 MSS ועתה = 𝔊ᴸ A *al.*; similar text variations below.—**21.** עתה: 𝔊 𝔏 𝔖 Is. om.—לך: the ethical dative, as at v.²⁴, is ignored by Is.—הקנה הרצוץ: Marti, on Is., argues that the figure of the broken reed was taken from Eze. 29⁶ᶠ·; but the figure of the reed was common (*e.g.*, Mt. 11⁷).—**22.** תאמרון: coll. pl.; Is. as sing. = VSS, exc. 𝔗 and Theodoret; for such indifferent use *cf.* cases in v.²⁷.—בירושלם: Is. om.—**23.** התערב = Is., 6 Gr. MSS, 𝔈 𝔗; *al.* as pl.—את: את מלך אשור is redundant; Is. the ungrammatical הם' 'א את; the phrase to be omitted, or 'ט 'א to be read; *BH* proposes here and at v.³¹ to read simply המלך.—**24.** פחת אחד עבדי: the clumsy construct construction is defended by Burn.; but rather, with St., 'פ has been introduced as an antiquarian note.—**25.** המקום הזה: Is., 'this land,' by conformation with the foll. phrase.—**26.** בן הלקיהו: Is., 𝔏 om., prob. arbitrarily. ארמית, יהורית: for the former word see Montg. on Dan. 2⁴. The two forms, 'aramaice,' 'iudaice,' are Aramaic; for the widespread use of the adverbial form see Duval, *Traité de grammaire syriaque*, 281.—**27.** אליהם: Is. avoids; אליו is demanded.—העל: read with Is. האל; the like change demanded in [האנשים] על, where Is. = Ki.—חריהם: 3 MSS, Is., חראיהם (see Note, 6²⁵); Ḳr. צוֹאָתָם.—שיניהם Kt.: Lexx. point the noun as שֵׁן, but שִׁין is preferable, *cf.* Akk. *šināti* (pl. as here). Note now the Ugaritic root *ṯyn* (Gordon, *Ugar. Handbook*, 3, 2154). Ḳr. כִּי רַגְלֵיהֶם: *cf.* similar suppression of indelicate terms in 6²⁵. *N.b.* the remarkable rewriting in Ch.—**28.** וידבר: 6 MSS, Is., 𝔙 om.— דבר [המלך]: 3 MSS את ד', 4 MSS דברי את = Is., Grr. 𝔙; for omission of את *cf.* GK §117, a.—**29.** מירו: absent in Is.; *ca.* 30 MSSᵒʳ מידי (see deR.'s long note); of Grr. B†, and 𝔗 = 𝔚; other VSS = מְיָדִי, which is required, the vocable being legalistic.—**30.** תנתן את העיר: for the construction see GK §121, a; 30 MSS, Is. om. את. —**31.** מלך אשור: Is. again with the ungrammatical הם' 'א.—**32.** [ארץ] לחם [וכרמים]: at first sight the combination appears odd, and was so felt by 𝔗, translating with חלקין, as though for Heb. חלקים, 'fields,' which Meinh., Šanda adopt; but such a text corruption is most unlikely, and the combination of 'bread and wine' is quite in place.—חזקיהו . . . ארץ 3⁰: absent in Is., which adds 'Hezekiah' as subj. of יסית, *inf.*; the later Jews at least knew that Babylonia was not a land of the olive.—וית יצהר: 2 MSS ויצהר '᾽ (= 𝔙); 1 MS om. וית, and so St.—כי: Is., פן, an intentional change (St.).—**34.** אלהי *bis*: Grr. (exc. 𝔊ᴸ), 𝔖ᴴ as sing.—הגיע ועוה: the nouns, lacking here in 𝔊 𝔊ᴸ and in Is., appear to have been introduced from 19¹³ where Grr. and Is. read them. 𝔗 developed the nouns into verbal expression, playing on the roots: " Has he not dispersed and carried them captive ? " —כי: B†=Is., וכי.—מירי שמרון את הצילו כי: as noted above Klost. rewrites the prefixed plus of OGrr. with 'ש ארץ אלהי ואיה, generally accepted by scholars, e.g., Kit., Burn., St., Šanda, BH, Eissf. For Rahlfs's criticism see SS 3, 278 ; Orlinsky's reply (*JQR* 30 [1939], 46) on score of his objection to ' the land of (Samaria) ' is valid. But the v. is an accretion, which lent itself to further manipulation by Lucian.—**35.** הארצות: 1 MS, Is.+האלה—unnecessary (St.).— ארצם את הצילו אשר: 𝔊ᴸ with sing. verb, improving the ungrammatical τις . . . οι of 𝔊.—**36.** והחרישו: read 'וַיֵּ with Is.—העם: Grr., Is. om., and so Orlinsky, ib., 47; but ' the people ' has definite political sense.—**37.** *N.b.* the formal repetition of the full titulars.

Ch. 19. **1.** Duhm regards the v. as intruded conformation with vv.¹⁴ᶠᶠ·, but note the appointment of priests in the commission.— **2.** After ' Shebna the scribe ' Gr. MS b' (HP 19) inserts κ. τον Σαιτην κ. τ. Σουμαιησουμαι κ. τ. Μακραπην τ. γεροντα, which Lagarde adopted in his Lucianic text, for which Rahlfs (*SS* 3, 25) criticizes his lack of judgment; for attempts at explanation see Burn., Haupt.—אמוץ בן הנביא ישעיהו: Is. correctly 'הנ' א בן 'יש'=𝔊ᴸ here ; the patronymic need not be secondary, *vs.* St. ; the title may be, since it fails in the rest of the ch. The father's name occurs on a seal (*IAE* 235).—**3.** ל[לְ]דָה: for the form see GK §69, m; 𝔖 𝔓 understand לְדָי, with Hos. 13¹³ in mind.—**4.** כל: 71 MSS, 𝔊ᴸ MS A, Is. om., חי [להרף] אלהים :=v.¹⁶; otherwise חיים 'א; 𝔗 euphemistically, ' the people of God.'—**8.** לבנה: Grr., Λοβνα, Λομνα, cases of phonetic dissimilation; *cf.* Grr. 8²².—**9.** תרהקה אל: for the prep. 3 MSS, Ḳr.ᵒʳ, Is. correctly על. For the name Hex. Θαρακα is the closest Gr. transcription. *Thrḳ* is demanded, and so תהרקא appears in an Eg. tomb inscr. (followed with (?) כושיא די מלכא, also naming Necho and Psammatichos), published by Giron in *Ancient Egypt*, pt. 2 (1923), 38 ff.; *cf.* Akk. *Tarḳu*; the nearest Gr. rendering is that of Strabo, Τεαρκων (i, 61).—וישב: MS L properly pref. a *pisḳah*; Is. erroneously, וישמע; *cf.* St.—**10.** לאמר . . . כה: 𝔊 (𝔖ᴴ ※) om., by parablepsis. acc. to Burn.; St. accepts the omission as original, arguing that in this case also a letter was sent; but this may have been the ground for the Gr. elision; diplomatic dispatches always have their oral presentation. —**11.** להחרימם: the root should be changed to חרב, ' to devastate,' as in v.¹⁷, with Joüon, Šanda; the Assyrians did not put conquered lands under the ban; see GB for cases of confusion of the two roots. The contrary suggestion to revise the verb in v.¹⁷ to הרם is amiss; see St. The suffix is grammatically incorrect, but *ad sensum*.—**12.** שהתו: 4 MSS, Is., השח(י)תו.—הלאשר: Is., תלשר; Hex. texts alone transliterate correctly. All the proper names are generally abused by the Grr. *N.b.* the use of preceding אשר like Akk. *ša*.—**13.** ומלך לעיר ספרוים הגע ועיה : the three city-names are secondary, and then prefixed with a gloss = ' a king to each city.' For לעיר Dussaud (*TH* 236) suggests rdg. לעש (of the Zakar inscr.), and is followed by Procksch on Is. See further Rosenthal's extensive note in his *Aram. Forschung*, 9, n. 3.—**14.** ויקראם . . . הספרים ויפרשהו . . . : VSS variously correct to consistent sings. or pls., as do most modern critics ; the pl., also at 20¹², was collective, then approached the notion of the sing. ; *cf.* Lat. ' litteræ.'—**15.** ויתפלל ח' לפני י" : 𝔊 (𝔖ᴴ ※) om.—to avoid ascription of such a sacred function to the king ?—יהוה : Is.+צבאות=𝔊ᴸ 𝔖.—**16.** דברי : Is. pref. כל =𝔗 𝔖 𝔙.—חֹלִ֑י: read with 6 MSS, Is., חֳלִי =VSS.— לחרף : 𝔗 the same variation as at v.⁴.—**17.** ואת ארצם : 𝔊 om. (𝔊ᴸ Hex., ' and all their land '), and so St., but his interpretation of the preceding verb here and in v.¹¹ appears inconsistent.—**18.** ונתנו : read וְנָתוֹן with Is.—אלהים: Is. om.—**20.** אל [סנחרב] : read על with MSSᵒʳ.—שמעתי : Is. om.—**21.** בתולת בת ציון : for the accumulated constructs see GK §130, e.—**22.** ועל מי הרימות קול : St. and Haupt variously attempt to ease the overburdened metre. —**23.** מלאכיך : Is., עבדיך=𝔙.—אדני : 14 MSS the original יהוה, and so MSS in Is.—ברכב: read בְּרֹב with very many MSS, Ḳr., and all VSS.—אני : 𝔊ᴸ+εποιησα δυναμιν=חיל עשיתי, as proposed by Graetz, accepted by St., *al*., and by Haupt with rearrangement of the whole metrical v. ; against the addition is the general unreliability of 𝔊ᴸ. *N.b.* the emphatic ego here and in v.²⁴.—ואחרב, ואבואה : VSS, exc. 𝔗, as of past time, and so critics generally correct to וָאָ֫, וָאָ֑ ; *cf.* ואחרב, v.²⁴, where the same change is proposed ; but the lively variation of pf. and impf. may not be ignored.—מבצור : as in the doubtful passage, 3¹⁹ ; Is., מִבְצָר, and so 6 MSS deR. here, which is to be accepted.—מלון [קצה] : 1 MS, Is., מרום=𝔖 𝔙 ; Grr. (exc. B, μεσον), μερος=𝔖ᴴ ; for the poetic phrase *cf.* Giesebrecht's correction of מלון ארחים, Jer. 9¹, to מ' אהרון.—**24.** קרתי : B†= εψυξα=ℭ, ' refreshed myself,' as from root קרר ; *al*. altered this into εφυλαξα=𝔖ᴴ, which also notes Aq.'s rendering with ' I cut.' *N.b.* the wild rendering of the v. in Gr. of Is.—ורים : Is. om. ; 𝔊 𝔙 properly, ἀλλότρια, ' alienae.'—כל יארי מצור : 𝔊ᴸ ignores כל (as exaggeration ?) ; for 'מ, 𝔊 𝔊ᴴ περιοχης, ' circumference '; 𝔊ᴸ συνεχεις, ' continuous ' ; 𝔖ᴴ 'uššānā', ' strength ' ; Sym., ' dense (rivers) ' ; 𝔗 𝔖 ' deep (rivers) ' ; 𝔙 ' (aquas) clausas ' ; AV ' besieged places.' The identification with ' Egypt ' first appears in Kimchi, noting that ' some interpreters ' have so understood it, and among modern VSS was first accepted by GV, followed by RVV JV. The same phrase appears in Is. 19⁶, as יארי מצרים, *cf.* Am. 8⁸, 9⁵, while Mic. 7¹² geographically contrasts Ashur and Masor. The latter word is paronomasia on the place-name (*cf.* בצל and בלל, Gen. 11⁹), Egypt possessing its fortified front against Asia since antiquity ; see Breasted, *HE* 447.—**25.** קדם . . . הלא : 𝔊 ℭ (𝔖ᴴ ※) om.—אתה : the fem. here and in the foll. pronom. suffixes as indefinite neuter is paralleled in Ex. 10[11], Is. 22[11], 30[8], Jer. 33[2] (on which see Graf in his Comm.); see GK §105, p, and cf. Note, 24[3].—[ויצרתיה]: Grr., Aq., 𝔖 𝔙 om., and so modern critics generally; but the consecution is that of parallelism, not of sequence, and 𝔐 may stand.—עתה: 1 MS ויתה:=𝔊[L] 𝔖 𝔙.—וּתְהִי: the tr. above follows AV RV; RV[Am] "that it should be thine"; JV, "yea, it is done," after the Grr.=וַתְּהִי. These trr. indicate the difficulty of interpretation. Poole notes Maius, citing scholars interpreting as of 2d pers., and so, e.g., Then.; Cheyne (on Is.), Burn.: "that thou becamest"; St., Šanda elide as 'metrically redundant.' Popper would rewrite. The interpretation as of 3d pers. might be kept with the preceding indefinite 'it' as subject, cf. a similar case, 24[3]. The pointing of $f\ddot{\imath}$ is to be kept as jussive of purpose; cf. Dr., Tenses, §63, and the Arabic use of fa with subjunctive, cf. Wright, Arab. Gram., 2, §15 (d).—לַהֲשׁוֹת: a remarkable punctuation; read with Is. לְהַשְׁאוֹת.— Inversion of the foll. accusatives is expected. BH suggests omission of נעים, 'metri causa.'—**26.** חתו ויבשו: Is., ובשו 'ח; either form is possible.—ירק: Dalman, A.u.S., 2, 345, explains as 'wild, edible vegetables.'—שרפה: Is., שדמה; the latter elsewhere='plantation,' exc. at 23[4], where the word is used as here in the sense of 'burning, blasting.'—לפני קמה: 'before standing corn,' as at Ex. 22[5], etc.; VSS treat it as a verb. For proposed corrections see Burn., Then., Haupt; e.g., לפני קֵמָה (Haupt after Orelli), לפני קָדִים 'before the east wind' (Then., Kit., Šanda, Popper). Quinta (cited by 𝔖[H]) has 'before thy standing up,' which suggested to Wellh. (Comp., 292, n. 1) the rdg. לְפְנֵי קָמְךָ, to be prefixed to v.[27], with the resultant parallelism of 'standing up' and 'sitting down,' a correction largely accepted, e.g., by Burn., Cheyne, St., Eissf. There remains the problem of the vacancy at end of v.[26], which St. leaves empty, while Haupt retains the text. Šanda, retaining that passage, avoids repetition of almost identical phrases by merely inserting at beginning of v.[27] קָמְךָ, which correction is given in tr. above.— **27.** ואת התרנוך אלי: the phrase has its duplicate immediately following in v.[28]; St. keeps the text here (eliding ואת), elides the duplicate; Šanda, BH, Eissf. make the reverse revision, which is preferable.—אלי: 3 MSS עלי, which is demanded, and so in v.[28].—**28.** שאננך: VSS='thy haughtiness,' RVV 'arrogancy,' marg., 'careless ease': AV JV 'thy tumult' (cf. FV)=שְׁאוֹנֵךְ, and this correction of text has been generally accepted since Benz. —עלה: Budde, St., Procksch cancel for metre's sake, Popper transfers to prec. hemistich.—**29.** ספיח: cf. Lev. 25[5, 11].—שחיש: Is., סחיש; the word a unicum.—זרעו וקצרו ונטעו: 𝔊 Hex. as nouns, hence possibility of original inf. abs. forms; but n.b. foll. ואכלו, where indeed Is. Kt. has ואכול, but this in conformation with אכול near the beginning of v.—**31.** יהוה: Is.+צבאות, which Ḳr. demands here, and so all VSS, exc. Gr. g, 𝔈.—**32.** [מלך] אל: על is again demanded.—**33.** יבא: 15 MSS Ken., deR., Is., בָא=VSS, EVV, and this appears to be demanded by the sequel, v.[35]; but the poem is independent of the prose sequel, and Senn.'s coming is regarded as in the future, cf. v.[32].—**34.** [העיר] אל: read על with MSS, Is.—**34.** להושיעה: OGrr. om., 𝕊[H] ⁛; it does not appear in the loose repetition, 20[6]; Haupt's metrical argument for its rejection is not of force in the tetrameter line.—**35.** ויהי בלילה ההוא: Is. om.; B 𝕲[L] κ. εγενετο νυκτος (al., κ. εγ. εως νυκτος); the Gr.=Engl. ' of a night '; see Comm., and cf. Orlinsky's extensive note, *JQR* 30 (1939), 43.—שמונים: 34 MSS, Is. plus conj.=𝕋.— **36.** ויסע וילך: as the subj. should have followed the first verb, St. elides these verbs (cf. Ch.); 𝕊 relieves the trouble with the pl. But with the common lack of explicitness as to subject the writer may have inserted it supplementarily.—וַיָּשָׁב: omission in 𝕲[L] is no authority for correction, vs. St., who then reads below וַיָּשָׁב נִינְוֵה, " and he returned to Nineveh." All these verbs are original in the text, and are not to be elided.—**37.** נסרך: identification with מרדך was made by Cheyne in *SBOT Is*, 114 f., Winckler (*KAT* 85), al.; the intentional alteration is similar to that in the names ' Shadrach<Marduk,' and ' Abed-nego<Abed-Nebo,' Dan. 1[7]. Other identifications have been proposed: Nusku, Nin-rag (see Cheyne, Haupt, Procksch), Nimurtu (Ungnad, *OLz*., 1917, 359). Legend may well have identified the god of the temple with Marduk; the particular Ass. deities are not known to the Canon.—אדרמלך: as a divine name at 17[31] (but see Comm. for correction to אדרמלך); Johns, Winckler (*KAT* 84, n. 2), Šanda suggest 'ארדם, ' Arad-malik,' cft. ' Arad-ellil,' name of one of Senn.'s sons; but Eusebius's ' Adramelus ' supports 𝕳.—שראצר: the name as element appears in *n. pr.*, Bethel-sar-'eṣer, Zech. 7[2] (see GB 792b). This name has plus בניו in Ḳr., 46 MSS Kt. (Ken., deR.), Is.=VSS. Ch. for ' his sons ' has מִיצָאֵי מֵעָיו, ' some offsprings of his bowels,' with which cf. the phrase in the Nabonidus cylinder cited in Comm. for the murderer, *māru ṣit libbišu*, repeating a common idiom.—ארכט: Grr., ' Ararat,' 𝕊[H] ' Armenia '=Gr. of Is.; 𝕋 ' Ḳardu,' cf. Gr. ' Kordyene '—' Kurd-land.'—אסרחדן: MSS and edd. vary in writing the name here and in Ezr. 4[2] as one word (so Ginsb.), or two (so L in *BH*); see Bär's note. The name now appears more exactly in Elephantine papp., אסרחאדן; it is rendered with ' Sacherdonos ' in Tob. 1[21].

Ch. 20[1-19]. Hezekiah's illness, and the attendant marvels and oracles effected by the prophet Isaiah. || Is. 38, 39; cf. 2 Ch. 32[24-26]. **1.** Upon the king's evidently mortal illness Isaiah announces to him by the word of YHWH his coming decease, and bids him: *Order thy household, i.e.,* make thy testament. **2.** The king *turned his face to the wall :* for private communion with his God (the same phrase in another connexion, I. 21[4]); 𝕋 interprets ' to the wall of the temple,' and so

II. 20¹⁻²¹

Kimchi. **3.** He recalls his merits before God. The *perfect heart* (so EVV; JV *whole heart*) may well be translated 'devoted heart,' the root of the adjective being that of the Muslim word *Islam*. *And Hezekiah wept with a great weeping:* according to Jos., the Talmud (Then., p. xxxii), and some later comm. (see Poole) the chief object of his grief was that he had no heir, Manasseh reaching the throne *ætat.* 12 years, and so born subsequently to this event. VV.⁴⁻⁸. There occurs the divine change of mind, for " the prayer of a righteous man availeth much " (Jam. 5¹⁶). **4.** *And it came to pass, Isaiah had not gone out to* [=GV EVV; FV JV *out of*] *the middle court* [with Ḳr.; Kt. *city*]——: for the variations of text and construction see Note. The middle court would be the complex of palace and temple; *cf.* I. 7⁸, and see Smith, *Jerusalem*, 2, 256 ff. The Heb. allows either construction for the object of 'going out'; in any case the point is the immediacy of the divine oracle; Is. omits this local item. —*and the word of* YHWH *came to him, to wit:* **5.** *Return, and say to Hezekiah, the prince of my people* [with use of the older title, which Is. om.] *: Thus has spoken* YHWH, *the God of David thy father : I have heard thy prayer, seen thy tears. Lo, I am healing thee. On the third day* (the day after the morrow) *thou shalt go up to the house of* YHWH. Hezekiah's affliction with an ulcer had debarred him from the temple. The reminiscence of David, repeated in v.⁶, is characteristic of Ki. (*e.g.*, I. 3⁶), is absent in Is. **6a.** *And I will add to thy days fifteen years:* for the figure see Comm. on 18¹³. **6b.** The promise of the rescue of the king and *this city from the palm of the king of Assyria*, with repetition of 19³¹, is obviously secondary. There is hardly reason, with Stade, to regard vv.⁵ᵇ·⁶ as metrical. **7.** *And Isaiah said : Take* [pl. verb] *a cake of figs ; and they took and applied it to the boil ; and he recovered.* According to the story Isaiah is in the line of Elisha (4⁸ᶠᶠ·, 5); Procksch *cft.* the medical allusions in Is., *e.g.*, 1⁵ᶠ·, 3¹⁷. For discussion of the disease see Ebstein, *Die Medizin im A.T.*, 99 ff. The Heb. word for *cake* appears in a veterinarian recipe for a horse-plaster in an Ugaritic text, 'a plaster of dried raisins' (see Note). In Is. as sequel to the long metrical " Writing of Hezekiah king of Judah, when he had been sick, and was recovered of his sickness," there follows the brief statement of Isaiah's recipe, an intruded note indeed! Ch. om. all reference to the medication.

VV.⁸⁻¹¹. The marvel of the sun-dial for Hezekiah's reassurance. This intruding story presents a later legend in the Isaianic cycle. The many-sided Isaiah appears here as a miracle-worker, like the earlier prophets, or, according to one school of interpretation, as an astronomer. The passage is indeed a belated postscript to the earlier statement that Hezekiah ' recovered.' Is. contains a much abbreviated form, leaving out the alternatives offered to the king in vv.⁹ᶠᶠ·. Ch., v.²⁴, reports only that Hezekiah was sick, prayed to YHWH, who " spoke to him, and gave him a sign." **8.** Hezekiah inquires of Isaiah : *Is there not a sign that YHWH will heal me, and I shall go upon the third day into the house of YHWH ?* **9.** *And Isaiah said : This is the sign for thee from YHWH, that YHWH will do this thing that he has spoken : Shall the shadow go on ten degrees, or shall it turn back ten degrees ?* **10.** *And Hezekiah said : It is an easy thing for the shadow to extend ten degrees ; not so, the shadow shall turn backwards ten degrees.* **11.** *And the prophet Isaiah called on YHWH, and he turned back the shadow in the degrees* (=dial) . . . *backwards ten degrees.* The four untranslated words mean *by which it went down in the degrees of Ahaz,* but the subject of the fem. verb. for ' went down ' cannot be the masc. noun for ' shadow '; see Note, arguing for interpolation from Is. We have here the only reference in the Bible to a horologe. Herodotus asserts that dial and gnomon came from Babylonia (ii, 109) ; the reference to Ahaz's instrument might connect with that king's other innovations from Assyria (16¹⁰ᶠᶠ·). For the Babylonian instrument see Meissner, *Bab. u. Ass.*, 2, 359 ; for the Egyptian, E. J. Pilcher, ' Portable Sundial from Gezer,' *QS* 1923, 85 ff., with full bibliography, and presenting a small portable sun-dial of Egyptian make of the first half of the 15th century B.C. found at Gezer ; *cf.* Gressmann, *ATB* 2, 39, and Abb. 110. For recent discoveries of such sun-dials may be noted the presentations by A. E. Mader, *JPOS* 1929, 122 ff. ; H. Ingholt, *Berytus,* 3 (1936), 112 ff. ; R. N. and M. L. Myall, *Sundials* (1938), give an admirable survey of the subject. For the *degrees* (the word is the same as *stairs,* 9¹³) Jos. thinks of the stairs of Hezekiah's palace, upon which the sun's rays could have moved as upon a rough-and-ready sun-dial. 𝕲 uses a technical term, אבן שעיא, 'hour-stone,' followed by 𝔙 with 'horologium.' An upright pillar for the gnomon surrounded with a dial (like the use of the Egyptian obelisk brought to Rome by Augustus) would have served the purpose. For the word 'step/stairs' thus technically used, *cf*. Lat. 'gradus,' Engl., 'degrees.' The king is pictured as viewing the afternoon phenomenon of the sun's shadow stretching out ; the parallel in Ch. states that " the sun went down." For presentation of exegetical interpretations of this marvel, see Keil, and Dillmann on Is. ; defenders of the alleged phenomenon have tried to connect it with known eclipses, so Bosanquet, for Jan. 11, 689 B.C., Mahler, for June 17, 679 ; *cf*. Thenius, *ad loc*. ; Rawlinson, *Comm*. ; Pinches, *DB* 4, 627 f. Delitzsch, on Is., holds that there was no change in the sun, only a miraculous optical illusion for Hezekiah's eyes. But to the naïve mind the claimed miracle was not impossible, *cf*. Josh. $10^{12\text{ff}}$.

VV.$^{12-19}$. The congratulatory embassy from the king of Babylon, Hezekiah's grandiose reception of it, and Isaiah's rebuke of him with dire prophecy. The section is a notable example of the construction of many of these prophetic stories ; it is based on an historic fact, while issuing in an apocryphal sequel. For Berodach-baladan, as the name is spelt here by current phonetic variation, Merodach-baladan of Is., the pugnacious opponent of Assyria, Marduk-apal-iddina, see the Histories cited in Additional Note, n. 1 ; as generally accepted, this diplomatic embassy may be placed *ca*. 705 B.C. The story gives a glimpse into the widespread diplomacy of the rebel movement. The king's father's name is given as Baladan ; in an inscription of Tiglath-pileser's the father is named Yakin (*ARA* I, §794) ; the name here may be an assumed patronymic to connect the king with his famous predecessor of the same name, towards 1500 B.C. ; *cf*. R. P. Dougherty, *The Sealand of Ancient Arabia* (1932), 44 f. **12.** The Babylonian king courteously *sent a letter and a present to Hezekiah, for he had heard that Hezekiah was sick.* **13.** *And Hezekiah rejoiced over them* [*i.e.*, the envoys ; so with Is. ; 𝔐 here *listened to them*], *and he showed them all* [Is. om.] *his store house, the silver and the gold and the spices and the oil of aroma and his* *armoury, and all that was found in his treasures,* with the extravagant sequel that he showed them everything *in his house and in all his dominion.* For the oil of aroma (*cf.* EVV) see Note; for the spices *cf.* the similar element of Solomon's wealth according to I. 10^{25}. The items well illustrate the Arabian trade, in which Hezekiah shared with profit; *cf.* the tradition of his wealth in 2 Ch. 32$^{27\text{ff.}}$. On Merodach-baladan's concern in that trade see Dougherty, as cited above. The two widely separated kingdoms circumvented Assyria's control by direct intercourse through the Arabian deserts. **14-16.** The courteous inquiry and response between Isaiah and his king concerning this diplomatic adventure is followed by a *word of* YHWH, that (**17**) *all that is in thy house and that thy fathers have stored up unto this day shall be carried to Babylon, there shall not be left a thing*—YHWH *has spoken.* **18.** *And of thy sons who shall issue from thee* [𝔥+repetitive *whom thou shalt beget*] *there shall be taken, and they shall become eunuchs* [with VSS, except 𝔗 *officers*=JV] *in the palace of the king of Babylon.* The prophet is correctly exhibited as opponent of such international alliances. The prediction is apocryphal, but the composition may not be dated much later than 597 B.C., when Jehoiachin and the royal family were carried off to Babylon, as there is no reference to the general exile. **19.** *And Hezekiah said to Isaiah: Good is the word of* YHWH *that thou hast spoken. And he said: Is it not* [sic 𝔥], *if peace and security be in my days?* Two independent responses of the king are here recorded, the first one of resignation, the second of self-congratulation. A tradition of OGr. omitted v.^{b}, and so since Duhm it has been generally cancelled as a late addition. But why such an obscure interpolation? The interrogative particle may be understood to mean, *If only peace and security be in my days!* The word translated *security* (EVV *truth*) refers to the divine faithfulness; *cf.* Ps. 132^{11}, etc. For such postponement of calamity for merit's sake *cf.* 22$^{18\text{ff.}}$, I. 21 $^{27\text{ff.}}$.

VV.$^{20.\ 21}$. The end of Hezekiah's reign, and summary. *Cf.* 2 Ch. 32$^{32.\ 33}$. **20.** *And the rest of the acts of Hezekiah, and all his might, and how he made the pool and the conduit, and brought the water into the city, are they not written in the book of the chronicles of the kings of Judah?* The royal *might* in this case is illustrated by 18$^{7.\ 8}$. For the excavation of the Siloam tunnel bringing the water of the Gihon spring, the 'Ain Sitti Maryam, on the east side of David's City to the inner pool of Siloam, cf. Ch. v.[30] : " (He) stopped the upper source of the water of Gihon and graded [so the Akk. correspondent of the root] it down to the west of David's City." The conduit was named Shîlôaḥ (root = 'mission,' 'emission') ; the name applied originally to the older conduit that ran around the Ophel to a pool to the south, appearing in Is. 7³. The reservoir at its outlet is called the Pool of Shelaḥ in Neh. 3[15], in the Gr. as Siloam, as also in the N.T. Ben Sira has a reminiscence of this construction, that it was worked with brass (48[17], see the Heb. text). The contemporary monumental record is the unique Siloam inscription, describing the remarkable feat of the operation of the tunnel from opposite ends with successful junction, so that " the water flowed from the source [the same word as in Ch.] to the pool [the word as here] for 1200 cubits [approximately 1775 ft.]." For this famous inscription see Driver, *Samuel*, pp. viii *seq.*, Cooke, *NSI* no 2 ; Lidzb., *HNE* 439 ; and *AT* 9 ; in tr. Barton, *AB* 476, *et al.* ; and for full discussion, Smith, *Jerusalem*, 1, 101 ff. ; Vincent, *Jérusalem Antique*, 1, 134 ff. For a review of Palestinian hydrography see Abel, *GP* 1, ch. 5. For similar operations cf. the deep tunnel (29 m. in depth) to a spring underlying Gezer (see R. A. S. Macalister, *Gezer*, 1, 256 ff., and pl. 52, cf. Gressmann, *ATB* 2, 177, and Abb. 635), and a like tunnel to an underground spring bored by workers from opposite ends at Megiddo (Breasted, *The Oriental Institute*, 1933, 255 ff.). There may be compared the Moabite Mesha's interest in such waterworks (ll. 22 ff. of his inscription). For a similar contemporary operation of great magnitude is to be noted the ' Sennacherib Canal,' as the royal author called it, a 30-mile long conduit to Nineveh (*ARA* 2, §§330–43), the remains of which great work were uncovered and announced by H. Frankfort (*ILN*, Aug. 1934, 294 ff. with 8 plates) ; see now T. Jacobsen and Seton Lloyd, *Sennacherib's Aqueduct at Jerwan, Or. Inst. Publ.*, 24 (1935). In connexion with Is. 22[9ff.], recording the scurry for the fortification of Jerusalem against an attacking army, with report of attempted water-works, it would appear that this new Siloam tunnel was subsequent to the year 701.

21. For fuller variants as to the burial, *e.g.*, Ch., see Note.

1. צו לביתך : the verb is used in sense of the parallel Arabic root, *wṣy*, e.g., *waṣīyatun*, 'testament.'—**2.** וַיָּשָׁב : Is.+חזקיהו=𝕲 𝔖 𝔄.—פניו את : B A, 𝔖^H text, om. ; St. follows suit with change of the prec. verb to וַיִּסֹּב ; but see Comm.—**3.** את אשר [התהלכתי] : for the adverbial character see examples given by C. Gaenssle on the rel. particle as ' a vague medium of relation,' *AJSL* 31, 46 ff.— לבב : Is., לב, but the phrase לבב שלם also elsewhere.—**4.** יצא : as followed with acc. of direction *cf.* Gen. 27³, etc., with acc. of object, Gen. 44⁴, etc.—העיר : 14 MSS, Ḳr., חצר=VSS, to be accepted ; for full treatment of the latter word see Orlinsky, *JAOS* 59 (1939), 22 ff. ; *cf. JQR* 30 (1939), 34 ff. For use of the article in התיכנה ה' *cf.* I. 7⁸. Is. om. this local note, along with a briefer text for vv.⁴⁻⁶.—**6.** ואת העיר הזאת : the phrase is *de trop*, is one layer in the stratification of the v., terminating in the citation of 19³⁴.—**7.** Ki. and Is. vary : ישאו ‖ קחו (Grr., 𝕮^W 𝔖 here=יקחו) ; ויקחו : 𝕲, Is. om. ; וישימו ‖ וימרחו (the latter a technical term, ' to plaster ') ; וַיְחִי ‖ וַיֶּחִי (=𝕲 𝔖 here).—דבלת האנים : *cf.* the Ugaritic parallel, *dblt ytnt wṣmqm ytnm*, ' an old plaster and old raisins,' Gordon, *Ugar. Handbook*, 2, 55 : 28.—**8.** מה אות : "what sign (is there) ? " ; *cf.* מה בצע, Gen. 37²⁶ ; but quite possibly מה = " (is there) not ? " *cf.* Arab. *mā*, ' not,' and see Lexx. for corresponding use in Heb. Haupt also notes the Arab. use of the construct with a foll. full sentence, for which see Wright, *Arab. Gr.*, 2, §78.— **9.** לך : Grr. om., exc. 𝕲^L.—הָלַךְ : the VSS as though interrog. future=הֲיֵלֵךְ , and so Rashi, Kimchi, modern VSS ; Jos. follows Is.'s omission of alternatives, and renders with " the sun has advanced, shall it return ? " Modern comm. generally make that correction (*cf. BH*) ; St. is dubious, holding that the verb " may reflect an older form of the story," along with suggested corrections from Is. ; Meinhold om. the passage, and tries to reconstruct on basis of Is. But the text can be retained by rdg. הָלֹךְ, the abs. inf. being used interrogatively.—**11.** אשר ירדה במעלות אחז : the clause appears along with a complicated expansion in Is., where appears at the end, מעלות אשר ירדה. But the clause here is absent in 𝕲 (B *al.*), and is a gloss from Is., with neglect of the necessary fem. subject to the verb. Meinhold continues rewriting on the basis of Is.—**12.** בְּרֹאדַךְ : MSS מראדך=Is. The *b* represents actual Bab. variety of pronunciation ; *cf.* foll. ' Baladan '=' Apal-iddina,' and the process *m>u* (Delitzsch, *Ass. Gram.*, §49, a) ; see Brock., *GVG* 1, §85, at length for labial dissimilation. Accordingly correction should not be made (as with St., *BH*, but see Haupt's note). The vocalization is abusive, prob. a diminutive form ; see Note on צעירה, 8²¹.—ספרים : the inconcinnity of the foll. עליהו induced the addition in 𝕲 of Is., ' and ambassadors ' ; deceived by this Duhm, *al.*, would correct to סריסים (' eunuchs '), which St. condemns.—מנחה : the Gr. renderings as at 8⁸.—חזקיהו 2⁰ ; Is., ויהק (=𝔖, 𝕲^L combining both rdgs.) ; St. rejoins that the root is never used in the sense required here.—

ADDITIONAL NOTE TO II. 18¹³–20¹⁹

13. וישמע : a few MSS, Is., וישמח =VSS (𝕮 ' received,' ' welcomed '), which is to be accepted.—כל : very many MSS, Ken., deR., 𝔖 𝔄 𝖁, Is. om.—נכחת [בית] : an Akkadism ; see GB.—שמן הטוב : Is., 'הש' הט, preferred here by St. ; but see Rhodokanakis, *Studien*, 4 f., identifying *ṭôb* with Arab. *ṭaib*, ' aroma,' and so nominal here, as at Jer. 6²⁰, Song 7¹⁰, etc.—**14.** אמרו : MS 93+לך=𝕮ᵂ 𝔖 𝔄 ; similarly below many MSS+אלי to באו =VSS, Is.—*N.b.* variation of aspect between אמרו and יבאו, like variation appearing in Ugaritic ; see *RSMT* 25.—**16.** יהוה : Is.+צבאות =𝕲ᴸ παντοκρατορος, y Σαβαωθ.—**17.** הנה ימים באים =Am. 8¹¹, 9¹³, etc. ; Grr., exc. B A+ ' said the Lord,' with reminiscence of such passages.—**18.** ממך : in this connexion unique, and St. would correct to מִמְּעֶיךָ (*cf.* Gen. 15⁴) ; but the vocable was ancient enough to induce the foll. gloss, אשר תוליד.—יקח : Grr., 𝕮 as יִקַּח ; Ḳr., some MSS, Is., יִקָּחוּ ; St. rightly retains Kt. as יִקָּח.—סריסים : *cf.* Note on Rabsaris, 18¹⁷ ; the orig. mng. is to be retained here with VSS, exc. 𝕮=JV.—**19.** ויאמר הלא אם שלום ואמת יהיה בימי : of Grr. B om (𝔖ᴴ ※), A alone tr. literally, μη ουν εαν, κ. τ. λ. (*cf.* 𝔖ᴴ) ; otherwise the VSS, exc. 𝕮, as precative, *e.g.*, 𝖁, " sit pax et veritas in diebus meis." Is. simplifies : 'ויאמר כי יהיה וג.—**21.** עם אבותיו : 𝕲ᴸ+" and was buried with his fathers in David's city " ; 𝕲ᴴ " and was buried in D.'s city." Ch. has an original and doubtless true tradition that " they buried him in the ascent of the tombs of David's sons."

ADDITIONAL NOTE ON EXTRACTS FROM CERTAIN ISAIANIC MEMOIRS AND ON THE RELATIONS OF HEZEKIAH AND SENNACHERIB, II. 18¹³–20¹⁹

In addition to the parallels in Ch., which goes its own way in deletion of diverse materials, these cc. appear in duplicate in Is. 37–39, the latter omitting 18¹⁴⁻¹⁶ (as not pertinent to the Isaiah story, and probably as derogatory to the fame of the king and the temple), and adding Hezekiah's prayer upon his illness, 38⁹⁻²⁰. The text of Is. is in briefer form, as against amplifications in Ki. ; *cf.* 38⁴⁻⁶ with Ki. 20⁴⁻⁶ ; 38⁷⁻⁹ with 20⁹⁻¹¹. The curt summary in Is. 38²¹⁻ ²², has been supplementarily added, and appears now to be universally regarded as secondary, and so, *e.g.*, by Kuenen (*Einl.*, 2, 84 ff., with full review of earlier literature) Stade (*Akad. Reden*, 214 ff.), Driver (*Int.*, 226 f.), Eissfeldt (*Einl.*, 369 ff.). With these duplicate texts, and still more with the complex of historical problems in view of the external history, no section of Ki. has produced more critical debate.[1]

---

[1] Most convenient for study of the parallel texts, Hebrew and Greek is Vanutelli's apparatus ; translation of the Hebrew texts is similarly presented by Klost., Kittel, Crockett, Kent. For specific studies of the parallel texts of Ki. and Is. (the MS variations are presented by Bär in his Appendix of ' Diversitates,' pp. 155 ff.) see the fundamental work of Gesenius, *Der Prophet Jesaja* (1820–21) ; Stade in *SBOT* ;

The narrative divides on the surface into five distinct sections. A. 18¹³⁻¹⁶ is an original historical notice of Hezekiah's capitulation to Sennacherib by payment of a heavy indemnity, a very remarkable domestic record of such a humiliation. B. 18¹⁷–19⁷. The demand of the Rab-shakeh, accompanied with a large army, for the surrender of Jerusalem is followed by the prophet Isaiah's comforting prediction upon Hezekiah's appeal to him. C. 19⁸⁻³⁷. Following the Rab-shakeh's return to him, being now engaged at Libnah, Sennacherib, disturbed

---

Cheyne on Is. in *SBOT*; Kuenen, *Einl.*, §45; Dr., *Int.*, 226 f. (a compact statement); Meinhold, *Die Jesaiaerzählungen* (1898—the most extensive monograph on the subject with full text-critical as well as historical discussion); J. Ziegler, *Untersuchungen zur Septuaginta d. Buches Isaias* (1934), also the elaborate corpus in his *Isaias* (1939) in the Göttingen *Septuaginta*; Orlinsky, 'The Kings-Isaiah Recensions of the Hezekiah Story,' Part I, *JQR* 30 (1939), 33 ff., with notable studies of the character and quantum of the Gr. texts and of particular critical questions; for inner textual variations see Sperber's monograph on *Hebrew . . . in Parallel Transmission*. The commentaries on Is., a book far more fully commented upon than Ki., are to be consulted; see Dr., p. 214, and the listing in Eissf., *Einl.*, 341; there is to be noted in this connexion the commentary of O. Procksch, *Jesaia I* (1930). For the historical background see the continuations of the Histories cited in Comm., n. 1, to ch. 17 (p. 464); in particular may be cited Kittel, *GVI* 1, 3, Beilage I, pp. 430–9. The following historical monographs are to be noted: J. V. Prašek, 'Sanheribs Feldzüge gegen Juda,' *MVG* 1903, pt. 4; Olmstead, 'Western Asia in the Reign of Sennacherib,' *Proc. Am. Hist. Assn.*, 1909, 94 ff.; Dhorme, *RB* 7 (1910), 501 ff. (on the Ass. campaigns); Rogers, 'Sennacherib and Judah,' *ZAW*, Beih. 27 (1914), 317 ff. (with extensive discussion of the development of historical criticism, this material summarized in his *CP* 336 ff.); L. L. Honor, *Sennacherib's Invasion of Palestine*, Columbia Univ. thesis, 1926; Wiener, 'Isaiah and the Siege of Jerusalem,' *JSOR* 1927, 195 ff. (with extensive reconstructions); W. Rudolph, 'Sanherib in Palästina,' *Pjb.*, 25 (1929), 59 ff.; C. Boutflower, *The Book of Isaiah I–XXXIX, in the Light of the Ass. Monuments*, 1930. For the illumination of the history from the book of Isaiah see also BDD *s.v.*; W. R. Smith, *The Prophets of Israel* (1882); G. A. Smith, *The Book of Isaiah* I (1927); Robinson, *Decline and Fall*, 73 ff., 138 ff.; James, *Personalities of the O.T.*, ch. 14. In some of the studies of text and history much labour has been lost in attempts at rewriting. *E.g.*, Klost. would read 'Sargon' for 'Sennacherib,' 18¹³, 'Ashdod' for 'Lachish,' v.¹⁴, 'Solomon' for 'Hezekiah,' v.¹⁶; Cheyne replaces 'Lachish' with 'Eshcol.' Meinh. om. 18²² (as not pertinent to the oration), and following Duhm, 18³²ᵇ⁻³⁵, also the phrase 'to reproach the Living God,' 19⁴, and rewrites the 'joint' in 19⁸·⁹. But it is in general impossible to rewrite such historical records, and in particular ancient rhetoric, in csnh arbitrary fashion.

by the report of Tirhakah's advance, sends to Hezekiah, demanding complete surrender; the latter presents the letter before YHWH; on divine motion Isaiah recited a defiant ode against Assyria (vv.$^{20-28}$), followed with more prosaic oracles (vv.$^{29-34}$); there ensues in that night the wholesale destruction of the great Assyrian army, followed by Sennacherib's return home and his murder by his sons. D. 20$^{1-11}$. Hezekiah's grievous illness is healed by Isaiah with a medical application, the prophet further reassuring him with the miracle of the sun-dial. E. 20$^{12-19}$. Isaiah's word of judgment upon Hezekiah for his courteous reception of the Babylonian embassy, foretelling the doom of his house at Babylon. A more critical division is to be made at the joint between B and C. Here, as Stade has argued, followed, *e.g.*, by Kittel, Skinner, Eissfeldt, and by Meinhold, Marti and Procksch on Isaiah, there is continuance of the theme of the 'rumour' which Sennacherib was to hear, to be followed by his return to his own land, where he is to 'fall by the sword' (v.^{7}), a rumour that is realized in the news he now 'hears' of Tirhakah's advance against him; the predicted doom appears in vv.$^{35-37}$, according to which the king of Assyria broke camp and returned to Nineveh, where he was murdered by his sons. There appears no motivation between Tirhakah's advance (v.^{9a}) and the demand for surrender of Jerusalem (v.$^{9bff.}$). That is, B, as thus extended and so to be understood below, comprises 18^{17}–19^{9a}, and its sequel is 19$^{36-37}$; and accordingly C, beginning with v.^{9b} ("And he sent ambassadors again to Hezekiah," etc.) is duplicate of B.

CC. 18–20 thus present three immediate contacts with the Assyrian empire, and an indirect contact in the reference to the rebel Merodachbaladan's embassy. Of these sections A is uniquely corroborated by an Assyrian inscription, even to the *minutiæ* of figures. B, despite lack of integration with the preceding story of the capitulation, has corroboration of 'the stout force' that accompanied the Rab-shakeh in Sennacherib's record of his blockade of Jerusalem, his statement recording Hezekiah's capitulation and the heavy ransom he paid, but without surrender. The list of Hezekiah's diplomatic commission of three officers of state for treating with the Assyrian includes the names of Hilkiah, Over-the-House, and Shebna, the Scribe, but in relations not dependent upon the Isaianic oracles referring to them (Is. 22$^{15ff.}$), according to which Shebna was to have disappeared in disgrace. The conclusion of B (19^{37}) is a datum of prime historical interest with its specific details of Sennacherib's murder. C duplicates B with the story of a further demand for surrender of Jerusalem, with only the king and the prophet as actors; it concludes (v.^{35}) with the legend of the miraculous destruction of the Assyrian army in one night, *en masse*, which has its traditional parallel in the Egyptian legend preserved by Herodotus of the plague of mice which upset Sennacherib's army.[2]

---

[2] The figure of '185,000' as smitten has its parallel in the Bab. tradition of Naram-sin's army of '180,000' which he lost (Güterbock, *ZA* 1938, 55).

D gives a personal story of Hezekiah and Isaiah ; the reference to the king of Assyria (20⁶) is doubtless an addition. E, while again a personal story of king and prophet, is of historical value and interest in presenting the widespread revolt against Assyria engineered by the persistent and crafty Merodach-baladan.

Criticism of these narratives is indeed confused by the interlocking of affairs of now approved accuracy with stories of a prophet, involving two cases of historically absurd statement, the one of the divine slaughter of 185,000 men in one night, the other of the recession of the solar shadow on the dial, as also Isaiah's alleged prediction of the Babylonian exile. Literary criticism is further complicated by the problem of the source of the material, evidently a collection of Memoirs of Isaiah, with oracles attributed to him, of the genuineness of which we may well be sceptical in view of the increasing accretion of attributions to the Prophets, as witnessed in the Prophetical books of the canon. We are here confronted for the first time with such memoirs of a canonical prophet, to be paralleled only by those of Jeremiah a century later. But the *genre* is not new ; it follows the literary tradition that had grown up in full form about the figures of Elijah and Elisha and other Sons of the Prophets ; similarly there had assembled about Isaiah a school of followers whom he specifically calls his ' disciples ' (Is. 8¹⁶). We may well assume that the literary richness which had marked the North wandered South to find a home and there express itself. Chronological order is not to be expected in such a series of stories, any more than in the editing of the Prophets. The humiliation of Hezekiah (A) is naturally made to precede the stories of his deliverance ; Merodach-baladan's mission is narrated at the end, as associated with Hezekiah's sickness unto death and the prophet's evil omen for the future of the dynasty. Similarly we may note that while Ki. records as one of ' acts of Hezekiah ' his water-works at Jerusalem, Ch. (II. 32¹⁻⁸) puts the ' stopping of the fountains ' of the city before the Assyrian approach. Accordingly the order of events is subject to revision. A should follow B, for sake of co-ordination with the Assyrian record. Kittel (*GVI* 2, 435) would preserve the order A B, suggesting that B followed a breach of faith on Sennacherib's part, *cft*. Is. 33¹ᶠᶠ·.[3]

In particular as to the relation of B and C—whether as parallel or independent stories—critical opinion remains divided. For the latter view there is the argument which would find historical background for the appearance of Tirhakah, who did not succeed to the Egyptian throne until 688-687 B.C., and for the asserted sequel at end of ch. 19 of Sennacherib's end. An explanation was first proposed by G. Rawlinson (according to Rogers), to wit, that Sennacherib campaigned in his latter

---

[3] The co-ordination and historical evaluation of the several narratives still remain an object of dispute. Honor presents (pp. xiii, xiv) six different hypotheses that have been offered by critics ; Stade uses six different colours for his critical presentation of the text.

ADDITIONAL NOTE TO II. 18¹³–20¹⁹

years against Tirhakah and that the second demand for Jerusalem's surrender was connected with this campaign. This argument is based upon denial of Tirhakah's importance before his accession; yet cf. Breasted, Alt, Meyer, as cited in connexion with 19⁹ᵃ. The view under discussion has been accepted by a large number of scholars, e.g., by Dhorme (pp. 516 ff.), Prašek, Jeremias, *ATLAO* 530; Šanda argues for progressive history in B and C, and S. Smith (pp. 13 ff.) and Robinson (*Decline and Fall*, 85 f.) allow or prefer the possibility of two events. On the other hand, Meinhold, Alt, Olmstead, Meyer, deny the historical independence of the two narratives. Stade treats the two narratives with equal scepticism, 'beide sind legendarisch' (*Akad. Reden*, 219). More light may yet be thrown upon the notable original data concerning Sennacherib's departure from Lachish to Libnah and the news of the advance of Tirhakah—a note which may be out of place. As we are dealing with a prophetic story-book based upon traditional acts and words of the prophet, it is far simpler to regard the two stories as variant traditions of Isaiah's part in the historical drama. Of the oracles only the ode, 19²¹⁻²⁸, can claim literary affinity to Isaiah, and so, e.g., Eissfeldt adjudges it as 'probably genuine' (*Einl.*, 371), and Šanda claims it as genuine. Whether the two following oracles, vv.²⁹⁻³¹, ³²⁻³⁴, rather prosaic pieces, have such affinity is dubious, although Isaianic origin is accepted, e.g., by Kittel (Comm.), Šanda, Procksch, Eissfeldt; the notion of a future 'sign' (v.²⁹) has its parallel in Is. 7¹⁴. [4] Cf. also the discussion between Burkitt (*JTS* 1933, 396 ff.) and Budde (*ib.*, 1934, 307 ff.). Of the two prophetic stories B doubtless deserves precedence with its content of exact historical detail; the historically colourless C is to be characterized in the words of the conservative Kittel as 'eine stark sagenhaft geartete Parallele zu der vorigen.'

---

[4] The problem of Isaiah's political position has been much discussed. K. Fullerton has at length denied Isaiah's part in the nationalistic politics of the day in the foll. articles: 'The Book of Isaiah: Critical Problems,' *HTR* 1913, 478 ff.; 'Viewpoints in the Discussion of Isaiah,' *JBL* 41 (1922), 1 ff.; 'Isaiah's Attitude in the Sennacherib Campaign,' *AJSL* 42 (1925), 1 ff. Subsequent literature is given by Kittel (*GVI* 2, 384, n. 3), he himself being in opposition to Fullerton, and by W. A. Irwin, with criticism of the preceding studies, who comes to the support of Fullerton, in 'Isaiah in the Crisis of 701,' *JR* 1936, 406 ff. The present writer finds himself cautious before doctrines based upon too idealistic conceptions of the prophets. Amos and Hosea were prophets of doom, and they predicted without restraint. Isaiah was in a different political and religious situation, and was doubtless a man of unique type. His partnership with Hezekiah, an able and ambitious king, by which he encouraged the monarch's faith in the God of Israel, is no stranger than that of Luther with Landgraf Philip of Hesse or of the English Reformers with Henry VIII, neither of which monarchs was a saint or even religious.

Finally, it is to be observed that these stories have full contemporary flavour, not only in the several historical details which they include, but also in their reflection of the times. We may compare the Elijah and Elisha cycles. The Assyrian Rab-shakeh might well have argued in such a blustering oration as is presented in 18$^{19\text{ff.}}$, even as a contemporary odist might have celebrated the fall of the tyrant as in 19$^{29\text{ff.}}$. The stories, if such they be rather than histories, were of early composition and within the Assyrian age—this judgment vs. Marti, who would assign the Rab-shakeh narrative to ca. 500 B.C., and its parallel to a still later date. Procksch pertinently remarks on the orations (p. 446) : " Die Rede des *Rabšaqe* in beiden Teilen ist geschickt angelegt, auch die Apostrophe von den Gesandten an das Volk sehr wirksam. Wenn sie auch wie die Reden bei Thukydides und Cäsar auf Rechnung des Schriftstellers kommt, so hält sie sich doch in den historischen Grenzen und verdient als rhetorische Leistung Anerkennung."

Ch. 21. The reigns of Manasseh and Amon. || 2 Ch. 33 ; *cf. Ant.*, x, 3-4, 1. Apart from the usual dynastic items the ch., covering over half a century, is devoted to the history of those kings' outrageous abandonment of the True Religion. But there was little else of national history to record in the two generations, when Judah was a pawn of Assyria under its conquering monarchs, Esarhaddon (681-669) and Ashurbanipal (669-626), who brought their empire to the pitch of its extent in enveloping Elam, Anatolia, Syria, Arabia, Egypt ; see the pertinent chapters in the Histories. ' Manasseh king of Judah ' (*Menaše šar Iaudi*) appears in a list of twenty-two named kings and their kingdoms in an inscription of Esarhaddon's (Prism B, col. 5, *KB* 2, 149, *ATB* 1, 357, *ARA* 2, §610, *AB* 476 f.). Ashurbanipal reports as among his vassals in his first campaign against Tirhakah, ' king of Egypt and Cush,' twenty-two kings, including Manasseh, *Minše ša Iaudi* (Prism C : *KB* 2, 238 f., *ARA* 2, §876). There are two late Biblical references to Assyrian deportations into Palestine, by Esarhaddon and by ' the noble Asenappar,' *i.e.*, Ashurbanipal (Ezra, 4$^{2. \ 9\text{ff.}}$). There is also the doubtless true tradition (*cf.* Eissfeldt, *Einl.*, 612), preserved in Ch. (vv.$^{11\text{-}13. \ 18. \ 19}$) of Manasseh's captivity in Babylon (taken thither ' with hooks,' *cf.* 19^{28}), in celebration of which and of the king's repentance the apocryphon of the Prayer of Manasseh was composed. Among such royal captives at his court Ashurbanipal lists kings of Egypt, among them Necho, whom he later restored, and large groups of royal hostages (*KB* 2, 167 ff., *ARA* 2, §§774, 779 ff.). For the religious retrogression of this period in face of the Assyrian terror and fascination, on which the prophet Zephaniah is the commentator, see Kittel, *GVI* 2, §48; Robinson, *HI* 401 ff.

VV.¹⁻¹⁸. The reign of Manasseh. After the preliminary data, stating the longest regnal term in the history of the dynasty, 55 years, the history is devoted to the king's apostasy. It is a homily of Deuteronomistic character (*cf.* Burney, Stade, *Akad. Reden*, 224 ff.), with a few original data, contained in vv.³⁻⁷, and v.¹⁸, a specific item as to his burial; v.¹⁶ may contain a true tradition of his bloody reign. The listing of abominations in vv.³ff. is largely independent of that in ch. 23, and has archival characteristics (see Notes).

3. *He built again the high-places that his father Hezekiah had destroyed, and he erected an altar* [𝔊 *altars*] *to the Baal, and made an Asherah, just as Ahab king of Israel had made, and he worshipped all the host of heaven, and served them.*

4. *And he built altars in the house of* YHWH, *as to which* YHWH *had said, In Jerusalem will I set my Name.*   **5.** *And he built altars for all the host of heaven in the two courts of the house of* YHWH.

6. *And he made his son to pass through the fire, and he practised augury and divination, and he made 'ôb and wizards—he increased in doing the evil in* YHWH's *eyes to provocation.* **7.** *And he set the image of the Asherah that he made in the house of which* YHWH *said to David and to his son Solomon: In this house and in Jerusalem, which I have chosen out of all the tribes of Israel, will I put my Name for ever.* VV.⁸·⁹ continue the homily on the tragedy.

V.³. For the sing. 'altar' of Baal see Note. The reference to 'an Asherah' depends upon the more explicit statement in v.⁷, where the Asherah is definitely an image. Of vv.⁴·⁵ the latter is generally assumed (*e.g.*, by Kittel, Stade) to be the secondary one, dependent on 23¹²; but the objective of the worship of the altars is required. Rather v.⁴ with its homiletic observation is secondary, and indeed a duplicate of v.⁷. For the problem of 'the two courts' (=23¹², *cf.* 'the middle court,' 20⁴) see Smith, *Jerusalem*, 2, 64, 256 ff., etc. This developed astral worship (see further Comm. on 23⁴ᶠᶠ·), popularized as Zephaniah records (1⁵), and referred to in Jeremiah's note of the popular worship of ' the queen of heaven ' (7¹⁸), came in with the Assyrian domination as part of the obligation of subject states to the empire ; *e.g.*, there were the ritual dues for ' Ashur and Bêlit, and the gods of Assyria,' required by Ashurbanipal ; so Luckenbill, *ARA* 2, §798, Schrader translating differently, *KB* 2, 195, as of imposition of their ' cults.' **6**. The v. lists autochthonous rites, paralleled in the condemnation of 17¹⁷. *He made his son to pass through the fire*, even as did Ahaz (16³), and a practice presented as usual in 23¹⁰. *And he practised augury and divination*. For the second term (root *nḥš*) *cf.* 17¹⁷, I. 20³³ ; the first term (root *'nn*) is explained by Dhorme as from *'ānān*, ' cloud,' *i.e.*, ' cloud-observer ' (*L'Évolution religieuse d'Israël*, 229 ff.). According to Is. 2⁶ this practice was introduced from Philistia. *And he made 'ôb and wizards ;* the double term occurs below, 23²⁴, in Is. 8¹⁹ (29⁴ *'ôb* alone), and in the anecdote, 1 Sam. 28³ᶠᶠ·, how Saul " removed the *'ôbôt* (fem. pl.) and wizards from the land." There Moffatt and Waterman translate the obscure word with ' medium,' evidently on basis of the feminine gender ; however the witch of Endor was specifically *ba'alat 'ôb*, ' possessed with an *'ôb*.' The word may have been transferred to the person possessed, just as possibly the word ' wizard ' may first have meant the ' knowing ' spirit ; see Burney. The double phrase here appears to be technical : *he practised the art of familiar spirit and wizard(s)*. *Cf.* the variations of translation in the VSS (with the notion of ventriloquism, will-control, etc.) and in modern trr. See Note, and at large Dhorme, pp. 234 ff., and T. W. Rosmarin's extensive Note in *REJ* 98 (1934), 95–9, with history of interpretation and essays at etymology. These superstitious rites were germane enough to Palestinian soil, but the fashion was re-introduced by the spell of the Babylonian religion.

VV.¹⁰⁻¹⁵. The doom of Jerusalem and Judah, put anonymously in the mouth of YHWH's *servants the prophets ; cf.* Dt. 28¹⁵ᶠᶠ·. **12.** *Whosoever hears of it, both his ears shall tingle :* the same phrase 1 Sam. 3¹¹, Jer. 19³. **13**. *I will stretch over Jerusalem the line of Samaria and the plummet of Ahab's house :* a rendering into historical terms of the ominous phrase, ' the

line of confusion and the plummet of emptiness ' (Is. 34^{11}).
The figurative declaration, *I will wipe Jerusalem, as a man
wipes a bowl, wiping it and turning it upside down*, is unique.
14. *I will cast off the remnant of mine inheritance*, etc. : cf.
Jer. 12^7. **16.** *Moreover innocent blood did Manasseh spill, very
much*, etc. : there may well be true tradition here of the
martyrdom of the faithful. There exist various forms of the
apocryphal ' Martyrdom ' or ' Ascension of Isaiah,' according
to which Isaiah was sawn asunder in this reign, reminiscence
of which appears in Heb. 11^{37} ; see R. H. Charles, *The Ascension of Isaiah* (1900), and Schürer, *GJV* 3, 386 ff. For these
two generations prophecy appears to have been silenced.
17. Among *the acts of Manasseh* recorded *in the chronicles*,
was *the sin that he sinned*, *i.e.*, an official record of his religious
innovations. **18.** Of *Uzzah's garden*, which the king had
acquired for his tomb, nothing further is known except for
his son Amon's interment there (v.^{26}).

For the extensive influence of this ch. on Ezekiel see Torrey,
Pseudo-Ezekiel (1930), 64 ff.

VV.$^{19-26}$. The reign of Amon. **19.** For his age at accession
see Comm. on 22^1. His mother's father's name, Harus, is
probably Arabic (see Note), and the place of his origin,
Yotebah, is to be identified with the place two stations from
Esyon-geber noted in Num. 33^{33}, Dt. 10^7. Jerome's *Onomasticon* places it in Judah, but it appears, listed next to
Aila-Elath in the fifth and sixth centuries as seat of a bishopric
(Abel, *GP* 2, 201). **23.** *And Amon's courtiers conspired against
him and killed the king in his house*. **24.** *And the people of the
land slew all the conspirators against king Amon. And the people
of the land made Josiah his son king in his stead*. It is pure
assumption to explain the assassination from popular political
grounds, as do Galling, *Die israelitische Staatsverfassung*, 33 f.,
Causse, *Du groupe ethnique*, 118 ff., for it was the *demos* that
at once took revenge upon the murderers. This interference
in the court by ' the people of the land ' is the most democratic
action recorded in the history ; *cf.* 11$^{13ff.}$, 23^{30}.

    1. מנשה : to list of extra-Israelite occurrences of the name in
GB is to be added Rhodian Μνασεως (Harris, *Gram*., 126) ; it
means ' causing to forget,' *i.e.*, an earlier loss in the family ;
similar affectional names are Menahem, ' consoler,' Tanhumath,

'consolation'; cf. Noth, IP 222.—3. מובחת : Grr., 𝔖ᴴ=רוֹבֵחַ, as at I. 16³², the pl. being induced by Ch., 'altars for the Baals.'—4. ובנה : cf. the four pfs. in similar usage in v.⁶ ; for the archival usage see on 14⁷.—מובחת : Grr. as sing.—יהוה 2⁰ : B A 𝔖ᴸ om., as redundant.—5. מובחות : Grr. (exc. 𝔖ᴸ), 𝔖ᴴ as sing.—בשתי : Hex., 𝔖 ' in all.'—6. בנו : Ch., בניו =Grr., 𝔖ᴴ ; but the use of the sing. is technical.—אוב : B† ελλην, early error (so an 𝕴 text, ℭ) for θελητην=A N and most MSS, even as Grr. at 23²⁴, θελητας ; cf. Aquila at Lev. 20⁶. This interpretation may have come by reference to root אבה (so Liddell and Scott) with association of the idea of 'will-control' over nature, spirits, even as θέλειν is used in Corpus Hermeticum, xiii, 7, θέλησον καὶ γίνεται, also the nouns θέλησις, θέλημα (C. Wesseley, Griechische Zauberpapyrus, in Denkschriften of the Vienna Academy, vol. 36, p. 151, and Neue griech. Zauberpapyri, ib., vol. 42, p. 86) ; for these reff. the writer is indebted to Prof. A. D. Nock. Lucian has εγγαστριμυθους, 'ventriloquists,' as at 23²⁴ ; 𝔖ᴴ zakkōrē=𝔖, 'remembrancers,' i.e., control by use of names or charm-words (?) 'pithones' of 𝔙 is the basis of EVV, 'familiar spirits.'—ידענים : 12 MSS as sing.=Ch., as though in the sequence the sing. were required ; cf. the rdgs. of the whole phrase at 23²⁴ and 1 Sam. 28³⁻⁹ with variations of the numbers. 'Wizards' of EVV (exc. JV, which paraphrases here) is an excellent etymological rendering. —להכעים : many MSS, Ch., להכעיסו =VSS ; but the absolute use appears also as at 23¹⁹ (where VSS+' the Lord '), and the phrase should be kept.—7. שמי : Grr. (exc. B=ℭ) as+שׁם.—8. ישמרו : 𝔖ᴸ ℭ Lucif. as though ישמעו.—כבל לעשות : OGrr. om. 'לע ; Hex., 'to do all '=Heb. MS 23.—ולכל : MS 70, Ch., לכל =Grr. (𝔖ᴴ 'like all '), to be preferred, the prep. continuing the acc. construction as at I. 1⁹ (cf. Haupt).—9. הרע : 𝔖+' in the Lord's eyes'; 𝔖ᴸ+' before the Lord.'—11. לפניו . . . הרע : 𝔖 om. הרע ; St. regards the asyndetic passage as duplication of v.⁸, cf. BH.—12. ויהודה : St. elides for lack of repeated prep. ; but 3 MSS have על =Grr., and so to be emended.—שמעיו : read with Kr., MSS שָׁמְעָה= Grr.—13. קו : so BH (MSS L C al.) ; but read קָו, as construct, with Mich., Bär, Ginsb.—צלחת : cf. צלחית, 2²⁰.—מָחֹה וְהַפֵּךְ : read as abs. infinitives, מָחֹה וְהָפֵךְ.—For v.ᵇ 𝔙 has an original interpretation : " et delebo Hierusalem, sicut deleri solent tabulæ ; delens vertam, et ducam crebrius stilum super faciem eius " ; this is defended by Joüon (Mél., 5, 483) with suggestion of לחות for צלחת.—16. לפה פה : פה לפה : 'level to the brim'; cf. 10²¹.—חטאתו : VSS here and at v.¹⁷ wrongly as pl.—18. בנן ביתו : 𝔖ᴸ om., prob. by parablepsis ; similar abbreviation in Heb. MSS.—19. אמון : the name at I. 22²⁶ ; 𝔖 Aμως.—משלמת : the name in the Elephantine papp. ; cf. מְשֶׁלֶם, 22³, שֶׁלֶם, 22¹⁴ ; for such names see Noth, IP 174. —חרוץ : a Phœn. name (Harris, Gram., 104) ; but in this connexion it is to be identified with Arab. names, Sinaitic חרוצו (Lidzb., HNE 280), Lihyanian חרוץ (NPS 1, 99).—יָפֶה : the closest Gr. tradition is Yetaba =𝔙 'Iethba'; the form has come by procession of the stem-vowel from yaṭûb, root טוב ; cf. קְאֵל, 14⁷.—22. יהוה 1⁰ : 2 MSS om. =𝔊ᴸ.—23. עבדי אמון : Ch., עבדיו =Gr. MSS, 𝔙.—וימיתו את המלך : Ch., וימיתהו =𝔊ᴸ 𝔖.—24. ויך : Ch., ויכו =𝔊ᴸ, ignoring the collective use of עם הארץ ; withal the pl. follows, וימליכו.—25. אשר עשה : 18 MSS pref. וכל =𝔊ᴸ 𝔗 𝔖 𝔄.—26. ויקבר : 22 MSS Ken., deR., ויקברו ; of the VSS 𝔗ᵂ alone has the sing. ; Haupt defends the sing. as impersonal, cf. 18⁴. VSS necessarily followed with their own idiom, and so EVV with the passive.—בקברתו : 𝔊ᴸ 'in his father's grave,' recalling v.¹⁸.

Ch. 22–23³⁰. The reign of Josiah. ‖ 2 Ch. 34–5 ; cf. Ant., x, 4–5, 1.

22¹·². Introduction. **1.** *Eight years old was Josiah when he began to reign.* Suspicion is cast upon the figure by the Hebrew grammar, which normally requires a numeral higher than ten with the sg. noun *šānāh* ; but see Note. Josiah's sons Jehoiakim and Jehoahaz were respectively 25 and 23 years old at the end of his life (*ca.* 38 years), and his father died in his 23d year, the present item making him a father in his 14th year—all cases of early paternity indeed, but not sufficient ground for correcting the father's given age (*vs.* Klostermann, Šanda). The reign may be dated *ca.* 639–608 B.C. With the death of Ashurbanipal in 626, and pending the doom of his empire, the subject provinces scented a fresh breath of liberty, and it was in these circumstances that in Josiah's 18th year (621 B.C.) a reform was effected based upon the nationalistic tradition and religion. There is no hint of international relations until the end of the reign with Josiah's tragic death in battle against the invader Pharaoh-Necho (23²⁹).

V.³–23²⁷. The great reformation. For criticism of this detailed history see Additional Note after 23³⁰. It opens with the account of an accidental discovery.

VV.³⁻⁷. Repairs ordered for the temple. **3.** *In the eighteenth year of king Josiah:* Ch. records that " in the eighth year of his reign, while he was yet young, he began to seek after the God of his father David ; and in the twelfth year he began to purge Judah and Jerusalem," etc., picking up our passage subsequently with " in the eighteenth year of his reign," etc.—altogether an attempt to display Josiah's early piety. He followed the precedent of his pious ancestor Jehoash

($12^{5ff.}$) in requiring careful handling of the temple receipts of loose silver, but his orders were more promptly carried out. He commissions for the purpose a high officer, *Shaphan ben Azaliah ben Meshullam, the secretary.* The name of Shaphan occurs in subsequent ancestries (25^{22}, Jer. $36^{11f.}$), but the relationships cannot be determined. Ch. 34^8 associates with Shaphan two others, 'Maaseiah, the governor of the city, and Joah ben Joahaz, the recorder.' **4.** Shaphan's commission is thus recorded: *Go up to Hilkiah the high priest, and have him smelt* [𝔥=EVV *sum up*] *the silver brought into the house of* Y*HWH, which the keepers of the threshold have collected from the people,* **5.** *and let them* (collective) *give it into the hand of those who do the work* (namely), *those in charge in the house of* Y*HWH, and let them give it to those who do the work in the house of* Y*HWH, to repair the dilapidation of the house.* VV.$^{4b-7}$ have close verbal parallelism with 12^{12-16}, and Stade properly eliminates the whole passage as secondary, clumsy as it is in its arrangement; it would expand in detail what is briefly reported to the king in v.^{9}. Hilkiah is called *high priest,* also at v.^{8} and 23^4, otherwise *inf.* simply *priest*; for the secondary character of the adj. see Comm., 12^{11}. Hilkiah was grandfather of Seraiah (25^{18}), father of Jehosadak, who went into captivity (1 Ch. $5^{40f.}$). Ancient tradition identified him with Jeremiah's father (Jer. 1^1), but the name was common (also Jer. 29^3), and the prophet, 'of the priests in Anathoth,' belonged to the line of Abiathar, not of Sadok (see Graf, *Jeremia*, 1862, 12 f.; Šanda). For the verb 'to smelt,' by slight correction of 𝔥, and so also in v.^{9}, see Note, and *cf.* similar terminology, also with correction of 𝔥, in 12^{11}.

VV.$^{8-13}$. The discovery of the book of the Law, and the effect upon the king. **8.** *And Hilkiah the high priest said to Shaphan the secretary: I have found the book of the Law in the house of* Y*HWH. And Hilkiah delivered the book to Shaphan, and he read it.* **9.** *And Shaphan the secretary came to the king, and he reported to the king and said: Thy servants have smelted the silver that was found in the house, and have given it into the hands of the workers in charge of the house of* Y*HWH.* **10.** *And Shaphan the secretary told the king, as follows: Hilkiah the priest has given me a book. And Shaphan read it before the king.* According to the dramatic story the scribe leaves it to the king to recognize the character of the book. **11.** *And it was, when the king heard the words of the book of the Law, that he rent his clothes.* **12.** *And the king gave orders to Hilkiah the priest, and Ahikam ben Shaphan, and Achbor ben Micaiah, and Shaphan the secretary, and Asaiah the king's minister, to wit:* ———. For the commission, properly headed by the priest, *cf.* 19². Ahikam was father of the notable Gedaliah, 25²²ᶠᶠ·. For listing of the many contemporary seals of officials with the title ' minister ' (Heb. ' slave '—*cf.* I. 1²) of the ' king ' see Albright, *JBL* 51 (1932), 79 f. ; A. Bergman, *ib.*, 55 (1936), 221 ff. **13.** *Go, inquire of YHWH on my behalf and on behalf of the people ⌐and on behalf of all Judah⌐* (secondary, see Note) *concerning the words of this book that has been found ; for great is YHWH's wrath that is kindled against us, because our fathers have not listened to the words of this book, to do according to all that is written in it* [𝕳 *against us ;* see Note]. The reader would recall the curses of Dt. 28¹⁵ᶠᶠ·, 29²¹ᶠᶠ·; *cf.* the report of Jeremiah's preaching of ' this covenant,' Jer. 11. ℭ to Eze. 1¹ knows the exact place and date of the discovery of the book.

VV.¹⁴⁻²⁰. The application of the commission to a prophetess and her direful response. **14.** The commission, headed by the priest, and of its own volition, *went to the prophetess Huldah, wife of Shallum ben Tikwah ben Harhas, keeper of the wardrobe* [Heb. *garments*] *; now she dwelt in Jerusalem, in the second quarter. And they told her.* Why did a chief priest inquire of a woman ? And who was she ? The question has been asked since at least Kimchi's day, and his explanations have been pursued by the comm. in Poole, that Jeremiah was not in the city, he had gone to warn the ten tribes, etc. Jeremiah was already a commissioned prophet since the 13th year of the reign, and Zephaniah must have preceded the Reformation (*cf.* Horst, Comm. in *HAT*, 1938). We have to remind ourselves that judgments upon personalities and their part in history vary between that of contemporaries and that of posterity. Indeed Jeremiah felt himself to be a forgotten man in his day. Huldah left no book. As prophetess she had predecessors in Miriam and Deborah ; later there appear in the rôle of prophetess one Noadiah, whom Nehemiah denounced (Neh. 6¹⁴), Anna, the pious aged saint of the temple (Luke 2³⁶), and that ' Jezebel of a prophetess ' (Rev. 2²⁰).

Two gates named after Huldah were at the south end of the temple, according to *Middoth* i, 2 (*cf.* Smith, *Jerusalem*, 2, 517). And why did not Josiah himself, as did Hezekiah (19$^{14ff.}$), go direct to the temple to receive comfort? Her husband's duty as *keeper of the wardrobe* is not specific for us, whether as officer of the king or of the temple (for the latter *cf.* 10^{22}). The *second quarter* (Heb. *mišnèh*) is generally taken as the expansion of Jerusalem towards the north; see Smith, *ib.*, 2, 202. According to Neh. 3$^{9, 12}$ there were two ' half-districts ' of Jerusalem; for discussion of possible identification of the word with the corrupted (?) *yĕšānāh*, translated ' the old city,' of Neh. 3^{6}, 12^{39}, see M. Burrows, *JBL* 54 (1935), 37. **15.** *And she said to them: Thus has spoken* YHWH *the God of Israel: Say to the man who sent you to me* (before God, the king is but a man)*:* **16.** *Thus has* YHWH *spoken: Behold, I am bringing evil upon this place and upon its citizens, all the words of the book which the king of Judah has read.* **17.** *Because they have deserted me, and burnt incense to other gods, so as to provoke me with all the work of their hands, my wrath is kindled against this place and shall not be quenched.* **18.** There follows a personal oracle of indulgence *to the king of Judah, who sent you to inquire of* YHWH*: Thus shall you say to him: Thus has spoken* YHWH *the God of Israel: as for the words that thou hast heard:* **19.** *Because thy heart is tender, and thou hast humbled thyself before* YHWH *upon hearing what I have said against this place and its inhabitants, that it should become an* [object of] *astonishment and curse* (the phrase at Jer. 44^{22}), *and thou hast rent thy clothes, and wept before me, I also have heard thee—oracle of* YHWH. **20***a. Therefore, behold, I will gather thee to thy fathers, and thou shalt be gathered to thy grave in peace, neither shall thy eyes see all the evil that I am bringing upon this place.* Cf. 23$^{29f.}$, whence the otiose *be gathered to thy grave* has been interpolated here. The prediction that he should *not see all the evil* was fulfilled, but not that he should die *in peace*. In this respect the prophecy was not *post eventum*. **20***b. And they brought back word to the king.*

1. שמנה שנה : MS 30 ש׳ עשרה ש׳=Gr. MSS 44, 71; see Note to 8^{17}, suggesting that in such cases the expected pl., שנים was written in abbreviated form.—ויאשיהו : the verbal root as in יהואש, 16^{1} (see Notes there and on 12^{1}), with the element in the jussive;

this overcomes the objection of Noth, *IP* 212.—עריה: for other *nn. pr.* with this verb see Noth, *ib.*, 182; עדאל occurs on a Palestinian seal (*JPOS* 1938, 114), is also S. Arab. (*NPS* 2, 104).—בצקת: listed by Josh. 15³⁹ between Lachish and Eglon.—**2.** ולא: 3 MSS לא= Gr. B i, original, as at I. 22⁴³.—**3.** יאשיהו: OGrr.+' in the 8th month,' 𝕲ᴴ ' in the seventh month ' (with attempt at dating at the New Year ?).—שפן: the name has been read erroneously in a seal-stamping, pl. VI to lecture by J. L. Starkey, *PEQ* 1936 178 ff.—אצליהו: Noth (*ib.*, 193) connects with אצילי, Ex. 24¹¹, and Arab. root, *'aṣula*, ' to be distinguished.'—**4.** חלקיהו: see Note, 18¹⁸.—**4.** ויתם: generally assumed as of ' summing up ' the account (so GV EVV); but 𝕲ᴸ χωνευσατε; 𝔙 ' confletur '=יַתֵּם, the verb as at v.⁹, the error through easy confusion of archaic כ and מ. For other suggested emendations see Burn., St.—**5.** ויתנה: a short spelling (but *cf.* MSS) for Ḳr. וַיִּתְּנֶהָ, which is supported by 𝕲, Hex.; 𝕲ᴸ 𝔙 tr. with the passive, which is interpretation.—'על יד ע: *cf.* Gen. 42³⁷.—המפקדים: so at v.⁹=הפקדים, 12¹².—בבית: Ḳr. בֵּית, as at v.⁹ and 12¹², the Kt. a prepositional phrase developed from the locative.—ויתנו: Grr., κ. εδωκαν (B -κεν); 𝕲ᴸ with plus, ' according to the king's command.'—**6.** נדרים: see Note, 12¹³.—הבית: 12 MSS pref. בדק=Grr., 𝕾ᴴ 𝕾.—**8.** [שפן] על: read with many MSS, Ch., אל.—' Shaphan the secretary '; Grr. (exc. 𝕲ᴸ), 𝕾ᴴ om.; the repetition was otiose to translators; similar avoidance of ' to the king ' *inf.* by 𝕲ᴸ with ' to him.'—**12.** עכבור: עכבר on a seal, *IAE* 185.—מיכיה: also MSS מיכיהו; see Note, I. 22⁸.—עשיה: the name on seals, עשיהו, עשיו, *ib.*, 187, 197, 218.—**13.** ובעד כל יהודה: some MSS have introduced various forms of plus from Ch. (which includes N. Israel); the phrase is redundant (St.); ' king and people ' is the sufficient constitutional term.—[שמעו א'] על: the prep. is careless, is so used in Jer. 26⁵.—[הספר] הזה: B i v om., 𝕾ᴴ ⁂; the Law was *the Book !*—עלינו: 3 MSS עליו, 𝕲ᴸ εν αυτω; *cf.* Ch. הזה על הספר, and *inf.*, 23³; the emendation is to be accepted.—**14.** חלדה: also name of the wife of Nabatæan Aretas IV, *CIS* II, no. 158. For its mng., ' snail,' *cf.* Shaphan, ' badger,' Achbor, ' field-mouse,' above; such animal names (*cf.* Noth, *ib.*, 230) appear to have been fashionable at this time.—אשת: B h i ℭ, ' mother of.'—שלם: primary name of Josiah's successor (Comm., 23³¹), also appearing in Lachish tablet iv: see Note, 21¹⁹.—תקוה: Ch. Kt., תוקהת, as from the common S. Arab. root *wḳh*, the form properly preferred here by Noth (*ib.*, 260).—חרחם: Ch., חסרה; VSS support the form here; some MSS חרהם, with which *cf.* S. Arab. *Ḥrḥ* (*NPS* 2, 266).—**15.** אליהם: B† om.—**16.** [המקום] אל: read על with Ch.—**17.** בכל מעשה: 2 MSS, Ch., במעשה=Grr., exc. 𝕲ᴸ.—ונצתה: for the irregular consecution *cf.* 23⁵.—**18.** הדברים אשר שמעת: of the Grr. 𝕲ᴸ, also the other VSS, exc. ℭ, paraphrase; Klost., *SBOT*, *al.* offer revisions; Gressmann (*ZAW* 1924, 319) proposes elision of something objectionable. But for such a break in construction *cf.* a case in 23¹⁷.—**19.** "מפני י: 𝕲ᴸ ' before me,' correcting the careless 3d pers.—וְקִלְלָה : 𝔊^L om. as blasphemy against the Holy City.—**20.** [אֲבֹתֶיךָ] עַל : MSS, Ch., אֶל, as also read *inf.*—קְבָרֹתֶיךָ : read קְבֻרָתוֹ ; *cf.* 23³⁰.—הַזֶּה הַמָּקוֹם עַל : Grr. (exc. B A), Ch. plus 'and upon its inhabitants.'

Ch. 23¹⁻³. The solemn covenant of king and people with YHWH. **1.** *And the king sent orders, and there were gathered to him all the elders of Judah and Jerusalem.* For *the elders*, a political term, see Comm. on 10¹, I. 8¹. **2.** *And the king went up to the house of YHWH, and all the men of Judah and all the citizens of Jerusalem with him, and the priests and the prophets, and all the people both small and great.* The extent of the congregation seems overdrawn in terms ; hence Stade, Eissfeldt would mark as secondary the final phrases, *and the priests*, etc., stylistically indeed a halting addition ; but the v. is a vivid statement of an enthusiastic occasion ; *cf.* I. 8¹ᶠᶠ·, Dt. 29⁹ᶠ·. The naming of *the prophets* has a contemporary ring, and their part as a guild in the reformation may not be ignored ; *cf.* Jer. 2⁸, where they and the priests are denounced, and for their perversion *cf.* Jer. 29. Ch. 34³⁰ replaces the item with ' the Levites ' (so 2 MSS here), 𝕮 with ' the scribes,' obvious corrections, like many by modern critics. *And he read in their ears all the words of the book of the covenant that was found in the house of YHWH.* The ' reading by the king ' is a formalism ; a scribe would have been the actual lector (*cf.* 22¹⁰). *The book of the covenant* is the most germane of the various titles that have come to be given to that book ; see Add. Note, II. **3.** *And the king stood by the pillar* [JV *on the platform*—see on 11¹⁴], *and he executed the covenant before YHWH, to go after YHWH, and to keep his commandments and his decrees* [EVV *testimonies*] *and his statutes* (*cf.* I. 2³, Dt. 4⁴⁴, etc.) *with whole heart and whole soul* (*cf.* Dt. 6⁵, etc.), *for ratification of the words of this covenant* (*cf.* Dt. 28⁶⁹), *as written in this book. And all the people took stand in* [EVV *stood to*] *the covenant.* The last expression, = " entered into the covenant," is a legal term ; *cf.* Dt. 29⁹ᶠᶠ·. For an earlier covenant of king and people with the Deity see 11¹⁷.

VV.⁴⁻¹⁴. The reformation in Jerusalem. **4a.** *And the king commanded Hilkiah the high priest and the priests* (25¹⁸ *priest*) *of second rank and the guards of the threshold* (*cf.* 12¹⁰, 22⁴) *to bring out from the hall of YHWH all the vessels made for* (*the*)

Baal and for (the) Asherah and for all the host of heaven; and he burned them outside of Jerusalem in the pyres [EVV *fields*—see Note] *of Kidron*. The early hierarchy of three orders is presented here, as at 25^{18}; for the official titles see Note. For the looting of such sacred vessels and the like in a temple *cf.* a record of Ashurbanipal's (*ARA* 2, §810). The pagan trinity of Baal, Asherah and the Heavenly Host is presented in due form: *cf.* 17^{16}, 21^3. Gressmann (' Josia u. das Deut.,' *ZAW* 1924, 324 f.) insists properly on Assyrianizing influences, and compares Ashurbanipal's requirement of ' revenues, dues, etc., for Assur and Bêlit, and the gods of Assyria ' (*cf.* Luckenbill, *ARA* 2, 798). But the terminology here is Syro-Palestinian. Baal and Asherah are coupled in the Ugaritic texts (exx. given by H. Bauer, *ZAW* 1933, 89, and in *RSMT* 92); in one Ugaritic text there is the pairing of ' El and Athirat ' (Dhorme, *Syria*, 1933, 39); for that field of mythology see the volumes of Nielsen and Schaeffer (the Schweich Lectures, ch. 4) cited in the Bibliography, and at large Dhorme, *L'Évolution religieuse d'Israël*, ch. 19. For the survival of these native Palestinian cults among the Israelite *émigrés* in Egypt see the discussions on the Elephantine papyri, and especially A. Vincent, *La religion des judéo-araméens d'Éléphantiné*. The stellar deities are named more exactly in v.⁵. **4b.** *And he carried their ashes unto Bethel:* this is an absurd addition, suggested by the story in vv.[15ff.]. **5.** *And he estopped the priestlings whom the kings of Judah had appointed ⸢to burn incense⸣* [with correction of 𐤉—all EVV *sotto voce* so correcting] *at the high-places in the cities of Judah and the suburbs of Jerusalem, and* (or *even*) *those who burned incense to* (*the*) *Baal, to the sun and the moon and the zodiacal-signs and all the host of heaven*. The v. is an intrusion with its reference to the provincial heathenish rites, interrupting the story of reform in Jerusalem. For *priestlings* (EVV *idolatrous priests*) see Note. The offering of incense, as distinct from sacrifice, to others than YHWH had been condoned by royal authority; *cf.* the distinction in the Church between the *latreia* of Deity and the *douleia* of the saints. The subordinate aspect of these provincial priests appears in vv.[8, 9]. For such celestial worship *cf.* Am. 5^{26}, presenting the names of two adopted astral deities, Sakkut (Heb. *sikkût*) and Kewan (Heb. *kîyûn*);

cf. Dt. 4¹⁹, 17³, Jer. 8², etc. The listing of Baal, sun and moon is typically Syrian. The Zakar inscription concludes with ascription to ' Baal of Heaven . . . and Sun and Moon and gods of heaven and gods of earth . . .' ; the Aramaic inscription at Tarsus has ascription to ' the Great Baal, Moon and Sun ' (Montgomery, *JAOS* 28 [1907], 104 ff. ; Lidzbarski, *Eph.*, 3, 1 ff.). For Baal of Heaven see Add. Note to I. 18. Under the Assyrian domination there arose a novel and extensive development of these cults ; *cf. KAT* 614 ff., Jastrow, *Religious Belief in Bab. and Ass.* (1911), ch. 4. Great as were the scientific results of Babylonian astronomy, the vulgar astrology that followed in its wake broke down the ethos of the simple folk-religions. As Jastrow remarks (p. 230) : " The more complicated the system, the greater its hold upon the masses." The Akk. term for the *zodiacal signs* (EVV variously, *planets, constellations, twelve signs*) is unique in the O.T., but is frequent in the later Jewish literature ; see Note. **6.** *And he brought out the Asherah from the house of* Yhwh *outside of Jerusalem to the valley of Kidron, and he burned it in the valley of Kidron, and ground it to powder, and cast its dust upon the graves of the common people* [Heb. *sons of the people*]. The v. is sequel to v.⁴. *The Asherah* was ' the graven image of the Asherah ' of 21⁷ ; *cf.* I. 15¹³ for Asa's removal of the like ' abominable ' object. The language used of its destruction is parallel to that for the fate of the golden calf, Ex. 32²⁰ ; the material, as in that case, was doubtless of wood with metal overlay, for which art *cf.* Dt. 7²⁵, Is. 30²², 40¹⁹. For the cemetery for the common people *cf.* the purchase of the Potter's Field, Mt. 27⁵ff.. The passage indicates the early general use of this rocky ravine E of Jerusalem not only for tombs of royalty and gentry but also as a common cemetery. The valley was to become a place of burial ' for lack of room ' according to Jer. 7³¹ff.. The tradition was continued by the great Jewish cemetery on the western slope of the Mount of Olives, complemented by the Muslim cemetery on the eastern face. The valley thus became the prospected scene of the final resurrection and the judgment of the world, and so, as Eusebius records, the novel name of the Valley of Jehoshaphat came to be applied to it, taken from Joel 4² (Engl. 3²). And the lower stretch of the Kidron valley bears the Arabic name

Wady en-Nār, 'Valley of (Hell-) Fire'; cf. Note to v.⁴. See Smith, *Jerusalem*, 1, bk. 1, ch. 7; Baedeker's *Pal. and Syria*, 72 ff.; Montgomery, 'The Holy City and Gehenna,' *JBL* 27 (1908), 24 ff.; and for the Arabic tradition G. Le Strange, *Palestine under the Moslems*, 218 ff. **7.** *And he broke down the houses of the sacred-prostitutes in* (the area of) *the house of* Y<small>HWH</small>, *where the women wove robes* [𝔥 *houses*, EVV *hangings/tents/coverings*—see Note] *for the Asherah*. For this depraved class, including both men and women (the word masc. here, as covering both sexes, and so the usual tr. here, 'sodomites,' is inexact), see Comm. on I. 14²¹. For women in the temple see Eze. 8¹⁴, and *cf.* the 'women's house' (*bit aštammi*) as a dependency of Babylonian temples (Meissner, *Bab. u. Ass.*, 2, 69; Bezold, *Glossar*, 79). For ritual vestments woven by women in the Babylonian temples see C. L. Woolley, *Antiquaries' Journal*, 5, 393 (cited by Robinson, *HI* 1, 419), and *cf.* the notice of such elaborate garments given by Lucian, *De Dea Syra*, 42. Gressmann (cited above) gives (pp. 325 ff.) several illustrative cases from the Greek field bearing upon these Oriental practices: a priestess who was περιάπτρια, 'dressmaker,' another κοσμητήρια, 'adorner,' etc. VV.⁸ᵃ·⁹ manifestly belong together, and like v.⁵ are out of place here. **8a.** *And he brought in all the priests from the cities of Judah, and he defiled the high-places where the priests burned incense, from Geba to Beer-sheba.* For Geba as the northern boundary of Judah see I. 15²². 'Priests' here is in contrast to 'priestlings,' v.⁵, but both are characterized as 'incense-burners.' **9.** *Only the priests of the high-places* (*cf.* I. 12³¹· ³²) *were not coming up to* (*i.e.*, serving at) *the altar of* Y<small>HWH</small> *in Jerusalem, but they ate unleaven among their brethren.* The provincial priests, now without local duty and support, were brought to Jerusalem, evidently for restraint and stipend; *cf.* Dt. 18⁶ᶠᶠ·. For the extreme of degradation to which they were subjected from a later point of view see Eze. 44¹⁰ᶠᶠ·. It is to be noted that these country clergy are called priests, not Levites, as Dt. has made the innovation. The eating of 'unleaven' remains a problem. Kittel and Šanda connect the reference with the subsequent Passover celebration (vv.²¹ᶠᶠ·). Kuenen's emendation to 'portions,' revision of the spelling of 'unleaven,' adjudged by Stade as 'not impossible,' is accepted positively by Gressmann (p. 327; *cf.* Eissfeldt). But such an early corruption of the familiar word is unaccountable, unless by intentional perversion. It may well be a technical term; those who might eat of the Paschal food were *ipso facto* admitted to all sacred foods; and so Rashi interprets. **8***b*. *And he broke down the high-places of the gates at the entrance of the gate of Joshua, commandant of the city, at one's left in the city-gate*: a most puzzling statement; with several *gate high-places* appearing at one spot! But true historical notes are preserved in the naming of the commandant Joshua (for the title *cf.* I. 22^{26}), and the exact location of the objects. A. Geiger's and G. Hoffman's ingenious proposition (*ZAW* 2, 175) to read *satyrs* in place of *gates* with change of two pointings in 𝔐, has been generally accepted. The word, also occurring at Lev. 17^7, 2 Ch. 11^{15}, Is. 13^{21}, 34^{14}, is translated with 'devils' by AV, 'he-goats' by RVV, 'satyrs' by JV. It might be best expressed in English with 'hobgoblins.' For such uncanny beings see Duhm, *Die bösen Geister im A.T.* (1904), 46 ff. The term is to be interpreted as a scoffing allusion to the debased ancient deities, as in the cited passages of Lev. and Ch. **10.** *And he defiled* (*the*) *Topheth in the vale of Ben-Hinnom* [=Ḳr.; Kt. *bnê-H.*], *that one should not pass his son and daughter in the fire to* (*the*) *Melek* [*the King*; 𝔐 *the Molek*, EVV *Molech*]. For etymology of 'Topheth,' still dubious, see Lexx., BDD, Smith, *Jerusalem*, 1, 197. For the deity see Comm. on I. 11^7, according to which his sanctuary was 'in the mount before Jerusalem.' The barbarous cult is condemned by the contemporary Dt. (12^{31}), and the unholy site execrated by Jer. (7$^{29ff.}$, 19); for a recent study see Torrey, *Pseudo-Ezekiel* (1930), ch.'3. For the *vale*, Heb. *gê*, in contrast to *naḥal*, 'wady,' used of the Kidron Valley, see Smith, vol. I, bk. 1, ch. 7, locating it on the south side of Jerusalem, and so in contradiction to the tradition identifying it with the Kidron valley, which became the seat of the apocalyptic Gehenna; see above on v.^{6}. **11.** *And he put away the horses which the kings of Judah had given to the sun at the entrance of the house of Y*HWH, *by the chamber of Nathan-melek the chamberlain* [or *eunuch*], *which was in the precincts; and the chariot* [with Grr.; 𝔥 pl.] *of the sun he burned with fire.* VV.$^{11,\,12}$ connect logically with vv.$^{4,\,5b}$. For *the sun's chariot* Dussaud *cft.*

(*RHR* 1931, 359, n. 2) the Akk. title of the sun, *rākib narkabti*, 'chariot-rider,' and the name of a deity at Senjirli, *Rkb-El*, 'Driver of El.' Graham and May cite (*Culture and Conscience*, 235, n. 2) an Akk. text detailing the 'charioteer of the deity,' and 'the sacred stable,' as also 'the sacred procession.' For an Assyrian relief exhibiting the procession of the gods, mounted on animals, one of them, presumably the sun, on a horse, see Jastrow, *Bildermappe zur Religion Babyloniens u. Assyriens* (1912), fig. 98; Gressmann, *ATB* 2, pl. cxxxv; *cf.* Rostovtzeff, 'Dieux et chevaux' (presenting bronze figurines), *Syria*, 1931, 48 ff. See also Gressmann, *ZAW* 1924, 323, n. 6; Langdon, *Semitic Mythology*, 54; F. J. Hollis in *Myth and Ritual* (S. H. Hooke ed.), Essay 5; H. G. May, 'Some Aspects of Solar Worship at Jerusalem,' *ZAW* 1937, 269 ff. For the naming of *the chamber of N.* Šanda *cft.* a similar personal tradition in the Mosque el-Akṣa. For the officer's ambiguous title *cf.* 18[17], 25[19]. For the word translated *precincts*, see Note. **12.** *And the altars on the roof—the upper chamber of Ahaz—that the kings of Judah had made, and the altars that Manasseh had made in the two courts of the house of* Y*HWH, did the king break down, and he* ⌜*broke them up there*⌝ [so with correction of impossible 𐤄—see Note], *and he cast their dust on the Kidron valley*. For this definite datum of stellar worship, expanding v.[5], *cf.* Zeph. 1[5] (see Horst, *HAT, ad loc.*), Jer. 19[13] (on the worship addressed to the host of heaven), and 32[29] (with Baal as object). The appositional phrase, *the upper chamber of Ahaz*, is regarded as secondary by Kittel, Stade; but even so, it is a worthy historical gloss. *Cf.* Ahaz's innovations recorded in 16[10ff.], and *n.b.* his sun-dial (20[11]); Šanda suggests reference to an observatory. The brief record is brilliantly illuminated by the Ugaritic legend (Gordon, *Ugar. Handbook*, 2, *Keret*), in which (lines 73 ff.) the hero is divinely bidden to ascend to the top of the tower, there to raise his hands towards the heavens, and to sacrifice to the Bull and to Baal, Ben-Dagan; his action in response is presented in identical terms below (lines 165 ff.). The notice of Manasseh's altars is citation of 21[5]. **13.** *And the high-places in front of Jerusalem on the right hand of the Mount of Destruction* [with sarcastic play on the original word 'oil,' *i.e.*, the **Mount of Olives**], *which Solomon king of Israel built to Ashtart*

[𝔐 *Ashtoreth*] *god*(*dess*) [𝔘 *abomination*] *of Sidonia, and to Chemosh god* [𝔘 *abomination*] *of Moab, and to Milkom god* [𝔘 *detestation*] *of the Bnê-Ammon, did the king defile.* For these pagan sanctuaries see Comm. on I. 11⁵ᶠᶠ·, of which this v. is pure repetition, with the additional note of their location at the southern end of the Mount of Olives. **14.** *And he broke in pieces the pillars, and cut down the Asherahs, and filled their place with men's bones:* another generalizing addition.

The specific details in the above confused account give clue to original materials. Of this order are, v.⁴, altars of Baal and Asherah ; v.⁶, destruction of the Asherah-image ; v.⁷, the sacred prostitutes' quarters ; v.⁸ᵇ, the satyr high-places ; v.¹¹, horses and chariot of the sun ; v.¹², the stellar altars. Of the remainder, vv.⁵· ⁸ᵃ· ⁹ concern the disposition of the provincial priests, v.⁵ indeed conflicting with vv.⁸ᵃ· ⁹ ; v.¹⁰, on the Melek-cult, is out of place, and may be secondary, as are vv.¹³· ¹⁴. *Cf.* the afterthought of the diviners below, v.²⁴.

VV.¹⁵⁻²⁰. The reformation outside of Judah. This passage of generalities, dependent upon the midrash in I. 13, is in absolute contrast to the historical details of vv.⁴⁻¹⁴. The desecration of the altar at Bethel may well be historical, but the murder of the priests of the high-places contradicts the treatment of the priestlings in v.⁵. **15.** *And moreover the altar at Bethel* [*the high-place which Jeroboam ben Nebat made, who entailed sin on Israel, moreover that altar and the high-place*] *he destroyed, and he ⌐broke up its stones⌐* [so at least the Grr., replacing impossible 𝔘 *burnt the high-place*]—*he stamped to dust ; and he burned Asherah.* Omission of the long bracketed section is necessary to reduce a most conflate passage (following *SBOT*). An altar can be destroyed, but hardly a high-place ; in the Jeroboam story the altar alone is the offensive object, references to high-places appearing there only in I. 12³¹, 13³²· ³³. The Grr. give at least a makeshift in place of the impossible burning of a high-place. The final reference to Asherah (here exceptionally without the article) is evidently secondary. **16.** *And Josiah faced about, and he saw the tombs that were there in the mount, and he gave orders, and took the bones from the tombs, and burned them upon the altar, and defiled it, according to the word of YHWH that the man of God* *proclaimed*, [*when Jeroboam stood at the Haj by the altar; and he faced about, and cast his eyes upon the tomb of the man of God*] [plus from Grr.], *who proclaimed these things*. The insertion from the Gr., itself clumsy, or the like is necessary, 𝔥 showing the result of parablepsis due to the double occurrence of *the man of God*. The original may have been simply: *And Josiah faced about, and he saw the tombs that were there in the mount, and he cast his eyes upon the tomb of the man of God, who proclaimed these things.* **17.** *And he said: What is that monument that I see?* For such a traditional sepulchral monument (*şîyûn*, the word also at Eze. 39^{15}), in modern Arabic the tomb of a *walī* (saint), *cf.* Rachel's 'pillar,' Gen. 35^{20} (with another word *maşşêbet*, as used in Phœn.). *And the men of the city said to him: The tomb!—The man of God who came from Judah, and proclaimed these things that thou hast done.* The initial exclamatory phrase is to be left despite critics; translations, *e.g.*, 𝔊^L EVV, naturally fill it out (see Note). **18.** *And he said: Let him be; none move his bones! And they left his bones alone, the bones of the prophet who came from Samaria.* The final clause is an absurd bit of carelessness, as the prophet came from Judah. 𝔊^L has a long insertion, introducing the elder prophet of the original midrash; but even he did not come from Samaria. **19.** *And moreover all the high-place houses in the cities of Samaria, which the kings of Israel had made for provocation, Josiah removed, and he did to them in accordance with all the things he had done at Bethel.* **20.** *And he sacrificed all the priests of the high-places, who were there, on the altars, and he burned men's bones upon them.* Notice of the *high-place houses* repeats I. 12^{31}. V.^{20} repeats I. 13^2.

VV.$^{21-23}$. The great Passover celebration in Jerusalem. **21.** *And the king commanded all the people, to wit: Celebrate Passover to YHWH your God, as is written in this book of the covenant.* **22.** *Indeed there was no celebration like this Passover since the days of the Judges, who judged Israel, and for all the days of the kings of Israel and of Judah.* **23.** *Just in the eighteenth year of king Josiah was this Passover celebrated to YHWH in Jerusalem.* The Passover was apparently chosen for this climax because it was the most distinctive Israelite feast, with the sacrifice of a lamb, distinctly nomadic and pastoral in character, and so peculiarly Judæan, the North Israelite element supplying the requirement of unleaven. *Cf.* Dt. 16[1ff.], and see Morgenstern in *HUCA* 10 (1935), 43 ff. Hempel finds here the statesmanlike combination of the festivals of the two regions (*Altheb. Lit.*, 142). The intensity of the reformation appears in the choice of the Passover for this demonstration, as that feast was one primarily of the family group, hence heretofore celebrated throughout the whole land. N. M. Nicolsky, in ' Pascha im Kulte des jerusalem. Tempels,' *ZAW* 1927, 171 ff., argues reasonably that this event was the innovating institution of a Passover Haj to the temple. *Cf.* the amplifications of this brief datum in 2 Ch. 35$^{1-19}$, 1 Esd. 1$^{1-22}$. The awkward repetition of the date as *in the eighteenth year* (*cf.* 22^3) appears secondary, an attempt to make the event initial in the reformation.

V.^{24}. A summary account of the purgation of various heathenish rites. For the ghostly rites as practised by Manasseh see Comm. on 21^6. For the *teraphim*, household gods, see Gressmann, *ZAW* 1924, 324 ff., and for the Akkadian background Sidney Smith, *Rev. d'Ass.*, 23 (1923), 127 ff. ; *JTS* 1932, 33 ff. ; and C. H. Gordon, *RB* 44 (1935), 35 ff.

VV.$^{25-27}$. The moralizing judgment. **25.** *And like him there was not before him a king, who* (so) *turned to YHWH with all his heart and all his soul and all his strength according to all the Law of Moses, and after him arose none like him.* Josiah's piety is expressed in terms of the Shema (Dt. 6^4), with its tripartite analysis of human nature, the intelligence, the feelings, the moral action. The statement contradicts the similar encomium given to Hezekiah (18^5). The one contemporary encomium of Josiah is from Jeremiah's hand (22$^{15, 16}$), but only lauding him as a just king (see Add. Note, n. 4). The encomium is given here, it would be out of place in connexion with the story of his tragic death. **26.** *Only YHWH turned not from the heat of his great anger, even as his anger was hot against Judah for all the provocations with which Manasseh provoked him.* **27.** *And YHWH said: Also Judah will I remove from my face, even as I removed Israel, and I will reject this city which I have chosen, Jerusalem, and the house of which I said, My Name shall be there.* As history proved, the reformation was not sufficient to thwart the original divine decree

(21¹⁰ᶠᶠ·). **28.** The usual formula of *the rest of the acts*, etc., is exceptionally placed before note of the king's death. VV.²⁹· ³⁰. The tragic end of the reign. For the history see Add. Note, §1. **29.** *In his days Pharaoh-Necho king of Egypt campaigned against the king of Assyria on the way to the river Euphrates; and king Josiah went to confront him. And he* (Pharaoh) *slew him at Megiddo, when he saw him*. **30.** *And his servants drove him, a dead man, from Megiddo, and brought him to Jerusalem. And they buried him in his tomb. And the people of the land took Jehoahaz ben Josiah, and they anointed him, and made him king in his father's stead.* 2 Ch. 35²⁰ (*cf.* 1 Esd. 1²³⁻³¹) makes Necho's objective Karkemish, but this is taken from the note, Jer. 46², of his subsequent campaign in 605 B.C. The identity of this Megiddo has been long in dispute. Herodotus reports (ii, 159) : " Necho, meeting the Syrians at Magdol, conquered them, and after the battle took Kadytis, a great city of Syria." Magdol is the Biblical Migdol on the Egyptian frontier (Ex. 14², Eze. 29¹⁰, *cf.* Abel, *GP* 2, 387) ; Kadytis has been identified with Gaza ; *cf.* Jer. 47¹. However, as now generally recognized, Magdol, better known to Herodotus, replaced the name Megiddo ; see Kittel, *GVI* 2, 417, n. 1, proposing also that Kadytis is Syrian, presumably Kadesh. Megiddo (*cf.* I. 9¹⁵) was the capital of the Assyrian district of Lower Galilee, which had now come into Josiah's hands.[1] It was at this strategic point that Josiah chose to meet the invader upon his entrance into the valley of Esdraelon. For the battle, in which he met his death, Ch. has a detailed and probably true tradition, which Jos. repeats (*Ant.*, x, 5, 1).[2] A novel view is that proposed by A. C. Welch, ' The Death of Josiah,' *ZAW* 1925, 255 ff., supported by Robinson (*HI* 424), that Josiah went ' to meet Necho ' at the latter's summons, and that the latter, without further detail, ' killed him.' The

---

[1] See Forrer, *Die Provinzeinteilung des ass. Reiches*, 27. Gressmann suggests (*ZAW* 1924, 336, n. 1) that ' Megiddo ' is abbreviation of ' Migdôl-'ēl,' which might account for Herodotus's place-name. For disruption of the traditional identification of Megiddo with Armageddon of Rev. 16¹⁶ see Torrey, ' Armageddon,' *HTR* 31 (1936), 237 ff., showing that the basis of the latter name is ' har mô'ēd ' of Is. 14¹³. For literature on Megiddo see Comm., I. 9¹⁵.

[2] See, especially for the parallel, B. Alfrink, ' Die Schlacht bei Megiddo u. der Tod des Josias (609),' *Biblica*, 15 (1934), 173 ff.

Hebrew statement is certainly terse beyond comparison ; yet the tragedy obscured all details to local historians. The military phrase ' to meet ' is used elsewhere (*e.g.*, Jos. 11²⁰), and ' to face the antagonist ' was a knightly expression (*cf.* 14⁸· ¹¹). *The people of the land* chose the successor, even as they had acted earlier upon similar tragedies of the throne (ch. 11, 21²⁴) ; see further Comm. on v.³¹.

Burkitt's Aquilanic Fragments appear for vv.¹¹⁻¹⁵· ¹⁹⁻²⁴· ²⁴⁻²⁷.
1. ויאספו : unless the verb is intransitive, it should be read as Nif. ; the rdg. by Ch., Grr. as sing. active with foll. acc. calls for the prep. את.—**2.** [כל] [ו]ישבי : Ch., 𝕲ʷ, of the Grr. B†, om.—as too extravagant ?—["י] בבית : 16 MSS בית, locative, as *e.g.*, v.²⁴— the older rdg.—**3.** [ו]לשמר : 2 MSS, Ch., B† om.—**4.** הכהן הגדול : 𝕾ᴴ ⁛, although in all Gr. MSS. For the adj. see Comm., 12¹¹, 22⁴⁻⁸.—כהני המשנה : 𝕿 the sing., and so at 25¹⁸, Jer. 52²⁴. For a possible similar Phœn. title see Harris, *Gram.*, 152, *s.v.* שני ; Lidzb. doubts the interpretation (*Eph.*, I, 248, n. 1) ; Eissf. accepts it (*ZAW* 1939, 6).—וישרפם : the pl. verb of 𝕲ᴸ 𝕾 is *ad sensum*.— בשרמות : Grr. transliterate, εν σαδημωθ (B† εν σαλημωθ ; *cf.* 𝕾ᴴ), exc. 𝕲ᴸ εν τω εμπυρισμω (+τ. χειμαρρου), and so Sym. (*cf.* Rahlfs, *SS* 3, 248) ; 𝕾 𝔙 ' in the valley,' 𝕿 ' in the plain,' EVV ' in the fields.' See Note on 19²⁶, where שרפה=שדמה of Is. ; but there are neither fields nor plains in that deep canyon. The word appears in Jer. 31⁴⁰, but miswritten שרמות, in similar connexion, ' the whole valley of the dead bodies and the ashes and השׁ unto the Wady Kidron ' ; the word in question is here again generally translated ' fields,' but see Graf, *ad loc.*, properly denying the pertinency. The interpretation of 𝕲ᴸ in both places is to the point, with שרם=שרף, ' to burn,' or better still, with rdg. of Sin for Shin, and so relating the root to that of שרף, ' the burnt city,' even as עירה is the ' sunken city ' (Arab. root *ġamara*, see Montg., *JQR* 25 [1935], 262). The word refers to the garbage fires in the valley, making it ultimately infamous as Gehenna ; *cf.* Comm. above. Klost., Kamph., Ehrl. would read משרפות, ' lime-kilns.' —ונשא : for the irregular consecution *cf.* the cases in vv.⁵· ⁸· ¹⁰· ¹⁵ ; Hölscher and Horst find critical basis in these cases for secondary character of the section (see Gressmann, *ZAW* 1924, 317, n. 2).— **5.** והשבית : 𝕿 correctly tr. with בטיל ; 𝔙 ' destroyed,' 𝕾 𝔄 ' killed ' ; original rdg. of 𝕲, κατεπαυσεν, preserved only by MS g and Aq., otherwise corrupted into κατεκαυσεν=𝕾ᴴ, an error suggested by v.²⁰.—כמרים : the word appears in the contemporary Zeph. 1⁴, and in Hos. 10⁵ ; earlier in Amarna tablets (*ḥamiru*), Egyptian (*kumru*) ; Phœn. and Punic כמר (in the Punic inscr. in parallelism with כהן, Harris, *Gram.*, 111) ; OAram. (two Nerab. inscriptions, ' to X priest of the Moon '—Lidzb., *HNE* 445 ; Cooke, *NSI* nos. 64, 65) ; the Elephantine papp. (of priests of an Egyptian god) ; Nabatæan,

Palmyrene (Lidzb., *ib.*, 297) ; Minæan (D. H. Müller, *Südarab. Altertümer*, 1899, 29 ; OArab. (C. Landberg, *Datina*, 1905–13, 965). For the most recent treatment see Albr., *SAC* 178, and notes. Mowinckel has attempted etymology, as ' der Heisse,' *i.e.*, ' machtbegabt ' (*ZAW* 1916, 238 f.) ; see also Dhorme, *RHR* 108 (1938), 118.—ויקטר : 𝔊ᴸ 𝔖 𝔙 read as לְקַטֵּר ; other Grr. 𝔖ᴴ 𝔗 = ויקטרו : the former is the preferable correction, and so EVV *sotto voce*. Gressmann (*ib.*, 326) would elide ויקטר . . . ירושלם as ' anstössig.' The Piel is used only of false worship.—מולות : properly ' stations ' ; *cf.* Phœn. נעם למול=ἀγαθῇ τύχῃ (Harris, *ib.*, 123). Grr. in general transliterate, with resultant corruptions, most correctly 𝔖ᴴ ; Aq., ' zodiacal constellations ' ; MS i ' stars ' ; MS p, ' the zodiacal signs.' Šanda gives an extensive study of Akk. *manzaltu*.—**6.** קבר=𝔊 𝔊ᴴ 𝔖ᴴ ; other VSS by necessity of translation as pl. ; but the construct phrase has pl. sense, *cf.* בית הבמות, 17²⁹.—**7.** בתי הקדשים : all Grr., 𝔖ᴴ as 'בית הק ; 'ק is common gender, *cf.* the collective קדש, I. 22⁴⁷.—[לאשרה] בתים : 𝔊 𝔊ᴴ 𝔖ᴴ transliterate, most texts having χεττιειμ/ν, but by error for βεττιειμ, as in x y, Theodoret ; 𝔊ᴸ Quinta, στολας=Lucif., ' ad stolas.' The Gr. transliteration has suggested to Klost., Benz., *al.*, כְּתָּנִים, ' tunics,' but the spelling χ- is secondary to β-, as Kit. observes. Šanda ingeniously connects the noun with Arab. *batt*, ' woven garment ' (and so G. R. Driver, *JBL* 55 [1936], 107), which interpretation is to be accepted, the corresponding Heb. root בדד representing the Arab. with voiced dentals after *b*, and so 𝔖 𝔄 tr.—**8.** שמה : for use of the form, which St. would correct, *cf.* Eze. 48³⁵, etc., and Arab. *tamma*.—נבע : B i Γαιβαλ=𝔈 ; most Hex. MSS, *e.g.*, N, have replaced with ' Dan.'—[באר] עד : 19 MSS ועד=Grr., 𝔖ᴴ 𝔗ᴸ 𝔖.— [השערים] במות : 𝔊 𝔊ᴴ=בית ; Klost., *al.* would read בְּכָח.—הַשְּׁעָרִים : איש בשער.—הַשְּׂעָרִים the correction accepted in Comm. would read 𝔊ᴸ 𝔗 read as though איש בָּא שער, accepted by many critics (*e.g.*, *BH*), but such translation is interpretative.—**9.** מצות : Kuenen's emendation to קְנָיוֹת, ' portions,' is attractive, but arbitrary ; see Kit., St., who leave the text with a question-mark.—**10.** הַתֹּפֶת : against the artificial Ḳr. (*cf.* ' Molek ') note the Gr. transliterations, *e.g.*, ταφεθ (B *al.*), θεφωθ (x y=𝔖ᴵᴵ), θοφθα (A†).—[הנם] בני : Ḳr. בֶּן, and so 50 MSS Ken., deR.=VSS ; elsewhere similar variations between Kt. and Ḳr. ; a variant form, Josh. 18¹⁶ om. בן. The name הנמי appears on a Judæan seal, *IAE* 246.—לבלתי : 2 MSS deR. om.=OGr. (B *al.*), some Luc. MSS, Hex. (𝔖ᴴ ※), 𝔖 𝔄 ; it appears to conflict with the prep. in foll. להעביר, (4 MSS העביר), but *cf.* 'למען ל, Eze. 21²⁰ ; the negative was probably introduced to express the royal intention (*cf.* St. *BH*).—**11.** מִבֹּא=' from entering ' ; but כְּבֹא or בְּבֹאָה must be read, as also implied by VSS EVV.—[לשכת] אל : so all MSS=Grr., 𝔗 ; 𝔙 ' iuxta,' EVV ' by,' as though על, which is required.—פרורים : also in sing., פַּרְבָּר, 1 Ch. 26¹⁸. The latter form now appears, with mng. as here, for a temple precinct in the Lydian Aramaic inscr. published by

E. Littmann in *Sardis*, vol. 6, pt. 1 (1916) ; *cf.* S. A. Cook, *Journ. Hell. Studies*, 1917, 77 ff., 219 ff. ; Torrey, *AJSL* 34 (1918), 185 ff., and at length P. Kahle and P. Sommer in *Kleinasiatische Forschungen*, vol. I (ed. by Sommer and H. Eheloff, 1930), 18 ff. For etymology as Persian see *SBOT*, GB. But a Bab. etymology has been proposed by T. Östreicher, p. 54, accepted by Gressmann, p. 323, and Procksch, p. 27 (for the titles see Add. Note, §2), identifying with Sumerian *ē-bar-bar*, ' shining house,' name of suntemples at Sippar, Babylon, etc. (Deimel, *Pantheon Bab.*, no. 3081). This etymology would obviate St.'s criticism of the word here as late because of Persian origin, but it is not used in the Bible of the temple but of its courts, as also in later Jewish use, and there also for ' suburbs ' (Jastrow, *Dict.*, 1218). VSS transliterate, exc. that Sym. Græcizes the transliteration into τ. φρουροῦ, ' the guard.' —מרכבות: MSS 1, 253 מרכבת : 𝔊 𝔊^H 𝔄 as sing.=מֶרְכָּבָה, to be accepted with St., *al.*—**12.** על הגג עלית אחז : see Comm. ; Šanda would elide the art. to obtain construct construction.—[יהודה] מלכי : B 𝔈 Lucif. as sing. by corruption of βασιλεις>-ευς, and then of prec. εποιησαν>-εν ; 𝔊^L followed suit, intruding with ' Ahaz (king of Judah).'—וירץ משם : Aq. used a rare verb of active sense, εδρομωσεν ; 𝔙 ' cucurrit ' (*cf.* mg. of EVV) ; other VSS, ' removed ' (=GV), 𝔊 𝔊^L with different verbs. Suggested emendations to וַיְצֵא (Benz., *al.*), וַיְרַקַּם (Ehrl., *al.*; *cf. BH*), with attachment of the foll. Mem to the verb have little textual basis. Kimchi suggested the verb רצץ ' to break up,' followed by FV EVV, and in suit correction to וַיְרֻצֵּם שָׁם is most plausible. St. and Haupt come to no definite conclusion.—**13.** הבמות : Grr. (not Aq.), 𝔖^H as הבית.—המשחית [להר] : Grr. (not Aq.) transliterate=𝔖^H ; 𝔙 ' (Montis) offensionis ' ; Aq., 𝔖 𝔄 as from root שחת, ' to destroy '; EVV ' destruction/corruption.' 𝔗 with ' Mount of Olives ' gives the right clue=הַר הַמִּשְׁחָה, ' Mount of (olive-) Oil ' ; the local application appears in the Mishna (Jastrow, *Dict.*, *s.v.* משחה), and such was the interpretation of Rashi, Kimchi. The original was early changed to the form here to verify Jer.'s prophecy (7³²) that the Kidron valley would be termed ' Valley of Slaughter ' (הרגה). Piscator (in Poole) early recognized the play on the word, comparing Hos. 10⁶. The noun of 𝔥 was recognized by Midrash as a demon, ' the Destroyer ' (Jastrow, *s.v.*).—שקץ : *bis* ; *cf.* I. 11⁵·⁷ ; also here מלכם תועבת *vs.* 'מ 'ש there.—**15.** הבמה 1⁰ ; secondary, as the asyndeton shows ; the insertion duplicated with the plus below, וישרף את הבמות.—ואת הבמה=Aq., 𝔖 𝔙 ; Grr., κ. συνετριψεν τ. λιθους αυτου=𝔈 𝔖^H, which Klost. rendered into וַיְשַׁבֵּר אֶת־אֲבָנֶיהָ for restoration of the original, followed by Burn., St., *al.*; *cf. BH* (Eissf. keeps 𝔥) ; ישבר is a possible textual corruption of the verb ; but the original may have been a careless bit of writing.—**16.** בהר : Grr. (exc. Aq., 𝔊^L), 𝔖^H, ' in the city,' as though בעיר.—See Comm. for acceptance of a long plus in Grr., 𝔖^H, proposed by Then., and accepted by almost all critics since ; for the re-written Heb.

see *BH*.—**17.** הֲלוֹ : also as fem. at 4^{25} ; the story is in Northern dialect.—הקבר : for the absolute noun, as rendered above, *cf.* similar cases at 9^{27} with corrected text, 22^{18b}, and see GK §167 ; *cf.* Wright, *Arab. Gr.*, 2, §35. Grr. om., exc. Aq., 𝕲^L, the latter as though for 'זֶה הַקּ, which St. adopts ; Benz., +קבר.—אשר עשית : Grr. (exc. Aq., 𝕲^L), 𝕊^H ' which he announced.'—[אל] הַמִּזְבֵּחַ בֵּית : read either 'מִזְבַּח ב' or 'הַמִּזְבֵּחַ ב, with 'ב understood as locative (some MSS 'בב), which construction was later ignored, and the Ḳr. attempted the construct ; for such cases of irregular Ḳr. see GK §127, f. St. regards the unnecessary בית אל as a gloss.—**18.** 𝕲^L adds to the v. a long exegetical plus, introducing ' the old prophet who dwelt at Bethel,' and ' the man of God from Judah ' ; see Rahlfs, *SS* 3, 279. St. retains 𝔐, as *vs.* Burn., *al.* Ehrl. would read here, " and his bones saved the prophet of Samaria," but there is no reference to the other prophet.—**19.** להכעים : 𝕊 corroborates 𝔐 ; the same absolute phrase at 21^6.—**20.** אשר שם : 𝕊 𝔄 interpret as אשר שמו, " who set incense" (*i.e.*, upon the altar) ; *cf.* Dt. 33^{10} for such use of the verb.—את עצמות אדם : the particle את, which critics would elide, introduces the direct citation of I. 13^2. **21.** הזה [ספר הברית] : 2 MSS הזאת=𝕲 Aq., 𝕊^H 𝕋 𝔙.—𝕲^L adds to the v., " and they did so," an example of translator's complement.—**22.** כפסח הזה : Grr. (not 𝕊^H)=הפסח הזה, which St. prefers, as though there had been no Passover celebration in Judah since the Judges ; but the point is the confinement of the celebration to Jerusalem.—וכל ימי מלכי ישראל ומלכי יהודה : acc. to 𝕊^H the first phrase is an Aquilanic addition to orig. 𝕲, but this leaves the second phrase in the air ; the whole expression may be dependent on 2 Ch. 35^{18}.—**23.** הזה [הפסח] : 𝕲 (B A *al.*) ℭ om.—**24.** אבות, ידענים : see Comm. on 21^6.—**25.** [תורת] ככל : MSS בכל.—ובכל.—**26.** כל [הכעסים] : Grr., exc. 𝕲^L, om. ; 𝕊^H has.—**27.** את ירושלם : noted by St. as ' scribal expansion ' ; but the city's name is parallel to the divine name of the temple.—**29.** פרעה נכה : Aimé-Giron has published an Eg. tomb inscr. naming פרעה נכו (*Anc. Egypt*, 1923, pt. 2, 38 ff.) ; the Gr. Νεχαω is closer to the Eg. name.—המלך [יאשיהו] : 𝕲 om. ; 𝕊^H ※ ; but repetition of the title is in place.—כראתו אתו : Joüon (*Mél.*, 483) regards as dittogr. of לקראתו : but see Comm.— **30.** בקברתו : Hex. (N *al.*, gloss in 𝕊^H)+' in the city of David.'

ADDITIONAL NOTE TO II. 22–23^{30}

§1. THE INTERNATIONAL HISTORY [1]

Josiah came to the throne in 639 B.C., when Ashurbanipal's empire was fast riding to its fall, in conflict with rebellious states, which

---

[1] See at large *CAH* 3, cc. 5, 9, 10, the Histories of Hall, ch. 11, Meyer, vol. 3, 139 ff. ; for Assyria and Babylonia, Rogers, vol. 2, bk. 3, ch. 11, bk. 4, ch. 1, Olmstead, *HA* ch. 48 ; for Egypt, Petrie, vol. 3, 312 ff., Breasted, ch. 27, Alt, *Israel u. Aegypten*, 87 ff. ; for Judah,

ultimately threw off the yoke, Media and Babylonia, the latter under Nabopolassar (ca. 609 B.C.), father of Nebuchadnezzar II, and in face of invading hordes of the northern Kimmerians and later the Scythians, the latter invasion probably in the notable year 626, the last sure dating for Ashurbanipal, and the year of the call of the prophet Jeremiah. For this last storm of barbarians, which swept as far as Egypt's borders, Herodotus gives a lengthy record (i, 103 ff.), while it is the background of prophecies of the contemporary Zephaniah and the young Jeremiah (Zeph. 1, 2; Jer. 1$^{13\text{ff.}}$, cc. 3–6, etc.).[2] The persistent combination of Media and Babylon brought Assyria to its end with the capture of Nineveh in the year 612, accompanied with the utter destruction of the capital and the neighbouring proud cities (cf. Nah. 2, 3). These two states now claimed and proceeded to divide the legacy of Assyria.

However there was a third nation, of far greater antiquity and imperial fame, which claimed its share of the spoils. Egypt had been conquered and despoiled by Ashurbanipal (ca. 660 B.C.). But there came the native revival under Psammetichos I (663–609) and his son Necho II (609–594). With the collapse of Assyria Egypt pressed again its ancient claims upon the Syrian coast-lands as far as the Euphrates. After the fall of Nineveh in 612 Necho advanced against the up-coming Neo-Babylonian empire, and Josiah met his death in opposing his progress through Israelite territory (608 B.C.). Our book records (23^{33}) Necho's subsequent sojourn at Syrian Riblah. But his control of Syria was ephemeral. There ensued the decisive battle with the crown-prince and future king of Babylon, Nebuchadnezzar II, at Karkemish in 605 (cf. the historical tradition at 2 Ch. 35^{20}), and the Pharaoh's empire was confined once more to Egypt. The decadent state of Judah became a pawn between the two empires.

The fresh Aryan nations were now entering upon the imperial map of south-western Asia. But before their time of empire arrived, occurred the spiritual revival of ancient Egypt and Babylonia, harking back to

---

Stade, vol. 1, 641 ff., Wellhausen, ch. 9, Sellin, vol. 1, 282 ff., Kittel, vol. 2, §49, Olmstead, *HPS* ch. 33, Robinson, vol. 1, ch. 20, Albright, 'The seal of Eliakim and the Latest Pre-exilic History,' *JBL* 51 (1932), 77 ff. For the major historical event are to be consulted C. J. Gadd, 'The Fall of Nineveh,' *Proc. Brit. Acad.*, 11 (1923), E. Florit, ' Ripercussioni immediate della caduta di Ninive sulla Palestina,' *Biblica*, 1932, 399 ff. A collection of pertinent Akkadian and Egyptian texts is given by Jirku, *AKAT* 184 ff. J. Lewy's extensive monograph, *Forschungen zur alten Geschichte*, includes a section on ' Das Datum der Schlacht bei Megiddo und die neubab. Synchronismen des A.T.,' with treatment of the Biblical texts (pp. 20 ff.) and presentation of Babylonian Chronicle G with commentary (pp. 68 ff.).

[2] For scepticism towards Herodotus's record of the Scythians and hence the removal of such a background for these prophecies see Eissf.'s argument in Horst's Comm. on Zeph. in *HAT* (1938), 184.

ancient times, in religion and art and literature. For Egypt see Breasted, ch. 27, and, succinctly, Meyer, 3, 149-51. The latter remarks that the foreign deity Seth was excluded from the pantheon, his name and statues obliterated, while the Syrian Anat and Astarte disappeared almost entirely—a close resemblance indeed to the Josianic reform! And similarly in Babylonia we find the revival of the religion and cult of the native god Marduk, along with the brilliant restoration of ancient sanctuaries; see A. Jeremias, *Monotheistische Strömungen innerhalb d. babylon. Religion* (1904), 23 ff., and Jastrow, *Rel. Bab. u. Ass.*, 1, ch. 14, remarking (p. 251), "Man kann die neubabylonische Periode als eine ausgesprochen religiöse bezeichnen," and his *Religious Belief in Bab. and Ass.*, 99 ff., noting 'the tendency towards monotheism' in Marduk's absorption of the powers and attributes of the other gods. Hall, in the opening of his chapter, observes that "the effect of the Egyptian renovation was but to intensify and emphasize the old age of Egypt," and similarly, "the restored kingdom of Nabopolassar . . . was marked, like the restored kingdom of Psamatik, by a revival of old days and old ways. . . . And Nabonidus, the last king of the last Babylonian dynasty, was, as we shall see, a learned archæologist, an enthusiastic collector of ancient divine images, and energetic preserver of the most ancient temples." And Albright in his *From the Stone Age*, pp. 240 ff., gives a graphic view of this widespreading wave of religious revival.

Judah in its repristination of traditional religion through the contemporary Deuteronomic reform was acting in consort with Egypt and Babylon for the national God and his people. Its action in part was of 'the spirit of the times.' But the document that underlay that reform was not archaizing, except in preservation of the proud traditional history; it was definitely prophetic, a programme for the future. And hence the permanent effect of the reformation for that people and its religion and for the world. Says Meyer (p. 158): "Dem Akt vom Jahre 621 stehen an Bedeutung wenig andere Begebenheiten der Weltgeschichte gleich: auf ihm beruht das Judentum und damit auch das Christentum wie der Islam." And Causse may be quoted in like strain (*Du groupe ethnique*, 175): "C'était un grand révolutionnaire que l'auteur de cette législation, un des plus grands révolutionnaires qui furent jamais. . . . Un point particulièrement significatif . . . c'est la manière dont s'effectue dans sa législation ce passage du collectivisme primitif à l'individualisme et à la religion intérieure que les prophètes de l'époque précédente avaient annoncés."

§2. The Book Found in the Temple

For the identity of the book found and its relation to Deuteronomy, a problem also involving the criticism of the book of Jeremiah, little more than reference may be made to the rapidly accumulating literature on the subject, in particular within the past two decades. Pfeiffer has presented an analytical bibliography for publications between 1914 and 1925 in his article, 'The History, Religion and Literature of

Israel,' *HTR* 27 (1934), 308 ff. There are to be noted the studies, with bibliographies, in the recent Introductions : Hempel, pp. 138 ff., Oesterley and Robinson, pp. 51 ff., Eissfeldt, §§22, 32, Pfeiffer, pp. 178 ff., with bibliography, pp. 867 ff. Two comprehensive treatments of recent date have appeared, with full bibliographies and criticism of the earlier literature : a Symposium on ' The Problem of Deuteronomy,' in *JBL* 47 (1928), 305–79, with discussion of the various date-themes, by J. A. Bewer, L. B. Paton, G. Dahl ; and A. R. Siebens, *L'Origine du code deutéronomique* (1928, pp. 251 ff.). Subsequent additions to the bibliography with digests are given by W. Baumgartner, *Theol. Rundschau*, 1929, 7 ff. ; A. Causse, in *Revue d'Histoire et de Philosophie Religieuses*, 1933, 1 ff., and *Du groupe ethnique*, ch. 5 ; A. Lods, *Les prophetes d'Israël et le début du judaisme* (1935), 157 ff. ; W. A. Irwin, ' An Objective Criterion for the Dating of Deut.,' *AJSL* 56 (1939), 337 ff. Noteworthy for the historical relations are : Östreicher, *Das deuteronomische Gesetz* (1923) ; Gressmann, ' Josia u. das Deut.,' *ZAW* 1924, 313 ff. ; Procksch, ' König Josia,' *Festgabe Th. Zahn* (1928), 19 ff. ; Sellin, *Gesch. d. isr.-jüd. Volkes*, 1, 289 ff. ; Kittel, *GVI* 2, Beil. II ; Robinson, *HI* 1, Note F, pp. 424 ff. ; also Dhorme, *L'Évolution religieuse d'Israël*, 1, 45 ff.

For the several theories concerning the origin of the book only brief references may be given here. Practically Mosaic origin has been claimed by H. M. Wiener in a series of articles in *Bibliotheca Sacra*, 1907 *et seq.* ; H. Junker, *Das Buch Deut.* (1933) ; J. Reider, in *JQR* 27 (1937), 349 ff. Most recently F. Dornseiff has argued for early composition of Dt. and D at large in the Pentateuch—for D a date *ca.* 830 B.C. (' Antikes zum A.T., 4 : Die Abfassungszeit des Pentateuchs u. die Deuteronomiumsfrage,' *ZAW* 1938, 64 ff., *e.g.*, p. 84). The theory of a Post-Exilic date has been propounded by G. R. Berry, *JBL* 39 (1920), 44 ff. ; 59 (1940), 133 ff. ; R. H. Kennett, *Deut. and the Decalogue* (1920) ; and most elaborately by G. Hölscher, ' Komposition u. Ursprung des Deuteronomiums,' *ZAW* 40 (1922), 161–255. For a comparatively early production, at least of the code in the book, argument has been made, *inter al.*, by Östreicher, *op. cit.*, A. C. Welch, *The Code of Deut.* (1924). Dhorme assigns the date of the book to the beginning of the seventh century or perhaps the end of the eighth. Irwin (*op. cit.*) denies the view of Post-Exilic origin, but remains uncertain as to the upper limit. As often with the composition of such programmatic theses, the dark age before the dawn is to be preferred for the origin of Dt. ; there may be noted the avoidance of political subjects, with only brief reference to the monarchy. The book ' found ' would be limited, as generally allowed by conservative critics, to cc. 5, 12–16, 28. Pfeiffer, in his *Int.*, 187, would extend this quantum to $4^{44}-8^{20}$, $10^{12}-11^{25}$, 12–26, $28^{1-24, 43-46, 69}$. There is to be noted Driver's still standard study of Dt. in his *Int.*, §5.

For the deposit and subsequent discovery of ancient temple archives, comparable with the present history, E. Naville first drew attention for Egypt in his article, 'Egyptian Writings in Foundation Walls and the Age of the Book of Deuteronomy,' *PSBA* 29 (1907), 232 ff. Similar references are found in Akkadian and Hittite records, citations of which are given by Jirku, *AKAT* 184 ff. But the book in question was not a foundation deposit; rather it was a document laid away in the temple library, perhaps for safe-keeping, even as such libraries existed in ancient temples. The book was, literally speaking, a pseudograph, although without a title in the modern sense of the word, and hence it is variously referred to, as 'the book of the Law,' 'the book of the Covenant,' 'the words of this Covenant written in this book' (II. 22^8, $23^{2,3}$). Moses' name is attached in the postscript, Dt. 31^{24}. *N.b.* Driver's apologetic for this ancient literary device of attribution to an ancient author, *Deut.*, pp. lv, *seq.*, and W. R. Smith, *The O.T. in the Jewish Church*, 363 ('not a forgery'). The composer may have had himself in mind with the words at 18^{18}: "I will raise them up a prophet from among their brethren like unto thee" (*cf.* v.^{15}—this in antagonism to the cults and prophets denounced). The book was a Utopian religious programme (Hempel, 'eine heilsprophetische Programmschrift').

The story of the finding of the book is the most detailed narrative in Ki., apart from stories of the prophets, since the history of Solomon. The petty details of the event, the personalities of the royal commission, in particular of 'Huldah the prophetess,' are striking proof of a story of real history (this *vs.* Winckler, *KAT* 277). It is a woman, not the priest Hilkiah, or another of the priests, or one of the many prophets of the day (*e.g.*, Zephaniah, Jeremiah), who gives the oracle on the event. The priest himself appears clear of connivance with the origin of the book in his resolve to appeal to a nonsacerdotal prophetess. By the latter the dynasty, as embodying the people, is denounced to the extreme; only with a second oracle, following Josiah's act of repentance, is he promised a death 'in peace' (22^{20}), a promise contradicted by his tragic death. Reliance may not be attributed to the report of the prophetess's words, but the alleged promise must have been anterior to the actual end. Also there is in Dt. no partisanship for the Davidic monarchy, no reference to the promises to David; for the first time in history we learn of a monarchy, which, if it is to be established, is to be constitutional: "He shall write him a copy of this law in a book," and "he shall read therein all the days of his life . . . that his heart be not lifted up above his brethren" (17$^{18\text{ff.}}$). Also of the primacy of Judah there is no hint. Similarly in the immediately following Law of the Priests (18$^{1-8}$), these are 'the priests, the Levites,' and the provincial Levites shall have full privilege, if they come up to the sanctuary. There is not a word about Sadokids, high-priesthood and the like, nor is Jerusalem named; there is only the indirect reference to "the place which YHWH shall choose." In literary style and theological character, in the line of the Elohist, the book may well have proceeded from a North Israelite, who had grasped in his convictions the historically proven necessity of a central sanctuary. We may compare the Prophet of Islam. The old Prophets of the North and Hosea had left a spiritual legacy to the South.

§3. THE REFORMATION [3]

The narrative in ch. 23 presents specific events almost only for Jerusalem and Judah ('from Geba to Beer-sheba'). The destruction of the altar at Bethel, while wholly probable, is involved in a lengthy midrash. The original material is interspersed with later intrusions. V.^{5a}, with contemptuous reference to 'the priestlings at the high-places,' contradicts the generous treatment given to 'the priests of the high-places,' according to v.^{9}. The summary of the stellar cults in v.^{5b}, while of contemporary flavour, is clumsily introduced. Both v.^{5} and v.^{8} interrupt the sequence of events in the purging of the temple, as does also v.^{10} with its datum on Topheth. V.^{13} is reproduction of I. 11$^{5\text{ff.}}$; v.^{24} is an afterthought, with 21^6 in mind.

As for the progress of the reform, which Ki. presents as one act, culminating in a great Passover festival, the fuller data of Ch. have been accepted by some scholars for defining certain stages in the process. According to 2 Ch. 34^3, "in the eighth year of his reign . . . he began to seek after the God of his father David; and in the twelfth year he began to purge Judah and Jerusalem," etc. There follows

---

[3] For recent criticism of the material in the composite story in ch. 23, along with mutual criticism, see Hölscher, 'Das Buch der Könige,' 206 ff., Östreicher, Gressmann, Kittel, Procksch, and *cf. SBOT*. Östreicher discovers two narratives, belonging severally to the two epochs that he assigns to the reformation. The data of the ch. are closely related to those in ch. 21, which gives the background of the present story.

(vv.⁸ff.) 'in his eighteenth year,' the discovery of 'the book of the Law of YHWH given by Moses,' continued by the story of the covenant of king and people, this leading up to the fulsome story of the great Passover (35¹⁻¹⁹). These epochal data are accepted by Östreicher (e.g., pp. 63 ff.), Procksch (pp. 20 ff.), and therewith a means of chronological analysis is claimed, chiming in with historical events; e.g., the king's twelfth year, 628 B.C., would be contemporaneous with the end of the known history of Ashurbanipal, the inroad of the Scythians, while the call of Jeremiah was approximate, in the thirteenth year. But the 'conversion' of the young king, *ætat.* 16, *i.e.*, at his coming of age, appears artificial.⁴ The immediate purgation of the whole land of Israel along with specification of certain tribe-lands follows, vv.⁶⁻⁷, although according to 2 Ch. 34³¹⁻³² only the citizens of Jerusalem and Benjamin took part in making a covenant before YHWH, so inconsistent is the story.

As for the spiritual progress of the reformation, apart from destruction of the heathenish cults and sanctuaries, we are left entirely in the dark. The prophets appear in the great act of the Covenant (v.²—there is no reason to excise the reference). Sellin has proposed the extravagant theory (p. 291) that the provincial priests were brought up to Jerusalem to learn the Law, and so to be sent forth as missionaries, 'as curates of souls and teachers of Torah.' The question of the relation of Jeremiah to the reform belongs primarily to the criticism of the book assigned to him. The discovery of the book occurred in the fifth year of his ministry (Jer. 1²). According to 11¹ff. Jeremiah was one of the preachers of 'the words of this covenant,' with initial stress on the curse lying upon those who 'hear not the words of this covenant,' and so preaching to 'the men of Judah and the citizens of Jerusalem,' and 'in the streets of Jerusalem.' But while our history records the prophets as abetting Josiah, and names a prophetess as a cardinal actor, it ignores Jeremiah. This omission is not cause for stringent criticism. But more remarkable is Jeremiah's entire ignoring of Josiah, with the one exception in his indirect reference to him in the threnody over his son and successor Shallum (22¹¹ff.) : " Did not thy father eat and drink and execute justice and right ? Then it was well with him. He judged the cause of the poor and needy. Then it was well. Is not this to know me ? " And apart from ch. 11 there is no reference to the reform. The problem of this offishness of the prophet has long been a troubled subject of discussion.⁵ Uniquely Torrey, holding to the late, pseudepigraphical origin of Ezekiel, and

---

⁴ The point would be made by the Chronicler that the young Josiah knew the Law, even if the original Book had been lost. For criticism of the above hypothesis see Gressmann, pp. 313 ff.

⁵ See, *e.g.*, Cheyne, *Jeremiah, His Life and Times* (*ca.* 1888), ch. 5; A. J. Puukko, 'Jeremias Stellung zum Deut. 8,' *BWAT* 13 (1913), 126 ff. ; G. A. Smith, *Jeremiah*⁴ (1929), ch. 4 ; Causse, *Du groupe ethnique*, 177 ff.

maintaining the full effect of Josiah's reformation, assigns similar late origin to Jer. 1–10.[6] But such extreme criticism of Jer. may be avoided by assuming a sharp cleavage between idealistic prophet and politically minded king.

§4. THE POLITICS OF JOSIAH'S REIGN

The interest of Biblical scholarship has naturally centred on the religious reformation, for which indeed we have data only for Judah. Josiah's confronting of Necho at Megiddo presents another phase of his reign, and that a secular one ; he attempted full recovery of the ancient bounds of All-Israel, and this as part of his duty as YHWH's Anointed.[7] For the political expansion of Josiah's kingdom with inclusion of the Israelite North Alt has proposed the interesting theory that the remains of the list of Josiah's territorial districting of the whole country are found in Josh. 18^{21-28}, $19^{2-8, 41-46}$.[8] There must have been some such political reorganization of his enlarged dominion to explain Josiah's defiance of Necho upon his intrusion into the strategic Jezreel Valley, and such secular causes may well have superseded those of religion. But there was the tragic collapse, which a Jeremiah may have feared, if not foreseen. The great prophets in general avoided 'entangling alliances' (cf. $20^{12\mathrm{ff.}}$), and demanded faith in the arm of the LORD alone. It was as in the age of the Protestant Reformation, when monarchs and reformers by no means saw alike ; the two groups worked together only when idealism and realism harmonized, though most often with a muddling of causes.

The last quarter of the seventh century was crucial in the world's history. The proud Assyrian empire fell into the dust. The nations of Egypt and Babylonia were revived with the hope of restoration of ancient empire. New kingdoms were established on the frontiers, Media and Lydia, and alien hordes of barbarous peoples, Kimmerians,

---

[6] See his *Pseudo-Ezekiel* (1930), ch. 3 (cf. review by S. Spiegel in *HTR* 24 [1931], 245 ff.), and 'The Background of Jer. 1–10,' *JBL* 56 (1937), 193 ff.

[7] Cf. the pertinent article by Olmstead, 'The Reform of Josiah and its Secular Aspects,' *AHR* 20 (1915), 566 ff.

[8] 'Judas Gaue unter Josia,' *Pjb.*, 21 (1925), 100 ff., and 'Eine galiläische Ortsliste in Jos. 19,' *ZAW* 1927, 59 ff. ; cf. Procksch, pp. 26 ff., and Noth, *Das Buch Josua*, *HAT* (1938), pp. ix ff., and Albright's review with archæological criticism in *JBL* 57 (1938), 226. A similar military reorganization of the kingdom has been proposed by E. Junge, 'Der Wiederaufbau des Heerwesens des Reiches Juda unter Josia,' *BWANT*, Folge IV, Heft 23 (1937). Vincent, in *La religion des judéo-araméens d'Éléphantiné*, 8 ff., 359 ff., holds that these early ' Jewish ' colonists were refugees from Josiah's purge of the North and from the Scythian invasion. The Jewish military colonies in Egypt may indeed go back to auxiliaries sent by Manasseh in his rebellion against Assyria, a practice condemned by Dt. 17^{16}.

II. 23³¹⁻³⁵   549

and Scythians, fanned an apocalyptic fervour. To Josiah's eye the God-given day had come with the destruction of Assyria, and so the divine opportunity for the political as well as the religious restoration of Israel. In modern terms, while religiously sincere, Josiah as king was a nationalist, a veritable King Arthur. He failed tragically in this rôle. Only ' the Book found,' which was published under his patronage, and the People of the Book survived.

VV.³¹⁻³⁵. *Judah a province of Egypt; the brief reign of Jehoahaz, and the Pharaoh's installation of his brother Eliakim-Jehoiakim as king.* || 2 Ch. 36¹⁻⁴, I Esd. 1³²⁻³⁶ ⁽³⁴⁻³⁸⁾ ; *cf. Ant.*, x, 5, 2. For the international history from this point to the end of the book see the continuations of the Histories listed in Additional Note above, §1. Between the events of the above section and those of the following chapters occurred, in 605 B.C., the momentous defeat of Necho at Karkemish, modern Jerablus, on the Euphrates at the NE point of Syria, by Nebuchadnezzar, the Babylonian crown-prince, who pursued the Egyptians to their frontiers, and then returned home to take the crown in succession to his father Nabopolassar. For the battle, with exact dating (' in Jehoiakim's fourth year ') and prophetic amplification, *cf.* Jer. 46. In this connexion is to be consulted the long extract from Berossos in *Ant.*, x, 11, 1, our prime authority for this western extension of Nebuchadnezzar's empire. For the subsequent history details are obscure. An anecdote from the beginning of Jehoiakim's reign reports his influence with the Egyptian government (Jer. 26²⁰ᶠᶠ·). He may have professed submission to the conqueror of Syro-Palestine (*cf.* 24⁷), but at heart have remained friendly to Egypt. The datum of 24¹ speaks of an undated advance by Nebuchadnezzar upon Jerusalem, Jehoiakim then becoming ' his servant ' for three years, and later ' rebelling.' See Kittel, *GVI* 2, 421, n. 1, for discussion of the chronology involved.

31. *Twenty-three years old was Jehoahaz when he began to reign, and for three months did he reign in Jerusalem. And his mother's name was Hamutal, daughter of Jeremiah of Libnah.* **32.** *And he did what was evil in the eyes of* YHWH, *like all that his fathers had done.* **33.** *And Pharaoh-Necho made him a prisoner at Riblah in the land of Hamath,* ⌜*so that he might not reign in Jerusalem*⌝ [secondary, Ḳr. correcting Kt.; see Note]. *And he put on the land a tribute of a hundred talents*

of silver and a [numeral evidently missing] *talent of gold.*
34. *And Pharaoh-Necho made Eliakim ben Josiah king in his father Josiah's stead* (*i.e.*, with legal ignoring of the predecessor), *and he changed his name to Jehoiakim. And Jehoahaz he took, and he* (Jehoahaz) *came to Egypt, and he died there.* **35.** *And the silver and the gold Jehoiakim gave to Pharaoh; he just taxed the land to give the money* [Heb. *silver*] *according to Pharaoh's command; of every one according to his rating did he exact the silver and the gold—' the people of the land '* [interpretative gloss]—*to give it to Pharaoh-Necho.* **31.** The new king evidently adopted a throne-name in place of the earlier ' Shallum,' by which he is known in Jeremiah's dirge (22$^{10\text{ff.}}$), and in the royal genealogy in 1 Ch. 3^{15}, according to which he was Josiah's fourth son, Jehoiakim being the second son ; in this case the selection of the younger prince would suggest a popular choice for some reason. But see Albright's argument (*JBL* 51 [1932], 92) that the figure would make Josiah only 14 years of age at Jehoiakim's birth (*cf.* however Comm., 22^1), and accordingly the figure is in error, and this prince was a younger brother. It may well be, with Albright, and Curtis *ad loc.*, that the family tree in 1 Ch. 3^{15} is wholly unreliable For the change of name, Shallum to Jehoahaz, there is to be noticed the extensive use of names with *yāhû* as component in this period, for which see Torczyner, *LL* 27 ff. The queen-mother's origin from rebellious Libnah (*cf.* 19^8) is of interest, and suggests a diplomatic marriage ; her name is of Arabic origin (see Note). **33.** For the importance of Riblah as capital of Cœle-Syria at the time, *cf.* 25$^{6\text{f.}\ 20\text{f.}}$. The place, with the name surviving, lies 34 km. S of Homs in the Orontes valley ; see Robinson, *LBR* 544 ff. (with full description of the now swampy terrain), Dussaud, *TH* 396 ff., Abel, *GP* 2, 436. *A talent of gold :* 𝔊 made the extravagant guess of ' 100 talents,' but 𝔊^L more reasonably ' 10 talents,' which is the proportion noted for the two metals in the tribute to Sennacherib, 18^{14} ' 300 of silver, and 30 of gold.' The figure in both cases is far below the 1000 talents stated to have been levied on Menahem of Israel (15^{19}). **34.** The change of name meant that the prince was created a new person by the Pharaoh. Similarly Nebuchadnezzar changed the subsequent king's name Mattaniah to Sedekiah (24^{17}). Šanda cites such cases

in Egypt; *e.g.*, Necho of Saïs gave his son Psammetichos I an Assyrian name, Nabū-šēzib-anni (*cf.* Rogers, *HBA* 2, 433). This ancient legality has survived in the Church, where historically a new name has been required at baptism, and so upon graduation to the priesthood, or to the papacy. This change of name suggested to Stade (*GVI* 1, 674) that it represented an understanding between the Deuteronomic reformers and Egypt, but this were absurd; Robinson remarks, far more to the point (*HI* 1, 431), that the change of name was 'perhaps a concession to Israelite feeling'; or rather there may have been a touch of satire on the Pharaoh's part, as though YHWH were actually on Egypt's side, *cf.* the Rab-shakeh's taunt, 18²⁵. For the death of Shallum in a strange land see Jeremiah's dirge, cited above. **35.** The v. presents universal taxation of the whole land, in contrast to the levy under Menahem, when only the men of wealth were assessed. The phrase, *the people of the land*, lacks construction (*n.b.* rewriting in EVV), but is a correct additional note. Critics (Klostermann, Stade, *al.*) have variously attempted improvement of the text. It would appear from Jeremiah's 'Woe' against Jehoiakim (22¹³ff·) that the king profited selfishly from this conscription of the wealth of all citizens—a common feature in Oriental handlings of money.

31. יהואחז=13¹; at 14¹ יואחז.—חמוטל: many MSS חטיטל=Kt. 24¹⁸, Jer. 52¹ (either vocalization possible); Grr., Jos., in the three cases=the latter form; *cf.* אביטל, 2 Sam. 3⁴, 1 Ch. 3³. For the first element, 'father-in-law,' *cf.* the name in 1 Ch. 4²⁶, to be read חֲמוּאֵל, and S. Arab. חמאל, and like combinations (*NPS* 1, 229). For the second element *cf.* יהוטל in Eleph. papp.; it means 'shade/shadow,' and appears in the repeated phrase of the Aram. copy of the Behistun inscription from the same quarter, בטלה די אהורמזד. Equivalent Heb. names are צַלְפָּחָר (with change of Ḳr.), צִלְצָאֵל (*cf.* Ps. 17⁸, etc.). The present name with ט for Heb. צ is doubtless Arabic. Noth (*IP* 39, 79) objects to this derivation, ignoring the S. Arab. names, and taking טל as 'dew' (!). —ירמיהו: on a seal and in a Lachish letter (*IAE* 215, Torczyner, *LL* no. 1), the full form in *-yāhû* is universal in these letters.— **33.** ויסירהו מלך מצרים: Ch., ויאסרהו פ' נ' ברבלה בארץ חמת במלך בירושלם; the verb in the latter affected the Gr. interpretation here, "and he removed him ... from reigning"=𝔖ᴴ, and the same influence induced the Ḳr. here, ממלך=ℭ𝔙; but the clumsy phrase במלך בי was an early accommodation with Ch., which ignores the item of the deposition at Riblah. Burn. unnecessarily finds

a reduction of two statements, "bound him at Riblah," and "removed him from reigning in Jerusalem."—עִנָּשׁ עַל הָאָרֶץ : 𝔊 om. through mistranslation of prec. יתן with εδωκεν (=𝔈).—[וֹהב] : ככר == N al.; 𝔊 (B A al.), 𝔈 '100 talents'; 𝔊ᴸ 𐤔 𐤀 'ten talents'; 𐤔ᴴ dubiously, 'talents.'—**34.** אליקים : see Note, 18¹⁸.—יהויקים : cf. ויקים, Neh. 12¹⁰, and so on a seal, *IAE* 197; יוקים, on a seal, Cooke, *NSI* 362.—וַיְבִּאֹ = 𝕿 𐤔 𐤀; other VSS as transitive = וַיָּבֵא ; 𝔊ᴸ as though ויביאהו = Ch.; 𝔓 is to be retained.—**35.** את עם הארץ : Grr. tr. the prep. with μετα = 𐤔ᴴ ; 𝕿 𝔙 𐤀 with 'from'; 𐤔 om. the phrase.

23³⁶–24⁷. The reign of Jehoiakim. ‖ 2 Ch. 36⁵⁻⁸ (where 𝔊, supplying lacuna of a parallel to Ki., vv.¹ᵇ⁻⁴, has a text parallel to, but differing from, 𝔊 of Ki.), 1 Esd. 1³⁷⁻⁴⁰ ⁽³⁹⁻⁴²⁾ ; *cf. Ant.*, x, 5, 2, 6. The historical data are few: the introductory formula to the reign, 23³⁶, the relations with Babylon, 24¹·²·⁷, the king's death and the succession, v.⁶. Ch. 24. **1.** *In his days Nebuchadnezzar king of Babylon came up, and Jehoiakim became his vassal for three years; then he turned and rebelled against him.* **2a.** *And YHWH sent against him the* (guerilla) *bands of Chaldæa and the bands of Aram and the bands of Moab and the bands of the Bnê-Ammon.* For these roving bands, always characteristic of those frontiers in unsettled times (*cf.* 5²), of Chaldæans (the first appearance of the word in the historical books) and Aramæan auxiliaries, *cf.* Jer. 35¹¹, where it is reported that the rustic Rechabites had to take refuge in Jerusalem from the depredations of invading troops, 'Chaldæans and Aramæans.' Nebuchadnezzar was otherwise occupied than to take a formal campaign, but he was now relieved of the Egyptian aggression (v.⁷). 𝔊 om. 'YHWH,' and it is secondary (so Stade, Eissfeldt, *cf. BH*), glossed in from the following moralizing section; but Nebuchadnezzar continues as subject of the foll verb. **2b.** *And he sent them into Judah ⸢to work destruction⸣* [=𝔊 Hex.; 𝔓 *to destroy him*] *according to the word of YHWH that he spoke through his ministers the prophets.* **3.** *Just according to the utterance* [Heb. *mouth*] *of YHWH was it in the case of Judah for removal from his face for the sin of Manasseh, according to all that he did;* **4.** ⸢*and also the innocent blood that he shed, and he filled Jerusalem with innocent blood*⸣ (the repetitive, unconstruable passage secondary) *and YHWH was unwilling to forgive.* The adverb *just* (EVV *only*), as common in Semitic syntax, relates to the climax of the period; in this case it was just Manasseh's sin that entailed the inevitable calamity, as foreordained ($21^{10\text{ff.}}$, $23^{26, 27}$). The long bracketed section is an intrusion suggested by 21^{16} for a more specific indictment. **5. 6.** In this postscript there is no reference to the king's burial. But 𝔊 in Ch., v.^{8} (where 𝔏 ignores the death), adds: "he was buried in the garden of Uzza" (cf. 21^{26}), which 𝔊$^\text{L}$ repeats here with plus, 'with his fathers.' It is attractive to regard this Gr. supplement as original, which would then have been elided to avoid clash with the Jeremianic prophecies of the king's being 'buried with an ass's burial,' 'cast forth beyond the gates of Jerusalem' (Jer. 22^{19}; cf. 36^{20}), on which matter Josephus expatiates; accordingly many critics restore the item to the text (so Stade, *GVI* 1, 679, n. 1, and *SBOT*, Wellhausen, *Comp.*, 359, Benzinger, Šanda, Eissfeldt). But Lucian's testimony is generally dubious, and 𝔊 of Ch. is certainly secondary, for according to Ch. v.^{6} Jehoiakim was taken prisoner to Babylon. If the king died in the siege by the roving bands, he could not have been accorded proper burial outside of the city's wall; hence the editor's ignorance is explainable. **7.** *And the king of Egypt came again no more out of his land; for the king of Babylon had taken, from the Wady of Egypt to the river Euphrates, all that belonged to the king of Egypt.* For historical order this detached item belongs to the beginning of the section. For an asserted capture of Jerusalem by Nebuchadnezzar in Jehoiakim's third year, with the latter's captivity in Babylon and the despoliation of the temple (Ch. v.^{6}, Dan. $1^{1\text{ff.}}$), see the writer's Comm. on Daniel at length. A study of the contemporary history has been given by G. R. Tabouis, *Nebuchadnezzar* (1931).

Ch. 23. **36.** וּבידה: MSS, Kr., וּבֻדָּה: the variant vowels are present Heb. and Aram. forms; the Grr. have amazing variations; other VSS=Kt., exc. 𝔗, also Jos.=Kr. For the name see Note, I. 4^5.—פריה=פריהו, 1 Ch. 27^{20}, and on a seal, *IAE* 203. Grr. again vary; *n.b.* Φαδαιλ/ιηλ in Hex. MSS. 𝔊$^\text{L}$ demanded that the mother of the other two brothers (23^{31}, 24^{18}) be mother of this prince, and altered the statement accordingly (see Rahlfs, *SS* 3, 279 f.—רומה: possibly Khan Rumeh, N of Sepphoris in Galilee, known to Jos. and Talmud (Abel, *GP* 2, 438) and =Aruma, mentioned along with Marum=Mezom in Tiglath-pileser's Annals (line 234, Rogers, *CP* 319). But *n.b.* דומה, var. רומה, in Judah, Josh. 15⁵².

Ch. 24. **1.** נבכדנאצר : for the various spellings here see Ken., and for the correct form, נבוכדראצר, in Jer. alone, the Lexx.—**2.** כשדים : without article, and so at 25⁵, otherwise at 25²⁵ ; *cf.* similar use of פלשתים.—ארם : 𝔖 𝔄 as 'Edom,' preferred by Grätz, Klost., Burn.—עמון : 𝔊ᴸ+' and from Samaria.'—להאבידו : 𝔊 Hex. =להאביד, preferable, with the absolute use of the verb ; *cf.* cases vv.³· ⁴, להכעיס 21⁶.—**3.** אך : the interpretation given above, following Ehrl., preserves the text, which has troubled critics ; see Kit.—פי [על] :=𝔙; other VSS as אף (𝔈 𝔖 𝔄 with indirect translation), and so=v.²⁰ ; St. allows the possibility of 𝔚, which indeed is fully supported by the argument of the period.—היתה : for the impersonal verb in the fem. see GK §144, b, c, as used of natural phenomena ; the same usage at large in Aram., see Nöld., *Syr. Gram.*, §254, also in Arab., *e.g.*, *ṭābat*, ' it was fine (weather) ' ; *cf.* also Note 19²⁵.

24⁸⁻¹⁷. The reign of Jehoiachin. || 2 Ch. 36⁹· ¹⁰, Jer. 29², 1 Esd. 1⁴¹⁻⁴⁴ ⁽⁴³⁻⁴⁶⁾ ; *cf. Ant.*, x, 6, 3 ; 7, 1.

8. *Eighteen years old was Jehoiachin when he began to reign, and three months did he reign in Jerusalem. And his mother's name was Nehushta bath Elnathan of Jerusalem.* **9.** *And he did what was evil in* Y*HWH*'*s eyes, like all that his father did.* **10.** *At that time came up the officers* [EVV *servants*] *of Nebuchadnezzar king of Babylon to Jerusalem, and the city entered into siege.* **11.** *And Nebuchadnezzar king of Babylon came against the city while his officers were besieging it ;* **12.** *and Jehoiachin king of Judah went out to the king of Babylon, he and his mother and his ministers* [EVV *servants*] *and captains and chamberlains* [Heb. primarily *eunuchs*]. *And the king of Babylon took him* (prisoner) *in the eighth year of his reign.*

13. *And he brought out thence all the treasures of the house of* Y*HWH and the treasures of the king's house ; and he cut up all the gold vessels which Solomon king of Israel had made, in the hall of* Y*HWH, even as* Y*HWH had said.*

15. *And he deported Jehoiachin to Babylon ; and the*

king's mother and the king's
wives and his chamberlains
and the nobles of the land he
took off, a deportation from
Jerusalem to Babylon.

14. And he deported all Jerusalem and all the captains

16. and all the soldiers, 7000, and the artisans and the smiths, 1000 the whole number, trained soldiers, fighting men; and the king of Babylon brought them, a deportation, to Babylon.

and all the trained men of the army, 10,000—a deportation—and all the artisans and smiths; there was none left except the humblest of the people of the land.

17. *And the king of Babylon made his uncle Mattaniah king in his stead; and he (i.e., the k. of B.) changed his name to Sedekiah.*

V.^{8}. The royal name has the Biblical variants ' Jeconiah,' ' Coniah '; it appears as ' Yochin ' on a local stamp of a royal ' page ' of the king, and now, most recently, as ' Yaukina king of Judah ' in a Babylonian inscription; see Note. VV.$^{10, 11}$. The siege was climaxed by the advent of Nebuchadnezzar for the surrender. V.^{12}. The surrender (they *went out*) of the king and royal personnel is well illustrated by the Assyrian picture of the surrender of Lachish (see Comm. on 18^{14}). The queen mother is included in Jeremiah's dirge (22$^{24\text{ff.}}$), and is pathetically referred to in 13^{18}, while 29^2 is a repetition, with variation, of the present v. The v. concludes with the first dating according to an extra-Israelite imperial system, in the year of the conqueror, ' the 8th of his reign.' In Jer. 52^{28} this deportation is dated ' in the 7th year '; the present dating follows the Jewish system of reckoning, that in Jer. the Babylonian, which regarded the fractional initial year as the *res šarrūti*, ' beginning of the reign,' a case of which is presented in 25^{27} (but see Note *ad loc.* for further discussion).

VV.$^{13-17}$. The most extensive criticism of this passage, following Thenius, Ewald (*HI* 4, 204), is that by Stade in *ZAW* 4 (1884), 271 ff. (with study of the deportation figures for the several captivities) ; *cf.* Begrich's summary agreement, *Chronologie*, 197. The critical display of the text given above may speak for itself. VV.$^{15, 17}$ are the straightforward sequence of vv.$^{8-12}$; it is the king and his court who are deported, the little state of Judah is left with an imperial appointee of the blood royal as king. V.^{15} is repetitive with a brief list of the officials, plus *the wives* (!) of the young king. The substance of these vv. appears to be of archival origin with their interest confined to the court. V.^{16}, out of place where it stands, supplies definite information on the other deported classes, the military, and the artisan guilds, with at least modest figures. However a much smaller figure is given for this deportation in Jer. 52$^{28ff.}$, namely 3023, while of the figures there listed for the three captivities the sum total is only 4600. The latter figure doubtless refers only to men, so that a much higher figure is to be assumed for the total of souls; *cf.* the figure of 27,290 captives taken by Sargon from Samaria. The two remaining vv. are definitely secondary. V.^{13} is out of place (' brought out thence,' with distant antecedent), and the account of the looting of all the treasures of temple and palace and of all Solomon's gold vessels in the temple-hall, ' according to the divine word,' is an expansive summary. It possesses no doubt a basis of real fact, and Torrey well makes the point (*Pseudo-Ezekiel*, 104) that according to this statement the conqueror converted ' into bullion ' the gold vessels, which therefore were not preserved intact as according to the tradition in 2 Ch. 36$^{7, 10, 18}$, Dan. 1^2. Below (25^{15}) only minor gold and silver vessels are named in the final looting. V.^{14} with its initial statement of the deportation of ' all Jerusalem ' (the adjective critically omitted by 𝕲) is extravagant, and the rest of the v. is a duplicate of v.^{16} with a large round number for the military deportees, and a conclusion for the remnant in the land that duplicates 25^{12}. Withal these additions have their contemporary interest. The military are variously referred to, with difficulty for English translation; *the soldiers* (𝔥 *men of war*) are paralleled with *the trained men of the army* (EVV *mighty men of valour*); for the latter see Comm. on 15^{20}, where they are the upper class of landed estate, who like the knights of later Europe led forth their clans to war. The repetition in v.^{16} of *trained* soldiers (גִּבֹּרִים *gibbôrîm*), fighting men (Heb. *makers of war*—cf. the EVV for these terms) is quite supernumerary. A matter of sociological interest appears in the words translated *artisans* and *smiths* (the latter word of uncertain denotation); the nouns are in the collective singular, denoting guilds; see Causse, *Du groupe ethnique*, 40 ff., and the archæologically based articles by I. Mendelsohn (see under Bibliography, xxvii). The parallel in Ch. and 𝕲 disputes the designation of Mattaniah as Jehoiachin's uncle; see Note. For the change of name *cf.* the case of Jehoiakim, 23³⁴.

8. ' 18 years ' : Ch., ' 8 ' ; but *n.b.* the ' wives,' *inf.*—יהויכין; *n.b.* the variations : יכניה, Jer. 24¹, 28⁴, 29², 1 Ch. 3¹⁶, ¹⁷, and כניהו, Jer. 22²⁴, ²⁸. The royal name appears in three contemporary identical jar-handle stamps, two from Tell Beit-Mirsim, one from Beth-Shemesh, with the text, אליקים נער יוכן, ' Eliakim steward [1] of Yochin ' ; see Albr., ' The Seal of Eliakim,' etc., *JBL* 51 (1932), 77 ff., and Diringer, *IAE* 126. Professor Albright also favoured the writer with copy of a communication he received from E. F. Weidner, reporting an Akk. inscription found in the royal palace in Babylon, later published by him in the *Mélanges Dussaud*, vol. 2. It details the payment of corn and oil to an encyclopædic list of persons, including ' Yaukinu šarru ša Yaḫudu.' *Cf.* the royal treatment subsequently given to the king acc. to 25²⁷ᶠᶠ, ². In the form given here the name means ' Y. establishes ' ; *cf.* the name ' Yachin,' I. 7²¹. The verb in the other two forms must be Ḳal, *i.e.*, ' Y. exists,' with the mng. of the verb as in Phœn., Akk., Arab. Noth assumes (*IP* 202, n. 1) the root כנן, ' to protect,' without good reason. Albr. proposes (*JBL* n. 13) as basis ' Yekenyahu,' with verb in Hif., ' Let Y. establish,' but without explanation of the verbal stem in the Biblical tradition, which is safer basis for etymology. There may well have been play upon the two verbal stems. Apart from a limited group of Gr. MSS (*e.g.*, g h n x y, but not consistently) the Grr., also 𝕮, and Esd. v.⁴³, by confusion with the preceding royal name, present the process Ιωακειν>Ιωακειμ, a confusion

---

[1] So Albr., with extensive treatment of the word, as also in *SAC* 153; the word has generally been translated above with ' page,' or ' squire,' *e.g.*, I. 20¹⁴.

[2] *P.S.*—Dr. Albright's information was published by him in an extensive article, ' King Joiachin in Exile,' *BA* 1942, 49 ff., to which the reader is referred for a summary review of a most interesting lot of nearly 300 cuneiform tablets, stating the rations to captives and artisans from many peoples. Five sons of the king are named; *cf.* the seven assigned to him in 1 Ch. 3¹⁷ᶠ.

persisting in the Christian tradition; cf. Mt. 1¹¹, and see Rahlfs, SS 3, 115, 122, 123.—' 3 months ': Ch.+' and 10 days.'—אלנתן: the name in the contemporary Lachish letter, no. 3.—**10**. עלה עבדי: Ḳr. of the verb עלי (and so 12 MSS), as demanded; MSS Ken. 70, 176, deR. 539 om. the noun, and so all VSS exc. 𝕿 𝔙; St., Eissf. prefer the elision; but the v. notes the investment of the city, v.¹¹ the advent of Neb. for the surrender.—**11**. על העיר: 𝕲 ' into the city.'—𝕲ᴸ reverses the two statements in the v.; see St., and Rahlfs, ib., 210.—**12**. [מלך] על: 13 MSS Ken., deR., אל, which is demanded, and so 𝕲ᴸ with πρos.—אתו: Gr. MSS with pl. pron., ad sensum.—**14**. והגלה: again the irregular consecution. —[ירושלם] כל : of Grr. only Hex. has (𝕾ᴴ ⁕).—עשרה: Ḳr. עשרת = MSS.—גוּלָה: 𝕲 for the phrase, αἰχμαλωσιαν (rdg. the sing. with MS j) δεκα χιλιαδες αἰχμαλωτισας (cf. 𝕾ᴴ), i.e., with double interpretation of the word as noun and ppl.; 𝕲ᴸ has the noun = גוּלָה, which is to be read. Joüon (Mél., 5, 485) supports Ḳr., endeavouring to discriminate between the masc. and fem. of the ppl.—המסגר: the unique noun only in the repetitions, v.¹⁶, Jer. 24¹, 29²; all VSS (exc. 𝕾 𝔄, which go their own way) as from the root 'ס, ' to shut up ': Grr., ' one who locks up,' and so 𝕿 𝔙, ' clusor,' Kimchi, ' locksmith ' (Jastrow, Dict., s.v.); but such mngs. would stand for very petty guilds. EVV simplify with ' smiths '=GV FV, and so obtain good sense. The Arab. root sajara, ' to roast in an oven,' is to be accepted for the mng., as of metal-smiths, in parallelism with the preceding guild of artisans, carpenters, and the like. This etymology may well explain the term זהב סגור I. 6²⁰, which is there translated with ' refined gold,' i.e., gold well smelted. The Arab. root has the primary mng. of ' to flow,' and this mng. appears for the same root in Heb. at Prov. 27¹⁵, ביום סגריר, ' in a day of downpour.' For further discussion see Then., the Commentaries of Graf and Giesebrecht on Jer. 24¹; Then. and Graf accept Hitzig's ingenious suggestion, understanding כֹּם גֵּר, and as parallel to עם עובד מם, I. 9²¹; but this is not to the point here.—דלת עם הארץ: the phrase as ד' הארץ only at 25¹² and parallel in Jer.—**15**. [הארץ] אולי: Ḳr. אֵילֵי (=many MSS), and so the Kt. in the same phrase at Eze. 17¹³; for the word see Lexx., roots אול, איל, and for a possible use of the word in the present sense in Phœn. see Harris, Gram., 77.—**16**. הכל: ' the sum total,' as at Ps. 14³=כֻּלוֹ Ps. 53⁴.—**17**. מתניה: מתניהו appears in Lachish letter no. 1; J. A. Thomson cft. Bab. ' Mattaniama,' AASOR 86 (1943), 24 f.—דדו: for the various denotations of the noun see Lexx.; Jer. 25¹ makes the king definitely uncle of Jehoiachin; Eze. 17¹³ refers to him indefinitely as ' one of the seed royal '; MS 70 om. (because of the dispute ?); Ch., ' his brother,' but 𝕲 there, ' his father's brother,' and so in the royal genealogy, 1 Ch. 3¹⁶. 𝕲 here (B A al.)=בנו, and so deR. 701; Šanda suggests that υιον is corruption of θειον; 1 Esd. om. See further Comm., 23³¹.

II. 24^{18}–25^{30}

Ch. 24^{18}–ch. 25. The last days of the nation. *Cf. Ant.*, x, 7, 2 ff. In addition to a moralizing summary in Ch. 36^{11-21} = I Esd. $1^{43\text{ff.}\;(45\text{ff.})}$, this section is paralleled by two sections of Jeremiah. Jer. 52 is a duplicate, with often better text, omitting the Judæan revolt (Ki. 25^{22-26}—for which see below). The text of 25^{1-12} is the original of the evident insertion in Jer. 39, vv.$^{1-10}$. On the other hand Jer. 40^7–41 is the basis of the brief summary contained here in vv.$^{22-26}$. The book, as also Jer. (52^{27}), originally concluded with the sombre statement (v.$^{21\text{b}}$), *And Judah went into exile from off its land.* To this were added postscripts (*cf.* the unique postscript in Jer. 52^{28-30}, with dates and census of the figures for the three captivities) : (1) vv.$^{22-26}$, the anecdote of Gedaliah's flight ; (2) vv.$^{27-30}$, the imperial benevolence to Jehoiachin, dated 37 years after his captivity, *i.e.*, *ca.* 560 B.C., and so terminus for the dating of the book. As a supplementary, but annalistically true statement, it gives an auspicious conclusion for the future with the note of the 'lifting up of the head' of the exiled king. *Cf.* Ch. with its postscript, taken from Ezra 1, giving Cyrus's proclamation of release.[1]

The primary editor, to his terminus at 25^{21}, knows only his people's sad history. He records nought of the international complications in which Sedekiah was involved, and of which the book of Jeremiah gives exposition.[2] The Pharaoh-Necho

---

[1] For the problem of the parallel narratives in Jer. see Commentaries on that book (in particular Cornill's) and Introductions. The text of Ki. has been much mutilated, as the VSS prove. For the inner-Hebrew variations see Sperber, *Hebrew . . . in Parallel Transmission.* The duplicates in Jer., for both Heb. and Gr., are presented fully in Vanutelli's volume, and the parallelisms in English by Kent, *SBOT.* For the Gr. text of the parallels in Jer. and its secondary origin see Olmstead, 'Source Study and the Biblical Text,' 1 ff. For an essay at precise dating see Albright's presentation cited in the Bibliography in Int., § 16, and for the light thrown by the Lachish letters upon these last days of Judah, Gordon, *The Living Past,* ch. 9.

[2] For the contemporary history involved in the rise of the Neo-Babylonian empire see Breasted, *HE* ch. 28 ; Alt, *Israel u. Aegypten,* 10 ff. ; Hall, *AHNE* ch. 12 ; Thompson, *CAH* 3, ch. 10 ; Kittel, *GVI* 2, §50 ; Olmstead, *HPS* ch. 35 ; Meyer, *GA* 3, 170 ff. ; Robinson, *HI* 1, 435 ff. For the citations in Josephus (*Ant.*, x, 11, 1) and Eusebius from Berossos, Abydenos, Polyhistor, see Schnabel, *Berossos,* 273 ff.

of ch. 23 died in 594 B.C., and was succeeded by his son Psammetichos II, and he by Apries of the Greek tradition, the Hophra of Jer. 44^{30} (588–569 B.C.). The last-named king took aggressive action against Babylon with an attack upon Philistia by sea. In opposition Nebuchadnezzar, probably fearing a direct attack upon the Syrian coast, and following Necho's example (23^{33}), established his military centre at Riblah (vv.$^{6, 20f.}$), and this notice has its correspondent in his inscription in the Wady Brisa in the Lebanon (Rogers, *CP* 365, Gressmann, *ATB* 1, 365). As Jeremiah shows, Sedekiah wavered in his allegiance, but finally declared for the pro-Egyptian party, and this brought upon him and his *entourage*, sacred and civil, the vengeance of his overlord. Our chronicler notes the exact dates of investment and capture of the city in Babylonian terms (vv.$^{1-3}$), the siege lasting from the royal 9th year, 10th month, 10th day, to the 11th year, 4th month, 9th day, *i.e.*, from *ca.* January, 587 B.C., to *ca.* July, 586; *cf.* the further exact dating in v.^{8}. The siege was one of starvation; the stout city might well have defied storming, and hence the final destruction of its walls (v.^{10}). *Cf.* Titus's five months' siege of the city. The minute details of the history, dates, events, personalities, vouch for the contemporary character of this notable document.

24^{18}–25^{7}. The reign of Sedekiah. **18.** The usual introductory data. **19-20***a*. The moral judgment, with reminiscence of v.^{3}. **20***b*. the history begins with the opening of the final catastrophe: *And Sedekiah rebelled against the king of Babylon.* Ch. gives the blame to the perfidious king, whom "Nebuchadnezzar had sworn by God." Ch. 25. **1.** *And it came to pass, in the ninth year of his reign, in the tenth month, on the tenth of the month, Nebuchadnezzar king of Babylon and all his army came against Jerusalem, and encamped against it, and built a siege-wall round about.* The naming of the Babylonian king as present in the investment of the city is incorrect, at the most a formal expression; *cf.* Jer. 38$^{17ff.}$, according to which surrender was to be made to 'the king of Babylon's princes,' and that king was actually at Riblah (v.^{6}). **2.** *And the city entered into siege, up to the eleventh year of king Sedekiah.*

II. 24^{18}–25^{30}

Ki. = Jer. 52^6 | Jer. 39^2

3. (Jer.+*in the fourth month*) *On the ninth of the month, and the famine was sore in the city, there was no food for the people of the land;* **4a.** *and the city was breached.* | *In the fourth month, and on the ninth of the month the city was breached.*

The consecution in Ki. is impossible; there has been intruded a reference to the historical famine; *cf.* Jer. 37^{21}. The specification of *the fourth month* must be restored from the parallels; this datum fails here also in all VSS exc. 𝔖 𝔄. For the later anniversary 'fast of the fourth month' and that of 'the fifth month' and two other ritual observances of the kind see Zech. 8^{19}; *cf.* Nowack, *Arch.*, 2, 270; *JE* 5, 347 ff. The dating is after Babylonian fashion, from Nisan. **4b.** *And all the men of war* [verb lacking, supplied by 4 MSS, ancient and modern VSS, *e.g.*, EVV *fled*] *by night by the gate between the double-walls* [Heb. a dual], *which was by the king's garden, while the Chaldæans were against the city round about; and he went out by the way of* (*i.e.*, to) *the Arabah.* **5.** *And the army of the Chaldæans pursued after the king and overtook him in the wastes of Jericho, all his army being scattered from him.* With this are to be compared the parallels in Jer. $39^{4,\ 5a}$: *And it came to pass that when Sedekiah king of Judah and all the men of war saw them* [with extensive antecedent in v.^{3}], *that they fled, and went out by night from the city by the way of the king's garden, by the gate between the double-walls, and he went out by the way of the Arabah. And the army of the Chaldæans pursued after them, and overtook Sedekiah in the wastes of Jericho.* Jer. 52^7 presents only the flight of the men of war, but v.^{8} centres on the king: *The army of the Chaldæans pursued after the king, and overtook Sedekiah in the wastes of Jericho, all his army being scattered from him.* The non-syntactical 'all the men of war' in v.^{4} is an evident intrusion from Jer. 52^7; the same intrusion has been made in Jer. 39. The original passage here was a reduction of the original longer form, and may once have simply read: *And he* [with antecedent understood] *went out by way of the Arabah. And the army of the Chaldæans overtook him*, etc. For location of *the gate cf.* Is. 22^{11}, "Ye made a basin between the double-walls";

the second wall was probably the circumvallation of the
Siloam pool (see Smith, *Jerusalem* 1, 225 f.). The *king's
garden* appears in Neh. 3^{15} as ' close by the wall of the pool of
haš-šèlaḥ,' *i.e.*, Siloam. The king's flight from the SE point of
the city, aiming for Jericho, was indeed ' through a desert,' as
Josephus remarks. *Cf.* the alleged presage of this flight in
Eze. $12^{1\text{ff.}}$. For *the wastes of Jericho cf.* Josh. 4^{13}, etc. **6.** *And
they seized the king, and brought him to the king of Babylon to
Riblah. And he* [so parallels in Jer., and also below ; 𝔥 *they*]
took process with him. **7.** *And Sedekiah's sons he slew before
his eyes, and Sedekiah's eyes he blinded. And he fettered him
in double-brass, and brought him to Babylon.* The translation
took process, the Heb., literally, *spoke judgment*, renders the
Babylonian juristic phrase, *dēna dabābu*; *cf.* Jer. 12^1, where
it is used of legal argument. Restoration in two cases of the
sing. pronoun *he* is necessary, *cf.* v.^{21} ; judicially the penalty
was the sovereign's action. The act of blinding captives
appears in Assyrian reliefs ; such mutilation destroyed the
royal potency. For the king's captivity *cf.* Jer. $34^{2\text{ff.}}$, with the
note, " thy eyes shall behold the eyes of the king of Babylon,"
and Eze. 12^{13}, according to which the king shall be brought to
Babylon, " yet shall he not see it, although he shall die there."

VV.$^{8\text{-}21}$. The end. The section is composite : vv.$^{8\text{-}12}$, the
destruction of the city and the exile ; vv.$^{13\text{-}17}$, an inventory
of the temple brass and vessels carried off to Babylon ;
vv.$^{18\text{-}21}$, the extreme penalty visited on the leaders of the
revolt, with repeated statement of the exile.

8. *And in the fifth month, on the seventh of the month—that
is the nineteenth year of king Nebuchadnezzar king of Babylon—
came Nebuzaradan, provost-marshal, minister of the king of
Babylon, to Jerusalem.* There is again a synchronism with
Babylonian chronology, *cf.* 24^{12}. The date is *ca.* July of
586 B.C. For variation of traditions as to the day-date see
Note. For the title of Nabū-zēr-iddina (so the Akk. name),
EVV ' chief of the guard ' (but at Gen. 37^{36} 𝔊 ' chief cook '),
properly ' chief-executioner,' see the writer's note in Comm.
on Daniel, 2^{14}. **9.** *And he burnt the house of* Y<small>HWH</small> *and the
king's house and all the houses of Jerusalem* [𝔥+the super-
fluous and ungrammatical clause, *and every magnate's house
he burnt with fire*]. **10.** *And the walls of Jerusalem round about*

⌜all⌝ [secondary?] *the Chaldæan army* [𝕳+gloss, *the provost-marshal's*] *broke down.* **11.** *And the rest of the people that were left in the city, and the deserters, who had deserted to the king of Babylon* [𝕳+*and the rest of the multitude*], *Nebuzaradan the provost-marshal took into exile.* The several bracketed sections are superfluous; the last one has given rise to various interpretations; see Note. The comment on the *deserters* is of interest. **12.** *And of the humble-folk of the land the provost-marshal left some for vinedressers and* ⌜*husbandmen*⌝ [?]. For these classes *cf.* 24^{14}. The mng. of the final term has only been guessed at; see Note.

VV.$^{13-17}$. An intruded antiquarian but historical note, presenting a summary of the valuable metal loot taken by the Babylonians. V.^{13}. The large pieces of brass they *broke up and carried their brass to Babylon.* V.^{14}. The small brazen vessels *they took away* intact. V.^{15}. The vessels of gold and silver the chief officer *took charge of*; these must have been small articles left over from the earlier looting (24^{13}). VV.$^{16, 17}$ are an added recapitulation based on I. 7$^{15\text{ff.}}$; for criticism, with parallel in Jer. 52$^{17-23}$, see Notes.

VV.$^{18-21a}$. The death-penalty inflicted upon selected Judæan notables. **18.** *And the provost-marshal took Seraiah the chief priest, and Sephaniah the priest of second rank, and the three threshold guardians;* **19.** *and from the city he took one chamberlain, the one in command of the men of war; and five men of those who saw the king's face, who were found in the city; and the secretary of* [so the genitive with Jer., and MSS and VSS here] *the commander of the host, who mustered the people of the land; and sixty men of the people of the land, who were found in the city.* **20.** *And Nebuzaradan the provost-marshal took them, and brought them to the king of Babylon to Riblah.* **21a.** *And the king of Babylon smote them and slew them at Riblah in the land of Hamath.* The summary punishment included, most exceptionally, the sacred *personnel* of the temple; apparently the hierarchy had led in the national cause. The three orders of the higher priesthood are presented as in 23^{4}, with the additional figure of *three* for the threshold-guardians, who, it may be assumed, were titularly in charge of the three temple gates (see Smith, *Jerusalem*, 2, 67, 257). The primate appears for the first time with the ancient title *kôhēn hā-rō'š* (also in Ch., Ezra), as over against *hak-kôhēn hag-gādôl*, literally ' the great priest ' ; see Comm. on 12¹¹. For Seraiah's genealogy see Comm., 22⁴. The second class of the condemned consisted of officers of state. The word translated *chamberlain* (primarily *eunuch*) is now applied to a generalissimo ; *cf.* the Assyrian military title *rab-sarīs* at 18¹⁷. Five courtiers are listed with a unique title, like the British ' privy councillors.' And an army adjutant appears in the person of a scribe/ secretary, charged with military enrolment, a secretary of war in modern terms ; the ' scribe ' appears in the mustering of Barak's forces, Jud. 5¹⁴, for which see Moore, *ad loc.*, and *cf.* the translations in EVV. The third estate is that of *the people of the land*, the country gentry ; see Comm. on 11¹⁷, and *cf.* Würthwein in his study there noted, p. 44 ; an exemplary number of these, *who were found in the city*, were included. The formality of the judgment, all according to law, appears in the transportation of the condemned to the royal assize at distant Riblah.

V.²¹ᵇ. The conclusion of the original book. *Cf.* the similar statement of the exile of North Israel, 17²³ᵇ. Jer. 52²⁸⁻³⁰ adds a list of numbered exiles in Nebuchadnezzar's several deportations ; *cf.* the higher figure given in 24¹⁴. The term ' exile ' is indeed a formal one ; the autonomy and so the existence of the nation were destroyed by the deportation of the upper classes. See Torrey, *Pseudo-Ezekiel*, ch. 6, for drastic criticism of the tradition of a total exile, although his criticism of the statements in Ki. should be much modified. *Cf.* S. Spiegel's rejoinder, ' Ezekiel or Pseudo-Ezekiel,' *HTR* 24 (1931), 245 ff. A very loose statement appears below, in v.²⁶, to the effect that *all the people, both small and great*, fled to Egypt, but this must be interpreted as referring particularly to the rebellious band congregated about all *the army captains*. Notable is the contention of the archæologist Albright, as against Torrey, based on his study of the ruined Judæan sites of this period, that there was a ' complete devastation ' during the exile ; see his *APB* 171 f., and his article, ' Recent Discoveries in Bible Lands,' ch. 17. However devastation does not involve deportation of all the inhabitants, even as the figures for the exiles in Jer. 52 are small.

VV.²²⁻²⁶. The Judæan revolt ; a postscript summary of

Jer. 40⁷⁻41. **22.** *And as for the people that were left in the land of Judah, whom Nebuchadnezzar king of Babylon had left, he appointed a governor over them, Gedaliah ben Ahikam ben Shaphan.* **23.** *And all the captains of the forces, they and ⌜their men⌝* [with Jer.; 𝔥 *the men*], *heard that the king of Babylon had appointed Gedaliah governor, and they came to Gedaliah to Mispah, even* [𝔥 *and*] *Ishmael ben Nethaniah and Johanan ben Kareah and Seraiah ben Tanhumeth the Netophathite and Jaazaniah ben ham-Maachathi, they and their men.* **24.** *And Gedaliah took oath with them and their men, and said to them: Be not afraid of the officials* [EVV *servants*] *of the Chaldæans. Dwell in the land, and serve the king of Babylon, and so it will be well with you.* **25.** *And it was in the seventh month, there came Ishmael ben Nethaniah ben Elishama, of the seed royal, and ten men with him, and they smote Gedaliah* [𝔥+*and he died*, not in Jer.] *and the Judæans and Chaldæans that were with him at Mispah.* **26.** *And all the people, both small and great, and the captains of the forces, rose up and came to Egypt, for they were afraid of the Chaldæans.*

The Babylonian king as a wise statesman arranged for the proper administration of his new fief-land, and diplomatically appointed a Judæan gentleman of high rank as his vizier, with seat at Mispah. But there remained a stiff-necked opposition to the new order of things, despite the fair promises given by their fellow-citizen, the new viceroy. It was the same spirit as that which animated the Maccabæan revolt and later the one against Rome. Gedaliah's father Ahikam had interfered in behalf of Jeremiah at the beginning of Jehoiakim's reign (Jer. 26²⁴), and had earlier served on Josiah's commission of inquiry concerning the Book of the Law (22¹²). The son was evidently a statesman of moderation, with the same attitude towards politics as Jeremiah's. Comparison with the present history may be made with conditions at the second destruction of the temple, when Josephus ' deserted ' to the Roman cause, and was exposed to the danger of assassination at the hand of fanatics, *e.g.*, his *Vita*, 48. Gedaliah was able to make a sworn settlement with some of the fugitive bands and their leaders that were still in defiance of the new *régime*. But he was attacked and murdered along with his *entourage* by a small party led by Ishmael, the latter with very personal concern, being one of the royal family. This high-handed crime terrified the whole group, and *they came to Egypt*, a statement of Egyptian provenance, as the verb shows. For their subsequent history the Jeremianic biography is to be consulted. Archæology has cast unexpected light on two of the persons involved. The seal ' of Gedaliahu Over-the-House,' לגדליהו על הבית, doubtless the person named here, has been discovered at Lachish ; see Starkey, *ILN* August, 1935, 241, S. H. Hooke, *QS* 1935, 195 ff., Diringer, *IAE* 257. Also the seal ' of Jaazaniahu servant of the king,' ליאזניהו עבד המלך, was discovered by Badè in 1932 at Tell en-Nasbeh ; see his article on the find in *ZAW* 1933, 150 ff., and his *Manual of Excavation in the Near East*, ch. 17, also Diringer, *ib.*, 181. The name also occurs on a seal published by Torrey in *AASOR* II–III (1922), 105. As the Notes show, several of the other names listed have contemporary illustration from seals, etc. For the identification of Mispah see Comm. on I. 15[22].

VV.[27-30]. The release and honouring of Jehoiachin. **27.** *And it was in the thirty-seventh year of the captivity of Jehoiachin king of Judah, in the twelfth month, on the twenty-seventh day of the month, that Evil-Merodach king of Babylon, in the year of his becoming king, lifted up the head (i.e., the person) of Jehoiachin king of Judah out of prison.* **28.** *And he spoke kindly with him, and set his throne above the throne(s) of the kings who were with him in Babylon.* **29.** *And he* (Jehoiachin) *changed his prison garments, and he ate bread before him* (Evil-Merodach) *continually all the days of his life.* **30.** *And for his allowance, a continual allowance was given him on the part of the king, every day a portion, all the days of his life.*

For this liberal treatment of the captive king, now corroborated by a Babylonian text, see Note to 24[8]. The date is given by the editor in Babylonia in Babylonian terms ; *in the year of his becoming king* apparently means the same as Akk. *ina rēš šarrūti*, generally interpreted as the initial portion of a year before the first full calendar year of the reign. A parallel appears in an Elephantine papyrus (Sachau, Pap. vi, Cowley, no. 6) : " ... in year 21 (*i.e.*, of Xerxes), the beginning of the reign when king Artaxerxes sat on his throne," *i.e.*, a double dating in throne-terms. But there is to be noted the discussion by Albright, *JBL* 51 (1932), 101 f., who, following J. Lewy, maintains that the term refers to the first full year. The 37th year, according to Albright 561/560 B.C., which is the first royal calendar year, dates from 597/596. The reason for the new king's favour to Jehoiachin is obscure; political motives in his short and troubled reign may have been the cause. Amel-Marduk is described by Berossos as one " who reigned unrighteously and luxuriously "; he was assassinated ' after two years ' by Nergal-šar-uṣur (560–556 B.C.), whose son and successor, Labāši-Marduk, was killed and succeeded by Nabū-na'id, the latter then confronted by Cyrus the Persian, the ultimate conqueror of the Babylonian realm (Berossos, cited by Josephus, *C. Ap.*, i, 20). This postscript reveals its dating; it was composed after Jehoiachin's death, but before the Persian conquest. The book is thus concluded with the theme of the continued dignity of the house of David, with what hope in mind we may only surmise.

Ch. 24. **18.** ואחת : A v 𝔖ᴴ om., but 𝔖 𝔄 have.—**20.** הִשְׁלִכוּ : inf. constr., 'הֻ' is demanded ; see Note, 3²⁵.—Ch. 25. **1.** בשנת התשיעית : the same construction at 17⁶, *q.v.* ; MSS and Jer. 39¹, בשנה הת'. A sherd of the ' ninth year,' presumably of Sedekiah, has been found at Lachish ; see *PEQ* 1938, 254.—[בחדש] העשירי : A ' the second,' rdg. δεκατω as δειτερω, hence N *al.*, ' the 12th ' ; but 𝔖 𝔄=𝔐.—[לחדש] בעשור : absent in Jer. ; most Grr. om. here ; A ' on the 14th,' Aq. in 𝔖ᴴ, ' the 11th ' ; a few MSS, *e.g.*, x y, also 𝔖 𝔄=𝔐.—**4***a.* הלילה :=' in that night ' ; Jer., לילה.— **4***b.* **5.** See Comm. for criticism of the passage ; rewritings can be attempted from the parallels in Jer. The lacuna of ' went out ' in v.⁴ᵇ was filled out not only by the VSS but also by 4 Heb. MSS : 93 168 insert יצאו, 180 250 ויברחו.—וילך : the persistence of the sing. (supported by B A 𝔖ᴴ) points to the king as the original stated subject through the preceding passage ; Jer. 52 has the pl., and so here 4 MSS.—כשדים *bis* : the absolute as at 24², varying with 'הכ', as at v.²⁴.—דרך הערבה : 𝔖ᴸ οδον τ. επι δυσμας ' the way to the west.'—**6.** רבלתה : Jer. 39 and 52+בארץ חמת= v.²¹, 23³³.—וידברו : this verb and שחטו, v.⁷, are to be corrected to the sing. (with Grr., 𝔖ᴴ, parallels in Jer.), as foll. עור and יאסרהו demand. Some MSS, Mich. read the last verb in v.⁷ as pl.—בבל : very many MSS, Jer. בבלה.—**8.** בשבעה : 3 MSS deR., בתשעה=𝔖ᴸ 𝔖 𝔄 (*cf.* Rahlfs, *SS* 3, 280, 291) ; Jer. 52, בעשור. The change to the ' 9th day ' was due to the celebration of the 9th of Ab. Kimchi resolved the variation of dates by asserting that the enemy entered the city on the 7th, set fire to it on the 9th, the conflagration ceasing on the 10th. Jos. dates the conflagration at the new moon of the 5th month.—נבוזראדן : the VSS bear early witness to the vocalization of 𐤉. The alleged appearance of the name in the Eleph. papp. is to be denied ; see Cowley, no. 9.—רב טבחים : Aq., 𐤔 𐤀 properly, 'chief of the lictors'; other Grr., αρχιμαγειρος, 'chief cook,' as at Gen. 37³⁶, etc.; Jos., στρατηγος. A seal found at Tell el-Kheleifeh, earlier read as עבד המלך, is read by Albright as טבח הט' (BASOR 71 [1938], 17).—עבד מלך בבל : Jer. 52, עבד לפני מ' ב', and so Grr., 𐤔ᴴ here, but rdg. as though עֶמֶד; but there is no reason for correction.—ירושלם : Jer. 52, בירושלם.—9. =ואת כל בית גדול Jer. 52, but rdg. הגדול ; Grr. (=𐤔ᴴ), 'every house,' exc. 𐤊ᴸ 'every great house'; Jer. 39 lacks the gloss.—10.. B A om. the v., exc. the final subject, רב טבחים.—חולה=Jer. 39, 52; all VSS, exc. 𐤂 𐤐, as sing.—[חיל]כל : 𐤊ᴸ om. ; prob. a gloss to חומת above, in agreement with Jer. 52.—אשר רב טבחים : Grr., Jer. 39 om. ; Jer. 52, אשר את ר' ט', and so many MSS here=𐤔ᴴ, other VSS, EVV, etc. ; but אשר=N. Israelite šě, see Note, 6¹¹.—11. על המלך בבל : Jer. 52, and so 5 MSS here, אל מלך ב' ; the original may have been אל המלך with 'Babylon' glossed in ; Jer. simply, עליו, i.e., which, corrected to אליו, i.e., to the officer, is the simplest correction, with St.— יתר ההמון : Grr., exc. 𐤊ᴸ, το λοιπον του στηριγματος=𐤔ᴴ, as from root אמן, and so=Jer. 52, but the noun treated not as 'artisan,' but as 'reliability,' as at Dt. 32²⁰; 𐤊ᴸ here=העם יתר.—12. מדלת הארץ : 𐤊ᴸ 𐤂 𐤔 𐤀='עם הא' מד', as at 24¹⁴.—:גֵּבִים=Jer. 52, and so here BH (L), Walton, Ginsb.; Mich., Ken., Bär the Kt. נבים ; see extensive note in deR. on variants and edd. 𐤊 Hex. transliterate with γαβειν (so N al., cf. 𐤔ᴴ—B by error ταβειν), which would represent גַּבִּים ; 𐤊ᴸ γεωργους=𐤔 𐤀 𐤐 ; cf. translation and order in 𐤕, 'farmers and vinedressers.' Jer. 39 gives an early perversion, ויתן להם כרמים ויגבים. The word has not been explained.—13. [ו"] בית : but בכ ת, inf., i.e., double rdgs.—For the pillars of brass, the bases, the sea of brass, cf. the summary, I. 7⁴¹⁻⁴⁴, which includes also the ten lavers, כיורות ; this has been suggested for correction of מכנות, since acc. to 16¹⁷ the bases had disappeared ; but the writer followed the original account.—14. הסירת, היעים, המזמרות, הכפות : a combination of I. 7⁴⁰, ⁵⁰, continued in v.¹⁵ with המחתות, המזרקות, הסירות חירות here corrects הכירות there. Jer. 52 adds five more items.—לקחו : Grr. (exc. 𐤊ᴸ=𐤔ᴴ) as sing., under influence of לקח, v.¹⁵.—16. האחד [הים] : 3 MSS אחד= Jer. 52 Ḳr., correctly, i.e., 'the pillars two, the sea one (piece),' as in epigraphic accounts, and similarly in v.¹⁹, 'a chamberlain, one (person).' Jer. has a plus of 'the oxen twelve.'—לא היה משקל: cf. Akk. ša mēnūtu lā išū (Šanda).—17. שלש אמה : the numeral to be corrected to חָמֵשׁ, with Jer. 52, cf. I. 7¹⁶ ; such nouns may have been written with numeral strokes, as in the papp., and hence easily miswritten or misread ; for the noun read pl., אמות, with many MSS, Ḳr., Jer. 52.—על השבכה : a gloss, parallel to על הכתרת, with reminiscence of I. 7¹⁸ ; it is basis of an expansion in Jer.52.—

II. 24^{18}–25^{30} 569

19. אשר הוא : Aramaism ; Jer. 52, אשר היה=Grr., in both cases by necessary rendering.—חמשה : Jer. 52, שבעה ; Hex. MSS, N al., 𝔖^H om.—הספר שר הצבא=𝔗, Gr. MS x ; Jer. 52, הצ' ספר ש', and so 3 MSS here=𝔊 𝔊^H 𝔖^H ; 𝔊^L gives a preceding doublet, τ. Σαφα τ. αρχιστρατηγον ; 𝔙 ' Sopher principem exercitus ' ; St. regards שר הצ' as a gloss ; however in our ignorance of ancient officialdom criticism is arbitrary. See Comm.—המצבא : the Hif. here and in Jer. 52 is unique. Albr. finds the noun as a military title in the Cyprian inscr. freshly interpreted by him in *BASOR* 83 (1941), 14 ff.—**20.** על : read אל with 12 MSS, Jer.—V.^{b}, רב טבחים, to v.^{29}, לפניו כל, fails in 𝔖^H through loss of a page.—**23.** והאנשים : read ואנשיהם, as below, and with 1 MS, Grr., 𝔗 𝔖 and Jer. 40^7.—המצפה : 4 MSS, Jer., המצפתה.—וישמעאל וג' : the conjunction is resumptive ; the name Ishmael occurs on two seals, *IAE* 203, 210.—נתניה : 2 MSS, Jer., נתניהו, and so on seals, *ib.* 191, 192.—יוחנן : the name as יוחנן on an Egyptian ostracon, Aimé-Giron, *Textes araméens*, no. 1.—תנחמת : = ' consolation ' ; *cf.* Note on ' Manasseh,' 21^1. The masc. name תנחם appears in a Lachish stamp (Diringer, *PEQ* 1941, 38 ff., no. 5).—הנטפתי : *i.e.*, of Netophah near Bethlehem, Ezr. 2^{22}, Neh. 7^{26}, earlier identified with Bait-naṭṭīf, now by Alt and others with ʽAin en-Naṭūf, 5 miles S of Bethlehem ; see Abel, *GP* 2, 399. Jer. prefixes ובני עופי.—יאוניהו : in a Lachish letter (Torczyner, no. 1), as son of מכשלם.—**24.** מעבדי : 4 MSS, Jer., מעבוד, and so here 𝔙, but this requires foll. את. St. would read מפני, as at v.^{26}, *cft.* some VSS. 𝔊 has here παροδον, *i.e.*, rdg. as מעבר, for which *cf.* אל עבר פניו, Eze. 1^9, etc. ; see Joüon, *Biblica*, 17, 345 ff., on use of עבר.—**25.** אלישמע : on seals, *IAE* 216, 257.—עשרה : B† om.—ויכו : B *al.* as sing.—ויתת : this interruption of the sequence of accusatives is to be omitted, with 𝔊, Jer. 41^2 (Gr. 48^2).—**27.** שבעה : 1 MS שמנה ; Jer. 52, חמשה ; Grr. there ' fourth ' —so scribes vary !—אויל מרדך : Schnabel (*Berossos*, 274, note) notes the old Latin version of Jos. for the first element as ' Amil,' and so revises the text of Jos.—מבית כלא : absolute, ' from prison ' ; it is unnecessary to read ' his prison,' with Grr. (exc. 𝔊^L), and so *BH*. Jer. pref. ויוצא אתו=3 MSS here, Grr., 𝔖 𝔄, exegetically. For the technical phrase, ' to lift up the head,' *cf.* Gen. 40^{13}.—**28.** מעל כסא : for the prep. Jer., ממעל ל', which is preferable. For the noun, VSS tr. as pl., but the construct phrase is treated as a composite noun ; *cf.* בית הבמות, etc.—**29.** ושנא : Jer. correctly, ושנה ; *n.b.* Aramaizing irregular construction, as also in foll. ואכל.—אכל לחם וג' : *i.e.*, he was his constant guest ; *cf.* Ps. 41^{10}, etc.—**30.** ארחתו : an Akk. word ; *cf. iaraḫtu*, Delitzsch, *Ass. Hwb.*, 310, ' wahrscheinlich Getreideportion,' and so from root ' to swallow ' ; *cf.* Bezold, *BAG* 67, listing also *arḫītu*, ' Monatsrate,' with a question-mark.— כל ימי חיי : Jer. 52 pref. עד יום מותו, a pure doublet ; but following Haupt and earlier critics cited by him, also Šanda, the phrase in Ki., concluding with ' his life ' is a euphemistic substitute for the original *finale* in ' his death.'

INDEXES

I. SELECT VOCABULARY OF HEBREW WORDS AND PHRASES

אבי, 378.
אביו, 273.
אבים, 273.
ארד, 244; cf. הדר.
אדרמלך, 479, 506.
אדרמלך, 479, 506.
אוב, 522; 'ôb, 520.
אופיר, 215.
אוריה, 463.
אחז, 230.
אחיה, 247.
אט, 335.
איזבל, 291.
איכבוד, 291.
איל, 159.
איתן, 132.
אליחרף, 113–15, 118.
אליקים, 552.
אלישמע, 569.
אל בית, 425.
אמון, 522.
אנכי, 98.
אסוך, 370.
אסף, 378.
ארות, 132.
ארון, 100.
ארמון, 290.
ארצא, 289.
אשנא (Ušna), 462.
אשר, 98, 258, 504, 512, 568.
אשר על העיר, 413.
אשרה, 280.
את, 328.
Achbor, 527.
Adad-melek, 476.
Adrammelek, 476, 498, 499.
'āz, 204.
'ălāh, 196.
Anammelek, 476.
Asherah, 233, 268, 275, 300, 411, 469, 530.
Ashima, 474–6.
Ashimat, 475.

ברא, 263.
בין, 406.
בית הבמות, 569.
בליעל, 334.
במות, 111.
בארך, 512.
Baal, 308.
Baal-zebub, 349.
Baladan, 509, 512.
Bathsheba, 84.
Beelzebul, 349.
Berodach-baladan, 509.
Beth-El, 475, 476.
Boaz, 170, 171.
brr, 383.

נהר, 372.
גלילה, 456.
גנבת, 246.
gĕbîrāh, 267, 274.
Gedaliahu Over-the-House, 566.

דבר, 263.
דוד, 81.
דומשק, 463.
ריב, 388.
דממה, 317.

הדר, 245, 280, 281.
הדר, 244, 280.
הושע, 456.
הימן, 132.
המזבח הנחשת, apposition of thing and material, 463.
הנה, 389.
הגם, 539.

וריר, 383.

זבל, 191, 192, 291.
זה הים, 272.
זמרי, 289.

חור, 124.
חיה, 371, 372.
חירם, 138.
חלוח, 527.

חלם, 329.
חלי, 352.
מחללים, חלל, 86.
חלקיהו, 527.
חמוטל, 551.
חסר, 202.
חפא, 478.
חפשי, 454.
חפשית, 454.
חרי, 86.
חרב, 365, 503.
חרוץ, 522.
חרחם, 527.
חרט, 380.
חרי, 388, 502.
חרם, 503.
ḥayl, 243.
ḥillôn, 349.

טברמן, 281.
טוב, 513.

יאזניהו, 569; cf. Jaazaniahu, 566.
יארי מצור, 504.
יאשיהו, 526.
יד, 426.
יהו, 404.
יהואש, 431.
יהויכין, 557.
יהויקים, 552.
יהונדב, 414.
יוכר, 433.
יוחנן, 569.
יום, conjunction of time, 397.
יטבה, 522.
ים סוף, 215.
יצא, with acc. 512.
יצא, Hiphil, 455.
יצע, 148.
יקר, 139.
ירמיהו, 551.
ירק, 505.
ישמעאל, 569.
יתר, 98.
Jeconiah, 555.
Yachin, 557.
Yākîn, 170.
Yochin, 555.
yôṣêr, 430.

כהן, 115.
כמר, 538.

כן, 330.
כרתי, 85, 86.
כתרת, 180.
kābôd, 108.
Kerêthîm, 78; cf. 86.
kĕrûb, 155, 156.
kiyôr, 178.
kôhēn, 115.
kôhēn hā-rôš, 429, 563.
korban, 428.

לול, 148.
לחש, 82, 329, 478; lḥš, 501.
לקח, Pual ppl., 356.

מרבר, 318.
מה, negative, 258, 512.
מועד, 371.
מופז, 230.
מות, Pual, Polal, 424.
מזבח, 522; mzbḥ, 474.
מיסך השבת, 464.
מכנה, 179.
מכר, 432.
ממלכה, 309.
מנשה, 521.
מסגר, 558.
מסגרת, 179.
מסח, 424.
מעלה, 404.
מצא, 265.
מקוה, 231.
משא, 406; cf. burden, 402.
משחה, 540.
משחית, 540.
משתין, 271.
massāḥ, 419.
maṣṣēbāh, 268, 358; maṣṣēbet, 535.
minḥāu, 362.
mišnêh, 526.
Molek, 232, 233.

נבות, 333.
נבחן, 479.
נגור, 425.
נחש, 82, 478.
ניר, 247.
נחשתן, 501; cf. Nehushtan, 481, 500.
נמשי, 404.
נסח, 424.
נסרך, 506.
נשא, נשא, 202.

INDEXES

נשא, נשׂה, 213.
נשׂי, 371.
נשׁף, 389.
נשׁק, 231.
נתיה, 569.
nbḥz (Nibhaz), 474.
nôḳēd, 359.

סוא, 477.
סנורים, 383.
סף, 184.
סכות בנות, 479.
סריס, 501.
sibbāh, 250.

עבד (of Baal), 415.
עבר, 569.
עד, 138.
עדות, 425.
עוד, 478,
עריה, 527.
עזב, 347.
עזוב, 271.
עזר, 477.
עלה המלחמה, 346; *cf.* 477.
עלית, 371.
עמור, 425.
עמורים, 165.
עצור, 271.
עשה, 330; 'celebrate,' 476.
עשתרת, 245.
עת, 371.
עתרקתה (Atargatis), 474, 475.
'am hā-'āreṣ, 422, 423.
'nn, 520.
'Ashtart, 233, 474, 475.

פריה, 553.
פז, 230.
פחה, 229, 230.
פלתי, 85.
פסח, 132, 310.
פקד, Hothpaal, 328.
פרבר, פרורים, 539.
פרשׁ, 82, 83, 327.
Pelēthîm, 78.
piskah, 264, 352, 405, 503.
pûk, 403.

צבר, 414.
צוה, 97.
צמר, 406.
צמל, apposition of material, 365.

ṣèdeḳ, 197.
ṣiyûn, 535.
ṣûr, 430.

קר, קור, 371.
(קמה) קום, 505.
ḳēn, 440.

רב טבחים, 568.
רב שקה, 501.
רוח, 357.
רומה, 553.
רחבעם, 248.
רכב, 405.
רפה, רפא, 357.
רתם, 317.

שׂ, 382.
שׂבכה, 351.
שׁבנה, 501, 502.
שׂרפה, שׂרמה, 505, 538.
שׂרדה, 425.
שׂחטו, 230.
שׂטן, 245; *cf.* Satan, 246.
שׂיג, 310.
שׂיח, 310.
שׂתן, 271, 502.
שׂכל, 357.
שׂלבים, 179.
שׂלח, Hiphil, 456.
שׂלם, 215, 527.
שׂלמה, 84.
שׂמרון, 290.
שׂנה, 477, 569.
שׂעלבין, 124.
שׂער, 390.
שׂפעה, 405.
שׂקפים, 147.
שׂר, 118.
Shaphan, 524, 527.
Shîlôaḥ, 511.

תור, 229.
תמם, 527.
תנחמת, 569.
תעלה, 311.
תפת, 539; *cf.* Topheth, 532.
תקוה, 527.
תרהקה, 503.
תרתק, 474.
תשׁובה, 328.

II. INDEX OF PLACES TREATED WITH ARCHÆOLOGICAL COMMENT

Abel-beth-Maachah, 278.
Adam, Adamah, 182.
Aphek, 324, 328.
Arubboth, 123.
Awwa, 472.

Baalath, 206.
Baal-shalisha, 370.
Ben-Hinnom, 532.
Beth-eked, 409.
Bethel, 257.
Beth-haggan, 402.
Beth-horon, 207.
Beth-shean, 119.
Beth-shemesh, 441.

Carmel, 300.
Cherith, 294.
Corner Gate, 441.

Dan, 278.
David's City, 90, 102.
double-walls, 561, 562.
Dragon Spring, 74.

Elisha's Spring, 355.
Eloth, 211, 212.
En-rogel, 73.
Entrance of Hamath, 200, 443.
Ephraim Gate, 441.
Esyon-geber, 211, 212, 270.

Gath, 430, 431.
Gaza, 129.
Gibeah, 276.
Gibeon, 104.
Gilgal, 353.
Gozan, 467.
Gur, 402.

Habor, 467.
Halah, 467.
Hamath, 200, 443.

Hasor, 206, 207.
Horeb, 313.
Horses' Gate, 422.

Iwwah, 472.
Iyon, 277.

Janoah, 451, 452.
Jehoshaphat, Valley of, 530.
Jericho, 287, 355.
Jezreel, 330.
Jibleam, 402.
Job's Well, 73, 74.

Kadytis, 537.
Kebul (Cabul), 205, 213.
Kedesh, 452.
Kidron, 530, 531.
king's garden, 562.
Kinneroth, 278.
Kir-hareseth, 363.
Kir-heres, 363.
Kue, 227, 459.
Kuthah, 472.

Lachish, 442.
Libnah, 396; cf. 398.

Maon, 239.
Megiddo, 207, 226, 270, 511, 537.
Midian, 246.
Migdol, 537.
Millo, 206, 243; cf. המלוא, 247.
Mispah, 276.
Musri, 227, 228.

Netophah, 569.

Ophir, 212.

Paran, 239.
Penuel, 254.
Petra, 439, 440.

Ramah, 276.
Ramoth-Gilead, 120, 337.
Reseph, 492.
Riblah, 550.
Rock, 439.

Sair, 396; cf. 398.
Samaria, 285, 341.
Sarephath, 294; cf. 297.
Sarethan, 120, 182.
Sepharwaim, 472.
Ṣerēdāh, 242.
Shechem, 249, 250.
Siloam, 511, 562.
Sinai, 313.
Socho, 123.
Steppe, 95.
Succoth, 182.

Tadmor, Tamar, 208.
Tarshish, 223.
Tell el-Ḳedaḥ, 207.
Tiphsah, 449, 450.
Tiphsah-Thapsacus, 129.
Tirsah, 281.
Tishbe, 293.
Tuleilat el-Ghassūl, 182.

Upper Pool, 486, 487.

Vale of Ben-Hinnom, 532.
Valley of Salt, 439.

Yānôaḥ, 452.
Ya'ūdi, 447.
Yotebah, 521.

Dark Peak Blues

an anthology

J Severn/James H Jones

*Copyright © 2020 J Severn/James H Jones
Kindle editions published by
James H Jones.
Paperback typeset in
Franklin Gothic Book 10.5pt*

All rights reserved. All characters, events, places and companies are either imaginary or are used fictitiously. This document may not be reproduced, used or broadcast, in any form, in whole or in part, without the prior written permission of the author. The right of J Severn/James H Jones to be identified as author of this work has been asserted by him under the Copyright, Designs and Patents Act, 1988.

J Severn is a pen name of James H Jones,
professional writer.
He lives in Thirsk, North Yorkshire, with his wife Maureen and their golden cocker spaniel, Bridget Jones.
James is a retired proofreader and editor.
He is a member of the prestigious writing group, ThirskWriteNow

By the same author

Jack Pays Back
Endgame
The House on Riverside Walk
Dead Man Walking
Jason's Luck
Errors of Judgment
(Un)Friendly Warning
The Lovesick Crow
Marmalade Thighs
Bad Day at Chester Odeon
A Ktima Too Far
Dragunov SVU
Someone Could Fall
He'll Have to Go

In progress:

Walker Unseen
Gone
A Mid-Reader's Tale
Hudson's Personal Services
4.54609
Rodney the Red Kite

Contents

Part One: Verse or Worse
Poems and Lyrics by J Severn

05. Dark Peak Blues
07. She Knows Me, She Knows Me Not
08. The Lovesick Crow
09. My Cocaine
10. Sweet, Sweet Love
11. My Grass is High
12. My Fickle Heart
13. Woman in Red
15. The Friendly Ghost
16. Michelin Un-Starred
17. Thank Goodness
18. Small Change
19. Hear No Evil
21. Willie's Small
22. Feeding Station
23. Sonnet for Emma
24. What's Fer Tea?
26. For Want of a Rhyme

Part Two: The Stories So Far:
Works in Progress by James H Jones

28. Walker Unseen
92. Gone
105. A Mind-Reader's Tale
120. Hudson's Personal Services
153. 4.54609
168. Rodney the Red Kite

185. Author's Note

dark peak blues

Part One: Verse or Worse
Poems and Lyrics by J Severn

Dark Peak Blues
J Severn
Copyright © 2020 J Severn

My woman done left me
And my dog up and died
Yeah, my woman done left me
And my dog up and died
My momma she hates me
And my pa's still inside

The roof's sprung a leak
And there's holes in my shoes
Yeah, the roof's sprung a leak
And there's holes in my shoes
Life's bleak on this peak
Got the Dark Peak Blues

So I'm leavin' Dark Peak
And I'm headin' put West
Yeah, I'm leaving Dark Peak
And headin' out West
I'm layin' those ol'
Dark Peak Blues to rest

This mornin' the postman
Brought wearisome news
Yeah, the postman done brought me
Some wearisome news
The damn bank's foreclosin'
'cause I ain't paid my dues

j severn

My daddy done told me
As they took him down
Yeah, my daddy done told me
As they took him on down
"Keep smiling, my son,
Don't show 'em a frown

Give the ol' finger
To the whole human race
Yeah, give the ol' finger
To the damn human race
An' make sure you do it
With a grin on your face"

So I'm leavin' Dark Peak
And I'm headin' out West
Yeah, I'm leavin' Dark Peak
And I'm headin' out West
I'm layin' those ol'
Dark Peak Blues to rest.

Yeah, I'm leavin' Dark Peak
'Cause it's sure for the best,
To be layin' those ol'
Dark Peak Blues to rest.
Yeah, I'm layin' those ol'
Dark Peak Blues to rest

Yeah, I'm layin' those ol'
Dark Peak Blues to rest

dark peak blues

She Knows Me, She Knows Me Not
J Severn
Copyright © 2020 J Severn

She knows my name, she knows my age
She knows the house I live in
She even knows where I was born
And the schooling I was given

She knows the places I have lived
She knows my resumé
She knows the ups and all the downs
I've lived through on my way

She knows what foods I like to eat
And the films I like to see
She knows what songs I love to hear
And sings them all - for me

She thinks she knows me well enough
She knows the things I favour
But she knows me not - she'll never know
Just how much I crave her

j severn

The Lovesick Crow
J Severn
Copyright © 2020 J Severn

"My love," cawed the crow. "Would you think it absurd
If I said you were the most beautiful bird?
The most beautiful bird I ever have seen
With your haunting eyes and your face so serene

There never could be a more wonderful sight
As you glide through the air so graceful in flight
If this old crow could just fly by your side
The heart of an eagle would be beating inside

Oh please let me show you how lovely you are
Please come to my nest for some R and R -
Dead Rats and Roadkill, my favourite fare -
What's mine is yours and I'll happily share

You have shown me, my love, what I knew not before
With you I have learned the true meaning of 'Caw'
My friends call me crazy, 'You've no chance,' they say
'For she flies by night and you by the day'

But I say let us negotiate
You could wake early and I'd stay up late
Then we would have all our evenings together
Soaring on high like birds of a feather."

"Oh you!" said the owl, blushing deep red
"I think you're just trying to turn my head."

My Cocaine
J Severn
Copyright © 2020 J Severn

You say it's not true that I really love you
But darling please let me explain
From the first time you looked
At me I've been hooked
My addiction my fix my cocaine

I try every day to find words to say
That'll make my feelings quite plain
What more can I do?
I can't live without you
My addiction my fix my cocaine

My love can't you see what you're doing to me?
You know you just drive me insane
And I need you again
And again and again
My addiction my fix my cocaine

j severn

Sweet, Sweet Love
J Severn
Copyright © 2020 J Severn

Oh sweet, sweet love,
it has to be said
You have what it takes
to knock a man dead

Oh sweet, sweet love,
when you walk down the street
The power of your beauty
sweeps me right off my feet

Oh sweet, sweet love,
when you come my way
In the midst of winter
'tis a summer's day

dark peak blues

My Grass is High
J Severn
Copyright © 2020 J Severn

When you left you took the lawnmower
And the vacuum cleaner too
Some carpets and some curtains
And the blind out of the loo

You even saw fit to take my tools
My Black & Decker drill
And some sentimental pieces
Left me in my mother's will

Now my grass is high but so am I
It was worth it all you see
For you've got the things but I've got the wings
I needed to fly free

j severn

My Fickle Heart
J Severn
Copyright © 2020 J Severn

"You hurt me," she said
And my heart filled with shame
She ran from the room
I called out her name

"Don't leave me," I wailed
And my heart filled with pain
She ran out on the roof
In the pouring rain

"Please wait – I love you
Don't do it!" I cried
As she launched into space
And my fickle heart – died

Woman in Red
J Severn
Copyright © 2020 J Severn

"Are you ready to order?" the waiter said,
To the plug-ugly man and the woman in red.
"Yes, my good man, I'm ready and able,"
Said the smug-faced fatso at the table.
"For starters, spaghetti with garlic bread,
No, wait, I'll have the paté instead,

"Then sirloin steak, nice and bloody and lean,
And tell the chef he's not to be mean
When he's dishing out the old French fries,
And make sure the mushrooms are a decent size,
And I'll have two portions of refried beans."
The woman in red sat still and serene.

"And bring some dips, mayonnaise and chilli
For dipping m'chips in, and don't be silly
By bringing 'em in those tiny pots,
Bring 'em in bowls - and bring me lots,
And I'll 'ave a big dish of piccalilli.
And you can cancel the paté, I'll 'ave the fusilli."

The waiter turned to the woman in red,
"And what would Madam like?" he said,
"She'll 'ave same as me," the man interjected,
"She can't disagree with what I've selected.
And don't go forgetting my garlic bread."
The woman in red quietly hung her head.

"Have you chosen a wine, Sir?" the waiter said,
"Yes," said the man, "I'll have the house red."
"And for Madam?" said the waiter, tongue in cheek,
But again, she wasn't allowed to speak.
"She'll 'ave same as me, lad, just like I said.
Best make it three bottles of red."

"Enough!" cried the woman. "I've something to say,
You've clearly forgotten it's Valentine's Day,
And you know I never eat meat, you swine,
You can stick your red wine where the sun don't shine.
I'm sick and tired of your bullying ways,
I'll choose my own food - and I'll drink the rosé."

The Friendly Ghost
J Severn
Copyright © 2020 J Severn

Oh look there's Casper
Coming down our street
What's he doing out
On Trick or Treat?

I know he's quite friendly
But surely he might
Give some of the kiddies
One helluva fright

And why is he wearing
Brown boots on his feet?
Oh I get it now –
It's just a boy in a sheet

Michelin Un-Starred
J Severn
Copyright © 2020 J Severn

The cook on the SS Invincible
Made meals which were nigh on invisible
His portions so small
They were no use at all
To the crew who found them quite risible

The cook on the SS Eugene
Was known for his lack of hygiene
His famous fish pie
Was one reason why
The pong below decks was obscene

But the cook on the SS Formidable
Served food which was chiefly inedible
When his dodgy beef stew
Ran straight through the crew
The demand for the heads was incredible.

NB: toilets on boats are called 'the heads'.

dark peak blues

Thank Goodness
J Severn
Copyright © 2020 J Severn

"Thank goodness that's over," the vicar said
As the guests filed out of the church
He'd seen many weddings but never like this
With the poor bride left in the lurch.

"Thank goodness that's over," the teacher said
When the end of term came around
She'd suffered the worst brats ever this year
And they'd run her right into the ground.

"Thank goodness that's over," the comedian said
When the curtain finally fell
He'd had some bad hecklers in his time
But tonight's was the heckler from Hell.

"Thank goodness that's over," the ringmaster said
Throwing his wet hankie down
He wondered, how come it was always him
Left drying the tears of a clown?

"Thank goodness that's over," the surgeon said
Wiping his scalpel clean
He'd done countless ops over the years
But this was the worst spleen he'd seen

"Thank goodness that's over," the writers cried
When Jay reached the end of his rhyme
They'd heard a lot worse but feared this verse
Might go on 'til the end of time

j severn

Small Change
J Severn
Copyright © 2020 J Severn

"Can you spare me some change?"
The homeless man cried
As we passed him by on the street
He was dirty, dishevelled
And stank of booze
And had cardboard shoes on his feet

"You're wasting your money,"
My girl-friend cried
As I threw some coins in his hat
"You know he'll just up
And spend it on drink."
I told her of course I knew that

I knew he'd be heading
Straight to the boozer
I knew how he spent his days
All that I wanted
Was to make him smile
I knew he'd not change his ways

But still she went on
All the way home
'Til I just couldn't take any more
It was time for a change
So I packed up her things
And quietly showed her the door

dark peak blues

Hear No Evil
J Severn
Copyright © 2020 J Severn

Simon was making such a dreadful din
He didn't hear his mum come in
"For goodness' sake," his mother said,
"Stop that racket and get to bed."

But Simon went on making a noise,
Clattering and banging his plastic toys
He heard not a single word she'd said,
And had no intention of going to bed

Going downstairs in total frustration
Mum apprised Dad of the situation,
"Piss off," said Dad. "I don't give a hoot,"
So she bloodied his nose with a riding boot

Then Mum and Dad had a terrible row
She called him a pillock, he called her a cow,
They each gave the other as good as they got
'Til he clubbed her to death with a cast-iron pot

They lived in a flat where the walls were thin,
Worried neighbours called the coppers in.
Detective Wilson and Inspector Bloom
Questioned young Simon up in his room

"Surely you heard all the noise they were making,
Shouting, screaming, crockery breaking?"
Said DC Wilson, shaking his head,
But Simon heard not a word they said

j severn

He just carried on as if they weren't there,
Whistling and playing without any care.
They quickly deduced 'twas because of his toys
He hadn't heard the unusual noise

Willie's Small
J Severn
Copyright © 2020 J Severn

I saw the writing on the wall
Proclaiming rudely 'Willie's Small
Now we all know that isn't true
For dear old Willie's six-foot-two

And if the writing on the wall
Is claiming Willie to be small
In other ways, it's without grounds
For Willie weighs three hundred pounds

Perhaps the words upon the wall
Mock not his height or girth at all
Perhaps they're being so unkind
About the size of Willie's mind

The wording makes no sense at all
It's just graffiti on the wall
I've covered height and girth and mind
Of 'small' there is no other kind

Thinking more about the scrawl
Upon the public toilet wall –
Could the message be incomplete
And the missing word be simply 'feet'?

Feeding Station
J Severn
Copyright © 2020 J Severn

All kinds of birds from across the nation
Flutter around our feeding station
Enjoying the wide variety of feeds
Like peanuts, fat balls and sunflower seeds

But there's one far greedier than all the rest
A bossy fat robin who puffs out his chest
As we're nearing Christmas he's growing so round
He can barely get himself off the ground

We're not surprised when the greedy prat
Catches the eye of next door's cat
It's nothing less than wildly hysterical
Watching the antics of a bird so spherical

Trying in vain to take to the skies
And deny the moggy his tasty prize
And I'm sure you don't need me, my friends
To tell you how this story ends.

Next Door's Cat 1, Round Robin 0.

Sonnet for Emma
J Severn
Copyright © 2020 J Severn

I find I'm in a bit of a pickle
Trying my best not to be so fickle
But you see, with my beloved Emma
I'm in a never-ending dilemma

Sometimes I think I should choose to stay
Sometimes I think I should fly away
Often, I think life might've been better
If in truth, perhaps, I'd never met her

Most of the time she just drives me crazy
She nags, she nit-picks, she calls me lazy
But once in a while, right out of the blue
She holds me so close and says, "I love you."

And those three little words quickly dissolve
All thoughts of leaving, all manly resolve.

What's Fer Tea?
J. Severn
Copyright © 2020 J Severn

Ma poked Pa in the arm pretty hard,
To be sure she had his attention.
"Our Jimmy's in trouble again," she cried,
"He's been kept back in detention."

"What for now?" Pa wanted to know,
"Will it make us late with us tea?"
"Get yer 'ead out yer belly, for once,"
said Ma, "And just try listening to me."

She sat her fat arse in a chair by the fire,
And gave him an old-fashioned look.
"The little bugger were caught bang to rights,
Defacing 'is geography book."

"He's away with the fairies, is all," said Pa,
"It's nothing to worry about."
"Fairies?" she cried. She leapt up alarmed,
And fetched him a rib-rattling clout.

"My son ain't no fairy, no way," she hissed,
"Go wash your mouth out with soap."
"Not that kind of fairy, my love," said Pa,
"It's just an old saying, you dope."

"*I'm* a dope?" she snapped, unappeased,
"It were you what called 'im a fairy."
Pa sat back to muster his thoughts,
He decided he'd better tread wary.

dark peak blues

"Away with the fairies," he said, real slow,
"Has nothing to do with queer.
It means distracted, like 'Head in the Clouds',
So, shut up and bring me a beer."

Just then young Jimmy came strolling in,
"Hi, folks," he said, "What's fer tea?
Oh, by the way, I'm in love with Paul
And Paul is in love with me.

"We both agree, it was meant to be,
A kind of Kismet, you see.
Now come on, Ma, you forgot to say –
What *are* we 'aving fer tea?"

For Want of a Rhyme
J Severn
Copyright © 2020 J Severn

It was a bright new day in the workhouse
And Fred thought he'd write him a rhyme,
But the warden barked, "Forget it, lad!
You simply don't have the time."

Poor Fred was assigned to the kitchen,
Where he set about peeling the spuds.
At the sink stood Molly, who as usual,
Was up to her oxsters in suds.

Our Fred had a crush on young Molly,
With her bottom so round and so wide.
He thought, 'Sod it! I'll write her a poem,'
But could think of no rhyme for 'backside'.

All day long he tried, how he tried,
'Til finally he thought, 'What a farce,'
And cried out to one of his workmates,
"Hey, buddy, what word rhymes with 'arse'?"

"Fred," his workmate cruelly replied
As he walked off with Molly in tow.
Fred looked on, crestfallen and sad
And cried out loud, full of woe,

"If only I'd thought of a rhyme for backside,
I'd be the one with that girl by my side,
I might even one day have made her my bride.
Still, I tried, oh boy, how I tried."

dark peak blues

He just couldn't hide the tears he cried,
And sighed as back to the spuds he hied.
He feared his true love would be ever denied,
All for the want of a rhyme for backside.

Part Two: The Stories So Far
Works in Progress by James H Jones

Walker Unseen
Copyright © 2020 James H Jones
A work of fiction

Chapter One
North York Moors, 2015
Dead Man Walking

"I – I – never knew - you - were this – this popular." She spoke so quietly, so faintly between desperate gasps for breath, he could barely hear her above all the clamour outside. There were more cars arriving and he could hear McLeod shouting instructions.

He pulled his darling Trish closer to him and kissed her forehead gently. She looked up at him. In the dim light from the fire he could see her lovely blue eyes fading slowly to grey, as he cradled her in his arms.

"I don't think popular's the right word, my angel," he said, caressing her cheek. She didn't answer. Her eyes closed as he watched, her failing breath hissing in her throat and blood foaming at her lips. The front of her pretty cream blouse was now almost completely red, the blood spreading outwards from the hole where a mother-of-pearl button had once been. Dead centre between her beautiful breasts.

Her breathing stopped and she went limp in his arms. He kissed her again, on the lips this time. After all, he wouldn't be impeding her breathing now, would he? He tasted her blood - and swore vengeance.

"Oh, my darling angel," he said, lowering her carefully to the floor in front of the old sofa. "I love you. I love you. I'm so sorry. I will make them pay for this, I promise you."

In the distance he could hear the deep rhythmic whump,

whump of an approaching helicopter. *It has to be McLeod's*, he thought, *no one else knows where the fuck I am*. He crept on all fours over to the window. Fragmented remains of the shattered windowpane lay beneath the ragged tears in the old yellow curtains where the bullets had ripped through.

The bastards had made a mistake. They had no way of knowing his angel was with him.

As darkness fell over the North York Moors, he and Patricia had finished their unpacking and lit a fire in the grate. She had collapsed gratefully on the comfy old sofa and he was in the kitchen making a brew, when they heard the sound of cars pulling up outside, and doors opening and slamming shut. He had run from the kitchen into the living room, shouting a warning and reaching for the light switch, but he was too late. Trish was already on her feet and heading towards the window. Her shadow fell across the curtain, and the bastards took their chances and opened fire.

Yes, they had made a mistake, all right. One which he swore they would pay for with their lives.

He peered out through the bottom corner of the window. It was too dark to make out much detail, but he could see the tops of a row of cars in the lane beyond the dry-stone garden wall, and shapes, a line of human shadows moving across the front lawn, creeping gradually closer to the farmhouse, some of them breaking ranks to run around to the back. The bastards thought they'd got him, and were closing in cautiously to finish him off - if he wasn't already dead. They were too many to count. *Bloody hell*, he thought, *how many goons has the bastard got on his payroll, for God's sake?*

Well, it made no difference how many. He vowed he would kill them all, every single one of them, and then he would kill McLeod. Slowly. The death of a thousand cuts. Easing away from the window, he checked his iPhone, even though he already knew there was no signal in this remote area. The farmhouse sat in a dip, surrounded by hills, and had no landline, no internet connection. He had no way of calling for back-up, even if he wanted to. Which he didn't. He reckoned he could handle it on his own.

The helicopter was much closer now. "It won't help you, McLeod," he whispered. "I'm coming for you."

But then the outside was flooded with light and the whump, whump of the helicopter was stationary, directly overhead. He crept along the wall to the window and peered out through its bottom corner again. In the cone of light shining down from the helicopter he saw the goons retreating to a safe distance.

What the fuck? What were they afraid of? They thought they'd got him, didn't they?

McLeod's big ugly head popped up from behind the wall. He held a bullhorn to his mouth.

"We know you're in there, Walker," came his amplified voice, competing with the unholy racket from above. "It's all over. The chopper's got you on thermal imaging, you fucking arsehole, so your fancy tricks won't help you now. And we've got you surrounded. You're a fucking dead man walking, Walker. Hey, that's funny. You get it, boys?"

Walker didn't find it funny. The moron thought he was living in some Ray Winstone movie, with his gangster wisecracks. He saw some of the goons laughing dutifully at their boss's feeble joke.

Thermal imaging? How the hell am I supposed to counter that? he thought, throwing himself quickly away from the window just as a burst of gunfire tore the tattered remnants of the curtains to shreds and completely destroyed what was left of the top half of the Welsh dresser which stood against the back wall, splintering the wood, sending fragmented shards of plates and Toby jugs flying in all directions, and shattering the single light-fitting which hung suspended from the ceiling. The same light-fitting which had thrown Trish's shadow across the curtains, before he'd had the chance to turn it off.

"Who's the stiff, Walker?" McLeod's voice broke into his thoughts. "I hope it was someone special. Whoever it was, we know they're dead, Walker. Chopper says their image is fading fast. You're all on your own, and pretty soon you'll be dead, as well, you fucking murdering piece of shit."

It was a little over two years since Walker had blown Gerry McLeod's low-life scum-bag of a brother Lennie off the face of the earth, and Gerry had been hunting him down ever since. Now he thought he had him well and truly cornered. Maybe he had. Walker couldn't see how he was going to escape a cordon of heavily armed goons and a helicopter equipped with thermal imaging.

But he swore he would find a way, and would kill every man Jack of them while he was at it.

For all they know, it might have been me they shot, he reasoned, *so McLeod has to be guessing. He can't be sure who he's dealing with. He'll find out soon enough, when I twist my knife in his gut.*

He wondered how the hell they had known where to find him, and decided it could only have been the Land Cruiser. Somehow, they must have found a way to plant a tracking device. He certainly hadn't been followed in the normal way, he would have known. And if they could plant a tracking device, why the hell hadn't they just planted a bomb instead? Most probably it was simply because McLeod wanted to be in the final act, to play a major role in Walker's downfall.

Whatever, the tech guys could sort the car out later. For now, he had a more pressing problem: what to do about the thermal imaging?

Then it dawned on him. He and Trish had rented this old farmhouse a few times over the years. They loved its remoteness, its isolation, hidden away high on the North York Moors, at the end of its own half-mile-long access lane, and he remembered something else about it. It had an attic. An attic with a skylight. And he had his 5-shot Browning shotgun, tucked away on top of the wardrobe upstairs. Goodbye helicopter. Goodbye thermal imaging. Then goodbye McLeod and Co.

He slid down in the corner as another burst of gunfire blew more chunks of wood out of the Welsh dresser. Reaching into his pocket he pulled out the small black plastic case and snapped it open. He took one of the capsules and bit into it, tilting his head back and feeling the bitter-sweet liquid slide down his throat.

Taking a deep breath, he got to his feet and ran, bent double, out into the hallway. He bounded up the stairs two at a time. Behind him, another burst of gunfire ripped through the glass and wood of the front door, bullets thudding into the staircase a few steps below him.

In the bedroom, he went straight to his Bergen for his Glock 17 and his FS commando knife, quickly strapping them to his belt. He stuffed his pockets with spare clips and the suppressor for the Glock. Reaching up, he took down the Browning from the top of the wardrobe, then stood in front of the long mirror, watching and waiting in the dim light.

His face and hands were the first to go, followed closely by his clothes. Briefly, his mobile phone, keys, loose change, spare clips for the Glock, the suppressor and his belt buckle appeared to be hovering in mid-air, then they too faded away. Finally, after another ten seconds or so, the Glock and knife disappeared, along with the middle section of the shotgun immediately around his hand. Apart from the extremities of the Browning, all he could see in the mirror was the room behind him. Looking down to where he knew his feet to be, he saw only the floorboards immediately beneath.

Five whole hours in an aura of invisibility. He had more than enough time, and plenty of ammo. And, especially for McLeod, he had the commando knife on his belt. Once the helicopter was dealt with he could discard the Browning, fit the suppressor to the Glock, and set about sending those goons to hell.

"Now we'll see who's the fucking dead man walking," he said quietly, as he headed for the stairs to the attic.

*Chapter Two
Lympstone, 2015
Another Fine Mess*

"Sorry to barge in, Sir, but there's something you need to know about. Urgently."

Warrant Officer Al Jackson had knocked and entered without waiting for an answer, something which he had never done before. Now he stood stiffly to attention in front of the boss's cluttered oak desk, clearly ill at ease.

"Well, what is it?" snapped the Brigadier, putting down the document he had been studying and nudging his glasses up his nose. "Spit it out, man."

"It's Walker, Sir," said Jackson. "We've had a call from him. Seems like he's in a spot of bother."

"Walker?" Brigadier Ridgway pushed his specs up his nose again, and Jackson thought, not for the first time, *I wish the cantankerous old bastard would get the bloody things adjusted, they're always slipping down his greasy conk*. "The man's on leave, isn't he? What the devil has he got himself into now, for Christ's sake? Is he okay?"

"Yes, he's okay, Sir, but he's as mad as a rabid dog," Jackson blurted out. "He needs the clean-up guys. It seems McLeod tracked him down to the farmhouse he'd rented, up in the North York Moors. Bit of a bloodbath, Sir, by the sound of things. Bodies everywhere, a downed helicopter in the field behind the house, a bunch of cars left at the scene. And sadly, Sir," Jackson took a deep breath and crossed his fingers before continuing. "It seems Walker's wife is dead, as well."

"Oh, dear God, not Patricia," the Brigadier sighed, holding a forefinger to the bridge of his sliding spectacles. He pushed his chair back, got to his feet and began pacing the office, hands clasped behind his back. He passed Walker's desk and glanced briefly at the framed wedding photo standing there. Through his second-storey window he could see the estuary beginning to take shape in the first grey light of dawn. "If there's anyone on this blighted planet guaranteed to bring a heap of trouble down on my head, it's Walker. The man is a veritable disaster-magnet. Dare I ask, is it contained?"

"Walker reckons so, Sir," Jackson replied. "For the time being, at least. He says the place is pretty remote. Oh, and he says he needs the tech guys, as well. He thinks McLeod must have tracked his car, somehow."

"Bloody hell, Jackson," the Brigadier moaned, his glasses slipping down again but going unnoticed. "Does he think we have unlimited resources? Why the devil does he have to spread death and mayhem everywhere he goes? Even when he's supposed to be on leave, for Christ's sake. Do you know how much it's going to cost, to ship all that manpower and equipment to some bloody isolated farmhouse in Yorkshire?"

"I don't know yet, Sir," answered an increasingly tense Jackson. "But I think we have to do it, Sir, I don't think we have any choice."

"Of course we *have to do it*, you blithering idiot," barked the Brigadier. "Did you think I was suggesting we just leave Walker to it, all on his own, for Christ's sake?"

"No, no, Sir, certainly not," said Jackson, a trifle stung by the 'blithering idiot' remark, even though he knew it was just the boss's way. "I'll go ahead and get things rolling, Sir. We need to move quickly if we are to keep it contained."

"Yes, yes, get on with it, man," the Brigadier replied, returning to his seat. "And keep me posted."

Jackson turned and headed for the door, breathing a sigh of relief, and began making his mental calculations. How many body bags would be needed? How many helicopter trips would it take to ship them out and dump them in the North Sea? How many cars would have to be transported and crushed? And how the blue blazes were they supposed to dispose of a downed helicopter, for fuck's sake? That would be a tricky one to cover up, and no mistake. It would almost certainly have to be dismantled on the spot and brought out on a low-loader.

And then there was the farmhouse itself to be cleaned up and damages repaired. And they'd need a coffin for Patricia Walker, and... *Bloody hell, Mike*, he thought, *another fine mess you've got me into.*

"*Wait*," the Brigadier called out, just as Jackson was about to close the door behind him. "You haven't told me if McLeod is amongst the dead. Please tell me he is."

"I'm sorry, Sir," said Jackson. "But Walker reckons McLeod and a handful of cronies must have fled the scene as soon as the helicopter went down. He left his men to die, Sir. I guess he knew they'd be no match for our Major Walker."

"Oh, dear God," groaned the Brigadier. "All this trouble and expense, and the bastard's still out there? Tell Walker I want to see him, here in my office, within the next twenty-four hours."

"Yes, Sir, but..." Jackson began.

"*But*?" his boss shouted. "But what, man? There are no *buts*."

"Yes, Sir, I mean, no, Sir," replied a slightly rattled Jackson. "I was just going to say, Sir, he is still on leave, officially. He's been awake all night, Sir, and it's a three-hundred-mile drive. And begging your pardon for reminding you, Sir, he has just lost his wife."

"Hm. Second thoughts," the Brigadier said quietly. "Make it twelve hours. Right here, in my office, in front of my desk, within twelve hours. Do I make myself understood?"

"Yes, Sir, loud and clear." Jackson retreated, at the double. He reminded himself that the boss's bad moods were down to nothing more than the frustration of being stuck behind a desk, after years of being on the front line. Not to mention a deep-seated concern for his team.

The Brigadier pushed his glasses back up his nose and picked up the document he had been studying before being so rudely interrupted. *Poor old Mike*, he thought. *He and Trish had such great plans. And how the devil am I supposed to break it to John and Val?*

In the event, it was a mere nine hours and fifteen minutes later when Jackson's announcement came over the intercom.

"Major Walker's here, Sir."

The Brigadier got up from his desk and crossed to the door. He threw a comforting arm around his visitor's shoulders. Walker's face was drawn and showing pale through the stubble, his eyes sunken in their sockets.

"I'm so sorry, Mike, old boy," Ridgway said, as he escorted his old friend to the chair in front of the desk. "Shocking news.

Dreadful. I have to say, you got here damn quickly, all things considered. Do you feel up to filling me in?"

"I'm okay, thanks, Edward," Walker replied, forcing a thin smile, as the Brigadier returned to his own seat. "I set off as soon as the team arrived. I left the Land Cruiser with the tech guys. They'll drive it back when they've finished checking it out. I borrowed one of the goons' cars. He won't be needing it again. Bloody awful Chrysler 300 thing, but it got us here pretty quick, all the same."

"Us?" queried the Brigadier, his specs sliding down his nose in equal and opposite reaction to the upwards motion of his eyebrows.

"Yeah, I kept one of the fuckers alive," said Walker. "I don't think he enjoyed the journey much, rolling around in the boot nursing two shattered kneecaps."

"*Bloody hell,*" Ridgway exclaimed. "Well done, Mike. Where is he now?"

"Jackson's taken charge of him," said Walker. "He's getting him patched up, ready for interrogation. I'm hoping he can tell us where McLeod might have gone to ground."

"Good," said Ridgway. "Let me know when he's ready. I want to be there. Tell me, Mike, how many dead?"

"I reckon about twenty-five," Walker replied. "I got most of the bastards with the Glock and a few with my knife. I couldn't believe it when I found McLeod had fucking scarpered. I've got to find that twisted little shit and kill him, Edward, you know that, don't you? You're not going to try and pull me off the case, are you?"

"What? No, of course not." Ridgway was quick to reassure him. "This isn't some corny Hollywood cop movie, Mike. McLeod is all yours and I wish you God speed. When you do catch up with him, make it slow and painful. Patricia was special to all of us, you know."

They fell silent for a while. The Brigadier buzzed Jackson and requested two coffees. The late afternoon sun was shining in through the window now, lighting up hovering dust motes, throwing long shadows across the carpet.

"I've broken the news to John and Valerie," said Ridgway quietly. "But they will need to see you, as well, you know. I will go with you, if you want me to." Walker acknowledged the offer with a nod of his head. "What's happening about her - her body, Mike?"

"They're bringing her home in the chopper," Walker replied. He shifted uncomfortably in his seat and fished in his pocket for a tissue. He got up and walked over to the window, dabbing at the corners of his eyes, gazing out at the estuary for a minute or so before continuing. "It's our anniversary tomorrow, you know. Six years, Edward, just six years, and that fucking animal has destroyed everything."

"I know, old boy, I know," said Ridgway. "And it can only be, what, eight years or so, since we rescued her from those blasted pirates?"

Chapter Three
Somalia, 2007
The Rescue Mission

Patricia Bradley came awake in pitch darkness, trying desperately but in vain to cling on to her dream, to keep at bay the nightmare which was her waking reality. Inevitably, the dream receded, as all dreams will, quickly fading away to nothing, trampled underfoot by the unstoppable advance of the conscious mind. She felt certain something had broken into her sleep and brought her awake prematurely, but she knew not what.

In her recurring dream, the Motor Yacht *Centenary* left Lympstone in fine weather and set off across the Channel to Honfleur, the first stop on its round-the-world voyage.

Trish and her best friend Paul Anderson had just finished university when they got the invitation to take a gap year and join her Uncle Richard and Aunt Louise, her mother's brother and sister-in-law, on the adventure of a lifetime.

When Colonel Richard Redfern retired from the Royal Marines, he and Louise ploughed all their savings into the MY *Centenary* and set about bringing to fruition their long-held ambition to sail around the world. A journey which they intended to undertake in the most leisurely fashion.

After a night in Honfleur, where, at a restaurant called *L'Assiette Gourmand*, they enjoyed the most fabulous meal Trish had ever experienced, they set off for the Med. Subsequent nights found them berthed in a string of romantic harbours dotted along the southern coasts of Spain and France. They sailed around the boot of Italy after stopping off at Sorrento and the Isle of Capri, and made their final European landfall at Agios Nikolaos in Crete.

By then, she and Paul had learned all they needed to know about navigation and seamanship, and that evening in the local taverna, Richard was lavish with his praise.

"A toast," he cried, raising his glass of Metaxa brandy. "To four seasoned old sea-dogs."

"Hey, less of the *old*," quipped Trish.

"Yes, and less of the *dogs*, as well, thank you," added Louise.

Paul, wise beyond his years, remained silent, hiding his amusement behind his brandy glass. Trish gazed appreciatively at her three companions, thinking how well they all looked, bronzed by the Mediterranean sun, relaxed and at ease, at one with the world.

In her dream, they made the fascinating trip through the Suez Canal and on down the Red Sea, coming out into the Gulf of Aden. From there, they successfully completed the three thousand kilometres voyage across the Indian Ocean to Malé in the Maldives, from where they planned to head south to Mauritius, then east to Perth in Western Australia.

But that was in the dream. In what became their terrifying reality, everything happened exactly the same, up to them leaving the Gulf of Aden. In actuality, they never made it to the Maldives. Or even anywhere near.

Their first night in the Indian Ocean, roughly one hundred and fifty kilometres east-south-east of the Gulf, they anchored up for the night. They enjoyed a meal and after-dinner drinks out on the open deck, under a clear starlit sky and the glow from the single white masthead light, the boat barely rocking on the calm dark sea. Conversation centred mainly on the joys to come, the sights they expected to see, the exotic far-flung places they planned to visit.

Later, about thirty minutes or so after she and Paul had made love and had retired to their separate bunks, Trish heard and felt a distinct *thump*.

Something had bumped into the starboard side of the boat, somewhere to the rear of her cabin.

Paul was the quickest to react. With a cry of "What the fuck?" he leapt from his bunk and, clad only in his boxers, headed for the deck. She followed as quickly as she could, stopping only to pull on her jeans and a tee-shirt.

The instant she emerged from the saloon she was grabbed roughly by both arms, forced to the deck and held face-down by two men.

She screamed when she saw Paul struggling valiantly to fight off a bunch of heavily-armed attackers. He managed to floor three of them with swinging roundhouse punches but as she watched, helpless and horrified, he was brutally clubbed by a rifle butt and fell to the deck, unconscious. One of the men raised a pistol and shot him in the belly.

She screamed again as, laughing with delight, four of them lifted his limp form by the arms and legs, swung him backwards and forwards a few times in an escalating rhythm, then flung him over the side, leaving a spattering of blood on the deck and up the railings.

She kicked and bucked and tossed, but the two men held her firm until she simply broke down and sobbed, drenching the decking with her tears, through which she saw her Uncle Richard and Aunt Louise being hauled out on to the deck, both of them stark naked.

Trish was pulled to her feet. All three of them were manhandled unceremoniously to the edge of the deck. For a heart-stopping moment, she was convinced they were about to join Paul in a watery grave, but they were simply forced into sitting positions, tied to the rail and left there.

The pirates up-anchored and the *Centenary* set off due west, following in the wake of the much smaller attack boat.

As dawn broke they were entering a river estuary on what Richard was certain had to be the eastern coast of Somalia.

"The bastards are obviously going to hold us for ransom," he muttered. "I dread to think what they might do if they find out who we really are."

The women were silent. Tears of sorrow ran down Trish's face as she thought of her poor darling Paul, lost forever somewhere in the depths of the Indian Ocean.

She mulled over her uncle's words, wondering how her parents would react to a ransom demand. She worried about what their captors might do if they found out Uncle Richard had been a Colonel in the Royal Marines Commando, and her father was Lieutenant Colonel Bradley, Commandant of CTCRM Lympstone.

So now, countless days later, when she woke from her dream in the filthy hut which had become their prison, she had no idea what time it was. All she knew was it was pitch dark, some ungodly time of the night and much earlier than she would

dark peak blues

normally have come reluctantly awake.

Something had definitely broken into her dreams, but she had no idea what. It certainly wasn't the usual urgent need to empty her churning bowels, tortured by the disgusting forced diet of boiled millet and an unpalatable flat bread the pirates called muufo.

It wasn't Uncle Richard's snoring or Aunt Louise's quiet sobbing, either, although she could hear them both well enough.

She lay still, holding her breath, listening. The only hint of light was a dim flickering from the dying campfire, barely visible through the slim gap at the bottom of the door. There were no windows. An occasional shadow told her their sentry was slowly pacing back and forth, no doubt determined to keep himself awake. She recalled the night when their guard had been caught sleeping, curled up outside the door. He had been beaten mercilessly for his sins.

But now, everything seemed normal, if this living nightmare could ever be described as such. Nonetheless, something had woken her, brought her fully alert, her every nerve tingling with anticipation.

Just as she was telling herself not to be silly, to calm down and try to get back to sleep, she heard a quiet *thud* and a short, muffled cry. The flimsy door burst open. Briefly silhouetted in the dim light from the campfire, a giant of a man came in backwards, dragging the limp body of the sentry by his ankles, then casting him to one side like some discarded bundle of rags.

"Good morning, Miss Bradley," the man said calmly, in perfect English, bending down to wipe his knife clean on the dead sentry's ragged shirt. Behind him Patricia could see more men moving stealthily from hut to hut. She heard what she later learned were the sounds of suppressed pistol shots. Across the room, the Redferns were now fully awake and propped up on their elbows. The man straightened up and slid his knife back into its sheath.

"Good morning Colonel, Mrs Redfern. Mister Anderson no longer with us, I see. Are we all set to go?"

"Bloody hell!" exclaimed Uncle Richard, now fully awake. "Mike Walker, as I live and die. Man, are we pleased to see you. How the devil did you find us?"

"A process of elimination, Sir," replied the man her uncle had addressed as Walker. "We must have sailed up just about every river on the east coast of Somalia, and let me tell you, there are bloody hundreds of 'em."

Through the doorway, Patricia saw the leader of the pirates emerging cautiously from the hut opposite, rifle at the ready. A figure rose up from the darkness behind him and, in what appeared to be one smooth movement, clamped an arm around the man's throat and, with his other hand, stuck a knife up and under the ribcage, straight into the heart. He let the body slump to the ground and strode across the clearing to their hut.

"All done, Captain," he said. Trish noticed sergeant's stripes on the sleeves of his battle fatigues. "I reckon thirteen dead. Unlucky for them, eh? All our men accounted for. No casualties."

"Thanks, Al," said Walker. "Let's get tidied up and get these good people out of here."

The 'tidying up' involved, firstly, dragging all the corpses over to the leader's hut and propping them up in sitting positions against the wall. The leader himself was placed dead centre and, as a clear signal to whoever found them, a green beret was placed on his head, at a rakish angle.

Secondly, the commandos gathered up all the pirates' weapons, a substantial collection of rifles, machine guns, pistols and grenades, carted them off and flung them into the river, which flowed past about one hundred metres from the collection of huts.

Tricia watched the one called Jackson keep back two of the rifles and a couple of pistols, dishing them out to his men. It was only then she realised there were just six commandos in all, including the captain and the sergeant, and she marvelled at how quickly and quietly they had overcome more than three times their number of pirates.

They left the camp, heading for the river. Richard and Patricia were okay to walk, but poor Louise, weakened by days of diarrhoea and vomiting, had to be carried. Captain Walker himself piggy-backed her down to the waiting Zodiac IRC.

A short trip down river took them to where the *Centenary* had been moored, well hidden from aerial view under an overhanging canopy of trees. Two commandos had been left in charge and helped Tricia and Richard to clamber aboard. Tricia couldn't help noticing some fresh bloodstains on the stern deck, and was careful to give them a wide berth.

"Sorry 'bout that, Miss," said one of the men, noticing. He spoke with a distinct Yorkshire accent. "The dozy fuckers – pardon my French, Miss – only left one man guarding t'boat. We fed 'im to t'fishes."

"That'll do, thank you, Ackroyd," said Walker sternly, failing to suppress the flicker of a grin as he carried Louise aboard and lowered her gently to her feet. "You can spare us the gory details."

In the inflatable, Sergeant Alec Jackson was on the radio. "Zodiac to Bluebell," he said. "Mission complete. All souls safe. *Centenary* recovered. On our way, over."

"Bluebell to Zodiac," came the reply. "Well done, men. Take care. Remember, it's not over until you're safely back with us. God speed. Out."

"It ain't over till the fat lady sings," quipped Jackson, chuckling to himself.

"Must he always bring God into it?" grumbled Walker simultaneously, so quietly only Tricia could hear him.

"Good Lord," exclaimed Richard, who had been listening intently to the radio conversation. "Was that who I think it was?"

"Yes, Sir," replied Walker. "Major Ridgway insisted on heading up the operation, the moment he heard who was involved. He's waiting for us now, on board FIC Bluebell. So, if you're feeling up to it, would you like to take back control of your boat and follow us out of this stinking river?" He jumped back into the inflatable, shouting out an order. "Sergeant Jackson, I want you, Ackroyd and Williams here, riding shotgun on board the *Centenary*. Watch our backs, lads."

Leaving the men to it, Tricia helped an exhausted but smiling Louise to her cabin. She was relieved to hear the engine bursting into life and to sense the boat beginning to move.

This time, as dawn was breaking, the *Centenary* headed east into the rising sun, sailing out of the estuary and back into the open sea, the three on-board commandos on look-out on the rear deck, the other five in the Zodiac inflatable riding point ahead of them.

By the time Tricia had rustled up breakfast and coffee for all on board, they had rendezvoused with FIC *Bluebell* and were heading north at maximum speed for the Gulf of Aden and the first safe harbour in the southern Red Sea. The sight of other vessels going about their normal everyday business brought it home to Tricia that the nightmare was finally over.

As they left the Indian Ocean in their wake, she thought wistfully of poor, brave Tom, lost forever beneath the waves.

On board the FIC, Major Ridgway and Captain Walker were closely examining the four weapons which Sergeant Jackson had kept back from being consigned to the river-bed.

"SA80 rifle, Sir," said Walker. "Which, as you know, is standard issue to our Regular Army. Though God knows why; not the most reliable of weapons. And 9mm Brownings, again standard British issue."

"Yes, yes, I know what they are," said the Major in his customary brusque manner, slapping his own Browning in its holster to emphasise his point. "And an AR15, as used by us and our friends in the SAS. Where the hell do you think the bastards got them from?"

"I don't know, Sir," said Walker quietly. "But we bloody well need to find out. They had the usual assortment of AK47s, some original Russian ones and some cheap Chinese copies, some genuine Israeli Uzis and the like, but these were in the majority, by far. Jackson reckons they threw over fifty of each in the river. One of the huts was used solely as an arsenal. We reckon our bunch of pirates was acting as the central arms distributor for the entire coast. Oh, I almost forgot. I brought you a present, Sir. Thought you might appreciate it." He reached into one of his capacious pockets and produced a gleaming SIG Sauer P227, quite obviously brand new. "Jackson took it from the pirates' leader. After he'd killed him, of course."

The Major pushed his glasses up his nose, took the pistol and studied it carefully, turning it over in his hands and testing its balance. He paced the width of his cramped quarters for a while, deep in thought.

"We'll have to take this business higher up, you know," he said, stopping and turning to look at Walker, frowning. "If those guns were sourced back home – and I know we both suspect they were - we'll have to get the MoD involved. And it will be taken straight out of our hands, then, for sure."

Chapter Four
Lympstone, 2010
The Old Ennui

Mike Walker got up from his desk and went and stood at the office window, watching the sun slowly lowering itself towards the hills on the far side of the estuary.

It was usually his favourite time of day, when the sun had finally swung round enough to shine in through his window and he could feel its warmth on his face, but he was in no mood to appreciate it. Days like the one he had just been through always found him, as the song says, *fighting vainly the old ennui*.

As senior training officer at CTCRM Lympstone, it had fallen to him, earlier in the afternoon, to inform two recruits they weren't going to make it through the rigorous commando training course. Having to be the bearer of bad news never failed to leave a nasty taste in his mouth.

Things were going to work out okay for one of the lads, whom Walker was happily recommending for reassignment and who would make an excellent Ordinary Seaman in the Royal Navy. The second one, however, was a definite no-hoper, and on being told he was headed straight back to Civvy Street, he'd broken down and cried like a baby.

Reading through the unfortunate recruit's progress report - or more realistically, no-progress report - Walker reckoned the somewhat accident-prone youth would represent considerably less of a threat to humanity behind the counter of a Starbucks, say, than he would if let loose on one of Her Majesty's ships. He most certainly should never be entrusted with a loaded weapon.

Not for the first time, he wondered how such an inept individual had managed to wangle his way on to the course. The selection process was pretty rigorous and was supposed to be foolproof, but once in a while some useless fish would slip through the net.

And now there was all the daily paperwork to plough through – an endless everyday succession of reports, assessments, recommendations, *ad* bloody *infinitum, ad* bloody *nauseam* - before he could even think of going home to his darling Trish.

Which reminded him; he had better not be late. It was their first wedding anniversary, and they had a table booked at the Swan Inn, their favourite eating place in Lympstone. He checked his watch and decided to give it another couple of hours, tops. If he hadn't finished the damned paperwork by then, it would have to wait until morning.

It was at times like this he yearned for the good old days, when he was Captain Walker, leading his own small elite troop of commandos, like when they'd rescued his darling Trish and the Redferns from those Somali pirates. She hadn't been his darling, then, of course. That came later. But it had definitely given them a conversation-stopping answer to the old question, "How did you two meet, then?"

Yes, he missed being out in the field, all right. It wasn't that he hadn't appreciated the promotion to Major, and he certainly knew his job was worthwhile. He even quite liked being under the command of his father-in-law – one of the best senior officers he had ever known - but at heart he had never been one for sitting behind a desk. And he could never entirely escape the notion that his current rank and position were, in no small measure, down to the influence of his wife's father, the eternally grateful Lt Col John Bradley, Commandant.

His thoughts were interrupted by the buzzing of the intercom. He strode back to his desk and leaned over to answer the call.

"Sorry to bother you, Sir," came the irritatingly fawning, nasal voice of the corporal from the outer office. The fellow made Walker's skin crawl. He often wished it could be legal to shoot someone for being an obnoxious little creep; but the man did a good enough job. "There's a Brigadier Ridgway here to see you, Sir, and another gentleman. They don't have an appointment, Sir, but the Brigadier says..."

"Stop blathering, man, I'll be right out," Walker interrupted and broke off the call. He moved to the door and threw it open, a big broad grin lighting up his face as his old friend approached. They met and shook hands warmly.

"Three coffees please, Corporal," said Walker, without

bothering to ask if coffee was what they all wanted. He ushered his guests through the door, not even troubling to ask after the identity of his other visitor.

"It's good to see you, Edward," he said, once they were seated. "Haven't seen you since our wedding. Don't tell me you've come all this way specially to bring us an anniversary present. A simple card would have sufficed."

"Good Lord, is it a year already?" the Brigadier replied. "Sorry, old chap, it had quite slipped my mind. Congratulations and God bless you. How is young Patricia? Married life suiting you both, I hope?"

"Trish is fine, thank you," Walker assured him, inwardly cringing a little at the God reference. "And married life is great. You should try it sometime. But that's not why you're here, is it?"

"Quite right, old boy," said the Brigadier. He half-turned to his companion, who had been sitting quietly, clutching a laptop case to his chest, as if frightened someone might come along at any moment and try to snatch it away. "Mike, allow me to introduce Richard Hopper, of the MoD. Richard, this is my old friend and colleague, Major Mike Walker who, as you know, is about to become the answer to all our prayers."

"What the...?" Walker began, but was interrupted by a light tap on the door signalling the arrival of their coffees. "Come in," he shouted, thinking *the toadying bastard even manages to make a knock on the door sound creepy.*

Once the corporal had left, the Brigadier stood up, pushed his glasses up his nose and began pacing back and forth, which Walker knew was just his old friend's way of gathering his thoughts before speaking out on some matter of great import.

Walker took the opportunity to study the man from the MoD, who smiled back at him a little nervously and shifted uneasily in his seat. He was a fairly nondescript individual, of indeterminate age, who was clothed in a manner which contributed in no small part to his eminently unmemorable appearance.

He wore a dark grey suit which had seen better days. White shirt, dark blue tie, slightly shabby black Oxfords, grey socks. His plain, pale, thin face was almost completely hidden behind an enormous pair of old-fashioned horn-rimmed spectacles, the unremarkable vision being topped off by an unruly mop of light brown hair, which looked as though it hadn't seen a brush or comb in a good long while.

Walker couldn't decide which word applied – nerd or geek? He had never been sure what the difference was, if any; nor did he care, really.

Realising he was making the poor man self-conscious, Walker smiled apologetically and turned his attention to his coffee. He waited patiently for his old friend to stop pacing and resume his seat. As he knew from experience, there was no point in trying to force the issue.

"Well now, Mike old boy," said the Brigadier, finally sitting back down and leaning his elbows on the desk. "I know you might think I've been on a cushy number since I've been at the MoD, but I'm here to tell you we have been extremely busy bees."

"I never thought any such thing, Edward," Walker protested, smiling. "In any case, you might say the same about me."

"*Touché*," said the Brigadier. "Anyway, getting down to business, I have a proposition for you, if you're interested, and I rather think you will be when you hear what it is. You might want to dismiss your corporal chappie out there, before I go on."

Walker buzzed his assistant and told him he could go home. The MoD man shuffled in his seat again and crossed his legs, hugging his laptop case even closer to his chest.

"You will remember the weapons we recovered in Somalia, of course," the Brigadier continued, receiving a nod in response. "I have to tell you, what we suspected at the time turned out to be true. They had come from the UK. My team at the MoD have been working on it ever since, in conjunction with Special Branch and the Security Services."

The Brigadier paused to take a drink of his coffee. Walker kept quiet. His curiosity was piqued, naturally, but he knew better than to start asking questions at this stage. He waited patiently while his old friend took a second sip of his drink, then wiped a finger across his lips.

"As it turns out, there's a great deal more involved than just one isolated bunch of Somali pirates," the Brigadier went on, sitting up a little straighter in his seat. "British military weapons have been cropping up all over the place. Afghanistan. Iraq. Palestine. Several African nations. And always in the hands of the wrong people. Terrorists. Insurgents. Extremists. So-called freedom fighters. Worst of all, bloody Al Qaeda and the Taliban."

Another pause. Walker held his hand up in a waiting gesture, crossed to the door and threw it open, making sure the corporal had actually left, and wasn't still lurking in the ante-room, earwigging. Satisfied, he sat back down, ready to hear more.

"It didn't take us too long to find out who's behind it all," the Brigadier said. "A real nasty pair of home-grown gangsters. The McLeod brothers. Gerry and Lennie. Based in Manchester. They are into everything you can imagine. Drugs. Armed robbery. Prostitution. Human trafficking. Protection. Loan-sharking. Extortion. You name it, they've been at it for years. They've recently moved into internet crime, which seems to be the up-and-coming thing nowadays. But the gun-running is the area which interests us the most, as you can imagine. It's another relatively recent addition to what might be called their portfolio, but one which slots in far too easily with their existing networks."

"Right, so, if you know who's behind it," said Walker, unable to keep silent any longer. "What do you need me for? Surely, between you all, I mean Special Branch, the MoD and, presumably, MI5 and 6, you must have enough to go ahead and shut them down."

"Oh, we've tried, all right," the Brigadier replied quietly. "But there's never enough hard evidence to bring them to justice in the normal manner. Three years we've been on this case, knowing all along who we were up against, but we've been frustrated at every turn. We've even managed to cut off a few of their lines of supply, but it doesn't seem to have had any effect. Cut off one arm, they quickly grow another, like some kind of blasted axolotl." He paused to push his glasses back up his nose and take another sip of his coffee. "They're a right clever pair of bastards, and know just how to keep themselves distanced and well protected every step of the way."

"What are their lines of supply, exactly?" asked Walker.

"Many and varied," came the reply. "Illegal arms trading, straightforward theft, armed robbery. Much of their materiel comes from the far east. Most worrying of all, though, is the involvement of MoD Kineton, which at least explains all the British military weapons you found in that Somali pirate camp."

"*What*?" Walker exclaimed, sitting bolt upright in his seat. "You mean to say they've actually been able to steal from the arsenal at Kineton?"

"No, no, not as such," the Brigadier said, holding up a calming hand. "Sorry, old boy, I didn't express myself very clearly, did I? No thefts from inside Kineton, as far as we can tell, but several consignments on their way to or from the arsenal have been waylaid. They are almost certainly getting inside information, but we haven't been able to pin it down. Yet. But we reckon they have at least one traitorous bastard on their payroll, probably more. And quite possibly at some of the highest levels."

They fell silent while Walker digested the information. He still hadn't learned what was expected of him, but having already raised the question he knew better than to ask again. In any case, he knew he was about to find out, because Richard Hopper was busy firing up his laptop, which was now open on a corner of the desk. Walker drained the last dregs of his coffee and waited patiently.

"I've been given the go-ahead to put together a deniable-ops team," the Brigadier said, finally cutting to the chase. He rose from his seat and began pacing the room, hands clasped behind his back, a habit which always reminded Walker of Prince Philip. "With a view to wiping out the McLeods and their operations, completely, once and for all, no questions asked. I want you to head it up, reporting directly, and exclusively, to me."

He paused for breath and stood at the window for a while, gazing at the sunset, gathering his thoughts. Walker sensed there was more to come and kept quiet, waiting for him to continue.

"You can choose your own team," the Brigadier spoke up again, turning from the window and resuming his pacing. "But armed with the unique resource which Mister Hopper here is about to show you, you'll find you won't be needing much help. Your old pal Warrant Officer Jackson and two or three others should be enough. Jackson's already on board, by the way, and keen as mustard, as you can imagine. In fact, he and Hopper here are staying with me, at my house in Lyme Regis. No doubt my dear sister will be spoiling him rotten as we speak, plying him with copious quantities of tea and home-made cake. So, what do you say? Interested?"

"On the face of it, it sounds like a great idea," said Walker, a gleam in his eye. "But why me, particularly? And what about my job here? And just what is this *unique resource*, exactly?"

"Your job's all taken care of, Mike," said the Brigadier, his eyes twinkling. "I've squared it with John and he's already busy organising a replacement for you. As of now, you are working for me. We'll be sharing this office, you and I, but you won't be needing it much after today. Your corporal chappie is being reassigned. Jackson will be taking over the outer office. We'll have our first strategy meeting right here, tomorrow morning, eleven hundred hours."

There was a pause. The Brigadier exchanged glances with Richard Hopper.

"So go on, then," Walker prompted. "Why me? And what *resource*?"

"You're an obvious choice, old boy," the Brigadier told him. "The right background, the right training and experience. Never forget, either, how it was you and your team who first brought all this to our attention in the first place. For that reason alone, you deserve to be the man. And, icing on the cake, you're the right blood group."

"What the hell has my blood group got to do with it?" Walker demanded, a note of anxiety creeping into his voice.

"Richard, if you would like to take over, now?" said the Brigadier, waving a hand at his companion. "I forgot to mention, young Richard here is an MoD boffin, a scientist, I should say. And a damned clever chap. Wait until you see what he and his team have come up with. Amazing stuff, truly amazing. You'll find it all hard to believe, I can tell you. It will answer all your questions. And needless to say, it's strictly hush-hush."

"Thank you, Brigadier," said Hopper, speaking for the first time, in what Walker thought was a much deeper voice than his geeky – or nerdy - appearance might have led one to expect. "Actually, my correct designation is physicist, but what's in a name, eh?"

He swivelled the laptop around so Walker could see there was a video set up, waiting to go. The opening-still showed a rather bare, utilitarian office. An old-fashioned desk and chair sitting on a faded grey carpet; two steel filing cabinets; an extremely dated coal-effect electric fire sitting in an ugly green-tiled fireplace. The top of the desk was cluttered with the usual office paraphernalia, including what looked like the very same laptop on which they were now viewing the video.

"Just to confirm, Major, before we continue," said Hopper. "You are blood group B Positive, are you not?" Walker responded with an affirmative grunt and a quick nod, as if to tell the man to get on with it. "Okay. Hit 'play' when you're ready, Major," Hopper continued. "But before you do, a word of warning. What you are about to see will undoubtedly seem completely unbelievable, but I can assure you, it is one hundred per cent genuine. There is no trick photography involved. No CGI. And I'm sure I don't need to remind you of your oath under the Official Secrets Act."

Having delivered his little speech, which Walker took without even blinking, he sat back in his seat and recrossed his legs, a self-satisfied smile playing around his lips. Edward Ridgway chuckled and came round the desk, to watch the video over Walker's shoulder.

"Go on, man, hit the button," urged the Brigadier. "I never tire of watching this."

When the film began rolling, Walker saw Richard Hopper himself appearing from the right. He was wearing the same suit. He went and sat behind the desk, on which, as well as the laptop, were a blotter, a phone, a stapler, a hole-punch, an old jam jar full of pens and pencils, and a nest of filing trays.

Hopper opened one of the desk drawers and, one at a time, produced three objects which he placed carefully on the blotter in front of him. A Browning 9mm pistol, a hunting knife and, finally, a black plastic case, about the size and shape of an old tobacco tin.

He opened the case, which had a hinged top, and swivelled it towards the camera, displaying its contents, which were nine fairly large capsules, nestling in what looked much like a miniature version of an egg-tray. Looking straight into the camera, he took one of the capsules, raised it slowly to his mouth, bit into it firmly and tilted his head back.

Picking up the pistol and the knife, one in each hand, he stood up and came round to the front of the desk, closer now to the camera but still fully in view.

"Now watch carefully," said the Brigadier, laying a hand on Walker's shoulder. "Don't even blink. You won't believe what happens next."

About half a minute went by, then Walker's mouth dropped open. Right in front of his eyes, Hopper began to disappear. First to go were his flesh and bones, his face, his head, his hands, leaving his glasses and the weapons eerily suspended in mid-air. Then his clothing and specs dissolved from view and for a brief moment Walker could see, as if they were floating, the man's watch, his keys, his loose change and mobile phone, then they went, too, followed shortly by the pistol and knife.

Finally, all Walker could see was an apparently empty office.

A few seconds later he saw the desk chair moving backwards. The gun and knife came into view on the desktop, followed by a bunch of keys, a mobile phone, a handful of coins and a watch. The video came to an end and the screen went black.

"Fucking hell!" said Walker, letting out the breath he hadn't realised he'd been holding. "Was that for real?"

"Absolutely, old boy," replied the Brigadier, laughing with delight at Walker's reaction. "Five whole hours of total invisibility, and no nasty side effects."

"How on Earth...?" Walker began, then fell speechless.

"I won't bore you with the details," said Hopper, looking extremely pleased with himself. "But it's all about light. In the simplest of terms, the chemical temporarily affects the physical nature of your aura. In normal circumstances, as I'm sure you are aware, light travels in straight lines. Light rays penetrate the aura, ignore it, say, and are stopped only when they hit the solid object which is your body. With this chemical coursing through your veins, when light hits the outer edge of the aura it is refracted, dispersed if you like, around its circumference and meets up again on the other side, forming an invisibility cloak around you. Hence material objects disappearing, as you witnessed, as well as human flesh and bones, just so long as they are within your aura."

"Jesus Christ!" muttered Walker. "This is pure science fiction gone bloody mad. You're breaking the laws of physics."

"Science fact, old boy," said the Brigadier, chuckling, as Walker hit 'play' to watch the video again from the beginning. "Take my word for it. I've seen it at first hand. I would have liked to try it out myself, but it only works properly with B Positive people, like you and Hopper, here. Anyone with any other blood group can still be seen, like some crazy see-through image. Truly disturbing to witness, let me tell you. Did you know, by the way, only nine per cent of the population share your blood group?"

"No, I didn't know that," Walker replied with a shake of the head. Not surprisingly, he had every appearance of a man in shock.

"And the real beauty of it is," the Brigadier went on, his eyes alight with boyish enthusiasm. "Thanks to the aura thing, one doesn't have to go around stark naked and unarmed. Unlike the poor chap in the H G Wells book, for example."

"If I remember correctly," said Walker, beginning to regain some of his customary composure. "That particular character went crazy. Lost his marbles completely."

"So he did, so he did," said the Brigadier, chuckling. "But he was purely fictional, after all. And even if he was real, running around stark naked in our lovely British weather would surely drive any man clean over the edge, eh?"

The two old friends fell silent and turned as one to the boffin.

"Everything begins to reappear after approximately five hours, give or take, depending on the individual's metabolism." Hopper continued his explanation as though he had not been interrupted. "But the chemical lingers in the bloodstream for roughly twenty-four hours, so you can't take another capsule within that period. Our experiments have shown the effects of exceeding the dose to be exponential. Taking a second capsule too soon after the five hours adds anything up to another ten hours of invisibility. Inconvenient, to say the least. And you can't carry a rifle, for example, because it would simply be too large. Its extremities would be completely visible beyond the limits of your aura."

"So here's the thing," said Walker, his mind working overtime. "If light gets refracted around the perimeter of your aura, how do you see? Because from what you're saying, light is deflected before it reaches your eyes."

"Good question," said Hopper, with a nod of acknowledgment. "In reality, what you see is the light arriving at your aura. For want of a better description, you find yourself looking out through a small area of nothing. Like watching a film really close up in a totally darkened room. And your vision is restricted, like tunnel vision. You can see clearly what is directly in your line of sight, but everything else becomes increasingly blurred as the light is bent around you. So your peripheral vision is pretty well zilch, unfortunately."

dark peak blues

"A bit like looking through night vision goggles, perhaps?" suggested the Brigadier, trying to relate to something with which he and Walker were already familiar.

"Sort of," said Hopper. "Not quite the same, but a reasonable enough comparison for our purposes."

He reached into his inside pocket and produced the black plastic case Walker had seen in the video.

"Care to try one, Major?" he said, smiling.

"Not now, man," the Brigadier barked. "It's Mike's wedding anniversary, remember? We'll call it a day and reconvene here tomorrow, eleven hundred hours, sharp. Sleep on it, Mike, and do feel free to discuss it with Patricia. Your new assignment, I mean. Just the bare bones of it, mind. Do not, under any circumstances, mention the invisibility thing."

"Of course not," said Walker. "As if she'd bloody well believe me, anyway. I still can't believe it, myself."

Chapter Five
Altrincham, 2010
Amber Alert

Neil McLeod lined himself up carefully on the pink, trying desperately to tune out his dad and his uncle, who were non-too-quietly arguing the toss behind him. For the first time in his young life he was on course for a one-four-seven break and was determined not to let anything distract him.

"What do you think, young 'un?" asked his uncle, giving him a poke in the ribs and making him miscue. The pink bounced harmlessly off the cushion and the cue ball sailed on its merry way and dropped cleanly into a corner pocket.

"Aha! Foul shot on the pink," cried his dad gleefully. "Six points to me, I think."

"For fuck's sake, Uncle Len," moaned Neil. "That was your fucking fault. I was on my way to a fucking one-four-fucking-seven."

"Hey, mind your language, lad," said his dad. He added his points to the scoreboard then retrieved the cue ball and placed it in the D. "You'll be in big fucking trouble if your mum hears you."

"The women can't hear us when we're in here," said Lennie. "In any case, they'll be upstairs trying on their new outfits. And stop leaning over my table with that big stinking cigar in your gob. Drop ash on my green baize and you'll find yourself smoking it through your arse."

Neil suppressed a giggle, the image of his dad with a smouldering cigar sticking out of his backside serving to make him forget all about his lost maximum break. His Uncle Len sure had a way with words. Lennie watched carefully while his brother Gerry stepped back from the table and placed the offending article in an ashtray on the bar-top.

"Make sure it won't fall out and burn my bar," said Lennie. "Same rule applies, except I'd shove it in lit end first."

Gerry just scowled and gave him the finger as he returned to the table to take his shot. Neil was no longer able to stifle his laughter and collapsed into a chair in hysterics. He made the mistake of picking his beer up before he'd stopped laughing, slopping some on the glass table-top.

"So, what do you think, then?" asked Uncle Len, sitting down at the other side of the table and rescuing his large whisky and soda from the spreading puddle of beer.

"About what, Uncle?" said Neil, pulling a tissue from his pocket to mop up the spillage. "I wasn't fucking listening, right? I was trying to concentrate on my fucking shot, before you nudged me and fucking spoilt everything."

"What do you think we should do about this latest bunch of nosy bastards?" said Lennie, ignoring his nephew's whingeing.

"What fucking nosy bastards?" queried Neil, peering over the lip of his beer mug with an expression of utter bafflement.

"Don't tell me your dad hasn't mentioned it," said Lennie. He turned to his younger brother, who was just lining up on the last red. "Gerry, why haven't you discussed it with Neil?"

"Why the fuck should I?" retorted Gerry. "It's nothing to do with him. He's just a lad."

"He's eighteen, Gerry," Lennie pointed out patiently. "He's a McLeod. He's your son and my nephew and he knows all about what we do for a living. What's more, he's one of the sharpest knives in the drawer. I value his opinion. So should you. It's time to make him a full member of the team."

"Whatever," said Gerry dismissively, taking a drag from his cigar and replacing it carefully in the ashtray before lining up on the black. He'd lost the game, but he wasn't about to give up on sinking the last ball.

Lennie shook his head in mock despair and turned back to his nephew.

"What your dad hasn't bothered to tell you," he said. "Is that we've been under constant observation recently, much more than ever before. And it's a team we've not seen before. Two cars, a Land Cruiser and a Mondeo. Always the same two blokes in each car. And passing our two houses at all hours of the day and night. Sometimes just sitting, parked up, a couple of hundred yards away."

"So the fuck what?" said Neil. "There's always some fucker or other watching us, isn't there?"

"Yes, there is," said Lennie. "But we've always known who they are. CID or Special Branch, usually. And not so flaming persistent, not like these bastards. For certain, they'll be logging our every move, all our comings and goings. For all we know, they might even have a team trying to follow us every time we go out. Not that they'd have much chance there, but still."

"What about the fucking cars?" asked Neil. "Haven't you tried tracing them?"

"Of course we have, lad," replied Lennie patiently, ignoring the sarcastic snort from his brother. "They are completely untraceable. So they have to be Special Branch, at the very least, or maybe some other covert mob."

"So what do you want from me?" asked Neil, for once omitting the eff word.

"We need to know who they are," his uncle explained. "And we need to decide how we're going to set about finding out. Once we've done that, we'll have a better idea of how to deal with them. That's where I thought you might come up with some original ideas."

There was a disdainful 'Hah!' from the other side of the room. Lennie shot his brother a warning look and turned back to his nephew.

"Can't we just take the fuckers out?" asked Neil.

"See, I told you he was just a lad," cried Gerry. "Sharpest knife in the drawer, eh? I think not."

"Shut up, Gerry," snapped Lennie. "No, Neil, we can't just take them out, as you put it. Not without knowing who they are, first. Who knows what shit we might bring down on our heads? So come on, what do you think? And be serious. We're not living in some Hollywood movie, here. But we need to go on amber alert, and we need a plan."

Neil took a long drink of his beer, draining his glass, playing for time.

We might not be living in a Hollywood movie, he thought, *but I've seen enough of them to know that's where the fucking answer lies*. He contemplated for a full minute before replying.

"Well, as I see it, we need to turn the fucking tables on them," he said. "Put our best fucking boys and girls on it and trail them back to wherever the fuck they're coming from."

"Good idea," said Lennie. "But we've already found they're as hard to follow as we are. Every time we've put a car or bike on them, they've managed to shake it off."

"Then don't use fucking cars or bikes," said Neil. "You must know which fucking direction they come from every time, so set up a chain of fucking pedestrians back along the route. Joggers, dog-walkers, fucking courting couples and the like. Keep working them further out, day by day, slowly but surely, and eventually you'll track the fuckers all the way back to their base. If they're around every fucking day, they must be fucking based somewhere not too fucking far away."

"You see, Gerry?" cried Lennie, smiling broadly. "I told you he was a sharp one."

"Hm, yes, fair enough," conceded Gerry. "Sounds like a good idea. He'd still better not let his mum catch him with all that fucking effing and blinding, though."

There was a knock at the door, which opened to reveal Lennie's wife Karen.

"Dinner's ready, boys," she announced and withdrew quietly.

"Right then," said Gerry. "We can discuss it further after we've eaten. We'll need to plan it carefully. Come on, Neil, you've earned your dinner tonight."

He gave his son a hearty slap on the back as they walked to the door.

"Yes, and we need to discuss that other matter," said Lennie, as they were crossing the music room. "Maybe that's another way for young Neil here to earn his salt – or 'make his bones', as our American friends say."

"Wow, Uncle Len," chirped up Neil, his eyes wide with excitement. "Sounds like you want me to take someone out or something."

Gerry, who was in the lead as usual when there was food in the offing, came to a standstill halfway across the library and turned to them, his arms held out sideways to bring them to a halt.

"Now hold on there, Lennie," he said, glaring at his older brother. "He's not ready for that yet. I don't want him getting mixed up in any killings, not until he's a lot older. If ever. We've got plenty of soldiers on the payroll for that kind of work, without involving my lad."

"Who is it?" piped up Neil, all agog. "Who do you need taking out? I'm up for it, Dad, honest. Just tell me who, where and when and give me a gun. I'm your man."

"All right, young 'un," said Lennie, putting a comforting arm around his nephew's shoulder. "Take it easy. We can talk about it after dinner."

"We are not involving Neil," snarled Gerry. "End of."

"Whatever," Lennie responded. "It's your shit what needs shovelling, whoever does it."

Neil was on tenterhooks all through dinner. He couldn't wait to find out who it was who needed taking out, and was hoping against hope that him and Uncle Len between 'em might be able to persuade his dad to let him do it. He knew he was more than ready to 'make his bones', as Uncle Len had called it. He liked that expression and knew where he'd heard it before. In his favourite film, 'The Godfather'.

Rules were rules, though. He knew better than to talk business at the dinner table, so had to grin and bear it while his mum and Aunt Karen prattled on and on about their latest purchases and his dad ploughed his way through second helpings – of all three courses.

It amused him to watch his Uncle Len giving the cook's arse a thorough goosing whenever she came within reach, and he marvelled at how his Aunt Karen didn't seem to mind. He could tell his mum didn't approve, though. He knew that look only too well. He wasn't sure how the cook felt about it. She showed no reaction whatsoever, managing to maintain a completely impassive expression on each and every occasion.

He chuckled inwardly at the thought of his dad trying to get away with similar behaviour with their cook at home. Mum would fucking kill him. If the cook didn't do it first. The woman was built like the proverbial brick shithouse and had arms like fucking Popeye.

From where he was sitting, he could see into the kitchen whenever the door was open, and had a clear view of the cook's shapely backside when she bent over to take stuff out of the oven. *You are such a lucky bastard, Uncle Len*, he thought. *What I wouldn't give to get my hands on that gorgeous fucking arse.*

His uncle caught him gaping and gave him a knowing wink.
I wish my dad could be more like Uncle Len, he thought. *And I*

wish our cook was more like this one and less like a fucking great big knobbly sack of potatoes.

After what seemed an eternity, dinner was finally over and the men returned to the games room to resume business.

Neil was delighted when his dad and uncle agreed to let him draw up a plan to backtrack the bastards in the Land Cruiser and Mondeo. He already had it all worked out in his head; it would be a piece of cake to lay it all out on paper for them.

The man they needed to get rid of was the manager of one of his dad's nightclubs, who had been dipping his sticky fingers into the takings – a capital offence where the McLeod brothers were concerned. No trial. No appeal. No mercy. Just a bullet to the head, a quick trip up to the Lake District and into a lake wearing concrete boots.

After a lengthy and heated discussion his dad finally compromised. He refused to allow Neil to carry out the actual execution, but decided the lad could go along as an observer. Not quite the 'making his bones' Neil had hoped for, but a major step along the way. And a massive vote of confidence from his dad.

He went to the jukebox and selected Johnny Cash's 'Folsom Prison Blues', setting it on 'repeat', just so he could hear his favourite line over and over again: 'I shot a man in Reno, just to watch him die.'

Chapter Six
Altrincham, 2010
Someone to Watch

Jackson's mobile rang. He picked it up off the table and answered with a curt "Yes?" He listened for a few seconds, Walker watching intently. "Okay, Owen, hold on. It's Williams," he said, picking up his cup of coffee, the phone still held to his ear. "McLeod's just arrived home. Driving his Range Rover, one lackey in the back. Floodlights are on all around the house and there are three goons patrolling the grounds, as usual, one of them with the Doberman."

Walker and Jackson were in the restaurant of the Cresta Court Hotel in Altrincham, having just finished a light early dinner. Sergeants Frank Ackroyd and Owen Williams were out in the Mondeo, assigned to keep watch on Lennie McLeod's house, a couple of miles away.

"Right. Tell them we'll be there in less than ten, Al," said Walker. "They can make another pass of Gerry's house, then come back in and have their turn at the feeding trough."

They drained their coffees and got up, waving their acknowledgments to the maître d' as they left the restaurant. Two minutes later they were in Walker's steel grey Land Cruiser, Jackson at the wheel.

Before they set off, Walker eased out of his bomber jacket. He unlocked the glovebox, from which, after a quick look around to make sure they weren't being watched, he retrieved the shoulder holster containing his 9mm Browning, and strapped it into place. He unfastened his belt and slid his sheathed commando knife into place, re-buckled and shrugged back into his jacket.

"Don't forget your box of tricks," said Jackson, digging into the driver's door pocket and handing him a small zipper case, about the size of an i-Pad, which he slipped inside his jacket. Finally, he pocketed the suppressor for the Browning and the black plastic

dark peak blues

case containing the capsules.

"Okay, Al, let's go," he said, fastening his seatbelt. He pulled his Blackberry out and hit speed-dial 3. "Five minutes, max," he said when Williams answered, then hung up.

It was little more than four minutes later when McLeod's house came into view. They were just in time to see the Mondeo disappearing around the bend up ahead, Ackroyd behind the wheel.

"How the other half lives, eh?" said Jackson, as they drove by the ornate electronic gates at the entrance to the driveway. A young couple jogged past in the opposite direction, a blur of pink and blue Lycra and matching bum-bags.

Walker clocked the cameras mounted on the gateposts and knew for certain they would be on film as usual as they drove past. Which meant the Mondeo had been observed, as well as the Land Cruiser.

Well, all the cameras in the world won't help you tonight, Lennie, he thought. He relaxed, remembering there was nothing in their files to suggest anything other than a standard CCTV set-up.

"Smile, Al," he said. "We're on Candid Camera again."

"I hope they've got my best side," quipped Jackson. "Tough on you, though, you're an ugly bastard from any angle."

"Such sparkling wit," quipped Walker in return. "You should do stand-up. Your face alone is good for a laugh."

Jackson chuckled and raised a finger.

Like most of the overpriced mansions in Altrincham, the McLeod residence shouted loudly of money, but even more loudly of bad taste. It reminded Walker of some southern States antebellum plantation house, with the row of four white columns planted along its frontage supporting a full width balcony above.

He wondered idly what its carbon footprint might be. He counted seven large sash windows along the front of the upper storey, and six on the ground floor, flanking the centrally placed palatial, double front door. To his knowledge, McLeod and his wife had no children, so this huge spread just housed the two of them. And possibly some domestic staff, although the team hadn't spotted any, so far. There was a small army of goons, as well, but they weren't accommodated in the main house.

The two-storey garage alone was bigger than Walker's house

back in Lympstone. He reckoned it would hold at least six cars. It had accommodation on its second floor, which their observations had shown to be the living quarters and command centre for the security team, no doubt equipped with full-time monitoring of the CCTV. Thinking of his house reminded him, he must not forget to phone his darling Tricia when they got back to the hotel, later.

"Anyway," he said, dismissing their idle banter and choosing instead to respond to Jackson's earlier comment. "Most of the so-called *other half* around here are probably footballers. Unlike their unsavoury neighbour, they're not quite so likely to end up residing in a cell in Strangeways."

"Or in an early coffin," Jackson remarked, giving way to a passing Bentley GT before turning the big Toyota around and heading back for another slow pass. "With any luck."

"Or in a coffin, as you say," Walker responded. "Either way suits me for the bastard McLeod brothers."

All of the houses in the area had electronic gates and security lighting, but McLeod's pile shone out brightest of all.

More bloody floodlighting than Old Trafford, thought Walker, referencing the famous football stadium which was only a few miles away.

Jackson slowed to give way to an elderly couple shuffling across the road in front of them, out on their evening constitutional, no doubt, and apparently sublimely oblivious to the big Toyota bearing down on them.

As they passed McLeod's pile again, Walker spotted two guards standing together near the front right-hand corner of the house, talking and smoking cigarettes. They were too far away for him to tell for sure, but he reckoned they would definitely be armed. As he watched, another man appeared, a Doberman pinscher at his heel.

"Looks like you might need the stun-gun, Mike," said Jackson, as they pulled out of sight of the house.

"Maybe," said Walker. "But with any luck I can be across the front lawn and in the house while the dog's around the back. I'll take it, anyway, just in case."

He took the stun-gun from the storage box between the seats and pocketed it. Pulling the plastic case from his pocket, he took out one of the capsules, bit into it and leaned his head back, letting the liquid trickle down.

dark peak blues

"Drop me off in another half mile or so, Al," he said. "Then drive around for a while. You could make a couple of passes of Gerry's house, see if there's anything happening there. I'll give you a call when I'm free and clear."

By the time Jackson brought the car to a halt, Walker had completely disappeared from view.

"Gawd," said Jackson. "That is so fucking spooky. I don't think I'll ever get used to it."

"How do you think I feel, then?" Walker responded. "It freaks me out no end. No matter how much the boffins keep telling me it's okay and there are no side effects, I can't help thinking about it. I keep worrying I might not come back, might end up permanently invisible, or the chemical might have some disastrous long-term effect, further down the line. Still, onward and upward, eh? Once more unto the breach, dear friends, and all that crap."

"Good luck, Mike," said Jackson, to an apparently self-opening passenger door. "I'll see you later, alligator. Well, about five hours later, anyway."

"Funny guy," retorted Walker. "I'll see *you* in less than two." *I'm a poet and I don't know it*, he thought, as he swung the door shut. He made a quick check of his equipment then slapped the side of the car to give Jackson the go ahead to pull away.

Five minutes later he was in front of McLeod's gates, having encountered nothing worse on the way than a seriously confused Jack Russell terrier. The little dog had clearly caught his scent but couldn't figure out why there was nothing to be seen. It kept looking back over its shoulder as its owner dragged it away.

He watched and waited for a minute or two. Just as he was readying himself to scale the gates, he was saved the trouble. A bright red Jaguar XK pulled into the entrance. Walker jumped out of the way in the nick of time, and the gates swung open.

Before the car disappeared up the driveway, he recognised Lennie's wife, Karen, whom he knew to be thirty-five. *She doesn't look a day over fifty*, he thought, noting her bleach-blonde hair and shovelled-on layers of make-up. The passenger seat and footwell were piled high with shopping bags from designer outlets.

Well now, Mrs McLeod, he thought, *been out spending hubby's ill-gotten gains, have we?* He followed through the gates just as they began their closing swing. Out of the corner of his eye he glimpsed the Jack Russell and its owner on their way back, moving at a much faster pace. Presumably the little dog had done its ones and twos and its master was anxious to get home. Maybe he was on a promise, lucky bastard. More likely, his dinner was waiting for him.

He set off up the drive and heard the deep metallic thud of the gates closing behind him, followed by the frenzied yapping of the little dog as, once again, it sensed his invisible presence.

"I definitely need to steer clear of the Doberman," he muttered quietly to himself. He turned and walked back to the gates, to distance himself as far from the house as possible, until he could be sure the big dog was well out of the way.

One of the guards was helping Karen McLeod carry her bags into the house. Job done, she went inside and the man slid in behind the wheel of the Jaguar and reversed it into the garage, one of its doors magically sliding up as he approached.

He came out of the side door of the garage just as his mate appeared around the left-hand corner of the house. They met near the front door. Once again, they stopped for a natter and lit up cigarettes. One of them pointed at the Jack Russell, which was still yapping and straining against its lead, as its owner tugged it gently away from the gates. Walker tensed, then relaxed when both guys burst out laughing.

He couldn't make out much of what was being said, but got the impression they were discussing the merits of the plucky little terrier as a possible ready meal for the Doberman. Right on cue, the dog and its handler came around the right-hand corner of the house, the man calling out in what was clearly an eastern European accent – Serbian, Walker guessed – wanting to know what all the jollity was about.

Walker deduced he was some kind of boss, because the other two immediately fell silent and set off in opposite directions, resuming their patrol duties. Doberman-bloke stood still for a while, watching them go, then stared at the gates. Walker could still hear the Jack Russell yapping, the sound gradually fading as it got further away.

Satisfied there was nothing to see, and no doubt reassured by the Doberman's complete lack of interest in proceedings, the man set off again, finally disappearing down the left-hand side of the house.

Walker set off at a run towards the front door, reaching it just as one of the guards came round the corner from his right. To his great relief, the door wasn't locked and he was inside before the guard had a chance to notice it opening and closing.

He stood still, getting his bearings. As was to be expected, it was a spacious hallway. There were four doors leading off, two to the left, one straight ahead to the left of the wide staircase, and one to the right, which was ajar and through which he could hear voices and some bloody awful rap music playing from a TV or sound system.

Immediately to his right was an ottoman, currently the resting place for most of Karen McLeod's designer shopping bags. The walls were adorned with reproductions of famous paintings; Walker clocked a Rubens nude, a Van Gogh sunflower and the inevitable Monet's garden.

Between the two left-hand doors there was a small ornate semi-circular table, serving as a stand for a modern cordless landline phone. Walker dug out the zipper case and extracted one of the tiny bugs. He fixed it underneath the table-top.

He glanced in the gold-framed mirror on the wall above the table and felt a slight tremor of shock when all he saw was the staircase behind him, set in the side of which was yet another door, presumably leading to a closet, or possibly to a basement. *Bloody hell*, he thought, *Al's not the only one who'll never get used to this invisibility thing.*

What he found most disconcerting was the small area of nothing-ness immediately in front of his eyes. He recalled Richard Hopper likening it to looking out through tunnel vision from a pitch-black room, at an extremely close-up screen. Hopper had explained the physics of it several times, but Walker still couldn't figure out how he could see at all, if light was being diverted around his aura.

"Silly boy," Hopper had said, as though speaking to a child. "You're seeing the light reaching your aura. You're looking out at it, so to speak, through what you so aptly call the nothing-ness, which is simply the small gap between your eyes and the extremity of your aura."

This was the first time he had used a capsule on an actual operation. The few months since his initial meeting with Hopper and Edward Ridgway had been spent almost entirely on planning. He had been invisible several times during that period, but always under the supervision of the boffin and his team, usually with Edward Ridgway watching closely from the sidelines.

There had been endless discussions, strategy meetings and exercises. There were several frustrating but necessary trials of various types of clothing and footwear, to establish which were best for moving around unheard. It had reminded him of a line from some otherwise long-forgotten book he had read as a boy: *...like a man in silent clothing in a city of the blind*. He'd taken easily to using odour-free shower gel, toothpaste and deodorant, for that was simply an old habit revisited.

There followed weeks of observations, watching the McLeod brothers, mainly at their houses in Altrincham; taking note of their routines; registering members of their households: family, staff, guards and guard-dogs, pets – of which Lennie and Karen had none, thankfully, unless you counted the ever-present Doberman; recording all their vehicles and keeping a log of all comings and goings; borrowing images from Google Earth, both satellite and street views, to supplement their own photographs and plan drawings.

During those weeks, Walker and his team soon discovered the truth of Edward Ridgway's assertion. The McLeod brothers were impossible to follow in the normal manner. They went nowhere without bodyguards, not even from their own front doors to their vehicles. They knew, and used, every trick in the book to lose a tail and avoid surveillance. They would drive into a multi-storey car park and magically disappear. They would make rapid switches from car to train or bus or taxi. On foot, they would step swiftly into a department store and vanish from view.

The same applied to their lackeys, who were clearly well-trained and equally impossible to follow. They checked all their vehicles regularly for bugs or tracking devices. They took meandering routes to and from every destination, making frequent and totally unpredictable changes of direction.

Whether or not the McLeods knew they were under observation was immaterial. They obviously acted under the assumption they were, at all times. In true modern gangster style, they only ever used cheap pay-as-you-go mobiles, which they changed as frequently as two or three times a week. Al

Jackson, an avid fan of American crime novels, called these phones 'burners', an expression happily adopted by the rest of the crew.

Walker froze as the sound of the TV grew louder when the door to the living room swung wider open and Karen McLeod appeared, clad only in her underwear, pale turquoise bra, panties and suspender belt and cream-coloured stockings. Now he could see for sure, she was definitely only thirty-five, her full figure shown off in all its glory. It was only the over-ambitious use of make-up and peroxide which made her appear older.

Scrape off the layers and she'd be quite pretty, he thought, *but you'd probably need a palette knife and a jar of white spirit.*

She grabbed one of the bags from the ottoman and disappeared back through the door, leaving it slightly more ajar than it had been. He decided she must be modelling her purchases for Lennie, and was proved right when he crept back up the hallway and eased himself through the gap into the living room. It was vast, taking up all of the front right-hand side of the house, heavy maroon velvet drapes drawn closed across all three windows.

Lennie McLeod was sprawled out on a huge red leather sofa, legs apart, glass of wine in one hand, cigarette in the other, a big grin lighting up his ugly mug. Close up, he was even fouler-looking than he appeared in the file photos. His obviously-dyed black hair was thick with grease or gel, and was long overdue a trip to the barbers. His jowls were pallid and sagging. His casual blue sweatshirt was far too large across the shoulders but was under severe challenge from his spreading midriff.

The files had him down as fifty-one, but he looked older. *A prime candidate for a heart attack*, thought Walker. *Assuming I don't kill him first.*

The huge wall-mounted plasma TV was tuned to some music channel, MTV Base or Kiss, Walker assumed, and Karen McLeod was gyrating in front of it to a 50 Cent song as she slipped into a green silk dress, which complemented her stunning figure beautifully. Walker guessed it probably cost more than he got paid in a year. Lennie let out a long, lustful groan as she swung around, bent over and waggled her ample bottom in time to the beat.

Lennie put his glass down on a side table, stubbed his

cigarette out in an enormous glass ashtray and began to unbuckle his belt. Walker decided it was time to leave the lovebirds to it and tiptoed silently back out into the hallway.

The room directly opposite turned out to be a library, with shelf-upon-shelf of leather-bound volumes, all looking suspiciously neat and tidy and almost certainly entirely unread. The furniture was a hotchpotch of reproduction antiques, including a large dark-oak desk, with an inlaid green leather top, on which stood a slightly incongruous Tiffany lamp. It was switched on, illuminating an open photo album. Walker took a look and wasn't surprised to discover the McLeods' idea of family snapshots was an endless succession of images of the lovely Karen, in various stages of undress.

He sat down in the black leather office chair and checked the drawers but found nothing of interest, unless one was into pornographic magazines. Nevertheless, he treated the underside of the desk to another of his bugs.

A door in the far wall led to a music room, the centrepiece of which was a Steinway grand, standing proud in front of the window. He wondered if it ever got played. There was certainly no sign of any sheet music. The back wall was given over to an enormous stereo system, while the one opposite him held a wall-to-wall, floor-to-ceiling collection of CDs, enough to put an HMV store to shame. Immediately to his left was a drum kit, beyond which a classic Fender guitar stood proudly on its stand. Movement caught his eye, as one of the guards walked past the window, shoulders slouched, cigarette dangling from his lips.

The far door led, unsurprisingly, to a games room. In pride of place was a full-size snooker table, with an adjacent rack of cues and a traditional wall-mounted sliding scoreboard. There were other items, too: table football, dartboard, table tennis. In the far left-hand corner stood a genuine old Wurlitzer jukebox, all lit up and ready to go. In the adjacent corner was a fully-equipped bar. This was a room which definitely got used, he reckoned, unlike the library and the music room, which were all show.

He supposed it must be enjoyed by Lennie and his brother, Gerry, and possibly Gerry's two teenage sons, Neil and Harry, whenever they came to visit. He could hardly see Lennie allowing any of his lackeys to use it, as it would involve them traipsing through his 'best' rooms to get to it. Maybe it came into play to

dark peak blues

entertain fellow members of the criminal fraternity from time to time. Important suppliers, valued customers, perhaps. He placed bugs under the snooker, table tennis and football tables, and tucked one well out of sight underneath the mahogany bar-top.

He retraced his steps. The space under the stairs turned out to be nothing more than a closet, coats hanging on wall hooks, an array of outdoor shoes stacked in a rack. No basement, then, apparently.

The facing door at the back of the hall led to an enormous kitchen, all lights blazing, illuminating gleaming stainless steel appliances, black granite worktops and shaker-style units, stretching all the way along to the right, behind the hall and the living room. At the far end the units gave way to a small dining area, a pine table with four chairs, next to patio doors. Something was roasting in the oven, lamb, for sure. The smell got Walker's juices flowing, even though he had already eaten. Three saucepans were simmering on the hob.

A panoramic picture window looked out on an acre or so of floodlit lawn, flanked by a pair of tennis courts on the left and perfectly maintained flower beds to the right. Walker spotted the man with the Doberman patrolling along the back fence, which was a good fifty yards away. And at least ten feet high. One of the guards walked past the window, close enough for Walker to see his five-o'clock shadow, illuminated by the floodlighting.

He jumped when a door opened to his left. A young black woman appeared, attractive, full-figured, wearing a smart black dress, white apron, white mob cap, black tights, sensible black shoes. Clearly, Mister and Mrs McLeod liked their cook to look the part. She could have stepped straight off a movie set. The ebony skin of her face shone with the heat from the oven. Walker couldn't help noticing a depth of sadness in her eyes.

He beat a hasty retreat to the far end of the kitchen when she came striding straight towards him, and relaxed when she stopped at the oven and gave her attention to the simmering pans.

From his new vantage point he could see the patio doors gave on to a stone-flagged area. There were two enormous stainless steel dog bowls to the right and a large floor-standing ashtray to the left, all confirming his guess that he was standing in the guards' dining area.

Beyond the cook he could see, through the open doorway, that she had come from what was, logically enough, the dining room. There was an enormous oak dining table, with seating for twelve, with just two places set ready at the nearest end, obviously for Lennie and Karen. The dining table was matched by a modern version of a Welsh dresser, displaying an impressive collection of porcelain of some brand or other. The room was softly lit by two silver candelabra on the table.

Walker's eye was drawn to a door in the far wall, beyond the table. He edged carefully past the cook, who was now bending down to inspect the meat roasting in the oven, her considerable rear end taking up a fair amount of the available space. He manfully resisted giving it a friendly nip as he squeezed through the gap. He chuckled inwardly, imagining her reaction if he'd given in to the temptation.

Entering the dining room, he saw a door immediately to his left, clearly the other door from the hallway. Stopping only to place a bug under each end of the dining table, he went quietly through the far door into a short passageway. There was a substantial downstairs bathroom and toilet to the right, followed by yet another clothes closet cum storeroom, and beyond that, finally, he found what he had been looking for. Lennie's den, what he no doubt called his office. A built-in workstation, with laptop, printer and another cordless phone. Two oak four-drawer filing cabinets – locked. A full-sized oak filing cupboard – locked. A glass-fronted drinks cabinet, also locked. Clearly Lennie was not the trusting type. Walker made a quick search without finding any keys, so had to be satisfied with placing a bug, this one beneath the desk.

There was another wall-mounted TV, a comparatively modest 32" Samsung, which Lennie could watch by swivelling round in his office chair.

He heard the murmur of voices, so moved swiftly back into the passageway, wondering how long he would be trapped there, unable to open the door to the dining room. Luck was with him, as Karen McLeod came through on her way to wash her hands, leaving the dining room door ajar behind her. He squeezed through and there was McLeod, already at the table, positively salivating in anticipation of the forthcoming feast. Through the kitchen doorway he could see the cook, busy dishing up.

dark peak blues

Not bothering to wash your hands, then, Lennie? thought Walker. *Goodness only knows where they've been in the last twenty minutes, although I might have a good idea.*

Right on cue, the cook came through and placed an enormous plate of food in front of her master, then was obliged to remain at his side while he put his arms around her and groped her ample backside with both hands, squeezing and kneading. To Walker's surprise, this continued when Karen reappeared and took her place opposite. She even smiled indulgently at her husband's antics. Obviously, this was a daily ritual, one which Walker seriously doubted was actually enjoyed by the cook, who remained impassive throughout.

McLeod finally let the woman go and she scuttled off to get Karen's food. Unbelievably, the long-suffering cook was subjected to much the same humiliation from her mistress, although just a single-handed grope this time, husband and wife now convulsed in fits of laughter.

Walker had seen enough. He wondered if the cook had to tolerate the same sort of treatment from the guards. He wouldn't be at all surprised. Perhaps she could be recruited to his cause. There was no mention of her in the files and he was pretty sure none of his team had ever seen her. He made a mental note to ask the lads later. Perhaps she lived in.

He still needed to recce the upstairs rooms but the door from the dining room to the hallway was closed. He resigned himself to waiting until the next time the cook came in, before he could make his escape into the kitchen and out to the hall that way. In the meantime, he stood still, breathing open-mouthed as he'd been taught, watching the McLeods eat their dinner and listening to Karen rabbiting on about all the clothes she'd bought.

He wondered how much Karen McLeod knew about her husband's business. *She must know he's a crook*, he thought, *but does she know the full extent of it? Does she know about the human trafficking and forced prostitution, the drug-dealing, the illegal and indiscriminate arms dealing? Even if she does know, does she actually care?*

Eventually, the cook came in, walking backwards, nudging the door out of the way with her bottom, her hands occupied with two steaming dishes of something with custard. Walker took his chance and darted into the kitchen and out through the other door into the hallway. Seconds later he was upstairs and began checking all the rooms off the upstairs hallway, which ran the full width of the house.

There were six bedrooms, four with *en suite* facilities, two guest bathrooms and a huge walk-in linen closet. To the left of the stairs was the master bedroom, complete with his and her dressing rooms and an enormous *en suite* bathroom. Walker couldn't help smiling at the sheer vulgarity of it. The space was dominated by a king-size bed, tastefully draped in frilly shocking pink. A mirror was fixed to the ceiling directly above. The furniture was shabby-chic, which even Walker knew was a bit *passé*, although he only knew because Patricia had told him so.

He planted a bug under Lennie's bedside table.

None of the other bedrooms were in use, although they were all fully-furnished and ready for guests.

There was a door at the far end of the passageway, which opened into a small apartment; combined bed-sitting room, shower room, toilet, kitchenette. It was sparsely but adequately furnished and equipped. He checked the wardrobe and drawers in the bed-sitting room and wasn't surprised to find a selection of black skirts and dresses, white blouses and aprons, black tights and two pairs of sensible black shoes. His quick but thorough search failed to reveal any clues to the woman's identity. No documents. No passport. No driving licence. No bank or credit cards. No purse or handbag. No photographs. No letters from home.

Conspicuously, the three windows, which all faced out to the side of the house and looked out on fully-grown trees, were barred. Now he knew why his team had never seen the cook. It all added up to one conclusion. She wasn't simply 'living in'. She was quite clearly being kept as a slave. There was no doubt she was a victim of one of the McLeods' human trafficking enterprises.

It struck him, the guards weren't just there to keep people out. For a moment, he considered speed-dialling 2 and asking Al Jackson to begin making enquiries about the poor woman, but decided it would be better to wait, rather than run even the slightest risk of being overheard.

He knew the McLeods were evil, of course. Edward Ridgway had made that abundantly clear to Mike and his team, but this development really brought it home to him. He made a vow, there and then, to make freeing this woman a personal priority in their quest to destroy the McLeod empire.

He left the apartment and quietly made his way back down to the hallway and into the library, from where he could watch out of the window, to get his timing right, Doberman-wise.

Right on cue, the dog and its handler passed by the window and disappeared off to his right. Giving them time to reach the far corner of the house, he nipped back into the hall and let himself out of the front door. One of the guards walked right in front of him, too absorbed in lighting up another cigarette to notice the door opening and closing.

james h jones

Chapter Seven
Altrincham, 2010
Urgent News

The side door to the garage was unlocked. It gave immediate access to a staircase to the upper floor. A wall-mounted light was bright enough for him to make out all the cars. Lennie's Range Rover, Karen's Jag, an Audi RS4 Avant, two VW Golf GTIs and, at the far end, a black Chrysler 300C. *Typical bloody gangster's car,* he thought, as he walked along, taking photos of them all on his Blackberry, which he'd had to learn to use by touch alone, like a blind man using Braille.

He climbed the stairs quietly, and ended up in a large room. This was quite clearly security HQ. A bank of CCTV monitors stood on a wide shelf under the window, watched over by a seedy-looking middle-aged man, slouched in an office chair, idly picking his nose as he gazed at the screens. He was wearing a headset which was connected to a radio transceiver on the desk in front of him. A battered Formica table stood against the back wall, flanked by four uncomfortable-looking metal frame chairs with thin plywood seats. In the far left-hand corner of the room was a door, with a small kitchen area along the wall to its right. Dirty plates and stained mugs littered the worktop, alongside a kettle and an old microwave oven. An open box of Tetley teabags, a half-used bag of sugar and a large jar of Kenco coffee served as a makeshift canister set.

Officers' Mess, thought Walker, chuckling silently, *with emphasis on the mess*. He went to the door at the other end of the room, which stood ajar. Easing through, he found it led to a short passageway, with a bathroom and toilet off to the right and sleeping quarters at the far end, boasting four untidy bunk beds, some cheap bedroom furniture and a couple of sagging armchairs.

Two of the beds were occupied. Stretched out asleep on one

of them was a skinny young man, wearing a dirty string vest, navy blue boxers and yellow socks featuring Road Runner and Wile E Coyote. The other occupant, in the bunk above him, was wearing a grubby tracksuit and was propped up on one elbow, reading a paperback. The night shift, Walker assumed. One of the armchairs was occupied by another man, this one fully dressed in suit and tie, as though in readiness for any call which might come through. He was reading a newspaper.

There was no sign of any other staff quarters, which confirmed the overall accuracy of his team's observations. They'd not known about the cook, of course, but that was hardly surprising.

Back in the main room he took out another bug and stuck it under the control desk, within inches of Mister Seedy, who had stopped picking his nose, in favour of scratching his groin. He appeared to be listening carefully to some incoming message, which Walker couldn't hear.

The monitors showed the entire perimeter of the house, including the street out front, the only sign of any activity being traffic passing the front gates. Interestingly, he saw that Mister Seedy was keeping a log of every vehicle, cyclist and pedestrian passing the gates.

Looking over the man's shoulder he saw each pass of his own Land Cruiser and the Mondeo had been recorded, with time, date and number of occupants carefully noted. Those entries were clearly differentiated from the rest by black ink asterisks, scruffily drawn in the margin alongside.

It didn't concern him unduly. Both the Land Cruiser and the Mondeo were untraceable in the normal way, and McLeod could only assume they were police or Special Branch officers on routine observations. Nonetheless, he thought it might be best to use a variety of vehicles in future, and maybe he and his men should get in the habit of using some basic disguises. He made a mental note to discuss it with Edward and the team.

Then he caught sight of a blue ring binder, lying on the desk to the right of Mister Seedy. It wasn't the binder itself which attracted his attention, so much as the label stuck to its front. 'Backtracking Log – Toyota/Mondeo'. It had a 'From' date of just two days earlier, which was a relief, to say the least. There was no way he could open it and look inside, not without alerting

Seedy, but the label alone told him all he needed to know. They were obviously taking serious steps to trace him and his team back to their base. Which wasn't that far away. Clearly, they would have to do more than simply change their vehicles and adopt disguises. New base required, *tout de suite*. New tactics needed. What a bummer.

He recalled the dog-walker, the joggers, the elderly couple all wrapped up in unseasonal hats, scarves and coats. Were they all on McLeod's payroll?

It was time to go. He went back down the stairs and paused at the door, his left hand on the knob. There was no window to look out of, so he stayed stock-still for a while, listening. Hearing nothing, he turned the knob and slowly inched the door open a fraction. There was still nothing to be seen or heard, although his zones of visibility were somewhat restricted.

He took a breath, opened the door all the way and stepped out. And found a snarling, slavering Doberman running straight at him from his right, its handler momentarily caught unawares, looking the other way. Reacting quickly, Walker stepped back inside the garage and held the door wide open with his left hand, his right hand reaching for the stun-gun. The dog came running in after him and skidded to a halt on the concrete floor, confused, clearly able to smell him but unable to see him. Following its nose, it swung towards him and Walker pressed the gun to its shoulder and squeezed the trigger. The poor creature gave a yelp which quickly became a whimper and sank to the floor.

From the doorway behind him, he heard an exclamation, definitely not Serbian. He recognised it as the Greek equivalent of "What the fuck...?" Turning, he grabbed the door and swung it full force into the man's face, sending him reeling backwards. The back of the man's head hit the house wall with a sickening crunch and he sank to the ground.

Walker heard the sounds of running feet approaching from both directions, and footsteps coming down the stairs, so he stepped carefully over the feet of the fallen dog-handler and slid along the garage wall in the direction of the front garden, then stood stock still, holding his breath, as one of the guards came tearing past him.

Curiosity got the better of him. He knew he should leave them to it and make his escape, but he couldn't resist the temptation to hang around and listen to them trying to figure out what the hell had just happened.

The dog-handler was coming round and, with help from one of the guards, got groggily back to his feet, gently fingering his bloodied nose and the back of his head. He remembered the dog going berserk and running into the garage. He recalled the door swinging hard into his face.

Behind them, the dog was still flat out on the floor, but was beginning to show signs of recovery, twitching and whimpering, like dogs do when they're dreaming of chasing rabbits.

Mister Seedy from the control room figured it out, and propounded his theory in a thick southern-Irish accent. He decided something must have spooked the dog, but God alone knew what. Who the hell knew what went through a dog's mind, anyway? It had run into the garage, setting the door swinging, had turned and jumped up, unintentionally catching the door on its inward swing and sending it smashing into the handler's face, knocking itself out in the process.

The Greek was not convinced. It wasn't quite how he remembered it. He swore the dog was already unconscious when he got to the door, and wanted to know why the door had been open, in the first place. Despite being reassured none of them had seen any sign of an intruder, he nonetheless ordered a full search of the garage and told Mister Seedy to go and take a look at everything the cameras might have recorded.

"Go take a look yourself," retorted Mister Seedy. "I've got some urgent news for the boss."

He headed off towards the back of the house.

The other two guards were making a poor job of trying to conceal their laughter, incurring some serious Greek cursing as they stepped into the garage to begin their fruitless search.

Satisfied, Walker strode across the front lawn, scaled the gates and ambled slowly away. He called speed-dial 3 on his Blackberry and told Williams and Ackroyd to check out of the hotel immediately and go and wait at the rendezvous point. And to make bloody sure they weren't followed. He switched to speed-dial 2 and called Al Jackson to arrange pick up.

"Don't drive past the house, Al," he cautioned. "Pick me up the same place you dropped me off."

He strolled to the pick-up point and leaned against a tree, thinking through everything he'd learned, waiting for the Land Cruiser to appear.

I could murder a bloody pint, he thought. *Or even two or three. But only after I'm sure we are all safely away. I've got to report in to Edward and speak to Trish, as well.*

Lady Luck stayed with him. The big Toyota swung to a halt right in front of him just as an approaching springer spaniel was beginning to show a doggy interest, tugging its complaining mistress along behind it. The woman, apparently distracted by the dog's antics, seemed to be taking no notice as Al got out of the car, came around to the nearside and opened the front passenger door. He pretended to be searching for something in the door pocket, giving Walker ample time to climb in.

Way up ahead, a young jogging couple had stopped for a breather and were sharing a bottle of water. He wondered if they were the same ones from earlier, and if so, how far they had run before turning around. He hoped it wasn't all the way to the hotel and back.

"Bad news, Al," he said, laying a restraining hand on Jackson's arm to stop him driving off immediately. "They're backtracking us with foot soldiers. We have to move base, immediately. And we need to come up with some fresh ideas. Like yesterday. I've already phoned Williams and Ackroyd and told them to check out, pronto. Head for the hotel, Al. We'll check out as well and catch up with them at the rendezvous point. And Code One evasion techniques essential, from here on in."

The unflappable Jackson responded in his customary manner – a sideways glance, the merest hint of a shrug and a barely perceptible nod of the head, as he slid the car into Drive and eased away from the kerb.

As he was pulling his phone out again to call the Brigadier, Walker glanced over his shoulder and noticed the dog-walking woman hadn't gone far and, unlike her dog, was trying much too hard to appear uninterested in the Land Cruiser.

"The dog lady's reporting in, Al," he said, as he hit speed-dial 1 on his Blackberry. "Look at the angle of her head. She's talking into lapel comms, for sure. Foot down, mate."

As they headed back to the hotel, Walker, with Jackson listening in intently, told Edward Ridgway everything that had happened in the house, up to and including the fun and games with the Doberman and its handler. He took extra care going over his discovery regarding the cook, and relating his disturbing findings in McLeod's control room.

"She's a prisoner, Al, for sure," said Walker, as he put his phone away. "A slave. Bars on the windows, no clothes other than working stuff. No documents, no handbag, nothing. God knows what other duties they force her to carry out. The mind boggles. I have to wonder, do they even let her into the garden to get some fresh air and some vitamin D?"

"The bastards," muttered Jackson.

"I tell you now," Walker said, quietly but firmly. "I'm going to get her out of there. Primarily for her sake, to get her to safety, obviously, but also, she could be of great help to us."

"Oh well now, that's a great idea, on the face of it," Jackson responded a mite cynically. "But just how, exactly, do you intend to go about it? Are you going to whisper in her ear, 'Don't be frightened, I'm an invisible man and I'm here to save you'? She'd scream the fucking place down, man. And even if she didn't, what could you do? Carry her past the guards, slung over your invisible shoulder?"

"I don't know how yet," said Walker, undeterred. "But I will. I have the bones of an idea. I need to bounce it off Edward first."

They were silent for a while, lost in their own thoughts.

"Let me guess," said Jackson, as they were swinging into the Cresta Court's car park. "You're going to force-feed her a capsule and bring her out invisible. Oh look, we're being watched by another dog walker. And there's that other jogging couple I saw earlier."

"Don't stop, Al," said Walker, pulling out his phone and feeling for speed-dial 3 again. "Keep going. Head straight for the rendezvous. We'll come back and check out later. I've got a bad feeling about this."

"What about the bug monitor?" Jackson protested, thinking of the essential piece of kit which was set up in his bedroom.

"Sod it for now," Walker told him, raising his phone to his ear and listening for a reply.

Chapter Eight
Altrincham, 2010
Red Alert

As Walker was crossing Lennie McLeod's front lawn, on his way to scale the gates, the man he'd named Mister Seedy, real name Sean O'Grady, entered the kitchen through the patio doors and strode purposefully past the cook. To her complete surprise – and delight - he didn't pause to give her one of his 'friendly' gropes. She let out a sigh of relief and her buttock muscles relaxed. They had automatically tensed the moment he'd appeared, in anticipation of his customary prodding and probing.

She lifted the carving knife out of the washing-up water and admired its gleaming stainless steel blade, dreaming.

Without even bothering to knock, O'Grady walked straight into the dining room. Lennie McLeod was just finishing his second helping of rhubarb crumble and custard, noisily scraping the dish clean. Karen was sipping her Irish coffee while flipping idly through a fashion catalogue.

"Good news, boss," said O'Grady. "We backtracked the Mondeo to the car park of the Cresta Court. The lads put a tracker on it. Just in time. Latest is, the two blokes came out of the hotel with their bags and drove off. Looks like they've checked out."

"Great work, Sean, thanks," said McLeod, carefully inspecting his pudding bowl, in case he'd missed any last residue of custard. "Sounds like they're shifting base." He paused, thinking, and gave his spoon a final lick before dropping it back in the bowl with a clatter. "We need to teach these bastards a lesson. I don't give a flying fuck who they are, I want them taken out. Get the Polish brothers on it."

"Already taken care of, boss," said O'Grady, glancing nervously at Mrs McLeod. He knew he should be used to it by now, but it never failed to unsettle him when his boss spoke so openly in front of her. As usual, she didn't even appear to be

dark peak blues

listening, seemingly still engrossed in her catalogue. "They're on their way. I guessed that's what you'd be wanting, and all."

"Good man," said McLeod, nodding his head in approval. "What about that fucking Land Cruiser?"

"Not been around here for a while," O'Grady told him. "Was seen passing your brother's house a couple of times, driver only, this time, no passenger. Not been back to the hotel, either."

"Right," said McLeod, fishing in his pocket for his phone. "Keep the ground team in place at the Cresta Court. The fuckers will show up there soon enough, and I want a tracker on them, as well. Now fuck off while I phone my brother."

"There was something else, boss," said O'Grady, a little hesitantly. McLeod listened, his phone in his hand, while the man related the strange incident with the Doberman and its handler, Vaz, full name Vasilios Voulgarakis.

"Very funny," said McLeod when O'Grady had told his tale. "Couldn't have happened to a nicer bloke. Give the Greek prick my sincerest indifference. Is Otto okay?"

"I think so, boss," said O'Grady. "He was just coming round when I left."

"Good!" said Lennie. "Now let's get on with it."

O'Grady hurried off back through the kitchen, just stopping long enough on his way to give the poor cook a thorough goosing as he passed. In the washing-up water, her Marigold-gloved hand tightened its grip on the handle of a cast-iron saucepan. *One of these days*, she thought, squeezing her thighs together tightly in defence.

McLeod went to his wife and gave her a quick kiss and a cheerful tweak of her right breast before retiring to his den to make the phone call. *I'm glad Otto's all right*, he thought. He really loved that dog, and spent many happy hours throwing a Frisbee for it in the back garden. No matter how far he threw it, the dog always got there first and caught the thing before it landed. He really didn't give a toss about the Greek arsehole, surly git that he was.

"Council of war, brother," he said. He idly swivelled his top-of-the-range leather executive chair while he brought Gerry up to date.

When he was fully in the picture, Gerry was in complete agreement with Lennie. Sending in the Kaczynski brothers was the right move. It was definitely time to send a clear message to whoever was controlling the snooping bastards. No matter who they were, they needed to be taught a lesson they would never forget.

Lennie and Gerry McLeod took great pride in their godlike power over life and death. They found it immensely satisfying to be able to reach out and kill by remote control, while remaining safe and sound in their ivory towers, with no fear of comeback. It didn't matter who their victims might be, they never hesitated to dish out their own particular form of rough justice.

"We gonna use the brothers for the twats in the Toyota as well?" asked Gerry.

"Maybe, maybe not. I've got some ideas about that," said Lennie. "Me and Karen will be with you in five. Is Neil there?"

"Yes, he is. Why?" said Gerry, a note of suspicion creeping into his voice. "What you asking about him for?"

"Maybe it's time for him to *make his bones*, as he likes to call it," said Lennie, and ended the call, cutting short his brother's angry protestations.

"Karen!" he yelled, as he made his way back to the dining room. "Get your knickers on, Hotlips, we're off to Gerry's."

Chapter Nine
Altrincham, 2010
Best Served Cold

"They don't look at all happy," said Jackson, looking in his rear view mirror as he headed the Land Cruiser straight for the exit from the hotel car park. He grinned happily. "They're all staring after us like we're the ones that got away."

"Let's hope we've all got away okay," said Walker, punching speed-dial 3 on his Blackberry. "And don't forget, they can't see me, so they're bound to be wondering where the hell I've got to."

Before Jackson could reply, the sound of Owen Williams' voice came over the Bluetooth connection.

"Yes, chief?"

"Owen, thank goodness," said Walker, clearly relieved. "Where are you, man? Is everything okay?"

"We're at the rendezvous, chief," came the reply. "And we're okay, no thanks to Frank's fucking driving. The fucking idiot thinks he's Jason Bourne, or something. We're right at the back of the car park, dead centre behind the pub, well out of sight of the road."

"Sit tight," said Walker. "We're on our way. Be with you in ten minutes or so. We drove straight through the hotel car park. It was crawling with McLeod's foot soldiers."

"You haven't checked out, then, chief?" asked Williams.

Walker braced himself on the armrest as Jackson made a swift left and right evasive manoeuvre, the big car's tyres squealing in protest.

"No, we'll go back and collect our stuff later," said Walker. "I'll give the hotel a call and tell 'em we'll be away overnight, and will be back tomorrow morning, or something."

"Right you are, chief," said Williams. "Where are we going from here? I'm dying to sit down with a decent pint."

"Like I said, sit tight," said Walker. "We'll speak to the

Brigadier when we get there, and sort something out then."

"Righto, chief," Williams replied, cheerfully enough for a bloke trapped in a Mondeo with a grumpy Yorkshireman. "Oh, got to go, chief, there's a police car pulling in."

"There's a what?" exclaimed Walker, anxiously.

"A police car, chief," said Williams. "One of those bloody awful Volvo estate things. Greater Manchester Police. Two bloody big brick shithouses inside. Looks like an armed response unit to me. They're giving us the evils. Reckon the pub landlord must have reported two suspicious looking blokes sitting in his car park. Yep, armed response, all right. They're coming over. Speak later."

"Owen, get the fuck out of there, now!" Walker yelled. He was too late. Williams had cut the connection. "Fuck! Fuck! Fuck!" he shouted, frantically reaching for his phone to redial. "Get us there, Al, forget evasion, just get us there."

As the Land Cruiser sped through the leafy streets of Altrincham at well over twice the legal limit, Walker and Jackson listened grimly to the sound of Owen Williams' phone ringing – and ringing – and ringing. Then it stopped, and they knew, whatever awaited them at the rendezvous, it wasn't going to be good news.

Five minutes later, Jackson swung the Toyota into the entrance to the pub car park and headed for the rear.

There was the Mondeo, dead centre, just as Owen Williams had described. As they rolled closer, their headlights lit up the occupants. Two men, apparently fast asleep in the front seats, their heads laid back against the headrests.

No sign of a police Volvo, naturally.

"Jesus H Christ," whispered Jackson, braking to a halt. "The poor bastards didn't stand a chance."

"Neither will we if we don't keep going," said Walker, hitting speed-dial 1. "Wait here while I make sure they're beyond help, then drive us away from here. We'll let the Brigadier sort this mess out."

He slid out of the car just as Edward Ridgway was answering his call. Jackson caught the beginning of the conversation over the Bluetooth before switching the engine off and going to help. Walker shot him a black look for not staying put, but said nothing about it.

Williams and Ackroyd had neat little holes in their temples, almost certainly from silenced .22s, fired at close range. Jackson checked their pockets while Walker continued a heated discussion with the Brigadier. He came up empty-handed. No phones, no wallets, nothing. Not that it worried him. None of them carried any genuine ID while they were on the job, and the 'burner' phones would not reveal much.

They climbed back into the Toyota, grim-faced. Jackson fired it up and eased it into Drive.

"Where to, Mike?" he asked quietly.

"Take me back to McLeod's, Al." said Walker, staring straight ahead. "The bastard is going to pay for this."

"What?" Jackson exclaimed, braking to a halt again before they'd even reached the exit. "Are you serious? You've got to be kidding me. What did the Brigadier say?"

"He said we should go to our second base and wait for further instructions," said Walker, calmly. "I told him we weren't about to do that. Just drive on, will you?"

Jackson stared at him for a few seconds, then pulled away again, turning left out of the exit, back towards Altrincham centre.

"Mike, I know you're hurting," said Jackson. "I am too. But the Brigadier was right. What did he say when you went against him?"

"He reminded me of the old saying about revenge," said Walker. "The one about it being a dish best served cold. I reminded him of the other old saying, strike while the iron's hot. How long have I been invisible, Al?"

"I'm not sure," said Jackson, shaking his head in resignation. He knew there was no stopping Mike once his mind was made up. "Two hours, maybe, more or less. Let's say you have no more than three hours left, to be on the safe side. What are you planning on doing, anyway?"

"Owen and Frank were more than just part of the team," said Walker. "They were our friends. We've been through hell together. But you know that, anyway." Jackson reached across and laid a hand on Walker's arm, signifying his understanding. "Now that bastard's taken them away. He thinks he's safe, tucked away in his mansion fortress. He thinks he's above the law, untouchable. Well, I've got a message for him. It begins with the words Royal

Marine Commandos and ends with the words Browning nine millimetre."

"You're going to kill him, then," said Jackson. It wasn't a question.

"I might just kill them all," said Walker, matter-of-factly. "Except the dog, maybe. And when I'm done, I'm going to open the gates and you can ride in like Sir fucking Galahad and rescue the cook."

"Hey," said Jackson, brightening up. "That's a great idea. Maybe we could even take over his house as our new base. That'd give his shit of a brother something to chew over. Wait a minute. When you say you might just kill them all, are you including his wife?"

"I'm not sure, Al," said Walker, thoughtfully. "We'll just have to see how it pans out. Maybe I'll leave her to the last and see what she has to say for herself."

"Jesus," said Jackson. "You mean it, don't you? If it's any consolation, I'm with you all the way. We can tell the Brigadier you *did* serve it cold. You're like a fucking glacier. Go dish it out, Mike, for Owen and Frank."

"For Owen and Frank," Walker echoed quietly.

Fifteen minutes later, Walker was scaling Lennie McLeod's gates. Inside, he took a few steps forwards then stood, watching and waiting. The floodlights were still blazing, but something was different. After a while, he realised what it was. There were only two guards circling the house. No Greek. No Doberman. All the better.

He took out his Browning and screwed the silencer into place. Its thirteen-shot magazine was loaded with subsonic rounds. He padded across the lawn and crept up behind the unsuspecting guard.

"For Owen and Frank," he said. The guard spun around, startled, and Walker hit him hard, right between his eyes, with the butt of the Browning.

Before the man hit the ground, Walker had him under the arms and dragged him into the shadow of the balcony, where he bound him hand and foot with cable-ties and gagged him with gaffer tape before propping him up against the wall, directly alongside the front door. Minutes later, his mate joined him, making them a neat matching pair, flanking the door.

"Count yourselves lucky I didn't shoot you in cold blood," he muttered at their inert forms, then turned and headed for the garage.

The first thing he noticed on entering was the expanse of bare concrete where Lennie's Range Rover should have been standing.

The second thing was a snarling Doberman pinscher coming pell-mell down the stairs to his left. He snatched the door open wider and, as soon as the dog reached the bottom of the steps he side-kicked the poor animal out through the door and slammed it shut behind it.

"Otto!" came a shout from upstairs. "What the 'ell is wrong with you, you stoopid dog?" The Greek emerged on the landing. "Otto! Where the fuck are you? Is there someone there? Is it you, Dave? 'Ave you let the dog out, you idiot?"

He was almost all the way down the stairs when the last thing he heard was, "For Owen and Frank," before Walker pistol-whipped him and he sank to the floor, out cold.

Mister Seedy was the next to appear at the head of the stairs.

"Oh, no, not again," he moaned, then turned to his left and yelled out. "Hey, lads! Come and give me a hand. The stupid Greek twat's only gone and fallen down the fecking stairs. With any luck, he'll have broken his ugly fat neck."

He bounded down the steps two at a time. When he reached the bottom, he bent over to inspect the crumpled form on the floor. Walker hit him with the stun gun, sending him sprawling face first over the Greek. Quickly, Walker pulled a hood over Seedy's head and cable-tied his wrists behind him. He finished just in time. The other two guards appeared at the top of the stairs, and stood gawping open-mouthed at the scene below them.

For Walker, it was like a turkey shoot. The bunk-bed guys cried out in agony when a couple of rounds from his silenced Browning took out their kneecaps. They tumbled down, adding to the misshapen pile at the foot of the stairs, screaming with pain and clutching at their shattered knees. Quickly, Walker cable-tied them and the Greek at their wrists and ankles, and gagged them with gaffer tape. He wrapped a couple of bands of tape around the outside of Seedy's hood while he was at it, not really caring too much if the man suffocated. Outside, the dog was barking furiously and scrabbling at the door.

One unaccounted for, thought Walker, and sprinted up the stairs. There was no sign of Suit, which meant he was either in the house, or had gone out with the Range Rover.

Back downstairs, he searched through two of the cars until he found what he was looking for in one of the Golfs. A remote control for the front gate. He ran back to the door and heaved the Greek and the two guards out of the way, oblivious to the blood and muffled screams and groaning. He yanked Seedy up into a fireman's lift and opened the door. The dog flew in and immediately stumbled over the three bound and gagged forms on the floor. Walker jumped out and pulled the door shut behind him.

"It's not your night, Otto," he said out loud. "At least you won't need to go hungry. Sweet dreams."

Seedy was beginning to moan and wriggle. Walker dumped him on the front porch and gave him another blast of the stun gun. For good measure, he cable-tied the man's ankles, before turning to the front door. It was locked and clearly impenetrable without a battering ram. He ran round to the patio doors at the back. They were also locked but proved to be no obstacle to a booted foot. Though he was fairly certain no one was home, he entered the kitchen cautiously, gun at the ready, aware that the noise he'd made shattering the patio doors had been enough to waken the dead.

It didn't take him long to establish Lennie and Karen were not at home. He carefully checked every room. The only sign of life was the sound of a television coming from the cook's apartment.

"They're not here," he told Al, speaking on his phone from outside the front door. "Lennie, Karen and one lackey missing, along with Lennie's Range Rover. Five bound and gagged. One hooded and trussed up, oven-ready, for us to take away and roast. Dog's shut in the garage. Come on in, Lancelot, and rescue your Guinevere. And make it quick, they could be back anytime. Which wouldn't worry me, particularly, but they might just wonder why there's a Land Cruiser in the driveway, with their comms man trussed up in the back seat, and two tied-up sentries flanking their front door."

While he was waiting for Al Jackson to appear, Walker called the Brigadier and brought him up-to-date. As he'd expected,

Edward Ridgway was less than pleased at Walker's blatant disregard for orders, but quickly moved on. He had already been in touch with Greater Manchester Police and told them they had two killers driving around in a police Volvo, passing themselves off as an armed response unit.

He was also quite excited at the prospect of receiving two unexpected guests, Seedy and the cook, and was keen to start pumping them for information.

Walker reminded him, the woman was a victim and would need handling gently. He didn't give a shit what they did with Seedy.

"I'm not an animal, thank you, Michael," the Brigadier responded gruffly. "She'll be well taken care of."

They hung up just as the Land Cruiser appeared at the gates. Walker clicked the remote.

james h jones

Gone
Copyright © 2020 James H Jones
A work of fiction

Chapter One
The Light

Rob came awake with a start, thinking he must have overslept. It was still relatively dark under the overpass, where seconds earlier he had been lost in dreams of better times, snug in his sleeping bag, his bedroll keeping him well insulated from the cold of the pavement.

Beyond the shade of the bridge, however, everywhere was bathed in an unimaginably bright white light. He dragged himself into a sitting position, his back against the stonework, tugging his poncho up under his chin for warmth. He tried to look out on Blakey Lane but the light, in both directions, was too bright and he was forced to avert his eyes.

A glance at his watch told him it was three o'clock. Surely he hadn't slept all the way through to mid-afternoon? It certainly didn't feel like it. But the light? Yet there was no sound, no rumble of traffic from the A168 overhead.

That was when he heard the scrabbling noise, close by. He soon located the source. It was a hedgehog. Well, what was left of one, anyway. Half a hedgehog, really. Its front half, legs scrabbling desperately for purchase on the tarmac surface of the footpath, was in the shade of the overpass. Its rear end, from just in front of where its little hind legs would have been, the end which had been exposed to the light, was missing. Gone. All that remained was the tiniest wisp of smoke and a slight scorch mark on the tarmac.

He was gaping at the dying creature, gobsmacked, when he heard the distinctly recognisable sound of a wagon on the A168, approaching from the north. As it got nearer he noticed its engine-note was fading, as if it was gradually coasting to a halt. Directly overhead it ran off the road and crashed into the steel parapet, the screeching of metal on metal almost deafening him, then he was subjected to the nerve-jangling sound of squealing tyres and complaining springs as it jackknifed across the carriageway. He heard its rear end smash into the central barrier, followed by an eerie silence.

"*Jesus Christ!*" he yelled. "I'd better get up there and help the poor bastard."

He scrambled the rest of the way out of his sleeping bag, got to his feet and took one stumbling step towards the light before remembering the hedgehog and stopping in his tracks. The creature was no longer scrabbling, its life-blood having ebbed away. He stared open-mouthed at the clearly defined point where its little half-body ended, right on the line between light and shade.

He stood still, confused, anxious to go and help the wagon driver, but scared shitless at the thought of ending up like the back end of that poor little hedgehog.

He nearly jumped out of his skin when the light disappeared, as abruptly as if someone had thrown a switch, plunging everything back into normal three a.m. darkness. Rob breathed a sigh of relief and took another step, but stopped himself, his self-preservation instincts going into overdrive. What if the light came back and caught him out in the open, halfway up the on-ramp or something?

He took several deep breaths and forced himself to count to fifty. It remained dark. Steeling himself, he stepped out from under the bridge and ran up the ramp as fast as his trembling legs would carry him.

The dual carriageway was empty except for the jackknifed artic on the bridge. Miles to the north he could see the bright light shining down on the landscape. It seemed to be illuminating a vast area, horizon to horizon, east to west, and was so high it seemed to become the sky.

What the hell was it? Where the hell was it coming from? Who, or what, was controlling it? Was it Armageddon? Would it keep moving north, or would it come back and get him?

He approached the crashed truck slowly. Its engine had

stalled and was making those characteristic ticking noises as it cooled, its offside headlight illuminating the scene. The front left corner of the tractor unit was smashed to pieces where it had ploughed into the unforgiving steel of the bridge parapet. He recalled having read somewhere how motorway bridges were almost always prefabricated in steel, before being transported to the site and mounted on stone buttresses, then finished off in tarmac or concrete. The rear end of the trailer unit had bent the central Armco crash barrier seriously out of shape. It was one of those big Morrison's Supermarket artics and had no problem completely blocking the two-lane carriageway. Not that there was any other traffic around.

Rob couldn't see into the cab from ground level, so he reached up, yanked the driver's door open and hauled himself up, expecting to find an injured, possibly unconscious driver slumped over the wheel.

Nothing. There was nobody there. He detected an unpleasant smell of burning, though, slightly reminiscent of overcooked pork, and noticed the driver's seat was scorched. He immediately thought of the half-hedgehog.

"I'll have to call for help," he said out loud, and cursed the misery of being homeless and no longer having the luxury of a mobile phone. Dismissing the idea of climbing into the cab and searching for the driver's phone, he set off at a run back down the ramp, heading for the detached houses in Blakey Lane, situated between the overpass and Thirsk Garden Centre.

The three houses were set back from the road. The first one had the unlikely name of 'Pharaoh's Rest', the words engraved in a miniature stone pyramid.

Must be Tutan-flippin-Khamun's house, he thought, as he ran up the drive, passing a Skoda Superb, smartly liveried as Black Arrow Private Hire and showing a local 01845 number. Continuing the Egyptian theme, the front door of the house boasted a large brass knocker in the shape of a scarab beetle. Gasping for breath and bent over with a stitch, Rob stretched an arm up and knocked loudly ten times. There was no response. He knocked again and yelled at the top of his voice, but still nothing.

Cursing, he ran to the next house. There was a brand-new silver Mercedes C-Class in the drive, wearing L-plates. Which probably explained why its nearside front wheel was sitting squarely in a flowerbed.

He pressed the illuminated doorbell and heard Friedland chimes echoing in the hallway beyond. Again, there was no response. He pressed the bell-push once more and banged his fist on the oak door, to no avail.

Drastic measures required, he decided, and picked up the largest stone from the adjacent rockery and flung it through the front window of, presumably, the living room.

He waited a few seconds, listening. Hearing nothing from within, he kicked the remains of the glass out of the way, climbed in, pushing the curtains to one side and headed straight for the hallway, not even registering the expensive furnishings.

He found a light switch, which revealed a landline phone sitting atop an ornate stand. Striding to it, he picked up the handset, checked for the dial-tone and punched in 999, at the same time shouting up the stairs, *"Hello! Is there anyone there?"*

He was disappointed on both counts. No response from upstairs. No answer to his 999 call. It just rang and rang – and rang.

Alongside the phone's docking station lay a set of car keys with a Mercedes fob. Above the table hung a gilt-framed mirror. Somewhat incongruously, a smiley face sticker grinned back at him from the bottom corner. Rob could see nothing to smile about. He gave it the finger, threw down the phone in disgust and headed up the stairs.

The first door he opened led to the master bedroom. The bed was empty but unmade, the pillows rumpled, the duvet higgledy-piggledy. There was a lingering smell of burnt pork. Closer inspection revealed scorch marks on the sheet and pillows, in two eerily human shapes.

Bloody hell, he thought, *two flippin' Turin shrouds.*

The next room along obviously belonged to a young woman, presumably the daughter of the house, and possibly the one responsible for the novel parking of the Merc. There was a predominance of pink, and an underlying aroma of cosmetics and hairspray, which failed to mask the roast meat smell coming from the unmade bed.

Rob didn't bother to check for scorch marks this time. In a rising panic, he ran back downstairs, gathered up the car keys and headed out to the Merc. If no one could be bloody well arsed to answer a 999 call, he'd just have to drive to the police station himself and rouse the useless idle buggers from their slumbers.

It was only after he'd driven into Thirsk town centre and parked up, that he began to realise the awful truth. He was alone. Completely and utterly alone.

There were two patrol cars and a Transit van outside the police station but he got no answer to the bell. There was no sign of life anywhere. He walked the streets, ringing doorbells, knocking knockers, banging on windows, shouting out, all to no avail. He didn't even raise a barking dog.

He ended up back in the market place, gazing around in despair. He saw nothing, heard nothing. Everyone, but everyone, was gone. Humans, animals, birds, insects. Vanished. Vaporised. It came to him, slowly, that he probably owed his life to the heavy steel construction of the bridge. Bricks and mortar hadn't saved those poor people lying in their beds, nor had the steel and glass of his cab been enough to protect the wagon driver.

As the first glimmerings of a new day began to dawn over an eerily silent Thirsk now devoid of life, he retired to the comfort and warmth of the Golden Fleece to make himself some breakfast and weigh up his options. As he'd expected, he had the entire hotel to himself.

Chapter Two
Goodbye, Robert Baker

Sitting down to his first decent breakfast in months, Rob wondered what the hell had happened. And what the hell was that light and where had it come from? And was there anyone else left alive? And how long would the electricity keep going if no one was manning the power stations? and what the devil should he do next?

I should go south, he decided. The bloody mysterious, deadly light was moving north, so south seemed an obvious choice, a no-brainer, in fact.

He wiped his last piece of fried bread around his plate then headed off to the bedrooms to seek out some decent clothing and a choice of car keys. The Merc was okay, but he had spotted a blue Jaguar XE-S parked directly in front of the hotel doors. Might as well travel in style.

It occurred to him: if the electricity failed, he wouldn't be able to get any petrol pumps to work. Then he realised it wouldn't matter, anyway. He could simply swap cars, whenever he wanted.

Nonetheless, he decided his first priority should be to acquire some jerry cans and fill them with petrol. Just in case the pumps stopped working and just in case he decided he'd like to keep the Jag. Assuming he could find the right keys.

As he wandered from empty room to empty room, kicking doors in as he went, gathering up clothes, toiletries and money and stuffing his ill-gotten gains into a borrowed suitcase, he gave some more thought to his immediate plans.

"I'll go to Harrogate first," he said to an empty bedroom, which, like all the others he'd been in, had that nasty lingering smell of roasted pork. "Maybe Al and Sue have managed to survive, somehow."

He realised it was unlikely, but knew he had to check. His

heart sank at the thought of finding nothing left of them but scorch marks in their bed. Alec and Sue Johnson had been his best friends for years. He had been too embarrassed, too foolishly proud, to let them know when he'd fallen on hard times, even though he knew they would have helped him. It had been his intention to get back on his feet, for his misfortune to be a thing of the past, before even thinking about telling them his tale of woe. *Now it's probably too late,* he thought, *they are almost certainly dead, like everyone else.*

And the worst thing was, he couldn't remember their phone number. Come to that, he couldn't remember anyone's number. Like most twenty-first century humans, he had stored all his contact numbers in his mobile. The one he'd had to give up when he'd lost everything else.

He picked up an expensive-looking leather wallet from the dressing table and found it stuffed with notes. At least two hundred pounds. From the pockets of his newly-acquired chinos, he pulled out the substantial bundle of cash he had already looted from other rooms and added it to the wallet, first emptying it of everything else. From his own well-worn faux-leather wallet he retrieved his few precious cards and documents, added them to his 'new' wallet and slid it into the right-hand pocket of his chinos.

That was when he spotted the bunch of keys at the far end of the dressing table, the Jaguar logo calling to him. The key ring was clipped in a carabiner, so he unbuckled his belt, fed the keys into place and re-buckled. Which gave him pause for thought.

I'm probably not going to need any of this cash, he reasoned. *It's most likely completely worthless now. But I may well need some believable identification, if I'm caught driving around in someone else's Jaguar.*

He went back to the items he had ejected from the wallet. Credit and debit cards. Other documents and cards, including AA Relay, Pets at Home, Jaguar Owners Club, and a driving licence, in both plastic and the now-outdated paper format. Rob realised he wasn't the only one to have hung on to the old paper licence counterpart.

Lying next to this pile of plastic and paper was a neat little business card case.

From this wealth of information, Rob gathered that the

dark peak blues

wallet's late owner was a man named Michael Forrest, who was the Managing Director of Forrest IT Systems, of Chester, Cheshire, with a home address in Neston, on the Wirral. His picture on the plastic driving licence showed him to be roughly the same age as Rob, who studied the image for a while, then threw it in the waste-bin. He took his own things back out of Michael Forrest's wallet and returned them to his old one, which he hid in a sock in the suitcase. Everything else belonging to Forrest, including the paper counterpart of the driving licence, he returned to the new wallet.

"Goodbye, Robert Baker," he said to his reflection in the dressing table mirror. "Hello, Michael Forrest."

When he finally left the Golden Fleece, he was freshly showered and shaved, and dressed in a new outfit, all top-of-the-range. Light blue Lacoste jacket and navy blue polo shirt. Navy blue chinos. Black and grey Adidas trainers. He had a backpack full of food and drink, courtesy of the hotel kitchen and bar, from which he had lifted, amongst other things, a couple of bottles of his favourite J&B Scotch. A roll-along suitcase trundled over the flagstones behind him. He unclipped the bunch of keys from the carabiner and aimed the remote at the beautiful metallic blue Jag, which opened up to him with a few welcoming blinks of its indicator lights.

He stood for a while, gazing around Thirsk market place, at the lovely old town which had been his home for so long, but which was now, in the pale early light of a new day, nothing more than a ghost town. He sighed, climbed into the Jaguar and started it up. To his relief, the fuel gauge needle swung immediately to 'full'. The radio, on the other hand, gave him nothing but static.

"If there's anyone else left alive, I'm coming to find you," he said out loud, as he left the market place and headed for the A168 southbound. "And if there is anyone, please let it be Al and Sue."

Chapter Three
Southbound

Travelling down the dual carriageway towards the A1, he passed a scattering of vehicles, mainly wagons and vans, some crashed into the central barrier or into the nearside embankment, some sitting as though they had simply coasted to a halt. There was no sign of human life – or death – anywhere. One vehicle he noticed, a bakery panel van, had suffered irreparable damage when it had run off the north-bound carriageway and collided head-on with an unyielding oak tree at the side of the road.

Which set him thinking. Not only had the oak tree been unaffected by the untimely onslaught of the bakery van, but apparently it had also come unscathed through the passing of the light. As had all plants, as far as he could see. Trees, hedges, grass, weeds, crops, all were still standing proud each side of the road, simply swaying in the breeze, just like they always had.

And thinking back, he remembered seeing hanging baskets and window boxes in Thirsk, all full of unaffected, thriving blooms. Just like any normal month of June. And there had been hanging baskets full of flowers on the front of the shop when he'd made a brief, futile stop at the services a mile or two back, hoping in vain to find some sign of life. Which there hadn't been, of course, so he'd robbed the shop of petrol cans and filled them all at the pumps.

Why, how, were plants unaffected? he wondered. His train of thought was interrupted by the need to make a decision. Should he head on to the A1, or take the exit which would keep him on the A168, going past the old RAF Dishforth airfield? He chose the latter, reasoning that when the light had passed on its way north, the A1 would likely have been a little busier than the A168, presenting him with more of an obstacle course.

Travelling along the stretch which ran parallel to the

dark peak blues

motorway, he could see he had made the right decision. The A1 was littered with crashed or stalled vehicles, again mainly wagons and vans, whereas the A168 remained relatively clear. Certainly, there was nothing to block his passage. Just the occasional empty, stationary vehicle to steer around.

Setting the cruise control to a comfortable 50mph, he directed his mind back to the matter of the unaffected plant-life. The more he thought about it, the more blindingly obvious it seemed. Whoever or whatever was behind the mysterious light, its death ray was clearly selective. Therefore, whether it be the handiwork of a foreign power or, more likely, of visitors from another planet, their aim was clear. Kill all fauna, preserve all flora. Which meant they wanted this country, or more likely this planet, to remain habitable. Which also meant, be they human or alien, they needed the plants for oxygen, or food, or both.

He wondered if fish had been affected. He hoped not, picturing the misery of a life without his beloved fish and chips.

He wondered how long he would have any life at all, with or without fish and chips. Assuming the light was the work of aliens, which to a lifelong sci-fi fan like him seemed the obvious explanation, he didn't think it would be long before they landed and began sweeping up any who, like him, had somehow escaped their death-light.

Yes, death-light. He decided that was what he would call it from then on. The Death-Light from Outer Space.

He turned off the A168 to make a detour through Boroughbridge. Not that he held much hope of finding anyone still alive, but the town held some fond memories for him. It was where his ex-wife had been brought up, and where his late in-laws had lived. He pulled to a halt outside Pybus's newsagents and climbed out of the Jaguar to stretch his legs and have a look around.

It was no more than he expected. The place was quiet as the grave. Even though the sun was now well above the horizon, there was no sign of life. No people, no dogs, no cats, no birds or bees. No sound of moving traffic. And that smell was hanging in the air. Only faint, a mere hint, but nonetheless enough to remind him of Sundays in the distant past, when the pork roast first went in the oven and the aroma would set his juices flowing. Now it served only to make him nauseous.

He began to wish he hadn't left the A168. For as he was standing there in the centre of a deathly-silent, empty Boroughbridge, he came to realise the sheer enormity of his situation and was overwhelmed by a dark cloud of loneliness.

He shook himself, as if by doing so he could dispel this unwelcome black mood, and climbed back into the car. He headed out of town and drove to Morrisons supermarket. He had a sudden urge for a bottle of Rington's iced tea.

It was after he had broken into Morrisons and was wandering the deserted aisles, dropping random items into a trolley, when another thought struck him. Like a thunderbolt.

He had been idly thinking about where to go, what to do, once he had been to Harrogate and inevitably found nothing remaining of his dear friends Al and Sue but scorch marks on their sheets. The obvious place, he reckoned, would be Leeds. Lots of homeless people in Leeds. Lots of underpasses, railway bridges and the like, under which some of those homeless may have been sleeping. Maybe even now, there were several of them roaming the city streets, wondering what the hell was happening.

His first thought was to drive into the city centre and pull up, perhaps on the Headrow near the town hall, and to blow his horn, and see who, if anyone, he might attract. Strength in numbers. If anyone did turn up, they could swap experiences, discuss options. They could even commandeer a posh hotel as their headquarters. If nothing else, he would at least have a decent bed for the night.

And that was when it hit him.

"You complete bloody idiot, Robert Baker," he shouted, his voice echoing in the empty supermarket. "How could you have been so stupid?"

For had he not just come from a posh hotel? A posh hotel devoid of life and rife with the stench of burnt pork? What if the aliens came back again with their deadly light and made another pass? Obviously, if they were able to travel across countless light-years of space, they were highly intelligent and technologically advanced beyond his imagination. Eons ahead of the Earth's naked apes. Therefore, they would not be so foolish as to assume that just one pass would be enough. They would expect there to be survivors. They would expect those survivors to be wandering around, disoriented, lost, numb with shock and almost certainly vulnerable to a second dose of the light.

He unscrewed the top off an iced tea and took a deep draught, revising his plans as he drank.

First of all, he concluded it would be suicidal to give in to the temptation of sleeping in a posh hotel bedroom. Or any normal bedroom, come to that. Which meant going back under steel bridges again. And sleeping in the Jaguar? Not the best idea. He figured his best move would be to ditch the car, in favour of a motorhome. At least then he could sleep in a comfortable bed while parked up under an overpass, safe from the death-light.

Which would mean emptying the cans of petrol and refilling them with diesel. Ah well.

But what of finding other survivors? The more he thought about it, the less appealing it became. He thought it best if he put that idea on hold, at least for the time being. Heartless though it made him feel, he decided self-preservation was his first duty. If he was going to get together with any survivors, it should be somewhere further down the line, when they were more likely to be people like him, who had been bright enough to reach the same conclusions he had. And once he'd got his hands on a decent motorhome, what then? Take on survivors, willy-nilly, or get the hell out of town and spend his nights alone under motorway bridges?

The longer he kept to himself, the more his chances of surviving any further passes of the death-light. If that meant he would be one of an ever-decreasing number of humans left alive, so be it. And if, or when, the aliens thought they'd made enough passes and decided to land, what then? Pointless to think about that. Pointless to think about anything, any more, beyond day-to-day survival.

And letting a load of deadbeats into his motorhome was a sure-fire recipe for disaster. He would probably end up dead at the hand of a fellow human being.

He chuckled at the presumption of calling a motorhome 'his' when he hadn't even acquired one yet. But he knew where there was one, a real beauty, and knew where he'd be heading for in Harrogate, after visiting Al and Sue's. Sue's brother and sister-in-law lived on the same estate and last time he had been to Harrogate they had been proudly showing off their latest acquisition. Self-contained living at its very best. A brand-new motorhome, built on a Fiat chassis, cleverly fitted out with all mod cons, even including central heating and satellite TV. The TV would be of no use now, but the heating definitely would. And the cooker and fridge. And the bed. Oh yes, the bed.

He could be dreaming sweet dreams of better times while The Death-Light from Outer Space was doing its worst.

As he was driving through Minskip he began to wonder what the aliens would be like. He knew it was yet another pointless mental exercise and that he should wait and see, but he couldn't help speculating. One thing for sure, he reasoned, they wouldn't be humanoid, or the 'grey men' of so many Hollywood movies.

He stopped himself thinking about alien life-forms and turned his mind to more positive, down-to-earth matters. Like where would people be most likely to have survived the Death-Light?

"London Underground!" he said out loud.

And thinking of trains led him, like the old song, to boats and planes. He felt sick at the thought, but knew it was only a matter of time before he came across a downed aeroplane, perhaps an easyJet, say, once full of happy holidaymakers, now nothing more than scorch marks on the seats.

Boats, though, were another matter entirely. In his mind's eye, he pictured container ships, decks piled high with protective steel, their bridges eerily lifeless, but the below-deck crews still working away, blissfully unaware, for the time being at least, of what had happened up above.

Sweeping through the curves on the way to Knaresborough, he revised his plans. First stop after Harrogate should be a container port. Like Hull. Or Immingham. Or Liverpool. Definitely not Leeds.

Driving through Knaresborough and on into Harrogate, he briefly enjoyed not having to worry about speed limits or red traffic lights. His enjoyment waned, the nearer he got to Jennyfield estate and Al and Sue's house.

dark peak blues

A Mind-Reader's Tale
Copyright © 2020 James H Jones
A work of fiction

Chapter One
Strictly See-Through

It came as no great shock to Steve Brown to discover his wife's mind was predominantly empty, occupied almost entirely by meaningless lists. Shopping lists. TV listings. Housekeeping schedules. Baking ingredients. After all, they had been husband and wife for almost fifteen years, and the realisation he had married an airhead, worse still, one afflicted with a mild form of OCD, had come to him fairly quickly after the honeymoon.

No, what was truly surprising, disturbingly, frighteningly so, was discovering he could actually hear her thoughts, swirling around in his own brain. Uninvited, and most definitely unwanted. And she didn't even have to be facing him. All he had to do was look at her.

He was sitting at the dining table in front of his closed laptop, feeling sorry for himself, nursing the painful, throbbing bump on his head. He should have known better. His ancient Citroen Xantia's rear hatch gas-struts had been weak for ages. He should have replaced them. Most certainly, he should not have trusted them in a high wind, therefore couldn't really complain when the full weight of the hatch came crashing down on the back of his head, stunning him and knocking him face-forwards into the luggage compartment of the car, his nose suffering minor carpet-burn in the process.

Perhaps it was time to think about getting a new car, but he loved his old Xantia and couldn't bear the thought of parting with it. A few years down the line it would be a classic. And in any case, replacement struts would be a much cheaper proposition than a new car, for sure.

He fingered the back of his head carefully. Fortunately, there was no sign of blood, but he reckoned he may well be mildly concussed. There was no point looking for sympathy from Angela. She was in her armchair, as usual, her back to him, TV remote on one arm, TV guide on the other, watching some boring tennis match. Her hero Nadal was getting a good thrashing from some bloke named Dustin Brown. *Good for him,* thought Steve, *more power to his elbow. Score one for the Browns.*

He was opening up his laptop, hoping his aching head would at least allow him to work on his novel, when he heard her cry out an anguished, "Oh no!" Nadal had apparently lost yet another point. He looked at her, well, at the back of her head, at least, and that was when they came crashing in. Her thoughts. *Her* thoughts? In *his* head? No, it couldn't be, he must be imagining it.

'Oh, Rafa, what's happening to you?' he heard her think, as clear as a bell, just as if she had spoken out loud. Steve stared, fascinated. 'Oh no! Another match point! You're going home, Rafa. What's that on the rug? Bloody hell, it's some muck out of Sacha's paws. Bloody dog! She's always trailing muck in.'

Steve switched his gaze to the rug, and the mind invasion stopped immediately. Sure enough, there was a tiny black speck of dirt, a few centimetres away from the front paws of their sleeping cocker spaniel. *Guilty as charged, Sacha old girl,* he thought, *the evidence is irrefutable.* Nadal lost the point, and the match and, muttering something unintelligible, Angela got up from her chair, bent down and picked up the miniscule bit of mud, pinched between finger and thumb.

He watched her as she walked through to the kitchen to deposit the offending article in the pedal bin, and she was right back in his head again. 'Bloody dog. You try to keep a clean house and all you get is people and dogs mucking it up all the time. I don't know why I bother.' She glanced his way. 'And look at him, sitting there watching me. What does he care? He thinks I'm crazy, always obsessing about cleaning, but what does he ever do? Just sits there in front of his laptop, writing his stupid stories, while I have to do all the work. He has no...'

Steve tore his eyes away, not wanting to hear any more of this vitriolic diatribe. Out of the corner of his eye he saw her go to the notepad she kept on top of the microwave. He risked another look in her direction, and got exactly what he expected. 'Cauliflower. Glade refill. Kippers. Wet-wipes. Bananas. Oh and I mustn't forget bleach, and...'

"What are you staring at?" she demanded, catching him watching her. "And when are you going to get off your arse and do some proper work, for a change?"

"Writing *is* proper work, darling," he replied, as patiently and politely as ever. Over the years, he had become accustomed to this regularly repeated exchange. Angela wasn't a reader, she would never understand. The only things she ever read were TV guides, catalogues and online shopping sites. "It's what I do, it's how I make a living, you have always known that."

She stared at him, thin-lipped, and what came next made him wish he'd looked away. 'Bloody useless bastard,' she thought. '*It's what I do*, indeed. Smarmy get. I wish I'd never met him. I should have married Johnny Williams, at least he's a proper man. He wouldn't...'

Steve dropped his eyes quickly. Who the hell was Johnny Williams? And what the hell was wrong with writing for a living, anyway? Didn't they have a decent enough lifestyle? Didn't it keep her in cleaning products and a never-ending variety of air-fresheners? Wasn't it good enough for her, watching her precious Wimbledon on a forty-two-inch 3D Samsung? Wasn't she happy with three holidays a year, and a wardrobe crammed with clothes? Not to mention the infinity of shoes and handbags. And her own brand-new Golf GTI in the double garage. Maybe it was time to think about a new car for himself, after all.

He didn't like what was happening to him, this unwanted, uninvited and decidedly distressing ability to read her thoughts. He had heard some things which he'd rather not know. He wondered if it was just Angela's thoughts he could hear. He hoped it wouldn't last, would soon prove to be no more than a temporary affliction brought on by the bump on his head, and would fade away as the swelling subsided, or the concussion passed.

He risked a look at Sacha. She was wide awake now and sitting up, and he was immensely relieved to find he wasn't picking up any doggy thoughts. Although there did seem to be a faint buzzing, a bit like a radio gives out when it's off-station.

Angela was back in her armchair now, her TV guide in hand. 'Oh no, I'm missing Come Dine With Me!' she thought, grabbing the remote and quickly changing to Channel 4. 'What a load of crap on tonight again. I wish Strictly Come Dancing was back on. I wonder who they'll have on this time? Can't wait. Although I wish Brucie was coming back. It won't be the same without...'

Steve looked away quickly and gazed instead at his laptop, barely registering the words on the screen in front of him, thinking, *Bruce flipping Forsyth, for goodness' sake? Heaven forbid they let that bloody awful man back again. If Room 101 was real, he'd be one of my first choices.*

He idly scratched Sacha's ears. She had stretched lazily, padded around the table and stuck her chin on his knee, like she always did when she wanted a bit of fuss.

"Come on, Sugar Lump, I'll take you for a walk," he said, and Sacha immediately began her customary ritual, spinning around and jumping up and down in eager anticipation.

When he stepped outside, their next-door neighbour, Sally, was in her front garden, watering the flowers. He marvelled, as always, at how pretty she looked. Not to mention what a stunning figure she had; something which he could hardly fail to notice on this particular occasion, with the bright sunlight filtering through her thin cotton dress, emphasising her every alluring curve.

Oh boy, she's such a stunner, he thought, as Sacha stopped, as usual, to give her undivided attention to the laurel bush at the bottom of their front path. *Such a shame she was widowed so young.*

She caught sight of him and gave him a wave as he eased Sacha away from the bush and headed in her direction.

"Hello, Steve, how are you?" she greeted him warmly, with a big beaming smile, putting her watering can down and coming over to him. She bent down to give Sacha some fuss, the front of her dress gapping and treating Steve to a clear view of her fetching cleavage and a tantalising glimpse of a flimsy white lace bra. "How are you getting on with your latest novel?"

"It's coming along, slowly but surely," he said, a little hoarsely, finding it extremely difficult to concentrate, distracted as he was by Sally's undeniable sexual magnetism, and the slight trembling of her bosom brought on by the physical exertion of caressing Sacha's ears. "Thank you for asking."

"I'm so looking forward to it," she said, straightening up. "I can't wait to read it. You know how much I love all your books."

And that was when Steve found out it wasn't just Angela's mind he could read.

'Oh my, what a lovely, lovely man,' he heard her thinking as she stood there, smiling at him, still rubbing Sacha's ears, the dog having jumped up, demanding more fuss. 'And so talented. I can't think what he sees in that miserable wife of his. He deserves someone so much nicer. Like me.'

Flustered, Steve bid her farewell and beat a hasty retreat, painfully aware that he must be blushing to his roots.

"Well now, Sacha old girl," he said out loud, as they wandered off down the path towards the beck. "I wonder if your mum will be able to read *my* mind, if I look her straight in the eye and think, 'I'm divorcing you, bitch, so you're free to go to your precious Johnny Williams, whoever he is. Assuming he would want you, anyway'. Or will I have to say it out loud? Better still, perhaps I should write it down for her. Writing *is* what I do, after all, smarmy get that I am."

Chapter Two
Ringing in an Empty Sky

Steve sat at the dining table, staring at the blank page of a new Word document. He knew he should be getting on with it. He was painfully aware of the pressing need to make a written record of what was happening to him, but where to begin?

It was two days since the rear hatch of his old Citroen Xantia had come crashing down on his head, and his whole world had changed.

Having convinced himself it could be nothing more than a passing phase, some strange side-effect of concussion, and feeling fairly certain it would fade away as the swelling went down, he had not bothered to discuss it with anyone.

How could one discuss such a thing, anyway? Who would ever believe he could 'hear' other people's thoughts inside his own head? Who would even want to know? Certainly not Angela. She would be horrified if she knew he could read her thoughts, as trivial and spiteful as they may be, and would in all probability try to have him certified. And may well succeed, come to that.

Most people, he suspected, would be mortified to discover he could read their deepest secrets. Sally, for example, would be deeply shocked and acutely embarrassed, and would probably hide herself away from him forever more.

And no, the phenomenon had not gone away. So yes, he needed to write it down but couldn't decide what route to take. Should he make it a true record of events, like a diary, say? Or would it perhaps be better to write it as fiction, a short story, or a screenplay, or even a novel?

More to the point, if the condition persisted, what was he going to do about it? Should he see his doctor? And if he did, what might happen then? Psychiatric assessments? Would he end up being sectioned and become nothing more than a guinea pig in some sinister, isolated research establishment?

Then all hope of concentration was shattered by the banging, clanging, intrusive sound of the bells of St Mary's church.

Bloody hell, he thought. *That's all I need. Don't they know it's Saturday? Oh, of course they do, silly me, it's bloody practice, again, as flaming usual. Which means they'll be at it for hours.*

There was no escape. It was a hot summer Saturday, so the patio doors were wide open behind him to capture what little breeze there might be, and the damn church was no more than half a mile away, so the noise was enough to make one's ribs rattle.

There was no point in retreating to his study upstairs, either, for he would still need to open the window. Bloody bell-ringers. Such mindless arrogance on their part, to think it acceptable to inflict their brain-numbing noise-pollution on an entire community, week after week, with total impunity.

Oh, how he hated religion. With a passion. All religions. And how frustrating it was, knowing there was little to be done about it, having to simply grin and bear it, through gritted teeth, waiting for the day of enlightenment which may well never dawn. Certainly not in his lifetime, anyway.

His mind wandered and all at once he was hearing another bell, one from his dim and distant past. He was back in his boyhood, a carefree teenager, kicking a football around with his mates on the playing field behind his old grammar school, and the bell he could hear was in the hand of their form-master, Charles Buyatt, known to one and all as Floggit, and it was signalling the end of break-time and summoning them back to their classrooms.

Floggit was Steve's favourite teacher, by far. As well as being their form-master, he was their English teacher, and a brilliant one, at that. What's more, he had taken Steve under his wing, recognising and encouraging his young pupil's blossoming skill as a writer.

"You have a God-given talent, Brown, S," Steve recalled him saying, as he signed off the boy's latest essay with a ten-out-of-ten. He used Steve's initial as usual to distinguish him from his classmate, Michael Brown, or Brown, M. "I know you don't believe in such a thing as God, my boy, and who's to say you are wrong? But this ability of yours must have come from somewhere."

"Thank you, Sir," Steve had replied. "I think it's most probably hereditary, Sir; from my mother's side. She's a pretty smart lady."

"Are you suggesting your father is, shall we say, a trifle lacking in the smart department, by any chance?" Floggit teased him, laughing at his own wit. "Well, from whomever it may have come," he went on, always the stickler for the correct placing of prepositions. "You must not let it go to waste. You must treasure it, nurture it, develop it, put it to good use."

And then Steve was coming out of his daydream, the sound of the old school hand-bell fading, driven from his thoughts by the continued all-pervading clamour of the church bells. A song came into his head, one he hadn't heard for a while, Kieran Kane's 'Bell Ringing in an Empty Sky', and he decided there and then to dig out the CD and play it loudly through his headphones. Then, at least, he would be rid of the dreadful, monotonous bing-bang-bing-bong going on outside.

And if he could only manage to keep his eyes averted from Angela, he would also be spared the everlasting stream of inanities tumbling around in her head. He had come to think of her mental processes as an endless succession of bees, as in bees in her bonnet, the latest one of which was the apparently burning need for a new three-piece suite. 'Need' being her choice of word, when what she really meant was 'want'. He had long since given up trying to explain the difference.

Back in his chair, having found the Kieran Kane CD and donned his headphones, he listened to the opening lines of his chosen track. 'There's a bell ringing in an empty sky, It's been the end of many men much better than I'. As the song played on, he reflected on some of his mind-reading experiences over the last couple of days, some more unsettling than others.

It had been a pleasant surprise, if a little embarrassing, to discover his neighbour, Sally Johnson, fancied him like mad, and not just because she was a fan of his books. It had been a great relief to discover his fellow writers were quite genuine in their praise of his latest short story, when he'd read it out at the writing-group meeting on Friday evening.

The young woman in the newsagents, however, had given him a bit of a shock earlier, when he had approached the counter clutching his Saturday Guardian. 'Here comes boring old Mister Two-Lucky-Dips-on-Tonight's-Thunderball-Please,' he heard her

dark peak blues

think, plain as day, her practised smile of welcome belying her veiled dislike. Stung, he paid for his paper and went elsewhere for his Lucky Dips, comforting himself with the thought that she probably viewed all her customers in the same dim light. He hoped.

Most unsettling of all, though, was the constant barrage of other people's thoughts which kept battling for space in his head as he passed them in the street. Harmless, everyday things, mainly, but they bounced around inside his head like a bucket full of rubber balls, driving out all rational thought. At first, he had tried to avoid looking at people, averting his eyes either down or skywards, but after a painful collision with a lamppost and tripping over an indignant woman's squealing Jack Russell, he considered it too dangerous. He tried concentrating instead on an imaginary horizon. Which seemed to work okay, up to a point.

He was still no nearer to deciding how to set about writing his story. What was abundantly clear, though, was the need to tell someone. If his condition persisted and he didn't unburden himself soon, he feared he may well end up actually going insane.

But who to tell? Not his doctor. Definitely not Angela. His solicitor, maybe?

Floggit Buyatt's words came back to him. "You have a God-given talent, Brown, S."

Maybe there lay the answer, after all. Maybe he should view it as a blessing, a gift, rather than a curse. He recalled several stories of people who had suffered a similar trauma and had strangely begun speaking in foreign accents, or even foreign languages. There was even one case he knew of, where a chap had banged his head on the bottom of a swimming pool and then found he could play the piano, even though he had never laid hands on one before. Surely, given careful thought and consideration, he should be able to apply his own 'gift' to something worthwhile?

Old Floggit's wise words of advice came to mind: Treasure. Nurture. Develop. Do not waste.

And then he knew exactly who he should talk to. His old pal, Alec Jackson, Big Al, who had been his best friend for more years than he cared to remember, and who, more to the point, had been a policeman, a Detective Inspector, no less. And Al's wife

Sue would be a good listener, as well.

Once – and if - he had managed to convince Al he was telling the truth, his old pal could surely put him in touch with the right people. After all, the police were said to sometimes use so-called psychics to assist them with their enquiries. What wouldn't they give for the help of a genuine, real-life mind-reader?

Mind made up, he stopped the CD, tugged his headphones off and was reaching for his phone when he realised the bloody church bells were still clanging away. *Bloody awful racket!* he thought, and decided he would have to go up to the front bedroom to make the call.

"Who are you phoning?" asked Angela, her voice full of suspicion as he headed for the door. "And why do you need to do it in secret?"

"Al and Sue," he replied and heard her think, 'Oh, his old cronies, I might have known.' "And it's not secret, I just need to get away from the noise of those blasted bells."

Strange, he thought as he climbed the stairs, *how her friends are called friends, while mine are all lumped under the derogatory classification of 'cronies'.*

It was always the same. Al and Sue – cronies. All twenty or so of his fellow-writers in the writing group – cronies. His long-time pals at his publishers – cronies. His author friends, Alan and Lois – cronies. The editorial staff at the magazine he wrote for – cronies. She had no idea how rude she was. He would never dream of referring to her friends in such a manner. Where Angela was concerned, it was just something you learned to live with. *Or to leave behind and move on*, he thought, *especially now I know what she really thinks of me.*

He sat on the bed, finding Al and Sue's number in his contact list, and remembered the things he had heard swirling around in Sally's head. He wondered how many other people thought he deserved much better. Maybe there were others who thought the same, and maybe they were right, but then again, better the devil...

"If I drive through to Harrogate tomorrow," he said when Sue answered the phone. "Will you be in? There's something I need to discuss with Al. With both of you, actually."

They arranged a time and Sue, full of concern as usual, pressed him for details. He assured her there was nothing to

dark peak blues

worry about, promised to bring cake – lemon drizzle, naturally – and laughed as he heard Al in the background, asking, "What does that grumpy old bastard want now? Tell him we've got nowt for him."

"Oh yes you have, Big Al," he said to himself as he disconnected the call. He absent-mindedly polished the screen of his phone on his jumper. "You've got a lifetime of experience to offer, and the kind of contacts I need."

A worry nagged at him, though. He knew it wouldn't take long to convince Al and Sue he was telling the truth about his newly acquired mind-reading abilities. That wasn't what was troubling him. What concerned him was, what thoughts might he hear in their heads which he would rather not know? He put it aside. He had to trust someone. Que sera, sera.

His spirits lifted when he walked back into the living room. The blasted bells had stopped ringing. Finally. And Angela had gone out with Sacha. Peace and quiet, for a little while at least.

He sat at his laptop, opened a new Word document and gave it the working title, 'A Mind-Reader's Tale'. He had made his mind up about one thing, at least. He would write it as fiction, maybe even make it a full-length novel.

Chapter Three
Heat

As Steve headed for Harrogate the following morning, his mind kept churning over the anonymous quotation he had come across on Facebook while he was enjoying his breakfast porridge. It read:
'When life is stressful, do something to lift your spirits. Go for a drive. Go two or three thousand miles away. Maybe change your name.'
Initially, it made him chuckle at the wit of it, but now he was beginning to appreciate its wisdom, too. After all, anyone who knew what he was going through at that time could hardly fail to agree he was under considerable stress. And no one did know. Not yet, anyway. Not until he reached Harrogate and unburdened himself on his old friends, Al and Sue.
"Why the urgent need to see your cronies, all of a sudden?" Angela had demanded when he'd told her he was heading off to Harrogate.
Naturally, he couldn't tell her the truth, so he'd fobbed her off with an excuse. He told her he needed to ask Al some serious questions about police procedure, to help with the book he was working on, and thought it would be better to speak to him face to face, maybe over some lunch and a pint of beer, rather than use the impersonal medium of the telephone or, worse still, email. He knew she wouldn't pursue the matter of the book; she never showed any interest in his work, even though it was their bread and butter.
'The bastard just wants to get away from me,' he heard her think. 'Well, that suits me fine. The sooner he pisses off, the better.'
Outwardly, she smiled at him benignly, and said, "Well, if you are going, why don't you take Sacha with you? It would give me the chance to go into town and do some shopping,

unencumbered."

Unencumbered? he thought. *Such a big word for her. I'm impressed.*

So now, as he eased the Xantia up to seventy on the A168, he reached out with his left hand and gave Sacha's ear a rub, and let his thoughts go back to the quotation.

It was obviously some American who had come up with it, otherwise the suggested mileage would have been in hundreds rather than thousands, but the principle was the same. Unless of course, one was prepared to drive all the way to, say, northern Greece.

In some weird way, the quotation reminded him of Neil Macauley, Robert de Niro's character in the movie, 'Heat'. Macauley, a career criminal, had a philosophy for survival. He maintained that when the chips were down you had to be prepared to walk away, at a moment's notice. You had to be ready and willing to leave everything behind. Everything and everyone, without hesitation and without looking back. In the end, it was Macauley's failure to stick to his own philosophy which led to his downfall. With the police closing in, the very moment when he should have been walking away, he simply could not resist taking the time to wreak vengeance on his betrayer.

Such thoughts had never occurred to Steve before. Why would they? It was only since the bump on his head had inflicted him with this unwelcome mind-reading ability, that he had come to know Angela's true nature. Her meanness of spirit. Her narrowness of mind. Her total lack of understanding of his driving passion for writing, what old Floggit Buyatt had called his 'God-given gift'.

He chose to stay on the A168 rather than filter on to the A1. It would be quieter, so he could allow his thoughts to develop freely as he drove. Sacha had climbed through to the back seat and was curled up asleep on her blanket. He glanced to his left at what had been RAF Dishforth, but was now occupied by some Army Logistics division.

Common sense told him simply walking away wasn't the right answer for him. Too messy. Too expensive. He didn't have the financial resources needed to carry out such a drastic manoeuvre.

Nevertheless, he knew, now, for certain, Angela and he were finished. He had to get away from her. He could not face living with her, knowing how much she loathed him. Separation and divorce offered the obvious solution, but that too would be messy and expensive.

So now, perhaps, he had two important matters to discuss with Al and Sue. What to do about his new-found ability to read people's minds. And how best to go about extricating himself from his marriage.

Turning off at Boroughbridge, to head for Harrogate via Minskip and Knaresborough, he decided he shouldn't burden his old friends with his Angela dilemma. He would make his own mind up. He was a writer, after all, so surely he should be able to come up with a sensible solution.

His mind drifted back to Neil Macauley. Steve knew exactly what Neil would do. He would have her killed. Or even kill her himself and bury her in the desert. He chuckled to himself, knowing full well it was only his writer's imagination running away with itself, as usual. There was no way he would ever use the 'Macauley solution' in real life. He only ever indulged such wild fantasies in his novels, where it was perfectly safe to wreak murder and mayhem, without fear of retribution.

And besides, there was no desert within reasonable driving distance of Thirsk. Although, come to think, the North Sea was only forty minutes' drive away, at Redcar.

Chapter Four
I Don't Know How

"How did you do that? How could you possibly know what I was thinking?" said Sue, wide-eyed and open-mouthed in amazement.

"I don't know *how*," I told her. "I just wish it would stop."

james h jones

*Hudson's Personal Services
Copyright © 2020 James H Jones
A work of fiction*

*Chapter One
Halifax Rain*

It was raining when Steve Hudson drove into Halifax. Typical. It was exactly how he always thought of it. Wet and miserable. He'd left Thirsk bathed in warm early morning sunshine, and now here he was driving through a torrential downpour, the windscreen wipers barely able to cope.

This was serious rain. The bouncing-off-the-tarmac, cats-and-dogs kind of rain. As if Halifax wasn't a depressing enough place to be on a Tuesday morning, anyway. It suited him fine, though. It meant people were too busy keeping their heads down and scurrying for shelter, to bother paying any attention to an anonymous dark blue Saab 9,5 rolling past.

The town hadn't changed much since his last visit, back in 2003, when brother-in-law Vinnie and his wife Julie had still lived here, before they moved to Oakwood. It was pretty much the same old, same old: oppressive, grey, run-down streets, now with a liberal sprinkling of bookmakers and charity shops. The same old smell, as well, an unpleasant blend of the local brewery and the carpet mill, with undertones of urban decay, held down by the all-pervading dampness of the atmosphere. The kind of smell you can taste in the back of your throat for hours afterwards.

"*SSDD,*" he thought, borrowing the expression from Stephen King. Same Shit, Different Day.

One thing which gave him a wry chuckle as he drove through the town centre, was the message emblazoned on a succession of banners strung across the streets, announcing the forthcoming 'Halifax Festival of Culture'.

"Yeah, right," he said out loud, to no one at all. "Halifax? Culture? Oxymoron, or what?"

First things first, he thought. *Locate the target house, recce the area, then think about getting some breakfast.*

While he waited at some traffic lights, he pulled on his plain navy-blue baseball cap and donned a pair of low-mag black-framed reading glasses, bought in Boots for the princely sum of £18.00. It paid to be extra careful, in this age of the omnipresent surveillance camera. He wasn't worried about the Saab; Terry had worked late in the workshop last night, making and fitting false plates, so the car was ready for him first thing this morning. The registration it was wearing for this trip matched an identical Saab, registered to some old bloke in Huddersfield, so there'd be no problems with any police ANPR cameras.

Tomorrow morning it would be back on the forecourt at Hudson Executive Cars in Thirsk, wearing its own plates and a fresh set of sale stickers. He reminded himself to give Terry a decent bonus for a job well done.

Fifteen minutes later, he was parked in a quiet, tree-lined avenue in the Savile Park area, about a hundred metres or so from the house in question, studying a detailed street map while appearing to be heavily absorbed in a phone call.

He realised it wasn't far from where Vinnie and Julie used to live, and where he had first met his darling Cindy. The houses in this street were very much the same style of imposing stone-built Victorian mansions, which probably began life as homes to rich mill-owners and textile merchants.

He couldn't help wondering what this Martin Perry bloke had done to incur Vinnie's wrath. He hadn't asked. It wasn't his business. And even with the 'family discount' he had given his brother-in-law, it was still a great little earner. There was definitely a long weekend in Paris coming up for him and Cindy.

Not to mention the added bonus of the help Vinnie had promised to give him later in the week, dealing with his own little family problem. Not direct personal help, as such. Old Vinnie never got his hands dirty. But he'd promised to let Terry help with the heavy lifting, which was all Steve needed, really. Good old Terry would do whatever was required and, as far as Steve was concerned, could be relied upon to keep his mouth shut. A Vinnie Wyte man, through and through.

Which thoughts conjured up an image of Vinnie and Julie, no doubt reclining right then by their pool on the Costa del Sol, sipping their first cocktails of the day and soaking up the sun. A careful man, Vinnie Wyte. Always sure to have a rock-solid alibi.

It looked like the job should be a piece of cake. Come nightfall, what few streetlamps there were would be rendered pretty much useless by the trees. He'd already eyeballed a suitable place to park on the next cross-street along, from where he could quickly walk to the victim's door, virtually unnoticed. Especially if it was still raining.

But never assume anything, as another old pal was fond of saying. Check and double check, then check again.

For the third time, he drove slowly past the Perrys' house. He'd already spotted some security lighting but, thankfully, there was no sign of any CCTV. Which had to be something of an oversight, if this Martin Perry was the kind of bigshot Vinnie had made him out to be. Perhaps he thought he was untouchable, tucked away in his Victorian mansion here in quiet Savile Park, Halifax, far from his field of operations in Leeds.

Which was where Vinnie operated.

Which, come to think of it, was probably more than enough explanation for this little trip. When it came to matters of business, Vinnie Wyte was famously territorial and had never cared much for anyone foolish enough to try encroaching on his turf.

It was time to move on, before he attracted the unwanted attention of any local residents. He drove out of Savile Park, then left Halifax behind for the time being, heading for the M62.

Late breakfast for Steve was an all-day at the motorway services, where everyone could see him but no one would remember, and where the Saab was just another unexceptional businessman's car, one among hundreds in the rain-drenched car park.

After breakfast, with bags of time to kill, he took the opportunity to head west, over the tops into Lancashire, somewhere else he hadn't been for a while. There was a place in Salford he needed to check out. One of Vinnie's 'business associates' – a Vinnie euphemism for fellow gangster - had a little job lined up there for Hudson's Personal Services. And there'd be no 'family discount' this time. It would earn him the

dark peak blues

means to buy in some more cars and have enough left over to take Cindy on a trip to her much-loved Lake Garda.

The big Saab virtually drove itself over the tops of the M62, allowing Steve's mind to drift back to their last little holiday in northern Italy, picturing Cindy reclining on the lake shore, all tanned and lovely in her tiny bikini.

He headed back for Halifax in the late afternoon, taking his time, a kind of nostalgia trip, following the old A58 through Bolton, Bury, Rochdale and up over the moors again to Ripponden and Sowerby Bridge, where he'd served his time as a policeman back in the nineties, and where he'd first come to know Vinnie Wyte. And of course where he'd met and fallen head-over-heels in love with Vinnie's beautiful sister, Cindy.

Dirty old Sowerby Bridge was another depressing shithole which hadn't improved much over the years. He thought briefly about the TV drama, Happy Valley, which had been filmed mainly in and around this very town and which he had liked for its gritty reality.

Not to mention the sterling performance of its star, Sarah Lancashire.

He climbed up into Halifax via Pye Nest, passing the famous landmark of Wainwright's Folly, just as darkness was falling. The rain was still coming down in buckets.

He pulled into a car park in King Cross, which he seemed to have all to himself. He retrieved his black nylon rucksack from the passenger footwell and made short work of the sandwiches and iced tea he'd bought at the services earlier. After placing the empty wrappings and the plastic bottle in a Tesco bag and cleaning his hands thoroughly with a wet-wipe, he fished out the Glock and screwed on its suppressor. Oh, how he loved the smell of gun oil. He double-checked the magazine, filled with seventeen rounds of subsonic 9mm ammo.

When he drove past the Perry house, the lights were on, and there was a bloody awful gangster-wannabe black Chrysler 300C parked in the drive, alongside a pearlescent purple Jeep Grand Cherokee. Appallingly bad taste. Not the sort of motors you would ever see on the forecourt of Hudson Executive Cars but good news for Steve, nonetheless. Their presence meant the Perrys were home, possibly enjoying what they couldn't know was to be their last supper.

Briefly, he wondered if there'd be any servants or young children in the house. Vinnie had said not, but you never knew. In any case, he was committed to leaving no witnesses. Vinnie had insisted on a complete wipeout. A clear message had to be sent out to anyone else who might be foolhardy enough to consider stepping on Vinnie Wyte's toes.

He parked in the cross-street, in his previously chosen spot and shrugged into his dark blue gaberdine raincoat, the one with the extra-deep pockets; plenty of room for the Glock, even with its suppressor fitted. Finally, he wriggled his fingers into tight-fitting latex gloves

It was still belting it down. The rain hadn't eased all day, which could only mean the gods were on his side. He turned his collar up, tugged the baseball cap lower over his eyes and stepped out of the car. As he had foreseen, the combination of rain and trees meant the streetlamps were throwing more shadow than light.

With any luck, he would be back in Thirsk by nine-thirty, in plenty of time to park the Saab in the workshop, stash his Glock away in its hidey-hole and switch to the Subaru Legacy he'd been using for a while. He could be home by ten. By ten-thirty he could be snug in his bed and deep in his darling Cindy. Job jobbed.

He walked past the cars in the driveway, climbed the two stone steps up to the double front door, rang the bell and waited.

The door was answered by a tall brassy-blonde woman, dressed in sluttish tight clothing and displaying an inordinate amount of patchily powdered cleavage, barely contained in a bra about two sizes too small.

Steve smiled at her pleasantly. "Lara Perry?" he said and when she began to reply, "Yes, who the fuck are...," he shot her right between her voluminous breasts. She crumpled silently on to the deep pile of the hall carpet.

He stepped past her fallen body, pushing the door closed behind him, and stood quietly in the hallway, getting his bearings.

Blood from the dead woman's bosom flowed freely, quickly forming a dark red patch in the cream-coloured carpet. Steve took extra care not to step in it.

A male voice called out from the room on the right.

"Who is it, honey-bun? If it's those flaming Jehovah's Witnesses again, tell 'em to fuck off and stick their bloody Watchtowers where the sun don't shine."

Those were to be the last words of the bigshot gangster Martin Perry.

Steve entered the room, gun raised.

"Hello, Martin," he said. "I have a message for you from Vinnie Wyte."

In the event, to Steve's great relief, there were no children in the house, just Martin and Lara Perry. She died in the hallway. He died at the dinner table, struggling desperately to rise from his seat. The subsonic 9mm round from the Glock 17 punched a neat hole through the front of his serviette, which he was wearing tucked into the top of his shirt, Italian-style. Their last supper had been tagliatelle carbonara.

Steve turned and left, carefully pulling the front door closed behind him.

"Thank you, Halifax rain," he said to himself quietly, as he unscrewed the suppressor from the Glock and walked back to his car. "You've been good to me today, but I hope I never have to pass this way again."

james h jones

Chapter Two
Have You Seen Your Dad?

On the afternoon of the Friday following his Tuesday trip to Halifax, Steve's desk phone rang. He picked it up and said, "Yes, Debbie?"

"It's your mum," she said. "She sounds a bit upset. Shall I put her through?"

Steve cursed under his breath. His dear old mum, the lovely Alice Hudson, was no doubt calling from the landline number at home in Headingley. She had never used a mobile phone in her entire life.

Briefly, he considered refusing the call; she should know better than to call him at work. And he already knew what the call would be about, anyway.

But he was in an expansive mood that Friday afternoon, having just sold the five-year-old Subaru Legacy estate which had been sitting on the forecourt for a while, and which he'd been using as his personal transport for several weeks. It had gone pretty damn quickly, once he'd dropped the price a couple of grand and given it pride of place as 'Deal of the Week'. As it turned out, the punter had been lusting after the Subaru for a while and had pounced the moment he saw the reduced price.

Which was a real bonus, coming as it had, so soon on the back of selling the Saab 9,5 he'd used for the Halifax run on Tuesday.

"Yes, put her through," he said to Debbie, then, cheerily, pretending he didn't know who was calling, "Stephen Hudson speaking. How may I help you?"

"Oh, Steve, thank God it's you. Have you seen your dad?" his mum blurted out, with none of her usual preamble, her voice all a-tremble.

"Not since Sunday, Mum," he told her. "But you know that anyway, you cooked the bloody dinner for us."

dark peak blues

"He's gone missing, Steve, he went to work yesterday as usual and never came home," she said. Her words came out all of a tumble and for once she didn't pull him up for swearing. "No one's seen him since he went out to get his sandwiches yesterday lunchtime, and he hasn't turned up at work again today. You haven't heard from him at all, have you?"

"No, I haven't. We were closed yesterday, because of the damned Tour de Yorkshire coming through, so Cindy and I had a trip to Redcar and Saltburn and took the boat out for a few hours. We made a day of it and stopped off for a meal on the way home. Naturally, we had our phones switched off, but I had no missed calls, anyway." The pre-planned lie tripped easily off his tongue. "I suppose you've tried calling his mobile?"

He was taken aback by the uncharacteristic vehemence of her reply.

"*Of course I have, you idiot*," she shouted. "It just goes to voicemail. And before you ask, I have checked with the police and the hospitals, and they have no record of him. Thank God for small mercies."

"What about his car?" Steve asked. "Has that been found?"

"It's still in the office car park," she told him. "You know he always walks to the sandwich shop at lunchtime. He never ever takes the Jag."

"Sorry, Mum, I should've known. What did the police say?" he asked. "Have they registered him as a missing person?"

"No, they haven't, the useless idle bastards." He was shocked; he'd never before heard her use such language. "They say it's too early, that he'll probably turn up soon enough with his tail between his legs. They obviously assume he's off somewhere with some tart or other, but they don't know him like I do. I told them, he'd never go with another woman and he's never failed to come home before."

And no other woman would ever have been daft enough to tolerate the evil, ham-fisted bastard, he thought to himself, being careful not to speak out loud.

"Well, don't worry too much, Mum," he said, trying to sound as calm and comforting as he could. "Keep trying his mobile. If he turns up here or I hear from him at all, I'll call you right away. I have to go now, I've got a customer."

You should be grateful, he thought as he ended the call. *It will give your bruises a chance to fade, once and for all.*

He sat back in his chair for a while, thinking over his story again, looking for any possible loopholes. He had taken the boat out but not with Cindy. The others on board had been his father and Terry. Derek Hudson was an unwilling passenger – until Steve and Terry fed him to the fishes.

Back in Thirsk he had dropped Terry off at his little terraced cottage then went and picked Cindy up. They enjoyed a great dinner out at the White Horse.

The Sunday dinner in Headingley had been the last straw. His mum had tried her best to hide the bruises, as usual, but he'd seen them, anyway. What really brought matters to a head, though, was Cindy spotting them, as well. He had told her many times what a monster his father was, but this was the first time she'd seen the evidence for herself.

She'd given him hell on the way home from Headingley, almost as if it was his own fault.

"Did you know your mum's breasts are a mass of bruises?" she yelled at him in the car. "I saw them when she bent down to get the roast out of the oven."

"Yes, I knew," he said.

"You *knew*?" she shouted, incredulous. "Why the hell didn't you do something? That smug bastard, just sitting there all smiles and self-satisfaction, singing his own praises, and that poor woman, putting on such a brave face. He's an animal. Why the hell is she still with him?"

"You think I haven't tried a thousand times to persuade her to leave him?" he said. "All my life I've been putting up with that evil bastard, and all she ever does is beg me not to interfere. It eats me up inside. He keeps on getting away with it, because she always forgives him, time after time."

A full minute passed before she spoke again.

"Then maybe, Steve, you should take the initiative," she said.

"What do you mean?" he asked, intrigued.

"I mean, if she won't leave him," she said, much quieter now. "Then maybe you should force the issue and have him taken out."

"Taken out? What? You mean have him killed?" he was shocked. He knew she was Vinnie Wyte's sister, he'd known that

dark peak blues

all along, even before he'd even asked her out. It was how he had come to meet her in the first place, after all. But this was the first time he'd heard her say anything like that. *Taken out*, for God's sake?

"We can speak to Vinnie tomorrow," she said, as they were pulling into their driveway in Riverside Walk. "Before he flies off to Spain. I know you're doing a little favour for him on Tuesday. I'm sure he'd be happy to give you any help you need, in return."

He couldn't help but chuckle at how she defined the killing of at least two people as a 'little favour'.

The conversation continued inside. She went on at him over their nightcaps and carried on all the way up the stairs and into the bedroom.

Her final shot came just before they turned the lights out.

"Has it never occurred to you," she said. "That she's simply too afraid to leave him? All that crap about loving him, forgiving him? You can bet your life that isn't the truth at all. She's just too damn scared of the consequences of going against him. You know there are refuges everywhere, don't you, full of terrified women, too scared to even go outside?"

He lay awake for ages, thinking about what she'd said. In the end, he decided she was right; it was way beyond the time for positive action. He also decided he would do the deed himself. Yes, he would take whatever help and advice he could get from Cindy's brother, but he wouldn't sit back and let someone else do his dirty work for him.

The next morning, they did speak to Vinnie. They caught him just in time, before he and Julie set off on their trip to the Costa del Sol.

So now, after hanging up on his mum and taking a minute or two to run through his story again, he sat back in his Mastermind chair, swivelling back and forth, reassuring himself he'd done the right thing.

His mum's line - *have you seen your dad?* - reminded him of the lovely old painting which had hung on his bedroom wall all through his childhood, and which had somehow helped him live through all the years of abuse. He remembered how he used to lie in bed, imagining himself to be the boy in the picture.

He swivelled his chair to the right and gazed at the much

larger reproduction of the very same painting, which now hung above his credenza. The English Civil War scene painted by William Frederick Yeames, depicting the young son of a Royalist being questioned by Parliamentarians. His eyes ran over the title plate, fixed in the bottom of the frame, 'And When Did You Last See Your Father?'

"I've got this one, lad," he said out loud, addressing the image of the boy, then turned to the inquisitor. "I last saw my father late yesterday afternoon, just before he sank below the surface of the North Sea, wrapped in chains and screaming for mercy."

He swivelled further round, to scan the rows of keys hanging on the board behind his desk. He had quite enjoyed taking the Subaru home every night, this last few weeks, but now it was being readied for its new owner, who would be collecting it Monday morning. He'd slipped Terry an extra fifty quid to give it a seriously thorough valeting. Not that Terry needed any extra incentive, being first and foremost one of Vinnie's men, and having helped Steve with the abduction and disposal of old man Hudson, as well. Steve just needed to be doubly sure there was absolutely no trace of the previous day's activities.

Even though Terry had done his usual job with the plates, it was a relief to know the car would be off his hands, well before any nosy coppers came sniffing around, asking about his missing dad. Ah well, maybe it was time to blow the cobwebs off the beautiful 2010 Jag XJR he'd bought in last week. It was on the forecourt, its dark blue metallic paintwork gleaming in the pale Spring sunshine.

"I'll leave you to it, Phil," he called to his sales manager as he headed for the exit. For the umpteenth time that day, Phil was lovingly polishing the silver Maserati Quattroporte which currently – and quite rightly - held centre stage in the showroom. "You might as well close up, once Terry has finished prepping the Legacy. See you tomorrow."

Boy, the Jag was one sweet motor. He decided to take it off the sales listing and keep it for a while. It'd be great on the run to Paris. And tonight, he'd take his darling Cindy out for a spin, up Sutton Bank and on to Helmsley, see if she liked the car, which he knew she would. Maybe treat her to a celebratory dinner at the Golden Fleece on the way home.

There was plenty to celebrate. Alice Hudson was finally free of

dark peak blues

the evil Derek – even if she didn't know it yet. Hudson Executive Cars was breaking all previous records, thank you. And as for Hudson's Personal Services, well let's just say, he'd be raising a glass to his brother-in-law tonight.

The Halifax job had worked a treat; disposing of his evil dad had gone like clockwork; and the Salford job was already lined up for next week. Another nice little earner, thank you very much.

He reckoned the grey BMW 3-series would be good for the Salford job, if it hadn't sold before then. Or one of the black Audi A6 Avants. Or something equally ten-a-penny inconspicuous. Definitely not the Nissan GTR, or the Maserati Quattroporte. And certainly not his new favourite, this beautiful Jag.

As he turned into Riverside Walk, he raised another imaginary glass to Vinnie, thanking him for allowing Terry to help, which had made yesterday's long round trip so much easier, so much more efficiently and quickly expedited. He smiled at the memory of the sheer terror on his father's face and his pathetic screams for mercy as they padlocked the chains around him and rolled him over the side of the boat.

When he pulled into the driveway, his darling Cindy came out to meet him. He was granted a cursory hug and a quick peck on the cheek, before she broke away from him and went and drooled all over the Jag. He followed along behind her, like a faithful puppy.

"I knew you'd like it," he said, as she slid into the cream leather front passenger seat, allowing him a tantalising glimpse of stocking tops, suspenders, silky-smooth thigh, and the briefest flash of turquoise from her satin knickers. "Fancy a spin, do we?"

He gave a friendly wave to Oliver Crompton across the way, who was just getting into his Prius and who had also, most likely, enjoyed the fine display of Cindy's attributes. No doubt the old bugger was off to meet his fancy woman at the Golden Fleece. Steve certainly couldn't blame him, not with a mind-numbingly boring hag of a wife like Marion.

"Come on then, Lewis bloody Hamilton," said Cindy. "Are we going for this spin, then, or what?"

james h jones

*Chapter Three
Lost Marbles*

In his office at Hudson Executive Cars, Steve was entertaining surprise guests. His neighbour Oliver Crompton, and Oliver's 'good friend' Kitty Updike.

Neither of them had ever been to the showroom before, even though Terry personally looked after Oliver's classic Alice-blue Alvis TE21. Steve always ferried the beautiful old car back and forth for him.

On this unprecedented occasion, Oliver and Kitty were taking a break from canvassing for the Green Party on Long Street.

"Green Party, Oliver?" Steve queried. He was at his credenza pouring three cups of coffee. "Somehow, I've always thought you'd be a Labour voter."

"I was," conceded Oliver. "Until bloody Corbyn and his cronies came on the scene. I'm a socialist, not a flaming Trotskyite."

"Language, please," Kitty scolded him.

Steve laughed as he served up the coffees and took his seat.

"It must be a bit soul-destroying, though," he said. "Supporting a party which only has one MP. And we hardly ever hear of them on TV."

Oliver scowled, growled and choked on his drink.

"Oh, please," cried Kitty, slapping Oliver on the back. "Please don't get him going on that subject. It drives him mad, the way UKIP gets all the telly time, when they don't even have one MP."

"It's that repellent little fascist Farage," grumbled Oliver. "It seems like the media can't get enough of the migrant-hating racist bastard. Don't ask me why."

Steve thought he had better change the subject.

"So, how's the lovely Maid Marion, then?" he asked, referring to Oliver's far-from-lovely fat little wife, and regretting his words as soon as they'd left his mouth.

Oliver glared at him. Kitty blushed and looked away, pretending to admire the painting hanging above the credenza.

"The lovely Maid Marion, as you call her," said Oliver, regaining his composure. "Is driving me further and further up the bloody wall with her never-ending religious bunkum. Thank you for asking. She's unbelievably obsessed with her medieval beliefs. With any luck, she'll bugger off one of these days and become a nun and leave me in peace. Come to think, a convent would be the best place for her. She could even cop off with Friar bloody Tuck, for all I care."

Steve's intercom buzzed. It was his office manager, Debbie Lee. Office manager was a bit of a misnomer, Debbie being the only one in the office, but appearances matter in the executive motor business. Which was why his only sales employee, Phil Ackroyd, carried the somewhat grandiose title of sales manager.

"There's a policewoman here, boss, wants to speak to you," said Debbie. "Shall I ask her to wait or tell her to come back later?"

Steve glanced out of his office window and saw a uniformed sergeant standing next to the Maserati, gazing at it in open admiration.

"Ask her to wait, if she wouldn't mind," said Steve. "Tell her I won't be long. Give her a coffee and tell Phil to sell her a car while she's waiting. Thanks, Debbie."

"We'd better get out of your hair, by the sound of things," said Oliver. "Nothing serious, I hope?"

"Oliver!" Kitty exclaimed, giving him a slap on the arm "Don't be so nosy."

"It's all right, Kitty, it's no great secret," said Steve. "It'll be about my dad. He's gone missing, I'm afraid."

"Oh, you poor thing," Kitty gushed, reaching across the desk and taking Steve by the hand, almost as though he was bereaved.

"Come on, Kitty," said Oliver. "It's time we were going, anyway."

Steve walked them to the showroom door then turned his attention to the policewoman, who turned out to be a sergeant by the unlikely name of Jolly. That he hadn't seen her locally was explained when she told him she had travelled down from Northallerton.

As he had expected, she was there on behalf of her

colleagues in Headlingley, making enquiries about his missing father. He assured her he had no idea what might have happened, that he had neither seen nor heard from his father since several days before he disappeared, and how he and his mother were in daily contact. He told her how they were all equally mystified, distraught, and lived in daily hope of his father's safe return.

Satisfied, Sergeant Jolly closed her notebook and was soon on her way. Naturally, she was not allowed to leave before agreeing to a guided tour of the stock and accepting one of his business cards.

As she was driving away, Phil and Debbie appeared at his side.

"Everything okay, boss?" asked Debbie, concerned.

"Absolutely fine, love, thanks," said Steve.

"Jolly fine, in fact," quipped Phil. Steve and Debbie shook their heads and walked away, leaving him giggling at his own schoolboy humour.

That evening, Cindy's brother Vinnie and his wife Julie, joined them for dinner. They would, as usual, be staying the night after an evening of fine dining and plenty to drink.

After dinner, the women wandered off together, leaving the men at the table.

Steve checked the ladies were out of earshot.

"I had a visit from a woman police sergeant this morning," he said. "Name of Sergeant Jolly, would you believe. Down from Northallerton, making enquiries on behalf of Headingley."

"They don't have any suspicions, I hope," said Vinnie.

"No, no, nothing like that," Steve assured him. "She just wanted to know if I had heard from him, at all."

"Good," said Vinnie. "There's no chance of them ever finding the bugger, is there?"

"Not unless they've got a bloody bathyscaphe, there isn't," said Steve, chuckling at the image. "And thanks again for letting Terry help me. It was definitely a two-man job, manhandling the old bugger on to the boat, then heaving him over the side."

They sat in silence for a while, enjoying their after-dinner whiskies.

"Got another little job for you, if you're interested," said Vinnie,

dark peak blues

lighting himself a big obnoxious cigar, a habit which Steve abhorred but knew better than to complain about.

"I'm listening," was all he said.

"My right-hand man, Paddy Ryan, is courting a Greek lady," said Vinnie, blowing big blue smoke rings at the ceiling. "Name of Vasiliki Voulgarakis. Lovely girl. A real Greek goddess, I can tell you. If I was single, I wouldn't mind having a go myself. But don't tell Julie, whatever you do."

He looked at Steve sideways and, getting no response, continued.

"She's the daughter of Vasilios Voulgarakis, one of the most successful businessmen in Leeds."

He paused again, and Steve knew he was expected to say something.

"Never heard of him," he said, knowing full well Vinnie would soon be putting him straight in that regard. "You want him killed, I take it?"

"No, no, not him!" Vinnie spluttered, swallowed some cigar smoke, went red in the face and suffered a short coughing fit. "Shut the fuck up and let me explain, for God's sake. You may not know it, but there is a huge Greek community in Leeds. They even have their very own Greek consul, would you believe. Vasiliki's dad supplies speciality foods to Greek restaurants. He started off in Leeds but has since expanded. He now supplies restaurants all across Yorkshire, Humberside, the North East, and parts of Lancashire and Derbyshire. You've probably seen his delivery vans around, Double V Foods, just never registered them."

Steve grunted an acknowledgement.

"Anyway," Vinnie continued, after taking a deep drink of his Scotch and soda and burping loudly. "He's recently expanded even further, venturing into Lincolnshire. And running straight into a fucking turf war. You see, there's this bloke Savidis, based in Nottingham..."

"Nottingham!" Steve interrupted. "That's the second time today I've been reminded of Robin bloody Hood. Don't tell me, his nickname's The Sheriff, and you want me to shoot him with a bow and arrow, right?"

Vinnie looked at him as if he'd lost his marbles.

"What the fuck are you on about?" said Vinnie. "Bow and

fucking arrow, for fuck's sake? Get a grip, man, for chrissake. Yes, I want him dead, but not with a frigging bow and arrow."

Steve laughed out loud.

"Sorry, Vinnie," he said. "Maid Marion and Friar Tuck were mentioned earlier today, and now you come up with Nottingham. Of course, I won't use a bow and arrow. Come to think, though, I'm a dab hand with a crossbow."

"A crossbow, for chrissake?" Vinnie exclaimed. "I want you to kill the bastard, not shoot a fucking apple off his head."

"That wasn't Robin Hood," said Steve. "That was William bloody Tell. You're getting your legends all mixed up."

"What's so funny?" asked Julie, coming into the room and finding them laughing at some shared joke.

Chapter Four
Reassignment

Vinnie Wyte's house – some might call it a villa – was situated in Oakwood, Leeds, on a quiet avenue which bordered the southern edge of Roundhay Park, allowing the houseowners open views from the fronts of their dwellings.

Late in the afternoon of the last Saturday before Christmas, a plain grey Ford Mondeo nestled in the shadows of some rhododendrons at the side of one of the park's access roads which conveniently fed into the avenue directly opposite the Wytes' house.

"Did you have to park actually in the bloody bushes?" grumbled DS Richard Turnbull of the NCA. "I can't open my bloody door. What if I need to get out for a pee?"

"Cross your legs?" suggested DS Les Broughton of West Yorkshire CID.

"Why are we here, anyway?" asked Turnbull, becoming increasingly grumpy. "There's fuck all happening."

"Stop moaning, will you? You know we had to be early. It'll all kick off soon enough, you'll see." Right on cue, a dark blue VW Passat pulled into Vinnie Wyte's entrance and pulled up at the entry-phone. "See, what'd I tell you? That's Vinnie's two chief enforcers, Ricky Patella and Danny the Dentist. Here first to make sure the party goes smoothly, no doubt."

"Great names," observed Turnbull. "Who do they think they are, the fucking Mafia?"

"Ricky likes to break kneecaps," said Broughton. "Uses a police truncheon, no less. Danny breaks jaws and knocks teeth out, leaving his victims living on soup. If they survive. Uses brass knuckles. Hey, look, see that GTI? That's Vinnie's cousin Gary. First time I've seen him at one of these do's. Son of Vinnie's auntie, Maggie Cooper."

"So, he's Gary Cooper, then?" said Turnbull. "For real? Like

'High Noon'?"

A black Audi A4 Avant pulled up at the gates, two men on board.

"Bloody hell, who's that?" Broughton exclaimed, grabbing for his notebook to quickly scribble down the reg number. "Not seen that car before. Must be a new boy. We'll soon find out."

He pulled out his phone.

In the passenger seat, Turnbull began singing quietly to himself in what was a quite pleasing baritone voice.

"Do not forsake me, oh my darlin', on this our wedding day-ay..."

"Tex Ritter," said Broughton.

"The very same," said Turnbull. "Now make the fucking call."

Inside the villa, Vinnie greeted his latest arrivals.

"Steve! Glad you could make it, and you've brought Terry, of course, like I asked. Ricky, Danny, show Terry here to his accommodation."

"Hey, I'm not staying ..." Terry began to protest but was cut short when the two apes took an arm each and led him away.

"What are you going to do with him?" Stephen asked.

"He's being reassigned to the farm tomorrow," said Vinnie.

Stephen grimaced. He knew what it meant. An unmarked grave on Vinnie's remote moorland farm at Norland.

"Hey, don't let it spoil our Christmas party," said Vinnie, putting a comforting arm around his brother-in-law's shoulders and steering him towards the dining room. "Bastard shouldn't have got drunk and started shooting his mouth off. Now you're sure your car won't be recognised? You know there's a couple of monkeys sitting in the bushes across the way."

"Yes, I'm sure. Terry cloned the plates before we left."

"Good. His last job for us. Now come and meet my cousin Gary. He'll be your new workshop technician, starting Monday morning. I've arranged for Rabbit Properties to go into Terry's house and clear it out. By this time tomorrow, our Gary'll be their new tenant."

"And if anyone asks about Terry?" said Stephen.

"Who knows?" said Vinnie, grinning. "He gave you his notice and wouldn't tell anyone where he was going. He'd only say he'd had a better offer." They strolled into the massive dining room.

"Julie, love, look who's here."

In the Mondeo, Broughton said "Thanks, Cliff," into his phone and closed the call.

"Got it," he announced. "Owner lives in Scarcroft. Name of Humphrey."

"Don't tell me," said Turnbull. "Bogart? Lyttleton?"

"Arnold," said Broughton. "Arnold Humphrey. The proud owner of a factory which makes fucking birdcages, of all things. I wonder what his connection with Vinnie Wyte might be?"

"Hah! Well," said Turnbull, chuckling. "We can rattle his cage tomorrow and find out."

They fell silent for a while. Turnbull turned his coat collar up and blew into his hands.

"Can you run the motor for a while?" he said. "I'm freezing my fucking balls off in here."

"Stop bleeding moaning, for God's sake. I told you to wear your thermals."

By now more guests had arrived, Broughton ticking them off in his notebook. He retrieved his Thermos flask from the back seat and they shared some lukewarm coffee.

"What's with all the VWs?" said Turnbull.

"It's the boss's rule," said Broughton. "VW, same as his initials. Drives one of those big ugly Touareg things himself, and his missus has a Golf R."

"Which means Mister Audi Birdcage isn't a member of Vinnie's gang, then," observed Turnbull. "Must be an associate. Or a special guest?"

"No shit, Sherlock."

In the house, the party was in full swing. The long oak dining table had been laid with a magnificent buffet, along with a good selection of strictly non-alcoholic drinks. Another of Vinnie's rules, and a sensible one, what with Old Bill always on the lookout for any opportunity to disrupt his organisation.

Vinnie beckoned to his right-hand man, Paddy Ryan.

"Paddy, lad," he said. "Time to dish out the envelopes."

Vinnie liked to reward loyalty with generous amounts of hard cash, so there were smiling faces all round. No one was getting reassigned to the farm. Except for the absent Terry. Stephen wondered what the poor bloke's overnight 'accommodation' was like. Probably some cold, remote room or maybe an outhouse tucked away at the back of the garden. He pictured Terry tied to a chair, tears running down his face, knowing this was his last night on earth. As opposed to being six feet under it.

It saddened him. Terry had been a great help to him. Still, stupid of him to get pissed and begin shooting his mouth off. Luckily, it had been Stephen's neighbour Oliver Crompton and his fancy piece who had been listening, otherwise Stephen might never have found out. Lucky, too, how Oliver had seemed to accept Stephen's explanation that Terry was no more than a sad little fantasist.

He hoped Vinnie's cousin Gary would turn out to be as useful. His first job on Monday morning would be to get the original plates back on the Audi, then Stephen could make it the latest 'Deal of the Week'.

"Nice fat envelope for you, Steve," Vinnie was saying. "Payment for the Bradford job, and a special bonus from Paddy here, personally, to say thank you for taking care of that Greek prick in Nottingham. Now make sure you give my sis a great Christmas, eh?"

Steve gave Paddy a thumbs-up, getting an American-style salute in return.

"Cheers, Vinnie. And you bet Cindy will be my number one priority, as ever. I've booked Christmas dinner at the Golden Fleece and in the new year we're off to Paris for a long weekend's shopping trip. Boy, does she love that Galeries Lafayette."

In the Mondeo, DS Turnbull had reached the end of his tether.

"Come on, Les, let's go," he said. "There's nothing more to see here, and I'm fucking busting for a piss."

"Yeah, and I'm fucking starving," said Broughton, firing up the engine. "Fancy a curry? It's on me."

The following morning, Turnbull and Broughton paid a visit to the home of Arnold Humphrey in Scarcroft, where they spoke to his wife.

Mrs Humphrey was a middle-aged woman who viewed officers of the law as the commonest of people, not worthy of the

dark peak blues

attention of a refined, upper-class lady such as she. At first, she kept them at the door, regarding them with a high degree of disdain and suspicion. Neither of the detective sergeants took it personally. They had both been around too long to be offended by a toffee-nosed old bat like her. Turnbull, being the slightly better-spoken of the two, took the lead and finally persuaded her to open up about the whereabouts of her husband on the previous evening.

They were disappointed with the answer. She assured them that she and her husband had hosted a dinner party, right there at their own home. A little reluctantly, she gave them a list of their guests. She told them her husband had not left the premises at any time during the evening and his Audi had remained in the impressive stone-built double garage throughout.

Back in the Mondeo, they headed for Arnold Humphrey's place of work, his birdcage manufacturing business on the south side of the city.

"Seems to me, we're on a wild goose chase," said Turnbull.

"I think you're wrong there," said Broughton. "They don't keep wild geese in cages."

"Ha-bloody-ha," said Turnbull. "You're about as funny as a fart in a phone box. But you know what I mean. I think Mrs Humphrey was telling us the absolute truth. A pound to a penny, her story will check out. Five'll get you ten, that Audi last night was a clone."

"You're spot on, old buddy," said Broughton. "Apart from the mixed betting metaphors. So, we'll go through the motions with Arnold then strike him off our list, okay? And start looking elsewhere for last night's mystery guest."

"Agreed," said Turnbull. "But can we stop somewhere for a full English first? I'm bloody starving.

james h jones

*Chapter Five
Wedding Plans*

In his study at 16 Riverside Walk, Oliver Crompton was on a Skype video call with his good friend, Kitty Updike. They were talking about the disappointing results suffered by the Greens in the recent local elections. It was a one-sided discussion; Kitty was simply lending a sympathetic ear to one of Oliver's rants. That there had been no council elections in their region on this occasion was no consolation to Oliver, who always viewed such matters from a national perspective.
"You're talking unusually quietly, darling," said Kitty. "Are you frightened of someone overhearing us?"
"Amelia and Stuart are here," he said. "They're in the front room with Marion, talking about their wedding."
As if on cue, he heard the living room door opening and the murmur of voices from within.
"Got to go, my love," he said quietly and cut the call. Kitty wouldn't mind, she was quite accustomed to such arbitrary treatment.
"*Oliver*," his wife called from the hallway. "You're needed."
"Coming, dear," he called back. He lumbered to his feet, muttering a curse at the painful protest from his knee. The ever-faithful black and white collie Moss raised himself from in front of the fire and followed his master from the room.
In the living room Oliver poured himself a coffee from the pot standing on the table and settled into his armchair. Moss lay down at his feet and, true to his doggy form, fell quickly back to sleep
"Now, pay attention, Oliver," said Marion. "We've been discussing the wedding arrangements and you need to fully understand your role on the day."
"My role?" said Oliver. "Are we planning a wedding or producing a Shakespeare play?"

Side by side on the sofa, Amelia and Stuart giggled. Marion frowned her disapproval.

"Don't be so flippant," she said. "This is serious. Now, very much against my wishes, Amelia and Stuart are still insisting upon going ahead with their plans for a civil ceremony at Hazlewood Castle. Goodness only knows how I'm supposed to explain their decision to the Reverend Parsons, especially after I had made provisional plans with him for a proper church wedding at St Joseph's."

"I've told you a thousand times, Mother," said Amelia, sitting up straight and speaking through gritted teeth. "We are not religious. The same goes for the vast majority of our guests."

"So you keep saying, dear," said Marion, with a dismissive wave. "But I brought you up as a Christian. You were christened in St Joseph's and it's only right you should get married there, as well. You might think you're an unbeliever just now, but you will come to realise the foolishness of it in time. Unlike your stubborn old heathen of a father who, I'm sorry to say, is way beyond hope and is destined to spend eternity in Hell. May God forgive him."

Amelia made no response. Her face was pale. Stuart wisely kept quiet, too, staring out of the window, pretending to be interested in the antics of the starlings at the feeding station. Oliver, more than accustomed to his wife's anachronistic views, what he called her medieval beliefs, merely sighed and shook his head.

"Anyway," Marion continued, undaunted. "You've made your minds up about Hazlewood Castle but I really think you should postpone it, now that we know Prince Harry and Meghan Markle are set to get married on the same day."

"We're not changing the date, Mother," said Amelia, quite firmly. "Just because you'd rather spend the entire day sitting gawping at the telly. Get over it. The date is fixed. Everything is arranged except for the bridal car. I still want Dad to drive me in his lovely Alvis."

"Happy to, my..." Oliver began.

"Out of the question," snapped Marion, with a dismissive wave of the hand. "Firstly, it's only got two doors, so you'd have trouble getting in and out. Secondly, it's only insured for your dad to drive and as father of the bride he has to travel in the back seat with you. But there's nothing to worry about. I've asked that nice

Mister Hudson if he will do the honours with his lovely Jaguar and he said he'd be delighted."

"What?" Oliver was flabbergasted. "You've asked that bloody used car salesman to drive my daughter and me to her wedding? How dare you? And without consulting me first. Bloody typical of you, woman. Blundering ahead without a moment's consideration for other peoples' feelings or opinions."

"Oh, for goodness' sake," Marion responded, her voice going up an octave or so. "Whatever's thé matter with you? It's a perfect solution. I don't know what you've got against Stephen. He's a lovely chap and his car is perfect for the occasion. What's more, he's happy to do it for free."

"I don't dislike him," said Oliver. "I simply don't trust him. I'm pretty sure he's a crook. There's something about him I can't put my finger on. And don't forget what that mechanic of his told me. I know I'm supposed to believe the chap was a drunken fantasist but wasn't it a bit strange how he suddenly disappeared soon afterwards?"

"What nonsense," said Marion. "You're just prejudiced because Stephen happens to sell used cars. You're a snob but you're too much of a coward to admit it. Well you'll just have to live with it. It's all arranged. And you'd better not go airing your silly unfounded suspicions in public, either. He could easily sue you for slander and who could blame him if he did?"

"What's all this about a mysterious disappearing mechanic?" asked Amelia, her journalistic instincts brought sharply awake. Alongside her, Stuart had turned his attention from the starlings and was also paying close attention.

"Technician," said Stuart. "We haven't called them mechanics for years."

"It was back before Christmas," said Oliver, ignoring his future son-in-law's grammatical pedantry. "I was having a drink with a friend in the Frankland Arms..."

"When he says *friend* he means his floozy, his fancy piece," Marion interrupted.

"As I was saying," Oliver went on, wisely not reacting to the jibe. "I was in the Frankland Arms and got talking to Hudson's then mechanic chappie. Terry, his name was. He'd had a skin-full and was running off at the mouth a bit. I asked him if he liked working for Hudson and he told me he didn't actually work for him. He said he was really employed by Hudson's brother-in-law, and he was on loan to Hudson. Well, I bought him a couple of drinks and before long he was boasting about the brother-in-law. Crowed about him being a high-flying Leeds gangster who had set Hudson up in his executive car business as a cover for the true nature of their relationship. Which he refused to discuss, drunk as he was. It all sounded too far-fetched to me. As if some Leeds Mister Big would want anything to do with a used car lot in Thirsk.

"Anyway, I bumped into Hudson the following lunchtime in the Golden Fleece and told him what Terry had been saying about him. He made a joke of it. Said the man was a drunken fool, making up wild stories when he'd had a few too many. He told me his wife's brother was a successful Leeds businessman who had, in fact, helped him out financially with setting up his car business, but certainly wasn't any kind of gangster. Which all made perfect sense at the time. Then the next I knew, Terry had disappeared. Hudson fed me some cock-and-bull story about him having had a better offer and leaving at short notice, but he seemed a bit evasive about it. I was disappointed because Terry had always made a great job of looking after my Alvis."

"So, what's his name?" asked Amelia.

"Stephen Hudson," said Oliver. "Lives directly opposite at number nineteen. Owns Hudson Executive Cars on Long Street."

"No, not him," she said, patiently. "The other fellow, the brother-in-law."

"Damned if I can remember," said Oliver. "Terry did let it slip, just the once, but..."

"It's Vincent," Marion interrupted. "He's Cindy Hudson's brother. Cindy introduced me to him and his wife one day when I was out with Moss. They'd just arrived for a visit. His wife's name is Julie, if I remember rightly. He was smoking a big fat cigar. He reminded me of that old film actor – oh, I can't remember his name. You'll know who I mean, Oliver. He played General Patton."

"George C Scott," said Oliver.

"Never heard of him," said Amelia.

"What sort of car were they in?" asked Stuart, now fully alert, he and Amelia perched on the edges of their seats.

"Oh, don't ask me, I don't know one car from another," said Marion. "It was one of those big ugly 4x4 things."

"Could it have been a VW Touareg, by any chance?" asked Stuart.

"What are you thinking?" said Amelia.

"I'm thinking Oliver could well be right about Stephen Hudson," said Stuart quietly. "I'm thinking this Vincent who Marion met is very likely to be none other than Vinnie Wyte, the biggest crime-lord in Leeds, In fact, I'm sure of it, because I know for a fact, his wife's name is Julie. And I know he drives a VW Touareg. He always drives a VW, because of his initials. And all his 'associates'," - he made air quotes with his fingers, which had Oliver wincing - "drive VWs as well. And he certainly does look remarkably like a young George C Scott. I also know a certain detective sergeant who will be more than interested to hear about all this. Assuming he's not already aware of the family connection."

"Oh, my goodness," said Marion.

"See? I bloody well knew it," said Oliver, pleased with himself. "Now you know Hudson's a crook, do you still want to involve him in our daughter's wedding?"

"No, not really," said Marion, frowning. "But just because his brother-in-law's a crook doesn't mean Stephen's one, does it? I happen to know, he's an ex-policeman. His wife let it slip one day. You're making him guilty by association, which doesn't seem fair to me."

"Have you not heard of bent coppers, Mother?" asked Amelia. "Does anyone know why he left the force?"

"Of course, I've heard of 'bent coppers', silly girl," Marion snapped. "But he's such a nice man. In any case, I wouldn't know how to go about turning down his kind offer, without giving something away."

"Don't worry, I'll do it," said Oliver. "I'll tell him Amelia wants it to be a private family affair and is insisting I drive her myself."

"Don't forget to thank him," said Marion. "Just because he *might* be a crook, there's no need for rudeness."

"Yes, dear, no, dear, of course, dear," said Oliver, rolling his eyes as he went to the table for more coffee.

Stuart was already on his phone, talking excitedly to his detective friend.

"Oh Lord, what have I done?" Marion muttered under her breath, gazing Heavenwards.

dark peak blues

Two days later, Steve Hudson was speaking to his brother-in-law. As usual, they were using burners, untraceable pay-as-you-go phones.

"A couple of things you need to know, Vinnie," said Steve, idly stirring his fourth coffee of the day.

"I'm listening," came the reply.

"Yesterday, my neighbour came to see me," said Steve. "You know the one, Oliver Crompton, the one whose daughter I was supposed to be chauffeuring to her wedding next month."

"Yeah, I know him," said Vinnie. "And you told me about the wedding thing weeks ago, remember? He lives across the way from you. I met his little fat wife a while back. She's the one with a face like a bag of spanners."

"The very same," said Steve, chuckling at Vinnie's coarse but on-the-button description of Marion Crompton. "Anyway, he came to tell me they won't be needing my services at the wedding, after all. He reckoned it was his daughter's idea, said she wants to keep it in the family and is insisting Oliver drives her in his Alvis."

"And that's something I *need to know*?" said Vinnie with barely concealed sarcasm.

"Not normally, no," said Steve. "But he seemed very sheepish about it to me, as if there was more to it. So, I pushed him a bit. I made out I was bitterly disappointed. I said I'd really been looking forward to doing the honours and that Cindy had already bought a new outfit. I said she was hoping to be asked to be maid of honour or whatever they call 'em these days. Not true, of course. I told him if they changed their minds, to just let me know. Which gave him verbal diarrhoea. He went all apologetic and red in the face, stumbling over a load of feeble excuses, babbling on about nothing much; but in amongst he let slip a bit of information which pricked my ears up. Turns out, his daughter Amelia and her boyfriend both work for the Yorkshire Post and the boyfriend, whose name is Stuart Teale, is their crime correspondent."

"Oh, him? He's a right little arsehole," said Vinnie. "Thinks he's a shit-hot investigative reporter but is about as much use as a frog in a jam jar. All wind and piss. Was that the big news you thought I'd need to know?"

"Not on its own, no," said Steve. "But you're the one who has always told me there's no such thing as coincidence, right?"

"Right enough," said Vinnie, his interest piqued. "Go on."

"This morning," said Steve, pausing to take a drink of his coffee. "No more than thirty minutes ago, we had a bloke wandering around the showroom. When Phil approached him, he shoo-ed him away, saying he was just having a look. He seemed to take a lot of interest in the two black A4 Avants I've got on show. One of which I drove to your house, remember? With cloned plates, of course, so no worries there. But still."

"But still?" said Vinnie. "What else?"

"After crawling all over the two Audis he made a phone call," said Steve. "Phil heard him telling someone about them. How there were two of them on show, either of which *fitted the bill*. Now, he could simply have been telling a mate that he'd found a car for him. Maybe it was just a coincidence, after all."

"Happenstance, maybe," muttered Vinnie. "Coincidence? Never. Did you get his name?"

"No, I didn't," said Steve. "But I clocked what he was driving. It was a plain grey Mondeo. Would you like the reg number?"

"Yes," said Vinnie. "Gimme it now, although I think I already know whose it'll turn out to be. I reckon I'll be having a word with my good friend Detective Superintendent Ron Pritchard, sooner rather then later. We need to put the kibosh on this PDQ. Sit tight. You'll be hearing from me."

Chapter Six
Trafficking

"The bastards are transferring me, Richard," DS Les Broughton was leaning forwards in his chair, his elbows planted firmly on his desk, his mobile phone pressed to his ear.

"Transferring you where to, for fuck's sake?" DS Turnbull wanted to know, his voice quiet but incredulous.

"County HQ in Wakefield," said Broughton. "I'm being promoted to Detective Inspector and they're putting me in charge of a team investigating a county-wide people-trafficking operation."

"Sounds a bit fishy to me," said Turnbull. "People-trafficking is very much in the NCA's remit, these days. It was taken out of the hands of local forces months ago, because it's a nationwide problem. People-traffickers have no respect or regard for county boundaries. We already have a terrific dedicated team in place, doing a great job."

"That's what I said to Pritchard," said Broughton, swapping his mobile to his other ear. "But he told me my new team is already working hand-in-glove with your lot."

"Do you believe him?" asked Turnbull.

"Don't see why not," said Broughton. "He's hardly likely to have invented an imaginary team. I'd very quickly find out if he had."

"I didn't mean that," said Turnbull quickly. "I should have said 'do you trust him?' I mean, do you trust his motives for giving you this new job just at this particular time?" He paused but getting no reply, he went on. "Let me ask you something. Is Vinnie Wyte involved in people-trafficking?"

"Not that I'm aware of," said Broughton. "Hold on a sec." He held the phone away from his ear. His door had opened and DC Mary Britten had taken a tentative step into his office.

"Yes, Mary, what can I do for you?" he said.

"Sorry to interrupt, Sarge," she said. "Stuart Teale from the

Yorkshire Post is at the front desk and is asking to see you."

Les Broughton heaved a frustrated sigh.

"Tell the little shit to fuck off and make an appointment, next time," Broughton snapped at her. "And when I say, 'fuck off', I mean tell him exactly that. No mincing your words, Mary, for all it might offend your delicate sensibilities."

"Righto, Sarge," said Mary and left the room quickly, but not so quickly Les Broughton didn't see the crimson blush rising up from her shirt collar. He chuckled to himself, only too aware of Mary Britten's hatred of bad language. He put the phone back to his ear.

"Sorry, Richard," he said, receiving a non-committal grunt in reply. "As I was saying. Wyte may be a pretty ruthless character but even he seems to draw the line at people-trafficking."

"As I thought," murmured Turnbull. "I couldn't help overhearing, you just sent young Teale away with a flea in his ear."

"Too fucking right, I did," said Broughton. "The little arsehole takes liberties. Needs bringing down a few pegs."

"Maybe so," observed Turnbull. "But have you thought about how your new job seems to have cropped up just after the aforementioned little arsehole passed on some interesting information about our friend Vinnie Wyte?"

"Bloody hell, Richard, what are you suggesting?" Broughton blustered.

"Not suggesting anything, really," said Turnbull. "But maybe we should be keeping a keen eye on that Super of yours. Maybe, just maybe, your sudden promotion was designed as a distraction more than a reward for a job well done. And maybe, just maybe, your equally sudden transfer was more down to string-pulling than you may care to imagine."

"God, Richard, have I ever told you what an old cynic you are?" said Broughton.

"Hey! Not so much of the 'old'," said Turrnbull, laughing. "And in my experience, a little cynicism can go a long way towards covering your arse, in the long run."

"Point taken, *old* lad," said Broughton, not labouring the 'old'. Well, not much, anyway.

At the same time as Broughton and Turnbull were having their conversation, Vinnie Wyte and Steve Hudson were on their burner phones again.

"Broughton's off the scene, you'll be pleased to hear," said Vinnie.

"What? You mean you've had him bumped off?" said Steve, only half joking. Through his interior window he watched Phil giving a punter a guided tour of the Quattroporte. He crossed his fingers. The bloody car had been there long enough. Maybe this time?

"Of course not, stupid boy," said Vinnie, chuckling. "Bad business to go around bumping off coppers. Pritchard's arranged for him to be promoted and transferred. Good fucking riddance, say I."

"That is good news," said Steve. "But no doubt there'll be somebody new on the case sooner rather than later, won't there?"

"Trouble is, old buddy, there already is," said Vinnie. "Always was, in fact. Turns out, Broughton was working with a Detective Sergeant from the NCA. One DS fucking Turnbull. And Pritchard can do fuck all about him."

"Shit!" said Steve.

"Shit indeed," said Vinnie. "And although it's kinda flattering to have drawn the attention of the NCA, it's attention we can well do without."

"So, what are we going to do about it?" said Steve. "Are you going to have to break your rule about not bumping off coppers?"

Vinnie was quiet for a while. Steve could almost hear the cogs whirring in his brother-in-law's brain. Finally, he spoke up.

"Not even thinking about breaking that particular rule," he said. "But I don't have an answer at the moment. I think we should just sit tight for now and be extra fucking careful until I can think of something. Killing a DS from the NCA would only bring a shitload of trouble down on our heads."

"Very wise, I'm sure," Steve agreed. "But I am also fairly certain, no one would miss an obnoxious little crime reporter from the Yorkshire Post. Apart from his girlfriend, maybe."

"Food for thought," said Vinnie. "I'll come back to you on that one."

Steve ended the call and pocketed his phone just as Phil came bursting into the office, all agog with the news that he had finally sold the Maserati.

"Without any haggling?" said Steve, reaching into his drawer for the bottle of J&B he kept for such auspicious occasions.

4.54609
Copyright © 2020 James H Jones
A work of fiction

Chapter One
Fossicking

"Why are you fossicking in the pedal bin?" asked Patrick, not unreasonably, he thought.

"I'm missing a teaspoon, if you must know," Julia snapped, without bothering to look up from her task. "I think I must've chucked it away last night, with my yoghurt pot. We're meant to have six but there are only five in the drawer, this morning. Anyway, what the hell does fossicking mean, when it's at home?"

"It means rummaging around looking for something," he said. "Not knowing what you might find. Australian gold mining slang, apparently. I picked it up during my time with the Anzacs in Gallipoli."

"Oh, no, not another of your silly time travelling stories again," said Julia, with a heartfelt sigh. "Darling, I know you're a writer but, for Heaven's sake, when are you ever going to grow up and stop spinning these ridiculous yarns? You have never been to Gallipoli in your entire life. And you weren't even born when the Anzacs were there."

"I'll prove it to you," said Patrick, aggrieved. "I'll go back to yesterday and watch you, see what you did with your precious teaspoon. Then, you will have to believe my 'silly time travel stories', once and for all."

"Whatever," said Julia dismissively. She resumed her rummaging in the pedal bin.

Patrick strode from the room, in what in the olden days would have been called high dudgeon. She heard him pounding up the stairs and entering his study. A few minutes later, she heard him coming down again. He strutted into the kitchen looking incredibly pleased with himself.

"It's in the cutlery tray," he announced. "But you dropped it in with the pudding spoons, by mistake. It's hidden, three or four spoons down."

Julia straightened up, looked at him sideways, rinsed her hands under the cold tap, wiped them on a tea towel and strode to the cutlery drawer. She lifted out three dessert spoons then gave a gasp.

Turning to him, she pointed the newly liberated teaspoon like an accusing finger.

"You did that on purpose," she growled, scowling at him. "You set it all up just to trick me."

"No, darling, I told you," he said quietly, his self-satisfied demeanour serving only to inflame her annoyance. "I went back to yesterday and watched you. I saw what you did with the teaspoon, like I said."

Julia drew breath as if about to protest further. She stopped short, her gaze drawn to his left arm.

"What on earth is that thing?" she demanded, once again using the teaspoon as a pointer.

He glanced down and saw, to his horror, he was still wearing his device, strapped firmly to his left arm, in plain view, around the outside of his shirt sleeve. He had been so anxious to tell her his news about the missing teaspoon, he had forgotten to take it off and stow it away safely in its hiding place, upstairs in his study.

He hesitated a moment, before deciding upon honesty. It was, after all, supposed to be the best policy.

"It's my time travel device," he explained, a little sheepishly. "It's how I travel through time."

"Yeah, right," scoffed Julia. "There you go again. You must think I'm an idiot. It's just your old scientific calculator, fitted with a strap."

"It was my old scientific calculator," Patrick admitted. "But I've adapted it. You key in the information to tell it the time and date you want to travel to and, hey presto. Look, I'll show you."

Julia decided to humour him, before calling for the men in white coats. She walked over to him. He held his arm up and, with his right hand, keyed in 173005112017<4.54609. He

dark peak blues

explained how it represented five-thirty PM on the fifth of November last year, then hit the enter key – and disappeared.

Julia stared, open-mouthed, at the empty space which, a moment before, had been occupied by her now missing husband. She was little more than halfway through crying out in surprise and alarm, when he reappeared, right in front of her eyes.

His face was split by the widest grin she had ever seen.

"Now do you believe me?" he said.

"What? How? Where did you disappear to?" she spluttered, reaching for the kitchen roll and tearing a piece off, to wipe away the tears.

"Right here, love, on the fifth of November last year," he said. "Fortunately, I remembered we were in here, preparing the bonfire buffet together. I watched us carrying it out to the picnic tables. I watched you hiding behind the hedge when the fireworks went off. I watched us clearing up the mess afterwards. I stayed long enough to see everyone else leave and us two getting undressed for bed. Then I thought I'd better leave, as well. As a general rule, I don't travel back to our own past and it was becoming a little bit embarrassing, to say the least."

Julia was now shaking, visibly, and he realised she was in shock. He put an arm around her and led her to the dining table. He sat her down and brought her a large J&B and water. Finally, he sat down beside her and explained how his device worked.

"You have to travel to the place from which you want to go back or forward in time," he said.

"You mean to say, you had to go all the way to Gallipoli," she said. "Before you could travel back to the time of the Anzacs?"

"Sad but true," he said.

"So how can you afford all the travel?" Julia wanted to know. "And how come you never seem to have been away from home? And if you were there at last year's bonfire, watching us, how come I didn't see two of you? This is all crazy."

"Apparently, time travel has its own set of unbreakable physical laws," said Patrick. "You can't change history, so it makes you invisible. I mean, you don't appear invisible to yourself. If you look down you can still see yourself. But people around you seem to be rendered completely unaware of your existence. Which means you have to be constantly on your guard, dodging contact with anyone.

"I think it's the butterfly effect thing. If you could be seen, you would have some effect, even if it was only slight. It's how I get to travel for free, you see. I slip a few minutes into the past or the future and I can get on and off trains, buses, 'planes, boats, completely unseen. It can be a bit hair-raising, at times, though, constantly dodging other people."

"The future?" Julia whispered, flabbergasted, as if it had only just registered.

"Yes, I just key in the 'greater than' symbol," he explained. "I haven't been far into the future, mind. Too scary. I really don't want to know what's ahead of us. To get back to the present, I use the equals key. 4.54609 means 'now'. The 'less than' symbol means before now, 'greater than' means after now. Weird, eh?"

"Why does that particular number mean 'now'?" she asked. "And how on earth did you come to discover it?"

"I don't know why it does," he said. "All I ever knew was, it's the number of litres in a gallon. I was playing around with the number one day, on an old calculator and the bloody thing disappeared, right in front of my eyes. I've never seen it since. It cost me an absolute fortune in calculators before I worked out what was happening."

"Gosh," she sighed, really intrigued now. "Where else have you been?"

"Oh, like the song says, I've been everywhere, man. I've seen the storming of the Bastille. I've seen Spitfires flying off to the Battle of Britain. I was standing in the Texas Book Depository in Dallas, when President Kennedy was shot. Whoever it was with the rifle, I can tell you it certainly wasn't Lee Harvey Oswald. He was what they call a patsy. The real shooter left him there with the smoking gun and scarpered, double quick. Oswald shouted after him, 'Don't forget, you promised to take care of my family.' I scarpered double quick after that, I can tell you, before I got trampled to death by a load of cops.

"Like I said, I've been everywhere, man."

"Oh wow! Can I go with you, next time?"

"I don't know, darling, I'll have to work on it."

"Work on it?" she said, a little miffed. "Surely, all you'd have to do is adapt another scientific calculator, just like you did with

dark peak blues

that one. Don't you want me to come with you?"

"Of course I do, darling," he said. "I just need to think through all the possible implications. And I would have to make sure we never, ever, got separated. And then there's the timing. You see, I worked out from the very beginning how important it is, not to reappear before I've actually disappeared. Which is why I always travel back to a few minutes after the time I left, to avoid any such calamity. Can you imagine how awkward it would be, dealing with two of me?"

"Hm," said Julia. "One of you can take some handling, at the best of times. Anyway, yes, I understand. We will have to plan carefully, if I am to join you on your travels."

Patrick gave her a hug and a big sloppy kiss.

"What would happen," she queried. "If you ended up somewhere you really liked and hit the equals symbol? I would lose you forever, wouldn't I?"

"No danger of that, my love," he replied. "There couldn't possibly be anywhere in the world, past, present or future, where I would rather be, than right here, with you, in our own special present."

"Aww," she said, with a smile and a sniffle.

Chapter Two
East End 1940

It took a while for Patrick to source the right kind of scientific calculator, which he could adapt to a time travel device for Julia.

A further three weeks went by before he felt comfortable enough to declare her fully trained and ready to accompany him on his travels through time.

By then, it was early November, with Remembrance Sunday fast approaching. They had both lost relatives in WWII. Patrick had lost a great uncle in the Normandy landings on the sixth of June 1944. Julia had lost her maternal grandmother and a great aunt, in the blitz on London in 1940. She was not sure of the actual date. Understandably, their conversation was full of talk about the eleventh of November.

On Saturday the ninth of November, the BBC screened the annual British Legion Festival of Remembrance, from the Albert Hall. Patrick and Julia were in full agreement, it was the best it had ever been. Brilliantly staged. Inspiring.

Far removed, indeed, from previous years, when it had been little more than an endless, dull procession of veterans, down a precarious set of stairs. All trying their best to keep in step, without falling flat on their faces. Or on their arses.

Patrick, for once, had no grumbles about it not being secular enough for his Humanist inclinations. The programme held his unwavering attention, almost to the very end, when he was finally driven from the room by the inevitable appearance of a bloke in a frock, who took centre stage to conduct the closing service.

Patrick departed with Bridget, their cocker spaniel, to take her on her last walk of the day. Julia chuckled when she heard him muttering something about it being 'too good to be bloody true. Why do they always have to spoil it by bringing on a bloody cleric?'

The following morning, Remembrance Sunday, they sat

together for breakfast. Which was when Julia told him where she wanted him to take her, on their first time travel adventure together.

"I would like to see where Grandma and Great Aunt Phyllis died," she said. "If you think we will be okay."

Patrick didn't reply straight away. He sat quietly for a while, contemplating her request, munching slowly on a slice of toast and marmalade.

"Righto, darling," he said after a while. "If it's what you want. Give me as much detail as you can come up with and I'll do some research. Just so long as you realise, it may turn out to be dangerous. I'm not sure if time travellers can consider themselves immune from the likes of German bombs. Or falling masonry and suchlike."

A few days later, Julia returned from a visit to her aunt and uncle in Eastbourne. She announced, with a big cheesy grin, that she had gleaned the necessary information.

"They were killed in a bombing raid during the night of thirteenth – fourteenth of November 1940," she told him. She went on to give him the house number and street name, in London's East End.

Patrick went to work on his laptop and, in no time, accumulated all the necessary information. The street still existed but modern-day images from Google Earth showed it bore little resemblance to the same street in the old black and white photos he managed to find elsewhere on the 'net. As usual, he used good old Wikipedia as his launch pad, from which he could quickly search for more detail around the Web.

Two days later, on Tuesday the twenty-sixth of November, they were standing hand in hand, in the East End street concerned. As they had already discovered on Google, it was a rather sad and depressing place to be. There was hardly anyone around, despite it being mid-morning. Property was mainly low-level commercial. A few nondescript shops, a pawnbroker, payday loan provider, a post office with so much external security it reminded Patrick of the movie 'Escape from New York'.

They walked to a deserted spot between a closed down BetFred and a boarded-up pizza joint. Patrick lifted his left arm, where his device was firmly strapped. He keyed in 100014111940<4.54609, then keyed the identical details into

Julia's device, which she also wore on her left sleeve.

Julia grimaced and hooked her free arm firmly through his.

"Are you sure you want to go through with this?" he asked. "You can change your mind, you know. I will understand."

"No, I'm okay," she said, her voice trembling slightly. "Let's go."

As soon as the street was free of traffic, he marched them to the white line.

"On three," he said. "One. Two. Three."

Simultaneously, they pressed their enter keys and disappeared from the street.

The scene which unfolded before them was one of unspeakable devastation. The entire street had been reduced to rubble. Black-grey smoke was still spiralling skywards from the ruins. Survivors, all clearly in shock, were either wandering aimlessly or standing stock still, gazing in despair at what used to be their homes.

The stench hit them, both of them reaching into their pockets for tissues and pressing them to their noses. The smell was a lethal combination of burned wood, charred masonry and smouldering cloth, all with a disturbing undercurrent of coppery blood and roasted human flesh.

Three ragged urchins, presumably a brother and his two sisters, were perched forlornly on a large lump of fallen masonry. All three were weeping and the two girls were crying out for their mummy. Patrick and Julia could only assume their mother was buried somewhere in the rubble behind them, most probably contributing to the eye-watering stink which had them gagging for fresh air. As for their father, who knew?

A hundred yards away, a bunch of ARP men fought valiantly to contain a raging fire, to no avail. Patrick concluded it was a fractured gas main, so they wouldn't be defeating it any time soon.

In the nick of time, he pulled Julia out of the way of a Hillman saloon. It was painted a dull shade of khaki and was driven by an army corporal. An officer sat in the back seat, his nose buried in some notes.

Patrick led them to the relative safety of the side of the street. He felt a shiver run down his spine when he noticed one of the young sisters was staring in their direction, almost as if she could see them, or had somehow sensed their presence.

It was only a fleeting thought, driven quickly from his mind when a Bedford ambulance came flying down the street. It swerved around piles of rubble which had spilled into its path, its bell ringing out stridently. When he looked again, the little girl was busy hugging her younger sister, wiping away her tears with a snotty handkerchief.

"Can you tell which house was your grandma's?" he asked.

"I have no idea," said Julia, weakly. He couldn't help noticing she was weeping, quietly. "How could I possibly find it, in all this?"

He led them to the quietest spot he could find, side-stepping several zombie-like survivors on the way.

"I don't think we should hang around any longer, darling," he said. "I know we don't exist here, really, and I know we can't change history and all that, but I'd rather not put it to the test, if you don't mind."

"You're right," she said. "Let's get out of here. I'm never going to find Grandma and I am really, really scared. Take us home, please, Patrick. We should never have come."

Patrick quickly keyed in the necessary parameters and, in no time, they were back in November 2019, in the same street, just five minutes ahead of the time they had left.

A passer-by looked at them strangely when they appeared in his path, as if from nowhere, then, with a dismissive shake of his head, went on his way.

"Thank goodness for that," said Patrick, letting out the breath he had been holding since 1940. "Come on, lover, let's go home."

"We did okay, though, didn't we?" said Julia. "I mean we came through it all unscathed, right?"

"We sure did," he agreed. "Where do you fancy next time? How about Arremanches on the sixth of June 1944?"

Julia said nothing in reply. His flippancy did nothing to lighten her sombre mood. She hooked up with him and they headed off down the street in the direction of the nearest tube station.

Chapter Three
Nightmares and Ghosts

Later that day, when they were finally home safely, relaxing with a bottle of Shiraz, Julia startled him when she let out a gasp and sat bolt upright in her chair.

"Whatever's the matter, darling?" Patrick asked, concerned.

"Oh, sorry, nothing to worry about," she said. "I've just remembered, it's your birthday in three days' time and I haven't even thought about what to get you, what with all this time travelling carry-on. Is there anything in particular you'd like?"

"Nothing special, my love," he said. "Just as long as you don't get me slippers again."

"Oh, no," she cried in mock alarm. "Slippers were number one on my list."

Patrick made no reply, settling instead for an old-fashioned look. In return, Julia gave him her best Mona Lisa smile.

"I wish I could get that awful stench out of my nostrils," she said, blowing her nose for the umpteenth time since their return. "I swear, I'm going to have nightmares for weeks to come."

They sat quietly for a while, each of them lost in their own thoughts.

"Did you notice the little girl back there?" Patrick said eventually, breaking the silence. "I mean, was it just me or was she actually aware of us?"

"Which little girl?" Julia asked, puzzled.

"The eldest of the two sisters, sitting on a lump of masonry with their brother," he said. "I swear, she looked straight at us when we walked to the roadside."

"Are you sure?" said Julia. "I thought she was watching the firefighters down the street."

"No, for sure, her eyes followed us as we walked. So, she could either see us or she was somehow aware of our presence."

Julia stared at him, temporarily speechless.

"I've been thinking about it ever since," said Patrick. "I think it might explain why people claim to have seen ghosts."

Still no response from an uncharacteristically muted Julia, so he went on to explain his theory.

"I had a dog bark at me in Dallas," he said. "And when I was at the storming of the Bastille, someone bumped into me. Quite hard. I stumbled and almost fell. But when I turned to look, there was no one there. No one anywhere near me.

"The more I think about it, the more it makes sense. I can't be the only one to have discovered time travel. I probably wasn't even the first. It stands to reason, there are countless others out there. And it would make perfect sense if we were invisible to each other, wouldn't it? So, it could explain ghosts. And it would also blow Stephen Hawkins's theory to smithereens."

"What theory would that be?" asked Julia, finally finding her voice.

"The one where he said, if time travel were ever to become possible, somewhere down the line, then we would know about it now, because we'd be inundated with visitors from the future. Maybe we already are but we just can't see them. How d'ya like them apples, kiddo?"

"Huh!" said Julia. "Someone's been reading too much Elmore Leonard again."

"There's no such thing as too much Elmore Leonard," Patrick stated firmly. "So, there's your answer as to what to get me for my birthday. Job jobbed."

"I don't follow," said Julia. "Kindly elucidate."

"Ha!" he exclaimed. "Sounds like someone I know has swallowed a dictionary. To elucidate, as you so pretentiously put it, for my birthday I would like the recently published omnibus editions of the complete writings of Elmore Leonard, please."

Julia laughed. "Consider it done," she said. "Now that's out of the way, what would you like for Christmas?"

"Are you kidding me?" he exclaimed. "You know I don't even think about Christmas before the twenty-fourth of December. If I even think about it at all."

"Sorry I spoke, Ebenezer," Julia retorted. "In which case, you won't mind if you never see so much as a ghost of a Christmas present."

"Oh, dear," he groaned. "The old jokes are still the best."

Chapter Four
Be Careful What You Wish For

Patrick's birthday on the twenty-ninth of November had come and gone, before the subject of time travel came up again.

It was the evening of the fifth of December. Patrick had his nose buried in a Lawrence Shames 'Key West' novel, the fourteenth in the series. Julia had bought him the Elmore Leonard Omnibus for his birthday, and he was well into it. The Key West novel was one to which he had treated himself and thought it was time to take a short break from the omnibus, so as not to overdose on Leonard.

Meanwhile, Julia was watching Eastenders on the telly.

He could never understand what she saw in it. He couldn't even watch a trailer for the dreadful programme. In fact, he thought the BBC should be ashamed of producing such garbage, never mind airing pretentious adverts for it.

'Drama? My foot!' he thought but didn't say out loud.

Finally, he heard the distinctive drumbeats, which he considered the best part of the show, signifying, as they did, the end.

"I've been thinking," said Julia.

Patrick immediately slid his bookmark into place and put Lawrence Shames to one side. He knew better than to not pay attention.

"Thinking about what, my love?" he said.

"About where we should go," she said, looking at him intently. "On our next time-travelling trip."

"Go on, I'm listening," he said.

Julia reached out and gripped his hand, so hard it made him wince. She took a deep breath and looked at him even more intently. 'Oh boy,' he thought, 'she really means business.'

"Darling, you know how much I miss my parents," she said quietly. "Well, with this time-travel thing, we could make it like they were still alive. Like they'd never died. We could go back and visit them any time we liked, as often as we liked. Whaddya think?"

Patrick didn't reply straight away. Slowly, he extracted his hand from her vice-like grip and rubbed it, gently coaxing back the lost circulation, staring back at her while he pondered her question.

"What do I think?" he said eventually. "I think you should be careful what you wish for, sweetheart. Remember how upset you were, after our trip back to the East End in the forties."

"That was different," she protested. "And you know it. Anyway, think about it. Just don't take too long."

Patrick made no reply. He went to the table and opened his laptop. Fifteen minutes later he went upstairs and reappeared with their two devices.

"Come on, then, missus," he said, striding towards the back door.

"Where are we going?" Julia wanted to know.

"Eastgate, Boroughbridge," he said, grinning.

Minutes later, they were in the Saab, heading for the dual carriageway.

As they headed north on the M1, an increasingly anxious Julia could restrain herself no longer.

"Listen, I know I told you not to take too long thinking about it," she said. "But isn't this just a teensy-weensy bit too hasty?"

"No worries, angel," he said. "I've got it covered. When we get to Eastgate, we'll go back to one p.m., on Thursday the twenty-fifth of July, nineteen ninety-one. Which was the hottest day of the year. A weekday means your mum will be home alone and a hot one means she'll have the back door open, with those old bead curtains hanging, to keep the flies out. So, we can sneak in and out without being detected."

"Clever clogs," muttered Julia, hiding a secret smile.

The terraced council houses on Eastgate had a private road running along the rear, separating their small back gardens from their much larger vegetable patches, which sloped gently, all the way down to the river.

When Patrick and Julia arrived behind what had been her parents' house, she almost wept at the way everything had been neglected. The gardens were overgrown with tall grass and weeds. The house was in dire need of some TLC.

"Not your problem, love," said Patrick. He set about strapping the adapted scientific calculators to their arms, then keyed in the parameters, 130025071991<4.54609.

They pressed their enter keys and the scene was instantly transformed to its former glory.

Behind them, a vast array of vegetables filled the space right down to the river. Patrick had never seen so many bumble bees in one place.

In front of them, the neat little garden was resplendent with roses, antirrhinums, begonias and, slap bang in the middle, reclining on a sun lounger on the tiny patch of lawn, lay Julia's mum, Marian.

The effect was quite stunning. She was wearing a one-piece bathing costume in a delicate shade of turquoise. A broad-brimmed straw sunhat threw her face into shadow but failed to hide her natural beauty and smooth-as-silk complexion.

She seemed to be asleep. A Mills & Boon novel lay face down on the gentle swell of her belly. Patrick was struck dumb. He had forgotten how much his late mother-in-law so closely resembled a slightly older version of his darling Julia.

"She's beautiful," Julia whispered, almost as if reading his thoughts. "Even more beautiful than I remember. Come on, let's go inside before she wakes up."

Patrick allowed himself to be led by the hand, past the recumbent Marian and in through the inevitable bead curtains.

Inside, Julia came to an abrupt halt.

"Oh my God," she exclaimed. "It's all so much smaller than I remember. The rooms are tiny. And the furniture has all shrunk. Look at the little table and chairs. It's like a doll's house."

Before Patrick could reply with his planned remark about memory playing tricks, they heard voices from outside. Julia stepped to the back door and peered through the bead curtains.

"It's their neighbour, David Whitham," she whispered. "I never liked him. He was a right randy old goat. Fancied himself as a bit of a lady-killer. When I was still at home, I could always feel his eyes following me around. Really, really creepy and... Oh no!"

"What's wrong?" said Patrick.

"He just said my mum should be wearing more sun cream and she's invited him in to rub it on for her. Oh. My. God. My mother was as bad as him. Quick, they're coming."

They retreated to a safe corner of the living room, from where they watched, spellbound, as a giggling Marian led her lover through the kitchen and living room, into the hallway and up the stairs to her bedroom.

"I never knew my mother was such a dirty cow," muttered Julia, tears running down her face. "Let's go home, please, Patrick."

"I did warn you, darling," he whispered, as they went back outside. "To be careful what you wish for."

james h jones

Rodney the Red Kite
Copyright © 2020 James H Jones
A work of fiction

Chapter One
Rodney and the Drone

Rodney was hovering over his favourite stretch of road, the first long straight on the back road from Kirkby Overblow to Wetherby. He was riding the thermals with his customary ease, his beady eyes fixed on the scene below.

It was just after daybreak on a lovely clear spring morning. He knew it was only a matter of time. The baby rabbits were already up and playing happily on the grass verges. Early commuter traffic was beginning to appear. All he had to do was maintain his hover – and keep watching.

Sooner or later - almost certainly sooner - one of the brainless little bunnies would dash out in front of an oncoming car and – splat – there would be Rodney's breakfast. All he would have to do was swoop down and grab it before other cars came along and pressed its lifeless body even flatter on the road surface. Or before those greedy crows could get there before him.

If the little ones were aware of his presence overhead, they showed no fear. Perhaps their mummies had explained how red kites were of no threat to living creatures, feeding only on carrion.

Either that or they were too young, too untrained to understand the meaning of fear. Rodney had long since decided it was the latter. A natural built-in ignorance which, thankfully, led them to playing too close to the road and running out blindly under the wheels of cars. Thus, providing him with an endless supply of tasty ready meals.

Sure enough, one of the bunnies pricked its ears and sat up

on its haunches, spying a playmate on the opposite verge. Rodney spotted a car coming fast from the direction of the village and got himself ready to dive. His tummy rumbled in anticipation.

Which was when he heard the strange whirring humming noise and sensed the shadow of something passing between him and the morning sun.

"Don't you be out more than ten minutes, young man," shouted Tommy's mum, as he shot off down the drive. "You have to get ready for school, remember, and breakfast's almost ready."

Tommy waved his hand to show he'd heard but neither turned nor replied. He was on a mission. He had little baby bunnies to save from being run over. And he was now more than ready, armed with his brand-new drone. The best birthday gift ever, thanks to his good old mum and dad.

He ran as fast as his little legs would carry him, out of the village and on to the long straight where he knew the babies would be out playing, completely unaware of the danger. His idea was to buzz them with his new drone and drive them away from the roadside, maybe even frighten them enough to keep them away forever.

As he approached, he saw the bunnies were already there, as he'd known they would be. Which was when he noticed the bird hovering overhead. He had no idea what kind of bird it was. It looked to him like some sort of giant hawk. Panicking, he skidded to a stop and quickly set about readying his drone. In his eyes, the hovering predator was more of a threat to the baby rabbits than any passing car.

Rodney found himself being dive-bombed by this strange black machine. It seemed able to mirror his every move. It flew around him, over and under him, forcing him to gain height. It came straight at him, head-on, and again he had to dodge it quickly to avoid a collision.

Out of the corner of his eye he saw the foolish bunny run into the road and, just as he had predicted, it got flattened by the speeding car. He also caught a fleeting glimpse of a young boy, who was watching his every move and who appeared to be clutching a small black box in both hands.

In the end, poor old Rodney was forced to turn tail and fly away. He went without breakfast that day.

Unlike young Tommy, who was back home in plenty of time to enjoy a steaming plate of sausages, egg and Italian plum peeled tomatoes. His absolute favourite. He told his mum all about how he had saved the baby bunnies from the nasty giant hawk, all thanks to his new drone, the best present ever.

His mum agreed, the drone was, without question, the best birthday present ever. She, too, wondered what kind of bird it had been.

dark peak blues

*Chapter Two
Rodney and the Scarecrow*

"Mornin', Mum, Dad," said Tommy, as he wandered into the kitchen. "What's for breakfast?"

It was Saturday morning. All three were in dressing gowns. Julia and Sean Delaney, Tommy's mum and dad, were at the table. Sean, busy inhaling a pint-sized, steaming mug of tea, acknowledged his son with his usual grunt and a wiggle of his fingers.

It was a standing family joke, how even Sean's grunts had an unmistakably Irish brogue.

Mum was staring at the screen of her laptop.

"Morning, sweetheart," she said. "I'll make your breakfast in a minute. Come and look at this, first. Tell me if it's the bird you saw yesterday morning."

Rubbing sleep from his eyes, Tommy looked over her shoulder.

"Yeah, that's the one," he cried. "What is it?"

"It's a red kite," she said. "Old Rogers next door told me all about them last night. They fly over the village regularly. They come from Harewood, apparently. The most important thing is, they're no danger to your baby bunnies. They only eat dead meat, like crows, so your bird was probably only waiting for breakfast. Like you, this morning. Porridge okay?"

Tommy felt a bit guilty now, for having driven the poor bird away with his drone. Not quite guilty enough, though, to spoil his enjoyment of the bowl of porridge which his mum cooked up.

Two mornings later, Rodney arrived at his favourite hovering place, at his usual time, only to find no bunnies playing on the grass verges and, to his further dismay, a constant flow of cars leaving the village and heading towards Wetherby.

He spied the remains of some dead bunnies on the road but there was nothing left for him. They had been picked clean by a bunch of crows. They were still around, perched in trees or on top of telephone poles, swooping down whenever there was a break in traffic, to peck at the last few morsels.

Rodney couldn't figure it out. Why were the villagers up and around so early? Had he overslept? He dismissed the idea instantly. His fellow kites had awoken at the same time and had flown off in different directions, heading for their favourite breakfast locations. It was a mystery.

He was puzzling over this when, from the corner of his eye, he saw the farmer, walking into the middle of the field alongside the road. He was carrying something which, to Rodney, looked like another man.

The morning was getting weirder and weirder. At least he wasn't being chased by some flying machine, like three mornings earlier. And the boy was nowhere to be seen.

Following the machine incident, he had enjoyed two mornings of relative peace. He had come to recognise those two days as the ones when humans slept in and didn't rush off in their cars. And when children also rose later and didn't go to school.

This may well turn out to be another morning when he might have to go without breakfast. Which prompted him to turn his attention to the field. There might be a dead vole or squirrel to be had. Not that he was particularly fond of squirrel, but needs must, eh?

The farmer had gone but the other man remained. He was standing there, stock still, arms straight out to his sides, slap bang in the centre of the field.

Rodney decided to wait until this man left, as well. He circled the field, looking for any tasty titbits which might be lying around.

There was nothing to be seen, other than the strange man, who was still standing there, motionless. He hadn't moved an inch since the farmer had left. The only thing moving was his big black coat, which flapped crazily in the brisk morning breeze.

Rodney took a calculated risk and swung lower for a closer look. Perhaps the man was dead, although, if he was, how come he hadn't fallen over? Didn't everything fall over when it died? Except for trees, maybe? Or squashed bunnies?

He glided lower and lower, so low in fact, he ran out of thermals and was forced to make an undignified landing, two lengths in front of the man.

dark peak blues

He was about to take off again, when the man chuckled. Or so it seemed to Rodney.

"Were you laughing at me?" said an aggrieved Rodney. He didn't really say it, as such. Red kites don't speak. They would if they could, but they can't, so they don't. No, he didn't say it, but he thought it, for sure.

"Sorry, old chap, no offence intended, but it was a somewhat ungainly landing," said the scarecrow, for scarecrow he was. He didn't really say it, as such. Scarecrows don't speak. They would if they could, but they can't, so they don't. No, he didn't say it, but he thought it, for sure.

Rodney regarded him intently. "What on earth are you?" he asked. "You're not a man, though you look like one. You're not alive, but you can speak, so you're not dead, either."

"I'm a scarecrow," said the scarecrow, proudly.

"A scarecrow?" said Rodney. "I've never heard of such a thing."

"Scarecrows scares the crows away, stopping them stealing the farmer's seeds," said the scarecrow. "The clue is in the name."

"It's not working out too well," said Rodney, as a crow promptly landed on the scarecrow's outstretched right arm.

"Shoo!" shouted the scarecrow and the crow flew away.

Rodney was impressed. "How come I haven't seen you before?" he asked.

"The farmer brings me out in spring, after he has planted his seeds," explained the scarecrow. "Usually just after the clocks go forward."

"Huh?" said Rodney. "What does that mean? What are clocks?"

"Oh, dear," sighed the scarecrow. "Don't you know anything? Humans measure the passing of time with devices called clocks. Every spring, they move them forward an hour. It's called daylight saving; it began during the war."

"War?" said Rodney, who was now seriously confused.

"Oh, never mind," said the scarecrow, exasperated. "Have you never heard of 'Spring forward, Fall back'? No, of course you haven't. You're far too young. Now shoo, the farmer's coming. I'll tell you more tomorrow."

Rodney took off and headed for home, his head spinning. He

noticed the young boy who was giving him a friendly wave as he flew over the road below.

His tummy was grumbling noisily, so he kept an eye out for breakfast as he went. By this time of day, he would even relish a dead hedgehog.

Chapter Three
Tommy, Rodney and Ed

The next morning, Rodney and his fellow red kites were up in the air an hour earlier, having learned their lesson the day before. Most of them had arrived back at base with empty stomachs and had spent the rest of the day searching for food. Mostly without success.

There was simply no substitute for a good breakfast, which invariably meant being up early enough to beat the crows to it.

However, on this particular morning, despite arriving at his favourite hovering place in good time and definitely being well ahead of the crows, Rodney was disappointed. Again.

There was not one single baby rabbit playing on the grass verges.

Instead, he spied the young boy, who was carrying the dreadful black flying machine which had driven Rodney away a few mornings earlier.

He decided he might as well try his luck over the big field. Maybe have a chat with his new friend, the scarecrow.

As he turned, the boy looked up. He gave a wave and shouted something which Rodney couldn't understand.

The scarecrow was in the same place, facing the same way, standing as still as ever.

As he circled the field, Rodney studied his friend with new eyes. He could see, now, how the poor old fellow was simply hanging from a crudely made wooden cross, which was driven into the ground. No wonder he never seemed to move.

At the far side of the field, he spotted it. Breakfast. Thank goodness. It was a dead squirrel. Not the best but it would have to do. He swooped down and was delighted to find it was still fresh and, best of all, had not yet been picked at by any other scavengers.

He picked it up in his talons and flew over to the scarecrow, planning to enjoy the company while he tucked in.

From the gateway to the field, Tommy watched the red kite circling. He saw it swoop down, pick something up in its talons and fly over and land directly in front of the scarecrow, where it began picking at what was, presumably, its breakfast.
The bird appeared to have no fear of the scarecrow, whatsoever. Neither did the crows and pigeons, apparently, who were busy pecking at the farmer's seeds, although, he noticed, they were all behind the scarecrow's back.
In fact, red kite apart, there wasn't a bird to be seen anywhere in front of the scarecrow. Which he found weird. Stranger still, the red kite kept looking up from his meal, almost as if he was carrying on a conversation with the scarecrow. Which was a daft idea, obviously.
He came to a decision. He would try to make friends with the bird, do his best to make amends for scaring it away the other morning. He tucked the drone and its remote control under the hedge, climbed the gate and set off across the field.
He was halfway there when the bird saw him and immediately took to the skies. Tommy stopped in his tracks.
"Wait!" he shouted. "I only want to tell you I'm sorry for driving you away. I didn't know you were a red kite. Please forgive me."
The bird continued to hover at a safe distance. Tommy walked on, slowly, keeping his hands firmly in his pockets, trying to appear as unthreatening as possible.
What happened next had him believing he was still in his bed, dreaming. As clear as a bell, he heard the scarecrow shouting up to the bird, repeating Tommy's message, pretty much word for word.
The scarecrow didn't really shout. Scarecrows don't shout. They would if they could, but they can't, so they don't. No, he didn't shout, but he thought extremely loudly, for sure.
The red kite squawked, as if in reply, and once again, Tommy heard the scarecrow's thoughts. Tommy pinched himself as hard as he could but failed to wake up in his bed.
"He's sorry," shouted the scarecrow. "He just wants to be your friend."
The bird squawked again but circled a little lower.
"Give him time," said the scarecrow, quietly. "You can't blame

him for being a trifle nervous."

"You can talk?" said Tommy, mouth agape. "For real? Or am I dreaming?"

"No, you are not dreaming, young man," said the scarecrow. "But you must swear to keep it secret. Not that anyone would believe you, anyway."

Tommy was so flabbergasted, he flopped down and sat cross-legged in front of the scarecrow. Above them, the kite came even lower, as if not wanting to be left out of their conversation.

"How can you possibly speak?" Tommy queried. "And how did you ever learn, in the first place? You don't even have a brain. Your head is just a carved turnip."

"There's no need to be so rude," said the scarecrow. "My head is brand new, I'll have you know. And my knowledge and memory are much, much older than you, you young whippersnapper."

"Sorry, sir, I didn't mean to be rude," said Tommy, noticing how the bird was now hovering behind the scarecrow's left shoulder. "I'm Tommy, by the way. Tommy Delaney. What's your name?"

"My name?" said the scarecrow. "I don't think I have one. The farmer just calls me Turnip 'Ead, if that's what you can call a name."

"Now that is rude," said Tommy and sat thinking for a while. "I know!" he cried. "I'll call you Ed, if that's okay with you."

The kite squawked.

"He says he's pleased to meet you, Tommy," said Ed. "And his name is Rodney. Sounds like he's forgiven you for whatever you did, after all."

"Gosh, you mean you can talk to birds, as well?" Tommy was even more flabbergasted now.

"Of course, I can," said Ed. "I can talk to all the animals and birds, naturally."

"So how come you didn't scare off all those crows and pigeons I saw in the field before?"

"Oh, them," said Ed. "Rodney was telling me about them when you came barging in. I hadn't scared them off because I hadn't seen them, had I? Because I can't turn around, can I?"

Tommy got up and walked slowly around Ed, taking in every detail.

"I see now," he said, circuit completed. "You're just sort of hung up on a wooden cross, like poor old Jesus. I bet my dad could fix that for you, dead easy."

"Who is poor old Jesus?" Ed wanted to know. "And how could your dad 'fix it', anyway?"

"My dad can turn his hand to anything," said Tommy, his chest swelling with pride. "He calls it his God-given skill set. Mum says it's the luck of the Irish. I'll speak to him about it. I bet he'll have an idea. Then we can approach the farmer, see what he thinks."

The bird squawked.

"He says, 'Good luck with that'," said Ed. "And don't forget our secret. Don't be telling anyone about how I can talk."

"Scout's honour," said Tommy. He gave a salute and headed for home, where he knew he's be in trouble for being late.

Chapter Four
Sean Solves the Problem

"Dere you go, our Tommy," said his dad, proudly. "Whaddya tink o' dat, den?"

"I think you need subtitles, for starters, Dad," said Tommy, grinning.

"And you need a clout, so you do, cheeky monkey," said Sean, throwing a pretend punch at his son.

It was the morning of Sunday, the first of April. The two of them were in the workshop at Delaney Fabrications, Sean's business, situated in a compact unit on the small industrial estate in Pannal, on the southern outskirts of Harrogate.

As usual, the place was a shambolic clutter of fabricating paraphernalia: Workbenches, welding equipment, steel offcuts, power tools. There were signs of works in progress but, taking pride of place, slap bang in the middle of the floor, was Sean's latest creation, the one which he had brought Tommy along to see.

It was standing in a large metal bucket, filled to the brim with soil, sticking out of which was an upright metal rod, reaching to a height approaching two metres. It had two arms, at what in a human would be shoulder height. It kind of resembled the wooden cross on which the farmer hung his scarecrow, But these arms looked real.

The left one hung down like a man's, angled from the shoulder and sticking out slightly backwards, like someone's arm swinging when they walked. Sean had even managed to give it a facsimile of a hand, complete with steel fingers.

The right arm was even more complex. It was crooked at the elbow. The hand curved upwards at the wrist and was holding a remarkably accurate copy of a shotgun, its barrels realistically pointing forwards and down

Tommy could see immediately how Ed would appear so much

more like a real man, once he was mounted on this magnificent creation.

"Gosh, Dad," he gasped in admiration. "It's incredible."

"You ain't seen nuttin' yet," said his dad. He stepped forward and gave the left arm a push and the entire assembly spun round and round.

"Wow!" Tommy exclaimed. "How did you do that, Dad?"

"Simple," said Sean. "I adapted one of those rotary washing line tings. A customer of mine had an old one dey never used, so it cost me nuttin' but a few bits o' scrap metal and some welding. De arms act like sails, catching the breeze and making it rotate slowly."

"Fantastic, Dad," cried Tommy, jumping up and down with enthusiasm. "Can we take it and show it to the farmer now? I'm sure he'll love it."

"Now?" said Sean. "You do know it's the first of April, don't you?"

"Yes, of course I do," said Tommy, puzzled. "Why? Are you worried he'll think it's an April Fool, or something?"

"No, lad," said his dad, grinning. "It's because I need a rest. I've just had a long March of thirty-one days."

Tommy groaned but laughed, anyway. More out of politeness than anything. His dad loved to crack a joke, no matter how old it might be.

"What if he won't buy it?" Tommy asked, concerned.

"No worries, lad," said Sean, giving him a slap on the back. "We'll make it a gift. Other farmers will see it and want one. Word will spread, you'll see. Orders will soon come flooding in. And you'll be on fifty per cent."

He knew he could never say anything to his dad but Tommy was really looking forward, most of all, to Ed's reaction. Once he was newly mounted on Sean Delaney's brilliant framework, Ed would no longer have to worry about birds landing behind him or, most humiliating of all, perching on his outstretched arms.

"Come on, young 'un," said Dad. "Help me get it loaded on the pick-up."

"Do you know where we're going, Dad?" Tommy asked, a worried frown creasing his brow.

"Course I do, son," Sean told him. "I've known old Bill Forrest

dark peak blues

for years. I redesigned his cowsheds for him, back before you were even born. Now, come on, shake a leg, me boyo."

Chapter Five
Ed in a Spin

Monday morning, Rodney found a new hovering spot, only a short distance from his usual but far enough away not to have young Tommy frightening the baby rabbits with his dratted flying machine.

Consequently, he was able to partake of an excellent tasty breakfast, undisturbed by anything more than the occasional passing car.

Full and contented, he resumed his hovering height while he pondered what to do next. It was far too early to be flying back home to Harewood.

From his new position, he could still see his friend, Ed the scarecrow, but from a greater distance and at a more acute angle than before. Nevertheless, he could see there was something different about his new buddy.

Ed's arms appeared to be much more man-like. Strangely, he appeared to be carrying a gun and, weirder still, he was turning around, slowly but surely.

The differences were so marked, Rodney couldn't help but wonder if the farmer had decided to get rid of Ed and had hired a real man to do the job, instead. Who could blame him, if he had? Poor old Ed could only ever do half a job, fixed in place like he was, unable to turn around and see the crows and pigeons happily stuffing themselves, behind him.

'Oh no,' thought Rodney. 'I hope he hasn't been chucked on a bonfire.'

Rodney decided to risk taking a closer look. He flew a bit higher and rode some thermals until he was circling directly above the new scarecrow, which was still rotating slowly below him.

He was debating whether or not to risk flying a little lower when he spotted young Tommy, coming up the road from the

dark peak blues

village. Without a moment's hesitation, the boy vaulted the gate and strode straight across the field, stopping directly in front of the man with the gun.

Tommy appeared to be talking to the man and pointed up at Rodney. Which was when Rodney got the shock of his life.

"Come on down here," shouted Ed. "Stop being such an old scaredy-kite."

Rodney was so taken aback, he lost his hover momentarily and plummeted a fair way downwards before recovering. By which time he had halved the distance between himself and the ground.

"That's better," shouted Ed, clearly mistaking Rodney's accidental manoeuvre for something deliberate, maybe even courageous. "Now come and see what Tommy's dad has made for me."

"Not just my dad," said Tommy. "My mum played a blinder as well. It was easy to fix you to the framework, with your belt and your tie and my grandad's old hat, but we couldn't figure out how to get your overcoat back on. It was Mum who cracked it. She cut it straight up the back and fitted it with two long strips of Velcro. Made it dead easy to pull it on in two halves and fasten it back together again. And it was Mum who came up with the idea of lashing the shotgun in place with an old leather bootlace."

All this time, Ed was rotating slowly. Tommy followed him, keeping him face to face while they spoke. Rodney landed and hopped along behind Tommy, keeping pace.

"Tell Rodney what you just told me," said Ed.

"I can't speak to him," Tommy protested. "I don't know how to speak bird."

"Yes, you do, silly boy," said Ed. "You just speak to him like you speak to me. Think really hard and concentrate. You'll be surprised."

"He's right, you know," said Rodney and, wonder of wonders, Tommy heard him, clear as a bell.

So, Tommy explained all about how his dad had designed and made Ed's wonderful new rotating frame and how they had taken it to farmer Bill and persuaded him to give it a try, for free.

"My dad's applied for a patent on the design," he said, which neither Ed nor Rodney understood. Tommy explained as best he could, leaving them none the wiser.

He gave up trying to teach them the intricacies of patent law and took out his iPhone.

"I'm going to make a video of you in action, Ed," he said. "Once Dad has his patent firmly in place, we can post it on social media and then sit back and watch the demand ramp up."

He was met by a stony silence.

"Never mind," he said with a deep sigh of resignation. "Neither of you have a clue what I'm on about but it doesn't matter. Dad has to have a patent so no one can steal his idea. Once he has that, we can really start to push for sales. I think there might be a job in it for you, Rodney."

"A job?" Rodney said, puzzled. "What's a job?"

"Work," said Tommy. "You know, something you do for pay, for reward. We could pay you in meat, if you want."

"Ooh, sounds good to me," Rodney replied, his interest aroused. "What would you want me to do?"

"You could scout out rotary washing lines for us," Tommy explained. "And maybe some other old-fashioned scarecrows, like Ed was."

"Hey, less of your cheek, young man," said Ed as he spun slowly around in the breeze.

dark peak blues

Author's Note

It may seem like having five novels on the go at once iis a bit of a tall order.

Normally, it would be. However, when one is stuck at home, hiding from the dreaded virus, then perhaps it is not such a daft idea, after all.

I am inspired by my membership of the fantastic writing group, ThirskWriteNow. My fellow writers are such a smart bunch, they know how to keep one another on their toes.

Wish me luck with the novels. I hope to finish at least two of them before the year is out. Fingers crossed.

James H Jones
Thirsk 2020

Printed in Poland
by Amazon Fulfillment
Poland Sp. z o.o., Wrocław